FEDERAL RULES
OF CIVIL PROCEDURE

As Amended to May 13, 2005

2005–2006 ABRIDGED EDUCATIONAL EDITION

THOMSON

WEST

Mat #40323091

© 2005 Thomson/West

Copyright is not claimed as to any part of the original work prepared by a United States Government officer or employee as part of that person's official duties.

Thomson/West have created this publication to provide you with accurate and authoritative information concerning the subject matter covered. However, this publication was not necessarily prepared by persons licensed to practice law in a particular jurisdiction. Thomson/West are not engaged in rendering legal or other professional advice, and this publication is not a substitute for the advice of an attorney. If you require legal or other expert advice, you should seek the services of a competent attorney or other professional

ISBN 0–314–15845–6

West's and Westlaw are registered in the U.S. Patent and Trademark Office.

TABLE OF CONTENTS

*

CONSTITUTION OF THE UNITED STATES

UNANNOTATED

PREAMBLE

WE THE PEOPLE of the United States, in Order to form a more perfect Union, establish Justice, insure domestic Tranquility, provide for the common defence, promote the general Welfare, and secure the Blessings of Liberty to ourselves and our Posterity, do ordain and establish this CONSTITUTION for the United States of America.

ARTICLE I

Section. 1. All legislative Powers herein granted shall be vested in a Congress of the United States, which shall consist of a Senate and House of Representatives.

Section. 2. The House of Representatives shall be composed of Members chosen every second Year by the People of the several States, and the Electors in each State shall have the Qualifications requisite for Electors of the most numerous Branch of the State Legislature.

No Person shall be a Representative who shall not have attained to the Age of twenty five Years, and been seven Years a Citizen of the United States, and who shall not, when elected, be an Inhabitant of that State in which he shall be chosen.

[Representatives and direct Taxes shall be apportioned among the several States which may be included within this Union, according to their respective Numbers, which shall be determined by adding to the whole Number of free Persons, including those bound to Service for a Term of Years, and excluding Indians not taxed, three fifths of all other Persons.] [1] The actual Enumeration shall be made within three Years after the first Meeting of the Congress of the United States, and within every subsequent Term of ten Years, in such Manner as they shall by Law direct. The Number of Representatives shall not exceed one for every thirty Thousand, but each State shall have at Least one Representative; and until such enumeration shall be made, the State of New Hampshire shall be entitled to chuse three, Massachusetts eight, Rhode-Island and Providence Plantations one, Connecticut five, New-York six, New Jersey four, Pennsylvania eight, Delaware one, Maryland six, Virginia ten, North Carolina five, South Carolina five, and Georgia three.

When vacancies happen in the Representation from any State, the Executive Authority thereof shall issue Writs of Election to fill such Vacancies.

The House of Representatives shall chuse their Speaker and other Officers; and shall have the sole Power of Impeachment.

[1] The clause of this paragraph inclosed in brackets was amended, as to the mode of apportionment of representatives among the several states, by the Fourteenth Amendment, § 2, and as to taxes on incomes without apportionment, by the Sixteenth Amendment.

Section. 3. [The Senate of the United States shall be composed of two Senators from each State, chosen by the Legislature thereof, for six Years; and each Senator shall have one Vote.] [1]

Immediately after they shall be assembled in Consequence of the first Election, they shall be divided as equally as may be into three Classes. The Seats of the Senators of the first Class shall be vacated at the Expiration of the second Year, of the second Class at the Expiration of the fourth Year, and of the third Class at the Expiration of the sixth Year, so that one third may be chosen every second Year; [and if Vacancies happen by Resignation, or otherwise, during the Recess of the Legislature of any State, the Executive thereof may make temporary Appointments until the next Meeting of the Legislature, which shall then fill such Vacancies.] [2]

No Person shall be a Senator who shall not have attained to the Age of thirty Years, and been nine Years a Citizen of the United States, and who shall not, when elected, be an Inhabitant of that State for which he shall be chosen.

The Vice President of the United States shall be President of the Senate, but shall have no Vote, unless they be equally divided.

The Senate shall chuse their other Officers, and also a President pro tempore, in the Absence of the Vice President, or when he shall exercise the Office of President of the United States.

The Senate shall have the sole Power to try all Impeachments. When sitting for that Purpose, they shall be on Oath or Affirmation. When the President of the United States is tried, the Chief Justice shall preside: And no Person shall be convicted without the Concurrence of two thirds of the Members present.

Judgment in Cases of Impeachment shall not extend further than to removal from Office, and disqualification to hold and enjoy any Office of honor, Trust or Profit under the United States: but the Party convicted shall nevertheless be liable and subject to Indictment, Trial, Judgment and Punishment, according to Law.

1 This paragraph, inclosed in brackets, was superseded by the Seventeenth Amendment.

2 The clause of this paragraph inclosed in brackets was superseded by the Seventeenth Amendment.

Section. 4.   The Times, Places and Manner of holding Elections for Senators and Representatives, shall be prescribed in each State by the Legislature thereof; but the Congress may at any time by Law make or alter such Regulations, except as to the Places of chusing Senators.

The Congress shall assemble at least once in every Year, and such Meeting shall be on the [first Monday in December],1 unless they shall by Law appoint a different Day.

1 The clause of this paragraph inclosed in brackets was superseded by the Twentieth Amendment.

Section. 5.   Each House shall be the Judge of the Elections, Returns and Qualifications of its own Members, and a Majority of each shall constitute a Quorum to do Business; but a smaller Number may adjourn from day to day, and may be authorized to compel the Attendance of absent Members, in such Manner, and under such Penalties as each House may provide.

Each House may determine the Rules of its Proceedings, punish its Members for disorderly Behaviour, and, with the Concurrence of two thirds, expel a Member.

Each House shall keep a Journal of its Proceedings, and from time to time publish the same, excepting such Parts as may in their Judgment require Secrecy; and the Yeas and Nays of the Members of either House on any question shall, at the Desire of one fifth of those Present, be entered on the Journal.

Neither House, during the Session of Congress, shall, without the Consent of the other, adjourn for more than three days, nor to any other Place than that in which the two Houses shall be sitting.

Section. 6.   The Senators and Representatives shall receive a Compensation for their Services, to be ascertained by Law, and paid out of the Treasury of the United States. They shall in all Cases, except Treason, Felony and Breach of the Peace, be privileged from Arrest during their Attendance at the Session of their respective Houses, and in going to and returning from the same; and for any Speech or Debate in either House, they shall not be questioned in any other Place.

No Senator or Representative shall, during the Time for which he was elected, be appointed to any civil Office under the Authority of the United States, which shall have been created, or the Emoluments whereof shall have been encreased during such time; and no Person holding any Office under the United States, shall be a Member of either House during his Continuance in Office.

Section. 7.   All Bills for raising Revenue shall originate in the House of Representatives; but the Senate may propose or concur with Amendments as on other Bills.

Every Bill which shall have passed the House of Representatives and the Senate, shall, before it becomes a Law, be presented to the President of the United States; If he approve he shall sign it, but if not he shall return it, with his Objections to that House in which it shall have originated, who shall enter the Objections at large on their Journal, and proceed to reconsider it. If after such Reconsideration two thirds of that House shall agree to pass the Bill, it shall be sent, together with the Objections, to the other House, by which it shall likewise be reconsidered, and if approved by two thirds of that House, it shall become a Law. But in all such Cases the Votes of both Houses shall be determined by Yeas and Nays, and the Names of the Persons voting for and against the Bill shall be entered on the Journal of each House respectively. If any Bill shall not be returned by the President within ten Days (Sundays excepted) after it shall have been presented to him, the Same shall be a Law, in like Manner as if he had signed it, unless the Congress by their Adjournment prevent its Return, in which Case it shall not be a Law.

Every Order, Resolution, or Vote to which the Concurrence of the Senate and House of Representatives may be necessary (except on a question of Adjournment) shall be presented to the President of the United States; and before the Same shall take Effect, shall be approved by him, or being disapproved by him, shall be repassed by two thirds of the Senate and House of Representatives, according to the Rules and Limitations prescribed in the Case of a Bill.

Section. 8. The Congress shall have Power To lay and collect Taxes, Duties, Imposts and Excises, to pay the Debts and provide for the common Defence and general Welfare of the United States; but all Duties, Imposts and Excises shall be uniform throughout the United States;

To borrow Money on the credit of the United States;

To regulate Commerce with foreign Nations, and among the several States, and with the Indian Tribes;

To establish an uniform Rule of Naturalization, and uniform Laws on the subject of Bankruptcies throughout the United States;

To coin Money, regulate the Value thereof, and of foreign Coin, and fix the Standard of Weights and Measures;

To provide for the Punishment of counterfeiting the Securities and current Coin of the United States;

To establish Post Offices and post Roads;

To promote the Progress of Science and useful Arts, by securing for limited Times to Authors and Inventors the exclusive Right to their respective Writings and Discoveries;

To constitute Tribunals inferior to the supreme Court;

To define and punish Piracies and Felonies committed on the high Seas, and Offences against the Law of Nations;

To declare War, grant Letters of Marque and Reprisal, and make Rules concerning Captures on Land and Water;

To raise and support Armies, but no Appropriation of Money to that Use shall be for a longer Term than two Years;

To provide and maintain a Navy;

To make Rules for the Government and Regulation of the land and naval Forces;

To provide for calling forth the Militia to execute the Laws of the Union, suppress Insurrections and repel Invasions;

To provide for organizing, arming, and disciplining, the Militia, and for governing such Part of them as may be employed in the Service of the United States, reserving to the States respectively, the Appointment of the Officers, and the Authority of training the Militia according to the discipline prescribed by Congress;

To exercise exclusive Legislation in all Cases whatsoever, over such District (not exceeding ten Miles square) as may, by Cession of particular States, and the Acceptance of Congress, become the Seat of the Government of the United States, and to exercise like Authority over all Places purchased by the Consent of the Legislature of the State in which the Same shall be, for the Erection of Forts, Magazines, Arsenals, dock-Yards, and other needful Buildings;—And

To make all Laws which shall be necessary and proper for carrying into Execution the foregoing Powers, and all other Powers vested by this Constitution in the Government of the United States, or in any Department or Officer thereof.

Section. 9. The Migration or Importation of such Persons as any of the States now existing shall think proper to admit, shall not be prohibited by the Congress prior to the Year one thousand eight hundred and eight, but a Tax or duty may be imposed on such Importation, not exceeding ten dollars for each Person.

The Privilege of the Writ of Habeas Corpus shall not be suspended, unless when in Cases of Rebellion or Invasion the public Safety may require it.

No Bill of Attainder or ex post facto Law shall be passed.

No Capitation, or other direct, Tax shall be laid, unless in Proportion to the Census or Enumeration herein before directed to be taken.[1]

No Tax or Duty shall be laid on Articles exported from any State.

No Preference shall be given by any Regulation of Commerce or Revenue to the Ports of one State over those of another; nor shall Vessels bound to, or from, one State, be obliged to enter, clear, or pay Duties in another.

No Money shall be drawn from the Treasury, but in Consequence of Appropriations made by Law; and a regular Statement and Account of the Receipts and Expenditures of all public Money shall be published from time to time.

No Title of Nobility shall be granted by the United States: And no Person holding any Office of Profit or Trust under them, shall, without the Consent of the Congress, accept of any present, Emolument, Office, or Title, of any kind whatever, from any King, Prince, or foreign State.

1 This paragraph has been affected by the Sixteenth Amendment.

Section. 10. No State shall enter into any Treaty, Alliance, or Confederation; grant Letters of Marque and Reprisal; coin Money; emit Bills of Credit; make any Thing but gold and silver Coin a Tender in Payment of Debts; pass any Bill of Attainder, ex post facto Law, or Law impairing the Obligation of Contracts, or grant any Title of Nobility.

No State shall, without the Consent of the Congress, lay any Imposts or Duties on Imports or Exports, except what may be absolutely necessary for executing it's inspection Laws: and the net Produce of all Duties and Imposts, laid by any State on Imports or Exports, shall be for the Use of the Treasury of the

United States; and all such Laws shall be subject to the Revision and Controul of the Congress.

No State shall, without the Consent of Congress, lay any Duty of Tonnage, keep Troops, or Ships of War in time of Peace, enter into any Agreement or Compact with another State, or with a foreign Power, or engage in War, unless actually invaded, or in such imminent Danger as will not admit of delay.

ARTICLE II

Section. 1. The executive Power shall be vested in a President of the United States of America. He shall hold his Office during the Term of four Years, and, together with the Vice President, chosen for the same Term, be elected, as follows:

Each State shall appoint, in such Manner as the Legislature thereof may direct, a Number of Electors, equal to the whole Number of Senators and Representatives to which the State may be entitled in the Congress: but no Senator or Representative, or Person holding an Office of Trust or Profit under the United States, shall be appointed an Elector.

[The Electors shall meet in their respective States, and vote by Ballot for two Persons, of whom one at least shall not be an Inhabitant of the same State with themselves. And they shall make a List of all the Persons voted for, and of the Number of Votes for each; which List they shall sign and certify, and transmit sealed to the Seat of the Government of the United States, directed to the President of the Senate. The President of the Senate shall, in the Presence of the Senate and House of Representatives, open all the Certificates, and the Votes shall then be counted. The Person having the greatest Number of Votes shall be the President, if such Number be a Majority of the whole Number of Electors appointed; and if there be more than one who have such Majority, and have an equal Number of Votes, then the House of Representatives shall immediately chuse by Ballot one of them for President; and if no Person have a Majority, then from the five highest on the List the said House shall in like Manner chuse the President. But in chusing the President, the Votes shall be taken by States, the Representation from each State having one Vote; A quorum for this Purpose shall consist of a Member or Members from two thirds of the States, and a Majority of all the States shall be necessary to a Choice. In every Case, after the Choice of the President, the Person having the greatest Number of Votes of the Electors shall be the Vice President. But if there should remain two or more who have equal Votes, the Senate shall chuse from them by Ballot the Vice President.] [1]

The Congress may determine the Time of chusing the Electors, and the Day on which they shall give their Votes; which Day shall be the same throughout the United States.

No Person except a natural born Citizen, or a Citizen of the United States, at the time of the Adoption of this Constitution, shall be eligible to the Office of President; neither shall any Person be eligible to that Office who shall not have attained to the Age of thirty five Years, and been fourteen Years a Resident within the United States.

In Case of the Removal of the President from Office, or of his Death, Resignation, or Inability to discharge the Powers and Duties of the said Office, the Same shall devolve on the Vice President, and the Congress may by Law provide for the Case of Removal, Death, Resignation or Inability, both of the President and Vice President, declaring what Officer shall then act as President, and such Officer shall act accordingly, until the Disability be removed, or a President shall be elected.

The President shall, at stated Times, receive for his Services, a Compensation, which shall neither be encreased nor diminished during the Period for which he shall have been elected, and he shall not receive within that Period any other Emolument from the United States, or any of them.

Before he enter on the Execution of his Office, he shall take the following Oath or Affirmation:—"I do solemnly swear (or affirm) that I will faithfully execute the Office of President of the United States, and will to the best of my Ability, preserve, protect and defend the Constitution of the United States."

[1] This paragraph, inclosed in brackets, was superseded by the Twelfth Amendment, post.

Section. 2. The President shall be Commander in Chief of the Army and Navy of the United States, and of the Militia of the several States, when called into the actual Service of the United States; he may require the Opinion, in writing, of the principal Officer in each of the executive Departments, upon any Subject relating to the Duties of their respective Offices, and he shall have Power to grant Reprieves and Pardons for Offences against the United States, except in Cases of Impeachment.

He shall have Power, by and with the Advice and Consent of the Senate, to make Treaties, provided two thirds of the Senators present concur; and he shall nominate, and by and with the Advice and Consent of the Senate, shall appoint Ambassadors, other public Ministers and Consuls, Judges of the supreme Court, and all other Officers of the United States, whose

Appointments are not herein otherwise provided for, and which shall be established by Law: but the Congress may by Law vest the Appointment of such inferior Officers, as they think proper, in the President alone, in the Courts of Law, or in the Heads of Departments.

The President shall have Power to fill up all Vacancies that may happen during the Recess of the Senate, by granting Commissions which shall expire at the End of their next Session.

Section. 3. He shall from time to time give to the Congress Information of the State of the Union, and recommend to their Consideration such Measures as he shall judge necessary and expedient; he may, on extraordinary Occasions, convene both Houses, or either of them, and in Case of Disagreement between them, with Respect to the Time of Adjournment, he may adjourn them to such Time as he shall think proper; he shall receive Ambassadors and other public Ministers; he shall take Care that the Laws be faithfully executed, and shall Commission all the Officers of the United States.

Section. 4. The President, Vice President and all civil Officers of the United States, shall be removed from Office on Impeachment for, and Conviction of, Treason, Bribery, or other high Crimes and Misdemeanors.

ARTICLE III

Section. 1. The judicial Power of the United States, shall be vested in one supreme Court, and in such inferior Courts as the Congress may from time to time ordain and establish. The Judges, both of the supreme and inferior Courts, shall hold their Offices during good Behaviour, and shall, at stated Times, receive for their Services, a Compensation, which shall not be diminished during their Continuance in Office.

Section. 2. The judicial Power shall extend to all Cases, in Law and Equity, arising under this Constitution, the Laws of the United States, and Treaties made, or which shall be made, under their Authority;—to all Cases affecting Ambassadors, other public Ministers and Consuls;—to all Cases of admiralty and maritime Jurisdiction;—to Controversies to which the United States shall be a Party;—to Controversies between two or more States;—between a State and Citizens of another State;—between citizens of different States;—between Citizens of the same State claiming Lands under Grants of different States, and between a State, or the Citizens thereof, and foreign States, Citizens or Subjects.[1]

In all Cases affecting Ambassadors, other public Ministers and Consuls, and those in which a State shall be Party, the supreme Court shall have original Jurisdiction. In all the other Cases before mentioned, the supreme Court shall have appellate Jurisdiction, both as to Law and Fact, with such Exceptions, and under such Regulations as the Congress shall make.

The Trial of all Crimes, except in Cases of Impeachment, shall be by Jury; and such Trial shall be held in the State where the said Crimes shall have been committed; but when not committed within any State, the Trial shall be at such Place or Places as the Congress may by Law have directed.

[1] This section has been affected by the Eleventh Amendment.

Section. 3. Treason against the United States, shall consist only in levying War against them, or in adhering to their Enemies, giving them Aid and Comfort. No Person shall be convicted of Treason unless on the Testimony of two Witnesses to the same overt Act, or on Confession in open Court.

The Congress shall have Power to declare the Punishment of Treason, but no Attainder of Treason shall work Corruption of Blood, or Forfeiture except during the Life of the Person attainted.

ARTICLE IV

Section. 1. Full Faith and Credit shall be given in each State to the public Acts, Records, and judicial Proceedings of every other State. And the Congress may by general Laws prescribe the Manner in which such Acts, Records and Proceedings shall be proved, and the Effect thereof.

Section. 2. The Citizens of each State shall be entitled to all Privileges and Immunities of Citizens in the several States.

A Person charged in any State with Treason, Felony, or other Crime, who shall flee from Justice, and be found in another State, shall on Demand of the executive Authority of the State from which he fled, be delivered up, to be removed to the State having Jurisdiction of the Crime.

No Person held to Service or Labour in one State, under the Laws thereof, escaping into another, shall, in Consequence of any Law or Regulation therein, be discharged from such Service or Labour, but shall be delivered up on Claim of the Party to whom such Service or Labour may be due.[1]

[1] This clause was affected by the Thirteenth Amendment.

Section. 3. New States may be admitted by the Congress into this Union; but no new State shall be formed or erected within the Jurisdiction of any other State; nor any State be formed by the Junction of two or more States, or Parts of States, without the Consent of the Legislatures of the States concerned as well as of the Congress.

The Congress shall have Power to dispose of and make all needful Rules and Regulations respecting the Territory or other Property belonging to the United States; and nothing in this Constitution shall be so construed as to Prejudice any Claims of the United States, or of any particular State.

Section. 4. The United States shall guarantee to every State in this Union a Republican Form of Government, and shall protect each of them against Invasion; and on Application of the Legislature, or of the Executive (when the Legislature cannot be convened) against domestic Violence.

ARTICLE V

The Congress, whenever two thirds of both Houses shall deem it necessary, shall propose Amendments to this Constitution, or, on the Application of the Legislatures of two thirds of the several States, shall call a Convention for proposing Amendments, which, in either Case, shall be valid to all Intents and Purposes, as Part of this Constitution, when ratified by the Legislatures of three fourths of the several States, or by Conventions in three fourths thereof, as the one or the other Mode of Ratification may be proposed by the Congress; Provided that no Amendment which may be made prior to the Year One thousand eight hundred and eight shall in any Manner affect the first and fourth Clauses in the Ninth Section of the first Article; and that no State, without its Consent, shall be deprived of its equal Suffrage in the Senate.

ARTICLE VI

All Debts contracted and Engagements entered into, before the Adoption of this Constitution, shall be as valid against the United States under this Constitution, as under the Confederation.

This Constitution, and the Laws of the United States which shall be made in Pursuance thereof; and all Treaties made, or which shall be made, under the Authority of the United States, shall be the supreme Law of the Land; and the Judges in every State shall be bound thereby, any Thing in the Constitution or Laws of any State to the Contrary notwithstanding.

The Senators and Representatives before mentioned, and the Members of the several State Legislatures, and all executive and judicial Officers, both of the United States and of the several States, shall be bound by Oath or Affirmation, to support this Constitution; but no religious Test shall ever be required as a Qualification to any Office or public Trust under the United States.

ARTICLE VII

The Ratification of the Conventions of nine States, shall be sufficient for the Establishment of this Constitution between the States so ratifying the Same.

DONE in Convention by the Unanimous Consent of the States present the Seventeenth Day of September in the Year of Our Lord one thousand seven hundred and Eighty seven and of the Independence of the United States of America the Twelfth. IN WITNESS whereof We have hereunto subscribed our Names.

Go. WASHINGTON—*Presidt.*
and deputy from Virginia

Attest WILLIAM JACKSON *Secretary*

New Hampshire

JOHN LANGDON	NICHOLAS GILMAN
Massachusetts	
NATHANIEL GORHAM	RUFUS KING
Connecticut	
WM. SAML. JOHNSON	ROGER SHERMAN
New York	
ALEXANDER HAMILTON	
New Jersey	
WIL: LIVINGSTON	WM. PATERSON.
DAVID BREARLEY.	JONA: DAYTON
Pennsylvania	
B FRANKLIN	THOS. FITZSIMONS
THOMAS MIFFLIN	JARED INGERSOLL
ROBT MORRIS	JAMES WILSON
GEO. CLYMER	GOUV MORRIS
Delaware	
GEO: READ	RICHARD BASSETT
GUNNING BEDFORD jun	JACO: BROOM
JOHN DICKINSON	

	Maryland	RICHD. DOBBS SPAIGHT	
JAMES MCHENRY	DANL CARROLL		*South Carolina*
DAN OF ST THOS. JENIFER		J. RUTLEDGE	CHARLES PINCKNEY
	Virginia	CHARLES COTESWORTH PINCKNEY	PIERCE BUTLER
JOHN BLAIR—	JAMES MADISON JR.		*Georgia*
	North Carolina	WILLIAM FEW	ABR BALDWIN
WM. BLOUNT	HU WILLIAMSON		

Articles in Addition to, and Amendment of, the Constitution of the United States of America, Proposed by Congress, and Ratified by the Legislatures of the Several States Pursuant to the Fifth Article of the Original Constitution

ARTICLE [I]

Congress shall make no law respecting an establishment of religion, or prohibiting the free exercise thereof; or abridging the freedom of speech, or of the press; or the right of the people peaceably to assemble, and to petition the Government for a redress of grievances.

ARTICLE [II]

A well regulated Militia, being necessary to the security of a free State, the right of the people to keep and bear Arms, shall not be infringed.

ARTICLE [III]

No Soldier shall, in time of peace be quartered in any house, without the consent of the Owner, nor in time of war, but in a manner to be prescribed by law.

ARTICLE [IV]

The right of the people to be secure in their persons, houses, papers, and effects, against unreasonable searches and seizures, shall not be violated, and no Warrants shall issue, but upon probable cause, supported by Oath or affirmation, and particularly describing the place to be searched, and the persons or things to be seized.

ARTICLE [V]

No person shall be held to answer for a capital, or otherwise infamous crime, unless on a presentment or indictment of a Grand Jury, except in cases arising in the land or naval forces, or in the Militia, when in actual service in time of War or public danger; nor shall any person be subject for the same offence to be twice put in jeopardy of life or limb; nor shall be compelled in any criminal case to be a witness against himself, nor be deprived of life, liberty, or property, without due process of law; nor shall private property be taken for public use, without just compensation.

ARTICLE [VI]

In all criminal prosecutions, the accused shall enjoy the right to a speedy and public trial, by an impartial jury of the State and district wherein the crime shall have been committed, which district shall have been previously ascertained by law, and to be informed of the nature and cause of the accusation; to be confronted with the witnesses against him; to have compulsory process for obtaining witnesses in his favor, and to have the Assistance of Counsel for his defence.

ARTICLE [VII]

In Suits at common law, where the value in controversy shall exceed twenty dollars, the right of trial by jury shall be preserved, and no fact tried by a jury, shall be otherwise reexamined in any Court of the United States, than according to the rules of the common law.

ARTICLE [VIII]

Excessive bail shall not be required, nor excessive fines imposed, nor cruel and unusual punishments inflicted.

ARTICLE [IX]

The enumeration in the Constitution, of certain rights, shall not be construed to deny or disparage others retained by the people.

ARTICLE [X]

The powers not delegated to the United States by the Constitution, nor prohibited by it to the States, are reserved to the States respectively, or to the people.

ARTICLE [XI]

The Judicial power of the United States shall not be construed to extend to any suit in law or equity, commenced or prosecuted against one of the United States by Citizens of another State, or by Citizens or Subjects of any Foreign State.

ARTICLE [XII]

The Electors shall meet in their respective states, and vote by ballot for President and Vice-President, one of whom, at least, shall not be an inhabitant of the same state with themselves; they shall name in their ballots the person voted for as President, and in distinct ballots the person voted for as Vice-President, and they shall make distinct lists of all persons voted for as President, and of all persons voted for as Vice-President, and of the number of votes for each, which lists they shall sign and certify, and transmit sealed to the seat of the government of the United States, directed to the President of the Senate;—The President of the Senate shall, in the presence of the Senate and House of Representatives, open all the certificates and the votes shall then be counted;—The person having the greatest number of votes for President, shall be the President, if such number be a majority of the whole number of Electors appointed; and if no person have such majority, then from the persons having the highest numbers not exceeding three on the list of those voted for as President, the House of Representatives shall choose immediately, by ballot, the President. But in choosing the President, the votes shall be taken by states, the representation from each state having one vote; a quorum for this purpose shall consist of a member or members from two-thirds of the states, and a majority of all the states shall be necessary to a choice. And if the House of Representatives shall not choose a President whenever the right of choice shall devolve upon them, before the fourth day of March next following, then the Vice-President shall act as President, as in the case of the death or other constitutional disability of the President.—The person having the greatest number of votes as Vice-President, shall be the Vice-President, if such number be a majority of the whole number of Electors appointed, and if no person have a majority, then from the two highest numbers on the list, the Senate shall choose the Vice-President; a quorum for the purpose shall consist of two-thirds of the whole number of Senators, and a majority of the whole number shall be necessary to a choice. But no person constitutionally ineligible to the office of President shall be eligible to that of Vice-President of the United States.[1]

[1] This Amendment was affected by the Twentieth Amendment.

ARTICLE XIII

Section 1. Neither slavery nor involuntary servitude, except as a punishment for crime whereof the party shall have been duly convicted, shall exist within the United States, or any place subject to their jurisdiction.

Section 2. Congress shall have power to enforce this article by appropriate legislation.

ARTICLE XIV

Section 1. All persons born or naturalized in the United States, and subject to the jurisdiction thereof, are citizens of the United States and of the State wherein they reside. No State shall make or enforce any law which shall abridge the privileges or immunities of citizens of the United States; nor shall any State deprive any person of life, liberty, or property, without due process of law; nor deny to any person within its jurisdiction the equal protection of the laws.

Section 2. Representatives shall be apportioned among the several States according to their respective numbers, counting the whole number of persons in each State, excluding Indians not taxed. But when the right to vote at any election for the choice of electors for President and Vice President of the United States, Representatives in Congress, the Executive and Judicial officers of a State, or the members of the Legislature thereof, is denied to any of the male inhabitants of such State, being twenty-one years of age, and citizens of the United States, or in any way abridged, except for participation in rebellion, or other crime, the basis of representation therein shall be reduced in the proportion which the number of such male citizens shall bear to the whole number of male citizens twenty-one years of age in such State.

Section 3. No person shall be a Senator or Representative in Congress, or elector of President and Vice President, or hold any office, civil or military, under the United States, or under any State, who, having previously taken an oath, as a member of Congress, or as an officer of the United States, or as a member of any State legislature, or as an executive or judicial officer of any State, to support the Constitution of the United States, shall have engaged in insurrection or rebellion against the same, or given aid or comfort to the enemies thereof. But Congress may by a vote of two-thirds of each House, remove such disability.

Section 4. The validity of the public debt of the United States, authorized by law, including debts incurred for payment of pensions and bounties for services in suppressing insurrection or rebellion, shall not be questioned. But neither the United States nor any State shall assume or pay any debt or obligation incurred in aid of insurrection or rebellion against the United States, or any claim for the loss or emancipation of any slave; but all such debts, obligations and claims shall be held illegal and void.

Section 5. The Congress shall have power to enforce, by appropriate legislation, the provisions of this article.

ARTICLE XV

Section 1. The right of citizens of the United States to vote shall not be denied or abridged by the United States or by any State on account of race, color, or previous condition of servitude.

Section 2. The Congress shall have power to enforce this article by appropriate legislation.

ARTICLE XVI

The Congress shall have power to lay and collect taxes on incomes, from whatever source derived, without apportionment among the several States, and without regard to any census or enumeration.

ARTICLE [XVII]

The Senate of the United States shall be composed of two Senators from each state, elected by the people thereof, for six years; and each Senator shall have one vote. The electors in each State shall have the qualifications requisite for electors of the most numerous branch of the State legislatures.

When vacancies happen in the representation of any State in the Senate, the executive authority of such State shall issue writs of election to fill such vacancies: *Provided*, That the legislature of any State may empower the executive thereof to make temporary appointments until the people fill the vacancies by election as the legislature may direct.

This amendment shall not be so construed as to affect the election or term of any Senator chosen before it becomes valid as part of the Constitution.

ARTICLE [XVIII]   [Repealed. See Article XXI]

Section 1. After one year from the ratification of this article the manufacture, sale, or transportation of intoxicating liquors within, the importation thereof into, or the exportation thereof from the United States and all territory subject to the jurisdiction thereof for beverage purposes is hereby prohibited.

Section 2. The Congress and the several States shall have concurrent power to enforce this article by appropriate legislation.

Section 3. This article shall be inoperative unless it shall have been ratified as an amendment to the Constitution by the legislatures of the several States, as provided in the Constitution, within seven years from the date of the submission hereof to the States by the Congress.

ARTICLE [XIX]

The right of citizens of the United States to vote shall not be denied or abridged by the United States or by any State on account of sex.

Congress shall have power to enforce this article by appropriate legislation.

ARTICLE [XX]

Section 1. The terms of the President and Vice President shall end at noon on the 20th day of January, and the terms of Senators and Representatives at noon on the 3d day of January, of the years in which such terms would have ended if this article had not been ratified; and the terms of their successors shall then begin.

Sec. 2. The Congress shall assemble at least once in every year, and such meeting shall begin at noon on the 3d day of January, unless they shall by law appoint a different day.

Sec. 3. If, at the time fixed for the beginning of the term of the President, the President elect shall have died, the Vice President elect shall become President. If a President shall not have been chosen before the time fixed for the beginning of his term, or if the President elect shall have failed to qualify, then the Vice President elect shall act as President until a President shall have qualified; and the Congress may by law provide for the case wherein neither a President elect nor a Vice President elect shall have qualified, declaring who shall then act as President, or the manner in which one who is to act shall be selected, and such person shall act accordingly until a President or Vice President shall have qualified.

Sec. 4. The Congress may by law provide for the case of the death of any of the persons from whom the House of Representatives may choose a President whenever the right of choice shall have devolved upon them, and for the case of the death of any of the persons from whom the Senate may choose a Vice President whenever the right of choice shall have devolved upon them.

Sec. 5. Sections 1 and 2 shall take effect on the 15th day of October following the ratification of this article.

Sec. 6. This article shall be inoperative unless it shall have been ratified as an amendment to the Constitution by the legislatures of three-fourths of the several States within seven years from the date of its submission.

ARTICLE [XXI]

Section 1. The eighteenth article of amendment to the Constitution of the United States is hereby repealed.

Sec. 2. The transportation or importation into any State, Territory, or possession of the United States for delivery or use therein of intoxicating liquors, in violation of the laws thereof, is hereby prohibited.

Sec. 3. This article shall be inoperative unless it shall have been ratified as an amendment to the Constitution by conventions in the several States, as provided in the Constitution, within seven years from the date of the submission hereof to the States by the Congress.

ARTICLE [XXII]

Section 1. No person shall be elected to the office of the President more than twice, and no person who has held the office of President, or acted as President, for more than two years of a term to which some other person was elected President shall be elected to the office of the President more than once. But this Article shall not apply to any person holding the office of President when this Article was proposed by the Congress, and shall not prevent any person who may be holding the office of President, or acting as Presi-

dent, during the term within which this Article becomes operative from holding the office of President or acting as President during the remainder of such term.

Sec. 2. This Article shall be inoperative unless it shall have been ratified as an amendment to the Constitution by the legislatures of three-fourths of the several States within seven years from the date of its submission to the States by the Congress.

ARTICLE [XXIII]

Section 1. The District constituting the seat of Government of the United States shall appoint in such manner as the Congress may direct:

A number of electors of President and Vice President equal to the whole number of Senators and Representatives in Congress to which the District would be entitled if it were a State, but in no event more than the least populous State; they shall be in

addition to those appointed by the States, but they shall be considered, for the purposes of the election of President and Vice President, to be electors appointed by a State; and they shall meet in the District and perform such duties as provided by the twelfth article of amendment.

Sec. 2. The Congress shall have power to enforce this article by appropriate legislation.

ARTICLE [XXIV]

Section 1. The right of citizens of the United States to vote in any primary or other election for President or Vice President, for electors for President or Vice President, or for Senator or Representative in Congress, shall not be denied or abridged by the

United States or any State by reason of failure to pay any poll tax or other tax.

Sec. 2. The Congress shall have power to enforce this article by appropriate legislation.

ARTICLE [XXV]

Section 1. In case of the removal of the President from office or of his death or resignation, the Vice President shall become President.

Sec. 2. Whenever there is a vacancy in the office of the Vice President, the President shall nominate a Vice President who shall take office upon confirmation by a majority vote of both Houses of Congress.

Sec. 3. Whenever the President transmits to the President pro tempore of the Senate and the Speaker of the House of Representatives his written declaration that he is unable to discharge the powers and duties of his office, and until he transmits to them a written declaration to the contrary, such powers and duties shall be discharged by the Vice President as Acting President.

Sec. 4. Whenever the Vice President and a majority of either the principal officers of the executive departments or of such other body as Congress may by law provide, transmit to the President pro tempore of the Senate and the Speaker of the House of Representatives their written declaration that the President is unable to discharge the powers and duties of his office, the Vice President shall immediately assume the powers and duties of the office as Acting President.

Thereafter, when the President transmits to the President pro tempore of the Senate and the Speaker of the House of Representatives his written declaration that no inability exists, he shall resume the powers and duties of his office unless the Vice President and a majority of either the principal officers of the executive department or of such other body as Congress may by law provide, transmit within four days to the President pro tempore of the Senate and the Speaker of the House of Representatives their written declaration that the President is unable to discharge the powers and duties of his office. Thereupon Congress shall decide the issue, assembling within forty-eight hours for that purpose if not in session. If the Congress, within twenty-one days after receipt of the latter written declaration, or, if Congress is not in session, within twenty-one days after Congress is required to assemble, determines by two-thirds vote of both Houses that the President is unable to discharge the powers and duties of his office, the Vice President shall continue to discharge the same as Acting President; otherwise, the President shall resume the powers and duties of his office.

ARTICLE [XXVI]

Section 1. The right of citizens of the United States, who are eighteen years of age or older, to vote shall not be denied or abridged by the United States or by any State on account of age.

Sec. 2. The Congress shall have power to enforce this article by appropriate legislation.

ARTICLE [XXVII][1]

[1] "Article [XXVII]" editorially added. Originally read "Article the second".

No law, varying the compensation for the services of the Senators and Representatives, shall take effect, until an election of Representatives shall have intervened.

FEDERAL
RULES OF CIVIL PROCEDURE
FOR THE
UNITED STATES DISTRICT COURTS

Amendments received to May 13, 2005

Complete Annotation Materials, see Title 28 U.S.C.A.

I. SCOPE OF RULES—ONE FORM OF ACTION

Rule 1. Scope and Purpose of Rules

These rules govern the procedure in the United States district courts in all suits of a civil nature whether cognizable as cases at law or in equity or in admiralty, with the exceptions stated in Rule 81. They shall be construed and administered to secure the just, speedy, and inexpensive determination of every action.

(As amended Dec. 29, 1948, eff. Oct. 20, 1949; Feb. 28, 1966, eff. July 1, 1966; Apr. 22, 1993, eff. Dec. 1, 1993.)

ADVISORY COMMITTEE NOTES

1937 Adoption

1. Rule 81 states certain limitations in the application of these rules to enumerated special proceedings.

2. The expression "district courts of the United States" appearing in the statute authorizing the Supreme Court of the United States to promulgate rules of civil procedure does not include the district courts held in the territories and insular possessions. See *Mookini et al. v. United States,* 1938, 58 S.Ct. 543, 303 U.S. 201, 82 L.Ed. 748.

3. These rules are drawn under the authority of the Act of June 19, 1934, U.S.C., Title 28, § 723b [see 2072] (Rules in actions at law; Supreme Court authorized to make), and § 723c [see 2072] (Union of equity and action at law rules; power of Supreme Court) and also other grants of rule making power to the Court. See Clark and Moore, *A New Federal Civil Procedure—I. The Background,* 44 Yale L.J. 387, 391 (1935). Under § 723b after the rules have taken effect all laws in conflict therewith are of no further force or effect. In accordance with § 723c the Court has united the general rules prescribed for cases in equity with those in actions at law so as to secure one form of civil action and procedure for both. See Rule 2 (One Form of Action). For the former practice in equity and at law see U.S.C.A., Title 28, §§ 723 and 730 [see 2071 et seq.] (conferring power on the Supreme Court to make rules of practice in equity) and the [former] Equity Rules promulgated thereunder; U.S.C., Title 28, [former] § 724 (Conformity act); [former] Equity Rule 22 (Action at Law Erroneously Begun as Suit in Equity—Transfer); [former] Equity Rule 23 (Matters Ordinarily Determinable at Law When Arising in Suit in Equity to be Disposed of Therein); U.S.C., Title 28, [former] §§ 397 (Amendments to pleadings when case brought to wrong side of court), and 398 (Equitable defenses and equitable relief in actions at law).

4. With the second sentence compare U.S.C., Title 28, [former] §§ 777 (Defects of form; amendments), [former] 767 (Amendment of process); [former] Equity Rule 19 (Amendments Generally).

1948 Amendment

The amendment effective Oct. 20, 1949, substituted the words "United States district courts" for the words "district courts of the United States."

1966 Amendment

This is the fundamental change necessary to effect unification of the civil and admiralty procedure. Just as the 1938 rules abolished the distinction between actions at law and suits in equity, this change would abolish the distinction between civil actions and suits in admiralty. See also Rule 81.

1993 Amendments

The purpose of this revision, adding the words "and administered" to the second sentence, is to recognize the affirmative duty of the court to exercise the authority conferred by these rules to ensure that civil litigation is resolved not only fairly, but also without undue cost or delay. As officers of the court, attorneys share this responsibility with the judge to whom the case is assigned.

Rule 2. One Form of Action

There shall be one form of action to be known as "civil action".

ADVISORY COMMITTEE NOTES

1937 Adoption

1. This rule modifies U.S.C., Title 28, [former] § 384 (Suits in equity, when not sustainable). U.S.C., Title 28, §§ 723 and 730 [sec. 2071, et seq.] (conferring power on the Supreme Court to make rules of practice in equity), are unaffected in so far as they relate to the rule making power in admiralty. These sections, together with § 723b [sec. 2072] (Rules in actions at law; Supreme Court authorized to make) are continued in so far as they are not inconsistent with § 2072, formerly § 723c (Union of equity and action at law rules; power of Supreme Court). See Note 3 to Rule 1. U.S.C., Title 28, [former] §§ 724 (Conformity act), 397

(Amendments to pleadings when case brought to wrong side of court) and 398 (Equitable defenses and equitable relief in actions at law) are superseded.

2. Reference to actions at law or suits in equity in all statutes should now be treated as referring to the civil action prescribed in these rules.

3. This rule follows in substance the usual introductory statements to code practices which provide for a single action and mode of procedure, with abolition of forms of action and procedural distinctions. Representative statutes are N.Y. Code 1848 (Laws 1848, ch. 379) § 62; N.Y.C.P.A. (1937) § 8; Calif.Code Civ.Proc. (Deering, 1937) § 307; 2 Minn.Stat.Ann. 1945 § 540.01; 2 Wash.Rev.Stat.Ann. (Remington, 1932) §§ 153, 255.

II. COMMENCEMENT OF ACTION; SERVICE OF PROCESS, PLEADINGS, MOTIONS, AND ORDERS

Rule 3.   Commencement of Action

A civil action is commenced by filing a complaint with the court.

ADVISORY COMMITTEE NOTES

1937 Adoption

1. Rule 5(e) defines what constitutes filing with the court.

2. This rule governs the commencement of all actions, including those brought by or against the United States or an officer or agency thereof, regardless of whether service is to be made personally pursuant to Rule 4(d), or otherwise pursuant to Rule 4(e).

3. With this rule compare [former] Equity Rule 12 (Issue of Subpoena—Time for Answer) and the following statutes (and other similar statutes) which provide a similar method for commencing an action:

U.S.C., Title 28:

     § 45 [former] (District courts; practice and procedure in certain cases under interstate commerce laws).

     § 762 [see 1402] (Petition in suit against United States).

     § 766 [see 2409] (Partition suits where United States is tenant in common or joint tenant).

4. This rule provides that the first step in an action is the filing of the complaint. Under Rule 4(a) this is to be followed forthwith by issuance of a summons and its delivery to an officer for service. Other rules providing for dismissal for failure to prosecute suggest a method available to attack unreasonable delay in prosecuting an action after it has been commenced. When a Federal or State statute of limitations is pleaded as a defense, a question may arise under this rule whether the mere filing of the complaint stops the running of the statute, or whether any further step is required, such as, service of the summons and complaint or their delivery to the marshal for service. The answer to this question may depend on whether it is competent for the Supreme Court, exercising the power to make rules of procedure without affecting substantive rights, to vary the operation of statutes of limitations. The requirement of rule 4(a) that the clerk shall forthwith issue the summons and deliver it to the marshal for service will reduce the chances of such a question arising.

Rule 4.   Summons

(a) Form. The summons shall be signed by the clerk, bear the seal of the court, identify the court and the parties, be directed to the defendant, and state the name and address of the plaintiff's attorney or, if unrepresented, of the plaintiff. It shall also state the time within which the defendant must appear and defend, and notify the defendant that failure to do so will result in a judgment by default against the defendant for the relief demanded in the complaint. The court may allow a summons to be amended.

(b) Issuance. Upon or after filing the complaint, the plaintiff may present a summons to the clerk for signature and seal. If the summons is in proper form, the clerk shall sign, seal, and issue it to the plaintiff for service on the defendant. A summons, or a copy of the summons if addressed to multiple defendants, shall be issued for each defendant to be served.

(c) Service with Complaint; by Whom Made.

(1) A summons shall be served together with a copy of the complaint. The plaintiff is responsible for service of a summons and complaint within the time allowed under subdivision (m) and shall furnish the person effecting service with the necessary copies of the summons and complaint.

(2) Service may be effected by any person who is not a party and who is at least 18 years of age. At the request of the plaintiff, however, the court may direct that service be effected by a United States marshal, deputy United States marshal, or other person or officer specially appointed by the court for that purpose. Such an appointment must be made when the plaintiff is authorized to proceed in forma pauperis pursuant to 28 U.S.C. § 1915 or is authorized to proceed as a seaman under 28 U.S.C. § 1916.

(d) Waiver of Service; Duty to Save Costs of Service; Request to Waive.

(1) A defendant who waives service of a summons does not thereby waive any objection to the venue or to the jurisdiction of the court over the person of the defendant.

(2) An individual, corporation, or association that is subject to service under subdivision (e), (f), or (h) and that receives notice of an action in the manner provided in this paragraph has a duty to avoid unnecessary costs of serving the summons. To

avoid costs, the plaintiff may notify such a defendant of the commencement of the action and request that the defendant waive service of a summons. The notice and request

(A) shall be in writing and shall be addressed directly to the defendant, if an individual, or else to an officer or managing or general agent (or other agent authorized by appointment or law to receive service of process) of a defendant subject to service under subdivision (h);

(B) shall be dispatched through first-class mail or other reliable means;

(C) shall be accompanied by a copy of the complaint and shall identify the court in which it has been filed;

(D) shall inform the defendant, by means of a text prescribed in an official form promulgated pursuant to Rule 84, of the consequences of compliance and of a failure to comply with the request;

(E) shall set forth the date on which the request is sent;

(F) shall allow the defendant a reasonable time to return the waiver, which shall be at least 30 days from the date on which the request is sent, or 60 days from that date if the defendant is addressed outside any judicial district of the United States; and

(G) shall provide the defendant with an extra copy of the notice and request, as well as a prepaid means of compliance in writing.

If a defendant located within the United States fails to comply with a request for waiver made by a plaintiff located within the United States, the court shall impose the costs subsequently incurred in effecting service on the defendant unless good cause for the failure be shown.

(3) A defendant that, before being served with process, timely returns a waiver so requested is not required to serve an answer to the complaint until 60 days after the date on which the request for waiver of service was sent, or 90 days after that date if the defendant was addressed outside any judicial district of the United States.

(4) When the plaintiff files a waiver of service with the court, the action shall proceed, except as provided in paragraph (3), as if a summons and complaint had been served at the time of filing the waiver, and no proof of service shall be required.

(5) The costs to be imposed on a defendant under paragraph (2) for failure to comply with a request to waive service of a summons shall include the costs subsequently incurred in effecting service under subdivision (e), (f), or (h), together with the costs, including a reasonable attorney's fee, of any motion required to collect the costs of service.

(e) Service Upon Individuals Within a Judicial District of the United States. Unless otherwise provided by federal law, service upon an individual from whom a waiver has not been obtained and filed, other than an infant or an incompetent person, may be effected in any judicial district of the United States:

(1) pursuant to the law of the state in which the district court is located, or in which service is effected, for the service of a summons upon the defendant in an action brought in the courts of general jurisdiction of the State; or

(2) by delivering a copy of the summons and of the complaint to the individual personally or by leaving copies thereof at the individual's dwelling house or usual place of abode with some person of suitable age and discretion then residing therein or by delivering a copy of the summons and of the complaint to an agent authorized by appointment or by law to receive service of process.

(f) Service Upon Individuals in a Foreign Country. Unless otherwise provided by federal law, service upon an individual from whom a waiver has not been obtained and filed, other than an infant or an incompetent person, may be effected in a place not within any judicial district of the United States:

(1) by any internationally agreed means reasonably calculated to give notice, such as those means authorized by the Hague Convention on the Service Abroad of Judicial and Extrajudicial Documents; or

(2) if there is no internationally agreed means of service or the applicable international agreement allows other means of service, provided that service is reasonably calculated to give notice:

(A) in the manner prescribed by the law of the foreign country for service in that country in an action in any of its courts of general jurisdiction; or

(B) as directed by the foreign authority in response to a letter rogatory or letter of request; or

(C) unless prohibited by the law of the foreign country, by

(i) delivery to the individual personally of a copy of the summons and the complaint; or

(ii) any form of mail requiring a signed receipt, to be addressed and dispatched by the clerk of the court to the party to be served; or

(3) by other means not prohibited by international agreement as may be directed by the court.

(g) Service Upon Infants and Incompetent Persons. Service upon an infant or an incompetent person in a judicial district of the United States shall be effected in the manner prescribed by the law of the state in which the service is made for the service of summons or other like process upon any such defendant in an action brought in the courts of general jurisdiction of that state. Service upon an infant or an incompetent person in a place not within any judicial district of the United States shall be effected in the manner prescribed by paragraph (2)(A) or (2)(B) of subdivision (f) or by such means as the court may direct.

(h) Service Upon Corporations and Associations. Unless otherwise provided by federal law, service upon a domestic or foreign corporation or upon a partnership or other unincorporated association that is subject to suit under a common name, and from which a waiver of service has not been obtained and filed, shall be effected:

(1) in a judicial district of the United States in the manner prescribed for individuals by subdivision (e)(1), or by delivering a copy of the summons and of the complaint to an officer, a managing or general agent, or to any other agent authorized by appointment or by law to receive service of process and, if the agent is one authorized by statute to receive service and the statute so requires, by also mailing a copy to the defendant, or

(2) in a place not within any judicial district of the United States in any manner prescribed for individuals by subdivision (f) except personal delivery as provided in paragraph (2)(C)(i) thereof.

(i) Serving the United States, Its Agencies, Corporations, Officers, or Employees.

(1) Service upon the United States shall be effected

  (A) by delivering a copy of the summons and of the complaint to the United States attorney for the district in which the action is brought or to an assistant United States attorney or clerical employee designated by the United States attorney in a writing filed with the clerk of the court or by sending a copy of the summons and of the complaint by registered or certified mail addressed to the civil process clerk at the office of the United States attorney and

  (B) by also sending a copy of the summons and of the complaint by registered or certified mail to the Attorney General of the United States at Washington, District of Columbia, and

  (C) in any action attacking the validity of an order of an officer or agency of the United States not made a party, by also sending a copy of the summons and of the complaint by registered or certified mail to the officer or agency.

(2)(A) Service on an agency or corporation of the United States, or an officer or employee of the United States sued only in an official capacity, is effected by serving the United States in the manner prescribed by Rule 4(i)(1) and by also sending a copy of the summons and complaint by registered or certified mail to the officer, employee, agency, or corporation.

  (B) Service on an officer or employee of the United States sued in an individual capacity for acts or omissions occurring in connection with the performance of duties on behalf of the United States—whether or not the officer or employee is sued also in an official capacity—is effected by serving the United States in the manner prescribed by Rule 4(i)(1) and by serving the officer or employee in the manner prescribed by Rule 4 (e), (f), or (g).

(3) The court shall allow a reasonable time to serve process under Rule 4(i) for the purpose of curing the failure to serve:

  (A) all persons required to be served in an action governed by Rule 4(i)(2)(A), if the plaintiff has served either the United States attorney or the Attorney General of the United States, or

  (B) the United States in an action governed by Rule 4(i)(2)(B), if the plaintiff has served an officer or employee of the United States sued in an individual capacity.

(j) Service Upon Foreign, State, or Local Governments.

(1) Service upon a foreign state or a political subdivision, agency, or instrumentality thereof shall be effected pursuant to 28 U.S.C. § 1608.

(2) Service upon a state, municipal corporation, or other governmental organization subject to suit shall be effected by delivering a copy of the summons and of the complaint to its chief executive officer or by serving the summons and complaint in the manner prescribed by the law of that state for the service of summons or other like process upon any such defendant.

(k) Territorial Limits of Effective Service.

(1) Service of a summons or filing a waiver of service is effective to establish jurisdiction over the person of a defendant

  (A) who could be subjected to the jurisdiction of a court of general jurisdiction in the state in which the district court is located, or

  (B) who is a party joined under Rule 14 or Rule 19 and is served at a place within a judicial district of the United States and not more than 100 miles from the place from which the summons issues, or

  (C) who is subject to the federal interpleader jurisdiction under 28 U.S.C. § 1335, or

  (D) when authorized by a statute of the United States.

(2) If the exercise of jurisdiction is consistent with the Constitution and laws of the United States, serving a summons or filing a waiver of service is also effective, with respect to claims arising under

federal law, to establish personal jurisdiction over the person of any defendant who is not subject to the jurisdiction of the courts of general jurisdiction of any state.

(*l*) **Proof of Service.** If service is not waived, the person effecting service shall make proof thereof to the court. If service is made by a person other than a United States marshal or deputy United States marshal, the person shall make affidavit thereof. Proof of service in a place not within any judicial district of the United States shall, if effected under paragraph (1) of subdivision (f), be made pursuant to the applicable treaty or convention, and shall, if effected under paragraph (2) or (3) thereof, include a receipt signed by the addressee or other evidence of delivery to the addressee satisfactory to the court. Failure to make proof of service does not affect the validity of the service. The court may allow proof of service to be amended.

(m) **Time Limit for Service.** If service of the summons and complaint is not made upon a defendant within 120 days after the filing of the complaint, the court, upon motion or on its own initiative after notice to the plaintiff, shall dismiss the action without prejudice as to that defendant or direct that service be effected within a specified time; provided that if the plaintiff shows good cause for the failure, the court shall extend the time for service for an appropriate period. This subdivision does not apply to service in a foreign country pursuant to subdivision (f) or (j)(1).

(n) **Seizure of Property; Service of Summons Not Feasible.**

(1) If a statute of the United States so provides, the court may assert jurisdiction over property. Notice to claimants of the property shall then be sent in the manner provided by the statute or by service of a summons under this rule.

(2) Upon a showing that personal jurisdiction over a defendant cannot, in the district where the action is brought, be obtained with reasonable efforts by service of summons in any manner authorized by this rule, the court may assert jurisdiction over any of the defendant's assets found within the district by seizing the assets under the circumstances and in the manner provided by the law of the state in which the district court is located.

(As amended Jan. 21, 1963, eff. July 1, 1963; Feb. 28, 1966, eff. July 1, 1966; Apr. 29, 1980, eff. Aug. 1, 1980; Jan. 12, 1983, Pub.L. 97–462, § 2, 96 Stat. 2527; Mar. 2, 1987, eff. Aug. 1, 1987; Apr. 22, 1993, eff. Dec. 1, 1993; Apr. 17, 2000, eff. Dec. 1, 2000.)

ADVISORY COMMITTEE NOTES

1937 Adoption

Note to Subdivision (a). With the provision permitting additional summons upon request of the plaintiff, compare former Equity Rule 14 (Alias Subpoena) and the last sentence of former Equity Rule 12 (Issue of Subpoena—Time for Answer).

Note to Subdivision (b). This rule prescribes a form of summons which follows substantially the requirements stated in former Equity Rules 12 (Issue of Subpoena—Time for Answer) and 7 (Process, Mesne and Final).

U.S.C., Title 28, § 721 [now 1691] (Sealing and testing of writs) is substantially continued insofar as it applies to a summons, but its requirements as to teste of process are superseded. U.S.C., Title 28, [former] § 722 (Teste of process, day of) is superseded.

See Rule 12(a) for a statement of the time within which the defendant is required to appear and defend.

Note to Subdivision (c). This rule does not affect U.S.C., Title 28, § 503 [see 566], as amended June 15, 1935 (Marshals; duties) and such statutes as the following insofar as they provide for service of process by a marshal, but modifies them in so far as they may imply service by a marshal only:

U.S.C., Title 15:

§ 5 (Bringing in additional parties) (Sherman Act)

§ 10 (Bringing in additional parties)

§ 25 (Restraining violations; procedure)

U.S.C., Title 28:

§ 45 [former] (Practice and procedure in certain cases under the interstate commerce laws)

Compare [former] Equity Rule 15 (Process, by Whom Served).

Note to Subdivision (d). Under this rule the complaint must always be served with the summons.

Paragraph (1). For an example of a statute providing for service upon an agent of an individual see U.S.C., Title 28, § 109 [now 1400, 1694] (Patent cases).

Paragraph (3). This enumerates the officers and agents of a corporation or of a partnership or other unincorporated association upon whom service of process may be made, and permits service of process only upon the officers, managing or general agents, or agents authorized by appointment or by law, of the corporation, partnership or unincorporated association against which the action is brought. See *Christian v. International Ass'n of Machinists*, 7 F.(2d) 481 (D.C.Ky. 1925) and *Singleton v. Order of Railway Conductors of America*, 9 F.Supp. 417 (D.C.Ill.1935). Compare *Operative Plasterers' and Cement Finishers' International Ass'n of the United States and Canada v. Case*, 93 F.(2d) 56 (App.D.C. 1937).

For a statute authorizing service upon a specified agent and requiring mailing to the defendant, see U.S.C., Title 6, § 7 (Surety companies as sureties; appointment of agents; service of process).

Paragraphs (4) and (5) provide a uniform and comprehensive method of service for all actions against the United States or an officer or agency thereof. For statutes providing for such service, see U.S.C., Title 7, §§ 217 (Proceedings for suspension of orders) 499k (Injunctions; application of injunction laws governing orders of Interstate Commerce Commission), 608c(15)(B) (Court review of ruling of Secretary of Agriculture), and 855 (making § 608c(15)(B) applicable to orders of the Secretary of Agriculture as to handlers of anti-hog-cholera serum and hog-cholera virus); U.S.C., Title

26, § 3679, (Bill in chancery to clear title to realty on which the United States has a lien for taxes); U.S.C., Title 28, former §§ 45, (District Courts; practice and procedure in certain cases under the interstate commerce laws), [former] 763 (Petition in suit against the United States; service; appearance by district attorney), 766 [now 2409] (Partition suits where United States is tenant in common or joint tenant), 902 [now 2410] (Foreclosure of mortgages or other liens on property in which the United States has an interest). These and similar statutes are modified in so far as they prescribe a different method of service or dispense with the service of a summons.

For the [former] Equity Rule on service, see [former] Equity Rule 13, Manner of Serving Subpoena.

Note to Subdivision (e). The provisions for the service of a summons or of notice or of an order in lieu of summons contained in U.S.C., Title 8, § 405 (Cancellation of certificates of citizenship fraudulently or illegally procured) (service by publication in accordance with State law); U.S.C., Title 28, § 118 [now 1655] (Absent defendants in suits to enforce liens); U.S.C., Title 35, § 72a [now 146, 291] (Jurisdiction of District Court of United States for the District of Columbia in certain equity suits where adverse parties reside elsewhere) (service by publication against parties residing in foreign countries); U.S.C., Title 38, § 445 [now 784] (Action against the United States on a veteran's contract of insurance) (parties not inhabitants of or not found within the district may be served with an order of the court, personally or by publication) and similar statutes are continued by this rule. Title 24, § 378 [now title 13, § 336] of the Code of the District of Columbia (Publication against non-resident; those absent for six months; unknown heirs or devisees; for divorce or in rem; actual service beyond District) is continued by this rule.

Note to Subdivision (f). This rule enlarges to some extent the present rule as to where service may be made. It does not, however, enlarge the jurisdiction of the district courts.

U.S.C., Title 28, §§ 113 [now 1392] (Suits in States containing more than one district) (where there are two or more defendants residing in different districts), [former] 115 (Suits of a local nature), 116 [now 1392] (Property in different districts in same state), [former] 838 (Executions run in all districts of state); U.S.C., Title 47, § 13 (Action for damages against a railroad or telegraph company whose officer or agent in control of a telegraph line refuses or fails to operate such line in a certain manner—"upon any agent of the company found in such state"); U.S.C., Title 49, § 321(c) [now 10330(b)] (Requiring designation of a process agent by interstate motor carriers and in case of failure so to do, service may be made upon any agent in the state) and similar statutes, allowing the running of process throughout a state, are substantially continued.

U.S.C., Title 15, §§ 5 (Bringing in additional parties) (Sherman Act), 25 (Restraining violations; procedure); U.S.C., Title 28, §§ 44 [now 2321] (Procedure in certain cases under interstate commerce laws; service of processes of court), 117 [now 754, 1692] (Property in different states in same circuit; jurisdiction of receiver), 839 [now 2413] (Executions; run in every State and Territory) and similar statutes, providing for the running of process beyond the territorial limits of a State, are expressly continued.

Note to Subdivision (g). With the second sentence compare [former] Equity Rule 15, (Process, by Whom Served).

Note to Subdivision (h). This rule substantially continues U.S.C., Title 28, [former] § 767 (Amendment of process).

1963 Amendment

Subdivision (b). Under amended subdivision (e) of this rule, an action may be commenced against a nonresident of the State in which the district court is held by complying with State procedures. Frequently the form of the summons or notice required in these cases by State law differs from the Federal form of summons described in present subdivision (b) and exemplified in Form 1. To avoid confusion, the amendment of subdivision (b) states that a form of summons or notice, corresponding "as nearly as may be" to the State form, shall be employed. See also a corresponding amendment of Rule 12(a) with regard to the time to answer.

Subdivision (d)(4). This paragraph, governing service upon the United States, is amended to allow the use of certified mail as an alternative to registered mail for sending copies of the papers to the Attorney General or to a United States officer or agency. Cf. N.J. Rule 4:5–2. See also the amendment of Rule 30(f)(1).

Subdivision (d)(7). Formerly a question was raised whether this paragraph, in the context of the rule as a whole, authorized service in original Federal actions pursuant to State statutes permitting service on a State official as a means of bringing a nonresident motorist defendant into court. It was argued in *McCoy v. Siler*, 205 F.2d 498, 501–2 (3d Cir.) (concurring opinion), cert. denied, 346 U.S. 872, 74 S.Ct. 120, 98 L.Ed. 380 (1953), that the effective service in those cases occurred not when the State official was served but when notice was given to the defendant outside the State, and that subdivision (f) (Territorial limits of effective service), as then worded, did not authorize out-of-State service. This contention found little support. A considerable number of cases held the service to be good, either by fixing upon the service on the official within the State as the effective service, thus satisfying the wording of subdivision (f) as it then stood, see *Holbrook v. Cafiero*, 18 F.R.D. 218 (D.Md. 1955); *Pasternack v. Dalo*, 17 F.R.D. 420 (W.D.Pa.1955); *Super Prods. Corp. v. Parkin*, 20 F.R.D. 377 (S.D.N.Y.1957), or by reading paragraph (7) as not limited by subdivision (f). See *Giffin v. Ensign*, 234 F.2d 307 (3d Cir. 1956); 2 Moore's *Federal Practice*, ¶4.19 (2d ed. 1948); 1 Barron & Holtzoff, *Federal Practice & Procedure* § 182.1 (Wright ed. 1960); Comment, 27 U. of Chi.L.Rev. 751 (1960). See also *Olberding v. Illinois Central R.R.*, 201 F.2d 582 (6th Cir.), rev'd on other grounds, 346 U.S. 338, 74 S.Ct. 83, 98 L.Ed. 39 (1953); *Feinsinger v. Bard*, 195 F.2d 45 (7th Cir. 1952).

An important and growing class of State statutes base personal jurisdiction over nonresidents on the doing of acts or on other contacts within the State, and permit notice to be given the defendant outside the State without any requirement of service on a local State official. See, e.g., Ill.Ann. Stat., c. 110, §§ 16, 17 (Smith–Hurd 1956); Wis.Stat. § 262.06 (1959). This service, employed in original Federal actions pursuant to paragraph (7), has also been held proper. See *Farr & Co. v. Cia. Intercontinental de Nav. de Cuba*, 243 F.2d 342 (2d Cir. 1957); *Kappus v. Western Hills Oil, Inc.*, 24 F.R.D. 123 (E.D.Wis.1959); *Star v. Rogalny*, 162 F.Supp. 181 (E.D.Ill.1957). It has also been held that the clause of paragraph (7) which permits service "in the manner prescribed by the law of the state," etc., is not limited by subdivision (c) requiring that service of all process be made by certain designated persons. See *Farr & Co. v. Cia. Intercontinental de Nav. de Cuba, supra.* But *cf. Sappia v. Lauro Lines,* 130 F.Supp. 810 (S.D.N.Y.1955).

The salutary results of these cases are intended to be preserved. See paragraph (7), with a clarified reference to State law, and amended subdivisions (e) and (f).

Subdivision (e). For the general relation between subdivisions (d) and (e), see 2 Moore, supra, ¶4.32.

The amendment of the first sentence inserting the word "thereunder" supports the original intention that the "order of court" must be authorized by a specific United States statute. See 1 Barron & Holtzoff, supra, at 731. The clause added at the end of the first sentence expressly adopts the view taken by commentators that, if no manner of service is prescribed in the statute or order, the service may be made in a manner stated in Rule 4. See 2 Moore, supra, ¶4.32, at 1004; Smit, *International Aspects of Federal Civil Procedure,* 61 Colum.L.Rev. 1031, 1036–39 (1961). But see Commentary, 5 Fed. Rules Serv. 791 (1942).

Examples of the statutes to which the first sentence relates are 28 U.S.C. § 2361 (Interpleader; process and procedure); 28 U.S.C. § 1655 (Lien enforcement; absent defendants).

The second sentence, added by amendment, expressly allows resort in original Federal actions to the procedures provided by State law for effecting service on nonresident parties (as well as on domiciliaries not found within the State). See, as illustrative, the discussion under amended subdivision (d)(7) of service pursuant to State nonresident motorist statutes and other comparable State statutes. Of particular interest is the change brought about by the reference in this sentence to State procedures for commencing actions against nonresidents by attachment and the like, accompanied by notice. Although an action commenced in a State court by attachment may be removed to the Federal court if ordinary conditions for removal are satisfied, see 28 U.S.C. § 1450; *Rorick v. Devon Syndicate, Ltd.,* 307 U.S. 299, 59 S.Ct. 877, 83 L.Ed. 1303 (1939); *Clark v. Wells,* 203 U.S. 164, 27 S.Ct. 43, 51 L.Ed. 138 (1906), there has heretofore been no provision recognized by the courts for commencing an original Federal civil action by attachment. See Currie, *Attachment and Garnishment in the Federal Courts,* 59 Mich.L.Rev. 337 (1961), arguing that this result came about through historical anomaly. Rule 64, which refers to attachment, garnishment, and similar procedures under State law, furnishes only provisional remedies in actions otherwise validly commenced. See *Big Vein Coal Co. v. Read,* 229 U.S. 31, 33 S.Ct. 694, 57 L.Ed. 1053 (1913); *Davis v. Ensign–Bickford Co.,* 139 F.2d 624 (8th Cir. 1944); 7 Moore's *Federal Practice* ¶64.05 (2d ed. 1954); 3 Barron & Holtzoff, *Federal Practice & Procedure* § 1423 (Wright ed. 1958); but *cf.* Note, 13 So.Calif.L.Rev. 361 (1940). The amendment will now permit the institution of original Federal actions against nonresidents through the use of familiar State procedures by which property of these defendants is brought within the custody of the court and some appropriate service is made upon them.

The necessity of satisfying subject-matter jurisdictional requirements and requirements of venue will limit the practical utilization of these methods of effecting service. Within those limits, however, there appears to be no reason for denying plaintiffs means of commencing actions in Federal courts which are generally available in the State courts. See 1 Barron & Holtzoff, supra, at 374–80; Nordbye, *Comments on Proposed Amendments to Rules of Civil Procedure for the United States District Courts,* 18 F.R.D. 105, 106 (1956); Note, 34 Corn.L.Q. 103 (1948); Note, 13 So.Calif.L.Rev. 361 (1940).

If the circumstances of a particular case satisfy the applicable Federal law (first sentence of Rule 4(e), as amended) and the applicable State law (second sentence), the party seeking to make the service may proceed under the Federal or the State law, at his option.

See also amended Rule 13(a), and the Advisory Committee's Note thereto.

Subdivision (f). The first sentence is amended to assure the effectiveness of service outside the territorial limits of the State in all the cases in which any of the rules authorize service beyond those boundaries. Besides the preceding provisions of Rule 4, see Rule 71A(d)(3). In addition, the new second sentence of the subdivision permits effective service within a limited area outside the State in certain special situations, namely, to bring in additional parties to a counterclaim or cross-claim (Rule 13 (h)), impleaded parties (Rule 14), and indispensable or conditionally necessary parties to a pending action (Rule 19); and to secure compliance with an order of commitment for civil contempt. In those situations effective service can be made at points not more than 100 miles distant from the courthouse in which the action is commenced, or to which it is assigned or transferred for trial.

The bringing in of parties under the 100-mile provision in the limited situations enumerated is designed to promote the objective of enabling the court to determine entire controversies. In the light of present-day facilities for communication and travel, the territorial range of the service allowed, analogous to that which applies to the service of a subpoena under Rule 45(e)(1), can hardly work hardship on the parties summoned. The provision will be especially useful in metropolitan areas spanning more than one State. Any requirements of subject-matter jurisdiction and venue will still have to be satisfied as to the parties brought in, although these requirements will be eased in some instances when the parties can be regarded as "ancillary." See *Pennsylvania R.R. v. Erie Avenue Warehouse Co.,* 5 F.R.Serv.2d 14a.62, Case 2 (3d Cir.1962); *Dery v. Wyer,* 265 F.2d 804 (2d Cir.1959); *United Artists Corp. v. Masterpiece Productions, Inc.,* 221 F.2d 213 (2d Cir.1955); *Lesnik v. Public Industrials Corp.,* 144 F.2d 968 (2d Cir.1944); *Vaughn v. Terminal Transp. Co.,* 162 F.Supp. 647 (E.D.Tenn.1957); and compare the fifth paragraph of the Advisory Committee's Note to Rule 4(e), as amended. The amendment is but a moderate extension of the territorial reach of Federal process and has ample practical justification. See 2 Moore, supra, § 4.01[13] (Supp. 1960); 1 Barron & Holtzoff, supra, § 184; Note, 51 Nw. U.L.Rev. 354 (1956). But *cf.* Nordbye, *Comments on Proposed Amendments to Rules of Civil Procedure for the United States District Courts,* 18 F.R.D. 105, 106 (1956).

As to the need for enlarging the territorial area in which orders of commitment for civil contempt may be served, see *Graber v. Graber,* 93 F.Supp. 281 (D.D.C.1950); *Teele Soap Mfg. Co. v. Pine Tree Products Co., Inc.,* 8 F.Supp. 546 (D.N.H.1934); *Mitchell v. Dexter,* 244 Fed. 926 (1st Cir. 1917); *In re Graves,* 29 Fed. 60 (N.D.Iowa 1886).

Complete Annotation Materials, see Title 28 U.S.C.A.

As to the Court's power to amend subdivisions (e) and (f) as here set forth, see *Mississippi Pub. Corp. v. Murphree,* 326 U.S. 438, 66 S.Ct. 242, 90 L.Ed. 185 (1946).

Subdivision (i). The continual increase of civil litigation having international elements makes it advisable to consolidate, amplify, and clarify the provisions governing service upon parties in foreign countries. See generally Jones, *International Judicial Assistance: Procedural Chaos and a Program for Reform,* 62 Yale L.J. 515 (1953); Longley, *Serving Process, Subpoenas and Other Documents in Foreign Territory,* Proc.A.B.A., Sec.Int'l & Comp.L. 34 (1959); Smit, *International Aspects of Federal Civil Procedure,* 61 Colum.L.Rev. 1031 (1961).

As indicated in the opening lines of new subdivision (i), referring to the provisions of subdivision (e), the authority for effecting foreign service must be found in a statute of the United States or a statute or rule of court of the State in which the district court is held providing in terms or upon proper interpretation for service abroad upon persons not inhabitants of or found within the State. See the Advisory Committee's Note to amended Rule 4(d)(7) and Rule 4(e). For examples of Federal and State statutes expressly authorizing such service, see 8 U.S.C. § 1451(b); 35 U.S.C. §§ 146, 293; Me.Rev.Stat., ch. 22, § 70 (Supp.1961); Minn.Stat.Ann. § 303.13 (1947); N.Y.Veh. & Tfc.Law § 253. Several decisions have construed statutes to permit service in foreign countries, although the matter is not expressly mentioned in the statutes. See, e.g., *Chapman v. Superior Court,* 162 Cal.App.2d 421, 328 P.2d 23 (Dist.Ct.App.1958); *Sperry v. Fliegers,* 194 Misc. 438, 86 N.Y.S.2d 830 (Sup.Ct.1949); *Ewing v. Thompson,* 233 N.C. 564, 65 S.E.2d 17 (1951); *Rushing v. Bush,* 260 S.W.2d 900 (Tex.Ct.Civ.App.1953). Federal and State statutes authorizing service on nonresidents in such terms as to warrant the interpretation that service abroad is permissible include 15 U.S.C. §§ 77v(a), 78aa, 79y; 28 U.S.C. § 1655; 38 U.S.C. § 784(a); Ill.Ann.Stat., c. 110, §§ 16, 17 (Smith–Hurd 1956); Wis.Stat. § 262.06 (1959).

Under subdivisions (e) and (i), when authority to make foreign service is found in a Federal statute or statute or rule of court of a State, it is always sufficient to carry out the service in the manner indicated therein. Subdivision (i) introduces considerable further flexibility by permitting the foreign service and return thereof to be carried out in any of a number of other alternative ways that are also declared to be sufficient. Other aspects of foreign service continue to be governed by the other provisions of Rule 4. Thus, for example, subdivision (i) effects no change in the form of the summons, or the issuance of separate or additional summons, or the amendment of service.

Service of process beyond the territorial limits of the United States may involve difficulties not encountered in the case of domestic service. Service abroad may be considered by a foreign country to require the performance of judicial, and therefore, "sovereign," acts within its territory, which that country may conceive to be offensive to its policy or contrary to its law. See Jones, supra, at 537. For example, a person not qualified to serve process according to the law of the foreign country may find himself subject to sanctions if he attempts service therein. See Inter-American Juridical Committee, *Report on Uniformity of Legislation on International Cooperation in Judicial Procedures* 20 (1952). The enforcement of a judgment in the foreign country in which the service was made may be embarrassed or prevented if the service did not comport with the law of that country. See ibid.

One of the purposes of subdivision (i) is to allow accommodation to the policies and procedures of the foreign country. It is emphasized, however, that the attitudes of foreign countries vary considerably and that the question of recognition of United States judgments abroad is complex. Accordingly, if enforcement is to be sought in the country of service, the foreign law should be examined before a choice is made among the methods of service allowed by subdivision (i).

Subdivision (i)(1). Subparagraph (a) of paragraph (1), permitting service by the method prescribed by the law of the foreign country for service on a person in that country in a civil action in any of its courts of general jurisdiction, provides an alternative that is likely to create least objection in the place of service and also is likely to enhance the possibilities of securing ultimate enforcement of the judgment abroad. See *Report on Uniformity of Legislation on International Cooperation in Judicial Procedures,* supra.

In certain foreign countries service in aid of litigation pending in other countries can lawfully be accomplished only upon request to the foreign courts, which in turn directs the service to be made. In many countries this has long been a customary way of accomplishing the service. See *In re Letters Rogatory out of First Civil Court of City of Mexico,* 261 Fed. 652 (S.D.N.Y.1919); Jones, supra, at 543; Comment, 44 Colum.L.Rev. 72 (1944); Note 58 Yale L.J. 1193 (1949). Subparagraph (B) of paragraph (1), referring to a letter rogatory, validates this method. A proviso, applicable to this subparagraph and the preceding one, requires, as a safeguard, that the service made shall be reasonably calculated to give actual notice of the proceedings to the party. See *Milliken v. Meyer,* 311 U.S. 457, 61 S.Ct. 339, 85 L.Ed. 278 (1940).

Subparagraph (C) of paragraph (1), permitting foreign service by personal delivery on individuals and corporations, partnerships, and associations, provides for a manner of service that is not only traditionally preferred, but also is most likely to lead to actual notice. Explicit provision for this manner of service was thought desirable because a number of Federal and State statutes permitting foreign service do not specifically provide for service by personal delivery abroad, see e.g., 35 U.S.C. §§ 146, 293; 46 U.S.C. § 1292; Calif.Ins.Code § 1612; N.Y.Veh. & Tfc. Law § 253, and it also may be unavailable under the law of the country in which the service is made.

Subparagraph (D) of paragraph (1), permitting service by certain types of mail, affords a manner of service that is inexpensive and expeditious, and requires a minimum of activity within the foreign country. Several statutes specifically provide for service in a foreign country by mail, e.g., Hawaii Rev.Laws §§ 230–31, 230–32 (1955); Minn.Stat.Ann. § 303.13 (1947); N.Y.Civ.Prac.Act, § 229–b; N.Y.Veh. & Tfc. Law § 253, and it has been sanctioned by the courts even in the absence of statutory provision specifying that form of service. *Zurini v. United States,* 189 F.2d 722 (8th Cir. 1951); *United States v. Cardillo,* 135 F.Supp. 798 (W.D.Pa. 1955); *Autogiro Co. v. Kay Gyroplanes, Ltd.,* 55 F.Supp. 919 (D.D.C.1944). Since the reliability of postal service may vary from country to country, service by mail is proper only when it is addressed to the party to be served and a form of mail requiring a signed receipt is used. An additional safeguard is provided by the requirement that the mailing be attended to by the clerk of the court. See also the provisions of paragraph (2) of this subdivision (i) regarding proof of service by mail.

Under the applicable law it may be necessary, when the defendant is an infant or incompetent person, to deliver the summons and complaint to a guardian, committee, or similar fiduciary. In such a case it would be advisable to make service under subparagraph (A), (B), or (E).

Subparagraph (E) of paragraph (1) adds flexibility by permitting the court by order to tailor the manner of service to fit the necessities of a particular case or the peculiar requirements of the law of the country in which the service is to be made. A similar provision appears in a number of statutes, e.g., 35 U.S.C. §§ 146, 293; 38 U.S.C. § 784(a); 46 U.S.C. § 1292.

The next-to-last sentence of paragraph (1) permits service under (C) and (E) to be made by any person who is not a party and is not less than 18 years of age or who is designated by court order or by the foreign court. Cf. Rule 45(c); N.Y.Civ.Prac.Act §§ 233, 235. This alternative increases the possibility that the plaintiff will be able to find a process server who can proceed unimpeded in the foreign country; it also may improve the changes of enforcing the judgment in the country of service. Especially is this alternative valuable when authority for the foreign service is found in a statute or rule of court that limits the group of eligible process servers to designated officials or special appointees who, because directly connected with another "sovereign," may be particularly offensive to the foreign country. See generally Smit, supra, at 1040–41. When recourse is had to subparagraph (A) or (B) the identity of the process server always will be determined by the law of the foreign country in which the service is made.

The last sentence of paragraph (1) sets forth an alternative manner for the issuance and transmission of the summons for service. After obtaining the summons from the clerk, the plaintiff must ascertain the best manner of delivering the summons and complaint to the person, court, or officer who will make the service. Thus the clerk is not burdened with the task of determining who is permitted to serve process under the law of a particular country or the appropriate governmental or nongovernmental channel for forwarding a letter rogatory. Under (D), however, the papers must always be posted by the clerk.

Subdivision (i)(2). When service is made in a foreign country, paragraph (2) permits methods for proof of service in addition to those prescribed by subdivision (g). Proof of service in accordance with the law of the foreign country is permitted because foreign process servers, unaccustomed to the form or the requirement of return of service prevalent in the United States, have on occasion been unwilling to execute the affidavit required by Rule 4(g). See Jones, supra, at 537; Longley, supra, at 35. As a corollary of the alternate manner of service in subdivision (i)(1)(E), proof of service as directed by order of the court is permitted. The special provision for proof of service by mail is intended as an additional safeguard when that method is used. On the type of evidence of delivery that may be satisfactory to a court in lieu of a signed receipt, see *Aero Associates, Inc. v. La Metropolitana*, 183 F.Supp. 357 (S.D.N.Y.1960).

1966 Amendment

The wording of Rule 4(f) is changed to accord with the amendment of Rule 13(h) referring to Rule 19 as amended.

1980 Amendment

Subdivision (a). This is a technical amendment to conform this subdivision with the amendment of subdivision (c).

Subdivision (c). The purpose of this amendment is to authorize service of process to be made by any person who is authorized to make service in actions in the courts of general jurisdiction of the state in which the district court is held or in which service is made.

There is a troublesome ambiguity in Rule 4. Rule 4(c) directs that all process is to be served by the marshal, by his deputy, or by a person specially appointed by the court. But Rule 4(d)(7) authorizes service in certain cases "in the manner prescribed by the law of the state in which the district court is held. . . ." And Rule 4(e), which authorizes service beyond the state and service in quasi in rem cases when state law permits such service, directs that "service may be made . . . under the circumstances and in the manner prescribed in the [state] statute or rule." State statutes and rules of the kind referred to in Rule 4(d)(7) and Rule 4(e) commonly designate the persons who are to make the service provided for, e.g., a sheriff or a plaintiff. When that is so, may the persons so designated by state law make service, or is service in all cases to be made by a marshal or by one specially appointed under present Rule 4(c)? The commentators have noted the ambiguity and have suggested the desirability of an amendment. See 2 Moore's *Federal Practice* ¶4.08 (1974); Wright & Miller, *Federal Practice and Procedure:* Civil § 1092 (1969). And the ambiguity has given rise to unfortunate results. See *United States for the use of Tanos v. St. Paul Mercury Ins. Co.*, 361 F.2d 838 (5th Cir. 1966); *Veeck v. Commodity Enterprises, Inc.*, 487 F.2d 423 (9th Cir.1973).

The ambiguity can be resolved by specific amendments to Rules 4(d)(7) and 4(e), but the Committee is of the view that there is no reason why Rule 4(c) should not generally authorize service of process in all cases by anyone authorized to make service in the courts of general jurisdiction of the state in which the district court is held or in which service is made. The marshal continues to be the obvious, always effective officer for service of process.

1987 Amendment

The amendments are technical. No substantive change is intended.

1993 Amendments

SPECIAL NOTE: Mindful of the constraints of the Rules Enabling Act, the Committee calls the attention of the Supreme Court and Congress to new subdivision (k)(2). Should this limited extension of service be disapproved, the Committee nevertheless recommends adoption of the balance of the rule, with subdivision (k)(1) becoming simply subdivision (k). The Committee Notes would be revised to eliminate references to subdivision (k)(2).

Purposes of Revision. The general purpose of this revision is to facilitate the service of the summons and complaint. The revised rule explicitly authorizes a means for service of

---

the summons and complaint on any defendant. While the methods of service so authorized always provide appropriate notice to persons against whom claims are made, effective service under this rule does not assure that personal jurisdiction has been established over the defendant served.

First, the revised rule authorizes the use of any means of service provided by the law not only of the forum state, but also of the state in which a defendant is served, unless the defendant is a minor or incompetent.

Second, the revised rule clarifies and enhances the cost-saving practice of securing the assent of the defendant to dispense with actual service of the summons and complaint. This practice was introduced to the rule in 1983 by an act of Congress authorizing "service-by-mail," a procedure that effects economic service with cooperation of the defendant. Defendants that magnify costs of service by requiring expensive service not necessary to achieve full notice of an action brought against them are required to bear the wasteful costs. This provision is made available in actions against defendants who cannot be served in the districts in which the actions are brought.

Third, the revision reduces the hazard of commencing an action against the United States or its officers, agencies, and corporations. A party failing to effect service on all the offices of the United States as required by the rule is assured adequate time to cure defects in service.

Fourth, the revision calls attention to the important effect of the Hague Convention and other treaties bearing on service of documents in foreign countries and favors the use of internationally agreed means of service. In some respects, these treaties have facilitated service in foreign countries but are not fully known to the bar.

Finally, the revised rule extends the reach of federal courts to impose jurisdiction over the person of all defendant against whom federal law claims are made and who can be constitutionally subjected to the jurisdiction of the courts of the United States. The present territorial limits on the effectiveness of service to subject a defendant to the jurisdiction of the court over the defendant's person are retained for all actions in which there is a state in which personal jurisdiction can be asserted consistently with state law and the Fourteenth Amendment. A new provision enables district courts to exercise jurisdiction, if permissible under the Constitution and not precluded by statute, when a federal claim is made against a defendant not subject to the jurisdiction of any single state.

The revised rule is reorganized to make its provisions more accessible to those not familiar with all of them. Additional subdivisions in this rule allow for more captions; several overlaps among subdivisions are eliminated; and several disconnected provisions are removed, to be relocated in a new Rule 4.1.

The Caption of the Rule. Prior to this revision, Rule 4 was entitled "Process" and applied to the service of not only the summons but also other process as well, although these are not covered by the revised rule. Service of process in eminent domain proceedings is governed by Rule 71A. Service of a subpoena is governed by Rule 45, and service of papers such as orders, motions, notices, pleadings, and other documents is governed by Rule 5.

The revised rule is entitled "Summons" and applies only to that form of legal process. Unless service of the summons is waived, a summons must be served whenever a person is joined as a party against whom a claim is made. Those few provisions of the former rule which relate specifically to service of process other than a summons are relocated in Rule 4.1 in order to simplify the text of this rule.

Subdivision (a). Revised subdivision (a) contains most of the language of the former subdivision (b). The second sentence of the former subdivision (b) has been stricken, so that the federal court summons will be the same in all cases. Few states now employ, distinctive requirements of form for a summons and the applicability of such a requirement in federal court can only serve as a trap for an unwary party or attorney. A sentence is added to this subdivision authorizing an amendment of a summons. This sentence replaces the rarely used former subdivision 4(h). See 4A Wright & Miller, Federal Practice and Procedure § 1131 (2d ed. 1987).

Subdivision (b). Revised subdivision (b) replaces the former subdivision (a). The revised text makes clear that the responsibility for filling in the summons falls on the plaintiff, not the clerk of the court. If there are multiple defendants, the plaintiff may secure issuance of a summons for each defendant, or may serve copies of a single original bearing the names of multiple defendants if the addressee of the summons is effectively identified.

Subdivision (c). Paragraph (1) of revised subdivision (c) retains language from the former subdivision (d)(1). Paragraph (2) retains language from the former subdivision (a), and adds an appropriate caution regarding the time limit for service set forth in subdivision (m).

The 1983 revision of Rule 4 relieved the marshals' offices of much of the burden of serving the summons. Subdivision (c) eliminates the requirement for service by the marshal's office in actions in which the party seeking service is the United States. The United States, like other civil litigants, is now permitted to designate any person who is 18 years of age and not a party to serve its summons.

The court remains obligated to appoint a marshal, a deputy, or some other person to effect service of a summons in two classes of cases specified by statute: actions brought in forma pauperis or by a seaman. 28 U.S.C. §§ 1915, 1916. The court also retains discretion to appoint a process server on motion of a party. If a law enforcement presence appears to be necessary or advisable to keep the peace, the court should appoint a marshal or deputy or other official person to make the service. The Department of Justice may also call upon the Marshals Service to perform services in actions brought by the United States. 28 U.S.C. § 651.

Subdivision (d). This text is new, but is substantially derived from the former subdivisions (c)(2)(C) and (D), added to the rule by Congress in 1983. The aims of the provision are to eliminate the costs of service of a summons on many parties and to foster cooperation among adversaries and counsel. The rule operates to impose upon the defendant those costs that could have been avoided if the defendant had cooperated reasonably in the manner prescribed. This device is useful in dealing with defendants who are furtive, or who reside in places not easily reached by process servers, or who are outside the United States and can be served only at substantial and unnecessary expense. Illustratively, there is no useful purpose achieved by requiring a plaintiff to comply with all the formalities of service in a foreign country, including costs of translation, when suing a defendant manufacturer, fluent in English, whose products are widely distributed in the United States. See Bankston v. Toyota Motor Corp., 889 F.2d 172 (8th Cir.1989).

The former text described this process as service-by-mail. This language misled some plaintiffs into thinking that service could be effected by mail without the affirmative cooperation of the defendant. E.g., Gulley v. Mayo Foundation, 886 F.2d 161 (8th Cir.1989). It is more accurate to describe the communication sent to the defendant as a request for a waiver of formal service.

The request for waiver of service may be sent only to defendants subject to service under subdivision (e), (f), or (h). The United States is not expected to waive service for the reason that its mail receiving facilities are inadequate to assure that the notice is actually received by the correct person in the Department of Justice. The same principle is applied to agencies, corporations, and officers of the United States and to other governments and entities subject to service under subdivision (j). Moreover, there are policy reasons why governmental entities should not be confronted with the potential for bearing costs of service in cases in which they ultimately prevail. Infants or incompetent persons likewise are not called upon to waive service because, due to their presumed inability to understand the request and its consequences, they must generally be served through fiduciaries.

It was unclear whether the former rule authorized, mailing of a request for "acknowledgement of service" to defendants outside the forum state. See 1 R. Casad, Jurisdiction in Civil Actions (2d Ed.) 5–29, 30 (1991) and cases cited. But, as Professor Casad observed, there was no reason not to employ this device in an effort to obtain service outside the state, and there are many instances in which it was in fact so used, with respect both to defendants within the United States and to defendants in other countries.

The opportunity for waiver has distinct advantages to a foreign defendant. By waiving service, the defendant can reduce the costs that may ultimately be taxed against it if unsuccessful in the lawsuit, including the sometimes substantial expense of translation that may be wholly unnecessary for defendants fluent in English. Moreover, a foreign defendant that waives service is afforded substantially more time to defend against the action than if it had been formally served: under Rule 12, a defendant ordinarily has only 20 days after service in which to file its answer or raise objections by motion, but by signing a waiver it is allowed 90 days after the date the request for waiver was mailed in which to submit its defenses. Because of the additional time needed for mailing and the unreliability of some foreign mail services, a period of 60 days (rather than the 30 days required for domestic transmissions) is provided for a return of a waiver sent to a foreign country.

It is hoped that, since transmission of the notice and waiver forms is a private nonjudicial act, does not purport to effect service, and is not accompanied by any summons or directive from a court, use of the procedure will not offend foreign sovereignties, even those that have withheld their assent to formal service by mail or have objected to the "service-by-mail" provisions of the former rule. Unless the addressee consents, receipt of the request under the revised rule does not give rise to any obligation to answer the lawsuit, does not provide a basis for default judgment, and does not suspend the statute of limitations in those states where the period continues to run until service. Nor are there any adverse consequences to a foreign defendant, since the provisions for shifting the expense of service to a defendant that declines to waive service apply only if the plaintiff and defendant are both located in the United States.

With respect to a defendant located in a foreign country like the United Kingdom, which accepts documents in English, whose Central Authority acts promptly in effecting service, and whose policies discourage its residents from waiving formal service, there will be little reason for a plaintiff to send the notice and request under subdivision (d) rather than use convention methods. On the other hand, the procedure offers significant potential benefits to a plaintiff when suing a defendant that, though fluent in English, is located in a country where, as a condition to formal service under a convention, documents must be translated into another language or where formal service will be otherwise costly or time-consuming.

Paragraph (1) is explicit that a timely waiver of service of a summons does not prejudice the right of a defendant to object by means of a motion authorized by Rule 12(b)(2) to the absence of jurisdiction over the defendant's person, or to assert other defenses that may be available. The only issues eliminated are those involving the sufficiency of the summons or the sufficiency of the method by which it is served.

Paragraph (2) states what the present rule implies: the defendant has a duty to avoid costs associated with the service of a summons not needed to inform the defendant regarding the commencement of an action. The text of the rule also sets forth the requirements for a Notice and Request for Waiver sufficient to put the cost-shifting provision in place. These requirements are illustrated in Forms 1A and 1B, which replace the former Form 18–A.

Paragraph (2)(A) is explicit that a request for waiver of service by a corporate defendant must be addressed to a person qualified to receive service. The general mail rooms of large organizations cannot be required to identify the appropriate individual recipient for an institutional summons.

Paragraph (2)(B) permits the use of alternatives to the United States mails in sending the Notice and Request. While private messenger services or electronic communications may be more expensive than the mail, they may be equally reliable and on occasion more convenient to the parties. Especially with respect to transmissions to foreign countries, alternative means may be desirable, for in some countries facsimile transmission is the most efficient and economical means of communication. If electronic means such as facsimile transmission are employed, the sender should maintain a record of the transmission to assure proof of transmission if receipt is denied, but a party receiving such a transmission has a duty to cooperate and cannot avoid liability for the resulting cost of formal service if the transmission is prevented at the point of receipt.

A defendant failing to comply with a request for waiver shall be given an opportunity to show good cause for the failure, but sufficient cause should be rare. It is not a good cause for failure to waive service that the claim is unjust or that the court lacks jurisdiction. Sufficient cause not to shift the cost of service would exist, however, if the defendant did not receive the request or was insufficiently literate in English to understand it. It should be noted that the provisions for shifting the cost of service apply only if the plaintiff and the defendant are both located in the United States, and accordingly a foreign defendant need not show "good cause" for its failure to waive service.

Paragraph (3) extends the time for answer if, before being served with process, the defendant waives formal service. The extension is intended to serve as an inducement to waive service and to assure that a defendant will not gain any delay be declining to waive service and thereby causing the additional time needed to effect service. By waiving service, a defendant is not called upon to respond to the complaint until 60 days from the date the notice was sent to it—90 days if the notice was sent to a foreign country—rather than within the 20 day period from date of service specified in Rule 12.

Paragraph (4) clarifies the effective date of service when service is waived; the provision is needed to resolve an issue arising when applicable law requires service of process to toll the statute of limitations. E.g., Morse v. Elmira Country Club, 752 F.2d 35 (2d Cir.1984). Cf. Walker v. Armco Steel Corp., 446 U.S. 740 (1980).

The provisions in former subdivision (c)(2)(C)(ii) of this rule may have been misleading to some parties. Some plaintiffs, not reading the rule carefully, supposed that receipt by the defendant of the mailed complaint had the effect both of establishing the jurisdiction of the court over the defendant's person and of tolling the statute of limitations in actions in which service of the summons is required to toll the limitations period. The revised rule is clear that, if the waiver is not returned and filed, the limitations period under such a law is not tolled and the action will not otherwise proceed until formal service of process is effected.

Some state limitations laws may toll an otherwise applicable statute at the time when the defendant receives notice of the action. Nevertheless, the device of requested waiver of service is not suitable if a limitations period which is about to expire is not tolled by filing the action. Unless there is ample time, the plaintiff should proceed directly to the formal methods for service identified in subdivisions (e), (f), or (h).

The procedure of requesting waiver of service should also not be used if the time for service under subdivision (m) will expire before the date on which the waiver must be returned. While a plaintiff has been allowed additional time for service in that situation, e.g., Prather v. Raymond Constr. Co., 570 F.Supp. 278 (N.D.Ga.1983), the court could refuse a request for additional time unless the defendant appears to have evaded service pursuant to subdivision (e) or (h). It may be noted that the presumptive time limit for service under subdivision (m) does not apply to service in a foreign country.

Paragraph (5) is a cost-shifting provision retained from the former rule. The costs that may be imposed on the defendant could include, for example, the cost of the time of a process server required to make contact with a defendant residing in a guarded apartment house or residential development. The paragraph is explicit that the costs of enforcing the cost-shifting provision are themselves recoverable from a defendant who fails to return the waiver. In the absence of such a provision, the purpose of the rule would be frustrated by the cost of its enforcement, which is likely to be high in relation to the small benefit secured by the plaintiff.

Some plaintiffs may send a notice and request for waiver and, without waiting for return of the waiver, also proceed with efforts to effect formal service on the defendant. To discourage this practice, the cost-shifting provisions in paragraphs (2) and (5) are limited to costs of effecting service incurred after the time expires for the defendant to return the waiver. Moreover, by returning the waiver within the time allowed and before being served with process, a defendant receives the benefit of the longer period for responding to the complaint afforded for waivers under paragraph (3).

Subdivision (e). This subdivision replaces former subdivisions (c)(2)(C)(i) and (d)(1). It provides a means for service of summons on individuals within a judicial district of the United States. Together with subdivision (f), it provides for service on persons anywhere, subject to constitutional and statutory constraints.

Service of the summons under this subdivision does not conclusively establish the jurisdiction of the court over the person of the defendant. A defendant may assert the territorial limits of the court's reach set forth in subdivision (k), including the constitutional limitations that may be imposed by the Due Process Clause of the Fifth Amendment.

Paragraph (1) authorizes service in any judicial district in conformity with state law. This paragraph sets forth the language of former subdivision (c)(2)(C)(i), which authorized the use of the law of the state in which the district court sits, but adds as an alternative the use of the law of the state in which the service is effected.

Paragraph (2) retains the text of the former subdivision (d)(1) and authorizes the use of the familiar methods of personal or abode service or service on an authorized agent in any judicial district.

To conform to these provisions, the former subdivision (e) bearing on proceedings against parties not found within the state is stricken. Likewise stricken is the first sentence of the former subdivision (f), which had restricted the authority of the federal process server to the state in which the district court sits.

Subdivision (f). This subdivision provides for service on individuals who are in a foreign country, replacing the former subdivision (i) that was added to Rule 4 in 1963. Reflecting the pattern of Rule 4 in incorporating state law limitations on the exercise of jurisdiction over persons, the former subdivision (i) limited service outside the United States to cases in which extraterritorial service was authorized by state or federal law. The new rule eliminates the requirement of explicit authorization. On occasion, service in a foreign country was held to be improper for lack of statutory authority. E.g., Martens v. Winder, 341 F.2d 197 (9th Cir.), cert. denied, 382 U.S. 937 (1965). This authority, however, was found to exist by implication. E.g., SEC v. VTR, Inc., 39 F.R.D. 19 (S.D.N.Y.1966). Given the substantial increase in the number of international transactions and events that are the subject of litigation in federal courts, it is appropriate to infer a general legislative authority to effect service on defendants in a foreign country.

A secondary effect of this provision for foreign service of a federal summons is to facilitate the use of federal long-arm law in actions brought to enforce the federal law against defendants who cannot be served under any state law but who can be constitutionally subjected to the jurisdiction of the federal court. Such a provision is set forth in paragraph (2) of subdivision (k) of this rule, applicable only to persons not subject to the territorial jurisdiction of any particular state.

Paragraph (1) gives effect to the Hague Convention on the Service Abroad of Judicial and Extrajudicial Documents, which entered into force for the United States on February 10, 1969. See 28 U.S.C.A., Fed.R.Civ.P. 4 (Supp.1986). This Convention is an important means of dealing with problems of service in a foreign country. See generally 1 B. Ristau, International Judicial Assistance §§ 4–1–1 to 4–5–2 (1990). Use of the Convention procedures, when available, is mandatory if documents must be transmitted abroad to effect service. See Volkswagenwerk Aktiengesellschaft v. Schlunk, 486 U.S. 694 (1988) (noting that voluntary use of these procedures may be desirable even when service could constitutionally be effected in another manner); J. Weis, The Federal Rules and the Hague Conventions: Concerns of Conformity and Comity, 50 U.Pitt.L.Rev. 903 (1989). Therefore, this paragraph provides that, when service is to be effected outside a judicial district of the United States, the methods of service appropriate under an applicable treaty shall be employed if available and if the treaty so requires.

The Hague Convention furnishes safeguards against the abridgment of rights of parties through inadequate notice. Article 15 provides for verification of actual notice or a demonstration that process was served by a method prescribed by the internal laws of the foreign state before a default judgment may be entered. Article 16 of the Convention also enables the judge to extend the time for appeal after judgment if the defendant shows a lack of adequate notice either to defend or to appeal the judgment, or has disclosed a prima facie case on the merits.

The Hague Convention does not specify a time within which a foreign country's Central Authority must effect service, but Article 15 does provide that alternate methods may be used if a Central Authority does not respond within six months. Generally, a Central Authority can be expected to respond much more quickly than that limit might permit, but there have been occasions when the signatory state was dilatory or refused to cooperate for substantive reasons. In such cases, resort may be had to the provision set forth in subdivision (f)(3).

Two minor changes in the text reflect the Hague Convention. First, the term "letter of request" has been added. Although these words are synonymous with "letter rogatory," "letter of request" is preferred in modern usage. The provision should not be interpreted to authorize use of a letter of request when there is in fact no treaty obligation on the receiving country to honor such a request from this country or when the United States does not extend diplomatic recognition to the foreign nation. Second, the passage formerly found in subdivision (i)(1)(B), "when service in either case is reasonably calculated to give actual notice," has been relocated.

Paragraph (2) provides alternative methods for use when internationally agreed methods are not intended to be exclusive, or where there is no international agreement applicable. It contains most of the language formerly set forth in subdivision (i) of the rule. Service by methods that would violate foreign law is not generally authorized. Subparagraphs (A) and (B) prescribe the more appropriate methods for conforming to local practice or using a local authority. Subparagraph (C) prescribes other methods authorized by the former rule.

Paragraph (3) authorizes the court to approve other methods of service not prohibited by international agreements.

The Hague Convention, for example, authorizes special forms of service in cases of urgency if convention methods will not permit service within the time required by the circumstances. Other circumstances that might justify the use of additional methods include the failure of the foreign country's Central Authority to effect service within the six-month period provided by the Convention, or the refusal of the Central Authority to serve a complaint seeking punitive damages or to enforce the antitrust laws of the United States. In such cases, the court may direct a special method of service not explicitly authorized by international agreement if not prohibited by the agreement. Inasmuch as our Constitution requires that reasonable notice be given, an earnest effort should be made to devise a method of communication that is consistent with due process and minimizes offense to foreign law. A court may in some instances specially authorize use of ordinary mail. Cf. Levin v. Ruby Trading Corp., 248 F.Supp. 537 (S.D.N.Y.1965).

Subdivision (g). This subdivision retains the text of former subdivision (d)(2). Provision is made for service upon an infant or incompetent person in a foreign country.

Subdivision (h). This subdivision retains the text of former subdivision (d)(3), with changes reflecting those made in subdivision (e). It also contains the provisions for service on a corporation or association in a foreign country, as formerly found in subdivision (i).

Frequent use should be made of the Notice and Request procedure set forth in subdivision (d) in actions against corporations. Care must be taken, however, to address the request to an individual officer or authorized agent of the corporation. It is not effective use of the Notice and Request procedure if the mail is sent undirected to the mail room of the organization.

Subdivision (i). This subdivision retains much of the text of former subdivisions (d)(4) and (d)(5). Paragraph (1) provides for service of a summons on the United States; it amends former subdivision (d)(4) to permit the United States attorney to be served by registered or certified mail. The rule does not authorize the use of the Notice and Request procedure of revised subdivision (d) when the United States is the defendant. To assure proper handling of mail in the United States attorney's office, the authorized mail service must be specifically addressed to the civil process clerk of the office of the United States attorney.

Paragraph (2) replaces former subdivision (d)(5). Paragraph (3) saves the plaintiff from the hazard of losing a substantive right because of failure to comply with the complex requirements of multiple service under this subdivision. That risk has proved to be more than nominal. E.g., Whale v. United States, 792 F.2d 951 (9th Cir.1986). This provision should be read in connection with the provisions of subdivision (c) of Rule 15 to preclude the loss of substantive rights against the United States or its agencies, corporations, or officers resulting from a plaintiff's failure to correctly identify and serve all the persons who should be named or served.

Subdivision (j). This subdivision retains the text of former subdivision (d)(6) without material change. The waiver-of-service provision is also inapplicable to actions against governments subject to service pursuant to this subdivision.

The revision adds a new paragraph (1) referring to the statute governing service of a summons on a foreign state and its political subdivisions, agencies, and instrumentalities, the Foreign Sovereign Immunities Act of 1976, 28 U.S.C. § 1608. The caption of the subdivision reflects that change.

Subdivision (k). This subdivision replaces the former subdivision (f), with no change in the title. Paragraph (1) retains the substance of the former rule in explicitly authorizing the exercise of personal jurisdiction over persons who can be reached under state long-arm law, the "100–mile bulge" provision added in 1963, or the federal interpleader act. Paragraph (1)(D) is new, but merely calls attention to federal legislation that may provide for nationwide or even world-wide service of process in cases arising under particular federal laws. Congress has provided for nationwide service of process and full exercise of territorial jurisdiction by all district courts with respect to specified federal actions. See 1 R. Casad, Jurisdiction in Civil Actions (2d Ed.) chap. 5 (1991).

Paragraph (2) is new. It authorizes the exercise of territorial jurisdiction over the person of any defendant against whom is made a claim arising under any federal law if that person is subject to personal jurisdiction in no state. This addition is a companion to the amendments made in revised subdivisions (e) and (f).

This paragraph corrects a gap in the enforcement of federal law. Under the former rule, a problem was presented when the defendant was a non-resident of the United States having contacts with the United States sufficient to justify the application of United States law and to satisfy federal standards of forum selection, but having insufficient contact with any single state to support jurisdiction under state long-arm legislation or meet the requirements of the Fourteenth Amendment limitation on state court territorial jurisdiction. In such cases, the defendant was shielded from the enforcement of federal law by the fortuity of a favorable limitation on the power of state courts, which was incorporated into the federal practice by the former rule. In this respect, the revision responds to the suggestion of the Supreme Court made in Omni Capital Int'l. v. Rudolf Wolff & Co., Ltd., 484 U.S. 97, 111 (1987).

There remain constitutional limitations on the exercise of territorial jurisdiction by federal courts over persons outside the United States. These restrictions arise from the Fifth Amendment rather than from the Fourteenth Amendment, which limits state-court reach and which was incorporated into federal practice by the reference to state law in the text of the former subdivision (e) that is deleted by this revision. The Fifth Amendment requires that any defendant have affiliating contacts with the United States sufficient to justify the exercise of personal jurisdiction over that party. Cf. Wells Fargo & Co. v. Wells Fargo Express Co., 556 F.2d 406, 418 (9th Cir.1977). There also may be a further Fifth Amendment constraint in that a plaintiff's forum selection might be so inconvenient to a defendant that it would be a denial of "fair play and substantial justice" required by the due process clause, even though the defendant had significant affiliating contacts with the United States. See De-James v. Magnificent Carriers, 654 F.2d 280, 286 n. 3 (3rd Cir.), cert. denied, 454 U.S. 1085 (1981). Compare World-Wide Volkswagen Corp. v. Woodson, 444 U.S. 286, 293–294 (1980); Insurance Corp. of Ireland v. Compagnie des Bauxites de Guinee, 456 U.S. 694, 702–03 (1982); Burger King Corp. v. Rudzewicz, 471 U.S. 462, 476–78 (1985); Asahi Metal Indus. v. Superior Court of Cal., Solano County, 480 U.S.

102, 108–13 (1987). See generally R. Lusardi, Nationwide Service of Process: Due Process Limitations on the Power of the Sovereign, 33 Vill.L.Rev. 1 (1988).

This provision does not affect the operation of federal venue legislation. See generally 28 U.S.C. § 1391. Nor does it affect the operation of federal law providing for the change of venue. 28 U.S.C. §§ 1404, 1406. The availability of transfer for fairness and convenience under § 1404 should preclude most conflicts between the full exercise of territorial jurisdiction permitted by this rule and the Fifth Amendment requirement of "fair play and substantial justice."

The district court should be especially scrupulous to protect aliens who reside in a foreign country from forum selections so onerous that injustice could result. "[G]reat care and reserve should be exercised when extending our notions of personal jurisdiction into the international field." Asahi Metal Indus. v. Superior Court of Cal., Solano County, 480 U.S. 102, 115 (1987), quoting United States v. First Nat'l City Bank, 379 U.S. 378, 404 (1965) (Harlan, J., dissenting).

This narrow extension of the federal reach applies only if a claim is made against the defendant under federal law. It does not establish personal jurisdiction if the only claims are those arising under state law or the law of another country, even though there might be diversity or alienage subject matter jurisdiction as to such claims. If, however, personal jurisdiction is established under this paragraph with respect to a federal claim, then 28 U.S.C. § 1367(a) provides supplemental jurisdiction over related claims against that defendant, subject to the court's discretion to decline exercise of that jurisdiction under 28 U.S.C. § 1367(c).

Subdivision (*l*). This subdivision assembles in one place all the provisions of the present rule bearing on proof of service. No material change in the rule is effected. The provision that proof of service can be amended by leave of court is retained from the former subdivision (h). See generally 4A Wright & Miller, Federal Practice and Procedure § 1132 (2d ed. 1987).

Subdivision (m). This subdivision retains much of the language of the present subdivision (j).

The new subdivision explicitly provides that the court shall allow additional time if there is good cause for the plaintiff's failure to effect service in the prescribed 120 days, and authorizes the court to relieve a plaintiff of the consequences of an application of this subdivision even if there is no good cause shown. Such relief formerly was afforded in some cases, partly in reliance on Rule 6(b). Relief may be justified, for example, if the applicable statute of limitations would bar the refiled action, or if the defendant is evading service or conceals a defect in attempted service. E.g., Ditkof v. Owens–Illinois, Inc., 114 F.R.D. 104 (E.D.Mich. 1987). A specific instance of good cause is set forth in paragraph (3) of this rule, which provides for extensions if necessary to correct oversights in compliance with the requirements of multiple service in actions against the United States or its officers, agencies, and corporations. The district court should also take care to protect pro se plaintiffs from consequences of confusion or delay attending the resolution of an in forma pauperis petition. Robinson v. America's Best Contacts & Eyeglasses, 876 F.2d 596 (7th Cir. 1989).

The 1983 revision of this subdivision referred to the "party on whose behalf such service was required," rather than to the "plaintiff," a term used generically elsewhere in this rule to refer to any party initiating a claim against a person who is not a party to the action. To simplify the text, the revision returns to the usual practice in the rule of referring simply to the plaintiff even though its principles apply with equal force to defendants who may assert claims against non-parties under Rules 13(h), 14, 19, 20, or 21.

Subdivision (n). This subdivision provides for in rem and quasi-in-rem jurisdiction. Paragraph (1) incorporates any requirements of 28 U.S.C. § 1655 or similar provisions bearing on seizures or liens.

Paragraph (2) provides for other uses of quasi-in-rem jurisdiction but limits its use to exigent circumstances. Provisional remedies may be employed as a means to secure jurisdiction over the property of a defendant whose person is not within reach of the court, but occasions for the use of this provision should be rare, as where the defendant is a fugitive or assets are in imminent danger of disappearing. Until 1963, it was not possible under Rule 4 to assert jurisdiction in a federal court over the property of a defendant not personally served. The 1963 amendment to subdivision (e) authorized the use of state law procedures authorizing seizures of assets as a basis for jurisdiction. Given the liberal availability of long-arm jurisdiction, the exercise of power quasi-in-rem has become almost an anachronism. Circumstances too spare to affiliate the defendant to the forum state sufficiently to support long-arm jurisdiction over the defendant's person are also inadequate to support seizure of the defendant's assets fortuitously found within the state. Shaffer v. Heitner, 433 U.S. 186 (1977).

2000 Amendment

Paragraph (2)(B) is added to Rule 4(i) to require service on the United States when a United States officer or employee is sued in an individual capacity for acts or omissions occurring in connection with duties performed on behalf of the United States. Decided cases provide uncertain guidance on the question whether the United States must be served in such actions. See *Vaccaro v. Dobre*, 81 F.3d 854, 856–857 (9th Cir.1996); *Armstrong v. Sears*, 33 F.3d 182, 185–187 (2d Cir.1994); *Ecclesiastical Order of the Ism of Am v. Chasin*, 845 F.2d 113, 116 (6th Cir.1988); *Light v. Wolf*, 816 F.2d 746 (D.C.Cir.1987); see also *Simpkins v. District of Columbia*, 108 F.3d 366, 368–369 (D.C.Cir.1997). Service on the United States will help to protect the interest of the individual defendant in securing representation by the United States, and will expedite the process of determining whether the United States will provide representation. It has been understood that the individual defendant must be served as an individual defendant, a requirement that is made explicit. Invocation of the individual service provisions of subdivisions (e), (f), and (g) invokes also the waiver- of-service provisions of subdivision (d).

Paragraph 2(B) reaches service when an officer or employee of the United States is sued in an individual capacity "for acts or omissions occurring in connection with the performance of duties on behalf of the United States." This phrase has been chosen as a functional phrase that can be applied without the occasionally distracting associations of such phrases as "scope of employment," "color of office," or "arising out of the employment." Many actions are brought against individual federal officers or employees of the United States for acts or omissions that have no connection whatev-

er to their governmental roles. There is no reason to require service on the United States in these actions. The connection to federal employment that requires service on the United States must be determined as a practical matter, considering whether the individual defendant has reasonable grounds to look to the United States for assistance and whether the United States has reasonable grounds for demanding formal notice of the action.

An action against a former officer or employee of the United States is covered by paragraph (2)(B) in the same way as an action against a present officer or employee. Termination of the relationship between the individual defendant and the United States does not reduce the need to serve the United States.

Paragraph (3) is amended to ensure that failure to serve the United States in an action governed by paragraph 2(B) does not defeat an action. This protection is adopted because there will be cases in which the plaintiff reasonably fails to appreciate the need to serve the United States . There is no requirement, however, that the plaintiff show that the failure to serve the United States was reasonable. A reasonable time to effect service on the United States must be allowed after the failure is pointed out. An additional change ensures that if the United States or United States attorney is served in an action governed by paragraph 2(A), additional time is to be allowed even though no officer, employee, agency, or corporation of the United States was served.

GAP Report

The most important changes were made to ensure that no one would read the seemingly independent provisions of paragraphs 2(A) and 2(B) to mean that service must be made twice both on the United States and on the United States employee when the employee is sued in both official and individual capacities. The word "only" was added in subparagraph (A) and the new phrase "whether or not the officer or employee is sued also in an individual capacity" was inserted in subparagraph (B).

Minor changes were made to include "Employees" in the catch-line for subdivision (i), and to add "or employee" in paragraph 2(A). Although it may seem awkward to think of suit against an employee in an official capacity, there is no clear definition that separates "officers" from "employees" for this purpose. The published proposal to amend Rule 12(a)(3) referred to actions against an employee sued in an official capacity, and it seemed better to make the rules parallel by adding "employee" to Rule 4(i)(2)(A) than by deleting it from Rule 12(a)(3)(A).

HISTORICAL NOTES

References in Text

Form 18–A, referred to in subsec. (c)(2)(C)(ii), was abrogated effective December 1, 1991, subject to contrary Congressional action.

Effective and Applicability Provisions

1983 Acts. Amendment by Pub.L. 97–462 effective 45 days after Jan. 12, 1983, see section 4 of Pub.L. 97–462, set out as a note under section 2071 of this title.

LEGISLATIVE STATEMENT

1983 Amendment

128 Congressional Record H 9848, Dec. 15, 1982. Mr. EDWARDS of California. Mr. Speaker, in July Mr. McClory and I brought before the House a bill to delay the effective date of proposed changes in rule 4 of the Federal Rules of Civil Procedure dealing with service of process. The Congress enacted that legislation and delayed the effective date so that we could cure certain problems in the proposed amendments to rule 4.

Since that time, Mr. McClory and I introduced a bill, H.R. 7154, that cures those problems. It was drafted in consultation with representatives of the Department of Justice, the Judicial Conference of the United States, and others.

The Department of Justice and the Judicial Conference have endorsed the bill and have urged its prompt enactment. Indeed, the Department of Justice has indicated that the changes occasioned by the bill will facilitate its collection of debts owed to the Government.

I have a letter from the Office of Legislative Affairs of the Department of Justice supporting the bill that I will submit for the Record. Also, I am submitting for the Record a section-by-section analysis of the bill.

H.R. 7154 makes much needed changes in rule 4 of the Federal Rules of Civil Procedure and is supported by all interested parties. I urge my colleagues to support it.

U.S. DEPARTMENT OF JUSTICE,
OFFICE OF LEGISLATIVE AFFAIRS,

Washington, D.C., December 10, 1982.
Hon. *Peter W. Rodino, Jr.*
Chairman, Committee on the Judiciary House of Representatives, Washington, D.C.

Dear Mr. Chairman: This is to proffer the views of the Department of Justice on H.R. 7154, the proposed Federal Rules of Civil Procedure Amendments Act of 1982. While the agenda is extremely tight and we appreciate that fact, we do reiterate that this Department strongly endorses the enactment of H.R. 7154. We would greatly appreciate your watching for any possible way to enact this legislation expeditiously.

H.R. 7154 would amend Rule 4 of the Federal Rules of Civil Procedure to relieve effectively the United States Marshals Service of the duty of routinely serving summonses and complaints for private parties in civil actions and would thus achieve a goal this Department has long sought. Experience has shown that the Marshals Service's increasing workload and limited budget require such major relief from the burdens imposed by its role as process-server in all civil actions.

The bill would also amend Rule 4 to permit certain classes of defendants to be served by first class mail with a notice and acknowledgment of receipt form enclosed. We have previously expressed a preference for the service-by-mail provisions of the proposed amendments to Rule 4 which the Supreme Court transmitted to Congress on April 28, 1982.

The amendments proposed by the Supreme Court would permit service by registered or certified mail, return receipt requested. We had regarded the Supreme Court proposal as the more efficient because it would not require an affirmative act of signing and mailing on the part of a defendant. Moreover, the Supreme Court proposal would permit the entry of a default judgment if the record contained a returned receipt showing acceptance by the defendant or a returned envelope showing refusal of the process by the defendant and subsequent service and notice by first class

mail. However, critics of that system of mail service have argued that certified mail is not an effective method of providing actual notice to defendants of claims against them because signatures may be illegible or may not match the name of the defendant, or because it may be difficult to determine whether mail has been "unclaimed" or "refused," the latter providing the sole basis for a default judgment.

As you know, in light of these criticisms the Congress enacted Public Law 97–227 (H.R. 6663) postponing the effective date of the proposed amendments to Rule 4 until October 1, 1983, so as to facilitate further review of the problem. This Department opposed the delay in the effective date, primarily because the Supreme Court's proposed amendments also contained urgently needed provisions designed to relieve the United States Marshals of the burden of serving summonses and complaints in private civil actions. In our view, these necessary relief provisions are readily separable from the issues of service by certified mail and the propriety of default judgment after service by certified mail which the Congress felt warranted additional review.

During the floor consideration of H.R. 6663 Congressman Edwards and other proponents of the delayed effective date pledged to expedite the review of the proposed amendments to Rule 4, given the need to provide prompt relief for the Marshals Service in the service of process area. In this spirit Judiciary Committee staff consulted with representatives of this Department, the Judicial Conference, and others who had voiced concern about the proposed amendments. H.R. 7154 is the product of those consultations and accommodated the concerns of the Department in a very workable and acceptable manner.

Accordingly, we are satisfied that the provisions of H.R. 7154 merit the support of all three branches of the Federal Government and everyone else who has a stake in the fair and efficient service of process in civil actions. We urge prompt consideration of H.R. 7154 by the Committee.[1]

The Office of Management and Budget has advised that there is no objection to the submission of this report from the standpoint of the Administration's program.

Sincerely,
ROBERT A. MCCONNELL,
Assistant Attorney General

[1] In addition to amending Rule 4, we have previously recommended: (a) amendments to 28 U.S.C. § 569(b) redefining the Marshals traditional role by eliminating the statutory requirement that they serve subpoenas, as well as summonses and complaints, and; (b) amendments to 28 U.S.C. § 1921 changing the manner and level in which marshal fees are charged for serving private civil process. These legislative changes are embodied in Section 10 of S. 2567 and the Department's proposed fiscal year 1983 Appropriations Authorization bill. If, in the Committee's judgment, efforts to incorporate these suggested amendments in H.R. 7154 would in any way impede consideration of the bill during the few remaining legislative days in the 97th Congress, we would urge that they be separately considered early in the 98th Congress.

H.R. 7154—Federal Rules of Civil Procedure Amendments Act of 1982

BACKGROUND

The Federal Rules of Civil Procedure set forth the procedures to be followed in civil actions and proceedings in

United States district courts. These rules are usually amended by a process established by 28 U.S.C. 2072, often referred to as the "Rules Enabling Act". The Rules Enabling Act provides that the Supreme Court can propose new rules of "practice and procedure" and amendments to existing rules by transmitting them to Congress after the start of a regular session but not later than May 1. The rules and amendments so proposed take effect 90 days after transmittal unless legislation to the contrary is enacted.[1]

On April 28, 1982, the Supreme Court transmitted to Congress several proposed amendments to the Federal Rules of Civil Procedure, the Federal Rules of Criminal Procedure (which govern criminal cases and proceedings in Federal courts), and the Rules and Forms Governing Proceedings in the United States District Courts under sections 2254 and 2255 of Title 28, United States Code (which govern habeas corpus proceedings). These amendments were to have taken effect on August 1, 1982.

The amendments to Rule 4 of the Federal Rules of Civil Procedure were intended primarily to relieve United States marshals of the burden of serving summonses and complaints in private civil actions. Appendix II, at 7 (Report of the Committee on Rules of Practice and Procedure), 16 (Advisory Committee Note). The Committee received numerous complaints that the changes not only failed to achieve that goal, but that in the process the changes saddled litigants with flawed mail service, deprived litigants of the use of effective local procedures for service, and created a time limit for service replete with ambiguities that could only be resolved by costly litigation. See House Report No. 97–662, at 2–4 (1982).

In order to consider these criticisms, Congress enacted Public Law 97–227, postponing the effective date of the proposed amendments to Rule 4 until October 1, 1983.[2] Accordingly, in order to help shape the policy behind, and the form of, the proposed amendments, Congress must enact legislation before October 1, 1983.[3]

With that deadline and purpose in mind, consultations were held with representatives of the Judicial Conference, the Department of Justice, and others who had voiced concern about the proposed amendments. H.R. 7154 is the product of those consultations. The bill seeks to effectuate the policy of relieving the Marshals Service of the duty of routinely serving summonses and complaints. It provides a system of service by mail modeled upon a system found to be effective in California, and finally, it makes appropriate stylistic, grammatical, and other changes in Rule 4.

NEED FOR THE LEGISLATION

1. CURRENT RULE 4

Rule 4 of the Federal Rules of Civil Procedure relates to the issuance and service of process. Subsection (c) authorizes service of process by personnel of the Marshals Service, by a person specially appointed by the Court, or "by a person authorized to serve process in an action brought in the courts of general jurisdiction of the state in which the district court is held or in which service is made." Subsection (d) describes how a summons and complaint must be served and designates those persons who must be served in cases involving specified categories of defendants. Mail service is not directly authorized. Subsection (d)(7), however, authorizes service under the law of the state in which the district court

sits upon defendants described in subsections (d)(1) (certain individuals) and (d)(3) (organizations). Thus, if state law authorizes service by mail of a summons and complaint upon an individual or organization described in subsections (d)(1) or (3), then subsection (d)(7) authorizes service by mail for United States district courts in that state.[4]

2. REDUCING THE ROLE OF MARSHALS

The Supreme Court's proposed modifications of Rule 4 were designed to alleviate the burden on the Marshals Service of serving summonses and complaints in private civil actions. Appendix II, at 7 (Report of the Committee on Rules of Practice and Procedure), 16 (Advisory Committee Note). While the Committee received no complaints about the goal of reducing the role of the Marshals Service, the Court's proposals simply failed to achieve that goal. See House Report No. 97–662, at 2–3 (1982).

The Court's proposed Rule 4(c)(2)(B) required the Marshals Service to serve summonses and complaints "pursuant to any statutory provision expressly providing for service by a United States Marshal or his deputy."[5] One such statutory provision is 28 U.S.C. 569(b), which compels marshals to "execute *all* lawful writs, process and orders issued under authority of the United States, *including those of the courts * * *.*" (emphasis added). Thus, any party could have invoked 28 U.S.C. 569(b) to utilize a marshal for service of a summons and complaint, thereby thwarting the intent of the new subsection to limit the use of marshals. The Justice Department acknowledges that the proposed subsection did not accomplish its objectives.[6]

Had 28 U.S.C. 569(b) been inconsistent with proposed Rule 4(c)(2)(B), the latter would have nullified the former under 28 U.S.C. 2072, which provides that "All laws in conflict with such rules shall be of no further force or effect after such rules have taken effect." Since proposed Rule 4(c)(2)(B) specifically referred to statutes such as 28 U.S.C. 569(b), however, the new subsection did not conflict with 28 U.S.C. 569(b) and did not, therefore, supersede it.

H.R. 7154 cures this problem and achieves the desired reduction in the role of the Marshals Service by authorizing marshals to serve summonses and complaints "on behalf of the United States". By so doing, H.R. 7154 eliminates the loophole in the Court's proposed language and still provides for service by marshals on behalf of the Government.[7]

3. MAIL SERVICE

The Supreme Court's proposed subsection (d)(7) and (8) authorized, as an alternative to personal service, mail service of summonses and complaints on individuals and organizations described in subsection (d)(1) and (3), but only through registered or certified mail, restricted delivery. Critics of that system of mail service argued that registered and certified mail were not necessarily effective methods of providing actual notice to defendants of claims against them. This was so, they argued, because signatures may be illegible or may not match the name of the defendant, or because it may be difficult to determine whether mail has been "unclaimed" or "refused", the latter apparently providing the sole basis for a default judgment.[8]

H.R. 7154 provides for a system of service by mail similar to the system now used in California. See Cal.Civ.Pro. § 415.30 (West 1973). Service would be by ordinary mail with a notice and acknowledgment of receipt form enclosed. If the defendant returns the acknowledgment form to the sender within 20 days of mailing, the sender files the return and service is complete. If the acknowledgment is not returned within 20 days of mailing, then service must be effected through some other means provided for in the Rules.

This system of mail service avoids the notice problems created by the registered and certified mail procedures proposed by the Supreme Court. If the proper person receives the notice and returns the acknowledgment, service is complete. If the proper person does not receive the mailed form, or if the proper person receives the notice but fails to return the acknowledgment form, another method of service authorized by law is required.[9] In either instance, however, the defendant will receive actual notice of the claim. In order to encourage defendants to return the acknowledgment form, the court can order a defendant who does not return it to pay the costs of service unless the defendant can show good cause for the failure to return it.

4. THE LOCAL OPTION

The Court's proposed amendments to Rule 4 deleted the provision in current subsection (d)(7) that authorizes service of a summons and complaint upon individuals and organizations "in the manner prescribed by the law of the state in which the district court is held for the service of summons or other like process upon any such defendant in an action brought in the courts of general jurisdiction of that state." The Committee received a variety of complaints about the deletion of this provision. Those in favor of preserving the local option saw no reason to forego systems of service that had been successful in achieving effective notice.[10]

H.R. 7154 carries forward the policy of the current rule and permits a party to serve a summons and complaint upon individuals and organizations described in Rule 4(d)(1) and (3) in accordance with the law of the state in which the district court sits. Thus, the bill authorizes four methods of serving a summons and complaint on such defendants: (1) service by a nonparty adult (Rule 4(c)(2)(A)); (2) service by personnel of the Marshals Service, if the party qualifies, such as because the party is proceeding in forma pauperis (Rule 4(c)(2)(B)); (3) service in any manner authorized by the law of the state in which the district court is held (Rule 4(c)(2)(C)(i)); or (4) service by regular mail with a notice and acknowledgment of receipt form enclosed (Rule 4(c)(2)(C)(ii)).[11]

5. TIME LIMITS

Rule 4 does not currently provide a time limit within which service must be completed. Primarily because United States marshals currently effect service of process, no time restriction has been deemed necessary, Appendix II, at 18 (Advisory Committee Note). Along with the proposed changes to subdivisions (c) and (d) to reduce the role of the Marshals Service, however, came new subdivision (j), requiring that service of a summons and complaint be made within 120 days of the filing of the complaint. If service were not accomplished within that time, proposed subdivision (j) required that the action "be dismissed as to that defendant without prejudice upon motion or upon the court's own initiative". Service by mail was deemed made for purposes of subdivi-

sion (j) "as of the date on which the process was accepted, refused, or returned as unclaimed".[12]

H.R. 7154 adopts a policy of limiting the time to effect service. It provides that if a summons and complaint have not been served within 120 days of the filing of the complaint and the plaintiff fails to show "good cause" for not completing service within that time, then the court must dismiss the action as to the unserved defendant. H.R. 7154 ensures that a plaintiff will be notified of an attempt to dismiss the action. If dismissal for failure to serve is raised by the court upon its own motion, the legislation requires that the court provide notice to the plaintiff. If dismissal is sought by someone else, Rule 5(a) of the Federal Rules of Civil Procedure requires that the motion be served upon the plaintiff.

Like proposed subsection (j), H.R. 7154 provides that a dismissal for failure to serve within 120 days shall be "without prejudice". Proposed subsection (j) was criticized by some for ambiguity because, it was argued, neither the text of subsection (j) nor the Advisory Committee Note indicated whether a dismissal without prejudice would toll a statute of limitation. *See* House Report 97–662, at 3–4 (1982). The problem would arise when a plaintiff files the complaint within the applicable statute of limitation period but does not effect service within 120 days. If the statute of limitation period expires during that period, and if the plaintiff's action is dismissed "without prejudice", can the plaintiff refile the complaint and maintain the action? The answer depends upon how the statute of limitation is tolled.[13]

If the law provides that the statute of limitation is tolled by filing and service of the complaint, then a dismissal under H.R. 7154 for failure to serve within the 120 days would, by the terms of the law controlling the tolling bar the plaintiff from later maintaining the cause of action.[14] If the law provides that the statute of limitation is tolled by filing alone, then the status of the plaintiff's cause of action turns upon the plaintiff's diligence. If the plaintiff has not been diligent, the court will dismiss the complaint for failure to serve within 120 days, and the plaintiff will be barred from later maintaining the cause of action because the statute of limitation has run. A dismissal without prejudice does not confer upon the plaintiff any rights that the plaintiff does otherwise possess and leaves a plaintiff whose action has been dismissed in the same position as if the action had never been filed.[15] If, on the other hand, the plaintiff has made reasonable efforts to effect service, then the plaintiff can move under Rule 6(b) to enlarge the time within which to serve or can oppose dismissal for failure to serve. A court would undoubtedly permit such a plaintiff additional time within which to effect service. Thus, a diligent plaintiff can preserve the cause of action. This result is consistent with the policy behind the time limit for service and with statutes of limitation, both of which are designed to encourage prompt movement of civil actions in the federal courts.

6. CONFORMING AND CLARIFYING SUBSECTIONS (D)(4) AND (5)

Current subsections (d)(4) and (5) prescribe which persons must be served in cases where an action is brought against the United States or an officer or agency of the United States. Under subsection (d)(4), where the United States is the named defendant, service must be made as follows: (1) personal service upon the United States attorney, an assistant United States attorney, or a designated clerical employee of the United States attorney in the district in which the action is brought; (2) registered or certified mail service to the Attorney General of the United States in Washington, D.C.; and (3) registered or certified mail service to the appropriate officer or agency if the action attacks an order of that officer or agency but does not name the officer or agency as a defendant. Under subsection (d)(5), where an officer or agency of the United States is named as a defendant, service must be made as in subsection (d)(4), except that personal service upon the officer or agency involved is required.[16]

The time limit for effecting service in H.R. 7154 would present significant difficulty to a plaintiff who has to arrange for personal service upon an officer or agency that may be thousands of miles away. There is little reason to require different types of service when the officer or agency is named as a party, and H.R. 7154 therefore conforms the manner of service under subsection (d)(5) to the manner of service under subsection (d)(4).

Section-By-Section Analysis

Section 1

Section 1 provides that the short title of the bill is the "Federal Rules of Civil Procedure Amendments Act of 1982".

Section 2

Section 2 of the bill consists of 7 numbered paragraphs, each amending a different part of Rule 4 of the Federal Rules of Civil Procedure.

Paragraph (1) deletes the requirement in present Rule 4(a) that a summons be delivered for service to the marshal or other person authorized to serve it. As amended by the legislation, Rule 4(a) provides that the summons be delivered to "the plaintiff or the plaintiff's attorney, who shall be responsible for prompt service of the summons and complaint". This change effectuates the policy proposed by the Supreme Court. See Appendix II, at — (Advisory Committee Note).

Paragraph (2) amends current Rule 4(c), which deals with the service of process. New Rule 4(c)(1) requires that all process, other than a subpoena or a summons and complaint, be served by the Marshals Service or by a person especially appointed for that purpose. Thus, the Marshals Service or persons specially appointed will continue to serve all process other than subpoenas and summonses and complaints, a policy identical to that proposed by the Supreme Court. See Appendix II, at 8 (Report of the Judicial Conference Committee on Rules of Practice and Procedure). The service of subpoenas is governed by Rule 45,[17] and the service of summonses and complaints is governed by new Rule 4(c)(2).

New Rule 4(c)(2)(A) sets forth the general rule that summonses and complaints shall be served by someone who is at least 18 years old and not a party to the action or proceeding. This is consistent with the Court's proposal. Appendix II, at 16 (Advisory Committee Note). Subparagraphs (B) and (C) of new Rule 4(c)(2) set forth exceptions to this general rule.

Subparagraph (B) sets forth 3 exceptions to the general rule. First, subparagraph (B)(i) requires the Marshals Service (or someone specially appointed by the court) to serve summonses and complaints on behalf of a party proceeding in forma pauperis or a seaman authorized to proceed under 28 U.S.C. 1916. This is identical to the Supreme Court's proposal. See Appendix II, at 3 (text of proposed rule), 16 (Advisory Committee Note). Second, subparagraph (B)(ii) requires the Marshals Service (or someone specially appointed by the court) to serve a summons and complaint when the court orders the marshals to do so in order properly to effect service in that particular action.[18] This, except for nonsubstantive changes in phrasing, is identical to the Supreme Court's proposal. See Appendix II, at 3 (text of proposed rule), 16 (Advisory Committee Note).

Subparagraph (C) of new Rule 4(c)(2) provides 2 exceptions to the general rule of service by a nonparty adult. These exceptions apply only when the summons and complaint is to be served upon persons described in Rule 4(d)(1) (certain individuals) or Rule 4(d)(3) (organizations).[19] First, subparagraph (C)(i) permits service of a summons and complaint in a manner authorized by the law of the state in which the court sits. This restates the option to follow local law currently found in Rule 4(d)(7) and would authorize service by mail if the state law so allowed. The method of mail service in that instance would, of course, be the method permitted by state law.

Second, subparagraph (C)(ii) permits service of a summons and complaint by regular mail. The sender must send to the defendant, by first-class mail, postage prepaid, a copy of the summons and complaint, together with 2 copies of a notice and acknowledgment of receipt of summons and complaint form and a postage prepaid return envelope addressed to the sender. If a copy of the notice and acknowledgment form is not received by the sender within 20 days after the date of mailing, then service must be made under Rule 4(c)(2)(A) or (B) (i.e., by a nonparty adult or, if the person qualifies,[20] by personnel of the Marshals Service or a person specially appointed by the court) in the manner prescribed by Rule 4(d)(1) or (3) (i.e., personal or substituted service).

New Rule 4(c)(2)(D) permits a court to penalize a person who avoids service by mail. It authorizes the court to order a person who does not return the notice and acknowledgment form within 20 days after mailing to pay the costs of service, unless that person can show good cause for failing to return the form. The purpose of this provision is to encourage the prompt return of the form so that the action can move forward without unnecessary delay. Fairness requires that a person who causes another additional and unnecessary expense in effecting service ought to reimburse the party who was forced to bear the additional expense.

Subparagraph (E) of Rule 4(c)(2) requires that the notice and acknowledgment form described in new Rule 4(c)(2)(C)(ii) be executed under oath or affirmation. This provision tracks the language of 28 U.S.C. 1746, which permits the use of unsworn declarations under penalty of perjury whenever an oath or affirmation is required. Statements made under penalty of perjury are subject to 18 U.S.C. 1621(2), which provides felony penalties for someone who "willfully subscribes as true any material matter which he does not believe to be true". The requirement that the form be executed under oath or affirmation is intended to encourage truthful submissions to the court, as the information contained in the form is important to the parties.[21]

New Rule 4(c)(3) authorizes the court freely to make special appointments to serve summonses and complaints under Rule 4(c)(2)(B) and all other process under Rule 4(c)(1). This carries forward the policy of present Rule 4(c).

Paragraph (3) of section 2 of the bill makes a non-substantive change in the caption of Rule 4(d) in order to reflect more accurately the provisions of Rule 4(d). Paragraph (3) also deletes a provision on service of a summons and complaint pursuant to state law. This provision is redundant in view of new Rule 4(c)(2)(C)(i).

Paragraph (4) of section 2 of the bill conforms Rule 4(d)(5) to present Rule 4(d)(4). Rule 4(d)(5) is amended to provide that service upon a named defendant agency or officer of the United States shall be made by "sending" a copy of the summons and complaint "by registered or certified mail" to the defendant.[22] Rule 4(d)(5) currently provides for service by "delivering" the copies to the defendant, but 28 U.S.C. 1391(e) authorizes delivery upon a defendant agency or officer outside of the district in which the action is brought by means of certified mail. Hence, the change is not a marked departure from current practice.

Paragraph (5) of section 2 of the bill amends the caption of Rule 4(e) in order to describe subdivision (e) more accurately.

Paragraph (6) of section 2 of the bill amends Rule 4(g), which deals with return of service. Present rule 4(g) is not changed except to provide that, if service is made pursuant to the new system of mail service (Rule 4(c)(2)(C)(ii)), the plaintiff or the plaintiff's attorney must file the court the signed acknowledgment form returned by the person served.

Paragraph (7) of section 2 of the bill adds new subsection (j) to provide a time limitation for the service of a summons and complaint. New Rule 4(j) retains the Supreme Court's requirement that a summons and complaint be served within 120 days of the filing of the complaint. See Appendix II, at 18 (Advisory Committee Note).[23] The plaintiff must be notified of an effort or intention to dismiss the action. This notification is mandated by subsection (j) if the dismissal is being raised on the court's own initiative and will be provided pursuant to Rule 5 (which requires service of motions upon the adverse party) if the dismissal is sought by someone else.[24] The plaintiff may move under Rule 6(b) to enlarge the time period. See Appendix II, at Id. (Advisory Committee Note). If service is not made within the time period or enlarged time period, however, and if the plaintiff fails to show "good cause" for not completing service, then the court must dismiss the action as to the unserved defendant. The dismissal is "without prejudice". The term "without prejudice" means that the dismissal does not constitute an adjudication of the merits of the complaint. A dismissal "without prejudice" leaves a plaintiff whose action has been dismissed in the position in which that person would have been if the action had never been filed.

SECTION 3

Section 3 of the bill amends the Appendix of Forms at the end of the Federal Rules of Civil Procedure by adding a new form 18A, "Notice and Acknowledgment for Service by Mail". This new form is required by new Rule 4(c)(2)(C)(ii), which requires that the notice and acknowledgment form used with service by regular mail conform substantially to Form 18A.

Form 18A as set forth in section 3 of the bill is modeled upon a form used in California.[25] It contains 2 parts. The first part is a notice to the person being served that tells that person that the enclosed summons and complaint is being served pursuant to Rule 4(c)(2)(C)(ii); advises that person to

sign and date the acknowledgment form and indicate the authority to receive service if the person served is not the party to the action (e.g., the person served is an officer of the organization being served); and warns that failure to return the form to the sender within 20 days may result in the court ordering the party being served to pay the expenses involved in effecting service. The notice also warns that if the complaint is not responded to within 20 days, a default judgment can be entered against the party being served. The notice is dated under penalty of perjury by the plaintiff or the plaintiff's attorney.[26]

The second part of the form contains the acknowledgment of receipt of the summons and complaint. The person served must declare on this part of the form, under penalty of perjury, the date and place of service and the person's authority to receive service.

SECTION 4

Section 4 of the bill provides that the changes in Rule 4 made by H.R. 7154 will take effect 45 days after enactment, thereby giving the bench and bar, as well as other interested persons and organizations (such as the Marshals Service), an opportunity to prepare to implement the changes made by the legislation. The delayed effective date means that service of process issued before the effective date will be made in accordance with current Rule 4. Accordingly, all process in the hands of the Marshals Service prior to the effective date will be served by the Marshals Service under the present rule.

SECTION 5

Section 5 of the bill provides that the amendments to Rule 4 proposed by the Supreme Court (whose effective date was postponed by Public Law 97–227) shall not take effect. This is necessary because under Public Law 97–227 the proposed amendments will take effect on October 1, 1983.

[1] The drafting of the rules and amendments is actually done by a committee of the Judicial Conference of the United States. In the case of the Federal Rules of Civil Procedure, the initial draft is prepared by the Advisory Committee on Civil Rules. The Advisory Committee's draft is then reviewed by the Committee on Rules of Practice and Procedure, which must give its approval to the draft. Any draft approved by that committee is forwarded to the Judicial Conference. If the Judicial Conference approves the draft, it forwards the draft to the Supreme Court. The Judicial Conference's role in the rule-making process is defined by 28 U.S.C. 331.

For background information about how the Judicial Conference committees operate, see Wright, "Procedural Reform: Its Limitation and Its Future," 1 Ga.L.Rev. 563, 565–66 (1967) (civil rules); statement of United States District Judge Roszel C. Thomsen, Hearings on Proposed Amendments to the Federal Rules of Criminal Procedure Before the Subcommittee on Criminal Justice of the House Committee on the Judiciary, 93d Cong., 2d Sess. at 25 (1974) (criminal rules); statement of United States Circuit Judge J. Edward Lumbard, id. at 203 (criminal rules); J. Weinstein, Reform of Federal Court Rulemaking Procedure (1977); Weinstein, "Reform of Federal Rulemaking Procedures," 76 Colum.L.Rev. 905 (1976).

[2] All of the other amendments, including all of the proposed amendments to the Federal Rules of Criminal Procedure and the Rules and Forms Governing Proceedings in the United States District Courts under sections 2254 and 2255 of Title 28, United States Code, took effect on August 1, 1982, as scheduled.

[3] The President has urged Congress to act promptly. See President's Statement on Signing H.R. 6663 into Law, 18 Weekly Comp. of Pres. Doc. 982 (August 2, 1982).

4 Where service of a summons is to be made upon a party who is neither an inhabitant of, nor found within, the state where the district court sits, subsection (e) authorizes service under a state statute or rule of court that provides for service upon such a party. This would authorize mail service if the state statute or rule of court provided for service by mail.

5 The Court's proposal authorized service by the Marshals Service in other situations. This authority, however, was not seen as thwarting the underlying policy of limiting the use of marshals. *See* Appendix II, at 16, 17 (Advisory Committee Note).

6 Appendix I, at 2 (letter of Assistant Attorney General Robert A. McConnell).

7 The provisions of H.R. 7154 conflict with 28 U.S.C. 569(b) because the latter is a broader command to marshals to serve all federal court process. As a later statutory enactment, however, H.R. 7154 supersedes 28 U.S.C. 569(b), thereby achieving the goal of reducing the role of marshals.

8 Proposed Rule 4(d)(8) provided that "Service . . . shall not be the basis for the entry of a default or a judgment by default unless the record contains a return receipt showing acceptance by the defendant or a returned envelope showing refusal of the process by the defendant." This provision reflects a desire to preclude default judgments on unclaimed mail. See Appendix II, at 7 (Report of the Committee on Rules of Practice and Procedure).

The interpretation of Rule 4(d)(8) to require a refusal of delivery in order to have a basis for a default judgment, while undoubtedly the interpretation intended and the interpretation that reaches the fairest result, may not be the only possible interpretation. Since a default judgment can be entered for defendant's failure to respond to the complaint once defendant has been served and the time to answer the complaint has run, it can be argued that a default judgment can be obtained where the mail was unclaimed because proposed subsection (j), which authorized dismissal of a complaint not served within 120 days, provided that mail service would be deemed made "on the date on which the process was accepted, refused, or *returned as unclaimed* " (emphasis added).

9 *See* p. 15 infra.

10 Proponents of the California system of mail service, in particular, saw no reason to supplant California's proven method of mail service with a certified mail service that they believed likely to result in default judgments without actual notice to defendants. See House Report No. 97–662, at 3 (1982).

11 The parties may, of course, stipulate to service, as is frequently done now.

12 While return of the letter as unclaimed was deemed service for the purpose of determining whether the plaintiff's action could be dismissed, return of the letter as unclaimed was not service for the purpose of entry of a default judgment against the defendant. See note 8 supra.

13 The law governing the tolling of a statute of limitation depends upon the type of civil action involved. In a diversity action, state law governs tolling. *Walker v. Armco Steel Corp.,* 446 U.S. 740 (1980). In *Walker,* plaintiff had filed his complaint and thereby commenced the action under Rule 3 of the Federal Rules of Civil Procedure within the statutory period. He did not, however, serve the summons and complaint until after the statutory period had run. The Court held that state law (which required both filing and service within the statutory period) governed, barring plaintiff's action.

In the federal question action, the courts of appeals have generally held that Rule 3 governs, so that the filing of the complaint tolls a statute of limitation. *United States v. Wahl,* 538 F.2d 285 (6th Cir. 1978); *Windbrooke Dev. Co. v. Environmental Enterprises Inc. of Fla.,* 524 F.2d 461 (5th Cir. 1975); *Metropolitan Paving Co. v. International Union of Operating Engineers,* 439 F.2d 300 (10th Cir. 1971); *Moore Co. v. Sid Richardson Carbon & Gasoline Co.,* 347 F.2d 921 (8th Cir.), cert. denied, 383 U.S. 925, reh. denied, 384 U.S. 914 (1965); *Hoffman v. Halden,* 268 F.2d 280 (9th Cir. 1959). The continued validity of this line of cases, however, must be questioned in light of the *Walker* case, even though the Court in that case expressly reserved judgment about

federal question actions, *see Walker v. Armco Steel Corp.,* 446 U.S. 741, 751 n.11 (1980).

14 The same result obtains even if service occurs within the 120 day period, if the service occurs after the statute of limitation has run.

15 See p. 19 infra.

16 See p. 17 infra.

17 Rule 45(c) provides that "A subpoena may be served by the marshal, by his deputy, or by any other person who is not a party and is not less than 18 years of age."

18 Some litigants have voiced concern that there may be situations in which personal service by someone other than a member of the Marshals Service may present a risk of injury to the person attempting to make the service. For example, a hostile defendant may have a history of injuring persons attempting to serve process. Federal judges undoubtedly will consider the risk of harm to private persons who would be making personal service when deciding whether to order the Marshals Service to make service under Rule 4(c)(2)(B)(iii).

19 The methods of service authorized by Rule 4(c)(2)(C) may be invoked by any person seeking to effect service. Thus, a nonparty adult who receives the summons and complaint for service under Rule 4(c)(1) may serve them personally or by mail in the manner authorized by Rule 4(c)(2)(C)(ii). Similarly, the Marshals Service may utilize the mail service authorized by Rule 4(c)(2)(C)(ii) when serving a summons and complaint under Rule 4(c)(2)(B)(i)(iii). When serving a summons and complaint under Rule 4(c)(2)(B)(ii), however, the Marshals Service must serve in the manner set forth in the court's order. If no particular manner of service is specified, then the Marshals Service may utilize Rule 4(c)(2)(C)(ii). It would not seem to be appropriate, however, for the Marshals Service to utilize Rule 4(c)(2)(C)(ii) in a situation where a previous attempt to serve by mail failed. Thus, it would not seem to be appropriate for the Marshals Service to attempt service by regular mail when serving a summons and complaint on behalf of a plaintiff who is proceeding in forma pauperis if that plaintiff previously attempted unsuccessfully to serve the defendant by mail.

20 To obtain service by personnel of the Marshals Service or someone specially appointed by the court, a plaintiff who has unsuccessfully attempted mail service under Rule 4(c)(2)(C)(ii) must meet the conditions of Rule 4(c)(2)(B)—for example, the plaintiff must be proceeding *in forma pauperis.*

21 For example, the sender must state the date of mailing on the form. If the form is not returned to the sender within 20 days of that date, then the plaintiff must serve the defendant in another manner and the defendant may be liable for the costs of such service. Thus, a defendant would suffer the consequences of a misstatement about the date of mailing.

22 See p. 12 supra.

23 The 120 day period begins to run upon the filing of each complaint. Thus, where a defendant files a cross-claim against the plaintiff, the 120 day period begins to run upon the filing of the cross-complaint, not upon the filing of the plaintiff's complaint initiating the action.

24 The person who may move to dismiss can be the putative defendant (i.e., the person named as defendant in the complaint filed with the court) or, in multi-party actions, another party to the action. (If the putative defendant moves to dismiss and the failure to effect service is due to that person's evasion of service, a court should not dismiss because the plaintiff has "good cause" for not completing service.)

25 See Cal.Civ.Pro. § 415.30 (West 1973).

26 See p. 16 supra.

Rule 4.1.   Service of Other Process

(a) Generally. Process other than a summons as provided in Rule 4 or subpoena as provided in Rule 45 shall be served by a United States marshal, a deputy United States marshal, or a person specially appointed for that purpose, who shall make proof of service as provided in Rule 4(1). The process may be served anywhere within the territorial limits of the state in which the district court is located, and, when authorized by a statute of the United States, beyond the territorial limits of that state.

(b) Enforcement of Orders: Commitment for Civil Contempt. An order of civil commitment of a person held to be in contempt of a decree or injunction issued to enforce the laws of the United States may be served and enforced in any district. Other orders in civil contempt proceedings shall be served in the state in which the court issuing the order to be enforced is located or elsewhere within the United States if not more than 100 miles from the place at which the order to be enforced was issued.
(Added Apr. 22, 1993, eff. Dec. 1, 1993.)

ADVISORY COMMITTEE NOTES
1993 Adoption

This is a new rule. Its purpose is to separate those few provisions of the former Rule 4 bearing on matters other than service of a summons to allow greater textual clarity in Rule 4. Subdivision (a) contains no new language.

Subdivision (b) replaces the final clause of the penultimate sentence of the former subdivision 4(f), a clause added to the rule in 1963. The new rule provides for nationwide service of orders of civil commitment enforcing decrees of injunctions issued to compel compliance with federal law. The rule makes no change in the practice with respect to the enforcement of injunctions or decrees not involving the enforcement of federally-created rights.

Service of process is not required to notify a party of a decree or injunction, or of an order that the party show cause why that party should not be held in contempt of such an order. With respect to a party who has once been served with a summons, the service of the decree or injunction itself or of an order to show cause can be made pursuant to Rule 5. Thus, for example, an injunction may be served on a party through that person's attorney. *Chagas v. United States,* 369 F.2d 643 (5th Cir.1966). The same is true for service of an order to show cause. *Waffenschmidt v. Mackay,* 763 F.2d 711 (5th Cir.1985).

The new rule does not affect the reach of the court to impose criminal contempt sanctions. Nationwide enforcement of federal decrees and injunctions is already available with respect to criminal contempt: a federal court may effect the arrest of a criminal contemnor anywhere in the United States, 28 U.S.C. § 3041, and a contemnor when arrested may be subject to removal to the district in which punishment may be imposed. Fed.R.Crim.P. 40. Thus, the present law permits criminal contempt enforcement against a contemnor wherever that person may be found.

The effect of the revision is to provide a choice of civil or criminal contempt sanctions in those situations to which it applies. Contempt proceedings, whether civil or criminal, must be brought in the court that was allegedly defied by a contumacious act. *Ex parte Bradley,* 74 U.S. 366 (1869). This is so even if the offensive conduct or inaction occurred outside the district of the court in which the enforcement proceeding must be conducted. *E.g., McCourtney v. United States,* 291 Fed. 497 (8th Cir.), *cert. denied,* 263 U.S. 714 (1923). For this purpose, the rule as before does not distinguish between parties and other persons subject to contempt sanctions by reason of their relation or connection to parties.

Rule 5. Serving and Filing Pleadings and Other Papers

(a) Service: When required. Except as otherwise provided in these rules, every order required by its terms to be served, every pleading subsequent to the original complaint unless the court otherwise orders because of numerous defendants, every paper relating to discovery required to be served upon a party unless the court otherwise orders, every written motion other than one which may be heard ex parte, and every written notice, appearance, demand, offer of judgment, designation of record on appeal, and similar paper shall be served upon each of the parties. No service need be made on parties in default for failure to appear except that pleadings asserting new or additional claims for relief against them shall be served upon them in the manner provided for service of summons in Rule 4.

In an action begun by seizure of property, in which no person need be or is named as defendant, any service required to be made prior to the filing of an answer, claim, or appearance shall be made upon the person having custody or possession of the property at the time of its seizure.

(b) Making Service.

(1) Service under Rules 5(a) and 77(d) on a party represented by an attorney is made on the attorney unless the court orders service on the party.

(2) Service under Rule 5(a) is made by:

(A) Delivering a copy to the person served by:
(i) handing it to the person;
(ii) leaving it at the person's office with a clerk or other person in charge, or if no one is in charge leaving it in a conspicuous place in the office; or
(iii) if the person has no office or the office is closed, leaving it at the person's dwelling house or usual place of abode with someone of suitable age and discretion residing there.

(B) Mailing a copy to the last known address of the person served. Service by mail is complete on mailing.

(C) If the person served has no known address, leaving a copy with the clerk of the court.

(D) Delivering a copy by any other means, including electronic means, consented to in writing by the person served. Service by electronic means is complete on transmission; service by other consented means is complete when the person making service delivers the copy to the agency designated to make delivery. If authorized by local rule, a party may make service under this subparagraph (D) through the court's transmission facilities.

(3) Service by electronic means under Rule 5(b)(2)(D) is not effective if the party making service learns that the attempted service did not reach the person to be served.

(c) Same: Numerous Defendants. In any action in which there are unusually large numbers of defendants, the court, upon motion or of its own initiative, may order that service of the pleadings of the defendants and replies thereto need not be made as between the defendants and that any cross-claim, counterclaim, or matter constituting an avoidance or affirmative defense contained therein shall be deemed to be denied or avoided by all other parties and that the filing of any such pleading and service thereof upon the plaintiff constitutes due notice of it to the parties. A copy of every such order shall be served upon the parties in such manner and form as the court directs.

(d) Filing; Certificate of Service. All papers after the complaint required to be served upon a party, together with a certificate of service, must be filed with the court within a reasonable time after service, but disclosures under Rule 26(a)(1) or (2) and the following discovery requests and responses must not be filed until they are used in the proceeding or the court orders filing: (i) depositions, (ii) interrogatories, (iii) requests for documents or to permit entry upon land, and (iv) requests for admission.

(e) Filing with the Court Defined. The filing of papers with the court as required by these rules shall be made by filing them with the clerk of court, except that the judge may permit the papers to be filed with the judge, in which event the judge shall note thereon the filing date and forthwith transmit them to the office of the clerk. A court may by local rule permit papers to be filed, signed, or verified by electronic means that are consistent with technical standards, if any, that the Judicial Conference of the United States establishes. A paper filed by electronic means in compliance with a local rule constitutes a written paper for the purpose of applying these rules. The clerk shall not refuse to accept for filing any paper presented for that purpose solely because it is not presented in proper form as required by these rules or any local rules or practices.

(As amended Jan. 21, 1963, eff. July 1, 1963; Mar. 30, 1970, eff. July 1, 1970; Apr. 29, 1980, eff. Aug. 1, 1980; Mar. 2, 1987, eff. Aug. 1, 1987; Apr. 30, 1991, eff. Dec. 1, 1991; Apr. 22, 1993, eff. Dec. 1, 1993; Apr. 23, 1996, eff. Dec. 1, 1996; Apr. 17, 2000, eff. Dec. 1, 2000; Apr. 23, 2001, eff. Dec. 1, 2001.)

ADVISORY COMMITTEE NOTES
1937 Adoption

Note to Subdivisions (a) and (b). Compare 2 Minn.Stat. (1927) §§ 9240, 9241, 9242; N.Y.C.P.A. (1937) §§ 163, 164 and N.Y.R.C.P. (1937) Rules 20, 21; 2 Wash.Rev.Stat.Ann. (Remington, 1932) §§ 244 to 249.

Note to Subdivision (d). Compare the present practice under former Equity Rule 12 (Issue of Subpoena—Time for Answer).

1963 Amendment

The words "affected thereby," stricken out by the amendment, introduced a problem of interpretation. See 1 Barron & Holtzoff, *Federal Practice & Procedure* 760–61 (Wright ed. 1960). The amendment eliminates this difficulty and promotes full exchange of information among the parties by requiring service of papers on all the parties to the action, except as otherwise provided in the rules. See also subdivision (c) of Rule 5. So, for example, a third-party defendant is required to serve his answer to the third-party complaint not only upon the defendant but also upon the plaintiff. See amended Form 22–A and the Advisory Committee's Note thereto.

As to the method of serving papers upon a party whose address is unknown, see Rule 5(b).

1970 Amendment

The amendment makes clear that all papers relating to discovery which are required to be served on any party must be served on all parties, unless the court orders otherwise. The present language expressly includes notices and demands, but it is not explicit as to answers or responses as provided in Rules 33, 34, and 36. Discovery papers may be voluminous or the parties numerous, and the court is empowered to vary the requirement if in a given case it proves needlessly onerous.

In actions begun by seizure of property, service will at times have to be made before the absent owner of the property has filed an appearance. For example, a prompt deposition may be needed in a maritime action in rem. See Rules 30(a) and 30(b)(2) and the related notes. A provision is added authorizing service on the person having custody or possession of the property at the time of its seizure.

1980 Amendment

Subdivision (d). By the terms of this rule and Rule 30(f)(1) discovery materials must be promptly filed, although it often happens that no use is made of the materials after they are filed. Because the copies required for filing are an added expense and the large volume of discovery filings presents serious problems of storage in some districts, the Committee in 1978 first proposed that discovery materials not be filed unless on order of the court or for use in the proceedings. But such materials are sometimes of interest to those who may have no access to them except by a requirement of filing, such as members of a class, litigants similarly situated, or the public generally. Accordingly, this amendment and a change in Rule 30(f)(1) continue the requirement of filing but make it subject to an order of the court that discovery materials not be filed unless filing is requested by the court or is effected by parties who wish to use the materials in the proceeding.

1987 Amendment

The amendments are technical. No substantive change is intended.

1991 Amendment

Subdivision (d). This subdivision is amended to require that the person making service under the rule certify that service has been effected. Such a requirement has generally been imposed by local rule.

Having such information on file may be useful for many purposes, including proof of service if an issue arises concerning the effectiveness of the service. The certificate will generally specify the date as well as the manner of service, but parties employing private delivery services may sometimes be unable to specify the date of delivery. In the latter circumstance, a specification of the date of transmission of the paper to the delivery service may be sufficient for the purposes of this rule.

Subdivision (e). The words *"pleading and other"* are stricken as unnecessary. Pleadings are papers within the meaning of the rule. The revision also accommodates the development of the use of facsimile transmission for filing.

Several local district rules have directed the office of the clerk to refuse to accept for filing papers not conforming to certain requirements of form imposed by local rules or practice. This is not a suitable role for the office of the clerk, and the practice exposes litigants to the hazards of time bars; for these reasons, such rules are proscribed by this revision. The enforcement of these rules and of the local rules is a role for a judicial officer. A clerk may of course advise a party or counsel that a particular instrument is not in proper form, and may be directed to so inform the court.

1993 Amendments

This is a technical amendment, using the broader language of Rule 25 of the Federal Rules of Appellate Procedure. The district court—and the bankruptcy court by virtue of a cross-reference in Bankruptcy Rule 7005—can, by local rule, permit filing not only by facsimile transmissions but also by other electronic means, subject to standards approved by the Judicial Conference.

1996 Amendments

The present Rule 5(e) has authorized filing by facsimile or other electronic means on two conditions. The filing must be authorized by local rule. Use of this means of filing must be authorized by the Judicial Conference of the United States and must be consistent with standards established by the Judicial Conference. Attempts to develop Judicial Conference standards have demonstrated the value of several adjustments in the rule.

The most significant change discards the requirement that the Judicial Conference authorize local electronic filing rules. As before, each district may decide for itself whether it has the equipment and personnel required to establish electronic filing, but a district that wishes to establish electronic filing need no longer await Judicial Conference action.

The role of Judicial Conference standards is clarified by specifying that the standards are to govern technical matters. Technical standards can provide nationwide uniformity, enabling ready use of electronic filing without pausing to adjust for the otherwise inevitable variations among local rules. Judicial Conference adoption of technical standards should prove superior to specification in these rules. Electronic technology has advanced with great speed. The process of adopting Judicial Conference standards should prove speedier and more flexible in determining the time for the first uniform standards, in adjusting standards at appropriate intervals, and in sparing the Supreme Court and Congress the need to consider technological details. Until Judicial Conference standards are adopted, however, uniformity will occur only to the extent that local rules deliberately seek to copy other local rules.

It is anticipated that Judicial Conference standards will govern such technical specifications as data formatting, speed of transmission, means to transmit copies of supporting documents, and security of communication. Perhaps more important, standards must be established to assure proper maintenance and integrity of the record and to provide appropriate access and retrieval mechanisms. Local rules must address these issues until Judicial Conference standards are adopted.

The amended rule also makes clear the equality of filing by electronic means with written filings. An electronic filing that complies with the local rule satisfies all requirements for filing on paper, signature, or verification. An electronic filing that otherwise satisfies the requirements of 28 U.S.C. § 1746 need not be separately made in writing. Public access to electronic filings is governed by the same rules as govern written filings.

The separate reference to filing by facsimile transmission is deleted. Facsimile transmission continues to be included as an electronic means.

2000 Amendment

Subdivision (d). Rule 5(d) is amended to provide that disclosures under Rule 26(a)(1) and (2), and discovery requests and responses under Rules 30, 31, 33, 34, and 36 must not be filed until they are used in the action. "Discovery requests" includes deposition notices and "discovery responses" includes objections. The rule supersedes and invalidates local rules that forbid, permit, or require filing of these materials before they are used in the action. The former Rule 26(a)(4) requirement that disclosures under Rule 26(a)(1) and (2) be filed has been removed. Disclosures under Rule 26(a)(3), however, must be promptly filed as provided in Rule 26(a)(3). Filings in connection with Rule 35 examinations, which involve a motion proceeding when the parties do not agree, are unaffected by these amendments.

Recognizing the costs imposed on parties and courts by required filing of discovery materials that are never used in an action, Rule 5(d) was amended in 1980 to authorize court orders that excuse filing. Since then, many districts have adopted local rules that excuse or forbid filing. In 1989 the Judicial Conference Local Rules Project concluded that these local rules were inconsistent with Rule 5(d), but urged the Advisory Committee to consider amending the rule. *Local Rules Project* at 92 (1989). The Judicial Conference of the Ninth Circuit gave the Committee similar advice in 1997. The reality of nonfiling reflected in these local rules has even been assumed in drafting the national rules. In 1993, Rule 30(f)(1) was amended to direct that the officer presiding at a deposition file it with the court or send it to the attorney who arranged for the transcript or recording. The Committee Note explained that this alternative to filing was designed for "courts which direct that depositions not be automatically filed." Rule 30(f)(1) has been amended to conform to this change in Rule 5(d).

Although this amendment is based on widespread experience with local rules, and confirms the results directed by these local rules, it is designed to supersede and invalidate local rules. There is no apparent reason to have different filing rules in different districts. Even if districts vary in present capacities to store filed materials that are not used in an action, there is little reason to continue expending court resources for this purpose. These costs and burdens would likely change as parties make increased use of audio- and videotaped depositions. Equipment to facilitate review and reproduction of such discovery materials may prove costly to acquire, maintain, and operate.

The amended rule provides that discovery materials and disclosures under Rule 26(a)(1) and (a)(2) must not be filed until they are "used in the proceeding." This phrase is meant to refer to proceedings in court. This filing requirement is not triggered by "use" of discovery materials in other discovery activities, such as depositions. In connection with proceedings in court, however, the rule is to be interpreted broadly; any use of discovery materials in court in connection with a motion, a pretrial conference under Rule 16, or otherwise, should be interpreted as use in the proceeding.

Once discovery or disclosure materials are used in the proceeding, the filing requirements of Rule 5(d) should apply to them. But because the filing requirement applies only with regard to materials that are used, only those parts of voluminous materials that are actually used need be filed. Any party would be free to file other pertinent portions of materials that are so used. *See* Fed. R. Evid. 106; *cf.* Rule 32(a)(4). If the parties are unduly sparing in their submissions, the court may order further filings. By local rule, a court could provide appropriate direction regarding the filing of discovery materials, such as depositions, that are used in proceedings.

"Shall" is replaced by "must" under the program to conform amended rules to current style conventions when there is no ambiguity.

GAP Report

The Advisory Committee recommends no changes to either the amendments to Rule 5(d) or the Committee Note as published.

2001 Amendments

Rule 5(b) is restyled.

Rule 5(b)(1) makes it clear that the provision for service on a party's attorney applies only to service made under Rules 5(a) and 77(d). Service under Rules 4, 4.1, 45(b), and 71A(d)(3)—as well as rules that invoke those rules—must be made as provided in those rules.

Subparagraphs (A), (B), and (C) of Rule 5(b)(2) carry forward the method-of-service provisions of former Rule 5(b).

Subparagraph (D) of Rule 5(b)(2) is new. It authorizes service by electronic means or any other means, but only if consent is obtained from the person served. The consent must be express, and cannot be implied from conduct. Early experience with electronic filing as authorized by Rule 5(d) is positive, supporting service by electronic means as well. Consent is required, however, because it is not yet possible to assume universal entry into the world of electronic communication. Subparagraph (D) also authorizes service by nonelectronic means. The Rule 5(b)(2)(B) provision making mail service complete on mailing is extended in subparagraph (D) to make service by electronic means complete on transmission; transmission is effected when the sender does the last act that must be performed by the sender. Service by other agencies is complete on delivery to the designated agency.

Finally, subparagraph (D) authorizes adoption of local rules providing for service through the court. Electronic case filing systems will come to include the capacity to make service by using the court's facilities to transmit all documents filed in the case. It may prove most efficient to establish an environment in which a party can file with the court, making use of the court's transmission facilities to serve the filed paper on all other parties. Transmission might be by such means as direct transmission of the paper, or by transmission of a notice of filing that includes an electronic link for direct access to the paper. Because service is under subparagraph (D), consent must be obtained from the persons served.

Consent to service under Rule 5(b)(2)(D) must be in writing, which can be provided by electronic means. Parties are encouraged to specify the scope and duration of the consent. The specification should include at least the persons to whom service should be made, the appropriate address or location for such service—such as the e-mail address or facsimile machine number, and the format to be used for attachments. A district court may establish a registry or other facility that allows advance consent to service by specified means for future actions.

Rule 6(e) is amended to allow additional time to respond when service is made under Rule 5(b)(2)(D). The additional time does not relieve a party who consents to service under Rule 5(b)(2)(D) of the responsibilities to monitor the facility designated for receiving service and to provide prompt notice of any address change.

Paragraph (3) addresses a question that may arise from a literal reading of the provision that service by electronic means is complete on transmission. Electronic communication is rapidly improving, but lawyers report continuing failures of transmission, particularly with respect to attachments. Ordinarily the risk of non-receipt falls on the person being served, who has consented to this form of service. But the risk should not extend to situations in which the person attempting service learns that the attempted service in fact did not reach the person to be served. Given actual knowledge that the attempt failed, service is not effected. The person attempting service must either try again or show circumstances that justify dispensing with service.

Paragraph (3) does not address the similar questions that may arise when a person attempting service learns that service by means other than electronic means in fact did not reach the person to be served. Case law provides few illustrations of circumstances in which a person attempting service actually knows that the attempt failed but seeks to act as if service had been made. This negative history suggests there is no need to address these problems in Rule 5(b)(3). This silence does not imply any view on these issues, nor on the circumstances that justify various forms of judicial action even though service has not been made.

Changes Made After Publication and Comments

Rule 5(b)(2)(D) was changed to require that consent be "in writing."

Rule 5(b)(3) is new. The published proposal did not address the question of failed service in the text of the rule. Instead, the Committee Note included this statement: "As with other modes of service, however, actual notice that the transmission was not received defeats the presumption of receipt that arises from the provision that service is complete on transmission. The sender must take additional steps to effect service. Service by other agencies is complete on delivery to the designated agency." The addition of paragraph (3) was prompted by consideration of the draft Appellate Rule 25(c) that was prepared for the meeting of the Appellate Rules Advisory Committee. This draft provided: "Service by electronic means is complete on transmission, unless the party making service is notified that the paper was not received." Although Appellate Rule 25(c) is being prepared for publication and comment, while Civil Rule 5(b) has been published and otherwise is ready to recommend for adoption, it seemed desirable to achieve some parallel between the two rules.

The draft Rule 5(b)(3) submitted for consideration by the Advisory Committee covered all means of service except for leaving a copy with the clerk of the court when the person to be served has no known address. It was not limited to electronic service for fear that a provision limited to electronic service might generate unintended negative implications as to service by other means, particularly mail. This concern was strengthened by a small number of opinions that say that service by mail is effective, because complete on mailing, even when the person making service has prompt actual notice that the mail was not delivered. The Advisory Committee voted to limit Rule 5(b)(3) to service by electronic means because this means of service is relatively new, and seems likely to miscarry more frequently than service by post. It was suggested during the Advisory Committee meeting that the question of negative implication could be addressed in the Committee Note. There was little discussion of this possibility. The Committee Note submitted above includes a "no negative implications" paragraph prepared by the Reporter for consideration by the Standing Committee.

The Advisory Committee did not consider at all a question that was framed during the later meeting of the Appellate Rules Advisory Committee. As approved by the Advisory Committee, Rule 5(b)(3) defeats service by electronic means "if the party making service learns that the attempted service did not reach the person to be served." It says nothing about the time relevant to learning of the failure. The omission may seem glaring. Curing the omission, however, requires selection of a time. As revised, proposed Appellate Rule 25(c) requires that the party making service learn of the failure within three calendar days. The Appellate Rules Advisory Committee will have the luxury of public comment and another year to consider the desirability of this short period. If Civil Rule 5(b) is to be recommended for adoption now, no such luxury is available. This issue deserves careful consideration by the Standing Committee.

Several changes are made in the Committee Note. (1) It requires that consent "be express, and cannot be implied from conduct." This addition reflects a more general concern stimulated by a reported ruling that an e-mail address on a firm's letterhead implied consent to e-mail service. (2) The paragraph discussing service through the court's facilities is expanded by describing alternative methods, including an "electronic link." (3) There is a new paragraph that states that the requirement of written consent can be satisfied by electronic means, and that suggests matters that should be addressed by the consent. (4) A paragraph is added to note the additional response time provided by amended Rule 6(e). (5) The final two paragraphs address newly added Rule 5(b)(3). The first explains the rule that electronic service is not effective if the person making service learns that it did not reach the person to be served. The second paragraph seeks to defeat any negative implications that might arise from limiting Rule 5(b)(3) to electronic service, not mail, not other means consented to such as commercial express service, and not service on another person on behalf of the person to be served.

Rule 6(e)

The Advisory Committee recommended that no change be made in Civil Rule 6(e) to reflect the provisions of Civil Rule 5(b)(2)(D) that, with the consent of the person to be served, would allow service by electronic or other means. Absent change, service by these means would not affect the time for acting in response to the paper served. Comment was requested, however, on the alternative that would allow an additional 3 days to respond. The alternative Rule 6(e) amendments are cast in a form that permits ready incorporation in the Bankruptcy Rules. Several of the comments suggest that the added three days should be provided. Electronic transmission is not always instantaneous, and may fail for any of a number of reasons. It may take three days to arrange for transmission in readable form. Providing added time to respond will not discourage people from asking for consent to electronic transmission, and may encourage people to give consent. The more who consent, the quicker will come the improvements that will make electronic service ever more attractive. Consistency with the Bankruptcy Rules will be a good thing, and the Bankruptcy Rules Advisory Committee believes the additional three days should be allowed.

Rule 6.   Time

(a) Computation. In computing any period of time prescribed or allowed by these rules, by the local rules of any district court, by order of court, or by any applicable statute, the day of the act, event, or default from which the designated period of time begins to run shall not be included. The last day of the period so computed shall be included, unless it is a Saturday, a Sunday, or a legal holiday, or, when the act to be done is the filing of a paper in court, a day on which weather or other conditions have made the office of the clerk of the district court inaccessible, in which event the period runs until the end of the next day which is not one of the aforementioned days. When the period of time prescribed or allowed is less than 11 days, intermediate Saturdays, Sundays, and legal holidays shall be excluded in the computation. As used in this rule and in Rule 77(c), "legal holiday"

includes New Year's Day, Birthday of Martin Luther King, Jr., Washington's Birthday, Memorial Day, Independence Day, Labor Day, Columbus Day, Veterans Day, Thanksgiving Day, Christmas Day, and any other day appointed as a holiday by the President or the Congress of the United States, or by the state in which the district court is held.

(b) Enlargement. When by these rules or by a notice given thereunder or by order of court an act is required or allowed to be done at or within a specified time, the court for cause shown may at any time in its discretion (1) with or without motion or notice order the period enlarged if request therefor is made before the expiration of the period originally prescribed or as extended by a previous order, or (2) upon motion made after the expiration of the specified period permit the act to be done where the failure to act was the result of excusable neglect; but it may not extend the time for taking any action under Rules 50(b) and (c)(2), 52(b), 59(b), (d) and (e), and 60(b), except to the extent and under the conditions stated in them.

[(c) Rescinded Feb. 28, 1966, eff. July 1, 1966]

(d) For Motions—Affidavits. A written motion, other than one which may be heard ex parte, and notice of the hearing thereof shall be served not later than 5 days before the time specified for the hearing, unless a different period is fixed by these rules or by order of the court. Such an order may for cause shown be made on ex parte application. When a motion is supported by affidavit, the affidavit shall be served with the motion; and, except as otherwise provided in Rule 59(c), opposing affidavits may be served not later than 1 day before the hearing, unless the court permits them to be served at some other time.

(e) Additional Time After Service under Rule 5(b)(2)(B), (C), or (D). Whenever a party has the right or is required to do some act or take some proceedings within a prescribed period after the service of a notice or other paper upon the party and the notice or paper is served upon the party under Rule 5(b)(2)(B), (C), or (D), 3 days shall be added to the prescribed period.

(As amended Dec. 27, 1946, eff. Mar. 19, 1948; Jan. 21, 1963, eff. July 1, 1963; Feb. 28, 1966, eff. July 1, 1966; Dec. 4, 1967, eff. July 1, 1968; Mar. 1, 1971, eff. July 1, 1971; Apr. 28, 1983, eff. Aug. 1, 1983; Apr. 29, 1985, eff. Aug. 1, 1985; Mar. 2, 1987, eff. Aug. 1, 1987; Apr. 29, 1999, eff. Dec. 1, 1999; Apr. 23, 2001, eff. Dec. 1, 2001.)

Proposed Amendment of Subdivision (e)

Effective December 1, 2005, absent contrary Congressional action, subdivision (e) of this rule is amended to read as follows:

*(e) **Additional Time After Certain Kinds of Service.** Whenever a party must or may act within a prescribed period after service and service is made*

under Rule 5(b)(2)(B), (C), or (D), 3 days are added after the prescribed period would otherwise expire under subdivision (a).

ADVISORY COMMITTEE NOTES

1937 Adoption

Note to Subdivisions (a) and (b). These are amplifications along lines common in state practices, of [former] Equity Rule 80 (Computation of Time—Sundays and Holidays) and of the provisions for enlargement of time found in [former] Equity Rules 8 (Enforcement of Final Decrees) and 16 (Defendant to Answer—Default—Decree Pro Confesso). See also Rule XIII, Rules and Forms in Criminal Cases, 1934, 292 U.S. 661, 666. Compare Ala.Code Ann. (Michie, 1928) § 13 and former Law Rule 8 of the Rules of the Supreme Court of the District of Columbia (1924), superseded in 1929 by Law Rule 8, Rules of the District Court of the United States for the District of Columbia (1937).

Note to Subdivision (c). This eliminates the difficulties caused by the expiration of terms of court. Such statutes as U.S.C., Title 28, [former] § 12 (Trials not discontinued by new term) are not affected. Compare Rules of the United States District Court of Minnesota, Rule 25 (Minn.Stat. (Mason, Supp.1936), p. 1089).

Note to Subdivision (d). Compare 2 Minn.Stat. (Mason, 1927) § 9246; N.Y.R.C.P. (1937) Rules 60 and 64.

1946 Amendment

Note to Subdivision (b). The purpose of the amendment is to clarify the finality of judgments. Prior to the advent of the Federal Rules of Civil Procedure, the general rule that a court loses jurisdiction to disturb its judgments, upon the expiration of the term at which they were entered, had long been the classic device which (together with the statutory limits on the time for appeal) gave finality to judgments. See note to rule 73(a). Rule 6(c) abrogates that limit on judicial power. That limit was open to many objections, one of them being inequality of operation because, under it, the time for vacating a judgment rendered early in a term was much longer than for a judgment rendered near the end of the term.

The question to be met under rule 6(b) is: how far should the desire to allow correction of judgments be allowed to postpone their finality? The rules contain a number of provisions permitting the vacation or modification of judgments on various grounds. Each of these rules contains express time limits on the motions for granting of relief. Rule 6(b) is a rule of general application giving wide discretion to the court to enlarge these time limits or revive them after they have expired, the only exceptions stated in the original rule being a prohibition against enlarging the time specified in Rule 59(b) and (d) for making motions for or granting new trials, and a prohibition against enlarging the time fixed by law for taking an appeal. It should also be noted that Rule 6(b) itself contains no limitation of time within which the court may exercise its discretion, and since the expiration of the term does not end its power, there is now no time limit on the exercise of its discretion under Rule 6(b).

Decisions of lower federal courts suggest that some of the rules containing time limits which may be set aside under Rule 6(b) are Rules 25, 50(b), 52(b), 60(b), and 73(g).

In a number of cases the effect of Rule 6(b) on the time limitations of these rules has been considered. Certainly the rule is susceptible of the interpretation that the court is given the power in its discretion to relieve a party from failure to act within the times specified in any of these other rules, with only the exceptions stated in Rule 6(b), and in some cases the rule has been so construed.

With regard to Rule 25(a) for substitution, it was held in *Anderson v. Brady,* Ky.1941, 1 F.R.D. 589, 4 Fed.Rules Service 25a.1, Case 1, and in *Anderson v. Yungkau,* C.C.A.6, 1946, 153 F.2d 685, certiorari granted 66 S.Ct. 1025, 328 U.S. 829, 90 L.Ed. 1606, that under Rule 6(b) the court had no authority to allow substitution of parties after the expiration of the limit fixed in Rule 25(a).

As to Rules 50(b) for judgments notwithstanding the verdict and 52(b) for amendment of findings and vacation of judgment, it was recognized in *Leishman v. Associated Wholesale Electric Co.,* 1943, 63 S.Ct. 543, 318 U.S. 203, 87 L.Ed. 714, that Rule 6(b) allowed the district court to enlarge the time to make a motion for amended findings and judgment beyond the limit expressly fixed in Rule 52(b). See *Coca-Cola v. Busch,* E.D.Pa.1943, 7 Fed.Rules Service, 59b.2, Case 4. Obviously, if the time limit in Rule 52(b) could be set aside under Rule 6(b), the time limit in Rule 50(b) for granting judgment notwithstanding the verdict (and thus vacating the judgment entered "forthwith" on the verdict) likewise could be set aside.

As to Rule 59 on motions for a new trial, it has been settled that the time limits in Rule 59(b) and (d) for making motions for or granting new trial could not be set aside under Rule 6(b), because Rule 6(b) expressly refers to Rule 59, and forbids it. See *Safeway Stores, Inc. v. Coe,* App.D.C. 1943, 136 F.2d 771, 78 U.S.App.D.C. 19; *Jusino v. Morales & Tio,* C.C.A.1, 1944, 139 F.2d 946; *Coca-Cola Co. v. Busch,* E.D.Pa.1943, 7 Fed.Rules Service 59b.2, Case 4; *Peterson v. Chicago Great Western Ry. Co.,* D.Neb.1943, 3 F.R.D. 346, 7 Fed.Rules Service 59b.2, Case 1; *Leishman v. Associated Wholesale Electric Co.,* 1943, 63 S.Ct. 543, 318 U.S. 203, 87 L.Ed. 714.

As to Rule 60(b) for relief from a judgment, it was held in *Schram v. O'Connor,* Mich.1941, 5 Fed.Rules Serv. 6b.31, Case 1, 2 F.R.D. 192, s.c. 5 Fed.Rules Serv. 6b.31, Case 2, 2 F.R.D. 192, that the six-months time limit in original rule 60(b) for making a motion for relief from a judgment for surprise, mistake, or excusable neglect could be set aside under Rule 6(b). The contrary result was reached in *Wallace v. United States,* C.C.A.2, 1944, 142 F.2d 240, certiorari denied 65 S.Ct. 37, 323 U.S. 712, 89 L.Ed. 573; *Reed v. South Atlantic Steamship Co. of Del.,* Del.1942, 2 F.R.D. 475, 6 Fed.Rules Serv. 60b.31, Case 1.

As to Rule 73(g), fixing the time for docketing an appeal, it was held in *Ains-worth v. Gill Glass & Fixture Co.,* C.C.A.3, 1939, 104 F.2d 83, that under Rule 6(b) the district court, upon motion made after the expiration of the forty-day period, stated in Rule 73(g), but before the expiration of the ninety-day period therein specified, could permit the docketing of the appeal on a showing of excusable neglect. The contrary was held in *Mutual Benefit Health & Accident Ass'n v. Snyder,* C.C.A.6, 1940, 109 F.2d 469 and in *Burke v. Canfield,* 1940, 111 F.2d 526, 72 App.D.C. 127.

The amendment of Rule 6(b) now proposed is based on the view that there should be a definite point where it can be said a judgment is final; that the right method of dealing with the problem is to list in Rule 6(b) the various other rules whose time limits may not be set aside, and then, if the time limit in any of those other rules is too short, to amend that other rule to give a longer time. The further argument is that Rule 6(c) abolished the long standing device to produce finality in judgments through expiration of the term, and since that limitation on the jurisdiction of courts to set aside their own judgments has been removed by Rule 6(c), some other limitation must be substituted or judgments never can be said to be final.

In this connection reference is made to the established rule that if a motion for new trial is seasonably made, the mere making or pendency of the motion destroys the finality of the judgment, and even though the motion is ultimately denied, the full time for appeal starts anew from the date of denial. Also, a motion to amend the findings under Rule 52(b) has the same effect on the time for appeal. *Leishman v. Associated Wholesale Electric Co.,* 1943, 63 S.Ct. 543, 318 U.S. 203, 87 L.Ed. 714. By the same reasoning a motion for judgment under Rule 50(b), involving as it does the vacation of a judgment entered "forthwith" on the verdict (Rule 58), operates to postpone, until an order is made, the running of the time for appeal. The Committee believes that the abolition by Rule 6(c) of the old rule that a court's power over its judgments ends with the term, requires a substitute limitation, and that unless Rule 6(b) is amended to prevent enlargement of the times specified in Rules 50(b), 52(b) and 60(b), and the limitation as to Rule 59(b) and (d) is retained, no one can say when a judgment is final. This is also true with regard to proposed Rule 59(e), which authorizes a motion to alter or amend a judgment, hence that rule is also included in the enumeration in amended Rule 6(b). In consideration of the amendment, however, it should be noted that Rule 60(b) is also to be amended so as to lengthen the six-months period originally prescribed in that rule to one year.

As to Rule 25 on substitution, while finality is not involved, the limit there fixed should be controlling. That rule, as amended, gives the court power, upon showing of a reasonable excuse, to permit substitution after the expiration of the two-year period.

As to Rule 73(g), it is believed that the conflict in decisions should be resolved and not left to further litigation, and that the rule should be listed as one whose limitation may not be set aside under Rule 6(b).

As to Rule 59(c), fixing the time for serving affidavits on motion for new trial, it is believed that the court should have authority under Rule 6(b) to enlarge the time, because, once the motion for new trial is made, the judgment no longer has finality, and the extension of time for affidavits thus does not of itself disturb finality.

Other changes proposed in Rule 6(b) are merely clarifying and conforming. Thus "request" is substituted for "application" in clause (1) because an application is defined as a motion under Rule 7(b). The phrase "extend the time" is substituted for "enlarge the period" because the former is a more suitable expression and relates more clearly to both clauses (1) and (2). The final phrase in Rule 6(b), "or the period for taking an appeal as provided by law", is deleted and a reference to Rule 73(a) inserted, since it is proposed to

state in that rule the time for appeal to a circuit court of appeals, which is the only appeal governed by the Federal Rules, and allows an extension of time. See Rule 72.

Subdivision (c). The purpose of this amendment is to prevent reliance upon the continued existence of a term as a source of power to disturb the finality of a judgment upon grounds other than those stated in these rules. See *Hill v. Hawes*, 1944, 64 S.Ct. 334, 320 U.S. 520, 88 L.Ed. 283; *Boaz v. Mutual Life Ins. Co. of New York*, C.C.A.8, 1944, 146 F.2d 321; *Bucy v. Nevada Construction Co.*, C.C.A.9, 1942, 125 F.2d 213.

1963 Amendment

Subdivision (a). This amendment is related to the amendment of Rule 77(c) changing the regulation of the days on which the clerk's office shall be open.

The wording of the first sentence of Rule 6(a) is clarified and the subdivision is made expressly applicable to computing periods of time set forth in local rules.

Saturday is to be treated in the same way as Sunday or a "legal holiday" in that it is not to be included when it falls on the last day of a computed period, nor counted as an intermediate day when the period is less than 7 days. "Legal holiday" is defined for purposes of this subdivision and amended Rule 77(c). Compare the definition of "holiday" in 11 U.S.C. § 1(18); also 5 U.S.C. § 86a; Executive Order No. 10358, *"Observance of Holidays,"* June 9, 1952, 17 Fed.Reg. 5269. In the light of these changes the last sentence of the present subdivision, dealing with half holidays, is eliminated.

With Saturdays and State holidays made "dies non" in certain cases by the amended subdivision, computation of the usual 5-day notice of motion or the 2-day notice to dissolve or modify a temporary restraining order may work out so as to cause embarrassing delay in urgent cases. The delay can be obviated by applying to the court to shorten the time, see Rules 6(d) and 65(b).

Subdivision (b). The prohibition against extending the time for taking action under Rule 25 (Substitution of parties) is eliminated. The only limitation of time provided for in amended Rule 25 is the 90-day period following a suggestion upon the record of the death of a party within which to make a motion to substitute the proper parties for the deceased party. See Rule 25(a)(1), as amended, and the Advisory Committee's Note thereto. It is intended that the court shall have discretion to enlarge that period.

1966 Amendment

P.L. 88–139, § 1, 77 Stat. 248, approved on October 16, 1963, amended 28 U.S.C. § 138 to read as follows: "The district court shall not hold formal terms." Thus Rule 6(c) is rendered unnecessary, and it is rescinded.

1967 Amendment

The amendment eliminates the references to Rule 73, which is to be abrogated.

1971 Amendment

The amendment adds Columbus Day to the list of legal holidays to conform the subdivision to the Act of June 28, 1968, 82 Stat. 250, which constituted Columbus Day a legal holiday effective after January 1, 1971.

The Act, which amended Title 5, U.S.C. § 6103(a), changes the day on which certain holidays are to be observed. Washington's Birthday, Memorial Day and Veterans Day are to be observed on the third Monday in February, the last Monday in May and the fourth Monday in October, respectively, rather than, as heretofore, on February 22, May 30, and November 11, respectively, Columbus Day is to be observed on the second Monday in October. New Year's Day, Independence Day, Thanksgiving Day and Christmas continue to be observed on the traditional days.

1983 Amendment

Subdivision (b). The amendment confers finality upon the judgments of magistrates by foreclosing enlargement of the time for appeal except as provided in new Rule 74(a) (20 day period for demonstration of excusable neglect).

1985 Amendment

Rule 6(a) is amended to acknowledge that weather conditions or other events may render the clerk's office inaccessible one or more days. Parties who are obliged to file something with the court during that period should not be penalized if they cannot do so. The amendment conforms to changes made in Federal Rule of Criminal Procedure 45(a), effective August 1, 1982.

The Rule also is amended to extend the exclusion of intermediate Saturdays, Sundays, and legal holidays to the computation of time periods less than 11 days. Under the current version of the Rule, parties bringing motions under rules with 10-day periods could have as few as 5 working days to prepare their motions. This hardship would be especially acute in the case of Rules 50(b) and (c)(2), 52(b), and 59(b), (d), and (e), which may not be enlarged at the discretion of the court. See Rule 6(b). If the exclusion of Saturdays, Sundays, and legal holidays will operate to cause excessive delay in urgent cases, the delay can be obviated by applying to the court to shorten the time. See Rule 6(b).

The Birthday of Martin Luther King, Jr., which becomes a legal holiday effective in 1986, has been added to the list of legal holidays enumerated in the Rule.

1987 Amendment

The amendments are technical. No substantive change is intended.

1999 Amendment

The reference to Rule 74(a) is stricken from the catalogue of time periods that cannot be extended by the district court. The change reflects the 1997 abrogation of Rule 74(a).

2001 Amendments

The additional three days provided by Rule 6(e) is extended to the means of service authorized by the new paragraph (D) added to Rule 5(b), including—with the consent of the person served—service by electronic or other means. The three-day addition is provided as well for service on a person with no known address by leaving a copy with the clerk of the court.

Changes Made After Publication and Comments

Proposed Rule 6(e) is the same as the "alternative proposal" that was published in August 1999.

2005 Amendments

[Effective December 1, 2005, absent contrary Congressional action.]

Rule 6(e) is amended to remove any doubt as to the method for extending the time to respond after service by mail, leaving with the clerk of court, electronic means, or other means consented to by the party served. Three days are added after the prescribed period otherwise expires under Rule 6(a). Intermediate Saturdays, Sundays, and legal holidays are included in counting these added three days. If the third day is a Saturday, Sunday, or legal holiday, the last day to act is the next day that is not a Saturday, Sunday, or legal holiday. The effect of invoking the day when the prescribed period would otherwise expire under Rule 6(a) can be illustrated by assuming that the thirtieth day of a thirty-day period is a Saturday. Under Rule 6(a) the period expires on the next day that is not a Sunday or legal holiday. If the following Monday is a legal holiday, under Rule 6(a) the period expires on Tuesday. Three days are then added— Wednesday, Thursday, and Friday as the third and final day

to act. If the period prescribed expires on a Friday, the three added days are Saturday, Sunday, and Monday, which is the third and final day to act unless it is a legal holiday. If Monday is a legal holiday, the next day that is not a legal holiday is the third and final day to act.

Application of Rule 6(e) to a period that is less than eleven days can be illustrated by a paper that is served by mailing on a Friday. If ten days are allowed to respond, intermediate Saturdays, Sundays, and legal holidays are excluded in determining when the period expires under Rule 6(a). If there is no legal holiday, the period expires on the Friday two weeks after the paper was mailed. The three added Rule 6(e) days are Saturday, Sunday, and Monday, which is the third and final day to act unless it is a legal holiday. If Monday is a legal holiday, the next day that is not a legal holiday is the final day to act.

HISTORICAL NOTES

Effective and Applicability Provisions

1946 Amendments. Effective date of amendment to this rule, see rule 86(b).

III. PLEADINGS AND MOTIONS

Rule 7.   Pleadings Allowed; Form of Motions

(a) Pleadings. There shall be a complaint and an answer; a reply to a counterclaim denominated as such; an answer to a cross-claim, if the answer contains a cross-claim; a third-party complaint, if a person who was not an original party is summoned under the provisions of Rule 14; and a third-party answer, if a third-party complaint is served. No other pleading shall be allowed, except that the court may order a reply to an answer or a third-party answer.

(b) Motions and Other Papers.

(1) An application to the court for an order shall be by motion which, unless made during a hearing or trial, shall be made in writing, shall state with particularity the grounds therefor, and shall set forth the relief or order sought. The requirement of writing is fulfilled if the motion is stated in a written notice of the hearing of the motion.

(2) The rules applicable to captions and other matters of form of pleadings apply to all motions and other papers provided for by these rules.

(3) All motions shall be signed in accordance with Rule 11.

(c) Demurrers, Pleas, etc., Abolished. Demurrers, pleas, and exceptions for insufficiency of a pleading shall not be used.

(As amended Dec. 27, 1946, eff. Mar. 19, 1948; Jan. 21, 1963, eff. July 1, 1963; Apr. 28, 1983, eff. Aug. 1, 1983.)

ADVISORY COMMITTEE NOTES

1937 Adoption

1. A provision designating pleadings and defining a motion is common in the state practice acts. See Smith-Hurd

Ill.Stats. ch. 110, § 156 (Designation and order of pleadings); 2 Minn.Stat. (Mason, 1927) § 9246 (Definition of motion); and N.Y.C.P.A. (1937) § 113 (Definition of motion). Former Equity Rules 18 (Pleadings—Technical Forms Abrogated), 29 (Defenses—How Presented), and 33 (Testing Sufficiency of Defense) abolished technical forms of pleading, demurrers and pleas, and exceptions for insufficiency of an answer.

2. **Note to Subdivision (a).** This preserves the substance of [former] Equity Rule 31 (Reply—When Required—When Cause at Issue). Compare the English practice, *English Rules under the Judicature Act* (The Annual Practice, 1937) O. 23, r.r. 1, 2 (Reply to counterclaim; amended, 1933, to be subject to the rules applicable to defenses, O. 21). See O. 21, r.r. 1–14; O. 27, r. 13 (When pleadings deemed denied and put in issue). Under the codes the pleadings are generally limited. A reply is sometimes required to an affirmative defense in the answer. 1 Colo.Stat.Ann. (1935) § 66; Ore. Code Ann. (1930) §§ 1–614, 1–616. In other jurisdictions no reply is necessary to an affirmative defense in the answer, but a reply may be ordered by the court. N.C.Code Ann. (1935) § 525; 1 S.D.Comp.Laws (1929) § 2357. A reply to a counterclaim is usually required. Ark.Civ.Code (Crawford, 1934) §§ 123 to 125; Wis.Stat. (1935) §§ 263.20, 263.21. U.S.C. Title 28, [former] § 45 (District courts; practice and procedure in certain cases) is modified insofar as it may dispense with a reply to a counterclaim.

For amendment of pleadings, see Rule 15 dealing with amended and supplemental pleadings.

3. All statutes which use the words "petition", "bill of complaint", "plea", "demurrer", and other such terminology are modified in form by this rule.

1946 Amendment

Note. This amendment eliminates any question as to whether the compulsory reply, where a counterclaim is pleaded, is a reply only to the counterclaim or is a general

---

reply to the answer containing the counterclaim. The Commentary, *Scope of Reply where Defendant Has Pleaded Counterclaim*, 1939, 1 Fed.Rules Serv. 672; *Fort Chartres and Ivy Landing Drainage and Levee District No. Five v. Thompson*, Ill.1945, 8 Fed.Rules Serv. 13.32, Case 1.

1963 Amendment

Certain redundant words are eliminated and the subdivision is modified to reflect the amendment of Rule 14(a) which in certain cases eliminates the requirement of obtaining leave to bring in a third-party defendant.

1983 Amendment

One of the reasons sanctions against improper motion practice have been employed infrequently is the lack of clarity of Rule 7. That rule has stated only generally that the pleading requirements relating to captions, signing, and other matters of form also apply to motions and other papers. The addition of Rule 7(b)(3) makes explicit the applicability of the signing requirement and the sanctions of Rule 11, which have been amplified.

HISTORICAL NOTES

Effective and Applicability Provisions

1946 Amendments. Effective date of amendment to this rule, see rule 86(b).

Rule 7.1. Disclosure Statement

(a) Who Must File: Nongovernmental Corporate Party. A nongovernmental corporate party to an action or proceeding in a district court must file two copies of a statement that identifies any parent corporation and any publicly held corporation that owns 10% or more of its stock or states that there is no such corporation.

(b) Time for Filing; Supplemental Filing. A party must:

(1) file the Rule 7.1(a) statement with its first appearance, pleading, petition, motion, response, or other request addressed to the court, and

(2) promptly file a supplemental statement upon any change in the information that the statement requires.

(Added Apr. 29, 2002, eff. Dec. 1, 2002.)

ADVISORY COMMITTEE NOTES

2002 Adoption

Rule 7.1 is drawn from Rule 26.1 of the Federal Rules of Appellate Procedure, with changes to adapt to the circumstances of district courts that dictate different provisions for the time of filing, number of copies, and the like. The information required by Rule 7.1(a) reflects the "financial interest" standard of Canon 3C(1)(c) of the Code of Conduct for United States Judges. This information will support properly informed disqualification decisions in situations that call for automatic disqualification under Canon 3C(1)(c). It does not cover all of the circumstances that may call for disqualification under the financial interest standard, and does not deal at all with other circumstances that may call for disqualification.

Although the disclosures required by Rule 7.1(a) may seem limited, they are calculated to reach a majority of the circumstances that are likely to call for disqualification on the basis of financial information that a judge may not know or recollect. Framing a rule that calls for more detailed disclosure will be difficult. Unnecessary disclosure requirements place a burden on the parties and on courts. Unnecessary disclosure of volumes of information may create a risk that a judge will overlook the one bit of information that might require disqualification, and also may create a risk that unnecessary disqualifications will be made rather than attempt to unravel a potentially difficult question. It has not been feasible to dictate more detailed disclosure requirements in Rule 7.1(a).

Rule 7.1 does not prohibit local rules that require disclosures in addition to those required by Rule 7.1. Developing experience with local disclosure practices and advances in electronic technology may provide a foundation for adopting more detailed disclosure requirements by future amendments of Rule 7.1.

Changes Made After Publication and Comment. The provisions that would require disclosure of additional information that may be required by the Judicial Conference have been deleted.

Rule 8. General Rules of Pleading

(a) Claims for Relief. A pleading which sets forth a claim for relief, whether an original claim, counterclaim, cross-claim, or third-party claim, shall contain (1) a short and plain statement of the grounds upon which the court's jurisdiction depends, unless the court already has jurisdiction and the claim needs no new grounds of jurisdiction to support it, (2) a short and plain statement of the claim showing that the pleader is entitled to relief, and (3) a demand for judgment for the relief the pleader seeks. Relief in the alternative or of several different types may be demanded.

(b) Defenses; Form of Denials. A party shall state in short and plain terms the party's defenses to each claim asserted and shall admit or deny the averments upon which the adverse party relies. If a party is without knowledge or information sufficient to form a belief as to the truth of an averment, the party shall so state and this has the effect of a denial. Denials shall fairly meet the substance of the averments denied. When a pleader intends in good faith to deny only a part or a qualification of an averment, the pleader shall specify so much of it as is true and material and shall deny only the remainder. Unless the pleader intends in good faith to controvert all the averments of the preceding pleading, the pleader may make denials as specific denials of designated averments or paragraphs or may generally deny all the averments except such designated averments or paragraphs as the pleader expressly admits; but, when the pleader does so intend to controvert all its averments,

including averments of the grounds upon which the court's jurisdiction depends, the pleader may do so by general denial subject to the obligations set forth in Rule 11.

(c) Affirmative Defenses. In pleading to a preceding pleading, a party shall set forth affirmatively accord and satisfaction, arbitration and award, assumption of risk, contributory negligence, discharge in bankruptcy, duress, estoppel, failure of consideration, fraud, illegality, injury by fellow servant, laches, license, payment, release, res judicata, statute of frauds, statute of limitations, waiver, and any other matter constituting an avoidance or affirmative defense. When a party has mistakenly designated a defense as a counterclaim or a counterclaim as a defense, the court on terms, if justice so requires, shall treat the pleading as if there had been a proper designation.

(d) Effect of Failure to Deny. Averments in a pleading to which a responsive pleading is required, other than those as to the amount of damage, are admitted when not denied in the responsive pleading. Averments in a pleading to which no responsive pleading is required or permitted shall be taken as denied or avoided.

(e) Pleading to be Concise and Direct; Consistency.

(1) Each averment of a pleading shall be simple, concise, and direct. No technical forms of pleading or motions are required.

(2) A party may set forth two or more statements of a claim or defense alternately or hypothetically, either in one count or defense or in separate counts or defenses. When two or more statements are made in the alternative and one of them if made independently would be sufficient, the pleading is not made insufficient by the insufficiency of one or more of the alternative statements. A party may also state as many separate claims or defenses as the party has regardless of consistency and whether based on legal, equitable, or maritime grounds. All statements shall be made subject to the obligations set forth in Rule 11.

(f) Construction of Pleadings. All pleadings shall be so construed as to do substantial justice.
(As amended Feb. 28, 1966, eff. July 1, 1966; Mar. 2, 1987, eff. Aug. 1, 1987.)

ADVISORY COMMITTEE NOTES

1937 Adoption

Note to Subdivision (a). See [former] Equity Rules 25 (Bill of Complaint—Contents), and 30 (Answer—Contents—Counterclaim). Compare 2 Ind.Stat.Ann. (Burns, 1933) §§ 2–1004, 2–1015; 2 Ohio Gen.Code Ann. (Page, 1926) §§ 11305, 11314; Utah Rev.Stat.Ann. (1933) §§ 104–7–2, 104–9–1.

See Rule 19(c) for the requirement of a statement in a claim for relief of the names of persons who ought to be parties and the reason for their omission.

See Rule 23(b) for particular requirements as to the complaint in a secondary action by shareholders.

Note to Subdivision (b). 1. This rule supersedes the methods of pleading prescribed in U.S.C., Title 19, § 508 (Persons making seizures pleading general issue and proving special matter); U.S.C. Title 35, [former] §§ 40d (Proving under general issue, upon notice, that a statement in application for an extended patent is not true), 69 [now 282] (Pleading and proof in actions for infringement) and similar statutes.

2. This rule is, in part, [former] Equity Rule 30 (Answer—Contents—Counterclaim), with the matter on denials largely from the Connecticut practice. See Conn. Practice Book (1934) §§ 107, 108, and 122; Conn.Gen.Stat. (1930) §§ 5508 to 5514. Compare the English practice, *English Rules Under the Judicature Act* (The Annual Practice, 1937) O. 19, r.r. 17–20.

Note to Subdivision (c). This follows substantially *English Rules Under the Judicature Act* (The Annual Practice, 1937) O. 19, r. 15 and N.Y.C.P.A. (1937) § 242, with "surprise" omitted in this rule.

Note to Subdivision (d). The first sentence is similar to former Equity Rule 30 (Answer—Contents—Counterclaim). For the second sentence see former Equity Rule 31 (Reply—When Required—When Cause at Issue). This is similar to *English Rules Under the Judicature Act* (The Annual Practice, 1937) O. 19, r.r. 13, 18; and to the practice of the States.

Note to Subdivision (e). This rule is an elaboration upon [former] Equity Rule 30 (Answer—Contents—Counterclaim), plus a statement of the actual practice under some codes. Compare also [former] Equity Rule 18 (Pleadings—Technical Forms Abrogated). See Clark, *Code Pleading* (1928), pp. 171–4, 432–5; Hankin, *Alternative and Hypothetical Pleading* (1924), 33 Yale L.J. 365.

Note to Subdivision (f). A provision of like import is of frequent occurrence in the codes. Smith-Hurd Ill.Stats. ch. 110, § 157(3); 2 Minn.Stat. (Mason, 1927) § 9266; N.Y.C.P.A. (1937) § 275; 2 N.D.Comp.Laws Ann. (1913) § 7458.

1966 Amendment

The change here is consistent with the broad purposes of unification.

1987 Amendment

The amendments are technical. No substantive change is intended.

Rule 9. Pleading Special Matters

(a) Capacity. It is not necessary to aver the capacity of a party to sue or be sued or the authority of a party to sue or be sued in a representative capacity or the legal existence of an organized association of persons that is made a party, except to the extent required to show the jurisdiction of the court. When a party desires to raise an issue as to the legal existence of any party or the capacity of any party to

sue or be sued or the authority of a party to sue or be sued in a representative capacity, the party desiring to raise the issue shall do so by specific negative averment, which shall include such supporting particulars as are peculiarly within the pleader's knowledge.

(b) Fraud, Mistake, Condition of the Mind. In all averments of fraud or mistake, the circumstances constituting fraud or mistake shall be stated with particularity. Malice, intent, knowledge, and other condition of mind of a person may be averred generally.

(c) Conditions Precedent. In pleading the performance or occurrence of conditions precedent, it is sufficient to aver generally that all conditions precedent have been performed or have occurred. A denial of performance or occurrence shall be made specifically and with particularity.

(d) Official Document or Act. In pleading an official document or official act it is sufficient to aver that the document was issued or the act done in compliance with law.

(e) Judgment. In pleading a judgment or decision of a domestic or foreign court, judicial or quasi-judicial tribunal, or of a board or officer, it is sufficient to aver the judgment or decision without setting forth matter showing jurisdiction to render it.

(f) Time and Place. For the purpose of testing the sufficiency of a pleading, averments of time and place are material and shall be considered like all other averments of material matter.

(g) Special Damage. When items of special damage are claimed, they shall be specifically stated.

(h) Admiralty and Maritime Claims. A pleading or count setting forth a claim for relief within the admiralty and maritime jurisdiction that is also within the jurisdiction of the district court on some other ground may contain a statement identifying the claim as an admiralty or maritime claim for the purposes of Rules 14(c), 38(e), 82, and the Supplemental Rules for Certain Admiralty and Maritime Claims. If the claim is cognizable only in admiralty, it is an admiralty or maritime claim for those purposes whether so identified or not. The amendment of a pleading to add or withdraw an identifying statement is governed by the principles of Rule 15. A case that includes an admiralty or maritime claim within this subdivision is an admiralty case within 28 U.S.C. § 1292(a)(3).

(As amended Feb. 28, 1966, eff. July 1, 1966; Dec. 4, 1967, eff. July 1, 1968; Mar. 30, 1970, eff. July 1, 1970; Mar. 2, 1987, eff. Aug. 1, 1987; April 11, 1997, eff. Dec. 1, 1997.)

ADVISORY COMMITTEE NOTES
1937 Adoption

Note to Subdivision (a). Compare [former] Equity Rule 25 (Bill of Complaint—Contents) requiring disability to be stated; Utah Rev.Stat.Ann. (1933) § 104–13–15, enumerating

a number of situations where a general averment of capacity is sufficient. For provisions governing averment of incorporation, see 2 Minn.Stat. (Mason, 1927) § 9271; N.Y.R.C.P. (1937) Rule 93; 2 N.D.Comp.Laws Ann. (1913) § 7981 et seq.

Note to Subdivision (b). See *English Rules Under the Judicature Act* (The Annual Practice, 1937) O. 19, r. 22.

Note to Subdivision (c). The codes generally have this or a similar provision. See *English Rules Under the Judicature Act* (The Annual Practice, 1937) O. 19, r. 14; 2 Minn. Stat. (Mason, 1927) § 9273; N.Y.R.C.P. (1937) Rule 92; 2 N.D.Comp.Laws Ann. (1913) § 7461; 2 Wash.Rev.Stat.Ann. (Remington, 1932) § 288.

Note to Subdivision (e). The rule expands the usual code provisions on pleading a judgment by including judgments or decisions of administrative tribunals and foreign courts. Compare Ark.Civ.Code (Crawford, 1934) § 141; 2 Minn.Stat. (Mason, 1927) § 9269; N.Y.R.C.P. (1937) Rule 95; 2 Wash. Rev.Stat.Ann. (Remington, 1932) § 287.

1966 Amendment

Certain distinctive features of the admiralty practice must be preserved for what are now suits in admiralty. This raises the question: After unification, when a single form of action is established, how will the counterpart of the present suit in admiralty be identifiable? In part the question is easily answered. Some claims for relief can only be suits in admiralty, either because the admiralty jurisdiction is exclusive or because no nonmaritime ground of federal jurisdiction exists. Many claims, however, are cognizable by the district courts whether asserted in admiralty or in a civil action, assuming the existence of a nonmaritime ground of jurisdiction. Thus at present the pleader has power to determine procedural consequences by the way in which he exercises the classic privilege given by the saving-to-suitors clause (28 U.S.C. § 1333) or by equivalent statutory provisions. For example, a longshoreman's claim for personal injuries suffered by reason of the unseaworthiness of a vessel may be asserted in a suit in admiralty or, if diversity of citizenship exists, in a civil action. One of the important procedural consequences is that in the civil action either party may demand a jury trial, while in the suit in admiralty there is no right to jury trial except as provided by statute.

It is no part of the purpose of unification to inject a right to jury trial into those admiralty cases in which that right is not provided by statute. Similarly as will be more specifically noted below, there is no disposition to change the present law as to interlocutory appeals in admiralty, or as to the venue of suits in admiralty; and, of course, there is no disposition to inject into the civil practice as it now is the distinctively maritime remedies (maritime attachment and garnishment, actions in rem, possessory, petitory and partition actions and limitation of liability). The unified rules must therefore provide some device for preserving the present power of the pleader to determine whether these historically maritime procedures shall be applicable to his claim or not; the pleader must be afforded some means of designating his claim as the counterpart of the present suit in admiralty, where its character as such is not clear.

The problem is different from the similar one concerning the identification of claims that were formerly suits in equity. While that problem is not free from complexities, it is broadly true that the modern counterpart of the suit in

equity is distinguishable from the former action at law by the character of the relief sought. This mode of identification is possible in only a limited category of admiralty cases. In large numbers of cases the relief sought in admiralty is simple money damages, indistinguishable from the remedy afforded by the common law. This is true, for example, in the case of the longshoreman's action for personal injuries stated above. After unification has abolished the distinction between civil actions and suits in admiralty, the complaint in such an action would be almost completely ambiguous as to the pleader's intentions regarding the procedure invoked. The allegation of diversity of citizenship might be regarded as a clue indicating an intention to proceed as at present under the saving-to-suitors clause; but this, too, would be ambiguous if there were also reference to the admiralty jurisdiction, and the pleader ought not be required to forego mention of all available jurisdictional grounds.

Other methods of solving the problem were carefully explored, but the Advisory Committee concluded that the preferable solution is to allow the pleader who now has power to determine procedural consequences by filing a suit in admiralty to exercise that power under unification, for the limited instances in which procedural differences will remain, by a simple statement in his pleading to the effect that the claim is an admiralty or maritime claim.

The choice made by the pleader in identifying or in failing to identify his claim as an admiralty or maritime claim is not an irrevocable election. The rule provides that the amendment of a pleading to add or withdraw an identifying statement is subject to the principles of Rule 15.

1968 Amendment

The amendment eliminates the reference to Rule 73 which is to be abrogated and transfers to Rule 9(h) the substance of Subsection (h) of Rule 73 which preserved the right to an interlocutory appeal in admiralty cases which is provided by 28 U.S.C. § 1292(a)(3).

1970 Amendment

The reference to Rule 26(a) is deleted, in light of the transfer of that subdivision to Rule 30(a) and the elimination of the de bene esse procedure therefrom. See the Advisory Committee's note to Rule 30(a).

1987 Amendment

The amendment is technical. No substantive change is intended.

1997 Amendment

Section 1292(a)(3) of the Judicial Code provides for appeal from "[i]nterlocutory decrees of * * * district courts * * * determining the rights and liabilities of the parties to admiralty cases in which appeals from final decrees are allowed."

Rule 9(h) was added in 1966 with the unification of civil and admiralty procedure. Civil Rule 73(h) was amended at the same time to provide that the § 1292(a)(3) reference "to admiralty cases shall be construed to mean admiralty and maritime claims within the meaning of Rule 9(h)." This provision was transferred to Rule 9(h) when the Appellate Rules were adopted.

A single case can include both admiralty or maritime claims and nonadmiralty claims or parties. This combination reveals an ambiguity in the statement in present Rule 9(h) that an admiralty "claim" is an admiralty "case." An order "determining the rights and liabilities of the parties" within the meaning of § 1292(a)(3) may resolve only a nonadmiralty claim, or may simultaneously resolve interdependent admiralty and nonadmiralty claims. Can appeal be taken as to the nonadmiralty matter, because it is part of a case that includes an admiralty claim, or is appeal limited to the admiralty claim?

The courts of appeals have not achieved full uniformity in applying the § 1292(a)(3) requirement that an order "determin[e] the rights and liabilities of the parties." It is common to assert that the statute should be construed narrowly, under the general policy that exceptions to the final judgment rule should be construed narrowly. This policy would suggest that the ambiguity should be resolved by limiting the interlocutory appeal right to orders that determine the rights and liabilities of the parties to an admiralty claim.

A broader view is chosen by this amendment for two reasons. The statute applies to admiralty "cases," and may itself provide for appeal from an order that disposes of a nonadmiralty claim that is joined in a single case with an admiralty claim. Although a rule of court may help to clarify and implement a statutory grant of jurisdiction, the line is not always clear between permissible implementation and impermissible withdrawal of jurisdiction. In addition, so long as an order truly disposes of the rights and liabilities of the parties within the meaning of § 1292(a)(3), it may prove important to permit appeal as to the nonadmiralty claim. Disposition of the nonadmiralty claim, for example, may make it unnecessary to consider the admiralty claim and have the same effect on the case and parties as disposition of the admiralty claim. Or the admiralty and nonadmiralty claims may be interdependent. An illustration is provided by Roco Carriers, Ltd. v. M/V Nurnberg Express, 899 F.2d 1292 (2d Cir.1990). Claims for losses of ocean shipments were made against two defendants, one subject to admiralty jurisdiction and the other not. Summary judgment was granted in favor of the admiralty defendant and against the nonadmiralty defendant. The nonadmiralty defendant's appeal was accepted, with the explanation that the determination of its liability was "integrally linked with the determination of non-liability" of the admiralty defendant, and that "section 1292(a)(3) is not limited to admiralty claims; instead, it refers to admiralty cases." 899 F.2d at 1297. The advantages of permitting appeal by the nonadmiralty defendant would be particularly clear if the plaintiff had appealed the summary judgment in favor of the admiralty defendant.

It must be emphasized that this amendment does not rest on any particular assumptions as to the meaning of the § 1292(a)(3) provision that limits interlocutory appeal to orders that determine the rights and liabilities of the parties. It simply reflects the conclusion that so long as the case involves an admiralty claim and an order otherwise meets statutory requirements, the opportunity to appeal should not turn on the circumstance that the order does—or does not—dispose of an admiralty claim. No attempt is made to invoke the authority conferred by 28 U.S.C. § 1292(e) to provide by rule for appeal of an interlocutory decision that is not otherwise provided for by other subsections of § 1292.

GAP Report on Rule 9(h). No changes have been made in the published proposal.

Rule 10. Form of Pleadings

(a) Caption; Names of Parties. Every pleading shall contain a caption setting forth the name of the court, the title of the action, the file number, and a designation as in Rule 7(a). In the complaint the title of the action shall include the names of all the parties, but in other pleadings it is sufficient to state the name of the first party on each side with an appropriate indication of other parties.

(b) Paragraphs; Separate Statements. All averments of claim or defense shall be made in numbered paragraphs, the contents of each of which shall be limited as far as practicable to a statement of a single set of circumstances; and a paragraph may be referred to by number in all succeeding pleadings. Each claim founded upon a separate transaction or occurrence and each defense other than denials shall be stated in a separate count or defense whenever a separation facilitates the clear presentation of the matters set forth.

(c) Adoption by Reference; Exhibits. Statements in a pleading may be adopted by reference in a different part of the same pleading or in another pleading or in any motion. A copy of any written instrument which is an exhibit to a pleading is a part thereof for all purposes.

ADVISORY COMMITTEE NOTES
1937 Adoption

The first sentence is derived in part from the opening statement of former Equity Rule 25 (Bill of Complaint—Contents). The remainder of the rule is an expansion in conformity with usual state provisions. For numbered paragraphs and separate statements, see Conn.Gen.Stat., 1930, § 5513; Smith-Hurd Ill.Stats. ch. 110, § 157(2); N.Y.R.C.P., (1937) Rule 90. For incorporation by reference, see N.Y.R.C.P., (1937) Rule 90. For written instruments as exhibits, see Smith-Hurd Ill.Stats. ch. 110, § 160.

Rule 11. Signing of Pleadings, Motions, and Other Papers; Representations to Court; Sanctions

(a) Signature. Every pleading, written motion, and other paper shall be signed by at least one attorney of record in the attorney's individual name, or, if the party is not represented by an attorney, shall be signed by the party. Each paper shall state the signer's address and telephone number, if any. Except when otherwise specifically provided by rule or statute, pleadings need not be verified or accompanied by affidavit. An unsigned paper shall be stricken unless omission of the signature is corrected promptly after being called to the attention of the attorney or party.

(b) Representations to Court. By presenting to the court (whether by signing, filing, submitting, or later advocating) a pleading, written motion, or other paper, an attorney or unrepresented party is certifying that to the best of the person's knowledge, information, and belief, formed after an inquiry reasonable under the circumstances,—

(1) it is not being presented for any improper purpose, such as to harass or to cause unnecessary delay or needless increase in the cost of litigation;

(2) the claims, defenses, and other legal contentions therein are warranted by existing law or by a nonfrivolous argument for the extension, modification, or reversal of existing law or the establishment of new law;

(3) the allegations and other factual contentions have evidentiary support or, if specifically so identified, are likely to have evidentiary support after a reasonable opportunity for further investigation or discovery; and

(4) the denials of factual contentions are warranted on the evidence or, if specifically so identified, are reasonably based on a lack of information or belief.

(c) Sanctions. If, after notice and a reasonable opportunity to respond, the court determines that subdivision (b) has been violated, the court may, subject to the conditions stated below, impose an appropriate sanction upon the attorneys, law firms, or parties that have violated subdivision (b) or are responsible for the violation.

(1) How Initiated.

(A) By Motion. A motion for sanctions under this rule shall be made separately from other motions or requests and shall describe the specific conduct alleged to violate subdivision (b). It shall be served as provided in Rule 5, but shall not be filed with or presented to the court unless, within 21 days after service of the motion (or such other period as the court may prescribe), the challenged paper, claim, defense, contention, allegation, or denial is not withdrawn or appropriately corrected. If warranted, the court may award to the party prevailing on the motion the reasonable expenses and attorney's fees incurred in presenting or opposing the motion. Absent exceptional circumstances, a law firm shall be held jointly responsible for violations committed by its partners, associates, and employees.

(B) On Court's Initiative. On its own initiative, the court may enter an order describing the specific conduct that appears to violate subdivision (b) and directing an attorney, law firm, or party to show cause why it has not violated subdivision (b) with respect thereto.

(2) Nature of Sanction; Limitations. A sanction imposed for violation of this rule shall be limited to what is sufficient to deter repetition of such conduct or comparable conduct by others similarly situated. Subject to the limitations in subparagraphs (A) and (B), the sanction may consist of, or include, directives of a nonmonetary nature, an order to pay a penalty into court, or, if imposed on motion and warranted for effective deterrence, an order directing payment to the movant of some or all of the reasonable attorneys' fees and other expenses incurred as a direct result of the violation.

(A) Monetary sanctions may not be awarded against a represented party for a violation of subdivision (b)(2).

(B) Monetary sanctions may not be awarded on the court's initiative unless the court issues its order to show cause before a voluntary dismissal or settlement of the claims made by or against the party which is, or whose attorneys are, to be sanctioned.

(3) Order. When imposing sanctions, the court shall describe the conduct determined to constitute a violation of this rule and explain the basis for the sanction imposed.

(d) Inapplicability to Discovery. Subdivisions (a) through (c) of this rule do not apply to disclosures and discovery requests, responses, objections, and motions that are subject to the provisions of Rules 26 through 37.

(As amended Apr. 28, 1983, eff. Aug. 1, 1983; Mar. 2, 1987, eff. Aug. 1, 1987; Apr. 22, 1993, eff. Dec. 1, 1993.)

ADVISORY COMMITTEE NOTES

1937 Adoption

This is substantially the content of [former] Equity Rules 24 (Signature of Counsel) and 21 (Scandal and Impertinence) consolidated and unified. Compare former Equity Rule 36 (Officers Before Whom Pleadings Verified). Compare to similar purposes, *English Rules Under the Judicature Act* (The Annual Practice, 1937) O. 19, r. 4, and *Great Australian Gold Mining Co. v. Martin,* L.R. 5 Ch.Div. 1, 10 (1877). Subscription of pleadings is required in many codes. 2 Minn.Stat. (Mason, 1927) § 9265; N.Y.R.C.P. (1937) Rule 91; 2 N.D.Comp.Laws Ann. (1913) § 7455.

This rule expressly continues any statute which requires a pleading to be verified or accompanied by an affidavit, such as: U.S.C., Title 28:

§ 381 [former] (Preliminary injunctions and temporary restraining orders)

§ 762 [now 1402] (Suit against the United States)

U.S.C., Title 28, § 829 [now 1927] (Costs; attorney liable for, when) is unaffected by this rule.

For complaints which must be verified under these rules, see Rules 23(b) (Secondary Action by Shareholders) and 65 (Injunctions).

For abolition of former rule in equity that the averments of an answer under oath must be overcome by the testimony of two witnesses or of one witness sustained by corroborating circumstances, see 12 P.S.Pa. § 1222; for the rule in equity itself, see *Greenfield v. Blumenthal,* C.C.A.3, 1934, 69 F.2d 294.

1983 Amendment

Since its original promulgation, Rule 11 has provided for the striking of pleadings and the imposition of disciplinary sanctions to check abuses in the signing of pleadings. Its provisions have always applied to motions and other papers by virtue of incorporation by reference in Rule 7(b)(2). The amendment and the addition of Rule 7(b)(3) expressly confirms this applicability.

Experience shows that in practice Rule 11 has not been effective in deterring abuses. See 6 Wright & Miller, *Federal Practice and Procedure: Civil* § 1334 (1971). There has been considerable confusion as to (1) the circumstances that should trigger striking a pleading or motion or taking disciplinary action, (2) the standard of conduct expected of attorneys who sign pleadings and motions, and (3) the range of available and appropriate sanctions. See Rodes, Ripple & Mooney, *Sanctions Imposable for Violations of the Federal Rules of Civil Procedure* 64–65, Federal Judicial Center (1981). The new language is intended to reduce the reluctance of courts to impose sanctions, see Moore, **Federal Practice** ¶ 7.05, at 1547, by emphasizing the responsibilities of the attorney and reenforcing those obligations by the imposition of sanctions.

The amended rule attempts to deal with the problem by building upon and expanding the equitable doctrine permitting the court to award expenses, including attorney's fees, to a litigant whose opponent acts in bad faith in instituting or conducting litigation. See, e.g., *Roadway Express, Inc. v. Piper,* 447 U.S. 752 (1980); *Hall v. Cole,* 412 U.S. 1, 5 (1973). Greater attention by the district courts to pleading and motion abuses and the imposition of sanctions when appropriate, should discourage dilatory or abusive tactics and help to streamline the litigation process by lessening frivolous claims or defenses.

The expanded nature of the lawyer's certification in the fifth sentence of amended Rule 11 recognizes that the litigation process may be abused for purposes other than delay. See, e.g., *Browning Debenture Holders' Committee v. DASA Corp.,* 560 F.2d 1078 (2d Cir.1977).

The words "good ground to support" the pleading in the original rule were interpreted to have both factual and legal elements. See, e.g., *Heart Disease Research Foundation v. General Motors Corp.,* 15 Fed.R.Serv.2d 1517, 1519 (S.D.N.Y.1972). They have been replaced by a standard of conduct that is more focused.

The new language stresses the need for some prefiling inquiry into both the facts and the law to satisfy the affirmative duty imposed by the rule. The standard is one of reasonableness under the circumstances. See *Kinee v. Abraham Lincoln Fed. Sav. & Loan Ass'n,* 365 F.Supp. 975 (E.D.Pa.1973). This standard is more stringent than the original good-faith formula and thus it is expected that a greater range of circumstances will trigger its violation. See *Nemeroff v. Abelson,* 620 F.2d 339 (2d Cir.1980).

The rule is not intended to chill an attorney's enthusiasm or creativity in pursuing factual or legal theories. The court is expected to avoid using the wisdom of hindsight and should test the signer's conduct by inquiring what was reasonable to believe at the time the pleading, motion, or other paper was submitted. Thus, what constitutes a reasonable inquiry may depend on such factors as how much time for investigation was available to the signer; whether he had to rely on a client for information as to the facts underlying the pleading, motion, or other paper; whether the pleading, motion, or other paper was based on a plausible view of the law; or whether he depended on forwarding counsel or another member of the bar.

The rule does not require a party or an attorney to disclose privileged communications or work product in order to show that the signing of the pleading, motion, or other paper is substantially justified. The provisions of Rule 26(c), including appropriate orders after *in camera* inspection by the court, remain available to protect a party claiming privilege or work product protection.

Amended Rule 11 continues to apply to anyone who signs a pleading, motion, or other paper. Although the standard is the same for unrepresented parties, who are obliged themselves to sign the pleadings, the court has sufficient discretion to take account of the special circumstances that often arise in *pro se* situations. See *Haines v. Kerner*, 404 U.S. 519 (1972).

The provision in the original rule for striking pleadings and motions as sham and false has been deleted. The passage has rarely been utilized, and decisions thereunder have tended to confuse the issue of attorney honesty with the merits of the action. See generally Risinger, *Honesty in Pleading and its Enforcement: Some "Striking" Problems with Fed.R.Civ.P. 11*, 61 Minn.L.Rev. 1 (1976). Motions under this provision generally present issues better dealt with under Rules 8, 12, or 56. See *Murchison v. Kirby*, 27 F.R.D. 14 (S.D.N.Y.1961); 5 Wright & Miller, *Federal Practice and Procedure: Civil* § 1334 (1969).

The former reference to the inclusion of scandalous or indecent matter, which is itself strong indication that an improper purpose underlies the pleading, motion, or other paper, also has been deleted as unnecessary. Such matter may be stricken under Rule 12(f) as well as dealt with under the more general language of amended Rule 11.

The text of the amended rule seeks to dispel apprehensions that efforts to obtain enforcement will be fruitless by insuring that the rule will be applied when properly invoked. The word "sanctions" in the caption, for example, stresses a deterrent orientation in dealing with improper pleadings, motions or other papers. This corresponds to the approach in imposing sanctions for discovery abuses. See *National Hockey League v. Metropolitan Hockey Club*, 427 U.S. 639 (1976) (per curiam). And the words "shall impose" in the last sentence focus the court's attention on the need to impose sanctions for pleading and motion abuses. The court, however, retains the necessary flexibility to deal appropriately with violations of the rule. It has discretion to tailor sanctions to the particular facts of the case, with which it should be well acquainted.

The references in the former text to wilfulness as a prerequisite to disciplinary action has been deleted. However, in considering the nature and severity of the sanctions to be imposed, the court should take account of the state of the attorney's or party's actual or presumed knowledge when the pleading or other paper was signed. Thus, for example, when a party is not represented by counsel, the absence of legal advice is an appropriate factor to be considered.

Courts currently appear to believe they may impose sanctions on their own motion. See *North American Trading Corp. v. Zale Corp.*, 73 F.R.D. 293 (S.D.N.Y.1979). Authority to do so has been made explicit in order to overcome the traditional reluctance of courts to intervene unless requested by one of the parties. The detection and punishment of a violation of the signing requirement, encouraged by the amended rule, is part of the court's responsibility for securing the system's effective operation.

If the duty imposed by the rule is violated, the court should have the discretion to impose sanctions on either the attorney, the party the signing attorney represents, or both, or on an unrepresented party who signed the pleading, and the new rule so provides. Although Rule 11 has been silent on the point, courts have claimed the power to impose sanctions on an attorney personally, either by imposing costs or employing the contempt technique. See 5 Wright & Miller, *Federal Practice and Procedure: Civil* § 1334 (1969); 2A Moore, *Federal Practice* ¶ 11.02, at 2104 n. 8. This power has been used infrequently. The amended rule should eliminate any doubt as to the propriety of assessing sanctions against the attorney.

Even though it is the attorney whose signature violates the rule, it may be appropriate under the circumstances of the case to impose a sanction on the client. See *Browning Debenture Holders' Committee v. DASA Corp.*, supra. This modification brings Rule 11 in line with practice under Rule 37, which allows sanctions for abuses during discovery to be imposed upon the party, the attorney, or both.

A party seeking sanctions should give notice to the court and the offending party promptly upon discovering a basis for doing so. The time when sanctions are to be imposed rests in the discretion of the trial judge. However, it is anticipated that in the case of pleadings the sanctions issue under Rule 11 normally will be determined at the end of the litigation, and in the case of motions at the time when the motion is decided or shortly thereafter. The procedure obviously must comport with due process requirements. The particular format to be followed should depend on the circumstances of the situation and the severity of the sanction under consideration. In many situations the judge's participation in the proceedings provides him with full knowledge of the relevant facts and little further inquiry will be necessary.

To assure that the efficiencies achieved through more effective operation of the pleading regimen will not be offset by the cost of satellite litigation over the imposition of sanctions, the court must to the extent possible limit the scope of sanction proceedings to the record. Thus, discovery should be conducted only by leave of the court, and then only in extraordinary circumstances.

Although the encompassing reference to "other papers" in new Rule 11 literally includes discovery papers, the certification requirement in that context is governed by proposed new Rule 26(g). Discovery motions, however, fall within the ambit of Rule 11.

1987 Amendment

The amendments are technical. No substantive change is intended.

1993 Amendments

Purpose of revision. This revision is intended to remedy problems that have arisen in the interpretation and application of the 1983 revision of the rule. For empirical examination of experience under the 1983 rule, see, *e.g.,* New York State Bar Committee on Federal Courts, *Sanctions and Attorneys' Fees* (1987); T. Willging, *The Rule 11 Sanctioning Process* (1989); American Judicature Society, *Report of the Third Circuit Task Force on Federal Rule of Civil Procedure 11* (S. Burbank ed., 1989); E. Wiggins, T. Willging, and D. Stienstra, *Report on Rule 11* (Federal Judicial Center 1991). For book-length analyses of the case law, see G. Joseph, *Sanctions: The Federal Law of Litigation Abuse* (1989); J. Solovy, *The Federal Law of Sanctions* (1991); G. Vairo, *Rule 11 Sanctions: Case Law Perspectives and Preventive Measures* (1991).

The rule retains the principle that attorneys and pro se litigants have an obligation to the court to refrain from conduct that frustrates the aims of Rule 1. The revision broadens the scope of this obligation, but places greater constraints on the imposition of sanctions and should reduce the number of motions for sanctions presented to the court. New subdivision (d) removes from the ambit of this rule all discovery requests, responses, objections, and motions subject to the provisions of Rule 26 through 37.

Subdivision (a). Retained in this subdivision are the provisions requiring signatures on pleadings, written motions, and other papers. Unsigned papers are to be received by the Clerk, but then are to be stricken if the omission of the signature is not corrected promptly after being called to the attention of the attorney or pro se litigant. Correction can be made by signing the paper on file or by submitting a duplicate that contains the signature. A court may require by local rule that papers contain additional identifying information regarding the parties or attorneys, such as telephone numbers to facilitate facsimile transmissions, though, as for omission of a signature, the paper should not be rejected for failure to provide such information.

The sentence in the former rule relating to the effect of answers under oath is no longer needed and has been eliminated. The provision in the former rule that signing a paper constitutes a certificate that it has been read by the signer also has been eliminated as unnecessary. The obligations imposed under subdivision (b) obviously require that a pleading, written motion, or other paper be read before it is filed or submitted to the court.

Subdivisions (b) and (c). These subdivisions restate the provisions requiring attorneys and pro se litigants to conduct a reasonable inquiry into the law and facts before signing pleadings, written motions, and other documents, and prescribing sanctions for violation of these obligations. The revision in part expands the responsibilities of litigants to the court, while providing greater constraints and flexibility in dealing with infractions of the rule. The rule continues to require litigants to "stop-and-think" before initially making legal or factual contentions. It also, however, emphasizes the duty of candor by subjecting litigants to potential sanctions for insisting upon a position after it is no longer tenable and by generally providing protection against sanctions if they withdraw or correct contentions after a potential violation is called to their attention.

The rule applies only to assertions contained in papers filed with or submitted to the court. It does not cover matters arising for the first time during oral presentations to the court, when counsel may make statements that would not have been made if there had been more time for study and reflection. However, a litigant's obligations with respect to the contents of these papers are not measured solely as of the time they are filed with or submitted to the court, but include reaffirming to the court and advocating positions contained in those pleadings and motions after learning that they cease to have any merit. For example, an attorney who during a pretrial conference insists on a claim or defense should be viewed as "presenting to the court" that contention and would be subject to the obligations of subdivision (b) measured as of that time. Similarly, if after a notice of removal is filed, a party urges in federal court the allegations of a pleading filed in state court (whether as claims, defenses, or in disputes regarding removal or remand), it would be viewed as "presenting"—and hence certifying to the district court under Rule 11—those allegations.

The certification with respect to allegations and other factual contentions is revised in recognition that sometimes a litigant may have good reason to believe that a fact is true or false but may need discovery, formal or informal, from opposing parties or third persons to gather and confirm the evidentiary basis for the allegation. Tolerance of factual contentions in initial pleadings by plaintiffs or defendants when specifically identified as made on information and belief does not relieve litigants from the obligation to conduct an appropriate investigation into the facts that is reasonable under the circumstances; it is not a license to join parties, make claims, or present defenses without any factual basis or justification. Moreover, if evidentiary support is not obtained after a reasonable opportunity for further investigation or discovery, the party has a duty under the rule not to persist with that contention. Subdivision (b) does not require a formal amendment to pleadings for which evidentiary support is not obtained, but rather calls upon a litigant not thereafter to advocate such claims or defenses.

The certification is that there is (or likely will be) "evidentiary support" for the allegation, not that the party will prevail with respect to its contention regarding the fact. That summary judgment is rendered against a party does not necessarily mean, for purposes of this certification, that it had no evidentiary support for its position. On the other hand, if a party has evidence with respect to a contention that would suffice to defeat a motion for summary judgment based thereon, it would have sufficient "evidentiary support" for purposes of Rule 11.

Denials of factual contentions involve somewhat different considerations. Often, of course, a denial is premised upon the existence of evidence contradicting the alleged fact. At other times a denial is permissible because, after an appropriate investigation, a party has no information concerning the matter or, indeed, has a reasonable basis for doubting the credibility of the only evidence relevant to the matter. A party should not deny an allegation it knows to be true; but it is not required, simply because it lacks contradictory evidence, to admit an allegation that it believes is not true.

The changes in subdivisions (b)(3) and (b)(4) will serve to equalize the burden of the rule upon plaintiffs and defendants, who under Rule 8(b) are in effect allowed to deny allegations by stating that from their initial investigation they lack sufficient information to form a belief as to the truth of the allegation. If, after further investigation or discovery, a denial is no longer warranted, the defendant should not continue to insist on that denial. While sometimes helpful, formal amendment of the pleadings to withdraw an allegation or denial is not required by subdivision (b).

Arguments for extensions, modifications, or reversals of existing law or for creation of new law do not violate subdivision (b)(2) provided they are "nonfrivolous." This establishes an objective standard, intended to eliminate any "empty-head pure-heart" justification for patently frivolous arguments. However, the extent to which a litigant has researched the issues and found some support for its theories even in minority opinions, in law review articles, or through consultation with other attorneys should certainly be taken into account in determining whether paragraph (2) has been violated. Although arguments for a change of law are not required to be specifically so identified, a contention that is so identified should be viewed with greater tolerance under the rule.

The court has available a variety of possible sanctions to impose for violations, such as striking the offending paper; issuing an admonition, reprimand, or censure; requiring participation in seminars or other educational programs; ordering a fine payable to the court; referring the matter to disciplinary authorities (or, in the case of government attorneys, to the Attorney General, Inspector General, or agency head), etc. *See Manual for Complex Litigation, Second,* § 42.3. The rule does not attempt to enumerate the factors a court should consider in deciding whether to impose a sanction or what sanctions would be appropriate in the circumstances; but, for emphasis, it does specifically note that a sanction may be nonmonetary as well as monetary. Whether the improper conduct was willful, or negligent; whether it was part of a pattern of activity, or an isolated event; whether it infected the entire pleading, or only one particular count or defense; whether the person has engaged in similar conduct in other litigation; whether it was intended to injure; what effect it had on the litigation process in time or expense; whether the responsible person is trained in the law; what amount, given the financial resources of the responsible person, is needed to deter that person from repetition in the same case; what amount is needed to deter similar activity by other litigants: all of these may in a particular case be proper considerations. The court has significant discretion in determining what sanctions, if any, should be imposed for a violation, subject to the principle that the sanctions should not be more severe than reasonably necessary to deter repetition of the conduct by the offending person or comparable conduct by similarly situated persons.

Since the purpose of Rule 11 sanctions is to deter rather than to compensate, the rule provides that, if a monetary sanction is imposed, it should ordinarily be paid into court as a penalty. However, under unusual circumstances, particularly for (b)(1) violations, deterrence may be ineffective unless the sanction not only requires the person violating the rule to make a monetary payment, but also directs that some or all of this payment be made to those injured by the violation. Accordingly, the rule authorizes the court, if requested in a motion and if so warranted, to award attorney's fees to another party. Any such award to another party, however, should not exceed the expenses and attorneys' fees

for the services directly and unavoidably caused by the violation of the certification requirement. If, for example, a wholly unsupportable count were included in a multi-count complaint or counterclaim for the purpose of needlessly increasing the cost of litigation to an impecunious adversary, any award of expenses should be limited to those directly caused by inclusion of the improper count, and not those resulting from the filing of the complaint or answer itself. The award should not provide compensation for services that could have been avoided by an earlier disclosure of evidence or an earlier challenge to the groundless claims or defenses. Moreover, partial reimbursement of fees may constitute a sufficient deterrent with respect to violations by persons having modest financial resources. In cases brought under statutes providing for fees to be awarded to prevailing parties, the court should not employ cost-shifting under this rule in a manner that would be inconsistent with the standards that govern the statutory award of fees, such as stated in *Christiansburg Garment Co. v. EEOC,* 434 U.S. 412 (1978).

The sanction should be imposed on the persons—whether attorneys, law firms, or parties—who have violated the rule or who may be determined to be responsible for the violation. The person signing, filing, submitting, or advocating a document has a nondelegable responsibility to the court, and in most situations is the person to be sanctioned for a violation. Absent exceptional circumstances, a law firm is to be held also responsible when, as a result of a motion under subdivision (c)(1)(A), one of its partners, associates, or employees is determined to have violated the rule. Since such a motion may be filed only if the offending paper is not withdrawn or corrected within 21 days after service of the motion, it is appropriate that the law firm ordinarily be viewed as jointly responsible under established principles of agency. This provision is designed to remove the restrictions of the former rule. *Cf. Pavelic & LeFlore v. Marvel Entertainment Group,* 493 U.S. 120 (1989) (1983 version of Rule 11 does not permit sanctions against law firm of attorney signing groundless complaint).

The revision permits the court to consider whether other attorneys in the firm, co-counsel, other law firms, or the party itself should be held accountable for their part in causing a violation. When appropriate, the court can make an additional inquiry in order to determine whether the sanction should be imposed on such persons, firms, or parties either in addition to or, in unusual circumstances, instead of the person actually making the presentation to the court. For example, such an inquiry may be appropriate in cases involving governmental agencies or other institutional parties that frequently impose substantial restrictions on the discretion of individual attorneys employed by it.

Sanctions that involve monetary awards (such as a fine or an award of attorney's fees) may not be imposed on a represented party for causing a violation of subdivision (b)(2), involving frivolous contentions of law. Monetary responsibility for such violations is more properly placed solely on the party's attorneys. With this limitation, the rule should not be subject to attack under the Rules Enabling Act. See *Willy v. Coastal Corp.,* — U.S. — (1992); *Business Guides, Inc. v. Chromatic Communications Enter. Inc.,* — U.S. — (1991). This restriction does not limit the court's power to impose sanctions or remedial orders that may have collateral financial consequences upon a party, such as dis-

---

missal of a claim, preclusion of a defense, or preparation of amended pleadings.

Explicit provision is made for litigants to be provided notice of the alleged violation and an opportunity to respond before sanctions are imposed. Whether the matter should be decided solely on the basis of written submissions or should be scheduled for oral argument (or, indeed, for evidentiary presentation) will depend on the circumstances. If the court imposes a sanction, it must, unless waived, indicate its reasons in a written order or on the record; the court should not ordinarily have to explain its denial of a motion for sanctions. Whether a violation has occurred and what sanctions, if any, to impose for a violation are matters committed to the discretion of the trial court; accordingly, as under current law, the standard for appellate review of these decisions will be for abuse of discretion. *See Cooter & Gell v. Hartmarx Corp.*, 496 U.S. 384 (1990) (noting, however, that an abuse would be established if the court based its ruling on an erroneous view of the law or on a clearly erroneous assessment of the evidence).

The revision leaves for resolution on a case-by-case basis, considering the particular circumstances involved, the question as to when a motion for violation of Rule 11 should be served and when, if filed, it should be decided. Ordinarily the motion should be served promptly after the inappropriate paper is filed, and, if delayed too long, may be viewed as untimely. In other circumstances, it should not be served until the other party has had a reasonable opportunity for discovery. Given the "safe harbor" provisions discussed below, a party cannot delay serving its Rule 11 motion until conclusion of the case (or judicial rejection of the offending contention).

Rule 11 motions should not be made or threatened for minor, inconsequential violations of the standards prescribed by subdivision (b). They should not be employed as a discovery device or to test the legal sufficiency or efficacy of allegations in the pleadings; other motions are available for those purposes. Nor should Rule 11 motions be prepared to emphasize the merits of a party's position, to exact an unjust settlement, to intimidate an adversary into withdrawing contentions that are fairly debatable, to increase the costs of litigation, to create a conflict of interest between attorney and client, or to seek disclosure of matters otherwise protected by the attorney-client privilege or the work-product doctrine. As under the prior rule, the court may defer its ruling (or its decision as to the identity of the persons to be sanctioned) until final resolution of the case in order to avoid immediate conflicts of interest and to reduce the disruption created if a disclosure of attorney-client communications is needed to determine whether a violation occurred or to identify the person responsible for the violation.

The rule provides that requests for sanctions must be made as a separate motion, *i.e.*, not simply included as an additional prayer for relief contained in another motion. The motion for sanctions is not, however, to be filed until at least 21 days (or such other period as the court may set) after being served. If, during this period, the alleged violation is corrected, as by withdrawing (whether formally or informally) some allegation or contention, the motion should not be filed with the court. These provisions are intended to provide a type of "safe harbor" against motions under Rule 11 in that a party will not be subject to sanctions on the basis of another party's motion unless, after receiving the motion, it

refuses to withdraw that position or to acknowledge candidly that it does not currently have evidence to support a specified allegation. Under the former rule, parties were sometimes reluctant to abandon a questionable contention lest that be viewed as evidence of a violation of Rule 11; under the revision, the timely withdrawal of a contention will protect a party against a motion for sanctions.

To stress the seriousness of a motion for sanctions and to define precisely the conduct claimed to violate the rule, the revision provides that the "safe harbor" period begins to run only upon service of the motion. In most cases, however, counsel should be expected to give informal notice to the other party, whether in person or by a telephone call or letter, of a potential violation before proceeding to prepare and serve a Rule 11 motion.

As under former Rule 11, the filing of a motion for sanctions is itself subject to the requirements of the rule and can lead to sanctions. However, service of a cross motion under Rule 11 should rarely be needed since under the revision the court may award to the person who prevails on a motion under Rule 11—whether the movant or the target of the motion—reasonable expenses, including attorney's fees, incurred in presenting or opposing the motion.

The power of the court to act on its own initiative is retained, but with the condition that this be done through a show cause order. This procedure provides the person with notice and an opportunity to respond. The revision provides that a monetary sanction imposed after a court-initiated show cause order be limited to a penalty payable to the court and that it be imposed only if the show cause order is issued before any voluntary dismissal or an agreement of the parties to settle the claims made by or against the litigant. Parties settling a case should not be subsequently faced with an unexpected order from the court leading to monetary sanctions that might have affected their willingness to settle or voluntarily dismiss a case. Since show cause orders will ordinarily be issued only in situations that are akin to a contempt of court, the rule does not provide a "safe harbor" to a litigant for withdrawing a claim, defense, etc., after a show cause order has been issued on the court's own initiative. Such corrective action, however, should be taken into account in deciding what—if any—sanction to impose if, after consideration of the litigant's response, the court concludes that a violation has occurred.

Subdivision (d). Rules 26(g) and 37 establish certification standards and sanctions that apply to discovery disclosures, requests, responses, objections, and motions. It is appropriate that Rules 26 through 37, which are specially designed for the discovery process, govern such documents and conduct rather than the more general provisions of Rule 11. Subdivision (d) has been added to accomplish this result.

Rule 11 is not the exclusive source for control of improper presentations of claims, defenses, or contentions. It does not supplant statutes permitting awards of attorney's fees to prevailing parties or alter the principles governing such awards. It does not inhibit the court in punishing for contempt, in exercising its inherent powers, or in imposing sanctions, awarding expenses, or directing remedial action authorized under other rules or under 28 U.S.C. § 1927. *See Chambers v. NASCO,* —— U.S. —— (1991). Chambers cautions, however, against reliance upon inherent powers if appropriate sanctions can be imposed under provisions such as Rule 11, and the procedures specified in Rule 11—notice, opportunity to respond, and findings—should ordinarily be employed when imposing a sanction under the court's inherent powers. Finally, it should be noted that Rule 11 does not preclude a party from initiating an independent action for malicious prosecution or abuse of process.

Rule 12. Defenses and Objections—When and How Presented—By Pleading or Motion—Motion for Judgment on Pleadings

(a) **When Presented.**

(1) Unless a different time is prescribed in a statute of the United States, a defendant shall serve an answer

(A) within 20 days after being served with the summons and complaint, or

(B) if service of the summons has been timely waived on request under Rule 4(d), within 60 days after the date when the request for waiver was sent, or within 90 days after that date if the defendant was addressed outside any judicial district of the United States.

(2) A party served with a pleading stating a cross-claim against that party shall serve an answer thereto within 20 days after being served. The plaintiff shall serve a reply to a counterclaim in the answer within 20 days after service of the answer, or, if a reply is ordered by the court, within 20 days after service of the order, unless the order otherwise directs.

(3)(A) The United States, an agency of the United States, or an officer or employee of the United States sued in an official capacity, shall serve an answer to the complaint or cross-claim— or a reply to a counterclaim—within 60 days after the United States attorney is served with the pleading asserting the claim.

(B) An officer or employee of the United States sued in an individual capacity for acts or omissions occurring in connection with the performance of duties on behalf of the United States shall serve an answer to the complaint or cross-claim—or a reply to a counterclaim—within 60 days after service on the officer or employee, or service on the United States attorney, whichever is later.

(4) Unless a different time is fixed by court order, the service of a motion permitted under this rule alters these periods of time as follows:

(A) if the court denies the motion or postpones its disposition until the trial on the merits, the responsive pleading shall be served within 10 days after notice of the court's action; or

(B) if the court grants a motion for a more definite statement, the responsive pleading shall be served within 10 days after the service of the more definite statement.

(b) **How Presented.** Every defense, in law or fact, to a claim for relief in any pleading, whether a claim, counterclaim, cross-claim, or third-party claim, shall be asserted in the responsive pleading thereto if one is required, except that the following defenses may at the option of the pleader be made by motion: (1) lack of jurisdiction over the subject matter, (2) lack of jurisdiction over the person, (3) improper venue, (4) insufficiency of process, (5) insufficiency of service of process, (6) failure to state a claim upon which relief can be granted, (7) failure to join a party under Rule 19. A motion making any of these defenses shall be made before pleading if a further pleading is permitted. No defense or objection is waived by being joined with one or more other defenses or objections in a responsive pleading or motion. If a pleading sets forth a claim for relief to which the adverse party is not required to serve a responsive pleading, the adverse party may assert at the trial any defense in law or fact to that claim for relief. If, on a motion asserting the defense numbered (6) to dismiss for failure of the pleading to state a claim upon which relief can be granted, matters outside the pleading are presented to and not excluded by the court, the motion shall be treated as one for summary judgment and disposed of as provided in Rule 56, and all parties shall be given reasonable opportunity to present all material made pertinent to such a motion by Rule 56.

(c) **Motion for Judgment on the Pleadings.** After the pleadings are closed but within such time as not to delay the trial, any party may move for judgment on the pleadings. If, on a motion for judgment on the pleadings, matters outside the pleadings are presented to and not excluded by the court, the motion shall be treated as one for summary judgment and disposed of as provided in Rule 56, and all parties shall be given reasonable opportunity to present all material made pertinent to such a motion by Rule 56.

(d) **Preliminary Hearings.** The defenses specifically enumerated (1)–(7) in subdivision (b) of this rule, whether made in a pleading or by motion, and the motion for judgment mentioned in subdivision (c) of this rule shall be heard and determined before trial on application of any party, unless the court orders that the hearing and determination thereof be deferred until the trial.

(e) **Motion for More Definite Statement.** If a pleading to which a responsive pleading is permitted is so vague or ambiguous that a party cannot reasonably be required to frame a responsive pleading, the party may move for a more definite statement before interposing a responsive pleading. The motion shall point out the defects complained of and the details desired. If the motion is granted and the order of the court is not obeyed within 10 days after notice of the order or within such other time as the court may fix, the court may strike the pleading to which the motion was directed or make such order as it deems just.

(f) Motion to Strike. Upon motion made by a party before responding to a pleading or, if no responsive pleading is permitted by these rules, upon motion made by a party within 20 days after the service of the pleading upon the party or upon the court's own initiative at any time, the court may order stricken from any pleading any insufficient defense or any redundant, immaterial, impertinent, or scandalous matter.

(g) Consolidation of Defenses in Motion. A party who makes a motion under this rule may join with it any other motions herein provided for and then available to the party. If a party makes a motion under this rule but omits therefrom any defense or objection then available to the party which this rule permits to be raised by motion, the party shall not thereafter make a motion based on the defense or objection so omitted, except a motion as provided in subdivision (h)(2) hereof on any of the grounds there stated.

(h) Waiver or Preservation of Certain Defenses.

(1) A defense of lack of jurisdiction over the person, improper venue, insufficiency of process, or insufficiency of service of process is waived (A) if omitted from a motion in the circumstances described in subdivision (g), or (B) if it is neither made by motion under this rule nor included in a responsive pleading or an amendment thereof permitted by Rule 15(a) to be made as a matter of course.

(2) A defense of failure to state a claim upon which relief can be granted, a defense of failure to join a party indispensable under Rule 19, and an objection of failure to state a legal defense to a claim may be made in any pleading permitted or ordered under Rule 7(a), or by motion for judgment on the pleadings, or at the trial on the merits.

(3) Whenever it appears by suggestion of the parties or otherwise that the court lacks jurisdiction of the subject matter, the court shall dismiss the action.

(As amended Dec. 27, 1946, eff. Mar. 19, 1948; Jan. 21, 1963, eff. July 1, 1963; Feb. 28, 1966, eff. July 1, 1966; Mar. 2, 1987, eff. Aug. 1, 1987; Apr. 22, 1993, eff. Dec. 1, 1993; Apr. 17, 2000, eff. Dec. 1, 2000.)

ADVISORY COMMITTEE NOTES

1937 Adoption

Note to Subdivision (a). 1. Compare [former] Equity Rules 12 (Issue of Subpoena—Time for Answer) and 31 (Reply—When Required—When Cause at Issue); 4 Mont. Rev.Codes Ann. (1935) §§ 9107, 9158; N.Y.C. P.A. (1937) § 263; N.Y.R.C.P. (1937) Rules 109–111.

2. U.S.C., Title 28, § 763 (now § 547) (Petition in action against United States; service; appearance by district attor-

ney) provides that the United States as a defendant shall have 60 days within which to answer or otherwise defend. This and other statutes which provide 60 days for the United States or an officer or agency thereof to answer or otherwise defend are continued by this rule. In so far as any statutes not excepted in rule 81 provide a different time for a defendant to defend, such statutes are modified. See U.S.C., Title 28, [former] § 45 (District courts; practice and procedure in certain cases under the interstate commerce laws) (30 days).

3. Compare the last sentence of [former] Equity Rule 29 (Defenses—How Presented) and N.Y.C.P.A. (1937) § 283. See Rule 15(a) for time within which to plead to an amended pleading.

Note to Subdivisions (b) and (d). 1. See generally [former] Equity Rules 29 (Defenses—How Presented), 33 (Testing Sufficiency of Defense), 43 (Defect of Parties—Resisting Objection), and 44 (Defect of Parties—Tardy Objection); N.Y.C.P.A. (1937) §§ 277–280; N.Y.R.C.P. (1937) Rules 106–112; *English Rules Under the Judicature Act* (The Annual Practice, 1937) O. 25, r.r. 1–4; Clark, *Code Pleading*, 1928, pp. 371–381.

2. For provisions authorizing defenses to be made in the answer or reply see *English Rules Under the Judicature Act*, (The Annual Practice, 1937) O. 25, r.r. 1–4; 1 Miss.Code Ann. (1930) §§ 378, 379. Compare Equity Rule 29 (Defenses—How Presented); U.S.C.A., Title 28, [former] § 45 (District Courts; practice and procedure in certain cases under the interstate commerce laws). U.S.C., Title 28, [former] § 45, substantially continued by this rule, provides: "No replication need be filed to the answer, and objections to the sufficiency of the petition or answer as not setting forth a cause of action or defense must be taken at the final hearing or by motion to dismiss the petition based on said grounds, which motion may be made at any time before answer is filed." Compare Calif.Code Civ.Proc., (Deering, 1937) § 433; 4 Nev.Comp.Laws (Hillyer, 1929) § 8600. For provisions that the defendant may demur and answer at the same time, see Calif.Code Civ.Proc. (Deering, 1937) § 431; 4 Nev.Comp. Laws (Hillyer, 1929) § 8598.

3. [Former] Equity Rule 29 (Defenses—How Presented) abolished demurrers and provided that defenses in point of law arising on the face of the bill should be made by motion to dismiss or in the answer, with further provision that every such point of law going to the whole or material part of the cause or causes stated might be called up and disposed of before final hearing "at the discretion of the court." Likewise many state practices have abolished the demurrer, or retain it only to attack substantial and not formal defects. See 6 Tenn.Code Ann. (Williams, 1934) § 8784; Ala.Code Ann. (Michie, 1928) § 9479; 2 Mass.Gen.Laws (Ter.Ed., 1932) ch. 231, §§ 15–18; Kansas Gen.Stat.Ann. (1935) §§ 60–705, 60–706.

Note to Subdivision (c). Compare [former] Equity Rule 33 (Testing Sufficiency of Defense); N.Y.R.C.P. (1937) Rules 111 and 112.

Note to Subdivisions (e) and (f). Compare [former] Equity Rules 20 (Further and Particular Statement in Pleading May be Required) and 21 (Scandal and Impertinence); *English Rules Under the Judicature Act* (The Annual Practice, 1937) O. 19, r.r. 7, 7a, 7b, 8; 4 Mont.Rev.Codes Ann. (1935) §§ 9166, 9167; N.Y.C.P.A. (1937) § 247; N.Y.C.P.A.

(1937) Rules 103, 115, 116, 117; Wyo.Rev.Stat.Ann. (Court-right, 1931) §§ 89–1033, 89–1034.

Note to Subdivision (g). Compare Rules of the District Court of the United States for the District of Columbia (1937) Equity Rule 11; N.M. Rules of Pleading, Practice and Procedure, 38 N.M.Rep. vii. [105–408] (1934); Wash.Gen. Rules of the Superior Courts, 1 Wash.Rev.Stat.Ann. (Remington, 1932) p. 160, Rule VI(e) and (f).

Note to Subdivision (h). Compare Calif.Code Civ.Proc. (Deering, 1937) § 434; 2 Minn.Stat. (Mason, 1927) § 9252; N.Y.C.P.A. (1937) §§ 278 and 279; Wash.Gen.Rules of the Superior Courts, 1 Wash.Rev.Stat.Ann. (Remington, 1932) p. 160, Rule VI(e). This rule continues U.S.C.A., Title 28, former § 80 [now 1359, 1447, 1919] (Dismissal or remand) (of action over which district court lacks jurisdiction), while U.S.C.A., Title 28, § 399 (Amendments to show diverse citizenship) is continued by Rule 15.

1946 Amendment

Note. Subdivision (a). Various minor alterations in language have been made to improve the statement of the rule. All references to bills of particulars have been stricken in accordance with changes made in subdivision (e).

Subdivision (b). The addition of defense (7), "failure to join an indispensable party", cures an omission in the rules which are silent as to the mode of raising such failure. See Commentary, *Manner of Raising Objection of Non-Joinder of Indispensable Party,* 1940, 2 Fed.Rules Serv. 658, and, 1942, 5 Fed.Rules Serv. 820. In one case, *United States v. Metropolitan Life Ins. Co.,* E.D.Pa.1941, 36 F.Supp. 399, the failure to join an indispensable party was raised under Rule 12(c).

Rule 12(b)(6), permitting a motion to dismiss for failure of the complaint to state a claim on which relief can be granted, is substantially the same as the old demurrer for failure of a pleading to state a cause of action. Some courts have held that as the rule by its terms refers to statements in the complaint, extraneous matter on affidavits, depositions or otherwise, may not be introduced in support of the motion, or to resist it. On the other hand, in many cases the district courts have permitted the introduction of such material. When these cases have reached circuit courts of appeals in situations where the extraneous material so received shows that there is no genuine issue as to any material question of fact and that on the undisputed facts as disclosed by the affidavits or depositions, one party or the other is entitled to judgment as a matter of law, the circuit courts, properly enough, have been reluctant to dispose of the case merely on the face of the pleading, and in the interest of prompt disposition of the action have made a final disposition of it. In dealing with such situations the Second Circuit has made the sound suggestion that whatever its label or original basis, the motion may be treated as a motion for summary judgment and disposed of as such. *Samara v. United States,* C.C.A.2, 1942, 129 F.2d 594, certiorari denied 63 S.Ct. 258, 317 U.S. 686, 87 L.Ed. 549; *Boro Hall Corp. v. General Motors Corp.,* C.C.A.2, 1942, 124 F.2d 822, certiorari denied 63 S.Ct. 436, 317 U.S. 695, 87 L.Ed. 556. See, also, *Kithcart v. Metropolitan Life Ins. Co.,* C.C.A.8, 1945, 150 F.2d 997.

It has also been suggested that this practice could be justified on the ground that the federal rules permit "speaking" motions. The Committee entertains the view that on

motion under Rule 12(b)(6) to dismiss for failure of the complaint to state a good claim, the trial court should have authority to permit the introduction of extraneous matter, such as may be offered on a motion for summary judgment, and if it does not exclude such matter the motion should then be treated as a motion for summary judgment and disposed of in the manner and on the conditions stated in Rule 56 relating to summary judgments, and, of course, in such a situation, when the case reaches the circuit court of appeals, that court should treat the motion in the same way. The Committee believes that such practice, however, should be tied to the summary judgment rule. The term "speaking motion" is not mentioned in the rules, and if there is such a thing its limitations are undefined. Where extraneous matter is received, by tying further proceedings to the summary judgment rule the courts have a definite basis in the rules for disposing of the motion.

The Committee emphasizes particularly the fact that the summary judgment rule does not permit a case to be disposed of by judgment on the merits on affidavits, which disclose a conflict on a material issue of fact, and unless this practice is tied to the summary judgment, rule, the extent to which a court, on the introduction of such extraneous matter, may resolve questions of fact on conflicting proof would be left uncertain.

The decisions dealing with this general situation may be generally grouped as follows: (1) cases dealing with the use of affidavits and other extraneous material on motions; (2) cases reversing judgments to prevent final determination on mere pleading allegations alone.

Under group (1) are: *Boro Hall Corp. v. General Motors Corp.,* C.C.A.2, 1942, 124 F.2d 822, certiorari denied 1943, 63 S.Ct. 436, 317 U.S. 695, 87 L.Ed. 556; *Gallup v. Caldwell,* C.C.A.3, 1941, 120 F.2d 90; *Central Mexico Light & Power Co. v. Munch,* C.C.A.2, 1940, 116 F.2d 85; *National Labor Relations Board v. Montgomery Ward & Co.,* 1944, 144 F.2d 528, 79 U.S.App.D.C. 200, certiorari denied 1944, 65 S.Ct. 134, 323 U.S. 774, 89 L.Ed. 619; *Urquhart v. American-La France Foamite Corp.,* 1944, 144 F.2d 542, 79 U.S.App.D.C. 219; *Samara v. United States,* C.C.A.2, 1942, 129 F.2d 594; *Cohen v. American Window Glass Co.,* C.C.A.2, 1942, 126 F.2d 111; *Sperry Products Inc. v. Association of American Railroads,* C.C.A.2, 1942, 132 F.2d 408; *Joint Council Dining Car Employees Local 370 v. Delaware, Lackawanna and Western R. Co.,* C.C.A.2, 1946, 157 F.2d 417; *Weeks v. Bareco Oil Co.,* C.C.A.7, 1941, 125 F.2d 84; *Carroll v. Morrison Hotel Corp.,* C.C.A.7, 1945, 149 F.2d 404; *Victory v. Manning,* C.C.A.3, 1942, 128 F.2d 415; *Locals No. 1470, No. 1469, and No. 1512 of International Longshoremen's Association v. Southern Pacific Co.,* C.C.A.5, 1942, 131 F.2d 605; *Lucking v. Delano,* C.C.A.6, 1942, 129 F.2d 283; *San Francisco Lodge No. 68 of International Association of Machinists v. Forrestal,* Cal.1944, 58 F.Supp. 466; *Benson v. Export Equipment Corp.,* 1945, 164 P.2d 380, 49 N.M. 356, construing New Mexico rule identical with Rule 12(b)(6); *F. E. Myers & Bros. Co. v. Gould Pumps, Inc.,* W.D.N.Y.1946, 9 Fed.Rules Serv. 12b.33, Case 2, 5 F.R.D. 132. Cf. *Kohler v. Jacobs,* C.C.A.5, 1943, 138 F.2d 440; *Cohen v. United States,* C.C.A.8, 1942, 129 F.2d 733.

Under group (2) are: *Sparks v. England,* C.C.A.8, 1940, 113 F.2d 579; *Continental Collieries, Inc. v. Shober,* C.C.A.3, 1942, 130 F.2d 631; *Downey v. Palmer,* C.C.A.2, 1940, 114 F.2d 116; *DeLoach v. Crowley's Inc.,* C.C.A.5, 1942, 128 F.2d

378; *Leimer v. State Mutual Life Assurance Co. of Worcester, Mass.*, C.C.A.8, 1940, 108 F.2d 302; *Rossiter v. Vogel,* C.C.A.2, 1943, 134 F.2d 908, compare s.c., C.C.A.2, 1945, 148 F.2d 292; *Karl Kiefer Machine Co. v. United States Bottlers Machinery Co.*, C.C.A.7, 1940, 113 F.2d 356; *Chicago Metallic Mfg. Co. v. Edward Katzinger Co.*, C.C.A.7, 1941, 123 F.2d 518; *Louisiana Farmers' Protective Union, Inc. v. Great Atlantic & Pacific Tea Co. of America, Inc.*, C.C.A.8, 1942, 131 F.2d 419; *Publicity Bldg. Realty Corp. v. Hannegan,* C.C.A.8, 1943, 139 F.2d 583; *Dioguardi v. Durning,* C.C.A.2, 1944, 139 F.2d 774; *Package Closure Corp. v. Sealright Co., Inc.*, C.C.A.2, 1944, 141 F.2d 972; *Tahir Erk v. Glenn L. Martin Co.*, C.C.A.4, 1941, 116 F.2d 865; *Bell v. Preferred Life Assurance Society of Montgomery, Ala.*, 1943, 64 S.Ct. 5, 320 U.S. 238, 88 L.Ed. 15.

The addition at the end of subdivision (b) makes it clear that on a motion under Rule 12(b)(6) extraneous material may not be considered if the court excludes it, but that if the court does not exclude such material the motion shall be treated as a motion for summary judgment and disposed of as provided in Rule 56. It will also be observed that if a motion under Rule 12(b)(6) is thus converted into a summary judgment motion, the amendment insures that both parties shall be given a reasonable opportunity to submit affidavits and extraneous proofs to avoid taking a party by surprise through the conversion of the motion into a motion for summary judgment. In this manner and to this extent the amendment regularizes the practice above described. As the courts are already dealing with cases in this way, the effect of this amendment is really only to define the practice carefully and apply the requirements of the summary judgment rule in the disposition of the motion.

Subdivision (c). The sentence appended to subdivision (c) performs the same function and is grounded on the same reasons as the corresponding sentence added in subdivision (b).

Subdivision (d). The change here was made necessary because of the addition of defense (7) in subdivision (b).

Subdivision (e). References in this subdivision to a bill of particulars have been deleted, and the motion provided for is confined to one for more definite statement to be obtained only in cases where the movant cannot reasonably be required to frame an answer or other responsive pleading to the pleading in question. With respect to preparations for trial, the party is properly relegated to the various methods of examination and discovery provided in the rules for that purpose. *Slusher v. Jones,* E.D.Ky.1943, 7 Fed.Rules Serv. 12e.231, Case 5, 3 F.R.D. 168; *Best Foods, Inc. v. General Mills, Inc.*, D.Del.1943, 7 Fed.Rules Serv. 12e.231, Case 7, 3 F.R.D. 275; *Braden v. Callaway,* E.D.Tenn.1943, 8 Fed. Rules Serv. 12e.231, Case 1 (". . . most courts . . . conclude that the definiteness required is only such as will be sufficient for the party to prepare responsive pleadings"). Accordingly, the reference to the 20 day time limit has also been eliminated, since the purpose of this present provision is to state a time period where the motion for a bill is made for the purpose of preparing for trial.

Rule 12(e) as originally drawn has been the subject of more judicial rulings than any other part of the rules, and has been much criticized by commentators, judges and members of the bar. See general discussion and cases cited in 1 Moore's *Federal Practice,* 1938, Cum.Supplement, § 12.07, under "Page 657"; also, Holtzoff, *New Federal Procedure*

and the Courts, 1940, 35–41. And compare vote of Second Circuit Conference of Circuit and District Judges, June 1940, recommending the abolition of the bill of particulars; *Sun Valley Mfg. Co. v. Mylish,* E.D.Pa.1944, 8 Fed.Rules Serv. 12e.231, Case 6 ("Our experience . . . has demonstrated not only that 'the office of the bill of particulars is fast becoming obsolete' . . . but that in view of the adequate discovery procedure available under the Rules, motions for bills of particulars should be abolished altogether."); *Walling v. American Steamship Co.*, W.D.N.Y.1945, 4 F.R.D. 355, 8 Fed.Rules Serv. 12e.244, Case 8 (". . . the adoption of the rule was ill advised. It has led to confusion, duplication and delay.") The tendency of some courts freely to grant extended bills of particulars has served to neutralize any helpful benefits derived from rule 8, and has overlooked the intended use of the rules on depositions and discovery. The words "or to prepare for trial"—eliminated by the proposed amendment—have sometimes been seized upon as grounds for compulsory statement in the opposing pleading of all the details which the movant would have to meet at the trial. On the other hand, many courts have in effect read these words out of the rule. See *Walling v. Alabama Pipe Co.*, W.D.Mo. 1942, 3 F.R.D. 159, 6 Fed.Rules Serv. 12e.244, Case 7; *Fleming v. Mason & Dixon Lines, Inc.*, E.D.Tenn.1941, 42 F.Supp. 230; *Kellogg Co. v. National Biscuit Co.*, D.N.J. 1941, 38 F.Supp. 643; *Brown v. H. L. Green Co.*, S.D.N.Y. 1943, 7 Fed.Rules Serv. 12e.231, Case 6; *Pedersen v. Standard Accident Ins. Co.*, W.D.Mo.1945, 8 Fed.Rules Serv. 12e.231, Case 8; *Bowles v. Ohse,* D.Neb.1945, 4 F.R.D. 403, 9 Fed.Rules Serv. 12e.231, Case 1; *Klages v. Cohen,* E.D.N.Y. 1945, 9 Fed.Rules Serv. 8a.25, Case 4; *Bowles v. Lawrence,* D.Mass.1945, 8 Fed.Rules Serv. 12e.231, Case 19; *McKinney Tool & Mfg. Co. v. Hoyt,* N.D.Ohio 1945, 9 Fed.Rules Serv. 12e.235, Case 1; *Bowles v. Jack,* D.Minn.1945, 5 F.R.D. 1, 9 Fed.Rules Serv. 12e.244, Case 9. And it has been urged from the bench that the phrase be stricken, *Poole v. White,* N.D.W.Va.1941, 5 Fed.Rules Serv. 12e.231, Case 4, 2 F.R.D. 40. See also *Bowles v. Gabel,* W.D.Mo.1946, 9 Fed.Rules Serv. 12e.244, Case 10. ("The courts have never favored that portion of the rules which undertook to justify a motion of this kind for the purpose of aiding counsel in preparing his case for trial.").

Subdivision (f). This amendment affords a specific method of raising the insufficiency of a defense, a matter which has troubled some courts, although attack has been permitted in one way or another. See *Dysart v. Remington-Rand, Inc.*, D.Conn.1939, 31 F.Supp. 296; *Eastman Kodak Co. v. McAuley,* S.D.N.Y.1941, 4 Fed.Rules Serv., 12f.21, Case 8, 2 F.R.D. 21; *Schenley Distillers Corp. v. Renken,* E.D.S.C. 1940, 34 F.Supp. 678; *Yale Transport Corp. v. Yellow Truck & Coach Mfg. Co.*, S.D.N.Y.1944, 3 F.R.D. 440; *United States v. Turner Milk Co.*, N.D.Ill.1941, 4 Fed.Rules Serv. 12b.51, Case 3, 1 F.R.D. 643; *Teiger v. Stephan Oderwald, Inc.*, S.D.N.Y.1940, 31 F.Supp. 626; *Teplitsky v. Pennsylvania R. Co.*, N.D.Ill.1941, 38 F.Supp. 535; *Callagher v. Carroll,* E.D.N.Y.1939, 27 F.Supp. 568; *United States v. Palmer,* S.D.N.Y.1939, 28 F.Supp. 936. And see *Indemnity Ins. Co. of North America v. Pan American Airways, Inc.*, S.D.N.Y. 1944, 58 F.Supp. 338; Commentary, *Modes of Attacking Insufficient Defenses in the Answer,* 901, 1939, 1 Fed.Rules Serv. 669, 1940, 2 Fed.Rules Serv. 640.

Subdivision (g). The change in title conforms with the companion provision in subdivision (h).

The alteration of the "except" clause requires that other than provided in subdivision (h) a party who resorts to a motion to raise defenses specified in the rule, must include in one motion all that are then available to him. Under the original rule defenses which could be raised by motion were divided into two groups which could be the subjects of two successive motions.

Subdivision (h). The addition of the phrase relating to indispensable parties is one of necessity.

1963 Amendment

This amendment conforms to the amendment of Rule 4(e). See also the Advisory Committee's Note to amended Rule 4(b).

1966 Amendment

Subdivision (b)(7). The terminology of this subdivision is changed to accord with the amendment of Rule 19. See the Advisory Committee's Note to Rule 19, as amended, especially the third paragraph therein before the caption "Subdivision (c)."

Subdivision (g). Subdivision (g) has forbidden a defendant who makes a preanswer motion under this rule from making a further motion presenting any defense or objection which was available to him at the time he made the first motion and which he could have included, but did not in fact include therein. Thus if the defendant moves before answer to dismiss the complaint for failure to state a claim, he is barred from making a further motion presenting the defense of improper venue, if that defense was available to him when he made his original motion. Amended subdivision (g) is to the same effect. This required consolidation of defenses and objections in a Rule 12 motion is salutary in that it works against piecemeal consideration of a case. For exceptions to the requirement of consolidation, see the last clause of subdivision (g), referring to new subdivision (h)(2).

Subdivision (h). The question has arisen whether an omitted defense which cannot be made the basis of a second motion may nevertheless be pleaded in the answer. Subdivision (h) called for waiver of "* * * defenses and objections which he [defendant] does not present * * * by motion * * * or, if he has made no motion, in his answer * * *." If the clause "if he has made no motion," was read literally, it seemed that the omitted defense was waived and could not be pleaded in the answer. On the other hand, the clause might be read as adding nothing of substance to the preceding words; in that event it appeared that a defense was not waived by reason of being omitted from the motion and might be set up in the answer. The decisions were divided. Favoring waiver, see *Keef v. Derounian,* 6 F.R.D. 11 (N.D.Ill.1946); *Elbinger v. Precision Metal Workers Corp.,* 18 F.R.D. 467 (E.D.Wis.1956); see also *Rensing v. Turner Aviation Corp.,* 166 F.Supp. 790 (N.D.Ill.1958); *P. Beiersdorf & Co. v. Duke Laboratories, Inc.,* 10 F.R.D. 282 (S.D.N.Y. 1950); *Neset v. Christensen,* 92 F.Supp. 78 (E.D.N.Y.1950). Opposing waiver, see *Phillips v. Baker,* 121 F.2d 752 (9th Cir.1941); *Crum v. Graham,* 32 F.R.D. 173 (D.Mont.1963) (regretfully following the Phillips case); see also *Birnbaum v. Birrell,* 9 F.R.D. 72 (S.D.N.Y.1948); *Johnson v. Joseph Schlitz Brewing Co.,* 33 F.Supp. 176 (E.D.Tenn.1940); cf. *Carter v. American Bus Lines, Inc.,* 22 F.R.D. 323 (D.Neb. 1958).

Amended subdivision (h)(1)(A) eliminates the ambiguity and states that certain specified defenses which were available to a party when he made a preanswer motion, but which he omitted from the motion, are waived. The specified defenses are lack of jurisdiction over the person, improper venue, insufficiency of process, and insufficiency of service of process (see Rule 12(b)(2)–(5)). A party who by motion invites the court to pass upon a threshold defense should bring forward all the specified defenses he then has and thus allow the court to do a reasonably complete job. The waiver reinforces the policy of subdivision (g) forbidding successive motions.

By amended subdivision (h)(1)(B), the specified defenses, even if not waived by the operation of (A), are waived by the failure to raise them by a motion under Rule 12 or in the responsive pleading or any amendment thereof to which the party is entitled as a matter of course. The specified defenses are of such a character that they should not be delayed and brought up for the first time by means of an application to the court to amend the responsive pleading.

Since the language of the subdivisions is made clear, the party is put on fair notice of the effect of his actions and omissions and can guard himself against unintended waiver. It is to be noted that while the defenses specified in subdivision (h)(1) are subject to waiver as there provided, the more substantial defenses of failure to state a claim upon which relief can be granted, failure to join a party indispensable under Rule 19, and failure to state a legal defense to a claim (see Rule 12(b)(6), (7), (f)), as well as the defense of lack of jurisdiction over the subject matter (see Rule 12(b)(1)), are expressly preserved against waiver by amended subdivision (h)(2) and (3).

1987 Amendment

The amendments are technical. No substantive change is intended.

1993 Amendment

Subdivision (a) is divided into paragraphs for greater clarity, and paragraph (1)(B) is added to reflect amendments to Rule 4. Consistent with Rule 4(d)(3), a defendant that timely waives service is allowed 60 days from the date the request was mailed in which to respond to the complaint, with an additional 30 days afforded if the request was sent out of the country. Service is timely waived if the waiver is returned within the time specified in the request (30 days after the request was mailed, or 60 days if mailed out of the country) and before being formally served with process. Sometimes a plaintiff may attempt to serve a defendant with process while also sending the defendant a request for waiver of service; if the defendant executes the waiver of service within the time specified and before being served with process, it should have the longer time to respond afforded by waiving service.

The date of sending the request is to be inserted by the plaintiff on the face of the request for waiver and on the waiver itself. This date is used to measure the return day for the waiver form, so that the plaintiff can know on a day certain whether formal service of process will be necessary; it is also a useful date to measure the time for answer when service is waived. The defendant who returns the waiver is given additional time for answer in order to assure that it loses nothing by waiving service of process.

2000 Amendment

Rule 12(a)(3)(B) is added to complement the addition of Rule 4(i)(2)(B). The purposes that underlie the requirement that service be made on the United States in an action that asserts individual liability of a United States officer or employee for acts occurring in connection with the performance of duties on behalf of the United States also require that the time to answer be extended to 60 days. Time is needed for the United States to determine whether to provide representation to the defendant officer or employee. If the United States provides representation, the need for an extended answer period is the same as in actions against the United States, a United States agency, or a United States officer sued in an official capacity.

An action against a former officer or employee of the United States is covered by subparagraph (3)(B) in the same way as an action against a present officer or employee. Termination of the relationship between the individual defendant and the United States does not reduce the need for additional time to answer.

GAP Report

No changes are recommended for Rule 12 as published.

Rule 13.   Counterclaim and Cross-Claim

(a) Compulsory Counterclaims. A pleading shall state as a counterclaim any claim which at the time of serving the pleading the pleader has against any opposing party, if it arises out of the transaction or occurrence that is the subject matter of the opposing party's claim and does not require for its adjudication the presence of third parties of whom the court cannot acquire jurisdiction. But the pleader need not state the claim if (1) at the time the action was commenced the claim was the subject of another pending action, or (2) the opposing party brought suit upon the claim by attachment or other process by which the court did not acquire jurisdiction to render a personal judgment on that claim, and the pleader is not stating any counterclaim under this Rule 13.

(b) Permissive Counterclaims. A pleading may state as a counterclaim any claim against an opposing party not arising out of the transaction or occurrence that is the subject matter of the opposing party's claim.

(c) Counterclaim Exceeding Opposing Claim. A counterclaim may or may not diminish or defeat the recovery sought by the opposing party. It may claim relief exceeding in amount or different in kind from that sought in the pleading of the opposing party.

(d) Counterclaim Against the United States. These rules shall not be construed to enlarge beyond the limits now fixed by law the right to assert counterclaims or to claim credits against the United States or an officer or agency thereof.

(e) Counterclaim Maturing or Acquired After Pleading. A claim which either matured or was acquired by the pleader after serving a pleading may, with the permission of the court, be presented as a counterclaim by supplemental pleading.

(f) Omitted Counterclaim. When a pleader fails to set up a counterclaim through oversight, inadvertence, or excusable neglect, or when justice requires, the pleader may by leave of court set up the counterclaim by amendment.

(g) Cross-Claim Against Co-Party. A pleading may state as a cross-claim any claim by one party against a co-party arising out of the transaction or occurrence that is the subject matter either of the original action or of a counterclaim therein or relating to any property that is the subject matter of the original action. Such cross-claim may include a claim that the party against whom it is asserted is or may be liable to the cross-claimant for all or part of a claim asserted in the action against the cross-claimant.

(h) Joinder of Additional Parties. Persons other than those made parties to the original action may be made parties to a counterclaim or cross-claim in accordance with the provisions of Rules 19 and 20.

(i) Separate Trials; Separate Judgments. If the court orders separate trials as provided in Rule 42(b), judgment on a counterclaim or cross-claim may be rendered in accordance with the terms of Rule 54(b) when the court has jurisdiction so to do, even if the claims of the opposing party have been dismissed or otherwise disposed of.

(As amended Dec. 27, 1946, eff. Mar. 19, 1948; Jan. 21, 1963, eff. July 1, 1963; Feb. 28, 1966, eff. July 1, 1966; Mar. 2, 1987, eff. Aug. 1, 1987.)

ADVISORY COMMITTEE NOTES

1937 Adoption

1. This is substantially [former] Equity Rule 30 (Answer—Contents—Counterclaim), broadened to include legal as well as equitable counterclaims.

2. Compare the English practice, *English Rules Under the Judicature Act* (The Annual Practice, 1937) O. 19, r.r. 2 and 3, and O. 21, r.r. 10–17; *Beddall v. Maitland*, L.R. 17 Ch.Div. 174, 181, 182 (1881).

3. Certain States have also adopted almost unrestricted provisions concerning both the subject matter of and the parties to a counterclaim. This seems to be the modern tendency. Ark.Civ.Code (Crawford, 1934) §§ 117 (as amended) and 118; N.J.Comp.Stat. (2 Cum.Supp. 1911–1924); N.Y.C.P.A. (1937) §§ 262, 266, 267 (all as amended, Laws of 1936, ch. 324), 268, 269, and 271; Wis.Stat. (1935) § 263.14(1)(c).

4. Most codes do not expressly provide for a counterclaim in the reply. Clark, *Code Pleading* (1928), p. 486. Ky.Codes (Carroll, 1932) Civ.Pract. § 98 does provide, however, for such counterclaim.

5. The provisions of this rule respecting counterclaims are subject to Rule 82 (Jurisdiction and Venue Unaffected). For a discussion of Federal jurisdiction and venue in regard to counterclaims and cross-claims, see Shulman and Jaegerman, *Some Jurisdictional Limitations in Federal Procedure* (1936), 45 Yale L.J. 393, 410 et seq.

6. This rule does not affect such statutes of the United States as U.S.C., Title 28, § 41(1) (now §§ 1332, 1345, 1359) (United States as plaintiff; civil suits at common law and in equity), relating to assigned claims in actions based on diversity of citizenship.

7. If the action proceeds to judgment without the interposition of a counterclaim as required by subdivision (a) of this rule, the counterclaim is barred. See *American Mills Co. v. American Surety Co.*, 260 U.S. 360, 43 S.Ct. 149, 67 L.Ed. 306 (1922); *Marconi Wireless Telegraph Co. v. National Electric Signalling Co.*, 206 Fed. 295 (E.D.N.Y., 1913); Hopkins, *Federal Equity Rules* (8th ed., 1933), p. 213; Simkins, *Federal Practice* (1934), p. 663.

8. For allowance of credits against the United States see U.S.C., Title 26, §§ 1672–1673 [sec. 7442] (Suits for refunds of internal revenue taxes—limitations); U.S.C., Title 28, § 774 (now § 2406) (Suits by United States against individuals; credits), [former] § 775 (Suits under postal laws; credits); U.S.C., Title 31, § 227 [now 3728] (Offsets against judgments and claims against United States).

1946 Amendment

Note. Subdivision (a). The use of the word "filing" was inadvertent. The word "serving" conforms with subdivision (e) and with usage generally throughout the rules.

The removal of the phrase "not the subject of a pending action" and the addition of the new clause at the end of the subdivision is designed to eliminate the ambiguity noted in *Prudential Insurance Co. of America v. Saxe*, App.D.C.1943, 77 U.S.App.D.C. 144, 134 F.2d 16, 33–34, cert. den., 1943, 319 U.S. 745, 63 S.Ct. 1033. The rewording of the subdivision in this respect insures against an undesirable possibility presented under the original rule whereby a party having a claim which would be the subject of a compulsory counterclaim could avoid stating it as such by bringing an independent action in another court after the commencement of the federal action but before serving his pleading in the federal action.

Subdivision (g). The amendment is to care for a situation such as where a second mortgagee is made defendant in a foreclosure proceeding and wishes to file a cross-complaint against the mortgagor in order to secure a personal judgment for the indebtedness and foreclose his lien. A claim of this sort by the second mortgagee may not necessarily arise out of the transaction or occurrence that is the subject matter of the original action under the terms of Rule 13(g).

Subdivision (h). The change clarifies the interdependence of Rules 13(i) and 54(b).

1963 Amendment

When a defendant, if he desires to defend his interest in property, is obliged to come in and litigate in a court to whose jurisdiction he could not ordinarily be subjected, fairness suggests that he should not be required to assert counterclaims, but should rather be permitted to do so at his election. If, however, he does elect to assert a counterclaim,

it seems fair to require him to assert any other which is compulsory within the meaning of Rule 13(a). Clause (2), added by amendment to Rule 13(a), carries out this idea. It will apply to various cases described in Rule 4(e), as amended, where service is effected through attachment or other process by which the court does not acquire jurisdiction to render a personal judgment against the defendant. Clause (2) will also apply to actions commenced in State courts jurisdictionally grounded on attachment or the like, and removed to the Federal courts.

1966 Amendment

Rule 13(h), dealing with the joinder of additional parties to a counterclaim or cross-claim, has partaken of some of the textual difficulties of Rule 19 on necessary joinder of parties. See Advisory Committee's Note to Rule 19, as amended; cf. 3 *Moore's Federal Practice*, par. 13.39 (2d ed. 1963), and Supp. thereto; 1A Barron & Holtzoff, *Federal Practice and Procedure* § 399 (Wright ed. 1960). Rule 13(h) has also been inadequate in failing to call attention to the fact that a party pleading a counterclaim or cross-claim may join additional persons when the conditions for permissive joinder of parties under Rule 20 are satisfied.

The amendment of Rule 13(h) supplies the latter omission by expressly referring to Rule 20, as amended, and also incorporates by direct reference the revised criteria and procedures of Rule 19, as amended. Hereafter, for the purpose of determining who must or may be joined as additional parties to a counterclaim or cross-claim, the party pleading the claim is to be regarded as a plaintiff and the additional parties as plaintiffs or defendants as the case may be, and amended Rules 19 and 20 are to be applied in the usual fashion. See also Rules 13(a) (compulsory counterclaims) and 22 (interpleader).

The amendment of Rule 13(h), like the amendment of Rule 19, does not attempt to regulate Federal jurisdiction or venue. See Rule 82. It should be noted, however, that in some situations the decisional law has recognized "ancillary" Federal jurisdiction over counterclaims and cross-claims and "ancillary" venue as to parties to these claims.

1987 Amendment

The amendments are technical. No substantive change is intended.

Rule 14. Third-Party Practice

(a) When Defendant May Bring in Third Party. At any time after commencement of the action a defending party, as a third-party plaintiff, may cause a summons and complaint to be served upon a person not a party to the action who is or may be liable to the third-party plaintiff for all or part of the plaintiff's claim against the third-party plaintiff. The third-party plaintiff need not obtain leave to make the service if the third-party plaintiff files the third-party complaint not later than 10 days after serving the original answer. Otherwise the third-party plaintiff must obtain leave on motion upon notice to all parties to the action. The person served with the summons and third-party complaint, hereinafter called the third-party defendant, shall make any defenses to the third-party plaintiff's claim as provided in Rule 12 and any counterclaims against the third-party plaintiff and cross-claims against other third-party defendants as provided in Rule 13. The third-party defendant may assert against the plaintiff any defenses which the third-party plaintiff has to the plaintiff's claim. The third-party defendant may also assert any claim against the plaintiff arising out of the transaction or occurrence that is the subject matter of the plaintiff's claim against the third-party plaintiff. The plaintiff may assert any claim against the third-party defendant arising out of the transaction or occurrence that is the subject matter of the plaintiff's claim against the third-party plaintiff, and the third-party defendant thereupon shall assert any defenses as provided in Rule 12 and any counterclaims and cross-claims as provided in Rule 13. Any party may move to strike the third-party claim, or for its severance or separate trial. A third-party defendant may proceed under this rule against any person not a party to the action who is or may be liable to the third-party defendant for all or part of the claim made in the action against the third-party defendant. The third-party complaint, if within the admiralty and maritime jurisdiction, may be in rem against a vessel, cargo, or other property subject to admiralty or maritime process in rem, in which case references in this rule to the summons include the warrant of arrest, and references to the third-party plaintiff or defendant include, where appropriate, a person who asserts a right under Supplemental Rule C(6)(b)(i) in the property arrested.

(b) When Plaintiff May Bring in Third Party. When a counterclaim is asserted against a plaintiff, the plaintiff may cause a third party to be brought in under circumstances which under this rule would entitle a defendant to do so.

(c) Admiralty and Maritime Claims. When a plaintiff asserts an admiralty or maritime claim within the meaning of Rule 9(h), the defendant or person who asserts a right under Supplemental Rule C(6)(b)(i), as a third-party plaintiff, may bring in a third-party defendant who may be wholly or partly liable, either to the plaintiff or to the third-party plaintiff, by way of remedy over, contribution, or otherwise on account of the same transaction, occurrence, or series of transactions or occurrences. In such a case the third-party plaintiff may also demand judgment against the third-party defendant in favor of the plaintiff, in which event the third-party defendant shall make any defenses to the claim of the plaintiff as well as to that of the third-party plaintiff in the manner provided in Rule 12 and the action shall proceed as if the plaintiff had commenced it against the third-party defendant as well as the third-party plaintiff.

(As amended Dec. 27, 1946, eff. Mar. 19, 1948; Jan. 21, 1963, eff. July 1, 1963; Feb. 28, 1966, eff. July 1, 1966; Mar. 2, 1987, eff. Aug. 1, 1987; Apr. 17, 2000, eff. Dec. 1, 2000.)

ADVISORY COMMITTEE NOTES

1937 Adoption

Third-party impleader is in some aspects a modern innovation in law and equity although well known in admiralty. Because of its many advantages a liberal procedure with respect to it has developed in England, in the federal admiralty courts, and in some American state jurisdictions. See *English Rules Under the Judicature Act* (The Annual Practice, 1937) O. 16A, r.r. 1–13; United States Supreme Court Admiralty Rules (1920), Rule 56 (Right to Bring in Party Jointly Liable); 12 P.S.Pa. § 141; Wis.Stat. (1935) §§ 260.19, 260.20; N.Y.C.P.A. (1937) §§ 193(2), 211(a). Compare La. Code Pract. (Dart, 1932) §§ 378–388. For the practice in Texas as developed by judicial decision, see *Lottman v. Cuilla*, Tex.1926, 288 S.W. 123, 126. For a treatment of this subject see Gregory, *Legislative Loss Distribution in Negligence Actions* (1936); *Shulman and Jaegerman, Some Jurisdictional Limitations on Federal Procedure (1936)*, 45 Yale L.J. 393, 417 et seq.

Third-party impleader under the-conformity act has been applied in actions at law in the Federal courts. *Lowry and Co., Inc. v. National City Bank of New York*, N.Y.1928, 28 F.2d 895; *Yellow Cab Co. of Philadelphia v. Rodgers*, C.C.A.3, 1932, 61 F.2d 729.

1946 Amendment

Note. The provisions in Rule 14(a) which relate to the impleading of a third party who is or may be liable to the plaintiff have been deleted by the proposed amendment. It has been held that under Rule 14(a) the plaintiff need not amend his complaint to state a claim against such third party if he does not wish to do so. *Satink v. Holland Township*, D.N.J.1940, 31 F.Supp. 229, noted, 1940, 88 U.Pa.L.Rev. 751; *Connelly v. Bender*, E.D.Mich.1941, 36 F.Supp. 368; *Whitmire v. Partin (Milton)*, E.D.Tenn.1941, 2 F.R.D. 83, 5 Fed.Rules Serv. 14a.513, Case 2; *Crim v. Lumbermen's Mutual Casualty Co.*, D.D.C.1939, 26 F.Supp. 715; *Carbola Chemical Co., Inc. v. Trundle*, S.D.N.Y.1943, 3 F.R.D. 502, 7 Fed.Rules Serv. 14a.224, Case 1; *Roadway Express, Inc. v. Automobile Ins. Co. of Hartford, Conn., (Providence Washington Ins. Co.)* N.D.Ohio 1945, 8 Fed.Rules Serv. 14a.513, Case 3. In *Delano v. Ives*, E.D.Pa.1941, 40 F.Supp. 672, the court said: ". . . the weight of authority is to the effect that a defendant cannot compel the plaintiff, who has sued him, to sue also a third party whom he does not wish to sue, by tendering in a third party complaint the third party as an additional defendant directly liable to the plaintiff." Thus impleader here amounts to no more than a mere offer of a party to the plaintiff, and if he rejects it, the attempt is a time-consuming futility. See *Satink v. Holland Township, supra; Malkin v. Arundel Corp.*, D.Md.1941, 36 F.Supp. 948; also Koenigsberger, *Suggestions for Changes in the Federal Rules of Civil Procedure*, 1941, 4 Fed.Rules Serv. 1010. But cf. *Atlantic Coast Line R. Co. v. United States Fidelity & Guaranty Co.*, Ga.1943, 52 F.Supp. 177. Moreover, in any case where the plaintiff could not have joined the third party originally because of jurisdictional limitations such as lack of diversity of citizenship, the majority view is that any attempt by the plaintiff to amend his complaint and assert a claim against the impleaded third party would be unavailing. *Hoskie v. Prudential Ins. Co. of America, (Lorrac Real Estate Corp.),* E.D.N.Y.1941, 39 F.Supp. 305; *Johnson v. G. J. Sherrard Co., (New England Telephone & Telegraph Co.),* D.Mass.1941, 5 Fed.Rules Serv. 14a.511, Case 1, 2 F.R.D. 164; *Thompson v. Cranston,* W.D.N.Y.1942, 6 Fed.Rules Serv. 14a.511, Case 1, 2 F.R.D. 270, affirmed CCA2d, 1942, 132 F.2d 631, certiorari denied 1945, 63 S.Ct. 1028, 319 U.S. 741, 87 L.Ed. 1698; *Friend v. Middle Atlantic Transportation Co.,* C.C.A.2, 1946, 153 F.2d 778, certiorari denied 1946, 66 S.Ct. 1370, 328 U.S. 865, 90 L.Ed. 1635; *Herrington v. Jones,* E.D.La.1941, 5 Fed.Rules Serv. 14a.511, Case 2, 2 F.R.D. 108; *Banks v. Employers' Liability Assurance Corp., (Central Surety & Ins. Corp.)* W.D.Mo.1943, 7 Fed.Rules Serv. 14a.11, Case 2; *Saunders v. Baltimore & Ohio R. Co.,* S.D.W.Va.1945, 9 Fed.Rules Serv. 14a.62, Case 2; *Hull v. United States Rubber Co. (Johnson Larsen and Co.),* E.D.Mich.1945, 9 Fed.Rules Serv. 14a.62, Case 3. See also concurring opinion of Circuit Judge Minton in *People of State of Illinois for Use of Trust Co. of Chicago v. Maryland Casualty Co.,* C.C.A.7, 1942, 132 F.2d 850, 853. Contra: *Sklar v. Hayes (Singer),* E.D.Pa.1941, 4 Fed.Rules Serv. 14a.511, Case 2, 1 F.R.D. 594. Discussion of the problem will be found in Commentary, *Amendment of Plaintiff's Pleading to Assert Claim Against Third-Party Defendant,* 1942, 5 Fed.Rules Serv. 811; Commentary, *Federal Jurisdiction in Third-Party Practice,* 1943, 6 Fed.Rules Serv. 766; Holtzoff, *Some Problems Under Federal Third-Party Practice,* 1941, 3 La.L.Rev. 408, 419–420; 1 Moore's *Federal Practice,* 1938, Cum.Supplement § 14.08. For these reasons therefore, the words "or to the plaintiff" in the first sentence of subdivision (a) have been removed by the amendment; and in conformance therewith the words "the plaintiff" in the second sentence of the subdivision, and the words "or to the third-party plaintiff" in the concluding sentence thereof have likewise been eliminated.

The third sentence of rule 14(a) has been expanded to clarify the right of the third-party defendant to assert any defenses which the third-party plaintiff may have to the plaintiff's claim. This protects the impleaded third-party defendant where the third-party plaintiff fails or neglects to assert a proper defense to the plaintiff's action. A new sentence has also been inserted giving the third-party defendant the right to assert directly against the original plaintiff any claim arising out of the transaction or occurrence that is the subject matter of the plaintiff's claim against the third-party plaintiff. This permits all claims arising out of the same transaction or occurrence to be heard and determined in the same action. See *Atlantic Coast Line R. Co. v. United States Fidelity & Guaranty Co.,* Ga.1943, 52 F.Supp. 177. Accordingly, the next to the last sentence of subdivision (a) has also been revised to make clear that the plaintiff may, if he desires, assert directly against the third-party defendant either by amendment or by a new pleading any claim he may have against him arising out of the transaction or occurrence that is the subject matter of the plaintiff's claim against the third-party plaintiff. In such a case, the third-party defendant then is entitled to assert the defenses, counter-claims and cross-claims provided in Rules 12 and 13.

The sentence reading "The third-party defendant is bound by the adjudication of the third-party plaintiff's liability to the plaintiff, as well as of his own to the plaintiff, or to the third-party plaintiff" has been stricken from Rule 14(a), not to change the law, but because the sentence states a rule of substantive law which is not within the scope of a procedural rule. It is not the purpose of the rules to state the effect of a judgment.

The elimination of the words "the third-party plaintiff, or any other party" from the second sentence of rule 14(a), together with the insertion of the new phrases therein, are not changes of substance but are merely for the purpose of clarification.

1963 Amendment

Under the amendment of the initial sentences of the subdivision, a defendant as a third-party plaintiff may freely and without leave of court bring in a third-party defendant if he files the third-party complaint not later than 10 days after he serves his original answer. When the impleader comes so early in the case, there is little value in requiring a preliminary ruling by the court on the propriety of the impleader.

After the third-party defendant is brought in, the court has discretion to strike the third-party claim if it is obviously unmeritorious and can only delay or prejudice the disposition of the plaintiff's claim, or to sever the third-party claim or accord it separate trial if confusion or prejudice would otherwise result. This discretion, applicable not merely to the cases covered by the amendment where the third-party defendant is brought in without leave, but to all impleaders under the rule, is emphasized in the next-to-last sentence of the subdivision, added by amendment.

In dispensing with leave of court for an impleader filed not later than 10 days after serving the answer, but retaining the leave requirement for impleaders sought to be effected thereafter, the amended subdivision takes a moderate position on the lines urged by some commentators, see Note, 43 Minn.L.Rev. 115 (1958); cf. Pa.R.Civ.P. 2252–53 (60 days after service on the defendant; Minn.R.Civ.P. 14.01 (45 days). Other commentators would dispense with the requirement of leave regardless of the time when impleader is effected, and would rely on subsequent action by the court to dismiss the impleader if it would unduly delay or complicate the litigation or would be otherwise objectionable. See 1A Barron & Holtzoff, *Federal Practice & Procedure* 649–50 (Wright ed. 1960); Comment, 58 Colum.L.Rev. 532, 546 (1958); cf. N.Y.Civ.Prac.Act § 193–a; Me.R.Civ.P. 14. The amended subdivision preserves the value of a preliminary screening, through the leave procedure, of impleaders attempted after the 10-day period.

The amendment applies also when an impleader is initiated by a third-party defendant against a person who may be liable to him, as provided in the last sentence of the subdivision.

1966 Amendment

Rule 14 was modeled on Admiralty Rule 56. An important feature of Admiralty Rule 56 was that it allowed impleader not only of a person who might be liable to the defendant by way of remedy over, but also of any person who might be liable to the plaintiff. The importance of this provision was that the defendant was entitled to insist that the plaintiff proceed to judgment against the third-party defendant. In certain cases this was a valuable implementation of a substantive right. For example, in a case of ship collision where a finding of mutual fault is possible, one shipowner, if sued alone, faces the prospect of an absolute judgment for the full amount of the damage suffered by an innocent third party; but if he can implead the owner of the other vessel, and if mutual fault is found, the judgment against the original defendant will be in the first instance only for a moiety of the damages; liability for the remainder will be conditioned on the plaintiff's inability to collect from the third-party defendant.

This feature was originally incorporated in Rule 14, but was eliminated by the amendment of 1946, so that under the amended rule a third party could not be impleaded on the basis that he might be liable to the plaintiff. One of the reasons for the amendment was that the Civil Rule, unlike the Admiralty Rule, did not require the plaintiff to go to judgment against the third-party defendant. Another reason was that where jurisdiction depended on diversity of citizenship the impleader of an adversary having the same citizenship as the plaintiff was not considered possible.

Retention of the admiralty practice in those cases that will be counterparts of a suit in admiralty is clearly desirable.

1987 Amendment

The amendments are technical. No substantive change is intended.

2000 Amendment

Subdivisions (a) and (c) are amended to reflect revisions in Supplemental Rule C(6).

GAP Report

Rule B(1)(a) was modified by moving "in an in personam action" out of paragraph (a) and into the first line of subdivision (1). This change makes it clear that all paragraphs of subdivision (1) apply when attachment is sought in an in personam action. Rule B(1)(d) was modified by changing the requirement that the clerk deliver the summons and process to the person or organization authorized to serve it. The new form requires only that the summons and process be delivered, not that the clerk effect the delivery. This change conforms to present practice in some districts and will facilitate rapid service. It matches the spirit of Civil Rule 4(b), which directs the clerk to issue the summons "to the plaintiff for service on the defendant." A parallel change is made in Rule C(3)(b).

Rule 15. Amended and Supplemental Pleadings

(a) Amendments. A party may amend the party's pleading once as a matter of course at any time before a responsive pleading is served or, if the pleading is one to which no responsive pleading is permitted and the action has not been placed upon the trial calendar, the party may so amend it at any time within 20 days after it is served. Otherwise a party may amend the party's pleading only by leave of court or by written consent of the adverse party; and leave shall be freely given when justice so requires. A party shall plead in response to an amended pleading within the time remaining for response to the original pleading or within 10 days after service of the amended pleading,

whichever period may be the longer, unless the court otherwise orders.

(b) Amendments to Conform to the Evidence. When issues not raised by the pleadings are tried by express or implied consent of the parties, they shall be treated in all respects as if they had been raised in the pleadings. Such amendment of the pleadings as may be necessary to cause them to conform to the evidence and to raise these issues may be made upon motion of any party at any time, even after judgment; but failure so to amend does not affect the result of the trial of these issues. If evidence is objected to at the trial on the ground that it is not within the issues made by the pleadings, the court may allow the pleadings to be amended and shall do so freely when the presentation of the merits of the action will be subserved thereby and the objecting party fails to satisfy the court that the admission of such evidence would prejudice the party in maintaining the party's action or defense upon the merits. The court may grant a continuance to enable the objecting party to meet such evidence.

(c) Relation Back of Amendments. An amendment of a pleading relates back to the date of the original pleading when

(1) relation back is permitted by the law that provides the statute of limitations applicable to the action, or

(2) the claim or defense asserted in the amended pleading arose out of the conduct, transaction, or occurrence set forth or attempted to be set forth in the original pleading, or

(3) the amendment changes the party or the naming of the party against whom a claim is asserted if the foregoing provision (2) is satisfied and, within the period provided by Rule 4(m) for service of the summons and complaint, the party to be brought in by amendment (A) has received such notice of the institution of the action that the party will not be prejudiced in maintaining a defense on the merits, and (B) knew or should have known that, but for a mistake concerning the identity of the proper party, the action would have been brought against the party.

The delivery or mailing of process to the United States Attorney, or United States Attorney's designee, or the Attorney General of the United States, or an agency or officer who would have been a proper defendant if named, satisfies the requirement of subparagraphs (A) and (B) of this paragraph (3) with respect to the United States or any agency or officer thereof to be brought into the action as a defendant.

(d) Supplemental Pleadings. Upon motion of a party the court may, upon reasonable notice and upon such terms as are just, permit the party to serve a supplemental pleading setting forth transactions or occurrences or events which have happened since the date of the pleading sought to be supplemented. Permission may be granted even though the original pleading is defective in its statement of a claim for relief or defense. If the court deems it advisable that the adverse party plead to the supplemental pleading, it shall so order, specifying the time therefor.

(As amended Jan. 21, 1963, eff. July 1, 1963; Feb. 28, 1966, eff. July 1, 1966; Mar. 2, 1987, eff. Aug. 1, 1987; Apr. 30, 1991, eff. Dec. 1, 1991; Dec. 9, 1991, Pub.L. 102–198, § 11(a), 105 Stat. 1626; Apr. 22, 1993, eff. Dec. 1, 1993.)

ADVISORY COMMITTEE NOTES

1937 Adoption

See generally for the present federal practice, [former] Equity Rules 19 (Amendments Generally), 28 (Amendment of Bill as of Course), 32 (Answer to Amended Bill), 34 (Supplemental Pleading), and 35 (Bills of Revivor and Supplemental Bills—Form); U.S.C. Title 28, § 399 [now 1653] (Amendments to show diverse citizenship) and [former] 777 (Defects of form; amendments). See *English Rules Under the Judicature Act* (The Annual Practice, 1937) O. 28, r. r. 1–13; O. 20, r. 4; O. 24, r. r. 1–3.

Note to Subdivision (a). The right to serve an amended pleading once as of course is common. 4 Mont.Rev.Codes Ann. (1935) § 9186; 1 Ore.Code Ann. (1930) § 1–904; 1 S.C.Code (Michie, 1932) § 493; *English Rules Under the Judicature Act* (The Annual Practice, 1937) O. 28, r. 2. Provision for amendment of pleading before trial, by leave of court, is in almost every code. If there is no statute the power of the court to grant leave is said to be inherent. Clark, *Code Pleading* (1928), pp. 498, 509.

Note to Subdivision (b). Compare [former] Equity Rule 19 (Amendments Generally) and code provisions which allow an amendment "at any time in furtherance of justice," (e.g., Ark.Civ.Code (Crawford, 1934) § 155) and which allow an amendment of pleadings to conform to the evidence, where the adverse party has not been misled and prejudiced (e.g., N.M.Stat.Ann. (Courtright, 1929) §§ 105–601, 105–602).

Note to Subdivision (c). "Relation back" is a well recognized doctrine of recent and now more frequent application. Compare Ala.Code Ann. (Michie, 1928) § 9513; Smith-Hurd Ill.Stats. ch. 110, § 170(2); 2 Wash.Rev.Stat.Ann. (Remington, 1932) § 308–3(4). See U.S.C., Title 28, § 399 [now 1653] (Amendments to show diverse citizenship) for a provision for "relation back".

Note to Subdivision (d). This is an adaptation of former Equity Rule 34 (Supplemental Pleading).

1963 Amendment

Rule 15(d) is intended to give the court broad discretion in allowing a supplemental pleading. However, some cases, opposed by other cases and criticized by the commentators, have taken the rigid and formalistic view that where the original complaint fails to state a claim upon which relief can be granted, leave to serve a supplemental complaint must be denied. See *Bonner v. Elizabeth Arden, Inc.,* 177 F.2d 703 (2d Cir. 1949); *Bowles v. Senderowitz,* 65 F.Supp. 548 (E.D.Pa.), rev'd on other grounds, 158 F.2d 435 (3d Cir. 1946), cert. denied, *Senderowitz v. Fleming,* 330 U.S. 848, 67 S.Ct. 1091, 91 L.Ed. 1292 (1947); cf. *LaSalle Nat. Bank v.*

222 East Chestnut St. Corp., 267 F.2d 247 (7th Cir.), cert. denied, 361 U.S. 836, 80 S.Ct. 88, 4 L.Ed.2d 77 (1959). But see *Camilla Cotton Oil Co. v. Spencer Kellogg & Sons,* 257 F.2d 162 (5th Cir. 1958); *Genuth v. National Biscuit Co.,* 81 F.Supp. 213 (S.D.N.Y.1948), app. dism., 177 F.2d 962 (2d Cir. 1949); 3 Moore's *Federal Practice* ¶15.01[5] (Supp.1960); 1A Barron & Holtzoff, *Federal Practice & Procedure* 820–21 (Wright ed. 1960). Thus plaintiffs have sometimes been needlessly remitted to the difficulties of commencing a new action even though events occurring after the commencement of the original action have made clear the right to relief.

Under the amendment the court has discretion to permit a supplemental pleading despite the fact that the original pleading is defective. As in other situations where a supplemental pleading is offered, the court is to determine in the light of the particular circumstances whether filing should be permitted, and if so, upon what terms. The amendment does not attempt to deal with such questions as the relation of the statute of limitations to supplemental pleadings, the operation of the doctrine of laches, or the availability of other defenses. All these questions are for decision in accordance with the principles applicable to supplemental pleadings generally. Cf. *Blau v. Lamb,* 191 F.Supp. 906 (S.D.N.Y.1961); *Lendonsol Amusement Corp. v. B. & Q. Assoc., Inc.,* 23 F.R.Serv. 15d.3, Case 1 (D.Mass.1957).

1966 Amendment

Rule 15(c) is amplified to state more clearly when an amendment of a pleading changing the party against whom a claim is asserted (including an amendment to correct a misnomer or misdescription of a defendant) shall "relate back" to the date of the original pleading.

The problem has arisen most acutely in certain actions by private parties against officers or agencies of the United States. Thus an individual denied social security benefits by the Secretary of Health, Education, and Welfare may secure review of the decision by bringing a civil action against that officer within sixty days. 42 U.S.C. § 405(g) (Supp. III, 1962). In several recent cases the claimants instituted timely action but mistakenly named as defendant the United States, the Department of HEW, the "Federal Security Administration" (a nonexistent agency), and a Secretary who had retired from the office nineteen days before. Discovering their mistakes, the claimants moved to amend their complaints to name the proper defendant; by this time the statutory sixty-day period had expired. The motions were denied on the ground that the amendment "would amount to the commencement of a new proceeding and would not relate back in time so as to avoid the statutory provision * * * that suit be brought within sixty days * * *" *Cohn v. Federal Security Adm.,* 199 F.Supp. 884, 885 (W.D.N.Y.1961); see also *Cunningham v. United States,* 199 F.Supp. 541 (W.D.Mo.1958); *Hall v. Department of HEW,* 199 F.Supp. 833 (S.D.Tex.1960); *Sandridge v. Folsom, Secretary of HEW,* 200 F.Supp. 25 (M.D.Tenn.1959). [The Secretary of Health, Education, and Welfare has approved certain ameliorative regulations under 42 U.S.C. § 405(g). See 29 Fed. Reg. 8209 (June 30, 1964); Jacoby, *The Effect of Recent Changes in the Law of "Nonstatutory" Judicial Review,* 53 Geo.L.J. 19, 42–43 (1964); see also *Simmons v. United States Dept. HEW,* 328 F.2d 86 (3d Cir. 1964).]

Analysis in terms of "new proceeding" is traceable to *Davis v. L. L. Cohen & Co.,* 268 U.S. 638 (1925), and *Mellon v. Arkansas Land & Lumber Co.*, 275 U.S. 460 (1928), but those cases antedate the adoption of the Rules which import different criteria for determining when an amendment is to "relate back". As lower courts have continued to rely on the *Davis* and *Mellon* cases despite the contrary intent of the Rules, clarification of Rule 15(c) is considered advisable.

Relation back is intimately connected with the policy of the statute of limitations. The policy of the statute limiting the time for suit against the Secretary of HEW would not have been offended by allowing relation back in the situations described above. For the government was put on notice of the claim within the stated period—in the particular instances, by means of the initial delivery of process to a responsible government official (see Rule 4(d)(4) and (5)). In these circumstances, characterization of the amendment as a new proceeding is not responsive to the realty [sic], but is merely question-begging; and to deny relation back is to defeat unjustly the claimant's opportunity to prove his case. See the full discussion by Byse, *Suing the "Wrong" Defendant in Judicial Review of Federal Administrative Action: Proposals for Reform*, 77 Harv.L.Rev. 40 (1963); see also Ill.Civ.P. Act § 46(4).

Much the same question arises in other types of actions against the government (see *Byse, supra,* at 45 n. 15). In actions between private parties, the problem of relation back of amendments changing defendants has generally been better handled by the courts, but incorrect criteria have sometimes been applied, leading sporadically to doubtful results. See 1A Barron & Holtzoff, *Federal Practice & Procedure* § 451 (Wright ed. 1960); 1 id. § 186 (1960); 2 id. § 543 (1961); 3 *Moore's Federal Practice*, par. 15.15 (Cum.Supp. 1962); Annot., *Change in Party After Statute of Limitations Has Run*, 8 A.L.R.2d 6 (1949). Rule 15(c) has been amplified to provide a general solution. An amendment changing the party against whom a claim is asserted relates back if the amendment satisfies the usual condition of Rule 15(c) of "arising out of the conduct * * * set forth * * * in the original pleading," and if, within the applicable limitations period, the party brought in by amendment, first, received such notice of the institution of the action—the notice need not be formal—that he would not be prejudiced in defending the action, and, second, knew or should have known that the action would have been brought against him initially had there not been a mistake concerning the identity of the proper party. Revised Rule 15(c) goes on to provide specifically in the government cases that the first and second requirements are satisfied when the government has been notified in the manner there described (see Rule 4(d)(4) and (5)). As applied to the government cases, revised Rule 15(c) further advances the objectives of the 1961 amendment of Rule 25(d) (substitution of public officers).

The relation back of amendments changing plaintiffs is not expressly treated in revised Rule 15(c) since the problem is generally easier. Again the chief consideration of policy is that of the statute of limitations, and the attitude taken in revised Rule 15(c) toward change of defendants extends by analogy to amendments changing plaintiffs. Also relevant is the amendment of Rule 17(a) (real party in interest). To avoid forfeitures of just claims, revised Rule 17(a) would provide that no action shall be dismissed on the ground that it is not prosecuted in the name of the real party in interest until a reasonable time has been allowed for correction of the defect in the manner there stated.

1987 Amendment

The amendments are technical. No substantive change is intended.

1991 Amendment

The rule has been revised to prevent parties against whom claims are made from taking unjust advantage of otherwise inconsequential pleading errors to sustain a limitations defense.

Paragraph (c)(1). This provision is new. It is intended to make it clear that the rule does not apply to preclude any relation back that may be permitted under the applicable limitations law. Generally, the applicable limitations law will be state law. If federal jurisdiction is based on the citizenship of the parties, the primary reference is the law of the state in which the district court sits. *Walker v. Armco Steel Corp.*, 446 U.S. 740 (1980). If federal jurisdiction is based on a federal question, the reference may be to the law of the state governing relations between the parties. *E.g., Board of Regents v. Tomanio*, 446 U.S. 478 (1980). In some circumstances, the controlling limitations law may be federal law. *E.g., West v. Conrail, Inc.*, 107 S.Ct. 1538 (1987). Cf. *Burlington Northern R. Co. v. Woods*, 480 U.S. 1 (1987); *Stewart Organization v. Ricoh*, 108 S.Ct. 2239 (1988). Whatever may be the controlling body of limitations law, if that law affords a more forgiving principle of relation back than the one provided in this rule, it should be available to save the claim. Accord, *Marshall v. Mulrenin*, 508 F.2d 39 (1st cir.1974). If *Schiavone v. Fortune*, 106 S.Ct. 2379 (1986) implies the contrary, this paragraph is intended to make a material change in the rule.

Paragraph (c)(3). This paragraph has been revised to change the result in *Schiavone v. Fortune, supra,* with respect to the problem of a misnamed defendant. An intended defendant who is notified of an action within the period allowed by Rule 4(m) [subdivision (m) in Rule 4 was a proposed subdivision which was withdrawn by the Supreme Court] for service of a summons and complaint may not under the revised rule defeat the action on account of a defect in the pleading with respect to the defendant's name, provided that the requirements of clauses (A) and (B) have been met. If the notice requirement is met within the Rule 4(m) [subdivision (m) in Rule 4 was a proposed subdivision which was withdrawn by the Supreme Court] period, a complaint may be amended at any time to correct a formal defect such as a misnomer or misidentification. On the basis of the text of the former rule, the Court reached a result in *Schiavone v. Fortune* that was inconsistent with the liberal pleading practices secured by Rule 8. See Bauer, *Schiavone: An Un-Fortune-ate Illustration of the Supreme Court's Role as Interpreter of the Federal Rules of Civil Procedure,* 63 Notre Dame L.Rev. 720 (1988); Brussack, *Outrageous Fortune: The Case for Amending Rule 15(c) Again,* 61 S.Cal. L.Rev. 671 (1988); Lewis, *The Excessive History of Federal Rule 15(c) and Its Lessons for Civil Rules Revision,* 86 Mich.L.Rev. 1507 (1987).

In allowing a name-correcting amendment within the time allowed by Rule 4(m), this rule allows not only the 120 days specified in that rule, but also any additional time resulting from any extension ordered by the court pursuant to that rule, as may be granted, for example, if the defendant is a fugitive from service of the summons.

This revision, together with the revision of Rule 4(i) with respect to the failure of a plaintiff in an action against the United States to effect timely service on all the appropriate officials, is intended to produce results contrary to those reached in *Gardner v. Gartman*, 880 F.2d 797 (4th Cir. 1989), *Rys v. U.S. Postal Service*, 886 F.2d 443 (1st Cir. 1989), *Martin's Food & Liquor, Inc. v. U.S. Dept. of Agriculture*, 14 F.R.D.3d 86 (N.D.Ill.1988). *But cf. Montgomery v. United States Postal Service*, 867 F.2d 900 (5th Cir. 1989), *Warren v. Department of the Army*, 867 F.2d 1156 (8th Cir. 1989); *Miles v. Department of the Army*, 881 F.2d 777 (9th Cir. 1989), *Barsten v. Department of the Interior*, 896 F.2d 422 (9th Cir. 1990); *Brown v. Georgia Dept. of Revenue*, 881 F.2d 1018 (11th Cir. 1989).

1993 Amendments

The amendment conforms the cross reference to Rule 4 to the revision of that rule.

HISTORICAL NOTES

Effective and Applicability Provisions

1991 Acts. Section 11(a) of Pub.L. 102–198 amended subd. (c)(3) of this rule, as transmitted to the Congress by the Supreme Court pursuant to section 2074 of title 28, United States Code, to become effective on December 1, 1991.

Rule 16. Pretrial Conferences; Scheduling; Management

(a) Pretrial Conferences; Objectives. In any action, the court may in its discretion direct the attorneys for the parties and any unrepresented parties to appear before it for a conference or conferences before trial for such purposes as

(1) expediting the disposition of the action;

(2) establishing early and continuing control so that the case will not be protracted because of lack of management;

(3) discouraging wasteful pretrial activities;

(4) improving the quality of the trial through more thorough preparation, and;

(5) facilitating the settlement of the case.

(b) Scheduling and Planning. Except in categories of actions exempted by district court rule as inappropriate, the district judge, or a magistrate judge when authorized by district court rule, shall, after receiving the report from the parties under Rule 26(f) or after consulting with the attorneys for the parties and any unrepresented parties by a scheduling conference, telephone, mail, or other suitable means, enter a scheduling order that limits the time

(1) to join other parties and to amend the pleadings;

(2) to file motions; and

(3) to complete discovery.

The scheduling order may also include

(4) modifications of the times for disclosures under Rules 26(a) and 26(e)(1) and of the extent of discovery to be permitted;

(5) the date or dates for conferences before trial, a final pretrial conference, and trial; and

(6) any other matters appropriate in the circumstances of the case.

The order shall issue as soon as practicable but in any event within 90 days after the appearance of a defendant and within 120 days after the complaint has been served on a defendant. A schedule shall not be modified except upon a showing of good cause and by leave of the district judge or, when authorized by local rule, by a magistrate judge.

(c) Subjects for Consideration at Pretrial Conferences. At any conference under this rule consideration may be given, and the court may take appropriate action, with respect to

(1) the formulation and simplification of the issues, including the elimination of frivolous claims or defenses;

(2) the necessity or desirability of amendments to the pleadings;

(3) the possibility of obtaining admissions of fact and of documents which will avoid unnecessary proof, stipulations regarding the authenticity of documents, and advance rulings from the court on the admissibility of evidence;

(4) the avoidance of unnecessary proof and of cumulative evidence, and limitations or restrictions on the use of testimony under Rule 702 of the Federal Rules of Evidence;

(5) the appropriateness and timing of summary adjudication under Rule 56;

(6) the control and scheduling of discovery, including orders affecting disclosures and discovery pursuant to Rule 26 and Rules 29 through 37;

(7) the identification of witnesses and documents, the need and schedule for filing and exchanging pretrial briefs, and the date or dates for further conferences and for trial;

(8) the advisability of referring matters to a magistrate judge or master;

(9) settlement and the use of special procedures to assist in resolving the dispute when authorized by statute or local rule;

(10) the form and substance of the pretrial order;

(11) the disposition of pending motions;

(12) the need for adopting special procedures for managing potentially difficult or protracted actions that may involve complex issues, multiple parties, difficult legal questions, or unusual proof problems;

(13) an order for a separate trial pursuant to Rule 42(b) with respect to a claim, counterclaim, cross-claim, or third-party claim, or with respect to any particular issue in the case;

(14) an order directing a party or parties to present evidence early in the trial with respect to a manageable issue that could, on the evidence, be the basis for a judgment as a matter of law under Rule 50(a) or a judgment on partial findings under Rule 52(c);

(15) an order establishing a reasonable limit on the time allowed for presenting evidence; and

(16) such other matters as may facilitate the just, speedy, and inexpensive disposition of the action. At least one of the attorneys for each party participating in any conference before trial shall have authority to enter into stipulations and to make admissions regarding all matters that the participants may reasonably anticipate may be discussed. If appropriate, the court may require that a party or its representative be present or reasonably available by telephone in order to consider possible settlement of the dispute.

(d) Final Pretrial Conference. Any final pretrial conference shall be held as close to the time of trial as reasonable under the circumstances. The participants at any such conference shall formulate a plan for trial, including a program for facilitating the admission of evidence. The conference shall be attended by at least one of the attorneys who will conduct the trial for each of the parties and by any unrepresented parties.

(e) Pretrial Orders. After any conference held pursuant to this rule, an order shall be entered reciting the action taken. This order shall control the subsequent course of the action unless modified by a subsequent order. The order following a final pretrial conference shall be modified only to prevent manifest injustice.

(f) Sanctions. If a party or party's attorney fails to obey a scheduling or pretrial order, or if no appearance is made on behalf of a party at a scheduling or pretrial conference, or if a party or party's attorney is substantially unprepared to participate in the conference, or if a party or party's attorney fails to participate in good faith, the judge, upon motion or the judge's own initiative, may make such orders with regard thereto as are just, and among others any of the orders provided in Rule 37(b)(2)(B), (C), (D). In lieu of or in addition to any other sanction, the judge shall require the party or the attorney representing the party or both to pay the reasonable expenses incurred because of any noncompliance with this rule, including attorney's fees, unless the judge finds that the noncompliance was substantially justified or that other circumstances make an award of expenses unjust.

(As amended Apr. 28, 1983, eff. Aug. 1, 1983; Mar. 2, 1987, eff. Aug. 1, 1987; Apr. 22, 1993, eff. Dec. 1, 1993.)

ADVISORY COMMITTEE NOTES

1937 Adoption

1. Similar rules of pre-trial procedure are now in force in Boston, Cleveland, Detroit, and Los Angeles, and a rule substantially like this one has been proposed for the urban centers of New York state. For a discussion of the successful operation of pre-trial procedure in relieving the congested condition of trial calendars of the courts in such cities and for the proposed New York plan, see *A Proposal for Minimizing Calendar Delay in Jury Cases* (Dec. 1936—published by the New York Law Society); *Pre-Trial Procedure and Administration,* Third Annual Report of the Judicial Council of the State of New York (1937), pages 207–243; *Report of the Commission on the Administration of Justice in New York State* (1934), pp. (288) to (290). See also *Pre-Trial Procedure in the Wayne Circuit Court,* Detroit, Michigan, Sixth Annual Report of the Judicial Council of Michigan (1936), pp. 63 to 75; and Sunderland, *The Theory and Practice of Pre-trial Procedure* (Dec. 1937) 36 Mich.L.Rev. 215–226, 21 J.Am.Jud. Soc. 125. Compare the English procedure known as the "summons for directions", *English Rules Under the Judicature Act* (The Annual Practice, 1937) O. 38a; and a similar procedure in New Jersey, N.J.S.A. 2:27–135, 2:27–136, 2:27–160; N.J. Supreme Court Rules, 2 N.J.Misc.Rep. (1924) 1230, Rules 94, 92, 93, 95 (the last three as amended 1933, 11 N.J.Misc.Rep. (1933) 955).

2. Compare the similar procedure under Rule 56(d) (Summary Judgment—Case Not Fully Adjudicated on Motion). Rule 12(g) (Consolidation of Motions), by requiring to some extent the consolidation of motions dealing with matters preliminary to trial, is a step in the same direction. In connection with clause (5) of this rule, see Rules 53(b) (Masters; Reference) and 53(e)(3) (Master's Report; In Jury Actions).

1983 Amendment

Introduction

Rule 16 has not been amended since the Federal Rules were promulgated in 1938. In many respects, the rule has been a success. For example, there is evidence that pretrial conferences may improve the quality of justice rendered in the federal courts by sharpening the preparation and presentation of cases, tending to eliminate trial surprise, and improving, as well as facilitating, the settlement process. See 6 Wright & Miller, *Federal Practice and Procedure:* Civil § 1522 (1971). However, in other respects particularly with regard to case management, the rule has not always been as helpful as it might have been. Thus there has been a widespread feeling that amendment is necessary to encourage pretrial management that meets the needs of modern litigation. See *Report of the National Commission for the Review of Antitrust Laws and Procedures* (1979).

Major criticism of Rule 16 has centered on the fact that its application can result in over-regulation of some cases and under-regulation of others. In simple, run-of-the-mill cases, attorneys have found pretrial requirements burdensome. It is claimed that over-administration leads to a series of mini-trials that result in a waste of an attorney's time and needless expense to a client. Pollack, *Pretrial Procedures*

More Effectively Handled, 65 F.R.D. 475 (1974). This is especially likely to be true when pretrial proceedings occur long before trial. At the other end of the spectrum, the discretionary character of Rule 16 and its orientation toward a single conference late in the pretrial process has led to under-administration of complex or protracted cases. Without judicial guidance beginning shortly after institution, these cases often become mired in discovery.

Four sources of criticism of pretrial have been identified. First, conferences often are seen as a mere exchange of legalistic contentions without any real analysis of the particular case. Second, the result frequently is nothing but a formal agreement on minutiae. Third, the conferences are seen as unnecessary and time-consuming in cases that will be settled before trial. Fourth, the meetings can be ceremonial and ritualistic, having little effect on the trial and being of minimal value, particularly when the attorneys attending the sessions are not the ones who will try the case or lack authority to enter into binding stipulations. See generally *McCargo v. Hedrick,* 545 F.2d 393 (4th Cir.1976); Pollack, *Pretrial Procedures More Effectively Handled,* 65 F.R.D. 475 (1974); Rosenberg, *The Pretrial Conference and Effective Justice* 45 (1964).

There also have been difficulties with the pretrial orders that issue following Rule 16 conferences. When an order is entered far in advance of trial, some issues may not be properly formulated. Counsel naturally are cautious and often try to preserve as many options as possible. If the judge who tries the case did not conduct the conference, he could find it difficult to determine exactly what was agreed to at the conference. But any insistence on a detailed order may be too burdensome, depending on the nature or posture of the case.

Given the significant changes in federal civil litigation since 1938 that are not reflected in Rule 16, it has been extensively rewritten and expanded to meet the challenges of modern litigation. Empirical studies reveal that when a trial judge intervenes personally at an early stage to assume judicial control over a case and to schedule dates for completion by the parties of the principal pretrial steps, the case is disposed of by settlement or trial more efficiently and with less cost and delay than when the parties are left to their own devices. Flanders, *Case Management and Court Management in United States District Courts* 17, Federal Judicial Center (1977). Thus, the rule mandates a pretrial scheduling order. However, although scheduling and pretrial conferences are encouraged in appropriate cases, they are not mandated.

Discussion

Subdivision (a); Pretrial Conferences; Objectives. The amended rule makes scheduling and case management an express goal of pretrial procedure. This is done in Rule 16(a) by shifting the emphasis away from a conference focused solely on the trial and toward a process of judicial management that embraces the entire pretrial phase, especially motions and discovery. In addition, the amendment explicitly recognizes some of the objectives of pretrial conferences and the powers that many courts already have assumed. Rule 16 thus will be a more accurate reflection of actual practice.

Subdivision (b); Scheduling and Planning. The most significant change in Rule 16 is the mandatory scheduling order described in Rule 16(b), which is based in part on

Wisconsin Civil Procedure Rule 802.10. The idea of scheduling orders is not new. It has been used by many federal courts. See, *e.g.,* Southern District of Indiana, Local Rule 19.

Although a mandatory scheduling order encourages the court to become involved in case management early in the litigation, it represents a degree of judicial involvement that is not warranted in many cases. Thus, subdivision (b) permits each district court to promulgate a local rule under Rule 83 exempting certain categories of cases in which the burdens of scheduling orders exceed the administrative efficiencies that would be gained. See Eastern District of Virginia, Local Rule 12(1). Logical candidates for this treatment include social security disability matters, habeas corpus petitions, forfeitures, and reviews of certain administrative actions.

A scheduling conference may be requested either by the judge, a magistrate when authorized by district court rule, or a party within 120 days after the summons and complaint are filed. If a scheduling conference is not arranged within that time and the case is not exempted by local rule, a scheduling order must be issued under Rule 16(b), after some communication with the parties, which may be by telephone or mail rather than in person. The use of the term "judge" in subdivision (b) reflects the Advisory Committee's judgment that it is preferable that this task should be handled by a district judge rather than a magistrate, except when the magistrate is acting under 28 U.S.C. § 636(c). While personal supervision by the trial judge is preferred, the rule, in recognition of the impracticality or difficulty of complying with such a requirement in some districts, authorizes a district by local rule to delegate the duties to a magistrate. In order to formulate a practicable scheduling order, the judge, or a magistrate when authorized by district court rule, and attorneys are required to develop a timetable for the matters listed in Rule 16(b)(1)–(3). As indicated in Rule 16(b)(4)–(5), the order may also deal with a wide range of other matters. The rule is phrased permissively as to clauses (4) and (5), however, because scheduling these items at an early point may not be feasible or appropriate. Even though subdivision (b) relates only to scheduling, there is no reason why some of the procedural matters listed in Rule 16(c) cannot be addressed at the same time, at least when a scheduling conference is held.

Item (1) assures that at some point both the parties and the pleadings will be fixed, by setting a time within which joinder of parties shall be completed and the pleadings amended.

Item (2) requires setting time limits for interposing various motions that otherwise might be used as stalling techniques.

Item (3) deals with the problem of procrastination and delay by attorneys in a context in which scheduling is especially important-discovery. Scheduling the completion of discovery can serve some of the same functions as the conference described in Rule 26(f).

Item (4) refers to setting dates for conferences and for trial. Scheduling multiple pretrial conferences may well be desirable if the case is complex and the court believes that a more elaborate pretrial structure, such as that described in the *Manual for Complex Litigation,* should be employed. On the other hand, only one pretrial conference may be necessary in an uncomplicated case.

As long as the case is not exempted by local rule, the court must issue a written scheduling order even if no scheduling conference is called. The order, like pretrial orders under the former rule and those under new Rule 16(c), normally will "control the subsequent course of the action." See Rule 16(e). After consultation with the attorneys for the parties and any unrepresented parties-a formal motion is not necessary-the court may modify the schedule on a showing of good cause if it cannot reasonably be met despite the diligence of the party seeking the extension. Since the scheduling order is entered early in the litigation, this standard seems more appropriate than a "manifest injustice" or "substantial hardship" test. Otherwise, a fear that extensions will not be granted may encourage counsel to request the longest possible periods for completing pleading, joinder, and discovery. Moreover, changes in the court's calendar sometimes will oblige the judge or magistrate when authorized by district court rule to modify the scheduling order.

The district courts undoubtedly will develop several prototype scheduling orders for different types of cases. In addition, when no formal conference is held, the court may obtain scheduling information by telephone, mail, or otherwise. In many instances this will result in a scheduling order better suited to the individual case than a standard order, without taking the time that would be required by a formal conference.

Rule 16(b) assures that the judge will take some early control over the litigation, even when its character does not warrant holding a scheduling conference. Despite the fact that the process of preparing a scheduling order does not always bring the attorneys and judge together, the fixing of time limits serves

> to stimulate litigants to narrow the areas of inquiry and advocacy to those they believe are truly relevant and material. Time limits not only compress the amount of time for litigation, they should also reduce the amount of resources invested in litigation. Litigants are forced to establish discovery priorities and thus to do the most important work first.

Report of the National Commission for the Review of Antitrust Laws and Procedures 28 (1979).

Thus, except in exempted cases, the judge or a magistrate when authorized by district court rule will have taken some action in every case within 120 days after the complaint is filed that notifies the attorneys that the case will be moving toward trial. Subdivision (b) is reenforced by subdivision (f), which makes it clear that the sanctions for violating a scheduling order are the same as those for violating a pretrial order.

Subdivision (c); Subjects to be Discussed at Pretrial Conferences. This subdivision expands upon the list of things that may be discussed at a pretrial conference that appeared in original Rule 16. The intention is to encourage better planning and management of litigation. Increased judicial control during the pretrial process accelerates the processing and termination of cases. Flanders, *Case Management and Court Management in United States District Courts*, 39 Federal Judicial Center (1977). See also *Report of the National Commission for the Review of Antitrust Laws and Procedures* (1979).

The reference in Rule 16(c)(1) to "formulation" is intended to clarify and confirm the court's power to identify the litigable issues. It has been added in the hope of promoting efficiency and conserving judicial resources by identifying the real issues prior to trial, thereby saving time and expense for everyone. See generally *Meadow Gold Prods. Co. v. Wright*, 278 F.2d 867 (D.C.Cir.1960). The notion is emphasized by expressly authorizing the elimination of frivolous claims or defenses at a pretrial conference. There is no reason to require that this await a formal motion for summary judgment. Nor is there any reason for the court to wait for the parties to initiate the process called for in Rule 16(c)(1).

The timing of any attempt at issue formulation is a matter of judicial discretion. In relatively simple cases it may not be necessary or may take the form of a stipulation between counsel or a request by the court that counsel work together to draft a proposed order.

Counsel bear a substantial responsibility for assisting the court in identifying the factual issues worthy of trial. If counsel fail to identify an issue for the court, the right to have the issue tried is waived. Although an order specifying the issues is intended to be binding, it may be amended at trial to avoid manifest injustice. See Rule 16(e). However, the rule's effectiveness depends on the court employing its discretion sparingly.

Clause (6) acknowledges the widespread availability and use of magistrates. The corresponding provision in the original rule referred only to masters and limited the function of the reference to the making of "findings to be used as evidence" in a case to be tried to a jury. The new text is not limited and broadens the potential use of a magistrate to that permitted by the Magistrate's Act.

Clause (7) explicitly recognizes that it has become commonplace to discuss settlement at pretrial conferences. Since it obviously eases crowded court dockets and results in savings to the litigants and the judicial system, settlement should be facilitated at as early a stage of the litigation as possible. Although it is not the purpose of Rule 16(b)(7) to impose settlement negotiations on unwilling litigants, it is believed that providing a neutral forum for discussing the subject might foster it. See Moore's *Federal Practice* ¶ 16.17; 6 Wright & Miller, *Federal Practice and Procedure: Civil* § 1522 (1971). For instance, a judge to whom a case has been assigned may arrange, on his own motion or at a party's request, to have settlement conferences handled by another member of the court or by a magistrate. The rule does not make settlement conferences mandatory because they would be a waste of time in many cases. See Flanders, *Case Management and Court Management in the United States District Courts*, 39 Federal Judicial Center (1977). Requests for a conference from a party indicating a willingness to talk settlement normally should be honored, unless thought to be frivolous or dilatory.

A settlement conference is appropriate at any time. It may be held in conjunction with a pretrial or discovery conference, although various objectives of pretrial management, such as moving the case toward trial, may not always be compatible with settlement negotiations, and thus a separate settlement conference may be desirable. See 6 Wright & Miller, *Federal Practice and Procedure: Civil* § 1522, at p. 571 (1971).

In addition to settlement, Rule 16(c)(7) refers to exploring the use of procedures other than litigation to resolve the dispute. This includes urging the litigants to employ adjudicatory techniques outside the courthouse. See, for example, the experiment described in *Green, Marks & Olson, Settling*

Large Case Litigation: An Alternative Approach, 11 Loyola of L.A.L.Rev. 493 (1978).

Rule 16(c)(10) authorizes the use of special pretrial procedures to expedite the adjudication of potentially difficult or protracted cases. Some district courts obviously have done so for many years. See Rubin, *The Managed Calendar: Some Pragmatic Suggestions About Achieving the Just, Speedy and Inexpensive Determination of Civil Cases in Federal Courts*, 4 Just.Sys.J. 135 (1976). Clause 10 provides an explicit authorization for such procedures and encourages their use. No particular techniques have been described; the Committee felt that flexibility and experience are the keys to efficient management of complex cases. Extensive guidance is offered in such documents as the *Manual for Complex Litigation*.

The rule simply identifies characteristics that make a case a strong candidate for special treatment. The four mentioned are illustrative, not exhaustive, and overlap to some degree. But experience has shown that one or more of them will be present in every protracted or difficult case and it seems desirable to set them out. See Kendig, *Procedures for Management of Non-Routine Cases*, 3 Hofstra L.Rev. 701 (1975).

The last sentence of subdivision (c) is new. See Wisconsin Civil Procedure Rule 802.11(2). It has been added to meet one of the criticisms of the present practice described earlier and insure proper preconference preparation so that the meeting is more than a ceremonial or ritualistic event. The reference to "authority" is not intended to insist upon the ability to settle the litigation. Nor should the rule be read to encourage the judge conducting the conference to compel attorneys to enter into stipulations or to make admissions that they consider to be unreasonable, that touch on matters that could not normally have been anticipated to arise at the conference, or on subjects of a dimension that normally require prior consultation with and approval from the client.

Subdivision (d); Final Pretrial Conference. This provision has been added to make it clear that the time between any final pretrial conference (which in a simple case may be the **only** pretrial conference) and trial should be as short as possible to be certain that the litigants make substantial progress with the case and avoid the inefficiency of having that preparation repeated when there is a delay between the last pretrial conference and trial. An optimum time of 10 days to two weeks has been suggested by one federal judge. Rubin, *The Managed Calendar: Some Pragmatic Suggestions About Achieving the Just, Speedy and Inexpensive Determination of Civil Cases in Federal Courts*, 4 Just. Sys.J. 135, 141 (1976). The Committee, however, concluded that it would be inappropriate to fix a precise time in the rule, given the numerous variables that could bear on the matter. Thus the timing has been left to the court's discretion.

At least one of the attorneys who will conduct the trial for each party must be present at the final pretrial conference. At this late date there should be no doubt as to which attorney or attorneys this will be. Since the agreements and stipulations made at this final conference will control the trial, the presence of lawyers who will be involved in it is especially useful to assist the judge in structuring the case, and to lead to a more effective trial.

Subdivision (e); Pretrial Orders. Rule 16(e) does not substantially change the portion of the original rule dealing with pretrial orders. The purpose of an order is to guide the course of the litigation and the language of the original rule making that clear has been retained. No compelling reason has been found for major revision, especially since this portion of the rule has been interpreted and clarified by over forty years of judicial decisions with comparatively little difficulty. See 6 Wright & Miller, *Federal Practice and Procedure: Civil* §§ 1521–30 (1971). Changes in language therefore have been kept to a minimum to avoid confusion.

Since the amended rule encourages more extensive pretrial management than did the original, two or more conferences may be held in many cases. The language of Rule 16(e) recognizes this possibility and the corresponding need to issue more than one pretrial order in a single case.

Once formulated, pretrial orders should not be changed lightly; but total inflexibility is undesirable. See, *e.g., Clark v. Pennsylvania R.R. Co.*, 328 F.2d 591 (2d Cir.1964). The exact words used to describe the standard for amending the pretrial order probably are less important than the meaning given them in practice. By not imposing any limitation on the ability to modify a pretrial order, the rule reflects the reality that in any process of continuous management, what is done at one conference may have to be altered at the next. In the case of the final pretrial order, however, a more stringent standard is called for and the words "to prevent manifest injustice," which appeared in the original rule, have been retained. They have the virtue of familiarity and adequately describe the restraint the trial judge should exercise.

Many local rules make the plaintiff's attorney responsible for drafting a proposed pretrial order, either before or after the conference. Others allow the court to appoint any of the attorneys to perform the task, and others leave it to the court. See Note, *Pretrial Conference: A Critical Examination of Local Rules Adopted by Federal District Courts*, 64 Va.L.Rev. 467 (1978). Rule 16 has never addressed this matter. Since there is no consensus about which method of drafting the order works best and there is no reason to believe that nationwide uniformity is needed, the rule has been left silent on the point. See *Handbook for Effective Pretrial Procedure*, 37 F.R.D. 225 (1964).

Subdivision (f); Sanctions. Original Rule 16 did not mention the sanctions that might be imposed for failing to comply with the rule. However, courts have not hesitated to enforce it by appropriate measures. See, e.g., *Link v. Wabash R. Co.*, 370 U.S. 628 (1962) (district court's dismissal under Rule 41(b) after plaintiff's attorney failed to appear at a pretrial conference upheld); *Admiral Theatre Corp. v. Douglas Theatre*, 585 F.2d 877 (8th Cir.1978) (district court has discretion to exclude exhibits or refuse to permit the testimony of a witness not listed prior to trial in contravention of its pretrial order).

To reflect that existing practice, and to obviate dependence upon Rule 41(b) or the court's inherent power to regulate litigation, *cf. Societe Internationale Pour Participations Industrielles et Commerciales, S.A. v. Rogers*, 357 U.S. 197 (1958), Rule 16(f) expressly provides for imposing sanctions on disobedient or recalcitrant parties, their attorneys, or both in four types of situations. Rodes, Ripple & Mooney, *Sanctions Imposable for Violations of the Federal Rules of Civil Procedure* 65–67, 80–84, Federal Judicial Center (1981). Furthermore, explicit reference to sanctions reinforces the rule's intention to encourage forceful judicial management.

Rule 16(f) incorporates portions of Rule 37(b)(2), which prescribes sanctions for failing to make discovery. This should facilitate application of Rule 16(f), since courts and lawyers already are familiar with the Rule 37 standards. Among the sanctions authorized by the new subdivision are: preclusion order, striking a pleading, staying the proceeding, default judgment, contempt, and charging a party, his attorney, or both with the expenses, including attorney's fees, caused by noncompliance. The contempt sanction, however, is only available for a violation of a court order. The references in Rule 16(f) are not exhaustive.

As is true under Rule 37(b)(2), the imposition of sanctions may be sought by either the court or a party. In addition, the court has discretion to impose whichever sanction it feels is appropriate under the circumstances. Its action is reviewable under the abuse-of-discretion standard. See *National Hockey League v. Metropolitan Hockey Club, Inc.*, 427 U.S. 639 (1976).

1987 Amendment

The amendments are technical. No substantive change is intended.

1993 Amendments

Subdivision (b). One purpose of this amendment is to provide a more appropriate deadline for the initial scheduling order required by the rule. The former rule directed that the order be entered within 120 days from the filing of the complaint. This requirement has created problems because Rule 4(m) allows 120 days for service and ordinarily at least one defendant should be available to participate in the process of formulating the scheduling order. The revision provides that the order is to be entered within 90 days after the date a defendant first appears (whether by answer or by a motion under Rule 12) or, if earlier (as may occur in some actions against the United States or if service is waived under Rule 4), within 120 days after service of the complaint on a defendant. The longer time provided by the revision is not intended to encourage unnecessary delays in entering the scheduling order. Indeed, in most cases the order can and should be entered at a much earlier date. Rather, the additional time is intended to alleviate problems in multi-defendant cases and should ordinarily be adequate to enable participation by all defendants initially named in the action.

In many cases the scheduling order can and should be entered before this deadline. However, when setting a scheduling conference, the court should take into account the effect this setting will have in establishing deadlines for the parties to meet under revised Rule 26(f) and to exchange information under revised Rule 26(a)(1). While the parties are expected to stipulate to additional time for making their disclosures when warranted by the circumstances, a scheduling conference held before defendants have had time to learn much about the case may result in diminishing the value of the Rule 26(f) meeting, the parties' proposed discovery plan, and indeed the conference itself.

New paragraph (4) has been added to highlight that it will frequently be desirable for the scheduling order to include provisions relating to the timing of disclosures under Rule 26(a). While the initial disclosures required by Rule 26(a)(1) will ordinarily have been made before entry of the scheduling order, the timing and sequence for disclosure of expert testimony and of the witnesses and exhibits to be used at trial should be tailored to the circumstances of the case and is a matter that should be considered at the initial scheduling conference. Similarly, the scheduling order might contain provisions modifying the extent of discovery (*e.g.*, number and length of depositions) otherwise permitted under these rules or by a local rule.

The report from the attorneys concerning their meeting and proposed discovery plan, as required by revised Rule 26(f), should be submitted to the court before the scheduling order is entered. Their proposals, particularly regarding matters on which they agree, should be of substantial value to the court in setting the timing and limitations on discovery and should reduce the time of the court needed to conduct a meaningful conference under Rule 16(b). As under the prior rule, while a scheduling order is mandated, a scheduling conference is not. However, in view of the benefits to be derived from the litigants and a judicial officer meeting in person, a Rule 16(b) conference should, to the extent practicable, be held in all cases that will involve discovery.

This subdivision, as well as subdivision (c)(8), also is revised to reflect the new title of United States Magistrate Judges pursuant to the Judicial Improvements Act of 1990.

Subdivision (c). The primary purposes of the changes in subdivision (c) are to call attention to the opportunities for structuring of trial under Rules 42, 50, and 52 and to eliminate questions that have occasionally been raised regarding the authority of the court to make appropriate orders designed either to facilitate settlement or to provide for an efficient and economical trial. The prefatory language of this subdivision is revised to clarify the court's power to enter appropriate orders at a conference notwithstanding the objection of a party. Of course settlement is dependent upon agreement by the parties and, indeed, a conference is most effective and productive when the parties participate in a spirit of cooperation and mindful of their responsibilities under Rule 1.

Paragraph (4) is revised to clarify that in advance of trial the court may address the need for, and possible limitations on, the use of expert testimony under Rule 702 of the Federal Rules of Evidence. Even when proposed expert testimony might be admissible under the standards of Rules 403 and 702 of the evidence rules, the court may preclude or limit such testimony if the cost to the litigants—which may include the cost to adversaries of securing testimony on the same subjects by other experts—would be unduly expensive given the needs of the case and the other evidence available at trial.

Paragraph (5) is added (and the remaining paragraphs renumbered) in recognition that use of Rule 56 to avoid or reduce the scope of trial is a topic that can, and often should, be considered at a pretrial conference. Renumbered paragraph (11) enables the court to rule on pending motions for summary adjudication that are ripe for decision at the time of the conference. Often, however, the potential use of Rule 56 is a matter that arises from discussions during a conference. The court may then call for motions to be filed.

Paragraph (6) is added to emphasize that a major objective of pretrial conferences should be to consider appropriate controls on the extent and timing of discovery. In many cases the court should also specify the times and sequence for disclosure of written reports from experts under revised Rule 26(a)(2)(B) and perhaps direct changes in the types of experts from whom written reports are required. Consideration should also be given to possible changes in the timing or form of the disclosure of trial witnesses and documents under Rule 26(a)(3).

Paragraph (9) is revised to describe more accurately the various procedures that, in addition to traditional settlement conferences, may be helpful in settling litigation. Even if a case cannot immediately be settled, the judge and attorneys can explore possible use of alternative procedures such as mini-trials, summary jury trials, mediation, neutral evaluation, and nonbinding arbitration that can lead to consensual resolution of the dispute without a full trial on the merits. The rule acknowledges the presence of statutes and local rules or plans that may authorize use of some of these procedures even when not agreed to by the parties. See 28 U.S.C. §§ 473(a)(6), 473(b)(4), 651–58; Section 104(b)(2), Pub.L. 101–650. The rule does not attempt to resolve questions as to the extent a court would be authorized to require such proceedings as an exercise of its inherent powers.

The amendment of paragraph (9) should be read in conjunction with the sentence added to the end of subdivision (c), authorizing the court to direct that, in appropriate cases, a responsible representative of the parties be present or available by telephone during a conference in order to discuss possible settlement of the case. The sentence refers to participation by a party or its representative. Whether this would be the individual party, an officer of a corporate party, a representative from an insurance carrier, or someone else would depend on the circumstances. Particularly in litigation in which governmental agencies or large amounts of money are involved, there may be no one with on-the-spot settlement authority, and the most that should be expected is access to a person who would have a major role in submitting a recommendation to the body or board with ultimate decision-making responsibility. The selection of the appropriate representative should ordinarily be left to the party and its counsel. Finally, it should be noted that the unwillingness of a party to be available, even by telephone, for a settlement conference may be a clear signal that the time and expense

involved in pursuing settlement is likely to be unproductive and that personal participation by the parties should not be required.

The explicit authorization in the rule to require personal participation in the manner stated is not intended to limit the reasonable exercise of the court's inherent powers, *e.g., G. Heileman Brewing Co. v. Joseph Oat Corp.,* 871 F.2d 648 (7th Cir.1989), or its power to require party participation under the Civil Justice Reform Act of 1990. See 28 U.S.C. § 473(b)(5) (civil justice expense and delay reduction plans adopted by district courts may include requirement that representatives "with authority to bind [parties] in settlement discussions" be available during settlement conferences).

New paragraphs (13) and (14) are added to call attention to the opportunities for structuring of trial under Rule 42 and under revised Rules 50 and 52.

Paragraph (15) is also new. It supplements the power of the court to limit the extent of evidence under Rules 403 and 611(a) of the Federal Rules of Evidence, which typically would be invoked as a result of developments during trial. Limits on the length of trial established at a conference in advance of trial can provide the parties with a better opportunity to determine priorities and exercise selectivity in presenting evidence than when limits are imposed during trial. Any such limits must be reasonable under the circumstances, and ordinarily the court should impose them only after receiving appropriate submissions from the parties outlining the nature of the testimony expected to be presented through various witnesses, and the expected duration of direct and cross-examination.

HISTORICAL NOTES

Change of Name

Reference to United States magistrate or to magistrate deemed to refer to United States magistrate judge pursuant to section 321 of Pub.L. 101–650, set out as a note under section 631 of this title.

IV. PARTIES

Rule 17. Parties Plaintiff and Defendant; Capacity

(a) **Real Party in Interest.** Every action shall be prosecuted in the name of the real party in interest. An executor, administrator, guardian, bailee, trustee of an express trust, a party with whom or in whose name a contract has been made for the benefit of another, or a party authorized by statute may sue in that person's own name without joining the party for whose benefit the action is brought; and when a statute of the United States so provides, an action for the use or benefit of another shall be brought in the name of the United States. No action shall be dismissed on the ground that it is not prosecuted in the name of the real party in interest until a reasonable time has been allowed after objection for ratification of commencement of the action by, or joinder or substitution of, the real party in interest; and such

ratification, joinder, or substitution shall have the same effect as if the action had been commenced in the name of the real party in interest.

(b) **Capacity to Sue or be Sued.** The capacity of an individual, other than one acting in a representative capacity, to sue or be sued shall be determined by the law of the individual's domicile. The capacity of a corporation to sue or be sued shall be determined by the law under which it was organized. In all other cases capacity to sue or be sued shall be determined by the law of the state in which the district court is held, except (1) that a partnership or other unincorporated association, which has no such capacity by the law of such state, may sue or be sued in its common name for the purpose of enforcing for or against it a substantive right existing under the Constitution or laws of the United States, and (2) that the capacity of a receiver appointed by a court of the United States to sue or be sued in a court of the United States is governed by Title 28, U.S.C., Sections 754 and 959(a).

(c) Infants or Incompetent Persons. Whenever an infant or incompetent person has a representative, such as a general guardian, committee, conservator, or other like fiduciary, the representative may sue or defend on behalf of the infant or incompetent person. An infant or incompetent person who does not have a duly appointed representative may sue by a next friend or by a guardian ad litem. The court shall appoint a guardian ad litem for an infant or incompetent person not otherwise represented in an action or shall make such other order as it deems proper for the protection of the infant or incompetent person.

(As amended Dec. 27, 1946, eff. Mar. 19, 1948; Dec. 29, 1948, eff. Oct. 20, 1949; Feb. 28, 1966, eff. July 1, 1966; Mar. 2, 1987, eff. Aug. 1, 1987; Apr. 25, 1988, eff. Aug. 1, 1988; Nov. 18, 1988, Pub.L. 100–690, Title VII, § 7049, 102 Stat. 4401.)

ADVISORY COMMITTEE NOTES

1937 Adoption

Note to Subdivision (a). The real party in interest provision, except for the last clause which is new, is taken verbatim from [former] Equity Rule 37 (Parties Generally—Intervention), except that the word "expressly" has been omitted. For similar provisions see N.Y.C.P.A., (1937) § 210; Wyo.Rev.Stat.Ann. (1931) §§ 89–501, 89–502, 89–503; *English Rules Under the Judicature Act* (The Annual Practice, 1937) O. 16, r. 8. See, also Equity Rule 41 (Suit to Execute Trusts of Will—Heir as Party). For examples of statutes of the United States providing particularly for an action for the use or benefit of another in the name of the United States, see U.S.C., Title 40, § 270b [see now 40 U.S.C.A. § 3133(b)] (Suit by persons furnishing labor and material for work on public building contracts * * * may sue on a payment bond, "in the name of the United States for the use of the person suing"); and U.S.C., Title 25, § 201 (Penalties under laws relating to Indians—how recovered). Compare U.S.C., Title 26, Int.Rev.Code [1939], § 3745(c) [former § 1645(c)] (Suits for penalties, fines, and forfeitures, under this title, where not otherwise provided for, to be in name of United States).

Note to Subdivision (b). For capacity see generally Clark and Moore, *New Federal Civil Procedure*—II. Pleadings and Parties, 44 Yale L.J. 1291, 1312–1317 (1935) and specifically *Coppedge v. Clinton,* 72 F.2d 531 (C.C.A.10th, 1934) (natural person); *David Lupton's Sons Co. v. Automobile Club of America,* 225 U.S. 489, 32 S.Ct. 711, 56 L.Ed. 1177, Ann.Cas.1914A, 699 (1912) (corporation); *Puerto Rico v. Russell & Co.,* 288 U.S. 476, 53 S.Ct. 447, 77 L.Ed. 903 (1933) (unincorporated assn.); *United Mine Workers of America v. Coronado Coal Co.,* 259 U.S. 344, 42 S.Ct. 570, 66 L.Ed. 975, 27 A.L.R. 762 (1922) (federal substantive right enforced against unincorporated association by suit against the association in its common name without naming all its members as parties). This rule follows the existing law as to such associations, as declared in the case last cited above. Compare *Moffat Tunnel League v. United States,* 289 U.S. 113, 53 S.Ct. 543, 77 L.Ed. 1069 (1933). See note to Rule 23, clause (1).

Note to Subdivision (c). The provision for infants and incompetent persons is substantially former Equity Rule 70 (Suits by or Against Incompetents) with slight additions. Compare the more detailed English provisions, *English Rules Under the Judicature Act* (The Annual Practice, 1937) O. 16, r.r. 16–21.

1946 Amendment

Note. The new matter [in subdivision (b)] makes clear the controlling character of Rule 66 regarding suits by or against a federal receiver in a federal court.

1948 Amendment

The amendment effective October 20, 1949, deleted the words "Rule 66" at the end of subdivision (b) and substituted the words "Title 28, U.S.C., §§ 754 and 959(a)".

1966 Amendment

The minor change in the text of the rule is designed to make it clear that the specific instances enumerated are not exceptions to, but illustrations of, the rule. These illustrations, of course, carry no negative implication to the effect that there are not other instances of recognition as the real party in interest of one whose standing as such may be in doubt. The enumeration is simply of cases in which there might be substantial doubt as to the issue but for the specific enumeration. There are other potentially arguable cases that are not excluded by the enumeration. For example, the enumeration states that the promisee in a contract for the benefit of a third party may sue as real party in interest; it does not say, because it is obvious, that the third-party beneficiary may sue (when the applicable law gives him that right.)

The rule adds to the illustrative list of real parties in interest a bailee—meaning, of course, a bailee suing on behalf of the bailor with respect to the property bailed. (When the possessor of property other than the owner sues for an invasion of the possessory interest he is the real party in interest.) The word "bailee" is added primarily to preserve the admiralty practice whereby the owner of a vessel as bailee of the cargo, or the master of the vessel as bailee of both vessel and cargo, sues for damage to either property interest or both. But there is no reason to limit such a provision to maritime situations. The owner of a warehouse in which household furniture is stored is equally entitled to sue on behalf of the numerous owners of the furniture stored. Cf. *Gulf Oil Corp. v. Gilbert,* 330 U.S. 501 (1947).

The provision that no action shall be dismissed on the ground that it is not prosecuted in the name of the real party in interest until a reasonable time has been allowed, after the objection has been raised, for ratification, substitution, etc., is added simply in the interests of justice. In its origin the rule concerning the real party in interest was permissive in purpose: it was designed to allow an assignee to sue in his own name. That having been accomplished, the modern function of the rule in its negative aspect is simply to protect the defendant against a subsequent action by the party actually entitled to recover, and to insure generally that the judgment will have its proper effect as res judicata.

This provision keeps pace with the law as it is actually developing. Modern decisions are inclined to be lenient when an honest mistake has been made in choosing the party in whose name the action is to be filed—in both maritime and nonmaritime cases. See *Levinson v. Deupree*, 345 U.S. 648 (1953); *Link Aviation, Inc. v. Downs*, 325 F.2d 613 (D.C.Cir. 1963). The provision should not be misunderstood or distorted. It is intended to prevent forfeiture when determination of the proper party to sue is difficult or when an understandable mistake has been made. It does not mean, for example, that, following an airplane crash in which all aboard were killed, an action may be filed in the name of John Doe (a fictitious person), as personal representative of Richard Roe (another fictitious person), in the hope that at a later time the attorney filing the action may substitute the real name of the real personal representative of a real victim, and have the benefit of suspension of the limitation period. It does not even mean, when an action is filed by the personal representative of John Smith, of Buffalo, in the good faith belief that he was aboard the flight, that upon discovery that Smith is alive and well, having missed the fatal flight, the representative of James Brown, of San Francisco, an actual victim, can be substituted to take advantage of the suspension of the limitation period. It is, in cases of this sort, intended to insure against forfeiture and injustice—in short, to codify in broad terms the salutary principle of *Levinson v. Deupree*, 345 U.S. 648 (1953), and *Link Aviation, Inc. v. Downs*, 325 F.2d 613 (D.C.Cir. 1963).

1987 Amendment

The amendments are technical. No substantive change is intended.

1988 Amendment

The amendment is technical. No substantive change is intended.

Rule 18. Joinder of Claims and Remedies

(a) Joinder of Claims. A party asserting a claim to relief as an original claim, counterclaim, cross-claim, or third-party claim, may join, either as independent or as alternate claims, as many claims, legal, equitable, or maritime, as the party has against an opposing party.

(b) Joinder of Remedies; Fraudulent Conveyances. Whenever a claim is one heretofore cognizable only after another claim has been prosecuted to a conclusion, the two claims may be joined in a single action; but the court shall grant relief in that action only in accordance with the relative substantive rights of the parties. In particular, a plaintiff may state a claim for money and a claim to have set aside a conveyance fraudulent as to that plaintiff, without first having obtained a judgment establishing the claim for money.

(As amended Feb. 28, 1966, eff. July 1, 1966; Mar. 2, 1987, eff. Aug. 1, 1987.)

ADVISORY COMMITTEE NOTES

1937 Adoption

Note to Subdivision (a). 1. Recent development, both in code and common law states, has been toward unlimited joinder of actions. See Ill.Rev.Stat. (1937) ch. 110, § 168; N.J.S.A. 2:27–37, as modified by N.J.Sup.Ct.Rules, Rule 21, 2 N.J.Misc. 1208 (1924); N.Y.C.P.A. (1937) § 258 as amended by Laws of 1935, ch. 339.

2. This provision for joinder of actions has been patterned upon [former] Equity Rule 26 (Joinder of Causes of Action) and broadened to include multiple parties. Compare the English practice, *English Rules Under the Judicature Act* (The Annual Practice, 1937) O. 18, r.r. 1–9 (noting rules 1 and 6). The earlier American codes set forth classes of joinder, following the now abandoned New York rule. See N.Y.C.P.A. § 258 before amended in 1935; Compare Kan. Gen.Stat.Ann. (1935) § 60–601; Wis.Stat.(1935) § 263.04 for the more liberal practice.

3. The provisions of this rule for the joinder of claims are subject to Rule 82 (Jurisdiction and Venue Unaffected). For the jurisdictional aspects of joinder of claims, see Shulman and Jaegerman, *Some Jurisdictional Limitations on Federal Procedure* (1936), 45 Yale L.J. 393, 397–410. For separate trials of joined claims, see Rule 42(b).

Note to Subdivision (b). This rule is inserted to make it clear that in a single action a party should be accorded all the relief to which he is entitled regardless of whether it is legal or equitable or both. This necessarily includes a deficiency judgment in foreclosure actions formerly provided for in [former] Equity Rule 10 (Decree for Deficiency in Foreclosures, Etc.). In respect to fraudulent conveyances the rule changes the former rule requiring a prior judgment against the owner (*Braun v. American Laundry Mach. Co.*, 56 F.2d 197 (S.D.N.Y. 1932)) to conform to the provisions of the Uniform Fraudulent Conveyance Act, §§ 9 and 10. See McLaughlin, *Application of the Uniform Fraudulent Conveyance Act*, 46 Harv.L.Rev. 404, 444 (1933).

1966 Amendment

The Rules "proceed upon the theory that no inconvenience can result from the joinder of any two or more matters in the pleadings, but only from trying two or more matters together which have little or nothing in common." Sunderland, *The New Federal Rules*, 45 W.Va.L.Q. 5, 13 (1938); see Clark, Code Pleading 58 (2d ed. 1947). Accordingly, Rule 18(a) has permitted a party to plead multiple claims of all types against an opposing party, subject to the court's power to direct an appropriate procedure for trying the claims. See Rules 42(b), 20(b), 21.

The liberal policy regarding joinder of claims in the pleadings extends to cases with multiple parties. However, the language used in the second sentence of Rule 18(a)—"if the requirements of Rules 19 [necessary joinder of parties], 20 [permissive joinder of parties], and 22 [interpleader] are satisfied"—has led some courts to infer that the rules regulating joinder of parties are intended to carry back to Rule 18(a) and to impose some special limits on joinder of claims in multiparty cases. In particular, Rule 20(a) has been read as restricting the operation of Rule 18(a) in certain situations in which a number of parties have been permissively joined in an action. In *Federal Housing Admr. v. Christianson*, 26 F.Supp. 419 (D.Conn.1939), the indorsee of two notes sued the three comakers of one note, and sought to join in the action a count on a second note which had been made by two of the three defendants. There was no doubt about the propriety of the joinder of the three parties defendant, for a right to relief was being asserted against all three defendants which arose out of a single "transaction" (the first note) and a question of fact or law "common" to all three defendants would arise in the action. See the text of Rule 20(a). The court, however, refused to allow the joinder of the count on the second note, on the ground that this right to relief, assumed to arise from a distinct transaction, did not involve a question common to all the defendants but only two of them. For analysis of the *Christianson* case and other authorities, see 2 Barron & Holtzoff, *Federal Practice & Procedure,* § 533.1 (Wright ed. 1961); 3 Moore's *Federal Practice,* par. 18.04[3] (2d ed. 1963).

If the court's view is followed, it becomes necessary to enter at the pleading stage into speculations about the exact relation between the claim sought to be joined against fewer than all the defendants properly joined in the action, and the claims asserted against all the defendants. Cf. Wright, *Joinder of Claims and Parties Under Modern Pleading Rules,* 36 Minn.L.Rev. 580, 605–06 (1952). Thus if it could be found in the Christianson situation that the claim on the second note arose out of the same transaction as the claim on the first or out of a transaction forming part of a "series," and that any question of fact or law with respect to the second note also arose with regard to the first, it would be held that the claim on the second note could be joined in the complaint. See 2 Barron & Holtzoff, supra, at 109; see also id. at 198 n. 60.4; cf. 3 Moore's *Federal Practice,* supra, at 1811. Such pleading niceties provide a basis for delaying and wasteful maneuver. It is more compatible with the design of the Rules to allow the claim to be joined in the pleading, leaving the question of possible separate trial of that claim to be later decided. See 2 Barron & Holtzoff, supra, § 533.1; Wright, supra, 36 Minn.L.Rev. at 604–11; *Developments in the Law—Multiparty Litigation in the Federal Courts,* 71 Harv. 874, 970–71 (1958); Commentary, *Relation Between Joinder of Parties and Joinder of Claims,* 5 F.R.Serv. 822 (1942). It is instructive to note that the court in the *Christianson* case, while holding that the claim on the second note could not be joined as a matter of pleading, held open the possibility that both claims would later be consolidated for trial under Rule 42(a). See 26 F.Supp. 419.

Rule 18(a) is now amended not only to overcome the *Christianson* decision and similar authority, but also to state clearly as a comprehensive proposition, that a party asserting a claim (an original claim, counterclaim, cross-claim, or third-party claim) may join as many claims as he has against an opposing party. See *Noland Co., Inc. v. Graver Tank & Mfg. Co.,* 301 F.2d 43, 49–51 (4th Cir.1962); but cf. *C. W. Humphrey Co. v. Security Alum. Co.,* 31 F.R.D. 41 (E.D.Mich.1962). This permitted joinder of claims is not affected by the fact that there are multiple parties in the action. The joinder of parties is governed by other rules operating independently.

It is emphasized that amended Rule 18(a) deals only with pleading. As already indicated, a claim properly joined as a matter of pleading need not be proceeded with together with the other claims if fairness or convenience justifies separate treatment.

Amended Rule 18(a), like the rule prior to amendment, does not purport to deal with questions of jurisdiction or venue which may arise with respect to claims properly joined as a matter of pleading. See Rule 82.

See also the amendment of Rule 20(a) and the Advisory Committee's Note thereto.

Free joinder of claims and remedies is one of the basic purposes of unification of the admiralty and civil procedure. The amendment accordingly provides for the inclusion in the rule of maritime claims as well as those which are legal and equitable in character.

1987 Amendment

The amendments are technical. No substantive change is intended.

Rule 19. Joinder of Persons Needed for Just Adjudication

(a) Persons to be Joined if Feasible. A person who is subject to service of process and whose joinder will not deprive the court of jurisdiction over the subject matter of the action shall be joined as a party in the action if (1) in the person's absence complete relief cannot be accorded among those already parties, or (2) the person claims an interest relating to the subject of the action and is so situated that the disposition of the action in the person's absence may (i) as a practical matter impair or impede the person's ability to protect that interest or (ii) leave any of the persons already parties subject to a substantial risk of incurring double, multiple, or otherwise inconsistent obligations by reason of the claimed interest. If the person has not been so joined, the court shall order that the person be made a party. If the person should join as a plaintiff but refuses to do so, the person may be made a defendant, or, in a proper case, an involuntary plaintiff. If the joined party objects to venue and joinder of that party would render the venue of the action improper, that party shall be dismissed from the action.

(b) Determination by Court Whenever Joinder not Feasible. If a person as described in subdivision (a)(1)–(2) hereof cannot be made a party, the court shall determine whether in equity and good conscience the action should proceed among the parties before it, or should be dismissed, the absent person being thus regarded as indispensable. The factors to be considered by the court include: first, to what extent a judgment rendered in the person's absence might be prejudicial to the person or those already parties; second, the extent to which, by protective provisions in the judgment, by the shaping of relief, or other measures, the prejudice can be lessened or avoided; third, whether a judgment rendered in the person's absence will be adequate; fourth, whether the plaintiff will have an adequate remedy if the action is dismissed for nonjoinder.

(c) Pleading Reasons for Nonjoinder. A pleading asserting a claim for relief shall state the names, if known to the pleader, of any persons as prescribed in subdivision (a)(1)–(2) hereof who are not joined, and the reasons why they are not joined.

(d) Exception of Class Actions. This rule is subject to the provisions of Rule 23.

(As amended Feb. 28, 1966, eff. July 1, 1966; Mar. 2, 1987, eff. Aug. 1, 1987.)

ADVISORY COMMITTEE NOTES

1937 Adoption

Note to Subdivision (a). The first sentence with verbal differences (e.g., "united" interest for "joint" interest) is to be found in [former] Equity Rule 37 (Parties Generally—Intervention). Such compulsory joinder provisions are common. Compare Alaska Comp.Laws (1933) § 3392 (containing in same sentence a "class suit" provision); Wyo.Rev.Stat. Ann. (Courtright, 1931) § 89–515 (immediately followed by "class suit" provisions, § 89–516). See also former Equity Rule 42 (Joint and Several Demands). For example of a proper case for involuntary plaintiff, see *Independent Wireless Telegraph Co. v. Radio Corp. of America*, 269 U.S. 459, 46 S.Ct. 166, 70 L.Ed. 357 (1926).

The joinder provisions of this rule are subject to Rule 82 (Jurisdiction and Venue Unaffected).

Note to Subdivision (b). For the substance of this rule see [former] Equity Rule 39 (Absence of Persons Who Would be Proper Parties) and U.S.C., Title 28, § 111 [now § 1391] (When part of several defendants cannot be served); *Camp v. Gress*, 250 U.S. 308, 39 S.Ct. 478, 63 L.Ed. 997 (1919). See also the second and third sentences of [former] Equity Rule 37 (Parties Generally—Intervention).

Note to Subdivision (c). For the substance of this rule see the fourth subdivision of [former] Equity Rule 25 (Bill of Complaint—Contents).

1966 Amendment

General Considerations

Whenever feasible, the persons materially interested in the subject of an action—see the more detailed description of these persons in the discussion of new subdivision (a) below—should be joined as parties so that they may be heard and a complete disposition made. When this comprehensive joinder cannot be accomplished—a situation which may be encountered in Federal courts because of limitations on service of process, subject matter jurisdiction, and venue—the case should be examined pragmatically and a choice made between the alternatives of proceeding with the action in the absence of particular interested persons, and dismissing the action.

Even if the court is mistaken in its decision to proceed in the absence of an interested person, it does not by that token deprive itself of the power to adjudicate as between the parties already before it through proper service of process. But the court can make a legally binding adjudication only between the parties actually joined in the action. It is true that an adjudication between the parties before the court may on occasion adversely affect the absent person as a practical matter, or leave a party exposed to a later inconsistent recovery by the absent person. These are factors which should be considered in deciding whether the action should proceed, or should rather be dismissed; but they do not themselves negate the court's power to adjudicate as between the parties who have been joined.

Defects in the Original Rule

The foregoing propositions were well understood in the older equity practice, see Hazard, *Indispensable Party: The Historical Origin of a Procedural Phantom*, 61 Colum.L.Rev. 1254 (1961), and Rule 19 could be and often was applied in consonance with them. But experience showed that the rule was defective in its phrasing and did not point clearly to the proper basis of decision.

Textual defects.—(1) The expression "persons * * * who ought to be parties if complete relief is to be accorded between those already parties," appearing in original subdivision (b), was apparently intended as a description of the persons whom it would be desirable to join in the action, all questions of feasibility of joinder being put to one side; but it was not adequately descriptive of those persons.

(2) The word "indispensable," appearing in original subdivision (b), was apparently intended as an inclusive reference to the interested persons in whose absence it would be advisable, all factors having been considered, to dismiss the action. Yet the sentence implied that there might be interested persons, not "indispensable," in whose absence the action ought also to be dismissed. Further, it seemed at least superficially plausible to equate the word "indispensable" with the expression "having a joint interest," appearing in subdivision (a). See *United States v. Washington Inst. of Tech., Inc.*, 138 F.2d 25, 26 (3d Cir. 1943); cf. *Chidester v. City of Newark*, 162 F.2d 598 (3d Cir. 1947). But persons holding an interest technically "joint" are not always so related to an action that it would be unwise to proceed without joining all of them, whereas persons holding an interest not technically "joint" may have this relation to an action. See Reed, *Compulsory Joinder of Parties in Civil Actions*, 55 Mich.L.Rev. 327, 356 ff., 483 (1957).

(3) The use of "indispensable" and "joint interest" in the context of original Rule 19 directed attention to the technical or abstract character of the rights or obligations of the persons whose joinder was in question, and correspondingly distracted attention from the pragmatic considerations which should be controlling.

(4) The original rule, in dealing with the feasibility of joining a person as a party to the action, besides referring to whether the person was "subject to the jurisdiction of the court as to both service of process and venue," spoke of whether the person could be made a party "without depriving the court of jurisdiction of the parties before it." The second quoted expression used "jurisdiction" in the sense of the competence of the court over the subject matter of the action, and in this sense the expression was apt. However, by a familiar confusion, the expression seems to have suggested to some that the absence from the lawsuit of a person who was "indispensable" or "who ought to be [a] part[y]" itself deprived the court of the power to adjudicate as between the parties already joined. See *Samuel Goldwyn, Inc. v. United Artists Corp.*, 113 F.2d 703, 707 (3d Cir. 1940); *McArthur v. Rosenbaum Co. of Pittsburgh*, 180 F.2d 617, 621 (3d Cir. 1949); cf. *Calcote v. Texas Pac. Coal & Oil Co.*, 157 F.2d 216 (5th Cir. 1946), cert. denied, 329 U.S. 782 (1946), noted in 56 Yale L.J. 1088 (1947); Reed, supra, 55 Mich. L.Rev. at 332–34.

Failure to point to correct basis of decision. The original rule did not state affirmatively what factors were relevant in deciding whether the action should proceed or be dismissed when joinder of interested persons was infeasible. In some instances courts did not undertake the relevant inquiry or were misled by the "jurisdiction" fallacy. In other instances there was undue preoccupation with abstract classifications of rights or obligations, as against consideration of the particular consequences of proceeding with the action and the ways by which these consequences might be ameliorated by the shaping of final relief or other precautions.

Although these difficulties cannot be said to have been general analysis of the cases showed that there was good reason for attempting to strengthen the rule. The literature also indicated how the rule should be reformed. See Reed, supra (discussion of the important case of *Shields v. Barrow*, 17 How. (58 U.S.) 130 (1854), appears at 55 Mich.L.Rev., p. 340 ff.); Hazard, supra; N.Y. Temporary Comm. on Courts, First Preliminary Report, Legis.Doc.1957, No. 6(b), pp. 28, 233; N.Y. Judicial Council, Twelfth Ann.Rep., Legis.Doc.1946, No. 17, p. 163; Joint Comm. on Michigan Procedural Revision, Final Report, Pt. III, p. 69 (1960); Note, *Indispensable Parties in the Federal Courts*, 65 Harv.L.Rev. 1050 (1952); *Developments in the Law—Multiparty Litigation in the Federal Courts*, 71 Harv.L.Rev. 874, 879 (1958); Mich.Gen.Court Rules, R. 205 (effective Jan. 1, 1963); N.Y.Civ.Prac.Law & Rules, § 1001 (effective Sept. 1, 1963).

The Amended Rule

New subdivision (a) defines the persons whose joinder in the action is desirable. Clause (1) stresses the desirability of joining those persons in whose absence the court would be obliged to grant partial or "hollow" rather than complete relief to the parties before the court. The interests that are being furthered here are not only those of the parties, but also that of the public in avoiding repeated lawsuits on the same essential subject matter. Clause (2)(i) recognizes the importance of protecting the person whose joinder is in question against the practical prejudice to him which may arise through a disposition of the action in his absence. Clause (2)(ii) recognizes the need for considering whether a party may be left, after the adjudication, in a position where a person not joined can subject him to a double or otherwise inconsistent liability. See Reed, supra, 55 Mich.L.Rev. at 330, 338; Note, supra, 65 Harv.L.Rev. at 1052–57; *Developments in the Law*, supra, 71 Harv.L.Rev. at 881–85.

The subdivision (a) definition of persons to be joined is not couched in terms of the abstract nature of their interests— "joint," "united," "separable," or the like. See N.Y. Temporary Comm. on Courts, First Preliminary Report, supra; Developments in the Law, supra, at 880. It should be noted particularly, however, that the description is not at variance with the settled authorities holding that a tortfeasor with the usual "joint-and-several" liability is merely a permissive party to an action against another with like liability. See 3 Moore's *Federal Practice* 2153 (2d ed. 1963); 2 Barron & Holtzoff, *Federal Practice & Procedure* § 513.8 (Wright ed. 1961). Joinder of these tortfeasors continues to be regulated by Rule 20; compare Rule 14 on third-party practice.

If a person as described in subdivision (a)(1)(2) is amenable to service of process and his joinder would not deprive the court of jurisdiction in the sense of competence over the action, he should be joined as a party; and if he has not been joined, the court should order him to be brought into the action. If a party joined has a valid objection to the venue and chooses to assert it, he will be dismissed from the action.

Subdivision (b).—When a person as described in subdivision (a)(1)–(2) cannot be made a party, the court is to determine whether in equity and good conscience the action should proceed among the parties already before it, or should be dismissed. That this decision is to be made in the light of pragmatic considerations has often been acknowledged by the courts. See *Roos v. Texas Co.*, 23 F.2d 171 (2d Cir. 1927), cert. denied 277 U.S. 587 (1928); *Niles-Bement-Pond Co. v. Iron Moulders' Union*, 254 U.S. 77, 80 (1920). The subdivision sets out four relevant considerations drawn from the experience revealed in the decided cases. The factors are to a certain extent overlapping, and they are not intended to exclude other considerations which may be applicable in particular situations.

The first factor brings in a consideration of what a judgment in the action would mean to the absentee. Would the absentee be adversely affected in a practical sense, and if so, would the prejudice be immediate and serious, or remote and minor? The possible collateral consequences of the judgment upon the parties already joined are also to be appraised. Would any party be exposed to a fresh action by the absentee, and if so, how serious is the threat? See the elaborate discussion in Reed, supra; cf. *A. L. Smith Iron Co. v. Dickson*, 141 F.2d 3 (2d Cir. 1944); *Caldwell Mfg. Co. v. Unique Balance Co.*, 18 F.R.D. 258 (S.D.N.Y.1955).

The second factor calls attention to the measures by which prejudice may be averted or lessened. The "shaping of relief" is a familiar expedient to this end. See, e.g., the award of money damages in lieu of specific relief where the latter might affect an absentee adversely. *Ward v. Deavers*, 203 F.2d 72 (D.C.Cir.1953); *Miller & Lux, Inc. v. Nickel*, 141 F.Supp. 41 (N.D.Calif.1956). On the use of "protective provisions," see *Roos v. Texas Co.*, supra; *Atwood v. Rhode Island Hosp. Trust Co.*, 275 Fed. 513, 519 (1st Cir. 1921), cert. denied, 257 U.S. 661 (1922); cf. *Stumpf v. Fidelity Gas Co.*, 294 F.2d 886 (9th Cir. 1961); and the general statement in *National Licorice Co. v. Labor Board*, 309 U.S. 350, 363 (1940).

Sometimes the party is himself able to take measures to avoid prejudice. Thus a defendant faced with a prospect of a second suit by an absentee may be in a position to bring the latter into the action by defensive interpleader. See *Hudson v. Newell*, 172 F.2d 848, 852 mod., 176 F.2d 546 (5th Cir. 1949); *Gauss v. Kirk*, 198 F.2d 83, 86 (D.C.Cir. 1952); *Abel v. Brayton Flying Service, Inc.*, 248 F.2d 713, 716 (5th Cir. 1957) (suggestion of possibility of counter-claim under Rule 13(h)); cf. *Parker Rust-Proof Co. v. Western Union Tel. Co.*, 105 F.2d 976 (2d Cir. 1939), cert. denied, 308 U.S. 597 (1939). So also the absentee may sometimes be able to avert prejudice to himself by voluntarily appearing in the action or intervening on an ancillary basis. See *Developments in the Law*, supra, 71 Harv.L.Rev. at 882; Annot., *Intervention or Subsequent Joinder of Parties as Affecting Jurisdiction of Federal Court Based on Diversity of Citizenship*, 134 A.L.R. 335 (1941); *Johnson v. Middleton*, 175 F.2d 535 (7th Cir. 1949); *Kentucky Nat. Gas Corp. v. Duggins*, 165 F.2d 1011 (6th Cir. 1948); *McComb v. McCormack*, 159 F.2d 219 (5th Cir. 1947). The court should consider whether this, in turn, would impose undue hardship on the absentee. (For the possibility of the court's informing an absentee of the pendency of the action, see comment under subdivision (c) below.)

The third factor—whether an "adequate" judgment can be rendered in the absence of a given person—calls attention to the extent of the relief that can be accorded among the parties joined. It meshes with the other factors, especially the "shaping of relief" mentioned under the second factor. Cf. *Kroese v. General Steel Castings Corp.*, 179 F.2d 760 (3d Cir. 1949), cert. denied, 339 U.S. 983 (1950).

The fourth factor, looking to the practical effects of a dismissal, indicates that the court should consider whether there is any assurance that the plaintiff, if dismissed, could sue effectively in another forum where better joinder would be possible. See *Fitzgerald v. Haynes*, 241 F.2d 417, 420 (3d Cir. 1957); *Fouke v. Schenewerk*, 197 F.2d 234, 236 (5th Cir. 1952); cf. *Warfield v. Marks*, 190 F.2d 178 (5th Cir. 1951).

The subdivision uses the word "indispensable" only in a conclusory sense, that is, a person is "regarded as indispensable" when he cannot be made a party and, upon consideration of the factors above mentioned, it is determined that in his absence it would be preferable to dismiss the action, rather than to retain it.

A person may be added as a party at any stage of the action on motion or on the court's initiative (see Rule 21); and a motion to dismiss, on the ground that a person has not been joined and justice requires that the action should not proceed in his absence, may be made as late as the trial on the merits (see Rule 12(h)(2), as amended; cf. Rule 12(b)(7), as amended). However, when the moving party is seeking dismissal in order to protect himself against a later suit by the absent person (subdivision (a)(2)(ii)), and is not seeking vicariously to protect the absent person against a prejudicial judgment (subdivision (a)(2)(i)), his undue delay in making the motion can properly be counted against him as a reason for denying the motion. A joinder question should be decided with reasonable promptness, but decision may properly be deferred if adequate information is not available at the time. Thus the relationship of an absent person to the action, and the practical effects of an adjudication upon him and others, may not be sufficiently revealed at the pleading stage; in such a case it would be appropriate to defer decision until the action was further advanced. Cf. Rule 12(d).

The amended rule makes no special provision for the problem arising in suits against subordinate Federal officials where it has often been set up as a defense that some superior officer must be joined. Frequently this defense has been accompanied by or intermingled with defenses of sovereign community or lack of consent of the United States to suit. So far as the issue of joinder can be isolated from the rest, the new subdivision seems better adapted to handle it than the predecessor provision. See the discussion in *Johnson v. Kirkland*, 290 F.2d 440, 446–47 (5th Cir. 1961) (stressing the practical orientation of the decisions); *Shaughnessy v. Pedreiro*, 349 U.S. 48, 54 (1955). Recent legislation, P.L. 87–748, 76 Stat. 744, approved October 5, 1962, adding §§ 1361, 1391(e) to Title 28, U.S.C., vests original jurisdiction in the District Courts over actions in the nature of mandamus to compel officials of the United States to perform their legal duties, and extends the range of service of process and liberalizes venue in these actions. If, then, it is found that a particular official should be joined in the action, the legislation will make it easy to bring him in.

Subdivision (c) parallels the predecessor subdivision (c) of Rule 19. In some situations it may be desirable to advise a person who has not been joined of the fact that the action is pending, and in particular cases the court in its discretion may itself convey this information by directing a letter or other informal notice to the absentee.

Subdivision (d) repeats the exception contained in the first clause of the predecessor subdivision (a).

1987 Amendment

The amendments are technical. No substantive change is intended.

Rule 20. Permissive Joinder of Parties

(a) Permissive Joinder. All persons may join in one action as plaintiffs if they assert any right to relief jointly, severally, or in the alternative in respect of or arising out of the same transaction, occurrence, or series of transactions or occurrences and if any question of law or fact common to all these persons will arise in the action. All persons (and any vessel, cargo or other property subject to admiralty process in rem) may be joined in one action as defendants if there is asserted against them jointly, severally, or in the alternative, any right to relief in respect of or arising out of the same transaction, occurrence, or series of transactions or occurrences and if any question of law or fact common to all defendants will arise in the action. A plaintiff or defendant need not be interested in obtaining or defending against all the relief demanded. Judgment may be given for one or more of the plaintiffs according to their respective rights to relief, and against one or more defendants according to their respective liabilities.

(b) Separate Trials. The court may make such orders as will prevent a party from being embarrassed, delayed, or put to expense by the inclusion of a party against whom the party asserts no claim and who asserts no claim against the party, and may order separate trials or make other orders to prevent delay or prejudice.

(As amended Feb. 28, 1966, eff. July 1, 1966; Mar. 2, 1987, eff. Aug. 1, 1987.)

ADVISORY COMMITTEE NOTES

1937 Adoption

The provisions for joinder here stated are in substance the provisions found in England, California, Illinois, New Jersey, and New York. They represent only a moderate expansion of the present federal equity practice to cover both law and equity actions.

With this rule compare also [former] Equity Rules 26 (Joinder of Causes of Action), 37 (Parties Generally—Intervention), 40 (Nominal Parties), and 42 (Joint and Several Demands).

The provisions of this rule for the joinder of parties are subject to Rule 82 (Jurisdiction and Venue Unaffected).

Note to Subdivision (a). The first sentence is derived from *English Rules Under the Judicature Act* (The Annual Practice, 1937) O. 16, r. 1. Compare Calif.Code Civ.Proc. (Deering, 1937) §§ 378, 379a; Ill.Rev.Stat. (1937) ch. 110, § 147–148; N.J.Comp.Stat. (2 Cum.Supp., 1911–1924), N.Y.C.P.A. (1937) §§ 209, 211. The second sentence is derived from *English Rules Under the Judicature Act* (The Annual Practice, 1937) O. 16, r. 4. The third sentence is derived from O. 16, r. 5, and the fourth from O. 16, r.r. 1 and 4.

Note to Subdivision (b). This is derived from *English Rules Under the Judicature Act* (The Annual Practice, 1937) O. 16, r.r. 1 and 5.

1966 Amendment

See the amendment of Rule 18(a) and the Advisory Committee's Note thereto. It has been thought that a lack of clarity in the antecedent of the word "them," as it appeared in two places in Rule 20(a), contributed to the view, taken by some courts, that this rule limited the joinder of claims in certain situations of permissive party joinder. Although the amendment of Rule 18(a) should make clear that this view is untenable, it has been considered advisable to amend Rule 20(a) to eliminate any ambiguity. See 2 Barron & Holtzoff, *Federal Practice & Procedure* 202 (Wright Ed. 1961).

A basic purpose of unification of admiralty and civil procedure is to reduce barriers to joinder; hence the reference to "any vessel," etc.

1987 Amendment

The amendments are technical. No substantive change is intended.

Rule 21. Misjoinder and Non-Joinder of Parties

Misjoinder of parties is not ground for dismissal of an action. Parties may be dropped or added by order of the court on motion of any party or of its own initiative at any stage of the action and on such terms as are just. Any claim against a party may be severed and proceeded with separately.

ADVISORY COMMITTEE NOTES

1937 Adoption

See *English Rules Under the Judicature Act* (The Annual Practice, 1937) O. 16, r. 11. See also [former] Equity Rules 43 (Defect of Parties—Resisting Objection) and 44 (Defect of Parties—Tardy Objection).

For separate trials see Rules 13(i) (Counterclaims and Cross-Claims: Separate Trials; Separate Judgments), 20(b) (Permissive Joinder of Parties: Separate Trials), and 42(b) (Separate Trials, generally) and the note to the latter rule.

Rule 22. Interpleader

(1) Persons having claims against the plaintiff may be joined as defendants and required to interplead when their claims are such that the plaintiff is or may be exposed to double or multiple liability. It is not ground for objection to the joinder that the claims of the several claimants or the titles on which their claims depend do not have a common origin or are not identical but are adverse to and independent of one another, or that the plaintiff avers that the plaintiff is not liable in whole or in part to any or all of the claimants. A defendant exposed to similar liability may obtain such interpleader by way of cross-claim or counterclaim. The provisions of this rule supplement and do not in any way limit the joinder of parties permitted in Rule 20.

(2) The remedy herein provided is in addition to and in no way supersedes or limits the remedy provided by Title 28, U.S.C., §§ 1335, 1397, and 2361. Actions under those provisions shall be conducted in accordance with these rules.

(As amended Dec. 29, 1948, eff. Oct. 20, 1949; Mar. 2, 1987, eff. Aug. 1, 1987.)

ADVISORY COMMITTEE NOTES

1937 Adoption

The first paragraph provides for interpleader relief along the newer and more liberal lines of joinder in the alternative. It avoids the confusion and restrictions that developed around actions of strict interpleader and actions in the nature of interpleader. Compare *John Hancock Mutual Life Insurance Co. v. Kegan et al.*, 22 F.Supp. 326 (D.C.Md.1938). It does not change the rules on service of process, jurisdiction, and venue, as established by judicial decision.

The second paragraph allows an action to be brought under the recent interpleader statute when applicable. By this paragraph all remedies under the statute are continued, but the manner of obtaining them is in accordance with these rules. For temporary restraining orders and preliminary injunctions under this statute, see Rule 65(e).

This rule substantially continues such statutory provisions as U.S.C., Title 38, § 445 [now 784] (Actions on claims; jurisdiction; parties; procedure; limitation; witnesses; definitions) (actions upon veterans' contracts of insurance with the United States), providing for interpleader by the United States where it acknowledges indebtedness under a contract of insurance with the United States; U.S.C., Title 49, § 97 (Interpleader of conflicting claimants) (by carrier which has issued bill of lading). See Chaffee, *The Federal Interpleader Act of 1936: I and II* (1936), 45 Yale L.J. 963, 1161.

1948 Amendment

The amendment effective October 20, 1949, substituted the reference to "Title 28, U.S.C., §§ 1335, 1397, and 2361," at the end of the first sentence of paragraph (2), for the reference to "Section 24(26) of the Judicial Code, as amended, U.S.C., Title 28, § 41(26)." The amendment also substituted the words "those provisions" in the second sentence of paragraph (2) for the words "that section."

1987 Amendment

The amendment is technical. No substantive change is intended.

Rule 23. Class Actions

(a) Prerequisites to a Class Action. One or more members of a class may sue or be sued as representative parties on behalf of all only if (1) the class is so numerous that joinder of all members is impracticable, (2) there are questions of law or fact common to the class, (3) the claims or defenses of the representative parties are typical of the claims or defenses of the class, and (4) the representative parties will fairly and adequately protect the interests of the class.

(b) Class Actions Maintainable. An action may be maintained as a class action if the prerequisites of subdivision (a) are satisfied, and in addition:

(1) the prosecution of separate actions by or against individual members of the class would create a risk of

(A) inconsistent or varying adjudications with respect to individual members of the class which would establish incompatible standards of conduct for the party opposing the class, or

(B) adjudications with respect to individual members of the class which would as a practical matter be dispositive of the interests of the other members not parties to the adjudications or substantially impair or impede their ability to protect their interests; or

(2) the party opposing the class has acted or refused to act on grounds generally applicable to the class, thereby making appropriate final injunctive relief or corresponding declaratory relief with respect to the class as a whole; or

(3) the court finds that the questions of law or fact common to the members of the class predominate over any questions affecting only individual members, and that a class action is superior to other available methods for the fair and efficient adjudication of the controversy. The matters pertinent to the findings include: (A) the interest of members of the class in individually controlling the prosecution or defense of separate actions; (B) the extent and nature of any litigation concerning the controversy already commenced by or against members of the class; (C) the desirability or undesirability of concentrating the litigation of the claims in the particular forum; (D) the difficulties likely to be encountered in the management of a class action.

(c) Determining by Order Whether to Certify a Class Action; Appointing Class Counsel; Notice and Membership in Class; Judgment; Multiple Classes and Subclasses.

(1)(A) When a person sues or is sued as a representative of a class, the court must—at an early practicable time—determine by order whether to certify the action as a class action.

(B) An order certifying a class action must define the class and the class claims, issues, or defenses, and must appoint class counsel under Rule 23(g).

(C) An order under Rule 23(c)(1) may be altered or amended before final judgment.

(2)(A) For any class certified under Rule 23(b)(1) or (2), the court may direct appropriate notice to the class.

(B) For any class certified under Rule 23(b)(3), the court must direct to class members the best notice practicable under the circumstances, including individual notice to all members who can be identified through reasonable effort. The notice must concisely and clearly state in plain, easily understood language:

- the nature of the action,
- the definition of the class certified,
- the class claims, issues, or defenses,
- that a class member may enter an appearance through counsel if the member so desires,
- that the court will exclude from the class any member who requests exclusion, stating when and how members may elect to be excluded, and
- the binding effect of a class judgment on class members under Rule 23(c)(3).

(3) The judgment in an action maintained as a class action under subdivision (b)(1) or (b)(2), whether or not favorable to the class, shall include and describe those whom the court finds to be members of the class. The judgment in an action maintained as a class action under subdivision (b)(3), whether or not favorable to the class, shall include and specify or describe those to whom the notice provided in subdivision (c)(2) was directed, and who have not requested exclusion, and whom the court finds to be members of the class.

(4) When appropriate (A) an action may be brought or maintained as a class action with respect to particular issues, or (B) a class may be divided into subclasses and each subclass treated as a class, and the provisions of this rule shall then be construed and applied accordingly.

(d) Orders in Conduct of Actions. In the conduct of actions to which this rule applies, the court may make appropriate orders: (1) determining the course of proceedings or prescribing measures to prevent undue repetition or complication in the presentation of evidence or argument; (2) requiring, for the protection of the members of the class or otherwise for the fair conduct of the action, that notice be given in such manner as the court may direct to some or all of the members of any step in the action, or of the proposed extent of the judgment, or of the opportunity of members to signify whether they consider the representation fair and adequate, to intervene and present claims or defenses, or otherwise to come into the action; (3) imposing conditions on the representative parties or on intervenors; (4) requiring that the pleadings be amended to eliminate therefrom allegations as to representation of absent persons, and that the action proceed accordingly; (5) dealing with similar procedural matters. The orders may be combined with an order under Rule 16, and may be altered or amended as may be desirable from time to time.

(e) Settlement, Voluntary Dismissal, or Compromise.

(1)(A) The court must approve any settlement, voluntary dismissal, or compromise of the claims, issues, or defenses of a certified class.

(B) The court must direct notice in a reasonable manner to all class members who would be bound by a proposed settlement, voluntary dismissal, or compromise.

(C) The court may approve a settlement, voluntary dismissal, or compromise that would bind class members only after a hearing and on finding that the settlement, voluntary dismissal, or compromise is fair, reasonable, and adequate.

(2) The parties seeking approval of a settlement, voluntary dismissal, or compromise under Rule 23(e)(1) must file a statement identifying any agreement made in connection with the proposed settlement, voluntary dismissal, or compromise.

(3) In an action previously certified as a class action under Rule 23(b)(3), the court may refuse to approve a settlement unless it affords a new opportunity to request exclusion to individual class members who had an earlier opportunity to request exclusion but did not do so.

(4)(A) Any class member may object to a proposed settlement, voluntary dismissal, or compromise that requires court approval under Rule 23(e)(1)(A).

(B) An objection made under Rule 23(e)(4)(A) may be withdrawn only with the court's approval.

(f) Appeals. A court of appeals may in its discretion permit an appeal from an order of a district court granting or denying class action certification under this rule if application is made to it within ten days after entry of the order. An appeal does not stay proceedings in the district court unless the district judge or the court of appeals so orders.

(g) Class Counsel.

(1) Appointing Class Counsel.

(A) Unless a statute provides otherwise, a court that certifies a class must appoint class counsel.

(B) An attorney appointed to serve as class counsel must fairly and adequately represent the interests of the class.

(C) In appointing class counsel, the court

(i) must consider:

• the work counsel has done in identifying or investigating potential claims in the action,

• counsel's experience in handling class actions, other complex litigation, and claims of the type asserted in the action,

• counsel's knowledge of the applicable law, and

• the resources counsel will commit to representing the class;

(ii) may consider any other matter pertinent to counsel's ability to fairly and adequately represent the interests of the class;

(iii) may direct potential class counsel to provide information on any subject pertinent to the appointment and to propose terms for attorney fees and nontaxable costs; and

(iv) may make further orders in connection with the appointment.

(2) Appointment Procedure.

(A) The court may designate interim counsel to act on behalf of the putative class before determining whether to certify the action as a class action.

(B) When there is one applicant for appointment as class counsel, the court may appoint that applicant only if the applicant is adequate under Rule 23(g)(1)(B) and (C). If more than one adequate applicant seeks appointment as class counsel, the court must appoint the applicant best able to represent the interests of the class.

(C) The order appointing class counsel may include provisions about the award of attorney fees or nontaxable costs under Rule 23(h).

(h) Attorney Fees Award. In an action certified as a class action, the court may award reasonable attorney fees and nontaxable costs authorized by law or by agreement of the parties as follows:

(1) Motion for Award of Attorney Fees. A claim for an award of attorney fees and nontaxable costs must be made by motion under Rule 54(d)(2), subject to the provisions of this subdivision, at a time set by the court. Notice of the motion must be served on all parties and, for motions by class counsel, directed to class members in a reasonable manner.

(2) Objections to Motion. A class member, or a party from whom payment is sought, may object to the motion.

(3) Hearing and Findings. The court may hold a hearing and must find the facts and state its conclusions of law on the motion under Rule 52(a).

(4) Reference to Special Master or Magistrate Judge. The court may refer issues related to the amount of the award to a special master or to a magistrate judge as provided in Rule 54(d)(2)(D). (As amended Feb. 28, 1966, eff. July 1, 1966; Mar. 2, 1987, eff. Aug. 1, 1987; Apr. 24, 1998, eff. Dec. 1, 1998; Mar. 27, 2003, eff. Dec. 1, 2003.)

ADVISORY COMMITTEE NOTES

1937 Adoption

Note to Subdivision (a). This is a substantial restatement of [former] Equity Rule 38 (Representatives of Class) as that rule has been construed. It applies to all actions, whether formerly denominated legal or equitable. For a general analysis of class actions, effect of judgment, and requisites of jurisdiction see Moore, *Federal Rules of Civil Procedure: Some Problems Raised by the Preliminary Draft*, 25 Georgetown L.J. 551, 570 et seq. (1937); Moore and Cohn, *Federal Class Actions*, 32 Ill.L.Rev. 307 (1937); Moore and Cohn, *Federal Class Actions—Jurisdiction and Effect of Judgment*, 32 Ill.L.Rev. 555–567 (1938); Lesar, *Class Suits and the Federal Rules*, 22 Minn.L.Rev. 34 (1937); cf. Arnold and James, *Cases on Trials, Judgments and Appeals* (1936) 175; and see Blume, *Jurisdictional Amount in Representative Suits*, 15 Minn.L.Rev. 501 (1931).

The general test of [former] Equity Rule 38 (Representatives of Class) that the question should be "one of common or general interest to many persons constituting a class so numerous as to make it impracticable to bring them all before the court," is a common test. For states which require the two elements of a common or general interest and numerous persons, as provided for in [former] Equity Rule 38, see Del.Ch. Rule 113; Fla.Comp.Gen.Laws Ann. (Supp., 1936) § 4918(7); Georgia Code (1933) § 37–1002, and see *English Rules Under the Judicature Act* (The Annual Practice, 1937) O. 16, r. 9. For statutory provisions providing for class actions when the question is one of common or general interest or when the parties are numerous, see Ala.Code Ann. (Michie, 1928) § 5701; 2 Ind.Stat.Ann. (Burns, 1933) § 2–220; N.Y.C.P.A. (1937) 195; Wis.Stat. (1935) § 260.12. These statutes have, however, been uniformly construed as though phrased in the conjunctive. See *Garfein v. Stiglitz*, 260 Ky. 430, 86 S.W.2d 155 (1935). The rule adopts the test of [former] Equity Rule 38, but defines what constitutes a "common or general interest". Compare with code provisions which make the action dependent upon the propriety of joinder of the parties. See Blume, *The "Common Questions" Principle in the Code Provision for Representative Suits*, 30 Mich.L.Rev. 878 (1932). For discussion of what constitutes "numerous persons" see Wheaton, *Representative Suits Involving Numerous Litigants*, 19 Corn.L.Q. 399 (1934); Note, 36 Harv.L.Rev. 89 (1922).

Clause (1), Joint, Common, or Secondary Right. This clause is illustrated in actions brought by or against representatives of an unincorporated association. See *Oster v. Brotherhood of Locomotive Firemen and Enginemen*, 271 Pa. 419, 114 Atl. 377 (1921); *Pickett v. Walsh*, 192 Mass. 572, 78 N.E. 753, 6 L.R.A., N.S., 1067 (1906); *Colt v. Hicks*, 97 Ind.App. 177, 179 N.E. 335 (1932). Compare Rule 17(b) as to when an unincorporated association has capacity to sue or be sued in its common name; *United Mine Workers of America v. Coronado Coal Co.*, 42 S.Ct. 570, 259 U.S. 344, 66 L.Ed.

975, 27 A.L.R. 762 (1922) (an unincorporated association was sued as an entity for the purpose of enforcing against it a federal substantive right); Moore, *Federal Rules of Civil Procedure: Some Problems Raised by the Preliminary Draft*, 25 Georgetown L.J. 551, 566 (for discussion of jurisdictional requisites when an unincorporated association sues or is sued in its common name and jurisdiction is founded upon diversity of citizenship). For an action brought by representatives of one group against representatives of another group for distribution of a fund held by an unincorporated association, see *Smith v. Swormstedt*, 16 How. 288, 14 L.Ed. 942 (U.S. 1853). Compare *Christopher, et al. v. Brusselback*, 1938, 58 S.Ct. 350, 302 U.S. 500, 82 L.Ed. 388.

For an action to enforce rights held in common by policyholders against the corporate issuer of the policies, see *Supreme Tribe of Ben Hur v. Cauble*, 255 U.S. 356, 41 S.Ct. 338, 65 L.Ed. 673 (1921). See also *Terry v. Little*, 101 U.S. 216, 25 L.Ed. 864 (1880); *John A. Roebling's Sons Co. v. Kinnicutt*, 248 Fed. 596 (D.C.N.Y., 1917) dealing with the right held in common by creditors to enforce the statutory liability of stockholders.

Typical of a secondary action is a suit by stockholders to enforce a corporate right. For discussion of the general nature of these actions see *Ashwander v. Tennessee Valley Authority*, 297 U.S. 288, 56 S.Ct. 466, 80 L.Ed. 688 (1936); Glenn, *The Stockholder's Suit—Corporate and Individual Grievances*, 33 Yale L.J. 580 (1924); McLaughlin, *Capacity of Plaintiff-Stockholder to Terminate a Stockholder's Suit*, 46 Yale L.J. 421 (1937). See also Subdivision (b) of this rule which deals with Shareholder's Action; Note, 15 Minn.L.Rev. 453 (1931).

Clause (2). A creditor's action for liquidation or reorganization of a corporation is illustrative of this clause. An action by a stockholder against certain named defendants as representatives of numerous claimants presents a situation converse to the creditor's action.

Clause (3). See *Everglades Drainage League v. Napoleon Broward Drainage Dist.*, 253 Fed. 246 (D.C.Fla., 1918); *Gramling v. Maxwell*, 52 F.2d 256 (D.C.N.C., 1931), approved in 30 Mich.L.Rev. 624 (1932); *Skinner v. Mitchell*, 108 Kan. 861, 197 Pac. 569 (1921); *Duke of Bedford v. Ellis* (1901) A.C. 1, for class actions when there were numerous persons and there was only a question of law or fact common to them; and see Blume, *The "Common Questions" Principle in the Code Provision for Representative Suits*, 30 Mich. L.Rev. 878 (1932).

Note to Subdivision (b). This is [former] Equity Rule 27 (Stockholder's Bill) with verbal changes. See also *Hawes v. Oakland*, 104 U.S. 450, 26 L.Ed. 827 (1882) and former Equity Rule 94, promulgated January 23, 1882, 104 U.S. IX.

Note to Subdivision (c). See McLaughlin, *Capacity of Plaintiff-Stockholder to Terminate a Stockholder's Suit*, 46 Yale L.J. 421 (1937).

Supplementary Note

Note. Subdivision (b), relating to secondary actions by shareholders, provides among other things, that in such an action the complainant "shall aver (1) that the plaintiff was a shareholder at the time of the transaction of which he complains or that his share thereafter devolved on him by operation of law * * *".

As a result of the decision in *Erie R. Co. v. Tompkins,* 1938, 304 U.S. 64, 58 S.Ct. 817 (decided April 25, 1938, after this rule was promulgated by the Supreme Court, though before it took effect) a question has arisen as to whether the provision above quoted deals with a matter of substantive right or is a matter of procedure. If it is a matter of substantive law or right, then under *Erie R. Co. v. Tompkins* clause (1) may not be validly applied in cases pending in states whose local law permits a shareholder to maintain such actions, although not a shareholder at the time of the transactions complained of. The Advisory Committee, believing the question should be settled in the courts, proposes no change in Rule 23 but thinks rather that the situation should be explained in an appropriate note.

The rule has a long history. In *Hawes v. Oakland,* 1882, 104 U.S. 450, the Court held that a shareholder could not maintain such an action unless he owned shares at the time of the transactions complained of, or unless they devolved on him by operation of law. At that time the decision in *Swift v. Tyson,* 1842, 16 Peters 1, was the law, and the federal courts considered themselves free to establish their own principles of equity jurisprudence, so the Court was not in 1882 and has not been, until *Erie R. Co. v. Tompkins* in 1938, concerned with the question whether *Hawes v. Oakland* dealt with substantive right or procedure.

Following the decision in *Hawes v. Oakland,* and at the same term, the Court, to implement its decision, adopted [former] Equity Rule 94, which contained the same provision above quoted from Rule 23 F.R.C.P. The provision in [former] Equity Rule 94 was later embodied in [former] Equity Rule 27, of which the present Rule 23 is substantially a copy.

In *City of Quincy v. Steel,* 1887, 120 U.S. 241, 245, 7 S.Ct. 520, the Court referring to *Hawes v. Oakland* said: "In order to give effect to the principles there laid down, this Court at that term adopted Rule 94 of the rules of practice for courts of equity of the United States."

Some other cases dealing with [former] Equity Rules 94 or 27 prior to the decision in *Erie R. Co. v. Tompkins* are *Dimpfel v. Ohio & Miss. R.R.,* 1884, 3 S.Ct. 573, 110 U.S. 209, 28 L.Ed. 121; *Illinois Central R. Co. v. Adams,* 1901, 21 S.Ct. 251, 180 U.S. 28, 34, 45 L.Ed. 410; *Venner v. Great Northern Ry.,* 1908, 28 S.Ct. 328, 209 U.S. 24, 30, 52 L.Ed. 666; *Jacobson v. General Motors Corp.,* S.D.N.Y.1938, 22 F.Supp. 255, 257. These cases generally treat *Hawes v. Oakland* as establishing a "principle" of equity, or as dealing not with jurisdiction but with the "right" to maintain an action, or have said that the defense under the equity rule is analogous to the defense that the plaintiff has no "title" and results in a dismissal "for want of equity."

Those state decisions which held that a shareholder acquiring stock after the event may maintain a derivative action are founded on the view that it is a right belonging to the shareholder at the time of the transaction and which passes as a right to the subsequent purchaser. See *Pollitz v. Gould,* 1911, 202 N.Y. 11, 94 N.E. 1088.

The first case arising after the decision in *Erie R. Co. v. Tompkins,* in which this problem was involved, was *Summers v. Hearst,* S.D.N.Y.1938, 23 F.Supp. 986. It concerned [former] Equity Rule 27, as Federal Rule 23 was not then in effect. In a well considered opinion Judge Leibell reviewed the decisions and said: "The federal cases that discuss this section of [former] Rule 27 support the view that it states a principle of substantive law." He quoted *Pollitz v. Gould,* 1911, 202 N.Y. 11, 94 N.E. 1088, as saying that the United States Supreme Court "seems to have been more concerned with establishing this rule as one of practice than of substantive law" but that "whether it be regarded as establishing a principle of law or a rule of practice, this authority has been subsequently followed in the United States courts."

He then concluded that, although the federal decisions treat the equity rule as "stating a principle of substantive law", if "[former] Equity Rule 27 is to be modified or revoked in view of *Erie R. Co. v. Tompkins,* it is not the province of this Court to suggest it, much less impliedly to follow that course by disregarding the mandatory provisions of the Rule."

In *Piccard v. Sperry Corporation,* S.D.N.Y.1941, 36 F.Supp. 1006, 1009–10, affirmed without opinion, C.C.A.2d 1941, 120 F.2d 328, a shareholder, not such at the time of the transactions complained of, sought to intervene. The court held an intervenor was as much subject to Rule 23 as an original plaintiff; and that the requirement of Rule 23(b) was "a matter of practice," not substance, and applied in New York where the state law was otherwise, despite *Erie R. Co. v. Tompkins.* In *New York v. Guaranty Trust Co. of New York,* C.C.A.2, 1944, 143 F.2d 503, rev'd on other grounds, 1945, 65 S.Ct. 1464, the court said: "Restrictions on the bringing of stockholders' actions, such as those imposed by F.R.C.P. 23(b) or other state statutes are procedural," citing the *Piccard* and other cases.

Some other federal decisions since 1938 touch the question.

In *Gallup v. Caldwell,* C.C.A.3, 1941, 120 F.2d 90, 95 arising in New Jersey, the point was raised but not decided, the court saying that it was not satisfied that the then New Jersey rule differed from Rule 23(b), and that "under the circumstances the proper course was to follow Rule 23(b)."

In *Mullins v. DeSoto Securities Co.,* W.D.La.1942, 45 F.Supp. 871, 878, the point was not decided, because the court found the Louisiana rule to be the same as that stated in Rule 23(b).

In *Toebelman v. Missouri-Kansas Pipe Line Co.,* D.Del. 1941, 41 F.Supp. 334, 340, the court dealt only with another part of Rule 23(b), relating to prior demands on the stockholders and did not discuss *Erie R. Co. v. Tompkins,* or its effect on the rule.

In *Perrott v. United States Banking Corp.,* D.Del.1944, 53 F.Supp. 953, it appeared that the Delaware law does not require the plaintiff to have owned shares at the time of the transaction complained of. The court sustained Rule 23(b), after discussion of the authorities, saying:

"It seems to me the rule does not go beyond procedure. * * * Simply because a particular plaintiff cannot qualify as a proper party to maintain such an action does not destroy or even whittle at the cause of action. The cause of action exists until a qualified plaintiff can get it started in a federal court."

In *Bankers Nat. Corp. v. Barr,* S.D.N.Y.1945, 9 Fed.Rules Serv. 23b.11, Case 1, the court held Rule 23(b) to be one of procedure, but that whether the plaintiff was a stockholder was a substantive question to be settled by state law.

The New York rule, as stated in *Pollitz v. Gould,* supra, has been altered by an act of the New York Legislature, Chapter 667, Laws of 1944, effective April 9, 1944, General Corporation Law, § 61, which provides that "in any action brought by a shareholder in the right of a * * * corporation, it must appear that the plaintiff was a stockholder at the time of the transaction of which he complains, or that his stock thereafter devolved upon him by operation of law." At the same time a further and separate provision was enacted, requiring under certain circumstances the giving of security for reasonable expenses and attorney's fees, to which security the corporation in whose right the action is brought and the defendants therein may have recourse. (Chapter 668, Laws of 1944, effective April 9, 1944, General Corporation Law, § 61–b.) These provisions are aimed at so-called "strike" stockholders' suits and their attendant abuses. *Shielcrawt v. Moffett*, Ct.App.1945, 294 N.Y. 180, 61 N.E.2d 435, rev'g 51 N.Y.S.2d 188, aff'g 49 N.Y.S.2d 64; *Noel Associates, Inc. v. Merrill*, Sup.Ct.1944, 184 Misc. 646, 63 N.Y.S.2d 143.

Insofar as § 61 is concerned, it has been held that the section is procedural in nature. *Klum v. Clinton Trust Co.*, Sup.Ct.1944, 183 Misc. 340, 48 N.Y.S.2d 267; *Noel Associates, Inc. v. Merrill*, supra. In the latter case the court pointed out that "The 1944 amendment to Section 61 rejected the rule laid down in the Pollitz case and substituted, in place thereof, in its precise language, the rule which has long prevailed in the Federal Courts and which is now Rule 23(b) * * *". There is, nevertheless, a difference of opinion regarding the application of the statute to pending actions. See *Klum v. Clinton Trust Co.*, supra (applicable); *Noel Associates, Inc. v. Merrill*, supra (inapplicable).

With respect to § 61–b, which may be regarded as a separate problem, *Noel Associates, Inc. v. Merrill*, supra, it has been held that even though the statute is procedural in nature—a matter not definitely decided—the Legislature evinced no intent that the provisions should apply to actions pending when it became effective. *Shielcrawt v. Moffett*, supra. As to actions instituted after the effective date of the legislation, the constitutionality of § 61–b is in dispute. See *Wolf v. Atkinson*, Sup.Ct.1944, 182 Misc. 675, 49 N.Y.S.2d 703 (constitutional); *Citron v. Mangel Stores Corp.*, Sup.Ct. 1944, 50 N.Y.S.2d 416 (unconstitutional); Zlinkoff, *The American Investor and the Constitutionality of § 61–b of the New York General Corporation Law*, 1945, 54 Yale L.J. 352.

New Jersey also enacted a statute, similar to Chapters 667 and 668 of the New York law. See P.L.1945, Ch. 131, R.S.Cum.Supp. 14:3–15. The New Jersey provision similar to Chapter 668, § 61–b, differs, however, in that it specifically applies retroactively. It has been held that this provision is procedural and hence will not govern a pending action brought against a New Jersey corporation in the New York courts. *Shielcrawt v. Moffett*, Sup.Ct.N.Y.1945, 184 Misc. 1074, 56 N.Y.S.2d 134.

See, also generally, 2 Moore's *Federal Practice*, 1938, 2250–2253, and Cum.Supplement § 23.05.

The decisions here discussed show that the question is a debatable one, and that there is respectable authority for either view, with a recent trend towards the view that Rule 23(b)(1) is procedural. There is reason to say that the question is one which should not be decided by the Supreme Court ex parte, but left to await a judicial decision in a litigated case, and that in the light of the material in this note, the only inference to be drawn from a failure to amend Rule 23(b) would be that the question is postponed to await a litigated case.

The Advisory Committee is unanimously of the opinion that this course should be followed.

If, however, the final conclusion is that the rule deals with a matter of substantive right, then the rule should be amended by adding a provision that Rule 23(b)(1) does not apply in jurisdictions where state law permits a shareholder to maintain a secondary action, although he was not a shareholder at the time of the transactions of which he complains.

1966 Amendment

Difficulties with the original rule. The categories of class actions in the original rule were defined in terms of the abstract nature of the rights involved: the so-called "true" category was defined as involving "joint, common, or secondary rights"; the "hybrid" category, as involving "several" rights related to "specific property"; the "spurious" category, as involving "several" rights affected by a common question and related to common relief. It was thought that the definitions accurately described the situations amenable to the class-suit device, and also would indicate the proper extent of the judgment in each category, which would in turn help to determine the res judicata effect of the judgment if questioned in a later action. Thus the judgments in "true" and "hybrid" class actions would extend to the class (although in somewhat different ways); the judgment in a "spurious" class action would extend only to the parties including intervenors. See Moore, *Federal Rules of Civil Procedure: Some Problems Raised by the Preliminary Draft*, 25 Geo.L.J. 551, 570–76 (1937).

In practice the terms "joint," "common," etc., which were used as the basis of the Rule 23 classification proved obscure and uncertain. See Chafee, *Some Problems of Equity* 245–46, 256–57 (1950); Kalven & Rosenfield, *The Contemporary Function of the Class Suit*, 8 U. of Chi.L.Rev. 684, 707 & n. 73 (1941); Keeffe, Levy & Donovan, *Lee Defeats Ben Hur*, 33 Corn.L.Q. 327, 329–36 (1948); *Developments in the Law: Multiparty Litigation in the Federal Courts*, 71 Harv. L.Rev. 874, 931 (1958); Advisory Committee's Note to Rule 19, as amended. The courts had considerable difficulty with these terms. See, e.g., *Gullo v. Veterans' Coop. H. Assn.*, 13 F.R.D. 11 (D.D.C.1952); *Shipley v. Pittsburgh & L.E.R. Co.*, 70 F.Supp. 870 (W.D.Pa.1947); *Deckert v. Independence Shares Corp.*, 27 F.Supp. 763 (E.D.Pa.1939), rev'd 108 F.2d 51 (3d Cir. 1939), rev'd, 311 U.S. 282 (1940), on remand, 39 F.Supp. 592 (E.D.Pa.1941), rev'd sub nom. *Pennsylvania Co. for Ins. on Lives v. Deckert*, 123 F.2d 979 (3d Cir.1941) (see Chafee, supra, at 264–65).

Nor did the rule provide an adequate guide to the proper extent of the judgments in class actions. First, we find instances of the courts classifying actions as "true" or intimating that the judgments would be decisive for the class where these results seemed appropriate but were reached by dint of depriving the word "several" of coherent meaning. See, e.g., *System Federation No. 91 v. Reed*, 180 F.2d 991 (6th Cir.1950); *Wilson v. City of Paducah*, 100 F.Supp. 116 (W.D.Ky.1951); *Citizens Banking Co. v. Monticello State Bank*, 143 F.2d 261 (8th Cir.1944); *Redmond v. Commerce Trust Co.*, 144 F.2d 140 (8th Cir.1944), cert. denied, 323 U.S. 776 (1944); *United States v. American Optical Co.*, 97 F.Supp. 66 (N.D.Ill.1951); *National Hairdressers' & C. Assn. v. Philad Co.*, 34 F.Supp. 264 (D.Del.1940); 41 F.Supp. 701 (D.Del.1940), aff'd mem., 129 F.2d 1020 (3d Cir.1942). Second, we find cases classified by the courts as "spurious" in which, on a realistic view, it would seem fitting for the judgments to extend to the class. See, e.g., *Knapp v.*

Bankers Sec. Corp., 17 F.R.D. 245 (E.D.Pa.1954), aff'd 230 F.2d 717 (3d Cir.1956); *Giesecke v. Denver Tramway Corp.*, 81 F.Supp. 957 (D.Del.1949); *York v. Guaranty Trust Co.*, 143 F.2d 503 (2d Cir.1944), rev'd on grounds not here relevant, 326 U.S. 99 (1945) (see Chafee, supra, at 208); cf. *Webster Eisenlohr, Inc. v. Kalodner*, 145 F.2d 316, 320 (3d Cir.1944), cert. denied, 325 U.S. 867 (1945). But cf. the early decisions, *Duke of Bedford v. Ellis*, [1901] A.C. 1; *Sheffield Waterworks v. Yeomans*, L.R. 2 Ch.App. 8 (1866); *Brown v. Vermuden*, 1 Ch.Cas. 272, 22 Eng.Rep. 796 (1676).

The "spurious" action envisaged by original Rule 23 was in any event an anomaly because, although denominated a "class" action and pleaded as such, it was supposed not to adjudicate the rights or liabilities of any person not a party. It was believed to be an advantage of the "spurious" category that it would invite decisions that a member of the "class" could, like a member of the class in a "true" or "hybrid" action, intervene on an ancillary basis without being required to show an independent basis of Federal jurisdiction, and have the benefit of the date of the commencement of the action for purposes of the statute of limitations. See 3 Moore's *Federal Practice*, pars. 23.10[1], 23.12 (2d ed.1963). These results were attained in some instances but not in others. On the statute of limitations, see *Union Carbide & Carbon Corp. v. Nisley*, 300 F.2d 561 (10th Cir.1961), pet. cert. dism., 371 U.S. 801 (1963); but cf. *P. W. Husserl, Inc. v. Newman*, 25 F.R.D. 264 (S.D.N.Y.1960); *Athas v. Day*, 161 F.Supp. 916 (D.Colo.1958). On ancillary intervention, see *Amen v. Black*, 234 F.2d 12 (10th Cir.1956), cert. granted, 352 U.S. 888 (1956), dism. on stip., 355 U.S. 600 (1958); but cf. *Wagner v. Kemper*, 13 F.R.D. 128 (W.D.Mo.1952). The results, however, can hardly depend upon the mere appearance of a "spurious" category in the rule; they should turn on more basic considerations. See discussion of subdivision (c)(1) below.

Finally, the original rule did not squarely address itself to the question of the measures that might be taken during the course of the action to assure procedural fairness, particularly giving notice to members of the class, which may in turn be related in some instances to the extension of the judgment to the class. See Chafee, supra, at 230–31; Keeffe, Levy & Donovan, supra; *Developments in the law*, supra, 71 Harv. L.Rev. at 937–38; Note, *Binding Effect of Class Actions*, 67 Harv.L.Rev. 1059, 1062–65 (1954); Note, *Federal Class Actions: A Suggested Revision of Rule 23*, 46 Colum.L.Rev. 818, 833–36 (1946); Mich.Gen.Court R. 208.4 (effective Jan. 1, 1963); Idaho R.Civ.P. 23(d); Minn.R.Civ.P. 23.04; N.Dak.R.Civ.P. 23(d).

The amended rule describes in more practical terms the occasions for maintaining class actions; provides that all class actions maintained to the end as such will result in judgments including those whom the court finds to be members of the class, whether or not the judgment is favorable to the class; and refers to the measures which can be taken to assure the fair conduct of these actions.

Subdivision (a) states the prerequisites for maintaining any class action in terms of the numerousness of the class making joinder of the members impracticable, the existence of questions common to the class, and the desired qualifications of the representative parties. See Weinstein, *Revision of Procedure: Some Problems in Class Actions*, 9 Buffalo L.Rev. 433, 458–59 (1960); 2 Barron & Holtzoff, *Federal Practice & Procedure* § 562, at 265, § 572, at 351–52 (Wright

ed. 1961). These are necessary but not sufficient conditions for a class action. See, e.g., *Giordano v. Radio Corp. of Am.*, 183 F.2d 558, 560 (3d Cir.1950); *Zachman v. Erwin*, 186 F.Supp. 681 (S.D.Tex.1959); *Baim & Blank, Inc. v. Warren-Connelly Co., Inc.*, 19 F.R.D. 108 (S.D.N.Y.1956). Subdivision (b) describes the additional elements which in varying situations justify the use of a class action.

Subdivision (b)(1). The difficulties which would be likely to arise if resort were had to separate actions by or against the individual members of the class here furnish the reasons for, and the principal key to, the propriety and value of utilizing the class-action device. The considerations stated under clauses (A) and (B) are comparable to certain of the elements which define the persons whose joinder in an action is desirable as stated in Rule 19(a), as amended. See amended Rule 19(a)(2)(i) and (ii), and the Advisory Committee's Note thereto; Hazard, *Indispensable Party: The Historical Origin of a Procedural Phantom*, 61 Colum.L.Rev. 1254, 1259–60 (1961); cf. 3 Moore, supra, par. 23.08, at 3435.

Clause (A): One person may have rights against, or be under duties toward, numerous persons constituting a class, and be so positioned that conflicting or varying adjudications in lawsuits with individual members of the class might establish incompatible standards to govern his conduct. The class action device can be used effectively to obviate the actual or virtual dilemma which would thus confront the party opposing the class. The matter has been stated thus: "The felt necessity for a class action is greatest when the courts are called upon to order or sanction the alteration of the status quo in circumstances such that a large number of persons are in a position to call on a single person to alter the status quo, or to complain if it is altered, and the possibility exists that [the] actor might be called upon to act in inconsistent ways." Louisell & Hazard, *Pleading and Procedure: State and Federal* 719 (1962); see *Supreme Tribe of Ben-Hur v. Cauble*, 255 U.S. 356, 366–67 (1921). To illustrate: Separate actions by individuals against a municipality to declare a bond issue invalid or condition or limit it, to prevent or limit the making of a particular appropriation or to compel or invalidate an assessment, might create a risk of inconsistent or varying determinations. In the same way, individual litigations of the rights and duties of riparian owners, or of landowners' rights and duties respecting a claimed nuisance, could create a possibility of incompatible adjudications. Actions by or against a class provide a ready and fair means of achieving unitary adjudication. See *Maricopa County Mun. Water Con. Dist. v. Looney*, 219 F.2d 529 (9th Cir.1955); *Rank v. Krug*, 142 F.Supp. 1, 154–59 (S.D.Calif.1956), on app., *State of California v. Rank*, 293 F.2d 340, 348 (9th Cir.1961); *Gart v. Cole*, 263 F.2d 244 (2d Cir.1959), cert. denied 359 U.S. 978 (1959); cf. *Martinez v. Maverick Cty. Water Con. & Imp. Dist.*, 219 F.2d 666 (5th Cir.1955); 3 Moore, supra, par. 23.11[2], at 3458–59.

Clause (B): This clause takes in situations where the judgment in a nonclass action by or against an individual member of the class, while not technically concluding the other members, might do so as a practical matter. The vice of an individual action would lie in the fact that the other members of the class, thus practically concluded, would have had no representation in the lawsuit. In an action by policy holders against a fraternal benefit association attacking a financial reorganization of the society, it would hardly have been practical, if indeed it would have been possible, to confine the effects of a validation of the reorganization to the individual plaintiffs. Consequently a class action was called for with adequate representation of all members of the class. See *Supreme Tribe of Ben-Hur v. Cauble*, 255 U.S. 356 (1921); *Waybright v. Columbian Mut. Life Ins. Co.*, 30 F.Supp. 885 (W.D.Tenn.1939); cf. *Smith v. Swormstedt*, 16 How. (57 U.S.) 288 (1853). For much the same reason actions by shareholders to compel the declaration of a dividend[,] the proper recognition and handling of redemption or pre-emption rights, or the like (or actions by the corporation for corresponding declarations of rights), should ordinarily be conducted as class actions, although the matter has been much obscured by the insistence that each shareholder has an individual claim. See *Knapp v. Bankers Securities Corp.*, 17 F.R.D. 245 (E.D.Pa.1954), aff'd, 230 F.2d 717 (3d Cir. 1956); *Giesecke v. Denver Tramway Corp.*, 81 F.Supp. 957 (D.Del.1949); *Zahn v. Transamerica Corp.*, 162 F.2d 36 (3d Cir.1947); *Speed v. Transamerica Corp.*, 100 F.Supp. 461 (D.Del.1951); *Sobel v. Whittier Corp.*, 95 F.Supp. 643 (E.D.Mich.1951), app. dism., 195 F.2d 361 (6th Cir.1952); *Goldberg v. Whittier Corp.*, 111 F.Supp. 382 (E.D.Mich.1953); *Dann v. Studebaker-Packard Corp.*, 288 F.2d 201 (6th Cir. 1961); *Edgerton v. Armour & Co.*, 94 F.Supp. 549 (S.D.Calif.1950); *Ames v. Mengel Co.*, 190 F.2d 344 (2d Cir.1951). (These shareholders' actions are to be distinguished from derivative actions by shareholders dealt with in new Rule 23.1). The same reasoning applies to an action which charges a breach of trust by an indenture trustee or other fiduciary similarly affecting the members of a large class of security holders or other beneficiaries, and which requires an accounting or like measures to restore the subject of the trust. See *Boesenberg v. Chicago T. & T. Co.*, 128 F.2d 245 (7th Cir.1942); *Citizens Banking Co. v. Monticello State Bank*, 143 F.2d 261 (8th Cir.1944); *Redmond v. Commerce Trust Co.*, 144 F.2d 140 (8th Cir.1944), cert. denied, 323 U.S. 776 (1944); cf. *York v. Guaranty Trust Co.*, 143 F.2d 503 (2d Cir.1944), rev'd on grounds not here relevant, 326 U.S. 99 (1945).

In various situations an adjudication as to one or more members of the class will necessarily or probably have an adverse practical effect on the interests of other members who should therefore be represented in the lawsuit. This is plainly the case when claims are made by numerous persons against a fund insufficient to satisfy all claims. A class action by or against representative members to settle the validity of the claims as a whole, or in groups, followed by separate proof of the amount of each valid claim and proportionate distribution of the fund, meets the problem. Cf. *Dickinson v. Burnham*, 197 F.2d 973 (2d Cir.1952), cert. denied, 344 U.S. 875 (1952); 3 Moore, supra, at par. 23.09. The same reasoning applies to an action by a creditor to set aside a fraudulent conveyance by the debtor and to appropriate the property to his claim, when the debtor's assets are insufficient to pay all creditors' claims. See *Heffernan v. Bennett & Armour*, 110 Cal.App.2d 564, 243 P.2d 846 (1952); cf. *City & County of San Francisco v. Market Street Ry.*, 95 Cal.App.2d 648, 213 P.2d 780 (1950). Similar problems, however, can arise in the absence of a fund either present or potential. A negative or mandatory injunction secured by one of a numerous class may disable the opposing party from performing claimed duties toward the other members of the class or materially affect his ability to do so. An adjudication as to movie "clearances and runs" nominally affecting only one exhibitor would often have practical effects on all the exhibitors in the same territorial area. Cf. *United States v. Paramount Pictures, Inc.*, 66 F.Supp. 323, 341–46 (S.D.N.Y. 1946); 334 U.S. 131, 144–48 (1948). Assuming a sufficiently numerous class of exhibitors, a class action would be advisable. (Here representation of subclasses of exhibitors could become necessary; see subdivision (c)(3)(B).)

Subdivision (b)(2). This subdivision is intended to reach situations where a party has taken action or refused to take action with respect to a class, and final relief of an injunctive nature or of a corresponding declaratory nature, settling the legality of the behavior with respect to the class as a whole, is appropriate. Declaratory relief "corresponds" to injunctive relief when as a practical matter it affords injunctive relief or serves as a basis for later injunctive relief. The subdivision does not extend to cases in which the appropriate final relief relates exclusively or predominantly to money damages. Action or inaction is directed to a class within the meaning of this subdivision even if it has taken effect or is threatened only as to one or a few members of the class, provided it is based on grounds which have general application to the class.

Illustrative are various actions in the civil-rights field where a party is charged with discriminating unlawfully against a class, usually one whose members are incapable of specific enumeration. See *Potts v. Flax*, 313 F.2d 284 (5th Cir. 1963); *Bailey v. Patterson*, 323 F.2d 201 (5th Cir. 1963), cert. denied, 376 U.S. 910, (1964); *Brunson v. Board of Trustees of School District No. 1, Clarendon Cty., S.C.*, 311 F.2d 107 (4th Cir. 1962), cert. denied, 373 U.S. 933 (1963); *Green v. School Bd. of Roanoke, Va.*, 304 F.2d 118 (4th Cir. 1962); *Orleans Parish School Bd. v. Bush*, 242 F.2d 156 (5th Cir. 1957), cert. denied, 354 U.S. 921 (1957); *Mannings v. Board of Public Inst. of Hillsborough County, Fla.*, 277 F.2d 370 (5th Cir. 1960); *Northcross v. Board of Ed. of City of Memphis*, 302 F.2d 818 (6th Cir. 1962), cert. denied, 370 U.S. 944 (1962); *Frasier v. Board of Trustees of Univ. of N.C.*, 134 F.Supp. 589 (M.D.N.C.1955, 3-judge court), aff'd 350 U.S. 979 (1956). Subdivision (b)(2) is not limited to civil-rights cases. Thus an action looking to specific or declaratory relief could be brought by a numerous class of purchasers, say retailers of a given description, against a seller alleged to have undertaken to sell to that class at prices higher than those set for other purchasers, say retailers of another description, when the applicable law forbids such a pricing differential. So also a patentee of a machine, charged with selling or licensing the machine on condition that purchasers or licensees also purchase or obtain licenses to use an ancillary unpatented machine, could be sued on a class basis by a numerous group of purchasers or licensees, or by a numerous group of competing sellers or licensors of the unpatented machine, to test the legality of the "tying" condition.

Subdivision (b)(3). In the situations to which this subdivision relates, class-action treatment is not as clearly called for as in those described above, but it may nevertheless be convenient and desirable depending upon the particular facts. Subdivision (b)(3) encompasses those cases in which a class action would achieve economies of time, effort, and expense, and promote uniformity of decision as to persons similarly situated, without sacrificing procedural fairness or bringing about other undesirable results. Cf. Chafee, supra, at 201.

The court is required to find, as a condition of holding that a class action may be maintained under this subdivision, that the questions common to the class predominate over the questions affecting individual members. It is only where this predominance exists that economies can be achieved by means of the class-action device. In this view, a fraud perpetrated on numerous persons by the use of similar misrepresentations may be an appealing situation for a class action, and it may remain so despite the need, if liability is found, for separate determination of the damages suffered by individuals within the class. On the other hand, although having some common core, a fraud case may be unsuited for treatment as a class action if there was material variation in the representations made or in the kinds or degrees of reliance by the persons to whom they were addressed. See *Oppenheimer v. F. J. Young & Co., Inc.*, 144 F.2d 387 (2d Cir. 1944); *Miller v. National City Bank of N.Y.*, 166 F.2d 723 (2d Cir. 1948); and for like problems in other contexts, see *Hughes v. Encyclopaedia Britannica*, 199 F.2d 295 (7th Cir. 1952); *Sturgeon v. Great Lakes Steel Corp.*, 143 F.2d 819 (6th Cir. 1944). A "mass accident" resulting in injuries to numerous persons is ordinarily not appropriate for a class action because of the likelihood that significant questions, not only of damages but of liability and defenses of liability, would be present, affecting the individuals in different ways. In these circumstances an action conducted nominally as a class action would degenerate in practice into multiple lawsuits separately tried. See *Pennsylvania R.R. v. United States*, 111 F.Supp. 80 (D.N.J.1953); cf. Weinstein, supra, 9 Buffalo L.Rev. at 469. Private damage claims by numerous individuals arising out of concerted antitrust violations may or may not involve predominating common questions. See *Union Carbide & Carbon Corp. v. Nisley*, 300 F.2d 561 (10th Cir. 1961), pet. cert. dism., 371 U.S. 801 (1963); cf. *Weeks v. Bareco Oil Co.*, 125 F.2d 84 (7th Cir. 1941); *Kainz v. Anheuser-Busch, Inc.*, 194 F.2d 737 (7th Cir. 1952); *Hess v. Anderson, Clayton & Co.*, 20 F.R.D. 466 (S.D.Calif.1957).

That common questions predominate is not itself sufficient to justify a class action under subdivision (b)(3), for another method of handling the litigious situation may be available which has greater practical advantages. Thus one or more actions agreed to by the parties as test or model actions may be preferable to a class action; or it may prove feasible and preferable to consolidate actions. Cf. Weinstein, supra, 9 Buffalo L.Rev. at 438–54. Even when a number of separate actions are proceeding simultaneously, experience shows that the burdens on the parties and the courts can sometimes be reduced by arrangements for avoiding repetitious discovery or the like. Currently the Coordinating Committee on Multiple Litigation in the United States District Courts (a subcommittee of the Committee on Trial Practice and Technique of the Judicial Conference of the United States) is charged with developing methods for expediting such massive litigation. To reinforce the point that the court with the aid of the parties ought to assess the relative advantages of alternative procedures for handling the total controversy, subdivision (b)(3) requires, as a further condition of maintaining the class action, that the court shall find that that procedure is "superior" to the others in the particular circumstances.

Factors (A)–(D) are listed, non-exhaustively, as pertinent to the findings. The court is to consider the interests of individual members of the class in controlling their own litigations and carrying them on as they see fit. See *Weeks v. Bareco Oil Co.*, 125 F.2d 84, 88–90, 93–94 (7th Cir. 1941) (anti-trust action); see also *Pentland v. Dravo Corp.*, 152 F.2d 851 (3d Cir. 1945), and Chafee, supra, at 273–75,

regarding policy of Fair Labor Standards Act of 1938, § 16(b), 29 U.S.C. § 216(b), prior to amendment by Portal-to-Portal Act of 1947, § 5(a). [The present provisions of 29 U.S.C. § 216(b) are not intended to be affected by Rule 23, as amended.]

In this connection the court should inform itself of any litigation actually pending by or against the individuals. The interests of individuals in conducting separate lawsuits may be so strong as to call for denial of a class action. On the other hand, these interests may be theoretic rather than practical; the class may have a high degree of cohesion and prosecution of the action through representatives would be quite unobjectionable, or the amounts at stake for individuals may be so small that separate suits would be impracticable. The burden that separate suits would impose on the party opposing the class, or upon the court calendars, may also fairly be considered. (See the discussion, under subdivision (c)(2) below, of the right of members to be excluded from the class upon their request.)

Also pertinent is the question of the desirability of concentrating the trial of the claims in the particular forum by means of a class action, in contrast to allowing the claims to be litigated separately in forums to which they would ordinarily be brought. Finally, the court should consider the problems of management which are likely to arise in the conduct of a class action.

Subdivision (c)(1). In order to give clear definition to the action, this provision requires the court to determine, as early in the proceedings as may be practicable, whether an action brought as a class action is to be so maintained. The determination depends in each case on satisfaction of the terms of subdivision (a) and the relevant provisions of subdivision (b).

An order embodying a determination can be conditional; the court may rule, for example, that a class action may be maintained only if the representation is improved through intervention of additional parties of a stated type. A determination once made can be altered or amended before the decision on the merits if, upon fuller development of the facts, the original determination appears unsound. A negative determination means that the action should be stripped of its character as a class action. See subdivision (d)(4). Although an action thus becomes a nonclass action, the court may still be receptive to interventions before the decision on the merits so that the litigation may cover as many interests as can be conveniently handled; the questions whether the intervenors in the nonclass action shall be permitted to claim "ancillary" jurisdiction or the benefit of the date of the commencement of the action for purposes of the statute of limitations are to be decided by reference to the laws governing jurisdiction and limitations as they apply in particular contexts.

Whether the court should require notice to be given to members of the class of its intention to make a determination, or of the order embodying it, is left to the court's discretion under subdivision (d)(2).

Subdivision (c)(2) makes special provision for class actions maintained under subdivision (b)(3). As noted in the discussion of the latter subdivision, the interests of the individuals in pursing their own litigations may be so strong here as to warrant denial of a class action altogether. Even when a class action is maintained under subdivision (b)(3), this individual interest is respected. Thus the court is required to direct notice to the members of the class of the right of each member to be excluded from the class upon his request. A member who does not request exclusion may, if he wishes, enter an appearance in the action through his counsel; whether or not he does so, the judgment in the action will embrace him.

The notice[,] setting forth the alternatives open to the members of the class, is to be the best practicable under the circumstances, and shall include individual notice to the members who can be identified through reasonable effort. (For further discussion of this notice, see the statement under subdivision (d)(2) below.)

Subdivision (c)(3). The judgment in a class action maintained as such to the end will embrace the class, that is, in a class action under subdivision (b)(1) or (b)(2), those found by the court to be class members; in a class action under subdivision (b)(3), those to whom the notice prescribed by subdivision (c)(2) was directed, excepting those who requested exclusion or who are ultimately found by the court not to be members of the class. The judgment has this scope whether it is favorable or unfavorable to the class. In a (b)(1) or (b)(2) action the judgment "describes" the members of the class, but need not specify the individual members; in a (b)(3) action the judgment "specifies" the individual members who have been identified and described the others.

Compare subdivision (c)(4) as to actions conducted as class actions only with respect to particular issues. Where the class-action character of the lawsuit is based solely on the existence of a "limited fund," the judgment, while extending to all claims of class members against the fund, has ordinarily left unaffected the personal claims of nonappearing members against the debtor. See 3 Moore, supra, par. 23.11[4].

Hitherto, in a few actions conducted as "spurious" class actions and thus nominally designed to extend only to parties and others intervening before the determination of liability, courts have held or intimated that class members might be permitted to intervene after a decision on the merits favorable to their interests, in order to secure the benefits of the decision for themselves, although they would presumably be unaffected by an unfavorable decision. See, as to the propriety of this so-called "one-way" intervention in "spurious" actions, the conflicting views expressed in *Union Carbide & Carbon Corp. v. Nisley,* 300 F.2d 561 (10th Cir. 1961), pet. cert. dism., 371 U.S. 801 (1963); *York v. Guaranty Trust Co.,* 143 F.2d 503, 529 (2d Cir. 1944), rev'd on grounds not here relevant, 326 U.S. 99 (1945); *Pentland v. Dravo Corp.,* 152 F.2d 851, 856 (3d Cir. 1945); *Speed v. Transamerica Corp.,* 100 F.Supp. 461, 463 (D.Del.1951); *State Wholesale Grocers v. Great Atl. & Pac. Tea Co.,* 24 F.R.D. 510 (N.D.Ill.1959); *Alabama Ind. Serv. Stat. Assn. v. Shell Pet. Corp.,* 28 F.Supp. 386, 390 (N.D.Ala.1939); *Tolliver v. Cudahy Packing Co.,* 39 F.Supp. 337, 339 (E.D.Tenn.1941); Kalven & Rosenfield, supra, 8 U. of Chi.L.Rev. 684 (1941); Comment, 53 Nw.U.L.Rev. 627, 632–33 (1958); *Developments in the Law,* supra, 71 Harv.L.Rev. at 935; 2 Barron & Holtzoff, supra, § 568; but cf. *Lockwood v. Hercules Powder Co.,* 7 F.R.D. 24, 28–29 (W.D.Mo.1947); *Abram v. San Joaquin Cotton Oil Co.,* 46 F.Supp. 969, 976–77 (S.D.Calif.1942); Chafee, supra, at 280, 285; 3 Moore, supra, par. 23.12, at 3476. Under proposed subdivision (c)(3), one-way intervention is excluded; the action will have been early determined to be a class or nonclass action, and in the former case the judgment, whether or not favorable, will include the class, as above stated.

Although thus declaring that the judgment in a class action includes the class, as defined, subdivision (c)(3) does not disturb the recognized principle that the court conducting the action cannot predetermine the *res judicata* effect of the judgment; this can be tested only in a subsequent action. See Restatement, Judgments § 86, comment (h), § 116 (1942). The court, however, in framing the judgment in any suit brought as a class action, must decide what its extent or coverage shall be, and if the matter is carefully considered, questions of *res judicata* are less likely to be raised at a later time and if raised will be more satisfactorily answered. See Chafee, supra, at 294; Weinstein, supra, 9 Buffalo L.Rev. at 460.

Subdivision (c)(4). This provision recognizes that an action may be maintained as a class action as to particular issues only. For example, in a fraud or similar case the action may retain its "class" character only through the adjudication of liability to the class; the members of the class may thereafter be required to come in individually and prove the amounts of their respective claims.

Two or more classes may be represented in a single action. Where a class is found to include subclasses divergent in interest, the class may be divided correspondingly, and each subclass treated as a class.

Subdivision (d) is concerned with the fair and efficient conduct of the action and lists some types of orders which may be appropriate.

The court should consider how the proceedings are to be arranged in sequence, and what measures should be taken to simplify the proof and argument. See subdivision (d)(1). The orders resulting from this consideration, like the others referred to in subdivision (d), may be combined with a pretrial order under Rule 16, and are subject to modification as the case proceeds.

Subdivision (d)(2) sets out a non-exhaustive list of possible occasions for orders requiring notice to the class. Such notice is not a novel conception. For example, in "limited fund" cases, members of the class have been notified to present individual claims after the basic class decision. Notice has gone to members of a class so that they might express any opposition to the representation, see *United States v. American Optical Co.,* 97 F.Supp. 66 (N.D.Ill.1951), and 1950–51 CCH Trade Cases 64573–74 (par. 62869); cf. *Weeks v. Bareco Oil Co.,* 125 F.2d 84, 94 (7th Cir. 1941), and notice may encourage interventions to improve the representation of the class. Cf. *Oppenheimer v. F. J. Young & Co.,* 144 F.2d 387 (2d Cir. 1944). Notice has been used to poll members on a proposed modification of a consent decree. See record in *Sam Fox Publishing Co. v. United States,* 366 U.S. 683 (1961).

Subdivision (d)(2) does not require notice at any stage, but rather calls attention to its availability and invokes the court's discretion. In the degree that there is cohesiveness or unity in the class and the representation is effective, the need for notice to the class will tend toward a minimum. These indicators suggest that notice under subdivision (d)(2) may be particularly useful and advisable in certain class actions maintained under subdivision (b)(3), for example, to permit members of the class to object to the representation. Indeed, under subdivision (c)(2), notice must be ordered, and is not merely discretionary, to give the members in a subdivision (b)(3) class action an opportunity to secure exclusion from the class. This mandatory notice pursuant to subdivision (c)(2), together with any discretionary notice which the court may find it advisable to give under subdivision (d)(2), is designed to fulfill requirements of due process to which the class action procedure is of course subject. See *Hansberry v. Lee*, 311 U.S. 32 (1940); *Mullane v. Central Hanover Bank & Trust Co.*, 339 U.S. 306 (1950); cf. *Dickinson v. Burnham*, 197 F.2d 973, 979 (2d Cir. 1952), and studies cited at 979 in 4; see also *All American Airways, Inc. v. Elderd*, 209 F.2d 247, 249 (2d Cir. 1954); *Gart v. Cole*, 263 F.2d 244, 248–49 (2d Cir. 1959), cert. denied, 359 U.S. 978 (1959).

Notice to members of the class, whenever employed under amended Rule 23, should be accommodated to the particular purpose but need not comply with the formalities for service of process. See Chafee, supra, at 230–31; *Brendle v. Smith*, 7 F.R.D. 119 (S.D.N.Y.1946). The fact that notice is given at one stage of the action does not mean that it must be given at subsequent stages. Notice is available fundamentally "for the protection of the members of the class or otherwise for the fair conduct of the action" and should not be used merely as a device for the undesirable solicitation of claims. See the discussion in *Cherner v. Transitron Electronic Corp.*, 201 F.Supp. 934 (D.Mass.1962); *Hormel v. United States*, 17 F.R.D. 303 (S.D.N.Y.1955).

In appropriate cases the court should notify interested government agencies of the pendency of the action or of particular steps therein.

Subdivision (d)(3) reflects the possibility of conditioning the maintenance of a class action, e.g., on the strengthening of the representation, see subdivision (c)(1) above; and recognizes that the imposition of conditions on intervenors may be required for the proper and efficient conduct of the action.

As to orders under subdivision (d)(4), see subdivision (c)(1) above.

Subdivision (e) requires approval of the court, after notice, for the dismissal or compromise of any class action.

1987 Amendment

The amendments are technical. No substantive change is intended.

1998 Amendments

Subdivision (f). This permissive interlocutory appeal provision is adopted under the power conferred by 28 U.S.C. § 1292(e). Appeal from an order granting or denying class certification is permitted in the sole discretion of the court of appeals. No other type of Rule 23 order is covered by this provision. The court of appeals is given unfettered discretion whether to permit the appeal, akin to the discretion exercised by the Supreme Court in acting on a petition for certiorari. This discretion suggests an analogy to the provision in 28 U.S.C. § 1292(b) for permissive appeal on certification by a district court. Subdivision (f), however, departs from the § 1291(b) model in two significant ways. It does not require that the district court certify the certification ruling for appeal, although the district court often can assist the parties and court of appeals by offering advice on the desirability of appeal. And it does not include the potentially limiting requirements of § 1292(b) that the district court order "involve[] a controlling question of law as to which there is substantial ground for difference of opinion and that an immediate appeal from the order may materially advance the ultimate termination of the litigation.

The courts of appeals will develop standards for granting review that reflect the changing areas of uncertainty in class litigation. The Federal Judicial Center study supports the view that many suits with class-action allegations present familiar and almost routine issues that are no more worthy of immediate appeal than many other interlocutory rulings. Yet several concerns justify expansion of present opportunities to appeal. An order denying certification may confront the plaintiff with a situation in which the only sure path to appellate review is by proceeding to final judgment on the merits of an individual claim that, standing alone, is far smaller than the costs of litigation. An order granting certification, on the other hand, may force a defendant to settle rather than incur the costs of defending a class action and run the risk of potentially ruinous liability. These concerns can be met at low cost by establishing in the court of appeals a discretionary power to grant interlocutory review in cases that show appeal-worthy certification issues.

Permission to appeal may be granted or denied on the basis of any consideration that the court of appeals finds persuasive. Permission is most likely to be granted when the certification decision turns on a novel or unsettled question of law, or when, as a practical matter, the decision on certification is likely dispositive of the litigation.

The district court, having worked through the certification decision, often will be able to provide cogent advice on the factors that bear on the decision whether to permit appeal. This advice can be particularly valuable if the certification decision is tentative. Even as to a firm certification decision, a statement of reasons bearing on the probably benefits and costs of immediate appeal can help focus the court of appeals decision, and may persuade the disappointed party that an attempt to appeal would be fruitless.

The 10–day period for seeking permission to appeal is designed to reduce the risk that attempted appeals will disrupt continuing proceedings. It is expected that the courts of appeals will act quickly in making the preliminary determination whether to permit appeal. Permission to appeal does not stay trial court proceedings. A stay should be sought first from the trial court. If the trial court refuses a stay, its action and any explanation of its views should weigh heavily with the court of appeals.

Appellate Rule 5 has been modified to establish the procedure for petitioning for leave to appeal under subdivision (f).

2003 Amendments

Subdivision (c). Subdivision (c) is amended in several respects. The requirement that the court determine whether to certify a class "as soon as practicable after commencement of an action" is replaced by requiring determination "at an early practicable time." The notice provisions are substantially revised.

Paragraph (1). Subdivision (c)(1)(A) is changed to require that the determination whether to certify a class be made "at an early practicable time." The "as soon as practicable" exaction neither reflect s prevailing practice nor captures the many valid reasons that may justify deferring the initial certification decision. See Willging, Hooper & Niemic, *Empirical Study of Class Actions in Four Federal District Courts: Final Report to the Advisory Committee on Civil Rules 26–36* (Federal Judicial Center 1996).

Time may be needed to gather information necessary to make the certification decision. Although an evaluation of the probable outcome on the merits is not properly part of the certification decision, discovery in aid of the certification decision often includes information required to identify the nature of the issues that actually will be presented at trial. In this sense it is appropriate to conduct controlled discovery into the "merits," limited to those aspects relevant to making the certification decision on an informed basis. Active judicial supervision may be required to achieve the most effective balance that expedites an informed certification determination without forcing an artificial and ultimately wasteful division between "certification discovery" and "merits discovery." A critical need is to determine how the case will be tried. An increasing number of courts require a party requesting class certification to present a "trial plan" that describes the issues likely to be presented at trial and tests whether they are susceptible of class-wide proof. See Manual For Complex Litigation Third, § 21.213, p. 44; § 30.11, p. 214; § 30.12, p. 215.

Other considerations may affect the timing of the certification decision. The party opposing the class may prefer to win dismissal or summary judgment as to the individual plaintiffs without certification and without binding the class that might have been certified. Time may be needed to explore designation of class counsel under Rule 23(g), recognizing that in many cases the need to progress toward the certification determination may require designation of interim counsel under Rule 23(g)(2)(A).

Although many circumstances may justify deferring the certification decision, active management may be necessary to ensure that the certification decision is not unjustifiably delayed.

Subdivision (c)(1)(C) reflects two amendments. The provision that a class certification "may be conditional" is deleted. A court that is not satisfied that the requirements of Rule 23 have been met should refuse certification until they have been met. The provision that permits alteration or amendment of an order granting or denying class certification is amended to set the cut-off point at final judgment rather than "the decision on the merits." This change avoids the possible ambiguity in referring to "the decision on the merits." Following a determination of liability, for example, proceedings to define the remedy may demonstrate the need to amend the class definition or subdivide the class. In this setting the final judgment concept is pragmatic. It is not the same as the concept used for appeal purposes, but it should be flexible, particularly in protracted litigation.

The authority to amend an order under Rule 23(c)(1) before final judgment does not restore the practice of "one-way intervention" that was rejected by the 1966 revision of Rule 23. A determination of liability after certification, however, may show a need to amend the class definition. Decertification may be warranted after further proceedings.

If the definition of a class certified under Rule 23(b)(3) is altered to include members who have not been afforded notice and an opportunity to request exclusion, notice—including an opportunity to request exclusion—must be directed to the new class members under Rule 23(c)(2)(B).

Paragraph (2). The first change made in Rule 23(c)(2) is to call attention to the court's authority—already established in part by Rule 23(d)(2)—to direct notice of certification to a Rule 23(b)(1) or (b)(2) class. The present rule expressly requires notice only in actions certified under Rule 23(b)(3). Members of classes certified under Rules 23(b)(1) or (b)(2) have interests that may deserve protection by notice.

The authority to direct notice to class members in a (b)(1) or (b)(2) class action should be exercised with care. For several reasons, there may be less need for notice than in a (b)(3) class action. There is no right to request exclusion from a (b)(1) or (b)(2) class. The characteristics of the class may reduce the need for formal notice. The cost of providing notice, moreover, could easily cripple actions that do not seek damages. The court may decide not to direct notice after balancing the risk that notice costs may deter the pursuit of class relief against the benefits of notice.

When the court does direct certification notice in a (b)(1) or (b)(2) class action, the discretion and flexibility established by subdivision (c)(2)(A) extend to the method of giving notice. Notice facilitates the opportunity to participate. Notice calculated to reach a significant number of class members often will protect the interests of all. Informal methods may prove effective. A simple posting in a place visited by many class members, directing attention to a source of more detailed information, may suffice. The court should consider the costs of notice in relation to the probable reach of inexpensive methods.

If a Rule 23(b)(3) class is certified in conjunction with a (b)(2) class, the (c)(2)(B) notice requirements must be satisfied as to the (b)(3) class.

The direction that class-certification notice be couched in plain, easily understood language is a reminder of the need to work unremittingly at the difficult task of communicating with class members. It is difficult to provide information about most class actions that is both accurate and easily understood by class members who are not themselves lawyers. Factual uncertainty, legal complexity, and the complication of class-action procedure raise the barriers high. The Federal Judicial Center has created illustrative clear-notice forms that provide a helpful starting point for actions similar to those described in the forms.

Subdivision (e). Subdivision (e) is amended to strengthen the process of reviewing proposed class-action settlements. Settlement may be a desirable means of resolving a class action. But court review and approval are essential to assure adequate representation of class members who have not participated in shaping the settlement.

Paragraph (1). Subdivision (e)(1)(A) expressly recognizes the power of a class representative to settle class claims, issues, or defenses.

Rule 23(e)(1)(A) resolves the ambiguity in former Rule 23(e)'s reference to dismissal or compromise of "a class action." That language could be—and at times was—read to require court approval of settlements with putative class representatives that resolved only individual claims. See Manual for Complex Litigation Third, § 30.41. The new rule requires approval only if the claims, issues, or defenses of a certified class are resolved by a settlement, voluntary dismissal, or compromise.

Subdivision (e)(1)(B) carries forward the notice requirement of present Rule 23(e) when the settlement binds the class through claim or issue preclusion; notice is not required when the settlement binds only the individual class representatives. Notice of a settlement binding on the class is required either when the settlement follows class certification

---

or when the decisions on certification and settlement proceed simultaneously.

Reasonable settlement notice may require individual notice in the manner required by Rule 23(c)(2)(B) for certification notice to a Rule 23(b)(3) class. Individual notice is appropriate, for example, if class members are required to take action—such as filing claims—to participate in the judgment, or if the court orders a settlement opt-out opportunity under Rule 23(e)(3).

Subdivision (e)(1)(C) confirms and mandates the already common practice of holding hearings as part of the process of approving settlement, voluntary dismissal, or compromise that would bind members of a class.

Subdivision (e)(1)(C) states the standard for approving a proposed settlement that would bind class members. The settlement must be fair, reasonable, and adequate. A helpful review of many factors that may deserve consideration is provided by *In re: Prudential Ins. Co. America Sales Practice Litigation Agent Actions,* 148 F.3d 283, 316–324 (3d Cir. 1998). Further guidance can be found in the Manual for Complex Litigation.

The court must make findings that support the conclusion that the settlement is fair, reasonable, and adequate. The findings must be set out in sufficient detail to explain to class members and the appellate court the factors that bear on applying the standard.

Settlement review also may provide an occasion to review the cogency of the initial class definition. The terms of the settlement themselves, or objections, may reveal divergent interests of class members and demonstrate the need to redefine the class or to designate subclasses. Redefinition of a class certified under Rule 23(b)(3) may require notice to new class members under Rule 23(c)(2)(B). See Rule 23(c)(1)(C).

Paragraph (2). Subdivision (e)(2) requires parties seeking approval of a settlement, voluntary dismissal, or compromise under Rule 23(e)(1) to file a statement identifying any agreement made in connection with the settlement. This provision does not change the basic requirement that the parties disclose all terms of the settlement or compromise that the court must approve under Rule 23(e)(1). It aims instead at related undertakings that, although seemingly separate, may have influenced the terms of the settlement by trading away possible advantages for the class in return for advantages for others. Doubts should be resolved in favor of identification.

Further inquiry into the agreements identified by the parties should not become the occasion for discovery by the parties or objectors. The court may direct the parties to provide to the court or other parties a summary or copy of the full terms of any agreement identified by the parties. The court also may direct the parties to provide a summary or copy of any agreement not identified by the parties that the court considers relevant to its review of a proposed settlement. In exercising discretion under this rule, the court may act in steps, calling first for a summary of any agreement that may have affected the settlement and then for a complete version if the summary does not provide an adequate basis for review. A direction to disclose a summary or copy of an agreement may raise concerns of confidentiality. Some agreements may include information that merits protection against general disclosure. And the court must provide an opportunity to claim work-product or other protections.

Paragraph (3). Subdivision (e)(3) authorizes the court to refuse to approve a settlement unless the settlement affords class members a new opportunity to request exclusion from a class certified under Rule 23(b)(3) after settlement terms are known. An agreement by the parties themselves to permit class members to elect exclusion at this point by the settlement agreement may be one factor supporting approval of the settlement. Often there is an opportunity to opt out at this point because the class is certified and settlement is reached in circumstances that lead to simultaneous notice of certification and notice of settlement. In these cases, the basic opportunity to elect exclusion applies without further complication. In some cases, particularly if settlement appears imminent at the time of certification, it may be possible to achieve equivalent protection by deferring notice and the opportunity to elect exclusion until actual settlement terms are known. This approach avoids the cost and potential confusion of providing two notices and makes the single notice more meaningful. But notice should not be delayed unduly after certification in the hope of settlement.

Rule 23(e)(3) authorizes the court to refuse to approve a settlement unless the settlement affords a new opportunity to elect exclusion in a case that settles after a certification decision if the earlier opportunity to elect exclusion provided with the certification notice has expired by the time of the settlement notice. A decision to remain in the class is likely to be more carefully considered and is better informed when settlement terms are known.

The opportunity to request exclusion from a proposed settlement is limited to members of a (b)(3) class. Exclusion may be requested only by individual class members; no class member may purport to opt out other class members by way of another class action.

The decision whether to approve a settlement that does not allow a new opportunity to elect exclusion is confided to the court's discretion. The court may make this decision before directing notice to the class under Rule 23(e)(1)(B) or after the Rule 23(e)(1)(C) hearing. Many factors may influence the court's decision. Among these are changes in the information available to class members since expiration of the first opportunity to request exclusion, and the nature of the individual class members' claims.

The terms set for permitting a new opportunity to elect exclusion from the proposed settlement of a Rule 23(b)(3) class action may address concerns of potential misuse. The court might direct, for example, that class members who elect exclusion are bound by rulings on the merits made before the settlement was proposed for approval. Still other terms or conditions may be appropriate.

Paragraph (4). Subdivision (e)(4) confirms t he right of class members to object to a proposed settlement, voluntary dismissal, or compromise. The right is defined in relation to a disposition that, because it would bind the class, requires court approval under subdivision (e)(1)(C).

Subdivision (e)(4)(B) requires court approval for withdrawal of objections made under subdivision (e)(4)(A). Review follows automatically if the objections are withdrawn on terms that lead to modification of the settlement with the class. Review also is required if the objector formally withdraws the objections. If the objector simply abandons pursuit of the objection, the court may inquire into the circumstances.

Approval under paragraph (4)(B) may be given or denied with little need for further inquiry if the objection and the disposition go only to a protest that the individual treatment afforded the objector under the proposed settlement is unfair because of factors that distinguish the objector from other class members. Different considerations may apply if the objector has protested that the proposed settlement is not fair, reasonable, or adequate on grounds that apply generally to a class or subclass. Such objections, which purport to represent class-wide interests, may augment the opportunity for obstruction or delay. If such objections are surrendered on terms that do not affect the class settlement or the objector's participation in the class settlement, the court often can approve withdrawal of the objections without elaborate inquiry.

Once an objector appeals, control of the proceeding lies in the court of appeals. The court of appeals may undertake review and approval of a settlement with the objector, perhaps as part of appeal settlement procedures, or may remand to the district court to take advantage of the district court's familiarity with the action and settlement.

Subdivision (g). Subdivision (g) is new. It responds to the reality that the selection and activity of class counsel are often critically important to the successful handling of a class action. Until now, courts have scrutinized proposed class counsel as well as the class representative under Rule 23(a)(4). This experience has recognized the importance of judicial evaluation of the proposed lawyer for the class, and this new subdivision builds on that experience rather than introducing an entirely new element into the class certification process. Rule 23(a)(4) will continue to call for scrutiny of the proposed class representative, while this subdivision will guide the court in assessing proposed class counsel as part of the certification decision. This subdivision recognizes the importance of class counsel, states the obligation to represent the interests of the class, and provides a framework for selection of class counsel. The procedure and standards for appointment vary depending on whether there are multiple applicants to be class counsel. The new subdivision also provides a method by which the court may make directions from the outset about the potential fee award to class counsel in the event the action is successful.

Paragraph (1) sets out the basic requirement that class counsel be appointed if a class is certified and articulates the obligation of class counsel to represent the interests of the class, as opposed to the potentially conflicting interests of individual class members. It also sets out the factors the court should consider in assessing proposed class counsel.

Paragraph (1)(A) requires that the court appoint class counsel to represent the class. Class counsel must be appointed for all classes, including each subclass that the court certifies to represent divergent interests.

Paragraph (1)(A) does not apply if "a statute provides otherwise." This recognizes that provisions of the Private Securities Litigation Reform Act of 1995, Pub. L. No. 104–67, 109 Stat. 737 (1995) (codified in various sections of 15 U.S.C.), contain directives that bear on selection of a lead plaintiff and the retention of counsel. This subdivision does not purport to supersede or to affect the interpretation of those provisions, or any similar provisions of other legislation.

Paragraph 1(B) recognizes t hat t he primary responsibility of class counsel, resulting from appointment as class counsel, is to represent the best interests of the class. The rule thus establishes the obligation of class counsel, an obligation that may be different from the customary obligations of counsel to individual clients. Appointment as class counsel means that the primary obligation of counsel is to the class rather than to any individual members of it. The class representatives do not have an unfettered right to "fire" class counsel. In the same vein, the class representatives cannot command class counsel to accept or reject a settlement proposal. To the contrary, class counsel must determine whether seeking the court's approval of a settlement would be in the best interests of the class as a whole.

Paragraph (1)(C) articulates the basic responsibility of the court to appoint class counsel who will provide the adequate representation called for by paragraph (1)(B). It identifies criteria that must be considered and invites the court to consider any other pertinent matters. Although couched in terms of the court's duty, the listing also informs counsel seeking appointment about the topics that should be addressed in an application for appointment or in the motion for class certification.

The court may direct potential class counsel to provide additional information about the topics mentioned in paragraph (1)(C) or about any other relevant topic. For example, the court may direct applicants to inform the court concerning any agreements about a prospective award of attorney fees or nontaxable costs, as such agreements may sometimes be significant in the selection of class counsel. The court might also direct that potential class counsel indicate how parallel litigation might be coordinated or consolidated with t he action before the court.

The court may also direct counsel to propose terms for a potential award of attorney fees and nontaxable costs. Attorney fee awards are an important feature of class action practice, and attention to this subject from the outset may often be a productive technique. Paragraph (2)(C) therefore authorizes the court to provide directions about attorney fees and costs when appointing class counsel. Because there will be numerous class actions in which this information is not likely to be useful, the court need not consider it in all class actions.

Some information relevant to class counsel appointment may involve matters that include adversary preparation in a way that should be shielded from disclosure to other parties. An appropriate protective order may be necessary to preserve confidentiality.

In evaluating prospective class counsel, the court should weigh all pertinent factors. No single factor should necessarily be determinative in a given case. For example, the resources counsel will commit to the case must be appropriate to its needs, but the court should be careful not to limit consideration t o lawyers with the greatest resources.

If, after review of all applicants, the court concludes that none would be satisfactory class counsel, it may deny class certification, reject all applications, recommend that an application be modified, invite new applications, or make any other appropriate order regarding selection and appointment of class counsel.

Paragraph (2). This paragraph sets out the procedure that should be followed in appointing class counsel. Although it affords substantial flexibility, it provides the framework for appointment of class counsel in all class actions. For counsel who filed the action, the materials submitted in support of the motion for class certification may suffice to justify appointment so long as the information described in paragraph (g)(1)(C) is included. If there are other applicants, they ordinarily would file a formal application detailing their suitability for the position.

In a plaintiff class action the court usually would appoint as class counsel only an attorney or attorneys who have sought appointment. Different considerations may apply in defendant class actions.

The rule states that the court should appoint "class counsel." In many instances, the applicant will be an individual attorney. In other cases, however, an entire firm, or perhaps numerous attorneys who are not otherwise affiliated but are collaborating on the action will apply. No rule of thumb exists to determine when such arrangements are appropriate; the court should be alert to the need for adequate staffing of the case, but also to the risk of overstaffing or an ungainly counsel structure.

Paragraph (2)(A) authorizes the court to designate interim counsel during the pre-certification period if necessary to protect the interests of the putative class. Rule 23(c)(1)(B) directs that the order certifying the class include appointment of class counsel. Before class certification, however, it will usually be important for an attorney to take action to prepare for the certification decision. The amendment to Rule 23(c)(1) recognizes that some discovery is often necessary for that determination. It also may be important to make or respond to motions before certification. Settlement may be discussed before certification. Ordinarily, such work is handled by the lawyer who filed the action. In some cases, however, there may be rivalry or uncertainty that makes formal designation of interim counsel appropriate. Rule 23(g)(2)(A) authorizes the court to designate interim counsel to act on behalf of the putative class before the certification decision is made. Failure to make the formal designation does not prevent the attorney who filed the action from proceeding in it. Whether or not formally designated interim counsel, an attorney who acts on behalf of the class before certification must act in the best interests of the class as a whole. For example, an attorney who negotiates a pre-certification settlement must seek a settlement that is fair, reasonable, and adequate for the class.

Rule 23(c)(1) provides that the court should decide whether to certify the class "at an early practicable time," and directs that class counsel should be appointed in the order certifying the class. In some cases, it may be appropriate for the court to allow a reasonable period after commencement of the action for filing applications to serve as class counsel. The primary ground for deferring appointment would be that there is reason to anticipate competing applications to serve as class counsel. Examples might include instances in which more than one class action has been filed, or in which other attorneys have filed individual actions on behalf of putative class members. The purpose of facilitating competing applications in such a case is to afford the best possible representation for the class. Another possible reason for deferring appointment would be that the initial applicant was found inadequate, but it seems appropriate to permit additional applications rather than deny class certification.

Paragraph (2)(B) states the basic standard the court should use in deciding whether to certify the class and appoint class counsel in the single applicant situation—that the applicant be able to provide the representation called for by paragraph (1)(B) in light of the factors identified in paragraph (1)(C).

If there are multiple adequate applicants, paragraph (2)(B) directs the court to select the class counsel best able to represent the interests of the class. This decision should also be made using the factors outlined in paragraph (1)(C), but in the multiple applicant situation the court is to go beyond scrutinizing the adequacy of counsel and make a comparison of the strengths of the various applicants. As with the decision whether to appoint the sole applicant for the position, no single factor should be dispositive in selecting class counsel in cases in which there are multiple applicants. The fact that a given attorney filed the instant action, for example, might not weigh heavily in the decision if that lawyer had not done significant work identifying or investigating claims. Depending on the nature of the case, one important consideration might be the applicant's existing attorney-client relationship with the proposed class representative.

Paragraph (2)(C) builds on the appointment process by authorizing the court to include provisions regarding attorney fees in the order appointing class counsel. Courts may find it desirable to adopt guidelines for fees or nontaxable costs, or to direct class counsel to report to the court at regular intervals on the efforts undertaken in the action, to facilitate the court's later determination of a reasonable attorney fee.

Subdivision (h). Subdivision (h) is new. Fee awards are a powerful influence on the way attorneys initiate, develop, and conclude class actions. Class action attorney fee awards have heretofore been handled, along with all other attorney fee awards, under Rule 54(d)(2), but that rule is not addressed to the particular concerns of class actions. This subdivision is designed to work in tandem with new subdivision (g) on appointment of class counsel, which may afford an opportunity for the court to provide an early framework for an eventual fee award, or for monitoring the work of class counsel during the pendency of the action.

Subdivision (h) applies to "an action certified as a class action." This includes cases in which there is a simultaneous proposal for class certification and settlement even though technically the class may not be certified unless the court approves the settlement pursuant to review under Rule 23(e). When a settlement is proposed for Rule 23(e) approval, either after certification or with a request for certification, notice to class members about class counsel's fee motion would ordinarily accompany the notice to the class about the settlement proposal itself.

This subdivision does not undertake to create new grounds for an award of attorney fees or nontaxable costs. Instead, it applies when such awards are authorized by law or by agreement of the parties. Against that background, it provides a format for all awards of attorney fees and nontaxable costs in connection with a class action, not only the award to class counsel. In some situations, there may be a basis for making an award to other counsel whose work produced a beneficial result for the class, such as attorneys who acted for the class before certification but were not appointed class counsel, or attorneys who represented objectors to a proposed settlement under Rule 23(e) or to the fee motion of class counsel. Other situations in which fee awards are authorized by law or by agreement of the parties may exist.

This subdivision authorizes an award of "reasonable" attorney fees and nontaxable costs. This is the customary term for measurement of fee awards in cases in which counsel may obtain an award of fees under the "common fund" theory that applies in many class actions, and is used in many fee-shifting statutes. Depending on the circumstances, courts have approached the determination of what is reasonable in different ways. In particular, there is some variation among courts about whether in "common fund" cases the court should use the lodestar or a percentage method of determining what fee is reasonable. The rule does not attempt to resolve the question whether the lodestar or percentage approach should be viewed as preferable.

Active judicial involvement in measuring fee awards is singularly important to the proper operation of the class-action process. Continued reliance on caselaw development of fee-award measures does not diminish the court's responsibility. In a class action, the district court must ensure that the amount and mode of payment of attorney fees are fair and proper whether the fees come from a common fund or are otherwise paid. Even in the absence of objections, the court bears this responsibility.

Courts discharging this responsibility have looked to a variety of factors. One fundamental focus is the result actually achieved for class members, a basic consideration in any case in which fees are sought on the basis of a benefit achieved for class members. The Private Securities Litigation Reform Act of 1995 explicitly makes this factor a cap for a fee award in actions to which it applies. See 15 U.S.C. §§ 77z–1(a)(6); 78u–4(a)(6) (fee award should not exceed a "reasonable percentage of the amount of any damages and prejudgment interest actually paid to the class"). For a percentage approach to fee measurement, results achieved is the basic starting point.

In many instances, the court may need to proceed with care in assessing the value conferred on class members. Settlement regimes that provide for future payments, for example, may not result in significant actual payments to class members. In this connection, the court may need to scrutinize the manner and operation of any applicable claims procedure. In some cases, it may be appropriate to defer some portion of the fee award until actual payouts to class members are known. Settlements involving nonmonetary provisions for class members also deserve careful scrutiny to ensure that these provisions have actual value to the class. On occasion the court's Rule 23(e) review will provide a solid basis for this sort of evaluation, but in any event it is also important to assessing the fee award for the class.

At the same time, it is important to recognize that in some class actions the monetary relief obtained is not the sole determinant of an appropriate attorney fees award. Cf. *Blanchard v. Bergeron*, 489 U.S. 87, 95 (1989) (cautioning in an individual case against an "undesirable emphasis" on "the importance of the recovery of damages in civil rights litigation" that might "shortchange efforts to seek effective injunctive or declaratory relief").

Any directions or orders made by the court in connection with appointing class counsel under Rule 23(g) should weigh heavily in making a fee award under this subdivision.

Courts have also given weight to agreements among the parties regarding the fee motion, and to agreements between class counsel and others about the fees claimed by the motion. Rule 54(d)(2)(B) provides: "If directed by the court, the motion shall also disclose the terms of any agreement with respect to fees to be paid for the services for which claim is made." The agreement by a settling party not to oppose a fee application up to a certain amount, for example, is worthy of consideration, but the court remains responsible to determine a reasonable fee. "Side agreements" regarding fees provide at least perspective pertinent to an appropriate fee award.

In addition, courts may take account of the fees charged by class counsel or other attorneys for representing individual claimants or objectors in the case. In determining a fee for class counsel, the court's objective is to ensure an overall fee that is fair for counsel and equitable within the class. In some circumstances individual fee agreements between class counsel and class members might have provisions inconsistent with those goals, and the court might determine that adjustments in the class fee award were necessary as a result.

Finally, it is important to scrutinize separately the application for an award covering nontaxable costs. If costs were addressed in the order appointing class counsel, those directives should be a presumptive starting point in determining what is an appropriate award.

Paragraph (1). Any claim for an award of attorney fees must be sought by motion under Rule 54(d)(2), which invokes the provisions for timing of appeal in Rule 58 and Appellate Rule 4. Owing to the distinctive features of class action fee motions, however, the provisions of this subdivision control disposition of fee motions in class actions, while Rule 54(d)(2) applies to matters not addressed in this subdivision.

The court should direct when the fee motion must be filed. For motions by class counsel in cases subject to court review of a proposed settlement under 23(e), it would be important to require the filing of at least the initial motion in time for inclusion of information about the motion in the notice to the class about the proposed settlement that is required by Rule 23(e). In cases litigated to judgment, the court might also order class counsel's motion to be filed promptly so that notice to the class under this subdivision (h) can be given.

Besides service of the motion on all parties, notice of class counsel's motion for attorney fees must be "directed to the class in a reasonable manner." Because members of the class have an interest in the arrangements for payment of class counsel whether that payment comes from the class fund or is made directly by another party, notice is required in all instances. In cases in which settlement approval is contemplated under Rule 23(e), notice of class counsel's fee motion should be combined with notice of the proposed settlement, and the provision regarding notice to the class is parallel to the requirements for notice under Rule 23(e). In adjudicated class actions, the court may calibrate the notice to avoid undue expense.

Paragraph (2). A class member and any party from whom payment is sought may object to the fee motion. Other parties—for example, nonsettling defendants—may not object because they lack a sufficient interest in the amount the court awards. The rule does not specify a time limit for making an objection. In setting the date objections are due, the court should provide sufficient time after the full fee motion is on file to enable potential objectors to examine the motion.

The court may allow an objector discovery relevant to the objections. In determining whether to allow discovery, the court should weigh the need for the information against the cost and delay that would attend discovery. See Rule 26(b)(2). One factor in determining whether to authorize discovery is the completeness of the material submitted in support of the fee motion, which depends in part on the fee measurement standard applicable to the case. If the motion provides thorough information, the burden should be on the objector to justify discovery to obtain further information.

Paragraph (3). Whether or not there are formal objections, the court must determine whether a fee award is justified and, if so, set a reasonable fee. The rule does not require a formal hearing in all cases. The form and extent of a hearing depend on the circumstances of the case. The rule does require findings and conclusions under Rule 52(a).

Paragraph (4). By incorporating Rule 54(d)(2), this provision gives the court broad authority to obtain assistance in determining the appropriate amount to award. In deciding whether to direct submission of such questions to a special master or magistrate judge, the court should give appropriate consideration to the cost and delay that such a process might entail.

Rule 23.1.   Derivative Actions by Shareholders

In a derivative action brought by one or more shareholders or members to enforce a right of a corporation or of an unincorporated association, the corporation or association having failed to enforce a right which may properly be asserted by it, the complaint shall be verified and shall allege (1) that the plaintiff was a shareholder or member at the time of the transaction of which the plaintiff complains or that the plaintiff's share or membership thereafter devolved on the plaintiff by operation of law, and (2) that the action is not a collusive one to confer jurisdiction on a court of the United States which it would not otherwise have. The complaint shall also allege with particularity the efforts, if any, made by the plaintiff to obtain the action the plaintiff desires from the directors or comparable authority and, if necessary, from the shareholders or members, and the reasons for the plaintiff's failure to obtain the action or for not making the effort. The derivative action may not be maintained if it appears that the plaintiff does not fairly and adequately represent the interests of the shareholders or members similarly situated in enforcing the right of the corporation or association. The action shall not be dismissed or compromised without the approval of the court, and notice of the proposed dismissal or compromise shall be given to shareholders or members in such manner as the court directs. (Added Feb. 28, 1966, eff. July 1, 1966, and amended Mar. 2, 1987, eff. Aug. 1, 1987.)

ADVISORY COMMITTEE NOTES
1966 Addition

A derivative action by a shareholder of a corporation or by a member of an unincorporated association has distinctive aspects which require the special provisions set forth in the new rule. The next-to-the-last sentence recognizes that the question of adequacy of representation may arise when the plaintiff is one of a group of shareholders or members. Cf. 3 Moore's *Federal Practice*, par. 23.08 (2d ed. 1963).

The court has inherent power to provide for the conduct of the proceedings in a derivative action, including the power to determine the course of the proceedings and require that any appropriate notice be given to shareholders or members.

1987 Amendment

The amendments are technical. No substantive change is intended.

Rule 23.2.   Actions Relating to Unincorporated Associations

An action brought by or against the members of an unincorporated association as a class by naming certain members as representative parties may be maintained only if it appears that the representative parties will fairly and adequately protect the interests of the association and its members. In the conduct of the action the court may make appropriate orders corresponding with those described in Rule 23(d), and the procedure for dismissal or compromise of the action shall correspond with that provided in Rule 23(e). (Added Feb. 28, 1966, eff. July 1, 1966.)

ADVISORY COMMITTEE NOTES
1966 Addition

Although an action by or against representatives of the membership of an unincorporated association has often been viewed as a class action, the real or main purpose of this characterization has been to give "entity treatment" to the association when for formal reasons it cannot sue or be sued as a jural person under Rule 17(b). See Louisell & Hazard, *Pleading and Procedure: State and Federal* 718 (1962); 3 Moore's *Federal Practice*, par. 23.08 (2d ed. 1963); Story, J. in *West v. Randall*, 29 Fed.Cas. 718, 722–23, No. 17,424 (C.C.D.R.I.1820); and, for examples, *Gibbs v. Buck*, 307 U.S. 66 (1939); *Tunstall v. Brotherhood of Locomotive F. & E.*, 148 F.2d 403 (4th Cir. 1945); *Oskoian v. Canuel*, 269 F.2d 311 (1st Cir. 1959). Rule 23.2 deals separately with these actions, referring where appropriate to Rule 23.

Rule 24.   Intervention

(a) Intervention of Right. Upon timely application anyone shall be permitted to intervene in an action: (1) when a statute of the United States confers an unconditional right to intervene; or (2) when the applicant claims an interest relating to the property or transaction which is the subject of the action and the applicant is so situated that the disposition of the action may as a practical matter impair or impede the applicant's ability to protect that interest, unless the applicant's interest is adequately represented by existing parties.

(b) Permissive Intervention. Upon timely application anyone may be permitted to intervene in an action: (1) when a statute of the United States confers a conditional right to intervene; or (2) when an applicant's claim or defense and the main action have a question of law or fact in common. When a party to an action relies for ground of claim or defense upon any statute or executive order administered by a federal or state governmental officer or agency or upon any regulation, order, requirement, or agreement issued or made pursuant to the statute or executive order, the officer or agency upon timely application may be permitted to intervene in the action. In exercising its discretion the court shall consider whether the intervention will unduly delay or prejudice the adjudication of the rights of the original parties.

(c) Procedure. A person desiring to intervene shall serve a motion to intervene upon the parties as provided in Rule 5. The motion shall state the grounds therefor and shall be accompanied by a pleading setting forth the claim or defense for which intervention is sought. The same procedure shall be followed when a statute of the United States gives a right to intervene. When the constitutionality of an act of Congress affecting the public interest is drawn in question in any action in which the United States or an officer, agency, or employee thereof is not a party, the court shall notify the Attorney General of the United States as provided in Title 28, U.S.C. § 2403. When the constitutionality of any statute of a State affecting the public interest is drawn in question in any action in which that State or any agency, officer, or employee thereof is not a party, the court shall notify the attorney general of the State as provided in Title 28, U.S.C. § 2403. A party challenging the constitutionality of legislation should call the attention of the court to its consequential duty, but failure to do so is not a waiver of any constitutional right otherwise timely asserted.

(As amended Dec. 27, 1946, eff. Mar. 19, 1948; Dec. 29, 1948, eff. Oct. 20, 1949; Jan. 21, 1963, eff. July 1, 1963; Feb. 28, 1966, eff. July 1, 1966; Mar. 2, 1987, eff. Aug. 1, 1987; Apr. 30, 1991, eff. Dec. 1, 1991.)

ADVISORY COMMITTEE NOTES

1937 Adoption

The right to intervene given by the following and similar statutes is preserved, but the procedure for its assertion is governed by this rule:

U.S.C., Title 28 former sections:

45a [now 2323] (Special attorneys; participation by Interstate Commerce Commission; intervention) (in certain cases under interstate commerce laws)

48 [now 2322] (Suits to be against United States; intervention by United States)

401 [now 2403] (Intervention by United States; constitutionality of Federal statute)

U.S.C., Title 40:

276a–2(b) [now 3162(a)(2)] (Bonds of contractors for public buildings or works; rights of persons furnishing labor and materials).

Compare with the last sentence of [former] Equity Rule 37 (Parties Generally—Intervention). This rule amplifies and restates the present federal practice at law and in equity. For the practice in admiralty see Admiralty Rules 34 (How Third Party May Intervene) and 42 (Claims Against Proceeds in Registry). See generally Moore and Levi, *Federal Intervention: I The Right to Intervene and Reorganization* (1936), 45 Yale L.J. 565. Under the codes two types of intervention are provided, one for the recovery of specific real or personal property (2 Ohio Gen.Code Ann. (Page, 1926) § 11263; Wyo.Rev.Stat.Ann. (Courtright, 1931) § 89–522), and the other allowing intervention generally when the applicant has an interest in the matter in litigation (1 Colo.Stat.Ann. (1935) Code Civ.Proc. § 22; La.Code Pract. (Dart, 1932) Arts. 389–394; Utah Rev.Stat.Ann. (1933) § 104–3–24). The English intervention practice is based upon various rules and decisions and falls into the two categories of absolute right and discretionary right. For the absolute right see *English Rules Under the Judicature Act* (The Annual Practice, 1937) O. 12, r. 24 (admiralty), r. 25 (land), r. 23 (probate); O. 57, r. 12 (execution); J.A. (1925) §§ 181, 182, 183(2) (divorce); *In re Metropolitan Amalgamated Estates, Ltd.,* (1912) 2 Ch. 497 (receivership); *Wilson v. Church,* 9 Ch.D. 552 (1878) (representative action). For the discretionary right see O. 16, r. 11 (non-joinder) and *Re Fowler,* 142 L.T.Jo. 94 (Ch.1916), *Vavasseur v. Krupp,* 9 Ch.D. 351 (1878) (persons out of the jurisdiction).

1946 Amendment

Note. Subdivision (a). The addition to subdivision (a)(3) covers the situation where property may be in the actual custody of some other officer or agency—such as the Secretary of the Treasury—but the control and disposition of the property is lodged in the court wherein the action is pending.

Subdivision (b). The addition in subdivision (b) permits the intervention of governmental officers or agencies in proper cases and thus avoids exclusionary constructions of the rule. For an example of the latter, see *Matter of Bender Body Co.,* Ref. Ohio 1941, 47 F.Supp. 224, holding that the Administrator of the Office of Price Administration, then acting under the authority of an Executive Order of the President, could not intervene in a bankruptcy proceeding to protest the sale of assets above ceiling prices. Compare, however, *Securities and Exchange Commission v. United States Realty & Improvement Co.,* 1940, 310 U.S. 434, 60 S.Ct. 1044, where permissive intervention of the Commission to protect the public interest in an arrangement proceeding under Chapter XI of the Bankruptcy Act was upheld. See also dissenting opinion in *Securities and Exchange Commission v. Long Island Lighting Co.,* C.C.A.2d 1945, 148 F.2d 252, judgment vacated as moot and case remanded with direction to dismiss complaint, 1945, 325 U.S. 833, 65 S.Ct. 1085. For discussion see Commentary, *Nature of Permissive Intervention Under Rule 24b,* 1940, 3 Fed.Rules Serv. 704; Berger, *Intervention by Public Agencies in Private Litigation in the Federal Courts,* 1940, 50 Yale L.J. 65.

Regarding the construction of subdivision (b)(2), see *Allen Calculators, Inc. v. National Cash Register Co.,* 1944, 64 S.Ct. 905, 322 U.S. 137, 88 L.Ed. 1188.

1948 Amendment

The amendment effective Oct. 20, 1949, substituted the reference to "Title 28, U.S.C.A. § 2403" at the end of subdivision (c) for the reference to "the Act of August 24, 1937, c. 754, § 1."

1963 Amendment

This amendment conforms to the amendment of Rule 5(a). See the Advisory Committee's Note to that amendment.

1966 Amendment

In attempting to overcome certain difficulties which have arisen in the application of present Rule 24(a)(2) and (3), this amendment draws upon the revision of the related Rules 19 (joinder of persons needed for just adjudication) and 23 (class actions), and the reasoning underlying that revision.

Rule 24(a)(3) as amended in 1948 provided for intervention of right where the applicant established that he would be adversely affected by the distribution or disposition of property involved in an action to which he had not been made a party. Significantly, some decided cases virtually disregarded the language of this provision. Thus Professor Moore states: "The concept of a fund has been applied so loosely that it is possible for a court to find a fund in almost any in personam action." 4 Moore's *Federal Practice,* par. 24.09[3], at 55 (2d ed. 1962), and see, e.g., *Formulabs, Inc. v. Hartley Pen Co.,* 275 F.2d 52 (9th Cir.1960). This development was quite natural, for Rule 24(a)(3) was unduly restricted. If an absentee would be substantially affected in a practical sense by the determination made in an action, he should, as a general rule, be entitled to intervene, and his right to do so should not depend on whether there is a fund to be distributed or otherwise disposed of. Intervention of right is here seen to be a kind of counterpart to Rule 19(a)(2)(i) on joinder of persons needed for a just adjudication: where, upon motion of a party in an action, an absentee should be joined so that he may protect his interest which as a practical matter may be substantially impaired by the disposition of the action, he ought to have a right to intervene in the action on his own motion. See Louisell & Hazard, *Pleading and Procedure: State and Federal* 749–50 (1962).

The general purpose of original Rule 24(a)(2) was to entitle an absentee, purportedly represented by a party, to intervene in the action if he could establish with fair probability that the representation was inadequate. Thus, where an action is being prosecuted or defended by a trustee, a beneficiary of the trust should have a right to intervene if he can show that the trustee's representation of his interest probably is inadequate; similarly a member of a class should have the right to intervene in a class action if he can show the inadequacy of the representation of his interest by the representative parties before the court.

Original Rule 24(a)(2), however, made it a condition of intervention that "the applicant is or may be bound by a judgment in the action," and this created difficulties with intervention in class actions. If the "bound" language was read literally in the sense of res judicata, it could defeat intervention in some meritorious cases. A member of a class to whom a judgment in a class action extended by its terms (see Rule 23(c)(3), as amended) might be entitled to show in a later action, when the judgment in the class action was claimed to operate as res judicata against him, that the "representative" in the class action had not in fact adequately represented him. If he could make this showing, the class-action judgment might be held not to bind him. See *Hansberry v. Lee,* 311 U.S. 32 (1940). If a class member sought to intervene in the class action proper, while it was still pending, on grounds of inadequacy of representation, he could be met with the argument: if the representation was in fact inadequate, he would not be "bound" by the judgment when it was subsequently asserted against him as res judicata, hence he was not entitled to intervene; if the representation was in fact adequate, there was no occasion or ground for intervention. See *Sam Fox Publishing Co. v. United States,* 366 U.S. 683 (1961); cf. *Sutphen Estates, Inc. v. United States,* 342 U.S. 19 (1951). This reasoning might be linguistically justified by original Rule 24(a)(2); but it could lead to poor results. Compare the discussion in *International M. & I. Corp. v. Von Clemm,* 301 F.2d 857 (2d Cir.1962); *Atlantic Refining Co. v. Standard Oil Co.,* 304 F.2d 387 (D.C.Cir. 1962). A class member who claims that his "representative" does not adequately represent him, and is able to establish that proposition with sufficient probability, should not be put to the risk of having a judgment entered in the action which by its terms extends to him, and be obliged to test the validity of the judgment as applied to his interest by a later collateral attack. Rather he should, as a general rule, be entitled to intervene in the action.

The amendment provides that an applicant is entitled to intervene in an action when his position is comparable to that of a person under Rule 19(a)(2)(i), as amended, unless his interest is already adequately represented in the action by existing parties. The Rule 19(a)(2)(i) criterion imports practical considerations, and the deletion of the "bound" language similarly frees the rule from undue preoccupation with strict considerations of res judicata.

The representation whose adequacy comes into question under the amended rule is not confined to formal representation like that provided by a trustee for his beneficiary or a representative party in a class action for a member of the class. A party to an action may provide practical representation to the absentee seeking intervention although no such formal relationship exists between them, and the adequacy of this practical representation will then have to be weighed. See *International M. & I. Crop. v. Von Clemm,* and *Atlantic Refining Co. v. Standard Oil Co.,* both supra; *Wolpe v. Poretsky,* 144 F.2d 505 (D.C.Cir.1944), cert. denied, 323 U.S. 777 (1944); cf. *Ford Motor Co. v. Bisanz Bros.,* 249 F.2d 22 (8th Cir.1957); and generally, Annot., 84 A.L.R.2d 1412 (1961).

An intervention of right under the amended rule may be subject to appropriate conditions or restrictions responsive among other things to the requirements of efficient conduct of the proceedings.

1987 Amendment

The amendments are technical. No substantive change is intended.

1991 Amendment

Language is added to bring Rule 24(c) into conformity with the statute cited, resolving some confusion reflected in district court rules. As the text provides, counsel challenging the constitutionality of legislation in an action in which the appropriate government is not a party should call the attention of the court to its duty to notify the appropriate governmental officers. The statute imposes the burden of notification on the court, not the party making the constitutional challenge, partly in order to protect against any possible waiver of constitutional rights by parties inattentive to the need for notice. For this reason, the failure of a party to call the court's attention to the matter cannot be treated as a waiver.

Rule 25. Substitution of Parties

(a) Death.

(1) If a party dies and the claim is not thereby extinguished, the court may order substitution of the proper parties. The motion for substitution may be made by any party or by the successors or representatives of the deceased party and, together with the notice of hearing, shall be served on the parties as provided in Rule 5 and upon persons not parties in the manner provided in Rule 4 for the service of a summons, and may be served in any judicial district. Unless the motion for substitution is made not later than 90 days after the death is suggested upon the record by service of a statement of the fact of the death as provided herein for the service of the motion, the action shall be dismissed as to the deceased party.

(2) In the event of the death of one or more of the plaintiffs or of one or more of the defendants in an action in which the right sought to be enforced survives only to the surviving plaintiffs or only against the surviving defendants, the action does not abate. The death shall be suggested upon the record and the action shall proceed in favor of or against the surviving parties.

(b) Incompetency.
If a party becomes incompetent, the court upon motion served as provided in subdivision (a) of this rule may allow the action to be continued by or against the party's representative.

(c) Transfer of Interest.
In case of any transfer of interest, the action may be continued by or against the original party, unless the court upon motion directs the person to whom the interest is transferred to be substituted in the action or joined with the original party. Service of the motion shall be made as provided in subdivision (a) of this rule.

(d) Public Officers; Death or Separation from Office.

(1) When a public officer is a party to an action in his official capacity and during its pendency dies, resigns, or otherwise ceases to hold office, the action does not abate and the officer's successor is automatically substituted as a party. Proceedings following the substitution shall be in the name of the substituted party, but any misnomer not affecting the substantial rights of the parties shall be disregarded. An order of substitution may be entered at any time, but the omission to enter such an order shall not affect the substitution.

(2) A public officer who sues or is sued in an official capacity may be described as a party by the officer's official title rather than by name; but the court may require the officer's name to be added.

(As amended Dec. 29, 1948, eff. Oct. 20, 1949; Apr. 17, 1961, eff. July 19, 1961; Jan. 21, 1963, eff. July 1, 1963; Mar. 2, 1987, eff. Aug. 1, 1987.)

ADVISORY COMMITTEE NOTES

1937 Adoption

Note to Subdivision (a). 1. The first paragraph of this rule is based upon [former] Equity Rule 45 (Death of Party—Revivor) and U.S.C., Title 28, former § 778 (Death of parties; substitution of executor or administrator). The *scire facias* procedure provided for in the statute cited is superseded and the writ is abolished by Rule 81(b). Paragraph two states the content of U.S.C., Title 28, former § 779 (Death of one of several plaintiffs or defendants). With these two paragraphs compare generally *English Rules Under the Judicature Act* (The Annual Practice, 1937) O. 17, r.r. 1–10.

2. This rule modifies U.S.C., Title 28, [former] §§ 778 (Death of parties; substitution of executor or administrator), 779 (Death of one of several plaintiffs or defendants), and 780 (Survival of actions, suits, or proceedings, etc.), in so far as they differ from it.

Note to Subdivisions (b) and (c). These are a combination and adaptation of N.Y.C.P.A. (1937) § 83 and Calif.Code Civ.Proc. (1937) § 385; see also 4 Nev.Comp.Laws (Hillyer, 1929) § 8561.

Note to Subdivision (d). With the first and last sentences compare U.S.C.A., Title 28, former § 780 (Survival of actions, suits, or proceedings, etc.). With the second sentence of this subdivision compare *Ex parte La Prade*, 1933, 53 S.Ct. 682, 289 U.S. 444, 77 L.Ed. 1311.

1948 Amendment

The amendment effective October 19, 1949, inserted the words, "the Canal Zone, a territory, an insular possession," in the first sentence of subdivision (d), and, in the same sentence, after the phrase "or other governmental agency," deleted the words, "or any other officer specified in the Act of February 13, 1925, c. 229, § 11 (43 Stat. 941), formerly section 780 of this title."

1961 Amendment

Subdivision (d)(1). Present Rule 25(d) is generally considered to be unsatisfactory. 4 Moore's *Federal Practice* ¶25.01[7] (2d ed. 1950); Wright, *Amendments to the Federal Rules: The Function of a Continuing Rules Committee*, 7 Vand.L.Rev. 521, 529 (1954); *Developments in the Law— Remedies Against the United States and Its Officials*, 70 Harv.L.Rev. 827, 931–34 (1957). To require, as a condition of substituting a successor public officer as a party to a pending action, that an application be made with a showing that there is substantial need for continuing the litigation, can rarely serve any useful purpose and fosters a burdensome formality. And to prescribe a short, fixed time period for substitution which cannot be extended even by agreement, see *Snyder v. Buck,* 340 U.S. 15, 19 (1950), with the penalty of dismissal of the action, "makes a trap for unsuspecting litigants which seems unworthy of a great government." *Vibra Brush Corp. v. Schaffer,* 256 F.2d 681, 684 (2d Cir. 1958). Although courts have on occasion found means of undercutting the rule, e.g. *Acheson v. Furusho,* 212 F.2d 284 (9th Cir.1954) (substitution of defendant officer unnecessary on theory that only a declaration of status was sought), it has operated harshly in many instances, e.g. *Snyder v. Buck,* supra; *Poindexter v. Folsom,* 242 F.2d 516 (3d Cir.1957).

Under the amendment, the successor is automatically substituted as a party without an application or showing of need to continue the action. An order of substitution is not required, but may be entered at any time if a party desires or the court thinks fit.

The general term "public officer" is used in preference to the enumeration which appears in the present rule. It comprises Federal, State, and local officers.

The expression "in his official capacity" is to be interpreted in its context as part of a simple procedural rule for substitution; care should be taken not to distort its meaning by mistaken analogies to the doctrine of sovereign immunity from suit or the Eleventh Amendment. The amended rule will apply to all actions brought by public officers for the government, and to any action brought in form against a named officer, but intrinsically against the government or the office or the incumbent thereof whoever he may be from time to time during the action. Thus the amended rule will apply to actions against officers to compel performance of official duties or to obtain judicial review of their orders. It will also apply to actions to prevent officers from acting in excess of their authority or under authority not validly conferred, cf. *Philadelphia Co. v. Stimson,* 223 U.S. 605 (1912), or from enforcing unconstitutional enactments, cf. *Ex parte Young,* 209 U.S. 123 (1908); *Ex parte La Prade,* 289 U.S. 444 (1933). In general it will apply whenever effective relief would call for corrective behavior by the one then having official status and power, rather than one who has lost that status and power through ceasing to hold office. Cf. *Land v. Dollar,* 330 U.S. 731 (1947); *Larson v. Domestic & Foreign Commerce Corp.,* 337 U.S. 682 (1949). Excluded from the operation of the amended rule will be the relatively infrequent actions which are directed to securing money judgments against the named officers enforceable against their personal assets; in these cases Rule 25(a)(1), not Rule 25(d), applies to the question of substitution. Examples are actions against officers seeking to make them pay damages out of their own pockets for defamatory utterances or other misconduct in some way related to the office, see *Barr v. Matteo,* 360 U.S. 564 (1959); *Howard v. Lyons,* 360 U.S. 593 (1959); *Gregoire v. Biddle,* 177 F.2d 579 (2d Cir.1949). cert. denied, 339 U.S. 949 (1950). Another example is the anomalous action for a tax refund against a collector of internal revenue, see *Ignelzi v. Granger,* 16 F.R.D. 517 (W.D.Pa.1955), 28 U.S.C. § 2006, 4 Moore, supra, ¶25.05, p. 531; but see 28 U.S.C. § 1346(a)(1), authorizing the bringing of such suits against the United States rather than the officer.

Automatic substitution under the amended rule, being merely a procedural device for substituting a successor for a past officeholder as a party, is distinct from and does not affect any substantive issues which may be involved in the action. Thus a defense of immunity from suit will remain in the case despite a substitution.

Where the successor does not intend to pursue the policy of his predecessor which gave rise to the lawsuit, it will be open to him, after substitution, as plaintiff to seek voluntary dismissal of the action, or as defendant to seek to have the action dismissed as moot or to take other appropriate steps to avert a judgment or decree. Contrast *Ex parte La Prade,* supra; *Allen v. Regents of the University System,* 304 U.S. 439 (1938); *McGrath v. National Assn. of Mfgrs.,* 344 U.S. 804 (1952); *Danenberg v. Cohen,* 213 F.2d 944 (7th Cir.1954).

As the present amendment of Rule 25(d)(1) eliminates a specified time period to secure substitution of public officers, the reference in Rule 6(b) (regarding enlargement of time) to Rule 25 will no longer apply to these public-officer substitutions.

As to substitution on appeal, the rules of the appellate courts should be consulted.

Subdivision (d)(2). This provision, applicable in "official capacity" cases as described above, will encourage the use of the official title without any mention of the officer individually, thereby recognizing the intrinsic character of the action and helping to eliminate concern with the problem of substitution. If for any reason it seems desirable to add the individual's name, this may be done upon motion or on the court's initiative; thereafter the procedure of amended Rule 25(d)(1) will apply if the individual named ceases to hold office.

For examples of naming the officer or title rather than the officeholder, see *Annot.,* 102 A.L.R. 943, 948–52; *Comment,* 50 Mich.L.Rev. 443, 450 (1952); cf. 26 U.S.C. § 7484. Where an action is brought by or against a board or agency with continuity of existence, it has been often decided that there is no need to name the individual members and substitution is unnecessary when the personnel changes. 4 Moore, supra, ¶25.09, p. 536. The practice encouraged by amended Rule 25(d)(2) is similar.

1963 Amendment

Present Rule 25(a)(1), together with present Rule 6(b), results in an inflexible requirement that an action be dismissed as to a deceased party if substitution is not carried out within a fixed period measured from the time of the death. The hardships and inequities of this unyielding requirement plainly appear from the cases. See, e.g., *Anderson v. Yungkau,* 329 U.S. 482, 67 S.Ct. 428, 91 L.Ed. 436 (1947); *Iovino v. Waterson,* 274 F.2d 41 (1959), cert. denied, *Carlin v. Sovino,* 362 U.S. 949, 80 S.Ct. 860, 4 L.Ed.2d 867 (1960); *Perry v. Allen,* 239 F.2d 107 (5th Cir.1956); *Starnes v. Pennsylvania R.R.,* 26 F.R.D. 625 (E.D.N.Y.), aff'd per curiam, 295 F.2d 704 (2d Cir.1961), cert. denied, 369 U.S. 813, 82 S.Ct. 688, 7 L.Ed.2d 612 (1962); *Zdanok v. Glidden Co.,* 28 F.R.D. 346 (S.D.N.Y.1961). See also 4 Moore's *Federal Practice* ¶25.01[9] (Supp.1960); 2 Barron & Holtzoff, *Federal Practice & Procedure* § 621, at 420–21 (Wright ed.1961).

The amended rule establishes a time limit for the motion to substitute based not upon the time of the death, but rather upon the time information of the death is provided by means of a suggestion of death upon the record, i.e. service of a statement of the fact of the death. Cf. Ill.Ann.Stat., c. 110, § 54(2) (Smith-Hurd 1956). The motion may not be made later than 90 days after the service of the statement unless the period is extended pursuant to Rule 6(b), as amended. See the Advisory Committee's Note to amended Rule 6(b). See also the new Official Form 30.

A motion to substitute may be made by any party or by the representative of the deceased party without awaiting the suggestion of death. Indeed, the motion will usually be so made. If a party or the representative of the deceased party desires to limit the time within which another may make the motion, he may do so by suggesting the death upon the record.

A motion to substitute made within the prescribed time will ordinarily be granted, but under the permissive language of the first sentence of the amended rule ("the court may order") it may be denied by the court in the exercise of a sound discretion if made long after the death—as can occur if the suggestion of death is not made or is delayed—and circumstances have arisen rendering it unfair to allow substitution. Cf. *Anderson v. Yungkau,* supra, 329 U.S. at 485,

486, 67 S.Ct. at 430, 431, 91 L.Ed. 436, where it was noted under the present rule that settlement and distribution of the estate of a deceased defendant might be so far advanced as to warrant denial of a motion for substitution even though made within the time limit prescribed by that rule. Accordingly, a party interested in securing substitution under the amended rule should not assume that he can rest indefinitely awaiting the suggestion of death before he makes his motion to substitute.

1987 Amendment

The amendments are technical. No substantive change is intended.

HISTORICAL NOTES

Effective and Applicability Provisions

1961 Amendments. Amendment adopted on Apr. 17, 1961, effective July 19, 1961, see rule 86(d).

V. DEPOSITIONS AND DISCOVERY

ADVISORY COMMITTEE'S EXPLANATORY STATEMENT CONCERNING 1970 AMENDMENTS TO DISCOVERY RULES

This statement is intended to serve as a general introduction to the amendments of Rules 26–37, concerning discovery, as well as related amendments of other rules. A separate note of customary scope is appended to amendments proposed for each rule. This statement provides a framework for the consideration of individual rule changes.

Changes in the Discovery Rules

The discovery rules, as adopted in 1938, were a striking and imaginative departure from tradition. It was expected from the outset that they would be important, but experience has shown them to play an even larger role than was initially foreseen. Although the discovery rules have been amended since 1938, the changes were relatively few and narrowly focused, made in order to remedy specific defects. The amendments now proposed reflect the first comprehensive review of the discovery rules undertaken since 1938. These amendments make substantial changes in the discovery rules. Those summarized here are among the more important changes.

Scope of Discovery. New provisions are made and existing provisions changed affecting the scope of discovery: (1) The contents of insurance policies are made discoverable (Rule 26(b)(2)). (2) A showing of good cause is no longer required for discovery of documents and things and entry upon land (Rule 34). However, a showing of need is required for discovery of "trial preparation" materials other than a party's discovery of his own statement and a witness' discovery of his own statement; and protection is afforded against disclosure in such documents of mental impressions, conclusions, opinions, or legal theories concerning the litigation. (Rule 26(b)(3)). (3) Provision is made for discovery with respect to experts retained for trial preparation, and particularly those experts who will be called to testify at trial (Rule 26(b)(4)). (4) It is provided that interrogatories and requests for admission are not objectionable simply because

they relate to matters of opinion or contention, subject of course to the supervisory power of the court (Rules 33(b), 36(a)). (5) Medical examination is made available as to certain nonparties. (Rule 35(a)).

Mechanics of Discovery. A variety of changes are made in the mechanics of the discovery process, affecting the sequence and timing of discovery, the respective obligations of the parties with respect to requests, responses, and motions for court orders, and the related powers of the court to enforce discovery requests and to protect against their abusive use. A new provision eliminates the automatic grant of priority in discovery to one side (Rule 26(d)). Another provides that a party is not under a duty to supplement his responses to requests for discovery, except as specified (Rule 26(e)).

Other changes in the mechanics of discovery are designed to encourage extrajudicial discovery with a minimum of court intervention. Among these are the following: (1) The requirement that a plaintiff seek leave of court for early discovery requests is eliminated or reduced, and motions for a court order under Rule 34 are made unnecessary. Motions under Rule 35 are continued. (2) Answers and objections are to be served together and an enlargement of the time for response is provided. (3) The party seeking discovery, rather than the objecting party, is made responsible for invoking judicial determination of discovery disputes not resolved by the parties. (4) Judicial sanctions are tightened with respect to unjustified insistence upon or objection to discovery. These changes bring Rules 33, 34, and 36 substantially into line with the procedure now provided for depositions.

Failure to amend Rule 35 in the same way is based upon two considerations. First, the Columbia Survey (described below) finds that only about 5 percent of medical examinations require court motions, of which about half result in court orders. Second and of greater importance, the interest of the person to be examined in the privacy of his person was recently stressed by the Supreme Court in *Schlagenhauf v. Holder,* 379 U.S. 104 (1964). The court emphasized the trial judge's responsibility to assure that the medical examination was justified, particularly as to its scope.

Rearrangement of Rules. A limited rearrangement of the discovery rules has been made, whereby certain provisions are transferred from one rule to another. The reasons for this rearrangement are discussed below in a separate section of this statement and the details are set out in a table at the end of this statement.

Optional Procedures. In two instances, new optional procedures have been made available. A new procedure is provided to a party seeking to take the deposition of a corporation or other organization (Rule 30(b)(6)). A party on whom interrogatories have been served requesting information derivable from his business records may under specified circumstances produce the records rather than give answers (Rule 33(c)).

Other Changes. This summary of changes is by no means exhaustive. Various changes have been made in order to improve, tighten, or clarify particular provisions, to resolve conflicts in the case law, and to improve language. All changes, whether mentioned here or not, are discussed in the appropriate note for each rule.

A Field Survey of Discovery Practice

Despite widespread acceptance of discovery as an essential part of litigation, disputes have inevitably arisen concerning the values claimed for discovery and abuses alleged to exist. Many disputes about discovery relate to particular rule provisions or court decisions and can be studied in traditional fashion with a view to specific amendment. Since discovery is in large measure extra-judicial, however, even these disputes may be enlightened by a study of discovery "in the field." And some of the larger questions concerning discovery can be pursued only by a study of its operation at the law office level and in unreported cases.

The Committee, therefore, invited the Project for Effective Justice of Columbia Law School to conduct a field survey of discovery. Funds were obtained from the Ford Foundation and the Walter E. Meyer Research Institute of Law, Inc. The survey was carried on under the direction of Prof. Maurice Rosenberg of Columbia Law School. The Project for Effective Justice has submitted a report to the Committee entitled "Field Survey of Federal Pretrial Discovery" (hereafter referred to as the Columbia Survey). The Committee is deeply grateful for the benefit of this extensive undertaking and is most appreciative of the cooperation of the Project and the funding organizations. The Committee is particularly grateful to Professor Rosenberg who not only directed the survey but has given much time in order to assist the Committee in assessing the results.

The Columbia Survey concludes, in general, that there is no empirical evidence to warrant a fundamental change in the philosophy of the discovery rules. No widespread or profound failings are disclosed in the scope or availability of discovery. The costs of discovery do not appear to be oppressive, as a general matter, either in relation to ability to pay or to the stakes of the litigation. Discovery frequently provides evidence that would not otherwise be available to the parties and thereby makes for a fairer trial or settlement. On the other hand, no positive evidence is found that discovery promotes settlement.

More specific findings of the Columbia Survey are described in other Committee notes, in relation to particular rule provisions and amendments. Those interested in more detailed information may obtain it from the Project for Effective Justice.

Rearrangement of the Discovery Rules

The present discovery rules are structured entirely in terms of individual discovery devices, except for Rule 27 which deals with perpetuation of testimony, and Rule 37 which provides sanctions to enforce discovery. Thus, Rules 26 and 28 to 32 are in terms addressed only to the taking of a deposition of a party or third person. Rules 33 to 36 then deal in succession with four additional discovery devices: Written interrogatories to parties, production for inspection of documents and things, physical or mental examination and requests for admission.

Under the rules as promulgated in 1938, therefore, each of the discovery devices was separate and self-contained. A defect of this arrangement is that there is no natural location in the discovery rules for provisions generally applicable to all discovery or to several discovery devices. From 1938 until the present, a few amendments have applied a discovery provision to several rules. For example, in 1948, the scope of deposition discovery in Rule 26(b) and the provision for protective orders in Rule 30(b) were incorporated by reference in Rules 33 and 34. The arrangement was adequate so long as there were few provisions governing discovery generally and these provisions were relatively simple.

As will be seen, however, a series of amendments are now proposed which govern most or all of the discovery devices. Proposals of a similar nature will probably be made in the future. Under these circumstances, it is very desirable, even necessary, that the discovery rules contain one rule addressing itself to discovery generally.

Rule 26 is obviously the most appropriate rule for this purpose. One of its subdivisions, Rule 26(b), in terms governs only scope of deposition discovery, but it has been expressly incorporated by reference in Rules 33 and 34 and is treated by courts as setting a general standard. By means of a transfer to Rule 26 of the provisions for protective orders now contained in Rule 30(b), and a transfer from Rule 26 of provisions addressed exclusively to depositions, Rule 26 is converted into a rule concerned with discovery generally. It becomes a convenient vehicle for the inclusion of new provisions dealing with the scope, timing, and regulation of discovery. Few additional transfers are needed. See table showing rearrangement of rules, set out following this statement.

There are, to be sure, disadvantages in transferring any provision from one rule to another. Familiarity with the present pattern, reinforced by the references made by prior court decisions and the various secondary writings about the rules, is not lightly to be sacrificed. Revision of treatises and other reference works is burdensome and costly. Moreover, many States have adopted the existing pattern as a model for their rules.

On the other hand, the amendments now proposed will in any event require revision of texts and reference works as well as reconsideration by States following the Federal model. If these amendments are to be incorporated in an understandable way, a rule with general discovery provisions is needed. As will be seen, the proposed rearrangement produces a more coherent and intelligible pattern for the discovery rules taken as a whole. The difficulties described are those encountered whenever statutes are reexamined and revised. Failure to rearrange the discovery rules now would freeze the present scheme, making future change even more difficult.

Table Showing Rearrangement of Rules

Existing Rule No.	New Rule No.
26(a)	30(a), 31(a)
26(c)	30(c)
26(d)	32(a)
26(e)	32(b)
26(f)	32(c)
30(a)	30(b)
30(b)	26(c)
32	32(d)

Rule 26. General Provisions Governing Discovery; Duty of Disclosure

(a) Required Disclosures; Methods to Discover Additional Matter.

(1) Initial Disclosures. Except in categories of proceedings specified in Rule 26(a)(1)(E), or to the extent otherwise stipulated or directed by order, a party must, without awaiting a discovery request, provide to other parties:

(A) the name and, if known, the address and telephone number of each individual likely to have discoverable information that the disclosing party may use to support its claims or defenses, unless solely for impeachment, identifying the subjects of the information;

(B) a copy of, or a description by category and location of, all documents, data compilations, and tangible things that are in the possession, custody, or control of the party and that the disclosing party may use to support its claims or defenses, unless solely for impeachment;

(C) a computation of any category of damages claimed by the disclosing party, making available for inspection and copying as under Rule 34 the documents or other evidentiary material, not privileged or protected from disclosure, on which such computation is based, including materials bearing on the nature and extent of injuries suffered; and

(D) for inspection and copying as under Rule 34 any insurance agreement under which any person carrying on an insurance business may be liable to satisfy part or all of a judgment which may be entered in the action or to indemnify or reimburse for payments made to satisfy the judgment.

(E) The following categories of proceedings are exempt from initial disclosure under Rule 26(a)(1):

(i) an action for review on an administrative record;

(ii) a petition for habeas corpus or other proceeding to challenge a criminal conviction or sentence;

(iii) an action brought without counsel by a person in custody of the United States, a state, or a state subdivision;

(iv) an action to enforce or quash an administrative summons or subpoena;

(v) an action by the United States to recover benefit payments;

(vi) an action by the United States to collect on a student loan guaranteed by the United States;

(vii) a proceeding ancillary to proceedings in other courts; and

(viii) an action to enforce an arbitration award.

These disclosures must be made at or within 14 days after the Rule 26(f) conference unless a different time is set by stipulation or court order, or unless a party objects during the conference that initial disclosures are not appropriate in the circumstances of the action and states the objection in the Rule 26(f) discovery plan. In ruling on the objection, the court must determine what disclosures—if any—are to be made, and set the time for disclosure. Any party first served or otherwise joined after the Rule 26(f) conference must make these disclosures within 30 days after being served or joined unless a different time is set by stipulation or court order. A party must make its initial disclosures based on the information then reasonably available to it and is not excused from making its disclosures because it has not fully completed its investigation of the case or because it challenges the sufficiency of another party's disclosures or because another party has not made its disclosures.

(2) Disclosure of Expert Testimony.

(A) In addition to the disclosures required by paragraph (1), a party shall disclose to other parties the identity of any person who may be used at trial to present evidence under Rules 702, 703, or 705 of the Federal Rules of Evidence.

(B) Except as otherwise stipulated or directed by the court, this disclosure shall, with respect to a witness who is retained or specially employed to provide expert testimony in the case or whose duties as an employee of the party regularly involve giving expert testimony, be accompanied by a written report prepared and signed by the witness. The report shall contain a complete statement of all opinions to be expressed and the basis and reasons therefor; the data or other information considered by the witness in forming the opinions; any exhibits to be used as a summary of or support for the opinions; the qualifications of the witness, including a list of all publications authored by the witness within the preceding ten years; the compensation to be paid for the study and testimony; and a listing of any other cases in which the witness has testified as an expert at trial or by deposition within the preceding four years.

(C) These disclosures shall be made at the times and in the sequence directed by the court. In the absence of other directions from the court or stipulation by the parties, the disclosures shall be made at least 90 days before the trial date or the date the case is to be ready for trial or, if the evidence is intended solely to contradict or rebut evidence on the same subject matter identified by another party under paragraph (2)(B), within 30 days after the disclosure made by the other party. The parties shall supplement these disclosures when required under subdivision (e)(1).

(3) Pretrial Disclosures. In addition to the disclosures required by Rule 26(a)(1) and (2), a party must provide to other parties and promptly file with the court the following information regarding the evidence that it may present at trial other than solely for impeachment:

(A) the name and, if not previously provided, the address and telephone number of each witness, separately identifying those whom the party expects to present and those whom the party may call if the need arises;

(B) the designation of those witnesses whose testimony is expected to be presented by means of a deposition and, if not taken stenographically, a transcript of the pertinent portions of the deposition testimony; and

(C) an appropriate identification of each document or other exhibit, including summaries of other evidence, separately identifying those which the party expects to offer and those which the party may offer if the need arises.

Unless otherwise directed by the court, these disclosures must be made at least 30 days before trial. Within 14 days thereafter, unless a different time is specified by the court, a party may serve and promptly file a list disclosing (i) any objections to the use under Rule 32(a) of a deposition designated by another party under Rule 26(a)(3)(B), and (ii) any objection, together with the grounds therefor, that may be made to the admissibility of materials identified under Rule 26(a)(3)(C). Objections not so disclosed, other than objections under Rules 402 and 403 of the Federal Rules of Evidence, are waived unless excused by the court for good cause.

(4) Form of Disclosures. Unless the court orders otherwise, all disclosures under Rules 26(a)(1) through (3) must be made in writing, signed, and served.

(5) Methods to Discover Additional Matter. Parties may obtain discovery by one or more of the following methods: depositions upon oral examination or written questions; written interrogatories; production of documents or things or permission to enter upon land or other property under Rule 34 or 45(a)(1)(C), for inspection and other purposes; physical and mental examinations; and requests for admission.

(b) Discovery Scope and Limits. Unless otherwise limited by order of the court in accordance with these rules, the scope of discovery is as follows:

(1) In General. Parties may obtain discovery regarding any matter, not privileged, that is relevant to the claim or defense of any party, including the existence, description, nature, custody, condition, and location of any books, documents, or other tangible things and the identity and location of persons having knowledge of any discoverable matter. For good cause, the court may order discovery of any matter relevant to the subject matter involved in the action. Relevant information need not be admissible at the trial if the discovery appears reasonably calculated to lead to the discovery of admissible evidence. All discovery is subject to the limitations imposed by Rule 26(b)(2)(i), (ii), and (iii).

(2) Limitations. By order, the court may alter the limits in these rules on the number of depositions and interrogatories or the length of depositions under Rule 30. By order or local rule, the court may also limit the number of requests under Rule 36. The frequency or extent of use of the discovery methods otherwise permitted under these rules and by any local rule shall be limited by the court if it determines that: (i) the discovery sought is unreasonably cumulative or duplicative, or is obtainable from some other source that is more convenient, less burdensome, or less expensive; (ii) the party seeking discovery has had ample opportunity by discovery in the action to obtain the information sought; or (iii) the burden or expense of the proposed discovery outweighs its likely benefit, taking into account the needs of the case, the amount in controversy, the parties' resources, the importance of the issues at stake in the litigation, and the importance of the proposed discovery in resolving the issues. The court may act upon its own initiative after reasonable notice or pursuant to a motion under Rule 26(c).

(3) Trial Preparation: Materials. Subject to the provisions of subdivision (b)(4) of this rule, a party may obtain discovery of documents and tangible things otherwise discoverable under subdivision (b)(1) of this rule and prepared in anticipation of litigation or for trial by or for another party or by or for that other party's representative (including the other party's attorney, consultant, surety, indemnitor, insurer, or agent) only upon a showing that the party seeking discovery has substantial need of the materials in the preparation of the party's case and that the party is unable without undue hardship to obtain the substantial equivalent of the materials by other means. In ordering discovery of such materials when the required showing has been made, the court shall protect against disclosure of the mental impressions, conclusions, opinions, or legal theories of an attorney or other representative of a party concerning the litigation.

A party may obtain without the required showing a statement concerning the action or its subject matter previously made by that party. Upon request, a person not a party may obtain without the required showing a statement concerning the action or its subject matter previously made by that person. If the request is refused, the person may move for a court order. The provisions of Rule 37(a)(4) apply to the award of expenses incurred in relation to the motion. For purposes of this paragraph, a statement previously made is (A) a written statement signed or otherwise adopted or approved by the person making it, or (B) a stenographic, mechanical, electrical, or other recording, or a transcription thereof, which is a substantially verbatim recital of an oral statement by the person making it and contemporaneously recorded.

(4) Trial Preparation: Experts.

(A) A party may depose any person who has been identified as an expert whose opinions may be presented at trial. If a report from the expert is required under subdivision (a)(2)(B), the deposition shall not be conducted until after the report is provided.

(B) A party may, through interrogatories or by deposition, discover facts known or opinions held by an expert who has been retained or specially employed by another party in anticipation of litigation or preparation for trial and who is not expected to be called as a witness at trial, only as provided in Rule 35(b) or upon a showing of exceptional circumstances under which it is impracticable for the party seeking discovery to obtain facts or opinions on the same subject by other means.

(C) Unless manifest injustice would result, (i) the court shall require that the party seeking discovery pay the expert a reasonable fee for time spent in responding to discovery under this subdivision; and (ii) with respect to discovery obtained under subdivision (b)(4)(B) of this rule the court shall require the party seeking discovery to pay the other party a fair portion of the fees and expenses reasonably incurred by the latter party in obtaining facts and opinions from the expert.

(5) Claims of Privilege or Protection of Trial Preparation Materials. When a party withholds information otherwise discoverable under these rules by claiming that it is privileged or subject to protection as trial preparation material, the party shall make the claim expressly and shall describe the nature of the documents, communications, or things not produced or disclosed in a manner that, without revealing information itself privileged or protected, will enable other parties to assess the applicability of the privilege or protection.

(c) Protective Orders. Upon motion by a party or by the person from whom discovery is sought, accompanied by a certification that the movant has in good faith conferred or attempted to confer with other affected parties in an effort to resolve the dispute without court action, and for good cause shown, the court in which the action is pending or alternatively, on matters relating to a deposition, the court in the district where the deposition is to be taken may make any order which justice requires to protect a party or person from annoyance, embarrassment, oppression, or undue burden or expense, including one or more of the following:

(1) that the disclosure or discovery not be had;

(2) that the disclosure or discovery may be had only on specified terms and conditions, including a designation of the time or place;

(3) that the discovery may be had only by a method of discovery other than that selected by the party seeking discovery;

(4) that certain matters not be inquired into, or that the scope of the disclosure or discovery be limited to certain matters;

(5) that discovery be conducted with no one present except persons designated by the court;

(6) that a deposition, after being sealed, be opened only by order of the court;

(7) that a trade secret or other confidential research, development, or commercial information not be revealed or be revealed only in a designated way; and

(8) that the parties simultaneously file specified documents or information enclosed in sealed envelopes to be opened as directed by the court.

If the motion for a protective order is denied in whole or in part, the court may, on such terms and conditions as are just, order that any party or other person provide or permit discovery. The provisions of Rule 37(a)(4) apply to the award of expenses incurred in relation to the motion.

after a reasonable inquiry, the request, response, or objection is:

(A) consistent with these rules and warranted by existing law or a good faith argument for the extension, modification, or reversal of existing law;

(B) not interposed for any improper purpose, such as to harass or to cause unnecessary delay or needless increase in the cost of litigation; and

(C) not unreasonable or unduly burdensome or expensive, given the needs of the case, the discovery already had in the case, the amount in controversy, and the importance of the issues at stake in the litigation.

If a request, response, or objection is not signed, it shall be stricken unless it is signed promptly after the omission is called to the attention of the party making the request, response, or objection, and a party shall not be obligated to take any action with respect to it until it is signed.

(3) If without substantial justification a certification is made in violation of the rule, the court, upon motion or upon its own initiative, shall impose upon the person who made the certification, the party on whose behalf the disclosure, request, response, or objection is made, or both, an appropriate sanction, which may include an order to pay the amount of the reasonable expenses incurred because of the violation, including a reasonable attorney's fee.

(As amended Dec. 27, 1946, eff. Mar. 19, 1948; Jan. 21, 1963, eff. July 1, 1963; Feb. 28, 1966, eff. July 1, 1966; Mar. 30, 1970, eff. July 1, 1970; Apr. 29, 1980, eff. Aug. 1, 1980; Apr. 28, 1983, eff. Aug. 1, 1983; Mar. 2, 1987, eff. Aug. 1, 1987; Apr. 22, 1993, eff. Dec. 1, 1993; Apr. 17, 2000, eff. Dec. 1, 2000.)

ADVISORY COMMITTEE NOTES
1937 Adoption

Note to Subdivision (a). This rule freely authorizes the taking of depositions under the same circumstances and by the same methods whether for the purpose of discovery or for the purpose of obtaining evidence. Many states have adopted this practice on account of its simplicity and effectiveness, safeguarding it by imposing such restrictions upon the subsequent use of the deposition at the trial or hearing as are deemed advisable. See Ark.Civ.Code (Crawford, 1934) §§ 606 to 607; Calif.Code Civ.Proc. (Deering, 1937) § 2021; 1 Colo.Stat.Ann. (1935) Code Civ.Proc. § 376; Idaho Code Ann. (1932) § 16–906; Ill.Rules of Pract.Rule 19 (Smith-Hurd Ill.Stats. c. 110, § 259.19); Smith-Hurd Ill.Stats. c. 51, § 24; 2 Ind.Stat.Ann. (Burns, 1933) §§ 2–1501, 2–1506; Ky. Codes (Carroll, 1932) Civ.Pract. § 557; 1 Mo.Rev.Stat. (1929) § 1753; 4 Mont.Rev.Codes Ann. (1935) § 10645; Neb.Comp. Stat. (1929) ch. 20, §§ 1246–7; 4 Nev.Comp.Laws (Hillyer, 1929) § 9001; 2 N.H.Pub.Laws (1926) ch. 337, § 1; N.C.Code Ann. (1935) § 1809; 2 N.D.Comp.Laws Ann. (1913) §§ 7889 to 7897; 2 Ohio Gen.Code Ann. (Page, 1926) §§ 11525–6; 1 Ore.Code Ann. (1930) Tit. 9, § 1503; 1 S.D.Comp.Laws (1929) §§ 2713–16; Vernon's Ann.Civ.Stats. Tex. arts. 3738, 3752, 3769; Utah Rev.Stat.Ann. (1933)

§ 104–51–7; Wash.Rules of Practice adopted by the Supreme Ct., Rule 8, 2 Wash.Rev.Stat.Ann. (Remington, 1932) § 308–8; W.Va.Code (1931) ch. 57, art. 4, § 1. Compare [former] Equity Rules 47 (Depositions—To be Taken in Exceptional Instances); 54 (Depositions Under Revised Statutes, §§ 863, 865, 866, 867—Cross Examination); 58 (Discovery—Interrogatories—Inspection and Production of Documents—Admission of Execution or Genuineness).

This and subsequent rules incorporate, modify, and broaden the provisions for depositions under U.S.C., Title 28, [former] §§ 639 (Depositions *de bene esse;* when and where taken; notice), 640 (Same; mode of taking), 641 (Same; transmission to court), 644 (Depositions under *dedimus potestatem* and *in perpetuam*), 646 (Deposition under *dedimus potestatem;* how taken). These statutes are superseded in so far as they differ from this and subsequent rules. U.S.C. Title 28, [former] § 643 (Depositions; taken in mode prescribed by State laws) is superseded by the third sentence of Subdivision (a).

While a number of states permit discovery only from parties or their agents, others either make no distinction between parties or agents of parties and ordinary witnesses, or authorize the taking of ordinary depositions, without restriction, from any persons who have knowledge of relevant facts. See Ark.Civ.Code (Crawford, 1934) §§ 606 to 607; 1 Idaho Code Ann. (1932) § 16–906; Ill.Rules of Pract., Rule 19 (Smith-Hurd Ill.Stats. c. 110, § 259.19); Smith-Hurd Ill.Stats. c. 51, § 24; 2 Ind.Stat.Ann. (Burns, 1933) § 2–1501; Ky.Codes (Carroll, 1932) Civ.Pract. §§ 554 to 558; 2 Md. Ann.Code (Bagby, 1924) Art. 35, § 21; 2 Minn.Stat. (Mason, 1927) § 9820; Mo.St.Ann. §§ 1753, 1759, pp. 4023, 4026; Neb.Comp.Stat. (1929) ch. 20, §§ 1246–7; 2 N.H.Pub.Laws (1926) ch. 337, § 1; 2 N.D.Comp.Laws Ann. (1913) § 7897; 2 Ohio Gen.Code Ann. (Page, 1926) §§ 11525–6; 1 S.D.Comp. Laws (1929) §§ 2713–16; Vernon's Ann.Civil Stats.Tex. arts. 3738, 3752, 3769; Utah Rev.Stat.Ann. (1933) § 104–51–7; Wash.Rules of Practice adopted by Supreme Ct., Rule 8, 2 Wash.Rev.Stat.Ann. (Remington, 1932) § 308–8; W.Va.Code (1931) ch. 57, art. 4, § 1.

The more common practice in the United States is to take depositions on notice by the party desiring them, without any order from the court, and this has been followed in these rules. See Calif.Code Civ.Proc. (Deering, 1937) § 2031; 2 Fla.Comp.Gen.Laws Ann. (1927) §§ 4405–7; 1 Idaho Code Ann. (1932) § 16–902; Ill.Rules of Pract., Rule 19 (Smith-Hurd Ill.Stats. c. 110, § 259.19); Smith-Hurd Ill.Stats. c. 51, § 24; 2 Ind.Stat.Ann. (Burns, 1933) § 2–1502; Kan.Gen.Stat. Ann. (1935) § 60–2827; Ky.Codes (Carroll, 1932) Civ.Pract. § 565; 2 Minn.Stat. (Mason, 1927) § 9820; Mo.St.Ann. § 1761, p. 4029; 4 Mont.Rev.Codes Ann. (1935) § 10651; Nev.Comp.Laws (Hillyer, 1929) § 9002; N.C.Code Ann. (1935) § 1809; 2 N.D.Comp.Laws Ann. (1913) § 7895; Utah Rev.Stat.Ann. (1933) § 104–51–8.

Note to Subdivision (b). While the old chancery practice limited discovery to facts supporting the case of the party seeking it, this limitation has been largely abandoned by modern legislation. See Ala.Code Ann. (Michie, 1928) §§ 7764 to 7773; 2 Ind.Stat.Ann. (Burns, 1933) §§ 2–1028, 2–1506, 2–1728–2–1732; Iowa Code (1935) § 11185; Ky. Codes (Carroll, 1932) Civ.Pract. §§ 557, 606(8); La.Code Pract. (Dart, 1932) arts. 347–356; 2 Mass.Gen.Laws (Ter.Ed., 1932) ch. 231, §§ 61 to 67; Mo.St.Ann. §§ 1753, 1759, pp. 4023, 4026; Neb.Comp.Stat. (1929) §§ 20–1246, 20–1247; 2

N.H.Pub.Laws (1926) ch. 337, § 1; 2 Ohio Gen.Code Ann. (Page, 1926) §§ 11497, 11526; Vernon's Ann.Civ.Stats.Tex. arts. 3738, 3753, 3769; Wis.Stat. (1935) § 326.12; Ontario Consol.Rules of Pract. (1928) Rules 237–347; Quebec Code of Civ.Proc. (Curran, 1922) §§ 286 to 290.

Note to Subdivisions (d), (e), and (f). The restrictions here placed upon the use of depositions at the trial or hearing are substantially the same as those provided in U.S.C., Title 28, [former] § 641, for depositions taken, *de bene esse*, with the additional provision that any deposition may be used when the court finds the existence of exceptional circumstances. Compare English Rules Under the Judicature Act (The Annual Practice, 1937) O. 37, r. 18 (with additional provision permitting use of deposition by consent of the parties). See also [former] Equity Rule 64 (Former Depositions, Etc. May be Used Before Master); and 2 Minn. Stat. (Mason, 1927) § 9835 (Use in a subsequent action of a deposition filed in a previously dismissed action between the same parties and involving the same subject matter).

1946 Amendment

Note. Subdivision (a). The amendment eliminates the requirement of leave of court for the taking of a deposition except where a plaintiff seeks to take a deposition within 20 days after the commencement of the action. The retention of the requirement where a deposition is sought by a plaintiff within 20 days of the commencement of the action protects a defendant who has not had an opportunity to retain counsel and inform himself as to the nature of the suit; the plaintiff, of course, needs no such protection. The present rule forbids the plaintiff to take a deposition, without leave of court, before the answer is served. Sometimes the defendant delays the serving of an answer for more than 20 days, but as 20 days are sufficient time for him to obtain a lawyer, there is no reason to forbid the plaintiff to take a deposition without leave merely because the answer has not been served. In all cases, Rule 30(a) empowers the court, for cause shown, to alter the time of the taking of a deposition, and Rule 30(b) contains provisions giving ample protection to persons who are unreasonably pressed. The modified practice here adopted is along the line of that followed in various states. See e.g., 8 Mo.Rev.Stat.Ann.1939, § 1917; 2 Burns' Ind.Stat.Ann.1933, § 2–1506.

Subdivision (b). The amendments to subdivision (b) make clear the broad scope of examination and that it may cover not only evidence for use at the trial but also inquiry into matters in themselves inadmissible as evidence but which will lead to the discovery of such evidence. The purpose of discovery is to allow a broad search for facts, the names of witnesses, or any other matters which may aid a party in the preparation or presentation of his case. *Engl v. Aetna Life Ins. Co.,* C.C.A.2, 1943, 139 F.2d 469; *Mahler v. Pennsylvania R. Co.,* E.D.N.Y.1945, 8 Fed.Rules Serv. 33.351, Case 1. In such a preliminary inquiry admissibility at trial should not be the test as to whether the information sought is within the scope of proper examination. Such a standard unnecessarily curtails the utility of discovery practice. Of course, matters entirely without bearing either as direct evidence or as leads to evidence are not within the scope of inquiry, but to the extent that the examination develops useful information, it functions successfully as an instrument of discovery, even if it produces no testimony directly admissible. *Lewis v. United Air Lines Transporta-*

tion Corp., D.Conn.1939, 27 F.Supp. 946; *Engl v. Aetna Life Ins. Co.,* supra; *Mahler v. Pennsylvania R. Co.,* supra; *Bloomer v. Sirian Lamp Co.,* D.Del.1944, 8 Fed.Rules Serv. 26b.31, Case 3; *Rosseau v. Langley,* N.Y.1945, 9 Fed.Rules Serv. 34.41, Case 1 (Rule 26 contemplates "examinations not merely for the narrow purpose of adducing testimony which may be offered in evidence but also for the broad discovery of information which may be useful in preparation for trial."); *Olson Transportation Co. v. Socony-Vacuum Co.,* E.D.Wis. 1944, 8 Fed.Rules Serv. 34.41, Case 2 (". . . the Rules . . . permit 'fishing' for evidence as they should."); Note, 1945, 45 Col.L.Rev. 482. Thus hearsay, while inadmissible itself, may suggest testimony which properly may be proved. Under Rule 26(b) several cases, however, have erroneously limited discovery on the basis of admissibility, holding that the word "relevant" in effect meant "material and competent under the rules of evidence". *Poppino v. Jones Store Co.,* W.D.Mo.1940, 1 F.R.D. 215, 3 Fed.Rules Serv. 26b.5, Case 1; *Benevento v. A. & P. Food Stores, Inc.,* E.D.N.Y.1939, 26 F.Supp. 424. Thus it has been said that inquiry might not be made into statements or other matters which, when disclosed, amounted only to hearsay. *See Maryland for use of Montvila v. Pan-American Bus Lines, Inc.,* D.Md.1940, 1 F.R.D. 213, 3 Fed.Rules Serv. 26b.211, Case 3; *Gitto v. "Italia," Societa Anonima Di Navigazione,* E.D.N.Y.1940, 31 F.Supp. 567; *Rose Silk Mills, Inc. v. Insurance Co. of North America,* S.D.N.Y.1939, 29 F.Supp. 504; *Colpak v. Hetterick,* E.D.N.Y.1941, 40 F.Supp. 350; *Matthies v. Peter F. Connolly Co.,* E.D.N.Y.1941, 6 Fed.Rules Serv. 30a.22, Case 1, 2 F.R.D. 277; *Matter of Examination of Citizens Casualty Co. of New York,* S.D.N.Y.1942, 3 F.R.D. 171, 7 Fed.Rules Serv. 26b.211, Case 1; *United States v. Silliman,* D.C.N.J.1944, 8 Fed.Rules Serv. 26b.52, Case 1. The contrary and better view, however, has often been stated. See, e.g., *Engl v. Aetna Life Ins. Co.,* supra; *Stevenson v. Melady,* S.D.N.Y. 1940, 3 Fed.Rules Serv. 26b.31, Case 1, 1 F.R.D. 329; *Lewis v. United Air Lines Transport Corp.,* supra; *Application of Zenith Radio Corp.,* E.D.Pa.1941, 4 Fed.Rules Serv. 30b.21, Case 1, 1 F.R.D. 627; *Steingut v. Guaranty Trust Co. of New York,* S.D.N.Y.1941, 1 F.R.D. 723, 4 Fed.Rules Serv. 26b.5, Case 2; *DeSeversky v. Republic Aviation Corp.,* E.D.N.Y.1941, 2 F.R.D. 183, 5 Fed.Rules Serv. 26b.31, Case 5; *Moore v. George A. Hormel & Co.,* S.D.N.Y.1942, 6 Fed.Rules Serv. 30b.41, Case 1, 2 F.R.D. 340; *Hercules Powder Co. v. Rohm & Haas Co.,* D.Del.1943, 7 Fed.Rules Serv. 45b.311, Case 2, 3 F.R.D. 302; *Bloomer v. Sirian Lamp Co.,* supra; *Crosby Steam Gage & Valve Co. v. Manning, Maxwell & Moore, Inc.,* D.Mass.1944, 8 Fed.Rules Serv. 26b.31, Case 1; *Patterson Oil Terminals, Inc. v. Charles Kurz & Co., Inc.,* E.D.Pa.1945, 9 Fed.Rules Serv. 33.321, Case 2; *Pueblo Trading Co. v. Reclamation Dist. No. 1500,* N.D.Cal.1945, 9 Fed.Rules Serv. 33.321, Case 4, 4 F.R.D. 471. See also discussion as to the broad scope of discovery in *Hoffman v. Palmer,* C.C.A.2, 1942, 129 F.2d 976, 995–997, affirmed 63 S.Ct. 477, 318 U.S. 109, 87 L.Ed. 645; Note, 1945, 45 Col.L.Rev. 482.

1963 Amendment

This amendment conforms to the amendment of Rule 28(b). See the next-to-last paragraph of the Advisory Committee's Note to that amendment.

1966 Amendment

The requirement that the plaintiff obtain leave of court in order to serve notice of taking of a deposition within 20 days after commencement of the action gives rise to difficulties when the prospective deponent is about to become unavailable for examination. The problem is not confined to admiralty, but has been of special concern in that context because of the mobility of vessels and their personnel. When Rule 26 was adopted as Admiralty Rule 30A in 1961, the problem was alleviated by permitting depositions *de bene esse*, for which leave of court is not required. See Advisory Committee's Note to Admiralty Rule 30A (1961).

A continuing study is being made in the effort to devise a modification of the 20-day rule appropriate to both the civil and admiralty practice to the end that Rule 26(a) shall state a uniform rule applicable alike to what are now civil actions and suits in admiralty. Meanwhile, the exigencies of maritime litigation require preservation, for the time being at least, of the traditional *de bene esse* procedure for the post-unification counterpart of the present suit in admiralty. Accordingly, the amendment provides for continued availability of that procedure in admiralty and maritime claims within the meaning of Rule 9(h).

1970 Amendment

A limited rearrangement of the discovery rules is made, whereby certain rule provisions are transferred, as follows: Existing Rule 26(a) is transferred to Rules 30(a) and 31(a). Existing Rule 26(c) is transferred to Rule 30(c). Existing Rules 26(d), (e), and (f) are transferred to Rule 32. Revisions of the transferred provisions, if any, are discussed in the notes appended to Rules 30, 31, and 32. In addition, Rule 30(b) is transferred to Rule 26(c). The purpose of this rearrangement is to establish Rule 26 as a rule governing discovery in general. (The reasons are set out in the Advisory Committee's explanatory statement.)

Subdivision (a)—Discovery Devices. This is a new subdivision listing all of the discovery devices provided in the discovery rules and establishing the relationship between the general provisions of Rule 26 and the specific rules for particular discovery devices. The provision that the frequency of use of these methods is not limited confirms existing law. It incorporates in general form a provision now found in Rule 33.

Subdivision (b)—Scope of Discovery. This subdivision is recast to cover the scope of discovery generally. It regulates the discovery obtainable through any of the discovery devices listed in Rule 26(a).

All provisions as to scope of discovery are subject to the initial qualification that the court may limit discovery in accordance with these rules. Rule 26(c) (transferred from 30(b)) confers broad powers on the courts to regulate or prevent discovery even though the materials sought are within the scope of 26(b), and these powers have always been freely exercised. For example, a party's income tax return is generally held not privileged, 2A Barron & Holtzoff, *Federal Practice and Procedure*, § 651.2 (Wright ed. 1961), and yet courts have recognized that interests in privacy may call for a measure of extra protection. E.g., *Wiesenberger v. W. E. Hutton & Co.*, 35 F.R.D. 556 (S.D.N.Y.1964). Similarly, the courts have in appropriate circumstances protected materials that are primarily of an impeaching character.

These two types of materials merely illustrate the many situations, not capable of governance by precise rule, in which courts must exercise judgment. The new subsections in Rule 26(b) do not change existing law with respect to such situations.

Subdivision (b)(1)—In General. The language is changed to provide for the scope of discovery in general terms. The existing subdivision, although in terms applicable only to depositions, is incorporated by reference in existing Rules 33 and 34. Since decisions as to relevance to the subject matter of the action are made for discovery purposes well in advance of trial, a flexible treatment of relevance is required and the making of discovery, whether voluntary or under court order, is not a concession or determination of relevance for purposes of trial. *Cf.* 4 *Moore's Federal Practice* ¶26–16[1] (2d ed. 1966).

Subdivision (b)(2)—Insurance Policies. Both the cases and commentators are sharply in conflict on the question whether defendant's liability insurance coverage is subject to discovery in the usual situation when the insurance coverage is not itself admissible and does not bear on another issue in the case. Examples of Federal cases requiring disclosure and supporting comments: *Cook v. Welty*, 253 F.Supp. 875 (D.D.C.1966) (cases cited); *Johanek v. Aberle*, 27 F.R.D. 272 (D.Mont.1961); Williams, *Discovery of Dollar Limits in Liability Policies in Automobile Tort Cases*, 10 Ala.L.Rev. 355 (1958); Thode, *Some Reflections on the 1957 Amendments to the Texas Rules*, 37 Tex.L.Rev. 33, 40–42 (1958). Examples of Federal cases refusing disclosure and supporting comments: *Bisserier v. Manning*, 207 F.Supp. 476 (D.N.J.1962); *Cooper v. Stender*, 30 F.R.D. 389 (E.D.Tenn.1962); Frank, *Discovery and Insurance, Coverage*, 1959 Ins.L.J. 281; Fournier, *Pre-trial Discovery of Insurance Coverage and Limits*, 28 Ford.L.Rev. 215 (1959).

The division in reported cases is close. State decisions based on provisions similar to the federal rules are similarly divided. See cases collected in 2A Barron & Holtzoff, *Federal Practice and Procedure* § 647.1, nn. 45.5, 45.6 (Wright ed. 1961). It appears to be difficult if not impossible to obtain appellate review of the issue. Resolution by rule amendment is indicated. The question is essentially procedural in that it bears upon preparation for trial and settlement before trial, and courts confronting the question, however they have decided it, have generally treated it as procedural and governed by the rules.

The amendment resolves this issue in favor of disclosure. Most of the decisions denying discovery, some explicitly, reason from the text of Rule 26(b) that it permits discovery only of matters which will be admissible in evidence or appear reasonably calculated to lead to such evidence; they avoid considerations of policy, regarding them as foreclosed. See *Bisserier v. Manning, supra*. Some note also that facts about a defendant's financial status are not discoverable as such, prior to judgment with execution unsatisfied, and fear that, if courts hold insurance coverage discoverable, they must extend the principle to other aspects of the defendant's financial status. The cases favoring disclosure rely heavily on the practical significance of insurance in the decisions lawyers make about settlement and trial preparation. In *Clauss v. Danker*, 264 F.Supp. 246 (S.D.N.Y.1967), the court held that the rules forbid disclosure but called for an amendment to permit it.

Disclosure of insurance coverage will enable counsel for both sides to make the same realistic appraisal of the case, so that settlement and litigation strategy are based on knowledge and not speculation. It will conduce to settlement and avoid protracted litigation in some cases, though in others it may have an opposite effect. The amendment is limited to insurance coverage, which should be distinguished from any other facts concerning defendant's financial status (1) because insurance is an asset created specifically to satisfy the claim; (2) because the insurance company ordinarily controls the litigation; (3) because information about coverage is available only from defendant or his insurer; and (4) because disclosure does not involve a significant invasion of privacy.

Disclosure is required when the insurer "may be liable" on part or all of the judgment. Thus, an insurance company must disclose even when it contests liability under the policy, and such disclosure does not constitute a waiver of its claim. It is immaterial whether the liability is to satisfy the judgment directly or merely to indemnify or reimburse another after he pays the judgment.

The provision applies only to persons "carrying on an insurance business" and thus covers insurance companies and not the ordinary business concern that enters into a contract of indemnification. *Cf.* N.Y.Ins.Law § 41. Thus, the provision makes no change in existing law on discovery of indemnity agreements other than insurance agreements by persons carrying on an insurance business. Similarly, the provision does not cover the business concern that creates a reserve fund for purposes of self-insurance.

For some purposes other than discovery, an application for insurance is treated as a part of the insurance agreement. The provision makes clear that, for discovery purposes, the application is not to be so treated. The insurance application may contain personal and financial information concerning the insured, discovery of which is beyond the purpose of this provision.

In no instance does disclosure make the facts concerning insurance coverage admissible in evidence.

Subdivision (b)(3)—Trial Preparation: Materials. Some of the most controversial and vexing problems to emerge from the discovery rules have arisen out of requests for the production of documents or things prepared in anticipation of litigation or for trial. The existing rules make no explicit provision for such materials. Yet, two verbally distinct doctrines have developed, each conferring a qualified immunity on these materials—the "good cause" requirement in Rule 34 (now generally held applicable to discovery of documents via deposition under Rule 45 and interrogatories under Rule 33) and the work-product doctrine of *Hickman v. Taylor,* 329 U.S. 495 (1947). Both demand a showing of justification before production can be had, the one of "good cause" and the other variously described in the *Hickman* case: "necessity or justification," "denial * * * would unduly prejudice the preparation of petitioner's case," or "cause hardship or injustice" 329 U.S. at 509–510.

In deciding the *Hickman* case, the Supreme Court appears to have expressed a preference in 1947 for an approach to the problem of trial preparation materials by judicial decision rather than by rule. Sufficient experience has accumulated, however, with lower court applications of the *Hickman* decision to warrant a reappraisal.

The major difficulties visible in the existing case law are (1) confusion and disagreement as to whether "good cause" is made out by a showing of relevance and lack of privilege, or requires an additional showing of necessity, (2) confusion and disagreement as to the scope of the *Hickman* work-product doctrine, particularly whether it extends beyond work actually performed by lawyers, and (3) the resulting difficulty of relating the "good cause" required by Rule 34 and the "necessity or justification" of the work-product doctrine, so that their respective roles and the distinctions between them are understood.

Basic Standard.—Since Rule 34 in terms requires a showing of "good cause" for the production of all documents and things, whether or not trial preparation is involved, courts have felt that a single formula is called for and have differed over whether a showing of relevance and lack of privilege is enough or whether more must be shown. When the facts of the cases are studied, however, a distinction emerges based upon the type of materials. With respect to documents not obtained or prepared with an eye to litigation, the decisions, while not uniform, reflect a strong and increasing tendency to relate "good cause" to a showing that the documents are relevant to the subject matter of the action. *E.g., Connecticut Mutual Life Ins. Co. v. Shields,* 17 F.R.D. 273 (S.D.N.Y. 1959), with cases cited; *Houdry Process Corp. v. Commonwealth Oil Refining Co.,* 24 F.R.D. 58 (S.D.N.Y.1955); see *Bell v. Commercial Ins. Co.,* 280 F.2d 514, 517 (3d Cir. 1960). When the party whose documents are sought shows that the request for production is unduly burdensome or oppressive, courts have denied discovery for lack of "good cause", although they might just as easily have based their decision on the protective provisions of existing Rule 30(b) (new Rule 26(c)). *E.g., Lauer v. Tankrederi,* 39 F.R.D. 334 (E.D.Pa. 1966).

As to trial-preparation materials, however, the courts are increasingly interpreting "good cause" as requiring more than relevance. When lawyers have prepared or obtained the materials for trial, all courts require more than relevance; so much is clearly commanded by *Hickman.* But even as to the preparatory work of nonlawyers, while some courts ignore work-product and equate "good cause" with relevance, *e.g., Brown v. New York, N.H. & H.R.R.,* 17 F.R.D. 324 (S.D.N.Y.1955), the more recent trend is to read "good cause" as requiring inquiry into the importance of and need for the materials as well as into alternative sources for securing the same information. In *Guilford Nat'l Bank v. Southern Ry.,* 297 F.2d 921 (4th Cir. 1962), statements of witnesses obtained by claim agents were held not discoverable because both parties had had equal access to the witnesses at about the same time, shortly after the collision in question. The decision was based solely on Rule 34 and "good cause"; the court declined to rule on whether the statements were work-products. The court's treatment of "good cause" is quoted at length and with approval in *Schlagenhauf v. Holder,* 379 U.S. 104, 117–118 (1964). See also *Mitchell v. Bass,* 252 F.2d 513 (8th Cir. 1958); *Hauger v. Chicago, R.I. & Pac. R.R.,* 216 F.2d 501 (7th Cir. 1954); *Burke v. United States,* 32 F.R.D. 213 (E.D.N.Y.1963). While the opinions dealing with "good cause" do not often draw an explicit distinction between trial preparation materials and other materials, in fact an overwhelming proportion of the cases in which a special showing is required are cases involving trial preparation materials.

The rules are amended by eliminating the general requirement of "good cause" from Rule 34 but retaining a requirement of a special showing for trial preparation materials in this subdivision. The required showing is expressed, not in terms of "good cause" whose generality has tended to encourage confusion and controversy, but in terms of the elements of the special showing to be made: substantial need of the materials in the preparation of the case and inability without undue hardship to obtain the substantial equivalent of the materials by other means.

These changes conform to the holdings of the cases, when viewed in light of their facts. Apart from trial preparation, the fact that the materials sought are documentary does not in and of itself require a special showing beyond relevance and absence of privilege. The protective provisions are of course available, and if the party from whom production is sought raises a special issue of privacy (as with respect to income tax returns or grand jury minutes) or points to evidence primarily impeaching, or can show serious burden or expense, the court will exercise its traditional power to decide whether to issue a protective order. On the other hand, the requirement of a special showing for discovery of trial preparation materials reflects the view that each side's informal evaluation of its case should be protected, that each side should be encouraged to prepare independently, and that one side should not automatically have the benefit of the detailed preparatory work of the other side. See Field and McKusick, *Maine Civil Practice* 264 (1959).

Elimination of a "good cause" requirement from Rule 34 and the establishment of a requirement of a special showing in this subdivision will eliminate the confusion caused by having two verbally distinct requirements of justification that the courts have been unable to distinguish clearly. Moreover, the language of the subdivision suggests the factors which the courts should consider in determining whether the requisite showing has been made. The importance of the materials sought to the party seeking them in preparation of his case and the difficulty he will have obtaining them by other means are factors noted in the *Hickman* case. The courts should also consider the likelihood that the party, even if he obtains the information by independent means, will not have the substantial equivalent of the documents the production of which he seeks.

Consideration of these factors may well lead the court to distinguish between witness statements taken by an investigator, on the one hand, and other parts of the investigative file, on the other. The court in *Southern Ry. v. Lanham*, 403 F.2d 119 (5th Cir. 1968), while it naturally addressed itself to the "good cause" requirements of Rule 34, set forth as controlling considerations the factors contained in the language of this subdivision. The analysis of the court suggests circumstances under which witness statements will be discoverable. The witness may have given a fresh and contemporaneous account in a written statement while he is available to the party seeking discovery only a substantial time thereafter. *Lanham, supra* at 127–128; *Guilford, supra* at 926. Or he may be reluctant or hostile. *Lanham, supra* at 128–129; *Brookshire v. Pennsylvania RR*, 14 F.R.D. 154 (N.D.Ohio 1953); *Diamond v. Mohawk Rubber Co.*, 33 F.R.D. 264 (D.Colo.1963). Or he may have a lapse of memory. *Tannenbaum v. Walker*, 16 F.R.D. 570 (E.D.Pa. 1954). Or he may probably be deviating from his prior statement. *Cf. Hauger v. Chicago, R.I. & Pac. RR*, 216 F.2d

501 (7th Cir. 1954). On the other hand, a much stronger showing is needed to obtain evaluative materials in an investigator's reports. *Lanham, supra* at 131–133; *Pickett v. L. R. Ryan, Inc.*, 237 F.Supp. 198 (E.D.S.C.1965).

Materials assembled in the ordinary course of business, or pursuant to public requirements unrelated to litigation, or for other nonlitigation purposes are not under the qualified immunity provided by this subdivision. *Goosman v. A. Duie Pyle, Inc.*, 320 F.2d 45 (4th Cir. 1963); *cf. United States v. New York Foreign Trade Zone Operators, Inc.*, 304 F.2d 792 (2d Cir. 1962). No change is made in the existing doctrine, noted in the *Hickman* case, that one party may discover relevant facts known or available to the other party, even though such facts are contained in a document which is not itself discoverable.

Treatment of Lawyers; Special Protection of Mental Impressions, Conclusions, Opinions, and Legal Theories Concerning the Litigation.—The courts are divided as to whether the work-product doctrine extends to the preparatory work only of lawyers. The *Hickman* case left this issue open since the statements in that case were taken by a lawyer. As to courts of appeals compare *Alltmont v. United States*, 177 F.2d 971, 976 (3d Cir. 1949), cert. denied, 339 U.S. 967 (1950) (*Hickman* applied to statements obtained by FBI agents on theory it should apply to "all statements of prospective witnesses which a party has obtained for his trial counsel's use"), with *Southern Ry. v. Campbell*, 309 F.2d 569 (5th Cir. 1962) (Statements taken by claim agents not workproduct), and *Guilford Nat'l Bank v. Southern Ry.*, 297 F.2d 921 (4th Cir. 1962) (avoiding issue of work-product as to claim agents, deciding case instead under Rule 34 "good cause"). Similarly, the district courts are divided on statements obtained by claim agents, compare, e.g., *Brown v. New York, N.H. & H.R.R.*, 17 F.R.D. 324 (S.D.N.Y.1955) with *Hanke v. Milwaukee Electric Ry. & Transp. Co.*, 7 F.R.D. 540 (E.D.Wis.1947); investigators, compare *Burke v. United States*, 32 F.R.D. 213 (E.D.N.Y.1963) with *Snyder v. United States*, 20 F.R.D. 7 (E.D.N.Y.1956); and insurers, compare *Gottlieb v. Bresler*, 24 F.R.D. 371 (D.D.C.1959) with *Burns v. Mulder*, 20 F.R.D. 605 (E.D.Pa.1957). See 4 Moore's *Federal Practice* ¶26.23[8.1] (2d ed. 1966); 2A Barron & Holtzoff, *Federal Practice and Procedure* § 652.2 (Wright ed. 1961).

A complication is introduced by the use made by courts of the "good cause" requirement of Rule 34, as described above. A court may conclude that trial preparation materials are not work-product because not the result of lawyer's work and yet hold that they are not producible because "good cause" has not been shown. *Cf. Guilford Nat'l Bank v. Southern Ry.*, 297 F.2d 921 (4th Cir. 1962), cited and described above. When the decisions on "good cause" are taken into account, the weight of authority affords protection of the preparatory work of both lawyers and nonlawyers (though not necessarily to the same extent) by requiring more than a showing of relevance to secure production.

Subdivision (b)(3) reflects the trend of the cases by requiring a special showing, not merely as to materials prepared by an attorney, but also as to materials prepared in anticipation of litigation or preparation for trial by or for a party or any representative acting on his behalf. The subdivision then goes on to protect against disclosure the mental impressions, conclusions, opinions, or legal theories concerning the litigation of an attorney or other representative of a party. The *Hickman* opinion drew special attention to the need for protecting an attorney against discovery of memoranda prepared from recollection of oral interviews. The courts have steadfastly safeguarded against disclosure of lawyers' mental impressions and legal theories, as well as mental impressions and subjective evaluations of investigators and claim-agents. In enforcing this provision of the subdivision, the courts will sometimes find it necessary to order disclosure of a document but with portions deleted.

Rules 33 and 36 have been revised in order to permit discovery calling for opinions, contentions, and admissions relating not only to fact but also to the application of law to fact. Under those rules, a party and his attorney or other representative may be required to disclose, to some extent, mental impressions, opinions, or conclusions. But documents or parts of documents containing these matters are protected against discovery by this subdivision. Even though a party may ultimately have to disclose in response to interrogatories or requests to admit, he is entitled to keep confidential documents containing such matters prepared for internal use.

Party's Right to Own Statement—An exception to the requirement of this subdivision enables a party to secure production of his own statement without any special showing. The cases are divided. Compare, *e.g., Safeway Stores, Inc. v. Reynolds,* 176 F.2d 476 (D.C. Cir.1949); *Shupe v. Pennsylvania R.R.,* 19 F.R.D. 144 (W.D.Pa.1956); with *e.g., New York Central R.R. v. Carr,* 251 F.2d 433 (4th Cir. 1957); *Belback v. Wilson Freight Forwarding Co.,* 40 F.R.D. 16 (W.D.Pa.1966).

Courts which treat a party's statement as though it were that of any witness overlook the fact that the party's statement is, without more, admissible in evidence. Ordinarily, a party gives a statement without insisting on a copy because he does not yet have a lawyer and does not understand the legal consequences of his actions. Thus, the statement is given at a time when he functions at a disadvantage. Discrepancies between his trial testimony and earlier statement may result from lapse of memory or ordinary inaccuracy; a written statement produced for the first time at trial may give such discrepancies a prominence which they do not deserve. In appropriate cases the court may order a party to be deposed before his statement is produced. *E.g., Smith v. Central Linen Service Co.,* 39 F.R.D. 15 (D.Md.1966); *McCoy v. General Motors Corp.,* 33 F.R.D. 354 (W.D.Pa. 1963).

Commentators strongly support the view that a party be able to secure his statement without a showing. 4 *Moore's Federal Practice* ¶26.23[8.4] (2d ed. 1966); 2A Barron & Holtzoff, *Federal Practice and Procedure* § 652.3 (Wright ed. 1961); see also Note, *Developments in the Law—Discovery,* 74 Harv.L.Rev. 940, 1039 (1961). The following states have by statute or rule taken the same position: *Statutes:* Fla.Stat.Ann. § 92.33; Ga.Code Ann. § 38–2109(b); La.Stat. Ann.R.S. 13:3732; Mass.Gen.Laws Ann. c. 271, § 44; Minn. Stat.Ann. § 602.01; N.Y.C.P.L.R. § 3101(e); *Rules:* Mo. R.C.P. 56.01(a); N.Dak.R.C.P. 34(b); Wyo.R.C.P. 34(b); *cf.* Mich.G.C.R. 306.2.

In order to clarify and tighten the provision on statements by a party, the term "statement" is defined. The definition is adapted from 18 U.S.C. § 3500(e) (Jencks Act). The statement of a party may of course be that of plaintiff or defendant, and it may be that of an individual or of a corporation or other organization.

Witness' Right to Own Statement.—A second exception to the requirement of this subdivision permits a non-party witness to obtain a copy of his own statement without any special showing. Many, though not all, of the considerations supporting a party's right to obtain his statement apply also to the non-party witness. Insurance companies are increasingly recognizing that a witness is entitled to a copy of his statement and are modifying their regular practice accordingly.

Subdivision (b)(4)—Trial Preparation: Experts. This is a new provision dealing with discovery of information (including facts and opinions) obtained by a party from an expert retained by that party in relation to litigation or obtained by the expert and not yet transmitted to the party. The subdivision deals separately with those experts whom the party expects to call as trial witnesses and with those experts who have been retained or specially employed by the party but who are not expected to be witnesses. It should be noted that the subdivision does not address itself to the expert whose information was not acquired in preparation for trial but rather because he was an actor or viewer with respect to transactions or occurrences that are part of the subject matter of the lawsuit. Such an expert should be treated as an ordinary witness.

Subsection (b)(4)(A) deals with discovery of information obtained by or through experts who will be called as witnesses at trial. The provision is responsive to problems suggested by a relatively recent line of authorities. Many of these cases present intricate and difficult issues as to which expert testimony is likely to be determinative. Prominent among them are food and drug, patent, and condemnation cases. See, *e.g., United States v. Nysco Laboratories, Inc.,* 26 F.R.D. 159, 162 (E.D.N.Y.1960) (food and drug); *E. I. du Pont de Nemours & Co. v. Phillips Petroleum Co.,* 24 F.R.D. 416, 421 (D.Del.1959) (patent); *Cold Metal Process Co. v. Aluminum Co. of America,* 7 F.R.D. 425 (N.D.Ohio 1947), aff'd, *Sachs v. Aluminum Co. of America,* 167 F.2d 570 (6th Cir. 1948) (same); *United States v. 50.34 Acres of Land,* 13 F.R.D. 19 (E.D.N.Y.1952) (condemnation).

In cases of this character, a prohibition against discovery of information held by expert witnesses produces in acute form the very evils that discovery has been created to prevent. Effective cross-examination of an expert witness requires advance preparation. The lawyer even with the help of his own experts frequently cannot anticipate the particular approach his adversary's expert will take or the data on which he will base his judgment on the stand. McGlothlin, *Some Practical Problems in Proof of Economic, Scientific, and Technical Facts,* 23 F.R.D. 467, 478 (1958). A California study of discovery and pretrial in condemnation cases notes that the only substitute for discovery of experts' valuation materials is "lengthy—and often fruitless—cross-examination during trial," and recommends pretrial exchange of such material. Calif.Law Rev.Comm'n, Discovery in Eminent Domain Proceedings 707–710 (Jan. 1963). Similarly, effective rebuttal requires advance knowledge of the line of testimony of the other side. If the latter is foreclosed by a rule against discovery, then the narrowing of issues and elimination of surprise which discovery normally produces are frustrated.

These considerations appear to account for the broadening of discovery against experts in the cases cited where expert testimony was central to the case. In some instances, the opinions are explicit in relating expanded discovery to improved cross-examination and rebuttal at trial. *Franks v. National Dairy Products Corp.*, 41 F.R.D. 234 (W.D.Tex. 1966); *United States v. 23.76 Acres*, 32 F.R.D. 593 (D.Md. 1963); see also an unpublished opinion of Judge Hincks, quoted in *United States v. 48 Jars, etc.*, 23 F.R.D. 192, 198 (D.D.C.1958). On the other hand, the need for a new provision is shown by the many cases in which discovery of expert trial witnesses is needed for effective cross-examination and rebuttal, and yet courts apply the traditional doctrine and refuse disclosure. *E.g., United States v. Certain Parcels of Land*, 25 F.R.D. 192 (N.D.Cal.1959); *United States v. Certain Acres*, 18 F.R.D. 98 (M.D.Ga.1955).

Although the trial problems flowing from lack of discovery of expert witnesses are most acute and noteworthy when the case turns largely on experts, the same problems are encountered when a single expert testifies. Thus, subdivision (b)(4)(A) draws no line between complex and simple cases, or between cases with many experts and those with but one. It establishes by rule substantially the procedure adopted by decision of the court in *Knighton v. Villian & Fassio*, 39 F.R.D. 11 (D.Md.1965). For a full analysis of the problem and strong recommendations to the same effect, see Friedenthal, *Discovery and Use of an Adverse Party's Expert Information*, 14 Stan.L.Rev. 455, 485–488 (1962); Long, *Discovery and Experts under the Federal Rules of Civil Procedure*, 38 F.R.D. 111 (1965).

Past judicial restrictions on discovery of an adversary's expert, particularly as to his opinions, reflect the fear that one side will benefit unduly from the other's better preparation. The procedure established in subsection (b)(4)(A) holds the risk to a minimum. Discovery is limited to trial witnesses, and may be obtained only at a time when the parties know who their expert witnesses will be. A party must as a practical matter prepare his own case in advance of that time, for he can hardly hope to build his case out of his opponent's experts.

Subdivision (b)(4)(A) provides for discovery of an expert who is to testify at the trial. A party can require one who intends to use the expert to state the substance of the testimony that the expert is expected to give. The court may order further discovery, and it has ample power to regulate its timing and scope and to prevent abuse. Ordinarily, the order for further discovery shall compensate the expert for his time, and may compensate the party who intends to use the expert for past expenses reasonably incurred in obtaining facts or opinions from the expert. Those provisions are likely to discourage abusive practices.

Subdivision (b)(4)(B) deals with an expert who has been retained or specially employed by the party in anticipation of litigation or preparation for trial (thus excluding an expert who is simply a general employee of the party not specially employed on the case), but who is not expected to be called as a witness. Under its provisions, a party may discover facts known or opinions held by such an expert only on a showing of exceptional circumstances under which it is impracticable for the party seeking discovery to obtain facts or opinions on the same subject by other means.

Subdivision (b)(4)(B) is concerned only with experts retained or specially consulted in relation to trial preparation. Thus the subdivision precludes discovery against experts who were informally consulted in preparation for trial, but not retained or specially employed. As an ancillary procedure, a party may on a proper showing require the other party to name experts retained or specially employed, but not those informally consulted.

These new provisions of subdivision (b)(4) repudiate the few decisions that have held an expert's information privileged simply because of his status as an expert, *e.g., American Oil Co. v. Pennsylvania Petroleum Products Co.*, 23 F.R.D. 680, 685–686 (D.R.I.1959). See *Louisell, Modern California Discovery* 315–316 (1963). They also reject as ill-considered the decisions which have sought to bring expert information within the work-product doctrine. See *United States v. McKay*, 372 F.2d 174, 176–177 (5th Cir. 1967). The provisions adopt a form of the more recently developed doctrine of "unfairness". See *e.g., United States v. 23.76 Acres of Land*, 32 F.R.D. 593, 597 (D.Md.1963); Louisell, *supra*, at 317–318; 4 *Moore's Federal Practice* 26.24 (2d ed. 1966).

Under subdivision (b)(4)(C), the court is directed or authorized to issue protective orders, including an order that the expert be paid a reasonable fee for time spent in responding to discovery, and that the party whose expert is made subject to discovery be paid a fair portion of the fees and expenses that the party incurred in obtaining information from the expert. The court may issue the latter order as a condition of discovery, or it may delay the order until after discovery is completed. These provisions for fees and expenses meet the objection that it is unfair to permit one side to obtain without cost the benefit of an expert's work for which the other side has paid, often a substantial sum. E.g., *Lewis v. United Air Lines Transp. Corp.*, 32 F.Supp. 21 (W.D.Pa.1940); *Walsh v. Reynolds Metal Co.*, 15 F.R.D. 376 (D.N.J.1954). On the other hand, a party may not obtain discovery simply by offering to pay fees and expenses. Cf. *Boynton v. R. J. Reynolds Tobacco Co.*, 36 F.Supp. 593 (D.Mass.1941).

In instances of discovery under subdivision (b)(4)(B), the court is directed to award fees and expenses to the other party, since the information is of direct value to the discovering party's preparation of his case. In ordering discovery under (b)(4)(A)(ii), the court has discretion whether to award fees and expenses to the other party; its decision should depend upon whether the discovering party is simply learning about the other party's case or is going beyond this to develop his own case. Even in cases where the court is directed to issue a protective order, it may decline to do so if it finds that manifest injustice would result. Thus, the court can protect, when necessary and appropriate, the interests of an indigent party.

Subdivision (c)—Protective Orders. The provisions of existing Rule 30(b) are transferred to this subdivision (c), as part of the rearrangement of Rule 26. The language has been changed to give it application to discovery generally. The subdivision recognizes the power of the court in the district where a deposition is being taken to make protective orders. Such power is needed when the deposition is being taken far from the court where the action is pending. The court in the district where the deposition is being taken may, and frequently will, remit the deponent or party to the court where the action is pending.

In addition, drafting changes are made to carry out and clarify the sense of the rule. Insertions are made to avoid any possible implication that a protective order does not extend to "time" as well as to "place" or may not safeguard against "undue burden or expense."

The new reference to trade secrets and other confidential commercial information reflects existing law. The courts have not given trade secrets automatic and complete immunity against disclosure, but have in each case weighed their claim to privacy against the need for disclosure. Frequently, they have been afforded a limited protection. See, *e.g., Covey Oil Co. v. Continental Oil Co.,* 340 F.2d 993 (10th Cir. 1965); *Julius M. Ames Co. v. Bostitch, Inc.,* 235 F.Supp. 856 (S.D.N.Y.1964).

The subdivision contains new matter relating to sanctions. When a motion for a protective order is made and the court is disposed to deny it, the court may go a step further and issue an order to provide or permit discovery. This will bring the sanctions of Rule 37(b) directly into play. Since the court has heard the contentions of all interested persons, an affirmative order is justified. See *Rosenberg, Sanctions to Effectuate Pretrial Discovery,* 58 Col.L.Rev. 480, 492–493 (1958). In addition, the court may require the payment of expenses incurred in relation to the motion.

Subdivision (d)—Sequence and Priority. This new provision is concerned with the sequence in which parties may proceed with discovery and with related problems of timing. The principal effects of the new provision are first, to eliminate any fixed priority in the sequence of discovery, and second, to make clear and explicit the court's power to establish priority by an order issued in a particular case.

A priority rule developed by some courts, which confers priority on the party who first serves notice of taking a deposition, is unsatisfactory in several important respects:

First, this priority rule permits a party to establish a priority running to all depositions as to which he has given earlier notice. Since he can on a given day serve notice of taking many depositions he is in a position to delay his adversary's taking of depositions for an inordinate time. Some courts have ruled that deposition priority also permits a party to delay his answers to interrogatories and production of documents. *E.g., E. I. du Pont de Nemours & Co. v. Phillips Petroleum Co.,* 23 F.R.D. 237 (D.Del.1959); *but cf. Sturdevant v. Sears, Roebuck & Co.,* 32 F.R.D. 426 (W.D.Mo. 1963).

Second, since notice is the key to priority, if both parties wish to take depositions first a race results. See *Caldwell-Clements, Inc. v. McGraw-Hill Pub. Co.,* 11 F.R.D. 156 (S.D.N.Y.1951) (description of tactics used by parties). But the existing rules on notice of deposition create a race with runners starting from different positions. The plaintiff may not give notice without leave of court until 20 days after commencement of the action, whereas the defendant may serve notice at any time after commencement. Thus, a careful and prompt defendant can almost always secure priority. This advantage of defendants is fortuitous, because the purpose of requiring plaintiff to wait 20 days is to afford defendant an opportunity to obtain counsel, not to confer priority.

Third, although courts have ordered a change in the normal sequence of discovery on a number of occasions, *e.g., Kaeppler v. James H. Matthews & Co.,* 200 F.Supp. 229 (E.D.Pa.1961); *Park & Tilford Distillers Corp. v. Distillers Co.,* 19 F.R.D. 169 (S.D.N.Y.1956), and have at all times avowed discretion to vary the usual priority, most commenta-

tors are agreed that courts in fact grant relief only for "the most obviously compelling reasons." 2A Barron & Holtzoff, *Federal Practice and Procedure* 44–47 (Wright ed. 1961); see also Younger, *Priority of Pretrial Examination in the Federal Courts—A Comment,* 34 N.Y.U.L.Rev. 1271 (1959); Freund, *The Pleading and Pretrial of an Antitrust Claim,* 46 Corn.L.Q. 555, 564 (1964). Discontent with the fairness of actual practice has been evinced by other observers. Comments, 59 Yale L.J. 117, 134–136 (1949); Yudkin, *Some Refinements in Federal Discovery Procedure,* 11 Fed.B.J. 289, 296–297 (1951); *Developments in the Law-Discovery,* 74 Harv.L.Rev. 940, 954–958 (1961).

Despite these difficulties, some courts have adhered to the priority rule, presumably because it provides a test which is easily understood and applied by the parties without much court intervention. It thus permits deposition discovery to function extrajudicially, which the rules provide for and the courts desire. For these same reasons, courts are reluctant to make numerous exceptions to the rule.

The Columbia Survey makes clear that the problem of priority does not affect litigants generally. It found that most litigants do not move quickly to obtain discovery. In over half of the cases, both parties waited at least 50 days. During the first 20 days after commencement of the action—the period when defendant might assure his priority by noticing depositions—16 percent of the defendants acted to obtain discovery. A race could not have occurred in more than 16 percent of the cases and it undoubtedly occurred in fewer. On the other hand, five times as many defendants as plaintiffs served notice of deposition during the first 19 days. To the same effect, see Comment, *Tactical Use and Abuse of Depositions Under the Federal Rules,* 59 Yale L.J. 117, 134 (1949).

These findings do not mean, however, that the priority rule is satisfactory or that a problem of priority does not exist. The court decisions show that parties do battle on this issue and carry their disputes to court. The statistics show that these court cases are not typical. By the same token, they reveal that more extensive exercise of judicial discretion to vary the priority will not bring a flood of litigation, and that a change in the priority rule will in fact affect only a small fraction of the cases.

It is contended by some that there is no need to alter the existing priority practice. In support, it is urged that there is no evidence that injustices in fact result from present practice and that, in any event, the courts can and do promulgate local rules, as in New York, to deal with local situations and issue orders to avoid possible injustice in particular cases.

Subdivision (d) is based on the contrary view that the rule of priority based on notice is unsatisfactory and unfair in its operation. Subdivision (d) follows an approach adapted from Civil Rule 4 of the District Court for the Southern District of New York. That rule provides that starting 40 days after commencement of the action, unless otherwise ordered by the court, the fact that one party is taking a deposition shall not prevent another party from doing so "concurrently." In practice, the depositions are not usually taken simultaneously; rather, the parties work out arrangements for alternation in the taking of depositions. One party may take a complete deposition and then the other, or, if the depositions are extensive, one party deposes for a set time, and then the other. See *Caldwell-Clements, Inc. v. McCraw-Hill Pub. Co.*, 11 F.R.D. 156 (S.D.N.Y.1951).

In principle, one party's initiation of discovery should not wait upon the other's completion, unless delay is dictated by special considerations. Clearly the principle is feasible with respect to all methods of discovery other than depositions. And the experience of the Southern District of New York shows that the principle can be applied to depositions as well. The courts have not had an increase in motion business on this matter. Once it is clear to lawyers that they bargain on an equal footing, they are usually able to arrange for an orderly succession of depositions without judicial intervention. Professor Moore has called attention to Civil Rule 4 and suggested that it may usefully be extended to other areas. 4 *Moore's Federal Practice* 1154 (2d ed. 1966).

The court may upon motion and by order grant priority in a particular case. But a local court rule purporting to confer priority in certain classes of cases would be inconsistent with this subdivision and thus void.

Subdivision (e)—Supplementation of Responses. The rules do not now state whether interrogatories (and questions at deposition as well as requests for inspection and admissions) impose a "continuing burden" on the responding party to supplement his answers if he obtains new information. The issue is acute when new information renders substantially incomplete or inaccurate an answer which was complete and accurate when made. It is essential that the rules provide an answer to this question. The parties can adjust to a rule either way, once they know what it is. See 4 *Moore's Federal Practice* ¶33.25[4] (2d ed. 1966).

Arguments can be made both ways. Imposition of a continuing burden reduces the proliferation of additional sets of interrogatories. Some courts have adopted local rules establishing such a burden. *E.g.*, E.D.Pa.R. 20(f), quoted in *Taggart v. Vermont Transp. Co.*, 32 F.R.D. 587 (E.D.Pa. 1963); D.Me.R. 15(c). Others have imposed the burden by decision. *E.g.*, *Chenault v. Nebraska Farm Products, Inc.*, 9 F.R.D. 529, 533 (D.Nebr.1949). On the other hand, there are serious objections to the burden, especially in protracted cases. Although the party signs the answers, it is his lawyer who understands their significance and bears the responsibility to bring answers up to date. In a complex case all sorts of information reaches the party, who little understands its bearing on answers previously given to interrogatories. In practice, therefore, the lawyer under a continuing burden must periodically recheck all interrogatories and canvass all new information. But a full set of new answers may no longer be needed by the interrogating party. Some issues will have been dropped from the case, some questions are now seen as unimportant, and other questions must in any event be reformulated. See *Novick v. Pennsylvania R.R.*, 18 F.R.D. 296, 298 (W.D.Pa.1955).

Subdivision (e) provides that a party is not under a continuing burden except as expressly provided. Cf. Note, 68 Harv.L.Rev. 673, 677 (1955). An exception is made as to the identity of persons having knowledge of discoverable matters, because of the obvious importance to each side of knowing all witnesses and because information about witnesses routinely comes to each lawyer's attention. Many of the decisions on the issue of a continuing burden have in fact concerned the identity of witnesses. An exception is also made as to expert trial witnesses in order to carry out the

provisions of Rule 26(b)(4). See *Diversified Products Corp. v. Sports Center Co.*, 42 F.R.D. 3 (D.Md.1967).

Another exception is made for the situation in which a party, or more frequently his lawyer, obtains actual knowledge that a prior response is incorrect. This exception does not impose a duty to check the accuracy of prior responses, but it prevents knowing concealment by a party or attorney. Finally, a duty to supplement may be imposed by order of the court in a particular case (including an order resulting from a pretrial conference) or by agreement of the parties. A party may of course make a new discovery request which requires supplementation of prior responses.

The duty will normally be enforced, in those limited instances where it is imposed, through sanctions imposed by the trial court, including exclusion of evidence, continuance, or other action, as the court may deem appropriate.

1980 Amendment

Subdivision (f). This subdivision is new. There has been widespread criticism of abuse of discovery. The Committee has considered a number of proposals to eliminate abuse, including a change in Rule 26(b)(1) with respect to the scope of discovery and a change in Rule 33(a) to limit the number of questions that can be asked by interrogatories to parties.

The Committee believes that abuse of discovery, while very serious in certain cases, is not so general as to require such basic changes in the rules that govern discovery in all cases. A very recent study of discovery in selected metropolitan districts tends to support its belief. P. Connolly, E. Holleman, & M. Kuhlman, *Judicial Controls and the Civil Litigative Process: Discovery* (Federal Judicial Center, 1978). In the judgment of the Committee abuse can best be prevented by intervention by the court as soon as abuse is threatened.

To this end this subdivision provides that counsel who has attempted without success to effect with opposing counsel a reasonable program or plan for discovery is entitled to the assistance of the court.

It is not contemplated that requests for discovery conferences will be made routinely. A relatively narrow discovery dispute should be resolved by resort to Rules 26(c) or 37(a), and if it appears that a request for a conference is in fact grounded in such a dispute, the court may refer counsel to those rules. If the court is persuaded that a request is frivolous or vexatious, it can strike it. See Rules 11 and 7(b)(2).

A number of courts routinely consider discovery matters in preliminary pretrial conferences held shortly after the pleadings are closed. This subdivision does not interfere with such a practice. It authorizes the court to combine a discovery conference with a pretrial conference under Rule 16 if a pretrial conference is held sufficiently early to prevent or curb abuse.

1983 Amendment

Excessive discovery and evasion or resistance to reasonable discovery requests pose significant problems. Recent studies have made some attempt to determine the sources and extent of the difficulties. See Brazil, *Civil Discovery: Lawyers' Views of its Effectiveness, Principal Problems and Abuses*, American Bar Foundation (1980); Connolly, Holle-

---

man & Kuhlman, *Judicial Controls and the Civil Litigative Process: Discovery*, Federal Judicial Center (1978); Ellington, *A Study of Sanctions for Discovery Abuse*, Department of Justice (1979); Schroeder & Frank, *The Proposed Changes in the Discovery Rules*, 1978 Ariz.St.L.J. 475.

The purpose of discovery is to provide a mechanism for making relevant information available to the litigants. "Mutual knowledge of all the relevant facts gathered by both parties is essential to proper litigation." *Hickman v. Taylor*, 329 U.S. 495, 507 (1947). Thus the spirit of the rules is violated when advocates attempt to use discovery tools as tactical weapons rather than to expose the facts and illuminate the issues by overuse of discovery or unnecessary use of defensive weapons or evasive responses. All of this results in excessively costly and time-consuming activities that are disproportionate to the nature of the case, the amount involved, or the issues or values at stake.

Given our adversary tradition and the current discovery rules, it is not surprising that there are many opportunities, if not incentives, for attorneys to engage in discovery that, although authorized by the broad, permissive terms of the rules, nevertheless results in delay. See Brazil, *The Adversary Character of Civil Discovery: A Critique and Proposals for Change*, 31 Vand.L.Rev. 1259 (1978). As a result, it has been said that the rules have "not infrequently [been] exploited to the disadvantage of justice." *Herbert v. Lando*, 441 U.S. 153, 179 (1979) (Powell, J., concurring). These practices impose costs on an already overburdened system and impede the fundamental goal of the "just, speedy, and inexpensive determination of every action." Fed.R.Civ.P. 1.

Subdivision (a); Discovery Methods. The deletion of the last sentence of Rule 26(a)(1), which provided that unless the court ordered otherwise under Rule 26(c) "the frequency of use" of the various discovery methods was not to be limited, is an attempt to address the problem of duplicative, redundant, and excessive discovery and to reduce it. The amendment, in conjunction with the changes in Rule 26(b)(1), is designed to encourage district judges to identify instances of needless discovery and to limit the use of the various discovery devices accordingly. The question may be raised by one of the parties, typically on a motion for a protective order, or by the court on its own initiative. It is entirely appropriate to consider a limitation on the frequency of use of discovery at a discovery conference under Rule 26(f) or at any other pretrial conference authorized by these rules. In considering the discovery needs of a particular case, the court should consider the factors described in Rule 26(b)(1).

Subdivision (b); Discovery Scope and Limits. Rule 26(b)(1) has been amended to add a sentence to deal with the problem of over-discovery. The objective is to guard against redundant or disproportionate discovery by giving the court authority to reduce the amount of discovery that may be directed to matters that are otherwise proper subjects of inquiry. The new sentence is intended to encourage judges to be more aggressive in identifying and discouraging discovery overuse. The grounds mentioned in the amended rule for limiting discovery reflect the existing practice of many courts in issuing protective orders under Rule 26(c). See, e.g., *Carlson Cos. v. Sperry & Hutchinson Co.*, 374 F.Supp. 1080 (D.Minn.1974); *Dolgow v. Anderson*, 53 F.R.D. 661 (E.D.N.Y.1971); *Mitchell v. American Tobacco Co.*, 33 F.R.D. 262 (M.D.Pa.1963); *Welty v. Clute*, 1 F.R.D. 446 (W.D.N.Y.1941). On the whole, however, district judges

have been reluctant to limit the use of the discovery devices. See, e.g., *Apco Oil Co. v. Certified Transp., Inc.*, 46 F.R.D. 428 (W.D.Mo.1969). See generally 8 Wright & Miller, *Federal Practice and Procedure: Civil* §§ 2036, 2037, 2039, 2040 (1970).

The first element of the standard, Rule 26(b)(1)(i), is designed to minimize redundancy in discovery and encourage attorneys to be sensitive to the comparative costs of different methods of securing information. Subdivision (b)(1)(ii) also seeks to reduce repetitiveness and to oblige lawyers to think through their discovery activities in advance so that full utilization is made of each deposition, document request, or set of interrogatories. The elements of Rule 26(b)(1)(iii) address the problem of discovery that is disproportionate to the individual lawsuit as measured by such matters as its nature and complexity, the importance of the issues at stake in a case seeking damages, the limitations on a financially weak litigant to withstand extensive opposition to a discovery program or to respond to discovery requests, and the significance of the substantive issues, as measured in philosophic, social, or institutional terms. Thus the rule recognizes that many cases in public policy spheres, such as employment practices, free speech, and other matters, may have importance far beyond the monetary amount involved. The court must apply the standards in an even-handed manner that will prevent use of discovery to wage a war of attrition or as a device to coerce a party, whether financially weak or affluent.

The rule contemplates greater judicial involvement in the discovery process and thus acknowledges the reality that it cannot always operate on a self-regulating basis. See Connolly, Holleman & Kuhlman, *Judicial Controls and the Civil Litigative Process: Discovery* 77, Federal Judicial Center (1978). In an appropriate case the court could restrict the number of depositions, interrogatories, or the scope of a production request. But the court must be careful not to deprive a party of discovery that is reasonably necessary to afford a fair opportunity to develop and prepare the case.

The court may act on motion, or its own initiative. It is entirely appropriate to resort to the amended rule in conjunction with a discovery conference under Rule 26(f) or one of the other pretrial conferences authorized by the rules.

Subdivision (g); Signing of Discovery Requests, Responses, and Objections. Rule 26(g) imposes an affirmative duty to engage in pretrial discovery in a responsible manner that is consistent with the spirit and purposes of Rules 26 through 37. In addition, Rule 26(g) is designed to curb discovery abuse by explicitly encouraging the imposition of sanctions. The subdivision provides a deterrent to both excessive discovery and evasion by imposing a certification requirement that obliges each attorney to stop and think about the legitimacy of a discovery request, a response thereto, or an objection. The term "response" includes answers to interrogatories and to requests to admit as well as responses to production requests.

If primary responsibility for conducting discovery is to continue to rest with the litigants, they must be obliged to act responsibly and avoid abuse. With this in mind, Rule 26(g), which parallels the amendments to Rule 11, requires an attorney or unrepresented party to sign each discovery request, response, or objection. Motions relating to discovery are governed by Rule 11. However, since a discovery request, response, or objection usually deals with more specific subject matter than motions or papers, the elements that must be certified in connection with the former are spelled out more completely. The signature is a certification of the elements set forth in Rule 26(g).

Although the certification duty requires the lawyer to pause and consider the reasonableness of his request, response, or objection, it is not meant to discourage or restrict necessary and legitimate discovery. The rule simply requires that the attorney make a reasonable inquiry into the factual basis of his response, request, or objection.

The duty to make a "reasonable inquiry" is satisfied if the investigation undertaken by the attorney and the conclusions drawn therefrom are reasonable under the circumstances. It is an objective standard similar to the one imposed by Rule 11. See the Advisory Committee Note to Rule 11. See also *Kinee v. Abraham Lincoln Fed. Sav. & Loan Ass'n*, 365 F.Supp. 975 (E.D.Pa.1973). In making the inquiry, the attorney may rely on assertions by the client and on communications with other counsel in the case as long as that reliance is appropriate under the circumstances. Ultimately, what is reasonable is a matter for the court to decide on the totality of the circumstances.

Rule 26(g) does not require the signing attorney to certify the truthfulness of the client's factual responses to a discovery request. Rather, the signature certifies that the lawyer has made a reasonable effort to assure that the client has provided all the information and documents available to him that are responsive to the discovery demand. Thus, the lawyer's certification under Rule 26(g) should be distinguished from other signature requirements in the rules, such as those in Rules 30(e) and 33.

Nor does the rule require a party or an attorney to disclose privileged communications or work product in order to show that a discovery request, response, or objection is substantially justified. The provisions of Rule 26(c), including appropriate orders after *in camera* inspection by the court, remain available to protect a party claiming privilege or work product protection.

The signing requirement means that every discovery request, response, or objection should be grounded on a theory that is reasonable under the precedents or a good faith belief as to what should be the law. This standard is heavily dependent on the circumstances of each case. The certification speaks as of the time it is made. The duty to supplement discovery responses continues to be governed by Rule 26(e).

Concern about discovery abuse has led to widespread recognition that there is a need for more aggressive judicial control and supervision. *ACF Industries, Inc. v. EEOC*, 439 U.S. 1081 (1979) (certiorari denied) (Powell, J., dissenting). Sanctions to deter discovery abuse would be more effective if they were diligently applied "not merely to penalize those whose conduct may be deemed to warrant such a sanction, but to deter those who might be tempted to such conduct in the absence of such a deterrent." *National Hockey League v. Metropolitan Hockey Club*, 427 U.S. 639, 643 (1976). See also Note, *The Emerging Deterrence Orientation in the Imposition of Discovery Sanctions*, 91 Harv.L.Rev. 1033 (1978). Thus the premise of Rule 26(g) is that imposing sanctions on attorneys who fail to meet the rule's standards will significantly reduce abuse by imposing disadvantages therefor.

Because of the asserted reluctance to impose sanctions on attorneys who abuse the discovery rules, see Brazil, *Civil Discovery: Lawyers' Views of its Effectiveness, Principal Problems and Abuses*, American Bar Foundation (1980); Ellington, *A Study of Sanctions for Discovery Abuse*, Department of Justice (1979), Rule 26(g) makes explicit the authority judges now have to impose appropriate sanctions and requires them to use it. This authority derives from Rule 37, 28 U.S.C. § 1927, and the court's inherent power. See *Roadway Express, Inc. v. Piper*, 447 U.S. 752 (1980); *Martin v. Bell Helicopter Co.*, 85 F.R.D. 654, 661–62 (D.Col. 1980); Note, *Sanctions Imposed by Courts on Attorneys Who Abuse the Judicial Process*, 44 U.Chi.L.Rev. 619 (1977). The new rule mandates that sanctions be imposed on attorneys who fail to meet the standards established in the first portion of Rule 26(g). The nature of the sanction is a matter of judicial discretion to be exercised in light of the particular circumstances. The court may take into account any failure by the party seeking sanctions to invoke protection under Rule 26(c) at an early stage in the litigation.

The sanctioning process must comport with due process requirements. The kind of notice and hearing required will depend on the facts of the case and the severity of the sanction being considered. To prevent the proliferation of the sanction procedure and to avoid multiple hearings, discovery in any sanction proceeding normally should be permitted only when it is clearly required by the interests of justice. In most cases the court will be aware of the circumstances and only a brief hearing should be necessary.

1987 Amendment

The amendments are technical. No substantive change is intended.

1993 Amendments

Subdivision (a). Through the addition of paragraphs (1)–(4), this subdivision imposes on parties a duty to disclose, without awaiting formal discovery requests, certain basic information that is needed in most cases to prepare for trial or make an informed decision about settlement. The rule requires all parties (1) early in the case to exchange information regarding potential witnesses, documentary evidence, damages, and insurance, (2) at an appropriate time during the discovery period to identify expert witnesses and provide a detailed written statement of the testimony that may be offered at trial through specially retained experts, and (3) as the trial date approaches to identify the particular evidence that may be offered at trial. The enumeration in Rule 26(a) of items to be disclosed does not prevent a court from requiring by order or local rule that the parties disclose additional information without a discovery request. Nor are parties precluded from using traditional discovery methods to obtain further information regarding these matters, as for example asking an expert during a deposition about testimony given in other litigation beyond the four-year period specified in Rule 26(a)(2)(B).

A major purpose of the revision is to accelerate the exchange of basic information about the case and to eliminate the paper work involved in requesting such information, and the rule should be applied in a manner to achieve those objectives. The concepts of imposing a duty of disclosure were set forth in Brazil, *The Adversary Character of Civil*

Discovery: A Critique and Proposals for Change, 31 *Vand. L.Rev.* 1348 (1978), and Schwarzer, *The Federal Rules, the Adversary Process, and Discovery Reform,* 50 *U.Pitt.L.Rev.* 703, 721–23 (1989).

The rule is based upon the experience of district courts that have required disclosure of some of this information through local rules, court-approved standard interrogatories, and standing orders. Most have required pretrial disclosure of the kind of information described in Rule 26(a)(3). Many have required written reports from experts containing information like that specified in Rule 26(a)(2)(B). While far more limited, the experience of the few state and federal courts that have required pre-discovery exchange of core information such as is contemplated in Rule 26(a)(1) indicates that savings in time and expense can be achieved, particularly if the litigants meet and discuss the issues in the case as a predicate for this exchange and if a judge supports the process, as by using the results to guide further proceedings in the case. Courts in Canada and the United Kingdom have for many years required disclosure of certain information without awaiting a request from an adversary.

Paragraph (1). As the functional equivalent of court-ordered interrogatories, this paragraph requires early disclosure, without need for any request, of four types of information that have been customarily secured early in litigation through formal discovery. The introductory clause permits the court, by local rule, to exempt all or particular types of cases from these disclosure requirement *[sic]* or to modify the nature of the information to be disclosed. It is expected that courts would, for example, exempt cases like Social Security reviews and government collection cases in which discovery would not be appropriate or would be unlikely. By order the court may eliminate or modify the disclosure requirements in a particular case, and similarly the parties, unless precluded by order or local rule, can stipulate to elimination or modification of the requirements for that case. The disclosure obligations specified in paragraph (1) will not be appropriate for all cases, and it is expected that changes in these obligations will be made by the court or parties when the circumstances warrant.

Authorization of these local variations is, in large measure, included in order to accommodate the Civil Justice Reform Act of 1990, which implicitly directs districts to experiment during the study period with differing procedures to reduce the time and expense of civil litigation. The civil justice delay and expense reduction plans adopted by the courts under the Act differ as to the type, form, and timing of disclosures required. Section 105(c)(1) of the Act calls for a report by the Judicial Conference to Congress by December 31, 1995, comparing experience in twenty of these courts; and section 105(c)(2)(B) contemplates that some changes in the Rules may then be needed. While these studies may indicate the desirability of further changes in Rule 26(a)(1), these changes probably could not become effective before December 1998 at the earliest. In the meantime, the present revision puts in place a series of disclosure obligations that, unless a court acts affirmatively to impose other requirements or indeed to reject all such requirements for the present, are designed to eliminate certain discovery, help focus the discovery that is needed, and facilitate preparation for trial or settlement.

Subparagraph (A) requires identification of all persons who, based on the investigation conducted thus far, are likely to have discoverable information relevant to the factual disputes between the parties. All persons with such information should be disclosed, whether or not their testimony will be supportive of the position of the disclosing party. As officers of the court, counsel are expected to disclose the identity of those persons who may be used by them as witnesses or who, if their potential testimony were known, might reasonably be expected to be deposed or called as a witness by any of the other parties. Indicating briefly the general topics on which such persons have information should not be burdensome, and will assist other parties in deciding which depositions will actually be needed.

Subparagraph (B) is included as a substitute for the inquiries routinely made about the existence and location of documents and other tangible things in the possession, custody, or control of the disclosing party. Although, unlike subdivision (a)(3)(C), an itemized listing of each exhibit is not required, the disclosure should describe and categorize, to the extent identified during the initial investigation, the nature and location of potentially relevant documents and records, including computerized data and other electronically-recorded information, sufficiently to enable opposing parties (1) to make an informed decision concerning which documents might need to be examined, at least initially, and (2) to frame their document requests in a manner likely to avoid squabbles resulting from the wording of the requests. As with potential witnesses, the requirement for disclosure of documents applies to all potentially relevant items then known to the party, whether or not supportive of its contentions in the case.

Unlike subparagraphs (C) and (D), subparagraph (B) does not require production of any documents. Of course, in cases involving few documents a disclosing party may prefer to provide copies of the documents rather than describe them, and the rule is written to afford this option to the disclosing party. If, as will be more typical, only the description is provided, the other parties are expected to obtain the documents desired by proceeding under Rule 34 or through informal requests. The disclosing party does not, by describing documents under subparagraph (B), waive its right to object to production on the basis of privilege or work product protection, or to assert that the documents are not sufficiently relevant to justify the burden or expense of production.

The initial disclosure requirements of subparagraphs (A) and (B) are limited to identification of potential evidence "relevant to disputed facts alleged with particularity in the pleadings." There is no need for a party to identify potential evidence with respect to allegations that are admitted. Broad, vague, and conclusory allegations sometimes tolerated in notice pleading—for example, the assertion that a product with many component parts is defective in some unspecified manner—should not impose upon responding parties the obligation at that point to search for and identify all persons possibly involved in, or all documents affecting, the design, manufacture, and assembly of the product. The greater the specificity and clarity of the allegations in the pleadings, the more complete should be the listing of potential witnesses and types of documentary evidence. Although paragraphs (1)(A) and (1)(B) by their terms refer to the factual disputes defined in the pleadings, the rule contemplates that these issues would be informally refined and clarified during the meeting of the parties under subdivision (f) and that the disclosure obligations would be adjusted in the light of these discussions. The disclosure requirements should, in short, be applied with common sense in light of the principles of Rule 1, keeping in mind the salutary purposes that the rule is intended to accomplish. The litigants should not indulge in gamesmanship with respect to the disclosure obligations.

Subparagraph (C) imposes a burden of disclosure that includes the functional equivalent of a standing Request for Production under Rule 34. A party claiming damages or other monetary relief must, in addition to disclosing the calculation of such damages, make available the supporting documents for inspection and copying as if a request for such materials had been made under Rule 34. This obligation applies only with respect to documents then reasonably available to it and not privileged or protected as work product. Likewise, a party would not be expected to provide a calculation of damages which, as in many patent infringement actions, depends on information in the possession of another party or person.

Subparagraph (D) replaces subdivision (b)(2) of Rule 26, and provides that liability insurance policies be made available for inspection and copying. The last two sentences of that subdivision have been omitted as unnecessary, not to signify any change of law. The disclosure of insurance information does not thereby render such information admissible in evidence. See Rule 411, Federal Rules of Evidence. Nor does subparagraph (D) require disclosure of applications for insurance, though in particular cases such information may be discoverable in accordance with revised subdivision (a)(5).

Unless the court directs a different time, the disclosures required by subdivision (a)(1) are to be made at or within 10 days after the meeting of the parties under subdivision (f). One of the purposes of this meeting is to refine the factual disputes with respect to which disclosures should be made under paragraphs (1)(A) and (1)(B), particularly if an answer has not been filed by a defendant, or, indeed, to afford the parties an opportunity to modify by stipulation the timing or scope of these obligations. The time of this meeting is generally left to the parties provided it is held at least 14 days before a scheduling conference is held or before a scheduling order is due under Rule 16(b). In cases in which no scheduling conference is held, this will mean that the meeting must ordinarily be held within 75 days after a defendant has first appeared in the case and hence that the initial disclosures would be due no later than 85 days after the first appearance of a defendant.

Before making its disclosures, a party has the obligation under subdivision (g)(1) to make a reasonable inquiry into the facts of the case. The rule does not demand an exhaustive investigation at this stage of the case, but one that is reasonable under the circumstances, focusing on the facts that are alleged with particularity in the pleadings. The type of investigation that can be expected at this point will vary based upon such factors as the number and complexity of the issues; the location, nature, number, and availability of potentially relevant witnesses and documents; the extent of past working relationships between the attorney and the client, particularly in handling related or similar litigation; and of course how long the party has to conduct an investigation, either before or after filing of the case. As provided in the last sentence of subdivision (a)(1), a party is not excused from the duty of disclosure merely because its investigation

is incomplete. The party should make its initial disclosures based on the pleadings and the information then reasonably available to it. As its investigation continues and as the issues in the pleadings are clarified, it should supplement its disclosures as required by subdivision (e)(1). A party is not relieved from its obligation of disclosure merely because another party has not made its disclosures or has made an inadequate disclosure.

It will often be desirable, particularly if the claims made in the complaint are broadly stated, for the parties to have their Rule 26(f) meeting early in the case, perhaps before a defendant has answered the complaint or had time to conduct other than a cursory investigation. In such circumstances, in order to facilitate more meaningful and useful initial disclosures, they can and should stipulate to a period of more than 10 days after the meeting in which to make these disclosures, at least for defendants who had no advance notice of the potential litigation. A stipulation at an early meeting affording such a defendant at least 60 days after receiving the complaint in which to make its disclosures under subdivision (a)(1)—a period that is two weeks longer than the time formerly specified for responding to interrogatories served with a complaint—should be adequate and appropriate in most cases.

Paragraph (2). This paragraph imposes an additional duty to disclose information regarding expert testimony sufficiently in advance of trial that opposing parties have a reasonable opportunity to prepare for effective cross examination and perhaps arrange for expert testimony from other witnesses. Normally the court should prescribe a time for these disclosures in a scheduling order under Rule 16(b), and in most cases the party with the burden of proof on an issue should disclose its expert testimony on that issue before other parties are required to make their disclosures with respect to that issue. In the absence of such a direction, the disclosures are to be made by all parties at least 90 days before the trial date or the date by which the case is to be ready for trial, except that an additional 30 days is allowed (unless the court specifies another time) for disclosure of expert testimony to be used solely to contradict or rebut the testimony that may be presented by another party's expert. For a discussion of procedures that have been used to enhance the reliability of expert testimony, see M. Graham, *Expert Witness Testimony and the Federal Rules of Evidence: Insuring Adequate Assurance of Trustworthiness,* 1986 U.Ill.L.Rev. 90.

Paragraph (2)(B) requires that persons retained or specially employed to provide expert testimony, or whose duties as an employee of the party regularly involve the giving of expert testimony, must prepare a detailed and complete written report, stating the testimony the witness is expected to present during direct examination, together with the reasons therefor. The information disclosed under the former rule in answering interrogatories about the "substance" of expert testimony was frequently so sketchy and vague that it rarely dispensed with the need to depose the expert and often was even of little help in preparing for a deposition of the witness. Revised Rule 37(c)(1) provides an incentive for full disclosure; namely, that a party will not ordinarily be permitted to use on direct examination any expert testimony not so disclosed. Rule 26(a)(2)(B) does not preclude counsel from providing assistance to experts in preparing the reports, and indeed, with experts such as automobile mechanics, this assistance may be needed. Nevertheless, the report, which is intended to set forth the substance of the direct examination, should be written in a manner that reflects the testimony to be given by the witness and it must be signed by the witness.

The report is to disclose the data and other information considered by the expert and any exhibits or charts that summarize or support the expert's opinions. Given this obligation of disclosure, litigants should no longer be able to argue that materials furnished to their experts to be used in forming their opinions—whether or not ultimately relied upon by the expert—are privileged or otherwise protected from disclosure when such persons are testifying or being deposed.

Revised subdivision (b)(4)(A) authorizes the deposition of expert witnesses. Since depositions of experts required to prepare a written report may be taken only after the report has been served, the length of the deposition of such experts should be reduced, and in many cases the report may eliminate the need for a deposition. Revised subdivision (e)(1) requires disclosure of any material changes made in the opinions of an expert from whom a report is required, whether the changes are in the written report or in testimony given at a deposition.

For convenience, this rule and revised Rule 30 continue to use the term "expert" to refer to those persons who will testify under Rule 702 of the Federal Rules of Evidence with respect to scientific, technical, and other specialized matters. The requirement of a written report in paragraph (2)(B), however, applies only to those experts who are retained or specially employed to provide such testimony in the case or whose duties as an employee of a party regularly involve the giving of such testimony. A treating physician, for example, can be deposed or called to testify at trial without any requirement for a written report. By local rule, order, or written stipulation, the requirement of a written report may be waived for particular experts or imposed upon additional persons who will provide opinions under Rule 702.

Paragraph (3). This paragraph imposes an additional duty to disclose, without any request, information customarily needed in final preparation for trial. These disclosures are to be made in accordance with schedules adopted by the court under Rule 16(b) or by special order. If no such schedule is directed by the court, the disclosures are to be made at least 30 days before commencement of the trial. By its terms, rule 26(a)(3) does not require disclosure of evidence to be used solely for impeachment purposes; however, disclosure of such evidence—as well as other items relating to conduct of trial—may be required by local rule or a pretrial order.

Subparagraph (A) requires the parties to designate the persons whose testimony they may present as substantive evidence at trial, whether in person or by deposition. Those who will probably be called as witnesses should be listed separately from those who are not likely to be called but who are being listed in order to preserve the right to do so if needed because of developments during trial. Revised Rule 37(c)(1) provides that only persons so listed may be used at trial to present substantive evidence. This restriction does not apply unless the omission was "without substantial justification" and hence would not bar an unlisted witness if the need for such testimony is based upon developments during

trial that could not reasonably have been anticipated—*e.g.*, a change of testimony.

Listing a witness does not obligate the party to secure the attendance of the person at trial, but should preclude the party from objecting if the person is called to testify by another party who did not list the person as a witness.

Subparagraph (B) requires the party to indicate which of these potential witnesses will be presented by deposition at trial. A party expecting to use at trial a deposition not recorded by stenographic means is required by revised Rule 32 to provide the court with a transcript of the pertinent portions of such depositions. This rule requires that copies of the transcript of a nonstenographic deposition be provided to other parties in advance of trial for verification, an obvious concern since counsel often utilize their own personnel to prepare transcripts from audio or video tapes. By order or local rule, the court may require that parties designate the particular portions of stenographic depositions to be used at trial.

Subparagraph (C) requires disclosure of exhibits, including summaries (whether to be offered in lieu of other documentary evidence or to be used as an aid in understanding such evidence), that may be offered as substantive evidence. The rule requires a separate listing of each such exhibit, though it should permit voluminous items of a similar or standardized character to be described by meaningful categories. For example, unless the court has otherwise directed, a series of vouchers might be shown collectively as a single exhibit with their starting and ending dates. As with witnesses, the exhibits that will probably be offered are to be listed separately from those which are unlikely to be offered but which are listed in order to preserve the right to do so if needed because of developments during trial. Under revised Rule 37(c)(1) the court can permit use of unlisted documents the need for which could not reasonably have been anticipated in advance of trial.

Upon receipt of these final pretrial disclosures, other parties have 14 days (unless a different time is specified by the court) to disclose any objections they wish to preserve to the usability of the deposition testimony or to the admissibility of the documentary evidence (other than under Rules 402 and 403 of the Federal Rules of Evidence). Similar provisions have become commonplace either in pretrial orders or by local rules, and significantly expedite the presentation of evidence at trial, as well as eliminate the need to have available witnesses to provide "foundation" testimony for most items of documentary evidence. The listing of a potential objection does not constitute the making of that objection or require the court to rule on the objection; rather, it preserves the right of the party to make the objection when and as appropriate during trial. The court may, however, elect to treat the listing as a motion "in limine" and rule upon the objections in advance of trial to the extent appropriate.

The time specified in the rule for the final pretrial disclosures is relatively close to the trial date. The objective is to eliminate the time and expense in making these disclosures of evidence and objections in those cases that settle shortly before trial, while affording a reasonable time for final preparation for trial in those cases that do not settle. In many cases, it will be desirable for the court in a scheduling or pretrial order to set an earlier time for disclosures of evidence and provide more time for disclosing potential objections.

Paragraph (4). This paragraph prescribes the form of disclosures. A signed written statement is required, reminding the parties and counsel of the solemnity of the obligations imposed; and the signature on the initial or pretrial disclosure is a certification under subdivision (g)(1) that it is complete and correct as of the time when made. Consistent with Rule 5(d), these disclosures are to be filed with the court unless otherwise directed. It is anticipated that many courts will direct that expert reports required under paragraph (2)(B) not be filed until needed in connection with a motion or for trial.

Paragraph (5). This paragraph is revised to take note of the availability of revised Rule 45 for inspection from nonparties of documents and premises without the need for a deposition.

Subdivision (b). This subdivision is revised in several respects. First, former paragraph (1) is subdivided into two paragraphs for ease of reference and to avoid renumbering of paragraphs (3) and (4). Textual changes are then made in new paragraph (2) to enable the court to keep tighter rein on the extent of discovery. The information explosion of recent decades has greatly increased both the potential cost of wide-ranging discovery and the potential for discovery to be used as an instrument for delay or oppression. Amendments to Rules 30, 31, and 33 place presumptive limits on the number of depositions and interrogatories, subject to leave of court to pursue additional discovery. The revisions in Rule 26(b)(2) are intended to provide the court with broader discretion to impose additional restrictions on the scope and extent of discovery and to authorize courts that develop case tracking systems based on the complexity of cases to increase or decrease by local rule the presumptive number of depositions and interrogatories allowed in particular types or classifications of cases. The revision also dispels any doubt as to the power of the court to impose limitations on the length of depositions under Rule 30 or on the number of requests for admission under Rule 36.

Second, former paragraph (2), relating to insurance, has been relocated as part of the required initial disclosures under subdivision (a)(1)(D), and revised to provide for disclosure of the policy itself.

Third, paragraph (4)(A) is revised to provide that experts who are expected to be witnesses will be subject to deposition prior to trial, conforming the norm stated in the rule to the actual practice followed in most courts, in which depositions of experts have become standard. Concerns regarding the expense of such depositions should be mitigated by the fact that the expert's fees for the deposition will ordinarily be borne by the party taking the deposition. The requirement under subdivision (a)(2)(B) of a complete and detailed report of the expected testimony of certain forensic experts may, moreover, eliminate the need for some such depositions or at least reduce the length of the depositions. Accordingly, the deposition of an expert required by subdivision (a)(2)(B) to provide a written report may be taken only after the report has been served.

Paragraph (4)(C), bearing on compensation of experts, is revised to take account of the changes in paragraph (4)(A).

Paragraph (5) is a new provision. A party must notify other parties if it is withholding materials otherwise subject to disclosure under the rule or pursuant to a discovery request because it is asserting a claim of privilege or work product protection. To withhold materials without such notice is contrary to the rule, subjects the party to sanctions under Rule 37(b)(2), and may be viewed as a waiver of the privilege or protection.

The party must also provide sufficient information to enable other parties to evaluate the applicability of the claimed privilege or protection. Although the person from whom the discovery is sought decides whether to claim a privilege or protection, the court ultimately decides whether, if this claim is challenged, the privilege or protection applies. Providing information pertinent to the applicability of the privilege or protection should reduce the need for in camera examination of the documents.

The rule does not attempt to define for each case what information must be provided when a party asserts a claim of privilege or work product protection. Details concerning time, persons, general subject matter, etc., may be appropriate if only a few items are withheld, but may be unduly burdensome when voluminous documents are claimed to be privileged or protected, particularly if the items can be described by categories. A party can seek relief through a protective order under subdivision (c) if compliance with the requirement for providing this information would be an unreasonable burden. In rare circumstances some of the pertinent information affecting applicability of the claim, such as the identity of the client, may itself be privileged; the rule provides that such information need not be disclosed.

The obligation to provide pertinent information concerning withheld privileged materials applies only to items "otherwise discoverable." If a broad discovery request is made— for example, for all documents of a particular type during a twenty year period—and the responding party believes in good faith that production of documents for more than the past three years would be unduly burdensome, it should make its objection to the breadth of the request and, with respect to the documents generated in that three year period, produce the unprivileged documents and describe those withheld under the claim of privilege. If the court later rules that documents for a seven year period are properly discoverable, the documents for the additional four years should then be either produced (if not privileged) or described (if claimed to be privileged).

Subdivision (c). The revision requires that before filing a motion for a protective order the movant must confer—either in person or by telephone—with the other affected parties in a good faith effort to resolve the discovery dispute without the need for court intervention. If the movant is unable to get opposing parties even to discuss the matter, the efforts in attempting to arrange such a conference should be indicated in the certificate.

Subdivision (d). This subdivision is revised to provide that formal discovery—as distinguished from interviews of potential witnesses and other informal discovery—not commence until the parties have met and conferred as required by subdivision (f). Discovery can begin earlier if authorized under Rule 30(a)(2)(C) (deposition of person about to leave the country) or by local rule, order, or stipulation. This will be appropriate in some cases, such as those involving requests for a preliminary injunction or motions challenging personal jurisdiction. If a local rule exempts any types of cases in which discovery may be needed from the requirement of a meeting under Rule 26(f), it should specify when discovery may commence in those cases.

The meeting of counsel is to take place as soon as practicable and in any event at least 14 days before the date of the scheduling conference under Rule 16(b) or the date a scheduling order is due under Rule 16(b). The court can assure that discovery is not unduly delayed either by entering a special order or by setting the case for a scheduling conference.

Subdivision (e). This subdivision is revised to provide that the requirement for supplementation applies to all disclosures required by subdivisions (a)(1)–(3). Like the former rule, the duty, while imposed on a "party," applies whether the corrective information is learned by the client or by the attorney. Supplementations need not be made as each new item of information is learned but should be made at appropriate intervals during the discovery period, and with special promptness as the trial date approaches. It may be useful for the scheduling order to specify the time or times when supplementations should be made.

The revision also clarifies that the obligation to supplement responses to formal discovery requests applies to interrogatories, requests for production, and requests for admissions, but not ordinarily to deposition testimony. However, with respect to experts from whom a written report is required under subdivision (a)(2)(B), changes in the opinions expressed by the expert whether in the report or at a subsequent deposition are subject to a duty of supplemental disclosure under subdivision (e)(1).

The obligation to supplement disclosures and discovery responses applies whenever a party learns that its prior disclosures or responses are in some material respect incomplete or incorrect. There is, however, no obligation to provide supplemental or corrective information that has been otherwise made known to the parties in writing or during the discovery process, as when a witness not previously disclosed is identified during the taking of a deposition or when an expert during a deposition corrects information contained in an earlier report.

Subdivision (f). This subdivision was added in 1980 to provide a party threatened with abusive discovery with a special means for obtaining judicial intervention other than through discrete motions under Rules 26(c) and 37(a). The amendment envisioned a two-step process: first, the parties would attempt to frame a mutually agreeable plan; second, the court would hold a "discovery conference" and then enter an order establishing a schedule and limitations for the conduct of discovery. It was contemplated that the procedure, an elective one triggered on request of a party, would be used in special cases rather than as a routine matter. As expected, the device has been used only sparingly in most courts, and judicial controls over the discovery process have ordinarily been imposed through scheduling orders under Rule 16(b) or through rulings on discovery motions.

The provisions relating to a conference with the court are removed from subdivision (f). This change does not signal any lessening of the importance of judicial supervision. Indeed, there is a greater need for early judicial involvement to consider the scope and timing of the disclosure requirements of Rule 26(a) and the presumptive limits on discovery imposed under these rules or by local rules. Rather, the change is made because the provisions addressing the use of conferences with the court to control discovery are more properly included in Rule 16, which is being revised to highlight the court's powers regarding the discovery process.

The desirability of some judicial control of discovery can hardly be doubted. Rule 16, as revised, requires that the court set a time for completion of discovery and authorizes various other orders affecting the scope, timing, and extent of discovery and disclosures. Before entering such orders, the court should consider the views of the parties, preferably by means of a conference, but at the least through written submissions. Moreover, it is desirable that the parties' proposals regarding discovery be developed through a process where they meet in person, informally explore the nature and basis of the issues, and discuss how discovery can be conducted most efficiently and economically.

As noted above, former subdivision (f) envisioned the development of proposed discovery plans as an optional procedure to be used in relatively few cases. The revised rule directs that in all cases not exempted by local rule or special order the litigants must meet in person and plan for discovery. Following this meeting, the parties submit to the court their proposals for a discovery plan and can begin formal discovery. Their report will assist the court in seeing that the timing and scope of disclosures under revised Rule 26(a) and the limitations on the extent of discovery under these rules and local rules are tailored to the circumstances of the particular case.

To assure that the court has the litigants' proposals before deciding on a scheduling order and that the commencement of discovery is not delayed unduly, the rule provides that the meeting of the parties take place as soon as practicable and in any event at least 14 days before a scheduling conference is held or before a scheduling order is due under Rule 16(b). (Rule 16(b) requires that a scheduling order be entered within 90 days after the first appearance of a defendant or, if earlier, within 120 days after the complaint has been served on any defendant.) The obligation to participate in the planning process is imposed on all parties that have appeared in the case, including defendants who, because of a pending Rule 12 motion, may not have yet filed an answer in the case. Each such party should attend the meeting, either through one of its attorneys or in person if unrepresented. If more parties are joined or appear after the initial meeting, an additional meeting may be desirable.

Subdivision (f) describes certain matters that should be accomplished at the meeting and included in the proposed discovery plan. This listing does not exclude consideration of other subjects, such as the time when any dispositive motions should be filed and when the case should be ready for trial.

The parties are directed under subdivision (a)(1) to make the disclosures required by that subdivision at or within 10 days after this meeting. In many cases the parties should use the meeting to exchange, discuss, and clarify their respective disclosures. In other cases, it may be more useful if the disclosures are delayed until after the parties have discussed at the meeting the claims and defenses in order to define the issues with respect to which the initial disclosures should be made. As discussed in the Notes to subdivision (a)(1), the parties may also need to consider whether a stipulation extending this 10–day period would be appropriate, as when a defendant would otherwise have less than 60 days after being served in which to make its initial disclosure. The parties should also discuss at the meeting what additional information, although not subject to the disclosure requirements, can be made available informally without the necessity for formal discovery requests.

The report is to be submitted to the court within 10 days after the meeting and should not be difficult to prepare. In most cases counsel should be able to agree that one of them will be responsible for its preparation and submission to the court. Form 35 has been added in the Appendix to the Rules, both to illustrate the type of report that is contemplated and to serve as a checklist for the meeting.

The litigants are expected to attempt in good faith to agree on the contents of the proposed discovery plan. If they cannot agree on all aspects of the plan, their report to the court should indicate the competing proposals of the parties on those items, as well as the matters on which they agree. Unfortunately, there may be cases in which, because of disagreements about time or place or for other reasons, the meeting is not attended by all parties or, indeed, no meeting takes place. In such situations, the report—or reports— should describe the circumstances and the court may need to consider sanctions under Rule 37(g).

By local rule or special order, the court can exempt particular cases or types of cases from the meet-and-confer requirement of subdivision (f). In general this should include any types of cases which are exempted by local rule from the requirement for a scheduling order under Rule 16(b), such as cases in which there will be no discovery (e.g., bankruptcy appeals and reviews of social security determinations). In addition, the court may want to exempt cases in which discovery is rarely needed (e.g., government collection cases and proceedings to enforce administrative summonses) or in which a meeting of the parties might be impracticable (e.g., actions by unrepresented prisoners). Note that if a court exempts from the requirements for a meeting any types of cases in which discovery may be needed, it should indicate when discovery may commence in those cases.

Subdivision (g). Paragraph (1) is added to require signatures on disclosures, a requirement that parallels the provisions of paragraph (2) with respect to discovery requests, responses, and objections. The provisions of paragraph (3) have been modified to be consistent with Rules 37(a)(4) and 37(c)(1); in combination, these rules establish sanctions for violation of the rules regarding disclosures and discovery matters. Amended Rule 11 no longer applies to such violations.

2000 Amendment

Purposes of amendments. The Rule 26(a)(1) initial disclosure provisions are amended to establish a nationally uniform practice. The scope of the disclosure obligation is narrowed to cover only information that the disclosing party may use to support its position. In addition, the rule exempts specified categories of proceedings from initial disclosure, and permits a party who contends that disclosure is not appropriate in the circumstances of the case to present its objections to the court, which must then determine whether disclosure should be made. Related changes are made in Rules 26(d) and (f).

The initial disclosure requirements added by the 1993 amendments permitted local rules directing that disclosure would not be required or altering its operation. The inclusion of the "opt out" provision reflected the strong opposition to initial disclosure felt in some districts, and permitted experimentation with differing disclosure rules in those districts that were favorable to disclosure. The local option also recognized that—partly in response to the first publication in 1991 of a proposed disclosure rule—many districts had

adopted a variety of disclosure programs under the aegis of the Civil Justice Reform Act. It was hoped that developing experience under a variety of disclosure systems would support eventual refinement of a uniform national disclosure practice. In addition, there was hope that local experience could identify categories of actions in which disclosure is not useful.

A striking array of local regimes in fact emerged for disclosure and related features introduced in 1993. *See* D. Stienstra, *Implementation of Disclosure in United States District Courts, With Specific Attention to Courts' Responses to Selected Amendments to Federal Rule of Civil Procedure 26* (Federal Judicial Center, March 30, 1998) (describing and categorizing local regimes). In its final report to Congress on the CJRA experience, the Judicial Conference recommended reexamination of the need for national uniformity, particularly in regard to initial disclosure. Judicial Conference, *Alternative Proposals for Reduction of Cost and Delay: Assessment of Principles, Guidelines and Techniques*, 175 F.R.D. 62, 98 (1997).

At the Committee's request, the Federal Judicial Center undertook a survey in 1997 to develop information on current disclosure and discovery practices. *See* T. Willging, J. Shapard, D. Stienstra & D. Miletich, *Discovery and Disclosure Practice, Problems, and Proposals for Change* (Federal Judicial Center, 1997). In addition, the Committee convened two conferences on discovery involving lawyers from around the country and received reports and recommendations on possible discovery amendments from a number of bar groups. Papers and other proceedings from the second conference are published in 39 Boston Col. L. Rev. 517–840 (1998).

The Committee has discerned widespread support for national uniformity. Many lawyers have experienced difficulty in coping with divergent disclosure and other practices as they move from one district to another. Lawyers surveyed by the Federal Judicial Center ranked adoption of a uniform national disclosure rule second among proposed rule changes (behind increased availability of judges to resolve discovery disputes) as a means to reduce litigation expenses without interfering with fair outcomes. *Discovery and Disclosure Practice, supra*, at 44–45. National uniformity is also a central purpose of the Rules Enabling Act of 1934, as amended, 28 U.S.C. §§ 2072–2077.

These amendments restore national uniformity to disclosure practice. Uniformity is also restored to other aspects of discovery by deleting most of the provisions authorizing local rules that vary the number of permitted discovery events or the length of depositions. Local rule options are also deleted from Rules 26(d) and (f).

Subdivision (a)(1). The amendments remove the authority to alter or opt out of the national disclosure requirements by local rule, invalidating not only formal local rules but also informal "standing" orders of an individual judge or court that purport to create exemptions from—or limit or expand—the disclosure provided under the national rule. *See* Rule 83. Case-specific orders remain proper, however, and are expressly required if a party objects that initial disclosure is not appropriate in the circumstances of the action. Specified categories of proceedings are excluded from initial disclosure under subdivision (a)(1)(E). In addition, the parties can stipulate to forgo disclosure, as was true before. But even in a case excluded by subdivision (a)(1)(E) or in which the parties stipulate to bypass disclosure, the court can order exchange of similar information in managing the action under Rule 16.

The initial disclosure obligation of subdivisions (a)(1)(A) and (B) has been narrowed to identification of witnesses and documents that the disclosing party may use to support its claims or defenses. "Use" includes any use at a pretrial conference, to support a motion, or at trial. The disclosure obligation is also triggered by intended use in discovery, apart from use to respond to a discovery request; use of a document to question a witness during a deposition is a common example. The disclosure obligation attaches both to witnesses and documents a party intends to use and also to witnesses and to documents the party intends to use if—in the language of Rule 26(a)(3)—"the need arises."

A party is no longer obligated to disclose witnesses or documents, whether favorable or unfavorable, that it does not intend to use. The obligation to disclose information the party may use connects directly to the exclusion sanction of Rule 37(c)(1). Because the disclosure obligation is limited to material that the party may use, it is no longer tied to particularized allegations in the pleadings. Subdivision (e)(1), which is unchanged, requires supplementation if information later acquired would have been subject to the disclosure requirement. As case preparation continues, a party must supplement its disclosures when it determines that it may use a witness or document that it did not previously intend to use.

The disclosure obligation applies to "claims and defenses," and therefore requires a party to disclose information it may use to support its denial or rebuttal of the allegations, claim, or defense of another party. It thereby bolsters the requirements of Rule 11(b)(4), which authorizes denials "warranted on the evidence," and disclosure should include the identity of any witness or document that the disclosing party may use to support such denials.

Subdivision (a)(3) presently excuses pretrial disclosure of information solely for impeachment. Impeachment information is similarly excluded from the initial disclosure requirement.

Subdivisions (a)(1)(C) and (D) are not changed. Should a case be exempted from initial disclosure by Rule 26(a)(1)(E) or by agreement or order, the insurance information described by subparagraph (D) should be subject to discovery, as it would have been under the principles of former Rule 26(b)(2), which was added in 1970 and deleted in 1993 as redundant in light of the new initial disclosure obligation.

New subdivision (a)(1)(E) excludes eight specified categories of proceedings from initial disclosure. The objective of this listing is to identify cases in which there is likely to be little or no discovery, or in which initial disclosure appears unlikely to contribute to the effective development of the case. The list was developed after a review of the categories excluded by local rules in various districts from the operation of Rule 16(b) and the conference requirements of subdivision (f). Subdivision (a)(1)(E) refers to categories of "proceedings" rather than categories of "actions" because some might not properly be labeled " actions." Case designations made by the parties or the clerk's office at the time of filing do not control application of the exemptions. The descriptions in the rule are generic and are intended to be administered by the parties—and, when needed, the courts—with the flexibility needed to adapt to gradual evolution in the types of proceedings that fall within these general categories. The exclusion

of an action for review on an administrative record, for example, is intended to reach a proceeding that is framed as an " appeal" based solely on an administrative record. The exclusion should not apply to a proceeding in a form that commonly permits admission of new evidence to supplement the record. Item (vii), excluding a proceeding ancillary to proceedings in other courts, does not refer to bankruptcy proceedings; application of the Civil Rules to bankruptcy proceedings is determined by the Bankruptcy Rules.

Subdivision (a)(1)(E) is likely to exempt a substantial proportion of the cases in most districts from the initial disclosure requirement. Based on 1996 and 1997 case filing statistics, Federal Judicial Center staff estimate that, nationwide, these categories total approximately one-third of all civil filings.

The categories of proceedings listed in subdivision (a)(1)(E) are also exempted from the subdivision (f) conference requirement and from the subdivision (d) moratorium on discovery. Although there is no restriction on commencement of discovery in these cases, it is not expected that this opportunity will often lead to abuse since there is likely to be little or no discovery in most such cases. Should a defendant need more time to respond to discovery requests filed at the beginning of an exempted action, it can seek relief by motion under Rule 26(c) if the plaintiff is unwilling to defer the due date by agreement.

Subdivision (a)(1)(E)'s enumeration of exempt categories is exclusive. Although a case-specific order can alter or excuse initial disclosure, local rules or "standing" orders that purport to create general exemptions are invalid. *See* Rule 83.

The time for initial disclosure is extended to 14 days after the subdivision (f) conference unless the court orders otherwise. This change is integrated with corresponding changes requiring that the subdivision (f) conference be held 21 days before the Rule 16(b) scheduling conference or scheduling order, and that the report on the subdivision (f) conference be submitted to the court 14 days after the meeting. These changes provide a more orderly opportunity for the parties to review the disclosures, and for the court to consider the report. In many instances, the subdivision (f) conference and the effective preparation of the case would benefit from disclosure before the conference, and earlier disclosure is encouraged.

The presumptive disclosure date does not apply if a party objects to initial disclosure during the subdivision (f) conference and states its objection in the subdivision (f) discovery plan. The right to object to initial disclosure is not intended to afford parties an opportunity to "opt out" of disclosure unilaterally. It does provide an opportunity for an objecting party to present to the court its position that disclosure would be "inappropriate in the circumstances of the action." Making the objection permits the objecting party to present the question to the judge before any party is required to make disclosure. The court must then rule on the objection and determine what disclosures—if any—should be made. Ordinarily, this determination would be included in the Rule 16(b) scheduling order, but the court could handle the matter in a different fashion. Even when circumstances warrant suspending some disclosure obligations, others—such as the damages and insurance information called for by subdivisions (a)(1)(C) and (D)—may continue to be appropriate.

The presumptive disclosure date is also inapplicable to a party who is "first served or otherwise joined" after the subdivision (f) conference. This phrase refers to the date of service of a claim on a party in a defensive posture (such as a defendant or third-party defendant), and the date of joinder of a party added as a claimant or an intervenor. Absent court order or stipulation, a new party has 30 days in which to make its initial disclosures. But it is expected that later-added parties will ordinarily be treated the same as the original parties when the original parties have stipulated to forgo initial disclosure, or the court has ordered disclosure in a modified form.

Subdivision (a)(3). The amendment to Rule 5(d) forbids filing disclosures under subdivisions (a)(1) and (a)(2) until they are used in the proceeding, and this change is reflected in an amendment to subdivision (a)(4) . Disclosures under subdivision (a)(3), however, may be important to the court in connection with the final pretrial conference or otherwise in preparing for trial. The requirement that objections to certain matters be filed points up the court's need to be provided with these materials. Accordingly, the requirement that subdivision (a)(3) materials be filed has been moved from subdivision (a)(4) to subdivision (a)(3), and it has also been made clear that they—and any objections—should be filed "promptly."

Subdivision (a)(4). The filing requirement has been removed from this subdivision. Rule 5(d) has been amended to provide that disclosures under subdivisions (a)(1) and (a)(2) must not be filed until used in the proceeding. Subdivision (a)(3) has been amended to require that the disclosures it directs, and objections to them, be filed promptly. Subdivision (a)(4) continues to require that all disclosures under subdivisions (a)(1), (a)(2), and (a)(3) be in writing, signed, and served.

"Shall" is replaced by "must" under the program to conform amended rules to current style conventions when there is no ambiguity.

GAP Report

The Advisory Committee recommends that the amendments to Rules 26(a)(1)(A) and (B) be changed so that initial disclosure applies to information the disclosing party "may use to support" its claims or defenses. It also recommends changes in the Committee Note to explain that disclosure requirement. In addition, it recommends inclusion in the Note of further explanatory matter regarding the exclusion from initial disclosure provided in new Rule 26(a)(1)(E) for actions for review on an administrative record and the impact of these exclusions on bankruptcy proceedings. Minor wording improvements in the Note are also proposed.

Subdivision (b)(1). In 1978, the Committee published for comment a proposed amendment, suggested by the Section of Litigation of the American Bar Association, to refine the scope of discovery by deleting the "subject matter" language. This proposal was withdrawn, and the Committee has since then made other changes in the discovery rules to address concerns about overbroad discovery. Concerns about costs and delay of discovery have persisted nonetheless, and other bar groups have repeatedly renewed similar proposals for amendment to this subdivision to delete the "subject matter" language. Nearly one-third of the lawyers surveyed in 1997 by the Federal Judicial Center endorsed narrowing the scope of discovery as a means of reducing litigation expense without interfering with fair case resolutions. *Discovery and Disclosure Practice, supra,* at 44–45 (1997). The Committee has heard that in some instances, particularly cases involving large quantities of discovery, parties seek to justify discovery requests that sweep far beyond the claims and defenses of the parties on the ground that they nevertheless have a bearing on the "subject matter" involved in the action.

The amendments proposed for subdivision (b)(1) include one element of these earlier proposals but also differ from these proposals in significant ways. The similarity is that the amendments describe the scope of party- controlled discovery in terms of matter relevant to the claim or defense of any party. The court, however, retains authority to order discovery of any matter relevant to the subject matter involved in the action for good cause. The amendment is designed to involve the court more actively in regulating the breadth of sweeping or contentious discovery. The Committee has been informed repeatedly by lawyers that involvement of the court in managing discovery is an important method of controlling problems of inappropriately broad discovery. Increasing the availability of judicial officers to resolve discovery disputes and increasing court management of discovery were both strongly endorsed by the attorneys surveyed by the Federal Judicial Center. *See Discovery and Disclosure Practice, supra,* at 44. Under the amended provisions, if there is an objection that discovery goes beyond material relevant to the parties' claims or defenses, the court would become involved to determine whether the discovery is relevant to the claims or defenses and, if not, whether good cause exists for authorizing it so long as it is relevant to the subject matter of the action. The good-cause standard warranting broader discovery is meant to be flexible.

The Committee intends that the parties and the court focus on the actual claims and defenses involved in the action. The dividing line between information relevant to the claims and defenses and that relevant only to the subject matter of the action cannot be defined with precision. A variety of types of information not directly pertinent to the incident in suit could be relevant to the claims or defenses raised in a given action. For example, other incidents of the same type, or involving the same product, could be properly discoverable under the revised standard. Information about organizational arrangements or filing systems of a party could be discoverable if likely to yield or lead to the discovery of admissible information. Similarly, information that could be used to impeach a likely witness, although not otherwise relevant to the claims or defenses, might be properly discoverable. In each instance, the determination whether such information is discoverable because it is relevant to the claims or defenses depends on the circumstances of the pending action.

The rule change signals to the court that it has the authority to confine discovery to the claims and defenses asserted in the pleadings, and signals to the parties that they have no entitlement to discovery to develop new claims or defenses that are not already identified in the pleadings. In general, it is hoped that reasonable lawyers can cooperate to manage discovery without the need for judicial intervention. When judicial intervention is invoked, the actual scope of discovery should be determined according to the reasonable needs of the action. The court may permit broader discovery in a particular case depending on the circumstances of the case, the nature of the claims and defenses, and the scope of the discovery requested.

The amendments also modify the provision regarding discovery of information not admissible in evidence. As added in 1946, this sentence was designed to make clear that otherwise relevant material could not be withheld because it was hearsay or otherwise inadmissible. The Committee was concerned that the "reasonably calculated to lead to the discovery of admissible evidence" standard set forth in this sentence might swallow any other limitation on the scope of discovery. Accordingly, this sentence has been amended to clarify that information must be relevant to be discoverable, even though inadmissible, and that discovery of such material is permitted if reasonably calculated to lead to the discovery of admissible evidence. As used here, "relevant" means within the scope of discovery as defined in this subdivision, and it would include information relevant to the subject matter involved in the action if the court has ordered discovery to that limit based on a showing of good cause.

Finally, a sentence has been added calling attention to the limitations of subdivision (b)(2)(i), (ii), and (iii). These limitations apply to discovery that is otherwise within the scope of subdivision (b)(1). The Committee has been told repeatedly that courts have not implemented these limitations with the vigor that was contemplated. *See 8 Federal Practice & Procedure* § 2008.1 at 121. This otherwise redundant cross-reference has been added to emphasize the need for active judicial use of subdivision (b)(2) to control excessive discovery. *Cf. Crawford-El v. Britton*, 118 S. Ct. 1584, 1597 (1998) (quoting Rule 26(b)(2)(iii) and stating that "Rule 26 vests the trial judge with broad discretion to tailor discovery narrowly").

GAP Report

The Advisory Committee recommends changing the rule to authorize the court to expand discovery to any "matter"—not "information"—relevant to the subject matter involved in the action. In addition, it recommends additional clarifying material in the Committee Note about the impact of the change on some commonly disputed discovery topics, the relationship between cost-bearing under Rule 26(b)(2) and expansion of the scope of discovery on a showing of good cause, and the meaning of "relevant" in the revision to the last sentence of current subdivision (b)(1). In addition, some minor clarifications of language changes have been proposed for the Committee Note .

Subdivision (b)(2). Rules 30, 31, and 33 establish presumptive national limits on the numbers of depositions and interrogatories. New Rule 30(d)(2) establishes a presumptive limit on the length of depositions. Subdivision (b)(2) is amended to remove the previous permission for local rules that establish different presumptive limits on these discovery activities. There is no reason to believe that unique circumstances justify varying these nationally-applicable presumptive limits in certain districts. The limits can be modified by court order or agreement in an individual action, but "standing" orders imposing different presumptive limits are not authorized. Because there is no national rule limiting the number of Rule 36 requests for admissions, the rule continues to authorize local rules that impose numerical limits on them. This change is not intended to interfere with differentiated case management in districts that use this technique by case-specific order as part of their Rule 16 process.

Subdivision (d). The amendments remove the prior authority to exempt cases by local rule from the moratorium on discovery before the subdivision (f) conference, but the categories of proceedings exempted from initial disclosure under subdivision (a)(1)(E) are excluded from subdivision (d). The parties may agree to disregard the moratorium where it applies, and the court may so order in a case, but "standing" orders altering the moratorium are not authorized.

Subdivision (f). As in subdivision (d), the amendments remove the prior authority to exempt cases by local rule from the conference requirement. The Committee has been informed that the addition of the conference was one of the most successful changes made in the 1993 amendments, and it therefore has determined to apply the conference requirement nationwide. The categories of proceedings exempted from initial disclosure under subdivision (a)(1)(E) are exempted from the conference requirement for the reasons that warrant exclusion from initial disclosure. The court may order that the conference need not occur in a case where otherwise required, or that it occur in a case otherwise exempted by subdivision (a)(1)(E). "Standing" orders altering the conference requirement for categories of cases are not authorized.

The rule is amended to require only a "conference" of the parties, rather than a "meeting." There are important benefits to face-to-face discussion of the topics to be covered in the conference, and those benefits may be lost if other means of conferring were routinely used when face-to- face meetings would not impose burdens. Nevertheless, geographic conditions in some districts may exact costs far out of proportion to these benefits. The amendment allows the court by case-specific order to require a face-to- face meeting, but "standing" orders so requiring are not authorized.

As noted concerning the amendments to subdivision (a)(1), the time for the conference has been changed to at least 21 days before the Rule 16 scheduling conference, and the time for the report is changed to no more than 14 days after the Rule 26(f) conference. This should ensure that the court will have the report well in advance of the scheduling conference or the entry of the scheduling order.

Since Rule 16 was amended in 1983 to mandate some case management activities in all courts, it has included deadlines for Completing these tasks to ensure that all courts do so within a reasonable time. Rule 26(f) was fit into this scheme when it was adopted in 1993. It was never intended, however, that the national requirements that certain activities be completed by a certain time should delay case management in districts that move much faster than the national rules direct, and the rule is therefore amended to permit such a court to adopt a local rule that shortens the period specified for the completion of these tasks.

"Shall" is replaced by "must," "does," or an active verb under the program to conform amended rules to current style conventions when there is no ambiguity.

GAP Report

The Advisory Committee recommends adding a sentence to the published amendments to Rule 26(f) authorizing local rules shortening the time between the attorney conference and the court's action under Rule 16(b), and addition to the Committee Note of explanatory material about this change to the rule. This addition can be made without republication in response to public comments.

Rule 27.   Depositions Before Action or Pending Appeal

(a) Before Action.

---

(1) **Petition.** A person who desires to perpetuate testimony regarding any matter that may be cognizable in any court of the United States may file a verified petition in the United States district court in the district of the residence of any expected adverse party. The petition shall be entitled in the name of the petitioner and shall show: 1, that the petitioner expects to be a party to an action cognizable in a court of the United States but is presently unable to bring it or cause it to be brought, 2, the subject matter of the expected action and the petitioner's interest therein, 3, the facts which the petitioner desires to establish by the proposed testimony and the reasons for desiring to perpetuate it, 4, the names or a description of the persons the petitioner expects will be adverse parties and their addresses so far as known, and 5, the names and addresses of the persons to be examined and the substance of the testimony which the petitioner expects to elicit from each, and shall ask for an order authorizing the petitioner to take the depositions of the persons to be examined named in the petition, for the purpose of perpetuating their testimony.

(2) **Notice and Service.** The petitioner shall thereafter serve a notice upon each person named in the petition as an expected adverse party, together with a copy of the petition, stating that the petitioner will apply to the court, at a time and place named therein, for the order described in the petition. At least 20 days before the date of hearing the notice shall be served either within or without the district or state in the manner provided in Rule 4(d) for service of summons; but if such service cannot with due diligence be made upon any expected adverse party named in the petition, the court may make such order as is just for service by publication or otherwise, and shall appoint, for persons not served in the manner provided in Rule 4(d), an attorney who shall represent them, and, in case they are not otherwise represented, shall cross-examine the deponent. If any expected adverse party is a minor or incompetent the provisions of Rule 17(c) apply.

(3) **Order and Examination.** If the court is satisfied that the perpetuation of the testimony may prevent a failure or delay of justice, it shall make an order designating or describing the persons whose depositions may be taken and specifying the subject matter of the examination and whether the depositions shall be taken upon oral examination or written interrogatories. The depositions may then be taken in accordance with these rules; and the court may make orders of the character provided for by Rules 34 and 35. For the purpose of applying these rules to depositions for perpetuating testimony, each reference therein to the court in which the action is pending shall be deemed to refer to the court in which the petition for such deposition was filed.

(4) **Use of Deposition.** If a deposition to perpetuate testimony is taken under these rules or if, although not so taken, it would be admissible in evidence in the courts of the state in which it is taken, it may be used in any action involving the same subject matter subsequently brought in a United States district court, in accordance with the provisions of Rule 32(a).

(b) **Pending Appeal.** If an appeal has been taken from a judgment of a district court or before the taking of an appeal if the time therefor has not expired, the district court in which the judgment was rendered may allow the taking of the depositions of witnesses to perpetuate their testimony for use in the event of further proceedings in the district court. In such case the party who desires to perpetuate the testimony may make a motion in the district court for leave to take the depositions, upon the same notice and service thereof as if the action was pending in the district court. The motion shall show (1) the names and addresses of persons to be examined and the substance of the testimony which the party expects to elicit from each; (2) the reasons for perpetuating their testimony. If the court finds that the perpetuation of the testimony is proper to avoid a failure or delay of justice, it may make an order allowing the depositions to be taken and may make orders of the character provided for by Rules 34 and 35, and thereupon the depositions may be taken and used in the same manner and under the same conditions as are prescribed in these rules for depositions taken in actions pending in the district court.

(c) **Perpetuation by Action.** This rule does not limit the power of a court to entertain an action to perpetuate testimony.

(As amended Dec. 27, 1946, eff. Mar. 19, 1948; Dec. 29, 1948, eff. Oct. 20, 1949; Mar. 1, 1971, eff. July 1, 1971; Mar. 2, 1987, eff. Aug. 1, 1987.)

Proposed Amendment of Subdivision (a)(2)

Effective December 1, 2005, absent contrary Congressional action, subdivision (a)(2) of this rule is amended to read as follows:

*(2) **Notice and Service.** At least 20 days before the hearing date, the petitioner must serve each expected adverse party with a copy of the petition and a notice stating the time and place of the hearing. The notice may be served either inside or outside the district or state in the manner provided in Rule 4. If that service cannot be made with due diligence on an expected adverse party, the court may order service by publication or otherwise. The court must appoint an attorney to represent persons not served in the manner provided by Rule 4 and to cross-examine the deponent if an*

unserved person is not otherwise represented. Rule 17(c) applies if any expected adverse party is a minor or is incompetent.

ADVISORY COMMITTEE NOTES

1937 Adoption

Note to Subdivision (a). This rule offers a simple method of perpetuating testimony in cases where it is usually allowed under equity practice or under modern statutes. See *Arizona v. California*, 1934, 54 S.Ct. 735, 292 U.S. 341, 78 L.Ed. 1298; *Todd Engineering Dry Dock and Repair Co. v. United States*, C.C.A.5, 1929, 32 F.2d 734; *Hall v. Stout*, 4 Del.Ch. 269 (1871). For comparable state statutes see Ark.Civ.Code (Crawford, 1934) §§ 666 to 670; Calif.Code Civ.Proc. (Deering, 1937) 2083–2089; Smith-Hurd Ill.Stats. c. 51, §§ 39 to 46; Iowa Code (1935) §§ 11400 to 11407; 2 Mass.Gen.Laws (Ter.Ed., 1932) ch. 233, §§ 46 to 63; N.Y.C.P.A. (1937) § 295; Ohio Gen.Code Ann. (Throckmorton, 1936) §§ 12216 to 12222; Va.Code Ann. (Michie, 1936) § 6235; Wis.Stat. (1935) §§ 326.27 to 326.29. The appointment of an attorney to represent absent parties or parties not personally notified, or a guardian ad litem to represent minors and incompetents, is provided for in several of the above statutes.

Note to Subdivision (b). This follows the practice approved in *Richter v. Union Trust Co.*, 1885, 5 S.Ct. 1162, 115 U.S. 55, 29 L.Ed. 345, by extending the right to perpetuate testimony to cases pending an appeal.

Note to Subdivision (c). This preserves the right to employ a separate action to perpetuate testimony under U.S.C., Title 28, [former] § 644 (Depositions under *dedimus potestatem* and *in perpetuam*) as an alternate method.

1946 Amendment

Note. Since the second sentence in subdivision (a)(3) refers only to depositions, it is arguable that Rules 34 and 35 are inapplicable in proceedings to perpetuate testimony. The new matter [in subdivisions (a)(3) and (b)] clarifies. A conforming change is also made in subdivision (b).

1948 Amendment

The amendment effective October 1949, substituted the words "United States district court" in subdivision (a)(1) and (4) for "district court of the United States."

1971 Amendment

The reference intended in this subdivision is to the rule governing the use of depositions in court proceedings. Formerly Rule 26(d), that rule is now Rule 32(a). The subdivision is amended accordingly.

1987 Amendment

The amendments are technical. No substantive change is intended.

2005 Amendments

[Effective December 1, 2005, absent contrary Congressional action.]

The outdated cross-reference to former Rule 4(d) is corrected to incorporate all Rule 4 methods of service. Former Rule 4(d) has been allocated to many different subdivisions of Rule 4. Former Rule 4(d) did not cover all categories of defendants or modes of service, and present Rule 4 reaches further than all of former Rule 4. But there is no reason to distinguish between the different categories of defendants and modes of service encompassed by Rule 4. Rule 4 service provides effective notice. Notice by such means should be provided to any expected adverse party that comes within Rule 4.

Other changes are made to conform Rule 27(a)(2) to current style conventions.

HISTORICAL NOTES

References in Text

"Rule 4(d)", referred to in subd. (a)(2), is Rule 4(d) prior to amendment by Supreme Court of the United States order dated Apr. 22, 1993, which failed to make conforming amendments to subd. (a)(2) of this rule. Rule 4(d) does not relate to manner of service which is provided for in Rule 4(e)(2) and (g) to (j).

Rule 28. Persons Before Whom Depositions may be Taken

(a) Within the United States. Within the United States or within a territory or insular possession subject to the jurisdiction of the United States, depositions shall be taken before an officer authorized to administer oaths by the laws of the United States or of the place where the examination is held, or before a person appointed by the court in which the action is pending. A person so appointed has power to administer oaths and take testimony. The term officer as used in Rules 30, 31 and 32 includes a person appointed by the court or designated by the parties under Rule 29.

(b) In Foreign Countries. Depositions may be taken in a foreign country (1) pursuant to any applicable treaty or convention, or (2) pursuant to a letter of request (whether or not captioned a letter rogatory), or (3) on notice before a person authorized to administer oaths in the place where the examination is held, either by the law thereof or by the law of the United States, or (4) before a person commissioned by the court, and a person so commissioned shall have the power by virtue of the commission to administer any necessary oath and take testimony. A commission or a letter of request shall be issued on application and notice and on terms that are just and appropriate. It is not requisite to the issuance of a commission or a letter of request that the taking of the deposition in any other manner is impracticable or inconvenient; and both a commission and a letter of request may be issued in proper cases. A notice or commission may designate the person before whom the deposition is to be taken either by name or descriptive title. A letter of request may be addressed "To the Appropriate Authority in [here name the country]." When a letter of request or any other device is used pursuant to any applicable treaty or convention, it shall be captioned in the form prescribed by that treaty or convention. Evidence obtained in response to a letter of request need not be excluded merely because it is not a verbatim transcript, because the testimony was not taken under oath, or because of any similar departure from the requirements for depositions taken within the United States under these rules.

(c) Disqualification for Interest. No deposition shall be taken before a person who is a relative or employee or attorney or counsel of any of the parties, or is a relative or employee of such attorney or counsel, or is financially interested in the action.

(As amended Dec. 27, 1946, eff. Mar. 19, 1948; Jan. 21, 1963, eff. July 1, 1963; Apr. 29, 1980, eff. Aug. 1, 1980; Mar. 2, 1987, eff. Aug. 1, 1987; Apr. 22, 1993, eff. Dec. 1, 1993.)

ADVISORY COMMITTEE NOTES

1937 Adoption

In effect this rule is substantially the same as U.S.C., Title 28, [former] § 639 (Depositions *de bene esse*; when and where taken; notice). U.S.C., Title 28, [former] § 642 (Depositions, acknowledgments, and affidavits taken by notaries public) does not conflict with subdivision (a).

1946 Amendments

Note. The added language [in subdivision (a)] provides for the situation, occasionally arising, when depositions must be taken in an isolated place where there is no one readily available who has the power to administer oaths and take testimony according to the terms of the rule as originally stated. In addition, the amendment affords a more convenient method of securing depositions in the case where state lines intervene between the location of various witnesses otherwise rather closely grouped. The amendment insures that the person appointed shall have adequate power to perform his duties. It has been held that a person authorized to act in the premises, as, for example, a master, may take testimony outside the district of his appointment. *Consolidated Fastener Co. v. Columbian Button & Fastener Co.*, C.C.N.D.N.Y.1898, 85 Fed. 54; *Mathieson Alkali Works v. Arnold, Hoffman & Co.*, C.C.A.1, 1929, 31 F.2d 1.

1963 Amendments

The amendment of clause (1) is designed to facilitate depositions in foreign countries by enlarging the class of persons before whom the depositions may be taken on notice. The class is no longer confined, as at present, to a secretary of embassy or legation, consul general, consul, vice consul, or consular agent of the United States. In a country that regards the taking of testimony by a foreign official in aid of litigation pending in a court of another country as an infringement upon its sovereignty, it will be expedient to notice depositions before officers of the country in which the examination is taken. See generally *Symposium, Letters Rogatory* (Grossman ed. 1956); Doyle, *Taking Evidence by Deposition and Letters Rogatory and Obtaining Documents in Foreign Territory*, Proc.A.B.A., Sec.Int'l & Comp.L. 37 (1959); Heilpern, *Procuring Evidence Abroad*, 14 Tul.L.Rev.

29 (1939); Jones, *International Judicial Assistance: Procedural Chaos and a Program for Reform*, 62 Yale L.J. 515, 526–29 (1953); Smit, *International Aspects of Federal Civil Procedure*, 61 Colum.L.Rev. 1031, 1056–58 (1961).

Clause (2) of amended subdivision (b), like the corresponding provision of subdivision (a) dealing with depositions taken in the United States, makes it clear that the appointment of a person by commission in itself confers power upon him to administer any necessary oath.

It has been held that a letter rogatory will not be issued unless the use of a notice or commission is shown to be impossible or impractical. See, e.g., *United States v. Matles*, 154 F.Supp. 574 (E.D.N.Y.1957); *The Edmund Fanning*, 89 F.Supp. 282 (E.D.N.Y.1950); *Branyan v. Koninklijke Luchtvaart Maatschappij*, 13 F.R.D. 425 (S.D.N.Y.1953). See also *Ali Akber Kiachif v. Philco International Corp.*, 10 F.R.D. 277 (S.D.N.Y.1950). The intent of the fourth sentence of the amended subdivision is to overcome this judicial antipathy and to permit a sound choice between depositions under a letter rogatory and on notice or by commission in the light of all the circumstances. In a case in which the foreign country will compel a witness to attend or testify in aid of a letter rogatory but not in aid of a commission, a letter rogatory may be preferred on the ground that it is less expensive to execute, even if there is plainly no need for compulsive process. A letter rogatory may also be preferred when it cannot be demonstrated that a witness will be recalcitrant or when the witness states that he is willing to testify voluntarily, but the contingency exists that he will change his mind at the last moment. In the latter case, it may be advisable to issue both a commission and a letter rogatory, the latter to be executed if the former fails. The choice between a letter rogatory and a commission may be conditioned by other factors, including the nature and extent of the assistance that the foreign country will give to the execution of either.

In executing a letter rogatory the courts of other countries may be expected to follow their customary procedure for taking testimony. See *United States v. Paraffin Wax*, 2255 Bags, 23 F.R.D. 289 (E.D.N.Y.1959). In many noncommon-law countries the judge questions the witness, sometimes without first administering an oath, the attorneys put any supplemental questions either to the witness or through the judge, and the judge dictates a summary of the testimony, which the witness acknowledges as correct. See *Jones, supra*, at 530–32; *Doyle, supra*, at 39–41. The last sentence of the amended subdivision provides, contrary to the implications of some authority, that evidence recorded in such a fashion need not be excluded on that account. See *The Mandu*, 11 F.Supp. 845 (E.D.N.Y.1935). But *cf. Nelson v. United States*, 17 Fed.Cas. 1340 (No. 10,116) (C.C.D.Pa. 1816); *Winthrop v. Union Ins. Co.*, 30 Fed.Cas. 376 (No. 17901) (C.C.D.Pa.1807). The specific reference to the lack of an oath or a verbatim transcript is intended to be illustrative. Whether or to what degree the value or weight of the evidence may be affected by the method of taking or recording the testimony is left for determination according to the circumstances of the particular case, *cf. Uebersee Finanz-Korporation, A.G. v. Brownell*, 121 F.Supp. 420 (D.D.C. 1954); *Danisch v. Guardian Life Ins. Co.*, 19 F.R.D. 235 (S.D.N.Y.1956); the testimony may indeed be so devoid of substance or probative value as to warrant its exclusion altogether.

Some foreign countries are hostile to allowing a deposition to be taken in their country, especially by notice or commission, or to lending assistance in the taking of a deposition. Thus compliance with the terms of amended subdivision (b) may not in all cases ensure completion of a deposition abroad. Examination of the law and policy of the particular foreign country in advance of attempting a deposition is therefore advisable. See 4 *Moore's Federal Practice* ¶¶28.05–28.08 (2d ed. 1950).

1980 Amendments

The amendments are clarifying.

1987 Amendments

The amendment is technical. No substantive change is intended.

1993 Amendments

This revision is intended to make effective use of the Hague Convention on the Taking of Evidence Abroad in Civil or Commercial Matters, and of any similar treaties that the United States may enter into in the future which provide procedures for taking depositions abroad. The party taking the deposition is ordinarily obliged to conform to an applicable treaty or convention if an effective deposition can be taken by such internationally approved means, even though a verbatim transcript is not available or testimony cannot be taken under oath. For a discussion of the impact of such treaties upon the discovery process, and of the application of principles of comity upon discovery in countries not signatories to a convention, see *Société Nationale Industrielle Aérospatiale v. United States District Court*, 482 U.S. 522 (1987).

The term "letter of request" has been substituted in the rule for the term "letter rogatory" because it is the primary method provided by the Hague Convention. A letter rogatory is essentially a form of letter of request. There are several other minor changes that are designed merely to carry out the intent of the other alterations.

HISTORICAL NOTES

Treaties and Conventions; Taking of Evidence Abroad in Civil or Commercial Matters; Observance On and After Oct. 7, 1972, by United States and Citizens and Persons Subject to Jurisdiction of United States

For text of Convention, see provisions set out as a note under section 1781 of this title.

Rule 29.　Stipulations Regarding Discovery Procedure

Unless otherwise directed by the court, the parties may by written stipulation (1) provide that depositions may be taken before any person, at any time or place, upon any notice, and in any manner and when so taken may be used like other depositions, and (2) modify other procedures governing or limitations placed upon discovery, except that stipulations extending the time provided in Rules 33, 34, and 36 for responses to discovery may, if they would interfere with any time set for completion of discovery, for

hearing of a motion, or for trial, be made only with the approval of the court.

(As amended Mar. 30, 1970, eff. July 1, 1970; Apr. 22, 1993, eff. Dec. 1, 1993.)

ADVISORY COMMITTEE NOTES

1970 Amendment

There is no provision for stipulations varying the procedures by which methods of discovery other than depositions are governed. It is common practice for parties to agree on such variations, and the amendment recognizes such agreements and provides a formal mechanism in the rules for giving them effect. Any stipulation varying the procedures may be superseded by court order, and stipulations extending the time for response to discovery under Rules 33, 34, and 36 require court approval.

1993 Amendments

This rule is revised to give greater opportunity for litigants to agree upon modifications to the procedures governing discovery or to limitations upon discovery. Counsel are encouraged to agree on less expensive and time-consuming methods to obtain information, as through voluntary exchange of documents, use of interviews in lieu of depositions, etc. Likewise, when more depositions or interrogatories are needed than allowed under these rules or when more time is needed to complete a deposition than allowed under a local rule, they can, by agreeing to the additional discovery, eliminate the need for a special motion addressed to the court.

Under the revised rule, the litigants ordinarily are not required to obtain the court's approval of these stipulations. By order or local rule, the court can, however, direct that its approval be obtained for particular types of stipulations; and, in any event, approval must be obtained if a stipulation to extend the 30–day period for responding to interrogatories, requests for production, or requests for admissions would interfere with dates set by the court for completing discovery, for hearing of a motion, or for trial.

Rule 30.　Depositions Upon Oral Examination

(a) When Depositions May Be Taken; When Leave Required.

(1) A Party may take the testimony of any person, including a party, by deposition upon oral examination without leave of court except as provided in paragraph (2). The attendance of witnesses may be compelled by subpoena as provided in Rule 45.

(2) A party must obtain leave of court, which shall be granted to the extent consistent with the principles stated in Rule 26(b)(2), if the person to be examined is confined in prison or if, without the written stipulation of the parties,

　(A) a proposed deposition would result in more than ten depositions being taken under this rule or Rule 31 by the plaintiffs, or by the defendants, or by third-party defendants;

(B) the person to be examined already has been deposed in the case; or

(C) a party seeks to take a deposition before the time specified in Rule 26(d) unless the notice contains a certification, with supporting facts, that the person to be examined is expected to leave the United States and be unavailable for examination in this country unless deposed before that time.

(b) Notice of Examination: General Requirements; Method of Recording; Production of Documents and Things; Deposition of Organization; Deposition by Telephone.

(1) A party desiring to take the deposition of any person upon oral examination shall give reasonable notice in writing to every other party to the action. The notice shall state the time and place for taking the deposition and the name and address of each person to be examined, if known, and, if the name is not known, a general description sufficient to identify the person or the particular class or group to which the person belongs. If a subpoena duces tecum is to be served on the person to be examined, the designation of the materials to be produced as set forth in the subpoena shall be attached to, or included in, the notice.

(2) The party taking the deposition shall state in the notice the method by which the testimony shall be recorded. Unless the court orders otherwise, it may be recorded by sound, sound-and-visual, or stenographic means, and the party taking the deposition shall bear the cost of the recording. Any party may arrange for a transcription to be made from the recording of a deposition taken by non-stenographic means.

(3) With prior notice to the deponent and other parties, any party may designate another method to record the deponent's testimony in addition to the method specified by the person taking the deposition. The additional record or transcript shall be made at that party's expense unless the court otherwise orders.

(4) Unless otherwise agreed by the parties, a deposition shall be conducted before an officer appointed or designated under Rule 28 and shall begin with a statement on the record by the officer that includes (A) the officer's name and business address; (B) the date, time, and place of the deposition; (C) the name of the deponent; (D) the administration of the oath or affirmation to the deponent; and (E) an identification of all persons present. If the deposition is recorded other than stenographically, the officer shall repeat items (A) through (C) at the beginning of each unit of recorded tape or other recording medium. The appearance or demeanor of deponents or attorneys shall not be dis-

torted through camera or sound-recording techniques. At the end of the deposition, the officer shall state on the record that the deposition is complete and shall set forth any stipulations made by counsel concerning the custody of the transcript or recording and the exhibits, or concerning other pertinent matters.

(5) The notice to a party deponent may be accompanied by a request made in compliance with Rule 34 for the production of documents and tangible things at the taking of the deposition. The procedure of Rule 34 shall apply to the request.

(6) A party may in the party's notice and in a subpoena name as the deponent a public or private corporation or a partnership or association or governmental agency and describe with reasonable particularity the matters on which examination is requested. In that event, the organization so named shall designate one or more officers, directors, or managing agents, or other persons who consent to testify on its behalf, and may set forth, for each person designated, the matters on which the person will testify. A subpoena shall advise a non-party organization of its duty to make such a designation. The persons so designated shall testify as to matters known or reasonably available to the organization. This subdivision (b)(6) does not preclude taking a deposition by any other procedure authorized in these rules.

(7) The parties may stipulate in writing or the court may upon motion order that a deposition be taken by telephone or other remote electronic means. For the purposes of this rule and Rules 28(a), 37(a)(1), and 37(b)(1), a deposition taken by such means is taken in the district and at the place where the deponent is to answer questions.

(c) Examination and Cross–Examination; Record of Examination; Oath; Objections.

Examination and cross-examination of witnesses may proceed as permitted at the trial under the provisions of the Federal Rules of Evidence except Rules 103 and 615. The officer before whom the deposition is to be taken shall put the witness on oath or affirmation and shall personally, or by someone acting under the officer's direction and in the officer's presence, record the testimony of the witness. The testimony shall be taken stenographically or recorded by any other method authorized by subdivision (b)(2) of this rule. All objections made at the time of the examination to the qualifications of the officer taking the deposition, to the manner of taking it, to the evidence presented, to the conduct of any party, or to any other aspect of the proceedings shall be noted by the officer upon the record of the deposition; but the examination shall proceed, with the testimony being taken subject to the objections. In lieu of participating in the oral examination, parties may serve written questions in a sealed envelope on the party taking the deposition and the party taking the deposition shall transmit them to the officer, who shall propound them to the witness and record the answers verbatim.

(d) Schedule and Duration; Motion to Terminate or Limit Examination.

(1) Any objection during a deposition must be stated concisely and in a non-argumentative and non-suggestive manner. A person may instruct a deponent not to answer only when necessary to preserve a privilege, to enforce a limitation directed by the court, or to present a motion under Rule 30(d) (4).

(2) Unless otherwise authorized by the court or stipulated by the parties, a deposition is limited to one day of seven hours. The court must allow additional time consistent with Rule 26(b)(2) if needed for a fair examination of the deponent or if the deponent or another person , or other circumstance, impedes or delays the examination.

(3) If the court finds that any impediment, delay, or other conduct has frustrated the fair examination of the deponent, it may impose upon the persons responsible an appropriate sanction, including the reasonable costs and attorney's fees incurred by any parties as a result thereof.

(4) At any time during a deposition, on motion of a party or of the deponent and upon a showing that the examination is being conducted in bad faith or in such manner as unreasonably to annoy, embarrass, or oppress the deponent or party, the court in which the action is pending or the court in the district where the deposition is being taken may order the officer conducting the examination to cease forthwith from taking the deposition, or may limit the scope and manner of the taking of the deposition as provided in Rule 26(c). If the order made terminates the examination, it may be resumed thereafter only upon the order of the court in which the action is pending. Upon demand of the objecting party or deponent, the taking of the deposition must be suspended for the time necessary to make a motion for an order. The provisions of Rule 37(a)(4) apply to the award of expenses incurred in relation to the motion.

(e) Review by Witness; Changes; Signing.

If requested by the deponent or a party before completion of the deposition, the deponent shall have 30 days after being notified by the officer that the transcript or recording is available in which to review the transcript or recording and, if there are changes in form or substance, to sign a statement reciting such changes and the reasons given by the

deponent for making them. The officer shall indicate in the certificate prescribed by subdivision (f)(1) whether any review was requested and, if so, shall append any changes made by the deponent during the period allowed.

(f) Certification and Delivery by Officer; Exhibits; Copies.

(1) The officer must certify that the witness was duly sworn by the officer and that the deposition is a true record of the testimony given by the witness. This certificate must be in writing and accompany the record of the deposition. Unless otherwise ordered by the court, the officer must securely seal the deposition in an envelope or package indorsed with the title of the action and marked "Deposition of [here insert name of witness]" and must promptly send it to the attorney who arranged for the transcript or recording, who must store it under conditions that will protect it against loss, destruction, tampering, or deterioration. Documents and things produced for inspection during the examination of the witness must, upon the request of a party, be marked for identification and annexed to the deposition and may be inspected and copied by any party, except that if the person producing the materials desires to retain them the person may (A) offer copies to be marked for identification and annexed to the deposition and to serve thereafter as originals if the person affords to all parties fair opportunity to verify the copies by comparison with the originals, or (B) offer the originals to be marked for identification, after giving to each party an opportunity to inspect and copy them, in which event the materials may then be used in the same manner as if annexed to the deposition. Any party may move for an order that the original be annexed to and returned with the deposition to the court, pending final disposition of the case.

(2) Unless otherwise ordered by the court or agreed by the parties, the officer shall retain stenographic notes of any deposition taken stenographically or a copy of the recording of any deposition taken by another method. Upon payment of reasonable charges therefor, the officer shall furnish a copy of the transcript or other recording of the deposition to any party or to the deponent.

(3) The party taking the deposition shall give prompt notice of its filing to all other parties.

(g) Failure to Attend or to Serve Subpoena; Expenses.

(1) If the party giving the notice of the taking of a deposition fails to attend and proceed therewith and another party attends in person or by attorney pursuant to the notice, the court may order the party giving the notice to pay to such other party the reasonable expenses incurred by that party and that party's attorney in attending, including reasonable attorney's fees.

(2) If the party giving the notice of the taking of a deposition of a witness fails to serve a subpoena upon the witness and the witness because of such failure does not attend, and if another party attends in person or by attorney because that party expects the deposition of that witness to be taken, the court may order the party giving the notice to pay to such other party the reasonable expenses incurred by that party and that party's attorney in attending, including reasonable attorney's fees.

(As amended Jan. 21, 1963, eff. July 1, 1963; Mar. 30, 1970, eff. July 1, 1970; Mar. 1, 1971, eff. July 1, 1971; Nov. 20, 1972, eff. July 1, 1975; Apr. 29, 1980, eff. Aug. 1, 1980; Mar. 2, 1987, eff. Aug. 1, 1987; Apr. 22, 1993, eff. Dec. 1, 1993; Apr. 17, 2000, eff. Dec. 1, 2000.)

ADVISORY COMMITTEE NOTES

1937 Adoption

Note to Subdivision (a). This is in accordance with common practice. See U.S.C., Title 28, [former] § 639 (Depositions *de bene esse*; when and where taken; notice), the relevant provisions of which are incorporated in this rule; West's Ann.Code Civ.Proc. § 2031; and statutes cited in respect to notice in the Note to Rule 26(a). The provision for enlarging or shortening the time of notice has been added to give flexibility to the rule.

Note to Subdivisions (b) and (d). These are introduced as a safeguard for the protection of parties and deponents on account of the unlimited right of discovery given by Rule 26.

Note to Subdivisions (c) and (e). These follow the general plan of [former] Equity Rule 51 (Evidence Taken Before Examiners, Etc.) and U.S.C., Title 28, [former] §§ 640 (Depositions *de bene esse*; mode of taking), and [former] 641 (Same; transmission to court), but are more specific. They also permit the deponent to require the officer to make changes in the deposition if the deponent is not satisfied with it. See also [former] Equity Rule 50 (Stenographer—Appointment—Fees.)

Note to Subdivision (f). Compare [former] Equity Rule 55 (Depositions Deemed Published When Filed.)

Note to Subdivision (g). This is similar to 2 Minn.Stat. (Mason, 1927) § 9833, but is more extensive.

1963 Amendments

This amendment corresponds to the change in Rule 4(d)(4). See Advisory Committee's Note to that amendment.

1970 Amendments

Subdivision (a). This subdivision contains the provisions of existing Rule 26(a), transferred here as part of the rearrangement relating to Rule 26. Existing Rule 30(a) is transferred to 30(b). Changes in language have been made to conform to the new arrangement.

This subdivision is further revised in regard to the requirement of leave of court for taking a deposition. The present procedure, requiring a plaintiff to obtain leave of court if he serves notice of taking a deposition within 20 days after commencement of the action, is changed in several respects. First, leave is required by reference to the time the deposition is to be taken rather than the date of serving notice of taking. Second, the 20-day period is extended to 30 days and runs from the service of summons and complaint on any defendant, rather than the commencement of the action. *Cf.* Ill.S.Ct.R. 19–1 S–H Ill.Ann.Stat. § 101.19–1. Third, leave is not required beyond the time that defendant initiates discovery, thus showing that he has retained counsel. As under the present practice, a party not afforded a reasonable opportunity to appear at a deposition, because he has not yet been served with process, is protected against use of the deposition at trial against him. See Rule 32(a), transferred from 26(d). Moreover, he can later redepose the witness if he so desires.

The purpose of requiring the plaintiff to obtain leave of court is, as stated by the Advisory Committee that proposed the present language of Rule 26(a), to protect "a defendant who has not had an opportunity to retain counsel and inform himself as to the nature of the suit." Note to 1948 amendment of Rule 26(a), quoted in 3A Barron & Holtzoff, *Federal Practice and Procedure* 455–456 (Wright ed. 1958). In order to assure defendant of this opportunity, the period is lengthened to 30 days. This protection, however, is relevant to the time of taking the deposition, not to the time that notice is served. Similarly, the protective period should run from the service of process rather than the filing of the complaint with the court. As stated in the note to Rule 26(d), the courts have used the service of notice as a convenient reference point for assigning priority in taking depositions, but with the elimination of priority in new Rule 26(d) the reference point is no longer needed. The new procedure is consistent in principle with the provisions of Rules 33, 34, and 36 as revised.

Plaintiff is excused from obtaining leave even during the initial 30-day period if he gives the special notice provided in subdivision (b)(2). The required notice must state that the person to be examined is about to go out of the district where the action is pending and more than 100 miles from the place of trial, or out of the United States, or on a voyage to sea, and will be unavailable for examination unless deposed within the 30-day period. These events occur most often in maritime litigation, when seamen are transferred from one port to another or are about to go to sea. Yet, there are analogous situations in nonmaritime litigation, and although the maritime problems are more common, a rule limited to claims in the admiralty and maritime jurisdiction is not justified.

In the recent unification of the civil and admiralty rules, this problem was temporarily met through addition in Rule 26(a) of a provision that depositions *de bene esse* may continue to be taken as to admiralty and maritime claims within the meaning of Rule 9(h). It was recognized at the time that "a uniform rule applicable alike to what are now civil actions and suits in admiralty" was clearly preferable, but the de bene esse procedure was adopted "for the time being at least." See Advisory Committee's Note in Report of the Judicial Conference: Proposed Amendments to Rules of Civil Procedure 43–44 (1966).

The changes in Rule 30(a) and the new Rule 30(b)(2) provide a formula applicable to ordinary civil as well as maritime claims. They replace the provision for depositions *de bene esse*. They authorize an early deposition without leave of court where the witness is about to depart and, unless his deposition is promptly taken, (1) it will be impossible or very difficult to depose him before trial or (2) his deposition can later be taken but only with substantially increased effort and expense. *Cf. S.S. Hai Chang*, 1966 A.M.C. 2239 (S.D.N.Y.1966), in which the deposing party is required to prepay expenses and counsel fees of the other party's lawyer when the action is pending in New York and depositions are to be taken on the West Coast. Defendant is protected by a provision that the deposition cannot be used against him if he was unable through exercise of diligence to obtain counsel to represent him.

The distance of 100 miles from place of trial is derived from the *de bene esse* provision and also conforms to the reach of a subpoena of the trial court, as provided in Rule 45(e). See also S.D.N.Y. Civ.R. 5(a). Some parts of the *de bene esse* provision are omitted from Rule 30(b)(2). Modern deposition practice adequately covers the witness who lives more than 100 miles away from place of trial. If a witness is aged or infirm, leave of court can be obtained.

Subdivision (b). Existing Rule 30(b) on protective orders has been transferred to Rule 26(c), and existing Rule 30(a) relating to the notice of taking deposition has been transferred to this subdivision. Because new material has been added, subsection numbers have been inserted.

Subdivision (b)(1). If a subpoena duces tecum is to be served, a copy thereof or a designation of the materials to be produced must accompany the notice. Each party is thereby enabled to prepare for the deposition more effectively.

Subdivision (b)(2). This subdivision is discussed in the note to subdivision (a), to which it relates.

Subdivision (b)(3). This provision is derived from existing Rule 30(a), with a minor change of language.

Subdivision (b)(4). In order to facilitate less expensive procedures, provision is made for the recording of testimony by other than stenographic means—*e.g.*, by mechanical, electronic, or photographic means. Because these methods give rise to problems of accuracy and trustworthiness, the party taking the deposition is required to apply for a court order. The order is to specify how the testimony is to be recorded, preserved, and filed, and it may contain whatever additional safeguards the court deems necessary.

Subdivision (b)(5). A provision is added to enable a party, through service of notice, to require another party to produce documents or things at the taking of his deposition. This may now be done as to a nonparty deponent through use of a subpoena duces tecum as authorized by Rule 45, but some courts have held that documents may be secured from a party only under Rule 34. See 2A Barron & Holtzoff, *Federal Practice and Procedure* § 644.1 n. 83.2, § 792 n. 16 (Wright ed. 1961). With the elimination of "good cause" from Rule 34, the reason for this restrictive doctrine has disappeared. *Cf.* N.Y.C.P.L.R. § 3111.

Whether production of documents or things should be obtained directly under Rule 34 or at the deposition under this rule will depend on the nature and volume of the documents or things. Both methods are made available. When the documents are few and simple, and closely related to the oral examination, ability to proceed via this rule will facilitate discovery. If the discovering party insists on examining many and complex documents at the taking of the deposition, thereby causing undue burdens on others, the

latter may, under Rules 26(c) or 30(d), apply for a court order that the examining party proceed via Rule 34 alone.

Subdivision (b)(6). A new provision is added, whereby a party may name a corporation, partnership, association, or governmental agency as the deponent and designate the matters on which he requests examination, and the organization shall then name one or more of its officers, directors, or managing agents, or other persons consenting to appear and testify on its behalf with respect to matters known or reasonably available to the organization. *Cf.* Alberta Sup.Ct.R. 255. The organization may designate persons other than officers, directors, and managing agents, but only with their consent. Thus, an employee or agent who has an independent or conflicting interest in the litigation—for example, in a personal injury case—can refuse to testify on behalf of the organization.

This procedure supplements the existing practice whereby the examining party designates the corporate official to be deposed. Thus, if the examining party believes that certain officials who have not testified pursuant to this subdivision have added information, he may depose them. On the other hand, a court's decision whether to issue a protective order may take account of the availability and use made of the procedures provided in this subdivision.

The new procedure should be viewed as an added facility for discovery, one which may be advantageous to both sides as well as an improvement in the deposition process. It will reduce the difficulties now encountered in determining, prior to the taking of a deposition, whether a particular employee or agent is a "managing agent." See Note, *Discovery Against Corporations Under the Federal Rules*, 47 Iowa L.Rev. 1006–1016 (1962). It will curb the "bandying" by which officers or managing agents of a corporation are deposed in turn but each disclaims knowledge of facts that are clearly known to persons in the organization and thereby to it. *Cf. Haney v. Woodward & Lothrop, Inc.*, 330 F.2d 940, 944 (4th Cir. 1964). The provision should also assist organizations which find that an unnecessarily large number of their officers and agents are being deposed by a party uncertain of who in the organization has knowledge. Some courts have held that under the existing rules a corporation should not be burdened with choosing which person is to appear for it. E.g., *United States v. Gahagan Dredging Corp.*, 24 F.R.D. 328, 329 (S.D.N.Y.1958). This burden is not essentially different from that of answering interrogatories under Rule 33, and is in any case lighter than that of an examining party ignorant of who in the corporation has knowledge.

Subdivision (c). A new sentence is inserted at the beginning, representing the transfer of existing Rule 26(c) to this subdivision. Another addition conforms to the new provision in subdivision (b)(4).

The present rule provides that transcription shall be carried out unless all parties waive it. In view of the many depositions taken from which nothing useful is discovered, the revised language provides that transcription is to be performed if any party requests it. The fact of the request is relevant to the exercise of the court's discretion in determining who shall pay for transcription.

Parties choosing to serve written questions rather than participate personally in an oral deposition are directed to serve their questions on the party taking the deposition, since the officer is often not identified in advance. Confidentiality is preserved, since the questions may be served in a sealed envelope.

Subdivision (d). The assessment of expenses incurred in relation to motions made under this subdivision (d) is made subject to the provisions of Rule 37(a). The standards for assessment of expenses are more fully set out in Rule 37(a), and these standards should apply to the essentially similar motions of this subdivision.

Subdivision (e). The provision relating to the refusal of a witness to sign his deposition is tightened through insertion of a 30-day time period.

Subdivision (f)(1). A provision is added which codifies in a flexible way the procedure for handling exhibits related to the deposition and at the same time assures each party that he may inspect and copy documents and things produced by a nonparty witness in response to a subpoena duces tecum. As a general rule and in the absence of agreement to the contrary or order of the court, exhibits produced without objection are to be annexed to and returned with the deposition, but a witness may substitute copies for purposes of marking and he may obtain return of the exhibits. The right of the parties to inspect exhibits for identification and to make copies is assured. *Cf.* N.Y.C.P.L.R. § 3116(c).

1971 Amendments

The subdivision permits a party to name a corporation or other form of organization as a deponent in the notice of examination and to describe in the notice the matters about which discovery is desired. The organization is then obliged to designate natural persons to testify on its behalf. The amendment clarifies the procedure to be followed if a party desires to examine a non-party organization through persons designated by the organization. Under the rules, a subpoena rather than a notice of examination is served on a non-party to compel attendance at the taking of a deposition. The amendment provides that a subpoena may name a non-party organization as the deponent and may indicate the matters about which discovery is desired. In that event, the non-party organization must respond by designating natural persons, who are then obliged to testify as to matters known or reasonably available to the organization. To insure that a non-party organization that is not represented by counsel has knowledge of its duty to designate, the amendment directs the party seeking discovery to advise of the duty in the body of the subpoena.

1972 Amendments

Subdivision (c). Existing Rule 43(b), which is to be abrogated, deals with the use of leading questions, the calling, interrogation, impeachment, and scope of cross-examination of adverse parties, officers, etc. These topics are dealt with in many places in the Rules of Evidence. Moreover, many pertinent topics included in the Rules of Evidence are not mentioned in Rule 43(b), e.g. privilege. A reference to the Rules of Evidence generally is therefore made in subdivision (c) of Rule 30.

1980 Amendments

Subdivision (b)(4). It has been proposed that electronic recording of depositions be authorized as a matter of course, subject to the right of a party to seek an order that a deposition be recorded by stenographic means. The Com-

mittee is not satisfied that a case has been made for a reversal of present practice. The amendment is made to encourage parties to agree to the use of electronic recording of depositions so that conflicting claims with respect to the potential of electronic recording for reducing costs of depositions can be appraised in the light of greater experience. The provision that the parties may stipulate that depositions may be recorded by other than stenographic means seems implicit in Rule 29. The amendment makes it explicit. The provision that the stipulation or order shall designate the person before whom the deposition is to be taken is added to encourage the naming of the recording technician as that person, eliminating the necessity of the presence of one whose only function is to administer the oath. See Rules 28(a) and 29.

Subdivision (b)(7). Depositions by telephone are now authorized by Rule 29 upon stipulation of the parties. The amendment authorizes that method by order of the court. The final sentence is added to make it clear that when a deposition is taken by telephone it is taken in the district and at the place where the witness is to answer the questions rather than that where the questions are propounded.

Subdivision (f)(1). For the reasons set out in the Note following the amendment of Rule 5(d), the court may wish to permit the parties to retain depositions unless they are to be used in the action. The amendment of the first paragraph permits the court to so order.

The amendment of the second paragraph is clarifying. The purpose of the paragraph is to permit a person who produces materials at a deposition to offer copies for marking and annexation to the deposition. Such copies are a "substitute" for the originals, which are not to be marked and which can thereafter be used or even disposed of by the person who produces them. In the light of that purpose, the former language of the paragraph had been justly termed "opaque." Wright & Miller, *Federal Practice and Procedure: Civil* § 2114.

1987 Amendments

The amendments are technical. No substantive change is intended.

1993 Amendments

Subdivision (a). Paragraph (1) retains the first and third sentences from the former subdivision (a) without significant modification. The second and fourth sentences are relocated.

Paragraph (2) collects all provisions bearing on requirements of leave of court to take a deposition.

Paragraph (2)(A) is new. It provides a limit on the number of depositions the parties may take, absent leave of court or stipulation with the other parties. One aim of this revision is to assure judicial review under the standards stated in Rule 26(b)(2) before any side will be allowed to take more than ten depositions in a case without agreement of the other parties. A second objective is to emphasize that counsel have a professional obligation to develop a mutual cost-effective plan for discovery in the case. Leave to take additional depositions should be granted when consistent with the principles of Rule 26(b)(2), and in some cases the ten-per-side limit should be reduced in accordance with those same principles. Consideration should ordinarily be given at the planning meeting of the parties under Rule 26(f) and at the time of a scheduling conference under Rule 16(b) as to enlargements or reductions in the number of depositions, eliminating the need for special motions.

A deposition under Rule 30(b)(6) should, for purposes of this limit, be treated as a single deposition even though more than one person may be designated to testify.

In multi-party cases, the parties on any side are expected to confer and agree as to which depositions are most needed, given the presumptive limit on the number of depositions they can take without leave of court. If these disputes cannot be amicably resolved, the court can be requested to resolve the dispute or permit additional depositions.

Paragraph (2)(B) is new. It requires leave of court if any witness is to be deposed in the action more than once. This requirement does not apply when a deposition is temporarily recessed for convenience of counsel or the deponent or to enable additional materials to be gathered before resuming the deposition. If significant travel costs would be incurred to resume the deposition, the parties should consider the feasibility of conducting the balance of the examination by telephonic means.

Paragraph (2)(C) revises the second sentence of the former subdivision (a) as to when depositions may be taken. Consistent with the changes made in Rule 26(d), providing that formal discovery ordinarily not commence until after the litigants have met and conferred as directed in revised Rule 26(f), the rule requires leave of court or agreement of the parties if a deposition is to be taken before that time (except when a witness is about to leave the country).

Subdivision (b). The primary change in subdivision (b) is that parties will be authorized to record deposition testimony by nonstenographic means without first having to obtain permission of the court or agreement from other counsel.

Former subdivision (b)(2) is partly relocated in subdivision (a)(2)(C) of this rule. The latter two sentences of the first paragraph are deleted, in part because they are redundant to Rule 26(g) and in part because Rule 11 no longer applies to discovery requests. The second paragraph of the former subdivision (b)(2), relating to use of depositions at trial where a party was unable to obtain counsel in time for an accelerated deposition, is relocated in Rule 32.

New paragraph (2) confers on the party taking the deposition the choice of the method of recording, without the need to obtain prior court approval for one taken other than stenographically. A party choosing to record a deposition only by videotape or audiotape should understand that a transcript will be required by Rule 26(a)(3)(B) and Rule 32(c) if the deposition is later to be offered as evidence at trial or on a dispositive motion under Rule 56. Objections to the nonstenographic recording of a deposition, when warranted by the circumstances, can be presented to the court under Rule 26(c).

Paragraph (3) provides that other parties may arrange, at their own expense, for the recording of a deposition by a means (stenographic, visual, or sound) in addition to the method designated by the person noticing the deposition. The former provisions of this paragraph, relating to the court's power to change the date of a deposition, have been eliminated as redundant in view of Rule 26(c)(2).

Revised paragraph (4) requires that all depositions be recorded by an officer designated or appointed under Rule 28 and contains special provisions designed to provide basic safeguards to assure the utility and integrity of recordings taken other than stenographically.

Paragraph (7) is revised to authorize the taking of a deposition not only by telephone but also by other remote electronic means, such as satellite television, when agreed to by the parties or authorized by the court.

Subdivision (c). Minor changes are made in this subdivision to reflect those made in subdivision (b) and to complement the new provisions of subdivision (d)(1), aimed at reducing the number of interruptions during depositions.

In addition, the revision addresses a recurring problem as to whether other potential deponents can attend a deposition. Courts have disagreed, some holding that witnesses should be excluded through invocation of Rule 615 of the evidence rules, and others holding that witnesses may attend unless excluded by an order under Rule 26(c)(5). The revision provides that other witnesses are not automatically excluded from a deposition simply by the request of a party. Exclusion, however, can be ordered under Rule 26(c)(5) when appropriate; and, if exclusion is ordered, consideration should be given as to whether the excluded witnesses likewise should be precluded from reading, or being otherwise informed about, the testimony given in the earlier depositions. The revision addresses only the matter of attendance by potential deponents, and does not attempt to resolve issues concerning attendance by others, such as members of the public or press.

Subdivision (d). The first sentence of new paragraph (1) provides that any objections during a deposition must be made concisely and in a non-argumentative and non-suggestive manner. Depositions frequently have been unduly prolonged, if not unfairly frustrated, by lengthy objections and colloquy, often suggesting how the deponent should respond. While objections may, under the revised rule, be made during a deposition, they ordinarily should be limited to those that under Rule 32(d)(3) might be waived if not made at that time, *i.e.*, objections on grounds that might be immediately obviated, removed, or cured, such as to the form of a question or the responsiveness of an answer. Under Rule 32(b), other objections can, even without the so-called "usual stipulation" preserving objections, be raised for the first time at trial and therefore should be kept to a minimum during a deposition.

Directions to a deponent not to answer a question can be even more disruptive than objections. The second sentence of new paragraph (1) prohibits such directions except in the three circumstances indicated: to claim a privilege or protection against disclosure (*e.g.*, as work product), to enforce a court directive limiting the scope or length of permissible discovery, or to suspend a deposition to enable presentation of a motion under paragraph (3).

Paragraph (2) is added to this subdivision to dispel any doubts regarding the power of the court by order or local rule to establish limits on the length of depositions. The rule also explicitly authorizes the court to impose the cost resulting from obstructive tactics that unreasonably prolong a deposition on the person engaged in such obstruction. This sanction may be imposed on a non-party witness as well as a party or attorney, but is otherwise congruent with Rule 26(g).

It is anticipated that limits on the length of depositions prescribed by local rules would be presumptive only, subject to modification by the court or by agreement of the parties. Such modifications typically should be discussed by the parties in their meeting under Rule 26(f) and included in the scheduling order required by Rule 16(b). Additional time, moreover, should be allowed under the revised rule when justified under the principles stated in Rule 26(b)(2). To reduce the number of special motions, local rules should ordinarily permit—and indeed encourage—the parties to agree to additional time, as when, during the taking of a deposition, it becomes clear that some additional examination is needed.

Paragraph (3) authorizes appropriate sanctions not only when a deposition is unreasonably prolonged, but also when an attorney engages in other practices that improperly frustrate the fair examination of the deponent, such as making improper objections or giving directions not to answer prohibited by paragraph (1). In general, counsel should not engage in any conduct during a deposition that would not be allowed in the presence of a judicial officer. The making of an excessive number of unnecessary objections may itself constitute sanctionable conduct, as may the refusal of an attorney to agree with other counsel on a fair apportionment of the time allowed for examination of a deponent or a refusal to agree to a reasonable request for some additional time to complete a deposition, when that is permitted by the local rule or order.

Subdivision (e). Various changes are made in this subdivision to reduce problems sometimes encountered when depositions are taken stenographically. Reporters frequently have difficulties obtaining signatures—and the return of depositions—from deponents. Under the revision pre-filing review by the deponent is required only if requested before the deposition is completed. If review is requested, the deponent will be allowed 30 days to review the transcript or recording and to indicate any changes in form or substance. Signature of the deponent will be required only if review is requested and changes are made.

Subdivision (f). Minor changes are made in this subdivision to reflect those made in subdivision (b). In courts which direct that depositions not be automatically filed, the reporter can transmit the transcript or recording to the attorney taking the deposition (or ordering the transcript or record), who then becomes custodian for the court of the original record of the deposition. Pursuant to subdivision (f)(2), as under the prior rule, any other party is entitled to secure a copy of the deposition from the officer designated to take the deposition; accordingly, unless ordered or agreed, the officer must retain a copy of the recording or the stenographic notes.

2000 Amendment

Subdivision (d). Paragraph (1) has been amended to clarify the terms regarding behavior during depositions. The references to objections " to evidence" and limitations "on evidence" have been removed to avoid disputes about what is "evidence" and whether an objection is to, or a limitation is on, discovery instead. It is intended that the rule apply to any objection to a question or other issue arising during a deposition, and to any limitation imposed by the court in connection with a deposition, which might relate to duration or other matters.

The current rule places limitations on instructions that a witness not answer only when the instruction is made by a "party." Similar limitations should apply with regard to anyone who might purport to instruct a witness not to answer a question. Accordingly, the rule is amended to apply the limitation to instructions by any person. The amendment is not intended to confer new authority on nonparties to instruct witnesses to refuse to answer deposition questions. The amendment makes it clear that, whatever the legitimacy of giving such instructions, the nonparty is subject to the same limitations as parties.

Paragraph (2) imposes a presumptive durational limitation of one day of seven hours for any deposition. The Committee has been informed that overlong depositions can result in undue costs and delays in some circumstances. This limitation contemplates that there will be reasonable breaks during the day for lunch and other reasons, and that the only time to be counted is the time occupied by the actual deposition. For purposes of this durational limit, the deposition of each person designated under Rule 30(b)(6) should be considered a separate deposition. The presumptive duration may be extended, or otherwise altered, by agreement. Absent agreement, a court order is needed. The party seeking a court order to extend the examination, or otherwise alter the limitations, is expected to show good cause to justify such an order.

Parties considering extending the time for a deposition—and courts asked to order an extension—might consider a variety of factors. For example, if the witness needs an interpreter, that may prolong the examination. If the examination will cover events occurring over a long period of time, that may justify allowing additional time. In cases in which the witness will be questioned about numerous or lengthy documents, it is often desirable for the interrogating party to send copies of the documents to the witness sufficiently in advance of the deposition so that the witness can become familiar with them. Should the witness nevertheless not read the documents in advance, thereby prolonging the deposition, a court could consider that a reason for extending the time limit. If the examination reveals that documents have been requested but not produced, that may justify further examination once production has occurred. In multi-party cases, the need for each party to examine the witness may warrant additional time, although duplicative questioning should be avoided and parties with similar interests should strive to designate one lawyer to question about areas of common interest. Similarly, should the lawyer for the witness want to examine the witness, that may require additional time. Finally, with regard to expert witnesses, there may more often be a need for additional time—even after the submission of the report required by Rule 26(a)(2)—for full exploration of the theories upon which the witness relies.

It is expected that in most instances the parties and the witness will make reasonable accommodations to avoid the need for resort to the court. The limitation is phrased in terms of a single day on the assumption that ordinarily a single day would be preferable to a deposition extending over multiple days; if alternative arrangements would better suit the parties, they may agree to them. It is also assumed that there will be reasonable breaks during the day. Preoccupation with timing is to be avoided.

The rule directs the court to allow additional time where consistent with Rule 26(b)(2) if needed for a fair examination of the deponent. In addition, if the deponent or another person impedes or delays the examination, the court must authorize extra time. The amendment makes clear that additional time should also be allowed where the examination is impeded by an "other circumstance," which might include a power outage, a health emergency, or other event.

In keeping with the amendment to Rule 26(b)(2), the provision added in 1993 granting authority to adopt a local rule limiting the time permitted for depositions has been removed. The court may enter a case-specific order directing shorter depositions for all depositions in a case or with regard to a specific witness. The court may also order that a deposition be taken for limited periods on several days.

Paragraph (3) includes sanctions provisions formerly included in paragraph (2). It authorizes the court to impose an appropriate sanction on any person responsible for an impediment that frustrated the fair examination of the deponent. This could include the deponent, any party, or any other person involved in the deposition. If the impediment or delay results from an "other circumstance" under paragraph (2), ordinarily no sanction would be appropriate.

Former paragraph (3) has been renumbered (4) but is otherwise unchanged .

Subdivision (f)(1): This subdivision is amended because Rule 5(d) has been amended to direct that discovery materials, including depositions, ordinarily should not be filed. The rule already has provisions directing that the lawyer who arranged for the transcript or recording preserve the deposition. Rule 5(d) provides that, once the deposition is used in the proceeding, the attorney must file it with the court.

"Shall" is replaced by "must" or "may" under the program to conform amended rules to current style conventions when there is no ambiguity.

GAP Report

The Advisory Committee recommends deleting the requirement in the published proposed amendments that the deponent consent to extending a deposition beyond one day, and adding an amendment to Rule 30(f)(1) to conform to the published amendment to Rule 5(d) regarding filing of depositions. It also recommends conforming the Committee Note with regard to the deponent veto, and adding material to the Note to provide direction on computation of the durational limitation on depositions, to provide examples of situations in which the parties might agree—or the court order—that a deposition be extended, and to make clear that no new authority to instruct a witness is conferred by the amendment. One minor wording improvement in the Note is also suggested.

HISTORICAL NOTES

Effective Date of Amendment Proposed November 20, 1972

Amendment of this rule embraced by the order entered by the Supreme Court of the United States on November 20, 1972, effective on the 180th day beginning after January 2, 1975, see section 3 of Pub.L. 93–595, Jan. 2, 1975, 88 Stat. 1959, set out as a note under section 2071 of Title 28.

Rule 31. Depositions Upon Written Questions

(a) Serving Questions; Notice.

(1) A party may take the testimony of any person, including a party, by deposition upon written questions without leave of court except as provided in paragraph (2). The attendance of witnesses may be compelled by the use of subpoena as provided in Rule 45.

(2) A party must obtain leave of court, which shall be granted to the extent consistent with the principles stated in Rule 26(b)(2), if the person to be examined is confined in prison or if, without the written stipulation of the parties.

(A) a proposed deposition would result in more than ten depositions being taken under this rule or Rule 30 by the plaintiffs, or by the defendants, or by third-party defendants;

(B) the person to be examined has already been deposed in the case; or

(C) a party seeks to take a deposition before the time specified in Rule 26(d).

(3) A party desiring to take a deposition upon written questions shall serve them upon every other party with a notice stating (1) the name and address of the person who is to answer them, if known, and if the name is not known, a general description sufficient to identify the person or the particular class or group to which the person belongs, and (2) the name or descriptive title and address of the officer before whom the deposition is to be taken. A deposition upon written questions may be taken of a public or private corporation or a partnership or association or governmental agency in accordance with the provisions of Rule 30(b)(6).

(4) Within 14 days after the notice and written questions are served, a party may serve cross questions upon all other parties. Within 7 days after being served with cross questions, a party may serve redirect questions upon all other parties. Within 7 days after being served with redirect questions, a party may serve recross questions upon all other parties. The court may for cause shown enlarge or shorten the time.

(b) **Officer to Take Responses and Prepare Record.** A copy of the notice and copies of all questions served shall be delivered by the party taking the deposition to the officer designated in the notice, who shall proceed promptly, in the manner provided by Rule 30(c), (e), and (f), to take the testimony of the witness in response to the questions and to prepare, certify, and file or mail the deposition, attaching thereto the copy of the notice and the questions received by the officer.

(c) **Notice of Filing.** When the deposition is filed the party taking it shall promptly give notice thereof to all other parties.

(As amended Mar. 30, 1970, eff. July 1, 1970; Mar. 2, 1987, eff. Aug. 1, 1987; Apr. 22, 1993, eff. Dec. 1, 1993.)

1937 Adoption

This rule is in accordance with common practice. In most of the states listed in the Note to Rule 26(a), provisions similar to this rule will be found in the statutes which in their respective statutory compilations follow those cited in the Note to Rule 26(a).

1970 Amendment

Confusion is created by the use of the same terminology to describe both the taking of a deposition upon "written interrogatories" pursuant to this rule and the serving of "written interrogatories" upon parties pursuant to Rule 33. The distinction between these two modes of discovery will be more readily and clearly grasped through substitution of the word "questions" for "interrogatories" throughout this rule.

Subdivision (a). A new paragraph is inserted at the beginning of this subdivision to conform to the rearrangement of provisions in Rules 26(a), 30(a), and 30(b).

The revised subdivision permits designation of the deponent by general description or by class or group. This conforms to the practice for depositions on oral examination.

The new procedure provided in Rule 30(b)(6) for taking the deposition of a corporation or other organization through persons designated by the organization is incorporated by reference.

The service of all questions, including cross, redirect, and recross, is to be made on all parties. This will inform the parties and enable them to participate fully in the procedure.

The time allowed for service of cross, redirect, and recross questions has been extended. Experience with the existing time limits shows them to be unrealistically short. No special restriction is placed on the time for serving the notice of taking the deposition and the first set of questions. Since no party is required to serve cross questions less than 30 days after the notice and questions are served, the defendant has sufficient time to obtain counsel. The court may for cause shown enlarge or shorten the time.

Subdivision (d). Since new Rule 26(c) provides for protective orders with respect to all discovery, and expressly provides that the court may order that one discovery device be used in place of another, subdivision (d) is eliminated as unnecessary.

1987 Amendment

The amendments are technical. No substantive change is intended.

1993 Amendments

Subdivision (a). The first paragraph of subdivision (a) is divided into two subparagraphs, with provisions comparable to those made in the revision of Rule 30. Changes are made in the former third paragraph, numbered in the revision as paragraph (4), to reduce the total time for developing cross-examination, redirect, and recross questions from 50 days to 28 days.

Rule 32. Use of Depositions in Court Proceedings

(a) Use of Depositions. At the trial or upon the hearing of a motion or an interlocutory proceeding, any part or all of a deposition, so far as admissible under the rules of evidence applied as though the witness were then present and testifying, may be used against any party who was present or represented at the taking of the deposition or who had reasonable notice thereof, in accordance with any of the following provisions:

(1) Any deposition may be used by any party for the purpose of contradicting or impeaching the testimony of deponent as a witness, or for any other purpose permitted by the Federal Rules of Evidence.

(2) The deposition of a party or of anyone who at the time of taking the deposition was an officer, director, or managing agent, or a person designated under Rule 30(b)(6) or 31(a) to testify on behalf of a public or private corporation, partnership or association or governmental agency which is a party may be used by an adverse party for any purpose.

(3) The deposition of a witness, whether or not a party, may be used by any party for any purpose if the court finds:

(A) that the witness is dead; or

(B) that the witness is at a greater distance than 100 miles from the place of trial or hearing, or is out of the United States, unless it appears that the absence of the witness was procured by the party offering the deposition; or

(C) that the witness is unable to attend or testify because of age, illness, infirmity, or imprisonment; or

(D) that the party offering the deposition has been unable to procure the attendance of the witness by subpoena; or

(E) upon application and notice, that such exceptional circumstances exist as to make it desirable, in the interest of justice and with due regard to the importance of presenting the testimony of witnesses orally in open court, to allow the deposition to be used.

A deposition taken without leave of court pursuant to a notice under Rule 30(a)(2)(C) shall not be used against a party who demonstrates that, when served with the notice, it was unable through the exercise of diligence to obtain counsel to represent it at the taking of the deposition; nor shall a deposition be used against a party who, having received less than 11 days notice of a deposition, has promptly upon receiving such notice filed a motion for a protective order under Rule 26(c)(2) requesting that the deposition not be held or be held at a different time or place and such motion is pending at the time the deposition is held.

(4) If only part of a deposition is offered in evidence by a party, an adverse party may require the offeror to introduce any other part which ought in fairness to be considered with the part introduced, and any party may introduce any other parts.

Substitution of parties pursuant to Rule 25 does not affect the right to use depositions previously taken; and, when an action has been brought in any court of the United States or of any State and another action involving the same subject matter is afterward brought between the same parties or their representatives or successors in interest, all depositions lawfully taken and duly filed in the former action may be used in the latter as if originally taken therefor. A deposition previously taken may also be used as permitted by the Federal Rules of Evidence.

(b) Objections to Admissibility. Subject to the provisions of Rule 28(b) and subdivision (d)(3) of this rule, objection may be made at the trial or hearing to receiving in evidence any deposition or part thereof for any reason which would require the exclusion of the evidence if the witness were then present and testifying.

(c) Form of Presentation. Except as otherwise directed by the court, a party offering deposition testimony pursuant to this rule may offer it in stenographic or nonstenographic form, but, if in nonstenographic form, the party shall also provide the court with a transcript of the portions so offered. On request of any party in a case tried before a jury, deposition testimony offered other than for impeachment purposes shall be presented in nonstenographic form, if available, unless the court for good cause orders otherwise.

(d) Effect of Errors and Irregularities in Depositions.

(1) **As to Notice.** All errors and irregularities in the notice for taking a deposition are waived unless written objection is promptly served upon the party giving the notice.

(2) **As to Disqualification of Officer.** Objection to taking a deposition because of disqualification of the officer before whom it is to be taken is waived unless made before the taking of the deposition begins or as soon thereafter as the disqualification becomes known or could be discovered with reasonable diligence.

(3) **As to Taking of Deposition.**

(A) Objections to the competency of a witness or to the competency, relevancy, or materiality of testimony are not waived by failure to make them

before or during the taking of the deposition, unless the ground of the objection is one which might have been obviated or removed if presented at that time.

(B) Errors and irregularities occurring at the oral examination in the manner of taking the deposition, in the form of the questions or answers, in the oath or affirmation, or in the conduct of parties, and errors of any kind which might be obviated, removed, or cured if promptly presented, are waived unless seasonable objection thereto is made at the taking of the deposition.

(C) Objections to the form of written questions submitted under Rule 31 are waived unless served in writing upon the party propounding them within the time allowed for serving the succeeding cross or other questions and within 5 days after service of the last questions authorized.

(4) **As to Completion and Return of Deposition.** Errors and irregularities in the manner in which the testimony is transcribed or the deposition is prepared, signed, certified, sealed, indorsed, transmitted, filed, or otherwise dealt with by the officer under Rules 30 and 31 are waived unless a motion to suppress the deposition or some part thereof is made with reasonable promptness after such defect is, or with due diligence might have been, ascertained.

(As amended Mar. 30, 1970, eff. July 1, 1970; Nov. 20, 1972, eff. July 1, 1975; Apr. 29, 1980, eff. Aug. 1, 1980; Mar. 2, 1987, eff. Aug. 1, 1987; Apr. 22, 1993, eff. Dec. 1, 1993.)

ADVISORY COMMITTEE NOTES
1937 Adoption

This rule is in accordance with common practice. In most of the states listed in the note to rule 26, provisions similar to this rule will be found in the statutes which in their respective statutory compilations follow those cited in the Note to Rule 26.

1970 Amendment

As part of the rearrangement of the discovery rules, existing subdivisions (d), (e), and (f) of Rule 26 are transferred to Rule 32 as new subdivisions (a), (b), and (c). The provisions of Rule 32 are retained as subdivision (d) of Rule 32 with appropriate changes in the lettering and numbering of subheadings. The new rule is given a suitable new title. A beneficial byproduct of the rearrangement is that provisions which are naturally related to one another are placed in one rule.

A change is made in new Rule 32(a), whereby it is made clear that the rules of evidence are to be applied to depositions offered at trial as though the deponent were then present and testifying at trial. This eliminates the possibility of certain technical hearsay objections which are based, not on the contents of deponent's testimony, but on his absence from court. The language of present Rule 26(d) does not appear to authorize these technical objections, but it is not entirely clear. Note present Rule 26(e), transferred to Rule 32(b); see 2A Barron & Holtzoff, *Federal Practice and Procedure* 164–166 (Wright ed. 1961).

An addition in Rule 32(a)(2) provides for use of a deposition of a person designated by a corporation or other organization, which is a party, to testify on its behalf. This complements the new procedure for taking the deposition of a corporation or other organization provided in Rules 30(b)(6) and 31(a). The addition is appropriate, since the deposition is in substance and effect that of the corporation or other organization which is a party.

A change is made in the standard under which a party offering part of a deposition in evidence may be required to introduce additional parts of the deposition. The new standard is contained in a proposal made by the Advisory Committee on Rules of Evidence. See Rule 1–07 and accompanying Note, *Preliminary Draft of Proposed Rules of Evidence for the United States District Courts and Magistrates* 21–22 (March, 1969).

References to other rules are changed to conform to the rearrangement, and minor verbal changes have been made for clarification. The time for objecting to written questions served under Rule 31 is slightly extended.

1972 Amendment

Subdivision (c). The concept of "making a person one's own witness" appears to have had significance principally in two respects: impeachment and waiver of incompetency. Neither retains any vitality under the Rules of Evidence. The old prohibition against impeaching one's own witness is eliminated by Evidence Rule 607. The lack of recognition in the Rules of Evidence of state rules of incompetency in the Dead Man's area renders it unnecessary to consider aspects of waiver arising from calling the incompetent party-witness. Subdivision (c) is deleted because it appears to be no longer necessary in the light of the Rules of Evidence.

1980 Amendment

Subdivision (a)(1). Rule 801(d) of the Federal Rules of Evidence permits a prior inconsistent statement of a witness in a deposition to be used as substantive evidence. And Rule 801(d)(2) makes the statement of an agent or servant admissible against the principal under the circumstances described in the Rule. The language of the present subdivision is, therefore, too narrow.

Subdivision (a)(4). The requirement that a prior action must have been dismissed before depositions taken for use in it can be used in a subsequent action was doubtless an oversight, and the courts have ignored it. See Wright & Miller, *Federal Practice and Procedure: Civil* § 2150. The final sentence is added to reflect the fact that the Federal Rules of Evidence permit a broader use of depositions previously taken under certain circumstances. For example, Rule 804(b)(1) of the Federal Rules of Evidence provides that if a witness is unavailable, as that term is defined by the rule, his deposition in any earlier proceeding can be used against a party to the prior proceeding who had an opportunity and similar motive to develop the testimony of the witness.

1987 Amendment

The amendment is technical. No substantive change is intended.

1993 Amendments

Subdivision (a). The last sentence of revised subdivision (a) not only includes the substance of the provisions formerly contained in the second paragraph of Rule 30(b)(2), but adds a provision to deal with the situation when a party, receiving minimal notice of a proposed deposition, is unable to obtain a court ruling on its motion for a protective order seeking to delay or change the place of the deposition. Ordinarily a party does not obtain protection merely by the filing of a motion for a protective order under Rule 26(c); any protection is dependent upon the court's ruling. Under the revision, a party receiving less than 11 days notice of a deposition can, provided its motion for a protective order is filed promptly, be spared the risks resulting from nonattendance at the deposition held before its motion is ruled upon. Although the revision of Rule 32(a) covers only the risk that the deposition could be used against the non-appearing movant, it should also follow that, when the proposed deponent is the movant, the deponent would have "just cause" for failing to appear for purposes of Rule 37(d)(1). Inclusion of this provision is not intended to signify that 11 days' notice is the minimum advance notice for all depositions or that greater than 10 days should necessarily be deemed sufficient in all situations.

Subdivision (c). This new subdivision, inserted at the location of a subdivision previously abrogated, is included in view of the increased opportunities for video-recording and audio-recording of depositions under revised Rule 30(b). Under this rule a party may offer deposition testimony in any of the forms authorized under Rule 30(b) but, if offering it in a nonstenographic form, must provide the court with a transcript of the portions so offered. On request of any party in a jury trial, deposition testimony offered other than for impeachment purposes is to be presented in a nonstenographic form if available, unless the court directs otherwise. Note that under Rule 26(a)(3)(B) a party expecting to use nonstenographic deposition testimony as substantive evidence is required to provide other parties with a transcript in advance of trial.

HISTORICAL NOTES

References in Text

The Federal Rules of Evidence, referred to in subd. (a)(1), (4), are set out in this title.

Effective Date of Amendment Proposed November 20, 1972

Amendment of this rule embraced by the order entered by the Supreme Court of the United States on November 20, 1972, effective on the 180th day beginning after January 2, 1975, see section 3 of Pub.L. 93–595, Jan. 2, 1975, 88 Stat. 1959, set out as a note under section 2071 of Title 28.

Rule 33. Interrogatories to Parties

(a) Availability. Without leave of court or written stipulation, any party may serve upon any other party written interrogatories, not exceeding 25 in number including all discrete subparts, to be answered by the party served or, if the party served is a public or private corporation or a partnership or association or governmental agency, by any officer or agent, who shall furnish such information as is available to the party. Leave to serve additional interrogatories shall be granted to the extent consistent with the principles of Rule 26(b)(2). Without leave of court or written stipulation, interrogatories may not be served before the time specified in Rule 26(d).

(b) Answers and Objections.

(1) Each interrogatory shall be answered separately and fully in writing under oath, unless it is objected to, in which event the objecting party shall state the reasons for objection and shall answer to the extent the interrogatory is not objectionable.

(2) The answers are to be signed by the person making them, and the objections signed by the attorney making them.

(3) The party upon whom the interrogatories have been served shall serve a copy of the answers, and objections if any, within 30 days after the service of the interrogatories. A shorter or longer time may be directed by the court or, in the absence of such an order, agreed to in writing by the parties subject to Rule 29.

(4) All grounds for an objection to an interrogatory shall be stated with specificity. Any ground not stated in a timely objection is waived unless the party's failure to object is excused by the court for good cause shown.

(5) The party submitting the interrogatories may move for an order under Rule 37(a) with respect to any objection to or other failure to answer an interrogatory.

(c) Scope; Use at Trial. Interrogatories may relate to any matters which can be inquired into under Rule 26(b)(1), and the answers may be used to the extent permitted by the rules of evidence.

An interrogatory otherwise proper is not necessarily objectionable merely because an answer to the interrogatory involves an opinion or contention that relates to fact or the application of law to fact, but the court may order that such an interrogatory need not be answered until after designated discovery has been completed or until a pre-trial conference or other later time.

(d) Option to Produce Business Records.

Where the answer to an interrogatory may be derived or ascertained from the business records of the party upon whom the interrogatory has been served or from an examination, audit or inspection of such business records, including a compilation, abstract or summary thereof, and the burden of deriving or ascertaining the answer is substantially the same for the party serving the interrogatory as for the party served, it is a sufficient answer to such interrogatory to specify the records from which the answer may be derived or ascertained and to afford to the party serving the interrogatory reasonable opportunity to examine, audit or inspect such records and to make copies, compilations, abstracts or summaries. A specification shall be in sufficient detail to permit the interrogating party to locate and to identify, as readily as can the party served, the records from which the answer may be ascertained.

(As amended Dec. 27, 1946, eff. Mar. 19, 1948; Mar. 30, 1970, eff. July 1, 1970; Apr. 29, 1980, eff. Aug. 1, 1980; Apr. 22, 1993, eff. Dec. 1, 1993.)

ADVISORY COMMITTEE NOTES

1937 Adoption

This rule restates the substance of [former] Equity Rule 58 (Discovery—Interrogatories—Inspection and Production of Documents—Admission of Execution or Genuineness), with modifications to conform to these rules.

1946 Amendment

Note. The added second sentence in the first paragraph of Rule 33 conforms with a similar change in Rule 26(a) and will avoid litigation as to when the interrogatories may be served. Original Rule 33 does not state the times at which parties may serve written interrogatories upon each other. It has been the accepted view, however, that the times were the same in Rule 33 as those stated in Rule 26(a). *United States v. American Solvents & Chemical Corp. of California,* D.Del.1939, 30 F.Supp. 107; *Sheldon v. Great Lakes Transit Corp.,* W.D.N.Y.1942, 2 F.R.D. 272, 5 Fed.Rules Serv. 33.11, Case 3; *Musher Foundation, Inc., v. Alba Trading Co.,* S.D.N.Y.1941, 42 F.Supp. 281; 2 *Moore's Federal Practice,* 1938, 2621. The time within which leave of court must be secured by a plaintiff has been fixed at 10 days, in view of the fact that a defendant has 10 days within which to make objections in any case, which should give him ample time to engage counsel and prepare.

Further in the first paragraph of Rule 33, the word "service" is substituted for "delivery" in conformance with the use of the word "serve" elsewhere in the rule and generally throughout the rules. See also Note to Rule 13(a) herein. The portion of the rule dealing with practice on objections has been revised so as to afford a clearer statement of the procedure. The addition of the words "to interrogatories to which objection is made" insures that only the answers to the objectionable interrogatories may be deferred, and that the answers to interrogatories not objectionable shall be forthcoming within the time prescribed in the rule. Under the original wording, answers to all interrogatories may be withheld until objections, sometimes to but a few interrogatories, are determined. The amendment expedites the procedure of the rule and serves to eliminate the strike value of objections to minor interrogatories. The elimination of the last sentence of the original rule is in line with the policy stated subsequently in this note.

The added second paragraph in Rule 33 contributes clarity and specificity as to the use and scope of interrogatories to the parties. The field of inquiry will be as broad as the scope of examination under Rule 26(b). There is no reason why interrogatories should be more limited than depositions, particularly when the former represent an inexpensive means of securing useful information. See *Hoffman v. Wilson Line, Inc.*, E.D.Pa.1946, 9 Fed.Rules Serv. 33.514, Case 2; *Brewster v. Technicolor, Inc.*, N.Y.1941, 2 F.R.D. 186, 5 Fed.Rules Serv. 33.319, Case 3; *Kingsway Press, Inc. v. Farrell Publishing Corp.*, S.D.N.Y.1939, 30 F.Supp. 775. Under present Rule 33 some courts have unnecessarily restricted the breadth of inquiry on various grounds. See *Auer v. Hershey Creamery Co.*, D.N.J.1939, 2 Fed.Rules Serv. 33.31, Case 2, 1 F.R.D. 14; *Tudor v. Leslie*, D.Mass.1940, 1 F.R.D. 448, 4 Fed.Rules Serv. 33.324, Case 1. Other courts have read into the rule the requirement that interrogation should be directed only towards "important facts", and have tended to fix a more or less arbitrary limit as to the number of interrogatories which could be asked in any case. See *Knox v. Alter*, W.D.Pa.1942, 2 F.R.D. 337, 6 Fed.Rules Serv. 33.352, Case 1; *Byers Theaters, Inc. v. Murphy*, W.D.Va.1940, 3 Fed.Rules Serv. 33.31, Case 3, 1 F.R.D. 286; *Coca-Cola Co. v. Dixi-Cola Laboratories, Inc.*, D.Md.1939, 30 F.Supp. 275. See also comment on these restrictions in Holtzoff, *Instruments of Discovery under Federal Rules of Civil Procedure*, 1942, 41 Mich.L.Rev. 205, 216–217. Under amended Rule 33, the party interrogated is given the right to invoke such protective orders under Rule 30(b) as are appropriate to the situation. At the same time, it is provided that the number of or number of sets of interrogatories to be served may not be limited arbitrarily or as a general policy to any particular number, but that a limit may be fixed only as justice requires to avoid annoyance, expense, embarrassment or oppression in individual cases. The party interrogated, therefore, must show the necessity for limitation on that basis. It will be noted that in accord with this change the last sentence of the present rule, restricting the sets of interrogatories to be served, has been stricken. In *J. Schoeneman, Inc. v. Brauer*, W.D.Mo.1940, 1 F.R.D. 292, 3 Fed.Rules Serv. 33.31, Case 2, the court said: "Rule 33 * * * has been interpreted * * * as being just as broad in its implications as in the case of depositions * * * It makes no difference therefore, how many interrogatories are propounded. If the inquiries are pertinent the opposing party cannot complain." To the same effect, see *Canuso v. City of Niagara Falls*, W.D.N.Y.1945, 8 Fed.Rules Serv. 33.352, Case 1; *Hoffman v. Wilson Line, Inc.*, supra.

By virtue of express language in the added second paragraph of Rule 33, as amended, any uncertainty as to the use of the answers to interrogatories is removed. The omission of a provision on this score in the original rule has caused some difficulty. See, e.g., *Bailey v. New England Mutual Life Ins. Co.*, S.D.Cal.1940, 1 F.R.D. 494, 4 Fed.Rules Serv. 33.46, Case 1.

The second sentence of the second paragraph in Rule 33, as amended, concerns the situation where a party wishes to serve interrogatories on a party after having taken his deposition, or vice versa. It has been held that an oral examination of a party, after the submission to him and answer of interrogatories, would be permitted. *Howard v. State Marine Corp.*, S.D.N.Y.1940, 4 Fed.Rules Serv. 33.62, Case 1, 1 F.R.D. 499; *Stevens v. Minder Construction Co.*, S.D.N.Y.1943, 3 F.R.D. 498, 7 Fed.Rules Serv. 30b.31, Case 2. But objections have been sustained to interrogatories served after the oral deposition of a party had been taken. *McNally v. Simons*, S.D.N.Y.1940, 3 Fed.Rules Serv. 33.61,

Case 1, 1 F.R.D. 254; *Currier v. Currier*, S.D.N.Y.1942, 3 F.R.D. 21, 6 Fed.Rules Serv. 33.61, Case 1. Rule 33, as amended, permits either interrogatories after a deposition or a deposition after interrogatories. It may be quite desirable or necessary to elicit additional information by the inexpensive method of interrogatories where a deposition has already been taken. The party to be interrogated, however, may seek a protective order from the court under Rule 30(b) where the additional deposition or interrogation works a hardship or injustice on the party from whom it is sought.

1970 Amendment

Subdivision (a). The mechanics of the operation of Rule 33 are substantially revised by the proposed amendment, with a view to reducing court intervention. There is general agreement that interrogatories spawn a greater percentage of objections and motions than any other discovery device. The Columbia Survey shows that, although half of the litigants resorted to depositions and about one-third used interrogatories, about 65 percent of the objections were made with respect to interrogatories and 26 percent related to depositions. See also Speck, *The Use of Discovery in United States District Courts*, 60 Yale L.J. 1132, 1144, 1151 (1951); Note, 36 Minn.L.Rev. 364, 379 (1952).

The procedures now provided in Rule 33 seem calculated to encourage objections and court motions. The time periods now allowed for responding to interrogatories—15 days for answers and 10 days for objections—are too short. The Columbia Survey shows that tardy response to interrogatories is common, virtually expected. The same was reported in Speck, *supra*, 60 Yale L.J. 1132, 1144. The time pressures tend to encourage objections as a means of gaining time to answer.

The time for objections is even shorter than for answers, and the party runs the risk that if he fails to object in time he may have waived his objections. *E.g., Cleminshaw v. Beech Aircraft Corp.*, 21 F.R.D. 300 (D.Del.1957); See 4 *Moore's Federal Practice*, ¶33.27 (2d ed. 1966); 2A Barron & Holtzoff, *Federal Practice and Procedure* 372–373 (Wright ed. 1961). It often seems easier to object than to seek an extension of time. Unlike Rules 30(d) and 37(a), Rule 33 imposes no sanction of expenses on a party whose objections are clearly unjustified.

Rule 33 assures that the objections will lead directly to court, through its requirement that they be served with a notice of hearing. Although this procedure does not preclude an out-of-court resolution of the dispute, the procedure tends to discourage informal negotiations. If answers are served and they are thought inadequate, the interrogating party may move under Rule 37(a) for an order compelling adequate answers. There is no assurance that the hearing on objections and that on inadequate answers will be heard together.

The amendment improves the procedure of Rule 33 in the following respects:

(1) The time allowed for response is increased to 30 days and this time period applies to both answers and objections, but a defendant need not respond in less than 45 days after service of the summons and complaint upon him. As is true under existing law, the responding party who believes that some parts or all of the interrogatories are objectionable may choose to seek a protective order under new Rule 26(c) or

may serve objections under this rule. Unless he applies for a protective order, he is required to serve answers or objections in response to the interrogatories, subject to the sanctions provided in Rule 37(d). Answers and objections are served together, so that a response to each interrogatory is encouraged, and any failure to respond is easily noted.

(2) In view of the enlarged time permitted for response, it is no longer necessary to require leave of court for service of interrogatories. The purpose of this requirement—that defendant have time to obtain counsel before a response must be made—is adequately fulfilled by the requirement that interrogatories be served upon a party with or after service of the summons and complaint upon him.

Some would urge that the plaintiff nevertheless not be permitted to serve interrogatories with the complaint. They fear that a routine practice might be invited, whereby form interrogatories would accompany most complaints. More fundamentally, they feel that, since very general complaints are permitted in present-day pleading, it is fair that the defendant have a right to take the lead in serving interrogatories. (These views apply also to Rule 36.) The amendment of Rule 33 rejects these views, in favor of allowing both parties to go forward with discovery, each free to obtain the information he needs respecting the case.

(3) If objections are made, the burden is on the interrogating party to move under Rule 37(a) for a court order compelling answers, in the course of which the court will pass on the objections. The change in the burden of going forward does not alter the existing obligation of an objecting party to justify his objections. *E.g., Pressley v. Bochlke,* 33 F.R.D. 316 (W.D.N.C. 1963). If the discovering party asserts that an answer is incomplete or evasive, again he may look to Rule 37(a) for relief, and he should add this assertion to his motion to overrule objections. There is no requirement that the parties consult informally concerning their differences, but the new procedure should encourage consultation, and the court may by local rule require it.

The proposed changes are similar in approach to those adopted by California in 1961. See Calif.Code Civ.Proc. § 2030(a). The experience of the Los Angeles Superior Court is informally reported as showing that the California amendment resulted in a significant reduction in court motions concerning interrogatories. Rhode Island takes a similar approach. See R. 33, *R.I.R. Civ.Proc. Official Draft,* p. 74 (Boston Law Book Co.).

A change is made in subdivision (a) which is not related to the sequence of procedures. The restriction to "adverse" parties is eliminated. The courts have generally construed this restriction as precluding interrogatories unless an issue between the parties is disclosed by the pleadings—even though the parties may have conflicting interests. E.g., *Mozeika v. Kaufman Construction Co.,* 25 F.R.D. 233 (E.D.Pa.1960) (plaintiff and third-party defendant); *Biddle v. Hutchinson,* 24 F.R.D. 256 (M.D.Pa.1959) (codefendants). The resulting distinctions have often been highly technical. In *Schlagenhauf v. Holder,* 379 U.S. 104 (1964), the Supreme Court rejected a contention that examination under Rule 35 could be had only against an "opposing" party, as not in keeping "with the aims of a liberal, nontechnical application of the Federal Rules." 379 U.S. at 116. Eliminating the requirement of "adverse" parties from Rule 33 brings it into line with all other discovery rules.

A second change in subdivision (a) is the addition of the term "governmental agency" to the listing of organizations whose answers are to be made by any officer or agent of the organization. This does not involve any change in existing law. Compare the similar listing in Rule 30(b)(6).

The duty of a party to supplement his answers to interrogatories is governed by a new provision in Rule 26(e).

Subdivision (b). There are numerous and conflicting decisions on the question whether and to what extent interrogatories are limited to matters "of fact," or may elicit opinions, contentions, and legal conclusions. Compare, e.g., *Payer, Hewitt & Co. v. Bellanca Corp.,* 26 F.R.D. 219 (D.Del.1960) (opinions bad); *Zinsky v. New York Central R.R.,* 36 F.R.D. 680 (N.D.Ohio 1964) (factual opinion or contention good, but legal theory bad); *United States v. Carter Products, Inc.,* 28 F.R.D. 373 (S.D.N.Y.1961) (factual contentions and legal theories bad) with *Taylor v. Sound Steamship Lines, Inc.,* 100 F.Supp. 388 (D.Conn.1951) (opinions good); *Bynum v. United States,* 36 F.R.D. 14 (E.D.La.1964) (contentions as to facts constituting negligence good). For lists of the many conflicting authorities, see 4 *Moore's Federal Practice* ¶33.17 (2d ed. 1966); 2A Barron & Holtzoff, *Federal Practice and Procedure* § 768 (Wright ed. 1961).

Rule 33 is amended to provide that an interrogatory is not objectionable merely because it calls for an opinion or contention that relates to fact or the application of law to fact. Efforts to draw sharp lines between facts and opinions have invariably been unsuccessful, and the clear trend of the cases is to permit "factual" opinions. As to requests for opinions or contentions that call for the application of law to fact, they can be most useful in narrowing and sharpening the issues, which is a major purpose of discovery. See *Diversified Products Corp. v. Sports Center Co.,* 42 F.R.D. 3 (D.Md. 1967); Moore, *supra;* Field & McKusick, *Maine Civil Practice* § 26.18 (1959). On the other hand, under the new language interrogatories may not extend to issues of "pure law," i.e., legal issues unrelated to the facts of the case. Cf. *United States v. Maryland & Va. Milk Producers Assn., Inc.,* 22 F.R.D. 300 (D.D.C.1958).

Since interrogatories involving mixed questions of law and fact may create disputes between the parties which are best resolved after much or all of the other discovery has been completed, the court is expressly authorized to defer an answer. Likewise, the court may delay determination until pretrial conference, if it believes that the dispute is best resolved in the presence of the judge.

The principal question raised with respect to the cases permitting such interrogatories is whether they reintroduce undesirable aspects of the prior pleading practice, whereby parties were chained to misconceived contentions or theories, and ultimate determination on the merits was frustrated. See James, *The Revival of Bills of Particulars under the Federal Rules,* 71 Harv.L.Rev. 1473 (1958). But there are few if any instances in the recorded cases demonstrating that such frustration has occurred. The general rule governing the use of answers to interrogatories is that under ordinary circumstances they do not limit proof. See, e.g., *McElroy v. United Air Lines, Inc.,* 21 F.R.D. 100 (W.D.Mo.1967); *Pressley v. Boehlke,* 33 F.R.D. 316, 317 (W.D.N.C.1963). Although in exceptional circumstances reliance on an answer may cause such prejudice that the court will hold the answering party bound to his answer, e.g., *Zielinski v. Philadelphia Piers, Inc.,* 139 F.Supp. 408 (E.D.Pa.1956), the interrogating party will ordinarily not be entitled to rely on the unchanging character of the answers he receives and cannot base prejudice on such reliance. The rule does not affect the power of a court to permit withdrawal or amendment of answers to interrogatories.

The use of answers to interrogatories at trial is made subject to the rules of evidence. The provisions governing use of depositions, to which Rule 33 presently refers, are not entirely apposite to answers to interrogatories, since deposition practice contemplates that all parties will ordinarily participate through cross-examination. See 4 *Moore's Federal Practice* ¶33.29[1] (2d ed. 1966).

Certain provisions are deleted from subdivision (b) because they are fully covered by new Rule 26(c) providing for protective orders and Rules 26(a) and 26(d). The language of the subdivision is thus simplified without any change of substance.

Subdivision (c). This is a new subdivision, adapted from Calif.Code Civ.Proc. § 2030(c), relating especially to interrogatories which require a party to engage in burdensome or expensive research into his own business records in order to give an answer. The subdivision gives the party an option to make the records available and place the burden of research of the party who seeks the information. "This provision, without undermining the liberal scope of interrogatory discovery, places the burden of discovery upon its potential benefittee," Louisell, *Modern California Discovery*, 124–125 (1963), and alleviates a problem which in the past has troubled Federal courts. See Speck, *The Use of Discovery in United States District Courts*, 60 Yale L.J. 1132, 1142–1144 (1951). The interrogating party is protected against abusive use of this provision through the requirement that the burden of ascertaining the answer be substantially the same for both sides. A respondent may not impose on an interrogating party a mass of records as to which research is feasible only for one familiar with the records. At the same time, the respondent unable to invoke this subdivision does not on that account lose the protection available to him under new Rule 26(c) against oppressive or unduly burdensome or expensive interrogatories. And even when the respondent successfully invokes the subdivision, the court is not deprived of its usual power, in appropriate cases, to require that the interrogating party reimburse the respondent for the expense of assembling his records and making them intelligible.

1980 Amendment

Subdivision (c). The Committee is advised that parties upon whom interrogatories are served have occasionally responded by directing the interrogating party to a mass of business records or by offering to make all of their records available, justifying the response by the option provided by this subdivision. Such practices are an abuse of the option. A party who is permitted by the terms of this subdivision to offer records for inspection in lieu of answering an interrogatory should offer them in a manner than permits the same direct and economical access that is available to the party. If the information sought exists in the form of compilations, abstracts or summaries then available to the responding party, those should be made available to the interrogating party. The final sentence is added to make it clear that a responding party has the duty to specify, by category and location, the records from which answers to interrogatories can be derived.

1993 Amendments

Purpose of Revision. The purpose of this revision is to reduce the frequency and increase the efficiency of interrogatory practice. The revision is based on experience with local rules. For ease of reference, subdivision (a) is divided into two subdivisions and the remaining subdivisions renumbered.

Subdivision (a). Revision of this subdivision limits interrogatory practice. Because Rule 26(a)(1)–(3) requires disclosure of much of the information previously obtained by this form of discovery, there should be less occasion to use it. Experience in over half of the district courts has confirmed that limitations on the number of interrogatories are useful and manageable. Moreover, because the device can be costly and may be used as a means of harassment, it is desirable to subject its use to the control of the court consistent with the principles stated in Rule 26(b)(2), particularly in multi-party cases where it has not been unusual for the same interrogatory to be propounded to a party by more than one of its adversaries.

Each party is allowed to serve 25 interrogatories upon any other party, but must secure leave of court (or a stipulation from the opposing party) to serve a larger number. Parties cannot evade this presumptive limitation through the device of joining as "subparts" questions that seek information about discrete separate subjects. However, a question asking about communications of a particular type should be treated as a single interrogatory even though it requests that the time, place, persons present, and contents be stated separately for each such communication.

As with the number of depositions authorized by Rule 30, leave to serve additional interrogatories is to be allowed when consistent with Rule 26(b)(2). The aim is not to prevent needed discovery, but to provide judicial scrutiny before parties make potentially excessive use of this discovery device. In many cases it will be appropriate for the court to permit a larger number of interrogatories in the scheduling order entered under Rule 16(b).

Unless leave of court is obtained, interrogatories may not be served prior to the meeting of the parties under Rule 26(f).

When a case with outstanding interrogatories exceeding the number permitted by this rule is removed to federal court, the interrogating party must seek leave allowing the additional interrogatories, specify which twenty-five are to be answered, or resubmit interrogatories that comply with the rule. Moreover, under Rule 26(d), the time for response would be measured from the date of the parties' meeting under Rule 26(f). See Rule 81(c), providing that these rules govern procedures after removal.

Subdivision (b). A separate subdivision is made of the former second paragraph of subdivision (a). Language is added to paragraph (1) of this subdivision to emphasize the duty of the responding party to provide full answers to the extent not objectionable. If, for example, an interrogatory seeking information about numerous facilities or products is deemed objectionable, but an interrogatory seeking information about a lesser number of facilities or products would not have been objectionable, the interrogatory should be answered with respect to the latter even though an objection is raised as to the balance of the facilities or products. Similarly, the fact that additional time may be needed to respond to some questions (or to some aspects of questions) should not

---

justify a delay in responding to those questions (or other aspects of questions) that can be answered within the prescribed time.

Paragraph (4) is added to make clear that objections must be specifically justified, and that unstated or untimely grounds for objection ordinarily are waived. Note also the provisions of revised Rule 26(b)(5), which require a responding party to indicate when it is withholding information under a claim of privilege or as trial preparation materials.

These provisions should be read in light of Rule 26(g), authorizing the court to impose sanctions on a party and attorney making an unfounded objection to an interrogatory.

Subdivisions (c) and (d). The provisions of former subdivisions (b) and (c) are renumbered.

Rule 34. Production of Documents and Things and Entry Upon Land for Inspection and Other Purposes

(a) Scope. Any party may serve on any other party a request (1) to produce and permit the party making the request, or someone acting on the requestor's behalf, to inspect and copy, any designated documents (including writings, drawings, graphs, charts, photographs, phonorecords, and other data compilations from which information can be obtained, translated, if necessary, by the respondent through detection devices into reasonably usable form), or to inspect and copy, test, or sample any tangible things which constitute or contain matters within the scope of Rule 26(b) and which are in the possession, custody or control of the party upon whom the request is served; or (2) to permit entry upon designated land or other property in the possession or control of the party upon whom the request is served for the purpose of inspection and measuring, surveying, photographing, testing, or sampling the property or any designated object or operation thereon, within the scope of Rule 26(b).

(b) Procedure. The request shall set forth, either by individual item or by category, the items to be inspected and describe each with reasonable particularity. The request shall specify a reasonable time, place, and manner of making the inspection and performing the related acts. Without leave of court or written stipulation, a request may not be served before the time specified in Rule 26(d).

The party upon whom the request is served shall serve a written response within 30 days after the service of the request. A shorter or longer time may be directed by the court or, in the absence of such an order, agreed to in writing by the parties, subject to Rule 29. The response shall state, with respect to each item or category, that inspection and related activities will be permitted as requested, unless the request is objected to, in which event the reasons for the objection shall be stated. If objection is made to part of an item or category, the part shall be specified and inspection permitted of the remaining parts. The

party submitting the request may move for an order under Rule 37(a) with respect to any objection to or other failure to respond to the request or any part thereof, or any failure to permit inspection as requested.

A party who produces documents for inspection shall produce them as they are kept in the usual course of business or shall organize and label them to correspond with the categories in the request.

(c) Persons Not Parties. A person not a party to the action may be compelled to produce documents and things or to submit to an inspection as provided in Rule 45.

(As amended Dec. 27, 1946, effective March 19, 1948; Mar. 30, 1970, eff. July 1, 1970; Apr. 29, 1980, eff. Aug. 1, 1980; Mar. 2, 1987, eff. Aug. 1, 1987; Apr. 30, 1991, eff. Dec. 1, 1991; Apr. 22, 1993, eff. Dec. 1, 1993.)

ADVISORY COMMITTEE NOTES

1937 Adoption

In England orders are made for the inspection of documents, *English Rules Under the Judicature Act (The Annual Practice,* 1937) O. 31, r.r. 14, et seq., or for the inspection of tangible property or for entry upon land, O. 50, r. 3. Michigan provides for inspection of damaged property when such damage is the ground of the action. Mich.Court Rules Ann. (Searl, 1933) Rule 41, § 2.

Practically all states have statutes authorizing the court to order parties in possession or control of documents to permit other parties to inspect and copy them before trial. See Ragland, *Discovery Before Trial* (1932) Appendix, p. 267, setting out the statutes.

Compare [former] Equity Rule 58 (Discovery—Interrogatories—Inspection and Production of Documents—Admission of Execution or Genuineness) (fifth paragraph).

1946 Amendment

Note. The changes in clauses (1) and (2) correlate the scope of inquiry permitted under Rule 34 with that provided in Rule 26(b), and thus remove any ambiguity created by the former differences in language. As stated in *Olson Transportation Co. v. Socony-Vacuum Oil Co.,* E.D.Wis.1944, 8 Fed.Rules Serv. 34.41, Case 2, "* * * Rule 34 is a direct and simple method of discovery." At the same time the addition of the words following the term "parties" makes certain that the person in whose custody, possession, or control the evidence reposes may have the benefit of the applicable protective orders stated in Rule 30(b). This change should be considered in the light of the proposed expansion of Rule 30(b).

An objection has been made that the word "designated" in Rule 34 has been construed with undue strictness in some district court cases so as to require great and impracticable specificity in the description of documents, papers, books, etc., sought to be inspected. The Committee, however, believes that no amendment is needed, and that the proper meaning of "designated" as requiring specificity has already been delineated by the Supreme Court. *See Brown v. United States,* 1928, 48 S.Ct. 288, 276 U.S. 134, 143, 72 L.Ed. 500 ("The subpoena * * * specifies * * * with reasonable particularity the subjects to which the documents called for related."); *Consolidated Rendering Co. v. Vermont,* 1908, 28 S.Ct. 178, 207 U.S. 541, 543–544, 52 L.Ed. 327 ("We see no reason why all such books, papers and correspondence which related to the subject of inquiry, and were described with reasonable detail, should not be called for and the company directed to produce them. Otherwise, the State would be compelled to designate each particular paper which it desired, which presupposes an accurate knowledge of such papers, which the tribunal desiring the papers would probably rarely, if ever, have.").

1970 Amendment

Rule 34 is revised to accomplish the following major changes in the existing rule: (1) to eliminate the requirement of good cause; (2) to have the rule operate extrajudicially; (3) to include testing and sampling as well as inspecting or photographing tangible things; and (4) to make clear that the rule does not preclude an independent action for analogous discovery against persons not parties.

Subdivision (a). Good cause is eliminated because it has furnished an uncertain and erratic protection to the parties from whom production is sought and is now rendered unnecessary by virtue of the more specific provisions added to Rule 26(b) relating to materials assembled in preparation for trial and to experts retained or consulted by parties.

The good cause requirement was originally inserted in Rule 34 as a general protective provision in the absence of experience with the specific problems that would arise thereunder. As the note to Rule 26(b)(3) on trial preparation materials makes clear, good cause has been applied differently to varying classes of documents, though not without confusion. It has often been said in court opinions that good cause requires a consideration of need for the materials and of alternative means of obtaining them, i.e., something more than relevance and lack of privilege. But the overwhelming proportion of the cases in which the formula of good cause has been applied to require a special showing are those involving trial preparation. In practice, the courts have not treated documents as having a special immunity to discovery simply because of their being documents. Protection may be afforded to claims of privacy or secrecy or of undue burden or expense under what is now Rule 26(c) (previously Rule 30(b)). To be sure, an appraisal of "undue" burden inevitably entails consideration of the needs of the party seeking discovery. With special provisions added to govern trial preparation materials and experts, there is no longer any occasion to retain the requirement of good cause.

The revision of Rule 34 to have it operate extrajudicially, rather than by court order, is to a large extent a reflection of existing law office practice. The Columbia Survey shows that of the litigants seeking inspection of documents or things, only about 25 percent filed motions for court orders. This minor fraction nevertheless accounted for a significant number of motions. About half of these motions were uncontested and in almost all instances the party seeking production ultimately prevailed. Although an extrajudicial procedure will not drastically alter existing practice under Rule 34—it will conform to it in most cases—it has the potential of saving court time in a substantial though proportionately small number of cases tried annually.

The inclusion of testing and sampling of tangible things and objects or operations on land reflects a need frequently encountered by parties in preparation for trial. If the operation of a particular machine is the basis of a claim for negligent injury, it will often be necessary to test its operating parts or to sample and test the products it is producing. *Cf.* Mich.Gen.Ct.R. 310.1(1) (1963) (testing authorized).

The inclusive description of "documents" is revised to accord with changing technology. It makes clear that Rule 34 applies to electronics data compilations from which information can be obtained only with the use of detection devices, and that when the data can as a practical matter be made usable by the discovering party only through respondent's devices, respondent may be required to use his devices to translate the data into usable form. In many instances, this means that respondent will have to supply a print-out of computer data. The burden thus placed on respondent will vary from case to case, and the courts have ample power under Rule 26(c) to protect respondent against undue burden or expense, either by restricting discovery or requiring that the discovering party pay costs. Similarly, if the discovering party needs to check the electronic source itself, the court may protect respondent with respect to preservation of his records, confidentiality of nondiscoverable matters, and costs.

Subdivision (b). The procedure provided in Rule 34 is essentially the same as that in Rule 33, as amended, and the discussion in the note appended to that rule is relevant to Rule 34 as well. Problems peculiar to Rule 34 relate to the specific arrangements that must be worked out for inspection and related acts of copying, photographing, testing, or sampling. The rule provides that a request for inspection shall set forth the items to be inspected either by item or category, describing each with reasonable particularity, and shall specify a reasonable time, place, and manner of making the inspection.

Subdivision (c). Rule 34 as revised continues to apply only to parties. Comments from the bar make clear that in the preparation of cases for trial it is occasionally necessary to enter land or inspect large tangible things in the possession of a person not a party, and that some courts have dismissed independent actions in the nature of bills in equity for such discovery on the ground that Rule 34 is preemptive. While an ideal solution to this problem is to provide for discovery against persons not parties in Rule 34, both the jurisdictional and procedural problems are very complex. For the present, this subdivision makes clear that Rule 34 does not preclude independent actions for discovery against persons not parties.

1980 Amendment

Subdivision (b). The Committee is advised that, "It is apparently not rare for parties deliberately to mix critical documents with others in the hope of obscuring significance." *Report of the Special Committee for the Study of Discovery Abuse, Section of Litigation of the American Bar Association* (1977) 22. The sentence added by this subdivision follows the recommendation of the *Report.*

1987 Amendment

The amendment is technical. No substantive change is intended.

1991 Amendment

This amendment reflects the change effected by revision of Rule 45 to provide for subpoenas to compel non-parties to produce documents and things and to submit to inspections of premises. The deletion of the text of the former paragraph is not intended to preclude an independent action for production of documents or things or for permission to enter upon land, but such actions may no longer be necessary in light of this revision.

1993 Amendments

The rule is revised to reflect the change made by Rule 26(d), preventing a party from seeking formal discovery prior to the meeting of the parties required by Rule 26(f). Also, like a change made in Rule 33, the rule is modified to make clear that, if a request for production is objectionable only in part, production should be afforded with respect to the unobjectionable portions.

When a case with outstanding requests for production is removed to federal court, the time for response would be measured from the date of the parties' meeting. See Rule 81(c), providing that these rules govern procedures after removal.

Rule 35. Physical and Mental Examinations of Persons

(a) Order for Examination. When the mental or physical condition (including the blood group) of a party or of a person in the custody or under the legal control of a party, is in controversy, the court in which the action is pending may order the party to submit to a physical or mental examination by a suitably licensed or certified examiner or to produce for examination the person in the party's custody or legal control. The order may be made only on motion for good cause shown and upon notice to the person to be examined and to all parties and shall specify the time, place, manner, conditions, and scope of the examination and the person or persons by whom it is to be made.

(b) Report of Examiner.

(1) If requested by the party against whom an order is made under Rule 35(a) or the person examined, the party causing the examination to be made shall deliver to the requesting party a copy of the detailed written report of the examiner setting out the examiner's findings, including results of all tests made, diagnoses and conclusions, together with like reports of all earlier examinations of the same condition. After delivery the party causing the examination shall be entitled upon request to receive from the party against whom the order is made a like report of any examination, previously or thereafter made, of the same condition, unless, in the case of a report of examination of a person not a party, the party shows that the party is unable to obtain it. The court on motion may make an order against a party requiring delivery of a report on such terms as are just, and if an examiner fails or refuses to make a report the court may exclude the examiner's testimony if offered at trial.

(2) By requesting and obtaining a report of the examination so ordered or by taking the deposition of the examiner, the party examined waives any privilege the party may have in that action or any other involving the same controversy, regarding the testimony of every other person who has examined or may thereafter examine the party in respect of the same mental or physical condition.

(3) This subdivision applies to examinations made by agreement of the parties, unless the agreement expressly provides otherwise. This subdivision does not preclude discovery of a report of an examiner or the taking of a deposition of the examiner in accordance with the provisions of any other rule.

(As amended Mar. 30, 1970, eff. July 1, 1970; Mar. 2, 1987, eff. Aug. 1, 1987; Nov. 18, 1988, Pub.L. 100–690, Title VII, § 7047(b), 102 Stat. 4401; Apr. 30, 1991, eff. Dec. 1, 1991.)

ADVISORY COMMITTEE NOTES

1937 Adoption

Physical examination of parties before trial is authorized by statute or rule in a number of states. See Ariz.Rev. Code Ann. (Struckmeyer, 1928) § 4468; Mich. Court Rules Ann. (Searl, 1933) Rule 41, § 2; 2 N.J.Comp.Stat. (1910); N.Y.C.P.A. (1937) § 306; 1 S.D.Comp.Laws (1929) § 2716A; 3 Wash.Rev.Stat.Ann. (Remington, 1932) § 1230–1.

Mental examination of parties is authorized in Iowa. Iowa Code (1935) ch. 491–F1. See McCash, *The Evolution of the Doctrine of Discovery and Its Present Status in Iowa*, 20 Ia.L.Rev. 68 (1934).

The constitutionality of legislation providing for physical examination of parties was sustained in *Lyon v. Manhattan Railway Co.*, 1894, 37 N.E. 113, 142 N.Y. 298, and *McGovern v. Hope*, 1899, 42 A. 830, 63 N.J.L. 76. In *Union Pacific Ry. Co. v. Botsford*, 1891, 11 S.Ct. 1000, 141 U.S. 250, 35 L.Ed. 734, it was held that the court could not order the physical examination of a party in the absence of statutory authority. But in *Camden and Suburban Ry. Co. v. Stetson*, 1900, 20 S.Ct. 617, 177 U.S. 172, 44 L.Ed. 721 where there was statutory authority for such examination, derived from a state statute made operative by the conformity act, the practice was sustained. Such authority is now found in the present rule made operative by the Act of June 19, 1934, c. 651, U.S.C., Title 28, § 2072, formerly §§ 723b (Rules in actions at law; Supreme Court authorized to make) and 723c (Union of equity and action at law rules; power of Supreme Court).

1970 Amendment

Subdivision (a). Rule 35(a) has hitherto provided only for an order requiring a party to submit to an examination. It is desirable to extend the rule to provide for an order against the party for examination of a person in his custody or under his legal control. As appears from the provisions of amended Rule 37(b)(2) and the comment under that rule, an order to "produce" the third person imposes only an obligation to use good faith efforts to produce the person.

The amendment will settle beyond doubt that a parent or guardian suing to recover for injuries to a minor may be ordered to produce the minor for examination. Further, the amendment expressly includes blood examination within the kinds of examinations that can be ordered under the rule. See *Beach v. Beach*, 114 F.2d 479 (D.C. Cir. 1940). Provisions similar to the amendment have been adopted in at least 10 States: Calif. Code Civ.Proc. § 2032; Ida.R.Civ.P. 35; Ill. S–H Ann. c. 110A, § 215; Md.R.P. 420; Mich.Gen.Ct.R. 311; Minn.R.Civ.P. 35; Mo.Vern.Ann.R.Civ.p. 60.01; N.Dak.R.Civ.P. 35; N.Y.C.P.L. § 3121; Wyo.R.Civ.P. 35.

The amendment makes no change in the requirements of Rule 35 that, before a court order may issue, the relevant physical or mental condition must be shown to be "in controversy" and "good cause" must be shown for the examination. Thus, the amendment has no effect on the recent decision of the Supreme Court in *Schlagenhauf v. Holder*, 379 U.S. 104 (1964), stressing the importance of these requirements and applying them to the facts of the case. The amendment makes no reference to employees of a party. Provisions relating to employees in the State statutes and rules cited above appear to have been virtually unused.

Subdivision (b)(1). This subdivision is amended to correct an imbalance in Rule 35(b)(1) as heretofore written. Under that text, a party causing a Rule 35(a) examination to be made is required to furnish to the party examined, on request, a copy of the examining physician's report. If he delivers this copy, he is in turn entitled to receive from the party examined reports of all examinations of the same condition previously or later made. But the rule has not in terms entitled the examined party to receive from the party causing the Rule 35(a) examination any reports of earlier examinations of the same condition to which the latter may have access. The amendment cures this defect. See La. Stat.Ann., Civ.Proc. art 1495 (1960); Utah R.Civ.P. 35(c).

The amendment specifies that the written report of the examining physician includes results of all tests made, such as results of X-rays and cardiograms. It also embodies changes required by the broadening of Rule 35(a) to take in persons who are not parties.

Subdivision (b)(3). This new subdivision removes any possible doubt that reports of examination may be obtained although no order for examination has been made under Rule 35(a). Examinations are very frequently made by agreement, and sometimes before the party examined has an attorney. The courts have uniformly ordered that reports be supplied, see 4 *Moore's Federal Practice* ¶35.06, n. 1 (2d ed. 1966); 2A Barron & Holtzoff, *Federal Practice and Procedure* § 823, n. 22 (Wright ed. 1961), and it appears best to fill the technical gap in the present rule.

The subdivision also makes clear that reports of examining physicians are discoverable not only under Rule 35(b), but under other rules as well. To be sure, if the report is privileged, then discovery is not permissible under any rule other than Rule 35(b) and it is permissible under Rule 35(b) only if the party requests a copy of the report of examination made by the other party's doctor. *Sher v. De Haven*, 199 F.2d 777 (D.C. Cir. 1952), *cert. denied* 345 U.S. 936 (1953). But if the report is unprivileged and is subject to discovery under the provisions of rules other than Rule 35(b)—such as Rules 34 or 26(b)(3) or (4)—discovery should not depend

upon whether the person examined demands a copy of the report. Although a few cases have suggested the contrary, *e.g., Galloway v. National Dairy Products Corp.*, 24 F.R.D. 362 (E.D.Pa.1959), the better considered district court decisions hold that Rule 35(b) is not preemptive. *E.g., Leszynski v. Russ*, 29 F.R.D. 10, 12 (D.Md.1961) and cases cited. The question was recently given full consideration in *Buffington v. Wood*, 351 F.2d 292 (3d Cir. 1965), holding that Rule 35(b) is not preemptive.

1987 Amendment

The amendments are technical. No substantive change is intended.

1991 Amendment

The revision authorizes the court to require physical or mental examinations conducted by any person who is suitably licensed or certified.

The rule was revised in 1988 by Congressional enactment to authorize mental examinations by licensed clinical psychologists. This revision extends that amendment to include other certified or licensed professionals, such as dentists or occupational therapists, who are not physicians or clinical psychologists, but who may be well-qualified to give valuable testimony about the physical or mental condition that is the subject of dispute.

The requirement that the examiner be *suitably* licensed or certified is a new requirement. The court is thus expressly authorized to assess the credentials of the examiner to assure that no person is subjected to a court-ordered examination by an examiner whose testimony would be of such limited value that it would be unjust to require the person to undergo the invasion of privacy associated with the examination. This authority is not wholly new, for under the former rule, the court retained discretion to refuse to order an examination, or to restrict an examination. 8 WRIGHT & MILLER, FEDERAL PRACTICE & PROCEDURE § 2234 (1986 Supp.). The revision is intended to encourage the exercise of this discretion, especially with respect to examinations by persons having narrow qualifications.

The court's responsibility to determine the suitability of the examiner's qualifications applies even to a proposed examination by a physician. If the proposed examination and testimony calls for an expertise that the proposed examiner does not have, it should not be ordered, even if the proposed examiner is a physician. The rule does not, however, require that the license or certificate be conferred by the jurisdiction in which the examination is conducted.

Rule 36. Requests for Admission

(a) Request for Admission. A party may serve upon any other party a written request for the admission, for purposes of the pending action only, of the truth of any matters within the scope of Rule 26(b)(1) set forth in the request that relate to statements or opinions of fact or of the application of law to fact, including the genuineness of any documents described in the request. Copies of documents shall be served with the request unless they have been or are otherwise furnished or made available for inspection and

---

copying. Without leave of court or written stipulation, requests for admission may not be served before the time specified in Rule 26(d).

Each matter of which an admission is requested shall be separately set forth. The matter is admitted unless, within 30 days after service of the request, or within such shorter or longer time as the court may allow or as the parties may agree to in writing, subject to Rule 29, the party to whom the request is directed serves upon the party requesting the admission a written answer or objection addressed to the matter, signed by the party or by the party's attorney. If objection is made, the reasons therefor shall be stated. The answer shall specifically deny the matter or set forth in detail the reasons why the answering party cannot truthfully admit or deny the matter. A denial shall fairly meet the substance of the requested admission, and when good faith requires that a party qualify an answer or deny only a part of the matter of which an admission is requested, the party shall specify so much of it as is true and qualify or deny the remainder. An answering party may not give lack of information or knowledge as a reason for failure to admit or deny unless the party states that the party has made reasonable inquiry and that the information known or readily obtainable by the party is insufficient to enable the party to admit or deny. A party who considers that a matter of which an admission has been requested presents a genuine issue for trial may not, on that ground alone, object to the request; the party may, subject to the provisions of Rule 37(c), deny the matter or set forth reasons why the party cannot admit or deny it.

The party who has requested the admissions may move to determine the sufficiency of the answers or objections. Unless the court determines that an objection is justified, it shall order that an answer be served. If the court determines that an answer does not comply with the requirements of this rule, it may order either that the matter is admitted or that an amended answer be served. The court may, in lieu of these orders, determine that final disposition of the request be made at a pre-trial conference or at a designated time prior to trial. The provisions of Rule 37(a)(4) apply to the award of expenses incurred in relation to the motion.

(b) Effect of Admission. Any matter admitted under this rule is conclusively established unless the court on motion permits withdrawal or amendment of the admission. Subject to the provision of Rule 16 governing amendment of a pre-trial order, the court may permit withdrawal or amendment when the presentation of the merits of the action will be subserved thereby and the party who obtained the admission fails to satisfy the court that withdrawal or amendment will prejudice that party in maintaining the action or defense on the merits. Any admission made

by a party under this rule is for the purpose of the pending action only and is not an admission for any other purpose nor may it be used against the party in any other proceeding.

(As amended Dec. 27, 1946, effective Mar. 19, 1948; Mar. 30, 1970, eff. July 1, 1970; Mar. 2, 1987, eff. Aug. 1, 1987; Apr. 22, 1993, eff. Dec. 1, 1993.)

ADVISORY COMMITTEE NOTES

1937 Adoption

Compare similar rules: [Former] Equity Rule 58 (last paragraph, which provides for the admission of the execution and genuineness of documents); *English Rules Under the Judicature Act* (The Annual Practice, 1937) O. 32; Ill.Rev. Stat. (1937) ch. 110, § 182 and Rule 18 (Ill.Rev.Stat. (1937) ch. 110, § 259.18); 2 Mass.Gen.Laws (Ter.Ed., 1932) ch. 231, § 69; Mich. Court Rules Ann. (Searl, 1933) Rule 42; N.J. Comp.Stat. (2 Cum.Supp. 1911–1924); N.Y.C.P.A. (1937) §§ 322, 323; Wis.Stat. (1935) § 327.22.

1946 Amendment

Note. The first change in the first sentence of Rule 36(a) and the addition of the new second sentence, specifying when requests for admissions may be served, bring Rule 36 in line with amended Rules 26(a) and 33. There is no reason why these rules should not be treated alike. Other provisions of Rule 36(a) give the party whose admissions are requested adequate protection.

The second change in the first sentence of the rule [subdivision (a)] removes any uncertainty as to whether a party can be called upon to admit matters of fact other than those set forth in relevant documents described in and exhibited with the request. In *Smyth v. Kaufman*, C.C.A.2, 1940, 114 F.2d 40, it was held that the word "therein", now stricken from the rule [said subdivision] referred to the request and that a matter of fact not related to any document could be presented to the other party for admission or denial. The rule of this case is now clearly stated.

The substitution of the word "served" for "delivered" in the third sentence of the amended rule [said subdivision] is in conformance with the use of the word "serve" elsewhere in the rule and generally throughout the rules. See also Notes to Rules 13(a) and 33 herein. The substitution [in said subdivision] of "shorter or longer" for "further" will enable a court to designate a lesser period than 10 days for answer. This conforms with a similar provision already contained in Rule 33.

The addition of clause (1) [in said subdivision] specifies the method by which a party may challenge the propriety of a request to admit. There has been considerable difference of judicial opinion as to the correct method, if any, available to secure relief from an allegedly improper request. See Commentary, *Methods of Objecting to Notice to Admit*, 1942, 5 Fed.Rules Serv. 835; *International Carbonic Engineering Co. v. Natural Carbonic Products, Inc.*, S.D.Cal.1944, 57 F.Supp. 248. The changes in clause (1) are merely of a clarifying and conforming nature.

The first of the added last two sentences [in said subdivision] prevents an objection to a part of a request from holding up the answer, if any, to the remainder. See similar proposed change in Rule 33. The last sentence strengthens the rule by making the denial accurately reflect the party's position. It is taken, with necessary changes, from Rule 8(b).

1970 Amendment

Rule 36 serves two vital purposes, both of which are designed to reduce trial time. Admissions are sought, first to facilitate proof with respect to issues that cannot be eliminated from the case, and secondly, to narrow the issues by eliminating those that can be. The changes made in the rule are designed to serve these purposes more effectively. Certain disagreements in the courts about the proper scope of the rule are resolved. In addition, the procedural operation of the rule is brought into line with other discovery procedures, and the binding effect of an admission is clarified. See generally Finman, *The Request for Admissions in Federal Civil Procedure*, 71 Yale L.J. 371 (1962).

Subdivision (a). As revised, the subdivision provides that a request may be made to admit any matters within the scope of Rule 26(b) that relate to statements or opinions of fact or of the application of law to fact. It thereby eliminates the requirement that the matters be "of fact." This change resolves conflicts in the court decisions as to whether a request to admit matters of "opinion" and matters involving "mixed law and fact" is proper under the rule. As to "opinion," compare, *e.g., Jackson Buff Corp. v. Marcelle*, 20 F.R.D. 139 (E.D.N.Y.1957); *California v. The S. S. Jules Fribourg*, 19 F.R.D. 432 (N.D.Calif.1955), with *e.g., Photon, Inc. v. Harris Intertype, Inc.*, 28 F.R.D. 327 (D.Mass.1961); *Hise v. Lockwood Grader Corp.*, 153 F.Supp. 276 (D.Nebr.1957). As to "mixed law and fact" the majority of courts sustain objections, *e.g., Minnesota Mining and Mfg. Co. v. Norton Co.*, 36 F.R.D. 1 (N.D.Ohio 1964), but *McSparran v. Hanigan*, 225 F.Supp. 628 (E.D.Pa.1963) is to the contrary.

Not only is it difficult as a practical matter to separate "fact" from "opinion," see 4 *Moore's Federal Practice* ¶36.04 (2d ed. 1966); cf. 2A Barron & Holtzoff, *Federal Practice and Procedure* 317 (Wright ed. 1961), but an admission on a matter of opinion may facilitate proof or narrow the issues or both. An admission of a matter involving the application of law to fact may, in a given case, even more clearly narrow the issues. For example, an admission that an employee acted in the scope of his employment may remove a major issue from the trial. In *McSparran v. Hanigan, supra*, plaintiff admitted that "the premises on which said accident occurred, were occupied or under the control" of one of the defendants, 225 F.Supp. at 636. This admission, involving law as well as fact, removed one of the issues from the lawsuit and thereby reduced the proof required at trial. The amended provision does not authorize requests for admissions of law unrelated to the facts of the case.

Requests for admission involving the application of law to fact may create disputes between the parties which are best resolved in the presence of the judge after much or all of the other discovery has been completed. Power is therefore expressly conferred upon the court to defer decision until a pretrial conference is held or until a designated time prior to trial. On the other hand, the court should not automatically defer decision; in many instances, the importance of the admission lies in enabling the requesting party to avoid the burdensome accumulation of proof prior to the pretrial conference.

Courts have also divided on whether an answering party may properly object to request for admission as to matters which that party regards as "in dispute." Compare, *e.g., Syracuse Broadcasting Corp. v. Newhouse*, 271 F.2d 910, 917 (2d Cir. 1959); *Driver v. Gindy Mfg. Corp.*, 24 F.R.D. 473 (E.D.Pa.1959); with, *e.g., McGonigle v. Baxter*, 27 F.R.D. 504 (E.D.Pa.1961); *United States v. Ehbauer*, 13 F.R.D. 462 (W.D.Mo.1952). The proper response in such cases is an answer. The very purpose of the request is to ascertain whether the answering party is prepared to admit or regards the matter as presenting a genuine issue for trial. In his answer, the party may deny, or he may give as his reason for inability to admit or deny the existence of a genuine issue. The party runs no risk of sanctions if the matter is genuinely in issue, since Rule 37(c) provides a sanction of costs only when there are no good reasons for a failure to admit.

On the other hand, requests to admit may be so voluminous and so framed that the answering party finds the task of identifying what is in dispute and what is not unduly burdensome. If so, the responding party may obtain a protective order under Rule 26(c). Some of the decisions sustaining objections on "disputability" grounds could have been justified by the burdensome character of the requests. See, *e.g., Syracuse Broadcasting Corp. v. Newhouse, supra.*

Another sharp split of authority exists on the question whether a party may base his answer on lack of information or knowledge without seeking out additional information. One line of cases has held that a party may answer on the basis of such knowledge as he has at the time he answers. *E.g., Jackson Buff Corp. v. Marcelle*, 20 F.R.D. 139 (E.D.N.Y.1957); *Sladek v. General Motors Corp.*, 16 F.R.D. 104 (S.D.Iowa 1954). A larger group of cases, supported by commentators, has taken the view that if the responding party lacks knowledge, he must inform himself in reasonable fashion. *E.g., Hise v. Lockwood Grader Corp.*, 153 F.Supp. 276 (D.Nebr. 1957); *E. H. Tate Co. v. Jiffy Enterprises, Inc.*, 16 F.R.D. 571 (E.D.Pa.1954); Finman, *supra*, 71 Yale L.J. 371, 404–409; 4 *Moore's Federal Practice* ¶36.04 (2d ed. 1966); 2A Barron & Holtzoff, *Federal Practice and Procedure* 509 (Wright ed. 1961).

The rule as revised adopts the majority view, as in keeping with a basic principle of the discovery rules that a reasonable burden may be imposed on the parties when its discharge will facilitate preparation for trial and ease the trial process. It has been argued against this view that one side should not have the burden of "proving" the other side's case. The revised rule requires only that the answering party make reasonable inquiry and secure such knowledge and information as are readily obtainable by him. In most instances, the investigation will be necessary either to his own case or to preparation for rebuttal. Even when it is not, the information may be close enough at hand to be "readily obtainable." Rule 36 requires only that the party state that he has taken these steps. The sanction for failure of a party to inform himself before he answers lies in the award of costs after trial, as provided in Rule 37(c).

The requirement that the answer to a request for admission be sworn is deleted, in favor of a provision that the answer be signed by the party or by his attorney. The provisions of Rule 36 make it clear that admissions function very much as pleadings do. Thus, when a party admits in part and denies in part, his admission is for purposes of the pending action only and may not be used against him in any other proceeding. The broadening of the rule to encompass mixed questions of law and fact reinforces this feature. Rule 36 does not lack a sanction for false answers; Rule 37(c) furnishes an appropriate deterrent.

The existing language describing the available grounds for objection to a request for admission is eliminated as neither necessary nor helpful. The statement that objection may be made to any request which is "improper" adds nothing to the provisions that the party serve an answer or objection addressed to each matter and that he state his reasons for any objection. None of the other discovery rules sets forth grounds for objection, except so far as all are subject to the general provisions of Rule 26.

Changes are made in the sequence of procedures in Rule 36 so that they conform to the new procedures in Rules 33 and 34. The major changes are as follows:

(1) The normal time for response to a request for admissions is lengthened from 10 to 30 days, conforming more closely to prevailing practice. A defendant need not respond, however, in less than 45 days after service of the summons and complaint upon him. The court may lengthen or shorten the time when special situations require it.

(2) The present requirement that the plaintiff wait 10 days to serve requests without leave of court is eliminated. The revised provision accords with those in Rules 33 and 34.

(3) The requirement that the objecting party move automatically for a hearing on his objection is eliminated, and the burden is on the requesting party to move for an order. The change in the burden of going forward does not modify present law on burden of persuasion. The award of expenses incurred in relation to the motion is made subject to the comprehensive provisions of Rule 37(a)(4).

(4) A problem peculiar to Rule 36 arises if the responding party serves answers that are not in conformity with the requirements of the rule—for example, a denial is not "specific," or the explanation of inability to admit or deny is not "in detail." Rule 36 now makes no provision for court scrutiny of such answers before trial, and it seems to contemplate that defective answers bring about admissions just as effectively as if no answer had been served. Some cases have so held. *E.g., Southern Ry. Co. v. Crosby*, 201 F.2d 878 (4th Cir. 1953); *United States v. Laney*, 96 F.Supp. 482 (E.D.S.C.1951).

Giving a defective answer the automatic effect of an admission may cause unfair surprise. A responding party who purported to deny or to be unable to admit or deny will for the first time at trial confront the contention that he has made a binding admission. Since it is not always easy to know whether a denial is "specific" or an explanation is "in detail," neither party can know how the court will rule at trial and whether proof must be prepared. Some courts, therefore, have entertained motions to rule on defective answers. They have at times ordered that amended answers be served, when the defects were technical, and at other times have declared that the matter was admitted. *E.g., Woods v. Stewart*, 171 F.2d 544 (5th Cir. 1948); *SEC v. Kaye, Real & Co.*, 122 F.Supp. 639 (S.D.N.Y.1954); *Sieb's Hatcheries, Inc. v. Lindley*, 13 F.R.D. 113 (W.D.Ark.1952). The rule as revised conforms to the latter practice.

Subdivision (b). The rule does not how indicate the extent to which a party is bound by his admission. Some courts view admissions as the equivalent of sworn testimony.

E.g., Ark–Tenn Distributing Corp. v. Breidt, 209 F.2d 359 (3d Cir. 1954); *United States v. Lemons*, 125 F.Supp. 686 (W.D.Ark.1954); 4 *Moore's Federal Practice* ¶36.08 (2d ed. 1966 Supp.). At least in some jurisdictions a party may rebut his own testimony, *e.g., Alamo v. Del Rosario*, 98 F.2d 328 (D.C.Cir.1938), and by analogy an admission made pursuant to Rule 36 may likewise be thought rebuttable. The courts in *Ark–Tenn* and *Lemons, supra*, reasoned in this way, although the results reached may be supported on different grounds. In *McSparran v. Hanigan*, 225 F.Supp. 628, 636–637 (E.D.Pa.1963), the court held that an admission is conclusively binding, though noting the confusion created by prior decisions.

The new provisions give an admission a conclusively binding effect, for purposes only of the pending action, unless the admission is withdrawn or amended. In form and substance a Rule 36 admission is comparable to an admission in pleadings or a stipulation drafted by counsel for use at trial, rather than to an evidentiary admission of a party. Louisell, *Modern California Discovery* § 8.07 (1963); 2A Barron & Holtzoff, *Federal Practice and Procedure* § 838 (Wright ed. 1961). Unless the party securing an admission can depend on its binding effect, he cannot safely avoid the expense of preparing to prove the very matters on which he has secured the admission, and the purpose of the rule is defeated. Field v. McKusick, *Maine Civil Practice* § 36.4 (1959); Finman, *supra*, 71 Yale L.J. 371, 418–426; Comment, 56 Nw.U.L.Rev. 679, 682–683 (1961).

Provision is made for withdrawal or amendment of an admission. This provision emphasizes the importance of having the action resolved on the merits, while at the same time assuring each party that justified reliance on an admission in preparation for trial will not operate to his prejudice. *Cf. Moosman v. Joseph P. Blitz, Inc.*, 358 F.2d 686 (2d Cir. 1966).

1987 Amendment

The amendments are technical. No substantive change is intended.

1993 Amendments

The rule is revised to reflect the change made by Rule 26(d), preventing a party from seeking formal discovery until after the meeting of the parties required by Rule 26(f).

Rule 37. Failure to Make Disclosure or Cooperate in Discovery; Sanctions

(a) Motion For Order Compelling Disclosure or Discovery. A party, upon reasonable notice to other parties and all persons affected thereby, may apply for an order compelling disclosure or discovery as follows:

(1) Appropriate Court. An application for an order to a party shall be made to the court in which the action is pending. An application for an order to a person who is not a party shall be made to the court in the district where the discovery is being, or is to be, taken.

(2) Motion.

(A) If a party fails to make a disclosure required by Rule 26(a), any other party may move to compel disclosure and for appropriate sanctions. The motion must include a certification that the movant has in good faith conferred or attempted to confer with the party not making the disclosure in an effort to secure the disclosure without court action.

(B) If a deponent fails to answer a question propounded or submitted under Rules 30 or 31, or a corporation or other entity fails to make a designation under Rule 30(b)(6) or 31(a), or a party fails to answer an interrogatory submitted under Rule 33, or if a party, in response to a request for inspection submitted under Rule 34, fails to respond that inspection will be permitted as requested or fails to permit inspection as requested, the discovering party may move for an order compelling an answer, or a designation, or an order compelling inspection in accordance with the request. The motion must include a certification that the movant has in good faith conferred or attempted to confer with the person or party failing to make the discovery in an effort to secure the information or material without court action. When taking a deposition on oral examination, the proponent of the question may complete or adjourn the examination before applying for an order.

(3) Evasive or Incomplete Disclosure, Answer, or Response. For purposes of this subdivision an evasive or incomplete disclosure, answer, or response is to be treated as a failure to disclose, answer, or respond.

(4) Expenses and Sanctions.

(A) If the motion is granted or if the disclosure or requested discovery is provided after the motion was filed, the court shall, after affording an opportunity to be heard, require the party or deponent whose conduct necessitated the motion or the party or attorney advising such conduct or both of them to pay to the moving party the reasonable expenses incurred in making the motion, including attorney's fees, unless the court finds that the motion was filed without the movant's first making a good faith effort to obtain the disclosure or discovery without court action, or that the opposing party's nondisclosure, response, or objection was substantially justified, or that other circumstances make an award of expenses unjust.

(B) If the motion is denied, the court may enter any protective order authorized under Rule 26(c) and shall, after affording an opportunity to be heard, require the moving party or the attorney filing the motion or both of them to pay to the party or deponent who opposed the motion the reasonable expenses incurred in opposing the motion, including attorney's fees, unless the court finds that the making of the motion was substantially justified or that other circumstances make an award of expenses unjust.

(C) If the motion is granted in part and denied in part, the court may enter any protective order authorized under Rule 26(c) and may, after affording an opportunity to be heard, apportion the reasonable expenses incurred in relation to the motion among the parties and persons in a just manner.

(b) Failure to Comply With Order.

(1) Sanctions by Court in District Where Deposition is Taken. If a deponent fails to be sworn or to answer a question after being directed to do so by the court in the district in which the deposition is being taken, the failure may be considered a contempt of that court.

(2) Sanctions by Court in Which Action is Pending. If a party or an officer, director, or managing agent of a party or a person designated under Rule 30(b)(6) or 31(a) to testify on behalf of a party fails to obey an order to provide or permit discovery, including an order made under subdivision (a) of this rule or Rule 35, or if a party fails to obey an order entered under Rule 26(f), the court in which the action is pending may make such orders in regard to the failure as are just, and among others the following:

(A) An order that the matters regarding which the order was made or any other designated facts shall be taken to be established for the purposes of the action in accordance with the claim of the party obtaining the order;

(B) An order refusing to allow the disobedient party to support or oppose designated claims or defenses, or prohibiting that party from introducing designated matters in evidence;

(C) An order striking out pleadings or parts thereof, or staying further proceedings until the order is obeyed, or dismissing the action or proceeding or any part thereof, or rendering a judgment by default against the disobedient party;

(D) In lieu of any of the foregoing orders or in addition thereto, an order treating as a contempt of court the failure to obey any orders except an order to submit to a physical or mental examination;

(E) Where a party has failed to comply with an order under Rule 35(a) requiring that party to produce another for examination, such orders as are listed in paragraphs (A), (B), and (C) of this subdivision, unless the party failing to comply shows that that party is unable to produce such person for examination.

In lieu of any of the foregoing orders or in addition thereto, the court shall require the party failing to obey the order or the attorney advising that party or both to pay the reasonable expenses, including attorney's fees, caused by the failure, unless the court finds that the failure was substantially justified or that other circumstances make an award of expenses unjust.

(c) Failure to Disclose; False or Misleading Disclosure; Refusal to Admit.

(1) A party that without substantial justification fails to disclose information required by Rule 26(a) or 26(e)(1), or to amend a prior response to discovery as required by Rule 26(e)(2), is not, unless such failure is harmless, permitted to use as evidence at a trial, at a hearing, or on a motion any witness or information not so disclosed. In addition to or in lieu of this sanction, the court, on motion and after affording an opportunity to be heard, may impose other appropriate sanctions. In addition to requiring payment of reasonable expenses, including attorney's fees, caused by the failure, these sanctions may include any of the actions authorized under Rule 37(b)(2)(A), (B), and (C) and may include informing the jury of the failure to make the disclosure.

(2) If a party fails to admit the genuineness of any document or the truth of any matter as requested under Rule 36, and if the party requesting the admissions thereafter proves the genuineness of the document or the truth of the matter, the requesting party may apply to the court for an order requiring the other party to pay the reasonable expenses incurred in making that proof, including reasonable attorney's fees. The court shall make the order unless it finds that (A) the request was held objectionable pursuant to Rule 36(a), or (B) the admission sought was of no substantial importance, or (C) the party failing to admit had reasonable ground to believe that the party might prevail on the matter, or (D) there was other good reason for the failure to admit.

(d) Failure of Party to Attend at Own Deposition or Serve Answers to Interrogatories or Respond to Request for Inspection. If a party or an officer, director, or managing agent of a party or a person designated under Rule 30(b)(6) or 31(a) to testify on behalf of a party fails (1) to appear before the officer who is to take the deposition, after being served with a proper notice, or (2) to serve answers or objections to interrogatories submitted under Rule 33, after proper service of the interrogatories, or (3) to serve a written response to a request for inspection submitted under Rule 34, after proper service of the request, the court in which the action is pending on motion may make such orders in regard to the failure

as are just, and among others it may take any action authorized under subparagraphs (A), (B), and (C) of subdivision (b)(2) of this rule. Any motion specifying a failure under clause (2) or (3) of this subdivision shall include a certification that the movant has in good faith conferred or attempted to confer with the party failing to answer or respond in an effort to obtain such answer or response without court action. In lieu of any order or in addition thereto, the court shall require the party failing to act or the attorney advising that party or both to pay the reasonable expenses, including attorney's fees, caused by the failure unless the court finds that the failure was substantially justified or that other circumstances make an award of expenses unjust.

The failure to act described in this subdivision may not be excused on the ground that the discovery sought is objectionable unless the party failing to act has a pending motion for a protective order as provided by Rule 26(c).

(e) [Abrogated]

(f) [Repealed. Pub.L. 96–481, Title II, § 205(a), Oct. 21, 1980, 94 Stat. 2330]

(g) Failure to Participate in the Framing of a Discovery Plan. If a party or a party's attorney fails to participate in good faith in the development and submission of a proposed discovery plan as required by Rule 26(f), the court may, after opportunity for hearing, require such party or attorney to pay to any other party the reasonable expenses, including attorney's fees, caused by the failure.

(As amended Dec. 29, 1948, eff. Oct. 20, 1949; Mar. 30, 1970, eff. July 1, 1970; Apr. 29, 1980, eff. Aug. 1, 1980; Pub.L. 96–481, Title II, § 205(a), Oct. 21, 1980, 94 Stat. 2330; Mar. 2, 1987, eff. Aug. 1, 1987; Apr. 22, 1993, eff. Dec. 1, 1993; Apr. 17, 2000, eff. Dec. 1, 2000.)

ADVISORY COMMITTEE NOTES

1937 Adoption

The provisions of this rule authorizing orders establishing facts or excluding evidence or striking pleadings, or authorizing judgments of dismissal or default, for refusal to answer questions or permit inspection or otherwise make discovery, are in accord with *Hammond Packing Co. v. Arkansas*, 1909, 29 S.Ct. 370, 212 U.S. 322, 53 L.Ed. 530, 15 Ann.Cas. 645, which distinguishes between the justifiable use of such measures as a means of compelling the production of evidence, and their unjustifiable use, as in *Hovey v. Elliott*, 1897, 17 S.Ct. 841, 167 U.S. 409, 42 L.Ed. 215, for the mere purpose of punishing for contempt.

1948 Amendment

The amendment effective October 1949, substituted the reference to "Title 28, U.S.C., § 1783" in subdivision (e) for the reference to "the Act of July 3, 1926, c. 762, § 1 (44 Stat. 835), U.S.C., Title 28, § 711."

1970 Amendment

Rule 37 provides generally for sanctions against parties or persons unjustifiably resisting discovery. Experience has brought to light a number of defects in the language of the rule as well as instances in which it is not serving the purposes for which it was designed. See Rosenberg, *Sanctions to Effectuate Pretrial Discovery,* 58 Col.L.Rev. 480 (1958). In addition, changes being made in other discovery rules require conforming amendments to Rule 37.

Rule 37 sometimes refers to a "failure" to afford discovery and at other times to a "refusal" to do so. Taking note of this dual terminology, courts have imported into "refusal" a requirement of "wilfullness." See *Roth v. Paramount Pictures Corp.,* 8 F.R.D. 31 (W.D.Pa.1948); *Campbell v. Johnson,* 101 F.Supp. 705, 707 (S.D.N.Y.1951). In *Societe Internationale v. Rogers,* 357 U.S. 197 (1958), the Supreme Court concluded that the rather random use of these two terms in Rule 37 showed no design to use them with consistently distinctive meanings, that "refused" in Rule 37(b)(2) meant simply a failure to comply, and that wilfullness was relevant only to the selection of sanctions, if any, to be imposed. Nevertheless, after the decision in *Societe,* the court in *Hinson v. Michigan Mutual Liability Co.,* 275 F.2d 537 (5th Cir. 1960) once again ruled that "refusal" required wilfullness. Substitution of "failure" for "refusal" throughout Rule 37 should eliminate this confusion and bring the rule into harmony with the *Societe Internationale* decision. See Rosenberg, *supra,* 58 Col.L.Rev. 480, 489–490 (1958).

Subdivision (a). Rule 37(a) provides relief to a party seeking discovery against one who, with or without stated objections, fails to afford the discovery sought. It has always fully served this function in relation to depositions, but the amendments being made to Rules 33 and 34 give Rule 37(a) added scope and importance. Under existing Rule 33, a party objecting to interrogatories must make a motion for court hearing on his objections. The changes now made in Rules 33 and 37(a) make it clear that the interrogating party must move to compel answers, and the motion is provided for in Rule 37(a). Existing Rule 34, since it requires a court order prior to production of documents or things or permission to enter on land, has no relation to Rule 37(a). Amendments of Rules 34 and 37(a) create a procedure similar to that provided for Rule 33.

Subdivision (a)(1). This is a new provision making clear to which court a party may apply for an order compelling discovery. Existing Rule 37(a) refers only to the court in which the deposition is being taken; nevertheless, it has been held that the court where the action is pending has "inherent power" to compel a party deponent to answer. *Lincoln Laboratories, Inc. v. Savage Laboratories, Inc.,* 27 F.R.D. 476 (D.Del.1961). In relation to Rule 33 interrogatories and Rule 34 requests for inspection, the court where the action is pending is the appropriate enforcing tribunal. The new provision eliminates the need to resort to inherent power by spelling out the respective roles of the court where the action is pending and the court where the deposition is taken. In some instances, two courts are available to a party seeking to compel answers from a party deponent. The party seeking discovery may choose the court to which he will apply, but the court has power to remit the party to the other court as a more appropriate forum.

Subdivision (a)(2). This subdivision contains the substance of existing provisions of Rule 37(a) authorizing motions to compel answers to questions put at depositions and to interrogatories. New provisions authorize motions for orders compelling designation under Rules 30(b)(6) and 31(a) and compelling inspection in accordance with a request made under Rule 34. If the court denies a motion, in whole or part, it may accompany the denial with issuance of a protective order. Compare the converse provision in Rule 26(c).

Subdivision (a)(3). This new provision makes clear that an evasive or incomplete answer is to be considered, for purposes of subdivision (a), a failure to answer. The courts have consistently held that they have the power to compel adequate answers. *E.g., Cone Mills Corp. v. Joseph Bancroft & Sons Co.,* 33 F.R.D. 318 (D.Del.1963). This power is recognized and incorporated into the rule.

Subdivision (a)(4). This subdivision amends the provisions for award of expenses, including reasonable attorney's fees, to the prevailing party or person when a motion is made for an order compelling discovery. At present, an award of expenses is made only if the losing party or person is found to have acted without substantial justification. The change requires that expenses be awarded unless the conduct of the losing party or person is found to have been substantially justified. The test of "substantial justification" remains, but the change in language is intended to encourage judges to be more alert to abuses occurring in the discovery process.

On many occasions, to be sure, the dispute over discovery between the parties is genuine, though ultimately resolved one way or the other by the court. In such cases, the losing party is substantially justified in carrying the matter to court. But the rules should deter the abuse implicit in carrying or forcing a discovery dispute to court when no genuine dispute exists. And the potential or actual imposition of expenses is virtually the sole formal sanction in the rules to deter a party from pressing to a court hearing frivolous requests for or objections to discovery.

The present provision of Rule 37(a) that the court shall require payment if it finds that the defeated party acted without "substantial justification" may appear adequate, but in fact it has been little used. Only a handful of reported cases include an award of expenses, and the Columbia Survey found that in only one instance out of about 50 motions decided under Rule 37(a) did the court award expenses. It appears that the courts do not utilize the most important available sanction to deter abusive resort to the judiciary.

The proposed change provides in effect that expenses should ordinarily be awarded unless a court finds that the losing party acted justifiably in carrying his point to court. At the same time, a necessary flexibility is maintained, since the court retains the power to find that other circumstances make an award of expenses unjust—as where the prevailing party also acted unjustifiably. The amendment does not significantly narrow the discretion of the court, but rather presses the court to address itself to abusive practices. The present provision that expenses may be imposed upon either the party or his attorney or both is unchanged. But it is not contemplated that expenses will be imposed upon the attorney merely because the party is indigent.

Subdivision (b). This subdivision deals with sanctions for failure to comply with a court order. The present captions for subsections (1) and (2) entitled, "Contempt" and "Other Consequences," respectively, are confusing. One of the consequences listed in (2) is the arrest of the party, representing the exercise of the contempt power. The contents of the subsections show that the first authorizes the sanction of contempt (and no other) by the court in which the deposition is taken, whereas the second subsection authorizes a variety of sanctions, including contempt, which may be imposed by the court in which the action is pending. The captions of the subsections are changed to reflect their contents.

The scope of Rule 37(b)(2) is broadened by extending it to include any order "to provide or permit discovery," including orders issued under Rules 37(a) and 35. Various rules authorize orders for discovery—e.g., Rule 35(b)(1), Rule 26(c) as revised, Rule 37(d). See Rosenberg, *supra*, 58 Col.L.Rev. 480, 484–486. Rule 37(b)(2) should provide comprehensively for enforcement of all these orders. *Cf. Societe Internationale v. Rogers*, 357 U.S. 197, 207 (1958). On the other hand, the reference to Rule 34 is deleted to conform to the changed procedure in that rule.

A new subsection (E) provides that sanctions which have been available against a party for failure to comply with an order under Rule 35(a) to submit to examination will now be available against him for his failure to comply with a Rule 35(a) order to produce a third person for examination, unless he shows that he is unable to produce the person. In this context, "unable" means in effect "unable in good faith." See *Societe Internationale v. Rogers*, 357 U.S. 197 (1958).

Subdivision (b)(2) is amplified to provide for payment of reasonable expenses caused by the failure to obey the order. Although Rules 37(b)(2) and 37(d) have been silent as to award of expenses, courts have nevertheless ordered them on occasion. *E.g., United Sheeplined Clothing Co. v. Arctic Fur Cap Corp.*, 165 F.Supp. 193 (S.D.N.Y.1958); *Austin Theatre, Inc. v. Warner Bros. Pictures, Inc.*, 22 F.R.D. 302 (S.D.N.Y. 1958). The provision places the burden on the disobedient party to avoid expenses by showing that his failure is justified or that special circumstances make an award of expenses unjust. Allocating the burden in this way conforms to the changed provisions as to expenses in Rule 37(a), and is particularly appropriate when a court order is disobeyed.

An added reference to directors of a party is similar to a change made in subdivision (d) and is explained in the note to that subdivision. The added reference to persons designated by a party under Rules 30(b)(6) or 31(a) to testify on behalf of the party carries out the new procedure in those rules for taking a deposition of a corporation or other organization.

Subdivision (c). Rule 37(c) provides a sanction for the enforcement of Rule 36 dealing with requests for admission. Rule 36 provides the mechanism whereby a party may obtain from another party in appropriate instances either (1) an admission, or (2) a sworn and specific denial or (3) a sworn statement "setting forth in detail the reasons why he cannot truthfully admit or deny." If the party obtains the second or third of these responses, in proper form, Rule 36 does not provide for a pretrial hearing on whether the response is warranted by the evidence thus far accumulated. Instead, Rule 37(c) is intended to provide posttrial relief in the form of a requirement that the party improperly refusing the admission pay the expenses of the other side in making the necessary proof at trial.

Rule 37(c), as now written, addresses itself in terms only to the sworn denial and is silent with respect to the statement of reasons for an inability to admit or deny. There is no apparent basis for this distinction, since the sanction provided in Rule 37(c) should deter all unjustified failures to admit.

This omission in the rule has caused confused and diverse treatment in the courts. One court has held that if a party give inadequate reasons, he should be treated before trial as having denied the request, so that Rule 37(c) may apply. *Bertha Bldg. Corp. v. National Theatres Corp.*, 15 F.R.D. 339 (E.D.N.Y.1954). Another has held that the party should be treated as having admitted the request. *Heng Hsin Co. v. Stern, Morgenthau & Co.*, 20 Fed.Rules Serv. 36a.52, Case 1 (S.D.N.Y. Dec. 10, 1954). Still another has ordered a new response, without indicating what the outcome should be if the new response were inadequate. *United States Plywood Corp. v. Hudson Lumber Co.*, 127 F.Supp. 489, 497–498 (S.D.N.Y.1954). See generally Finman, *The Request for Admissions in Federal Civil Procedure*, 71 Yale L.J. 371, 426–430 (1962). The amendment eliminates this defect in Rule 37(c) by bringing within its scope all failures to admit.

Additional provisions in Rule 37(c) protect a party from having to pay expenses if the request for admission was held objectionable under Rule 36(a) or if the party failing to admit had reasonable ground to believe that he might prevail on the matter. The latter provision emphasizes that the true test under Rule 37(c) is not whether a party prevailed at trial but whether he acted reasonably in believing that he might prevail.

Subdivision (d). The scope of subdivision (d) is broadened to include responses to requests for inspection under Rule 34, thereby conforming to the new procedures of Rule 34.

Two related changes are made in subdivision (d): the permissible sanctions are broadened to include such orders "as are just"; and the requirement that the failure to appear or respond be "wilful" is eliminated. Although Rule 37(d) in terms provides for only three sanctions, all rather severe, the courts have interpreted it as permitting softer sanctions than those which it sets forth. E.g., *Gill v. Stolow*, 240 F.2d 669 (2d Cir.1957); *Saltzman v. Birrell*, 156 F.Supp. 538 (S.D.N.Y.1957); 2A Barron & Holtzoff, *Federal Practice and Procedure* 554–557 (Wright ed. 1961). The rule is changed to provide the greater flexibility as to sanctions which the cases show is needed.

The resulting flexibility as to sanctions eliminates any need to retain the requirement that the failure to appear or respond be "wilful." The concept of "wilful failure" is at best subtle and difficult, and the cases do not supply a bright line. Many courts have imposed sanctions without referring to wilfullness. E.g., *Milewski v. Schneider Transportation Co.*, 238 F.2d 397 (6th Cir.1956); *Dictograph Products, Inc. v. Kentworth Corp.*, 7 F.R.D. 543 (W.D.Ky.1947). In addition, in view of the possibility of light sanctions, even a negligent failure should come within Rule 37(d). If default is caused by counsel's ignorance of Federal practice, cf. *Dunn v. Pa. R.R.*, 96 F.Supp. 597 (N.D.Ohio 1951), or by his preoccupation with another aspect of the case, cf. *Maurer–Neuer, Inc. v. United Packinghouse Workers*, 26 F.R.D. 139 (D.Kans.1960), dismissal of the action and default judgment are not justified, but the imposition of expenses and fees may well be. "Wilfullness" continues to play a role, along with various other factors, in the choice of sanctions. Thus, the scheme conforms to Rule 37(b) as construed by the Supreme Court in *Societe Internationale v. Rogers*, 357 U.S. 197, 208 (1958).

A provision is added to make clear that a party may not properly remain completely silent even when he regards a notice to take his deposition or a set of interrogatories or requests to inspect as improper and objectionable. If he desires not to appear or not to respond, he must apply for a protective order. The cases are divided on whether a protective order must be sought. Compare *Collins v. Wayland,* 139 F.2d 677 (9th Cir. 1944), *cert. den.* 322 U.S. 744; *Bourgeois v. El Paso Natural Gas Co.,* 20 F.R.D. 358 (S.D.N.Y. 1957); *Loosley v. Stone,* 15 F.R.D. 373 (S.D.Ill.1954), with *Scarlatos v. Kulukundis,* 21 F.R.D. 185 (S.D.N.Y.1957); *Ross v. True Temper Corp.,* 11 F.R.D. 307 (N.D.Ohio 1951). Compare also Rosenberg, *supra,* 58 Col.L.Rev. 480, 496 (1958) with 2A Barron & Holtzoff, *Federal Practice and Procedure* 530–531 (Wright ed. 1961). The party from whom discovery is sought is afforded, through Rule 26(c), a fair and effective procedure whereby he can challenge the request made. At the same time, the total noncompliance with which Rule 37(d) is concerned may impose severe inconvenience or hardship on the discovering party and substantially delay the discovery process. Cf. 2B Barron & Holtzoff, *Federal Practice and Procedure* 306–307 (Wright ed. 1961) (response to a subpoena).

The failure of an officer or managing agent of a party to make discovery as required by present Rule 37(d) is treated as the failure of the party. The rule as revised provides similar treatment for a director of a party. There is slight warrant for the present distinction between officers and managing agents on the one hand and directors on the other. Although the legal power over a director to compel his making discovery may not be as great as over officers or managing agents, *Campbell v. General Motors Corp.,* 13 F.R.D. 331 (S.D.N.Y.1952), the practical differences are negligible. That a director's interests are normally aligned with those of his corporation is shown by the provisions of old Rule 26(d)(2), transferred to 32(a)(2) (deposition of director of party may be used at trial by an adverse party for any purpose) and of Rule 43(b) (director of party may be treated at trial as a hostile witness on direct examination by any adverse party). Moreover, in those rare instances when a corporation is unable through good faith efforts to compel a director to make discovery, it is unlikely that the court will impose sanctions. Cf. *Societe Internationale v. Rogers,* 357 U.S. 197 (1958).

Subdivision (e). The change in the caption conforms to the language of 28 U.S.C. § 1783, as amended in 1964.

Subdivision (f). Until recently, costs of a civil action could be awarded against the United States only when expressly provided by Act of Congress, and such provision was rarely made. See H.R.Rep.No. 1535, 89th Cong., 2d Sess., 2–3 (1966). To avoid any conflict with this doctrine, Rule 37(f) has provided that expenses and attorney's fees may not be imposed upon the United States under Rule 37. See 2A Barron & Holtzoff, *Federal Practice and Procedure* 857 (Wright ed. 1961).

A major change in the law was made in 1966, 80 Stat. 308, 28 U.S.C. § 2412 (1966), whereby a judgment for costs may ordinarily be awarded to the prevailing party in any civil action brought by or against the United States. Costs are not to include the fees and expenses of attorneys. In light of this legislative development, Rule 37(f) is amended to permit the award of expenses and fees against the United States under Rule 37, but only to the extent permitted by statute. The amendment brings Rule 37(f) into line with present and future statutory provisions.

1980 Amendment

Subdivision (b)(2). New Rule 26(f) provides that if a discovery conference is held, at its close the court shall enter an order respecting the subsequent conduct of discovery. The amendment provides that the sanctions available for violation of other court orders respecting discovery are available for violation of the discovery conference order.

Subdivision (e). Subdivision (e) is stricken. Title 28, U.S.C. § 1783 no longer refers to sanctions. The subdivision otherwise duplicates Rule 45(e)(2).

Subdivision (g). New Rule 26(f) imposes a duty on parties to participate in good faith in the framing of a discovery plan by agreement upon the request of any party. This subdivision authorizes the court to award to parties who participate in good faith in an attempt to frame a discovery plan the expenses incurred in the attempt if any party or his attorney fails to participate in good faith and thereby causes additional expense.

Failure of United States to Participate in Good Faith in Discovery. Rule 37 authorizes the court to direct that parties or attorneys who fail to participate in good faith in the discovery process pay the expenses, including attorneys' fees, incurred by other parties as a result of that failure. Since attorneys' fees cannot ordinarily be awarded against the United States (28 U.S.C. § 2412), there is often no practical remedy for the misconduct of its officers and attorneys. However, in the case of a government attorney who fails to participate in good faith in discovery, nothing prevents a court in an appropriate case from giving written notification of that fact to the Attorney General of the United States and other appropriate heads of offices or agencies thereof.

1987 Amendment

The amendments are technical. No substantive change is intended.

1993 Amendments

Subdivision (a). This subdivision is revised to reflect the revision of Rule 26(a), requiring disclosure of matters without a discovery request.

Pursuant to new subdivision (a)(2)(A), a party dissatisfied with the disclosure made by an opposing party may under this rule move for an order to compel disclosure. In providing for such a motion, the revised rule parallels the provisions of the former rule dealing with failures to answer particular interrogatories. Such a motion may be needed when the information to be disclosed might be helpful to the party seeking the disclosure but not to the party required to make the disclosure. If the party required to make the disclosure would need the material to support its own contentions, the more effective enforcement of the disclosure requirement will be to exclude the evidence not disclosed, as provided in subdivision (c)(1) of this revised rule.

Language is included in the new paragraph and added to the subparagraph (B) that requires litigants to seek to resolve discovery disputes by informal means before filing a motion with the court. This requirement is based on successful experience with similar local rules of court promulgated pursuant to Rule 83.

The last sentence of paragraph (2) is moved into paragraph (4).

Under revised paragraph (3), evasive or incomplete disclosures and responses to interrogatories and production requests are treated as failures to disclose or respond. Interrogatories and requests for production should not be read or interpreted in an artificially restrictive or hypertechnical manner to avoid disclosure of information fairly covered by the discovery request, and to do so is subject to appropriate sanctions under subdivision (a).

Revised paragraph (4) is divided into three subparagraphs for ease of reference, and in each the phrase "after opportunity for hearing" is changed to "after affording an opportunity to be heard" to make clear that the court can consider such questions on written submissions as well as on oral hearings.

Subparagraph (A) is revised to cover the situation where information that should have been produced without a motion to compel is produced after the motion is filed but before it is brought on for hearing. The rule also is revised to provide that a party should not be awarded its expenses for filing a motion that could have been avoided by conferring with opposing counsel.

Subparagraph (C) is revised to include the provision that formerly was contained in subdivision (a)(2) and to include the same requirement of an opportunity to be heard that is specified in subparagraphs (A) and (B).

Subdivision (c). The revision provides a self-executing sanction for failure to make a disclosure required by Rule 26(a), without need for a motion under subdivision (a)(2)(A).

Paragraph (1) prevents a party from using as evidence any witnesses or information that, without substantial justification, has not been disclosed as required by Rules 26(a) and 26(e)(1). This automatic sanction provides a strong inducement for disclosure of material that the disclosing party would expect to use as evidence, whether at a trial, at a hearing, or on a motion, such as one under Rule 56. As disclosure of evidence offered solely for impeachment purposes is not required under those rules, this preclusion sanction likewise does not apply to that evidence.

Limiting the automatic sanction to violations "without substantial justification," coupled with the exception for violations that are "harmless," is needed to avoid unduly harsh penalties in a variety of situations: *e.g.,* the inadvertent omission from a Rule 26(a)(1)(A) disclosure of the name of a potential witness known to all parties; the failure to list as a trial witness a person so listed by another party; or the lack of knowledge of a pro se litigant of the requirement to make disclosures. In the latter situation, however, exclusion would be proper if the requirement for disclosure had been called to the litigant's attention by either the court or another party.

Preclusion of evidence is not an effective incentive to compel disclosure of information that, being supportive of the position of the opposing party, might advantageously be concealed by the disclosing party. However, the rule provides the court with a wide range of other sanctions—such as declaring specified facts to be established, preventing contradictory evidence, or, like spoliation of evidence, allowing the jury to be informed of the fact of nondisclosure—that, though not self-executing, can be imposed when found to be warranted after a hearing. The failure to identify a witness or document in a disclosure statement would be admissible under the Federal Rules of Evidence under the same principles that allow a party's interrogatory answers to be offered against it.

Subdivision (d). This subdivision is revised to require that, where a party fails to file any response to interrogatories or a Rule 34 request, the discovering party should informally seek to obtain such responses before filing a motion for sanctions.

The last sentence of this subdivision is revised to clarify that it is the pendency of a motion for protective order that may be urged as an excuse for a violation of subdivision (d). If a party's motion has been denied, the party cannot argue that its subsequent failure to comply would be justified. In this connection, it should be noted that the filing of a motion under Rule 26(c) is not self-executing—the relief authorized under that rule depends on obtaining the court's order to that effect.

Subdivision (g). This subdivision is modified to conform to the revision of Rule 26(f).

2000 Amendment

Subdivision (c)(1). When this subdivision was added in 1993 to direct exclusion of materials not disclosed as required, the duty to supplement discovery responses pursuant to Rule 26(e)(2) was omitted. In the face of this omission, courts may rely on inherent power to sanction for failure to supplement as required by Rule 26(e)(2), *see 8 Federal Practice & Procedure* § 2050 at 607–09, but that is an uncertain and unregulated ground for imposing sanctions. There is no obvious occasion for a Rule 37(a) motion in connection with failure to supplement, and ordinarily only Rule 37(c)(1) exists as rule-based authority for sanctions if this supplementation obligation is violated.

The amendment explicitly adds failure to comply with Rule 26(e)(2) as a ground for sanctions under Rule 37(c)(1), including exclusion of withheld materials. The rule provides that this sanction power only applies when the failure to supplement was "without substantial justification." Even if the failure was not substantially justified, a party should be allowed to use the material that was not disclosed if the lack of earlier notice was harmless.

"Shall" is replaced by "is" under the program to conform amended rules to current style conventions when there is no ambiguity.

GAP Report

The Advisory Committee recommends that the published amendment proposal be modified to state that the exclusion sanction can apply to failure "to amend a prior response to discovery as required by Rule 26(e)(2)." In addition, one minor phrasing change is recommended for the Committee Note.

HISTORICAL NOTES

Effective and Applicability Provisions

1980 Acts. Amendment by Pub.L. 96–481 effective Oct. 1, 1981, and applicable to adversary adjudication defined in section 504(b)(1)(C) of Title 5, and to civil actions and adversary adjudications described in section 2412 of Title 28, Judiciary and Judicial Procedure, which are pending on, or commenced on or after Oct. 1, 1981, see section 208 of Pub.L.

96–481, set out as an Effective Date note under section 504 of Title 5, Government Organization and Employees.

VI. TRIALS

Rule 38.   Jury Trial of Right

(a) Right Preserved. The right of trial by jury as declared by the Seventh Amendment to the Constitution or as given by a statute of the United States shall be preserved to the parties inviolate.

(b) Demand. Any party may demand a trial by jury of any issue triable of right by a jury by (1) serving upon the other parties a demand therefor in writing at any time after the commencement of the action and not later than 10 days after the service of the last pleading directed to such issue, and (2) filing the demand as required by Rule 5(d). Such demand may be indorsed upon a pleading of the party.

(c) Same: Specification of Issues. In the demand a party may specify the issues which the party wishes so tried; otherwise the party shall be deemed to have demanded trial by jury for all the issues so triable. If the party has demanded trial by jury for only some of the issues, any other party within 10 days after service of the demand or such lesser time as the court may order, may serve a demand for trial by jury of any other or all of the issues of fact in the action.

(d) Waiver. The failure of a party to serve and file a demand as required by this rule constitutes a waiver by the party of trial by jury. A demand for trial by jury made as herein provided may not be withdrawn without the consent of the parties.

(e) Admiralty and Maritime Claims. These rules shall not be construed to create a right to trial by jury of the issues in an admiralty or maritime claim within the meaning of Rule 9(h).

(As amended Feb. 28, 1966, eff. July 1, 1966; Mar. 2, 1987, eff. Aug. 1, 1987; Apr. 22, 1993, eff. Dec. 1, 1993.)

ADVISORY COMMITTEE NOTES
1937 Adoption

This rule provides for the preservation of the constitutional right of trial by jury as directed in the enabling act (act of June 19, 1934, 48 Stat. 1064, U.S.C., Title 28, § 723c [sec. 2072]), and it and the next rule make definite provision for claim and waiver of jury trial, following the method used in many American states and in England and the British Dominions. Thus the claim must be made at once on initial pleading or appearance under Ill.Rev.Stat. (1937) ch. 110, § 188; 6 Tenn.Code Ann. (Williams, 1934) § 8734; compare Wyo.Rev.Stat.Ann. (1931) § 89–1320 (with answer or reply); within 10 days after the pleadings are completed or the case is at issue under 2 Conn.Gen.Stat. (1930) § 5624; Hawaii Rev.Laws (1935) § 4101; 2 Mass.Gen.Laws (Ter.Ed.1932) ch. 231, § 60; 3 Mich.Comp.Laws (1929) § 14263; Mich. Court

Rules Ann. (Searl, 1933) Rule 33 (15 days); England (until 1933) O. 36, r.r. 2 and 6; and Ontario Jud. Act (1927) § 57(1) (4 days, or, where prior notice of trial, 2 days from such notice); or at a definite time varying under different codes, from 10 days before notice of trial to 10 days after notice, or, as in many, when the case is called for assignment, Ariz.Rev. Code Ann. (Struckmeyer, 1928) § 3802; Calif. Code Civ.Proc. (Deering, 1937) § 631, par. 4; Iowa Code (1935) § 10724; 4 Nev.Comp.Laws (Hillyer, 1929) § 8782; N.M. Stat.Ann. (Courtright, 1929) § 105–814; N.Y.C.P.A. (1937) § 426, subdivision 5 (applying to New York, Bronx, Richmond, Kings, and Queens Counties); R.I. Pub. Laws (1929), ch. 1327, amending R.I. Gen.Laws (1923) ch. 337, § 6; Utah Rev.Stat. Ann. (1933) § 104–23–6; 2 Wash.Rev.Stat.Ann. (Remington, 1932) § 316; England (4 days after notice of trial), Administration of Justice Act (1933) § 6 and amended rule under the Judicature Act (The Annual Practice, 1937), O. 36, r. 1; Australia High Court Procedure Act (1921) § 12, Rules, O. 33, r. 2; Alberta Rules of Ct. (1914) 172, 183, 184; British Columbia Sup.Ct.Rules (1925) O. 36, r.r. 2, 6, 11, and 16; New Brunswick Jud. Act (1927) O. 36, r.r. 2 and 5. See James, Trial by Jury and the New Federal Rules of Procedure (1936), 45 Yale L.J. 1022.

Rule 81(c) provides for claim for jury trial in removed actions.

The right to trial by jury as declared in U.S.C., Title 28, § 770 (Trial of issues of fact; by jury; exceptions), and similar statutes, is unaffected by this rule. This rule modifies U.S.C., Title 28, [former] § 773 (Trial of issues of fact; by court).

1966 Amendments

See Note to Rule 9(h), supra.

1987 Amendments

The amendments are technical. No substantive change is intended.

1993 Amendments

Language requiring the filing of a jury demand as provided in subdivision (d) is added to subdivision (b) to eliminate an apparent ambiguity between the two subdivisions. For proper scheduling of cases, it is important that jury demands not only be served on other parties, but also be filed with the court.

Rule 39.   Trial by Jury or by the Court

(a) By Jury. When trial by jury has been demanded as provided in Rule 38, the action shall be designated upon the docket as a jury action. The trial of all issues so demanded shall be by jury, unless (1) the parties or their attorneys of record, by written stipulation filed with the court or by an oral stipulation made in open court and entered in the record, consent to trial by the court sitting without a jury or (2) the court upon motion or of its own initiative finds that a right of trial by jury of some or all of those issues does not exist under the Constitution or statutes of the United States.

(b) By the Court. Issues not demanded for trial by jury as provided in Rule 38 shall be tried by the court; but, notwithstanding the failure of a party to demand a jury in an action in which such a demand might have been made of right, the court in its discretion upon motion may order a trial by a jury of any or all issues.

(c) Advisory Jury and Trial by Consent. In all actions not triable of right by a jury the court upon motion or of its own initiative may try any issue with an advisory jury or, except in actions against the United States when a statute of the United States provides for trial without a jury, the court, with the consent of both parties, may order a trial with a jury whose verdict has the same effect as if trial by jury had been a matter of right.

ADVISORY COMMITTEE NOTES
1937 Adoption

The provisions for express waiver of jury trial found in U.S.C., Title 28, [former] § 773 (Trial of issues of fact; by court) are incorporated in this rule. See Rule 38, however, which extends the provisions for waiver of jury. U.S.C., Title 28, [former] § 772 (Trial of issues of fact; in equity in patent causes) is unaffected by this rule. When certain of the issues are to be tried by jury and others by the court, the court may determine the sequence in which such issues shall be tried. *See Liberty Oil Co. v. Condon Nat. Bank*, 260 U.S. 235, 43 S.Ct. 118, 67 L.Ed. 232 (1922).

A discretionary power in the courts to send issues of fact to the jury is common in state procedure. Compare Calif. Code Civ.Proc. (Deering, 1937) § 592; 1 Colo.Stat.Ann. (1935) Code Civ.Proc., ch. 12, § 191; Conn.Gen.Stat. (1930) § 5625; 2 Minn.Stat. (Mason, 1927) § 9288; 4 Mont.Rev. Codes Ann. (1935) § 9327; N.Y.C.P.A. (1937) § 430; 2 Ohio Gen.Code Ann. (Page, 1926) § 11380; 1 Okla.Stat.Ann. (Harlow, 1931) § 351 [12 Okl.St.Ann. § 557]; Utah Rev.Stat.Ann. (1933) § 104–23–5; 2 Wash.Rev.Stat.Ann. (Remington, 1932) § 315; Wis.Stat. (1935) § 270.07. See [former] Equity Rule 23 (Matters Ordinarily Determinable at Law When Arising in Suit in Equity to be Disposed of Therein) and U.S.C., Title 28 [former] § 772 (Trial of issues of fact; in equity in patent causes); *Colleton Merc. Mfg. Co. v. Savannah River Lumber Co.*, C.C.A.4, 1922, 280 F. 358; *Fed. Res. Bk. of San Francisco v. Idaho Grimm Alfalfa Seed Growers' Ass'n*, C.C.A.9, 1925, 8 F.2d 922, certiorari denied 46 S.Ct. 347, 270 U.S. 646, 70 L.Ed. 778 (1926); *Watt v. Starke*, 1879, 101 U.S. 247, 25 L.Ed. 826.

Rule 40. Assignment of Cases for Trial

The district courts shall provide by rule for the placing of actions upon the trial calendar (1) without request of the parties or (2) upon request of a party and notice to the other parties or (3) in such other manner as the courts deem expedient. Precedence shall be given to actions entitled thereto by any statute of the United States.

ADVISORY COMMITTEE NOTES
1937 Adoption

U.S.C., Title 28, [former] § 769 (Notice of case for trial) is modified. See former Equity Rule 56 (On Expiration of Time for Depositions, Case Goes on Trial Calendar). See also [former] Equity Rule 57 (Continuances).

For examples of statutes giving precedence, see U.S.C., Title 28, § 47 (now §§ 1253, 2101, 2325) (Injunctions as to orders of Interstate Commerce Commission); § 380 (now §§ 1253, 2101, 2284) (Injunctions; alleged unconstitutionality of state statutes); § 380a (now §§ 1253, 2101, 2284) (Same; Constitutionality of federal statute); [former] § 768 (Priority of cases where a state is party); Title 15, § 28 (Antitrust laws; suits against monopolies expedited); Title 22, § 240 (Petition for restoration of property seized as munitions of war, etc.); and Title 49, [former] § 44 (Proceedings in equity under interstate commerce laws; expedition of suits).

Rule 41. Dismissal of Actions
(a) Voluntary Dismissal: Effect Thereof.

(1) By Plaintiff; by Stipulation. Subject to the provisions of Rule 23(e), of Rule 66, and of any statute of the United States, an action may be dismissed by the plaintiff without order of court (i) by filing a notice of dismissal at any time before service by the adverse party of an answer or of a motion for summary judgment, whichever first occurs, or (ii) by filing a stipulation of dismissal signed by all parties who have appeared in the action. Unless otherwise stated in the notice of dismissal or stipulation, the dismissal is without prejudice, except that a notice of dismissal operates as an adjudication upon the merits when filed by a plaintiff who has once dismissed in any court of the United States or of any state an action based on or including the same claim.

(2) By Order of Court. Except as provided in paragraph (1) of this subdivision of this rule, an action shall not be dismissed at the plaintiff's instance save upon order of the court and upon such terms and conditions as the court deems proper. If a counterclaim has been pleaded by a defendant prior to the service upon the defendant of the plaintiff's motion to dismiss, the action shall not be dismissed against the defendant's objection unless the counterclaim can remain pending for independent adjudication by the court. Unless otherwise specified in the order, a dismissal under this paragraph is without prejudice.

(b) Involuntary Dismissal: Effect Thereof. For failure of the plaintiff to prosecute or to comply with these rules or any order of court, a defendant may move for dismissal of an action or of any claim against the defendant. Unless the court in its order for dismissal otherwise specifies, a dismissal under this subdivision and any dismissal not provided for in this rule, other than a dismissal for lack of jurisdiction, for improper venue, or for failure to join a party under Rule 19, operates as an adjudication upon the merits.

(c) Dismissal of Counterclaim, Cross-Claim, or Third-Party Claim. The provisions of this rule apply to the dismissal of any counterclaim, cross-claim, or third-party claim. A voluntary dismissal by the claimant alone pursuant to paragraph (1) of subdivision (a) of this rule shall be made before a responsive pleading is served or, if there is none, before the introduction of evidence at the trial or hearing.

(d) Costs of Previously-Dismissed Action. If a plaintiff who has once dismissed an action in any court commences an action based upon or including the same claim against the same defendant, the court may make such order for the payment of costs of the action previously dismissed as it may deem proper and may stay the proceedings in the action until the plaintiff has complied with the order.

(As amended Dec. 27, 1946, eff. Mar. 19, 1948; Jan. 21, 1963, eff. July 1, 1963; Feb. 28, 1966, eff. July 1, 1966; Dec. 4, 1967, eff. July 1, 1968; Mar. 2, 1987, eff. Aug. 1, 1987; Apr. 30, 1991, eff. Dec. 1, 1991.)

ADVISORY COMMITTEE NOTES

1937 Adoption

Note to Subdivision (a). Compare Ill.Rev.Stat. (1937) c. 110, § 176, and *English Rules Under the Judicature Act* (The Annual Practice, 1937) O. 26.

Provisions regarding dismissal in such statutes as U.S.C., Title 8, § 164 [see 1329] (Jurisdiction of district courts in immigration cases) and U.S.C., Title 31, § 232 [now 3730] (Liability of persons making false claims against United States; suits) are preserved by paragraph (1).

Note to Subdivision (b). This provides for the equivalent of a nonsuit on motion by the defendant after the completion of the presentation of evidence by the plaintiff. Also, for actions tried without a jury, it provides the equivalent of the directed verdict practice for jury actions which is regulated by Rule 50.

1946 Amendment

Note. Subdivision (a). The insertion of the reference to Rule 66 correlates Rule 41(a)(1) with the express provisions concerning dismissal set forth in amended Rule 66 on receivers.

The change in Rule 41(a)(1)(i) gives the service of a motion for summary judgment by the adverse party the same effect in preventing unlimited dismissal as was originally given only to the service of an answer. The omission of reference to a motion for summary judgment in the original rule was subject to criticism. 3 *Moore's Federal Practice*, 1938, 3037–3038, n. 12. A motion for summary judgment may be forthcoming prior to answer, and if well taken will eliminate the necessity for an answer. Since such a motion may require even more research and preparation than the answer

itself, there is good reason why the service of the motion, like that of the answer, should prevent a voluntary dismissal by the adversary without court approval.

The word "generally" has been stricken from Rule 41(a)(1)(ii) in order to avoid confusion and to conform with the elimination of the necessity for special appearance by original Rule 12(b).

Subdivision (b). In some cases tried without a jury, where at the close of plaintiff's evidence the defendant moves for dismissal under Rule 41(b) on the ground that plaintiff's evidence is insufficient for recovery, the plaintiff's own evidence may be conflicting or present questions of credibility. In ruling on the defendant's motion, questions arise as to the function of the judge in evaluating the testimony and whether findings should be made if the motion is sustained. Three circuits hold that as the judge is the trier of the facts in such a situation his function is not the same as on a motion to direct a verdict, where the jury is the trier of the facts, and that the judge in deciding such a motion in a non-jury case may pass on conflicts of evidence and credibility, and if he performs that function of evaluating the testimony and grants the motion on the merits, findings are required. *Young v. United States*, C.C.A.9, 1940, 111 F.2d 823; *Gary Theatre Co. v. Columbia Pictures Corporation*, C.C.A.7, 1941, 120 F.2d 891; *Bach v. Friden Calculating Machine Co., Inc.*, C.C.A.6, 1945, 148 F.2d 407. Cf. *Mateas v. Fred Harvey, a Corporation*, C.C.A.9, 1945, 146 F.2d 989. The Third Circuit has held that on such a motion the function of the court is the same as on a motion to direct in a jury case, and that the court should only decide whether there is evidence which would support a judgment for the plaintiff, and therefore, findings are not required by Rule 52. *Federal Deposit Insurance Corp. v. Mason*, C.C.A.3, 1940, 115 F.2d 548; *Schad v. Twentieth Century-Fox Film Corp.*, C.C.A.3, 1943, 136 F.2d 991. The added sentence in Rule 41(b) incorporates the view of the Sixth, Seventh and Ninth Circuits. See also 3 *Moore's Federal Practice*, 1938, Cum.Supplement § 41.03, under "Page 3045"; Commentary, *The Motion to Dismiss in Non-Jury Cases*, 1946, 9 Fed.Rules Serv., Comm.Pg. 41b.14.

1963 Amendment

Under the present text of the second sentence of this subdivision, the motion for dismissal at the close of the plaintiff's evidence may be made in a case tried to a jury as well as in a case tried without a jury. But, when made in a jury-tried case, this motion overlaps the motion for a directed verdict under Rule 50(a), which is also available in the same situation. It has been held that the standard to be applied in deciding the Rule 41(b) motion at the close of the plaintiff's evidence in a jury-tried case is the same as that used upon a motion for a directed verdict made at the same stage; and, just as the court need not make findings pursuant to Rule 52(a) when it directs a verdict, so in a jury-tried case it may omit these findings in granting the Rule 41(b) motion. See generally *O'Brien v. Westinghouse Electric Corp.*, 293 F.2d 1, 5–10 (3d Cir. 1961).

As indicated by the discussion in the *O'Brien* case, the overlap has caused confusion. Accordingly, the second and third sentences of Rule 41(b) are amended to provide that the motion for dismissal at the close of the plaintiff's evidence shall apply only to nonjury cases (including cases tried with an advisory jury). Hereafter the correct motion in jury-tried cases will be the motion for a directed verdict. This involves no change of substance. It should be noted that the court upon a motion for a directed verdict may in appropriate circumstances deny that motion and grant instead a new trial, or a voluntary dismissal without prejudice under Rule 41(a)(2). See 6 *Moore's Federal Practice* ¶59.08[5] (2d ed. 1954); *cf. Cone v. West Virginia Pulp & Paper Co.,* 330 U.S. 212, 217, 67 S.Ct. 752, 91 L.Ed. 849 (1947).

The first sentence of Rule 41(b), providing for dismissal for failure to prosecute or to comply with the Rules or any order of court, and the general provisions of the last sentence remain applicable in jury as well as nonjury cases.

The amendment of the last sentence of Rule 41(b) indicates that a dismissal for lack of an indispensable party does not operate as an adjudication on the merits. Such a dismissal does not bar a new action, for it is based merely "on a plaintiff's failure to comply with a precondition requisite to the Court's going forward to determine the merits of his substantive claim." See *Costello v. United States,* 365 U.S. 265, 284–288, 81 S.Ct. 534, 5 L.Ed.2d 551 & n. 5 (1961); *Mallow v. Hinde,* 12 Wheat. (25 U.S.) 193, 6 L.Ed. 599 (1827); Clark, *Code Pleading* 602 (2d ed. 1947); *Restatement of Judgments* § 49, comm. a, b (1942). This amendment corrects an omission from the rule and is consistent with an earlier amendment, effective in 1948, adding "the defense of failure to join an indispensable party" to clause (1) of Rule 12(h).

1966 Amendment

The terminology is changed to accord with the amendment of Rule 19. See that amended rule and the Advisory Committee's Note thereto.

1968 Amendment

The amendment corrects an inadvertent error in the reference to amended Rule 23.

1987 Amendment

The amendment is technical. No substantive change is intended.

1991 Amendment

Language is deleted that authorized the use of this rule as a means of terminating a non-jury action on the merits when the plaintiff has failed to carry a burden of proof in presenting the plaintiff's case. The device is replaced by the new provisions of Rule 52(c), which authorize entry of judgment against the defendant as well as the plaintiff, and earlier than the close of the case of the party against whom judgment is rendered. A motion to dismiss under Rule 41 on the ground that a plaintiff's evidence is legally insufficient should now be treated as a motion for judgment on partial findings as provided in Rule 52(c).

Rule 42.   Consolidation; Separate Trials

(a) **Consolidation.** When actions involving a common question of law or fact are pending before the court, it may order a joint hearing or trial of any or all the matters in issue in the actions; it may order all the actions consolidated; and it may make such orders

concerning proceedings therein as may tend to avoid unnecessary costs or delay.

(b) **Separate Trials.** The court, in furtherance of convenience or to avoid prejudice, or when separate trials will be conducive to expedition and economy, may order a separate trial of any claim, cross-claim, counterclaim, or third-party claim, or of any separate issue or of any number of claims, cross-claims, counterclaims, third-party claims, or issues, always preserving inviolate the right of trial by jury as declared by the Seventh Amendment to the Constitution or as given by a statute of the United States.
(As amended Feb. 28, 1966, eff. July 1, 1966.)

ADVISORY COMMITTEE NOTES

1937 Adoption

Subdivision (a) is based upon U.S.C., Title 28, [former] § 734 (Orders to save costs; consolidation of causes of like nature) but in so far as the statute differs from this rule, it is modified.

For comparable statutes dealing with consolidation see Ark.Dig.Stat. (Crawford & Moses, 1921) § 1081; Calif.Code Civ.Proc. (Deering, 1937) § 1048; N.M.Stat.Ann. (Courtright, 1929) § 105–828; N.Y.C.P.A. (1937) §§ 96, 96a, and 97; American Judicature Society, Bulletin XIV, (1919) Art. 26.

For severance or separate trials see Calif.Code Civ.Proc. (Deering, 1937) § 1048; N.Y.C.P.A. (1937) § 96; American Judicature Society, Bulletin XIV (1919) Art. 3, § 2 and Art. 10, § 10. See also the third sentence of Equity Rule 29 (Defenses—How Presented) providing for discretionary separate hearing and disposition before trial of pleas in bar or abatement, and see also Rule 12(d) of these rules for preliminary hearings of defenses and objections.

For the entry of separate judgments, see Rule 54(b) (Judgment at Various Stages).

1966 Amendment

In certain suits in admiralty separation for trial of the issues of liability and damages (or of the extent of liability other than damages, such as salvage and general average) has been conducive to expedition and economy, especially because of the statutory right to interlocutory appeal in admiralty cases (which is of course preserved by these Rules). While separation of issues for trial is not to be routinely ordered, it is important that it be encouraged where experience has demonstrated its worth. Cf. Weinstein, *Routine Bifurcation of Negligence Trials,* 14 Vand. L.Rev. 831 (1961).

In cases (including some cases within the admiralty and maritime jurisdiction) in which the parties have a constitutional or statutory right of trial by jury, separation of issues may give rise to problems. See *e.g., United Air Lines, Inc. v. Wiener,* 286 F.2d 302 (9th Cir.1961). Accordingly, the proposed change in Rule 42 reiterates the mandate of Rule 38 respecting preservation of the right to jury trial.

Rule 43.   Taking of Testimony

(a) **Form.** In every trial, the testimony of witnesses shall be taken in open court, unless a federal law, these rules, the Federal Rules of Evidence, or other rules adopted by the Supreme Court provide otherwise. The court may, for good cause shown in compelling circumstances and upon appropriate safeguards, permit presentation of testimony in open court by contemporaneous transmission from a different location.

[(b), (c) Abrogated]

(d) Affirmation in Lieu of Oath. Whenever under these rules an oath is required to be taken, a solemn affirmation may be accepted in lieu thereof.

(e) Evidence on Motions. When a motion is based on facts not appearing of record the court may hear the matter on affidavits presented by the respective parties, but the court may direct that the matter be heard wholly or partly on oral testimony or deposition.

(f) Interpreters. The court may appoint an interpreter of its own selection and may fix the interpreter's reasonable compensation. The compensation shall be paid out of funds provided by law or by one or more of the parties as the court may direct, and may be taxed ultimately as costs, in the discretion of the court.

(As amended Feb. 28, 1966, eff. July 1, 1966; Nov. 20, 1972, and Dec. 18, 1972, eff. July 1, 1975; Mar. 2, 1987, eff. Aug. 1, 1987; Apr. 23, 1996, eff. Dec. 1, 1996.)

ADVISORY COMMITTEE NOTES
1937 Adoption

Note to Subdivision (a). The first sentence is a restatement of the substance of U.S.C., Title 28, § 635 (Proof in common-law actions), [former] § 637 (see §§ 2072, 2073) (Proof in equity and admiralty), and [former] Equity Rule 46 (Trial—Testimony Usually Taken in Open Court—Rulings on Objections to Evidence). This rule abolishes in patent and trademark actions, the practice under [former] Equity Rule 48 of setting forth in affidavits the testimony in chief of expert witnesses whose testimony is directed to matters of opinion. The second and third sentences on admissibility of evidence and Subdivision (b) on contradiction and cross-examination modify U.S.C., Title 28, § 725 (now 1652) (Laws of states as rules of decision) insofar as that statute has been construed to prescribe conformity to state rules of evidence. Compare Callahan and Ferguson, *Evidence and the New Federal Rules of Civil Procedure*, 45 Yale L.J. 622 (1936), and *Same: 2*, 47 Yale L.J. 195 (1937). The last sentence modifies to the extent indicated U.S.C., Title 28, [former] § 631 (Competency of witnesses governed by State laws).

Note to Subdivision (b). See 4 *Wigmore on Evidence* (2d ed., 1923) § 1885 et seq.

Note to Subdivision (c). See [former] Equity Rule 46 (Trial—Testimony Usually Taken in Open Court-Rulings on Objections to Evidence). With the last sentence compare *Dowagiac v. Lochren*, 143 Fed. 211 (C.C.A. 8th, 1906). See also *Blease v. Garlington*, 92 U.S. 1, 23 L.Ed. 521 (1876); *Nelson v. United States*, 201 U.S. 92, 114, 26 S.Ct. 358, 50 L.Ed. 673 (1906); *Unkle v. Wills*, 281 Fed. 29 (C.C.A. 8th, 1922).

See Rule 61 for harmless error in either the admission or exclusion of evidence.

Note to Subdivision (d). See [former] Equity Rule 78 (Affirmation in Lieu of Oath) and U.S.C., Title 1, § 1 (Words importing singular number, masculine gender, etc.; extended application), providing for affirmation in lieu of oath.

Supplementary Note on Advisory Committee Regarding Rules 43 and 44

Note. These rules have been criticized and suggested improvements offered by commentators. 1 *Wigmore on Evidence*, 3d ed. 1940, 200–204; Green, *The Admissibility of Evidence Under the Federal Rules*, 1941, 55 Harv.L.Rev. 197. Cases indicate, however, that the rule is working better than these commentators had expected. *Boerner v. United States*, C.C.A.2d, 1941, 117 F.2d 387, cert. den., 1941, 313 U.S. 587, 61 S.Ct. 1120; *Mosson v. Liberty Fast Freight Co.*, C.C.A.2d, 1942, 124 F.2d, 448; *Hartford Accident & Indemnity Co. v. Olivier*, C.C.A. 5th, 1941, 123 F.2d 709; *Anzano v. Metropolitan Life Ins. Co. of New York*, C.C.A.3d, 1941, 118 F.2d 430; *Franzen v. E. I. DuPont De Nemours & Co.*, C.C.A.3d, 1944, 146 F.2d 837; *Fakouri v. Cadais*, C.C.A. 5th, 1945, 147 F.2d 667; *In re C. & P. Co.*, S.D.Cal.1945, 63 F.Supp. 400, 408. But cf. *United States v. Aluminum Co. of America*, S.D.N.Y.1938, 1 Fed.Rules Serv. 43a.3, Case 1; Note, 1946, 46 Col.L.Rev. 267. While consideration of a comprehensive and detailed set of rules of evidence seems very desirable, it has not been feasible for the Committee so far to undertake this important task. Such consideration should include the adaptability to federal practice of all or parts of the proposed Code of Evidence of the American Law Institute. See Armstrong, *Proposed Amendments to Federal Rules of Civil Procedure*, 4 F.R.D. 124, 137–138.

1966 Amendment

Note to Subdivision (f). This new subdivision [subdivision (f)] authorizes the court to appoint interpreters (including interpreters for the deaf), to provide for their compensation, and to tax the compensation as costs. Compare proposed subdivision (b) of Rule 28 of the Federal Rules of Criminal Procedure.

1972 Amendment

Rule 43, entitled Evidence, has heretofore served as the basic rule of evidence for civil cases in federal courts. Its very general provisions are superseded by the detailed provisions of the new Rules of Evidence. The original title and many of the provisions of the rule are, therefore, no longer appropriate.

Subdivision (a). The provision for taking testimony in open court is not duplicated in the Rules of Evidence and is retained. Those dealing with admissibility of evidence and competency of witnesses, however, are no longer needed or appropriate since those topics are covered at large in the Rules of Evidence. They are accordingly deleted. The language is broadened, however, to take account of acts of Congress dealing with the taking of testimony, as well as of the Rules of Evidence and any other rules adopted by the Supreme Court.

Subdivision (b). The subdivision is no longer needed or appropriate since the matters with which it deals are treated in the Rules of Evidence. The use of leading questions, both generally and in the interrogation of an adverse party or witness identified with him, is the subject of Evidence Rule 611(c). Who may impeach is treated in Evidence Rule 601 [sic; probably means 607], and scope of cross-examination is covered in Evidence Rule 611(b). The subdivision is accordingly deleted.

Subdivision (c). Offers of proof and making a record of excluded evidence are treated in Evidence Rule 103. The subdivision is no longer needed or appropriate and is deleted.

1987 Amendment

The amendment is technical. No substantive change is intended.

1996 Amendment

Rule 43(a) is revised to conform to the style conventions adopted for simplifying the present Civil Rules. The only intended changes of meaning are described below.

The requirement that testimony be taken "orally" is deleted. The deletion makes it clear that testimony of a witness may be given in open court by other means if the witness is not able to communicate orally. Writing or sign language are common examples. The development of advanced technology may enable testimony to be given by other means. A witness unable to sign or write by hand may be able to communicate through a computer or similar device.

Contemporaneous transmission of testimony from a different location is permitted only on showing good cause in compelling circumstances. The importance of presenting live testimony in court cannot be forgotten. The very ceremony of trial and the presence of the factfinder may exert a powerful force for truthtelling. The opportunity to judge the demeanor of a witness face-to-face is accorded great value in our tradition. Transmission cannot be justified merely by showing that it is inconvenient for the witness to attend the trial.

The most persuasive showings of good cause and compelling circumstances are likely to arise when a witness is unable to attend trial for unexpected reasons, such as accident or illness, but remains able to testify from a different place. Contemporaneous transmission may be better than an attempt to reschedule the trial, particularly if there is a risk that other—and perhaps more important—witnesses might not be available at a later time.

Other possible justifications for remote transmission must be approached cautiously. Ordinarily depositions, including video depositions, provide a superior means of securing the testimony of a witness who is beyond the reach of a trial subpoena, or of resolving difficulties in scheduling a trial that can be attended by all witnesses. Deposition procedures ensure the opportunity of all parties to be represented while the witness is testifying. An unforeseen need for the testimony of a remote witness that arises during trial, however, may establish good cause and compelling circumstances. Justification is particularly likely if the need arises from the interjection of new issues during trial or from the unexpected inability to present testimony as planned from a different witness.

Good cause and compelling circumstances may be established with relative ease if all parties agree that testimony should be presented by transmission. The court is not bound by a stipulation, however, and can insist on live testimony.

Rejection of the parties' agreement will be influenced, among other factors, by the apparent importance of the testimony in the full context of the trial.

A party who could reasonably foresee the circumstances offered to justify transmission of testimony will have special difficulty in showing good cause and the compelling nature of the circumstances. Notice of a desire to transmit testimony from a different location should be given as soon as the reasons are known, to enable other parties to arrange a deposition, or to secure an advance ruling on transmission so as to know whether to prepare to be present with the witness while testifying.

No attempt is made to specify the means of transmission that may be used. Audio transmission without video images may be sufficient in some circumstances, particularly as to less important testimony. Video transmission ordinarily should be preferred when the cost is reasonable in relation to the matters in dispute, the means of the parties, and the circumstances that justify transmission. Transmission that merely produces the equivalent of a written statement ordinarily should not be used.

Safeguards must be adopted that ensure accurate identification of the witness and that protect against influence by persons present with the witness. Accurate transmission likewise must be assured.

Other safeguards should be employed to ensure that advance notice is given to all parties of foreseeable circumstances that may lead the proponent to offer testimony by transmission. Advance notice is important to protect the opportunity to argue for attendance of the witness at trial. Advance notice also ensures an opportunity to depose the witness, perhaps by video record, as a means of supplementing transmitted testimony.

HISTORICAL NOTES

References in Text

The Federal Rules of Evidence, referred to in subd. (a), are set out in this title.

Effective Date of Amendments Proposed November 20, 1972, and December 18, 1972

Amendments of this rule embraced by orders entered by the Supreme Court of the United States on November 20, 1972, and December 18, 1972, effective on the 180th day beginning after January 2, 1975, see section 3 of Pub.L. 93–595, Jan. 2, 1975, 88 Stat. 1959, set out as a note under section 2071 of Title 28.

Rule 44. Proof of Official Record

(a) Authentication.

(1) Domestic. An official record kept within the United States, or any state, district, or commonwealth, or within a territory subject to the administrative or judicial jurisdiction of the United States, or an entry therein, when admissible for any purpose, may be evidenced by an official publication thereof or by a copy attested by the officer having the legal custody of the record, or by the officer's deputy, and accompanied by a certificate that such officer has the custody. The certificate may be made by a judge of a court of record of the district or political subdivision in which the record is kept, authenticated by the seal of the court, or may be made by any public officer having a seal of office and having official duties in the district or political subdivision in which the record is kept, authenticated by the seal of the officer's office.

(2) Foreign. A foreign official record, or an entry therein, when admissible for any purpose, may be evidenced by an official publication thereof; or a copy thereof, attested by a person authorized to make the attestation, and accompanied by a final certification as to the genuineness of the signature and official position (i) of the attesting person, or (ii) of any foreign official whose certificate of genuineness of signature and official position relates to the attestation or is in a chain of certificates of genuineness of signature and official position relating to the attestation. A final certification may be made by a secretary of embassy or legation, consul general, vice consul, or consular agent of the United States, or a diplomatic or consular official of the foreign country assigned or accredited to the United States. If reasonable opportunity has been given to all parties to investigate the authenticity and accuracy of the documents, the court may, for good cause shown, (i) admit an attested copy without final certification or (ii) permit the foreign official record to be evidenced by an attested summary with or without a final certification. The final certification is unnecessary if the record and the attestation are certified as provided in a treaty or convention to which the United States and the foreign country in which the official record is located are parties.

(b) Lack of Record. A written statement that after diligent search no record or entry of a specified tenor is found to exist in the records designated by the statement, authenticated as provided in subdivision (a)(1) of this rule in the case of a domestic record, or complying with the requirements of subdivision (a)(2) of this rule for a summary in the case of a foreign record, is admissible as evidence that the records contain no such record or entry.

(c) Other Proof. This rule does not prevent the proof of official records or of entry or lack of entry therein by any other method authorized by law.
(As amended Feb. 28, 1966, eff. July 1, 1966; Mar. 2, 1987, eff. Aug. 1, 1987; Apr. 30, 1991, eff. Dec. 1, 1991.)

ADVISORY COMMITTEE NOTES

1937 Adoption

This rule provides a simple and uniform method of proving public records, and entry or lack of entry therein, in all cases including those specifically provided for by statutes of the United States. Such statutes are not superseded, however, and proof may also be made according to their provisions whenever they differ from this rule. Some of those statutes are:

U.S.C., Title 28 [former sections]:
§ 661[now 1733] (Copies of department or corporation records and papers; admissibility; seal)
§ 662[now 1733] (Same; in office of General Counsel of the Treasury)
§ 663[now 1733] (Instruments and papers of Comptroller of Currency; admissibility)
§ 664[now 1733] (Organization certificates of national banks; admissibility)
§ 665[now 1733] (Transcripts from books of Treasury in suits against delinquents; admissibility)
§ 666[now 1733] (Same; certificate by Secretary or Assistant Secretary)
§ 670[now 1743] (Admissibility of copies of statements of demands by Post Office Department)
§ 671[now 1733] (Admissibility of copies of post office records and statement of accounts)
§ 672[former] (Admissibility of copies of records in General Land Office)
§ 673[now 1744] (Admissibility of copies of records, and so forth, of Patent Office)
§ 674[now 1745] (Copies of foreign letters patent as prima facie evidence)
§ 675[former] (Copies of specifications and drawings of patents admissible)
§ 676[now 1736] (Extracts from Journals of Congress admissible when injunction of secrecy removed)
§ 677[now 1740] (Copies of records in offices of United States consuls admissible)
§ 678[former] (Books and papers in certain district courts)
§ 679[former] (Records in clerks' offices, western district of North Carolina)
§ 680[former] (Records in clerks' offices of former district of California)
§ 681[now 1734] (Original records lost or destroyed; certified copy admissible)
§ 682[now 1734] (Same; when certified copy not obtainable)
§ 685[now 1735] (Same; certified copy of official papers)
§ 687[now 1738] (Authentication of legislative acts; proof of judicial proceedings of State)
§ 688[now 1739] (Proofs of records in offices not pertaining to courts)
§ 689[now 1742] (Copies of foreign records relating to land titles)
§ 695[now 1732] (Writings and records made in regular course of business; admissibility)
§ 695e[now 1741] (Foreign documents on record in public offices; certification)

U.S.C., Title 1:
§ 30[now 112] (Statutes at large; contents; admissibility in evidence)
§ 30a[now 113] ("Little and Brown's" edition of laws and treaties competent evidence of Acts of Congress)
§ 54[now 204] (Codes and supplements as establishing prima facie the laws of United States and District of Columbia, etc.)
§ 55[now 208] (Copies of supplements to Code of Laws of United States and of District of Columbia Code and supplements; conclusive evidence of original)

U.S.C., Title 5:

§ 490[former] (Records of Department of Interior; authenticated copies as evidence)

U.S.C., Title 6:

§ 7[now Title 31, § 9306] (Surety Companies as sureties; appointment of agents; service of process)

U.S.C., Title 8:

§ 9a[see 1435(c)] (Citizenship of children of persons naturalized under certain laws; repatriation of native-born women married to aliens prior to September 22, 1922; copies of proceedings)

§ 356[see 1443] (Regulations for execution of naturalization laws; certified copies of papers as evidence)

§ 399b(d)[see 1443] (Certifications of naturalization records; authorization; admissibility as evidence)

U.S.C., Title 11:

§ 44(d), (e), (f), (g)[former] (Bankruptcy court proceedings and orders as evidence)

§ 204[former] (Extensions extended, etc.; evidence of confirmation)

§ 207(j)[former] (Corporate reorganizations; certified copy of decree as evidence)

U.S.C., Title 15:

§ 127 (Trade-mark records in Patent Office; copies as evidence)

U.S.C., Title 20:

§ 52 (Smithsonian Institution; evidence of title to site and buildings)

U.S.C., Title 25:

§ 6 (Bureau of Indian Affairs; seal; authenticated and certified documents; evidence)

U.S.C., Title 31:

§ 46[now 704] (Laws governing General Accounting Office; copies of books, records, etc., thereof as evidence)

U.S.C., Title 38:

§ 11g[see 202] (Seal of Veterans' Administration; authentication of copies of records)

U.S.C., Title 40:

§ 238 [former 44 U.S.C.A. § 300h] (National Archives; seal; reproduction of archives; fee; admissibility in evidence of reproductions)

§ 270c [see now 40 U.S.C.A. § 3133(a)] (Bonds of contractors for public works; right of person furnishing labor or material to copy of bond)

U.S.C., Title 43:

§§ 57–59 (Copies of land surveys, etc., in certain states and districts admissible as evidence)

§ 83 (General Land Office registers and receivers; transcripts of records as evidence)

U.S.C., Title 46:

§ 823 (Records of Maritime Commission; copies; publication of reports; evidence)

U.S.C., Title 47:

§ 154(m) (Federal Communications Commission; copies of reports and decisions as evidence)

§ 412 (Documents filed with Federal Communications Commission as public records; prima facie evidence; confidential records)

U.S.C., Title 49:

§ 14(3)[now 10310] (Interstate Commerce Commission reports and decisions; printing and distribution of copies)

§ 16(13)[now 10303(b)] (Copies of schedules, tariffs, etc. filed with Interstate Commerce Commission as evidence)

§ 19a(i)[now 10785(c)] (Valuation of property of carriers by Interstate Commerce Commission; final published valuations as evidence)

Supplementary Note of Advisory Committee Regarding Rules 43 and 44.

For supplementary note of Advisory Committee on this rule, see note under Rule 43.

1966 Amendment

Note to Subdivision (a)(1). These provisions on proof of official records kept within the United States are similar in substance to those heretofore appearing in Rule 44. There is a more exact description of the geographical areas covered. An official record kept in one of the areas enumerated qualifies for proof under subdivision (a)(1) even though it is not a United States official record. For example, an official record kept in one of these areas by a government in exile falls within subdivision (a)(1). It also falls within subdivision (a)(2) which may be availed of alternatively. Cf. *Banco de Espana v. Federal Reserve Bank*, 114 F.2d 438 (2d Cir. 1940).

Note to Subdivision (a)(2). Foreign official records may be proved, as heretofore, by means of official publications thereof. See *United States v. Aluminum Co. of America*, 1 F.R.D. 71 (S.D.N.Y.1939). Under this rule, a document that, on its face, appears to be an official publication, is admissible, unless a party opposing its admission into evidence shows that it lacks that character.

The rest of subdivision (a)(2) aims to provide greater clarity, efficiency, and flexibility in the procedure for authenticating copies of foreign official records.

The reference to attestation by "the officer having the legal custody of the record," hitherto appearing in Rule 44, has been found inappropriate for official records kept in foreign countries where the assumed relation between custody and the authority to attest does not obtain. See 2B Barron & Holtzoff, Federal Practice & Procedure § 992 (Wright ed. 1961). Accordingly it is provided that an attested copy may be obtained from any person authorized by the law of the foreign country to make the attestation without regard to whether he is charged with responsibility for maintaining the record or keeping it in his custody.

Under Rule 44 a United States foreign service officer has been called on to certify to the authority of the foreign official attesting the copy as well as the genuineness of his signature and his official position. See Schlesinger, *Comparative Law 57* (2d ed. 1959); Smit. *International Aspects of Federal Civil Procedure*, 61 Colum.L.Rev. 1031, 1063 (1961); 22 C.F.R. § 92.41(a), (e) (1958). This has created practical difficulties. For example, the question of the authority of the foreign officer might raise issues of foreign law which were beyond the knowledge of the United States officer. The difficulties are met under the amended rule by eliminating the element of the authority of the attesting foreign official from the scope of the certifying process, and by specifically permitting use of the chain-certificate method. Under this method, it is sufficient if the original attestation purports to have been issued by an authorized person and is accompanied by a certificate of another foreign official whose certificate may in turn be followed by that of a foreign official of higher rank. The process continues until a foreign official is reached as to whom the United States foreign service official (or a diplomatic or consular officer of the foreign country assigned or accredited to the United States) has adequate information upon which to base a "final certification." See *New York Life Ins. Co. v. Aronson,* 38 F.Supp. 687 (W.D.Pa.1941); 22 C.F.R. § 92.37 (1958).

The final certification (a term used in contradistinction to the certificates prepared by the foreign officials in a chain) relates to the incumbency and genuineness of signature of the foreign official who attested the copy of the record or, where the chain-certificate method is used, of a foreign official whose certificate appears in the chain, whether that certificate is the last in the chain or not. A final certification may be prepared on the basis of material on file in the consulate or any other satisfactory information.

Although the amended rule will generally facilitate proof of foreign official records, it is recognized that in some situations it may be difficult or even impossible to satisfy the basic requirements of the rule. There may be no United States consul in a particular foreign country; the foreign officials may not cooperate, peculiarities may exist or arise hereafter in the law or practice of a foreign country. See *United States v. Grabina,* 119 F.2d 863 (2d Cir. 1941); and, generally, Jones, *International Judicial Assistance: Procedural Chaos and a Program for Reform,* 62 Yale L.J. 515, 548–49 (1953). Therefore the final sentence of subdivision (a)(2) provides the court with discretion to admit an attested copy of a record without a final certification, or an attested summary of a record with or without a final certification. See Rep. of Comm. on Comparative Civ.Proc. & Prac., Proc. A.B.A., Sec. Int'l & Comp.L. 123, 130–31 (1952); Model Code of Evidence §§ 517, 519 (1942). This relaxation should be permitted only when it is shown that the party has been unable to satisfy the basic requirements of the amended rule despite his reasonable efforts. Moreover it is specially provided that the parties must be given a reasonable opportunity in these cases to examine into the authenticity and accuracy of the copy or summary.

Note to Subdivision (b). This provision relating to proof of lack of record is accommodated to the changes made in subdivision (a).

Note to Subdivision (c). The amendment insures that international agreements of the United States are unaffected by the rule. Several consular conventions contain provisions for reception of copies or summaries of foreign official records. See, e.g., Consular Conv. with Italy, May 8, 1878, art. X, 20 Stat. 725, T.S. No. 178 (Dept. State 1878). See also 28 U.S.C. §§ 1740–42, 1745; *Fakouri v. Cadais,* 149 F.2d 321 (5th Cir.1945), cert. denied 326 U.S. 742 (1945); 5 *Moore's Federal Practice,* par. 44.05 (2d ed. 1951).

1987 Amendment

The amendments are technical. No substantive change is intended.

1991 Amendment

The amendment to paragraph (a)(1) strikes the references to specific territories, two of which are no longer subject to the jurisdiction of the United States, and adds a generic term to describe governments having a relationship with the United States such that their official records should be treated as domestic records.

The amendment to paragraph (a)(2) adds a sentence to dispense with the final certification by diplomatic officers when the United States and the foreign country where the record is located are parties to a treaty or convention that abolishes or displaces the requirement. In that event the treaty or convention is to be followed. This changes the former procedure for authenticating foreign official records only with respect to records from countries that are parties to the Hague Convention Abolishing the Requirement of Legalization for Foreign Public Documents. Moreover, it does not affect the former practice of attesting the records, but only changes the method of certifying the attestation.

The Hague Public Documents Convention provides that the requirement of a final certification is abolished and replaced with a model *apostille,* which is to be issued by officials of the country where the records are located. See Hague Public Documents Convention, Arts. 2–4. The *apostille* certifies the signature, official position, and seal of the attesting officer. The authority who issues the *apostille* must maintain a register or card index showing the serial number of the *apostille* and other relevant information recorded on it. A foreign court can then check the serial number and information on the *apostille* with the issuing authority in order to guard against the use of fraudulent *apostilles.* This system provides a reliable method for maintaining the integrity of the authentication process, and the *apostille* can be accorded greater weight than the normal authentication procedure because foreign officials are more likely to know the precise capacity under their law of the attesting officer than would an American official. See generally Comment, *The United States and the Hague Convention Abolishing the Requirement of Legalization for Foreign Public Documents,* 11 HARV. INT'L L.J. 476, 482, 488 (1970).

TREATIES AND CONVENTIONS

CONVENTION ABOLISHING THE REQUIREMENT OF LEGALISATION FOR FOREIGN PUBLIC DOCUMENTS

The States signatory to the present Convention,

Desiring to abolish the requirement of diplomatic or consular legalisation for foreign public documents,

Have resolved to conclude a Convention to this effect and have agreed upon the following provisions:

ARTICLE 1

The present Convention shall apply to public documents which have been executed in the territory of one contracting State and which have to be produced in the territory of another contracting State.

For the purposes of the present Convention, the following are deemed to be public documents:

 (a) Documents emanating from an authority or an official connected with the courts or tribunals of the State, including those emanating from a public prosecutor, a clerk of a court or a process server ("huissier de justice");

 (b) Administrative documents;

(c) Notarial acts;

(d) Official certificates which are placed on documents signed by persons in their private capacity, such as official certificates recording the registration of a document or the fact that it was in existence on a certain date and official and notarial authentications of signatures.

However, the present Convention shall not apply:

(a) To documents executed by diplomatic or consular agents;

(b) To administrative documents dealing directly with commercial or customs operations.

ARTICLE 2

Each contracting State shall exempt from legalisation documents to which the present Convention applies and which have to be produced in its territory. For the purposes of the present Convention, legalisation means only the formality by which the diplomatic or consular agents of the country in which the document has to be produced certify the authenticity of the signature, the capacity in which the person signing the document has acted and, where appropriate, the identity of the seal or stamp which it bears.

ARTICLE 3

The only formality that may be required in order to certify the authenticity of the signature, the capacity in which the person signing the document has acted and, where appropriate, the identity of the seal or stamp which it bears, is the addition of the certificate described in Article 4, issued by the competent authority of the State from which the document emanates.

However, the formality mentioned in the preceding paragraph cannot be required when either the laws, regulations, or practice in force in the State where the document is produced or an agreement between two or more contracting States have abolished or simplified it, or exempt the document itself from legalisation.

ARTICLE 4

The certificate referred to in the first paragraph of Article 3 shall be placed on the document itself or on an "allonge"; it shall be in the form of the model annexed to the present Convention.

It may, however, be drawn up in the official language of the authority which issues it. The standard terms appearing therein may be in a second language also. The title "Apostille (Convention de La Haye du 5 octobre 1961)" shall be in the French language.

ARTICLE 5

The certificate shall be issued at the request of the person who has signed the document or of any bearer.

When properly filled in, it will certify the authenticity of the signature, the capacity in which the person signing the document has acted and, where appropriate, the identity of the seal or stamp which the document bears.

The signature, seal and stamp on the certificate are exempt from all certification.

ARTICLE 6

Each contracting State shall designate by reference to their official function, the authorities who are competent to issue the certificate referred to in the first paragraph of Article 3.

It shall give notice of such designation to the Ministry of Foreign Affairs of the Netherlands at the time it deposits its instrument of ratification or of accession or its declaration of extension. It shall also give notice of any change in the designated authorities.

ARTICLE 7

Each of the authorities designated in accordance with Article 6 shall keep a register or card index in which it shall record the certificates issued, specifying:

(a) The number and date of the certificate,

(b) The name of the person signing the public document and the capacity in which he has acted, or in the case of unsigned documents, the name of the authority which has affixed the seal or stamp.

At the request of any interested person, the authority which has issued the certificate shall verify whether the particulars in the certificate correspond with those in the register or card index.

ARTICLE 8

When a treaty, convention or agreement between two or more contracting States contains provisions which subject the certification of a signature, seal or stamp to certain formalities, the present Convention will only override such provisions if those formalities are more rigorous than the formality referred to in Articles 3 and 4.

ARTICLE 9

Each contracting State shall take the necessary steps to prevent the performance of legalisations by its diplomatic or consular agents in cases where the present Convention provides for exemption.

ARTICLE 10

The present Convention shall be open for signature by the States represented at the Ninth session of the Hague Conference on Private International Law and Iceland, Ireland, Liechtenstein and Turkey.

It shall be ratified, and the instruments of ratification shall be deposited with the Ministry of Foreign Affairs of the Netherlands.

ARTICLE 11

The present Convention shall enter into force on the sixtieth day after the deposit of the third instrument of ratification referred to in the second paragraph of Article 10.

The Convention shall enter into force for each signatory State which ratifies subsequently on the sixtieth day after the deposit of its instrument of ratification.

ARTICLE 12

Any State not referred to in Article 10 may accede to the present Convention after it has entered into force in accordance with the first paragraph of Article 11. The instrument of accession shall be deposited with the Ministry of Foreign Affairs of the Netherlands.

Such accession shall have effect only as regards the relations between the acceding State and those contracting States which have not raised an objection to its accession in the six months after the receipt of the notification referred to in sub-paragraph (d) of Article 15. Any such objection shall be notified to the Ministry of Foreign Affairs of the Netherlands.

The Convention shall enter into force as between the acceding State and the States which have raised no objection to its accession on the sixtieth day after the expiry of the period of six months mentioned in the preceding paragraph.

ARTICLE 13

Any State may, at the time of signature, ratification or accession, declare that the present Convention shall extend to all the territories for the international relations of which it is responsible, or to one or more of them. Such a declaration shall take effect on the date of entry into force of the Convention for the State concerned.

At any time thereafter, such extension shall be notified to the Ministry of Foreign Affairs of the Netherlands.

When the declaration of extension is made by a State which has signed and ratified, the Convention shall enter into force for the territories concerned in accordance with Article 11. When the declaration of extension is made by a State which has acceded, the Convention shall enter into force for the territories concerned in accordance with Article 12.

ARTICLE 14

The present Convention shall remain in force for five years from the date of its entry into force in accordance with the first paragraph of Article 11, even for States which have ratified it or acceded to it subsequently.

If there has been no denunciation, the Convention shall be renewed tacitly every five years.

Any denunciation shall be notified to the Ministry of Foreign Affairs of the Netherlands at least six months before the end of the five year period.

It may be limited to certain of the territories to which the Convention applies.

The denunciation will only have effect as regards the State which has notified it. The Convention shall remain in force for the other contracting States.

ARTICLE 15

The Ministry of Foreign Affairs of the Netherlands shall give notice to the States referred to in Article 10, and to the States which have acceded in accordance with Article 12, of the following:

(a) The notifications referred to in the second paragraph of Article 6;

(b) The signatures and ratifications referred to in Article 10;

(c) The date on which the present Convention enters into force in accordance with the first paragraph of Article 11;

(d) The accessions and objections referred to in Article 12 and the date on which such accessions take effect;

(e) The extensions referred to in Article 13 and the date on which they take effect;

(f) The denunciations referred to in the third paragraph of Article 14.

In witness whereof the undersigned, being duly authorised thereto, have signed the present Convention.

Done at The Hague the 5th October 1961, in French and in English, the French text prevailing in case of divergence between the two texts, in a single copy which shall be deposited in the archives of the Government of the Netherlands, and of which a certified copy shall be sent, through the diplomatic channel, to each of the States represented at the Ninth session of the Hague Conference on Private International Law and also to Iceland, Ireland, Liechtenstein and Turkey.

[Signatures omitted.]

ANNEX TO THE CONVENTION
Model of certificate

The certificate will be in the form of a square with sides at least 9 centimetres long

APOSTILLE
(Convention de La Haye du 5 octobre 1961)

1. Country: . . . .
   This public document
2. has been signed by . . . .
3. acting in the capacity of . . . .
4. bears the seal/stamp of . . . .
   . . . .
                          Certified
5. at . . . .   6.   the . . . .
7. by . . . .
8. N° . . . .
9. Seal/stamp: 10.   Signature:
   . . . .

Convention abolishing the requirement of legalization for foreign public documents, with annex. Done at The Hague October 5, 1961; entered into force for the United States October 15, 1981. (TIAS 10072; 527 UNTS 189).

Parties to the Convention

In addition to the United States, the following are parties to the Convention:

Contracting State	Territories to which Extended
Andorra [1]	
Antigua and Barbuda	
Argentina [1a]	
Armenia	
Australia [1b]	All the territories for the international relations of which it is responsible
Austria	
Bahamas	
Barbados	
Belarus [1c]	
Belgium	
Belize [1d]	
Bosnia-Herzegovina	

Contracting State	Territories to which Extended
Botswana	
Brunei	
China, Hong Kong Special Administrative Region only 1e	
Croatia	
Cyprus	
El Salvador	
Fiji	
Finland	
France	Entire territory of the French Republic
	Anglo-French Condominium of the New Hebrides (Vanuatu)*
Germany, Federal Republic of 1f	
Greece	
Hungary	
Israel	
Italy	
Japan	
Latvia	
Lesotho	
Liberia 1g	
Liechtenstein	
Lithuania	
Luxembourg	
Macedonia, former Yugoslav Republic of	
Malawi	
Malta	
Marshall Islands 2	
Mauritius	
Mexico	
Netherlands	the Kingdom in Europe
	Netherlands Antilles and Aruba
Norway	
Panama	
Portugal	Angola*
	Mozambique*
	and other overseas departments
Russian Federation 3	
San Marino	
Seychelles	
Slovenia	
South Africa	
Spain	
St. Kitts & Nevis	
Suriname	
Swaziland	
Switzerland	
Tonga	
Turkey	
United Kingdom of Great Britain and Northern Ireland	
	Anguilla
	the Bailiwick of Guernsey
	Barbados*
	Bermuda
	British Antarctic Territory
	British Guiana (Guyana)*
	British Solomon Islands Protectorate (Solomon Islands)*
	Cayman Islands
	Dominica*
	Falkland Islands
	Gibraltar
	Gilbert and Ellice Islands (Kiribati/Tuvalu)*
	Grenada*
	the Isle of Man
	Jersey
	Montserrat
	New Hebrides (Vanuatu)*

Contracting State	Territories to which Extended
	St. Helena
	Saint Christopher and Nevis*
	Saint Lucia*
	Saint Vincent*
	Southern Rhodesia (Zimbabwe)*
	Turks and Caicos Islands
	British Virgin Islands
United States	Those territories for the foreign relations of which the United States is responsible
Yugoslavia 4	

* Now independent and no confirmation issued by the newly independent country that the Convention is deemed to apply.

1 *Notification in conformity with Article 15 of the Convention*

On 15 April 1996 the Ministry of Foreign Affairs of the Kingdom of the Netherlands received the instrument of accession of the Principality of Andorra to the above-mentioned Convention in accordance with Article 12, first paragraph, of the Convention.

In accordance with the terms of Article 12, paragraph 1, of the Convention any State not mentioned in Article 10 may accede to this Convention. In accordance with Article 12, paragraph 2, such accession shall have effect only as regards the relations between the Principality of Andorra and those contracting States (at present: Anitgua and Barbuda, Argentina, Armenia, Australia, Austria, Bahamas, Barbados, Belgium, Belize, Byelorus, Bosnia and Herzegovina, Botswana, Brunei, Darussalam, Croatia, Cyprus, El Salvador, Fiji, Finland, France, Germany, Greece, Hungary, Israel, Italy, Japan, the Kingdom of the Netherlands, Lesotho, Liechtenstein, Luxembourg, the former Yugoslav Republic of Macedonia, Malawi, Malta, Marshall Islands, Mauritius, Mexico, Norway, Panama, Portugal, Russia, Saint Kitts and Nevis, San Marino, Seychelles, Slovenia, South Africa, Spain, Surinam, Swaziland, Switerland, Tonga, Turkey, the United Kingdom of Great Britain and Northern Ireland and the United States of America) which have not raised an objection to its accession in the six months after receipt of this notification. For practical reasons this six months' period will run from 1 May 1996 till 1 November 1996.

1a In accordance with Article 12, paragraph 1, the instrument of accession by the Argentine Republic to the above-mentioned Convention was deposited with the Ministry of Foreign Affairs of the Kingdom of the Netherlands on 8 May 1987.

The instrument of accession contains the declaration annexed to this notification.

"In accordance with the terms of Article 12, paragraph 1, of the Convention any State not mentioned in Article 10 may accede to this Convention. In accordance with Article 12, paragraph 2, such accession shall have effect only as regards the relations between the Argentine Republic and those contracting States (at present: Antigua and Barbuda, Austria, Bahamas, Belgium, Botswana, Brunei Darussalam, Cyprus, Fiji, Finland, France, the Federal Republic of Germany, Greece, Hungary, Israel, Italy, Japan, Lesotho, Liechtenstein, Luxembourg, Malawi, Malta, Mauritius, the Kingdom of the Netherlands, Norway, Portugal, Seychelles, Spain, Surinam, Swaziland, Switzerland, Tonga, Turkey, the United Kingdom of Great Britain and Northern Ireland, the United States of America and Yugoslavia) which have not raised an objection to its accession in the six months after the receipt of this notification. For practical reasons this six months' period will extend from 20 June 1987 till 20 December 1987."

"The Argentine Republic rejects the extension of the application of the Convention Abolishing the Requirement of Legalization for Foreign Public Documents, concluded at The Hague on October 5, 1961, to the Malvinas, South Georgia, and South Sandwich Islands, as notified by the United Kingdom of Great Britain and Northern Ireland to the Ministry of Foreign Affairs of the Kingdom of the Netherlands on February 24, 1965, and reaffirms its sovereign rights over the Malvinas, South Georgia, and South Sandwich Islands, which form an integral part of its national territory.

"The United Nations General Assembly has adopted resolutions 2065(XX), 3160(XXVIII), 31/49, 37/9, 38/12, 39/6, 40/21, and 41/40, acknowledging the existence of a sovereignty dispute with respect to the question of the Malvinas Islands, and urging the Argentine Republic and the United Kingdom of Great Britain and Northern Ireland to continue negotiating in order to reach a peaceful and definitive solution to the dispute as soon as possible, through the good offices of the United Nations Secretary General, who is to inform the General Assembly of the progress achieved.

"The Argentine Republic also rejects the extension of the Convention, notified on the same date as above, to the so-called "British Antarctic Territory," and thereby reaffirms the rights of the Republic to the Argentine Antarctic Sector, including those relating to its corresponding maritime sovereignty or jurisdiction. It further recalls the safeguards on claims of territorial sovereignty in Antarctica set forth in Article IV of the Antarctic Treaty, done at Washington on December 1, 1959, to which the Argentine Republic and the United Kingdom of Great Britain and Northern Ireland are parties." (Translation provided by the Division of Language Services, Department of State)

1b *Notification in conformity with Article 15 of the Convention*

On 11 July 1994 Australia deposited its instrument of accession at the Ministry of Foreign Affairs of the Kingdom of the Netherlands to the above-mentioned Convention in accordance with Article 12, first paragraph, of the Convention.

Australia made the following declarations:

"—pursuant to the second paragraph of Article 6, the Secretary to the Department of Foreign Affairs and Trade of the Commonwealth will be its competent authority for the purpose of that Article; and

—pursuant to Article 13, the Convention shall extend to all the territories for the international relations of which it is responsible."

In accordance with the terms of Article 12, paragraph 1, of the Convention any State not mentioned in Article 10 may accede to this Convention. In accordance with Article 12, paragraph 2, such accession shall have effect only as regards the relations between Australia and those contracting States (at present: Antigua and Barbuda, Argentina, Armenia, Austria, Bahamas, Belgium, Belize, Byelorus, Bosnia and Herzegovina, Botswana, Brunei Darussalam, Croatia, Cyprus, Fiji, Finland, France, Germany, Greece, Hungary, Israel, Italy, Japan, the Kingdom of the Netherlands, Lesotho, Liechtenstein, Luxemburg, The former Yugoslav Republic of Macedonia, Malawi, Malta, Marshall Islands, Mauritius, Norway, Panama, Portugal, Russia, Seychelles, Slovenia, Spain, Surinam, Swaziland, Switzerland, Tonga, Turkey, the United Kingdom of Great Britain and Northern Ireland and the United States of America) which have not raised an objection to its accession in the six months after receipt of this notification. For practical reasons this six months' period will run from 15 July 1994 till 15 January 1995.

1c The Ministry of Foreign Affairs of the Byelorussian Republic communicated the following by Note of 8 February 1993:

Translation

. . . .the Ministry would advise that in accordance with Article 6 of the Convention and in accordance with the Decree issued by the Government of the Byelorussian Republic on 1 January 1993, official documents issued by the government agencies of the Byelorussian Republic for use in the territories of contracting States of the Hague Convention, repealing the necessity of legalisation of foreign official documents, are now authorised only by an apostille written on these documents.

1d *Notification in conformity with Article 15 of the Convention*

On 17 July 1992 the Ministry of Foreign Affairs of the Kingdom of the Netherlands received the instrument of accession by Belize to the above–mentioned Convention in accordance with Article 12, first paragraph, of the Convention.

In accordance with the terms of Article 12, paragraph 1, of the Convention any State not mentioned in Article 10 may accede to this Convention. In accordance with Article 12, paragraph 2, such accession shall have effect only as regards the relations between Belize and those contracting States (at present Antigua and Barbuda, Argentina, Austria, Bahamas, Belgium, Botswana, Brunei Darussalam, Cyprus, Fiji, Finland, France, the Federal Republic of Germany, Greece, Hungary, Israel, Italy, Japan, Lesotho, Liechtenstein, Luxembourg, Malawi, Malta, Marshall Islands, Mauritius, the Kingdom of the Netherlands, Norway, Panama, Portugal, Russia, Seychelles, Spain, Surinam, Swaziland, Switzerland, Tonga, Turkey, the United Kingdom of Great Britain and Northern Ireland, the United States of America and Yugoslavia) which have not raised an objection to its accession in the six months after the receipt of this notification. For practical reasons this six months' period will extend from 10 August 1992 till 10 February 1993.

The Contracting States were notified by the depositary of the accession on 10 August 1992. None of these States raised an objection to the accession within the period of six months specified in Article 12, paragraph 2, which period expired on 10 February 1993.

The provisions of the Convention will enter into force between Belize and the Contracting States on 11 April 1993.

1e "The Embassy of the People's Republic of China in the Kingdom of the Netherlands

No. He Wai Fa (97)–54 (Translation)

The Hague, June 3, 1997

Your Excellency,

In accordance with the Joint Declaration of the Government of the People's Republic of China and the Government of the United Kingdom of Great Britain and Northern Ireland on the Question of Hong Kong signed on 19 December 1984 (hereinafter referred to as the "Joint Declaration"), the People's Republic of China will resume the exercise of sovereignty over Hong Kong with effect from 1 July 1997. Hong Kong will, with effect from that date, become a Special Administrative Region of the People's Republic of China and will enjoy a high degree of autonomy, except in foreign and defence affairs which are the responsibilities of the Central People's Government of the People's Republic of China.

It is provided both in Section XI of Annex I to the Joint Declaration, "Elaboration by the Government of the People's Republic of China of its Basic Policies Regarding Hong Kong", and Article 153 of the Basic Law of the Hong Kong Special Administrative Region of the People's Republic of China, which was adopted on 4 April 1990 by the National People's Congress of the People's Republic of China, that international agreements to which the People's Republic of China is not a party but which are implemented in Hong Kong may continue to be implemented in the Hong Kong Special Administrative Region.

In accordance with the above provisions, I am instructed by the Minister of Foreign Affairs of the People's Republic of China to make the following notification:

The Convention Abolishing the Requirement of Legalization for Foreign Public Documents done at the Hague on 5 October 1961 (hereinafter referred to as the "Convention"), by which the Government of the Kingdom of the Netherlands is designated as the depository, which applies to Hong Kong at present, will continue to apply to the Hong Kong Special Administrative Region with effect from 1 July 1997. The Government of the People's Republic of China also makes the following declaration:

In accordance with Article 6 of the Convention, it designates each of the following as the competent authorities in the Hong Kong Special Administrative Region to issue the certificates referred to in Paragraph 1 of Article 3 of the Convention for the Hong Kong Special Administrative Region: the Administrative Secretary, the Registrar of the High Court, the Deputy Registrar of the High Court and the Assistant Registrar of the High Court.

Within the above ambit, responsibility for the international rights and obligations of a party to the Convention will be assumed by the Government of the People's Republic of China. ..."

1f On October 3, 1990 the German Democratic Republic acceded to the Federal Republic of Germany.

1g *Ed. Note*—The Government of the United States of America does not accept the accession of the Government of Liberia to the Convention. The Convention is not in force between the Government of the United States of America and the Government of Liberia.

2 *Notification in conformity with Article 15 of the Convention*

The Government of the Marshall Islands deposited its instrument of accession to the Convention with the Ministry of Foreign Affairs of the Kingdom of the Netherlands on 18 November 1991 in accordance with Article 12, first paragraph, of the Convention.

The Contracting States were notified by the depositary of the accession on 25 November 1991. None of these States raised an objection to the accession within the period of six months specified in Article 12, paragraph 2, which period expired on 15 June 1992.

The provisions of the Convention entered into force between the Marshall Islands and the Contracting States on 14 August 1992.

3 . . . the Convention entered into force between the Russian Federation and the Contracting States on 31 May 1992. The status of the Republics with respect to this Convention is under review by the Depositary.

4 [Ed. Note—The U.S. view is that the Socialist Federal Republic of Yugoslavia has dissolved and no successor state represents its continuation.]

Authorities in the United States of America Competent to Issue the Certificate Referred to in Article 3 of the Convention

I. Authentication Officer and Acting Authentication Officer, United States Department of State

II. Clerks and deputy clerks of the following: The Supreme Court of the United States, the Courts of Appeals for the First through the Eleventh Circuits, the District of Columbia Circuit and the Federal Circuit; the United States District Courts; the United States Court of International Trade; the United States Claims Court; the District Court of Guam, the District Court of the Virgin Islands, and the District Court for the Northern Mariana Islands.

The District Court for the District of the Canal Zone ceased to exist on Mar. 31, 1982. Its records have been transferred to the National Archives which will certify those records.

III. Officers of the individual States and other subdivisions as indicated:

States:

Alabama: Secretary of State

Alaska: Lieutenant Governor; Attorney General; Clerk of the Appellate Court

Arizona: Secretary of State; Assistant Secretary of State

Arkansas: Secretary of State; Chief Deputy Secretary of State

California: Secretary of State; any Assistant Secretary of State; any Deputy Secretary of State

Colorado: Secretary of State; Deputy Secretary of State

Connecticut: Secretary of the State; Deputy Secretary of the State

Delaware: Secretary of State; Acting Secretary of State

Florida: Secretary of State

Georgia: Georgia Superior Court Clerks' Cooperative Authority

Hawaii: Lieutenant Governor of the State of Hawaii

Idaho: Secretary of State; Chief Deputy Secretary of State; Deputy Secretary of State; Notary Public Clerk

Illinois: Secretary of State; Assistant Secretary of State; Deputy Secretary of State

Indiana: Secretary of State; Deputy Secretary of State

Iowa: Secretary of State; Deputy Secretary of State

Kansas: Secretary of State; Assistant Secretary of State; any Deputy Assistant Secretary of State

Kentucky: Secretary of State; Assistant Secretary of State

Louisiana: Secretary of State

Maine: Secretary of State; Deputy Secretary of State

Maryland: Secretary of State

Massachusetts: Deputy Secretary of the Commonwealth of Massachusetts for Public Records (beginning in 1981 through January 13, 1995); Deputy Secretary of State of the Commonwealth of Massachusetts (beginning January 16, 1995, through November 16, 1995); Secretary of the Commonwealth of Massachusetts (from November 17, 1995)

Michigan: Secretary of State; Deputy Secretary of State

Minnesota: Secretary of State; Deputy Secretary of State

Mississippi: Secretary of State; any Assistant Secretary of State

Missouri: Secretary of State; Deputy Secretary of State

Montana: Secretary of State; Chief Deputy Secretary of State; Government Affairs Bureau Chief

Nebraska: Secretary of State; Deputy Secretary of State

Nevada: Secretary of State; Chief Deputy Secretary of State; Deputy Secretary of State

New Hampshire: Secretary of State; Deputy Secretary of State

New Jersey: Secretary of State; Assistant Secretary of State

New Mexico: Secretary of State

New York: Secretary of State; Executive Deputy Secretary of State; any Deputy Secretary of State; any Special Deputy Secretary of State

North Carolina: Secretary of State; Deputy Secretary of State

North Dakota: Secretary of State; Deputy Secretary of State

Ohio: Secretary of State; Assistant Secretary of State

Oklahoma: Secretary of State; Assistant Secretary of State; Budget Officer of the Secretary of State

Oregon: Secretary of State; Deputy Secretary of State; Acting Secretary of State; Assistant to the Secretary of State

Pennsylvania: Secretary of the Commonwealth; any Deputy Secretary of the Commonwealth

Rhode Island: Secretary of State; First Deputy Secretary of State; Second Deputy Secretary of State

South Carolina: Secretary of State

South Dakota: Secretary of State; Deputy Secretary of State

Tennessee: Secretary of State

Texas: Secretary of State; Assistant Secretary of State

Utah: Lieutenant Governor; Deputy Lieutenant Governor; Administrative Assistant

Vermont: Secretary of State; Deputy Secretary of State

Virginia: Secretary of the Commonwealth; Chief Clerk, Office of the Secretary of the Commonwealth

---

Washington (State): Secretary of State; Assistant Secretary of State; Director, Department of Licensing

West Virginia: Secretary of State; Under Secretary of State; any Deputy Secretary of State

Wisconsin: Secretary of State; Assistant Secretary of State

Wyoming: Secretary of State; Deputy Secretary of State

Other Subdivisions:

American Samoa: Secretary of American Samoa; Attorney General of American Samoa

District of Columbia (Washington, D.C.): Executive Secretary; Assistant Executive Secretary; Mayor's Special Assistant and Assistant to the Executive Secretary; Secretary of the District of Columbia

Guam (Territory of): Director, Department of Administration; Acting Director, Department of Administration; Deputy Director, Department of Administration; Acting Deputy Director, Department of Administration

Northern Mariana Islands (Commonwealth of the): Attorney General; Acting Attorney General; Clerk of the Court, Commonwealth Trial Court; Deputy Clerk, Commonwealth Trial Court

Puerto Rico (Commonwealth of): Under Secretary of State; Assistant Secretary of State for External Affairs; Assistant Secretary of State; Chief, Certifications Office; Director, Office of Protocol; Assistant Secretary of State for International Affairs; Chief Certification Office

Virgin Islands of the United States: no authority designated

Rule 44.1. Determination of Foreign Law

A party who intends to raise an issue concerning the law of a foreign country shall give notice by pleadings or other reasonable written notice. The court, in determining foreign law, may consider any relevant material or source, including testimony, whether or not submitted by a party or admissible under the Federal Rules of Evidence. The court's determination shall be treated as a ruling on a question of law.

(Added Feb. 28, 1966, eff. July 1, 1966, and amended Nov. 20, 1972, eff. July 1, 1975; Mar. 2, 1987, eff. Aug. 1, 1987.)

ADVISORY COMMITTEE NOTES

1966 Adoption

Rule 44.1 is added by amendment to furnish Federal courts with a uniform and effective procedure for raising and determining an issue concerning the law of a foreign country.

To avoid unfair surprise, the *first sentence* of the new rule requires that a party who intends to raise an issue of foreign law shall give notice thereof. The uncertainty under Rule 8(a) about whether foreign law must be pleaded—compare *Siegelman v. Cunard White Star, Ltd.,* 221 F.2d 189 (2d Cir.1955), and *Pedersen v. United States,* 191 F.Supp. 95 (D. Guam 1961), with *Harrison v. United Fruit Co.,* 143 F.Supp. 598 (S.D.N.Y.1956)—is eliminated by the provision that the notice shall be "written" and "reasonable." It may, but need not be, incorporated in the pleadings. In some situations the

pertinence of foreign law is apparent from the outset; accordingly the necessary investigation of that law will have been accomplished by the party at the pleading stage, and the notice can be given conveniently in the pleadings. In other situations the pertinence of foreign law may remain doubtful until the case is further developed. A requirement that notice of foreign law be given only through the medium of the pleadings would tend in the latter instances to force the party to engage in a peculiarly burdensome type of investigation which might turn out to be unnecessary; and correspondingly the adversary would be forced into a possible wasteful investigation. The liberal provisions for amendment of the pleadings afford help if the pleadings are used as the medium of giving notice of the foreign law; but it seems best to permit a written notice to be given outside of and later than the pleadings, provided the notice is reasonable.

The new rule does not attempt to set any definite limit on the party's time for giving the notice of an issue of foreign law; in some cases the issue may not become apparent until the trial and notice then given may still be reasonable. The stage which the case had reached at the time of the notice, the reason proffered by the party for his failure to give earlier notice, and the importance to the case as a whole of the issue of foreign law sought to be raised, are among the factors which the court should consider in deciding a question of the reasonableness of a notice. If notice is given by one party it need not be repeated by any other and serves as a basis for presentation of material on the foreign law by all parties.

The *second sentence* of the new rule describes the materials to which the court may resort in determining an issue of foreign law. Heretofore the district courts, applying Rule 43(a), have looked in certain cases to State law to find the rules of evidence by which the content of foreign-country law is to be established. The State laws vary; some embody procedures which are inefficient, time consuming and expensive. See, generally, Nussbaum, *Proving the Law of Foreign Countries,* 3 Am. J. Comp. L. 60 (1954). In all events the ordinary rules of evidence are often inapposite to the problem of determining foreign law and have in the past prevented examination of material which could have provided a proper basis for the determination. The new rule permits consideration by the court of any relevant material, including testimony, without regard to its admissibility under Rule 43. Cf. N.Y. Civ. Prac. Law & Rules, R. 4511 (effective Sept. 1, 1963); 2 Va. Code Ann. tit. 8, § 8–273; 2 W. Va. Code Ann. § 5711.

In further recognition of the peculiar nature of the issue of foreign law, the new rule provides that in determining this law the court is not limited by material presented by the parties; it may engage in its own research and consider any relevant material thus found. The court may have at its disposal better foreign law materials than counsel have presented, or may wish to reexamine and amplify material that has been presented by counsel in partisan fashion or in insufficient detail. On the other hand, the court is free to insist on a complete presentation by counsel.

There is no requirement that the court give formal notice to the parties of its intention to engage in its own research on an issue of foreign law which has been raised by them, or of its intention to raise and determine independently an issue not raised by them. Ordinarily the court should inform the parties of material it has found diverging substantially from the material which they have presented; and in general the court should give the parties an opportunity to analyze and counter new points upon which it proposes to rely. See Schlesinger, *Comparative Law* 142 (2d ed. 1959); Wyzanski, *A Trial Judge's Freedom and Responsibility,* 65 Harv. L.Rev. 1281, 1296 (1952); cf. *Siegelman v. Cunard White Star, Ltd.,* supra, 221 F.2d at 197. To require, however, that the court give formal notice from time to time as it proceeds with its study of the foreign law would add an element of undesirable rigidity to the procedure for determining issues of foreign law.

The new rule refrains from imposing an obligation on the court to take "judicial notice" of foreign law because this would put an extreme burden on the court in many cases; and it avoids use of the concept of "judicial notice" in any form because of the uncertain meaning of that concept as applied to foreign law. See, e.g., Stern, *Foreign Law in the Courts: Judicial Notice and Proof,* 45 Calif.L.Rev. 23, 43 (1957). Rather the rule provides flexible procedures for presenting and utilizing material on issues of foreign law by which a sound result can be achieved with fairness to the parties.

Under the *third sentence*, the court's determination of an issue of foreign law is to be treated as a ruling on a question of "law," not "fact," so that appellate review will not be narrowly confined by the "clearly erroneous" standard of Rule 52(a). *Cf. Uniform Judicial Notice of Foreign Law Act* § 3; Note, 72 Harv.L.Rev. 318 (1958).

The new rule parallels Article IV of the Uniform Interstate and International Procedure Act, approved by the Commissioners on Uniform State Laws in 1962, except that § 4.03 of Article IV states that "[t]he court, not the jury" shall determine foreign law. The new rule does not address itself to this problem, since the Rules refrain from allocating functions as between the court and the jury. See Rule 38(a). It has long been thought, however, that the jury is not the appropriate body to determine issues of foreign law. See, e.g., Story, *Conflict of Laws,* § 638 (1st ed. 1834, 8th ed. 1883); 1 Greenleaf, *Evidence,* § 486 (1st ed. 1842, 16th ed. 1899); 4 Wigmore, *Evidence* § 2558 (1st ed. 1905); 9 id. § 2558 (3d ed. 1940). The majority of the States have committed such issues to determination by the court. See Article 5 of the Uniform Judicial Notice of Foreign Law Act, adopted by twenty-six states, 9A U.L.A. 318 (1957) (Suppl.1961, at 134); N.Y.Civ.Prac.Law & Rules, R. 4511 (effective Sept. 1, 1963); Wigmore, loc. cit. And Federal courts that have considered the problem in recent years have reached the same conclusion without reliance on statute. See *Jansson v. Swedish American Line,* 185 F.2d 212, 216 (1st Cir.1950); *Bank of Nova Scotia v. San Miguel,* 196 F.2d 950, 957, n. 6 (1st Cir.1952); *Liechti v. Roche,* 198 F.2d 174 (5th Cir.1952); *Daniel Lumber Co. v. Empresas Hondurenas, S.A.,* 215 F.2d 465 (5th Cir.1954).

1972 Amendment

Since the purpose of the provision is to free the judge, in determining foreign law, from any restrictions imposed by evidence rules, a general reference to the Rules of Evidence is appropriate and is made.

1987 Amendment

The amendment is technical. No substantive change is intended.

HISTORICAL NOTES

References in Text

The Federal Rules of Evidence, referred to in text, are set out in this title.

Effective Date of Amendment Proposed November 20, 1972

Amendment of this rule embraced by the order entered by the Supreme Court of the United States on November 20, 1972, effective on the 180th day beginning after January 2, 1975, see section 3 of Pub.L. 93–595, Jan. 2, 1975, 88 Stat. 1959, set out as a note under section 2071 of Title 28.

Rule 45. Subpoena

(a) Form; Issuance.

(1) Every subpoena shall

(A) state the name of the court from which it is issued; and

(B) state the title of the action, the name of the court in which it is pending, and its civil action number; and

(C) command each person to whom it is directed to attend and give testimony or to produce and permit inspection and copying of designated books, documents or tangible things in the possession, custody or control of that person, or to permit inspection of premises, at a time and place therein specified; and

(D) set forth the text of subdivisions (c) and (d) of this rule.

A command to produce evidence or to permit inspection may be joined with a command to appear at trial or hearing or at deposition, or may be issued separately.

(2) A subpoena commanding attendance at a trial or hearing shall issue from the court for the district in which the hearing or trial is to be held. A subpoena for attendance at a deposition shall issue from the court for the district designated by the notice of deposition as the district in which the deposition is to be taken. If separate from a subpoena commanding the attendance of a person, a subpoena for production or inspection shall issue from the court for the district in which the production or inspection is to be made.

(3) The clerk shall issue a subpoena, signed but otherwise in blank, to a party requesting it, who shall complete it before service. An attorney as officer of the court may also issue and sign a subpoena on behalf of

(A) a court in which the attorney is authorized to practice; or

(B) a court for a district in which a deposition or production is compelled by the subpoena, if the deposition or production pertains to an action pending in a court in which the attorney is authorized to practice.

(b) Service.

(1) A subpoena may be served by any person who is not a party and is not less than 18 years of age. Service of a subpoena upon a person named therein shall be made by delivering a copy thereof to such person and, if the person's attendance is commanded, by tendering to that person the fees for one day's attendance and the mileage allowed by law. When the subpoena is issued on behalf of the United States or an officer or agency thereof, fees and mileage need not be tendered. Prior notice of any commanded production of documents and things or inspection of premises before trial shall be served on each party in the manner prescribed by Rule 5(b).

(2) Subject to the provisions of clause (ii) of subparagraph (c)(3)(A) of this rule, a subpoena may be served at any place within the district of the court by which it is issued, or at any place without the district that is within 100 miles of the place of the deposition, hearing, trial, production, or inspection specified in the subpoena or at any place within the state where a state statute or rule of court permits service of a subpoena issued by a state court of general jurisdiction sitting in the place of the deposition, hearing, trial, production, or inspection specified in the subpoena. When a statute of the United States provides therefor, the court upon proper application and cause shown may authorize the service of a subpoena at any other place. A subpoena directed to a witness in a foreign country who is a national or resident of the United States shall issue under the circumstances and in the manner and be served as provided in Title 28, U.S.C. § 1783.

(3) Proof of service when necessary shall be made by filing with the clerk of the court by which the subpoena is issued a statement of the date and manner of service and of the names of the persons served, certified by the person who made the service.

(c) Protection of Persons Subject to Subpoenas.

(1) A party or an attorney responsible for the issuance and service of a subpoena shall take reasonable steps to avoid imposing undue burden or expense on a person subject to that subpoena. The court on behalf of which the subpoena was issued shall enforce this duty and impose upon the party or attorney in breach of this duty an appropriate sanction, which may include, but is not limited to, lost earnings and a reasonable attorney's fee.

(2)(A) A person commanded to produce and permit inspection and copying of designated books, papers, documents or tangible things, or inspection of premises need not appear in person at the place of production or inspection unless commanded to appear for deposition, hearing or trial.

(B) Subject to paragraph (d)(2) of this rule, a person commanded to produce and permit inspection and copying may, within 14 days after service of the subpoena or before the time specified for compliance if such time is less than 14 days after service, serve upon the party or attorney designated in the subpoena written objection to inspection or copying of any or all of the designated materials or of the premises. If objection is made, the party serving the subpoena shall not be entitled to inspect and copy the materials or inspect the premises except pursuant to an order of the court by which the subpoena was issued. If objection has been made, the party serving the subpoena may, upon notice to the person commanded to produce, move at any time for an order to compel the production. Such an order to compel production shall protect any person who is not a party or an officer of a party from significant expense resulting from the inspection and copying commanded.

(3)(A) On timely motion, the court by which a subpoena was issued shall quash or modify the subpoena if it

(i) fails to allow reasonable time for compliance;

(ii) requires a person who is not a party or an officer of a party to travel to a place more than 100 miles from the place where that person resides, is employed or regularly transacts business in person, except that, subject to the provisions of clause (c)(3)(B)(iii) of this rule, such a person may in order to attend trial be commanded to travel from any such place within the state in which the trial is held, or

(iii) requires disclosure of privileged or other protected matter and no exception or waiver applies, or

(iv) subjects a person to undue burden.

(B) If a subpoena

(i) requires disclosure of a trade secret or other confidential research, development, or commercial information, or

(ii) requires disclosure of an unretained expert's opinion or information not describing specific events or occurrences in dispute and resulting from the expert's study made not at the request of any party, or

(iii) requires a person who is not a party or an officer of a party to incur substantial expense to travel more than 100 miles to attend trial, the court may, to protect a person subject to or affected by the subpoena, quash or modify the subpoena or, if the party in whose behalf the subpoena is issued shows a substantial need for the testimony or material that cannot be otherwise met without undue hardship and assures that the person to whom the subpoena is addressed will be reasonably compensated, the court may order appearance or production only upon specified conditions.

(d) Duties in Responding to Subpoena.

(1) A person responding to a subpoena to produce documents shall produce them as they are kept in the usual course of business or shall organize and label them to correspond with the categories in the demand.

(2) When information subject to a subpoena is withheld on a claim that it is privileged or subject to protection as trial preparation materials, the claim shall be made expressly and shall be supported by a description of the nature of the documents, communications, or things not produced that is sufficient to enable the demanding party to contest the claim.

(e) Contempt. Failure by any person without adequate excuse to obey a subpoena served upon that person may be deemed a contempt of the court from which the subpoena issued. An adequate cause for failure to obey exists when a subpoena purports to require a non-party to attend or produce at a place not within the limits provided by clause (ii) of subparagraph (c)(3)(A).

(As amended Dec. 27, 1946, eff. Mar. 19, 1948; Dec. 29, 1948, eff. Oct. 20, 1949; Mar. 30, 1970, eff. July 1, 1970; Apr. 29, 1980, eff. Aug. 1, 1980; Apr. 29, 1985, eff. Aug. 1, 1985; Mar. 2, 1987, eff. Aug. 1, 1987; Apr. 30, 1991, eff. Dec. 1, 1991.)

Proposed Amendment of Subdivision (a)(2)

Effective December 1, 2005, absent contrary Congressional action, subdivision (a)(2) of this rule is amended to read as follows:

(2) A subpoena must issue as follows:

(A) for attendance at a trial or hearing, from the court for the district where the trial or hearing is to be held;

(B) for attendance at a deposition, from the court for the district where the deposition is to be taken, stating the method for recording the testimony; and

(C) for production and inspection, if separate from a subpoena commanding a person's attendance, from the court for the district where the production or inspection is to be made.

ADVISORY COMMITTEE NOTES
1937 Adoption

This rule applies to subpoenas ad testificandum and duces tecum issued by the district courts for attendance at a hearing or a trial, or to take depositions. It does not apply to the enforcement of subpoenas issued by administrative officers and commissions pursuant to statutory authority. The enforcement of such subpoenas by the district courts is regulated by appropriate statutes. Many of these statutes do not place any territorial limits on the validity of subpoenas so issued, but provide that they may be served anywhere within the United States. Among such statutes are the following:

U.S.C., Title 7, §§ 222 and 511n (Secretary of Agriculture)

U.S.C., Title 15, § 49 (Federal Trade Commission)

U.S.C., Title 15, §§ 77v(b), 78u(c), 79r(d) (Securities and Exchange Commission)

U.S.C., Title 16, §§ 797(g) and 825f (Federal Power Commission)

U.S.C., Title 19, § 1333(b) (Tariff Commission)

U.S.C., Title 22, §§ 268, 270d and 270e (International Commissions, etc.)

U.S.C., Title 26, §§ 614, 619(b) [see 7456] (Board of Tax Appeals)

U.S.C., Title 26, § 1523(a) [see 7608] (Internal Revenue Officers)

U.S.C., Title 29, § 161 (Labor Relations Board)

U.S.C., Title 33, § 506 (Secretary of Army)

U.S.C., Title 35, §§ 54 to 56 [now 24] (Patent Office proceedings)

U.S.C., Title 38, [former] § 133 (Veterans' Administration)

U.S.C., Title 41, § 39 (Secretary of Labor)

U.S.C., Title 45, § 157 Third. (h) (Board of Arbitration under Railway Labor Act)

U.S.C., Title 45, § 222(b) (Investigation Commission under Railroad Retirement Act of 1935)

U.S.C., Title 46, § 1124(b) (Maritime Commission)

U.S.C., Title 47, § 409(c) and (d) (Federal Communications Commission)

U.S.C., Title 49, § 12(2) and (3) [now 10321] (Interstate Commerce Commission)

U.S.C., Title 49, § 173a [see 1484] (Secretary of Commerce)

Note to Subdivisions (a) and (b). These simplify the form of subpoena as provided in U.S.C., Title 28, [former] § 655 (Witnesses; subpoena; form; attendance under); and broaden U.S.C, Title 28, [former] § 636 (Production for books and writings) to include all actions, and to extend to any person. With the provision for relief from an oppressive or unreasonable subpoena duces tecum, compare N.Y.C.P.A. (1937) § 411.

Note to Subdivision (c). This provides for the simple and convenient method of service permitted under many state codes; e.g., N.Y.C.P.A. (1937) §§ 220, 404, J.Ct.Act, § 191; 3 Wash.Rev.Stat.Ann. (Remington, 1932) § 1218. Compare former Equity Rule 15 (Process, by Whom Served).

For statutes governing fees and mileage of witnesses see:

U.S.C., Title 28 former sections:

600a[now 1871] (Per diem; mileage)

600c[now 1821, 1823] (Amount per diem and mileage for witnesses; subsistence)

600d[former] (Fees and mileage in certain states)

601[former] (Witnesses' fees; enumeration)

602[now 1824] (Fees and mileage of jurors and witnesses)

603[see Title 5, §§ 5515, 5537] (No officer of court to have witness fees)

Note to Subdivision (d). The method provided in paragraph (1) for the authorization of the issuance of subpoenas has been employed in some districts. See *Henning v. Boyle,* S.D.N.Y.1901, 112 F. 397. The requirement of an order for the issuance of a subpoena duces tecum is in accordance with U.S.C., Title 28, [former] § 647 (Deposition under dedimus potestatem; subpoena duces tecum). The provisions of paragraph (2) are in accordance with common practice. See U.S.C., Title 28, former § 648 (Deposition under dedimus potestatem; witnesses, when required to attend); N.Y.C.P.A. (1937) § 300; 1 N.J.Rev.Stat. (1937) 2:27–174.

Note to Subdivision (e). The first paragraph continues the substance of U.S.C., Title 28, [former] § 654 (Witnesses; subpoenas; may run into another district). Compare U.S.C., Title 11, [former] § 69 (Referees in bankruptcy; contempts before) (production of books and writings) which is not affected by this rule. For examples of statutes which allow the court, upon proper application and cause shown, to authorize the clerk of the court to issue a subpoena for a witness who lives in another district and at a greater distance than 100 miles from the place of the hearing or trial, see:

U.S.C., Title 15:

§ 23 (Suits by United States; subpoenas for witnesses) (under antitrust laws).

U.S.C., Title 38:

§ 445[now 784] (Actions on claims; jurisdiction; parties; procedure; limitation; witnesses; definitions) (Veterans' insurance contracts).

The second paragraph continues the present procedure applicable to certain witnesses who are in foreign countries. See U.S.C., Title 28, §§ 711 [now 1783] (Letters rogatory to take testimony of witness, addressed to court of foreign country; failure of witness to appear; subpoena) and 713 [now 1783] (Service of Subpoena on witness in foreign country).

Note to Subdivision (f). Compare [former] Equity Rule 52 (Attendance of Witnesses Before Commissioner, Master, or Examiner).

1946 Amendment

Note to Subdivision (b). The added words, "or tangible things" in subdivision (b) merely make the rule for the subpoena duces tecum at the trial conform to that of subdivision (d) for the subpoena at the taking of depositions. The insertion of the words "or modify" in clause (1) affords desirable flexibility.

Subdivision (d). The added last sentence of amended subdivision (d)(1) properly gives the subpoena for documents or tangible things the same scope as provided in Rule 26(b), thus promoting uniformity. The requirement in the last sentence of original Rule 45(d)(1)—to the effect that leave of court should be obtained for the issuance of such a subpoena—has been omitted. This requirement is unnecessary and oppressive on both counsel and court, and it had been criticized by district judges. There is no satisfactory reason

for a differentiation between a subpoena for the production of documentary evidence by a witness at a trial (Rule 45(a)) and for the production of the same evidence at the taking of a deposition. Under this amendment, the person subpoenaed may obtain the protection afforded by any of the orders permitted under Rule 30(b) or Rule 45(b). See *Application of Zenith Radio Corp.,* E.D.Pa.1941, 4 F.Rules Serv. 30b.21. Case 1, 1 F.R.D. 627; *Fox v. House,* Okla.1939, 29 F.Supp. 673; *United States of America for the Use of Tilo Roofing Co., Inc. v. J. Slotnik Co.,* Conn.1944, 3 F.R.D. 408.

The changes in subdivisions (d)(2) give the court the same power in the case of residents of the district as is conferred in the case of non-residents, and permit the court to fix a place for attendance which may be more convenient and accessible for the parties than that specified in the rule.

1948 Amendment

The amendment effective October 1949, substituted the reference to "Title 28, U.S.C., § 1783" at the end of subdivision (e)(2) for the reference to "the Act of July 3, 1926, c. 762, §§ 1, 3 (44 Stat. 835), U.S.C., Title 28, § 713."

1970 Amendment

At present, when a subpoena duces tecum is issued to a deponent, he is required to produce the listed materials at the deposition, but is under no clear compulsion to permit their inspection and copying. This results in confusion and uncertainty before the time the deposition is taken, with no mechanism provided whereby the court can resolve the matter. Rule 45(d)(1), as revised, makes clear that the subpoena authorizes inspection and copying of the materials produced. The deponent is afforded full protection since he can object, thereby forcing the party serving the subpoena to obtain a court order if he wishes to inspect and copy. The procedure is thus analogous to that provided in Rule 34.

The changed references to other rules conform to changes made in those rules. The deletion of words in the clause describing the proper scope of the subpoena conforms to a change made in the language of Rule 34. The reference to Rule 26(b) is unchanged but encompasses new matter in that subdivision. The changes make it clear that the scope of discovery through a subpoena is the same as that applicable to Rule 34 and the other discovery rules.

1980 Amendment

Subdivision (d)(1). The amendment defines the term "proof of service" as used in the first sentence of the present subdivision. For want of a definition, the district court clerks have been obliged to fashion their own, with results that vary from district to district. All that seems required is a simple certification on a copy of the notice to take a deposition that the notice has been served on every other party to the action. That is the proof of service required by Rule 25(d) of both the Federal Rules of Appellate Procedure and the Supreme Court Rules.

Subdivision (e)(1). The amendment makes the reach of a subpoena of a district court at least as extensive as that of the state courts of general jurisdiction in the state in which the district court is held. Under the present rule the reach of a district court subpoena is often greater, since it extends throughout the district. No reason appears why it should be less, as it sometimes is because of the accident of district lines. Restrictions upon the reach of subpoenas are imposed to prevent undue inconvenience to witnesses. State statutes and rules of court are quite likely to reflect the varying degrees of difficulty and expense attendant upon local travel.

1985 Amendment

Present Rule 45(d)(2) has two sentences setting forth the territorial scope of deposition subpoenas. The first sentence is directed to depositions taken in the judicial district in which the deponent resides; the second sentence addresses situations in which the deponent is not a resident of the district in which the deposition is to take place. The Rule, as currently constituted, creates anomalous situations that often cause logistical problems in conducting litigation.

The first sentence of the present Rule states that a deponent may be required to attend only in the *county* wherein that person resides or is employed or transacts business in person, that is, where the person lives or works. Under this provision a deponent can be compelled, without court order, to travel from one end of that person's home county to the other, no matter how far that may be. The second sentence of the Rule is somewhat more flexible, stating that someone who does not reside in the district in which the deposition is to be taken can be required to attend in the county where the person is served with the subpoena, *or* within 40 miles from the place of service.

Under today's conditions there is no sound reason for distinguishing between residents of the district or county in which a deposition is to be taken and nonresidents, and the Rule is amended to provide that any person may be subpoenaed to attend a deposition within a specified radius from that person's residence, place of business, or where the person was served. The 40-mile radius has been increased to 100 miles.

1987 Amendment

The amendments are technical. No substantive change is intended.

1991 Amendment

Purposes of Revision. The purposes of this revision are (1) to clarify and enlarge the protections afforded persons who are required to assist the court by giving information or evidence; (2) to facilitate access outside the deposition procedure provided by Rule 30 to documents and other information in the possession of persons who are not parties; (3) to facilitate service of subpoenas for depositions or productions of evidence at places distant from the district in which an action is proceeding; (4) to enable the court to compel a witness found within the state in which the court sits to attend trial; (5) to clarify the organization of the text of the rule.

Subdivision (a). This subdivision is amended in seven significant respects.

First, Paragraph (a)(3) modifies the requirement that a subpoena be issued by the clerk of court. Provision is made for the issuance of subpoenas by attorneys as officers of the court. This revision perhaps culminates an evolution. Subpoenas were long issued by specific order of the court. As this became a burden to the court, general orders were made authorizing clerks to issue subpoenas on request. Since 1948, they have been issued in blank by the clerk of any federal court to any lawyer, the clerk serving as stationer to the bar. In allowing counsel to issue the subpoena, the rule is merely a recognition of present reality.

Although the subpoena is in a sense the command of the attorney who completes the form, defiance of a subpoena is nevertheless an act in defiance of a court order and exposes the defiant witness to contempt sanctions. In *ICC v. Brimson*, 154 U.S. 447 (1894), the Court upheld a statute directing federal courts to issue subpoenas to compel testimony before the ICC. In *CAB v. Hermann*, 353 U.S. 322 (1957), the Court approved as established practice the issuance of administrative subpoenas as a matter of absolute agency right. And in *NLRB v. Warren Co.*, 350 U.S. 107 (1955), the Court held that the lower court had no discretion to withhold sanctions against a contemnor who violated such subpoenas. The 1948 revision of Rule 45 put the attorney in a position similar to that of the administrative agency, as a public officer entitled to use the court's contempt power to investigate facts in dispute. Two courts of appeals have touched on the issue and have described lawyer-issued subpoenas as mandates of the court. *Waste Conversion, Inc. v. Rollins Environmental Services (NJ), Inc.*, 893 F.2d 605 (3d cir. 1990); *Fisher v. Marubent Cotton Corp.*, 526 F.2d 1338, 1340 (8th cir., 1975). Cf. *Young v. United States ex rel Vuitton et Fils S.A.*, 481 U.S. 787, 821 (1987) (Scalia, J., concurring). This revision makes the rule explicit that the attorney acts as an officer of the court in issuing and signing subpoenas.

Necessarily accompanying the evolution of this power of the lawyer as officer of the court is the development of increased responsibility and liability for the misuse of this power. The latter development is reflected in the provisions of subdivision (c) of this rule, and also in the requirement imposed by paragraph (3) of this subdivision that the attorney issuing a subpoena must sign it.

Second, Paragraph (a)(3) authorizes attorneys in distant districts to serve as officers authorized to issue commands in the name of the court. Any attorney permitted to represent a client in a federal court, even one admitted pro haec vice, has the same authority as a clerk to issue a subpoena from any federal court for the district in which the subpoena is served and enforced. In authorizing attorneys to issue subpoenas from distant courts, the amended rule effectively authorizes service of a subpoena anywhere in the United States by an attorney representing any party. This change is intended to ease the administrative burdens of interdistrict law practice. The former rule resulted in delay and expense caused by the need to secure forms from clerks' offices some distance from the place at which the action proceeds. This change does not enlarge the burden on the witness.

Pursuant to Paragraph (a)(2), a subpoena for a deposition must still issue from the court in which the deposition or production would be compelled. Accordingly, a motion to quash such a subpoena if it overbears the limits of the subpoena power must, as under the previous rule, be presented to the court for the district in which the deposition would occur. Likewise, the court in whose name the subpoena is issued is responsible for its enforcement.

Third, in order to relieve attorneys of the need to secure an appropriate seal to affix to a subpoena issued as an officer of a distant court, the requirement that a subpoena be under seal is abolished by the provisions of Paragraph (a)(1).

Fourth, Paragraph (a)(1) authorizes the issuance of a subpoena to compel a non-party to produce evidence independent of any deposition. This revision spares the necessity of a deposition of the custodian of evidentiary material required to be produced. A party seeking additional production from a person subject to such a subpoena may serve an additional subpoena requiring additional production at the same time and place.

Fifth, Paragraph (a)(2) makes clear that the person subject to the subpoena is required to produce materials in that person's control whether or not the materials are located within the district or within the territory within which the subpoena can be served. The non-party witness is subject to the same scope of discovery under this rule as that person would be as a party to whom a request is addressed pursuant to Rule 34.

Sixth, Paragraph (a)(1) requires that the subpoena include a statement of the rights and duties of witnesses by setting forth in full the text of the new subdivisions (c) and (d).

Seventh, the revised rule authorizes the issuance of a subpoena to compel the inspection of premises in the possession of a non-party. Rule 34 has authorized such inspections of premises in the possession of a party as discovery compelled under Rule 37, but prior practice required an independent proceeding to secure such relief ancillary to the federal proceeding when the premises were not in the possession of a party. Practice in some states has long authorized such use of a subpoena for this purpose without apparent adverse consequence.

Subdivision (b). Paragraph (b)(1) retains the text of the former subdivision (c) with minor changes.

The reference to the United States marshal and deputy marshal is deleted because of the infrequency of the use of these officers for this purpose. Inasmuch as these officers meet the age requirement, they may still be used if available.

A provision requiring service of prior notice pursuant to Rule 5 of compulsory pretrial production or inspection has been added to paragraph (b)(1). The purpose of such notice is to afford other parties an opportunity to object to the production or inspection, or to serve a demand for additional documents or things. Such additional notice is not needed with respect to a deposition because of the requirement of notice imposed by Rule 30 or 31. But when production or inspection is sought independently of a deposition, other parties may need notice in order to monitor the discovery and in order to pursue access to any information that may or should be produced.

Paragraph (b)(2) retains language formerly set forth in subdivision (e) and extends its application to subpoenas for depositions or production.

Paragraph (b)(3) retains language formerly set forth in paragraph (d)(1) and extends its applications to subpoenas for trial or hearing or production.

Subdivision (c). This provision is new and states the rights of witnesses. It is not intended to diminish rights conferred by Rules 26–37 or any other authority.

Paragraph (c)(1) gives specific application to the principle stated in Rule 26(g) and specifies liability for earnings lost by a non-party witness as a result of a misuse of the subpoena. No change in existing law is thereby effected. Abuse of a subpoena is an actionable tort, *Board of Ed. v. Farmingdale Classroom Teach. Ass'n*, 38 N.Y.2d 397, 380 N.Y.S.2d 635,

343 N.E.2d 278 (1975), and the duty of the attorney to the non-party is also embodied in Model Rule of Professional Conduct 4.4. The liability of the attorney is correlative to the expanded power of the attorney to issue subpoenas. The liability may include the cost of fees to collect attorneys' fees owed as a result of a breach of this duty.

Paragraph (c)(2) retains language from the former subdivision (b) and paragraph (d)(1). The 10–day period for response to a subpoena is extended to 14 days to avoid the complex calculations associated with short time periods under Rule 6 and to allow a bit more time for such objections to be made.

A non-party required to produce documents or materials is protected against significant expense resulting from involuntary assistance to the court. This provision applies, for example, to a non-party required to provide a list of class members. The court is not required to fix the costs in advance of production, although this will often be the most satisfactory accommodation to protect the party seeking discovery from excessive costs. In some instances, it may be preferable to leave uncertain costs to be determined after the materials have been produced, provided that the risk of uncertainty is fully disclosed to the discovering party. See, *e.g., United States v. Columbia Broadcasting Systems, Inc.,* 666 F.2d 364 (9th Cir.1982).

Paragraph (c)(3) explicitly authorizes the quashing of a subpoena as a means of protecting a witness from misuse of the subpoena power. It replaces and enlarges on the former subdivision (b) of this rule and tracks the provisions of Rule 26(c). While largely repetitious, this rule is addressed to the witness who may read it on the subpoena, where it is required to be printed by the revised paragraph (a)(1) of this rule.

Subparagraph (c)(3)(A) identifies those circumstances in which a subpoena must be quashed or modified. It restates the former provisions with respect to the limits of mandatory travel that are set forth in the former paragraphs (d)(2) and (e)(1), with one important change. Under the revised rule, a federal court can compel a witness to come from any place in the state to attend trial, whether or not the local state law so provides. This extension is subject to the qualification provided in the next paragraph, which authorizes the court to condition enforcement of a subpoena compelling a non-party witness to bear substantial expense to attend trial. The traveling non-party witness may be entitled to reasonable compensation for the time and effort entailed.

Clause (c)(3)(A)(iv) requires the court to protect all persons from undue burden imposed by the use of the subpoena power. Illustratively, it might be unduly burdensome to compel an adversary to attend trial as a witness if the adversary is known to have no personal knowledge of matters in dispute, especially so if the adversary would be required to incur substantial travel burdens.

Subparagraph (c)(3)(B) identifies circumstances in which a subpoena should be quashed unless the party serving the subpoena shows a substantial need and the court can devise an appropriate accommodation to protect the interests of the witness. An additional circumstance in which such action is required is a request for costly production of documents; that situation is expressly governed by subparagraph (b)(2)(B)[1].

Clause (c)(3)(B)(i) authorizes the court to quash, modify, or condition a subpoena to protect the person subject to or affected by the subpoena from unnecessary or unduly harmful disclosures of confidential information. It corresponds to Rule 26(c)(7).

Clause (c)(3)(B)(ii) provides appropriate protection for the intellectual property of the non-party witness; it does not apply to the expert retained by a party, whose information is subject to the provisions of Rule 26(b)(4). A growing problem has been the use of subpoenas to compel the giving of evidence and information by unretained experts. Experts are not exempt from the duty to give evidence, even if they cannot be compelled to prepare themselves to give effective testimony, *e.g.*, *Carter–Wallace, Inc. v. Otte*, 474 F.2d 529 (2d Cir.1972), but compulsion to give evidence may threaten the intellectual property of experts denied the opportunity to bargain for the value of their services. See generally Maurer, *Compelling the Expert Witness: Fairness and Utility Under the Federal Rules of Civil Procedure*, 19 GA.L.REV. 71 (1984); Note, *Discovery and Testimony of Unretained Experts*, 1987 DUKE L.J. 140. Arguably the compulsion to testify can be regarded as a "taking" of intellectual property. The rule establishes the right of such persons to withhold their expertise, at least unless the party seeking it makes the kind of showing required for a conditional denial of a motion to quash as provided in the final sentence of subparagraph (c)(3)(B); that requirement is the same as that necessary to secure work product under Rule 26(b)(3) and gives assurance of reasonable compensation. The Rule thus approves the accommodation of competing interests exemplified in *United States v. Columbia Broadcasting Systems Inc.*, 666 F.2d 364 (9th Cir.1982). See also *Wright v. Jeep Corporation*, 547 F.Supp. 871 (E.D.Mich.1982).

As stated in *Kaufman v. Edelstein*, 539 F.2d 811, 822 (2d Cir.1976), the district court's discretion in these matters should be informed by "the degree to which the expert is being called because of his knowledge of facts relevant to the case rather than in order to give opinion testimony; the difference between testifying to a previously formed or expressed opinion and forming a new one; the possibility that, for other reasons, the witness is a unique expert; the extent to which the calling party is able to show the unlikelihood that any comparable witness will willingly testify; and the degree to which the witness is able to show that he has been oppressed by having continually to testify...."

Clause (c)(3)(B)(iii) protects non-party witnesses who may be burdened to perform the duty to travel in order to provide testimony at trial. The provision requires the court to condition a subpoena requiring travel of more than 100 miles on reasonable compensation.

Subdivision (d). This provision is new. Paragraph (d)(1) extends to non-parties the duty imposed on parties by the last paragraph of Rule 34(b), which was added in 1980.

Paragraph (d)(2) is new and corresponds to the new Rule 26(b)(5) [paragraph (5) in Rule 26(b) was a proposed paragraph which was withdrawn by the Supreme Court]. Its purpose is to provide a party whose discovery is constrained by a claim of privilege or work product protection with information sufficient to evaluate such a claim and to resist if it seems unjustified. The person claiming a privilege or protection cannot decide the limits of that party's own entitlement.

A party receiving a discovery request who asserts a privilege or protection but fails to disclose that claim is at risk of waiving the privilege or protection. A person claiming a privilege or protection who fails to provide adequate information about the privilege or protection claim to the party seeking the information is subject to an order to show cause why the person should not be held in contempt under subdivision (e). Motions for such orders and responses to motions are subject to the sanctions provisions of Rules 7 and 11.

A person served a subpoena that is too broad may be faced with a burdensome task to provide full information regarding all that person's claims to privilege or work product protection. Such a person is entitled to protection that may be secured through an objection made pursuant to paragraph (c)(2).

Subdivision (e). This provision retains most of the language of the former subdivision (f).

"Adequate cause" for a failure to obey a subpoena remains undefined. In at least some circumstances, a non-party might be guilty of contempt for refusing to obey a subpoena even though the subpoena manifestly overreaches the appropriate limits of the subpoena power. *E.g.*, *Walker v. City of Birmingham*, 388 U.S. 307 (1967). But, because the command of the subpoena is not in fact one uttered by a judicial officer, contempt should be very sparingly applied when the non-party witness has been overborne by a party or attorney. The language added to subdivision (f) is intended to assure that result where a non-party has been commanded, on the signature of an attorney, to travel greater distances than can be compelled pursuant to this rule.

1 So in original. Probably should be "subparagraph (c)(2)(B)".

2005 Amendments

[Effective December 1, 2005, absent contrary Congressional action.]

This amendment closes a small gap in regard to notifying witnesses of the manner for recording a deposition. A deposition subpoena must state the method for recording the testimony.

Rule 30(b)(2) directs that the party noticing a deposition state in the notice the manner for recording the testimony, but the notice need not be served on the deponent. The deponent learns of the recording method only if the deponent is a party or is informed by a party. Rule 30(b)(3) permits another party to designate an additional method of recording with prior notice to the deponent and the other parties. The deponent thus has notice of the recording method when an additional method is designated. This amendment completes the notice provisions to ensure that a nonparty deponent has notice of the recording method when the recording method is described only in the deposition notice.

A subpoenaed witness does not have a right to refuse to proceed with a deposition due to objections to the manner of recording. But under rare circumstances, a nonparty witness might have a ground for seeking a protective order under Rule 26(c) with regard to the manner of recording or the use of the deposition if recorded in a certain manner. Should such a witness not learn of the manner of recording until the deposition begins, undesirable delay or complication might result. Advance notice of the recording method affords an opportunity to raise such protective issues.

Other changes are made to conform Rule 45(a)(2) to current style conventions.

HISTORICAL NOTES

Treaties and Conventions; Taking of Evidence Abroad in Civil or Commercial Matters; Observance On and After Oct. 7, 1972, by United States and Citizens and Persons Subject to Jurisdiction of United States

For text of Convention, see provisions set out as a note under section 1781 of this title.

Rule 46.   Exceptions Unnecessary

Formal exceptions to rulings or orders of the court are unnecessary; but for all purposes for which an exception has heretofore been necessary it is sufficient that a party, at the time the ruling or order of the court is made or sought, makes known to the court the action which the party desires the court to take or the party's objection to the action of the court and the grounds therefor; and, if a party has no opportunity to object to a ruling or order at the time it is made, the absence of an objection does not thereafter prejudice the party.

(As amended Mar. 2, 1987, eff. Aug. 1, 1987.)

ADVISORY COMMITTEE NOTES

1937 Adoption

Abolition of formal exceptions is often provided by statute. See Ill.Rev.Stat. (1937), ch. 110, § 204; Neb.Comp.Stat. (1929) § 20–1139; N.M.Stat.Ann. (Courtright, 1929) § 105–830; 2 N.D.Comp.Laws Ann. (1913) § 7653; Ohio Code Ann. (Throckmorton, 1936) § 11560; 1 S.D.Comp.Laws (1929) § 2542; Utah Rev.Stat.Ann. (1933) §§ 104–39–2, 104–24–18; Va.Rules of Court, Rule 22, 163 Va. v. xii (1935); Wis.Stat. (1935) § 270.39. Compare N.Y.C.P.A. (1937) §§ 583, 445, and 446, all as amended by L.1936, ch. 915. Rule 51 deals with objections to the court's instructions to the jury.

U.S.C., Title 28, [former] § 776 (Bill of exceptions; authentication; signing of by judge) and [former] § 875 (Review of findings in cases tried without a jury) are superseded insofar as they provide for formal exceptions, and a bill of exceptions.

1987 Amendment

The amendments are technical. No substantive change is intended.

Rule 47.   Selection of Jurors

(a) Examination of Jurors. The court may permit the parties or their attorneys to conduct the examination of prospective jurors or may itself conduct the examination. In the latter event, the court shall permit the parties or their attorneys to supplement the examination by such further inquiry as it deems proper or shall itself submit to the prospective jurors such additional questions of the parties or their attorneys as it deems proper.

(b) Peremptory Challenges. The court shall allow the number of peremptory challenges provided by 28 U.S.C. § 1870.

(c) Excuse. The court may for good cause excuse a juror from service during trial or deliberation.

(As amended Feb. 28, 1966, eff. July 1, 1966; Apr. 30, 1991, eff. Dec. 1, 1991.)

ADVISORY COMMITTEE NOTES

1937 Adoption

Note to Subdivision (a). This permits a practice found very useful by Federal trial judges. For an example of a state practice in which the examination by the court is supplemented by further inquiry by counsel, see Rule 27 of the Code of Rules for the District Courts of Minnesota, 186 Minn. xxxiii (1932), 3 Minn.Stat. (Mason, Supp.1936) Appendix 4, p. 1062.

Note to Subdivision (b). The provision for an alternate juror is one often found in modern state codes. See N.C.Code (1935) § 2330(a); Ohio Gen.Code Ann. (Page, Supp.1926–1935) § 11419–47; Pa.Stat.Ann. (Purdon, Supp. 1936) Title 17, § 1153; compare U.S.C., Title 28, [former] § 417a (Alternate jurors in criminal trials); 1 N.J.Rev.Stat. (1937) 2:91A–1, 2:91A–2, 2:91A–3.

Provisions for qualifying, drawing, and challenging of jurors are found in U.S.C., Title 28:

- § 411 [now 1861] (Qualifications and exemptions)
- § 412 [now 1864] (Manner of drawing)
- § 413 [now 1865] (Apportioned in district)
- § 415 [see 1862] (Not disqualified because of race or color)
- § 416 [now 1867] (Venire; service and return)
- § 417 [now 1866] (Talesmen for petit jurors)
- § 418 [now 1866] (Special juries)
- § 423 [now 1869] (Jurors not to serve more than once a year)
- § 424 [now 1870] (Challenges)

and D.C.Code (1930) Title 18, §§ 341 to 360 (Juries and Jury Commission) and Title 6, § 366 (Peremptory challenges).

1966 Amendment

The revision of this subdivision brings it into line with the amendment of Rule 24(c) of this Federal Rules of Criminal Procedure. That rule previously allowed four alternate jurors, as contrasted with the two allowed in civil cases, and the amendments increase the number to a maximum of six in all cases. The Advisory Committee's Note to amended Criminal Rule 24(c) points to experience demonstrating that four alternates may not be enough in some lengthy criminal trials; and the same may be said of civil trials. The Note adds:

"The words 'or are found to be' are added to the second sentence to make clear that an alternate juror may be called in the situation where it is first discovered during the trial that a juror was unable or disqualified to perform his duties at the time he was sworn."

1991 Amendment

Subdivision (b). The former provision for alternate jurors is stricken and the institution of the alternate juror abolished.

The former rule reflected the long-standing assumption that a jury would consist of exactly twelve members. It provided for additional jurors to be used as substitutes for jurors who are for any reason excused or disqualified from service after the commencement of the trial. Additional jurors were traditionally designated at the outset of the trial, and excused at the close of the evidence if they had not been promoted to full service on account of the elimination of one of the original jurors.

The use of alternate jurors has been a source of dissatisfaction with the jury system because of the burden it places on alternates who are required to listen to the evidence but denied the satisfaction of participating in its evaluation.

Subdivision (c). This provision makes it clear that the court may in appropriate circumstances excuse a juror during the jury deliberations without causing a mistrial. Sickness, family emergency or juror misconduct that might occasion a mistrial are examples of appropriate grounds for excusing a juror. It is not grounds for the dismissal of a juror that the juror refuses to join with fellow jurors in reaching a unanimous verdict.

Rule 48. Number of Jurors—Participation in Verdict

The court shall seat a jury of not fewer than six and not more than twelve members and all jurors shall participate in the verdict unless excused from service by the court pursuant to Rule 47(c). Unless the parties otherwise stipulate, (1) the verdict shall be unanimous and (2) no verdict shall be taken from a jury reduced in size to fewer than six members. (As amended Apr. 30, 1991, eff. Dec. 1, 1991.)

ADVISORY COMMITTEE NOTES

1937 Adoption

For provisions in state codes, compare Utah Rev.Stat.Ann. (1933) § 48–0–5 (In civil cases parties may agree in open court on lesser number of jurors); 2 Wash.Rev.Stat.Ann. (Remington, 1932) § 323 (Parties may consent to any number of jurors not less than three).

1991 Amendment

The former rule was rendered obsolete by the adoption in many districts of local rules establishing six as the standard size for a civil jury.

It appears that the minimum size of a jury consistent with the Seventh Amendment is six. Cf. *Ballew v. Georgia*, 435 U.S. 223 (1978) (holding that a conviction based on a jury of less than six is a denial of due process of law). If the parties agree to trial before a smaller jury, a verdict can be taken, but the parties should not other than in exceptional circumstances be encouraged to waive the right to a jury of six, not only because of the constitutional stature of the right, but also because smaller juries are more erratic and less effective in serving to distribute responsibility for the exercise of judicial power.

Because the institution of the alternate juror has been abolished by the proposed revision of Rule 47, it will ordinarily be prudent and necessary, in order to provide for sickness or disability among jurors, to seat more than six jurors. The use of jurors in excess of six increases the representativeness of the jury and harms no interest of a party. *Ray v. Parkside Surgery Center*, 13 F.R.Serv. 585 (6th Cir.1989).

If the court takes the precaution of seating a jury larger than six, an illness occurring during the deliberation period will not result in a mistrial, as it did formerly, because all seated jurors will participate in the verdict and a sufficient number will remain to render a unanimous verdict of six or more.

In exceptional circumstances, as where a jury suffers depletions during trial and deliberation that are greater than can reasonably be expected, the parties may agree to be bound by a verdict rendered by fewer than six jurors. The court should not, however, rely upon the availability of such an agreement, for the use of juries smaller than six is problematic for reasons fully explained in *Ballew v. Georgia*, supra.

Rule 49. Special Verdicts and Interrogatories

(a) Special Verdicts. The court may require a jury to return only a special verdict in the form of a special written finding upon each issue of fact. In that event the court may submit to the jury written questions susceptible of categorical or other brief answer or may submit written forms of the several special findings which might properly be made under the pleadings and evidence; or it may use such other method of submitting the issues and requiring the written findings thereon as it deems most appropriate. The court shall give to the jury such explanation and instruction concerning the matter thus submitted as may be necessary to enable the jury to make its findings upon each issue. If in so doing the court omits any issue of fact raised by the pleadings or by the evidence, each party waives the right to a trial by jury of the issue so omitted unless before the jury retires the party demands its submission to the jury. As to an issue omitted without such demand the court may make a finding; or, if it fails to do so, it shall be deemed to have made a finding in accord with the judgment on the special verdict.

(b) General Verdict Accompanied by Answer to Interrogatories. The court may submit to the jury, together with appropriate forms for a general verdict, written interrogatories upon one or more issues of fact the decision of which is necessary to a verdict. The court shall give such explanation or instruction as may be necessary to enable the jury both to make answers to the interrogatories and to render a general verdict, and the court shall direct the jury both to make written answers and to render a general verdict. When the general verdict and the answers are harmonious, the appropriate judgment upon the verdict and answers shall be entered pursuant to Rule 58. When the answers are consistent with each other but one or more is inconsistent with the general verdict, judgment may be entered pursuant to Rule 58 in accordance with the answers, notwithstanding the general verdict, or the court may return the jury for further consideration of its answers and verdict or may order a new trial. When the answers are inconsistent with each other and one or more is likewise inconsistent with the general verdict, judgment shall not be entered, but the court shall return the jury for further consideration of its answers and verdict or shall order a new trial.

(As amended Jan. 21, 1963, eff. July 1, 1963; Mar. 2, 1987, eff. Aug. 1, 1987.)

ADVISORY COMMITTEE NOTES

1937 Adoption

The Federal courts are not bound to follow state statutes authorizing or requiring the court to ask a jury to find a special verdict or to answer interrogatories. *Victor American Fuel Co. v. Peccarich,* 209 Fed. 568 (C.C.A.8th, 1913), cert. den. 232 U.S. 727, 34 S.Ct. 603, 58 L.Ed. 817 (1914); *Spokane and I.E.R. Co. v. Campbell,* 217 Fed. 518 (C.C.A.9th, 1914), affd. 241 U.S. 497, 36 S.Ct. 683, 60 L.Ed. 1125 (1916); Simkins, *Federal Practice* (1934) § 186. The power of a territory to adopt by statute the practice under Subdivision (b) has been sustained. *Walker v. New Mexico and Southern Pacific R.R.,* 165 U.S. 593, 17 S.Ct. 421, 41 L.Ed. 837 (1897); *Southwestern Brewery and Ice Co. v. Schmidt,* 226 U.S. 162, 33 S.Ct. 68, 57 L.Ed. 170 (1912).

Compare Wis.Stat. (1935) §§ 270.27, 270.28 and 270.30; Green, *A New Development in Jury Trial* (1927), 13 A.B.A.J. 715; Morgan, *A Brief History of Special Verdicts and Special Interrogatories,* 1923, 32 Yale L.J. 575.

The provisions of U.S.C., Title 28, [former] § 400(3) (now §§ 2201, 2202) (Declaratory judgments authorized; procedure) permitting the submission of issues of fact to a jury are covered by this rule.

1963 Amendment

This amendment conforms to the amendment of Rule 58. See the Advisory Committee's Note to Rule 58, as amended.

1987 Amendment

The amendments are technical. No substantive change is intended.

Rule 50. Judgment as a Matter of Law in Jury Trials; Alternative Motion for New Trial; Conditional Rulings

(a) Judgment as a Matter of Law.

(1) If during a trial by jury a party has been fully heard on an issue and there is no legally sufficient evidentiary basis for a reasonable jury to find for that party on that issue, the court may determine the issue against that party and may grant a motion for judgment as a matter of law against that party with respect to a claim or defense that cannot under the controlling law be maintained or defeated without a favorable finding on that issue.

(2) Motions for judgment as a matter of law may be made at any time before submission of the case to the jury. Such a motion shall specify the judgment sought and the law and the facts on which the moving party is entitled to the judgment.

(b) Renewing Motion for Judgment After Trial; Alternative Motion for New Trial. If, for any reason, the court does not grant a motion for judgment as a matter of law made at the close of all the evidence, the court is considered to have submitted the action to the jury subject to the court's later deciding the legal questions raised by the motion. The movant may renew its request for judgment as a matter of law by filing a motion no later than 10 days after entry of judgment— and may alternatively request a new trial or join a motion for a new trial under Rule 59. In ruling on a renewed motion, the court may:

(1) if a verdict was returned:

(A) allow the judgment to stand,

(B) order a new trial, or

(C) direct entry of judgment as a matter of law; or

(2) if no verdict was returned;

(A) order a new trial, or

(B) direct entry of judgment as a matter of law.

(c) Granting Renewed Motion for Judgment as a Matter of Law; Conditional Rulings; New Trial Motion

(1) If the renewed motion for judgment as a matter of law is granted, the court shall also rule on the motion for a new trial, if any, by determining whether it should be granted if the judgment is thereafter vacated or reversed, and shall specify the grounds for granting or denying the motion for the new trial. If the motion for a new trial is thus conditionally granted, the order thereon does not affect the finality of the judgment. In case the motion for a new trial has been conditionally granted and the judgment is reversed on appeal, the new trial shall proceed unless the appellate court has otherwise ordered. In case the motion for a new trial has been conditionally denied, the appellee on appeal may assert error in that denial; and if the judgment is reversed on appeal, subsequent proceedings shall be in accordance with the order of the appellate court.

(2) Any motion for a new trial under Rule 59 by a party against whom judgment as a matter of law is rendered shall be filed no later than 10 days after entry of the judgment.

(d) Same: Denial of Motion for Judgment as a Matter of Law. If the motion for judgment as a matter of law is denied, the party who prevailed on that motion may, as appellee, assert grounds entitling the party to a new trial in the event the appellate court concludes that the trial court erred in denying the motion for judgment. If the appellate court reverses the judgment, nothing in this rule precludes it from determining that the appellee is entitled to a new trial, or from directing the trial court to determine whether a new trial shall be granted.

(As amended Jan. 21, 1963, eff. July 1, 1963; Mar. 2, 1987, eff. Aug. 1, 1987; Apr. 30, 1991, eff. Dec. 1, 1991; Apr. 22, 1993, eff. Dec. 1, 1993; Apr. 27, 1995, eff. Dec. 1, 1995.)

ADVISORY COMMITTEE NOTES

1937 Adoption

Note to Subdivision (a). The present federal rule is changed to the extent that the formality of an express reservation of rights against waiver is no longer necessary. See *Sampliner v. Motion Picture Patents Co.*, 41 S.Ct. 79, 254 U.S. 233, 65 L.Ed. 240 (1920); *Union Indemnity Co. v. United States*, 74 F.2d 645 (C.C.A. 6th, 1935). The requirement that specific grounds for the motion for a directed verdict must be stated settles a conflict in the federal cases. See Simkins, *Federal Practice* (1934) § 189.

Note to Subdivision (b). For comparable state practice upheld under the conformity act, see *Baltimore and Carolina Line v. Redman*, 55 S.Ct. 890, 295 U.S. 654, 79 L.Ed. 1636 (1935); compare *Slocum v. New York Life Ins. Co.*, 33 S.Ct. 523, 228 U.S. 364, 57 L.Ed. 879, Ann.Cas.1914D, 1029 (1913).

See *Northern Ry. Co. v. Page*, 47 S.Ct. 491, 274 U.S. 65, 71 L.Ed. 929 (1927), following the Massachusetts practice of alternative verdicts, explained in Thorndike, *Trial by Jury in United States Courts*, 26 Harv.L.Rev. 732 (1913). See also Thayer, *Judicial Administration*, 63 U. of Pa.L.Rev. 585, 600–601, and note 32 (1915); Scott, *Trial by Jury and the Reform of Civil Procedure*, 31 Harv.L.Rev. 669, 685 (1918); Comment, 34 Mich.L.Rev. 93, 98 (1935).

1963 Amendment

Subdivision (a). The practice, after the court has granted a motion for a directed verdict, of requiring the jury to express assent to a verdict they did not reach by their own deliberations serves no useful purpose and may give offense to the members of the jury. See 2B Barron & Holtzoff, *Federal Practice & Procedure* § 1072, at 367 (Wright ed. 1961); Blume, *Origin and Development of the Directed Verdict*, 48 Mich.L.Rev. 555, 582–85, 589–90 (1950). The final sentence of the subdivision, added by amendment, provides that the court's order granting a motion for a directed verdict is effective in itself, and that no action need be taken by the foreman or other members of the jury. See Ariz. R.Civ.P. 50(c); cf. Fed.R.Crim.P. 29(a). No change is intended in the standard to be applied in deciding the motion. To assure this interpretation, and in the interest of simplicity, the traditional term, "directed verdict," is retained.

Subdivision (b). A motion for judgment notwithstanding the verdict will not lie unless it was preceded by a motion for a directed verdict made at the close of all the evidence.

The amendment of the second sentence of this subdivision sets the time limit for making the motion for judgment n.o.v.

at 10 days after the entry of judgment, rather than 10 days after the reception of the verdict. Thus the time provision is made consistent with that contained in Rule 59(b) (time for motion for new trial) and Rule 52(b) (time for motion to amend findings by the court).

Subdivision (c) deals with the situation where a party joins a motion for a new trial with his motion for judgment n.o.v., or prays for a new trial in the alternative, and the motion for judgment n.o.v. is granted. The procedure to be followed in making rulings on the motion for the new trial, and the consequences of the rulings thereon, were partly set out in *Montgomery Ward & Co. v. Duncan*, 311 U.S. 243, 253, 61 S.Ct. 189, 85 L.Ed. 147 (1940), and have been further elaborated in later cases. See *Cone v. West Virginia Pulp & Paper Co.*, 330 U.S. 212, 67 S.Ct. 752, 91 L.Ed. 849 (1947); *Globe Liquor Co., Inc. v. San Roman*, 332 U.S. 571, 68 S.Ct. 246, 92 L.Ed. 177 (1948); *Fountain v. Filson*, 336 U.S. 681, 69 S.Ct. 754, 93 L.Ed. 971 (1949); *Johnson v. New York, N.H. & H.R.R. Co.*, 344 U.S. 48, 73 S.Ct. 125, 97 L.Ed. 77 (1952). However, courts as well as counsel have often misunderstood the procedure, and it will be helpful to summarize the proper practice in the text of the rule. The amendments do not alter the effects of a jury verdict or the scope of appellate review.

In the situation mentioned, subdivision (c)(1) requires that the court make a "conditional" ruling on the new-trial motion, i.e., a ruling which goes on the assumption that the motion for judgment n.o.v. was erroneously granted and will be reversed or vacated; and the court is required to state its grounds for the conditional ruling. Subdivision (c)(1) then spells out the consequences of a reversal of the judgment in the light of the conditional ruling on the new-trial motion.

If the motion for new trial has been conditionally granted, and the judgment is reversed, "the new trial shall proceed unless the appellate court has otherwise ordered." The party against whom the judgment n.o.v. was entered below may, as appellant, besides seeking to overthrow that judgment, also attack the conditional grant of the new trial. And the appellate court, if it reverses the judgment n.o.v., may in an appropriate case also reverse the conditional grant of the new trial and direct that judgment be entered on the verdict. See *Bailey v. Slentz*, 189 F.2d 406 (10th Cir. 1951); *Moist Cold Refrigerator Co. v. Lou Johnson Co.*, 249 F.2d 246 (9th Cir. 1957), cert. denied, 356 U.S. 968, 78 S.Ct. 1008, 2 L.Ed.2d 1074 (1958); *Peters v. Smith*, 221 F.2d 721 (3d Cir. 1955); *Dailey v. Timmer*, 292 F.2d 824 (3d Cir. 1961), explaining *Lind v. Schenley Industries, Inc.*, 278 F.2d 79 (3d Cir.), cert. denied, 364 U.S. 835, 81 S.Ct. 58, 5 L.Ed.2d 60 (1960); *Cox v. Pennsylvania R.R.*, 120 A.2d 214 (D.C.Mun. Ct.App.1956); 3 Barron & Holtzoff, *Federal Practice & Procedure* § 1302.1 at 346–47 (Wright ed. 1958); 6 *Moore's Federal Practice* ¶59.16 at 3915 n. 8a (2d ed. 1954).

If the motion for a new trial has been conditionally denied, and the judgment is reversed, "subsequent proceedings shall be in accordance with the order of the appellate court." The party in whose favor judgment n.o.v. was entered below may, as appellee, besides seeking to uphold that judgment, also urge on the appellate court that the trial court committed error in conditionally denying the new trial. The appellee may assert this error in his brief, without taking a cross-appeal. Cf. *Patterson v. Pennsylvania R.R.*, 238 F.2d 645, 650 (6th Cir. 1956); *Hughes v. St. Louis Nat. L. Baseball Club, Inc.*, 359 Mo. 993, 997, 224 S.W.2d 989, 992 (1949). If the appellate court concludes that the judgment cannot stand, but accepts the appellee's contention that there was error in the conditional denial of the new trial, it may order a new trial in lieu of directing the entry of judgment upon the verdict.

Subdivision (c)(2), which also deals with the situation where the trial court has granted the motion for judgment n.o.v., states that the verdict-winner may apply to the trial court for a new trial pursuant to Rule 59 after the judgment n.o.v. has been entered against him. In arguing to the trial court in opposition to the motion for judgment n.o.v., the verdict-winner may, and often will, contend that he is entitled, at the least, to a new trial, and the court has a range of discretion to grant a new trial or (where plaintiff won the verdict) to order a dismissal of the action without prejudice instead of granting judgment n.o.v. See *Cone v. West Virginia Pulp & Paper Co.,* supra, 330 U.S. at 217, 218, 67 S.Ct. at 755, 756, 91 L.Ed. 849. Subdivision (c)(2) is a reminder that the verdict-winner is entitled, even after entry of judgment n.o.v. against him, to move for a new trial in the usual course. If in these circumstances the motion is granted, the judgment is superseded.

In some unusual circumstances, however, the grant of the new-trial motion may be only conditional, and the judgment will not be superseded. See the situation in *Tribble v. Bruin,* 279 F.2d 424 (4th Cir. 1960) (upon a verdict for plaintiff, defendant moves for and obtains judgment n.o.v.; plaintiff moves for a new trial on the ground of inadequate damages; trial court might properly have granted plaintiff's motion, conditional upon reversal of the judgment n.o.v.).

Even if the verdict-winner makes no motion for a new trial, he is entitled upon his appeal from the judgment n.o.v. not only to urge that that judgment should be reversed and judgment entered upon the verdict, but that errors were committed during the trial which at the least entitle him to a new trial.

Subdivision (d) deals with the situation where judgment has been entered on the jury verdict, the motion for judgment n.o.v. and any motion for a new trial having been denied by the trial court. The verdict-winner, as appellee, besides seeking to uphold the judgment may urge upon the appellate court that in case the trial court is found to have erred in entering judgment on the verdict, there are grounds for granting him a new trial instead of directing the entry of judgment for his opponent. In appropriate cases the appellate court is not precluded from itself directing that a new trial be had. See *Weade v. Dichmann, Wright & Pugh, Inc.,* 337 U.S. 801, 69 S.Ct. 1326, 93 L.Ed. 1704 (1949). Nor is it precluded in proper cases from remanding the case for a determination by the trial court as to whether a new trial should be granted. The latter course is advisable where the grounds urged are suitable for the exercise of trial court discretion.

Subdivision (d) does not attempt a regulation of all aspects of the procedure where the motion for judgment n.o.v. and any accompanying motion for a new trial are denied, since the problems have not been fully canvassed in the decisions and the procedure is in some respects still in a formative stage. It is, however, designed to give guidance on certain important features of the practice.

1987 Amendment

The amendments are technical. No substantive change is intended.

1991 Amendment

Subdivision (a). The revision of this subdivision aims to facilitate the exercise by the court of its responsibility to assure the fidelity of its judgment to the controlling law, a responsibility imposed by the Due Process Clause of the Fifth Amendment. *Cf. Galloway v. United States,* 319 U.S. 372 (1943).

The revision abandons the familiar terminology of *direction of verdict* for several reasons. The term is misleading as a description of the relationship between judge and jury. It is also freighted with anachronisms some of which are the subject of the text of former subdivision (a) of this rule that is deleted in this revision. Thus, it should not be necessary to state in the text of this rule that a motion made pursuant to it is not a waiver of the right to jury trial, and only the antiquities of directed verdict practice suggest that it might have been. The term "judgment as a matter of law" is an almost equally familiar term and appears in the text of Rule 56; its use in Rule 50 calls attention to the relationship between the two rules. Finally, the change enables the rule to refer to preverdict and post-verdict motions with a terminology that does not conceal the common identity of two motions made at different times in the proceeding.

If a motion is denominated a motion for directed verdict or for judgment notwithstanding the verdict, the party's error is merely formal. Such a motion should be treated as a motion for judgment as a matter of law in accordance with this rule.

Paragraph (a)(1) articulates the standard for the granting of a motion for judgment as a matter of law. It effects no change in the existing standard. That existing standard was not expressed in the former rule, but was articulated in long-standing case law. *See generally* Cooper, *Directions for Directed Verdicts: A Compass for Federal Courts,* 55 MINN.L.REV. 903 (1971). The expressed standard makes clear that action taken under the rule is a performance of the court's duty to assure enforcement of the controlling law and is not an intrusion on any responsibility for factual determinations conferred on the jury by the Seventh Amendment or any other provision of federal law. Because this standard is also used as a reference point for entry of summary judgment under 56(a), it serves to link the two related provisions.

The revision authorizes the court to perform its duty to enter judgment as a matter of law at any time during the trial, as soon as it is apparent that either party is unable to carry a burden of proof that is essential to that party's case. Thus, the second sentence of paragraph (a)(1) authorizes the court to consider a motion for judgment as a matter of law as soon as a party has completed a presentation on a fact essential to that party's case. Such early action is appropriate when economy and expedition will be served. In no event, however, should the court enter judgment against a party who has not been apprised of the materiality of the dispositive fact and been afforded an opportunity to present any available evidence bearing on that fact. In order further to facilitate the exercise of the authority provided by this rule, Rule 16 is also revised to encourage the court to schedule an order of trial that proceeds first with a presentation on an issue that is likely to be dispositive, if such an issue is identified in the course of pretrial. Such scheduling can be appropriate where the court is uncertain whether favorable action should be taken under Rule 56. Thus, the revision affords the court the alternative of denying a motion for summary judgment while scheduling a separate trial of the issue under Rule 42(b) or scheduling the trial to begin with a presentation on that essential fact which the opposing party seems unlikely to be able to maintain.

Paragraph (a)(2) retains the requirement that a motion for judgment be made prior to the close of the trial, subject to renewal after a jury verdict has been rendered. The purpose of this requirement is to assure the responding party an opportunity to cure any deficiency in that party's proof that may have been overlooked until called to the party's attention by a late motion for judgment. Cf. *Farley Transp. Co. v. Santa Fe Trail Transp. Co.*, 786 F.2d 1342 (9th Cir.1986) ("If the moving party is then permitted to make a later attack on the evidence through a motion for judgment notwithstanding the verdict or an appeal, the opposing party may be prejudiced by having lost the opportunity to present additional evidence before the case was submitted to the jury"); *Benson v. Allphin*, 786 F.2d 268 (7th Cir.1986) ("the motion for directed verdict at the close of all the evidence provides the nonmovant an opportunity to do what he can to remedy the deficiencies in his case . . ."); *McLaughlin v. The Fellows Gear Shaper Co.*, 4 F.R.Serv.3d 607 (3d Cir.1986) (per Adams, J., dissenting: "This Rule serves important practical purposes in ensuring that neither party is precluded from presenting the most persuasive case possible and in preventing unfair surprise after a matter has been submitted to the jury"). At one time, this requirement was held to be of constitutional stature, being compelled by the Seventh Amendment. Cf. *Slocum v. New York Insurance Co.*, 228 U.S. 364 (1913). But cf. *Baltimore & Carolina Line v. Redman*, 295 U.S. 654 (1935).

The second sentence of paragraph (a)(2) does impose a requirement that the moving party articulate the basis on which a judgment as a matter of law might be rendered. The articulation is necessary to achieve the purpose of the requirement that the motion be made before the case is submitted to the jury, so that the responding party may seek to correct any overlooked deficiencies in the proof. The revision thus alters the result in cases in which courts have used various techniques to avoid the requirement that a motion for a directed verdict be made as a predicate to a motion for judgment notwithstanding the verdict. E.g., *Benson v. Allphin*, 788 F.2d 268 (7th Cir.1986) ("this circuit has allowed something less than a formal motion for directed verdict to preserve a party's right to move for judgment notwithstanding the verdict"). *See generally* 9 WRIGHT & MILLER, FEDERAL PRACTICE AND PROCEDURE § 2537 (1971 and Supp.). The information required with the motion may be supplied by explicit reference to materials and argument previously supplied to the court.

This subdivision deals only with the entry of judgment and not with the resolution of particular factual issues as a matter of law. The court may, as before, properly refuse to instruct a jury to decide an issue if a reasonable jury could on the evidence presented decide that issue in only one way.

Subdivision (b). This provision retains the concept of the former rule that the post-verdict motion is a renewal of an earlier motion made at the close of the evidence. One purpose of this concept was to avoid any question arising

under the Seventh Amendment. *Montgomery Ward & Co. v. Duncan*, 311 U.S. 243 (1940). It remains useful as a means of defining the appropriate issue posed by the post-verdict motion. A post-trial motion for judgment can be granted only on grounds advanced in the pre-verdict motion. *E.g.*, *Kutner Buick, Inc. v. American Motors Corp.*, 848 F.2d 614 (3d Cir.1989).

Often it appears to the court or to the moving party that a motion for judgment as a matter of law made at the close of the evidence should be reserved for a post-verdict decision. This is so because a jury verdict for the moving party moots the issue and because a preverdict ruling gambles that a reversal may result in a new trial that might have been avoided. For these reasons, the court may often wisely decline to rule on a motion for judgment as a matter of law made at the close of the evidence, and it is not inappropriate for the moving party to suggest such a postponement of the ruling until after the verdict has been rendered.

In ruling on such a motion, the court should disregard any jury determination for which there is no legally sufficient evidentiary basis enabling a reasonable jury to make it. The court may then decide such issues as a matter of law and enter judgment if all other material issues have been decided by the jury on the basis of legally sufficient evidence, or by the court as a matter of law.

The revised rule is intended for use in this manner with Rule 49. Thus, the court may combine facts established as a matter of law either before trial under Rule 56 or at trial on the basis of the evidence presented with other facts determined by the jury under instructions provided under Rule 49 to support a proper judgment under this rule.

This provision also retains the former requirement that a post-trial motion under the rule must be made within 10 days after entry of a contrary judgment. The renewed motion must be served and filed as provided by Rule 5. A purpose of this requirement is to meet the requirements of F.R.App.P. 4(a)(4).

Subdivision (c). Revision of this subdivision conforms the language to the change in diction set forth in subdivision (a) of this revised rule.

Subdivision (d). Revision of this subdivision conforms the language to that of the previous subdivisions.

1993 Amendments

This technical amendment corrects an ambiguity in the text of the 1991 revision of the rule, which, as indicated in the Notes, was not intended to change the existing standards under which "directed verdicts" could be granted. This amendment makes clear that judgments as a matter of law in jury trials may be entered against both plaintiffs and defendants and with respect to issues or defenses that may not be wholly dispositive of a claim or defense.

1995 Amendments

The only change, other than stylistic, intended by this revision is to prescribe a uniform explicit time for filing of post-judgment motions under this rule—no later than 10 days after entry of the judgment. Previously, there was an inconsistency in the wording of Rules 50, 52, and 59 with respect to whether certain post-judgment motions had to be filed, or merely served, during that period. This inconsistency caused special problems when motions for a new trial were joined with other post-judgment motions. These motions affect the finality of the judgment, a matter often of importance to third persons as well as the parties and the court. The Committee believes that each of these rules should be revised to require filing before end of the 10–day period. Filing is an event that can be determined with certainty from court records. The phrase "no later than" is used—rather than "within"—to include post-judgment motions that sometimes are filed before actual entry of the judgment by the clerk. It should be noted that under Rule 6(a) Saturdays, Sundays, and legal holidays are excluded in measuring the 10–day period, and that under Rule 5 the motions when filed are to contain a certificate of service on other parties.

Rule 51. Instructions to Jury; Objections; Preserving a Claim of Error

(a) Requests.

(1) A party may, at the close of the evidence or at an earlier reasonable time that the court directs, file and furnish to every other party written requests that the court instruct the jury on the law as set forth in the requests.

(2) After the close of the evidence, a party may:

(A) file requests for instructions on issues that could not reasonably have been anticipated at an earlier time for requests set under Rule 51(a)(1), and

(B) with the court's permission file untimely requests for instructions on any issue.

(b) Instructions. The court:

(1) must inform the parties of its proposed instructions and proposed action on the requests before instructing the jury and before final jury arguments;

(2) must give the parties an opportunity to object on the record and out of the jury's hearing to the proposed instructions and actions on requests before the instructions and arguments are delivered; and

(3) may instruct the jury at any time after trial begins and before the jury is discharged.

(c) Objections.

(1) A party who objects to an instruction or the failure to give an instruction must do so on the record, stating distinctly the matter objected to and the grounds of the objection.

(2) An objection is timely if:

(A) a party that has been informed of an instruction or action on a request before the jury is instructed and before final jury arguments, as provided by Rule 51(b)(1), objects at the opportunity for objection required by Rule 51(b)(2); or

(B) a party that has not been informed of an instruction or action on a request before the time for objection provided under Rule 51(b)(2) objects promptly after learning that the instruction or request will be, or has been, given or refused.

(d) Assigning Error; Plain Error.

(1) A party may assign as error:

(A) an error in an instruction actually given if that party made a proper objection under Rule 51(c), or

(B) a failure to give an instruction if that party made a proper request under Rule 51(a), and—unless the court made a definitive ruling on the record rejecting the request—also made a proper objection under Rule 51(c).

(2) A court may consider a plain error in the instructions affecting substantial rights that has not been preserved as required by Rule 51(d)(1)(A) or (B).

(As amended Mar. 2, 1987, eff. Aug. 1, 1987; Mar. 27, 2003, eff. Dec. 1, 2003.)

ADVISORY COMMITTEE NOTES

1937 Adoption

Supreme Court Rule 8 requires exceptions to the charge of the court to the jury which shall distinctly state the several matters of law in the charge to which exception is taken. Similar provisions appear in the rules of the various Circuit Courts of Appeals.

1987 Amendment

Although Rule 51 in its present form specifies that the court shall instruct the jury only after the arguments of the parties are completed, in some districts (typically those in states where the practice is otherwise) it is common for the parties to stipulate to instruction before the arguments. The purpose of the amendment is to give the court discretion to instruct the jury either before or after argument. Thus, the rule as revised will permit resort to the long-standing federal practice or to an alternative procedure, which has been praised because it gives counsel the opportunity to explain the instructions, argue their application to the facts and thereby give the jury the maximum assistance in determining the issues and arriving at a good verdict on the law and the evidence. As an ancillary benefit, this approach aids counsel by supplying a natural outline so that arguments may be directed to the essential fact issues which the jury must decide. See generally Raymond, *Merits and Demerits of the Missouri System of Instructing Juries*, 5 St. Louis U.L.J. 317 (1959). Moreover, if the court instructs before an argument, counsel then know the precise words the court has chosen and need not speculate as to the words the court will later use in its instructions. Finally, by instructing ahead of argument the court has the attention of the jurors when they are fresh and can give their full attention to the court's instructions. It is more difficult to hold the attention of jurors after lengthy arguments.

2003 Amendments

Rule 51 is revised to capture many of the interpretations that have emerged in practice. The revisions in text will make uniform the conclusions reached by a majority of decisions on each point. Additions also are made to cover some practices that cannot now be anchored in the text of Rule 51.

Scope. Rule 51 governs instructions to the trial jury on the law that governs the verdict. A variety of other instructions cannot practicably be brought within Rule 51. Among these instructions are preliminary instructions to a venire, and cautionary or limiting instructions delivered in immediate response to events at trial.

Requests. Subdivision (a) governs requests. Apart from the plain error doctrine recognized in subdivision (d)(2), a court is not obliged to instruct the jury on issues raised by the evidence unless a party requests an instruction. The revised rule recognizes the court's authority to direct that requests be submitted before trial.

The close-of-the-evidence deadline may come before trial is completed on all potential issues. Trial may be formally bifurcated or may be sequenced in some less formal manner. The close of the evidence is measured by the occurrence of two events: completion of all intended evidence on an identified phase of the trial and impending submission to the jury with instructions.

The risk in directing a pretrial request deadline is that trial evidence may raise new issues or reshape issues the parties thought they had understood. Courts need not insist on pretrial requests in all cases. Even if the request time is set before trial or early in the trial, subdivision (a)(2)(A) permits requests after the close of the evidence to address issues that could not reasonably have been anticipated at the earlier time for requests set by the court.

Subdivision (a)(2)(B) expressly recognizes the court's discretion to act on an untimely request. The most important consideration in exercising the discretion confirmed by subdivision (a)(2)(B) is the importance of the issue to the case—the closer the issue lies to the "plain error" that would be recognized under subdivision (d)(2), the better the reason to give an instruction. The cogency of the reason for failing to make a timely request also should be considered. To be considered under subdivision (a)(2)(B) a request should be made before final instructions and before final jury arguments. What is a "final" instruction and argument depends on the sequence of submitting the case to the jury. If separate portions of the case are submitted to the jury in sequence, the final arguments and final instructions are those made on submitting to the jury the portion of the case addressed by the arguments and instructions.

Instructions. Subdivision (b)(1) requires the court to inform the parties, before instructing the jury and before final jury arguments related to the instruction, of the proposed instructions as well as the proposed action on instruction requests. The time limit is addressed to final jury arguments to reflect the practice that allows interim argument s during trial in complex cases; it may not be feasible to develop final instructions before such interim arguments. It is enough that counsel know of the intended instructions before making final arguments addressed to the issue. If the trial is sequenced or bifurcated, the final arguments addressed to an issue may occur before the close of the entire trial.

Subdivision (b)(2) complements subdivision (b)(1) by carrying forward the opportunity to object established by present Rule 51. It makes explicit the opportunity to object on the record, ensuring a clear memorial of the objection.

Subdivision (b)(3) reflects common practice by authorizing instructions at any time after trial begins and before the jury is discharged.

Objections. Subdivision (c) states the right to object to an instruction or the failure to give an instruction. It carries forward the formula of present Rule 51 requiring that the objection state distinctly the matter objected to and the grounds of the objection, and makes explicit the requirement that the objection be made on the record. The provisions on the time to object make clear that it is timely to object promptly after learning of an instruction or action on a request when the court has not provided advance information as required by subdivision (b)(1). The need to repeat a request by way of objection is continued by new subdivision (d)(1)(B) except where the court made a definitive ruling on the record.

Preserving a claim of error and plain error. Many cases hold that a proper request for a jury instruction is not alone enough to preserve the right to appeal failure to give the instruction. The request must be renewed by objection. This doctrine is appropriate when the court may not have sufficiently focused on the request, or may believe that the request has been granted in substance although in different words. But this doctrine may also prove a trap for the unwary who fail to add an objection after the court has made it clear that the request has been considered and rejected on the merits. Subdivision (d)(1)(B) establishes authority to review the failure to grant a timely request, despite a failure to add an objection, when the court has made a definitive ruling on the record rejecting the request.

Many circuits have recognized that an error not preserved under Rule 51 may be reviewed in exceptional circumstances. The language adopted to capture these decisions in subdivision (d)(2) is borrowed from Criminal Rule 52. Although the language is the same, the context of civil litigation often differs from the context of criminal prosecution; actual application of the plain-error standard takes account of the differences. The Supreme Court has summarized application of Criminal Rule 52 as involving four elements: (1) there must be an error; (2) the error must be plain; (3) the error must affect substantial rights; and (4) the error must seriously affect the fairness, integrity, or public reputation of judicial proceedings. Johnson v. U.S., 520 U.S. 461, 466–467, 469–470 (1997). (The Johnson case quoted the fourth element from its decision in a civil action, U.S. v. Atkinson, 297 U.S. 157, 160 (1936): "In exceptional circumstances, especially in criminal cases, appellate courts, in the public interest, may, of their own motion, notice errors to which no exception has been taken, if the errors are obvious, or if they otherwise substantially affect the fairness, integrity, or public reputation of judicial proceedings.")

The court's duty to give correct jury instructions in a civil action is shaped by at least four factors.

The factor most directly implied by a "plain" error rule is the obviousness of the mistake. The importance of the error is a second major factor. The costs of correcting an error reflect a third factor that is affected by a variety of circumstances. In a case that seems close to the fundamental error line, account also may be taken of the impact a verdict may have on nonparties.

Rule 52. Findings by the Court; Judgment on Partial Findings

(a) Effect. In all actions tried upon the facts without a jury or with an advisory jury, the court shall find the facts specially and state separately its conclusions of law thereon, and judgment shall be entered pursuant to Rule 58; and in granting or refusing interlocutory injunctions the court shall similarly set forth the findings of fact and conclusions of law which constitute the grounds of its action. Requests for findings are not necessary for purposes of review. Findings of fact, whether based on oral or documentary evidence, shall not be set aside unless clearly erroneous, and due regard shall be given to the opportunity of the trial court to judge of the credibility of the witnesses. The findings of a master, to the extent that the court adopts them, shall be considered as the findings of the court. It will be sufficient if the findings of fact and conclusions of law are stated orally and recorded in open court following the close of the evidence or appear in an opinion or memorandum of decision filed by the court. Findings of fact and conclusions of law are unnecessary on decisions of motions under Rule 12 or 56 or any other motion except as provided in subdivision (c) of this rule.

(b) Amendment. On a party's motion filed no later than 10 days after entry of judgment, the court may amend its findings—or make additional findings—and may amend the judgment accordingly. The motion may accompany a motion for a new trial under Rule 59. When findings of fact are made in actions tried without a jury, the sufficiency of the evidence supporting the findings may be later questioned whether or not in the district court the party raising the question objected to the findings, moved to amend them, or moved for partial findings.

(c) Judgment on Partial Findings. If during a trial without a jury a party has been fully heard on an issue and the court finds against the party on that issue, the court may enter judgment as a matter of law against that party with respect to a claim or defense that cannot under the controlling law be maintained or defeated without a favorable finding on that issue, or the court may decline to render any judgment until the close of all the evidence. Such a judgment shall be supported by findings of fact and conclusions of law as required by subdivision (a) of this rule.

(As amended Dec. 27, 1946, eff. Mar. 19, 1948; Jan. 21, 1963, eff. July 1, 1963; Apr. 28, 1983, eff. Aug. 1, 1983; Apr. 29, 1985, eff. Aug. 1, 1985; Apr. 30, 1991, eff. Dec. 1, 1991; Apr. 22, 1993, eff. Dec. 1, 1993; Apr. 27, 1995, eff. Dec. 1, 1995.)

ADVISORY COMMITTEE NOTES

1937 Adoption

See [former] Equity Rule 70½, as amended Nov. 25, 1935, (Findings of Fact and Conclusions of Law) and U.S.C., Title 28, [former] § 764 (Opinion, findings, and conclusions in action against United States) which are substantially continued in this rule. The provisions of U.S.C., Title 28, [former] §§ 773 (Trial of issues of fact; by court) and [former] 875 (Review in cases tried without a jury) are superseded in so far as they provide a different method of finding facts and a different method of appellate review. The rule stated in the third sentence of Subdivision (a) accords with the decisions on the scope of the review in modern federal equity practice. It is applicable to all classes of findings in cases tried without a jury whether the finding is of a fact concerning which there was conflict of testimony, or of a fact deduced or inferred from uncontradicted testimony. See *Silver King Coalition Mines Co. v. Silver King Consolidated Mining Co.*, C.C.A.8, 1913, 204 F. 166, certiorari denied 33 S.Ct. 1051, 229 U.S. 624, 57 L.Ed. 1356; *Warren v. Keep*, 1894, 15 S.Ct. 83, 155 U.S. 265, 39 L.Ed. 144; *Furrer v. Ferris*, 1892, 12 S.Ct. 821, 145 U.S. 132, 36 L.Ed. 649; *Tilghman v. Proctor*, 1888, 8 S.Ct. 894, 125 U.S. 136, 149, 31 L.Ed. 664; *Kimberly v. Arms*, 1889, 9 S.Ct. 355, 129 U.S. 512, 524, 32 L.Ed. 764. Compare *Kaeser & Blair Inc. v. Merchants' Ass'n*, C.C.A.6, 1933, 64 F.2d 575, 576; *Dunn v. Trefry*, C.C.A.1, 1919, 260 F. 147.

In the following states findings of fact are required in all cases tried without a jury (waiver by the parties being permitted as indicated at the end of the listing): Arkansas, Civ.Code (Crawford, 1934) § 364; California, Code Civ.Proc. (Deering, 1937) §§ 632, 634; Colorado, 1 Stat.Ann. (1935) Code Civ.Proc. §§ 232, 291 (in actions before referees or for possession of and damages to land); Connecticut, Gen.Stats. §§ 5660, 5664; Idaho, 1 Code Ann. (1932) §§ 7–302 through 7–305; Massachusetts (equity cases), 2 Gen.Laws (Ter.Ed., 1932) ch. 214, § 23; Minnesota, 2 Stat. (Mason, 1927) § 9311; Nevada, 4 Comp.Laws (Hillyer, 1929) §§ 8783–8784; New Jersey, Sup.Ct.Rule 113, 2 N.J.Misc. 1197, 1239 (1924); New Mexico, Stat.Ann. (Courtright, 1929) §§ 105–813; North Carolina, Code (1935) § 569; North Dakota, 2 Comp.Laws Ann. (1913) § 7641; Oregon, 2 Code Ann. (1930) §§ 2–502; South Carolina, Code (Michie, 1932) § 649; South Dakota, 1 Comp. Laws (1929) §§ 2525–2526; Utah, Rev.Stat.Ann. (1933) §§ 104–26–2, 104–26–3; Vermont (where jury trial waived), Pub.Laws (1933) § 2069; Washington, 2 Rev.Stat.Ann. (Remington, 1932) § 367; Wisconsin, Stat. (1935) § 270.33. The parties may waive this requirement for findings in California, Idaho, North Dakota, Nevada, New Mexico, Utah, and South Dakota.

In the following states the review of findings of fact in all non-jury cases, including jury waived cases, is assimilated to the equity review: Alabama, Code Ann. (Michie, 1928) §§ 9498, 8599; California, Code Civ.Proc. (Derring, 1937) § 956a; but see 20 Calif.Law Rev. 171 (1932); Colorado, *Johnson v. Kountze*, 1895, 43 P. 445, 21 Colo. 486, semble; Illinois, *Baker v. Hinricks*, 1934, 194 N.E. 284, 359 Ill. 138; *Weininger v. Metropolitan Fire Ins. Co.*, 1935, 195 N.E. 420, 359 Ill. 584, 98 A.L.R. 169; Minnesota, *State Bank of Gibbon v. Walter*, 1926, 208 N.W. 423, 167 Minn. 37; *Waldron v. Page*, 1934, 253 N.W. 894, 191 Minn. 302; New Jersey N.J.S.A. 2:27–241, 2:27–363, as interpreted in *Bussy v. Hatch*, 1920, 111 A. 546, 95 N.J.L. 56; New York, *York Mortgage Corporation v. Clotar Const. Corp.*, 1930, 172 N.E. 265, 254 N.Y. 128; North Dakota, Comp.Laws Ann. (1913) § 7846, as amended by N.D.Laws 1933, c. 208; *Milnor Holding Co. v. Holt*, 1933, 248 N.W. 315, 63 N.D. 362, 370; Oklahoma, *Wichita Mining and Improvement Co. v. Hale*,

1908, 94 P. 530, 20 Okl. 159; South Dakota, *Randall v. Burk Township*, 4 S.D. 337, 57 N.W. 4 (1893); Texas, *Custard v. Flowers*, 1929, 14 S.W.2d 109; Utah, Rev.Stat.Ann. (1933) § 104–41–5; Vermont, *Roberge v. Troy*, 1933, 163 A. 770, 105 Vt. 134; Washington, 2 Rev.Stat.Ann. (Remington, 1932) §§ 309–316; *McCullough v. Puget Sound Realty Associates*, 1913, 136 Pac. 1146, 76 Wash. 700, but see *Cornwall v. Anderson*, 1915, 148 P. 1, 85 Wash. 369; West Virginia, *Kinsey v. Carr*, 1906, 55 S.E. 1004, 60 W.Va. 449, semble; Wisconsin, Stat. (1935) § 251.09; *Campbell v. Sutliff*, 1927, 214 N.W. 374, 193 Wis. 370; *Gessler v. Erwin Co.*, 1924, 193 N.W. 303, 182 Wis. 315.

For examples of an assimilation of the review of findings of fact in cases tried without a jury to the review at law as made in several states, see Clark and Stone, *Review of Findings of Fact*, 4 U. of Chi.L.Rev. 190, 215 (1937).

1946 Amendment

Note to Subdivision (a). The amended rule makes clear that the requirement for findings of fact and conclusions of law thereon applies in a case with an advisory jury. This removes an ambiguity in the rule as originally stated, but carries into effect what has been considered its intent. 3 *Moore's Federal Practice*, 1938, 3119. *Hurwitz v. Hurwitz*, 1943, 136 F.2d 796, 78 U.S.App.D.C. 66.

The two sentences added at the end of Rule 52(a) eliminate certain difficulties which have arisen concerning findings and conclusions. The first of the two sentences permits findings of fact and conclusions of law to appear in an opinion or memorandum of decision. See, e.g., *United States v. One 1941 Ford Sedan*, S.D.Tex.1946, 65 F.Supp. 84. Under original Rule 52(a) some courts have expressed the view that findings and conclusions could not be incorporated in an opinion. *Detective Comics, Inc. v. Bruns Publications*, S.D.N.Y.1939, 28 F.Supp. 399; *Pennsylvania Co. for Insurance on Lives & Granting Annuities v. Cincinnati & L.E.R. Co.*, S.D.Ohio 1941, 43 F.Supp. 5; *United States v. Aluminum Co. of America*, S.D.N.Y.1941, 2 F.R.D. 224, 5 Fed. Rules Serv. 52a.11, Case 3; see also s.c., 44 F.Supp. 97. But, to the contrary, see *Wellman v. United States*, D.Mass.1938, 25 F.Supp. 868; *Cook v. United States*, D.Mass.1939, 26 F.Supp. 253; *Proctor v. White*, D.Mass.1939, 28 F.Supp. 161; *Green Valley Creamery, Inc. v. United States*, C.C.A.1, 1939, 108 F.2d 342. See also *Matton Oil Transfer Corp. v. The Dynamic*, C.C.A.2, 1941, 123 F.2d 999; *Carter Coal Co. v. Litz*, C.C.A.4, 1944, 140 F.2d 934; *Woodruff v. Heiser*, C.C.A.10, 1945, 150 F.2d 869; *Coca Cola Co. v. Busch*, Pa.1943, 7 Fed. Rules Serv. 59b.2, Case 4; Oglebay, *Some Developments in Bankruptcy Law*, 1944, 18 J. of Nat'l Ass'n of Ref. 68, 69. Findings of fact aid in the process of judgment and in defining for future cases the precise limitations of the issues and the determination thereon. Thus they not only aid the appellate court on review, *Hurwitz v. Hurwitz*, App.D.C.1943, 136 F.2d 796, 78 U.S.App.D.C. 66, but they are an important factor in the proper application of the doctrines of res judicata and estoppel by judgment. Nordbye, *Improvements in Statement of Findings of Fact and Conclusions of Law*, 1 F.R.D. 25, 26–27; *United States v. Forness*, C.C.A.2, 1942, 125 F.2d 928, certiorari denied 1942, 62 S.Ct. 1293, 316 U.S. 694, 86 L.Ed. 1764. These findings should represent the judge's own determination and not the long, often argumentative statements of successful counsel. *United States v. Forness*, supra; *United States v.*

Crescent Amusement Co., 1944, 1945, 65 S.Ct. 254, 323 U.S. 173, 89 L.Ed. 160. Consequently, they should be a part of the judge's opinion and decision, either stated therein or stated separately. *Matton Oil Transfer Corp. v. The Dynamic*, supra. But the judge need only make brief, definite, pertinent findings and conclusions upon the contested matters; there is no necessity for over-elaboration of detail or particularization of facts. *United States v. Forness*, supra; *United States v. Crescent Amusement Co.*, supra. See also *Petterson Lighterage & Towing Corp. v. New York Central R. Co.*, C.C.A.2, 1942, 126 F.2d 992; *Brown Paper Mill Co., Inc. v. Irwin*, C.C.A.8, 1943, 134 F.2d 337; *Allen Bradley Co. v. Local Union No. 3, I.B.E.W.*, C.C.A.2, 1944, 145 F.2d 215, reversed on other grounds 65 S.Ct. 1533, 325 U.S. 797; *Young v. Murphy*, Ohio 1946, 9 Fed.Rules Serv. 52a.11, Case 2.

The last sentence of Rule 52(a) as amended will remove any doubt that findings and conclusions are unnecessary upon decision of a motion, particularly one under Rule 12 or Rule 56, except as provided in amended Rule 41(b). As so holding, see *Thomas v. Peyser*, App.D.C.1941, 118 F.2d 369; *Schad v. Twentieth Century-Fox Corp.*, C.C.A.3, 1943, 136 F.2d 991; *Prudential Ins. Co. of America v. Goldstein*, N.Y.1942, 43 F.Supp. 767; *Somers Coal Co. v. United States*, N.D.Ohio 1942, 2 F.R.D. 532, 6 Fed.Rules Serv. 52a.1, Case 1; *Pen-Ken Oil & Gas Corp. v. Warfield Natural Gas Co.*, E.D.Ky.1942, 2 F.R.D. 355, 5 Fed. Rules Serv. 52a.1, Case 3; also Commentary, *Necessity of Findings of Fact*, 1941, 4 Fed. Rules Serv. 936.

1963 Amendment

This amendment conforms to the amendment of Rule 58. See the Advisory Committee's Note to Rule 58, as amended.

1983 Amendment

Rule 52(a) has been amended to revise its penultimate sentence to provide explicitly that the district judge may make the findings of fact and conclusions of law required in nonjury cases orally. Nothing in the prior text of the rule forbids this practice, which is widely utilized by district judges. See Christensen, *A Modest Proposal for Immeasurable Improvement*, 64 A.B.A.J. 693 (1978). The objective is to lighten the burden on the trial court in preparing findings in nonjury cases. In addition, the amendment should reduce the number of published district court opinions that embrace written findings.

1985 Amendment

Rule 52(a) has been amended (1) to avoid continued confusion and conflicts among the circuits as to the standard of appellate review of findings of fact by the court, (2) to eliminate the disparity between the standard of review as literally stated in Rule 52(a) and the practice of some courts of appeals, and (3) to promote nationwide uniformity. See Note, *Rule 52(a): Appellate Review of Findings of Fact Based on Documentary or Undisputed Evidence*, 49 Va. L.Rev. 506, 536 (1963).

Some courts of appeal have stated that when a trial court's findings do not rest on demeanor evidence and evaluation of a witness' credibility, there is no reason to defer to the trial court's findings and the appellate court more readily can find them to be clearly erroneous. See, e.g., *Marcum v. United*

States, 621 F.2d 142, 144–45 (5th Cir.1980). Others go further, holding that appellate review may be had without application of the "clearly erroneous" test since the appellate court is in as good a position as the trial court to review a purely documentary record. See, *e.g.*, *Atari, Inc. v. North American Philips Consumer Electronics Corp.*, 672 F.2d 607, 614 (7th Cir.), cert. denied, 459 U.S. 880 (1982); *Lydle v. United States*, 635 F.2d 763, 765 n. 1 (6th Cir.1981); *Swanson v. Baker Indus., Inc.*, 615 F.2d 479, 483 (8th Cir.1980); *Taylor v. Lombard*, 606 F.2d 371, 372 (2d Cir.1979), cert. denied, 445 U.S. 946 (1980); *Jack Kahn Music Co. v. Baldwin Piano & Organ Co.*, 604 F.2d 755, 758 (2d Cir.1979); *John R. Thompson Co. v. United States*, 477 F.2d 164, 167 (7th Cir.1973).

A third group has adopted the view that the "clearly erroneous" rule applies in all nonjury cases even when findings are based solely on documentary evidence or on inferences from undisputed facts. See, *e.g.*, *Maxwell v. Sumner*, 673 F.2d 1031, 1036 (9th Cir.), *cert. denied*, 459 U.S. 976 (1982); *United States v. Texas Education Agency*, 647 F.2d 504, 506–07 (5th Cir.1981), *cert. denied*, 454 U.S. 1143 (1982); *Constructora Maza, Inc. v. Banco de Ponce*, 616 F.2d 573, 576 (1st Cir.1980); *In re Sierra Trading Corp.*, 482 F.2d 333, 337 (10th Cir.1973); *Case v. Morrisette*, 475 F.2d 1300, 1306–07 (D.C.Cir.1973).

The commentators also disagree as to the proper interpretation of the Rule. *Compare* Wright, *The Doubtful Omniscience of Appellate Courts*, 41 Minn.L.Rev. 751, 769–70 (1957) (language and intent of Rule support view that "clearly erroneous" test should apply to all forms of evidence), *and* 9 C. Wright & A. Miller, *Federal Practice and Procedure: Civil § 2587*, at 740 (1971) (language of the Rule is clear), *with* 5A J. Moore, *Federal Practice* ¶ 52.04, 2687–88 (2d ed. 1982) (Rule as written supports broader review of findings based on non-demeanor testimony).

The Supreme Court has not clearly resolved the issue. See, *Bose Corp. v. Consumers Union of United States, Inc.*, 466 U.S. 485, 104 S.Ct. 1949, 1958 (1984); *Pullman Standard v. Swint*, 456 U.S. 273, 293 (1982); *United States v. General Motors Corp.*, 384 U.S. 127, 141 n. 16 (1966); *United States v. United States Gypsum Co.*, 333 U.S. 364, 394–96 (1948).

The principal argument advanced in favor of a more searching appellate review of findings by the district court based solely on documentary evidence is that the rationale of Rule 52(a) does not apply when the findings do not rest on the trial court's assessment of credibility of the witnesses but on an evaluation of documentary proof and the drawing of inferences from it, thus eliminating the need for any special deference to the trial court's findings. These considerations are outweighed by the public interest in the stability and judicial economy that would be promoted by recognizing that the trial court, not the appellate tribunal, should be the finder of the facts. To permit courts of appeals to share more actively in the fact-finding function would tend to undermine the legitimacy of the district courts in the eyes of litigants, multiply appeals by encouraging appellate retrial of some factual issues, and needlessly reallocate judicial authority.

1991 Amendment

Subdivision (c) is added. It parallels the revised Rule 50(a), but is applicable to non-jury trials. It authorizes the court to enter judgment at any time that it can appropriately make a dispositive finding of fact on the evidence.

The new subdivision replaces part of Rule 41(b), which formerly authorized a dismissal at the close of the plaintiff's case if the plaintiff had failed to carry an essential burden of proof. Accordingly, the reference to Rule 41 formerly made in subdivision (a) of this rule is deleted.

As under the former Rule 41(b), the court retains discretion to enter no judgment prior to the close of the evidence.

Judgment entered under this rule differs from a summary judgment under Rule 56 in the nature of the evaluation made by the court. A judgment on partial findings is made after the court has heard all the evidence bearing on the crucial issue of fact, and the finding is reversible only if the appellate court finds it to be "clearly erroneous." A summary judgment, in contrast, is made on the basis of facts established on account of the absence of contrary evidence or presumptions; such establishments of fact are rulings on questions of law as provided in Rule 56(a) and are not shielded by the "clear error" standard of review.

1993 Amendments

This technical amendment corrects an ambiguity in the text of the 1991 revision of the rule, similar to the revision being made to Rule 50. This amendment makes clear that judgments as a matter of law in nonjury trials may be entered against both plaintiffs and defendants and with respect to issues or defenses that may not be wholly dispositive of a claim or defense.

1995 Amendments

The only change, other than stylistic, intended by this revision is to require that any motion to amend or add findings after a nonjury trial must be filed no later than 10 days after entry of the judgment. Previously, there was an inconsistency in the wording of Rules 50, 52, and 59 with respect to whether certain post-judgment motions had to be filed, or merely served, during that period. This inconsistency caused special problems when motions for a new trial were joined with other post-judgment motions. These motions affect the finality of the judgment, a matter often of importance to third persons as well as the parties and the court. The Committee believes that each of these rules should be revised to require filing before end of the 10–day period. Filing is an event that can be determined with certainty from court records. The phrase "no later than" is used—rather than "within"—to include post-judgment motions that sometimes are filed before actual entry of the judgment by the clerk. It should be noted that under Rule 6(a) Saturdays, Sundays, and legal holidays are excluded in measuring the 10–day period, and that under Rule 5 the motions when filed are to contain a certificate of service on other parties.

Rule 53. Masters

(a) Appointment.

(1) Unless a statute provides otherwise, a court may appoint a master only to:

    (A) perform duties consented to by the parties;

    (B) hold trial proceedings and make or recommend findings of fact on issues to be decided by the court without a jury if appointment is warranted by

    (i) some exceptional condition, or

    (ii) the need to perform an accounting or resolve a difficult computation of damages; or

    (C) address pretrial and post-trial matters that cannot be addressed effectively and timely by an available district judge or magistrate judge of the district.

(2) A master must not have a relationship to the parties, counsel, action, or court that would require disqualification of a judge under 28 U.S.C. § 455 unless the parties consent with the court's approval to appointment of a particular person after disclosure of any potential grounds for disqualification.

(3) In appointing a master, the court must consider the fairness of imposing the likely expenses on the parties and must protect against unreasonable expense or delay.

(b) Order Appointing Master.

(1) **Notice.** The court must give the parties notice and an opportunity to be heard before appointing a master. A party may suggest candidates for appointment.

(2) **Contents.** The order appointing a master must direct the master to proceed with all reasonable diligence and must state:

    (A) the master's duties, including any investigation or enforcement duties, and any limits on the master's authority under Rule 53(c);

    (B) the circumstances—if any—in which the master may communicate ex parte with the court or a party;

    (C) the nature of the materials to be preserved and filed as the record of the master's activities;

    (D) the time limits, method of filing the record, other procedures, and standards for reviewing the master's orders, findings, and recommendations; and

    (E) the basis, terms, and procedure for fixing the master's compensation under Rule 53(h).

(3) **Entry of Order.** The court may enter the order appointing a master only after the master has filed an affidavit disclosing whether there is any ground for disqualification under 28 U.S.C. § 455 and, if a ground for disqualification is disclosed, after the parties have consented with the court's approval to waive the disqualification.

(4) **Amendment.** The order appointing a master may be amended at any time after notice to the parties, and an opportunity to be heard.

(c) Master's Authority. Unless the appointing order expressly directs otherwise, a master has authority to regulate all proceedings and take all appropriate measures to perform fairly and efficiently the assigned duties. The master may by order impose upon a party any noncontempt sanction provided by Rule 37 or 45, and may recommend a contempt sanction against a party and sanctions against a nonparty.

(d) Evidentiary Hearings. Unless the appointing order expressly directs otherwise, a master conducting an evidentiary hearing may exercise the power of the appointing court to compel, take, and record evidence.

(e) Master's Orders. A master who makes an order must file the order and promptly serve a copy on each party. The clerk must enter the order on the docket.

(f) Master's Reports. A master must report to the court as required by the order of appointment. The master must file the report and promptly serve a copy of the report on each party unless the court directs otherwise.

(g) Action on Master's Order, Report, or Recommendations.

(1) **Action.** In acting on a master's order, report, or recommendations, the court must afford an opportunity to be heard and may receive evidence, and may: adopt or affirm; modify; wholly or partly reject or reverse; or resubmit to the master with instructions.

(2) **Time To Object or Move.** A party may file objections to—or a motion to adopt or modify—the master's order, report, or recommendations no later than 20 days from the time the master's order, report, or recommendations are served, unless the court sets a different time.

(3) **Fact Findings.** The court must decide de novo all objections to findings of fact made or recommended by a master unless the parties stipulate with the court's consent that:

    (A) the master's findings will be reviewed for clear error, or

    (B) the findings of a master appointed under Rule 53(a)(1)(A) or (C) will be final.

(4) **Legal Conclusions.** The court must decide de novo all objections to conclusions of law made or recommended by a master.

(5) **Procedural Matters.** Unless the order of appointment establishes a different standard of review, the court may set aside a master's ruling on a procedural matter only for an abuse of discretion.

(h) Compensation.

(1) **Fixing Compensation.** The court must fix the master's compensation before or after judgment on the basis and terms stated in the order of appointment, but the court may set a new basis and terms after notice and an opportunity to be heard.

(2) **Payment.** The compensation fixed under Rule 53(h)(1) must be paid either:

    (A) by a party or parties; or

(B) from a fund or subject matter of the action within the court's control.

(3) Allocation. The court must allocate payment of the master's compensation among the parties after considering the nature and amount of the controversy, the means of the parties, and the extent to which any party is more responsible than other parties for the reference to a master. An interim allocation may be amended to reflect a decision on the merits.

(i) Appointment of Magistrate Judge. A magistrate judge is subject to this rule only when the order referring a matter to the magistrate judge expressly provides that the reference is made under this rule.

(As amended Feb. 28, 1966, eff. July 1, 1966; Apr. 28, 1983, eff. Aug. 1, 1983; Mar. 2, 1987, eff. Aug. 1, 1987; Apr. 30, 1991, eff. Dec. 1, 1991; Apr. 22, 1993, eff. Dec. 1, 1993; Mar. 27, 2003, eff. Dec. 1, 2003.)

ADVISORY COMMITTEE NOTES

1937 Adoption

Note to Subdivision (a). This is a modification of former Equity Rule 68 (Appointment and Compensation of Masters).

Note to Subdivision (b). This is substantially the first sentence of [former] Equity Rule 59 (Reference to Master—Exceptional, Not Usual) extended to actions formerly legal. See *Ex parte Peterson,* 1920, 40 S.Ct. 543, 253 U.S. 300, 64 L.Ed. 919.

Note to Subdivision (c). This is [former] Equity Rules 62 (Powers of Master) and 65 (Claimants Before Master Examinable by Him) with slight modifications. Compare [former] Equity Rules 49 (Evidence Taken Before Examiners, Etc.) and 51 (Evidence Taken Before Examiners, Etc.).

Note to Subdivision (d). (1) This is substantially a combination of the second sentence of [former] Equity Rule 59 (Reference to Master—Exceptional, Not Usual) and [former] Equity Rule 60 (Proceedings Before Master). Compare [former] Equity Rule 53 (Notice of Taking Testimony Before Examiner, Etc.).

(2) This is substantially [former] Equity Rule 52 (Attendance of Witnesses Before Commissioner, Master, or Examiner).

(3) This is substantially [former] Equity Rule 63 (Form of Accounts Before Master).

Note to Subdivision (e). This contains the substance of [former] Equity Rules 61 (Master's Report—Documents Identified but not Set Forth), 61½ (Master's Report—Presumption as to Correctness—Review), and 66 (Return of Master's Report—Exceptions—Hearing), with modifications as to the form and effect of the report and for inclusion of reports by auditors, referees, and examiners, and references in actions formerly legal. Compare [former] Equity Rules 49 (Evidence Taken Before Examiners, Etc.) and 67 (Costs on Exceptions to Master's Report). See *Camden v. Stuart,* 144 U.S. 104, 12 S.Ct. 585, 36 L.Ed. 363 (1892); *Ex parte Peterson,* 253 U.S. 300, 40 S.Ct. 543, 64 L.Ed. 919 (1920).

1966 Amendment

These changes are designed to preserve the admiralty practice whereby difficult computations are referred to a commissioner or assessor, especially after an interlocutory judgment determining liability. As to separation of issues for trial see Rule 42(b).

1983 Amendment

Subdivision (a). The creation of full-time magistrates, who serve at government expense and have no nonjudicial duties competing for their time, eliminates the need to appoint standing masters. Thus the prior provision in Rule 53(a) authorizing the appointment of standing masters is deleted. Additionally, the definition of "master" in subdivision (a) now eliminates the superseded office of commissioner.

The term "special master" is retained in Rule 53 in order to maintain conformity with 28 U.S.C. § 636(b)(2), authorizing a judge to designate a magistrate "to serve as a special master pursuant to the applicable provisions of this title and the Federal Rules of Civil Procedure for the United States District Courts." Obviously, when a magistrate serves as a special master, the provisions for compensation of masters are inapplicable, and the amendment to subdivision (a) so provides.

Although the existence of magistrates may make the appointment of outside masters unnecessary in many instances, see, e.g., *Gautreaux v. Chicago Housing Authority,* 384 F.Supp. 37 (N.D.Ill.1974), mandamus denied *sub nom., Chicago Housing Authority v. Austin,* 511 F.2d 82 (7th Cir. 1975); *Avco Corp. v. American Tel. & Tel. Co.,* 68 F.R.D. 532 (S.D.Ohio 1975), such masters may prove useful when some special expertise is desired or when a magistrate is unavailable for lengthy and detailed supervision of a case.

Subdivision (b). The provisions of 28 U.S.C. § 636(b)(2) not only permit magistrates to serve as masters under Rule 53(b) but also eliminate the exceptional condition requirement of Rule 53(b) when the reference is made with the consent of the parties. The amendment to subdivision (b) brings Rule 53 into harmony with the statute by exempting magistrates, appointed with the consent of the parties, from the general requirement that some exceptional condition requires the reference. It should be noted that subdivision (b) does not address the question, raised in recent decisional law and commentary, as to whether the exceptional condition requirement is applicable when *private masters* who are not magistrates are appointed with the consent of the parties. See Silberman, *Masters and Magistrates Part II: The American Analogue,* 50 N.Y.U.L.Rev. 1297, 1354 (1975).

Subdivision (c). The amendment recognizes the abrogation of Federal Rule 43(c) by the Federal Rules of Evidence.

Subdivision (f). The new subdivision responds to confusion flowing from the dual authority for references of pretrial matters to magistrates. Such references can be made, with or without the consent of the parties, pursuant to Rule 53 or under 28 U.S.C. § 636(b)(1)(A) and (b)(1)(B). There are a number of distinctions between references made under the statute and under the rule. For example, under the statute nondispositive pretrial matters may be referred to a magistrate, without consent, for final determination with reconsideration by the district judge if the magistrate's order is clearly erroneous or contrary to law. Under the rule, however, the appointment of a master, without consent of the parties, to supervise discovery would require some exceptional condition (Rule 53(b)) and would subject the proceedings to the report procedures of Rule 53(e). If an order of reference does not clearly articulate the source of the court's authority the resulting proceedings could be subject to attack on grounds of the magistrate's noncompliance with the provisions of Rule 53. This subdivision therefore establishes a presumption that the limitations of Rule 53 are not applicable unless the reference is specifically made subject to Rule 53.

A magistrate serving as a special master under 28 U.S.C. § 636(b)(2) is governed by the provisions of Rule 53, with the exceptional condition requirement lifted in the case of a consensual reference.

1987 Amendment

The amendments are technical. No substantive change is intended.

1991 Amendment

The purpose of the revision is to expedite proceedings before a master. The former rule required only a filing of the master's report, with the clerk then notifying the parties of the filing. To receive a copy, a party would then be required to secure it from the clerk. By transmitting directly to the parties, the master can save some efforts of counsel. Some local rules have previously required such action by the master.

1993 Amendments

This revision is made to conform the rule to changes made by the Judicial Improvements Act of 1990.

2003 Amendments

Rule 53 is revised extensively to reflect changing practices in using masters. From the beginning in 1938, Rule 53 focused primarily on special masters who perform trial functions. Since then, however, courts have gained experience with masters appointed to perform a variety of pretrial and post-trial functions. See Willging, Hooper, Leary, Miletich, Reagan, & Shapard, *Special Masters' Incidence and Activity* (Federal Judicial Center 2000). This revised Rule 53 recognizes that in appropriate circumstances masters may properly be appointed to perform these functions and regulates such appointments. Rule 53 continues to address trial masters as well, but permits appointment of a trial master in an action to be tried to a jury only if the parties consent. The new rule clarifies the provisions that govern the appointment and function of masters for all purposes. Rule 53(g) also changes the standard of review for findings of fact made or recommended by a master. The core of the original Rule 53 remains, including its prescription that appointment of a master must be the exception and not the rule.

Special masters are appointed in many circumstances outside the Civil Rules. Rule 53 applies only to proceedings that Rule 1 brings within its reach.

Subdivision (a)(1)

District judges bear primary responsibility for the work of their courts. A master should be appointed only in limited circumstances. Subdivision (a)(1) describes three different standards, relating to appointments by consent of the parties,

appointments for trial duties, and appointments for pretrial or post-trial duties.

Consent Masters. Subparagraph (a)(1)(A) authorizes appointment of a master with the parties' consent. Party consent does not require that the court make the appointment; the court retains unfettered discretion to refuse appointment.

Trial Masters. Use of masters for the core functions of trial has been progressively limited. These limits are reflected in the provisions of subparagraph (a)(1)(B) that restrict appointments to exercise trial functions. The Supreme Court gave clear direction to this trend in *La Buy v. Howes Leather Co.*, 352 U.S. 249 (1957); earlier roots are sketched in *Los Angeles Brush Mfg. Corp. v. James*, 272 U.S. 701 (1927). As to nonjury trials, this trend has developed through elaboration of the "exceptional condition" requirement in present Rule 53(b). This phrase is retained, and will continue to have the same force as it has developed. Although the provision that a reference "shall be the exception and not the rule" is deleted, its meaning is embraced for this setting by the exceptional condition requirement.

Subparagraph (a)(1)(B)(ii) carries forward the approach of present Rule 53(b), which exempts from the "exceptional condition" requirement "matters of account and of difficult computation of damages." This approach is justified only as to essentially ministerial determinations that require mastery of much detailed information but that do not require extensive determinations of credibility. Evaluations of witness credibility should only be assigned to a trial master when justified by an exceptional condition.

The use of a trial master without party consent is abolished as to matters to be decided by a jury unless a statute provides for this practice.

Abolition of the direct power to appoint a trial master as t o issues to be decided by a jury leaves the way free to appoint a trial master with the consent of all parties. A trial master should be appointed in a jury case, with consent of the parties and concurrence of the court, only if the parties waive jury trial with respect to the issues submitted to the master or if the master's findings are to be submitted to the jury as evidence in the manner provided by former Rule 53(e)(3). In no circumstance may a master be appointed to preside at a jury trial.

The central function of a trial master is to preside over an evidentiary hearing on the merits of the claims or defenses in the action. This function distinguishes the trial master from most functions of pretrial and post-trial masters. If any master is to be used for such matters as a preliminary injunction hearing or a determination of complex damages issues, for example, the master should be a trial master. The line, however, is not distinct. A pretrial master might well conduct an evidentiary hearing on a discovery dispute, and a post-trial master might conduct evidentiary hearings on questions of compliance.

Rule 53 has long provided authority to report the evidence without recommendations in nonjury trials. This authority is omitted from Rule 53(a)(1)(B). In some circumstances a master may be appointed under Rule 53(a)(1)(A) or (C) to take evidence and report without recommendations.

For nonjury cases, a master also may be appointed to assist the court in discharging trial duties other than conducting an evidentiary hearing.

Pretrial and Post–Trial Masters. Subparagraph (a)(1)(C) authorizes appointment of a master to address pretrial or post-trial matters. Appointment is limited to matters that cannot be addressed effectively and in a timely fashion by an available district judge or magistrate judge of the district. A master's pretrial or post-trial duties may include matters that could be addressed by a judge, such as reviewing discovery documents for privilege, or duties that might not be suitable for a judge. Some forms of settlement negotiations, investigations, or administration of an organization are familiar examples of duties that a judge might not feel free to undertake.

Magistrate Judges. Particular attention should be paid to the prospect that a magistrate judge may be available for special assignments. United States magistrate judges are authorized by statute to perform many pretrial functions in civil actions. 28 U.S.C. § 636(b)(1). Ordinarily a district judge who delegates these functions should refer them to a magistrate judge acting as magistrate judge.

There is statutory authority to appoint a magistrate judge as special master. 28 U.S.C. § 636(b)(2). In special circumstances, or when expressly authorized by a statute other than § 636(b)(2), it may be appropriate to appoint a magistrate judge as a master when needed to perform functions outside those listed in § 636(b)(1). There is no apparent reason to appoint a magistrate judge to perform as master duties that could be performed in the role of magistrate judge. Party consent is required for trial before a magistrate judge, moreover, and this requirement should not be undercut by resort to Rule 53 unless specifically authorized by statute; see 42 U.S.C. § 2000e–5(f)(5).

Pretrial Masters. The appointment of masters to participate in pretrial proceedings has developed extensively over the last two decades as some district courts have felt the need for additional help in managing complex litigation. This practice is not well regulated by present Rule 53, which focuses on masters as trial participants. Rule 53 is amended to confirm the authority to appoint—and to regulate the use of—pretrial masters.

A pretrial master should be appointed only when the need is clear. Direct judicial performance of judicial functions may be particularly important in cases that involve important public issues or many parties. At the extreme, a broad delegation of pretrial responsibility as well as a delegation of trial responsibilities can run afoul of Article III.

A master also may be appointed to address matters that blur the divide between pretrial and trial functions. The court's responsibility to interpret patent claims as a matter of law, for example, may be greatly assisted by appointing a master who has expert knowledge of the field in which the patent operates. Review of the master's findings will be de novo under Rule 53(g)(4), but the advantages of initial determination by a master may make the process more effective and timely than disposition by the judge acting alone. Determination of foreign law may present comparable difficulties. The decision whether to appoint a master to address such matters is governed by subdivision (a)(1)(C), not the trial-master provisions of subdivision (a)(1)(B).

Post–Trial Masters. Courts have come to rely on masters to assist in framing and enforcing complex decrees. Present Rule 53 does not directly address this practice. Amended Rule 53 authorizes appointment of post-trial masters for these and similar purposes. The constraint of subdivision (a)(1)(C) limits this practice to cases in which the master's duties cannot be performed effectively and in a timely fashion by an available district judge or magistrate judge of the district.

Reliance on a master is appropriate when a complex decree requires complex policing, particularly when a party has proved resistant or intransigent. This practice has been recognized by the Supreme Court, see *Local 28, Sheet Metal Workers' Internat. Assn. v. EEOC*, 478 U.S. 421, 481–482 (1986). The master's role in enforcement may extend to investigation in ways that are quite unlike the traditional role of judicial officers in an adversary system.

Expert Witness Overlap. This rule does not address the difficulties that arise when a single person is appointed to perform overlapping roles as master and as court-appointed expert witness under Evidence Rule 706. Whatever combination of functions is involved, the Rule 53(a)(1)(B) limit that confines trial masters to issues to be decided by the court does not apply to a person who also is appointed as an expert witness under Evidence Rule 706.

Subdivision (a)(2) and (3)

Masters are subject to the Code of Conduct for United States Judges, with exceptions spelled out in the Code. Special care must be taken to ensure that there is no actual or apparent conflict of interest involving a master. The standard of disqualification is established by 28 U.S.C. § 455. The affidavit required by Rule 53(b)(3) provides an important source of information about possible grounds for disqualification, but careful inquiry should be made at the time of making the initial appointment. The disqualification standards established by § 455 are strict. Because a master is not a public judicial officer, it may be appropriate to permit the parties to consent to appointment of a particular person as master in circumstances that would require disqualification of a judge. The judge must be careful to ensure that no party feels any pressure to consent, but with such assurances—and with the judge's own determination that there is no troubling conflict of interests or disquieting appearance of impropriety—consent may justify an otherwise barred appointment.

One potential disqualification issue is peculiar to the master's role. It may happen that a master who is an attorney represents a client whose litigation is assigned to the judge who appointed the attorney as master. Other parties to the litigation may fear that the attorney-master will gain special respect from the judge. A flat prohibition on appearance before the appointing judge during the time of service as master, however, might in some circumstances unduly limit the opportunity to make a desirable appointment. These matters may be regulated to some extent by state rules of professional responsibility. The question of present conflicts, and the possibility of future conflicts, can be considered at the time of appointment. Depending on the circumstances, the judge may consider it appropriate to impose a non-appearance condition on the lawyer-master, and perhaps on the master's firm as well.

Subdivision (b)

The order appointing a pretrial master is vitally important in informing the master and the parties about the nature and extent of the master's duties and authority. Care must be taken to make the order as precise as possible. The parties must be given notice and opportunity to be heard on the question whether a master should be appointed and on the terms of the appointment. To the extent possible, the notice should describe the master's proposed duties, time to complete the duties, standards of review, and compensation. Often it will be useful to engage the parties in the process of identifying the master, inviting nominations, and reviewing potential candidates. Party involvement may be particularly useful if a pretrial master is expected to promote settlement.

The hearing requirement of Rule 53(b)(1) can be satisfied by an opportunity to make written submissions unless the circumstances require live testimony.

Rule 53(b)(2) requires precise designation of the master's duties and authority. Clear identification of any investigating or enforcement duties is particularly important. Clear delineation of topics for any reports or recommendations is also an important part of this process. And it is important to protect against delay by establishing a time schedule for performing the assigned duties. Early designation of the procedure for fixing the master's compensation also may provide useful guidance to the parties.

Ex parte communications between a master and the court present troubling questions. Ordinarily the order should prohibit such communications, assuring that the parties know where authority is lodged at each step of the proceedings. Prohibiting ex parte communications between master and court also can enhance the role of a settlement master by assuring the parties that settlement can be fostered by confidential revelations that will not be shared with the court. Yet there may be circumstances in which the master's role is enhanced by the opportunity for ex parte communications with the court. A master assigned to help coordinate multiple proceedings, for example, may benefit from off-the-record exchanges with the court about logistical matters. The rule does not directly regulate these matters. It requires only that the court exercise its discretion and address the topic in the order of appointment.

Similarly difficult questions surround ex parte communications between a master and the parties. Ex parte communications may be essential in seeking to advance settlement. Ex parte communications also may prove useful in other settings, as with in camera review of documents to resolve privilege questions. In most settings, however, ex parte communications with the parties should be discouraged or prohibited. The rule requires that the court address the topic in the order of appointment.

Subdivision (b)(2)(C) provides that the appointment order must state the nature of the materials to be preserved and filed as the record of the master's activities, and (b)(2)(D) requires that the order state the method of filing the record. It is not feasible to prescribe the nature of the record without regard to the nature of the master's duties. The records appropriate to discovery duties may be different from those appropriate to encouraging settlement, investigating possible violations of a complex decree, or making recommendations for trial findings. A basic requirement, however, is that the master must make and file a complete record of the evidence considered in making or recommending findings of fact on the basis of evidence. The order of appointment should routinely include this requirement unless the nature of the appointment precludes any prospect that the master will make or recommend evidence-based findings of fact. In some circumstances it may be appropriate for a party to file materials directly with the court as provided by Rule 5(e),

but in many circumstances filing with the court may be inappropriate. Confidentiality is important with respect to many materials that may properly be considered by a master. Materials in the record can be transmitted to the court, and filed, in connection with review of a master's order, report, or recommendations under subdivisions (f) and (g). Independently of review proceedings, the court may direct filing of any materials that it wishes to make part of the public record.

The provision in subdivision (b)(2)(D) that the order must state the standards for reviewing the master's orders, findings, or recommendations is a reminder of the provisions of subdivision (g)(3) that recognize stipulations for review less searching than the presumptive requirement of de novo decision by the court. Subdivision (b)(2)(D) does not authorize the court to supersede the limits of subdivision (g)(3).

In setting the procedure for fixing the master's compensation, it is useful at the outset to establish specific guidelines to control total expense. The court has power under subdivision (h) to change the basis and terms for determining compensation after notice to the parties.

Subdivision (b)(3) permits entry of the order appointing a master only after the master has filed an affidavit disclosing whether there is any ground for disqualification under 28 U.S.C. § 455. If the affidavit discloses a possible ground for disqualification, the order can enter only if the court determines that there is no ground for disqualification or if the parties, knowing of the ground for disqualification, consent with the court's approval to waive the disqualification.

The provision in Rule 53(b)(4) for amending the order of appointment is as import ant as the provisions for the initial order. Anything that could be done in the initial order can be done by amendment. The hearing requirement can be satisfied by an opportunity to make written submissions unless the circumstances require live testimony.

Subdivision (c)

Subdivision (c) is a simplification of the provisions scattered throughout present Rule 53. It is intended to provide the broad and flexible authority necessary to discharge the master's responsibilities. The most important delineation of a master's authority and duties is provided by the Rule 53(b) appointing order.

Subdivision (d)

The subdivision (d) provisions for evidentiary hearings are reduced from the extensive provisions in current Rule 53. This simplification of the rule is not intended to diminish the authority that may be delegated to a master. Reliance is placed on the broad and general terms of subdivision (c).

Subdivision (e)

Subdivision (e) provides that a master's order must be filed and entered on the docket. It must be promptly served on the parties, a task ordinarily accomplished by mailing or other means as permitted by Rule 5(b). In some circumstances it may be appropriate to have the clerk's office assist the master in mailing the order to the parties.

Subdivision (f)

Subdivision (f) restates some of the provisions of present Rule 53(e)(1). The report is the master's primary means of communication with the court. The materials to be provided to support review of the report will depend on the nature of the report. The master should provide all portions of the record preserved under Rule 53(b)(2)(C) that the master deems relevant to the report. The parties may designate additional materials from the record, and may seek permission to supplement the record with evidence. The court may direct that additional materials from the record be provided and filed. Given the wide array of tasks that may be assigned to a pretrial master, there may be circumstances that justify sealing a report or review record against public access—a report on continuing or failed settlement efforts is the most likely example. A post-trial master may be assigned duties in formulating a decree that deserve similar protection. Such circumstances may even justify denying access to the report or review materials by the parties, although this step should be taken only for the most compelling reasons. Sealing is much less likely to be appropriate with respect to a trial master's report.

Before formally making an order, report, or recommendations, a master may find it helpful to circulate a draft to the parties for review and comment. The usefulness of this practice depends on the nature of the master's proposed action.

Subdivision (g)

The provisions of subdivision (g)(1), describing the court's powers to afford a hearing, take evidence, and act on a master's order, report, or recommendations are drawn from present Rule 53(e)(2), but are not limited, as present Rule 53(e)(2) is limited, to the report of a trial master in a nonjury action. The requirement that the court must afford an opportunity to be heard can be satisfied by taking written submissions when the court acts on the report without taking live testimony.

The subdivision (g)(2) time limits for objecting to—or seeking adoption or modification of—a master's order, report, or recommendations, are important. They are not jurisdictional. Although a court may properly refuse to entertain untimely review proceedings, the court may excuse the failure to seek timely review. The basic time period is lengthened to 20 days because the present 10–day period may be too short to permit thorough study and response to a complex report dealing with complex litigation. If no party asks the court to act on a master's report, the court is free to adopt the master's action or to disregard it at any relevant point in the proceedings.

Subdivision (g)(3) establishes the standards of review for a master's findings of fact or recommended findings of fact. The court must decide de novo all objections to findings of fact made or recommended by the master unless the parties stipulate, with the court's consent, that the findings will be reviewed for clear error or—with respect to a master appointed on the parties' consent or appointed to address pretrial or post-trial matters—that the findings will be final. Clear-error review is more likely to be appropriate with respect to findings that do not go to the merits of the underlying claims or defenses, such as findings of fact bearing on a privilege objection to a discovery request. Even if no objection is made, the court is free to decide the facts de novo; to review for clear error if an earlier approved stipulation provided clear-error review; or to withdraw its consent to a stipulation for clear-error review or finality, and then to decide de novo. If the court withdraws its consent to a stipulation for finality or clear-error review, it may reopen the opportunity to object.

Under Rule 53(g)(4), the court must decide de novo all objections to conclusions of law made or recommended by a master. As with findings of fact, the court also may decide conclusions of law de novo when no objection is made.

Apart from factual and legal questions, masters often make determinations that, when made by a trial court, would be treated as matters of procedural discretion. The court may set a standard for review of such matters in the order of appointment, and may amend the order to establish the standard. If no standard is set by the original or amended order appointing the master, review of procedural matters is for abuse of discretion. The subordinate role of the master means that the trial court's review for abuse of discretion may be more searching than the review that an appellate court makes of a trial court.

If a master makes a recommendation on any matter that does not fall within Rule 53(g)(3), (4), or (5), the court may act on the recommendation under Rule 53(g)(1).

Subdivision (h)

The need to pay compensation is a substantial reason for care in appointing private persons as masters.

Payment of the master's fees must be allocated among the parties and any property or subject-matter within the court's control. The amount in controversy and the means of the parties may provide some guidance in making the allocation. The nature of the dispute also may be important—parties pursuing matters of public interest, for example, may deserve special protection. A party whose unreasonable behavior has occasioned the need to appoint a master, on the other hand, may properly be charged all or a major portion of the master's fees. It may be proper to revise an interim allocation after decision on the merits. The revision need not await a decision that is final for purposes of appeal, but may be made to reflect disposition of a substantial portion of the case.

The basis and terms for fixing compensation should be stated in the order of appointment. The court retains power to alter the initial basis and terms, after notice and an opportunity to be heard, but should protect the parties against unfair surprise.

The provision of former Rule 53(a) that the "provision for compensation shall not apply when a United States Magistrate Judge is designated to serve as a master" is deleted as unnecessary. Other provisions of law preclude compensation.

Subdivision (i)

Rule 53(i) carries forward unchanged former Rule 53(f).

HISTORICAL NOTES

References in Text

The Federal Rules of Evidence, referred to in subd. (d), are set out in this title.

Change of Name

United States magistrate appointed under section 631 of Title 28, Judiciary and Judicial Procedure, to be known as United States magistrate judge after Dec. 1, 1990, with any reference to United States magistrate or magistrate in Title 28, in any other Federal statute, etc., deemed a reference to United States magistrate judge appointed under section 631 of Title 28, see section 321 of Pub.L. 101–650, set out as a note under section 631 of Title 28.

VII. JUDGMENT

Rule 54. Judgments; Costs

(a) Definition; Form. "Judgment" as used in these rules includes a decree and any order from which an appeal lies. A judgment shall not contain a recital of pleadings, the report of a master, or the record of prior proceedings.

(b) Judgment Upon Multiple Claims or Involving Multiple Parties. When more than one claim for relief is presented in an action, whether as a claim, counterclaim, cross-claim, or third-party claim, or when multiple parties are involved, the court may direct the entry of a final judgment as to one or more but fewer than all of the claims or parties only upon an express determination that there is no just reason for delay and upon an express direction for the entry of judgment. In the absence of such determination and direction, any order or other form of decision, however designated, which adjudicates fewer than all the claims or the rights and liabilities of fewer than all the parties shall not terminate the action as to any of the claims or parties, and the order or other form of decision is subject to revision at any time before the entry of judgment adjudicating all the claims and the rights and liabilities of all the parties.

(c) Demand for Judgment. A judgment by default shall not be different in kind from or exceed in amount that prayed for in the demand for judgment. Except as to a party against whom a judgment is entered by default, every final judgment shall grant the relief to which the party in whose favor it is rendered is entitled, even if the party has not demanded such relief in the party's pleadings.

(d) Costs; Attorneys' Fees.

(1) Costs Other than Attorneys' Fees. Except when express provision therefor is made either in a statute of the United States or in these rules, costs other than attorneys' fees shall be allowed as of course to the prevailing party unless the court otherwise directs; but costs against the United States, its officers, and agencies shall be imposed only to the extent permitted by law. Such costs may be taxed by the clerk on one day's notice. On motion served within 5 days thereafter, the action of the clerk may be reviewed by the court.

(2) Attorneys' Fees.

(A) Claims for attorneys' fees and related non-taxable expenses shall be made by motion unless the substantive law governing the action provides for the recovery of such fees as an element of damages to be proved at trial.

(B) Unless otherwise provided by statute or order of the court, the motion must be filed no later than 14 days after entry of judgment; must specify the judgment and the statute, rule, or other grounds entitling the moving party to the award; and must state the amount or provide a fair estimate of the amount sought. If directed by the court, the motion shall also disclose the terms of any agreement with respect to fees to be paid for the services for which claim is made.

(C) On request of a party or class member, the court shall afford an opportunity for adversary submissions with respect to the motion in accordance with Rule 43(e) or Rule 78. The court may determine issues of liability for fees before receiving submissions bearing on issues of evaluation of services for which liability is imposed by the court. The court shall find the facts and state its conclusions of law as provided in Rule 52(a).

(D) By local rule the court may establish special procedures by which issues relating to such fees may be resolved without extensive evidentiary hearings. In addition, the court may refer issues relating to the value of services to a special master under Rule 53 without regard to the provisions of Rule 53(a)(1) and may refer a motion for attorneys' fees to a magistrate judge under Rule 72(b) as if it were a dispositive pretrial matter.

(E) The provisions of subparagraphs (A) through (D) do not apply to claims for fees and expenses as sanctions for violations of these rules or under 28 U.S.C. § 1927.

(As amended Dec. 27, 1946, eff. Mar. 19, 1948; Apr. 17, 1961, eff. July 19, 1961; Mar. 2, 1987, eff. Aug. 1, 1987; Apr. 22, 1993, eff. Dec. 1, 1993; Apr. 29, 2002, eff. Dec. 1, 2002; Mar. 27, 2003, eff. Dec. 1, 2003.)

ADVISORY COMMITTEE NOTES

1937 Adoption

Note to Subdivision (a). The second sentence is derived substantially from [former] Equity Rule 71 (Form of Decree).

Note to Subdivision (b). This provides for the separate judgment of equity and code practice. See Wis.Stat. (1935) § 270.54; Compare N.Y.C.P.A. (1937) § 476.

Note to Subdivision (c). For the limitation on default contained in the first sentence, see 2 N.D.Comp.Laws Ann. (1913) § 7680; N.Y.C.P.A. (1937) § 479. Compare *English Rules Under the Judicature Act* (The Annual Practice, 1937) O. 13, r.r. 3–12. The remainder is a usual code provision. It makes clear that a judgment should give the relief to which a party is entitled, regardless of whether it is legal or equitable or both. This necessarily includes the deficiency judgment in foreclosure cases formerly provided for by Equity Rule 10 (Decree for Deficiency in Foreclosures, Etc.).

Note to Subdivision (d). For the present rule in common law actions, see *Ex parte Peterson,* 253 U.S. 300, 40

S.Ct. 543, 64 L.Ed. 919 (1920); Payne, *Costs in Common Law Actions in the Federal Courts* (1935), 21 Va.L.Rev. 397.

The provisions as to costs in actions in forma pauperis contained in U.S.C., Title 28, former §§ 832–836 [now 1915] are unaffected by this rule. Other sections of U.S.C., Title 28, which are unaffected by this rule are: [former] §§ 815 (Costs; plaintiff not entitled to, when), 821 [now 1928] (Costs; infringement of patent; disclaimer), 825 (Costs; several actions), 829 [now 1927] (Costs; attorney liable for, when), and 830 [now 1920] (Costs; bill of; taxation).

The provisions of the following and similar statutes as to costs against the United States and its officers and agencies are specifically continued:

U.S.C., Title 15, §§ 77v(a), 78aa, 79y (Securities and Exchange Commission)

U.S.C., Title 16, § 825p (Federal Power Commission)

U.S.C., Title 26, [former] §§ 3679(d) and 3745(d) (Internal revenue actions)

U.S.C., Title 26, [former] § 3770(b)(2) (Reimbursement of costs of recovery against revenue officers)

U.S.C., Title 28, [former] § 817 (Internal revenue actions)

U.S.C., Title 28, § 836 [now 1915] (United States—actions in *forma pauperis*)

U.S.C., Title 28, § 842 [now 2006] (Actions against revenue officers)

U.S.C., Title 28, § 870 [now 2408] (United States—in certain cases)

U.S.C., Title 28, [former] § 906 (United States—foreclosure actions)

U.S.C., Title 47, § 401 (Communications Commission)

The provisions of the following and similar statutes as to costs are unaffected:

U.S.C., Title 7, § 210(f) (Actions for damages based on an order of the Secretary of Agriculture under Stockyards Act)

U.S.C., Title 7, § 499g(c) (Appeals from reparations orders of Secretary of Agriculture under Perishable Commodities Act)

U.S.C., Title 8, [former] § 45 (Action against district attorneys in certain cases)

U.S.C., Title 15, § 15 (Actions for injuries due to violation of antitrust laws)

U.S.C., Title 15, § 72 (Actions for violation of law forbidding importation or sale of articles at less than market value or wholesale prices)

U.S.C., Title 15, § 77k (Actions by persons acquiring securities registered with untrue statements under Securities Act of 1933)

U.S.C., Title 15, § 78i(e) (Certain actions under the Securities Exchange Act of 1934)

U.S.C., Title 15, § 78r (Similar to 78i(e))

U.S.C., Title 15, § 96 (Infringement of trade-mark—damages)

U.S.C., Title 15, § 99 (Infringement of trade-mark—injunctions)

U.S.C., Title 15, § 124 (Infringement of trade-mark—damages)

U.S.C., Title 19, § 274 (Certain actions under customs law)

U.S.C., Title 30, § 32 (Action to determine right to possession of mineral lands in certain cases)

U.S.C., Title 31, §§ 232 [now 3730] and 234 [former] (Action for making false claims upon United States)

U.S.C., Title 33, § 926 (Actions under Harbor Workers' Compensation Act)

U.S.C., Title 35, § 67 [now 281, 284] (Infringement of patent—damages)

U.S.C., Title 35, § 69 [now 282] (Infringement of patent—pleading and proof)

U.S.C., Title 35, § 71 [now 288] (Infringement of patent—when specification too broad)

U.S.C., Title 45, § 153p (Actions for non-compliance with an order of National R.R. Adjustment Board for payment of money)

U.S.C., Title 46, [former] § 38 (Action for penalty for failure to register vessel)

U.S.C., Title 46, § 829 (Action based on non-compliance with an order of Maritime Commission for payment of money)

U.S.C., Title 46, § 941 (Certain actions under Ship Mortgage Act)

U.S.C., Title 46, § 1227 (Actions for damages for violation of certain provisions of the Merchant Marine Act, 1936)

U.S.C., Title 47, § 206 (Actions for certain violations of Communications Act of 1934)

U.S.C., Title 49, § 16(2) [now 11705] (Action based on non-compliance with an order of I.C.C. for payment of money)

1946 Amendment

Note. The historic rule in the federal courts has always prohibited piecemeal disposal of litigation and permitted appeals only from final judgments except in those special instances covered by statute. *Hohorst v. Hamburg—American Packet Co.*, 1893, 13 S.Ct. 590, 148 U.S. 262, 37 L.Ed. 443; *Rexford v. Brunswick-Balke-Collender Co.*, 1913, 33 S.Ct. 515, 228 U.S. 339, 57 L.Ed. 864; *Collins v. Miller*, 1920, 40 S.Ct. 347, 252 U.S. 364, 64 L.Ed. 616. Rule 54(b) was originally adopted in view of the wide scope and possible content of the newly created "civil action" in order to avoid the possible injustice of a delay in judgment of a distinctly separate claim to await adjudication of the entire case. It was not designed to overturn the settled federal rule stated above, which, indeed, has more recently been reiterated in *Catlin v. United States*, 1945, 65 S.Ct. 631, 324 U.S. 229, 89 L.Ed. 911. See also *United States v. Florian*, 1941, 61 S.Ct. 713, 312 U.S. 656, 85 L.Ed. 1105; *Reeves v. Beardall*, 1942, 62 S.Ct. 1085, 316 U.S. 283, 86 L.Ed. 1478.

Unfortunately, this was not always understood, and some confusion ensued. Hence situations arose where district courts made a piecemeal disposition of an action and entered what the parties thought amounted to a judgment, although a trial remained to be had on other claims similar or identical with those disposed of. In the interim the parties did not know their ultimate rights, and accordingly took an appeal, thus putting the finality of the partial judgment in question. While most appellate courts have reached a result generally in accord with the intent of the rule, yet there have been divergent precedents and division of views which have served to render the issues more clouded to the parties appellant. It hardly seems a case where multiplicity of precedents will tend to remove the problem from debate. The problem is presented and discussed in the following cases: *Atwater v.*

North American Coal Corp., C.C.A.2, 1940, 111 F.2d 125; *Rosenblum v. Dingfelder,* C.C.A.2, 1940, 111 F.2d 406; *Audi-Vision, Inc. v. RCA Mfg. Co., Inc.,* C.C.A.2, 1943, 136 F.2d 621; *Zalkind v. Scheinman,* C.C.A.2, 1943, 139 F.2d 895; *Oppenheimer v. F. J. Young & Co., Inc.,* C.C.A.2, 1944, 144 F.2d 387; *Libbey-Owens-Ford Glass Co. v. Sylvania Industrial Corp.,* C.C.A.2, 1946, 154 F.2d 814, certiorari denied 1946, 66 S.Ct. 1353, 328 U.S. 859, 90 L.Ed. 1630; *Zarati Steamship Co. v. Park Bridge Corp.,* C.C.A.2, 1946, 154 F.2d 377; *Baltimore and Ohio R. Co. v. United Fuel Gas Co.,* C.C.A.4, 1946, 154 F.2d 545; *Jefferson Electric Co. v. Sola Electric Co.,* C.C.A.7, 1941, 122 F.2d 124; *Leonard v. Socony-Vacuum Oil Co.,* C.C.A.7, 1942, 130 F.2d 535; *Markham v. Kasper,* C.C.A.7, 1945, 152 F.2d 270; *Hanney v. Franklin Fire Ins. Co. of Philadelphia,* C.C.A.9, 1944, 142 F.2d 864; *Toomey v. Toomey,* App.D.C.1945, 149 F.2d 19, 80 U.S.App. D.C. 77.

In view of the difficulty thus disclosed, the Advisory Committee in its two preliminary drafts of proposed amendments attempted to redefine the original rule with particular stress upon the interlocutory nature of partial judgments which did not adjudicate all claims arising out of a single transaction or occurrence. This attempt appeared to meet with almost universal approval from those of the profession commenting upon it, although there were, of course, helpful suggestions for additional changes in language or clarification of detail. But cf. Circuit Judge Frank's dissenting opinion in *Libbey-Owens-Ford Glass Co. v. Sylvania Industrial Corp.,* supra, n. 21 of the dissenting opinion. The Committee, however, became convinced on careful study of its own proposals that the seeds of ambiguity still remained, and that it had not completely solved the problem of piecemeal appeals. After extended consideration, it concluded that a retention of the older federal rule was desirable, and that this rule needed only the exercise of a discretionary power to afford a remedy in the infrequent harsh case to provide a simple, definite, workable rule. This is afforded by amended Rule 54(b). It re-establishes an ancient policy with clarity and precision. For the possibility of staying execution where not all claims are disposed of under Rule 54(b), see amended Rule 62(h).

1961 Amendment

This rule permitting appeal, upon the trial court's determination of "no just reason for delay," from a judgment upon one or more but less than all the claims in an action, has generally been given a sympathetic construction by the courts and its validity is settled. *Reeves v. Beardall,* 316 U.S. 283 (1942); *Sears, Roebuck & Co. v. Mackey,* 351 U.S. 427 (1956); *Cold Metal Process Co. v. United Engineering & Foundry Co.,* 351 U.S. 445 (1956).

A serious difficulty has, however, arisen because the rule speaks of claims but nowhere mentions parties. A line of cases has developed in the circuits consistently holding the rule to be inapplicable to the dismissal, even with the requisite trial court determination, of one or more but less than all defendants jointly charged in an action, i.e. charged with various forms of concerted or related wrongdoing or related liability. See *Mull v. Ackerman,* 279 F.2d 25 (2d Cir. 1960); *Richards v. Smith,* 276 F.2d 652 (5th Cir. 1960); *Hardy v. Bankers Life & Cas. Co.,* 222 F.2d 827 (7th Cir. 1955); *Steiner v. 20th Century-Fox Film Corp.,* 220 F.2d 105 (9th Cir. 1955). For purposes of Rule 54(b) it was arguable that there were as many "claims" as there were parties defendant

and that the rule in its present text applied where less than all of the parties were dismissed, cf. *United Artists Corp. v. Masterpiece Productions, Inc.,* 221 F.2d 213, 215 (2d Cir. 1955); *Bowling Machines, Inc. v. First Nat. Bank,* 283 F.2d 39 (1st Cir. 1960); but the Courts of Appeals are now committed to an opposite view.

The danger of hardship through delay of appeal until the whole action is concluded may be at least as serious in the multiple-parties situations as in multiple-claims cases, see *Pabellon v. Grace Line, Inc.,* 191 F.2d 169, 179 (2d Cir. 1951), cert. denied, 342 U.S. 893 (1951), and courts and commentators have urged that Rule 54(b) be changed to take in the former. See *Reagan v. Traders & General Ins. Co.,* 255 F.2d 845 (5th Cir. 1958); *Meadows v. Greyhound Corp.,* 235 F.2d 233 (5th Cir. 1956); *Steiner v. 20th Century-Fox Film Corp.,* supra; 6 Moore's Federal Practice ¶54.34[2] (2d ed. 1953); 3 Barron & Holtzoff, *Federal Practice & Procedure* § 1193.2 (Wright ed. 1958); *Developments in the Law—Multiparty Litigation,* 71 Harv.L.Rev. 874, 981 (1958); Note, 62 Yale L.J. 263, 271 (1953); Ill.Ann.Stat. ch. 110, § 50(2) (Smith-Hurd 1956). The amendment accomplishes this purpose by referring explicitly to parties.

There has been some recent indication that interlocutory appeal under the provisions of 28 U.S.C. § 1292(b), added in 1958, may now be available for the multiple-parties cases here considered. See *Jaftex Corp. v. Randolph Mills, Inc.,* 282 F.2d 508 (2d Cir. 1960). The Rule 54(b) procedure seems preferable for those cases, and § 1292(b) should be held inapplicable to them when the rule is enlarged as here proposed. See *Luckenbach Steamship Co., Inc., v. H. Muehlstein & Co., Inc.,* 280 F.2d 755, 757 (2d Cir. 1960); 1 Barron & Holtzoff, supra, § 58.1, p. 321 (Wright ed. 1960).

1987 Amendment

The amendment is technical. No substantive change is intended.

1993 Amendments

Subdivision (d). This revision adds paragraph (2) to this subdivision to provide for a frequently recurring form of litigation not initially contemplated by the rules—disputes over the amount of attorneys' fees to be awarded in the large number of actions in which prevailing parties may be entitled to such awards or in which the court must determine the fees to be paid from a common fund. This revision seeks to harmonize and clarify procedures that have been developed through case law and local rules.

Paragraph (1). Former subdivision (d), providing for taxation of costs by the clerk, is renumbered as paragraph (1) and revised to exclude applications for attorneys' fees.

Paragraph (2). This new paragraph establishes a procedure for presenting claims for attorneys' fees, whether or not denominated as "costs." It applies also to requests for reimbursement of expenses, not taxable as costs, when recoverable under governing law incident to the award of fees. Cf. *West Virginia Univ. Hosp. v. Casey,* —— U.S. —— (1991), holding, prior to the Civil Rights Act of 1991, that expert witness fees were not recoverable under 42 U.S.C. § 1988. As noted in subparagraph (A), it does not, however, apply to fees recoverable as an element of damages, as when sought under the terms of a contract; such damages typically are to be claimed in a pleading and may involve issues to be resolved by a jury. Nor, as provided in subparagraph (E), does it apply to awards of fees as sanctions authorized or mandated under these rules or under 28 U.S.C. § 1927.

Subparagraph (B) provides a deadline for motions for attorneys' fees—14 days after final judgment unless the court or a statute specifies some other time. One purpose of this provision is to assure that the opposing party is informed of the claim before the time for appeal has elapsed. Prior law did not prescribe any specific time limit on claims for attorneys' fees. White v. New Hampshire Dep't of Employment Sec., 455 U.S. 445 (1982). In many nonjury cases the court will want to consider attorneys' fee issues immediately after rendering its judgment on the merits of the case. Note that the time for making claims is specifically stated in some legislation, such as the Equal Access to Justice Act, 28 U.S.C. § 2412(d)(1)(B) (30–day filing period).

Prompt filing affords an opportunity for the court to resolve fee disputes shortly after trial, while the services performed are freshly in mind. It also enables the court in appropriate circumstances to make its ruling on a fee request in time for any appellate review of a dispute over fees to proceed at the same time as review on the merits of the case.

Filing a motion for fees under this subdivision does not affect the finality or the appealability of a judgment, though revised Rule 58 provides a mechanism by which prior to appeal the court can suspend the finality to resolve a motion for fees. If an appeal on the merits of the case is taken, the court may rule on the claim for fees, may defer its ruling on the motion, or may deny the motion without prejudice, directing under subdivision (d)(2)(B) a new period for filing after the appeal has been resolved. A notice of appeal does not extend the time for filing a fee claim based on the initial judgment, but the court under subdivision (d)(2)(B) may effectively extend the period by permitting claims to be filed after resolution of the appeal. A new period for filing will automatically begin if a new judgment is entered following a reversal or remand by the appellate court or the granting of a motion under Rule 59.

The rule does not require that the motion be supported at the time of filing with the evidentiary material bearing on the fees. This material must of course be submitted in due course, according to such schedule as the court may direct in light of the circumstances of the case. What is required is the filing of a motion sufficient to alert the adversary and the court that there is a claim for fees, and the amount of such fees (or a fair estimate).

If directed by the court, the moving party is also required to disclose any fee agreement, including those between attorney and client, between attorneys sharing a fee to be awarded, and between adversaries made in partial settlement of a dispute where the settlement must be implemented by court action as may be required by Rules 23(e) and 23.1 or other like provisions. With respect to the fee arrangements requiring court approval, the court may also by local rule require disclosure immediately after such arrangements are agreed to. E.g., Rule 5 of United States District Court for the Eastern District of New York; cf. In re "Agent Orange" Product Liability Litigation (MDL 381), 611 F.Supp. 1452, 1464 (E.D.N.Y.1985).

In the settlement of class actions resulting in a common fund from which fees will be sought, courts frequently have required that claims for fees be presented in advance of hearings to consider approval of the proposed settlement.

The rule does not affect this practice, as it permits the court to require submissions of fee claims in advance of entry of judgment.

Subparagraph (C) assures the parties of an opportunity to make an appropriate presentation with respect to issues involving the evaluation of legal services. In some cases, an evidentiary hearing may be needed, but this is not required in every case. The amount of time to be allowed for the preparation of submissions both in support of and in opposition to awards should be tailored to the particular case.

The court is explicitly authorized to make a determination of the liability for fees before receiving submissions by the parties bearing on the amount of an award. This option may be appropriate in actions in which the liability issue is doubtful and the evaluation issues are numerous and complex.

The court may order disclosure of additional information, such as that bearing on prevailing local rates or on the appropriateness of particular services for which compensation is sought.

On rare occasion, the court may determine that discovery under Rules 26–37 would be useful to the parties. Compare Rules Governing Section 2254 Cases in the U.S. District Courts, Rule 6. See Note, Determining the Reasonableness of Attorneys' Fees—the Discoverability of Billing Records, 64 B.U.L.Rev. 241 (1984). In complex fee disputes, the court may use case management techniques to limit the scope of the dispute or to facilitate the settlement of fee award disputes.

Fee awards should be made in the form of a separate judgment under Rule 58 since such awards are subject to review in the court of appeals. To facilitate review, the paragraph provides that the court set forth its findings and conclusions as under Rule 52(a), though in most cases this explanation could be quite brief.

Subparagraph (D) explicitly authorizes the court to establish procedures facilitating the efficient and fair resolution of fee claims. A local rule, for example, might call for matters to be presented through affidavits, or might provide for issuance of proposed findings by the court, which would be treated as accepted by the parties unless objected to within a specified time. A court might also consider establishing a schedule reflecting customary fees or factors affecting fees within the community, as implicitly suggested by Justice O'Connor in Pennsylvania v. Delaware Valley Citizens' Council, 483 U.S. 711, 733 (1987) (O'Connor, J., concurring) (how particular markets compensate for contingency). Cf. Thompson v. Kennickell, 710 F.Supp. 1 (D.D.C.1989) (use of findings in other cases to promote consistency). The parties, of course, should be permitted to show that in the circumstances of the case such a schedule should not be applied or that different hourly rates would be appropriate.

The rule also explicitly permits, without need for a local rule, the court to refer issues regarding the amount of a fee award in a particular case to a master under Rule 53. The district judge may designate a magistrate judge to act as a master for this purpose or may refer a motion for attorneys' fees to a magistrate judge for proposed findings and recommendations under Rule 72(b). This authorization eliminates any controversy as to whether such references are permitted under Rule 53(b) as "matters of account and of difficult computation of damages" and whether motions for attorneys' fees can be treated as the equivalent of a dispositive pretrial matter that can be referred to a magistrate judge. For consistency and efficiency, all such matters might be referred to the same magistrate judge.

Subparagraph (E) excludes from this rule the award of fees as sanctions under these rules or under 28 U.S.C. § 1927.

2002 Amendments

Subdivision (d)(2)(C) is amended to delete the requirement that judgment on a motion for attorney fees be set forth in a separate document. This change complements the amendment of Rule 58(a)(1), which deletes the separate document requirement for an order disposing of a motion for attorney fees under Rule 54. These changes are made to support amendment of Rule 4 of the Federal Rules of Appellate Procedure. It continues to be important that a district court make clear its meaning when it intends an order to be the final disposition of a motion for attorney fees.

The requirement in subdivision (d)(2)(B) that a motion for attorney fees be not only filed but also served no later than 14 days after entry of judgment is changed to require filing only, to establish a parallel with Rules 50, 52, and 59. Service continues to be required under Rule 5(a).

2003 Amendments

Rule 54(d)(2)(D) is revised to reflect amendments to Rule 53.

HISTORICAL NOTES

Effective and Applicability Provisions

1961 Amendments. Amendment adopted on Apr. 17, 1961, effective July 19, 1961, see Rule 86(d).

Rule 55. Default

(a) Entry. When a party against whom a judgment for affirmative relief is sought has failed to plead or otherwise defend as provided by these rules and that fact is made to appear by affidavit or otherwise, the clerk shall enter the party's default.

(b) Judgment. Judgment by default may be entered as follows:

(1) By the Clerk. When the plaintiff's claim against a defendant is for a sum certain or for a sum which can by computation be made certain, the clerk upon request of the plaintiff and upon affidavit of the amount due shall enter judgment for that amount and costs against the defendant, if the defendant has been defaulted for failure to appear and is not an infant or incompetent person.

(2) By the Court. In all other cases the party entitled to a judgment by default shall apply to the court therefor; but no judgment by default shall be entered against an infant or incompetent person unless represented in the action by a general guardian, committee, conservator, or other such representative who has appeared therein. If the party against whom judgment by default is sought has appeared in the action, the party (or, if appearing by representative, the party's representative) shall be served with written notice of the application for judgment at least 3 days prior to the hearing on such application. If, in order to enable the court to enter judgment or to carry it into effect, it is necessary to take an account or to determine the amount of damages or to establish the truth of any averment by evidence or to make an investigation of any other matter, the court may conduct such hearings or order such references as it deems necessary and proper and shall accord a right of trial by jury to the parties when and as required by any statute of the United States.

(c) Setting Aside Default. For good cause shown the court may set aside an entry of default and, if a judgment by default has been entered, may likewise set it aside in accordance with Rule 60(b).

(d) Plaintiffs, Counterclaimants, Cross-Claimants. The provisions of this rule apply whether the party entitled to the judgment by default is a plaintiff, a third-party plaintiff, or a party who has pleaded a cross-claim or counterclaim. In all cases a judgment by default is subject to the limitations of Rule 54(c).

(e) Judgment Against the United States. No judgment by default shall be entered against the United States or an officer or agency thereof unless the claimant establishes a claim or right to relief by evidence satisfactory to the court.

(As amended Mar. 2, 1987, eff. Aug. 1, 1987.)

ADVISORY COMMITTEE NOTES

1937 Adoption

This represents the joining of the equity decree *pro confesso* (former Equity Rules 12 (Issue of Subpoena—Time for Answer), 16 (Defendant to Answer—Default—Decree *Pro Confesso*), 17 (Decree *Pro Confesso* to be Followed by Final Decree—Setting Aside Default), 29 (Defenses—How Presented), 31 (Reply—When Required—When Cause at Issue)) and the judgment by default now governed by U.S.C., Title 28, [former] § 724 (Conformity act). For dismissal of an action for failure to comply with these rules or any order of the court, see Rule 41(b).

Note to Subdivision (a). The provision for the entry of default comes from the Massachusetts practice, 2 Mass.Gen. Laws (Ter.Ed., 1932) ch. 231, § 57. For affidavit of default, see 2 Minn.Stat. (Mason, 1927) § 9256.

Note to Subdivision (b). The provision in paragraph (1) for the entry of judgment by the clerk when plaintiff claims a sum certain is found in the N.Y.C.P.A. (1937) § 485, in Calif.Code Civ.Proc. (Deering, 1937) § 585(1), and in Conn.Practice Book (1934) § 47. For provisions similar to paragraph (2), compare Calif.Code, *supra*, § 585(2); N.Y.C.P.A. (1937) § 490; 2 Minn.Stat. (Mason, 1927) § 9256(3); 2 Wash.Rev.Stat.Ann. (Remington, 1932) § 411(2). U.S.C., Title 28, § 1874, formerly § 785 (Action to recover forfeiture in bond) and similar statutes are preserved by the last clause of paragraph (2).

Note to Subdivision (e). This restates substantially the last clause of U.S.C., Title 28, [former] § 763 (Action against the United States under the Tucker Act). As this rule governs in all actions against the United States, U.S.C., Title 28, [former] § 45 (Practice and procedure in certain cases under the interstate commerce laws) and similar statutes are modified insofar as they contain anything inconsistent therewith.

Supplementary Note

Note. The operation of Rule 55(b) (Judgment) is directly affected by the Soldiers' and Sailors' Civil Relief Act of 1940, 50 U.S.C. Appendix, § 501 et seq. Section 200 of the Act [50 U.S.C. Appendix, § 520] imposes specific requirements which must be fulfilled before a default judgment can be entered, e.g., *Ledwith v. Storkan*, D.Neb.1942, 6 Fed.Rules Serv. 60b.24, Case 2, 2 F.R.D. 539, and also provides for the vacation of a judgment in certain circumstances. See discussion in Commentary, Effect of Conscription Legislation on the Federal Rules, 1940, 3 Fed.Rules Serv. 725; 3 *Moore's Federal Practice*, 1938, Cum.Supplement § 55.02.

1987 Amendment

The amendments are technical. No substantive change is intended.

Rule 56. Summary Judgment

(a) For Claimant. A party seeking to recover upon a claim, counterclaim, or cross-claim or to obtain a declaratory judgment may, at any time after the expiration of 20 days from the commencement of the action or after service of a motion for summary judgment by the adverse party, move with or without supporting affidavits for a summary judgment in the party's favor upon all or any part thereof.

(b) For Defending Party. A party against whom a claim, counterclaim, or cross-claim is asserted or a declaratory judgment is sought may, at any time, move with or without supporting affidavits for a summary judgment in the party's favor as to all or any part thereof.

(c) Motion and Proceedings Thereon. The motion shall be served at least 10 days before the time fixed for the hearing. The adverse party prior to the day of hearing may serve opposing affidavits. The judgment sought shall be rendered forthwith if the pleadings, depositions, answers to interrogatories, and admissions on file, together with the affidavits, if any, show that there is no genuine issue as to any material fact and that the moving party is entitled to a judgment as a matter of law. A summary judgment, interlocutory in character, may be rendered on the issue of liability alone although there is a genuine issue as to the amount of damages.

(d) Case Not Fully Adjudicated on Motion. If on motion under this rule judgment is not rendered upon the whole case or for all the relief asked and a trial is necessary, the court at the hearing of the motion, by examining the pleadings and the evidence before it and by interrogating counsel, shall if practicable ascertain what material facts exist without substantial controversy and what material facts are actually and in good faith controverted. It shall thereupon make an order specifying the facts that appear without substantial controversy, including the extent to which the amount of damages or other relief is not in controversy, and directing such further proceedings in the action as are just. Upon the trial of the action the facts so specified shall be deemed established, and the trial shall be conducted accordingly.

(e) Form of Affidavits; Further Testimony; Defense Required. Supporting and opposing affidavits shall be made on personal knowledge, shall set forth such facts as would be admissible in evidence, and shall show affirmatively that the affiant is competent to testify to the matters stated therein. Sworn or certified copies of all papers or parts thereof referred to in an affidavit shall be attached thereto or served therewith. The court may permit affidavits to be supplemented or opposed by depositions, answers to interrogatories, or further affidavits. When a motion for summary judgment is made and supported as provided in this rule, an adverse party may not rest upon the mere allegations or denials of the adverse party's pleading, but the adverse party's response, by affidavits or as otherwise provided in this rule, must set forth specific facts showing that there is a genuine issue for trial. If the adverse party does not so respond, summary judgment, if appropriate, shall be entered against the adverse party.

(f) When Affidavits are Unavailable. Should it appear from the affidavits of a party opposing the motion that the party cannot for reasons stated present by affidavit facts essential to justify the party's opposition, the court may refuse the application for judgment or may order a continuance to permit affidavits to be obtained or depositions to be taken or discovery to be had or may make such other order as is just.

(g) Affidavits Made in Bad Faith. Should it appear to the satisfaction of the court at any time that any of the affidavits presented pursuant to this rule are presented in bad faith or solely for the purpose of delay, the court shall forthwith order the party employing them to pay to the other party the amount of the reasonable expenses which the filing of the affidavits caused the other party to incur, including reasonable attorney's fees, and any offending party or attorney may be adjudged guilty of contempt.

(As amended Dec. 27, 1946, eff. Mar. 19, 1948; Jan. 21, 1963, eff. July 1, 1963; Mar. 2, 1987, eff. Aug. 1, 1987.)

ADVISORY COMMITTEE NOTES
1937 Adoption

This rule is applicable to all actions, including those against the United States or an officer or agency thereof.

Summary judgment procedure is a method for promptly disposing of actions in which there is no genuine issue as to any material fact. It has been extensively used in England for more than 50 years and has been adopted in a number of American states. New York, for example, has made great use of it. During the first nine years after its adoption there, the records of New York county alone show 5,600 applications for summary judgments. Report of the Commission on the Administration of Justice in New York State (1934), p. 383. See also *Third Annual Report of the Judicial Council of the State of New York* (1937), p. 30.

In England it was first employed only in cases of liquidated claims, but there has been a steady enlargement of the scope of the remedy until it is now used in actions to recover land or chattels and in all other actions at law, for liquidated or unliquidated claims, except for a few designated torts and breach of promise of marriage. *English Rules Under the Judicature Act* (The Annual Practice, 1937) O. 3, r. 6; Orders 14, 14A, and 15; see also O. 32, r. 6, authorizing an application for judgment at any time upon admissions. In Michigan (3 Comp.Laws (1929) § 14260) and Illinois (Smith-Hurd Ill.Stats. c. 110, §§ 181, 259.15, 259.16), it is not limited to liquidated demands. New York (N.Y.R.C.P. (1937) Rule 113; see also Rule 107) has brought so many classes of actions under the operation of the rule that the Commission on Administration of Justice in New York State (1934) recommend that all restrictions be removed and that the remedy be available "in any action" (p. 287). For the history and nature of the summary judgment procedure and citations of state statutes, see Clark and Samenow, *The Summary Judgment* (1929), 38 Yale L.J. 423.

Note to Subdivision (d). See Rule 16 (Pre-Trial Procedure; Formulating Issues) and the Note thereto.

Note to Subdivisions (e) and (f). These are similar to rules in Michigan. Mich.Court Rules Ann. (Searl, 1933) Rule 30.

1946 Amendment

Note to Subdivision (a). The amendment allows a claimant to move for a summary judgment at any time after the expiration of 20 days from the commencement of the action or after service of a motion for summary judgment by the adverse party. This will normally operate to permit an earlier motion by the claimant than under the original rule, where the phrase "at any time after the pleading in answer thereto has been served" operates to prevent a claimant from moving for summary judgment, even in a case clearly proper for its exercise, until a formal answer has been filed. Thus in *Peoples Bank v. Federal Reserve Bank of San Francisco*, N.D.Cal.1944, 58 F.Supp. 25, the plaintiff's countermotion for a summary judgment was stricken as premature, because the defendant had not filed an answer. Since Rule 12(a) allows at least 20 days for an answer, that time plus the 10 days required in Rule 56(c) means that under original Rule 56(a) a minimum period of 30 days necessarily has to elapse in every case before the claimant can be heard on his right to a summary judgment. An extension of time by the court or the service of preliminary motions of any kind will prolong that period even further. In many cases this merely represents unnecessary delay. See *United States v. Adler's Creamery, Inc.*, C.C.A.2, 1939, 107 F.2d 987. The changes are in the interest of more expeditious litigation. The 20-day period, as provided, gives the defendant an opportunity to secure counsel and determine a course of action. But in a case where the defendant himself makes a motion for summary judgment within that time, there is no reason to restrict the plaintiff and the amended rule so provides.

Subdivision (c). The amendment of Rule 56(c), by the addition of the final sentence, resolves a doubt expressed in *Sartor v. Arkansas Natural Gas Corp.*, 1944, 64 S.Ct. 724, 321 U.S. 620, 88 L.Ed. 967. See also Commentary, Summary Judgment as to Damages, 1944, 7 Fed.Rules Serv. 974; *Madeirense Do Brasil S/A v. Stulman-Emrick Lumber Co.*, C.C.A.2d, 1945, 147 F.2d 399, certiorari denied 1945, 65 S.Ct. 1201, 325 U.S. 861, 89 L.Ed. 1982. It makes clear that although the question of recovery depends on the amount of damages, the summary judgment rule is applicable and summary judgment may be granted in a proper case. If the case is not fully adjudicated it may be dealt with as provided in subdivision (d) of Rule 56, and the right to summary recovery determined by a preliminary order, interlocutory in character, and the precise amount of recovery left for trial.

Subdivision (d). Rule 54(a) defines "judgment" as including a decree and "any order from which an appeal lies." Subdivision (d) of Rule 56 indicates clearly, however, that a partial summary "judgment" is not a final judgment, and, therefore, that it is not appealable, unless in the particular case some statute allows an appeal from the interlocutory order involved. The partial summary judgment is merely a pretrial adjudication that certain issues shall be deemed established for the trial of the case. This adjudication is more nearly akin to the preliminary order under Rule 16, and likewise serves the purpose of speeding up litigation by eliminating before trial matters wherein there is no genuine issue of fact. See *Leonard v. Socony-Vacuum Oil Co.*, C.C.A.7, 1942, 130 F.2d 535; *Biggins v. Oltmer Iron Works*, C.C.A.7, 1946, 154 F.2d 214; 3 *Moore's Federal Practice*, 1938, 3190–3192. Since interlocutory appeals are not allowed, except where specifically provided by statute, see 3 Moore, op. cit. supra, 3155–3156, this interpretation is in line with that policy, *Leonard v. Socony-Vacuum Oil Co.*, supra. See also *Audi Vision Inc. v. RCA Mfg. Co.*, C.C.A.2, 1943, 136 F.2d 621; *Toomey v. Toomey*, 1945, 149 F.2d 19, 80 U.S.App.D.C. 77; *Biggins v. Oltmer Iron Works*, supra; *Catlin v. United States*, 1945, 65 S.Ct. 631, 324 U.S. 229, 89 L.Ed. 911.

1963 Amendment

Subdivision (c). By the amendment "answers to interrogatories" are included among the materials which may be considered on motion for summary judgment. The phrase was inadvertently omitted from the rule, see 3 Barron & Holtzoff, *Federal Practice & Procedure* 159–60 (Wright ed. 1958), and the courts have generally reached by interpretation the result which will hereafter be required by the text of the amended rule. See Annot., 74 A.L.R.2d 984 (1960).

Subdivision (e). The words "answers to interrogatories" are added in the third sentence of this subdivision to conform to the amendment of subdivision (c).

The last two sentences are added to overcome a line of cases, chiefly in the Third Circuit, which has impaired the utility of the summary judgment device. A typical case is as follows: A party supports his motion for summary judgment by affidavits or other evidentiary matter sufficient to show that there is no genuine issue as to a material fact. The adverse party, in opposing the motion, does not produce any evidentiary matter, or produces some but not enough to establish that there is a genuine issue for trial. Instead, the adverse party rests on averments of his pleadings which on their face present an issue. In this situation Third Circuit cases have taken the view that summary judgment must be denied, at least if the averments are "well-pleaded," and not suppositious, conclusory, or ultimate. See *Frederick Hart & Co., Inc. v. Recordgraph Corp.*, 169 F.2d 580 (3d Cir. 1948); *United States ex rel. Kolton v. Halpern*, 260 F.2d 590 (3d Cir. 1958); *United States ex rel. Nobles v. Ivey Bros. Constr. Co., Inc.*, 191 F.Supp. 383 (D.Del.1961); *Jamison v. Pennsylvania Salt Mfg. Co.*, 22 F.R.D. 238 (W.D.Pa.1958); *Bunny Bear, Inc. v. Dennis Mitchell Industries*, 139 F.Supp. 542 (E.D.Pa.1956); *Levy v. Equitable Life Assur. Society*, 18 F.R.D. 164 (E.D.Pa.1955).

The very mission of the summary judgment procedure is to pierce the pleadings and to assess the proof in order to see whether there is a genuine need for trial. The Third Circuit doctrine, which permits the pleadings themselves to stand in the way of granting an otherwise justified summary judgment, is incompatible with the basic purpose of the rule. See 6 *Moore's Federal Practice* 2069 (2d ed. 1953); 3 Barron & Holtzoff, supra, § 1235.1.

It is hoped that the amendment will contribute to the more effective utilization of the salutary device of summary judgment.

The amendment is not intended to derogate from the solemnity of the pleadings. Rather it recognizes that, despite the best efforts of counsel to make his pleadings accurate, they may be overwhelmingly contradicted by the proof available to his adversary.

Nor is the amendment designed to affect the ordinary standards applicable to the summary judgment motion. So, for example: Where an issue as to a material fact cannot be resolved without observation of the demeanor of witnesses in order to evaluate their credibility, summary judgment is not appropriate. Where the evidentiary matter in support of the motion does not establish the absence of a genuine issue, summary judgment must be denied even if no opposing evidentiary matter is presented. And summary judgment may be inappropriate where the party opposing it shows under subdivision (f) that he cannot at the time present facts essential to justify his opposition.

1987 Amendment

The amendments are technical. No substantive change is intended.

Rule 57. Declaratory Judgments

The procedure for obtaining a declaratory judgment pursuant to Title 28, U.S.C., § 2201, shall be in accordance with these rules, and the right to trial by jury may be demanded under the circumstances and in the manner provided in Rules 38 and 39. The existence of another adequate remedy does not preclude a judgment for declaratory relief in cases where it is appropriate. The court may order a speedy hearing of an action for a declaratory judgment and may advance it on the calendar.

(As amended Dec. 29, 1948, eff. Oct. 20, 1949.)

ADVISORY COMMITTEE NOTES

1937 Adoption

The fact that a declaratory judgment may be granted "whether or not further relief is or could be prayed" indicates that declaratory relief is alternative or cumulative and not exclusive or extraordinary. A declaratory judgment is appropriate when it will "terminate the controversy" giving rise on undisputed or relatively undisputed facts, it operates frequently as a summary proceeding, justifying docketing the case for early hearing as on a motion, as provided for in California (Code Civ.Proc. (Deering, 1937) § 1062a), Michigan (3 Comp.Laws (1929) § 13904), and Kentucky (Codes (Carroll, 1932) Civ.Pract. § 639a–3).

The "controversy" must necessarily be "of a justiciable nature, thus excluding an advisory decree upon a hypothetical state of facts." *Ashwander v. Tennessee Valley Authority*, 1936, 56 S.Ct. 466, 473, 297 U.S. 288, 80 L.Ed. 688. The existence or non-existence of any right, duty, power, liability, privilege, disability, or immunity or of any fact upon which such legal relations depend, or of a status, may be declared. The petitioner must have a practical interest in the declaration sought and all parties having an interest therein or adversely affected must be made parties or be cited. A declaration may not be rendered if a special statutory proceeding has been provided for the adjudication of some special type of case, but general ordinary or extraordinary legal remedies, whether regulated by statute or not, are not deemed special statutory proceedings.

When declaratory relief will not be effective in settling the controversy, the court may decline to grant it. But the fact that another remedy would be equally effective affords no ground for declining declaratory relief. The demand for relief shall state with precision the declaratory judgment relief, cumulatively or in the alternative; but when coercive relief only is sought but is deemed ungrantable, or inappropriate, the court may *sua sponte*, if it serves a useful purpose, grant instead a declaration of rights. *Hasselbring v. Koepke*, 1933, 248 N.W. 869, 263 Mich. 466, 93 A.L.R. 1170. Written instruments, including ordinances and statutes, may be construed before or after breach at the petition of a properly interested party, process being served on the private parties or public officials interested. In other respects the Uniform Declaratory Judgment Act affords a guide to the scope and function of the Federal act. Compare *Aetna Life Insurance Co. v. Haworth*, 1937, 57 S.Ct. 461, 300 U.S. 227, 81 L.Ed. 617, 108 A.L.R. 1000; *Nashville, Chattanooga & St. Louis Ry. v. Wallace*, 1933, 53 S.Ct. 345, 288 U.S. 249, 77 L.Ed. 730, 87 A.L.R. 1191; *Gully, Tax Collector v. Interstate Natural Gas Co.*, 82 F.2d 145 (C.C.A.5, 1936); *Ohio Casualty Ins. Co. v. Plummer*, Tex.1935, 13 F.Supp. 169; Borchard, Declaratory Judgments (1934), *passim*.

1948 Amendment

The amendment effective October 1949, substituted the reference to "Title 28, U.S.C., § 2201" in the first sentence for the reference to "Section 274(d) of the Judicial Code, as amended, U.S.C., Title 28, § 400".

Rule 58. Entry of Judgment

(a) Separate Document.

(1) Every judgment and amended judgment must be set forth on a separate document, but a separate document is not required for an order disposing of a motion:

(A) for judgment under Rule 50(b);

(B) to amend or make additional findings of fact under Rule 52(b);

(C) for attorney fees under Rule 54;

(D) for a new trial, or to alter or amend the judgment, under Rule 59; or

(E) for relief under Rule 60.

(2) Subject to Rule 54(b):

(A) unless the court orders otherwise, the clerk must, without awaiting the court's direction, promptly prepare, sign, and enter the judgment when:

(i) the jury returns a general verdict,

(ii) the court awards only costs or a sum certain, or

(iii) the court denies all relief;

(B) the court must promptly approve the form of the judgment, which the clerk must promptly enter, when:

(i) the jury returns a special verdict or a general verdict accompanied by interrogatories, or

(ii) the court grants other relief not described in Rule 58(a)(2).

(b) Time of Entry. Judgment is entered for purposes of these rules:

(1) if Rule 58(a)(1) does not require a separate document, when it is entered in the civil docket under Rule 79(a), and

(2) if Rule 58(a)(1) requires a separate document, when it is entered in the civil docket under Rule 79(a) and when the earlier of these events occurs:

(A) when it is set forth on a separate document, or

(B) when 150 days have run from entry in the civil docket under Rule 79(a).

(c) Cost or Fee Awards.

(1) Entry of judgment may not be delayed, nor the time for appeal extended, in order to tax costs or award fees, except as provided in Rule 58(c)(2).

(2) When a timely motion for attorney fees is made under Rule 54(d)(2), the court may act before a notice of appeal has been filed and has become effective to order that the motion have the same effect under Federal Rule of Appellate Procedure 4(a)(4) as a timely motion under Rule 59.

(d) Request for Entry. A party may request that judgment be set forth on a separate document as required by Rule 58(a)(1).

(As amended Dec. 27, 1946, eff. Mar. 19, 1948; Jan. 21, 1963, eff. July 1, 1963; Apr. 22, 1993, eff. Dec. 1, 1993; Apr. 29, 2002, eff. Dec. 1, 2002.)

ADVISORY COMMITTEE NOTES

1937 Adoption

See Wis.Stat. (1935) § 270.31 (judgment entered forthwith on verdict of jury unless otherwise ordered), § 270.65 (where trial is by the court, entered by direction of the court), § 270.63 (entered by clerk on judgment on admitted claim for money). Compare 1 Idaho Code Ann. (1932) § 7–1101, and 4 Mont.Rev.Codes Ann. (1935) § 9403, which provide that judgment in jury cases be entered by clerk within 24 hours after verdict unless court otherwise directs. Conn.Practice Book (1934), § 200, provides that all judgments shall be entered within one week after rendition. In some States such as Washington, 2 Rev.Stat.Ann. (Remington, 1932), § 431, in jury cases the judgment is entered two days after the return of verdict to give time for making motion for new trial; § 435 (*ibid.*), provides that all judgments shall be entered by the clerk, subject to the court's direction.

1946 Amendment

Note. The reference to Rule 54(b) is made necessary by the amendment of that rule.

Two changes have been made in Rule 58 in order to clarify the practice. The substitution of the more inclusive phrase "all relief be denied" for the words "there be no recovery", makes it clear that the clerk shall enter the judgment forthwith in the situations specified without awaiting the filing of a formal judgment approved by the court. The phrase "all relief be denied" covers cases such as the denial of a bankrupt's discharge and similar situations where the relief sought is refused but there is literally no denial of a "recovery".

The addition of the last sentence in the rule emphasizes that judgments are to be entered promptly by the clerk without waiting for the taxing of costs. Certain district court rules, for example, Civil Rule 22 of the Southern District of New York—until its annulment Oct. 1, 1945, for conflict with this rule—and the like rule of the Eastern District of New York, are expressly in conflict with this provision, although the federal law is of long standing and well settled. *Fowler v. Hamill*, 1891, 11 S.Ct. 663, 139 U.S. 549, 35 L.Ed. 266; *Craig v. The Hartford*, C.C.Cal.1856, Fed.Cas. No. 3,333; *Tuttle v. Claflin*, C.C.A.2, 1895, 60 F. 7, certiorari denied 1897; 17 S.Ct. 992, 166 U.S. 721, 41 L.Ed. 1188; *Prescott & A.C. Ry. Co. v. Atchison, T. & S.F.R. Co.*, C.C.A.2, 1897, 84 F. 213; *Stallo v. Wagner*, C.C.A.2, 1917, 245 F. 636, 639–40; *Brown v. Parker*, C.C.A.8, 1899, 97 F. 446; *Allis-Chalmers v. United States*, C.C.A.7, 1908, 162 F. 679. And this applies even though state law is to the contrary. *United States v. Nordbye*, C.C.A.8, 1935, 75 F.2d 744, certiorari denied 56 S.Ct. 103, 296 U.S. 572, 80 L.Ed. 404. Inasmuch as it has been held that failure of the clerk thus to enter judgment is a "misprision" "not to be excused", *The Washington*, C.C.A.2, 1926, 16 F.2d 206, such a district court rule may have serious consequences for a district court clerk. Rules of this sort also provide for delay in entry of the judgment contrary to Rule 58. See *Commissioner of Internal Revenue v. Bed-*

ford's Estate, 1945, 65 S.Ct. 1157, 325 U.S. 283, 91 L.Ed. 1611.

1963 Amendment

Under the present rule a distinction has sometimes been made between judgments on general jury verdicts, on the one hand, and, on the other, judgments upon decisions of the court that a party shall recover only money or costs or that all relief shall be denied. In the first situation, it is clear that the clerk should enter the judgment without awaiting a direction by the court unless the court otherwise orders. In the second situation it was intended that the clerk should similarly enter the judgment forthwith upon the court's decision; but because of the separate listing in the rule, and the use of the phrase "upon receipt . . . of the direction," the rule has sometimes been interpreted as requiring the clerk to await a separate direction of the court. All these judgments are usually uncomplicated, and should be handled in the same way. The amended rule accordingly deals with them as a single group in clause (1) (substituting the expression "only a sum certain" for the present expression "only money"), and requires the clerk to prepare, sign and enter them forthwith, without awaiting court direction, unless the court makes a contrary order. (The clerk's duty is ministerial and may be performed by a deputy clerk in the name of the clerk. See 28 U.S.C. § 956; cf. *Gilbertson v. United States,* 168 Fed. 672 (7th Cir. 1909).) The more complicated judgments described in clause (2) must be approved by the court before they are entered.

Rule 58 is designed to encourage all reasonable speed in formulating and entering the judgment when the case has been decided. Participation by the attorneys through the submission of forms of judgment involves needless expenditure of time and effort and promotes delay, except in special cases where counsel's assistance can be of real value. See *Matteson v. United States,* 240 F.2d 517, 518–19 (2d Cir. 1956). Accordingly, the amended rule provides that attorneys shall not submit forms of judgment unless directed to do so by the court. This applies to the judgments mentioned in clause (2) as well as clause (1).

Hitherto some difficulty has arisen, chiefly where the court has written an opinion or memorandum containing some apparently directive or dispositive words, e.g., "the plaintiff's motion [for summary judgment] is granted," see *United States v. F. & M. Schaefer Brewing Co.,* 356 U.S. 227, 229, 78 S.Ct. 674, 2 L.Ed.2d 721 (1958). Clerks on occasion have viewed these opinions or memoranda as being in themselves a sufficient basis for entering judgment in the civil docket as provided by Rule 79(a). However, where the opinion or memorandum has not contained all the elements of a judgment, or where the judge has later signed a formal judgment, it has become a matter of doubt whether the purported entry of judgment was effective, starting the time running for post-verdict motions and for the purpose of appeal. See id.; and compare *Blanchard v. Commonwealth Oil Co.,* 294 F.2d 834 (5th Cir. 1961); *United States v. Higginson,* 238 F.2d 439 (1st Cir. 1956); *Danzig v. Virgin Isle Hotel, Inc.,* 278 F.2d 580 (3d Cir. 1960); *Sears v. Austin,* 282 F.2d 340 (9th Cir. 1960), with *Matteson v. United States,* supra; *Erstling v. Southern Bell Tel. & Tel. Co.,* 255 F.2d 93 (5th Cir. 1958); *Barta v. Oglala Sioux Tribe,* 259 F.2d 553 (8th Cir. 1958) cert. denied, 358 U.S. 932, 79 S.Ct. 320, 3 L.Ed.2d 304 (1959); *Beacon Fed. S. & L. Assn. v. Federal Home L. Bank*

Bd., 266 F.2d 246 (7th Cir.), cert. denied, 361 U.S. 823, 80 S.Ct. 70, 4 L.Ed.2d 67 (1959); *Ram v. Paramount Film D. Corp.,* 278 F.2d 191 (4th Cir. 1960).

The amended rule eliminates these uncertainties by requiring that there be a judgment set out on a separate document—distinct from any opinion or memorandum—which provides the basis for the entry of judgment. That judgment shall be on separate documents is also indicated in Rule 79(b); and see General Rule 10 of the U.S. District Courts for the Eastern and Southern Districts of New York; *Ram v. Paramount Film D. Corp.,* supra, at 194.

See the amendment of Rule 79(a) and the new specimen forms of judgment, Forms 31 and 32.

See also Rule 55(b)(1) and (2) covering the subject of judgments by default.

1993 Amendments

Ordinarily the pendency or post-judgment filing of a claim for attorney's fees will not affect the time for appeal from the underlying judgment. See Budinich v. Becton Dickinson & Co., 486 U.S. 196 (1988). Particularly if the claim for fees involves substantial issues or is likely to be affected by the appellate decision, the district court may prefer to defer consideration of the claim for fees until after the appeal is resolved. However, in many cases it may be more efficient to decide fee questions before an appeal is taken so that appeals relating to the fee award can be heard at the same time as appeals relating to the merits of the case. This revision permits, but does not require, the court to delay the finality of the judgment for appellate purposes under revised Fed.R.App.P. 4(a) until the fee dispute is decided. To accomplish this result requires entry of an order by the district court before the time a notice of appeal becomes effective for appellate purposes. If the order is entered, the motion for attorney's fees is treated in the same manner as a timely motion under Rule 59.

2002 Amendments

Rule 58 has provided that a judgment is effective only when set forth on a separate document and entered as provided in Rule 79(a). This simple separate document requirement has been ignored in many cases. The result of failure to enter judgment on a separate document is that the time for making motions under Rules 50, 52, 54(d)(2)(B), 59, and some motions under Rule 60, never begins to run. The time to appeal under Appellate Rule 4(a) also does not begin to run. There have been few visible problems with respect to Rule 50, 52, 54(d)(2)(B), 59, or 60 motions, but there have been many and horridly confused problems under Appellate Rule 4(a). These amendments are designed to work in conjunction with Appellate Rule 4(a) to ensure that appeal time does not linger on indefinitely, and to maintain the integration of the time periods set for Rules 50, 52, 54(d)(2)(B), 59, and 60 with Appellate Rule 4(a).

Rule 58(a) preserves the core of the present separate document requirement, both for the initial judgment and for any amended judgment. No attempt is made to sort through the confusion that some courts have found in addressing the elements of a separate document. It is easy to prepare a separate document that recites the terms of the judgment without offering additional explanation or citation of authority. Forms 31 and 32 provide examples.

Rule 58 is amended, however, to address a problem that arises under Appellate Rule 4(a). Some courts treat such orders as those that deny a motion for new trial as a "judgment," so that appeal time does not start to run until the order is entered on a separate document. Without attempting to address the question whether such orders are appealable, and thus judgments as defined by Rule 54(a), the amendment provides that entry on a separate document is not required for an order disposing of the motions listed in Appellate Rule 4(a). The enumeration of motions drawn from the Appellate Rule 4(a) list is generalized by omitting details that are important for appeal time purposes but that would unnecessarily complicate the separate document requirement. As one example, it is not required that any of the enumerated motions be timely. Many of the enumerated motions are frequently made before judgment is entered. The exemption of the order disposing of the motion does not excuse the obligation to set forth the judgment itself on a separate document. And if disposition of the motion results in an amended judgment, the amended judgment must be set forth on a separate document.

Rule 58(b) discards the attempt to define the time when a judgment becomes "effective." Taken in conjunction with the Rule 54(a) definition of a judgment to include "any order from which an appeal lies," the former Rule 58 definition of effectiveness could cause strange difficulties in implementing pretrial orders that are appealable under interlocutory appeal provisions or under expansive theories of finality. Rule 58(b) replaces the definition of effectiveness with a new provision that defines the time when judgment is entered. If judgment is promptly set forth on a separate document, as should be done when required by Rule 58(a)(1), the new provision will not change the effect of Rule 58. But in the cases in which court and clerk fail to comply with this simple requirement, the motion time periods set by Rules 50, 52, 54, 59, and 60 begin to run after expiration of 150 days from entry of the judgment in the civil docket as required by Rule 79(a).

A companion amendment of Appellate Rule 4(a)(7) integrates these changes with the time to appeal.

The new all-purpose definition of the entry of judgment must be applied with common sense to other questions that may turn on the time when judgment is entered. If the 150-day provision in Rule 58(b)(2)(B)—designed to integrate the time for post-judgment motions with appeal time—serves no purpose, or would defeat the purpose of another rule, it should be disregarded. In theory, for example, the separate document requirement continues to apply to an interlocutory order that is appealable as a final decision under collateral-order doctrine. Appealability under collateral-order doctrine should not be complicated by failure to enter the order as a judgment on a separate document—there is little reason to force trial judges to speculate about the potential appealability of every order, and there is no means to ensure that the trial judge will always reach the same conclusion as the court of appeals. Appeal time should start to run when the collateral order is entered without regard to creation of a separate document and without awaiting expiration of the 150 days provided by Rule 58(b)(2). Drastic surgery on Rules 54(a) and 58 would be required to address this and related issues, however, and it is better to leave this conundrum to the pragmatic disregard that seems its present fate. The present amendments do not seem to make matters worse, apart from one false appearance. If a pretrial order is set forth on a separate document that meets the requirements of Rule 58(b), the time to move for reconsideration seems to begin to run, perhaps years before final judgment. And even if there is no separate document, the time to move for reconsideration seems to begin 150 days after entry in the civil docket. This apparent problem is resolved by Rule 54(b), which expressly permits revision of all orders not made final under Rule 54(b) "at any time before the entry of judgment adjudicating all the claims and the rights and liabilities of all the parties."

New Rule 58(d) replaces the provision that attorneys shall not submit forms of judgment except on direction of the court. This provision was added to Rule 58 to avoid the delays that were frequently encountered by the former practice of directing the attorneys for the prevailing party to prepare a form of judgment, and also to avoid the occasionally inept drafting that resulted from attorney-prepared judgments. See *11 Wright, Miller & Kane, Federal Practice & Procedure: Civil 2d, § 2786.* The express direction in Rule 58(a)(2) for prompt action by the clerk, and by the court if court action is required, addresses this concern. The new provision allowing any party to move for entry of judgment on a separate document will protect all needs for prompt commencement of the periods for motions, appeals, and execution or other enforcement.

Changes Made After Publication and Comment Minor style changes were made. The definition of the time of entering judgment in Rule 58(b) was extended to reach all Civil Rules, not only the Rules described in the published version—Rules 50, 52, 54(d)(2)(B), 59, 60, and 62. And the time of entry was extended from 60 days to 150 days after entry in the civil docket without a required separate document.

Rule 59. New Trials; Amendment of Judgments

(a) Grounds. A new trial may be granted to all or any of the parties and on all or part of the issues (1) in an action in which there has been a trial by jury, for any of the reasons for which new trials have heretofore been granted in actions at law in the courts of the United States; and (2) in an action tried without a jury, for any of the reasons for which rehearings have heretofore been granted in suits in equity in the courts of the United States. On a motion for a new trial in an action tried without a jury, the court may open the judgment if one has been entered, take additional testimony, amend findings of fact and conclusions of law or make new findings and conclusions, and direct the entry of a new judgment.

(b) Time for Motion. Any motion for a new trial shall be filed no later than 10 days after entry of the judgment.

(c) Time for Serving Affidavits. When a motion for new trial is based on affidavits, they shall be filed with the motion. The opposing party has 10 days after service to file opposing affidavits, but that period may be extended for up to 20 days, either by the court for good cause or by the parties' written stipulation. The court may permit reply affidavits.

(d) On Court's Initiative; Notice; Specifying Grounds. No later than 10 days after entry of judgment the court, on its own, may order a new trial for any reason that would justify granting one on a party's motion. After giving the parties notice and an opportunity to be heard, the court may grant a timely motion for a new trial for a reason not stated in the motion. When granting a new trial on its own initiative or for a reason not stated in a motion, the court shall specify the grounds in its order.

(e) Motion to Alter or Amend Judgment. Any motion to alter or amend a judgment shall be filed no later than 10 days after entry of the judgment.

(As amended Dec. 27, 1946, eff. Mar. 19, 1948; Feb. 28, 1966, eff. July 1, 1966; Apr. 27, 1995, eff. Dec. 1, 1995.)

ADVISORY COMMITTEE NOTES

1937 Adoption

This rule represents an amalgamation of the petition for rehearing of [former] Equity Rule 69 (Petition for Rehearing) and the motion for new trial of 28 U.S.C., § 2111, formerly § 391 (New trials; harmless error), made in the light of the experience and provision of the code States. Compare Calif.Code Civ.Proc., Deering, 1937, §§ 656 to 663a, 28 U.S.C., § 2111, formerly § 391 (New trials; harmless error) is thus substantially continued in this rule. U.S.C., Title 28, [former] § 840 (Executions; stay on conditions) is modified insofar as it contains time provisions inconsistent with Subdivision (b). For the effect of the motion for new trial upon the time for taking an appeal see *Morse v. United States*, 1926, 46 S.Ct. 241, 270 U.S. 151, 70 L.Ed. 518; *Aspen Mining and Smelting Co. v. Billings*, 1893, 14 S.Ct. 4, 150 U.S. 31, 37 L.Ed. 986.

For partial new trials which are permissible under Subdivision (a), see *Gasoline Products Co., Inc. v. Champlin Refining Co.*, 1931, 51 S.Ct. 513, 283 U.S. 494, 75 L.Ed. 1188; *Schuerholz v. Roach*, C.C.A.4, 1932, 58 F.2d 32; *Simmons v. Fish*, 1912, 97 N.E. 102, 210 Mass. 563, Ann.Cas.1912D, 588 (sustaining and recommending the practice and citing federal cases and cases in accord from about sixteen States and contra from three States). The procedure in several States provides specifically for partial new trials. Ariz.Rev.Code Ann., Struckmeyer, 1928, § 3852; Calif.Code Civ.Proc., Deering, 1937, §§ 657, 662; Smith-Hurd Ill.Stats., 1937, c. 110, § 216 (Par. (f)); Md.Ann.Code, Bagby, 1924, Art. 5, §§ 25, 26; Mich.Court Rules Ann., Searl, 1933, Rule 47, § 2; Miss.Sup.Ct.Rule 12, 161 Miss. 903, 905, 1931; N.J.Sup.Ct. Rules 131, 132, 147, 2 N.J.Misc. 1197, 1246–1251, 1255, 1924; 2 N.D.Comp.Laws Ann., 1913, § 7844, as amended by N.D.Laws 1927, ch. 214.

1946 Amendment

Note. Subdivision (b). With the time for appeal to a circuit court of appeals reduced in general to 30 days by the proposed amendment of Rule 73(a), the utility of the original "except" clause, which permits a motion for a new trial on the ground of newly discovered evidence to be made before the expiration of the time for appeal, would have been seriously restricted. It was thought advisable, therefore, to take care of this matter in another way. By amendment of Rule 60(b), newly discovered evidence is made the basis for relief from a judgment, and the maximum time limit has been extended to one year. Accordingly the amendment of Rule 59(b) eliminates the "except" clause and its specific treatment of newly discovered evidence as a ground for a motion for new trial. This ground remains, however, as a basis for a motion for new trial served not later than 10 days after the entry of judgment. See also Rule 60(b).

As to the effect of a motion under subdivision (b) upon the running of appeal time, see amended Rule 73(a) and Note.

Note to Subdivision (e). This subdivision has been added to care for a situation such as that arising in *Boaz v. Mutual Life Ins. Co. of New York*, C.C.A.8, 1944, 146 F.2d 321, and makes clear that the district court possesses the power asserted in that case to alter or amend a judgment after its entry. The subdivision deals only with alteration or amendment of the original judgment in a case and does not relate to a judgment upon motion as provided in Rule 50(b). As to the effect of a motion under subdivision (e) upon the running of appeal time, see amended Rule 73(a) and Note.

The title of Rule 59 has been expanded to indicate the inclusion of this subdivision.

1966 Amendment

By narrow interpretation of Rule 59(b) and (d), it has been held that the trial court is without power to grant a motion for a new trial, timely served, by an order made more than 10 days after the entry of judgment, based upon a ground not stated in the motion but perceived and relied on by the trial court sua sponte. *Freid v. McGrath*, 133 F.2d 350 (D.C.Cir. 1942); *National Farmers Union Auto. & Cas. Co. v. Wood*, 207 F.2d 659 (10th Cir. 1953); *Bailey v. Slentz*, 189 F.2d 406 (10th Cir. 1951); *Marshall's U.S. Auto Supply, Inc. v. Cashman*, 111 F.2d 140 (10th Cir. 1940), cert. denied, 311 U.S. 667 (1940); but see *Steinberg v. Indemnity Ins. Co.*, 36 F.R.D. 253 (E.D.La.1964).

The result is undesirable. Just as the court has power under Rule 59(d) to grant a new trial of its own initiative within the 10 days, so it should have power, when an effective new trial motion has been made and is pending, to decide it on grounds thought meritorious by the court although not advanced in the motion. The second sentence added by amendment to Rule 59(d) confirms the court's power in the latter situation, with provision that the parties be afforded a hearing before the power is exercised. See 6 *Moore's Federal Practice*, par. 59.09[2] (2d ed. 1953).

In considering whether a given ground has or has not been advanced in the motion made by the party, it should be borne in mind that the particularity called for in stating the grounds for a new trial motion is the same as that required for all motions by Rule 7(b)(1). The latter rule does not require ritualistic detail but rather a fair indication to court and counsel of the substance of the grounds relied on. See *Lebeck v. William A. Jarvis Co.*, 250 F.2d 285 (3d Cir. 1957); *Tsai v. Rosenthal*, 297 F.2d 614 (8th Cir. 1961); *General Motors Corp. v. Perry*, 303 F.2d 544 (7th Cir. 1962); cf. *Grimm v. California Spray-Chemical Corp.*, 264 F.2d 145 (9th Cir. 1959); *Cooper v. Midwest Feed Products Co.*, 271 F.2d 177 (8th Cir. 1959).

1995 Amendments

The only change, other than stylistic, intended by this revision is to add explicit time limits for filing motions for a new trial, motions to alter or amend a judgment, and affidavits opposing a new trial motion. Previously, there was an inconsistency in the wording of Rules 50, 52, and 59 with respect to whether certain post-judgment motions had to be filed, or merely served, during the prescribed period. This inconsistency caused special problems when motions for a new trial were joined with other post-judgment motions. These motions affect the finality of the judgment, a matter often of importance to third persons as well as the parties and the court. The Committee believes that each of these rules should be revised to require filing before end of the 10–day period. Filing is an event that can be determined with certainty from court records. The phrase "no later than" is used—rather than "within"—to include post-judgment motions that sometimes are filed before actual entry of the judgment by the clerk. It should be noted that under Rule 5 the motions when filed are to contain a certificate of service on other parties. It also should be noted that under Rule 6(a) Saturdays, Sundays, and legal holidays are excluded in measuring the 10–day period, but that Bankruptcy Rule 9006(a) excludes intermediate Saturdays, Sundays, and legal holidays only in computing periods less than 8 days.

Rule 60. Relief From Judgment or Order

(a) Clerical Mistakes. Clerical mistakes in judgments, orders or other parts of the record and errors therein arising from oversight or omission may be corrected by the court at any time of its own initiative or on the motion of any party and after such notice, if any, as the court orders. During the pendency of an appeal, such mistakes may be so corrected before the appeal is docketed in the appellate court, and thereafter while the appeal is pending may be so corrected with leave of the appellate court.

(b) Mistakes; Inadvertence; Excusable Neglect; Newly Discovered Evidence; Fraud, Etc. On motion and upon such terms as are just, the court may relieve a party or a party's legal representative from a final judgment, order, or proceeding for the following reasons: (1) mistake, inadvertence, surprise, or excusable neglect; (2) newly discovered evidence which by due diligence could not have been discovered in time to move for a new trial under Rule 59(b); (3) fraud (whether heretofore denominated intrinsic or extrinsic), misrepresentation, or other misconduct of an adverse party; (4) the judgment is void; (5) the judgment has been satisfied, released, or discharged, or a prior judgment upon which it is based has been reversed or otherwise vacated, or it is no longer equitable that the judgment should have prospective application; or (6) any other reason justifying relief from the operation of the judgment. The motion shall be made within a reasonable time, and for reasons (1), (2), and (3) not more than one year after the judgment, order, or proceeding was entered or taken. A motion under this subdivision (b) does not affect the finality of a judgment or suspend its operation. This rule does not limit the power of a court to entertain an independent action to relieve a party from a judgment, order, or proceeding, or to grant relief to a defendant not actually personally notified as provided in Title 28, U.S.C., § 1655, or to set aside a judgment for fraud upon the court. Writs of coram nobis, coram vobis, audita querela, and bills of review and bills in the nature of a bill of review, are abolished, and the procedure for obtaining any relief from a judgment shall be by motion as prescribed in these rules or by an independent action.

(As amended Dec. 27, 1946, eff. Mar. 19, 1948; Dec. 29, 1948, eff. Oct. 20, 1949; Mar. 2, 1987, eff. Aug. 1, 1987.)

ADVISORY COMMITTEE NOTES

1937 Adoption

Note to Subdivision (a). See [former] Equity Rule 72 (Correction of Clerical Mistakes in Orders and Decrees); Mich.Court Rules Ann. (Searl, 1933) Rule 48, § 3; 2 Wash. Rev.Stat.Ann. (Remington, 1932) § 464(3); Wyo.Rev.Stat. Ann. (Courtright, 1931) § 89–2301(3). For an example of a very liberal provision for the correction of clerical errors and for amendment after judgment, see Va.Code Ann. (Michie, 1936) §§ 6329, 6333.

Note to Subdivision (b). Application to the court under this subdivision does not extend the time for taking an appeal, as distinguished from the motion for new trial. This section is based upon Calif.Code Civ.Proc. (Deering, 1937) § 473. See also N.Y.C.P.A. (1937) § 108; 2 Minn.Stat. (Mason, 1927) § 9283.

For the independent action to relieve against mistake, etc., see Dobie, *Federal Procedure*, pages 760 to 765, compare 639; and Simkins, *Federal Practice*, ch. CXXI (pp. 820 to 830) and ch. CXXII (pp. 831 to 834), compare § 214.

1946 Amendment

Note. Subdivision (a). The amendment incorporates the view expressed in *Perlman v. 322 West Seventy-Second Street, Co., Inc.*, C.C.A.2d, 1942, 127 F.2d 716; 3 *Moore's Federal Practice*, 1938, 3276, and further permits correction after docketing, with leave of the appellate court. Some courts have thought that upon the taking of an appeal the district court lost its power to act. See *Schram v. Safety Investment Co.*, E.D.Mich.1942, 45 F.Supp. 636; also *Miller v. United States*, C.C.A.7th, 1940, 114 F.2d 267.

Subdivision (b). When promulgated, the rules contained a number of provisions, including those found in Rule 60(b), describing the practice by a motion to obtain relief from judgments, and these rules, coupled with the reservation in Rule 60(b) of the right to entertain a new action to relieve a party from a judgment, were generally supposed to cover the field. Since the rules have been in force, decisions have been rendered that the use of bills of review, coram nobis, or audita querela to obtain relief from final judgments is still proper, and that various remedies of this kind still exist although they are not mentioned in the rules and the practice is not prescribed in the rules. It is obvious that the rules should be complete in this respect and define the practice with respect to any existing rights or remedies to obtain relief from final judgments. For extended discussion of the old common law writs and equitable remedies, the interpretation of Rule 60, and proposals for change, see Moore and Rogers, *Federal Relief from Civil Judgments*, 1946, 55 Yale L.J. 623. See also 3 *Moore's Federal Practice*, 1938, 3254 et seq.; Commentary, *Effect of Rule 60b on Other Methods of Relief From Judgment*, 1941, 4 Fed.Rules Serv. 942, 945; *Wallace v. United States*, C.C.A.2d, 1944, 142 F.2d 240, certiorari denied 65 S.Ct. 37, 323 U.S. 712, 89 L.Ed. 573.

The reconstruction of Rule 60(b) has for one of its purposes a clarification of this situation. Two types of procedure to obtain relief from judgments are specified in the rules as it is proposed to amend them. One procedure is by motion in the court and in the action in which the judgment was rendered. The other procedure is by a new or independent action to obtain relief from a judgment, which action may or may not be begun in the court which rendered the judgment. Various rules, such as the one dealing with a motion for new trial and for amendment of judgments, Rule 59, one for amended findings, Rule 52, and one for judgment notwithstanding the verdict, Rule 50(b), and including the provisions of Rule 60(b) as amended, prescribe the various types of cases in which the practice by motion is permitted. In each case there is a limit upon the time within which resort to a motion is permitted, and this time limit may not be enlarged under Rule 6(b). If the right to make a motion is lost by the expiration of the time limits fixed in these rules, the only other procedural remedy is by a new or independent action to set aside a judgment upon those principles which have heretofore been applied in such an action. Where the independent action is resorted to, the limitations of time are those of laches or statutes of limitations. The Committee has endeavored to ascertain all the remedies and types of relief heretofore available by coram nobis, coram vobis, audita querela, bill of review, or bill in the nature of a bill of review. See Moore and Rogers, *Federal Relief from Civil Judgments*, 1946, 55 Yale L.J. 623, 659 to 682. It endeavored then to amend the rules to permit, either by motion or by independent action, the granting of various kinds of relief from judgments which were permitted in the federal courts prior to the adoption of these rules, and the amendment concludes with a provision abolishing the use of bills of review and the other common law writs referred to, and requiring the practice to be by motion or by independent action.

To illustrate the operation of the amendment, it will be noted that under Rule 59(b) as it now stands, without amendment, a motion for new trial on the ground of newly discovered evidence is permitted within ten days after the entry of the judgment, or after that time upon leave of the court. It is proposed to amend Rule 59(b) by providing that under that rule a motion for new trial shall be served not later than ten days after the entry of the judgment, whatever the ground be for the motion, whether error by the court or newly discovered evidence. On the other hand, one of the purposes of the bill of review in equity was to afford relief on the ground of newly discovered evidence long after the entry of the judgment. Therefore, to permit relief by a motion similar to that heretofore obtained on bill of review, Rule 60(b) as amended permits an application for relief to be made by motion, on the ground of newly discovered evidence, within one year after judgment. Such a motion under Rule 60(b) does not affect the finality of the judgment, but a motion under Rule 59, made within 10 days, does affect finality and the running of the time for appeal.

If these various amendments, including principally those to Rule 60(b), accomplish the purpose for which they are intended, the federal rules will deal with the practice in every sort of case in which relief from final judgments is asked, and prescribe the practice. With reference to the question whether, as the rules now exist, relief by coram nobis, bills of review, and so forth, is permissible, the generally accepted view is that the remedies are still available, although the precise relief obtained in a particular case by use of these ancillary remedies is shrouded in ancient lore and mystery. See *Wallace v. United States*, C.C.A.2d, 1944, 142 F.2d 240, certiorari denied 65 S.Ct. 37, 323 U.S. 712, 89 L.Ed. 573; *Fraser v. Doing*, App.D.C.1942, 130 F.2d 617; *Jones v. Watts*, C.C.A.5th, 1944, 142 F.2d 575; *Preveden v. Hahn*, S.D.N.Y.1941, 36 F.Supp. 952; *Cavallo v. Agwilines, Inc.*, S.D.N.Y.1942, 6 Fed.Rules Serv. 60b.31, Case 2, 2 F.R.D. 526; *McGinn v. United States*, D.C.Mass.1942, 6 Fed.Rules Serv. 60b.51, Case 3, 2 F.R.D. 562; *City of Shattuck, Oklahoma ex rel. Versluis v. Oliver*, W.D.Okl.1945, 8 Fed.Rules Serv. 60b.31, Case 3; Moore and Rogers, *Federal Relief from Civil Judgments*, 1946, 55 Yale L.J. 623, 631 to 653; 3 *Moore's Federal Practice*, 1938, 3254 et seq.; Commentary, *Effect of Rule 60b on Other Methods of Relief From Judgment*, op. cit. supra. Cf. *Norris v. Camp*, C.C.A.10th, 1944, 144 F.2d 1; Reed v. South Atlantic Steamship Co. of Delaware, *D.Del.1942, 2 F.R.D. 475, 6 Fed.Rules Serv. 60b.31, Case 1;* Laughlin v. Berens, *D.D.C.1945, 8 Fed.Rules Serv. 60b.51, Case 1, 73 W.L.R. 209.*

The transposition of the words "the court" and the addition of the word "and" at the beginning of the first sentence are merely verbal changes. The addition of the qualifying word "final" emphasizes the character of the judgments, orders or proceedings from which Rule 60(b) affords relief; and hence interlocutory judgments are not brought within the restrictions of the rule, but rather they are left subject to the complete power of the court rendering them to afford such relief from them as justice requires.

The qualifying pronoun "his" has been eliminated on the basis that it is too restrictive, and that the subdivision should include the mistake or neglect of others which may be just as material and call just as much for supervisory jurisdiction as where the judgment is taken against the party through *his* mistake, inadvertence, etc.

Fraud, whether intrinsic or extrinsic, misrepresentation, or other misconduct of an adverse party are express grounds for relief by motion under amended subdivision (b). There is no sound reason for their exclusion. The incorporation of fraud and the like within the scope of the rule also removes confusion as to the proper procedure. It has been held that relief from a judgment obtained by extrinsic fraud could be secured by motion within a "reasonable time," which might be after the time stated in the rule had run. *Fiske v. Buder*, C.C.A.8th, 1942, 125 F.2d 841; see also inferentially *Bucy v. Nevada Construction Co.*, C.C.A.9th, 1942, 125 F.2d 213. On the other hand, it has been suggested that in view of the fact that fraud was omitted from original Rule 60(b) as a ground for relief, an independent action was the only proper remedy. Commentary, *Effect of Rule 60b on Other Methods of Relief From Judgment*, 1941, 4 Fed.Rules Serv. 942, 945. The amendment settles this problem by making fraud an express ground for relief by motion; and under the saving clause, fraud may be urged as a basis for relief by independent action insofar as established doctrine permits. See Moore and Rogers, *Federal Relief from Civil Judgments,* 1946, 55 Yale L.J. 623, 653 to 659; 3 Moore's Federal Practice, 1938, 3267 et seq. And the rule expressly does not limit the power of the court, when fraud has been perpetrated upon it, to give relief under the saving clause. As an illustration of this situation, see *Hazel-Atlas Glass Co. v. Hartford Empire Co.,* 1944, 64 S.Ct. 997, 322 U.S. 238, 88 L.Ed. 1250.

The time limit for relief by motion in the court and in the action in which the judgment was rendered has been enlarged from six months to one year.

It should be noted that Rule 60(b) does not assume to define the substantive law as to the grounds for vacating judgments, but merely prescribes the practice in proceedings to obtain relief. It should also be noted that under § 200(4) of the Soldiers' and Sailors' Civil Relief Act of 1940, § 501 et seq. [§ 520(4)] of the Appendix to Title 50, a judgment rendered in any action or proceeding governed by the section may be vacated under certain specified circumstances upon proper application to the court.

1948 Amendment

The amendment effective October, 1949 substituted the reference to "Title 28, U.S.C. § 1655," in the next to the last sentence of subdivision (b), for the reference to "Section 57 of the Judicial Code, U.S.C., Title 28, § 118".

1987 Amendment

The amendment is technical. No substantive change is intended.

Rule 61. Harmless Error

No error in either the admission or the exclusion of evidence and no error or defect in any ruling or order or in anything done or omitted by the court or by any of the parties is ground for granting a new trial or for setting aside a verdict or for vacating, modifying, or otherwise disturbing a judgment or order, unless refusal to take such action appears to the court inconsistent with substantial justice. The court at every stage of the proceeding must disregard any error or defect in the proceeding which does not affect the substantial rights of the parties.

ADVISORY COMMITTEE NOTES

1937 Adoption

A combination of U.S.C., Title 28, § 2111, [former] § 391 (New trials; harmless error) and [former] § 777 (Defects of form; amendments) with modifications. See *McCandless v. United States,* 1936, 56 S.Ct. 764, 298 U.S. 342, 80 L.Ed. 1205. Compare [former] Equity Rule 72 (Correction of Clerical Mistakes in Orders and Decrees); and last sentence of [former] Equity Rule 46 (Trial—Testimony Usually Taken in Open Court—Rulings on Objections to Evidence). For the last sentence see the last sentence of [former] Equity Rule 19 (Amendments Generally).

Rule 62. Stay of Proceedings to Enforce a Judgment

(a) **Automatic Stay; Exceptions—Injunctions, Receiverships, and Patent Accountings.** Except as stated herein, no execution shall issue upon a judgment nor shall proceedings be taken for its enforcement until the expiration of 10 days after its entry. Unless otherwise ordered by the court, an interlocutory or final judgment in an action for an injunction or in a receivership action, or a judgment or order directing an accounting in an action for infringement of letters patent, shall not be stayed during the period after its entry and until an appeal is taken or during the pendency of an appeal. The provisions of subdivision (c) of this rule govern the suspending, modifying, restoring, or granting of an injunction during the pendency of an appeal.

(b) **Stay on Motion for New Trial or for Judgment.** In its discretion and on such conditions for the security of the adverse party as are proper, the court may stay the execution of or any proceedings to enforce a judgment pending the disposition of a motion for a new trial or to alter or amend a judgment made pursuant to Rule 59, or of a motion for relief from a judgment or order made pursuant to Rule 60, or of a motion for judgment in accordance with a motion for a directed verdict made pursuant to Rule 50, or of a motion for amendment to the findings or for additional findings made pursuant to Rule 52(b).

(c) **Injunction Pending Appeal.** When an appeal is taken from an interlocutory or final judgment granting, dissolving, or denying an injunction, the court in its discretion may suspend, modify, restore, or grant an injunction during the pendency of the appeal upon such terms as to bond or otherwise as it considers proper for the security of the rights of the adverse party. If the judgment appealed from is rendered by a district court of three judges specially constituted pursuant to a statute of the United States, no such order shall be made except (1) by such court sitting in open court or (2) by the assent of all the judges of such court evidenced by their signatures to the order.

(d) **Stay Upon Appeal.** When an appeal is taken the appellant by giving a supersedeas bond may obtain a stay subject to the exceptions contained in subdivision (a) of this rule. The bond may be given at or after the time of filing the notice of appeal or of procuring the order allowing the appeal, as the case may be. The stay is effective when the supersedeas bond is approved by the court.

(e) **Stay in Favor of the United States or Agency Thereof.** When an appeal is taken by the United States or an officer or agency thereof or by direction of any department of the Government of the United States and the operation or enforcement of the judgment is stayed, no bond, obligation, or other security shall be required from the appellant.

(f) Stay According to State Law. In any state in which a judgment is a lien upon the property of the judgment debtor and in which the judgment debtor is entitled to a stay of execution, a judgment debtor is entitled, in the district court held therein, to such stay as would be accorded the judgment debtor had the action been maintained in the courts of that state.

(g) Power of Appellate Court Not Limited. The provisions in this rule do not limit any power of an appellate court or of a judge or justice thereof to stay proceedings during the pendency of an appeal or to suspend, modify, restore, or grant an injunction during the pendency of an appeal or to make any order appropriate to preserve the status quo or the effectiveness of the judgment subsequently to be entered.

(h) Stay of Judgment as to Multiple Claims or Multiple Parties. When a court has ordered a final judgment under the conditions stated in Rule 54(b), the court may stay enforcement of that judgment until the entering of a subsequent judgment or judgments and may prescribe such conditions as are necessary to secure the benefit thereof to the party in whose favor the judgment is entered.

(As amended Dec. 27, 1946, eff. Mar. 19, 1948; Dec. 29, 1948, eff. Oct. 20, 1949; Apr. 17, 1961, eff. July 19, 1961; Mar. 2, 1987, eff. Aug. 1, 1987.)

ADVISORY COMMITTEE NOTES
1937 Adoption

Note to Subdivision (a). The first sentence states the substance of the last sentence of U.S.C., Title 28, [former] § 874 (Supersedeas). The remainder of the subdivision states the substance of the last clause of U.S.C., Title 28, § 1292, [formerly] § 227 (Appeals in proceedings for injunctions; receivers; and admiralty), and of §§ 1292, 2107, [formerly] § 227a (Appeals in suits in equity for infringement of letters patent for inventions; stay of proceedings for accounting), but extended to include final as well as interlocutory judgments.

Note to Subdivision (b). This modifies U.S.C., Title 28, [former] § 840 (Executions; stay on conditions).

Note to Subdivision (c). Compare [former] Equity Rule 74 (Injunction Pending Appeal); and *Cumberland Telephone and Telegraph Co. v. Louisiana Public Service Commission,* 1922, 43 S.Ct. 75, 260 U.S. 212, 67 L.Ed. 217. See Simkins, Federal Practice (1934), § 916, in regard to the effect of appeal on injunctions and the giving of bonds. See U.S.C., [former] Title 6 (Official and Penal Bonds) for bonds by surety companies. For statutes providing for a specially constituted district court of three judges, see:

U.S.C., Title 7:

§ 217 (Proceedings for suspension of orders of Secretary of Agriculture under Stockyards Act)—by reference.

§ 499k (Injunctions; application of injunction laws governing orders of Interstate Commerce Commission to orders of Secretary of Agriculture under Perishable Commodities Act)—by reference.

U.S.C., Title 15:

§ 28 (Antitrust laws; suits against monopolies expedited)

U.S.C., Title 28, former:

§ 47 [now 2325 (repealed)] (Injunctions as to orders of Interstate Commerce Commission, etc.)

§ 380 [now 2284] (Injunctions; alleged unconstitutionality of State statutes)

§ 380a [now 2284] (Same; constitutionality of federal statute)

U.S.C., Title 49:

§ 44 [former] (Suits in equity under interstate commerce laws; expedition of suits)

Note to Subdivision (d). This modifies U.S.C., Title 28, [former] § 874 (Supersedeas). See Rule 36(2), Rules of the Supreme Court of the United States, which governs supersedeas bonds on direct appeals to the Supreme Court, and Rule 73(d), of these rules, which governs supersedeas bonds on appeals to a circuit court of appeals. The provisions governing supersedeas bonds in both kinds of appeals are substantially the same.

Note to Subdivision (e). This states the substance of U.S.C., Title 28, § 2408, formerly § 870 (Bond; not required of the United States).

Note to Subdivision (f). This states the substance of U.S.C., Title 28, [former] § 841 (Executions; stay of one term) with appropriate modification to conform to the provisions of Rule 6(c) as to terms of court.

1946 Amendment

Note. Subdivision (a). [This subdivision not amended]. Sections 203 and 204 of the Soldiers' and Sailors' Civil Relief Act of 1940, 50 U.S.C., Appendix, § 501 et seq. [§§ 523, 524], provide under certain circumstances for the issuance and continuance of a stay of execution of any judgment or order entered against a person in military service. See *Bowsman v. Peterson,* D.Neb.1942, 45 F.Supp. 741. Section 201 of the Act [50 U.S.C. App. § 521] permits under certain circumstances the issuance of a stay of any action or proceeding at any stage thereof, where either the plaintiff or defendant is a person in military service. See also note to Rule 64 herein.

Subdivision (b). This change was necessary because of the proposed addition to Rule 59 of subdivision (e).

Subdivision (h). In proposing to revise Rule 54(b), the Committee thought it advisable to include a separate provision in Rule 62 for stay of enforcement of a final judgment in cases involving multiple claims.

1948 Amendment

The amendment effective October 1949 deleted at the end of subdivision (g) the following language which originally appeared after the word "entered": "and these rules do not supersede the provisions of Section 210 of the Judicial Code, as amended, U.S.C., Title 28, [former] § 47a, or of other statutes of the United States to the effect that stays pending appeals to the Supreme Court may be granted only by that court or a justice thereof."

1961 Amendment

The amendment adopted Apr. 17, 1961, effective July 19, 1961, eliminated words "on some but not all of the claims presented in the action" which followed "final judgment".

1987 Amendment

The amendment is technical. No substantive change is intended.

Rule 63.   Inability of a Judge to Proceed

If a trial or hearing has been commenced and the judge is unable to proceed, any other judge may proceed with it upon certifying familiarity with the record and determining that the proceedings in the case may be completed without prejudice to the parties. In a hearing or trial without a jury, the successor judge shall at the request of a party recall any witness whose testimony is material and disputed and who is available to testify again without undue burden. The successor judge may also recall any other witness.

(As amended Mar. 2, 1987, eff. Aug. 1, 1987; Apr. 30, 1991, eff. Dec. 1, 1991.)

ADVISORY COMMITTEE NOTES

1937 Adoption

This rule adapts and extends the provisions of U.S.C., Title 28, [former] § 776 (Bill of exceptions; authentication; signing of by judge) to include all duties to be performed by the judge after verdict or judgment. The statute is therefore superseded.

1987 Amendment

The amendments are technical. No substantive change is intended.

1991 Amendment

The revision substantially displaces the former rule. The former rule was limited to the disability of the judge, and made no provision for disqualification or possible other reasons for the withdrawal of the judge during proceedings. In making provision for other circumstances, the revision is not intended to encourage judges to discontinue participation in a trial for any but compelling reasons. Cf. *United States v. Lane*, 708 F.2d 1394, 1395–1397 (9th Cir.1983). Manifestly, a substitution should not be made for the personal convenience of the court, and the reasons for a substitution should be stated on the record.

The former rule made no provision for the withdrawal of the judge during the trial, but was limited to disqualification after trial. Several courts concluded that the text of the former rule prohibited substitution of a new judge prior to the points described in the rule, thus requiring a new trial, whether or not a fair disposition was within reach of a substitute judge. *E.g., Whalen v. Ford Motor Credit Co.*, 684 F.2d 272 (4th Cir.1982, en banc) *cert. denied*, 459 U.S. 910 (1982) (jury trial); *Arrow–Hart, Inc. v. Philip Carey Co.*, 552 F.2d 711 (6th Cir.1977) (non-jury trial). *See generally* Comment, *The Case of the Dead Judge: Fed.R.Civ.P. 63: Whalen v. Ford Motor Credit Co.*, 67 MINN.L.REV. 827 (1983).

The increasing length of federal trials has made it likely that the number of trials interrupted by the disability of the judge will increase. An efficient mechanism for completing these cases without unfairness is needed to prevent unnecessary expense and delay. To avoid the injustice that may result if the substitute judge proceeds despite unfamiliarity with the action, the new Rule provides, in language similar to Federal Rule of Criminal Procedure 25(a), that the successor judge must certify familiarity with the record and determine that the case may be completed before that judge without prejudice to the parties. This will necessarily require that there be available a transcript or a videotape of the proceedings prior to substitution. If there has been a long but incomplete jury trial, the prompt availability of the transcript or videotape is crucial to the effective use of this rule, for the jury cannot long be held while an extensive transcript is prepared without prejudice to one or all parties.

The revised text authorizes the substitute judge to make a finding of fact at a bench trial based on evidence heard by a different judge. This may be appropriate in limited circumstances. First, if a witness has become unavailable, the testimony recorded at trial can be considered by the successor judge pursuant to F.R.Ev. 804, being equivalent to a recorded deposition available for use at trial pursuant to Rule 32. For this purpose, a witness who is no longer subject to a subpoena to compel testimony at trial is unavailable. Secondly, the successor judge may determine that particular testimony is not material or is not disputed, and so need not be reheard. The propriety of proceeding in this manner may be marginally affected by the availability of a videotape record; a judge who has reviewed a trial on videotape may be entitled to greater confidence in his or her ability to proceed.

The court would, however, risk error to determine the credibility of a witness not seen or heard who is available to be recalled. Cf. *Anderson v. City of Bessemer City NC*, 470 U.S. 564, 575 (1985); *Marshall v. Jerrico Inc.*, 446 U.S. 238, 242 (1980). See also *United States v. Radatz*, 447 U.S. 667 (1980).

VIII.   PROVISIONAL AND FINAL REMEDIES

ADVISORY COMMITTEE NOTES

1991 Amendment

The purpose of the revision is to divide this chapter of the Rules into two. No substantive change is effected.

Rule 64.   Seizure of Person or Property

At the commencement of and during the course of an action, all remedies providing for seizure of person or property for the purpose of securing satisfaction of the judgment ultimately to be entered in the action are available under the circumstances and in the manner provided by the law of the state in which the district court is held, existing at the time the remedy is sought, subject to the following qualifications: (1) any existing statute of the United States governs to the extent to which it is applicable; (2) the action in which any of the foregoing remedies is used shall be commenced and prosecuted or, if removed from a state court, shall be prosecuted after removal, pursuant to these rules. The remedies thus available include arrest, attachment, garnishment, replevin, sequestration, and other corresponding or equivalent remedies, however designated and regardless of whether by state procedure the remedy is ancillary to an action or must be obtained by an independent action.

ADVISORY COMMITTEE NOTES

1937 Adoption

This rule adopts the existing Federal law, except that it specifies the applicable State law to be that of the time when the remedy is sought. Under U.S.C., Title 28, [former] § 726 (Attachments as provided by State laws) the plaintiff was entitled to remedies by attachment or other process which were on June 1, 1872, provided by the applicable State law, and the district courts might, from time to time, by general rules, adopt such State laws as might be in force. This statute is superseded as are district court rules which are rendered unnecessary by the rule.

Lis pendens. No rule concerning lis pendens is stated, for this would appear to be a matter of substantive law affecting State laws of property. It has been held that in the absence of a State statute expressly providing for the recordation of notice of the pendency of Federal actions, the commencement of a Federal action is notice to all persons affected. *King v. Davis*, 137 F. 198 (W.D.Va., 1903). It has been held, however, that when a state statute does so provide expressly, its provisions are binding. *United States v. Calcasieu Timber Co.*, 236 F. 196 (C.C.A.5th, 1916).

For statutes of the United States on attachment, see, e.g.: U.S.C., Title 28 former:

§ 737 [now 2710] (Attachment in postal suits)

§ 738 [now 2711] (Attachment; application for warrant)

§ 739 [now 2712] (Attachment; issue of warrant)

§ 740 [now 2713] (Attachment; trial of ownership of property)

§ 741 [now 2714] (Attachment; investment of proceeds of attached property)

§ 742 [now 2715] (Attachment; publication of attachment)

§ 743 [now 2716] (Attachment; personal notice of attachment)

§ 744 [now 2717] (Attachment; discharge; bond)

§ 745 [former] (Attachment; accrued rights not affected)

§ 746 (Attachments dissolved in conformity with State laws)

For statutes of the United States on garnishment, see, e.g.: U.S.C., Title 28, former:

§ 748 [now 2405] (Garnishees in suits by United States against a corporation)

§ 749 [now 2405] (Same; issue tendered on denial of indebtedness)

§ 750 [now 2405] (Same; garnishee failing to appear)

For statutes of the United States on arrest, see, e.g.: U.S.C., Title 28 former:

§ 376 [now 1651] (Writs of ne exeat)

§ 755 [former] (Special bail in suits for duties and penalties)

§ 756 [former] (Defendant giving bail in one district and committed in another)

§ 757 [former] (Defendant giving bail in one district and committed in another; defendant held until judgment in first suit)

§ 758 [former] (Bail and affidavits; taking by commissioners)

§ 759 [former] (Calling of bail in Kentucky)

§ 760 [former] (Clerks may take bail de bene esse)

§ 843 [now 2007] (Imprisonment for debt)

§ 844 [now 2007] (Imprisonment for debt; discharge according to State laws)

§ 845 [now 2007] (Imprisonment for debt; jail limits)

For statutes of the United States on replevin, see, e.g.: U.S.C., Title 28:

§ 2463, formerly § 747 (Replevy of property taken under revenue laws).

Supplementary Note

Note. Sections 203 and 204 of the Soldiers' and Sailors' Civil Relief Act of 1940, 50 U.S.C.Appendix, § 501 et seq. [§§ 523 and 524], provide under certain circumstances for the issuance and continuance of a stay of the execution of any judgment entered against a person in military service, or the vacation or stay of any attachment or garnishment directed against such person's property, money, or debts in the hands of another. See also Note to Rule 62 herein.

Rule 65. Injunctions

(a) Preliminary Injunction.

(1) *Notice.* No preliminary injunction shall be issued without notice to the adverse party.

(2) *Consolidation of Hearing With Trial on Merits.* Before or after the commencement of the hearing of an application for a preliminary injunction, the court may order the trial of the action on the merits to be advanced and consolidated with the hearing of the application. Even when this consolidation is not ordered, any evidence received upon an application for a preliminary injunction which would be admissible upon the trial on the merits becomes part of the record on the trial and need not be repeated upon the trial. This subdivision (a)(2) shall be so construed and applied as to save to the parties any rights they may have to trial by jury.

(b) Temporary Restraining Order; Notice; Hearing; Duration. A temporary restraining order may be granted without written or oral notice to the ad-

verse party or that party's attorney only if (1) it clearly appears from specific facts shown by affidavit or by the verified complaint that immediate and irreparable injury, loss, or damage will result to the applicant before the adverse party or that party's attorney can be heard in opposition, and (2) the applicant's attorney certifies to the court in writing the efforts, if any, which have been made to give the notice and the reasons supporting the claim that notice should not be required. Every temporary restraining order granted without notice shall be indorsed with the date and hour of issuance; shall be filed forthwith in the clerk's office and entered of record; shall define the injury and state why it is irreparable and why the order was granted without notice; and shall expire by its terms within such time after entry, not to exceed 10 days, as the court fixes, unless within the time so fixed the order, for good cause shown, is extended for a like period or unless the party against whom the order is directed consents that it may be extended for a longer period. The reasons for the extension shall be entered of record. In case a temporary restraining order is granted without notice, the motion for a preliminary injunction shall be set down for hearing at the earliest possible time and takes precedence of all matters except older matters of the same character; and when the motion comes on for hearing the party who obtained the temporary restraining order shall proceed with the application for a preliminary injunction and, if the party does not do so, the court shall dissolve the temporary restraining order. On 2 days' notice to the party who obtained the temporary restraining order without notice or on such shorter notice to that party as the court may prescribe, the adverse party may appear and move its dissolution or modification and in that event the court shall proceed to hear and determine such motion as expeditiously as the ends of justice require.

(c) Security. No restraining order or preliminary injunction shall issue except upon the giving of security by the applicant, in such sum as the court deems proper, for the payment of such costs and damages as may be incurred or suffered by any party who is found to have been wrongfully enjoined or restrained. No such security shall be required of the United States or of an officer or agency thereof.

The provisions of Rule 65.1 apply to a surety upon a bond or undertaking under this rule.

(d) Form and Scope of Injunction or Restraining Order. Every order granting an injunction and every restraining order shall set forth the reasons for its issuance; shall be specific in terms; shall describe in reasonable detail, and not by reference to the complaint or other document, the act or acts sought to be restrained; and is binding only upon the parties to the action, their officers, agents, servants, employees, and attorneys, and upon those persons in active concert or participation with them who receive actual notice of the order by personal service or otherwise.

(e) Employer and Employee; Interpleader; Constitutional Cases. These rules do not modify any statute of the United States relating to temporary restraining orders and preliminary injunctions in actions affecting employer and employee; or the provisions of Title 28, U.S.C., § 2361, relating to preliminary injunctions in actions of interpleader or in the nature of interpleader; or Title 28, U.S.C., § 2284, relating to actions required by Act of Congress to be heard and determined by a district court of three judges.

(f) Copyright Impoundment. This rule applies to copyright impoundment proceedings.

(As amended Dec. 27, 1946, eff. Mar. 19, 1948; Dec. 29, 1948, eff. Oct. 20, 1949; Feb. 28, 1966, eff. July 1, 1966; Mar. 2, 1987, eff. Aug. 1, 1987; Apr. 23, 2001, eff. Dec. 1, 2001.)

ADVISORY COMMITTEE NOTES

1937 Adoption

Note to Subdivisions (a) and (b). These are taken from U.S.C., Title 28, [former] § 381 (Injunctions; preliminary injunctions and temporary restraining orders).

Note to Subdivision (c). Except for the last sentence, this is substantially U.S.C., Title 28, [former] § 382 (Injunctions; security on issuance of). The last sentence continues the following and similar statutes which expressly except the United States or an officer or agency thereof from such security requirements: U.S.C. Title 15, §§ 77t(b), 78u(e), and 79r(f) (Securities and Exchange Commission). It also excepts the United States or an officer or agency thereof from such security requirements in any action in which a restraining order or interlocutory judgment of injunction issues in its favor whether there is an express statutory exception from such security requirements or not.

See U.S.C., [former] Title 6 (Official and Penal Bonds) for bonds by surety companies.

Note to Subdivision (d). This is substantially U.S.C., Title 28, [former] § 383 (Injunctions; requisites of order; binding effect).

Note to Subdivision (e). The words "relating to temporary restraining orders and preliminary injunctions in actions affecting employer and employee" are words of description and not of limitation.

Compare [former] Equity Rule 73 (Preliminary Injunctions and Temporary Restraining Orders) which is substantially equivalent to the statutes.

For other statutes dealing with injunctions which are continued, see e.g.:

U.S.C., Title 28 former:
- § 46 [now 2324] (Suits to enjoin orders of Interstate Commerce Commission to be against United States)
- § 47 [now 2325] (Injunctions as to orders of Interstate Commerce Commission; appeal to Supreme Court; time for taking)
- § 378 [former] (Injunctions; when granted)
- § 379 [now 2283] (Injunctions; stay in State courts)

§ 380 [now 1253, 2101, 2281, 2284] (Injunctions; alleged unconstitutionality of State statutes; appeal to Supreme Court)

§ 380a [now 1253, 2101, 2281, 2284] (Injunctions; constitutionality of Federal statute; application for hearing; appeal to Supreme Court)

U.S.C., Title 7:

§ 216 (Court proceedings to enforce orders; injunction)

§ 217 (Proceedings for suspension of orders)

U.S.C., Title 15:

§ 4 (Jurisdiction of courts; duty of district attorney; procedure)

§ 25 (Restraining violations; procedure)

§ 26 (Injunctive relief for private parties; exceptions)

§ 77t(b) (Injunctions and prosecution of offenses)

1946 Amendment

Note. It has been held that in actions on preliminary injunction bonds the district court has discretion to grant relief in the same proceeding or to require the institution of a new action on the bond. *Russell v. Farley*, 1881, 105 U.S. 433, 466. It is believed, however, that in all cases the litigant should have a right to proceed on the bond in the same proceeding, in the manner provided in Rule 73(f) for a similar situation. The paragraph added to Rule 65(c) insures this result and is in the interest of efficiency. There is no reason why Rules 65(c) and 73(f) should operate differently. Compare § 50, sub. n of the Bankruptcy Act, 11 U.S.C. § 78, sub. n, under which actions on all bonds furnished pursuant to the Act may be proceeded upon summarily in the bankruptcy court. See 2 *Collier on Bankruptcy*, 14th ed. by Moore and Oglebay, 1853–1854.

1948 Amendment

The amendment effective October 1949, changed subdivision (e) in the following respects: in the first clause the amendment substituted the words "any statute of the United States" for the words "the Act of October 15, 1914, c. 323, §§ 1 and 20 (38 Stat. 730), U.S.C., Title 29, §§ 52 and 53, or the Act of March 23, 1932, c. 90 (47 Stat. 70), U.S.C., Title 29, c. 6"; in the second clause of subdivision (e) the amendment substituted the reference to "Title 28, U.S.C., § 2361" for the reference to "Section 24(26) of the Judicial Code as amended, U.S.C., Title 28, § 41(26)"; and the third clause was amended to read "Title 28, U.S.C., § 2284," etc., as at present, instead of "the Act of August 24, 1937, c. 754, § 3, relating to actions to enjoin the enforcement of acts of Congress."

1966 Amendment

Subdivision (a)(2). This new subdivision provides express authority for consolidating the hearing of an application for a preliminary injunction with the trial on the merits. The authority can be exercised with particular profit when it appears that a substantial part of the evidence offered on the application will be relevant to the merits and will be presented in such form as to qualify for admission on the trial proper. Repetition of evidence is thereby avoided. The fact that the proceedings have been consolidated should cause no delay in the disposition of the application for the preliminary injunction, for the evidence will be directed in the first instance to that relief, and the preliminary injunction, if justified by the proof, may be issued in the course of the consolidated proceedings. Furthermore, to consolidate the proceedings will tend to expedite the final disposition of the action. It is believed that consolidation can be usefully availed of in many cases.

The subdivision further provides that even when consolidation is not ordered, evidence received in connection with an application for a preliminary injunction which would be admissible on the trial on the merits forms part of the trial record. This evidence need not be repeated on the trial. On the other hand, repetition is not altogether prohibited. That would be impractical and unwise. For example, a witness testifying comprehensively on the trial who has previously testified upon the application for a preliminary injunction might sometimes be hamstrung in telling his story if he could not go over some part of his prior testimony to connect it with his present testimony. So also, some repetition of testimony may be called for where the trial is conducted by a judge who did not hear the application for the preliminary injunction. In general, however, repetition can be avoided with an increase of efficiency in the conduct of the case and without any distortion of the presentation of evidence by the parties.

Since an application for a preliminary injunction may be made in an action in which, with respect to all or part of the merits, there is a right to trial by jury, it is appropriate to add the caution appearing in the last sentence of the subdivision. In such a case the jury will have to hear all the evidence bearing on its verdict, even if some part of the evidence has already been heard by the judge alone on the application for the preliminary injunction.

The subdivision is believed to reflect the substance of the best current practice and introduces no novel conception.

Subdivision (b). In view of the possibly drastic consequences of a temporary restraining order, the opposition should be heard, if feasible, before the order is granted. Many judges have properly insisted that, when time does not permit of formal notice of the application to the adverse party, some expedient, such as telephonic notice to the attorney for the adverse party, be resorted to if this can reasonably be done. On occasion, however, temporary restraining orders have been issued without any notice when it was feasible for some fair, although informal, notice to be given. See the emphatic criticisms in *Pennsylvania Rd. Co. v. Transport Workers Union*, 278 F.2d 693, 694 (3d Cir. 1960); *Arvida Corp. v. Sugarman*, 259 F.2d 428, 429 (2d Cir. 1958); *Lummus Co. v. Commonwealth Oil Ref. Co., Inc.*, 297 F.2d 80, 83 (2d Cir. 1961), cert. denied, 368 U.S. 986 (1962).

Heretofore the first sentence of subdivision (b), in referring to a notice "served" on the "adverse party" on which a "hearing" could be held, perhaps invited the interpretation that the order might be granted without notice if the circumstances did not permit of a formal hearing on the basis of a formal notice. The subdivision is amended to make it plain that informal notice, which may be communicated to the attorney rather than the adverse party, is to be preferred to no notice at all.

Before notice can be dispensed with, the applicant's counsel must give his certificate as to any efforts made to give notice and the reasons why notice should not be required. This certificate is in addition to the requirement of an affidavit or verified complaint setting forth the facts as to the irreparable injury which would result before the opposition could be heard.

The amended subdivision continues to recognize that a temporary restraining order may be issued without any notice when the circumstances warrant.

Subdivision (c). Original Rules 65 and 73 contained substantially identical provisions for summary proceedings against sureties on bonds required or permitted by the rules. There was fragmentary coverage of the same subject in the Admiralty Rules. Clearly, a single comprehensive rule is required, and is incorporated as Rule 65.1.

1987 Amendment

The amendments are technical. No substantive change is intended.

2001 Amendments

New subdivision (f) is added in conjunction with abrogation of the antiquated Copyright Rules of Practice adopted for proceedings under the 1909 Copyright Act. Courts have naturally turned to Rule 65 in response to the apparent inconsistency of the former Copyright Rules with the discretionary impoundment procedure adopted in 1976, 17 U.S.C. § 503(a). Rule 65 procedures also have assuaged well-founded doubts whether the Copyright Rules satisfy more contemporary requirements of due process. See, e.g., *Religious Technology Center v. Netcom On–Line Communications Servs., Inc.*, 923 F.Supp. 1231, 1260–1265 (N.D.Cal.1995); *Paramount Pictures Corp. v. Doe*, 821 F.Supp. 82 (E.D.N.Y. 1993); *WPOW, Inc. v. MRLJ Enterprises*, 584 F.Supp. 132 (D.D.C.1984).

A common question has arisen from the experience that notice of a proposed impoundment may enable an infringer to defeat the court's capacity to grant effective relief. Impoundment may be ordered on an ex parte basis under subdivision (b) if the applicant makes a strong showing of the reasons why notice is likely to defeat effective relief. Such no-notice procedures are authorized in trademark infringement proceedings, see 15 U.S.C. § 1116(d), and courts have provided clear illustrations of the kinds of showings that support ex parte relief. See *Matter of Vuitton et Fils S.A.*, 606 F.2d 1 (2d Cir.1979); *Vuitton v. White*, 945 F.2d 569 (3d Cir.1991). In applying the tests for no-notice relief, the court should ask whether impoundment is necessary, or whether adequate protection can be had by a less intrusive form of no-notice relief shaped as a temporary restraining order.

This new subdivision (f) does not limit use of trademark procedures in cases that combine trademark and copyright claims. Some observers believe that trademark procedures should be adopted for all copyright cases, a proposal better considered by Congressional processes than by rulemaking processes.

Changes Made After Publication and Comments

No change has been made.

Rule 65.1. Security: Proceedings Against Sureties

Whenever these rules, including the Supplemental Rules for Certain Admiralty and Maritime Claims, require or permit the giving of security by a party, and security is given in the form of a bond or stipula-

tion or other undertaking with one or more sureties, each surety submits to the jurisdiction of the court and irrevocably appoints the clerk of the court as the surety's agent upon whom any papers affecting the surety's liability on the bond or undertaking may be served. The surety's liability may be enforced on motion without the necessity of an independent action. The motion and such notice of the motion as the court prescribes may be served on the clerk of the court, who shall forthwith mail copies to the sureties if their addresses are known.

(Added Feb. 28, 1966, eff. July 1, 1966, and amended Mar. 2, 1987, eff. Aug. 1, 1987.)

ADVISORY COMMITTEE NOTES

1966 Addition

See Note to Rule 65.

1987 Amendment

The amendments are technical. No substantive change is intended.

Rule 66. Receivers Appointed by Federal Courts

An action wherein a receiver has been appointed shall not be dismissed except by order of the court. The practice in the administration of estates by receivers or by other similar officers appointed by the court shall be in accordance with the practice heretofore followed in the courts of the United States or as provided in rules promulgated by the district courts. In all other respects the action in which the appointment of a receiver is sought or which is brought by or against a receiver is governed by these rules.

(As amended Dec. 27, 1946, eff. Mar. 19, 1948; Dec. 29, 1948, eff. Oct. 20, 1949.)

ADVISORY COMMITTEE NOTES

1946 Amendment

Note. The title of Rule 66 has been expanded to make clear the subject of the rule, i.e., federal equity receivers.

The first sentence added to Rule 66 prevents a dismissal by any party, after a federal equity receiver has been appointed, except upon leave of court. A party should not be permitted to oust the court and its officer without the consent of that court. See Civil Rule 31(e), Eastern District of Washington.

The second sentence added at the beginning of the rule deals with suits by or against a federal equity receiver. The first clause thereof eliminates the formal ceremony of an ancillary appointment before suit can be brought by a receiver, and is in accord with the more modern state practice, and with more expeditious and less expensive judicial administration. 2 *Moore's Federal Practice*, 1938, 2088–2091. For the rule necessitating ancillary appointment, see *Sterrett v. Second Nat. Bank*, 1918, 39 S.Ct. 27, 248 U.S. 73, 63 L.Ed. 135; *Kelley v. Queeney*, W.D.N.Y.1941, 41 F.Supp. 1015; see also *McCandless v. Furlaud*, 1934, 55 S.Ct. 42, 293 U.S. 67, 79

L.Ed. 202. This rule has been extensively criticized. First, *Extraterritorial Powers of Receivers*, 1932, 27 Ill.L.Rev. 271; Rose, *Extraterritorial Actions by Receivers*, 1933, 17 Minn. L.Rev. 704; Laughlin, *The Extraterritorial Powers of Receivers*, 1932, 45 Harv.L.Rev. 429; Clark and Moore, *A New Federal Civil Procedure—II, Pleadings and Parties*, 1935, 44 Yale L.J. 1291, 1312–1315; Note, 1932, 30 Mich.L.Rev. 1322. See also comment in *Bicknell v. Lloyd-Smith*, C.C.A.2d, 1940, 109 F.2d 527, certiorari denied 61 S.Ct. 15, 311 U.S. 650, 85 L.Ed. 416. The second clause of the sentence merely incorporates the well-known and general rule that, absent statutory authorization, a federal receiver cannot be sued without leave of the court which appointed him, applied in the federal courts since *Barton v. Barbour*, 1881, 104 U.S. 126. See also 1 *Clark on Receivers*, 2d ed., § 549. Under [§ 959 of this title, formerly] 28 U.S.C. § 125 leave of court is unnecessary when a receiver is sued "in respect of any act or transaction of his in carrying on the business" connected with the receivership property, but such suit is subject to the general equity jurisdiction of the court in which the receiver was appointed, so far as justice necessitates.

Capacity of a state court receiver to sue or be sued in Federal court is governed by Rule 17(b).

The last sentence added to Rule 66 assures the application of the rules in all matters except actual administration of the receivership estate itself. Since this implicitly carries with it the applicability of those rules relating to appellate procedure, the express reference thereto contained in Rule 66 has been stricken as superfluous. Under Rule 81(a)(1) the rules do not apply to bankruptcy proceedings except as they may be made applicable by order of the Supreme Court. Rule 66 is applicable to what is commonly known as a federal "chancery" or "equity" receiver, or similar type of court officer. It is not designed to regulate or affect receivers in bankruptcy, which are governed by the Bankruptcy Act and the General Orders. Since the Federal Rules are applicable in bankruptcy by virtue of General Orders in Bankruptcy 36 and 37 [see Appendix II following Rules of Bankruptcy Procedure, Title 11] only to the extent that they are not inconsistent with the Bankruptcy Act or the General Orders, Rule 66 is not applicable to bankruptcy receivers. See 1 *Collier on Bankruptcy*, 14th ed. by Moore and Oglebay, ¶¶2.23–2.36.

1948 Amendment

The amendment effective October 1949 deleted a sentence which formerly appeared immediately following the first sentence and which read as follows: "A receiver shall have the capacity to sue in any district court without ancillary appointment; but actions against a receiver may not be commenced without leave of the court appointing him except when authorized by a statute of the United States."

Rule 67. Deposit in Court

In an action in which any part of the relief sought is a judgment for a sum of money or the disposition of a sum of money or the disposition of any other thing capable of delivery, a party, upon notice to every other party, and by leave of court, may deposit with the court all or any part of such sum or thing, whether or not that party claims all or any part of the sum or thing. The party making the deposit shall serve the order permitting deposit on the clerk of the court. Money paid into court under this rule shall be deposited and withdrawn in accordance with the provisions of Title 28, U.S.C., §§ 2041, and 2042; the Act of June 26, 1934, c. 756, § 23, as amended (48 Stat. 1236, 58 Stat. 845), U.S.C., Title 31, § 725v; or any like statute. The fund shall be deposited in an interest-bearing account or invested in an interest-bearing instrument approved by the court.

(As amended Dec. 29, 1948, eff. Oct. 20, 1949; Apr. 28, 1983, eff. Aug. 1, 1983.)

ADVISORY COMMITTEE NOTES

1937 Adoption

This rule provides for deposit in court generally, continuing similar special provisions contained in such statutes as U.S.C., Title 28, [§§ 1335, 1397, 2361, formerly] § 41(26) (Original jurisdiction of bills of interpleader, and of bills in the nature of interpleader). See generally *Howard v. United States*, 1902, 22 S.Ct. 543, 184 U.S. 676, 46 L.Ed. 754; United States Supreme Court Admiralty Rules (1920), Rules 37 (Bringing Funds into Court), 41 (Funds in Court Registry), and 42 (Claims Against Proceeds in Registry). With the first sentence, compare *English Rules Under the Judicature Act* (The Annual Practice, 1937) O. 22, r. 1(1).

1948 Amendment

The amendment effective October 1949 substituted the reference to "Title 28, U.S.C.A., §§ 2041, and 2042" for the reference to "Sections 995 and 996, Revised Statutes, as amended, U.S.C.A., Title 28, §§ 851, 852." The amendment also added the words "as amended" following the citation of the Act of June 26, 1934, c. 756, § 23, and, in the parenthetical citation immediately following, added the reference to "58 Stat. 845".

1983 Amendment

Rule 67 has been amended in three ways. The first change is the addition of the clause in the first sentence. Some courts have construed the present rule to permit deposit only when the party making it claims no interest in the fund or thing deposited. E.g., *Blasin-Stern v. Beech-Nut Life Savers Corp.*, 429 F.Supp. 533 (D. Puerto Rico 1975); *Dinkins v. General Aniline & Film Corp.*, 214 F.Supp. 281 (S.D.N.Y.1963). However, there are situations in which a litigant may wish to be relieved of responsibility for a sum or thing, but continue to claim an interest in all or part of it. In these cases the deposit-in-court procedure should be available; in addition to the advantages to the party making the deposit, the procedure gives other litigants assurance that any judgment will be collectable. The amendment is intended to accomplish that.

The second change is the addition of a requirement that the order of deposit be served on the clerk of the court in which the sum or thing is to be deposited. This is simply to assure that the clerk knows what is being deposited and what his responsibilities are with respect to the deposit. The latter point is particularly important since the rule as amended contemplates that deposits will be placed in interest-bearing accounts; the clerk must know what treatment has been ordered for the particular deposit.

Complete Annotation Materials, see Title 28 U.S.C.A.

The third change is to require that any money be deposited in an interest-bearing account or instrument approved by the court.

HISTORICAL NOTES

References in Text

The Act of June 26, 1934, c. 756, § 23, as amended (48 Stat. 1236, 58 Stat. 845), 31 U.S.C. § 725v, referred to in text, was repealed by Pub.L. 97–258, § 5(b), Sept. 13, 1982, 96 Stat. 1074, the first section of which enacted Title 31, Money and Finance. Insofar as not superseded by sections 2041 and 2042 of Title 28, Judiciary and Judicial Procedure, the Act of June 26, 1934, § 23, as amended (31 U.S.C. 725v) was reenacted as sections 572a and 2043 of Title 28 by Pub.L. 97–258, § 2(g)(3), (4).

Rule 68.   Offer of Judgment

At any time more than 10 days before the trial begins, a party defending against a claim may serve upon the adverse party an offer to allow judgment to be taken against the defending party for the money or property or to the effect specified in the offer, with costs then accrued. If within 10 days after the service of the offer the adverse party serves written notice that the offer is accepted, either party may then file the offer and notice of acceptance together with proof of service thereof and thereupon the clerk shall enter judgment. An offer not accepted shall be deemed withdrawn and evidence thereof is not admissible except in a proceeding to determine costs. If the judgment finally obtained by the offeree is not more favorable than the offer, the offeree must pay the costs incurred after the making of the offer. The fact that an offer is made but not accepted does not preclude a subsequent offer. When the liability of one party to another has been determined by verdict or order or judgment, but the amount or extent of the liability remains to be determined by further proceedings, the party adjudged liable may make an offer of judgment, which shall have the same effect as an offer made before trial if it is served within a reasonable time not less than 10 days prior to the commencement of hearings to determine the amount or extent of liability.

(As amended Dec. 27, 1946, eff. Mar. 19, 1948; Feb. 28, 1966, eff. July 1, 1966; Mar. 2, 1987, eff. Aug. 1, 1987.)

ADVISORY COMMITTEE NOTES

1937 Adoption

See 2 Minn.Stat. (Mason, 1927) § 9323; 4 Mont.Rev.Codes Ann. (1935) § 9770; N.Y.C.P.A. (1937) § 177.

For the recovery of costs against the United States, see Rule 54(d).

1946 Amendment

Note. The third sentence of Rule 68 has been altered to make clear that evidence of an unaccepted offer is admissible in a proceeding to determine the costs of the action but is not otherwise admissible.

The two sentences substituted for the deleted last sentence of the rule assure a party the right to make a second offer where the situation permits—as, for example, where a prior offer was not accepted but the plaintiff's judgment is nullified and a new trial ordered, whereupon the defendant desires to make a second offer. It is implicit, however, that as long as the case continues—whether there be a first, second or third trial—and the defendant makes no further offer, his first and only offer will operate to save him the costs from the time of that offer if the plaintiff ultimately obtains a judgment less than the sum offered. In the case of successive offers not accepted, the offeror is saved the costs incurred after the making of the offer which was equal to or greater than the judgment ultimately obtained. These provisions should serve to encourage settlements and avoid protracted litigation.

The phrase "before the trial begins", in the first sentence of the rule, has been construed in *Cover v. Chicago Eye Shield Co.*, C.C.A.7th, 1943, 136 F.2d 374, certiorari denied 64 S.Ct. 53, 320 U.S. 749, 88 L.Ed. 445.

1966 Amendment

This logical extension of the concept of offer of judgment is suggested by the common admiralty practice of determining liability before the amount of liability is determined.

1987 Amendment

The amendments are technical. No substantive change is intended.

Rule 69.   Execution

(a) In General. Process to enforce a judgment for the payment of money shall be a writ of execution, unless the court directs otherwise. The procedure on execution, in proceedings supplementary to and in aid of a judgment, and in proceedings on and in aid of execution shall be in accordance with the practice and procedure of the state in which the district court is held, existing at the time the remedy is sought, except that any statute of the United States governs to the extent that it is applicable. In aid of the judgment or execution, the judgment creditor or a successor in interest when that interest appears of record, may obtain discovery from any person, including the judgment debtor, in the manner provided in these rules or in the manner provided by the practice of the state in which the district court is held.

(b) Against Certain Public Officers. When a judgment has been entered against a collector or other officer of revenue under the circumstances stated in Title 28, U.S.C., § 2006, or against an officer of Congress in an action mentioned in the Act of March 3, 1875, ch. 130, § 8 (18 Stat. 401), U.S.C., Title 2, § 118, and when the court has given the certificate of probable cause for the officer's act as provided in those statutes, execution shall not issue against the officer or the officer's property but the final judgment shall be satisfied as provided in such statutes.

(As amended Dec. 29, 1948, eff. Oct. 20, 1949; Mar. 30, 1970, eff. July 1, 1970; Mar. 2, 1987, eff. Aug. 1, 1987.)

ADVISORY COMMITTEE NOTES

1937 Adoption

Note to Subdivision (a). This follows in substance U.S.C. Title 28, [former] §§ 727 (Executions as provided by State laws) and [former 729] [now Title 42, § 1988] (Proceedings in vindication of civil rights), except that, as in the similar case of attachments (see note to Rule 64), the rule specifies the applicable state law to be that of the time when the remedy is sought, and thus renders unnecessary, as well as supersedeas, local district court rules.

Statutes of the United States on execution, when applicable, govern under this rule. Among these are:

U.S.C., Title 12:

§ 91 (Transfers by bank and other acts in contemplation of insolvency)

§ 632 (Jurisdiction of United States district courts in cases arising out of foreign banking jurisdiction where Federal reserve bank a party)

U.S.C., Title 19:

§ 199 (Judgments for customs duties, how payable)

U.S.C., Title 26 [I.R.C.1939]:

§ 1610(a) [former] (Surrender of property subject to distraint)

U.S.C., Title 28 former:

§ 122 [now 1656] (Creation of new district or transfer of territory; lien)

§ 350 [now 2101] (Time for making application for appeal or certiorari; stay pending application for certiorari)

§ 489 [now 547] (District Attorneys; reports to Department of Justice)

§ 574 [now 1921] (Marshals, fees enumerated)

§ 786 [former] (Judgments for duties; collected in coin)

§ 811 [now 1961] (Interest on judgments)

§ 838 [former] (Executions; run in all districts of State)

§ 839 [now 2413] (Executions; run in every State and Territory)

§ 840 [former] (Executions; stay on conditions), as modified by Rule 62(b)

§ 841 [former] (Executions; stay of one term), as modified by Rule 62(f)

§ 842 [now 2006] (Executions; against officers of revenue in cases of probable cause), as incorporated in Subdivision (b) of this rule

§ 843 [now 2007] (Imprisonment for debt)

§ 844 [now 2007] (Imprisonment for debt; discharge according to State laws)

§ 845 [now 2007] (Imprisonment for debt; jail limits)

§ 846 [now 2005] (Fieri Facias; appraisal of goods; appraisers)

§ 847 [now 2001] (Sales; real property under order or decree)

§ 848 [now 2004] (Sales; personal property under order or decree)

§ 849 [now 2002] (Sales; necessity of notice)

§ 850 [now 2003] (Sales; death of marshall after levy or after sale)

§ 869 [former] (Bond in former error and on appeal), as incorporated in Rule 73(c)

§ 874 [former] (Supersedeas), as modified by Rules 62(d) and 73(d)

U.S.C., Title 31:

§ 195 [now 3715] (Purchase on execution)

U.S.C., Title 33:

§ 918 (Collection of defaulted payments)

U.S.C., Title 49:

§ 74(g) [former] (Causes of action arising out of Federal control of railroads; execution and other process)

Special statutes of the United States on exemption from execution are also continued. Among these are:

U.S.C., Title 2:

§ 118 (Actions against officers of Congress for official acts)

U.S.C., Title 5 former:

§ 729 [see 8346, 8470] (Federal employees retirement annuities not subject to assignment, execution, levy or other legal process)

U.S.C., Title 10 former:

§ 610 [now 3690, 8690] (Exemption of enlisted men from arrest on civil process)

U.S.C., Title 22 former:

§ 21(h) [see 4060] (Foreign service retirement and disability system; establishment; rules and regulations; annuities; nonassignable; exemption from legal process)

U.S.C., Title 33:

§ 916 (Assignment and exemption from claims of creditors) (Longshoremen's and Harborworkers' Compensation Act)

U.S.C., Title 38 former:

§ 54 [see 3101] (Attachment, levy or seizure of moneys due pensioners prohibited)

§ 393 [former] (Army and Navy Medal of Honor Roll; pensions additional to other pensions; liability to attachment, etc.) Compare [former] Title 34, § 365(c) (Medal of Honor Roll; special pension to persons enrolled)

§ 618 [see 3101] (Benefits exempt from seizure under process and taxation; no deductions for indebtedness to United States)

U.S.C., Title 43:

§ 175 (Exemption from execution of homestead land)

U.S.C., Title 48 former:

§ 1371o (Panama canal and railroad retirement annuities, exemption from execution and so forth.)

Supplementary Note

Note. With respect to the provisions of the Soldiers' and Sailors' Civil Relief Act of 1940, 50 U.S.C. Appendix, § 501 et seq., see notes to Rules 62 and 64 herein.

1948 Amendment

The amendment effective October 1949, substituted the citation of "Title 28, U.S.C., § 2006" in subdivision (b) in place of the citation to "Section 989, Revised Statutes, U.S.C., Title 28, § 842".

Complete Annotation Materials, see Title 28 U.S.C.A.

1970 Amendment

The amendment assures that, in aid of execution on a judgment, all discovery procedures provided in the rules are available and not just discovery via the taking of a deposition. Under the present language, one court had held that Rule 34 discovery is unavailable to the judgment creditor. *M. Lowenstein & Sons, Inc. v. American Underwear Mfg. Co.*, 11 F.R.D. 172 (E.D.Pa.1951). Notwithstanding the language, and relying heavily on legislative history referring to Rule 33, the Fifth Circuit has held that a judgment creditor may invoke Rule 33 interrogatories. *United States v. McWhirter*, 376 F.2d 102 (5th Cir. 1967). But the court's reasoning does not extend to discovery except as provided in Rules 26–33. One commentator suggests that the existing language might properly be stretched to all discovery, 7 *Moore's Federal Practice* ¶69.05[1] (2d ed. 1966), but another believes that a rules amendment is needed. 3 Barron & Holtzoff, *Federal Practice and Procedure* 1484 (Wright ed. 1958). Both commentators and the court in *McWhirter* are clear that, as a matter of policy, Rule 69 should authorize the use of all discovery devices provided in the rules.

1987 Amendment

The amendments are technical. No substantive change is intended.

Rule 70. Judgment for Specific Acts; Vesting Title

If a judgment directs a party to execute a conveyance of land or to deliver deeds or other documents or to perform any other specific act and the party fails to comply within the time specified, the court may direct the act to be done at the cost of the disobedient party by some other person appointed by the court and the act when so done has like effect as if done by the party. On application of the party entitled to performance, the clerk shall issue a writ of attachment or sequestration against the property of the disobedient party to compel obedience to the judgment. The court may also in proper cases adjudge the party in contempt. If real or personal property is within the district, the court in lieu of directing a conveyance thereof may enter a judgment divesting the title of any party and vesting it in others and such judgment has the effect of a conveyance executed in due form of law. When any order or judgment is for the delivery of possession, the party in whose favor it is entered is entitled to a writ of execution or assistance upon application to the clerk.

ADVISORY COMMITTEE NOTES

1937 Adoption

Compare [former] Equity Rules 7 (Process, Mesne and Final), 8 (Enforcement of Final Decrees), and 9 (Writ of Assistance). To avoid possible confusion, both old and new denominations for attachment (sequestration) and execution (assistance) are used in this rule. Compare with the provision in this rule that the judgment may itself vest title, 6 Tenn.Ann.Code (Williams, 1934), § 10594; 2 Conn.Gen.Stat. (1930), § 5455; N.M.Stat.Ann. (Courtright, 1929), § 117–117; 2 Ohio Gen.Code Ann. (Page, 1926), § 11590; and England, Supreme Court of Judicature Act (1925), § 47.

Rule 71. Process in Behalf of and Against Persons not Parties

When an order is made in favor of a person who is not a party to the action, that person may enforce obedience to the order by the same process as if a party; and, when obedience to an order may be lawfully enforced against a person who is not a party, that person is liable to the same process for enforcing obedience to the order as if a party.

(As amended Mar. 2, 1987, eff. Aug. 1, 1987.)

ADVISORY COMMITTEE NOTES

1937 Adoption

Compare [former] Equity Rule 11 (Process in Behalf of and Against Persons Not Parties). Compare also *Terrell v. Allison*, 1875, 21 Wall. 289, 22 L.Ed. 634; *Farmers' Loan and Trust Co. v. Chicago and A. Ry. Co.*, C.C.Ind.1890, 44 F. 653; *Robert Findlay Mfg. Co. v. Hygrade Lighting Fixture Corp.*, E.D.N.Y.1923, 288 F. 80; *Thompson v. Smith*, C.C.Minn.1870, Fed.Cas. No. 13,977.

1987 Amendment

The amendments are technical. No substantive change is intended.

IX. SPECIAL PROCEEDINGS [1]

[1] Another Chapter IX which was set out post has been abrogated.

ADVISORY COMMITTEE NOTES

1991 Addition

This chapter heading is to be inserted between Rule 71 and Rule 71A.

Rule 71A. Condemnation of Property

(a) **Applicability of Other Rules.** The Rules of Civil Procedure for the United States District Courts govern the procedure for the condemnation of real and personal property under the power of eminent domain, except as otherwise provided in this rule.

(b) **Joinder of Properties.** The plaintiff may join in the same action one or more separate pieces of property, whether in the same or different ownership and whether or not sought for the same use.

(c) **Complaint.**

RULES OF CIVIL PROCEDURE **Rule 71A**

(1) **Caption.** The complaint shall contain a caption as provided in Rule 10(a), except that the plaintiff shall name as defendants the property, designated generally by kind, quantity, and location, and at least one of the owners of some part of or interest in the property.

(2) **Contents.** The complaint shall contain a short and plain statement of the authority for the taking, the use for which the property is to be taken, a description of the property sufficient for its identification, the interests to be acquired, and as to each separate piece of property a designation of the defendants who have been joined as owners thereof or of some interest therein. Upon the commencement of the action, the plaintiff need join as defendants only the persons having or claiming an interest in the property whose names are then known, but prior to any hearing involving the compensation to be paid for a piece of property, the plaintiff shall add as defendants all persons having or claiming an interest in that property whose names can be ascertained by a reasonably diligent search of the records, considering the character and value of the property involved and the interests to be acquired, and also those whose names have otherwise been learned. All others may be made defendants under the designation "Unknown Owners." Process shall be served as provided in subdivision (d) of this rule upon all defendants, whether named as defendants at the time of the commencement of the action or subsequently added, and a defendant may answer as provided in subdivision (e) of this rule. The court meanwhile may order such distribution of a deposit as the facts warrant.

(3) **Filing.** In addition to filing the complaint with the court, the plaintiff shall furnish to the clerk at least one copy thereof for the use of the defendants and additional copies at the request of the clerk or of a defendant.

(d) **Process.**

(1) **Notice; Delivery.** Upon the filing of the complaint the plaintiff shall forthwith deliver to the clerk joint or several notices directed to the defendants named or designated in the complaint. Additional notices directed to defendants subsequently added shall be so delivered. The delivery of the notice and its service have the same effect as the delivery and service of the summons under Rule 4.

(2) **Same; Form.** Each notice shall state the court, the title of the action, the name of the defendant to whom it is directed, that the action is to condemn property, a description of the defendant's property sufficient for its identification, the interest to be taken, the authority for the taking, the uses for which the property is to be taken, that the defendant may serve upon the plaintiff's attorney an answer within 20 days after service of the notice, and that the failure so to serve an answer constitutes a consent to the taking and to the authority of the court to proceed to hear the action and to fix the compensation. The notice shall conclude with the name of the plaintiff's attorney and an address within the district in which action is brought where the attorney may be served. The notice need contain a description of no other property than that to be taken from the defendants to whom it is directed.

(3) **Service of Notice.**

(A) **Personal Service.** Personal service of the notice (but without copies of the complaint) shall be made in accordance with Rule 4 upon a defendant whose residence is known and who resides within the United States or a territory subject to the administrative or judicial jurisdiction of the United States.

(B) **Service by Publication.** Upon the filing of a certificate of the plaintiff's attorney stating that the attorney believes a defendant cannot be personally served, because after diligent inquiry within the state in which the complaint is filed the defendant's place of residence cannot be ascertained by the plaintiff or, if ascertained, that it is beyond the territorial limits of personal service as provided in this rule, service of the notice shall be made on this defendant by publication in a newspaper published in the county where the property is located, or if there is no such newspaper, then in a newspaper having a general circulation where the property is located, once a week for not less than three successive weeks. Prior to the last publication, a copy of the notice shall also be mailed to a defendant who cannot be personally served as provided in this rule but whose place of residence is then known. Unknown owners may be served by publication in like manner by a notice addressed to "Unknown Owners."

Service by publication is complete upon the date of the last publication. Proof of publication and mailing shall be made by certificate of the plaintiff's attorney, to which shall be attached a printed copy of the published notice with the name and dates of the newspaper marked thereon.

(4) **Return; Amendment.** Proof of service of the notice shall be made and amendment of the notice or proof of its service allowed in the manner provided for the return and amendment of the summons under Rule 4.

(e) **Appearance or Answer.** If a defendant has no objection or defense to the taking of the defendant's property, the defendant may serve a notice of appearance designating the property in which the defendant claims to be interested. Thereafter, the defendant shall receive notice of all proceedings affecting it. If a defendant has any objection or defense to the taking of the property, the defendant shall serve an answer within 20 days after the service of notice upon the defendant. The answer shall identify the property in which the defendant claims to have an interest, state the nature and extent of the interest claimed, and state all the defendant's objections and defenses to the taking of the property. A defendant waives all defenses and objections not so presented, but at the trial of the issue of just compensation, whether or not the defendant has previously appeared or answered, the defendant may present evidence as to the amount of the compensation to be paid for the property, and the defendant may share in the distribution of the award. No other pleading or motion asserting any additional defense or objection shall be allowed.

(f) Amendment of Pleadings. Without leave of court, the plaintiff may amend the complaint at any time before the trial of the issue of compensation and as many times as desired, but no amendment shall be made which will result in a dismissal forbidden by subdivision (i) of this rule. The plaintiff need not serve a copy of an amendment, but shall serve notice of the filing, as provided in Rule 5(b), upon any party affected thereby who has appeared and, in the manner provided in subdivision (d) of this rule, upon any party affected thereby who has not appeared. The plaintiff shall furnish to the clerk of the court for the use of the defendants at least one copy of each amendment and shall furnish additional copies on the request of the clerk or of a defendant. Within the time allowed by subdivision (e) of this rule a defendant may serve an answer to the amended pleading, in the form and manner and with the same effect as there provided.

(g) Substitution of Parties. If a defendant dies or becomes incompetent or transfers an interest after the defendant's joinder, the court may order substitution of the proper party upon motion and notice of hearing. If the motion and notice of hearing are to be served upon a person not already a party, service shall be made as provided in subdivision (d)(3) of this rule.

(h) Trial. If the action involves the exercise of the power of eminent domain under the law of the United States, any tribunal specially constituted by an Act of Congress governing the case for the trial of the issue of just compensation shall be the tribunal for the determination of that issue; but if there is no such specially constituted tribunal any party may have a trial by jury of the issue of just compensation by filing a demand therefor within the time allowed for answer or within such further time as the court may fix, unless the court in its discretion orders that, because of the character, location, or quantity of the property to be condemned, or for other reasons in the interest of justice, the issue of compensation shall be determined by a commission of three persons appointed by it.

In the event that a commission is appointed the court may direct that not more than two additional persons serve as alternate commissioners to hear the case and replace commissioners who, prior to the time when a decision is filed, are found by the court to be unable or disqualified to perform their duties. An alternate who does not replace a regular commissioner shall be discharged after the commission renders its final decision. Before appointing the members of the commission and alternates the court shall advise the parties of the identity and qualifications of each prospective commissioner and alternate and may permit the parties to examine each such designee. The parties shall not be permitted or required by the court to suggest nominees. Each party shall have the right to object for valid cause to the appointment of any person as a commissioner or alternate. If a commission is appointed it shall have the authority of a master provided in Rule 53(c) and proceedings before it shall be governed by the provisions of Rule 53(d). Its action and report shall be determined by a majority and its findings and report shall have the effect, and be dealt with by the court in accordance with the practice, prescribed in Rule 53(e), (f), and (g). Trial of all issues shall otherwise be by the court.

(i) Dismissal of Action.

(1) As of Right. If no hearing has begun to determine the compensation to be paid for a piece of property and the plaintiff has not acquired the title or a lesser interest in or taken possession, the plaintiff may dismiss the action as to that property, without an order of the court, by filing a notice of dismissal setting forth a brief description of the property as to which the action is dismissed.

(2) By Stipulation. Before the entry of any judgment vesting the plaintiff with title or a lesser interest in or possession of property, the action may be dismissed in whole or in part, without an order of the court, as to any property by filing a stipulation of dismissal by the plaintiff and the defendant affected thereby; and, if the parties so stipulate, the court may vacate any judgment that has been entered.

(3) By Order of the Court. At any time before compensation for a piece of property has been determined and paid and after motion and hearing, the court may dismiss the action as to that property, except that it shall not dismiss the action as to any part of the property of which the plaintiff has taken possession or in which the plaintiff has taken title or a lesser interest, but shall award just compensation for the possession, title or lesser interest so taken. The court at any time may drop a defendant unnecessarily or improperly joined.

(4) Effect. Except as otherwise provided in the notice, or stipulation of dismissal, or order of the court, any dismissal is without prejudice.

(j) Deposit and its Distribution. The plaintiff shall deposit with the court any money required by law as a condition to the exercise of the power of eminent domain; and, although not so required, may make a deposit when permitted by statute. In such cases the court and attorneys shall expedite the proceedings for the distribution of the money so deposited and for the ascertainment and payment of just compensation. If the compensation finally awarded to any defendant exceeds the amount which has been paid to that defendant on distribution of the deposit, the court shall enter judgment against the plaintiff and in favor of that defendant for the deficiency. If the compensation finally awarded to any defendant is less than the amount which has been paid to that defendant, the court shall enter judgment against that defendant and in favor of the plaintiff for the overpayment.

(k) Condemnation Under a State's Power of Eminent Domain. The practice as herein prescribed governs in actions involving the exercise of the power of eminent domain under the law of a state, provided that if the state law makes provision for trial of any issue by jury, or for trial of the issue of compensation by jury or commission or both, that provision shall be followed.

(*l*) Costs. Costs are not subject to Rule 54(d).
(Added Apr. 30, 1951, eff. Aug. 1, 1951, and amended Jan. 21, 1963, eff. July 1, 1963; Apr. 29, 1985, eff. Aug. 1, 1985; Mar. 2, 1987, eff. Aug. 1, 1987; Apr. 25, 1988, eff. Aug. 1, 1988; Nov. 18, 1988, Pub.L. 100–690, Title VII, § 7050, 102 Stat. 4401; Apr. 22, 1993, eff. Dec. 1, 1993; Mar. 27, 2003, eff. Dec. 1, 2003.)

ADVISORY COMMITTEE NOTES
1951 Addition
Supplementary Report

The Court will remember that at its conference on December 2, 1948, the discussion was confined to subdivision (h) of the rule (* * *), the particular question being whether the tribunal to award compensation should be a commission or a jury in cases where the Congress has not made specific provision on the subject. The Advisory Committee was agreed from the outset that a rule should not be promulgated which would overturn the decision of the Congress as to the kind of tribunal to fix compensation, provided that the system established by Congress was found to be working well. We found two instances where the Congress had specified the kind of tribunal to fix compensation. One case was the District of Columbia ([former] §§ 361 to 386 of Title 40 [now D.C. Code, Title 16, § 1301 et seq.]) where a rather unique system exists under which the court is required in all cases to order the selection of a "jury" of five from among not less than twenty names drawn from "the special box provided by law." They must have the usual qualifications of jurors and

in addition must be freeholders of the District and not in the service of the United States or the District. That system has been in effect for many years, and our inquiry revealed that it works well under the conditions prevailing in the District, and is satisfactory to the courts of the District, the legal profession and to property owners.

The other instance is that of the Tennessee Valley Authority, where the act of Congress (section 831x of Title 16) provides that compensation is fixed by three disinterested commissioners appointed by the court, whose award goes before the District Court for confirmation or modification. The Advisory Committee made a thorough inquiry into the practical operation of the TVA commission system. We obtained from counsel for the TVA the results of their experience, which afforded convincing proof that the commission system is preferable under the conditions affecting TVA and that the jury system would not work satisfactorily. We then, under date of February 6, 1947, wrote every Federal judge who had ever sat in a TVA condemnation case, asking his views as to whether the commission system is satisfactory and whether a jury system should be preferred. Of 21 responses from the judges 17 approved the commission system and opposed the substitution of a jury system for the TVA. Many of the judges went further and opposed the use of juries in any condemnation cases. Three of the judges preferred the jury system, and one dealt only with the TVA provision for a three judge district court. The Advisory Committee has not considered abolition of the three judge requirement of the TVA Act, because it seemed to raise a question of jurisdiction, which cannot be altered by rule. Nevertheless the Department of Justice continued its advocacy of the jury system for its asserted expedition and economy; and others favored a uniform procedure. In consequence of these divided counsels the Advisory Committee was itself divided, but in its May 1948 Report to the Court recommended the following rule as approved by a majority (* * *):

(h) Trial. If the action involves the exercise of the power of eminent domain under the law of the United States, any tribunal especially constituted by an Act of Congress governing the case for the trial of the issue of just compensation shall be the tribunal for the determination of that issue; but if there is no such specially constituted tribunal any party may have a trial by jury of the issue of just compensation by filing a demand therefor within the time allowed for answer or within such further time as the court may fix. Trial of all issues shall otherwise be by the court.

The effect of this was to preserve the existing systems in the District of Columbia and in TVA cases, but to provide for a jury to fix compensation in all other cases.

Before the Court's conference of December 2, 1948, the Chief Justice informed the Committee that the Court was particularly interested in the views expressed by Judge John Paul, Judge of the United States District Court for the Western District of Virginia, in a letter from him to the chairman of the Advisory Committee, dated February 13, 1947. Copies of all the letters from judges who had sat in TVA cases had been made available to the Court, and this letter from Judge Paul is one of them. Judge Paul strongly opposed jury trials and recommended the commission system in large projects like the TVA, and his views seemed to have impressed the Court and to have been the occasion for the conference.

Complete Annotation Materials, see Title 28 U.S.C.A.

The reasons which convinced the Advisory Committee that the use of commissioners instead of juries is desirable in TVA cases were these:

1. The TVA condemns large areas of land of similar kind, involving many owners. Uniformity in awards is essential. The commission system tends to prevent discrimination and provide for uniformity in compensation. The jury system tends to lack of uniformity. Once a reasonable and uniform standard of values for the area has been settled by a commission, litigation ends and settlements result.

2. Where large areas are involved many small landowners reside at great distances from the place where a court sits. It is a great hardship on humble people to have to travel long distances to attend a jury trial. A commission may travel around and receive the evidence of the owner near his home.

3. It is impracticable to take juries long distances to view the premises.

4. If the cases are tried by juries the burden on the time of the courts is excessive.

These considerations are the very ones Judge Paul stressed in his letter. He pointed out that they applied not only to the TVA but to other large governmental projects, such as flood control, hydroelectric power, reclamation, national forests, and others. So when the representatives of the Advisory Committee appeared at the Court's conference December 2, 1948, they found it difficult to justify the proposed provision in subdivision (h) of the rule that a jury should be used to fix compensation in all cases where Congress had not specified the tribunal. If our reasons for preserving the TVA system were sound, provision for a jury in similar projects of like magnitude seemed unsound.

Aware of the apparent inconsistency between the acceptance of the TVA system and the provision for a jury in all other cases, the members of the Committee attending the conference of December 2, 1948, then suggested that in the other cases the choice of jury or commission be left to the discretion of the District Court, going back to a suggestion previously made by Committee members and reported at page 15 of the Preliminary Draft of June 1947. They called the attention of the Court to the fact that the entire Advisory Committee had not been consulted about this suggestion and proposed that the draft be returned to the Committee for further consideration, and that was done.

The proposal we now make for subdivision (h) is as follows:

(h) Trial. If the action involves the exercise of the power of eminent domain under the law of the United States, any tribunal specially constituted by an Act of Congress governing the case for the trial of the issue of just compensation shall be the tribunal for the determination of that issue; but if there is no such specially constituted tribunal any party may have a trial by jury of the issue of just compensation by filing a demand therefor within the time allowed for answer or within such further time as the court may fix, unless the court in its discretion orders that, because of the character, location, or quantity of the property to be condemned, or for other reasons in the interest of justice, the issue of compensation shall be determined by a commission of three persons appointed by it. If a commission is appointed it shall have the powers of a master provided in subdivision (c) of Rule 53 and proceedings before it shall be governed by the provisions of

paragraphs (1) and (2) of subdivision (d) of Rule 53. Its action and report shall be determined by a majority and its findings and report shall have the effect, and be dealt with by the court in accordance with the practice, prescribed in paragraph (2) of subdivision (e) of Rule 53. Trial of all issues shall otherwise be by the court.

In the 1948 draft the Committee had been almost evenly divided as between jury or commission and that made it easy for us to agree on the present draft. It would be difficult to state in a rule the various conditions to control the District Court in its choice and we have merely stated generally the matters which should be considered by the District Court.

The rule as now drafted seems to meet Judge Paul's objection. In large projects like the TVA the court may decide to use a commission. In a great number of cases involving only sites for buildings or other small areas, where use of a jury is appropriate, a jury may be chosen. The District Court's discretion may also be influenced by local preference or habit, and the preference of the Department of Justice and the reasons for its preference will doubtless be given weight. The Committee is convinced that there are some types of cases in which use of a commission is preferable and others in which a jury may be appropriately used, and that it would be a mistake to provide that the same kind of tribunal should be used in all cases. We think the available evidence clearly leads to that conclusion.

When this suggestion was made at the conference of December 2, 1948, representatives of the Department of Justice opposed it, expressing opposition to the use of a commission in any case. Their principal ground for opposition to commissions was then based on the assertion that the commission system is too expensive because courts allow commissioners too large compensation. The obvious answer to that is that the compensation of commissioners ought to be fixed or limited by law, as was done in the TVA Act, and the agency dealing with appropriations—either the Administrative Office or some other interested department of the government—should correct that evil, if evil there be, by obtaining such legislation. Authority to promulgate rules of procedure does not include power to fix compensation of government employees. The Advisory Committee is not convinced that even without such legislation the commission system is more expensive than the jury system. The expense of jury trials includes not only the per diem and mileage of the jurors impaneled for a case but like items for the entire venire. In computing cost of jury trials, the salaries of court officials, judges, clerks, marshals and deputies must be considered. No figures have been given to the Committee to establish that the cost of the commission system is the greater.

We earnestly recommend the rule as now drafted for promulgation by the Court, in the public interest.

The Advisory Committee have given more time to this rule, including time required for conferences with the Department of Justice to hear statements of its representatives, than has been required by any other rule. The rule may not be perfect but if faults develop in practice they may be promptly cured. Certainly the present conformity system is atrocious.

Under state practices, just compensation is normally determined by one of three methods: by commissioners; by commissioners with a right of appeal to and trial de novo before a jury; and by a jury, without a commission. A trial to the court or to the court including a master are, however, other methods that are occasionally used. Approximately 5 states use only commissioners; 23 states use commissioners with a trial de novo before a jury; and 18 states use only the jury. This classification is advisedly stated in approximate terms, since the same state may utilize diverse methods, depending upon different types of condemnations or upon the locality of the property, and since the methods used in a few states do not permit of a categorical classification. To reject the proposed rule and leave the situation as it is would not satisfy the views of the Department of Justice. The Department and the Advisory Committee agree that the use of a commission, with appeal to a jury, is a wasteful system.

The Department of Justice has a voluminous "Manual on Federal Eminent Domain," the 1940 edition of which has 948 pages with an appendix of 73 more pages. The title page informs us the preparation of the manual was begun during the incumbency of Attorney General Cummings, was continued under Attorney General Murphy, and completed during the incumbency of Attorney General Jackson. The preface contains the following statement:

It should also be mentioned that the research incorporated in the manual would be of invaluable assistance in the drafting of a new uniform code, or rules of court, for federal condemnation proceedings, which are now greatly confused, not only by the existence of over seventy federal statutes governing condemnations for different purposes—statutes which sometimes conflict with one another—but also by the countless problems occasioned by the requirements of conformity to state law. Progress of the work has already demonstrated that the need for such reform exists.

It is not surprising that more than once Attorneys General have asked the Advisory Committee to prepare a federal rule and rescue the government from this morass.

The Department of Justice has twice tried and failed to persuade the Congress to provide that juries shall be used in all condemnation cases. The debates in Congress show that part of the opposition to the Department of Justice's bills came from representatives opposed to jury trials in all cases, and in part from a preference for the conformity system. Our present proposal opens the door for district judges to yield to local preferences on the subject. It does much for the Department's points of view. It is a great improvement over the present so-called conformity system. It does away with the wasteful "double" system prevailing in 23 states where awards by commissions are followed by jury trials.

Aside from the question as to the choice of a tribunal to award compensation, the proposed rule would afford a simple and improved procedure.

We turn now to an itemized explanation of the other changes we have made in the 1948 draft. Some of these result from recent amendments to the Judicial Code. Others result from a reconsideration by the Advisory Committee of provisions which we thought could be improved.

    1. In the amended Judicial Code, the district courts are designated as "United States District Courts" instead of "District Courts of the United States," and a corresponding change has been made in the rule.

    2. After the 1948 draft was referred back to the committee, the provision in subdivision (c)(2), relating to naming defendants, * * * which provided that the plaintiff shall add as defendants all persons having or claiming an interest in that property whose names can be ascertained by a search of the records to the extent commonly made by competent searchers of title in the vicinity "in light of the type and value of the property involved," the phrase in quotation marks was changed to read "in the light of the character and value of the property involved and the interests to be acquired."

The Department of Justice made a counter proposal * * * that there be substituted the words "reasonably diligent search of the records, considering the type." When the American Bar Association thereafter considered the draft, it approved the Advisory Committee's draft of this subdivision, but said that it had no objection to the Department's suggestion. Thereafter, in an effort to eliminate controversy, the Advisory Committee accepted the Department's suggestion as to (c)(2), using the word "character" instead of the word "type."

The Department of Justice also suggested that in subdivision (d)(3)(ii) relating to service by publication, the search for a defendant's residence as a preliminary to publication be limited to the state in which the complaint is filed. Here again the American Bar Association's report expressed the view that the Department's suggestion was unobjectionable and the Advisory Committee thereupon adopted it.

    3. Subdivision (k) of the 1948 draft is as follows:

    (k) Condemnation Under a State's Power of Eminent Domain. If the action involves the exercise of the power of eminent domain under the law of a state, the practice herein prescribed may be altered to the extent necessary to observe and enforce any condition affecting the substantial rights of a litigant attached by the state law to the exercise of the state's power of eminent domain.

Occasionally condemnation cases under a state's power of eminent domain reach a United States District Court because of diversity of citizenship. Such cases are rare, but provision should be made for them.

The 1948 draft of (k) required a district court to decide whether a provision of state law specifying the tribunal to award compensation is or is not a "condition" attached to the exercise of the state's power. On reconsideration we concluded that it would be wise to redraft (k) so as to avoid that troublesome question. As to conditions in state laws which affect the substantial rights of a litigant, the district courts would be bound to give them effect without any rule on the subject. Accordingly we present two alternative revisions. One suggestion supported by a majority of the Advisory Committee is as follows:

    (k) Condemnation Under a State's Power of Eminent Domain. The practice herein prescribed governs in actions involving the exercise of the power of eminent domain under the law of a state, provided that if the state law makes provision for trial of any issue by jury, or for trial of the issue of compensation by jury or commission or both, that provision shall be followed.

The other is as follows:

    (k) Condemnation Under a State's Power of Eminent Domain. The practice herein prescribed governs in actions involving the exercise of the power of eminent domain under the law of a state, provided that if the state law gives a right to a trial by jury such a trial shall in any case be allowed to the party demanding it within the time permitted by these rules, and in that event no hearing before a commission shall be had.

The first proposal accepts the state law as to the tribunals to fix compensation, and in that respect leaves the parties in precisely the same situation as if the case were pending in a state court, including the use of a commission with appeal to a jury, if the state law so provides. It has the effect of avoiding any question as to whether the decisions in *Erie R. Co. v. Tompkins* and later cases have application to a situation of this kind.

The second proposal gives the parties a right to a jury trial if that is provided for by state law, but prevents the use of both commission and jury. Those members of the Committee who favor the second proposal do so because of the obvious objections to the double trial, with a commission and appeal to a jury. As the decisions in *Erie R. Co. v. Tompkins* and later cases may have a bearing on this point, and the Committee is divided, we think both proposals should be placed before the Court.

4. The provision * * * of the 1948 draft * * * prescribing the effective date of the rule was drafted before the recent amendment of the Judicial Code on that subject. On May 10, 1950, the President approved an act which amended section 2072 of Title 28, United States Code, to read as follows:

Such rules shall not take effect until they have been reported to Congress by the Chief Justice at or after the beginning of a regular session thereof but not later than the first day of May, and until the expiration of ninety days after they have been thus reported.

To conform to the statute now in force, we suggest a provision as follows:

Effective Date. This Rule 71A and the amendment to Rule 81(a) will take effect on August 1, 1951. Rule 71A governs all proceedings in actions brought after it takes effect and also all further proceedings in actions then pending, except to the extent that in the opinion of the court its application in a particular action pending when the rule takes effect would not be feasible or would work injustice, in which event the former procedure applies.

If the rule is not reported to Congress by May 1, 1951, this provision must be altered.

[Par. 3 of Supreme Court Order adopted Apr. 30, 1951, setting out this rule and providing for the abrogation of par. (7) of Rule 81(a), and providing for the Effective Date, as stated herein, was transmitted to Congress on May 1, 1951 by the Chief Justice of the United States (House Document No. 121, May 1, 1951, 82nd Cong., 1st Sess.), in conformity with § 2072 of this title. As no action was taken by Congress within the 90-day period required by that section, this rule and the abrogation of par. (7) of Rule 81(a) took effect on Aug. 1, 1951, as provided in said order.]

5. We call attention to the fact that the proposed rule does not contain a provision for the procedure to be followed in order to exercise the right of the United States to take immediate possession or title, when the condemnation proceeding is begun. There are several statutes conferring such a right which are cited in the original notes to the May 1948 draft * * *. The existence of this right is taken into account in the rule. In subdivision (c)(2), * * * it is stated: "Upon the commencement of the action, the plaintiff need join as defendants only the per-

sons having or claiming an interest in the property whose names are then known." That is to enable the United States to exercise the right to immediate title or possession without the delay involved in ascertaining the names of all interested parties. The right is also taken into account in the provision relating to dismissal (paragraph (i), subdivisions (1), (2), and (3), * * *); also in paragraph (j) relating to deposits and their distribution.

The Advisory Committee considered whether the procedure for exercising the right should be specified in the rule and decided against it, as the procedure now being followed seems to be giving no trouble, and to draft a rule to fit all the statutes on the subject might create confusion.

The American Bar Association has taken an active interest in a rule for condemnation cases. In 1944 its House of Delegates adopted a resolution which among other things resolved:

That before adoption by the Supreme Court of the United States of any redraft of the proposed rule, time and opportunity should be afforded to the bar to consider and make recommendations concerning any such redraft.

Accordingly, in 1950 the revised draft was submitted to the American Bar Association and its section of real property, probate and trust law appointed a committee to consider it. That committee was supplied with copies of the written statement from the Department of Justice giving the reasons relied on by the Department for preferring a rule to use juries in all cases. The Advisory Committee's report was approved at a meeting of the section of real property law, and by the House of Delegates at the annual meeting of September 1950. The American Bar Association report gave particular attention to the question whether juries or commissions should be used to fix compensation, approved the Advisory Committee's solution appearing in their latest draft designed to allow use of commissions in projects comparable to the TVA, and rejected the proposal for use of juries in all cases.

In November 1950 a committee of the Federal Bar Association, the chairman of which was a Special Assistant to the Attorney General, made a report which reflected the attitude of the Department of Justice on the condemnation rule.

Aside from subdivision (h) about the tribunal to award compensation the final draft of the condemnation rule here presented has the approval of the American Bar Association and, we understand, the Department of Justice, and we do not know of any opposition to it. Subdivision (h) has the unanimous approval of the Advisory Committee and has been approved by the American Bar Association. The use of commissions in TVA cases, and, by fair inference, in cases comparable to the TVA, is supported by 17 out of 20 judges who up to 1947 had sat in TVA cases. The legal staff of the TVA has vigorously objected to the substitution of juries for commissions in TVA cases. We regret to report that the Department of Justice still asks that subdivision (h) be altered to provide for jury trials in an cases where Congress has not specified the tribunal. We understand that the Department approves the proposal that the system prevailing in 23 states for the "double" trial, by commission with appeal to and trial de novo before a jury, should be abolished, and also asks that on demand a jury should be substituted for a commission, in those states where use of a commission alone is now required. The Advisory Committee has no evidence that commissions do not operate satisfactorily in the case of projects comparable to the TVA.

Original Report

General Statement. 1. Background. When the Advisory Committee was formulating its recommendations to the Court concerning rules of procedure, which subsequently became the Federal Rules of 1938, the Committee concluded at an early stage not to fix the procedure in condemnation cases. This is a matter principally involving the exercise of the federal power of eminent domain, as very few condemnation cases involving the state's power reach the United States District Courts. The Committee's reasons at that time were that inasmuch as condemnation proceedings by the United States are governed by statutes of the United States, prescribing different procedure for various agencies and departments of the government, or, in the absence of such statutes, by local state practice under the Conformity Act (former § 258 of Title 40), it would be extremely difficult to draft a uniform rule satisfactory to the various agencies and departments of the government and to private parties; and that there was no general demand for a uniform rule. The Committee continued in that belief until shortly before the preparation of the April 1937 Draft of the Rules, when the officials of the Department of Justice having to do with condemnation cases urgently requested the Committee to propose rules on this subject. The Committee undertook the task and drafted a Condemnation Rule which appeared for the first time as Rule 74 of the April 1937 Draft. After the publication and distribution of this initial draft many objections were urged against it by counsel for various governmental agencies, whose procedure in condemnation cases was prescribed by federal statutes. Some of these agencies wanted to be excepted in whole or in part from the operation of the uniform rule proposed in April 1937. And the Department of Justice changed its position and stated that it preferred to have government condemnations conducted by local attorneys familiar with the state practice, which was applied under the Conformity Act where the Acts of Congress do not prescribe the practice; that it preferred to work under the Conformity Act without a uniform rule of procedure. The profession generally showed little interest in the proposed uniform rule. For these reasons the Advisory Committee in its Final Report to the Court in November 1937 proposed that all of Rule 74 be stricken and that the Federal Rules be made applicable only to appeals in condemnation cases. See note to Rule 74 of the Final Report.

Some of six or seven years later when the Advisory Committee was considering the subject of amendments to the Federal Rules both government officials and the profession generally urged the adoption of some uniform procedure. This demand grew out of the volume of condemnation proceedings instituted during the war, and the general feeling of dissatisfaction with the diverse condemnation procedures that were applicable in the federal courts. A strongly held belief was that both the sovereign's power to condemn and the property owner's right to compensation could be promoted by a simplified rule. As a consequence the Committee proposed a Rule 71A on the subject of condemnation in its Preliminary Draft of May 1944. In the Second Preliminary Draft of May 1945 this earlier proposed Rule 71A was, however, omitted. The Committee did not then feel that it had sufficient time to prepare a revised draft satisfactorily to

it which would meet legitimate objections made to the draft of May 1944. To avoid unduly delaying the proposed amendments to existing rules the Committee concluded to proceed in the regular way with the preparation of the amendments to these rules and deal with the question of a condemnation rule as an independent matter. As a consequence it made no recommendations to the Court on condemnation in its Final Report of Proposed Amendments of June 1946; and the amendments which the Court adopted in December 1946 did not deal with condemnation. After concluding its task relative to amendments, the Committee returned to a consideration of eminent domain, its proposed Rule 71A of May 1944, the suggestions and criticisms that had been presented in the interim, and in June 1947 prepared and distributed to the profession another draft of a proposed condemnation rule. This draft contained several alternative provisions, specifically called attention to and asked for opinion relative to these matters, and in particular as to the constitution of the tribunal to award compensation. The present draft was based on the June 1947 formulation, in light of the advice of the profession on both matters of substance and form.

2. Statutory Provisions. The need for a uniform condemnation rule in the federal courts arises from the fact that by various statutes Congress has prescribed diverse procedures for certain condemnation proceedings, and, in the absence of such statutes, has prescribed conformity to local state practice under former § 258 of Title 40. This general conformity adds to the diversity of procedure since in the United States there are multifarious methods of procedure in existence. Thus in 1931 it was said that there were 269 different methods of judicial procedure in different classes of condemnation cases and 56 methods of nonjudicial or administrative procedure. First Report of Judicial Council of Michigan, 1931, § 46, pp. 55 to 56. These numbers have not decreased. Consequently, the general requirement of conformity to state practice and procedure, particularly where the condemnor is the United States, leads to expense, delay and uncertainty. In advocacy of a uniform federal rule, see Armstrong, *Proposed Amendments to Federal Rules for Civil Procedure*, 1944, 4 F.R.D. 124, 134; id., *Report of the Advisory Committee on Federal Rules of Civil Procedure Recommending Amendments*, 1946, 5 F.R.D. 339, 357.

There are a great variety of Acts of Congress authorizing the exercise of the power of eminent domain by the United States and its officers and agencies. These statutes for the most part do not specify the exact procedure to be followed, but where procedure is prescribed, it is by no means uniform.

The following are instances of Acts which merely authorize the exercise of the power without specific declaration as to the procedure:

U.S.C., Title 16:

> § 404c–11 (Mammoth Cave National Park; acquisition of lands, interests in lands or other property for park by the Secretary of the Interior).
>
> § 426d (Stones River National Park; acquisition of land for parks by the Secretary of the Army).
>
> § 450aa (George Washington Carver National Monument; acquisition of land by the Secretary of the Interior).
>
> § 517 (National forest reservation; title to lands to be acquired by the Secretary of Agriculture).

U.S.C., Title 42:

§§ 1805(b)(5), 1813(b) [now §§ 2061 and 2112, and §§ 2221 to 2224, respectively, of Title 42] (Atomic Energy Act).

The following are instances of Acts which authorized condemnation and declare that the procedure is to conform what that of similar actions in state courts:

U.S.C., Title 16:

§ 423k (Richmond National Battlefield Park; acquisition of lands by the Secretary of the Interior).

§ 814 (Exercise by water power licensee of power of eminent domain).

U.S.C., Title 24:

§ 78 [Repealed] (Condemnation of land for the former National Home for Disabled Volunteer Soldiers).

U.S.C., Title 33:

§ 591 (Condemnation of lands and materials for river and harbor improvement by the Secretary of the Army).

U.S.C., Title 40:

§ 257 [now § 3113] (Condemnation of realty for sites for public building and for other public uses by the Secretary of the Treasury authorized).

§ 258 [Omitted as superseded by this rule] (Same procedure).

U.S.C., Title 50:

§ 171 [Repealed and is now covered by § 2663 of Title 10] (Acquisition of land by the Secretary of the Army for national defense).

§ 172 [Repealed and is now covered by §§ 2664 and 2665 of Title 10] (Acquisition of property by the Secretary of the Army, etc., for production of lumber).

§ 632 App. [Omitted as terminated by § 645 of the Appendix to Title 50] (Second War Powers Act, 1942; acquisition of real property for war purposes by the Secretary of Army, the Secretary of the Navy and others).

The following are Acts in which a more or less complete code of procedure is set forth in connection with the taking:

U.S.C., Title 16:

§ 831x (Condemnation by Tennessee Valley Authority).

U.S.C., Title 40:

§ 361–386 [Repealed] [now D.C.Code, Title 16, § 1301 et seq.] (Acquisition of lands in District of Columbia for use of United States; condemnation).

3. Adjustment of Rule to Statutory Provisions. While it was apparent that the principle of uniformity should be the basis for a rule to replace the multiple diverse procedures set out above, there remained a serious question as to whether an exception could properly be made relative to the method of determining compensation. Where Congress had provided for conformity to state law the following were the general methods in use: an initial determination by commissioners, with appeal to a judge; an initial award, likewise made by commissioners, but with the appeal to a jury; and determination by a jury without a previous award by commissioners. In two situations Congress had specified the tribunal to determine the issue of compensation: condemnation by the Tennessee Valley Authority; and condemnation in the District of Columbia. Under the TVA procedure the initial determination of value is by three disinterested commissioners, appointed by the court, from a locality other than the one in which the land lies. Either party may except to the award of the commission; in that case the exceptions are to be heard by three district judges (unless the parties stipulate for a lesser number), with a right of appeal to the circuit court of appeals. The TVA is a regional agency. It is faced with the necessity of acquiring a very substantial acreage within a relatively small area, and charged with the task of carrying on within the Tennessee Valley and in cooperation with the local people a permanent program involving navigation and flood control, electric power, soil conservation, and general regional development. The success of this program is partially dependent upon the good will and cooperation of the people of the Tennessee Valley, and this in turn partially depends upon the land acquisition program. Disproportionate awards among landowners would create dissatisfaction and ill will. To secure uniformity in treatment Congress provided the rather unique procedure of the three-judge court to review de novo the initial award of the commissioners. This procedure has worked to the satisfaction of the property owners and the TVA. A full statement of the TVA position and experience is set forth in Preliminary Draft of Proposed Rule to Govern Condemnation Cases (June, 1947) 15–19. A large majority of the district judges with experience under this procedure approve it, subject to some objection to the requirement for a three-judge district court to review commissioners' awards. A statutory three-judge requirement is, however, jurisdictional and must be strictly followed. *Stratton v. St. Louis, Southwestern Ry. Co.,* 1930, 51 S.Ct. 8, 282 U.S. 10, 75 L.Ed. 135; *Ayrshire Collieries Corp. v. United States,* 1947, 67 S.Ct. 1168, 331 U.S. 132, 91 L.Ed. 1391. Hence except insofar as the TVA statute itself authorizes the parties to stipulate for a court of less than three judges, the requirement must be followed, and would seem to be beyond alteration by court rule even if change were thought desirable. Accordingly the TVA procedure is retained for the determination of compensation in TVA condemnation cases. It was also thought desirable to retain the specific method Congress had prescribed for the District of Columbia, which is a so-called jury of five appointed by the court. This is a local matter and the specific treatment accorded by Congress has given local satisfaction.

Aside from the foregoing limited exceptions dealing with the TVA and the District of Columbia, the question was whether a uniform method for determining compensation should be a commission with appeal to a district judge, or a commission with appeal to a jury, or a jury without a commission. Experience with the commission on a nation-wide basis, and in particular with the utilization of a commission followed by an appeal to a jury, has been that the commission is time consuming and expensive. Furthermore, it is largely a futile procedure where it is preparatory to jury trial. Since in the bulk of states a land owner is entitled eventually to a jury trial, since the jury is a traditional tribunal for the determination of questions of value, and since experience with juries has proved satisfactory to both government and land owner, the right to jury trial is adopted as the general rule. Condemnation involving the TVA and the District of Columbia are the two exceptions. See Note to Subdivision (h), infra.

Note to Subdivision (a). As originally promulgated the Federal Rules governed appeals in condemnation proceedings but were not otherwise applicable. Rule 81(a)(7). Pre-appeal procedure, in the main, conformed to state procedure. See statutes and discussion, supra. The purpose of Rule 71A is to provide a uniform procedure for condemnation in the federal district courts, including the District of Columbia.

To achieve this purpose Rule 71A prescribes such specialized procedure as is required by condemnation proceedings, otherwise it utilizes the general framework of the Federal Rules where specific detail is unnecessary. The adoption of Rule 71A, of course, renders paragraph (7) of Rule 81(a) unnecessary.

The promulgation of a rule for condemnation procedure is within the rulemaking power. The Enabling Act [Act of June 19, 1934, c. 651, §§ 1, 2 (48 Stat. 1064), former §§ 723b, 723c, now § 2072, of this title] gives the Supreme Court "the power to prescribe, by general rules * * * the forms of process, writs, pleadings, and motions, and the practice and procedure in civil actions at law." Such rules, however, must not abridge, enlarge, or modify substantive rights. In *Kohl v. United States*, 1875, 91 U.S. 367, 23 L.Ed. 449, a proceeding instituted by the United States to appropriate land for a postoffice site under a statute enacted for such purpose, the Supreme Court held that "a proceeding to take land in virtue of the government's eminent domain, and determining the compensation to be made for it, is * * * a suit at common law, when initiated in a court." See, also, *Madisonville Traction Co. v. Saint Bernard Mining Co.*, 1905, 25 S.Ct. 251, 196 U.S. 239, 49 L.Ed. 462, infra, under subdivision (k). And the Conformity Act [former § 258 of Title 40], which is superseded by Rule 71A, deals only with "practice, pleadings, forms and proceedings and not with matters of substantive laws." *United States v. 243.22 Acres of Land in Village of Farmingdale, Town of Babylon, Suffolk County, N.Y.,* D.C.N.Y.1942, 43 F.Supp. 561, affirmed 129 F.2d 678, certiorari denied 63 S.Ct. 441, 317 U.S. 698, 87 L.Ed. 558.

Rule 71A affords a uniform procedure for all cases of condemnation invoking the national power of eminent domain, and, to the extent stated in subdivision (k), for cases invoking a state's power of eminent domain; and supplants all statutes prescribing a different procedure. While the almost exclusive utility of the rule is for the condemnation of real property, it also applies to the condemnation of personal property, either as an incident to real property or as the sole object of the proceeding, when permitted or required by statute. See former § 438j [now § 5001] of Title 38 (World War Veterans' Relief Act); former §§ 1805, 1811, and 1813 of Title 42 (Atomic Energy Act); former § 79 [now § 100] of Title 50 (Nitrates Act); former §§ 161 to 165 and § 166, of Title 50 (Helium Gas Act). Requisitioning of personal property with the right in the owner to sue the United States, where the compensation cannot be agreed upon (see former § 1813 [now §§ 2221 to 2224] of Title 42, for example) will continue to be the normal method of acquiring personal property and Rule 71A in no way interferes with or restricts any such right. Only where the law requires or permits the formal procedure of condemnation to be utilized will the rule have any applicability to the acquisition of personal property.

Rule 71A is not intended to and does not supersede the Act of February 26, 1931, c. 307, §§ 1 to 5 (46 Stat. 1421), §§ 258a to 258e of Title 40, which is a supplementary condemnation statute, permissive in its nature and designed to permit the prompt acquisition of title by the United States, pending the condemnation proceeding, upon a deposit in court. See *United States v. 76,800 Acres, More or Less, of Land, in Bryan and Liberty Counties, Ga.,* D.C.Ga.1942, 44 F.Supp. 653; *United States v. 17,280 Acres of Land, More or Less, Situated in Saunders County, Neb.,* D.C.Neb.1942, 47 F.Supp. 267. The same is true insofar as the following or any other statutes authorize the acquisition of title or the taking of immediate possession:

U.S.C., Title 33:

§ 594 (When immediate possession of land may be taken; for a work of river and harbor improvements.)

U.S.C., Title 42:

§ 1813(b) [now §§ 2221 to 2224 of Title 42] (When immediate possession may be taken under Atomic Energy Act).

U.S.C., Title 50:

§ 171 [Repealed and is now covered by § 2663 of Title 10] (Acquisition of land by the Secretary of the Army for national defense).

§ 632 App. [Omitted as terminated by § 645 of the Appendix to Title 50] (Second War Powers Act, 1942; acquisition of real property for war purposes by the Secretary of the Army, the Secretary of the Navy, and others).

Note to Subdivision (b). This subdivision provides for broad joinder in accordance with the tenor of other rules such as Rule 18. To require separate condemnation proceedings for each piece of property separately owned would be unduly burdensome and would serve no useful purpose. And a restriction that only properties may be joined which are to be acquired for the same public use would also cause difficulty. For example, a unified project to widen a street, construct a bridge across a navigable river, and for the construction of approaches to the level of the bridge on both sides of the river might involve acquiring property for different public uses. Yet it is eminently desirable that the plaintiff may in one proceeding condemn all the property interests and rights necessary to carry out this project. Rule 21 which allows the court to sever and proceed separately with any claim against a party, and Rule 42(b) giving the court broad discretion to order separate trials give adequate protection to all defendants in condemnation proceedings.

Note to Subdivision (c). Since a condemnation proceeding is in rem and since a great many property owners are often involved, paragraph (1) requires the property to be named and only one of the owners. In other respects and caption will contain the name of the court, the title of the action, file number, and a designation of the pleading as a complaint in accordance with Rule 10(a).

Since the general standards of pleading are stated in other rules, paragraph (2) prescribes only the necessary detail for condemnation proceedings. Certain statutes allow the United States to acquire title or possession immediately upon commencement of an action. See the Act of February 26, 1931, c. 307, §§ 1 to 5 (46 Stat. 1421), §§ 258a to 258e of Title 40; and § 594 of Title 33, former § 1813(b) of Title 42, former § 171 of Title 50, former § 632 of the Appendix to Title 50, supra. To carry out the purpose of such statutes and to aid the condemnor in instituting the action even where title is not acquired at the outset, the plaintiff is initially required to join as defendants only the persons having or claiming an interest in the property whose names are then known. This is no way prejudices the property owner, who must eventually be joined as a defendant, served with process, and allowed to answer before there can be any hearing involving the compensation to be paid for his piece of property. The rule requires the plaintiff to name all persons having or claiming an interest in the property of whom the plaintiff has learned and, more importantly, those appearing of record. By charging the plaintiff with the necessity to make "a search of the records of the extent commonly made by competent searches of title in the vicinity in light of the type and value of the property involved" both the plaintiff and property owner are protected. Where a short term interest in property of little value is involved, as a two or three year easement over a vacant land for purposes of ingress and egress to other property, a search of the records covering a long period of time is not required. Where on the other hand fee simple title in valuable property is being condemned the search must necessarily cover a much longer period of time and be commensurate with the interests involved. But even here the search is related to the type made by competent title searchers in the vicinity. A search that extends back to the original patent may be feasible in some midwestern and western states and be proper under certain circumstances. In the Atlantic seaboard states such a search is normally not feasible nor desirable. There is a common sense business accommodation of what title searchers can and should do. For state statutes requiring persons appearing as owners or otherwise interested in the property to be named as defendants, see 3 Colo.Stat.Ann., 1935, c. 61, § 2; Ill.Ann.Stat. (Smith-Hurd) c. 47, § 2; 1 Iowa Code, 1946, § 472.3; Kans.Stat.Ann., 1935, § 26–101; 2 Mass.Laws Ann., 1932, c. 80A, § 4; 7 Mich.Stat.Ann., 1936, § 8.2; 2 Minn.Stat., Mason 1927, § 6541; 20 N.J.Stat.Ann., 1939, § 1–2; 3 Wash.Revised Stat., Remington, 1932, Title 6, § 891. For state provisions allowing persons whose names are not known to be designated under the descriptive term of "unknown owner", see Hawaii Revised Laws, 1945, c. 8, § 310 ("such [unknown] defendant may be joined in the petition under a fictitious name."); Ill.Ann.Stat. (Smith-Hurd) c. 47, § 2 ("Persons interested, whose names are unknown, may be made parties defendant by the description of the unknown owners; * * *"); Maryland Code Ann., 1939, Art. 33A, § 1 ("In case any owner or owners is or are not known, he or they may be described in such petition as the unknown owner or owners, or the unknown heir or heirs of a deceased owner."); 2 Mass.Laws Ann., 1932, c. 80A, § 4 ("Persons not in being, unascertained or unknown who may have an interest in any of such land shall be made parties respondent by such description as seems appropriate, * * *"); New Mex.Stat.Ann., 1941, § 25–901 ("the owners * * * shall be parties defendant, by name, if the names are known, and by description of the unknown owners of the land therein described, if their names are unknown."); Utah Code Ann., 1943, § 104–61–7 ("The names of all owners and claimants of the property, if known, or a statement that they are unknown, who must be styled defendants").

The last sentence of paragraph (2) enables the court to expedite the distribution of a deposit, in whole or in part, as soon as pertinent facts of ownership, value and the like are established. See also subdivision (j).

The signing of the complaint is governed by Rule 11.

Note to Subdivision (d). In lieu of a summons, which is the initial process in other civil actions under Rule 4(a), subdivision (d) provides for a notice which is to contain sufficient information so that the defendant in effect obtains the plaintiff's statement of his claim against the defendant to whom the notice is directed. Since the plaintiff's attorney is an officer of the court and to prevent unduly burdening the clerk of the court, paragraph (1) of subdivision (d) provides that plaintiff's attorney shall prepare and deliver a notice or

notices to the clerk. Flexibility is provided by the provision for joint or several notices, and for additional notices. Where there are only a few defendants it may be convenient to prepare but one notice directed to all the defendants. In other cases where there are many defendants it will be more convenient to prepare two or more notices; but in any event a notice must be directed to each named defendant. Paragraph (2) provides that the notice is to be signed by the plaintiff's attorney. Since the notice is to be delivered to the clerk, the issuance of the notice will appear of record in the court. The clerk should forthwith deliver the notice or notices for service to the marshal or to a person specially appointed to serve the notice. Rule 4(a). The form of the notice is such that, in addition to informing the defendant of the plaintiff's statement of claim, it tells the defendant precisely what his rights are. Failure on the part of the defendant to serve an answer constitutes a consent to the taking and to the authority of the court to proceed to fix compensation therefor, but it does not preclude the defendant from presenting evidence as to the amount of compensation due him or in sharing the award of distribution. See subdivision (e); Form 28.

While under Rule 4(f) the territorial limits of a summons are normally the territorial limits of the state in which the district court is held, the territorial limits for personal service of a notice under Rule 71A(d)(3) are those of the nation. This extension of process is here proper since the aim of the condemnation proceeding is not to enforce any personal liability and the property owner is helped, not imposed upon, by the best type of service possible. If personal service cannot be made either because the defendant's whereabouts cannot be ascertained, or, if ascertained, the defendant cannot be personally served, as where he resides in a foreign country such as Canada or Mexico, then service by publication is proper. The provisions for this type of service are set forth in the rule and are in no way governed by § 118 [now § 1655] of this title.

Note to Subdivision (e). Departing from the scheme of Rule 12, subdivision (e) requires all defenses and objections to be presented in an answer and does not authorize a preliminary motion. There is little need for the latter in condemnation proceedings. The general standard of pleading is governed by other rules, particularly Rule 8, and this subdivision (e) merely prescribes what matters the answer should set forth. Merely by appearing in the action a defendant can receive notice of all proceedings affecting him. And without the necessity of answering a defendant may present evidence as to the amount of compensation due him, and he may share in the distribution of the award. See also subdivision (d)(2); Form 28.

Note to Subdivision (f). Due to the number of persons who may be interested in the property to be condemned, there is a likelihood that the plaintiff will need to amend his complaint, perhaps many times, to add new parties or state new issues. This subdivision recognizes that fact and does not burden the court with applications by the plaintiff for leave to amend. At the same time all defendants are adequately protected; and their need to amend the answer is adequately protected by Rule 15, which is applicable by virtue of subdivision (a) of this Rule 71A.

Note to Subdivision (g). A condemnation action is a proceeding in rem. Commencement of the action as against a defendant by virtue of his joinder pursuant to subdivision (c)(2) is the point of cut-off and there is no mandatory requirement for substitution because of a subsequent change of interest, although the court is given ample power to require substitution. Rule 25 is inconsistent with subdivision (g) and hence inapplicable. Accordingly, the time periods of Rule 25 do not govern to require dismissal nor to prevent substitution.

Note to Subdivision (h). This subdivision prescribes the method for determining the issue of just compensation in cases involving the federal power of eminent domain. The method of jury trial provided by subdivision (h) will normally apply in cases involving the state power by virtue of subdivision (k).

Congress has specially constituted a tribunal for the trial of the issue of just compensation in two instances: condemnation under the Tennessee Valley Authority Act; and condemnation in the District of Columbia. These tribunals are retained for reasons set forth in the General Statement: 3. Adjustment of Rule to Statutory Provisions, supra. Subdivision (h) also has prospective application so that if Congress should create another special tribunal, that tribunal will determine the issue of just compensation. Subject to these exceptions the general method of trial of that issue is to be by jury if any party demands it, otherwise that issue, as well as all other issues, are to be tried by the court.

As to the TVA procedure that is continued, § 831x of Title 16 requires that three commissioners be appointed to fix the compensation; that exceptions to their award are to be heard by three district judges (unless the parties stipulate for a lesser number) and that the district judges try the question de novo; that an appeal to the circuit court of appeals may be taken within 30 days from the filing of the decision of the district judges; and that the circuit court of appeals shall on the record fix compensation "without regard to the awards of findings theretofore made by the commissioners or the district judges." The mode of fixing compensation in the District of Columbia, which is also continued, is prescribed in former §§ 361 to 386 of Title 40. Under former § 371 the court is required in all cases to order the selection of a jury of five from among not less than 20 names, drawn "from the special box provided by law." They must have the usual qualifications of jurors and in addition must be freeholders of the District, and not in the service of the United States or the District. A special oath is administered to the chosen jurors. The trial proceeds in the ordinary way, except that the jury is allowed to separate after they have begun to consider their verdict.

There is no constitutional right to jury trial in a condemnation proceeding. *Bauman v. Ross*, 1897, 17 S.Ct. 966, 167 U.S. 548, 42 L.Ed. 270. See, also, Hines, *Does the Seventh Amendment to the Constitution of the United States Require Jury Trials in all Condemnation Proceedings?*, 1925, 11 Va.L.Rev. 505; Blair, *Federal Condemnation Proceedings and the Seventh Amendment*, 1927, 41 Harv.L.Rev. 29; 3 *Moore's Federal Practice*, 1938, 3007. Prior to Rule 71A, jury trial in federal condemnation proceedings was, however, enjoyed under the general conformity statute, former § 258 of Title 40, in states which provided for jury trial. See generally, 2 Lewis, *Eminent Domain*, 3d ed. 1909, §§ 509, 510; 3 Moore, op. cit. supra. Since the general conformity statute is superseded by Rule 71A, see supra under subdivision (a), and since it was believed that the rule to be substituted should likewise give a right to jury trial, subdivi-

sion (h) establishes that method as the general one for determining the issue of just compensation.

Note to Subdivision (i). Both the right of the plaintiff to dismiss by filing a notice of dismissal and the right of the court to permit a dismissal are circumscribed to the extent that where the plaintiff has acquired the title or a lesser interest or possession, viz., any property interest for which just compensation should be paid, the action may not be dismissed, without the defendant's consent, and the property owner remitted to another court, such as the Court of Claims, to recover just compensation for the property right taken. Circuity of action is thus prevented without increasing the liability of the plaintiff to pay just compensation for any interest that is taken. Freedom of dismissal is accorded, where both the condemnor and condemnee agree, up to the time of the entry of judgment vesting plaintiff with title. And power is given to the court, where the parties agree, to vacate the judgment and thus revest title in the property owner. In line with Rule 21, the court may at any time drop a defendant who has been unnecessarily or improperly joined as where it develops that he has no interest.

Note to Subdivision (j). Whatever the substantive law is concerning the necessity of making a deposit will continue to govern. For statutory provisions concerning deposit in court in condemnation proceedings by the United States, see § 258a of [former] Title 40; § 594 of Title 33; acquisition of title and possession statutes referred to in note to subdivision (a), supra. If the plaintiff is invoking the state's power of eminent domain the necessity of deposit will be governed by the state law. For discussion of such law, see 1 Nichols, Eminent Domain, 2d ed. 1917, §§ 209 to 216. For discussion of the function of deposit and the power of the court to enter judgment in cases both of deficiency and overpayment, see *United States v. Miller*, 1943, 63 S.Ct. 276, 317 U.S. 369, 87 L.Ed. 336, 147 A.L.R. 55, rehearing denied 63 S.Ct. 557, 318 U.S. 798, 87 L.Ed. 1162 (judgment in favor of plaintiff for overpayment ordered).

The court is to make distribution of the deposit as promptly as the facts of the case warrant. See also subdivision (c)(2).

Note to Subdivision (k). While the overwhelming number of cases that will be brought in the federal courts under this rule will be actions involving the federal power of eminent domain, a small percentage of cases may be instituted in the federal court or removed thereto on the basis of diversity or alienage which will involve the power of eminent domain under the law of a state. See *Boom Co. v. Patterson*, 1878, 98 U.S. 403, 25 L.Ed. 206; *Searl v. School District No. 2*, 1888, 8 S.Ct. 460, 124 U.S. 197, 31 L.Ed. 415; *Madisonville Traction Co. v. Saint Bernard Mining Co.*, 1905, 25 S.Ct. 251, 196 U.S. 239, 49 L.Ed. 462. In the Madisonville case, and in cases cited therein, it has been held that condemnation actions brought by state corporations in the exercise of a power delegated by the state might be governed by procedure prescribed by the laws of the United States, whether the cases were begun in or removed to the federal court. See, also, *Franzen v. Chicago, M. & St. P. Ry. Co.*, C.C.A.7th, 1921, 278 F. 370, 372.

Any condition affecting the substantial right of a litigant attached by state law is to be observed and enforced, such as making a deposit in court where the power of eminent domain is conditioned upon so doing. (See also subdivision (j). Subject to this qualification, subdivision (k) provides that in cases involving the state power of eminent domain, the practice prescribed by other subdivisions of Rule 71A shall govern.

Note to Subdivision (*l*). Since the condemnor will normally be the prevailing party and since he should not recover his costs against the property owner, Rule 54(d), which provides generally that costs shall go to the prevailing party, is made inapplicable. Without attempting to state what the rule on costs is, the effect of subdivision (*l*) is that costs shall be awarded in accordance with the law that has developed in condemnation cases. This has been summarized as follows: "Costs of condemnation proceedings are not assessable against the condemnee, unless by stipulation he agrees to assume some or all of them. Such normal expenses of the proceeding as bills for publication of notice, commissioners' fees, the cost of transporting commissioners and jurors to take a view, fees for attorneys to represent defendants who have failed to answer, and witness' fees, are properly charged to the government, though not taxed as costs. Similarly, if it is necessary that a conveyance be executed by a commissioner, the United States pay his fees and those for recording the deed. However, the distribution of the award is a matter in which the United States has no legal interest. Expenses incurred in ascertaining the identity of distributees and deciding between conflicting claimants are properly chargeable against the award, not against the United States, although United States attorneys are expected to aid the court in such matters as amici curiae." Lands Division Manual 861. For other discussion and citation, see *Grand River Dam Authority v. Jarvis*, C.C.A.10th, 1942, 124 F.2d 914. Costs may not be taxed against the United States except to the extent permitted by law. *United States v. 125.71 Acres of Land in Loyalhanna Tp., Westmoreland County, Pa.*, D.C.Pa.1944, 54 F.Supp. 193; Lands Division Manual 859. Even if it were thought desirable to allow the property owner's costs to be taxed against the United States, this is a matter for legislation and not court rule.

1963 Amendment

This amendment conforms to the amendment of Rule 4(f).

1985 Amendment

Rule 71A(h) provides that except when Congress has provided otherwise, the issue of just compensation in a condemnation case may be tried by a jury if one of the parties so demands, unless the court in its discretion orders the issue determined by a commission of three persons. In 1980, the Comptroller General of the United States in a Report to Congress recommended that use of the commission procedure should be encouraged in order to improve and expedite the trial of condemnation cases. The Report noted that long delays were being caused in many districts by such factors as crowded dockets, the precedence given criminal cases, the low priority accorded condemnation matters, and the high turnover of Assistant United States Attorneys. The Report concluded that revising Rule 71A to make the use of the commission procedure more attractive might alleviate the situation.

Accordingly, Rule 71A(h) is being amended in a number of respects designed to assure the quality and utility of a Rule 71A commission. First, the amended Rule will give the court discretion to appoint, in addition to the three members of a commission, up to two additional persons as alternate commissioners who would hear the case and be available, at any time up to the filing of the decision by the three-member commission, to replace any commissioner who becomes unable or disqualified to continue. The discretion to appoint alternate commissioners can be particularly useful in protracted cases, avoiding expensive retrials that have been required in some cases because of the death or disability of a commissioner. Prior to replacing a commissioner an alternate would not be present at, or participate in, the commission's deliberations.

Second, the amended Rule requires the court, before appointment, to advise the parties of the identity and qualifications of each prospective commissioner and alternate. The court then may authorize the examination of prospective appointees by the parties and each party has the right to challenge for cause. The objective is to insure that unbiased and competent commissioners are appointed.

The amended Rule does not prescribe a qualification standard for appointment to a commission, although it is understood that only persons possessing background and ability to appraise real estate valuation testimony and to award fair and just compensation on the basis thereof would be appointed. In most situations the chairperson should be a lawyer and all members should have some background qualifying them to weigh proof of value in the real estate field and, when possible, in the particular real estate market embracing the land in question.

The amended Rule should give litigants greater confidence in the commission procedure by affording them certain rights to participate in the appointment of commission members that are roughly comparable to the practice with regard to jury selection. This is accomplished by giving the court permission to allow the parties to examine prospective commissioners and by recognizing the right of each party to object to the appointment of any person for cause.

1987 Amendment

The amendments are technical. No substantive change is intended.

1988 Amendment

The amendment is technical. No substantive change is intended.

1993 Amendments

The references to the subdivisions of Rule 4 are deleted in light of the revision of that rule.

2003 Amendments

The references to specific subdivisions of Rule 53 are deleted or revised to reflect amendments of Rule 53.

Rule 72. Magistrate Judges; Pretrial Orders

(a) Nondispositive Matters. A magistrate judge to whom a pretrial matter not dispositive of a claim or defense of a party is referred to hear and determine shall promptly conduct such proceedings as are required and when appropriate enter into the record a written order setting forth the disposition of the matter. Within 10 days after being served with a copy of the magistrate judge's order, a party may serve and file objections to the order; a party may not thereafter assign as error a defect in the magistrate judge's order to which objection was not timely made. The district judge to whom the case is assigned shall consider such objections and shall modify or set aside any portion of the magistrate judge's order found to be clearly erroneous or contrary to law.

(b) Dispositive Motions and Prisoner Petitions. A magistrate judge assigned without consent of the parties to hear a pretrial matter dispositive of a claim or defense of a party or a prisoner petition challenging the conditions of confinement shall promptly conduct such proceedings as are required. A record shall be made of all evidentiary proceedings before the magistrate judge, and a record may be made of such other proceedings as the magistrate judge deems necessary. The magistrate judge shall enter into the record a recommendation for disposition of the matter, including proposed findings of fact when appropriate. The clerk shall forthwith mail copies to all parties.

A party objecting to the recommended disposition of the matter shall promptly arrange for the transcription of the record, or portions of it as all parties may agree upon or the magistrate judge deems sufficient, unless the district judge otherwise directs. Within 10 days after being served with a copy of the recommended disposition, a party may serve and file specific, written objections to the proposed findings and recommendations. A party may respond to another party's objections within 10 days after being served with a copy thereof. The district judge to whom the case is assigned shall make a de novo determination upon the record, or after additional evidence, of any portion of the magistrate judge's disposition to which specific written objection has been made in accordance with this rule. The district judge may accept, reject, or modify the recommended decision, receive further evidence, or recommit the matter to the magistrate judge with instructions.

(Added Apr. 28, 1983, eff. Aug. 1, 1983, and amended Apr. 30, 1991, eff. Dec. 1, 1991; Apr. 22, 1993, eff. Dec. 1, 1993.)

ADVISORY COMMITTEE NOTES

1983 Addition

Subdivision (a). This subdivision addresses court-ordered referrals of nondispositive matters under 28 U.S.C. § 636(b)(1)(A). The rule calls for a written order of the magistrate's disposition to preserve the record and facilitate review. An oral order read into the record by the magistrate will satisfy this requirement.

No specific procedures or timetables for raising objections to the magistrate's rulings on nondispositive matters are set forth in the Magistrates Act. The rule fixes a 10-day period in order to avoid uncertainty and provide uniformity that will eliminate the confusion that might arise if different periods

were prescribed by local rule in different districts. It also is contemplated that a party who is successful before the magistrate will be afforded an opportunity to respond to objections raised to the magistrate's ruling.

The last sentence of subdivision (a) specifies that reconsideration of a magistrate's order, as provided for in the Magistrates Act, shall be by the district judge to whom the case is assigned. This rule does not restrict experimentation by the district courts under 28 U.S.C. § 636(b)(3) involving references of matters other than pretrial matters, such as appointment of counsel, taking of default judgments, and acceptance of jury verdicts when the judge is unavailable.

Subdivision (b). This subdivision governs court-ordered referrals of dispositive pretrial matters and prisoner petitions challenging conditions of confinement, pursuant to statutory authorization in 28 U.S.C. § 636(b)(1)(B). This rule does not extend to habeas corpus petitions, which are covered by the specific rules relating to proceedings under Sections 2254 and 2255 of Title 28.

This rule implements the statutory procedures for making objections to the magistrate's proposed findings and recommendations. The 10–day period, as specified in the statute, is subject to Rule 6(e) which provides for an additional 3–day period when service is made by mail. Although no specific provision appears in the Magistrates Act, the rule specifies a 10–day period for a party to respond to objections to the magistrate's recommendation.

Implementing the statutory requirements, the rule requires the district judge to whom the case is assigned to make a de novo determination of those portions of the report, findings, or recommendations to which timely objection is made. The term "de novo" signifies that the magistrate's findings are not protected by the clearly erroneous doctrine, but does not indicate that a second evidentiary hearing is required. See *United States v. Raddatz*, 417 [447] U.S. 667 (1980). See also Silberman, *Masters and Magistrates Part II: The American Analogue*, 50 N.Y.U. L.Rev. 1297, 1367 (1975). When no timely objection is filed, the court need only satisfy itself that there is no clear error on the face of the record in order to accept the recommendation. See *Campbell v. United States Dist. Court*, 501 F.2d 196, 206 (9th Cir.1974), cert. denied, 419 U.S. 879, quoted in House Report No. 94–1609, 94th Cong.2d Sess. (1976) at 3. Compare *Park Motor Mart, Inc. v. Ford Motor Co.*, 616 F.2d 603 (1st Cir.1980). Failure to make timely objection to the magistrate's report prior to its adoption by the district judge may constitute a waiver of appellate review of the district judge's order. *See United States v. Walters*, 638 F.2d 947 (6th Cir.1981).

1991 Amendment

This amendment is intended to eliminate a discrepancy in measuring the 10 days for serving and filing objections to a magistrate's action under subdivisions (a) and (b) of this Rule. The rule as promulgated in 1983 required objections to the magistrate's handling of nondispositive matters to be served and filed within 10 days of entry of the order, but required objections to dispositive motions to be made within 10 days of being served with a copy of the recommended disposition. Subdivision (a) is here amended to conform to subdivision (b) to avoid any confusion or technical defaults, particularly in connection with magistrate orders that rule on both dispositive and nondispositive matters.

The amendment is also intended to assure that objections to magistrate's orders that are not timely made shall not be considered. *Compare* Rule 51.

1993 Amendments

This revision is made to conform the rule to changes made by the Judicial Improvements Act of 1990.

HISTORICAL NOTES

Change of Name

Reference to United States magistrate or to magistrate deemed to refer to United States magistrate judge pursuant to section 321 of Pub.L. 101–650, set out as a note under section 631 of this title.

Rule 73.   Magistrate Judges; Trial by Consent and Appeal Options

(a) Powers; Procedure. When specially designated to exercise such jurisdiction by local rule or order of the district court and when all parties consent thereto, a magistrate judge may exercise the authority provided by Title 28, U.S.C. § 636(c) and may conduct any or all proceedings, including a jury or nonjury trial, in a civil case. A record of the proceedings shall be made in accordance with the requirements of Title 28, U.S.C. § 636(c)(5).

(b) Consent. When a magistrate judge has been designated to exercise civil trial jurisdiction, the clerk shall give written notice to the parties of their opportunity to consent to the exercise by a magistrate judge of civil jurisdiction over the case, as authorized by Title 28, U.S.C. § 636(c). If, within the period specified by local rule, the parties agree to a magistrate judge's exercise of such authority, they shall execute and file a joint form of consent or separate forms of consent setting forth such election.

A district judge, magistrate judge, or other court official may again advise the parties of the availability of the magistrate judge, but, in so doing, shall also advise the parties that they are free to withhold consent without adverse substantive consequences. A district judge or magistrate judge shall not be informed of a party's response to the clerk's notification, unless all parties have consented to the referral of the matter to a magistrate judge.

The district judge, for good cause shown on the judge's own initiative, or under extraordinary circumstances shown by a party, may vacate a reference of a civil matter to a magistrate judge under this subdivision.

(c) Appeal. In accordance with Title 28, U.S.C. § 636(c)(3), appeal from a judgment entered upon direction of a magistrate judge in proceedings under this rule will lie to the court of appeals as it would from a judgment of the district court.

[(d) Optional Appeal Route.] **(Abrogated, April 11, 1997, eff. Dec. 1, 1997)**

(Added Apr. 28, 1983, eff. Aug. 1, 1983, and amended Mar. 2, 1987, eff. Aug. 1, 1987; Apr. 22, 1993, eff. Dec. 1, 1993; Apr. 11, 1997, eff. Dec. 1, 1997.)

ADVISORY COMMITTEE NOTES
1983 Addition

Subdivision (a). This subdivision implements the broad authority of the 1979 amendments to the Magistrates Act, 28 U.S.C. § 636(c), which permit a magistrate to sit in lieu of a district judge and exercise civil jurisdiction over a case, when the parties consent. See McCabe, *The Federal Magistrate Act of 1979*, 16 Harv.J.Legis. 343, 364–79 (1979). In order to exercise this jurisdiction, a magistrate must be specially designated under 28 U.S.C. § 636(c)(1) by the district court or courts he serves. The only exception to a magistrate's exercise of civil jurisdiction, which includes the power to conduct jury and nonjury trials and decide dispositive motions, is the contempt power. A hearing on contempt is to be conducted by the district judge upon certification of the facts and an order to show cause by the magistrate. See 28 U.S.C. § 639(e). In view of 28 U.S.C. § 636(c)(1) and this rule, it is unnecessary to amend Rule 58 to provide that the decision of a magistrate is a "decision by the court" for the purposes of that rule and a "final decision of the district court" for purposes of 28 U.S.C. § 1291 governing appeals.

Subdivision (b). This subdivision implements the blind consent provision of 28 U.S.C. § 636(c)(2) and is designed to ensure that neither the judge nor the magistrate attempts to induce a party to consent to reference of a civil matter under this rule to a magistrate. See House Rep. No. 96–444, 96th Cong. 1st Sess. 8 (1979).

The rule opts for a uniform approach in implementing the consent provision by directing the clerk to notify the parties of their opportunity to elect to proceed before a magistrate and by requiring the execution and filing of a consent form or forms setting forth the election. However, flexibility at the local level is preserved in that local rules will determine how notice shall be communicated to the parties, and local rules will specify the time period within which an election must be made.

The last paragraph of subdivision (b) reiterates the provision in 28 U.S.C. § 636(c)(6) for vacating a reference to the magistrate.

Subdivision (c). Under 28 U.S.C. § 636(c)(3), the normal route of appeal from the judgment of a magistrate—the only route that will be available unless the parties otherwise agree in advance—is an appeal by the aggrieved party "directly to the appropriate United States court of appeals from the judgment of the magistrate in the same manner as an appeal from any other judgment of a district court." The quoted statutory language indicates Congress' intent that the same procedures and standards of appealability that govern appeals from district court judgments govern appeals from magistrates' judgments.

Subdivision (d). 28 U.S.C. § 636(c)(4) offers parties who consent to the exercise of civil jurisdiction by a magistrate an alternative appeal route to that provided in subdivision (c) of this rule. This optional appellate route was provided by Congress in recognition of the fact that not all civil cases warrant the same appellate treatment. In cases where the amount in controversy is not great and there are no difficult questions of law to be resolved, the parties may desire to avoid the expense and delay of appeal to the court of appeals by electing an appeal to the district judge. See McCabe, *The Federal Magistrate Act of 1979*, 16 Harv.J.Legis, 343, 388 (1979). This subdivision provides that the parties may elect the optional appeal route at the time of reference to a magistrate. To this end, the notice by the clerk under subdivision (b) of this rule shall explain the appeal option and the corollary restriction on review by the court of appeals. This approach will avoid later claims of lack of consent to the avenue of appeal. The choice of the alternative appeal route to the judge of the district court should be made by the parties in their forms of consent. Special appellate rules to govern appeals from a magistrate to a district judge appear in new Rules 74 through 76.

1987 Amendment

The amendment is technical. No substantive change is intended.

1993 Amendments

This revision is made to conform the rule to changes made by the Judicial Improvements Act of 1990. The Act requires that, when being reminded of the availability of a magistrate judge, the parties be advised that withholding of consent will have no "adverse substantive consequences." They may, however, be advised if the withholding of consent will have the adverse procedural consequence of a potential delay in trial.

1997 Amendments

The Federal Courts Improvement Act of 1996 repealed the former provisions of 28 U.S.C. § 636(c)(4) and (5) that enabled parties that had agreed to trial before a magistrate judge to agree also that appeal should be taken to the district court. Rule 73 is amended to conform to this change. Rules 74, 75, and 76 are abrogated for the same reason. The portions of Form 33 and Form 34 that referred to appeals to the district court also are deleted.

HISTORICAL NOTES

Change of Name

Reference to United States magistrate or to magistrate deemed to refer to United States magistrate judge pursuant to section 321 of Pub.L. 101–650, set out as a note under section 631 of this title.

[Rule 74. Method of Appeal From Magistrate Judge to District Judge Under Title 28, U.S.C. § 636(c)(4) and Rule 73(d)] (Abrogated April 11, 1997, eff. Dec. 1, 1997)

ADVISORY COMMITTEE NOTES

1997 Amendment

Rule 74 is abrogated for the reasons described in the Note to Rule 73.

[Rule 75. Proceedings on Appeal From Magistrate Judge to District Judge Under Rule 73(d)] (Abrogated April 11, 1997, eff. Dec. 1, 1997)

ADVISORY COMMITTEE NOTES

1997 Amendment

Rule 75 is abrogated for the reasons described in the Note to Rule 73.

[Rule 76. Judgment of the District Judge on the Appeal Under Rule 73(d) and Costs] (Abrogated April 11, 1997, eff. Dec. 1, 1997)

ADVISORY COMMITTEE NOTES

1997 Amendment

Rule 76 is abrogated for the reasons described in the Note to Rule 73.

[IX. APPEALS [1] (Abrogated)]

[1] Another chapter IX is set out ante.

HISTORICAL NOTES

Prior Provisions

The heading "IX. APPEALS" and Rules 72 to 76, formerly constituting the provisions of IX, were abrogated Dec. 4, 1967, effective July 1, 1968. Former Rules 72 to 76 were the civil rules relating to appeals, the provisions of which, except for Rule 73(h), were transferred to and covered by the Federal Rules of Appellate Procedure and (in the case of Rule 72) the Rules of the Supreme Court. The substance of Rule 73(h) was transferred to Rule 9(h) of these Rules.

X. DISTRICT COURTS AND CLERKS

Rule 77. District Courts and Clerks

(a) District Courts Always Open. The district courts shall be deemed always open for the purpose of filing any pleading or other proper paper, of issuing and returning mesne and final process, and of making and directing all interlocutory motions, orders, and rules.

(b) Trials and Hearings; Orders in Chambers. All trials upon the merits shall be conducted in open court and so far as convenient in a regular court room. All other acts or proceedings may be done or conducted by a judge in chambers, without the attendance of the clerk or other court officials and at any place either within or without the district; but no hearing, other than one ex parte, shall be conducted outside the district without the consent of all parties affected thereby.

(c) Clerk's Office and Orders by Clerk. The clerk's office with the clerk or a deputy in attendance shall be open during business hours on all days except Saturdays, Sundays, and legal holidays, but a district court may provide by local rule or order that its clerk's office shall be open for specified hours on Saturdays or particular legal holidays other than New Year's Day, Birthday of Martin Luther King, Jr., Washington's Birthday, Memorial Day, Independence Day, Labor Day, Columbus Day, Veterans Day, Thanksgiving Day, and Christmas Day. All motions and applications in the clerk's office for issuing mesne process, for issuing final process to enforce and execute judgments, for entering defaults or judgments by default, and for other proceedings which do not require allowance or order of the court are grantable of course by the clerk; but the clerk's action may be suspended or altered or rescinded by the court upon cause shown.

(d) Notice of Orders or Judgments. Immediately upon the entry of an order or judgment the clerk shall serve a notice of the entry in the manner provided for in Rule 5(b) upon each party who is not in default for failure to appear, and shall make a note in the docket of the service. Any party may in addition serve a notice of such entry in the manner provided in Rule 5(b) for the service of papers. Lack of notice of the entry by the clerk does not affect the time to appeal or relieve or authorize the court to relieve a party for failure to appeal within the time allowed, except as permitted in Rule 4(a) of the Federal Rules of Appellate Procedure.

(As amended Dec. 27, 1946, eff. Mar. 19, 1948; Jan. 21, 1963, eff. July 1, 1963; Dec. 4, 1967, eff. July 1, 1968; Mar. 1, 1971, eff. July 1, 1971; Mar. 2, 1987, eff. Aug. 1, 1987; Apr. 30, 1991, eff. Dec. 1, 1991; Apr. 23, 2001, eff. Dec. 1, 2001.)

ADVISORY COMMITTEE NOTES

1937 Adoption

This rule states the substance of U.S.C., Title 28, § 452, formerly § 13 (Courts open as courts of admiralty and equity). Compare [former] Equity Rules 1 (District Court Always Open For Certain Purposes—Orders at Chambers), 2 (Clerk's Office Always Open, Except, Etc.), 4 (Notice of Orders), and 5 (Motions Grantable of Course by Clerk).

1946 Amendment

Note. Rule 77(d) has been amended to avoid such situations as the one arising in *Hill v. Hawes*, 1944, 64 S.Ct. 334, 320 U.S. 520, 88 L.Ed. 283. In that case, an action instituted in the District Court for the District of Columbia, the clerk failed to give notice of the entry of a judgment for defendant

as required by Rule 77(d). The time for taking an appeal then was 20 days under Rule 10 of the Court of Appeals (later enlarged by amendment to thirty days), and due to lack of notice of the entry of judgment the plaintiff failed to file his notice of appeal within the prescribed time. On this basis the trial court vacated the original judgment and then re-entered it, whereupon notice of appeal was filed. The Court of Appeals dismissed the appeal as taken too late. The Supreme Court, however, held that although rule 77(d) did not purport to attach any consequence to the clerk's failure to give notice as specified, the terms of the rule were such that the appellant was entitled to rely on it, and the trial court in such a case, in the exercise of a sound discretion, could vacate the former judgment and enter a new one, so that the appeal would be within the allowed time.

Because of Rule 6(c), which abolished the old rule that the expiration of the term ends a court's power over its judgment, the effect of the decision in *Hill v. Hawes* is to give the district court power, in its discretion and without time limit, and long after the term may have expired, to vacate a judgment and reenter it for the purpose of reviving the right of appeal. This seriously affects the finality of judgments. See also proposed Rule 6(c) and Note; proposed Rule 60(b) and Note; and proposed Rule 73(a) and Note.

Rule 77(d) as amended makes it clear that notification by the clerk of the entry of a judgment has nothing to do with the starting of the time for appeal; that time starts to run from the date of entry of judgment and not from the date of notice of the entry. Notification by the clerk is merely for the convenience of litigants. And lack of such notification in itself has no effect upon the time for appeal; but in considering an application for extension of time for appeal as provided in Rule 73(a), the court may take into account, as one of the factors affecting its decision, whether the clerk failed to give notice as provided in Rule 77(d) or the party failed to receive the clerk's notice. It need not, however, extend the time for appeal merely because the clerk's notice was not sent or received. It would, therefore, be entirely unsafe for a party to rely on absence of notice from the clerk of the entry of a judgment, or to rely on the adverse party's failure to serve notice of the entry of a judgment. Any party may, of course, serve timely notice of the entry of a judgment upon the adverse party and thus preclude a successful application, under Rule 73(a), for the extension of the time for appeal.

1963 Amendment

Subdivision (c). The amendment authorizes closing of the clerk's office on Saturday as far as civil business is concerned. However, a district court may require its clerk's office to remain open for specified hours on Saturdays or "legal holidays" other than those enumerated ("Legal holiday" is defined in Rule 6(a), as amended.) The clerk's offices of many district courts have customarily remained open on some of the days appointed as holidays by State law. This practice could be continued by local rule or order.

Subdivision (d). This amendment conforms to the amendment of Rule 5(a). See the Advisory Committee's Note to that amendment.

1968 Amendment

The provisions of Rule 73(a) are incorporated in Rule 4(a) of the Federal Rules of Appellate Procedure.

1971 Amendment

The amendment adds Columbus Day to the list of legal holidays. See the Note accompanying the amendment of Rule 6(a).

1987 Amendment

The amendments are technical. No substantive change is intended. The Birthday of Martin Luther King, Jr. is added to the list of national holidays in Rule 77.

1991 Amendment

This revision is a companion to the concurrent amendment to Rule 4 of the Federal Rules of Appellate Procedure. The purpose of the revisions is to permit district courts to ease strict sanctions now imposed on appellants whose notices of appeal are filed late because of their failure to receive notice of entry of a judgment. See, e.g. *Tucker v. Commonwealth Land Title Ins. Co.*, 800 F.2d 1054 (11th Cir.1986); *Ashby Enterprises, Ltd. v. Weitzman, Dym & Associates*, 780 F.2d 1043 (D.C.Cir.1986); *In re OPM Leasing Services, Inc.*, 769 F.2d 911 (2d Cir.1985); *Spika v. Village of Lombard, Ill.*, 763 F.2d 282 (7th Cir.1985); *Hall v. Community Mental Health Center of Beaver County*, 772 F.2d 42 (3d Cir.1985); *Wilson v. Atwood v. Stark*, 725 F.2d 255 (5th Cir. en banc), cert. dismissed, 105 S.Ct. 17 (1984); *Case v. BASF Wyandotte*, 727 F.2d 1034 (Fed.Cir.1984), cert. denied, 105 S.Ct. 386 (1984); *Hensley v. Chesapeake & Ohio R.R. Co.*, 651 F.2d 226 (4th Cir.1981); *Buckeye Cellulose Corp. v. Electric Construction Co.*, 569 F.2d 1036 (8th Cir.1978).

Failure to receive notice may have increased in frequency with the growth in the caseload in the clerks' offices. The present strict rule imposes a duty on counsel to maintain contact with the court while a case is under submission. Such contact is more difficult to maintain if counsel is outside the district, as is increasingly common, and can be a burden to the court as well as counsel.

The effect of the revisions is to place a burden on prevailing parties who desire certainty that the time for appeal is running. Such parties can take the initiative to assure that their adversaries receive effective notice. An appropriate procedure for such notice is provided in Rule 5.

The revised rule lightens the responsibility but not the workload of the clerk's offices, for the duty of that office to give notice of entry of judgment must be maintained.

2001 Amendments

Rule 77(d) is amended to reflect changes in Rule 5(b). A few courts have experimented with serving Rule 77(d) notices by electronic means on parties who consent to this procedure. The success of these experiments warrants express authorization. Because service is made in the manner provided in Rule 5(b), party consent is required for service by electronic or other means described in Rule 5(b)(2)(D). The same provision is made for a party who wishes to ensure actual communication of the Rule 77(d) notice by also serving notice.

Changes Made After Publication and Comments

Rule 77(d) was amended to correct an oversight in the published version. The clerk is to note "service," not "mailing," on the docket.

HISTORICAL NOTES

References in Text

The Federal Rules of Appellate Procedure, referred to in subd. (d), are set out in Title 28, U.S.C.A., Federal Rules of Appellate Procedure.

Rule 78. Motion Day

Unless local conditions make it impracticable, each district court shall establish regular times and places, at intervals sufficiently frequent for the prompt dispatch of business, at which motions requiring notice and hearing may be heard and disposed of; but the judge at any time or place and on such notice, if any, as the judge considers reasonable may make orders for the advancement, conduct, and hearing of actions.

To expedite its business, the court may make provision by rule or order for the submission and determination of motions without oral hearing upon brief written statements of reasons in support and opposition.

(As amended Mar. 2, 1987, eff. Aug. 1, 1987.)

ADVISORY COMMITTEE NOTES

1937 Adoption

Compare [former] Equity Rule 6 (Motion Day) with the first paragraph of this rule. The second paragraph authorizes a procedure found helpful for the expedition of business in some of the Federal and State courts. See Rule 43(e) of these rules dealing with evidence on motions. Compare *Civil Practice Rules of the Municipal Court of Chicago* (1935), Rules 269, 270, 271.

1987 Amendment

The amendment is technical. No substantive change is intended.

Rule 79. Books and Records Kept by the Clerk and Entries Therein

(a) Civil Docket. The clerk shall keep a book known as "civil docket" of such form and style as may be prescribed by the Director of the Administrative Office of the United States Courts with the approval of the Judicial Conference of the United States, and shall enter therein each civil action to which these rules are made applicable. Actions shall be assigned consecutive file numbers. The file number of each action shall be noted on the folio of the docket whereon the first entry of the action is made. All papers filed with the clerk, all process issued and returns made thereon, all appearances, orders, verdicts, and judgments shall be entered chronologically in the civil docket on the folio assigned to the action and shall be marked with its file number. These entries shall be brief but shall show the nature of each paper filed or writ issued and the substance of each order or judgment of the court and of the returns showing execution of process. The entry of an order or judgment shall show the date the entry is made. When in an action trial by jury has been properly demanded or ordered the clerk shall enter the word "jury" on the folio assigned to that action.

(b) Civil Judgments and Orders. The clerk shall keep, in such form and manner as the Director of the Administrative Office of the United States Courts with the approval of the Judicial Conference of the United States may prescribe, a correct copy of every final judgment or appealable order, or order affecting title to or lien upon real or personal property, and any other order which the court may direct to be kept.

(c) Indices; Calendars. Suitable indices of the civil docket and of every civil judgment and order referred to in subdivision (b) of this rule shall be kept by the clerk under the direction of the court. There shall be prepared under the direction of the court calendars of all actions ready for trial, which shall distinguish "jury actions" from "court actions."

(d) Other Books and Records of the Clerk. The clerk shall also keep such other books and records as may be required from time to time by the Director of the Administrative Office of the United States Courts with the approval of the Judicial Conference of the United States.

(As amended Dec. 27, 1946, eff. Mar. 19, 1948; Dec. 29, 1948, eff. Oct. 20, 1949; Jan. 21, 1963, eff. July 1, 1963.)

ADVISORY COMMITTEE NOTES

1937 Adoption

Compare [former] Equity Rule 3 (Books Kept by Clerk and Entries Therein). In connection with this rule, see also the following statutes of the United States:

U.S.C., Title 5 former:

§ 301 [See Title 28, § 526] (Officials for investigation of official acts, records and accounts of marshals, attorneys, clerks of courts, United States commissioners, referees and trustees)

§ 318 [former] (Accounts of district attorneys)

U.S.C., Title 28 former:

§ 556 [former] (Clerks of district courts; books open to inspection)

§ 567 [now 751] (Same; accounts)

§ 568 [now 751] (Same; reports and accounts of moneys received; dockets)

§ 813 [former] (Indices of judgment debtors to be kept by clerks)

And see "Instructions to United States Attorneys, Marshals, Clerks and Commissioners" issued by the Attorney General of the United States.

1946 Amendment

Note. Subdivision (a). The amendment substitutes the Director of the Administrative Office of the United States Courts, acting subject to the approval of the Judicial Conference of Senior Circuit Judges, in the place of the Attorney General as a consequence of and in accordance with the provisions of the act establishing the Administrative Office and transferring functions thereto. Act of August 7, 1939, c. 501, §§ 1 to 7, 53 Stat. 1223, 28 U.S.C.A. §§ 601 to 610, formerly §§ 444 to 450.

Subdivision (b). The change in this subdivision does not alter the nature of the judgments and orders to be recorded in permanent form but it does away with the express requirement that they be recorded in a book. This merely gives latitude for the preservation of court records in other than book form, if that shall seem advisable, and permits with the approval of the Judicial Conference the adoption of such modern, space-saving methods as microphotography. See *Proposed Improvements in the Administration of the Offices of Clerks of United States District Courts,* prepared by the Bureau of the Budget, 1941, 38–42. See also Rule 55, Federal Rules of Criminal Procedure.

Subdivision (c). The words "Separate and" have been deleted as unduly rigid. There is no sufficient reason for requiring that the indices in all cases be separate; on the contrary, the requirement frequently increases the labor of persons searching the records as well as the labor of the clerk's force preparing them. The matter should be left to administrative discretion.

The other changes in the subdivision merely conform with those made in subdivision (b) of the rule.

Subdivision (d). Subdivision (d) is a new provision enabling the Administrative Office, with the approval of the Judicial Conference, to carry out any improvements in clerical procedure with respect to books and records which may be deemed advisable. See report cited in Note to subdivision (b), supra.

1948 Amendment

The amendment effective October 1949, substituted the name, "Judicial Conference of the United States," for "Judicial Conference of Senior Circuit Judges," in the first sentence of subdivision (a), and in subdivisions (b) and (d).

1963 Amendment

The terminology is clarified without any change of the prescribed practice. See amended Rule 58, and the Advisory Committee's Note thereto.

Rule 80.   Stenographer; Stenographic Report or Transcript as Evidence

[(a) Abrogated (Dec. 27, 1946, eff. Mar. 19, 1948)].

[(b) Abrogated (Dec. 27, 1946, eff. Mar. 19, 1948)].

(c) Stenographic Report or Transcript as Evidence. Whenever the testimony of a witness at a trial or hearing which was stenographically reported is admissible in evidence at a later trial, it may be proved by the transcript thereof duly certified by the person who reported the testimony.

(As amended Dec. 27, 1946, eff. Mar. 19, 1948.)

Note to Subdivision (a). This follows substantially [former] Equity Rule 50 (Stenographer— Appointment— Fees). [This subdivision was abrogated. See amendment note of Advisory Committee below.]

Note to Subdivision (b). See *Reports of Conferences of Senior Circuit Judges with the Chief Justice of the United States* (1936), 22 A.B.A.J. 818, 819; (1937), 24 A.B.A.J. 75, 77. [This subdivision was abrogated. See amendment note of Advisory Committee below.]

Note to Subdivision (c). Compare Iowa Code (1935) § 11353.

1946 Amendment

Note. Subdivisions (a) and (b) of Rule 80 have been abrogated because of Public Law 222, 78th Cong., c. 3, 2d Sess., approved Jan. 20, 1944, 28 U.S.C. §§ 550, 604, 753, 1915, 1920, formerly § 9a, providing for the appointment of official stenographers for each district court, prescribing their duties, providing for the furnishing of transcripts, the taxation of the fees therefor as costs, and other related matters. This statute has now been implemented by Congressional appropriation available for the fiscal year beginning July 1, 1945.

Subdivision (c) of Rule 80 (Stenographic Report or Transcript as Evidence) has been retained unchanged.

XI. GENERAL PROVISIONS

Rule 81. Applicability in General

(a) To What Proceedings Applicable.

(1) These rules do not apply to prize proceedings in admiralty governed by Title 10, U.S.C., §§ 7651–7681. They do apply to proceedings in bankruptcy to the extent provided by the Federal Rules of Bankruptcy Procedure.

(2) These rules are applicable to proceedings for admission to citizenship, habeas corpus, and quo warranto, to the extent that the practice in such proceedings is not set forth in statutes of the United States, the Rules Governing Section 2254 Cases, or the Rules Governing Section 2255 Proceedings, and has heretofore conformed to the practice in civil actions.

(3) In proceedings under Title 9, U.S.C., relating to arbitration, or under the Act of May 20, 1926, ch. 347, § 9 (44 Stat. 585), U.S.C., Title 45, § 159, relating to boards of arbitration of railway labor disputes, these rules apply only to the extent that matters of procedure are not provided for in those statutes. These rules apply to proceedings to compel the giving of testimony or production of documents in accordance with a subpoena issued by an officer or agency of the United States under any statute of the United States except as otherwise provided by statute or by rules of the district court or by order of the court in the proceedings.

(4) These rules do not alter the method prescribed by the Act of February 18, 1922, ch. 57, § 2 (42 Stat. 388), U.S.C., Title 7, § 292; or by the Act of June 10, 1930, ch. 436, § 7 (46 Stat. 534), as amended, U.S.C., Title 7, § 499g(c), for instituting proceedings in the United States district courts to review orders of the Secretary of Agriculture; or prescribed by the Act of June 25, 1934, ch. 742, § 2 (48 Stat. 1214), U.S.C., Title 15, § 522, for instituting proceedings to review orders of the Secretary of the Interior; or prescribed by the Act of February 22, 1935, ch. 18, § 5 (49 Stat. 31), U.S.C., Title 15, § 715d(c), as extended, for instituting proceedings to review orders of petroleum control boards; but the conduct of such proceedings in the district courts shall be made to conform to these rules so far as applicable.

(5) These rules do not alter the practice in the United States district courts prescribed in the Act of July 5, 1935, ch. 372, §§ 9 and 10 (49 Stat. 453), as amended, U.S.C., Title 29, §§ 159 and 160, for beginning and conducting proceedings to enforce orders of the National Labor Relations Board; and in respects not covered by those statutes, the practice in the district courts shall conform to these rules so far as applicable.

(6) These rules apply to proceedings for enforcement or review of compensation orders under the Longshoremen's and Harbor Workers' Compensation Act, Act of March 4, 1927, c. 509, §§ 18, 21 (44 Stat. 1434, 1436), as amended, U.S.C., Title 33, §§ 918, 921, except to the extent that matters of procedure are provided for in that Act. The provisions for service by publication and for answer in proceedings to cancel certificates of citizenship under the Act of June 27, 1952, c. 477, Title III, c. 2, § 340 (66 Stat. 260), U.S.C., Title 8, § 1451, remain in effect.

[(7) Abrogated, effective Aug. 1, 1951. (Supreme Court Order, Apr. 30, 1951.)]

(b) Scire Facias and Mandamus. The writs of scire facias and mandamus are abolished. Relief heretofore available by mandamus or scire facias may be obtained by appropriate action or by appropriate motion under the practice prescribed in these rules.

(c) Removed Actions. These rules apply to civil actions removed to the United States district courts from the state courts and govern procedure after

removal.   Repleading is not necessary unless the
court so orders.   In a removed action in which the
defendant has not answered, the defendant shall answer or present the other defenses or objections
available under these rules within 20 days after the
receipt through service or otherwise of a copy of the
initial pleading setting forth the claim for relief upon
which the action or proceeding is based, or within 20
days after the service of summons upon such initial
pleading, then filed, or within 5 days after the filing of
the petition for removal, whichever period is longest.
If at the time of removal all necessary pleadings have
been served, a party entitled to trial by jury under
Rule 38 shall be accorded it, if the party's demand
therefor is served within 10 days after the petition for
removal is filed if the party is the petitioner, or if not
the petitioner within 10 days after service on the party
of the notice of filing the petition.   A party who, prior
to removal, has made an express demand for trial by
jury in accordance with state law, need not make a
demand after removal.   If state law applicable in the
court from which the case is removed does not require
the parties to make express demands in order to claim
trial by jury, they need not make demands after
removal unless the court directs that they do so within
a specified time if they desire to claim trial by jury.
The court may make this direction on its own motion
and shall do so as a matter of course at the request of
any party.   The failure of a party to make demand as
directed constitutes a waiver by that party of trial by
jury.

**[(d) Abrogated, effective Oct. 20, 1949. (Supreme
Court Order, Dec. 29, 1948)].**

(e) Law Applicable.   Whenever in these rules the
law of the state in which the district court is held is
made applicable, the law applied in the District of
Columbia governs proceedings in the United States
District Court for the District of Columbia.   When the
word "state" is used, it includes, if appropriate, the
District of Columbia.   When the term "statute of the
United States" is used, it includes, so far as concerns
proceedings in the United States District Court for
the District of Columbia, any Act of Congress locally
applicable to and in force in the District of Columbia.
When the law of a state is referred to, the word "law"
includes the statutes of that state and the state judicial decisions construing them.

(f) References to Officer of the United States.
Under any rule in which reference is made to an
officer or agency of the United States, the term
"officer" includes a district director of internal revenue, a former district director or collector of internal
revenue, or the personal representative of a deceased
district director or collector of internal revenue.
(As amended Dec. 28, 1939, eff. Apr. 3, 1941; Dec. 27, 1946,
eff. Mar. 19, 1948; Dec. 29, 1948, eff. Oct. 20, 1949; Apr. 30,
1951, eff. Aug. 1, 1951; Jan. 21, 1963, eff. July 1, 1963; Feb.

28, 1966, eff. July 1, 1966; Dec. 4, 1967, eff. July 1, 1968;
Mar. 1, 1971, eff. July 1, 1971; Mar. 2, 1987, eff. Aug. 1, 1987;
Apr. 23, 2001, eff. Dec. 1, 2001; Apr. 29, 2002, eff. Dec. 1,
2002.)

ADVISORY COMMITTEE NOTES
1937 Adoption

Note to Subdivision (a).   Paragraph (1): Compare the
enabling act, Act of June 19, 1934, U.S.C., Title 28, § 2072,
formerly § 723b (Rules in actions at law; Supreme Court
authorized to make) and § 2072, formerly § 723c (Union of
equity and action at law rules; power of Supreme Court).
For the application of these rules in bankruptcy and copyright proceedings, see Orders xxxvi and xxxvii in Bankruptcy
and Rule 1 of Rules of Practice and Procedure under § 25 of
the copyright act, Act of March 4, 1909, U.S.C., Title 17,
former § 25 [see 412, 501 et seq.]   (Infringement and rules
of procedure).

For examples of statutes which are preserved by paragraph (2) see: U.S.C., Title 8, [former] ch. 9 (Naturalization);
Title 28, former ch. 14 [now 153] (Habeas corpus); Title 28,
former §§ 377a to 377c [now D.C.Code, Title 16 § 3501 et
seq.] (Quo warranto); and such forfeiture statutes as U.S.C.,
Title 7, former § 116 (Misbranded seeds, confiscation), and
Title 21, § 334(b), formerly § 14 (Pure Food and Drug Act—
condemnation of adulterated or misbranded Food; procedure).   See also *443 Cans of Frozen Eggs Product v. U.S.,*
1912, 33 S.Ct. 50, 226 U.S. 172, 57 L.Ed. 174.

For examples of statutes which under paragraph (7) will
continue to govern procedure in condemnation cases, see
U.S.C. [former] Title 40, [former] § 258 (Condemnation of
realty for sites for public building, etc., procedure); U.S.C.,
Title 16, § 831x (Condemnation by Tennessee Valley Authority); U.S.C., [former] Title 40, § 120 (Acquisition of lands for
public use in District of Columbia); [former] Title 40, ch. 7
[now D.C.Code, Title 16, § 1301 et seq.] (Acquisition of lands
in District of Columbia for use of United States; condemnation).

Note to Subdivision (b).   Some statutes which will be
affected by this subdivision are;
U.S.C., Title 7:
§ 222 (Federal Trade Commission powers adopted for enforcement of Stockyards Act) (By reference to Title 15,
§ 49)
U.S.C., Title 15:
§ 49 (Enforcement of Federal Trade Commission orders
and antitrust laws)
§ 77t(c) (Enforcement of Securities and Exchange Commission orders and Securities Act of 1933)
§ 78u(f) (Same; Securities Exchange Act of 1934)
§ 79r(g) (Same; Public Utility Holding Company Act of
1935)
U.S.C., Title 16:
§ 820 (Proceedings in equity for revocation or to prevent
violations of license of Federal Power Commission licensee)
§ 825m(b) (Mandamus to compel compliance with Federal
Water Power Act, etc.)
U.S.C., Title 19:
§ 1333(c) (Mandamus to compel compliance with orders of
Tariff Commission, etc.)

U.S.C., Title 28, former:

§ 377 [now 1651] (Power to issue writs)

§ 572 [now 1923] (Fees, attorneys, solicitors and proctors)

§ 778 [former] (Death of parties; substitution of executor or administrator). Compare Rule 25(a) (Substitution of parties; death), and the note thereto.

U.S.C., Title 33:

§ 495 (Removal of bridges over navigable waters)

U.S.C., Title 45:

§ 88 (Mandamus against Union Pacific Railroad Company)

§ 153(p) (Mandamus to enforce orders of Adjustment Board under Railway Labor Act)

§ 185 (Same; National Air Transport Adjustment Board) (By reference to § 153)

U.S.C., Title 47:

§ 11 (Powers of Federal Communications Commission)

§ 401(a) (Enforcement of Federal Communications Act and orders of Commission)

§ 406 (Same; Compelling furnishing of facilities; mandamus)

U.S.C., Title 49:

§ 19a(l) [now 11703] (Mandamus to compel compliance with Interstate Commerce Act)

§ 20(9) [now 11703] (Jurisdiction to compel compliance with interstate commerce laws by mandamus)

For comparable provisions in state practice see Smith-Hurd Ill.Stats.c. 110, § 179 (1937); Calif.Code Civ.Proc. (Deering, 1937) § 802.

Note to Subdivision (c). Such statutes as the following dealing with the removal of actions are substantially continued and made subject to these rules:

U.S.C., Title 28 former:

§ 71 [now 1441, 1445, 1447] (Removal of suits from state courts)

§ 72 [now 1446, 1447] (Same; procedure)

§ 73 [former] (Same; suits under grants of land from different states)

§ 74 [now 1443, 1446, 1447] (Same; causes against persons denied civil rights)

§ 75 [now 1446] (Same; petitioner in actual custody of state court)

§ 76 [now 1442, 1446, 1447] (Same; suits and prosecutions against revenue officers)

§ 77 [now 1442] (Same; suits by aliens)

§ 78 [now 1449] (Same; copies of records refused by clerk of state court)

§ 79 [now 1450] (Same; previous attachment bonds or orders)

§ 80 [now 1359, 1447, 1919] (Same; dismissal or remand)

§ 81 [now 1447] (Same; proceedings in suits removed)

§ 82 [former] (Same; record; filing and return)

§ 83 [now 1447, 1448] (Service of process after removal)

U.S.C., Title 28, §§ 1446, 1447, formerly § 72, supra, however, is modified by shortening the time for pleading in removed actions.

Note to Subdivision (e). The last sentence of this subdivision modifies U.S.C., Title 28, § 1652, formerly § 725 (Laws of States as rules of decision) in so far as that statute

has been construed to govern matters of procedure and to exclude state judicial decisions relative thereto.

1946 Amendment

Note to Subdivision (a). Despite certain dicta to the contrary, *Lynn v. United States*, C.C.A.5th, 1940, 110 F.2d 586; *Mount Tivy Winery, Inc. v. Lewis*, N.D.Cal.1942, 42 F.Supp. 636, it is manifest that the rules apply to actions against the United States under the Tucker Act [28 U.S.C., §§ 41(20), 250, 251, 254, 257, 258, 287, 289, 292, 761–765 [now 791, 1346, 1401, 1402, 1491, 1493, 1496, 1501, 1503, 2071, 2072, 2411, 2412, 2501, 2506, 2509, 2510]]. See United States to use of *Foster Wheeler Corp. v. American Surety Co. of New York*, E.D.N.Y.1939, 25 F.Supp. 700; *Boerner v. United States*, E.D.N.Y.1939, 26 F.Supp. 769; *United States v. Gallagher*, C.C.A.9th, 1945, 151 F.2d 556. Rules 1 and 81 provide that the rules shall apply to all suits of a civil nature, whether cognizable as cases at law or in equity except those specifically excepted; and the character of the various proceedings excepted by express statement in Rule 81, as well as the language of the rules generally, shows that the term "civil action" [Rule 2] includes actions against the United States. Moreover, the rules in many places expressly make provision for the situation wherein the United States is a party as either plaintiff or defendant. See Rules 4(d)(4), 12(a), 13(d), 25(d), 37(f), 39(c), 45(c), 54(d), 55(e), 62(e), and 65(c). In *United States v. Sherwood*, 1941, 61 S.Ct. 767, 312 U.S. 584, 85 L.Ed. 1058, the Solicitor General expressly conceded in his brief for the United States that the rules apply to Tucker Act cases. The Solicitor General stated: "The Government, of course, recognizes that the Federal Rules of Civil Procedure apply to cases brought under the Tucker Act." (Brief for the United States, p. 31). Regarding *Lynn v. United States*, supra, the Solicitor General said: "In *Lynn v. United States* . . . the Circuit Court of Appeals for the Fifth Circuit went beyond the Government's contention there, and held that an action under the Tucker Act is neither an action at law nor a suit in equity and, seemingly, that the Federal Rules of Civil Procedure are, therefore, inapplicable. We think the suggestion is erroneous. Rules 4(d), 12(a), 39(c), and 55(e) expressly contemplate suits against the United States, and nothing in the enabling Act (48 Stat. 1064, 28 U.S.C. §§ 723b, 723c [see 2072]) suggests that the Rules are inapplicable to Tucker Act proceedings, which in terms are to accord with court rules and their subsequent modifications (Sec. 4, Act of March 3, 1887, 24 Stat. 505, 28 U.S.C. § 761 [see 2071, 2072])." (Brief for the United States, p. 31, n. 17.)

United States v. Sherwood, supra, emphasizes, however, that the application of the rules in Tucker Act cases affects only matters of procedure and does not operate to extend jurisdiction. See also Rule 82. In the Sherwood case, the New York Supreme Court, acting under § 795 of the New York Civil Practice Act, made an order, authorizing Sherwood, as a judgment creditor, to maintain a suit under the Tucker Act to recover damages from the United States for breach of its contract with the judgment debtor, Kaiser, for construction of a post office building. Sherwood brought suit against the United States and Kaiser in the District Court for the Eastern District of New York. The question before the United States Supreme Court was whether a United States District Court had jurisdiction to entertain a suit against the United States wherein private parties were joined as parties defendant. It was contended that either the Federal Rules of Civil Procedure or the Tucker Act, or both, embodied the consent of the United States to be sued in litigations in which issues between the plaintiff and third persons were to be adjudicated. Regarding the effect of the Federal Rules, the Court declared that nothing in the rules, so far as they may be applicable in Tucker Act cases, authorized the maintenance of any suit against the United States to which it had not otherwise consented. The matter involved was not one of procedure but of jurisdiction, the limits of which were marked by the consent of the United States to be sued. The jurisdiction thus limited is unaffected by the Federal Rules of Civil Procedure.

Subdivision (a)(2). The added sentence makes it clear that the rules have not superseded the requirements of U.S.C., Title 28, § 2253, formerly § 466. *Schenk v. Plummer,* C.C.A.9, 1940, 113 F.2d 726.

For correct application of the rules in proceedings for forfeiture of property for violation of a statute of the United States, such as under U.S.C., Title 22, § 405 (seizure of war materials intended for unlawful export) or U.S.C., Title 21, § 334(b) (Federal Food, Drug, and Cosmetic Act; formerly Title 21, U.S.C. § 14, Pure Food and Drug Act), see *Reynal v. United States,* C.C.A.5, 1945, 153 F.2d 929; *United States v. 108 Boxes of Cheddar Cheese,* S.D.Iowa 1943, 3 F.R.D. 40.

Subdivision (a)(3). The added sentence makes it clear that the rules apply to appeals from proceedings to enforce administrative subpoenas. See *Perkins v. Endicott Johnson Corp.,* C.C.A.2d 1942, 128 F.2d 208, affirmed on other grounds 63 S.Ct. 339, 317 U.S. 501, 87 L.Ed. 424; *Walling v. News Printing Inc.,* C.C.A.3, 1945, 148 F.2d 57; *McCrone v. United States,* 1939, 59 S.Ct. 685, 307 U.S. 61, 83 L.Ed. 1108. And, although the provision allows full recognition of the fact that the rigid application of the rules in the proceedings themselves may conflict with the summary determination desired, *Goodyear Tire & Rubber Co. v. National Relations Board,* C.C.A.6, 1941, 122 F.2d 450; *Cudahy Packing Co. v. National Labor Relations Board,* C.C.A.10, 1941, 117 F.2d 692, it is drawn so as to permit application of any of the rules in the proceedings whenever the district court deems them helpful. See, e.g., *Peoples Natural Gas Co. v. Federal Power Commission,* App.D.C.1942, 127 F.2d 153, certiorari denied 62 S.Ct. 1298, 316 U.S. 700, 86 L.Ed. 1769; *Martin v. Chandis Securities Co.,* C.C.A.9th, 1942, 128 F.2d 731. Compare the application of the rules in summary proceedings in bankruptcy under General Order 37. See 1 *Collier on Bankruptcy,* 14th ed. by Moore and Oglebay, 326–327; 2 Collier, op.cit.supra, 1401–1402; 3 Collier, op.cit.supra, 228–231; 4 Collier, op.cit.supra, 1199–1202.

Subdivision (a)(6). Section 405 of U.S.C., Title 8 originally referred to in the last sentence of paragraph (6), has been repealed and § 738 [now 1451], U.S.C., Title 8, has been enacted in its stead. The last sentence of paragraph (6) has, therefore, been amended in accordance with this change. The sentence has also been amended so as to refer directly to the statute regarding the provision of time for answer, thus avoiding any confusion attendant upon a change in the statute.

That portion of subdivision (a)(6) making the rules applicable to proceedings for enforcement or review of compensation orders under the Longshoremen's and Harbor Workers' Compensation Act [33 U.S.C. § 901 et seq.] was added by an amendment made pursuant to order of the Court, December 28, 1939, effective three months subsequent to the adjournment of the 76th Congress, January 3, 1941.

Subdivision (c). The change in subdivision (c) effects more speedy trials in removed actions. In some states many of the courts have only two terms a year. A case, if filed 20 days before a term, is returnable to that term, but if filed less than 20 days before a term, is returnable to the following term, which convenes six months later. Hence, under the original wording of Rule 81(c), where a case is filed less than 20 days before the term and is removed within a few days but before answer, it is possible for the defendant to delay interposing his answer or presenting his defenses by motion for six months or more. The rule as amended prevents this result.

Subdivision (f). The use of the phrase "the United States or an officer or agency thereof" in the rules (as e.g., in Rule 12(a) and amended Rule 73(a)) could raise the question of whether "officer" includes a collector of internal revenue, a former collector, or the personal representative of a deceased collector, against whom suits for tax refunds are frequently instituted. Difficulty might ensue for the reason that a suit against a collector or his representative has been held to be a personal action. *Sage v. United States,* 1919, 39 S.Ct. 415, 250 U.S. 33, 63 L.Ed. 828; *Smietanka v. Indiana Steel Co.,* 1921, 42 S.Ct. 1, 257 U.S. 1, 66 L.Ed. 99; *United States v. Nunnally Investment Co.,* 1942, 62 S.Ct. 1064, 316 U.S. 258, 86 L.Ed. 1455. The addition of subdivision (f) to Rule 81 dispels any doubts on the matter and avoids further litigation.

1948 Amendment

The amendment effective October 1949, substituted the words "United States District Court" for the words "District Court of the United States" in the last sentence of subdivision (a)(1) and in the first and third sentences of subdivision (e). The amendment substituted the words "United States district courts" in lieu of "district courts of the United States" in subdivision (a)(4) and (5) and in the first sentence of subdivision (c).

The amendment effective October 20, 1949, also made the following changes:

In subdivision (a)(1), the reference to "Title 17, U.S.C." was substituted for the reference to "the Act of March 4, 1909, c. 320, § 25 (35 Stat. 1081), as amended, U.S.C., Title 17, § 25."

In subdivision (a)(2), the reference to "Title 28, U.S.C., § 2253" was substituted for "U.S.C., Title 28, § 466."

In subdivision (a)(3), the reference in the first sentence to "Title 9, U.S.C.," was substituted for "the Act of February 12, 1925, c. 213 (43 Stat. 883), U.S.C., Title 9".

In subdivision (a)(5), the words "as amended" were inserted after the parenthetical citation of "(49 Stat. 453)," and after the citations of "Title 29, §§ 159 and 160," former references to subdivisions "(e), (g), and (i)" were deleted.

In subdivision (a)(6), after the words "These rules" at the beginning of the first sentence, the following words were deleted: "do not apply to proceedings under the Act of September 13, 1888, c. 1015, § 13 (25 Stat. 479), as amended, U.S.C., Title 8, [former] § 282, relating to deportation of Chinese; they". Also in the first sentence, after the parenthetical citation of "(44 Stat. 1434, 1436)," the words "as amended" were added. In the last sentence, the words

"October 14, 1940, c. 876, § 338 (54 Stat. 1158)" were inserted in lieu of the words "June 29, 1906, c. 3592, § 15 (34 Stat. 601), as amended."

In subdivision (c), the word "all" originally appearing in the first sentence between the words "govern" and "procedure" was deleted. In the third sentence, the portion beginning with the words "20 days after the receipt" and including all the remainder of that sentence was substituted for the following language: "the time allowed for answer by the law of the state or within 5 days after the filing of the transcript of the record in the district court of the United States, whichever period is longer, but in any event within 20 days after the filing of the transcript". In the fourth or last sentence, after the words at the beginning of the sentence, "If at the time of removal all necessary pleadings have been," the word "served" was inserted in lieu of the word "filed," and the concluding words of the sentence, "petition for removal is filed if he is the petitioner," together with the final clause immediately following, were substituted for the words "record of the action is filed in the district court of the United States."

1963 Amendment

Subdivision (a)(4). This change reflects the transfer of functions from the Secretary of Commerce to the Secretary of the Interior made by 1939 Reorganization Plan No. II, § 4(e), 53 Stat. 1433.

Subdivision (a)(6). The proper current reference is to the 1952 statute superseding the 1940 statute.

Subdivision (c). Most of the cases have held that a party who has made a proper express demand for jury trial in the State court is not required to renew the demand after removal of the action. *Zakoscielny v. Waterman Steamship Corp.*, 16 F.R.D. 314 (D.Md.1954); *Talley v. American Bakeries Co.*, 15 F.R.D. 391 (E.D.Tenn.1954); *Rehrer v. Service Trucking Co.*, 15 F.R.D. 113 (D.Del.1953); 5 *Moore's Federal Practice* ¶38.39[3] (2d ed. 1951); 1 Barron & Holtzoff, *Federal Practice & Procedure* § 132 (Wright ed. 1960). But there is some authority to the contrary. *Petsel v. Chicago, B. & Q.R. Co.*, 101 F.Supp. 1006 (S.D.Iowa 1951); *Nelson v. American Nat. Bank & Trust Co.*, 9 F.R.D. 680 (E.D.Tenn. 1950). The amendment adopts the preponderant view.

In order still further to avoid unintended waivers of jury trial, the amendment provides that where by State law applicable in the court from which the case is removed a party is entitled to jury trial without making an express demand, he need not make a demand after removal. However, the district court for calendar or other purposes may on its own motion direct the parties to state whether they demand a jury, and the court must make such a direction upon the request of any party. Under the amendment a district court may find it convenient to establish a routine practice of giving these directions to the parties in appropriate cases.

Subdivision (f). The amendment recognizes the change of nomenclature made by Treasury Dept. Order 150–26(2), 18 Fed.Reg. 3499 (1953).

As to a special problem arising under Rule 25 (Substitution of parties) in actions for refund of taxes, see the Advisory Committee's Note to the amendment of Rule 25(d), effective July 19, 1961; and 4 *Moore's Federal Practice* ¶25.09 at 531 (2d ed. 1950).

1966 Amendment

See Note to Rule 1, supra.

Statutory proceedings to forfeit property for violation of the laws of the United States, formerly governed by the admiralty rules, will be governed by the unified and supplemental rules. See Supplemental Rule A.

Upon the recommendation of the judges of the United States District Court for the District of Columbia, the Federal Rules of Civil Procedure are made applicable to probate proceedings in that court. The exception with regard to adoption proceedings is removed because the court no longer has jurisdiction of those matters; and the words "mental health" are substituted for "lunacy" to conform to the current characterization in the District.

The purpose of the amendment to paragraph (3) is to permit the deletion from Rule 73(a) of the clause "unless a shorter time is provided by law." The 10 day period fixed for an appeal under 45 U.S.C. § 159 is the only instance of a shorter time provided for appeals in civil cases. Apart from the unsettling effect of the clause, it is eliminated because its retention would preserve the 15 day period heretofore allowed by 28 U.S.C. § 2107 for appeals from interlocutory decrees in admiralty, it being one of the purposes of the amendment to make the time for appeals in civil and admiralty cases uniform under the unified rules. See Advisory Committee's Note to subdivision (a) of Rule 73.

1968 Amendment

The amendments eliminate inappropriate references to appellate procedure.

1971 Amendment

Title 28, U.S.C., § 2243 now requires that the custodian of a person detained must respond to an application for a writ of habeas corpus "within three days unless for good cause additional time, not exceeding twenty days, is allowed." The amendment increases to forty days the additional time that the district court may allow in habeas corpus proceedings involving persons in custody pursuant to a judgment of a state court. The substantial increase in the number of such proceedings in recent years has placed a considerable burden on state authorities. Twenty days has proved in practice too short a time in which to prepare and file the return in many such cases. Allowance of additional time should, of course, be granted only for good cause.

While the time allowed in such a case for the return of the writ may not exceed forty days, this does not mean that the state must necessarily be limited to that period of time to provide for the federal court the transcript of the proceedings of a state trial or plenary hearing if the transcript must be prepared after the habeas corpus proceeding has begun in the federal court.

1987 Amendment

The amendments are technical. No substantive change is intended.

2001 Amendments

Former Copyright Rule 1 made the Civil Rules applicable to copyright proceedings except to the extent the Civil Rules were inconsistent with Copyright Rules. Abrogation of the Copyright Rules leaves the Civil Rules fully applicable to copyright proceedings. Rule 81(a)(1) is amended to reflect this change.

The District of Columbia Court Reform and Criminal Procedure Act of 1970, Pub.L. 91–358, 84 Stat. 473, transferred mental health proceedings formerly held in the United States District Court for the District of Columbia to local District of Columbia courts. The provision that the Civil Rules do not apply to these proceedings is deleted as superfluous.

The reference to incorporation of the Civil Rules in the Federal Rules of Bankruptcy Procedure has been restyled.

Changes Made After Publication and Comments

The Committee Note was amended to correct the inadvertent omission of a negative. As revised, it correctly reflects the language that is stricken from the rule.

2002 Amendments

This amendment brings Rule 81(a)(2) into accord with the Rules Governing § 2254 and § 2255 proceedings. In its present form, Rule 81(a)(2) includes return-time provisions that are inconsistent with the provisions in the Rules Governing §§ 2254 and 2255. The inconsistency should be eliminated, and it is better that the time provisions continue to be set out in the other rules without duplication in Rule 81. Rule 81 also directs that the writ be directed to the person having custody of the person detained. Similar directions exist in the § 2254 and § 2255 rules, providing additional detail for applicants subject to future custody. There is no need for partial duplication in Rule 81.

The provision that the civil rules apply to the extent that practice is not set forth in the § 2254 and § 2255 rules dovetails with the provisions in Rule 11 of the § 2254 rules and Rule 12 of the § 2255 rules.

Changes Made After Publication and Comment The only change since publication is deletion of an inadvertent reference to § 2241 proceedings.

HISTORICAL NOTES

Effective Date of Abrogation

Abrogation of par. (7) of subdivision (a) of this rule as effective Aug. 1, 1951, see Effective Date note incorporated within the Supplementary Report set out under the heading 1951 Addition in the Advisory Committee Notes appearing under Rule 71A of these rules.

Pending Actions

For applicability of Supreme Court amendments to pending cases, see Orders of the Supreme Court of the United States Adopting and Amending Rules set out preceding Rule 1 of these rules.

Rule 82. Jurisdiction and Venue Unaffected

These rules shall not be construed to extend or limit the jurisdiction of the United States district courts or the venue of actions therein. An admiralty or maritime claim within the meaning of Rule 9(h) shall not be treated as a civil action for the purposes of Title 28, U.S.C., §§ 1391–1392.

(As amended Dec. 29, 1948, eff. Oct. 20, 1949; Feb. 28, 1966, eff. July 1, 1966; Apr. 23, 2001, eff. Dec. 1, 2001.)

ADVISORY COMMITTEE NOTES

1937 Adoption

These rules grant extensive power of joining claims and counterclaims in one action, but, as this rule states, such grant does not extend federal jurisdiction. The rule is declaratory of existing practice under the [former] Federal Equity Rules with regard to such provisions as [former] Equity Rule 26 on Joinder of Causes of Action and [former] Equity Rule 30 on Counterclaims. Compare Shulman and Jaegerman, *Some Jurisdictional Limitations on Federal Procedure*, 45 Yale L.J. 393 (1936).

1948 Amendment

The amendment effective October 1949, substituted the words "United States district courts" for "district courts of the United States."

1966 Amendment

Title 28, U.S.C., § 1391(b) provides: "A civil action wherein jurisdiction is not founded solely on diversity of citizenship may be brought only in the judicial district where all defendants reside, except as otherwise provided by law." This provision cannot appropriately be applied to what were formerly suits in admiralty. The rationale of decisions holding it inapplicable rests largely on the use of the term "civil action": i.e., a suit in admiralty is not a "civil action" within the statute. By virtue of the amendment to Rule 1, the provisions of Rule 2 convert suits in admiralty into civil actions. The added sentence is necessary to avoid an undesirable change in existing law with respect to venue.

2001 Amendments

The final sentence of Rule 82 is amended to delete the reference to 28 U.S.C. § 1393, which has been repealed.

Style Comment

The recommendation that the change be made without publication carries with it a recommendation that style changes not be made. Styling would carry considerable risks. The first sentence of Rule 82, for example, states that the Civil Rules do not "extend or limit the jurisdiction of the United States district courts." That sentence is a flat lie if "jurisdiction" includes personal or quasi-in rem jurisdiction. The styling project on this rule requires publication and comment.

Rule 83. Rules by District Courts; Judge's Directives

(a) Local Rules

(1) Each district court, acting by a majority of its district judges, may, after giving appropriate public notice and an opportunity for comment, make and amend rules governing its practice. A local rule shall be consistent with—but not duplicative of— Acts of Congress and rules adopted under 28 U.S.C. §§ 2072 and 2075, and shall conform to any uniform numbering system prescribed by the Judicial Con-

ference of the United States. A local rule takes effect on the date specified by the district court and remains in effect unless amended by the court or abrogated by the judicial council of the circuit. Copies of rules and amendments shall, upon their promulgation, be furnished to the judicial council and the Administrative Office of the United States Courts and be made available to the public.

(2) A local rule imposing a requirement of form shall not be enforced in a manner that causes a party to lose rights because of a nonwillful failure to comply with the requirement.

(b) Procedures When There is No Controlling Law. A judge may regulate practice in any manner consistent with federal law, rules adopted under 28 U.S.C. §§ 2072 and 2075, and local rules of the district. No sanction or other disadvantage may be imposed for noncompliance with any requirement not in federal law, federal rules, or the local district rules unless the alleged violator has been furnished in the particular case with actual notice of the requirement. (As amended Apr. 29, 1985, eff. Aug. 1, 1985; Apr. 27, 1995, eff. Dec. 1, 1995.)

ADVISORY COMMITTEE NOTES

1937 Adoption

This rule substantially continues U.S.C., Title 28, § 2071, formerly § 731 (Rules of practice in district courts) with the additional requirement that copies of such rules and amendments be furnished to the Supreme Court of the United States. See [former] Equity Rule 79 (Additional Rules by District Court). With the last sentence compare United States Supreme Court Admiralty Rules, 1920, Rule 44 (Right of Trial Courts to Make Rules of Practice) (originally promulgated in 1842).

1985 Amendment

Rule 83, which has not been amended since the Federal Rules were promulgated in 1938, permits each district to adopt local rules not inconsistent with the Federal Rules by a majority of the judges. The only other requirement is that copies be furnished to the Supreme Court.

The widespread adoption of local rules and the modest procedural prerequisites for their promulgation have led many commentators to question the soundness of the process as well as the validity of some rules. See 12 C. Wright & A. Miller, *Federal Practice and Procedure: Civil* § 3152, at 217 (1973); Caballero, *Is There an Over-Exercise of Local Rule-Making Powers by the United States District Courts?*, 24 Fed.Bar News 325 (1977). Although the desirability of local rules for promoting uniform practice within a district is widely accepted, several commentators also have suggested reforms to increase the quality, simplicity, and uniformity of the local rules. See Note, *Rule 83 and the Local Federal Rules,* 67 Colum.L.Rev. 1251 (1967), and Comment, *The Local Rules of Civil Procedure in the Federal District Courts—A Survey,* 1966 Duke L.J. 1011.

The amended Rule attempts, without impairing the procedural validity of existing local rules, to enhance the local rulemaking process by requiring appropriate public notice of proposed rules and an opportunity to comment on them. Although some district courts apparently consult the local bar before promulgating rules, many do not, which has led to criticism of a process that has district judges consulting only with each other. See 12 C. Wright & A. Miller, *supra,* § 3152, at 217; Blair, *The New Local Rules for Federal Practice in Iowa,* 23 Drake L.Rev. 517 (1974). The new language subjects local rulemaking to scrutiny similar to that accompanying the Federal Rules, administrative rulemaking, and legislation. It attempts to assure that the expert advice of practitioners and scholars is made available to the district court before local rules are promulgated. See Weinstein, *Reform of Court Rule-Making Procedures* 84–87, 127–37, 151 (1977).

The amended Rule does not detail the procedure for giving notice and an opportunity to be heard since conditions vary from district to district. Thus, there is no explicit requirement for a public hearing, although a district may consider that procedure appropriate in all or some rulemaking situations. See generally, Weinstein, *supra,* at 117–37, 151. The new Rule does not foreclose any other form of consultation. For example, it can be accomplished through the mechanism of an "Advisory Committee" similar to that employed by the Supreme Court in connection with the Federal Rules themselves.

The amended Rule provides that a local rule will take effect upon the date specified by the district court and will remain in effect unless amended by the district court or abrogated by the judicial council. The effectiveness of a local rule should not be deferred until approved by the judicial council because that might unduly delay promulgation of a local rule that should become effective immediately, especially since some councils do not meet frequently. Similarly, it was thought that to delay a local rule's effectiveness for a fixed period of time would be arbitrary and that to require the judicial council to abrogate a local rule within a specified time would be inconsistent with its power under 28 U.S.C. § 332 (1976) to nullify a local rule at any time. The expectation is that the judicial council will examine all local rules, including those currently in effect, with an eye toward determining whether they are valid and consistent with the Federal Rules, promote inter-district uniformity and efficiency, and do not undermine the basic objectives of the Federal Rules.

The amended Rule requires copies of local rules to be sent upon their promulgation to the judicial council and the Administrative Office of the United States Courts rather than to the Supreme Court. The Supreme Court was the appropriate filing place in 1938, when Rule 83 originally was promulgated, but the establishment of the Administrative Office makes it a more logical place to develop a centralized file of local rules. This procedure is consistent with both the Criminal and the Appellate Rules. See Fed.R.Crim.P. 57(a); Fed.R.App.P. 47. The Administrative Office also will be able to provide improved utilization of the file because of its recent development of a Local Rules Index.

The practice pursued by some judges of issuing standing orders has been controversial, particularly among members of the practicing bar. The last sentence in Rule 83 has been amended to make certain that standing orders are not inconsistent with the Federal Rules or any local district court rules. Beyond that, it is hoped that each district will adopt procedures, perhaps by local rule, for promulgating and reviewing single-judge standing orders.

1995 Amendments

Subdivision (a). This rule is amended to reflect the requirement that local rules be consistent not only with the national rules but also with Acts of Congress. The amendment also states that local rules should not repeat Acts of Congress or national rules.

The amendment also requires that the numbering of local rules conform with any uniform numbering system that may be prescribed by the Judicial Conference. Lack of uniform numbering might create unnecessary traps for counsel and litigants. A uniform numbering system would make it easier for an increasingly national bar and for litigants to locate a local rule that applies to a particular procedural issue.

Paragraph (2) is new. Its aim is to protect against loss of rights in the enforcement of local rules relating to matters of form. For example, a party should not be deprived of a right to a jury trial because its attorney, unaware of—or forgetting—a local rule directing that jury demands be noted in the caption of the case, includes a jury demand only in the body of the pleading. The proscription of paragraph (2) is narrowly drawn—covering only violations attributable to nonwillful failure to comply and only those involving local rules directed to matters of form. It does not limit the court's power to impose substantive penalties upon a party if it or its attorney contumaciously or willfully violates a local rule, even one involving merely a matter of form. Nor does it affect the court's power to enforce local rules that involve more than mere matters of form—for example, a local rule requiring parties to identify evidentiary matters relied upon to support or oppose motions for summary judgment.

Subdivision (b). This rule provides flexibility to the court in regulating practice when there is no controlling law. Specifically, it permits the court to regulate practice in any manner consistent with Acts of Congress, with rules adopted under 28 U.S.C. §§ 2072 and 2075, and with the district local rules.

This rule recognizes that courts rely on multiple directives to control practice. Some courts regulate practice through the published Federal Rules and the local rules of the court. Some courts also have used internal operating procedures, standing orders, and other internal directives. Although such directives continue to be authorized, they can lead to problems. Counsel or litigants may be unaware of various directives. In addition, the sheer volume of directives may impose an unreasonable barrier. For example, it may be difficult to obtain copies of the directives. Finally, counsel or litigants may be unfairly sanctioned for failing to comply with a directive. For these reasons, the amendment to this rule disapproves imposing any sanction or other disadvantage on a person for noncompliance with such an internal directive, unless the alleged violator has been furnished actual notice of the requirement in a particular case.

There should be no adverse consequence to a party or attorney for violating special requirements relating to practice before a particular court unless the party or attorney has actual notice of those requirements. Furnishing litigants with a copy outlining the judge's practices—or attaching instructions to a notice setting a case for conference or trial—would suffice to give actual notice, as would an order in a case specifically adopting by reference a judge's standing order and indicating how copies can be obtained.

HISTORICAL NOTES

Change of Name

Reference to United States magistrate or to magistrate deemed to refer to United States magistrate judge pursuant to section 321 of Pub.L. 101–650, set out as a note under section 631 of this title.

Rule 84. Forms

The forms contained in the Appendix of Forms are sufficient under the rules and are intended to indicate the simplicity and brevity of statement which the rules contemplate.

(As amended Dec. 27, 1946, eff. Mar. 19, 1948.)

ADVISORY COMMITTEE NOTES

1937 Adoption

In accordance with the practice found useful in many codes, provision is here made for a limited number of official forms which may serve as guides in pleading. Compare 2 Mass.Gen.Laws (Ter.Ed., 1932) ch. 231, § 147, Forms 1–47; *English Annual Practice* (1937) Appendix A to M, inclusive; *Conn.Practice Book* (1934) Rules, 47–68, pp. 123 to 427.

1946 Amendment

Note. The amendment serves to emphasize that the forms contained in the Appendix of Forms are sufficient to withstand attack under the rules under which they are drawn, and that the practitioner using them may rely on them to that extent. The circuit courts of appeals generally have upheld the use of the forms as promoting desirable simplicity and brevity of statement. *Sierocinski v. E. I. DuPont DeNemours & Co.,* C.C.A.3, 1939, 103 F.2d 843; *Swift & Co. v. Young,* C.C.A.4, 1939, 107 F.2d 170; *Sparks v. England,* C.C.A.8, 1940, 113 F.2d 579; *Ramsouer v. Midland Valley R. Co.,* C.C.A.8, 1943, 135 F.2d 101. And the forms as a whole have met with widespread approval in the courts. See cases cited in 1 Moore's Federal Practice, 1938, Cum. Supplement § 8.07, under "Page 554"; see also Commentary, The Official Forms, 1941, 4 Fed.Rules Serv. 954. In Cook, "Facts" and "Statements of Fact", 1937, 4 U.Chi.L.Rev. 233, 245–246, it is said with reference to what is now Rule 84: ". . . pleaders in the federal courts are not to be left to guess as to the meaning of [the] language" in Rule 8(a) regarding the form of the complaint. "All of which is as it should be. In no other way can useless litigation be avoided." Ibid. The amended rule will operate to discourage isolated results such as those found in *Washburn v. Moorman Mfg. Co.,* S.D.Cal. 1938, 25 F.Supp. 546; *Employers Mutual Liability Ins. Co. of Wisconsin v. Blue Line Transfer Co.,* W.D.Mo.1941, 2 F.R.D. 121, 5 Fed.Rules Serv. 12e.235, Case 2.

Rule 85. Title

These rules may be known and cited as the Federal Rules of Civil Procedure.

Rule 86. Effective Date

(a) [Effective Date of Original Rules].[1] These rules will take effect on the day which is 3 months subsequent to the adjournment of the second regular session of the 75th Congress, but if that day is prior to September 1, 1938, then these rules will take effect on September 1, 1938. They govern all proceedings in actions brought after they take effect and also all further proceedings in actions then pending, except to the extent that in the opinion of the court their application in a particular action pending when the rules take effect would not be feasible or would work injustice, in which event the former procedure applies.

(b) Effective Date of Amendments. The amendments adopted by the Supreme Court on December 27, 1946, and transmitted to the Attorney General on January 2, 1947, shall take effect on the day which is three months subsequent to the adjournment of the first regular session of the 80th Congress, but, if that day is prior to September 1, 1947, then these amendments shall take effect on September 1, 1947. They govern all proceedings in actions brought after they take effect and also all further proceedings in actions then pending, except to the extent that in the opinion of the court their application in a particular action pending when the amendments take effect would not be feasible or would work injustice, in which event the former procedure applies.

(c) Effective Date of Amendments. The amendments adopted by the Supreme Court on December 29, 1948, and transmitted to the Attorney General on December 31, 1948, shall take effect on the day following the adjournment of the first regular session of the 81st Congress.

(d) Effective Date of Amendments. The amendments adopted by the Supreme Court on April 17, 1961, and transmitted to the Congress on April 18, 1961, shall take effect on July 19, 1961. They govern all proceedings in actions brought after they take effect and also all further proceedings in actions then pending, except to the extent that in the opinion of the court their application in a particular action pending when the amendments take effect would not be feasible or would work injustice, in which event the former procedure applies.

(e) Effective Date of Amendments. The amendments adopted by the Supreme Court on January 21, 1963, and transmitted to the Congress on January 21, 1963, shall take effect on July 1, 1963. They govern all proceedings in actions brought after they take effect and also all further proceedings in actions then pending, except to the extent that in the opinion of the court their application in a particular action pending when the amendments take effect would not be feasible or would work injustice, in which event the former procedure applies.

(As amended Dec. 27, 1946, eff. Mar. 19, 1948; Dec. 29, 1948, eff. Oct. 20, 1949; Apr. 17, 1961, eff. July 19, 1961; Jan. 21 and Mar. 18, 1963, eff. July 1, 1963.)

1 Subdivision heading supplied editorially.

ADVISORY COMMITTEE NOTES

1937 Adoption

See former Equity Rule 81 (These Rules Effective February 1, 1913—Old Rules Abrogated).

HISTORICAL NOTES

Effective and Applicability Provisions

1948 Amendments. The first regular session of the 81st Congress adjourned sine die on Oct. 19, 1949, therefore the amendments to Rules 1, 17, 22, 24, 25, 27, 37, 45, 57, 60, 65, 66, 67, 69, 72–76, 79, 81, 82, and 86 and to forms 1, 19, 22, 23, and 27 became effective on Oct. 20, 1949, following the adjournment as provided for in subsection (c) of this rule.

1946 Amendments. The first regular session of the 80th Congress adjourned sine die on Friday, Dec. 19, 1947, therefore the amendments to Rules 6, 7, 12, 13, 14, 17, 24, 26, 27, 28, 33, 34, 36, 41, 45, 52, 54, 56, 58, 59, 60, 62, 65, 66, 68, 73, 75, 77, 79, 80, 81, 84, and 86, became effective Mar. 19, 1948 as provided for in subsection (b) of this rule.

Effective Date of 1970 Amendments; Transmission to Congress

Sections 2 and 3 of the Order of the Supreme Court, dated Mar. 30, 1970, provided:

"2. That the foregoing amendments to the Rules of Civil Procedure shall take effect on July 1, 1970, and shall govern all proceedings in actions brought thereafter and also in all further proceedings in actions then pending, except to the extent that in the opinion of the court their application in a particular action then pending would not be feasible or would work injustice, in which event the former procedure applies.

"3. That the Chief Justice be, and he hereby is, authorized to transmit to the Congress the foregoing amendments to the Rules of Civil Procedure in accordance with the provisions of Title 28, U.S.C. § 2072."

Effective Date of 1966 Amendment; Transmission to Congress; Rescission

Sections 2 to 4 of the Order of the Supreme Court, dated Feb. 28, 1966, 383 U.S. 1031, provided:

"2. That the foregoing amendments and additions to the Rules of Civil Procedure shall take effect on July 1, 1966, and shall govern all proceedings in actions brought thereafter and also in all further proceedings in actions then pending, except to the extent that in the opinion of the court their application in a particular action then pending would not be feasible or would work injustice, in which event the former procedure applies.

"3. That the Chief Justice be, and he hereby is, authorized to transmit to the Congress the foregoing amendments and additions to the Rules of Civil Procedure in accordance with the provisions of Title 28, U.S.C., §§ 2072 and 2073.

"4. That: (a) subdivision (c) of Rule 6 of the Rules of Civil Procedure for the United States District Courts promulgated by this court on December 20, 1937, effective September 16, 1938; (b) Rule 2 of the Rules for Practice and Procedure under section 25 of An Act To amend and consolidate the Acts respecting copyright, approved March 4, 1909, promulgated by this court on June 1, 1909, effective July 1, 1909; and (c) the Rules of Practice in Admiralty and Maritime Cases, promulgated by this court on December 6, 1920, effective March 7, 1921, as revised, amended and supplemented, be, and they hereby are, rescinded, effective July 1, 1966."

APPENDIX OF FORMS

(See Rule 84)

INTRODUCTORY STATEMENT

1. The following forms are intended for illustration only. They are limited in number. No attempt is made to furnish a manual of forms. Each form assumes the action to be brought in the Southern District of New York. If the district in which an action is brought has divisions, the division should be indicated in the caption.

2. Except where otherwise indicated each pleading, motion, and other paper should have a caption similar to that of the summons, with the designation of the particular paper substituted for the word "Summons." In the caption of the summons and in the caption of the complaint all parties must be named but in other pleadings and papers, it is sufficient to state the name of the first party on either side, with an appropriate indication of other parties. See Rules 4(b), 7(b)(2), and 10(a).

3. In Form 3 and the forms following, the words, "Allegation of jurisdiction," are used to indicate the appropriate allegation in Form 2.

4. Each pleading, motion, and other paper is to be signed in his individual name by at least one attorney of record (Rule 11). The attorney's name is to be followed by his address as indicated in Form 3. In forms following Form 3 the signature and address are not indicated.

5. If a party is not represented by an attorney, the signature and address of the party are required in place of those of the attorney.

Form 1. Summons

United States District Court for the
Southern District of New York

Civil Action, File Number _____

A. B., Plaintiff ⟩
    v. ⟩   *Summons*
C. D., Defendant ⟩

To the above-named Defendant:

You are hereby summoned and required to serve upon _____, plaintiff's attorney, whose address is _____, an answer to the complaint which is herewith served upon you, within 20 [1] days after service of this summons upon you, exclusive of the day of service. If you fail to do so, judgment by default will be taken against you for the relief demanded in the complaint.

_____,
Clerk of Court.

[Seal of the U.S. District Court]

Dated _____

(This summons is issued pursuant to Rule 4 of the Federal Rules of Civil Procedure)

(As amended Dec. 29, 1948, eff. Oct. 20, 1949.)

[1] If the United States or an officer or agency there of is a defendant, the time to be inserted as to it is 60 days.

Form 1A. Notice of Lawsuit and Request for Waiver of Service of Summons

TO: (A)

[as (B) of (C)]

A lawsuit has been commenced against you (or the entity on whose behalf you are addressed). A copy of the complaint is attached to this notice. It has been filed in the United States District Court for the (D) and has been assigned docket number (E).

This is not a formal summons or notification from the court, but rather my request that you sign and return the enclosed waiver of service in order to save the cost of serving you with a judicial summons and an additional copy of the complaint. The cost of service will be avoided if I receive a signed copy of the waiver within (F) days after the date designated below as the date on which this Notice and Request is sent. I enclose a stamped and addressed envelope (or other means of cost-free return) for your use. An extra copy of the waiver is also attached for your records.

If you comply with this request and return the signed waiver, it will be filed with the court and no summons will be served on you. The action will then proceed as if you had been served on the date the waiver is filed, except that you will not be obligated to answer the complaint before 60 days from the date designated below as the date on which this notice is sent (or before 90 days from that date if your address is not in any judicial district of the United States).

If you do not return the signed waiver within the time indicated, I will take appropriate steps to effect formal service in a manner authorized by the Federal

Rules of Civil Procedure and will then, to the extent authorized by those Rules, ask the court to require you (or the party on whose behalf you are addressed) to pay the full costs of such service. In that connection, please read the statement concerning the duty of parties to waive the service of the summons, which is set forth on the reverse side (or at the foot) of the waiver form.

I affirm that this request is being sent to you on behalf of the plaintiff, this ___ day of _____, _____.

Signature of Plaintiff's Attorney
or Unrepresented Plaintiff

Notes:

A—Name of individual defendant (or name of officer or agent of corporate defendant)

B—Title, or other relationship of individual to corporate defendant

C—Name of corporate defendants, if any

D—District

E—Docket number of action

F—Addresses must be given at least 30 days (60 days if located in foreign country) in which to return waiver

(Added Apr. 22, 1993, eff. Dec. 1, 1993.)

ADVISORY COMMITTEE NOTES
1993 Adoption

Forms 1A and 1B reflect the revision of Rule 4. They replace Form 18–A.

HISTORICAL NOTES

Effective and Applicability Provisions of Enactment and Abrogation

1991 Acts. Amendments by Supreme Court Order dated Apr. 30, 1991, adding Form 1A "Notice of Lawsuit and Request for Waiver of Service of Summons" and Form 1B "Waiver of Service of Summons" became effective Dec. 1, 1991. Pub.L. 102–198, § 11(b), Dec. 9, 1991, 105 Stat. 1626, set out as a note under section 2074 of Title 28, Judiciary and Judicial Procedure, provided that, effective Dec. 9, 1991, Forms 1A and 1B are not to be effective.

Form 1B. Waiver of Service of Summons

TO: (name of plaintiff's attorney or unrepresented plaintiff)

I acknowledge receipt of your request that I waive service of a summons in the action of (caption of action), which is case number (docket number) in the United States District Court for the (district). I have also received a copy of the complaint in the action, two copies of this instrument, and a means by which I can return the signed waiver to you without cost to me.

I agree to save the cost of service of a summons and an additional copy of the complaint in this lawsuit by not requiring that I (or the entity on whose behalf I am acting) be served with judicial process in the manner provided by Rule 4.

I (or the entity on whose behalf I am acting) will retain all defenses or objections to the lawsuit or to the jurisdiction or venue of the court except for objections based on a defect in the summons or in the service of the summons.

I understand that a judgment may be entered against me (or the party on whose behalf I am acting) if an answer or motion under Rule 12 is not served upon you within 60 days after (date request was sent), or within 90 days after that date if the request was sent outside the United States.

_____   _____
Date   Signature
Printed/typed name: _____
  [as _____]
  [of _____]

To be printed on reverse side of the waiver form or set forth at the foot of the form:

Duty to Avoid Unnecessary Costs of Service of Summons

Rule 4 of the Federal Rules of Civil Procedure requires certain parties to cooperate in saving unnecessary costs of service of the summons and complaint. A defendant located in the United States who, after being notified of an action and asked by a plaintiff located in the United States to waive service of a summons, fails to do so will be required to bear the cost of such service unless good cause be shown for its failure to sign and return the waiver.

It is not good cause for a failure to waive service that a party believes that the complaint is unfounded, or that the action has been brought in an improper place or in a court that lacks jurisdiction over the subject matter of the action or over its person or property. A party who waives service of the summons retains all defenses and objections (except any relating to the summons or the service of the summons), and may later object to the jurisdiction of the court or to the place where the action has been brought.

A defendant who waives service must within the time specified on the waiver form serve on the plaintiff's attorney (or unrepresented plaintiff) a response to the complaint and must also file a signed copy of the response with the court. If the answer or motion is not served within this time, a default judgment may be taken against that defendant. By waiving service, a defendant is allowed more time to answer than if the summons had been actually served when the request for waiver of service was received.

(Added Apr. 22, 1993, eff. Dec. 1, 1993.)

ADVISORY COMMITTEE NOTES

1993 Adoption

Forms 1A and 1B reflect the revision of Rule 4. They replace Form 18–A.

HISTORICAL NOTES

Effective and Applicability Provisions of Enactment and Abrogation

1991 Acts. Amendments by Supreme Court Order dated Apr. 30, 1991, adding Form 1A "Notice of Lawsuit and Request for Waiver of Service of Summons" and Form 1B "Waiver of Service of Summons" became effective Dec. 1, 1991. Pub.L. 102–198, § 11(b), Dec. 9, 1991, 105 Stat. 1626, set out as a note under section 2074 of Title 28, Judiciary and Judicial Procedure, provided that, effective Dec. 9, 1991, Forms 1A and 1B are not to be effective.

Congressional Action Contrary to Supreme Court Enactment of Form

Enactment of Form 1–B, relating to waiver of service of summons, as transmitted to Congress by the Supreme Court pursuant to section 2074 of this title, which was to take effect Dec. 1, 1991, was nullified by Congress, see section 11 of Pub.L. 102–198, set out as a note under section 2074 of this title.

Form 2.   Allegation of Jurisdiction

(a) Jurisdiction founded on diversity of citizenship and amount.

Plaintiff is a [citizen of the State of Connecticut][1] [corporation incorporated under the laws of the State of Connecticut having its principal place of business in the State of Connecticut] and defendant is a corporation incorporated under the laws of the State of New York having its principal place of business in a State other than the State of Connecticut. The matter in controversy exceeds, exclusive of interest and costs, the sum specified by 28 U.S.C. § 1332.

(b) Jurisdiction founded on the existence of a Federal question.

The action arises under [the Constitution of the United States, Article ___, Section ___]; [the ___ Amendment to the Constitution of the United States, Section ___]; [the Act of ___, ___ Stat. ___; U.S.C., Title ___, § ___]; [the Treaty of the United States (here describe the treaty)][2] as hereinafter more fully appears.

(c) Jurisdiction founded on the existence of a question arising under particular statutes.

The action arises under the Act of ___, ___ Stat. ___; U.S.C., Title ___, § ___, as hereinafter more fully appears.

(d) Jurisdiction founded on the admiralty or maritime character of the claim.

This is a case of admiralty and maritime jurisdiction, as hereinafter more fully appears. [If the pleader wishes to invoke the distinctively maritime procedures referred to in Rule 9(h), add the following or its substantial equivalent: This is an admiralty or maritime claim within the meaning of Rule 9(h).]

[1] Form for natural person.

[2] Use the appropriate phrase or phrases. The general allegation of the existence of a Federal question is ineffective unless the matters constituting the claim for relief as set forth in the complaint raise a Federal question.

NOTES

1. Diversity of citizenship. U.S.C., Title 28, § 1332 (Diversity of citizenship; amount in controversy; costs), as amended by PL 85–554, 72 Stat. 415, July 25, 1958, states in subsection (c) that "For the purposes of this section and section 1441 of this title [removable actions], a corporation shall be deemed a citizen of any State by which it has been incorporated and of the State where it has its principal place of business." Thus if the defendant corporation in Form 2(a) had its principal place of business in Connecticut, diversity of citizenship would not exist. An allegation regarding the principal place of business of each corporate party must be made in addition to an allegation regarding its place of incorporation.

2. Jurisdictional amount. U.S.C., Title 28, § 1331 (Federal question; amount in controversy; costs) and § 1332 (Diversity of citizenship; amount in controversy; costs), as amended by PL 85–554, 72 Stat. 415, July 25, 1958, require that the amount in controversy, exclusive of interest and costs, be in excess of $10,000. The allegation as to the amount in controversy may be omitted in any case where by law no jurisdictional amount is required. See, for example, U.S.C., Title 28, § 1338 (Patents, copyrights, trade-marks, and unfair competition), § 1343 (Civil rights and elective franchise).

3. Pleading venue. Since improper venue is a matter of defense, it is not necessary for plaintiff to include allegations showing the venue to be proper. See 1 *Moore's Federal Practice,* par. 0.140[1–4] (2d ed. 1959).

(As amended Apr. 17, 1961, eff. July 19, 1961; Feb. 28, 1966, eff. July 1, 1966; Apr. 22, 1993, eff. Dec. 1, 1993; Apr. 29, 1999, eff. Dec. 1, 1999.)

ADVISORY COMMITTEE NOTES

1966 Amendment

Since the Civil Rules have not heretofore been applicable to proceedings in Admiralty (Rule 81(a)(1)), Form 2 naturally has not contained a provision for invoking the admiralty jurisdiction. The form has never purported to be comprehensive, as making provision for all possible grounds of jurisdiction; but a provision for invoking the admiralty jurisdiction is particularly appropriate as an incident of unification.

Certain distinctive features of the admiralty practice must be preserved in unification, just as certain distinctive characteristics of equity were preserved in the merger of law and equity in 1938. Rule 9(h) provides the device whereby, after unification, with its abolition of the distinction between civil actions and suits in admiralty, the pleader may indicate his choice of the distinctively maritime procedures, and designates those features that are preserved. This form illustrates an appropriate way in which the pleader may invoke those procedures. Use of this device is not necessary if the claim is cognizable only by virtue of the admiralty and maritime jurisdiction, nor if the claim is within the exclusive admiralty jurisdiction of the district court.

Omission of a statement such as this from the pleading indicates the pleader's choice that the action proceed as a conventional civil action, if this is jurisdictionally possible, without the distinctive maritime remedies and procedures. It should be remembered, however, that Rule 9(h) provides that a pleading may be amended to add or withdraw such an identifying statement subject to the principles stated in Rule 15.

1993 Amendments

This form is revised to reflect amendments to 28 U.S.C. §§ 1331 and 1332 providing jurisdiction for federal questions without regard to the amount in controversy and raising the amount required to be in controversy in diversity cases to fifty thousand dollars.

HISTORICAL NOTES

Effective and Applicability Provisions

1961 Amendments. Amendment adopted on Apr. 17, 1961, effective July 19, 1961, see Rule 86(d).

Form 3. Complaint on a Promissory Note

1. Allegation of jurisdiction.

2. Defendant on or about June 1, 1935, executed and delivered to plaintiff a promissory note [in the following words and figures: (here set out the note verbatim)]; [a copy of which is hereto annexed as Exhibit A]; [whereby defendant promised to pay to plaintiff or order [1] on June 1, 1936 the sum of _____ dollars with interest thereon at the rate of six percent. per annum].

3. Defendant owes to plaintiff the amount of said note and interest.

Wherefore plaintiff demands judgment against defendant for the sum of _____ dollars, interest, and costs.

Signed: _____
Attorney for Plaintiff.
Address: _____

Notes

1. The pleader may use the material in one of the three sets of brackets. His choice will depend upon whether he desires to plead the document verbatim, or by exhibit, or according to its legal effect.

2. Under the rules free joinder of claims is permitted. See rules 8(e) and 18. Consequently the claims set forth in each and all of the following forms may be joined with this complaint or with each other. Ordinarily each claim should be stated in a separate division of the complaint, and the divisions should be designated as counts successively numbered. In particular the rules permit alternative and inconsistent pleading. See Form 10.

(As amended Jan. 21, 1963, eff. July 1, 1963.)

[1] So in original.

ADVISORY COMMITTEE NOTES

1963 Amendment

At various places, these Forms [Forms 3, 4, 5, 6, 7, 8, 9, 10, 11, 12, 13, 18, 21] allege or refer to damages of "ten thousand dollars, interest, and costs," or the like. The Forms were written at a time when the jurisdictional amount in ordinary "diversity" and "Federal question" cases was an amount in excess of $3,000, exclusive of interest and costs, so the illustrative amounts set out in the Forms were adequate for jurisdictional purposes. However, U.S.C. Title 28, § 1331 (Federal question; amount in controversy; costs) and § 1332 (Diversity of citizenship; amount in controversy; costs), as amended by Pub.L. 85–554, 72 Stat. 415, July 25, 1958, now require that the amount in controversy, exclusive of interest and costs, be in excess of $10,000. Accordingly the Forms are misleading. They are amended at appropriate places by deleting the stated dollar amount and substituting a blank, to be properly filled in by the pleader.

Form 4. Complaint on an Account

1. Allegation of jurisdiction.

2. Defendant owes plaintiff _____ dollars according to the account hereto annexed as Exhibit A.

Wherefore (etc. as in Form 3).

(As amended Jan. 21, 1963, eff. July 1, 1963.)

ADVISORY COMMITTEE NOTES

1963 Amendment

This form was amended in 1963 by deleting the stated dollar amount and substituting a blank, to be properly filled in by the pleader. See Note of Advisory Committee under Form 3.

Form 5. Complaint for Goods Sold and Delivered

1. Allegation of jurisdiction.

2. Defendant owes plaintiff _____ dollars for goods sold and delivered by plaintiff to defendant between June 1, 1936 and December 1, 1936.

Wherefore (etc. as in Form 3).

Note

This form may be used where the action is for an agreed price or for the reasonable value of the goods.

(As amended Jan. 21, 1963, eff. July 1, 1963.)

ADVISORY COMMITTEE NOTES

1963 Amendment

This form was amended in 1963 by deleting the stated dollar amount and substituting a blank, to be properly filled in by the pleader. See Note of Advisory Committee under Form 3.

Form 6. Complaint for Money Lent

1. Allegation of jurisdiction.

2. Defendant owes plaintiff _____ dollars for money lent by plaintiff to defendant on June 1, 1936.

Wherefore (etc. as in Form 3).

(As amended Jan. 21, 1963, eff. July 1, 1963.)

ADVISORY COMMITTEE NOTES

1963 Amendment

This form was amended in 1963 by deleting the stated dollar amount and substituting a blank, to be properly filled in by the pleader. See Note of Advisory Committee under Form 3.

Form 7. Complaint for Money Paid by Mistake

1. Allegation of jurisdiction.

2. Defendant owes plaintiff _____ dollars for money paid by plaintiff to defendant by mistake on June 1, 1936, under the following circumstances: [here state the circumstances with particularity—see Rule 9(b)].

Wherefore (etc. as in Form 3).

(As amended Jan. 21, 1963, eff. July 1, 1963.)

ADVISORY COMMITTEE NOTES

1963 Amendment

This form was amended in 1963 by deleting the stated dollar amount and substituting a blank, to be properly filled in by the pleader. See Note of Advisory Committee under Form 3.

Form 8. Complaint for Money Had and Received

1. Allegation of jurisdiction.

2. Defendant owes plaintiff _____ dollars for money had and received from one G. H. on June 1, 1936, to be paid by defendant to plaintiff.

Wherefore (etc. as in Form 3).

(As amended Jan. 21, 1963, eff. July 1, 1963.)

ADVISORY COMMITTEE NOTES

1963 Amendment

This form was amended in 1963 by deleting the stated dollar amount and substituting a blank, to be properly filled in by the pleader. See Note of Advisory Committee under Form 3.

Form 9. Complaint for Negligence

1. Allegation of jurisdiction.

2. On June 1, 1936, in a public highway called Boylston Street in Boston, Massachusetts, defendant negligently drove a motor vehicle against plaintiff who was then crossing said highway.

3. As a result plaintiff was thrown down and had his leg broken and was otherwise injured, was prevented from transacting his business, suffered great pain of body and mind, and incurred expenses for medical attention and hospitalization in the sum of one thousand dollars.

Wherefore plaintiff demands judgment against defendant in the sum of _____ dollars and costs.

NOTE

Since contributory negligence is an affirmative defense, the complaint need contain no allegation of due care of plaintiff.

(As amended Jan. 21, 1963, eff. July 1, 1963.)

ADVISORY COMMITTEE NOTES

1963 Amendment

This form was amended in 1963 by deleting the stated dollar amount and substituting a blank, to be properly filled in by the pleader. See Note of Advisory Committee under Form 3.

Form 10. Complaint for Negligence Where Plaintiff is Unable to Determine Definitely Whether the Person Responsible is C. D. or E. F. or Whether Both are Responsible and Where his Evidence may Justify a Finding of Wilfulness or of Recklessness or of Negligence

A. B., Plaintiff	)	
v.	)	*Complaint*
C. D. and E. F., Defendants	)	

1. Allegation of jurisdiction.

2. On June 1, 1936, in a public highway called Boylston Street in Boston, Massachusetts, defendant C. D. or defendant E. F., or both defendants C. D. and E. F. wilfully or recklessly or negligently drove or caused to be driven a motor vehicle against plaintiff who was then crossing said highway.

3. As a result plaintiff was thrown down and had his leg broken and was otherwise injured, was prevented from transacting his business, suffered great pain of body and mind, and incurred expenses for medical attention and hospitalization in the sum of one thousand dollars.

Wherefore plaintiff demands judgment against C. D. or against E. F. or against both in the sum of _____ dollars and costs.

(As amended Jan. 21, 1963, eff. July 1, 1963.)

ADVISORY COMMITTEE NOTES

1963 Amendment

This form was amended in 1963 by deleting the stated dollar amount and substituting a blank, to be properly filled in by the pleader. See Note of Advisory Committee under Form 3.

Form 11. Complaint for Conversion

1. Allegation of jurisdiction.

2. On or about December 1, 1936, defendant converted to his own use ten bonds of the _____ Company (here insert brief identification as by number and

issue) of the value of _____ dollars, the property of plaintiff.

Wherefore plaintiff demands judgment against defendant in the sum of _____ dollars, interest, and costs.

(As amended Jan. 21, 1963, eff. July 1, 1963.)

ADVISORY COMMITTEE NOTES

1963 Amendment

This form was amended in 1963 by deleting the stated dollar amount and substituting a blank, to be properly filled in by the pleader. See Note of Advisory Committee under Form 3.

Form 12. Complaint for Specific Performance of Contract to Convey Land

1. Allegation of jurisdiction.

2. On or about December 1, 1936, plaintiff and defendant entered into an agreement in writing a copy of which is hereto annexed as Exhibit A.

3. In accord with the provisions of said agreement plaintiff tendered to defendant the purchase price and requested a conveyance of the land, but defendant refused to accept the tender and refused to make the conveyance.

4. Plaintiff now offers to pay the purchase price.

Wherefore plaintiff demands (1) that defendant be required specifically to perform said agreement, (2) damages in the sum of one thousand dollars, and (3) that if specific performance is not granted plaintiff have judgment against defendant in the sum of _____ dollars.

NOTE

Here, as in Form 3, plaintiff may set forth the contract verbatim in the complaint or plead it, as indicated, by exhibit, or plead it according to its legal effect. Furthermore, plaintiff may seek legal or equitable relief or both even though this was impossible under the system in operation before these rules.

(As amended Jan. 21, 1963, eff. July 1, 1963.)

ADVISORY COMMITTEE NOTES

1963 Amendment

This form was amended in 1963 by deleting the stated dollar amount and substituting a blank, to be properly filled in by the pleader. See Note of Advisory Committee under Form 3.

Form 13. Complaint on Claim for Debt and to Set Aside Fraudulent Conveyance Under Rule 18(b)

A. B., Plaintiff   )
       v.   )   *Complaint*
C. D. and E. F., Defendants   )

1. Allegation of jurisdiction.

2. Defendant C. D. on or about _____ executed and delivered to plaintiff a promissory note [in the following words and figures: (here set out the note verbatim)]; [a copy of which is hereto annexed as Exhibit A]; [whereby defendant C. D. promised to pay to plaintiff or order [1] on _____ the sum of five thousand dollars with interest thereon at the rate of _____ percent. per annum].

3. Defendant C. D. owes to plaintiff the amount of said note and interest.

4. Defendant C. D. on or about _____ conveyed all his property, real and personal [or specify and describe] to defendant E. F. for the purpose of defrauding plaintiff and hindering and delaying the collection of the indebtedness evidenced by the note above referred to.

Wherefore plaintiff demands:

(1) That plaintiff have judgment against defendant C. D. for _____ dollars and interest; (2) that the aforesaid conveyance to defendant E. F. be declared void and the judgment herein be declared a lien on said property; (3) that plaintiff have judgment against the defendants for costs.

(As amended Jan. 21, 1963, eff. July 1, 1963.)

[1] So in original.

ADVISORY COMMITTEE NOTES

1963 Amendment

This form was amended in 1963 by deleting the stated dollar amount and substituting a blank, to be properly filled in by the pleader. See Note of Advisory Committee under Form 3.

Form 14. Complaint for Negligence Under Federal Employer's Liability Act

1. Allegation of jurisdiction.

2. During all the times herein mentioned defendant owned and operated in interstate commerce a railroad which passed through a tunnel located at _____ and known as Tunnel No. _____.

3. On or about June 1, 1936, defendant was repairing and enlarging the tunnel in order to protect interstate trains and passengers and freight from injury and in order to make the tunnel more conveniently usable for interstate commerce.

4. In the course of thus repairing and enlarging the tunnel on said day defendant employed plaintiff as one of its workmen, and negligently put plaintiff to work in a portion of the tunnel which defendant had left unprotected and unsupported.

5. By reason of defendant's negligence in thus putting plaintiff to work in that portion of the tunnel, plaintiff was, while so working pursuant to defendant's orders, struck and crushed by a rock, which fell from the unsupported portion of the tunnel, and was (here describe plaintiff's injuries).

6. Prior to these injuries, plaintiff was a strong, able-bodied man, capable of earning and actually earning ____ dollars per day. By these injuries he has been made incapable of any gainful activity, has suffered great physical and mental pain, and has incurred expense in the amount of ____ dollars for medicine, medical attendance, and hospitalization.

Wherefore plaintiff demands judgment against defendant in the sum of ____ dollars and costs.

Form 15. Complaint for Damages Under Merchant Marine Act

1. Allegation of jurisdiction. [If the pleader wishes to invoke the distinctively maritime procedures referred to in Rule 9(h), add the following or its substantial equivalent: This is an admiralty or maritime claim within the meaning of Rule 9(h).]

2. During all the times herein mentioned defendant was the owner of the steamship ____ and used it in the transportation of freight for hire by water in interstate and foreign commerce.

3. During the first part of (month and year) at ____ plaintiff entered the employ of defendant as an able seaman on said steamship under seamen's articles of customary form for a voyage from ____ ports to the Orient and return at a wage of ____ dollars per month and found, which is equal to a wage of ____ dollars per month as a shore worker.

4. On June 1, 1936, said steamship was about ____ days out of the port of ____ and was being navigated by the master and crew on the return voyage to ____ ports. (Here describe weather conditions and the condition of the ship and state as in an ordinary complaint for personal injuries the negligent conduct of defendant.)

5. By reason of defendant's negligence in thus (brief statement of defendant's negligent conduct) and the unseaworthiness of said steamship, plaintiff was (here describe plaintiff's injuries).

6. Prior to these injuries, plaintiff was a strong, able-bodied man, capable of earning and actually earning ____ dollars per day. By these injuries he has been made incapable of any gainful activity; has suffered great physical and mental pain, and has incurred expense in the amount of ____ dollars for medicine, medical attendance, and hospitalization.

Wherefore plaintiff demands judgment against defendant in the sum of ____ dollars and costs.
(As amended Feb. 28, 1966, eff. July 1, 1966.)

ADVISORY COMMITTEE NOTES
1966 Amendment

See Advisory Committee's Note to Form 2.

Form 16. Complaint for Infringement of Patent

1. Allegation of jurisdiction.

2. On May 16, 1934, United States Letters Patent No. ____ were duly and legally issued to plaintiff for an invention in an electric motor; and since that date plaintiff has been and still is the owner of those Letters Patent.

3. Defendant has for a long time past been and still is infringing those Letters Patent by making, selling, and using electric motors embodying the patented invention, and will continue to do so unless enjoined by this court.

4. Plaintiff has placed the required statutory notice on all electric motors manufactured and sold by him under said Letters Patent, and has given written notice to defendant of his said infringement.

Wherefore plaintiff demands a preliminary and final injunction against continued infringement, an accounting for damages, and an assessment of interest and costs against defendant.
(As amended Jan. 21, 1963, eff. July 1, 1963.)

ADVISORY COMMITTEE NOTES
1963 Amendment

The prayer for relief is amended to reflect the language of the present patent statute, Title 35, U.S.C., § 284 (Damages).

Form 17. Complaint for Infringement of Copyright and Unfair Competition

1. Allegation of jurisdiction.

2. Prior to March, 1936, plaintiff, who then was and ever since has been a citizen of the United States, created and wrote an original book, entitled ____.

3. This book contains a large amount of material wholly original with plaintiff and is copyrightable subject matter under the laws of the United States.

4. Between March 2, 1936, and March 10, 1936, plaintiff complied in all respects with the Act of (give citation) and all other laws governing copyright, and secured the exclusive rights and privileges in and to the copyright of said book, and received from the Register of Copyrights a certificate of registration, dated and identified as follows: "March 10, 1936, Class ____, No. ____."

5. Since March 10, 1936, said book has been published by plaintiff and all copies of it made by plaintiff or under his authority or license have been printed, bound, and published in strict conformity with the provisions of the Act of ____ and all other laws governing copyright.

6. Since March 10, 1936, plaintiff has been and still is the sole proprietor of all rights, title, and interest in and to the copyright in said book.

7. After March 10, 1936, defendant infringed said copyright by publishing and placing upon the market a book entitled _____, which was copied largely from plaintiff's copyrighted book, entitled _____.

8. A copy of plaintiff's copyrighted book is hereto attached as "Exhibit 1"; and a copy of defendant's infringing book is hereto attached as "Exhibit 2."

9. Plaintiff has notified defendant that defendant has infringed the copyright of plaintiff, and defendant has continued to infringe the copyright.

10. After March 10, 1936, and continuously since about _____, defendant has been publishing, selling and otherwise marketing the book entitled _____, and has thereby been engaging in unfair trade practices and unfair competition against plaintiff to plaintiff's irreparable damage.

Wherefore plaintiff demands:

(1) That defendant, his agents, and servants be enjoined during the pendency of this action and permanently from infringing said copyright of said plaintiff in any manner, and from publishing, selling, marketing or otherwise disposing of any copies of the book entitled _____.

(2) That defendant be required to pay to plaintiff such damages as plaintiff has sustained in consequence of defendant's infringement of said copyright and said unfair trade practices and unfair competition and to account for

(a) all gains, profits and advantages derived by defendant by said trade practices and unfair competition and

(b) all gains, profits, and advantages derived by defendant by his infringement of plaintiff's copyright or such damages as to the court shall appear proper within the provisions of the copyright statutes, but not less than two hundred and fifty dollars.

(3) That defendant be required to deliver up to be impounded during the pendency of this action all copies of said book entitled _____ in his possession or under his control and to deliver up for destruction all infringing copies and all plates, molds, and other matter for making such infringing copies.

(4) That defendant pay to plaintiff the costs of this action and reasonable attorney's fees to be allowed to the plaintiff by the court.

(5) That plaintiff have such other and further relief as is just.

(As amended Dec. 27, 1946, eff. Mar. 19, 1948.)

ADVISORY COMMITTEE NOTES
1946 Amendment

This form, as set out, incorporates amendments made at the same time certain rules of the Federal Rules of Civil Procedure were amended. See Rule 86(b) of such rules.

Form 18. Complaint for Interpleader and Declaratory Relief

1. Allegation of jurisdiction.

2. On or about June 1, 1935, plaintiff issued to G. H. a policy of life insurance whereby plaintiff promised to pay to K. L. as beneficiary the sum of _____ dollars upon the death of G. H. The policy required the payment by G. H. of a stipulated premium on June 1, 1936, and annually thereafter as a condition precedent to its continuance in force.

3. No part of the premium due June 1, 1936, was ever paid and the policy ceased to have any force or effect on July 1, 1936.

4. Thereafter, on September 1, 1936, G. H. and K. L. died as the result of a collision between a locomotive and the automobile in which G. H. and K. L. were riding.

5. Defendant C. D. is the duly appointed and acting executor of the will of G. H.; defendant E. F. is the duly appointed and acting executor of the will of K. L.; defendant X. Y. claims to have been duly designated as beneficiary of said policy in place of K. L.

6. Each of defendants, C. D., E. F., and X. Y. is claiming that the above-mentioned policy was in full force and effect at the time of the death of G. H.; each of them is claiming to be the only person entitled to receive payment of the amount of the policy and has made demand for payment thereof.

7. By reason of these conflicting claims of the defendants, plaintiff is in great doubt as to which defendant is entitled to be paid the amount of the policy, if it was in force at the death of G. H.

Wherefore plaintiff demands that the court adjudge:

(1) That none of the defendants is entitled to recover from plaintiff the amount of said policy or any part thereof.

(2) That each of the defendants be restrained from instituting any action against plaintiff for the recovery of the amount of said policy or any part thereof.

(3) That, if the court shall determine that said policy was in force at the death of G. H., the defendants be required to interplead and settle between themselves their rights to the money due under said policy, and that plaintiff be discharged from all liability in the premises except to the person whom the court shall adjudge entitled to the amount of said policy.

(4) That plaintiff recover its costs.

(As amended Jan. 21, 1963, eff. July 1, 1963.)

ADVISORY COMMITTEE NOTES
1963 Amendment

This form was amended in 1963 by deleting the stated dollar amount and substituting a blank, to be properly filled in by the pleader. See Note of Advisory Committee under Form 3.

Form 18–A.　[Abrogated]
ADVISORY COMMITTEE NOTES

This form is superseded by Forms 1A and 1B in view of the revision of Rule 4.

HISTORICAL NOTES
Effective Date of Abrogation

Abrogation effective Dec. 1, 1993, absent contrary Congressional action.

Form 19.　Motion to Dismiss, Presenting Defenses of Failure to State a Claim, of Lack of Service of Process, of Improper Venue, and of Lack of Jurisdiction Under Rule 12(b)

The defendant moves the court as follows:

1. To dismiss the action because the complaint fails to state a claim against defendant upon which relief can be granted.

2. To dismiss the action or in lieu thereof to quash the return of service of summons on the grounds (a) that the defendant is a corporation organized under the laws of Delaware and was not and is not subject to service of process within the Southern District of New York, and (b) that the defendant has not been properly served with process in this action, all of which more clearly appears in the affidavits of M. N. and X. Y. hereto annexed as Exhibit A and Exhibit B respectively.

3. To dismiss the action on the ground that it is in the wrong district because (a) the jurisdiction of this court is invoked solely on the ground that the action arises under the Constitution and laws of the United States and (b) the defendant is a corporation incorporated under the laws of the State of Delaware and is not licensed to do or doing business in the Southern District of New York, all of which more clearly appears in the affidavits of K. L. and V. W. hereto annexed as Exhibits C and D, respectively.

4. To dismiss the action on the ground that the court lacks jurisdiction because the amount actually in controversy is less than ten thousand dollars exclusive of interest and costs.

Signed: _____
Attorney for Defendant.
Address: _____

Notice of Motion

To: _____

Attorney for Plaintiff.

_____

Please take notice, that the undersigned will bring the above motion on for hearing before this Court at Room ___, United States Court House, Foley Square, City of New York, on the ___ day of ___, 20___, at 10 o'clock in the forenoon of that day or as soon thereafter as counsel can be heard.

Signed: _____
Attorney for Defendant.
Address: _____

NOTES

1. The above motion and notice of motion may be combined and denominated Notice of Motion. See Rule 7(b).

2. As to paragraph 3, see U.S.C., Title 28, § 1391 (Venue generally), subsections (b) and (c).

3. As to paragraph 4, see U.S.C., Title 28, § 1331 (Federal question; amount in controversy; costs), as amended by P.L. 85–554, 72 Stat. 415, July 25, 1958, requiring that the amount in controversy, exclusive of interest and costs, be in excess of $10,000. [Editor's note: This Note reflects U.S.C., Title 28, § 1331, prior to the 1976 and 1980 amendments eliminating the $10,000 jurisdictional amount. See U.S.C., Title 28, § 1332.]

(As amended Dec. 29, 1948, eff. Oct. 20, 1949; Apr. 17, 1961, eff. July 19, 1961; Mar. 27, 2003, eff. Dec. 1, 2003.)

Form 20.　Answer Presenting Defenses Under Rule 12(b)

First Defense

The complaint fails to state a claim against defendant upon which relief can be granted.

Second Defense

If defendant is indebted to plaintiffs for the goods mentioned in the complaint, he is indebted to them jointly with G. H. G. H. is alive; is a citizen of the State of New York and a resident of this district, is subject to the jurisdiction of this court, as to both service of process and venue; can be made a party without depriving this court of jurisdiction of the present parties, and has not been made a party.

Third Defense

Defendant admits the allegation contained in paragraphs 1 and 4 of the complaint; alleges that he is without knowledge or information sufficient to form a belief as to the truth of the allegations contained in paragraph 2 of the complaint; and denies each and every other allegation contained in the complaint.

Fourth Defense

The right of action set forth in the complaint did not accrue within six years next before the commencement of this action.

Counterclaim

(Here set forth any claim as a counterclaim in the manner in which a claim is pleaded in a complaint. No statement of the grounds on which the court's jurisdiction depends need be made unless the counterclaim requires independent grounds of jurisdiction.)

Cross-Claim Against Defendant M. N.

(Here set forth the claim constituting a cross-claim against defendant M. N. in the manner in which a claim is pleaded in a complaint. The statement of grounds upon which the court's jurisdiction depends need not be made unless the cross-claim requires independent grounds of jurisdiction.)

NOTE

The above form contains examples of certain defenses provided for in Rule 12(b). The first defense challenges the legal sufficiency of the complaint. It is a substitute for a general demurrer or a motion to dismiss.

The second defense embodies the old plea in abatement; the decision thereon, however, may well provide under Rules 19 and 21 for the citing in of the party rather than an abatement of the action.

The third defense is an answer on the merits.

The fourth defense is one of the affirmative defenses provided for in Rule 8(c).

The answer also includes a counterclaim and a cross-claim.

ADVISORY COMMITTEE NOTES

1946 Amendment

The explanatory note incorporates revisions made by the Advisory Committee at the same time amendments to certain rules of the Federal Rules of Civil Procedure were made. See also Rule 12(b) as amended.

Form 21. Answer to Complaint Set Forth in Form 8, With Counterclaim for Interpleader

Defense

Defendant admits the allegations stated in paragraph 1 of the complaint; and denies the allegations stated in paragraph 2 to the extent set forth in the counterclaim herein.

Counterclaim for Interpleader

1. Defendant received the sum of _____ dollars as a deposit from E. F.

2. Plaintiff has demanded the payment of such deposit to him by virtue of an assignment of it which he claims to have received from E. F.

3. E. F. has notified the defendant that he claims such deposit, that the purported assignment is not valid, and that he holds the defendant responsible for the deposit.

Wherefore defendant demands:

(1) That the court order E. F. to be made a party defendant to respond to the complaint and to this counterclaim.[1]

(2) That the court order the plaintiff and E. F. to interplead their respective claims.

(3) That the court adjudge whether the plaintiff or E. F. is entitled to the sum of money.

(4) That the court discharge defendant from all liability in the premises except to the person it shall adjudge entitled to the sum of money.

(5) That the court award to the defendant its costs and attorney's fees.

(As amended Jan. 21, 1963, eff. July 1, 1963.)

[1] Rule 13(h) provides for the court ordering parties to a counterclaim, but who are not parties to the original action, to be brought in as defendants.

ADVISORY COMMITTEE NOTES

1963 Amendment

This form was amended in 1963 by deleting the stated dollar amount and substituting a blank, to be properly filled in by the pleader. See Note of Advisory Committee under Form 3.

[Form 22.   Eliminated, eff. July 1, 1963]

HISTORICAL NOTES

Codifications

Form 22 for motion to bring in third-party defendant, setting out as an exhibit summons and third-party complaint, and for notice of motion, was superseded by Forms 22–A and 22–B, setting out summons and complaint against third-party defendant, and motion to bring in third-party defendant, effective July 1, 1963. See Advisory Committee notes under Forms 22–A and 22–B.

Form 22–A. Summons and Complaint Against Third-Party Defendant

United States District Court for the
Southern District of New York

Civil Action, File Number ____

A. B., Plaintiff	)	
v.	)	
C. D., Defendant and	)	
Third–Party Plaintiff	)	*Summons*
v.	)	
E. F., Third-Party Defendant	)	

To the above-named Third-Party Defendant:

You are hereby summoned and required to serve upon _____, plaintiff's attorney whose address is _____, and upon _____, who is attorney for C. D., defendant and third-party plaintiff, and whose address is _____, an answer to the third-party complaint which is herewith served upon you within 20 days after the service of this summons upon you exclusive of the day of service. If you fail to do so, judgment by default will be taken against you for the relief demanded in the third-party complaint. There is also served upon you herewith a copy of the complaint of the plaintiff which you may but are not required to answer.

_____,
Clerk of Court.

[Seal of District Court]

Dated _____

United States District Court for the
Southern District of New York

Civil Action, File Number ___

A. B., Plaintiff	)
v.	)
C. D., Defendant and	)
Third-Party Plaintiff	) *Third-Party Complaint*
v.	)
E. F., Third-Party Defendant	)

1. Plaintiff A. B. has filed against defendant C. D. a complaint, a copy of which is hereto attached as "Exhibit A."

2. (Here state the grounds upon which C. D. is entitled to recover from E. F., all or part of what A. B. may recover from C. D. The statement should be framed as in an original complaint.)

Wherefore C. D. demands judgment against third-party defendant E. F. for all sums [1] that may be adjudged against defendant C. D. in favor of plaintiff A. B.

Signed: _____,
Attorney for Defendant C. D.
Address: _____

Notice of Motion

(Contents the same as in Form 19. The notice should be addressed to all parties to the action.)

Exhibit X

(Contents the same as in Form 22–A.)

(Added Jan. 21, 1963, eff. July 1, 1963.)

ADVISORY COMMITTEE NOTES
1963 Adoption

Form 22–B is intended for use when, under amended Rule 14(a), leave of court is required to bring in a third-party defendant.

Signed: _____
Attorney for C. D.,
Third-Party Plaintiff
Address: _____

(Added Jan. 21, 1963, eff. July 1, 1963.)

[1] Make appropriate change where C. D. is entitled to only partial recovery-over against E. F.

ADVISORY COMMITTEE NOTES
1963 Adoption

Under the amendment of Rule 14(a), a defendant who files a third-party complaint not later than 10 days after serving his original answer need not obtain leave of court to bring in the third-party defendant by service under Rule 4. Form 22–A is intended for use in these cases.

The changes in the form of summons reflect an earlier amendment of Rule 14(a), effective in 1948, making it permissive, rather than mandatory, for the third-party defendant to answer the plaintiff's complaint. See *Cooper v. D/S A/S Progress,* 188 F.Supp. 578 (E.D.Pa.1960); 1A Barron & Holtzoff, *Federal Practice & Procedure* 696 (Wright ed. 1960).

Under the amendment of Rule 5(a) requiring, with certain exceptions, that papers be served upon all the parties to the action, the third-party defendant, even if he makes no answer to the plaintiff's complaint, is obliged to serve upon the plaintiff a copy of his answer to the third-party complaint. Similarly, the defendant is obliged to serve upon the plaintiff a copy of the summons and complaint against the third-party defendant.

Form 22–B. Motion to Bring in Third-Party Defendant

Defendant moves for leave, as third-party plaintiff, to cause to be served upon E. F. a summons and third-party complaint, copies of which are hereto attached as Exhibit X.

Form 23. Motion to Intervene as a Defendant Under Rule 24

(Based upon the complaint, Form 16)

United States District Court for the
Southern District of New York

Civil Action, File Number ___

A. B., plaintiff	)
v.	) *Motion to intervene*
	) *as a defendant*
C. D., defendant	)
E. F., applicant	)
for intervention	)

E. F. moves for leave to intervene as a defendant in this action, in order to assert the defenses set forth in his proposed answer, of which a copy is hereto attached, on the ground that he is the manufacturer and vendor to the defendant, as well as to others, of the articles alleged in the complaint to be an infringement of plaintiff's patent, and as such has a defense to plaintiff's claim presenting both questions of law and of fact which are common to the main action.[1]

Signed: _____,
Attorney for E. F.,
Applicant for Intervention.
Address: _____

Notice of Motion

(Contents the same as in Form 19)

United States District Court for the Southern District of New York

Civil Action, File Number ____

A. B., plaintiff)
)
        v.   )   *Intervener's Answer*
C. D., defendant)
E. F., intervener)

First Defense

Intervener admits the allegations stated in paragraphs 1 and 4 of the complaint; denies the allegations in paragraph 3, and denies the allegations in paragraph 2 in so far as they assert the legality of the issuance of the Letters Patent to plaintiff.

Second Defense

Plaintiff is not the first inventor of the articles covered by the Letters Patent specified in his complaint, since articles substantially identical in character were previously patented in Letters Patent granted to intervener on January 5, 1920.

Signed: _____,
Attorney for E. F.,
Intervener.
Address: _____

(As amended Dec. 29, 1948, eff. Oct. 20, 1949.)

[1] For other grounds of intervention, either of right or in the discretion of the court, see Rule 24(a) and (b).

Form 24. Request for Production of Documents, etc., Under Rule 34

Plaintiff A. B. requests defendant C. D. to respond within _____ days to the following requests:

(1) That defendant produce and permit plaintiff to inspect and to copy each of the following documents:

(Here list the documents either individually or by category and describe each of them.)

(Here state the time, place, and manner of making the inspection and performance of any related acts.)

(2) That defendant produce and permit plaintiff to inspect and to copy, test, or sample each of the following objects:

(Here list the objects either individually or by category and describe each of them.)

(Here state the time, place, and manner of making the inspection and performance of any related acts.)

(3) That defendant permit plaintiff to enter (here describe property to be entered) and to inspect and to photograph, test or sample (here describe the portion of the real property and the objects to be inspected).

(Here state the time, place, and manner of making the inspection and performance of any related acts.)

Signed: _____,
Attorney for Plaintiff.
Address: _____

(As amended Mar. 30, 1970, eff. July 1, 1970.)

ADVISORY COMMITTEE NOTES

1970 Amendment

Form 24 is revised to accord with the changes made in Rule 34.

Form 25. Request for Admission Under Rule 36

Plaintiff A. B. requests defendant C. D. within ____ days after service of this request to make the following admissions for the purpose of this action only and subject to all pertinent objections to admissibility which may be interposed at the trial:

1. That each of the following documents, exhibited with this request, is genuine.

(Here list the documents and describe each document.)

2. That each of the following statements is true.

(Here list the statements.)

Signed: _____,
Attorney for Plaintiff.
Address: _____

(As amended Dec. 27, 1946, eff. Mar. 19, 1948.)

Form 26. Allegation of Reason for Omitting Party

When it is necessary, under Rule 19(c), for the pleader to set forth in his pleading the names of persons who ought to be made parties, but who are not so made, there should be an allegation such as the one set out below:

John Doe named in this complaint is not made a party to this action [because he is not subject to the jurisdiction of this court]; [because he cannot be made a party to this action without depriving this court of jurisdiction].

Form 27. [Abrogated. Dec. 4, 1967, eff. July 1, 1968]

ADVISORY COMMITTEE NOTES

1967 Amendment

The form of notice of appeal is transferred to the Federal Rules of Appellate Procedure as Form 1.

Form 28. Notice: Condemnation

United States District Court for the
Southern District of New York

Civil Action, File Number ___

United States of America, plaintiff	)
v.	)
1,000 Acres of Land in [here insert a	) *Notice*
general location as "City of ___"	)
or "County of ___"], John Doe et	)
al., and Unknown Owners, Defendants	)

To (here insert the names of the defendants to whom the notice is directed):

You are hereby notified that a complaint in condemnation has heretofore been filed in the office of the clerk of the United States District Court for the Southern District of New York, in the United States Court House in New York City, New York, for the taking (here state the interest to be acquired, as "an estate in fee simple") for use (here state briefly the use, "as a site for a post-office building") of the following described property in which you have or claim an interest.

(Here insert brief description of the property in which the defendants, to whom the notice is directed, have or claim an interest.)

The authority for the taking is (here state briefly, as "the Act of ___, ___ Stat. ___, U.S.C., Title ___, § ___".)[1]

You are further notified that if you desire to present any objection or defense to the taking of your property you are required to serve your answer on the plaintiff's attorney at the address herein designated within twenty days after _____.[2]

Your answer shall identify the property in which you claim to have an interest, state the nature and extent of the interest you claim, and state all of your objections and defenses to the taking of your property. All defenses and objections not so presented are waived. And in case of your failure so to answer the complaint, judgment of condemnation of that part of the above-described property in which you have or claim an interest will be rendered.

But without answering, you may serve on the plaintiff's attorney a notice of appearance designating the property in which you claim to be interested. Thereafter you will receive notice of all proceedings affecting it. At the trial of the issue of just compensation, whether or not you have previously appeared or answered, you may present evidence as to the amount of the compensation to be paid for your property, and you may share in the distribution of the award.

United States Attorney.
Address _____

(Here state an address within the district where the United States Attorney may be served as "United States Court House, New York, N.Y.".)

Dated _____

(Added May 1, 1951, eff. Aug. 1, 1951.)

[1] And where appropriate add a citation to any applicable Executive Order.

[2] Here insert the words "personal service of this notice upon you," if personal service is to be made pursuant to subdivision (d)(3)(i) of this rule [Rule 71A]; or, insert the date of the last publication of notice, if service by publication is to be made pursuant to subdivision (d)(3)(ii) of this rule.

Form 29. Complaint: Condemnation

United States District Court for the
Southern District of New York

Civil Action, File Number ___

United States of America, Plaintiff	)
v.	)
1,000 Acres of Land in [here insert a	) *Complaint*
general location as "City of ___"	)
or "County of ___"], John Doe, et	)
al., and Unknown Owners, Defendants	)

1.   This is an action of a civil nature brought by the United States of America for the taking of property under the power of eminent domain and for the ascertainment and award of just compensation to the owners and parties in interest.[1]

2.   The authority for the taking is (here state briefly, as "the Act of ___, ___ Stat. ___, U.S.C., Title ___, § ___").[2]

3.   The use for which the property is to be taken is (here state briefly the use, "as a site for a post-office building").

4.   The interest to be acquired in the property is (here state the interest as "an estate in fee simple").

5.   The property so to be taken is (here set forth a description of the property sufficient for its identification) or (described in Exhibit A hereto attached and made a part hereof).

6.   The persons known to the plaintiff to have or claim an interest in the property[3] are:

(Here set forth the names of such persons and the interests claimed.)[4]

7.   In addition to the persons named, there are or may be others who have or may claim some interest in the property to be taken, whose names are unknown to the plaintiff and on diligent inquiry have not been ascertained. They are made parties to the action under the designation "Unknown Owners."

Complete Annotation Materials, see Title 28 U.S.C.A.

Wherefore the plaintiff demands judgment that the property be condemned and that just compensation for the taking be ascertained and awarded and for such other relief as may be lawful and proper.

_____
United States Attorney.
Address _____

(Here state an address within the district where the United States Attorney may be served, as "United States Court House, New York, N.Y.".)
(Added May 1, 1951, eff. Aug. 1, 1951.)

1 If the plaintiff is not the United States, but is, for example, a corporation invoking the power of eminent domain delegated to it by the state, then this paragraph 1 of the complaint should be appropriately modified and should be preceded by a paragraph appropriately alleging federal jurisdiction for the action, such as diversity. See Form 2.

2 And where appropriate add a citation to any applicable Executive Order.

3 At the commencement of the action the plaintiff need name as defendants only the persons having or claiming an interest in the property whose names are then known, but prior to any hearing involving the compensation to be paid for a particular piece of property the plaintiff must add as defendants all persons having or claiming an interest in that property whose names can be ascertained by an appropriate search of the records and also those whose names have otherwise been learned. See Rule 71A(c)(2).

4 The plaintiff should designate, as to each separate piece of property, the defendants who have been joined as owners thereof or of some interest therein. See Rule 71A(c)(2).

Form 30. Suggestion of Death Upon the Record Under Rule 25(a)(1)

A. B. [describe as a party, or as executor, administrator, or other representative or successor of C. D., the deceased party] suggests upon the record, pursuant to Rule 25(a)(1), the death of C. D. [describe as party] during the pendency of this action.
(Added Jan. 21, 1963, eff. July 1, 1963.)

Form 31. Judgment on Jury Verdict

United States District Court for the
Southern District of New York

Civil Action, File Number ___

A. B., Plaintiff   )
        v.   )   *Judgment*
C. D., Defendant)

This action came on for trial before the Court and a jury, Honorable John Marshall, District Judge, presiding, and the issues having been duly tried and the jury having duly rendered its verdict,

It is Ordered and Adjudged

[that the plaintiff A. B. recover of the defendant C. D. the sum of _____, with interest thereon at the rate of _____ percent as provided by law, and his costs of action.]

[that the plaintiff take nothing, that the action be dismissed on the merits, and that the defendant C. D. recover of the plaintiff A. B. his costs of action.]

Dated at New York, New York, this ___ day of _____, 20___.

_____,
Clerk of Court.

NOTE

1. This Form is illustrative of the judgment to be entered upon the general verdict of a jury. It deals with the cases where there is a general jury verdict awarding the plaintiff money damages or finding for the defendant, but is adaptable to other situations of jury verdicts.

2. The clerk, unless the court otherwise orders, is required forthwith to prepare, sign, and enter the judgment upon a general jury verdict without awaiting any direction by the court. The form of the judgment upon a special verdict or a general verdict accompanied by answers to interrogatories shall be promptly approved by the court, and the clerk shall thereupon enter it. See Rule 58, as amended.

3. The Rules contemplate a simple judgment promptly entered. See Rule 54(a). Every judgment shall be set forth on a separate document. See Rule 58, as amended.

4. Attorneys are not to submit forms of judgment unless directed in exceptional cases to do so by the court. See Rule 58, as amended.
(Added Jan. 21, 1963, eff. July 1, 1963, and amended Mar. 27, 2003, eff. Dec. 1, 2003.)

Form 32. Judgment on Decision by the Court

United States District Court for the
Southern District of New York

Civil Action, File Number ___

A. B., Plaintiff   )
        v.   )   *Judgment*
C. D., Defendant)

This action came on for [trial] [hearing] before the Court, Honorable John Marshall, District Judge, presiding, and the issues having been duly [tried] [heard] and a decision having been duly rendered,

It is Ordered and Adjudged

[that the plaintiff A. B. recover of the defendant C. D. the sum of _____, with interest thereon at the rate of _____ percent as provided by law, and his costs of action.]

[that the plaintiff take nothing, that the action be dismissed on the merits, and that the defendant C. D. recover of the plaintiff A. B. his costs of action.]

Dated at New York, New York, this ___ day of _____, 20___.

_____,
Clerk of Court.

NOTES

1. This Form is illustrative of the judgment to be entered upon a decision of the court. It deals with the cases of decisions by the court awarding a party only money damages or costs, but is adaptable to other decisions by the court.

2. The clerk, unless the court otherwise orders, is required forthwith, without awaiting any direction by the court, to prepare, sign, and enter the judgment upon a decision by the court that a party shall recover only a sum certain or costs or that all relief shall be denied. The form of the judgment upon a decision by the court granting other relief shall be promptly approved by the court, and the clerk shall thereupon enter it. See Rule 58, as amended.

3. See also paragraphs 3–4 of the Explanatory Note to Form 31.

(Added Jan. 21, 1963, eff. July 1, 1963, and amended Mar. 27, 2003, eff. Dec. 1, 2003.)

Form 33. Notice of Availability of Magistrate Judge to Exercise Jurisdiction

In accordance with the provisions of Title 28, U.S.C. § 636(c), you are hereby notified that a United States magistrate judge of this district court is available to exercise the court's jurisdiction and to conduct any or all proceedings in this case including a jury or nonjury trial, and entry of a final judgment. Exercise of this jurisdiction by a magistrate judge is, however, permitted only if all parties voluntarily consent.

You may, without adverse substantive consequences, withhold your consent, but this will prevent the court's jurisdiction from being exercised by a magistrate judge. If any party withholds consent, the identity of the parties consenting or withholding consent will not be communicated to any magistrate judge or to the district judge to whom the case has been assigned.

An appeal from a judgment entered by a magistrate judge may be taken directly to the United States court of appeals for this judicial circuit in the same manner as an appeal from any other judgment of a district court.

Copies of the Form for the "Consent to Jurisdiction by a United States Magistrate Judge" are available from the clerk of the court.

(Added Apr. 28, 1983, eff. Aug. 1, 1983, and amended Apr. 22, 1993, eff. Dec. 1, 1993; April 11, 1997, eff. Dec. 1, 1997.)

ADVISORY COMMITTEE NOTES

1993 Amendments

This form, together with Form 34, is revised in light of the Judicial Improvements Act of 1990. Section 308 modified 28 U.S.C. § 636(c)(2) to enhance the potential of parties consenting to trial before a magistrate judge. While the exercise of jurisdiction by a magistrate judge remains dependent on the voluntary consent of the parties, the statute provides that the parties should be advised, and may be reminded, of the availability of this option and eliminates the proscription against judicial suggestions of the potential benefits of referral provided the parties are also advised that they "are free to withhold consent without adverse substantive consequences." The parties may be advised if the withholding of consent will result in a potential delay in trial.

HISTORICAL NOTES

Change of Name

United States magistrate appointed under section 631 of Title 28, Judiciary and Judicial Procedure, to be known as United States magistrate judge after Dec. 1, 1990, with any reference to United States magistrate or magistrate in Title 28, in any other Federal statute, etc., deemed a reference to United States magistrate judge appointed under section 631 of Title 28, see section 321 of Pub.L. 101–650, set out as a note under section 631 of Title 28.

Form 34. Consent to Exercise of Jurisdiction by a United States Magistrate Judge

UNITED STATES DISTRICT COURT

_____ DISTRICT OF _____

```
                          )
            Plaintiff,    )
                          )
vs.                       )  Docket No. _____
                          )
            Defendant.    )
```

CONSENT TO JURISDICTION BY A UNITED STATES MAGISTRATE JUDGE

In accordance with the provisions of Title 28, U.S.C. § 636(c), the undersigned party or parties to the above-captioned civil matter hereby voluntarily consent to have a United States magistrate judge conduct any and all further proceedings in the case, including trial, and order the entry of a final judgment.

_____   _____
Date   Signature

Note: Return this form to the Clerk of the Court if you consent to jurisdiction by a magistrate judge. Do not send a copy of this form to any district judge or magistrate judge.

(Added Apr. 28, 1983, eff. Aug. 1, 1983, and amended Apr. 22, 1993, eff. Dec. 1, 1993; April 11, 1997, eff. Dec. 1, 1997.)

HISTORICAL NOTES

Change of Name

United States magistrate appointed under section 631 of Title 28, Judiciary and Judicial Procedure, to be known as United States magistrate judge after Dec. 1, 1990, with any reference to United States magistrate or magistrate in Title 28, in any other Federal statute, etc., deemed a reference to United States magistrate judge appointed under section 631 of Title 28, see section 321 of Pub.L. 101–650, set out as a note under section 631 of Title 28.

Form 34A. Order of Reference

UNITED STATES DISTRICT COURT

_____ DISTRICT OF _____

```
                          )
           Plaintiff,     )
                          )
vs.                       )  Docket No. _____
                          )
           Defendant.     )
```

ORDER OF REFERENCE

IT IS HEREBY ORDERED that the above-captioned matter be referred to United States Magistrate Judge for all further proceedings and entry of judgment in accordance with Title 28, U.S.C. § 636(c) and the consent of the parties.

_____
                           U.S. District Judge

(Added Apr. 22, 1993, eff. Dec. 1, 1993.)

Form 35. Report of Parties' Planning Meeting

[Caption and Names of Parties]

1. Pursuant to Fed.R.Civ.P. 26(f), a meeting was held on (date) at (place) and was attended by:

(name) for plaintiff(s)

(name) for defendant(s) (party name)

(name) for defendant(s) (party name)

2. Pre–Discovery Disclosures. The parties [have exchanged] [will exchange by (date)] the information required by [Fed.R.Civ.P. 26(a)(1)] [local rule ___].

3. Discovery Plan. The parties jointly propose to the court the following discovery plan: [Use separate paragraphs or subparagraphs as necessary if parties disagree.]

Discovery will be needed on the following subjects: (brief description of subjects on which discovery will be needed)

All discovery commenced in time to be completed by (date). [Discovery on (issue for early discovery) to be completed by (date).]

Maximum of ___ interrogatories by each party to any other party. [Responses due ___ days after service.]

Maximum of ___ requests for admission by each party to any other party. [Responses due ___ days after service.]

Maximum of ___ depositions by plaintiff(s) and ___ by defendant(s).

Each deposition [other than of _____] limited to maximum of ___ hours unless extended by agreement of parties.

Reports from retained experts under Rule 26(a)(2) due:

from plaintiff(s) by (date)

from defendant(s) by (date)

Supplementations under Rule 26(e) due (time(s) or interval(s)).

4. Other Items. [Use separate paragraphs or subparagraphs as necessary if parties disagree.]

The parties [request] [do not request] a conference with the court before entry of the scheduling order.

The parties request a pretrial conference in (month and year).

Plaintiff(s) should be allowed until (date) to join additional parties and until (date) to amend the pleadings.

Defendant(s) should be allowed until (date) to join additional parties and until (date) to amend the pleadings.

All potentially dispositive motions should be filed by (date).

Settlement [is likely] [is unlikely] [cannot be evaluated prior to (date)] [may be enhanced by use of the following alternative dispute resolution procedure: [_____].

Final lists of witnesses and exhibits under Rule 26(a)(3) should be due

from plaintiff(s) by (date)

from defendant(s) by (date)

Parties should have ___ days after service of final lists of witnesses and exhibits to list objections under Rule 26(a)(3).

The case should be ready for trial by (date) [and at this time is expected to take approximately (length of time)].

[Other matters.]

Date: _____
(Added Apr. 22, 1993, eff. Dec. 1, 1993.)

ADVISORY COMMITTEE NOTES

1993 Adoption

This form illustrates the type of report the parties are expected to submit to the court under revised Rule 26(f) and may be useful as a checklist of items to be discussed at the meeting.

TITLE 28

JUDICIARY AND JUDICIAL PROCEDURE

Act June 25, 1948, c. 646, § 1, 62 Stat. 869

SELECTED SECTIONS

HISTORICAL AND STATUTORY NOTES

Effective and Applicability Provisions

Section 38 of Act June 25, 1948, c. 646, 62 Stat. 992, provided that: "The provisions of this Act shall take effect on Sept. 1, 1948."

Separability of Provisions

Section 34 of Act June 25, 1948, c. 646, 62 Stat. 991, provided that: "If any part of Title 28, Judiciary and Judicial Procedure, as set out in section 1 of this Act, shall be held invalid, the remainder shall not be affected thereby."

Enactment into Law; Citation

Section 1 of Act June 25, 1948, c. 646, 62 Stat. 869, provided in part: "That title 28 of the United States Code, entitled 'Judicial Code and Judiciary' is hereby revised, codified, and enacted into law, and may be cited as 'Title 28, United States Code, section ____.'"

Miscellaneous Provisions

Sections 2 to 32 of Act June 25, 1948, c. 646, 62 Stat. 985 to 991 contained certain executing provisions and conforming amendments to sections in other titles of the United States Code. For text of sections 2 to 32, see "Act June 25, 1948, c. 646, §§ 2 to 39, 62 Stat. 985 to 991," set out following the last section of Title 28.

Section 35 of Act June 25, 1948, c. 646, 62 Stat. 991, was not classified to the United States Code. For text of section 35, see "Act June 25, 1948, c. 646, §§ 2 to 39, 62 Stat. 985 to 991" set out following the last section of Title 28.

Sections 36 and 37 of Act June 25, 1948, c. 646, 62 Stat. 991, 992, contained certain executing provisions and conforming amendments to sections in other titles of the United States Code. For text of sections 36 and 37, see "Act June 25, 1948, c. 646, §§ 2 to 39, 62 Stat. 985 to 991", set out following the last section of Title 28.

Legislative Construction

Section 33 of Act June 25, 1948, c. 646, 62 Stat. 991, provided that: "No inference of a legislative construction is to be drawn by reason of the chapter in Title 28, Judiciary and Judicial Procedure, as set out in section 1 of this Act, in which any section is placed, nor by reason of the catchlines used in such title."

Repeals; Rights and Liabilities Saved

Section 39 of Act June 25, 1948, c. 646, 62 Stat. 992, repealed the sections or parts thereof of the Revised Statutes of the United States, Statutes at Large, or the Revised Statutes of the District of Columbia covering provisions codified in this title, but saved any rights or liabilities then existing under said sections or parts thereof.

Writs of Error

Act Jan. 31, 1928, c. 14, § 1, 45 Stat. 54 [section 861a of former Title 28, Judicial Code and Judiciary], provided that: "The writ of error in cases, civil and criminal, is abolished. All relief which heretofore [Jan. 31, 1928] could be obtained by writ of error shall hereafter be obtainable by appeal." This provision was omitted from the 1948 Revised Judicial Code as obsolete, and repealed by Act June 25, 1948, c. 646, § 39, 62 Stat. 992.

R.S. § 1012 as affected by Act Mar. 3, 1911, c. 231, § 291, 36 Stat. 1167 [Section 880 of former Title 28, Judicial Code and Judiciary], provided that appeals from district courts shall be subject to the same rules, regulations, and restrictions as are or may be prescribed in law in cases of writs of error. This provision was repealed by Act June 25, 1948, c. 646, § 39, 62 Stat. 992. Section 2 of Act Jan. 31, 1928, c. 14, 45 Stat. 54, as amended Apr. 26, 1928, c. 440, 45 Stat. 466; June 25, 1948, c. 646, § 23, 62 Stat. 990 [section 861b of former Title 28, Judicial Code and Judiciary], provided that: "All Acts of Congress referring to writs of error shall be construed as amended to the extent necessary to substitute appeal for writ of error."

Title 28 as Continuation of Existing Law; Change of Name of Circuit Courts of Appeals

Section 2(b) of Act June 25, 1948, c. 646, 62 Stat. 985, provided that: "The provisions of Title 28, Judiciary and Judicial Procedure, of the United States Code, set out in section 1 of this Act, with respect to the organization of each of the several courts therein provided for and of the Administrative Office of the United States Courts, shall be construed as continuations of existing law, and the tenure of the judges, officers, and employees thereof and of the United States attorneys and marshals and their deputies and assistants, in office on the effective date of this Act [Sept. 1, 1948], shall not be affected by its enactment, but each of them shall continue to serve in the same capacity under the appropriate provisions of title 28, as set out in section 1 of this Act, pursuant to his prior appointment: *Provided, however,* That each circuit court of appeals shall, as in said title 28 set out, hereafter be known as a United States court of appeals. No loss of rights, interruption of jurisdiction, or prejudice to matters pending in any of such courts on the effective date of this Act shall result from its enactment."

PART IV—JURISDICTION AND VENUE

HISTORICAL AND STATUTORY NOTES

Codifications

The analysis of chapters comprising Part IV was amended by Pub.L. 95–598, Title II, § 241(b), Nov. 6, 1978, 92 Stat. 2671, effective June 28, 1984, pursuant to Pub.L. 95–598, Title IV, § 402(b), Nov. 6, 1978, 92 Stat. 2682, as amended by Pub.L. 98–249, § 1(a), Mar. 31, 1984, 98 Stat. 116; Pub.L. 98–271, § 1(a), Apr. 30, 1984, 98 Stat. 163; Pub.L. 98–299, § 1(a), May 25, 1984, 98 Stat. 214; Pub.L. 98–325, § 1(a),

June 20, 1984, 98 Stat. 268, set out as an Effective Date note preceding section 101 of Title 11, Bankruptcy, by adding:

Section 402(b) of Pub.L. 95–598 was amended by section 113 of Pub.L. 98–353, Title I, July 10, 1984, 98 Stat. 343, by substituting "shall not be effective" for "shall take effect on June 28, 1984", thereby eliminating the amendment by section 241(b) of Pub.L. 95–598, effective June 27, 1984, pursuant to section 122(c) of Pub.L. 98–353, set out as an Effective and Applicability Provisions note under section 151 of this title.

Section 121(a) of Pub.L. 98–353 directed that section 402(b) of Pub.L. 95–598 be amended by substituting "the date of enactment of the Bankruptcy Amendments and Federal Judgeship Act of 1984 [i.e. July 10, 1984]" for "June 28, 1984". This amendment was not executed in view of the prior amendment to section 402(b) of Pub.L. 95–598 by section 113 of Pub.L. 98–353.

Change of Name

References to United States Claims Court deemed to refer to United States Court of Federal Claims and references to Claims Court deemed to refer to Court of Federal Claims, see section 902(b) of Pub.L. 102–572, set out as a note under section 171 of Title 28, Judiciary and Judicial Procedure.

CHAPTER 81—SUPREME COURT

HISTORICAL AND STATUTORY NOTES

Definitions of Courts and Judges

Section 32 of Act June 25, 1948, as amended by Act May 24, 1949, c. 139, § 127, 63 Stat. 107, provided:

"(a) All laws of the United States in force on September 1, 1948, in which reference is made to a 'circuit court of appeals'; 'senior circuit judge'; 'senior district judge'; 'presiding judge'; 'chief justice', except when reference to the Chief Justice of the United States is intended; or 'justice', except when used with respect to a justice of the Supreme Court of the United States in his capacity as such or as a circuit justice, are hereby amended by substituting 'court of appeals' for 'circuit court of appeals'; 'chief judge of the circuit' for 'senior circuit judge'; 'chief judge of the district court' for 'senior district judge'; 'chief judge' for 'presiding judge'; 'chief judge' for 'chief justice', except when reference to the Chief Justice of the United States is intended; and 'judge' for 'justice', except when the latter term is used with

respect to a justice of the Supreme Court of the United States in his capacity as such or as a circuit justice.

"(b) All laws of the United States in force on September 1, 1948, in which reference is made to the Supreme Court of the District of Columbia or to the District Court of the United States for the District of Columbia are amended by substituting 'United States District Court for the District of Columbia' for such designations.

"(c) All laws of the United States in force on September 1, 1948, in which reference is made to the 'Conference of Senior Circuit Judges', or to the 'Judicial Conference of Senior Circuit Judges' are amended by substituting 'Judicial Conference of the United States' for such designations.

"(d) This section shall not be construed to amend historical references to courts or judicial offices which have no present or future application to such courts or offices."

§ 1251. Original jurisdiction

(a) The Supreme Court shall have original and exclusive jurisdiction of all controversies between two or more States.

(b) The Supreme Court shall have original but not exclusive jurisdiction of:

(1) All actions or proceedings to which ambassadors, other public ministers, consuls, or vice consuls of foreign states are parties;

(2) All controversies between the United States and a State;

(3) All actions or proceedings by a State against the citizens of another State or against aliens.

(June 25, 1948, c. 646, 62 Stat. 927; Sept. 30, 1978, Pub.L. 95–393, § 8(b), 92 Stat. 810.)

HISTORICAL AND STATUTORY NOTES

Effective and Applicability Provisions

1978 Acts. Amendment by Pub.L. 95–393 effective at the end of the 90-day period beginning on Sept. 30, 1978, see section 9 of Pub.L. 95–393, set out as a note under section 254a of Title 22, Foreign Relations and Intercourse.

Statutes Governing Writs of Error to Apply to Appeals

Act Jan. 31, 1928, c. 14, § 2, 45 Stat. 54, amended Apr. 26, 1928, c. 440, 45 Stat. 466; June 25, 1948, c. 646, § 23, 62 Stat. 990, provided that: "All Acts of Congress referring to writs of error shall be construed as amended to the extent necessary to substitute appeal for writ of error." See, also, notes preceding section 1 of this title.

[§ 1252. Repealed. Pub.L. 100–352, § 1, June 27, 1988, 102 Stat. 662]

HISTORICAL AND STATUTORY NOTES

Section, Acts June 25, 1948, c. 646, 62 Stat. 928; Oct. 31, 1951, c. 655, § 47, 65 Stat. 726; July 7, 1958, Pub.L. 85–508, § 12(e), (f), 72 Stat. 348; Mar. 18, 1959, Pub.L. 86–3, § 14(a), 73 Stat. 10, provided for direct appeals to Supreme Court from decisions invalidating Acts of Congress.

Effective Date of Repeal

Repeal of section effective ninety days after June 27, 1988, except that such repeal shall not apply to cases pending in the Supreme Court on such effective date or affect the right to review or the manner of reviewing the judgment or decree of a court which was entered before such effective date, see section 7 of Pub.L. 100–352, set out as a note under section 1254 of this title.

§ 1253. Direct appeals from decisions of three-judge courts

Except as otherwise provided by law, any party may appeal to the Supreme Court from an order granting or denying, after notice and hearing, an interlocutory or permanent injunction in any civil action, suit or proceeding required by any Act of Congress to be heard and determined by a district court of three judges.

(June 25, 1948, c. 646, 62 Stat. 928.)

§ 1254. Courts of appeals; certiorari; certified questions

Cases in the courts of appeals may be reviewed by the Supreme Court by the following methods:

(1) By writ of certiorari granted upon the petition of any party to any civil or criminal case, before or after rendition of judgment or decree;

(2) By certification at any time by a court of appeals of any question of law in any civil or criminal case as to which instructions are desired, and upon such certification the Supreme Court may give binding instructions or require the entire record to be sent up for decision of the entire matter in controversy.

(June 25, 1948, c. 646, 62 Stat. 928; June 27, 1988, Pub.L. 100–352, § 2(a), (b), 102 Stat. 662.)

HISTORICAL AND STATUTORY NOTES

Effective and Applicability Provisions

1988 Acts. Section 7 of Pub.L. 100–352 provided that: "The amendments made by this Act [amending this section by striking out 'appeal;' in heading and by striking out par. (2) and redesignating former par. (3) as (2), and amending sections 1257, 1258, 2101, 2104, and 2350 of this title, section 437h of Title 2, The Congress, section 136w of Title 7, Agriculture, section 1631e of Title 22, Foreign Relations and Intercourse, section 652 of Title 25, Indians, section 988 of Title 33, Navigation and Navigable Waters, section 1652 of Title 43, Public Lands, and sections 719, 743, and 1105 of Title 45, Railroads, and repealing sections 1252 and 2103 of this title] shall take effect ninety days after the date of the enactment of this Act [June 27, 1988], except that such amendments shall not apply to cases pending in the Supreme Court on the effective date of such amendments or affect the right to review or the manner of reviewing the judgment or decree of a court which was entered before such effective date."

[§§ 1255, 1256. Repealed. Pub.L. 97–164, Title I, § 123, Apr. 2, 1982, 96 Stat. 36]

HISTORICAL AND STATUTORY NOTES

Section 1255, Act June 25, 1948, c. 646, 62 Stat. 928, authorized the Supreme Court to review cases in the Court of Claims by writ of certiorari and by certification of questions of law.

Section 1256, Act June 25, 1948, c. 646, 62 Stat. 928, authorized the Supreme Court to review cases in the Court of Customs and Patent Appeals by writ of certiorari.

Effective Date of Repeal

Repeal effective Oct. 1, 1982, see section 402 of Pub.L. 97–164, set out as Effective and Applicability Provisions of 1982 Amendments note under section 171 of this title.

§ 1257. State courts; certiorari

(a) Final judgments or decrees rendered by the highest court of a State in which a decision could be had, may be reviewed by the Supreme Court by writ of certiorari where the validity of a treaty or statute of the United States is drawn in question or where the validity of a statute of any State is drawn in question on the ground of its being repugnant to the Constitution, treaties, or laws of the United States, or where any title, right, privilege, or immunity is specially set up or claimed under the Constitution or the treaties or statutes of, or any commission held or authority exercised under, the United States.

(b) For the purposes of this section, the term "highest court of a State" includes the District of Columbia Court of Appeals.

(June 25, 1948, c. 646, 62 Stat. 929; July 29, 1970, Pub.L. 91–358, Title I, § 172(a)(1), 84 Stat. 590; June 27, 1988, Pub.L. 100–352, § 3, 102 Stat. 662.)

HISTORICAL AND STATUTORY NOTES
Effective and Applicability Provisions

1988 Acts. Amendment by section 3 of Pub.L. 100–352 effective ninety days after June 27, 1988, except that such amendment not to apply to cases pending in the Supreme Court on such effective date or affect the right to review or the manner of reviewing the judgment or decree of a court which was entered before such effective date, see section 7 of Pub.L. 100–352, set out as a note under section 1254 of this title.

1970 Acts. Section 199(a) of Title 1 of Pub.L. 91–358 provided that: "The effective date of this title (and the amendments made by this title) [which enacted sections 1363, 1451, and 2113 of this title, and amended this section and sections 292 and 1869 of this title, section 5102 of Title 5, Government Organization and Employees, and section 260a of Title 42, the Public Health and Welfare] shall be the first day of the seventh calendar month which begins after the date of the enactment of this Act [July 29, 1970]."

§ 1258. Supreme Court of Puerto Rico; certiorari

Final judgments or decrees rendered by the Supreme Court of the Commonwealth of Puerto Rico may be reviewed by the Supreme Court by writ of certiorari where the validity of a treaty or statute of the United States is drawn in question or where the validity of a statute of the Commonwealth of Puerto Rico is drawn in question on the ground of its being repugnant to the Constitution, treaties, or laws of the United States, or where any title, right, privilege, or immunity is specially set up or claimed under the Constitution or the treaties or statutes of, or any commission held or authority exercised under, the United States.

(Added Pub.L. 87–189, § 1, Aug. 30, 1961, 75 Stat. 417, and amended, Pub.L. 100–352, § 4, June 27, 1988, 102 Stat. 662.)

HISTORICAL AND STATUTORY NOTES
Effective and Applicability Provisions

1988 Acts. Amendment by section 4 of Pub.L. 100–352 effective ninety days after June 27, 1988, except that such amendment not to apply to cases pending in the Supreme Court on such effective date or affect the right to review or the manner of reviewing the judgment or decree of a court which was entered before such effective date, pursuant to section 7 of Pub.L. 100–352, set out as a note under section 1254 of this title.

§ 1259. Court of Appeals for the Armed Forces; certiorari

Decisions of the United States Court of Appeals for the Armed Forces may be reviewed by the Supreme Court by writ of certiorari in the following cases:

(1) Cases reviewed by the Court of Appeals for the Armed Forces under section 867(a)(1) of title 10.

(2) Cases certified to the Court of Appeals for the Armed Forces by the Judge Advocate General under section 867(a)(2) of title 10.

(3) Cases in which the Court of Appeals for the Armed Forces granted a petition for review under section 867(a)(3) of title 10.

(4) Cases, other than those described in paragraphs (1), (2), and (3) of this subsection, in which the Court of Appeals for the Armed Forces granted relief.

(Added Pub.L. 98–209, § 10(a)(1), Dec. 6, 1983, 97 Stat. 1405, and amended Pub.L. 101–189, Div. A, Title XIII, § 1304(b)(3), Nov. 29, 1989, 103 Stat. 1577; Pub.L. 103–337, Div. A, Title IX, § 924(d)(1)(C), (2)(A), Oct. 5, 1994, 108 Stat. 2832.)

HISTORICAL AND STATUTORY NOTES
Effective and Applicability Provisions

1983 Acts. Section effective on the first day of the eighth calendar month beginning after Dec. 6, 1983, see section 12(a)(1) of Pub.L 98–209, set out as a note under section 801 of Title 10, Armed Forces.

CHAPTER 83—COURTS OF APPEALS

HISTORICAL AND STATUTORY NOTES
Codifications

The table of sections for chapter 83 was amended by Pub.L. 95–598, Title II, § 236(b), Nov. 6, 1978, 92 Stat. 2667,

effective June 28, 1984, pursuant to Pub.L. 95–598, Title IV, § 402(b), Nov. 6, 1978, 92 Stat. 2682, as amended by Pub.L. 98–249, § 1(a), Mar. 31, 1984, 98 Stat. 116; Pub.L. 98–271, § 1(a), Apr. 30, 1984, 98 Stat. 163; Pub.L. 98–299, § 1(a), May 25, 1984, 98 Stat. 214; Pub.L. 98–325, § 1(a), June 20, 1984, 98 Stat. 268, set out as an Effective and Applicability Provisions note preceding section 101 of Title 11, Bankruptcy, by adding:

"1293. Bankruptcy appeals.".

Section 402(b) of Pub.L. 95–598 was amended by section 113 of Pub.L. 98–353, Title I, July 10, 1984, 98 Stat. 343, by substituting "shall not be effective" for "shall take effect on June 28, 1984", thereby eliminating the amendment by section 236(a) of Pub.L. 95–598, effective June 27, 1984, pursuant to section 122(c) of Pub.L. 98–353, set out as an Effective and Applicability Provisions note under section 151 of this title.

Section 121(a) of Pub.L. 98–353 directed that section 402(b) of Pub.L. 95–598 be amended by substituting "the date of enactment of the Bankruptcy Amendments and Federal Judgeship Act of 1984 [i.e. July 10, 1984]" for "June 28, 1984". This amendment was not executed in view of the prior amendment to section 402(b) of Pub.L. 95–598 by section 113 of Pub.L. 98–353.

§ 1291. Final decisions of district courts

The courts of appeals (other than the United States Court of Appeals for the Federal Circuit) shall have jurisdiction of appeals from all final decisions of the district courts of the United States, the United States District Court for the District of the Canal Zone, the District Court of Guam, and the District Court of the Virgin Islands, except where a direct review may be had in the Supreme Court. The jurisdiction of the United States Court of Appeals for the Federal Circuit shall be limited to the jurisdiction described in sections 1292(c) and (d) and 1295 of this title.

(June 25, 1948, c. 646, 62 Stat. 929; Oct. 31, 1951, c. 655, § 48, 65 Stat. 726; July 7, 1958, Pub.L. 85–508, § 12(e), 72 Stat. 348; Apr. 2, 1982, Pub.L. 97–164, Title I, § 124, 96 Stat. 36.)

HISTORICAL AND STATUTORY NOTES

Effective and Applicability Provisions

1982 Acts. Amendment by Pub.L. 97–164 effective Oct. 1, 1982, see section 402 of Pub.L. 97–164, set out as a note under section 171 of this title.

1958 Acts. Amendment of section by Pub.L. 85–508 effective Jan. 3, 1959, upon admission of Alaska into the Union pursuant to Proc. No. 3269, Jan. 3, 1959, 24 F.R. 81, 73 Stat. c16, as required by sections 1 and 8(c) of Pub.L. 85–508, see notes set out under section 81A of this title and preceding section 21 of Title 48, Territories and Insular Possessions.

Termination of United States District Court for the District of the Canal Zone

For termination of the United States District Court for the District of the Canal Zone at end of the "transition period", being the 30–month period beginning Oct. 1, 1979, and ending midnight Mar. 31, 1982, see Paragraph 5 of Article XI of the Panama Canal Treaty of 1977 and sections 3831 and 3841 to 3843 of Title 22, Foreign Relations and Intercourse.

§ 1292. Interlocutory decisions

(a) Except as provided in subsections (c) and (d) of this section, the courts of appeals shall have jurisdiction of appeals from:

(1) Interlocutory orders of the district courts of the United States, the United States District Court for the District of the Canal Zone, the District Court of Guam, and the District Court of the Virgin Islands, or of the judges thereof, granting, continuing, modifying, refusing or dissolving injunctions, or refusing to dissolve or modify injunctions, except where a direct review may be had in the Supreme Court;

(2) Interlocutory orders appointing receivers, or refusing orders to wind up receiverships or to take steps to accomplish the purposes thereof, such as directing sales or other disposals of property;

(3) Interlocutory decrees of such district courts or the judges thereof determining the rights and liabilities of the parties to admiralty cases in which appeals from final decrees are allowed.

(b) When a district judge, in making in a civil action an order not otherwise appealable under this section, shall be of the opinion that such order involves a controlling question of law as to which there is substantial ground for difference of opinion and that an immediate appeal from the order may materially advance the ultimate termination of the litigation, he shall so state in writing in such order. The Court of Appeals which would have jurisdiction of an appeal of such action may thereupon, in its discretion, permit an appeal to be taken from such order, if application is made to it within ten days after the entry of the order: *Provided, however,* That application for an appeal hereunder shall not stay proceedings in the district court unless the district judge or the Court of Appeals or a judge thereof shall so order.

(c) The United States Court of Appeals for the Federal Circuit shall have exclusive jurisdiction—

(1) of an appeal from an interlocutory order or decree described in subsection (a) or (b) of this section in any case over which the court would have jurisdiction of an appeal under section 1295 of this title; and

(2) of an appeal from a judgment in a civil action for patent infringement which would otherwise be appealable to the United States Court of Appeals for the Federal Circuit and is final except for an accounting.

(d)(1) When the chief judge of the Court of International Trade issues an order under the provisions of section 256(b) of this title, or when any judge of the Court of International Trade, in issuing any other interlocutory order, includes in the order a statement that a controlling question of law is involved with respect to which there is a substantial ground for difference of opinion and that an immediate appeal from that order may materially advance the ultimate termination of the litigation, the United States Court of Appeals for the Federal Circuit may, in its discretion, permit an appeal to be taken from such order, if application is made to that Court within ten days after the entry of such order.

(2) When the chief judge of the United States Court of Federal Claims issues an order under section 798(b) of this title, or when any judge of the United States Court of Federal Claims, in issuing an interlocutory order, includes in the order a statement that a controlling question of law is involved with respect to which there is a substantial ground for difference of opinion and that an immediate appeal from that order may materially advance the ultimate termination of the litigation, the United States Court of Appeals for the Federal Circuit may, in its discretion, permit an appeal to be taken from such order, if application is made to that Court within ten days after the entry of such order.

(3) Neither the application for nor the granting of an appeal under this subsection shall stay proceedings in the Court of International Trade or in the Court of Federal Claims, as the case may be, unless a stay is ordered by a judge of the Court of International Trade or of the Court of Federal Claims or by the United States Court of Appeals for the Federal Circuit or a judge of that court.

(4)(A) The United States Court of Appeals for the Federal Circuit shall have exclusive jurisdiction of an appeal from an interlocutory order of a district court of the United States, the District Court of Guam, the District Court of the Virgin Islands, or the District Court for the Northern Mariana Islands, granting or denying, in whole or in part, a motion to transfer an action to the United States Court of Federal Claims under section 1631 of this title.

(B) When a motion to transfer an action to the Court of Federal Claims is filed in a district court, no further proceedings shall be taken in the district court until 60 days after the court has ruled upon the motion. If an appeal is taken from the district court's grant or denial of the motion, proceedings shall be further stayed until the appeal has been decided by the Court of Appeals for the Federal Circuit. The stay of proceedings in the district court shall not bar the granting of preliminary or injunctive relief, where appropriate and where expedition is reasonably necessary. However, during the period in which proceedings are stayed as provided in this subparagraph, no transfer to the Court of Federal Claims pursuant to the motion shall be carried out.

(e) The Supreme Court may prescribe rules, in accordance with section 2072 of this title, to provide for an appeal of an interlocutory decision to the courts of appeals that is not otherwise provided for under subsection (a), (b), (c), or (d).

(June 25, 1948, c. 646, 62 Stat. 929; Oct. 31, 1951, c. 655, § 49, 65 Stat. 726; July 7, 1958, Pub.L. 85–508, § 12(e), 72 Stat. 348; Sept. 2, 1958, Pub.L. 85–919, 72 Stat. 1770; Apr. 2, 1982, Pub.L. 97–164, Title I, § 125, 96 Stat. 36; Nov. 8, 1984, Pub.L. 98–620, Title IV, § 412, 98 Stat. 3362; Nov. 19, 1988, Pub.L. 100–702, Title V, § 501, 102 Stat. 4652; Oct. 29, 1992,

Pub.L. 102–572, Title I, § 101, Title IX, §§ 902(b), 906(c), 106 Stat. 4506, 4516, 4518.)

HISTORICAL AND STATUTORY NOTES

Effective and Applicability Provisions

1992 Acts. Amendment by sections 902(b) and 906(c) of Pub.L. 102–572 effective Oct. 29, 1992, see section 911 of Pub.L. 102–572, set out as a note under section 171 of this title.

Amendment by section 906(c) of Pub.L. 102–572 effective Oct. 29, 1992, see section 911 of Pub.L. 102–572, set out as a note under section 171 of Title 28, Judiciary and Judicial Procedure.

Amendment by section 101 of Pub.L. 102–572 effective Jan. 1, 1993, see section 1101(a) of Pub.L. 102–572, set out as a note under section 905 of Title 2, The Congress.

1988 Acts. Section 502 of Title V of Pub.L. 100–702 provided that: "The amendment made by section 501 [enacting subsec. (d)(4) of this section] shall apply to any action commenced in the district court on or after the date of enactment of this title [Nov. 19, 1988]."

1982 Acts. Amendment by Pub.L. 97–164 effective Oct. 1, 1982, see section 402 of Pub.L. 97–164, set out as a note under section 171 of this title.

1958 Acts. Amendment of section by Pub.L. 85–508 effective Jan. 3, 1959, upon admission of Alaska into the Union pursuant to Proc. No. 3269, Jan. 3, 1959, 24 F.R. 81, 73 Stat. c16, as required by Section 1 and 8(c) of Pub.L. 85–508, see notes set out under Section 81A of this title and preceding Section 21 of Title 48, Territories and Insular Possessions.

Change of Name

References to United States Claims Court deemed to refer to United States Court of Federal Claims and references to Claims Court deemed to refer to Court of Federal Claims, see section 902(b) of Pub.L. 102–572, set out as a note under section 171 of Title 28, Judiciary and Judicial Procedure.

Termination of United States District Court for the District of the Canal Zone

For termination of the United States District Court for the District of the Canal Zone at end of the "transition period", being the 30–month period beginning Oct. 1, 1979, and ending midnight Mar. 31, 1982, see Paragraph 5 of Article XI of the Panama Canal Treaty of 1977 and sections 3831 and 3841 to 3843 of Title 22, Foreign Relations and Intercourse.

[§ 1293. Repealed. Pub.L. 87–189, § 3, Aug. 30, 1961, 75 Stat. 417]

HISTORICAL AND STATUTORY NOTES

Section, Acts June 25, 1948, c. 646, 62 Stat. 929; Mar. 18, 1959, Pub.L. 86–3, § 14(b), 73 Stat. 10, provided for appeal from supreme court of Puerto Rico to court of appeals for first circuit. See section 1258 of this title.

Codifications

A subsequent section 1293, as added by Pub.L. 95–598, Title II, § 236a, Nov. 6, 1978, 92 Stat. 2667, effective June 28, 1984, pursuant to Pub.L. 95–598, Title IV, § 402(b), Nov. 6, 1978, 92 Stat. 2682, as amended by Pub.L. 98–249, § 1(a), Mar. 31, 1984, 98 Stat. 116; Pub.L. 98–271, § 1(a), Apr. 30,

1984, 98 Stat. 163; Pub.L. 98–299, § 1(a), May 25, 1984, 98 Stat. 214; Pub.L. 98–325, § 1(a), June 20, 1984, 98 Stat. 268, set out as an Effective and Applicability Provisions note preceding section 101 of Title 11, Bankruptcy, read as follows:

§ 1293. Bankruptcy appeals

(a) The courts of appeals shall have jurisdiction of appeals from all final decisions of panels designated under section 160(a) of this title.

(b) Notwithstanding section 1482 of this title, a court of appeals shall have jurisdiction of an appeal from a final judgment, order, or decree of an appellate panel created under section 160 or a District court of the United States or from a final judgment, order, or decree of a bankruptcy court of the United States if the parties to such appeal agree to a direct appeal to the court of appeals.

Section 402(b) of Pub.L. 95–598 was amended by section 113 of Pub.L. 98–353, Title I, July 10, 1984, 98 Stat. 343, by substituting "shall not be effective" for "shall take effect on June 28, 1984", thereby eliminating the addition of subsequent section 1293 by section 236(a) of Pub.L. 95–598, effective June 27, 1984, pursuant to section 122(c) of Pub.L. 98–353, set out as an Effective and Applicability Provisions note under section 151 of this title.

Section 121(a) of Pub.L. 98–353 directed that section 402(b) of Pub.L. 95–598 be amended by substituting "the date of enactment of the Bankruptcy Amendments and Federal Judgeship Act of 1984 [i.e. July 10, 1984]" for "June 28, 1984". This amendment was not executed in view of the prior amendment to section 402(b) of Pub.L. 95–598 by section 113 of Pub.L. 98–353.

§ 1294. Circuits in which decisions reviewable

Except as provided in sections 1292(c), 1292(d), and 1295 of this title, appeals from reviewable decisions of the district and territorial courts shall be taken to the courts of appeals as follows:

(1) From a district court of the United States to the court of appeals for the circuit embracing the district;

(2) From the United States District Court for the District of the Canal Zone, to the Court of Appeals for the Fifth Circuit;

(3) From the District Court of the Virgin Islands, to the Court of Appeals for the Third Circuit;

(4) From the District Court of Guam, to the Court of Appeals for the Ninth Circuit.

(June 25, 1948, c. 646, 62 Stat. 930; Oct. 31, 1951, c. 655, § 50(a), 65 Stat. 727; July 7, 1958, Pub.L. 85–508, § 12(g), 72 Stat. 348; Mar. 18, 1959, Pub.L. 86–3, § 14(c), 73 Stat. 10; Aug. 30, 1961, Pub.L. 87–189, § 5, 75 Stat. 417; Nov. 6, 1978, Pub.L. 95–598, Title II, § 237, 92 Stat. 2667; Apr. 2, 1982, Pub.L. 97–164, Title I, § 126, 96 Stat. 37.)

HISTORICAL AND STATUTORY NOTES

Codifications

This section was amended by Pub.L. 95–598, Title II, § 237, Nov. 6, 1978, 92 Stat. 2667, effective June 28, 1984, pursuant to Pub.L. 95–598, Title IV, § 402(b), Nov. 6, 1978,

92 Stat. 2682, as amended by Pub.L. 98–249, § 1(a), Mar. 31, 1984, 98 Stat. 116; Pub.L. 98–271, § 1(a), Apr. 30, 1984, 98 Stat. 163; Pub.L. 98–299, § 1(a), May 25, 1984, 98 Stat. 214; Pub.L. 98–325, § 1(a), June 20, 1984, 98 Stat. 268, set out as an Effective and Applicability Provisions note preceding section 101 of Title II, Bankruptcy, to read as follows:

§ 1294. Circuits in which decisions reviewable

Except as provided in sections 1292(c), 1292(d), and 1295 of this title, appeals from reviewable decisions of the district, bankruptcy, and territorial courts shall be taken to the courts of appeals as follows:

(1) From a district court of the United States to the court of appeals for the circuit embracing the district;

(2) From the United States District Court for the District of the Canal Zone, to the Court of Appeals for the Fifth Circuit;

(3) From the District Court of the Virgin Islands, to the Court of Appeals for the Third Circuit;

(4) From the District Court of Guam, to the Court of Appeals for the Ninth Circuit;

(5) From a panel designated under section 160(a) of this title to the court of appeals for the circuit in which the panel was so designated;

(6) From a bankruptcy court of the United States to the court of appeals for the circuit embracing the district in which the bankruptcy court is located.

Section 402(b) of Pub.L. 95–598 was amended by section 113 of Pub.L. 98–353, Title I, July 10, 1984, 98 Stat. 343, by substituting "shall not be effective" for "shall take effect on June 28, 1984", thereby eliminating the amendment by section 237 of Pub.L. 95–598, effective June 27, 1984, pursuant to section 122(c) of Pub.L. 98–353, set out as an Effective and Applicability Provisions note under section 151 of this title.

Section 121(a) of Pub.L. 98–353 directed that section 402(b) of Pub.L. 95–598 be amended by substituting "the date of enactment of the Bankruptcy Amendments and Federal Judgeship Act of 1984 [i.e. July 10, 1984]" for "June 28, 1984". This amendment was not executed in view of the prior amendment to section 402(b) of Pub.L. 95–598 by section 113 of Pub.L. 98–353.

Effective and Applicability Provisions

1982 Acts. Amendment by Pub.L. 97–164 effective Oct. 1, 1982, see section 402 of Pub.L. 97–164, set out as a note under section 171 of this title.

1959 Acts. Amendment of section by Pub.L. 86–3 effective upon the admission of the State of Hawaii into the Union, see note set out under section 91 of this title. Admission of Hawaii into the Union was accomplished Aug. 21, 1959 upon issuance of Proc. No. 3309, Aug. 21, 1959, 25 F.R. 6868, 73 Stat. c74, as required by sections 1 and 7(c) of Pub.L. 86–3, Mar. 18, 1959, 73 Stat. 4, set out as notes preceding section 491 of Title 48, Territories and Insular Possessions.

1958 Acts. Amendment of section by Pub.L. 85–508 effective Jan. 3, 1959, upon admission of Alaska into the Union pursuant to Proc. No. 3269, Jan. 3, 1959, 24 F.R. 81, 73 Stat. c16, as required by sections 1 and 8(c) of Pub.L. 85–508, see notes set out under section 81A of this title and preceding section 21 of Title 48, Territories and Insular Possessions.

Termination of United States District Court for the District of the Canal Zone

For termination of the United States District Court for the District of the Canal Zone at end of the "transition period", being the 30–month period beginning Oct. 1, 1979, and ending midnight Mar. 31, 1982, see Paragraph 5 of Article XI of the Panama Canal Treaty of 1977 and sections 3831 and 3841 to 3843 of Title 22, Foreign Relations and Intercourse.

§ 1295.　Jurisdiction of the United States Court of Appeals for the Federal Circuit

(a) The United States Court of Appeals for the Federal Circuit shall have exclusive jurisdiction—

(1) of an appeal from a final decision of a district court of the United States, the United States District Court for the District of the Canal Zone, the District Court of Guam, the District Court of the Virgin Islands, or the District Court for the Northern Mariana Islands, if the jurisdiction of that court was based, in whole or in part, on section 1338 of this title, except that a case involving a claim arising under any Act of Congress relating to copyrights, exclusive rights in mask works, or trademarks and no other claims under section 1338(a) shall be governed by sections 1291, 1292, and 1294 of this title;

(2) of an appeal from a final decision of a district court of the United States, the United States District Court for the District of the Canal Zone, the District Court of Guam, the District Court of the Virgin Islands, or the District Court for the Northern Mariana Islands, if the jurisdiction of that court was based, in whole or in part, on section 1346 of this title, except that jurisdiction of an appeal in a case brought in a district court under section 1346(a)(1), 1346(b), 1346(e), or 1346(f) of this title or under section 1346(a)(2) when the claim is founded upon an Act of Congress or a regulation of an executive department providing for internal revenue shall be governed by sections 1291, 1292, and 1294 of this title;

(3) of an appeal from a final decision of the United States Court of Federal Claims;

(4) of an appeal from a decision of—

(A) the Board of Patent Appeals and Interferences of the United States Patent and Trademark Office with respect to patent applications and interferences, at the instance of an applicant for a patent or any party to a patent interference, and any such appeal shall waive the right of such applicant or party to proceed under section 145 or 146 of title 35;

(B) the Under Secretary of Commerce for Intellectual Property and Director of the United States Patent and Trademark Office or the Trademark Trial and Appeal Board with respect to applications for registration of marks and other proceedings as provided in section 21 of the Trademark Act of 1946 (15 U.S.C. 1071); or

(C) a district court to which a case was directed pursuant to section 145, 146, or 154(b) of title 35;

(5) of an appeal from a final decision of the United States Court of International Trade;

(6) to review the final determinations of the United States International Trade Commission relating to unfair practices in import trade, made under section 337 of the Tariff Act of 1930 (19 U.S.C. 1337);

(7) to review, by appeal on questions of law only, findings of the Secretary of Commerce under U.S. note 6 to subchapter X of chapter 98 of the Harmonized Tariff Schedule of the United States (relating to importation of instruments or apparatus);

(8) of an appeal under section 71 of the Plant Variety Protection Act (7 U.S.C. 2461);

(9) of an appeal from a final order or final decision of the Merit Systems Protection Board, pursuant to sections 7703(b)(1) and 7703(d) of title 5;

(10) of an appeal from a final decision of an agency board of contract appeals pursuant to section 8(g)(1) of the Contract Disputes Act of 1978 (41 U.S.C. 607(g)(1));

(11) of an appeal under section 211 of the Economic Stabilization Act of 1970;

(12) of an appeal under section 5 of the Emergency Petroleum Allocation Act of 1973;

(13) of an appeal under section 506(c) of the Natural Gas Policy Act of 1978; and

(14) of an appeal under section 523 of the Energy Policy and Conservation Act.

(b) The head of any executive department or agency may, with the approval of the Attorney General, refer to the Court of Appeals for the Federal Circuit for judicial review any final decision rendered by a board of contract appeals pursuant to the terms of any contract with the United States awarded by that department or agency which the head of such department or agency has concluded is not entitled to finality pursuant to the review standards specified in section 10(b) of the Contract Disputes Act of 1978 (41 U.S.C. 609(b)). The head of each executive department or agency shall make any referral under this section within one hundred and twenty days after the receipt of a copy of the final appeal decision.

(c) The Court of Appeals for the Federal Circuit shall review the matter referred in accordance with the standards specified in section 10(b) of the Contract Disputes Act of 1978. The court shall proceed with judicial review on the administrative record made before the board of contract appeals on matters so referred as in other cases pending in such court, shall determine the issue of finality of the appeal decision, and shall, if appropriate, render judgment thereon, or remand the matter to any administrative or executive body or official with such direction as it may deem proper and just.

(Added Pub.L. 97–164, Title I, § 127(a), Apr. 2, 1982, 96 Stat. 37, and amended Pub.L. 98–622, Title II, § 205(a), Nov. 8, 1984, 98 Stat. 3388; Pub.L. 100–418, Title I, § 1214(a)(3), Aug. 23, 1988, 102 Stat. 1156; Pub.L. 100–702, Title X, § 1020(a)(3), Nov. 19, 1988, 102 Stat. 4671; Pub.L. 102–572, Title I, § 102(c), Title IX, § 902(b)(1), Oct. 29, 1992, 106 Stat. 4507, 4516; Pub.L. 106–113, Div. B, § 1000(a)(9) [Title IV, §§ 4402(b)(2), 4732(b)(14)], Nov. 29, 1999, 113 Stat. 1536, 1501A–560, 1501A–584.)

HISTORICAL AND STATUTORY NOTES

References in Text

The Harmonized Tariff Schedule of the United States, referred to in subsec. (a)(7), is not carried in the Code. See Publication of Harmonized Tariff Schedule note set out under section 1202 of Title 19, Customs Duties.

Section 211 of the Economic Stabilization Act of 1970, referred to in subsec. (a)(11), is section 211 of Pub.L. 91–379, Title II, Aug. 15, 1970, as added Pub.L. 92–210, § 2, Dec. 22, 1971, 85 Stat. 743, as amended, which is set out as a note under TECA Rule 3, this title, and in codified form under section 1904 of Title 12, Banks and Banking.

Section 5 of the Emergency Petroleum Allocation Act of 1973, referred to in subsec. (a)(12), is section 5 of Pub.L. 93–159, Nov. 27, 1973, 87 Stat. 633, as amended, which was classified to section 754 of Title 15, Commerce and Trade, prior to the omission of such section pursuant to section 760g of Title 15.

Section 506(c) of the Natural Gas Policy Act of 1978, referred to in subsec. (a)(13), is section 506(c) of Pub.L. 95–621, Title V, Nov. 9, 1978, 92 Stat. 3404, which is classified to section 3416(c) of Title 15, Commerce and Trade.

Section 523 of the Energy Policy and Conservation Act, referred to in subsec. (a)(14), is section 523 of Pub.L. 94–163, Title V, Dec. 22, 1975, 89 Stat. 962, which is classified to section 6393 of Title 42, The Public Health and Welfare.

Effective and Applicability Provisions

1999 Acts. Amendment by Pub.L. 106–113 [§ 4732], effective 4 months after Nov. 29, 1999, see Pub.L. 106–113 [§ 4731], set out as a note under section 1 of Title 35.

Amendment by Pub.L. 106–113 [§ 4402], to take effect on the date that is six months after Nov. 29, 1999 and, except for a design patent application filed under chapter 16 of Title 35, to be applicable to any application filed on or after the date that is six months after Nov. 29, 1999, see Pub.L. 106–113 [§ 4405], set out as a note under section 154 of Title 35.

1992 Acts. Amendment by section 902(b)(1) of Pub.L. 102–572 effective Oct. 29, 1992, see section 911 of Pub.L. 102–572, set out as a note under section 171 of this title.

Amendment by Pub.L. 102–572 effective Jan. 1, 1993, see section 1101(a) of Pub.L. 102–572, set out as a note under section 905 of Title 2, The Congress.

1988 Acts. Amendment by Pub.L. 100–418 effective Jan. 1, 1989, and applicable with respect to articles entered on or after such date, see section 1217(b)(1) of Pub.L. 100–418, set out as an Effective and Applicability Provisions note under section 3001 of Title 19, Customs Duties.

1984 Acts. Amendment by Pub.L. 98–622 applicable to all United States patents granted before, on, or after Nov. 8, 1984, and to all applications for United States patents pending on or filed after that date, except as otherwise provided, see section 106 of Pub.L. 98–622, set out as a note under section 103 of Title 35, Patents.

Amendment by Pub.L. 98–622, effective three months after Nov. 8, 1984, see section 207 of Pub.L. 98–622, set out as a note under section 7 of Title 35, Patents.

1982 Acts. Section effective Oct. 1, 1982, see section 402 of Pub.L. 97–164, set out as a note under section 171 of this title.

Abolition of Temporary Emergency Court of Appeals

Section 102(d), (e) of Pub.L. 102–572 provided that:

"**(d) Abolition of Court.**—The Temporary Emergency Court of Appeals created by section 211(b) of the Economic Stabilization Act of 1970 [set out as a note under TECA Rule 3, this title] is abolished, effective 6 months after the date of the enactment of this Act [Oct. 29, 1992].

"**(e) Pending cases.**—(1) Any appeal which, before the effective date of abolition described in subsection (d), is pending in the Temporary Emergency Court of Appeals but has not been submitted to a panel of such court as of that date shall be assigned to the United States Court of Appeals for the Federal Circuit as though the appeal had originally been filed in that court.

"**(2)** Any case which, before the effective date of abolition described in subsection (d), has been submitted to a panel of the Temporary Emergency Court of Appeals and as to which the mandate has not been issued as of that date shall remain with that panel for all purposes and, notwithstanding the provisions of sections 291 and 292 of title 28, United States Code [sections 291 and 292 of this title], that panel shall be assigned to the United States Court of Appeals for the Federal Circuit for the purpose of deciding such case."

Termination of United States District Court for the District of the Canal Zone

For termination of the United States District Court for the District of the Canal Zone at end of the "transition period", being the 30–month period beginning Oct. 1, 1979, and ending midnight Mar. 31, 1982, see Paragraph 5 of Article XI of the Panama Canal Treaty of 1977 and sections 3831 and 3841 to 3843 of Title 22, Foreign Relations and Intercourse.

Transfer of Cases and Petitions Pending in Court of Claims and in Court of Customs and Patent Appeals on October 1, 1982

For provisions directing that any case pending before the Court of Claims on Oct. 1, 1982, in which a report on the merits has been filed by a commissioner, or in which there is pending a request for review, and upon which the court has not acted, and any matter pending before the United States Court of Customs and Patent Appeals on Oct. 1, 1982, be transferred to the United States Court of Appeals for the Federal Circuit, and that any petition for rehearing, reconsideration, alteration, modification, or other change in any decision of the United States Court of Claims or the United States Court of Customs and Patent Appeals rendered prior to Oct. 1, 1982, that has not been determined by either of those courts on that date, or that is filed after that date, be determined by the United States Court of Appeals for the Federal Circuit, see section 403(a)–(c) of Pub.L. 97–164, set out as a note under section 171 of this title.

§ 1296. Review of certain agency actions

(a) **Jurisdiction.**—Subject to the provisions of chapter 179, the United States Court of Appeals for the Federal Circuit shall have jurisdiction over a petition for review of a final decision under chapter 5 of title 3 of—

(1) an appropriate agency (as determined under section 454 of title 3);

(2) the Federal Labor Relations Authority made under part D of subchapter II of chapter 5 of title 3, notwithstanding section 7123 of title 5; or

(3) the Secretary of Labor or the Occupational Safety and Health Review Commission, made under part C of subchapter II of chapter 5 of title 3.

(b) **Filing of petition.**—Any petition for review under this section must be filed within 30 days after the date the petitioner receives notice of the final decision.

(Added Pub.L. 104–331, § 3(a)(1), Oct. 26, 1996, 110 Stat. 4069.)

HISTORICAL AND STATUTORY NOTES

Effective and Applicability Provisions

1996 Acts. Section 3(d) of Pub.L. 104–331 provided that: "The amendments made by this section [enacting this section, sections 1413, and 3901 to 3908 of this title, and amending sections 1346 and 2402 of this title] shall take effect on October 1, 1997."

Prior Provisions

A prior section 1296, Pub.L. 97–164, Title I, § 127(a), Apr. 2, 1982, 96 Stat. 39, relating to precedence of cases in the United States Court of Appeals for the Federal Circuit, was repealed by Pub.L. 98–620, Title IV, § 402(29)(C), Nov. 8, 1984, 98 Stat. 3359.

CHAPTER 85—DISTRICT COURTS; JURISDICTION

HISTORICAL AND STATUTORY NOTES

Codifications

The table of sections for chapter 85 was amended by Pub.L. 95–598, Title II, § 238(b), Nov. 6, 1978, 92 Stat. 2668, effective June 28, 1984, pursuant to Pub.L. 95–598, Title IV, § 402(b), Nov. 6, 1978, 92 Stat. 2682, as amended by Pub.L. 98–249, § 1(a), Mar. 31, 1984, 98 Stat. 116; Pub.L. 98–271, § 1(a), Apr. 30, 1984, 98 Stat. 163; Pub.L. 98–299, § 1(a), May 25, 1984, 98 Stat. 214; Pub.L. 98–325, § 1(a), June 20, 1984, 98 Stat. 268, by substituting "1334. Bankruptcy appeals." for "1334. Bankruptcy matters and proceedings.".

Section 402(b) of Pub.L. 95–598 was amended by section 113 of Pub.L. 98–353, Title I, July 10, 1984, 98 Stat. 343, by substituting "shall not be effective" for "shall take effect on June 28, 1984", thereby eliminating the amendment by section 238(b) of Pub.L. 95–598, effective June 27, 1984, pursuant to section 122(c) of Pub.L. 98–353, set out as an Effective Date note under section 151 of this title.

Section 121(a) of Pub.L. 98–353 directed that section 402(b) of Pub.L. 95–598 be amended by substituting "the date of enactment of the Bankruptcy Amendments and Federal Judgeship Act of 1984 [i.e. July 10, 1984]" for "June 28, 1984". This amendment was not executed in view of the prior amendment to section 402(b) of Pub.L. 95–598 by section 113 of Pub.L. 98–353.

Effective and Applicability Provisions

2002 Acts. Amendments by section 11020(b) of Pub.L. 107–273 shall apply to a civil action if the accident giving rise to the cause of action occurred on or after the 90th day after Nov. 2, 2002, see section 11020(c) of Pub.L. 107–273, set out as a note under 28 U.S.C.A. § 1369.

§ 1330. Actions against foreign states

(a) The district courts shall have original jurisdiction without regard to amount in controversy of any nonjury civil action against a foreign state as defined in section 1603(a) of this title as to any claim for relief in personam with respect to which the foreign state is not entitled to immunity either under sections 1605–1607 of this title or under any applicable international agreement.

(b) Personal jurisdiction over a foreign state shall exist as to every claim for relief over which the district courts have jurisdiction under subsection (a) where service has been made under section 1608 of this title.

(c) For purposes of subsection (b), an appearance by a foreign state does not confer personal jurisdiction with respect to any claim for relief not arising out of any transaction or occurrence enumerated in sections 1605–1607 of this title.

(Added Pub.L. 94–583, § 2(a), Oct. 21, 1976, 90 Stat. 2891.)

HISTORICAL AND STATUTORY NOTES

Effective and Applicability Provisions

1976 Acts. Section effective 90 days after Oct. 21, 1976, see section 8 of Pub.L. 94–583, set out as a note under section 1602 of this title.

§ 1331. Federal question

The district courts shall have original jurisdiction of all civil actions arising under the Constitution, laws, or treaties of the United States.

(June 25, 1948, c. 646, 62 Stat. 930; July 25, 1958, Pub.L. 85–554, § 1, 72 Stat. 415; Oct. 21, 1976, Pub.L. 94–574, § 2, 90 Stat. 2721; Dec. 1, 1980, Pub.L. 96–486, § 2(a), 94 Stat. 2369.)

HISTORICAL AND STATUTORY NOTES

Effective and Applicability Provisions

1980 Acts. Section 4 of Pub.L. 96–486 provided: "This Act [amending this section and section 2072 of Title 15, Commerce and Trade, and enacting provisions set out as a note under section 1 of this title] shall apply to any civil action pending on the date of enactment of this Act [Dec. 1, 1980]."

1958 Acts. Section 3 of Pub.L. 85–554 provided that: "This Act [amending this section and sections 1332 and 1445 of this title] shall apply only in the case of actions commenced after the date of the enactment of this Act [July 25, 1958]."

§ 1332. Diversity of citizenship; amount in controversy; costs

(a) The district courts shall have original jurisdiction of all civil actions where the matter in controversy exceeds the sum or value of $75,000, exclusive of interest and costs, and is between—

    (1) citizens of different States;

    (2) citizens of a State and citizens or subjects of a foreign state;

    (3) citizens of different States and in which citizens or subjects of a foreign state are additional parties; and

    (4) a foreign state, defined in section 1603(a) of this title, as plaintiff and citizens of a State or of different States.

For the purposes of this section, section 1335, and section 1441, an alien admitted to the United States for permanent residence shall be deemed a citizen of the State in which such alien is domiciled.

(b) Except when express provision therefor is otherwise made in a statute of the United States, where the plaintiff who files the case originally in the Federal courts is finally adjudged to be entitled to recover less than the sum or value of $75,000, computed without regard to any setoff or counterclaim to which the defendant may be adjudged to be entitled, and exclusive of interest and costs, the district court may deny costs to the plaintiff and, in addition, may impose costs on the plaintiff.

(c) For the purposes of this section and section 1441 of this title—

    (1) a corporation shall be deemed to be a citizen of any State by which it has been incorporated and of the State where it has its principal place of business, except that in any direct action against the insurer of a policy or contract of liability insurance, whether incorporated or unincorporated, to which action the insured is not joined as a party-defendant, such insurer shall be deemed a citizen of the State of which the insured is a citizen, as well as of any State by which the insurer has been incorporated and of the State where it has its principal place of business; and

    (2) the legal representative of the estate of a decedent shall be deemed to be a citizen only of the same State as the decedent, and the legal representative of an infant or incompetent shall be deemed to be a citizen only of the same State as the infant or incompetent.

(d)(1) In this subsection—

(A) the term "class" means all of the class members in a class action;

(B) the term "class action" means any civil action filed under rule 23 of the Federal Rules of Civil Procedure or similar State statute or rule of judicial procedure authorizing an action to be brought by 1 or more representative persons as a class action;

(C) the term "class certification order" means an order issued by a court approving the treatment of some or all aspects of a civil action as a class action; and

(D) the term "class members" means the persons (named or unnamed) who fall within the definition of the proposed or certified class in a class action.

(2) The district courts shall have original jurisdiction of any civil action in which the matter in controversy exceeds the sum or value of $5,000,000, exclusive of interest and costs, and is a class action in which—

(A) any member of a class of plaintiffs is a citizen of a State different from any defendant;

(B) any member of a class of plaintiffs is a foreign state or a citizen or subject of a foreign state and any defendant is a citizen of a State; or

(C) any member of a class of plaintiffs is a citizen of a State and any defendant is a foreign state or a citizen or subject of a foreign state.

(3) A district court may, in the interests of justice and looking at the totality of the circumstances, decline to exercise jurisdiction under paragraph (2) over a class action in which greater than one-third but less than two-thirds of the members of all proposed plaintiff classes in the aggregate and the primary defendants are citizens of the State in which the action was originally filed based on consideration of—

(A) whether the claims asserted involve matters of national or interstate interest;

(B) whether the claims asserted will be governed by laws of the State in which the action was originally filed or by the laws of other States;

(C) whether the class action has been pleaded in a manner that seeks to avoid Federal jurisdiction;

(D) whether the action was brought in a forum with a distinct nexus with the class members, the alleged harm, or the defendants;

(E) whether the number of citizens of the State in which the action was originally filed in all proposed plaintiff classes in the aggregate is substantially larger than the number of citizens from any other State, and the citizenship of the other members of the proposed class is dispersed among a substantial number of States; and

(F) whether, during the 3–year period preceding the filing of that class action, 1 or more other class actions asserting the same or similar claims on behalf of the same or other persons have been filed.

(4) A district court shall decline to exercise jurisdiction under paragraph (2)—

(A)(i) over a class action in which—

(I) greater than two-thirds of the members of all proposed plaintiff classes in the aggregate are citizens of the State in which the action was originally filed;

(II) at least 1 defendant is a defendant—

    (aa) from whom significant relief is sought by members of the plaintiff class;

    (bb) whose alleged conduct forms a significant basis for the claims asserted by the proposed plaintiff class; and

    (cc) who is a citizen of the State in which the action was originally filed; and

(III) principal injuries resulting from the alleged conduct or any related conduct of each defendant were incurred in the State in which the action was originally filed; and

(ii) during the 3-year period preceding the filing of that class action, no other class action has been filed asserting the same or similar factual allegations against any of the defendants on behalf of the same or other persons; or

(B) two-thirds or more of the members of all proposed plaintiff classes in the aggregate, and the primary defendants, are citizens of the State in which the action was originally filed.

(5) Paragraphs (2) through (4) shall not apply to any class action in which—

(A) the primary defendants are States, State officials, or other governmental entities against whom the district court may be foreclosed from ordering relief; or

(B) the number of members of all proposed plaintiff classes in the aggregate is less than 100.

(6) In any class action, the claims of the individual class members shall be aggregated to determine whether the matter in controversy exceeds the sum or value of $5,000,000, exclusive of interest and costs.

(7) Citizenship of the members of the proposed plaintiff classes shall be determined for purposes of paragraphs (2) through (6) as of the date of filing of the complaint or amended complaint, or, if the case stated by the initial pleading is not subject to Federal jurisdiction, as of the date of service by plaintiffs of an amended pleading, motion, or other paper, indicating the existence of Federal jurisdiction.

(8) This subsection shall apply to any class action before or after the entry of a class certification order by the court with respect to that action.

(9) Paragraph (2) shall not apply to any class action that solely involves a claim—

(A) concerning a covered security as defined under 16(f)(3) [1] of the Securities Act of 1933 (15 U.S.C. 78p(f)(3)) and section 28(f)(5)(E) of the Securities Exchange Act of 1934 (15 U.S.C. 78bb(f)(5)(E));

(B) that relates to the internal affairs or governance of a corporation or other form of business enterprise and that arises under or by virtue of the laws of the State in which such corporation or business enterprise is incorporated or organized; or

(C) that relates to the rights, duties (including fiduciary duties), and obligations relating to or created by or pursuant to any security (as defined under section 2(a)(1) of the Securities Act of 1933 (15 U.S.C. 77b(a)(1)) and the regulations issued thereunder).

(10) For purposes of this subsection and section 1453, an unincorporated association shall be deemed to be a citizen of the State where it has its principal place of business and the State under whose laws it is organized.

(11)(A) For purposes of this subsection and section 1453, a mass action shall be deemed to be a class action removable under paragraphs (2) through (10) if it otherwise meets the provisions of those paragraphs.

(B)(i) As used in subparagraph (A), the term "mass action" means any civil action (except a civil action within the scope of section 1711(2)) in which monetary relief claims of 100 or more persons are proposed to be tried jointly on the ground that the plaintiffs' claims involve common questions of law or fact, except that jurisdiction shall exist only over those plaintiffs whose claims in a mass action satisfy the jurisdictional amount requirements under subsection (a).

(ii) As used in subparagraph (A), the term "mass action" shall not include any civil action in which—

(I) all of the claims in the action arise from an event or occurrence in the State in which the action was filed, and that allegedly resulted in injuries in that State or in States contiguous to that State;

(II) the claims are joined upon motion of a defendant;

(III) all of the claims in the action are asserted on behalf of the general public (and not on behalf of individual claimants or members of a purported class) pursuant to a State statute specifically authorizing such action; or

(IV) the claims have been consolidated or coordinated solely for pretrial proceedings.

(C)(i) Any action(s) removed to Federal court pursuant to this subsection shall not thereafter be transferred to any other court pursuant to section 1407, or the rules promulgated thereunder, unless a majority of the plaintiffs in the action request transfer pursuant to section 1407.

(ii) This subparagraph will not apply—

(I) to cases certified pursuant to rule 23 of the Federal Rules of Civil Procedure; or

(II) if plaintiffs propose that the action proceed as a class action pursuant to rule 23 of the Federal Rules of Civil Procedure.

(D) The limitations periods on any claims asserted in a mass action that is removed to Federal court pursuant to this subsection shall be deemed tolled during the period that the action is pending in Federal court.

(e) The word "States", as used in this section, includes the Territories, the District of Columbia, and the Commonwealth of Puerto Rico.

(June 25, 1948, c. 646, 62 Stat. 930; July 26, 1956, c. 740, 70 Stat. 658; July 25, 1958, Pub.L. 85–554, § 2, 72 Stat. 415; Aug. 14, 1964, Pub.L. 88–439, § 1, 78 Stat. 445; Oct. 21, 1976, Pub.L. 94–583, § 3, 90 Stat. 2891; Nov. 19, 1988, Pub.L. 100–702, Title II, §§ 201(a), 202(a), 203(a), 102 Stat. 4646; Oct. 19, 1996, Pub.L. 104–317, Title II, § 205(a), 110 Stat. 3850; Feb. 18, 2005, Pub.L. 109–2, § 4(a), 119 Stat. 9.)

[1] So in original. Reference to "16(f)(3)" probably should be preceded by "section".

HISTORICAL AND STATUTORY NOTES

References in Text

Rule 23 of the Federal Rules of Civil Procedure, referred to in subsec. (d)(1)(B) and (11)(C)(ii), is set out following the code sections of this title.

The reference to section 16(f)(3) of the Securities Act of 1933 in subsec. (d)(9)(A) means May 27, 1933, c. 38, Title I, § 16(f)(3), 48 Stat. 84, as amended, which is classified to 15 U.S.C.A. § 78p(f)(3).

Section 28(f)(5)(E) of the Securities Exchange Act of 1934, referred to in subsec. (d)(9)(A), is May 27, 1933, c. 38, Title I, § 2(f)(5)(E), 48 Stat. 74, as amended, which is classified to 15 U.S.C.A. § 78bb(f)(5)(E).

Section 2(a)(1) of the Securities Act of 1933, referred to in subsec. (d)(9)(C), is May 27, 1933, c. 38, Title I, § 2(a)(1), 48 Stat. 74, as amended, which is classified to 15 U.S.C.A. § 77b(a)(1).

Effective and Applicability Provisions

2005 Acts. Pub.L. 109–2, § 9, Feb. 18, 2005, 119 Stat. 14, provided that: "The amendments made by this Act [the Class Action Fairness Act of 2005, which enacted this note and 28 U.S.C.A. §§ 1453 and 1711 to 1715, amended 28 U.S.C.A. §§ 1332, 1335, and 1603, and enacted provisions set out as notes under 28 U.S.C.A. §§ 1711, 2071, and 2074] shall apply to any civil action commenced on or after the date of enactment of this Act [Feb. 18, 2005]."

1996 Acts. Section 205(b) of Pub.L. 104–317 provided that: "The amendment made by this section [amending this section] shall take effect 90 days after the date of enactment of this Act [Oct. 19, 1996]."

1988 Acts. Section 201(b) of Title II of Pub.L. 100–702 provided that: "The amendments made by this section [amending amount in controversy in subsecs. (a) and (b) of this section] shall apply to any civil action commenced on or after the 180th day after the date of enactment of this title [Nov. 19, 1988]."

Section 202(b) of Title II of Pub.L. 100–702 provided that: "The amendment made by this section [amending subsec. (c) of this section] shall apply to any civil action commenced in or removed to a United States district court on or after the 180th day after the date of enactment of this title [Nov. 19, 1988]."

Section 203(b) of Title II of Pub.L. 100–702 provided that: "The amendment made by this section [amending subsec. (a) of this section by enacting citizenship of permanent resident alien provision] shall apply to claims in civil actions commenced in or removed to the United States district courts on or after the 180th day after the date of enactment of this title [Nov. 19, 1988]."

1976 Acts. Amendment by Pub.L. 94–583 effective 90 days after Oct. 21, 1976, see section 8 of Pub.L. 94–583, set out as a note under section 1602 of this title.

1964 Acts. Section 2 of Pub.L. 88–439 provided that: "The amendment made by this Act to section 1332(c), title 28, United States Code [subsec. (c) of this section], applies only to causes of action arising after the date of enactment of this Act [Aug. 14, 1964]."

1958 Acts. Amendment of section by Pub.L. 85–554 applicable only in the case of actions commenced after July 25, 1958, see section 3 of Pub.L. 85–554, set out as a note under section 1331 of this title.

§ 1333. Admiralty, maritime and prize cases

The district courts shall have original jurisdiction, exclusive of the courts of the States, of:

   (1) Any civil case of admiralty or maritime jurisdiction, saving to suitors in all cases all other remedies to which they are otherwise entitled.

   (2) Any prize brought into the United States and all proceedings for the condemnation of property taken as prize.

(June 25, 1948, c. 646, 62 Stat. 931; May 24, 1949, c. 139, § 79, 63 Stat. 101.)

§ 1334. Bankruptcy cases and proceedings

(a) Except as provided in subsection (b) of this section, the district courts shall have original and exclusive jurisdiction of all cases under title 11.

(b) Notwithstanding any Act of Congress that confers exclusive jurisdiction on a court or courts other than the district courts, the district courts shall have original but not exclusive jurisdiction of all civil proceedings arising under title 11, or arising in or related to cases under title 11.

(c)(1) Nothing in this section prevents a district court in the interest of justice, or in the interest of comity with State courts or respect for State law, from abstaining from hearing a particular proceeding arising under title 11 or arising in or related to a case under title 11.

(2) Upon timely motion of a party in a proceeding based upon a State law claim or State law cause of action, related to a case under title 11 but not arising under title 11 or arising in a case under title 11, with respect to which an action could not have been commenced in a court of the United States absent jurisdiction under this section, the district court shall abstain from hearing such proceeding if an action is commenced, and can be timely adjudicated, in a State forum of appropriate jurisdiction.

(d) Any decision to abstain or not to abstain made under this subsection (other than a decision not to abstain in a proceeding described in subsection (c)(2)) is not reviewable by appeal or otherwise by the court of appeals under section 158(d), 1291, or 1292 of this title or by the Supreme Court of the United States under section 1254 of this title. This subsection [1] shall not be construed to limit the applicability of the stay provided for by section 362 of title 11, United States Code, as such section applies to an action affecting the property of the estate in bankruptcy.

(e) The district court in which a case under title 11 is commenced or is pending shall have exclusive jurisdiction of all of the property, wherever located, of the debtor as of the commencement of such case, and of property of the estate.

(June 25, 1948, c. 646, 62 Stat. 931; Nov. 6, 1978, Pub.L. 95–598, Title II, § 238(a), 92 Stat. 2667; July 10, 1984, Pub.L. 98–353, Title I, § 101(a), 98 Stat. 333; Oct. 27, 1986, Pub.L. 99–554, Title I, § 144(e), 100 Stat. 3096; Dec. 1, 1990, Pub.L. 101–650, Title III, § 309(b), 104 Stat. 5113; Oct. 22, 1994, Pub.L. 103–394, Title I, § 104(b), 108 Stat. 4109.)

[1] So in original. Probably should be a reference to subsection (c).

Amendment of Subsection (b)

Pub.L. 109–8, Title III, § 324(a)(1), (b), Title XV, § 1501, Apr. 20, 2005, 119 Stat. 98, 216, provided that, except as otherwise provided, effective 180 days after April 20, 2005, and only applicable with respect to cases filed under Title 11 before Apr. 20, 2005, subsection (b) is amended by striking "Notwithstanding" and inserting "Except as provided in subsection (e)(2), and notwithstanding".

Amendment of Subsection (c)

Pub.L. 109–8, Title VIII, § 802(c)(2), Title XV, § 1501, Apr. 20, 2005, 119 Stat. 145, 216, provided that, except as otherwise provided, effective 180 days after April 20, 2005, and inapplicable with respect to cases commenced under Title 11 before the effective date, subsection (c) of this section is amended by striking "Nothing in" and inserting "Except with respect to a case under chapter 15 of title 11, nothing in".

Amendment of Subsection (d)

Pub.L. 109–8, Title XII, § 1219, Title XV, § 1501, Apr. 20, 2005, 119 Stat. 195, 216, provided that, except as otherwise provided, effective 180 days after April 20, 2005, and inapplicable with respect to cases commenced under Title 11 before the effective date, subsection (d) of this section is amended by striking "made under this subsection" and inserting "made under subsection (c)", and by substituting "Subsection (c) and this subsection" for "This subsection".

Amendment of Subsection (e)

Pub.L. 109–8, Title III, § 324(a)(2), (b), Title XV, § 1501, Apr. 20, 2005, 119 Stat. 98, 216, provided that, except as otherwise provided, effective 180 days after April 20, 2005, and only applicable with respect to cases filed under Title 11 after Apr. 20, 2005, subsection (e) is amended to read as follows:

(e) The district court in which a case under title 11 is commenced or is pending shall have exclusive jurisdiction—

(1) of all the property, wherever located, of the debtor as of the commencement of such case, and of property of the estate; and

(2) over all claims or causes of action that involve construction of section 327 of title 11, United States Code, or rules relating to disclosure requirements under section 327.

HISTORICAL AND STATUTORY NOTES

Codifications

This section was amended by Pub.L. 95–598, Title II, § 238(a), Nov. 6, 1978, 92 Stat. 2668, effective June 28, 1984, pursuant to Pub.L. 95–598, Title IV, § 402(b), Nov. 6, 1978, 92 Stat. 2682, as amended by Pub.L. 98–249, § 1(a), Mar. 31, 1984, 98 Stat. 116; Pub.L. 98–271, § 1(a), Apr. 30, 1984, 98 Stat. 163; Pub.L. 98–299, § 1(a), May 25, 1984, 98 Stat. 214; Pub.L. 98–325, § 1(a), June 20, 1984, 98 Stat. 268, set out as an Effective and Applicability Provisions note preceding section 101 of Title 11, Bankruptcy, to read as follows:

"**§ 1334. Bankruptcy appeals**

"**(a)** The district courts for districts for which panels have not been ordered appointed under section 160 of this title shall have jurisdiction of appeals from all final judgments, orders, and decrees of bankruptcy courts.

"**(b)** The district courts for such districts shall have jurisdiction of appeals from interlocutory orders and decrees of bankruptcy courts, but only by leave of the district court to which the appeal is taken.

"**(c)** A district court may not refer an appeal under that section to a magistrate or to a special master."

Section 402(b) of Pub.L. 95–598 was amended by section 113 of Pub.L. 98–353 by substituting "shall not be effective" for "shall take effect on June 28, 1984", thereby eliminating the amendment by section 238(a) of Pub.L. 95–598, effective June 27, 1984, pursuant to section 122(c) of Pub.L. 98–353, set out as an Effective and Applicability Provisions note under 28 U.S.C.A. § 151.

Section 121(a) of Pub.L. 98–353 directed that section 402(b) of Pub.L. 95–598 be amended by substituting "the date of enactment of the Bankruptcy Amendments and Federal Judgeship Act of 1984 [i.e. July 10, 1984]" for "June 28, 1984". This amendment was not executed in view of the prior amendment to section 402(b) of Pub.L. 95–598 by section 113 of Pub.L. 98–353.

Effective and Applicability Provisions

2005 Acts. Pub.L. 109–8, Title III, § 324(b), Apr. 20, 2005, 119 Stat. 98, provided that: "This section [amending subsecs. (b) and (e) of this section] shall only apply to cases filed after the date of enactment of this Act [Apr. 20, 2005]."

Except as otherwise provided, amendments by Pub.L. 109–8 effective 180 days after April 20, 2005, and inapplicable with respect to cases commenced under Title 11 before the effective date, see Pub.L. 109–8, § 1501, set out as a note under 11 U.S.C.A. § 101.

1994 Acts. Amendment by Pub.L. 103–394 effective on Oct. 22, 1994, and not to apply with respect to cases commenced under Title 11 of the United States Code before Oct. 22, 1994, see section 702 of Pub.L. 103–394, set out as a note under section 101 of Title 11, Bankruptcy.

1986 Acts. Amendment by Pub.L. 99–554 effective 30 days after Oct. 27, 1986, except as otherwise provided for, see section 302(a) of Pub.L. 99–554, as amended, set out as a note under section 581 of this title.

1984 Acts. Amendment by Pub.L. 98–353, except for subsec. (c)(2), effective July 10, 1984, see section 122(a) of Pub.L. 98–353, set out as a note under section 151 of this title.

Subsec. (c)(2) not applicable with respect to cases under Title 11, Bankruptcy, that are pending on July 10, 1984, or to proceedings arising in or related to such cases, see section 122(b) of Pub.L. 98–353, set out as a note under section 151 of this title.

Separability of Provisions

If any provision of or amendment made by Pub.L. 103–394 or the application of such provision or amendment to any person or circumstance is held to be unconstitutional, the remaining provisions of and amendments made by Pub.L. 103–394 and the application of such provisions and amendments to any person or circumstance shall not be affected thereby, see section 701 of Pub.L. 103–394, set out as a note under section 101 of Title 11, Bankruptcy.

Jurisdiction Over and Transfer of Bankruptcy Cases and Proceedings

Section 115 of Pub.L. 98–353 provided that:

"**(a)** On the date of the enactment of this Act [July 10, 1984] the appropriate district court of the United States shall have jurisdiction of—

"**(1)** cases, and matters and proceedings in cases, under the Bankruptcy Act [former Title 11, Bankruptcy] that are pending immediately before such date in the bankruptcy courts continued by section 404(a) of the Act of November 6, 1978 (Public Law 95–598; 92 Stat. 2687) [Pub.L. 95–598, Title IV, § 404(a), Nov. 6, 1978, 92 Stat. 2683, formerly set out as a note preceding section 151 of this title], and

"**(2)** cases under title 11 of the United States Code [Title 11, Bankruptcy], and proceedings arising under title 11 of the United States Code or arising in or related to cases under title 11 of the United States Code, that are pending immediately before such date in the bankruptcy courts continued by section 404(a) of the Act of November 6, 1978 (Public Law 95–598; 92 Stat. 2687).

"**(b)** On the date of the enactment of this Act [July 10, 1984], there shall be transferred to the appropriate district court of the United States appeals from final judgments, orders, and decrees of the bankruptcy courts pending immediately before such date in the bankruptcy appellate panels appointed under section 405(c) of the Act of November 6, 1978 (Public Law 95–598; 92 Stat. 2685) [formerly set out as a note preceding section 1471 of this title]."

§ 1335. Interpleader

(a) The district courts shall have original jurisdiction of any civil action of interpleader or in the nature of interpleader filed by any person, firm, or corporation, association, or society having in his or its custody or possession money or property of the value of $500 or more, or having issued a note, bond, certificate, policy of insurance, or other instrument of value or amount of $500 or more, or providing for the delivery or payment or the loan of money or property of such amount or value, or being under any obligation written or unwritten to the amount of $500 or more, if

(1) Two or more adverse claimants, of diverse citizenship as defined in subsection (a) or (d) of section 1332 of this title, are claiming or may claim to be entitled to such money or property, or to any one or more of the benefits arising by virtue of any note, bond, certificate, policy or other instrument, or arising by virtue of any such obligation; and if (2) the plaintiff has deposited such money or property or has paid the amount of or the loan or other value of such instrument or the amount due under such obligation into the registry of the court, there to abide the judgment of the court, or has given bond payable to the clerk of the court in such amount and with such surety as the court or judge may deem proper, conditioned upon the compliance by the plaintiff with the future order or judgment of the court with respect to the subject matter of the controversy.

(b) Such an action may be entertained although the titles or claims of the conflicting claimants do not have a common origin, or are not identical, but are adverse to and independent of one another.

(June 25, 1948, c. 646, 62 Stat. 931; Feb. 18, 2005, Pub.L. 109–2, § 4(b)(1), 119 Stat. 12.)

HISTORICAL AND STATUTORY NOTES
Effective and Applicability Provisions

2005 Acts. Amendments by Class Action Fairness Act of 2005, Pub.L. 109–2, Feb. 18, 2005, 119 Stat. 4, applicable to any civil action commenced on or after Feb. 18, 2005, see Pub.L. 109–2, § 9, set out as a note under 28 U.S.C.A. § 1332.

§ 1336. Surface Transportation Board's orders

(a) Except as otherwise provided by Act of Congress, the district courts shall have jurisdiction of any civil action to enforce, in whole or in part, any order of the Surface Transportation Board, and to enjoin or suspend, in whole or in part, any order of the Surface Transportation Board for the payment of money or the collection of fines, penalties, and forfeitures.

(b) When a district court or the United States Court of Federal Claims refers a question or issue to the Surface Transportation Board for determination, the court which referred the question or issue shall have exclusive jurisdiction of a civil action to enforce, enjoin, set aside, annul, or suspend, in whole or in part, any order of the Surface Transportation Board arising out of such referral.

(c) Any action brought under subsection (b) of this section shall be filed within 90 days from the date that the order of the Surface Transportation Board becomes final.

(June 25, 1948, c. 646, 62 Stat. 931; Aug. 30, 1964, Pub.L. 88–513, § 1, 78 Stat. 695; Jan. 2, 1975, Pub.L. 93–584, § 1, 88 Stat. 1917; Apr. 2, 1982, Pub.L. 97–164, Title I, § 128, 96 Stat. 39; Oct. 29, 1992, Pub.L. 102–572, Title IX, § 902(b)(1), 106 Stat. 4516; Dec. 29, 1995, Pub.L. 104–88, Title III, § 305(a)(1), (2), 109 Stat. 944.)

HISTORICAL AND STATUTORY NOTES
Effective and Applicability Provisions

1995 Acts. Amendment by Pub.L. 104–88 effective Jan. 1, 1996, see section 2 of Pub.L. 104–88, set out as a note under section 701 of Title 49, Transportation.

1992 Acts. Amendment by Pub.L. 102–572 effective Oct. 29, 1992, see section 911 of Pub.L. 102–572, set out as a note under section 171 of this title.

1982 Acts. Amendment by Pub.L. 97–164 effective Oct. 1, 1982, see section 402 of Pub.L. 97–164, set out as a note under section 171 of this title.

1975 Acts. Amendment by Pub.L. 93–584 not applicable to actions commenced on or before the last day of the first month beginning after Jan. 2, 1975, and actions to enjoin or suspend orders of the Interstate Commerce Commission which are pending when this amendment becomes effective shall not be affected thereby, but shall proceed to final disposition under the law existing on the date they were commenced, see section 10 of Pub.L. 93–584, set out as a note under section 2321 of this title.

§ 1337. Commerce and antitrust regulations; amount in controversy, costs

(a) The district courts shall have original jurisdiction of any civil action or proceeding arising under any Act of Congress regulating commerce or protecting trade and commerce against restraints and monopolies: *Provided, however,* That the district courts shall have original jurisdiction of an action brought under section 11706 or 14706 of title 49, only if the matter in controversy for each receipt or bill of lading exceeds $10,000, exclusive of interest and costs.

(b) Except when express provision therefor is otherwise made in a statute of the United States, where a plaintiff who files the case under section 11706 or 14706 of title 49, originally in the Federal courts is finally adjudged to be entitled to recover less than the sum or value of $10,000, computed without regard to any setoff or counterclaim to which the defendant may be adjudged to be entitled, and exclusive of any interest and costs, the district court may deny costs to the plaintiff and, in addition, may impose costs on the plaintiff.

(c) The district courts shall not have jurisdiction under this section of any matter within the exclusive jurisdiction of the Court of International Trade under chapter 95 of this title.

(June 25, 1948, c. 646, 62 Stat. 931; Oct. 20, 1978, Pub.L. 95–486, § 9(a), 92 Stat. 1633; Oct. 10, 1980, Pub.L. 96–417, Title V, § 505, 94 Stat. 1743; Jan. 12, 1983, Pub.L. 97–449, § 5(f), 96 Stat. 2442; Dec. 29, 1995, Pub.L. 104–88, Title III, § 305(a)(3), 109 Stat. 944.)

HISTORICAL AND STATUTORY NOTES
Effective and Applicability Provisions

1995 Acts. Amendment by Pub.L. 104–88 effective Jan. 1, 1996, see section 2 of Pub.L. 104–88, set out as a note under section 701 of Title 49, Transportation.

1980 Acts. Amendment by Pub.L. 96–417 effective on Nov. 1, 1980 and applicable with respect to civil actions pending on or commenced on or after such date, see section 701(a) of Pub.L. 96–417, as amended, set out as a note under section 251 of this title.

§ 1338.   Patents, plant variety protection, copyrights, mask works, designs, trademarks, and unfair competition

(a) The district courts shall have original jurisdiction of any civil action arising under any Act of Congress relating to patents, plant variety protection, copyrights and trademarks. Such jurisdiction shall be exclusive of the courts of the states in patent, plant variety protection and copyright cases.

(b) The district courts shall have original jurisdiction of any civil action asserting a claim of unfair competition when joined with a substantial and related claim under the copyright, patent, plant variety protection or trademark laws.

(c) Subsections (a) and (b) apply to exclusive rights in mask works under chapter 9 of title 17, and to exclusive rights in designs under chapter 13 of title 17, to the same extent as such subsections apply to copyrights.

(June 25, 1948, c. 646, 62 Stat. 931; Dec. 24, 1970, Pub.L. 91–577, Title III, § 143(b), 84 Stat. 1559; Nov. 19, 1988, Pub.L. 100–702, Title X, § 1020(a)(4), 102 Stat. 4671; Oct. 28, 1998, Pub.L. 105–304, Title V, § 503(b)(1), (2)(A), 112 Stat.

2917; Nov. 29, 1999, Pub.L. 106–113, Div. B, § 1000(a)(9) [Title III, § 3009(1)], 113 Stat. 1536, 1501A–551.)

HISTORICAL AND STATUTORY NOTES
Effective and Applicability Provisions

1998 Acts. Amendment by Pub.L. 105–304, effective Oct. 28, 1998, see section 505 of Pub.L. 105–304, set out as a note under section 1301 of Title 17, Copyrights.

1970 Acts. Amendment by Pub.L. 91–577 effective Dec. 24, 1970, see section 141 of Pub.L. 91–577, set out as a note under section 2321 of Title 7, Agriculture.

§ 1339.   Postal matters

The district courts shall have original jurisdiction of any civil action arising under any Act of Congress relating to the postal service.
(June 25, 1948, c. 646, 62 Stat. 932.)

§ 1340.   Internal revenue; customs duties

The district courts shall have original jurisdiction of any civil action arising under any Act of Congress providing for internal revenue, or revenue from imports or tonnage except matters within the jurisdiction of the Court of International Trade.
(June 25, 1948, c. 646, 62 Stat. 932; Oct. 10, 1980, Pub.L. 96–417, Title V, § 501(21), 94 Stat. 1742.)

HISTORICAL AND STATUTORY NOTES
Effective and Applicability Provisions

1980 Acts. Amendment by Pub.L. 96–417 effective on Nov. 1, 1980 and applicable with respect to civil actions pending on or commenced on or after such date, see section 701(a) of Pub.L. 96–417, as amended, set out as a note under section 251 of this title.

§ 1341.   Taxes by States

The district courts shall not enjoin, suspend or restrain the assessment, levy or collection of any tax under State law where a plain, speedy and efficient remedy may be had in the courts of such State.
(June 25, 1948, c. 646, 62 Stat. 932.)

§ 1342.   Rate orders of State agencies

The district courts shall not enjoin, suspend or restrain the operation of, or compliance with, any order affecting rates chargeable by a public utility and made by a State administrative agency or a rate-making body of a State political subdivision, where:

(1) Jurisdiction is based solely on diversity of citizenship or repugnance of the order to the Federal Constitution; and,

(2) The order does not interfere with interstate commerce; and,

(3) The order has been made after reasonable notice and hearing; and,

(4) A plain, speedy and efficient remedy may be had in the courts of such State.

(June 25, 1948, c. 646, 62 Stat. 932.)

§ 1343.   Civil rights and elective franchise

(a) The district courts shall have original jurisdiction of any civil action authorized by law to be commenced by any person:

(1) To recover damages for injury to his person or property, or because of the deprivation of any right or privilege of a citizen of the United States, by any act done in furtherance of any conspiracy mentioned in section 1985 of Title 42;

(2) To recover damages from any person who fails to prevent or to aid in preventing any wrongs mentioned in section 1985 of Title 42 which he had knowledge were about to occur and power to prevent;

(3) To redress the deprivation, under color of any State law, statute, ordinance, regulation, custom or usage, of any right, privilege or immunity secured by the Constitution of the United States or by any Act of Congress providing for equal rights of citizens or of all persons within the jurisdiction of the United States;

(4) To recover damages or to secure equitable or other relief under any Act of Congress providing for the protection of civil rights, including the right to vote.

(b) For purposes of this section—

(1) the District of Columbia shall be considered to be a State; and

(2) any Act of Congress applicable exclusively to the District of Columbia shall be considered to be a statute of the District of Columbia.

(June 25, 1948, c. 646, 62 Stat. 932; Sept. 3, 1954, c. 1263, § 42, 68 Stat. 1241; Sept. 9, 1957, Pub.L. 85–315, Part III, § 121, 71 Stat. 637; Dec. 29, 1979, Pub.L. 96–170, § 2, 93 Stat. 1284.)

HISTORICAL AND STATUTORY NOTES

Effective and Applicability Provisions

1979 Acts. Section 3 of Pub.L. 96–170 provided that: "The amendments made by this Act [amending this section and section 1983 of Title 42, The Public Health and Welfare] shall apply with respect to any deprivation of rights, privileges, or immunities secured by the Constitution and laws occurring after the date of the enactment of this Act [Dec. 29, 1979]."

§ 1344.   Election disputes

The district courts shall have original jurisdiction of any civil action to recover possession of any office, except that of elector of President or Vice President, United States Senator, Representative in or delegate to Congress, or member of a state legislature, authorized by law to be commenced, wherein it appears that the sole question touching the title to office arises out of denial of the right to vote, to any citizen offering to vote, on account of race, color or previous condition of servitude.

The jurisdiction under this section shall extend only so far as to determine the rights of the parties to office by reason of the denial of the right, guaranteed by the Constitution of the United States and secured by any law, to enforce the right of citizens of the United States to vote in all the States.

(June 25, 1948, c. 646, 62 Stat. 932.)

§ 1345.   United States as plaintiff

Except as otherwise provided by Act of Congress, the district courts shall have original jurisdiction of all civil actions, suits or proceedings commenced by the United States, or by any agency or officer thereof expressly authorized to sue by Act of Congress.

(June 25, 1948, c. 646, 62 Stat. 933.)

§ 1346.   United States as defendant

(a) The district courts shall have original jurisdiction, concurrent with the United States Court of Federal Claims, of:

(1) Any civil action against the United States for the recovery of any internal-revenue tax alleged to have been erroneously or illegally assessed or collected, or any penalty claimed to have been collected without authority or any sum alleged to have been excessive or in any manner wrongfully collected under the internal-revenue laws;

(2) Any other civil action or claim against the United States, not exceeding $10,000 in amount, founded either upon the Constitution, or any Act of Congress, or any regulation of an executive department, or upon any express or implied contract with the United States, or for liquidated or unliquidated damages in cases not sounding in tort, except that the district courts shall not have jurisdiction of any civil action or claim against the United States founded upon any express or implied contract with the United States or for liquidated or unliquidated damages in cases not sounding in tort which are subject to sections 8(g)(1) and 10(a)(1) of the Contract Disputes Act of 1978. For the purpose of this paragraph, an express or implied contract with the Army and Air Force Exchange Service, Navy Exchanges, Marine Corps Exchanges, Coast Guard Exchanges, or Exchange Councils of the National Aeronautics and Space Administration shall be considered an express or implied contract with the United States.

(b)(1) Subject to the provisions of chapter 171 of this title, the district courts, together with the United States District Court for the District of the Canal Zone and the District Court of the Virgin Islands, shall have exclusive jurisdiction of civil actions on claims against the United States, for money damages, accruing on and after January 1, 1945, for injury or loss of property, or personal injury or death caused by the negligent or wrongful act or omission of any employee of the Government while acting within the scope of his office or employment, under circumstances where the United States, if a private person, would be liable to the claimant in accordance with the law of the place where the act or omission occurred.

(2) No person convicted of a felony who is incarcerated while awaiting sentencing or while serving a sentence may bring a civil action against the United States or an agency, officer, or employee of the Government, for mental or emotional injury suffered while in custody without a prior showing of physical injury.

(c) The jurisdiction conferred by this section includes jurisdiction of any set-off, counterclaim, or other claim or demand whatever on the part of the United States against any plaintiff commencing an action under this section.

(d) The district courts shall not have jurisdiction under this section of any civil action or claim for a pension.

(e) The district courts shall have original jurisdiction of any civil action against the United States provided in section 6226, 6228(a), 7426, or 7428 (in the case of the United States district court for the District of Columbia) or section 7429 of the Internal Revenue Code of 1986.

(f) The district courts shall have exclusive original jurisdiction of civil actions under section 2409a to quiet title to an estate or interest in real property in which an interest is claimed by the United States.

(g) Subject to the provisions of chapter 179, the district courts of the United States shall have exclusive jurisdiction over any civil action commenced under section 453(2) of title 3, by a covered employee under chapter 5 of such title.

(June 25, 1948, c. 646, 62 Stat. 933; Apr. 25, 1949, c. 92, § 2(a), 63 Stat. 62; May 24, 1949, c. 139, § 80(a), (b), 63 Stat. 101; Oct. 31, 1951, c. 655, § 50(b), 65 Stat. 727; July 30, 1954, c. 648, § 1, 68 Stat. 589; July 7, 1958, Pub.L. 85–508, § 12(e), 72 Stat. 348; Aug. 30, 1964, Pub.L. 88–519, 78 Stat. 699; Nov. 2, 1966, Pub.L. 89–719, Title II, § 202(a), 80 Stat. 1148; July 23, 1970, Pub.L. 91–350, § 1(a), 84 Stat. 449; Oct. 25, 1972, Pub.L. 92–562, § 1, 86 Stat. 1176; Oct. 4, 1976, Pub.L. 94–455, Title XII, § 1204(c) (1), Title XIII, § 1306(b) (7), 90 Stat. 1697, 1719; Nov. 1, 1978, Pub.L. 95–563, § 14(a), 92 Stat. 2389; Apr. 2, 1982, Pub.L. 97–164, Title I, § 129, 96 Stat. 39; Sept. 3, 1982, Pub.L. 97–248, Title IV, § 402(c) (17), 96 Stat. 669; Oct. 22, 1986, Pub.L. 99–514, § 2, 100 Stat. 2095; Oct. 29, 1992, Pub.L. 102–572, Title IX, § 902(b)(1), 106 Stat. 4516; Apr. 26, 1996, Pub.L. 104–134, Title I, § 101[(a)][Title VIII, § 806], 110 Stat. 1321–75; renumbered Title I May 2, 1996, Pub.L. 104–140, § 1(a), 110 Stat. 1327, and amended Oct. 26, 1996, Pub.L. 104–331, § 3(b)(1), 110 Stat. 4069.)

HISTORICAL AND STATUTORY NOTES

Senate Revision Amendment

The provisions of Title 28, U.S.C., section 932, which related to application of the Federal Rules of Civil Procedure, were originally set out in section 2676 of this revised title, but such section 2676 was eliminated by Senate amendment. See 80th Congress Senate Report No. 1559, amendment No. 61.

1949 Acts. This section corrects typographical errors in section 1346(a)(1) of Title 28, U.S.C., and in section 1346(b) of such title.

House Report No. 276, see 1949 U.S. Code Cong. Service, p. 1226.

Senate Report No. 303 and House Report No. 352, see 1949 U.S.Code Cong.Service, p. 1248.

1951 Acts. Senate Report No. 1020, see 1951 U.S. Code Cong. and Adm. Service, p. 2578.

1954 Acts. House Report No. 659 and Conference Report No. 2276, see 1954 U.S. Code Cong. and Adm. News, p. 2716.

1958 Acts. House Report No. 624, see 1958 U.S. Code Cong. and Adm. News, p. 2933.

1964 Acts. Senate Report No. 1390, see 1964 U.S. Code Cong. and Adm. News, p. 3254.

1966 Acts. Senate Report No. 1708, see 1966 U.S. Code Cong. and Adm. News, p. 3722.

1970 Acts. House Report No. 91–933, see 1970 U.S. Code Cong. and Adm. News, p. 3477.

1972 Acts. House Report No. 92–1559, see 1972 U.S. Code Cong. and Adm. News, p. 4547.

1976 Acts. House Report Nos. 94–658 and 94–1380, Senate Report No. 94–938(Parts I and II), and House Conference Report No. 94–1515, see 1976 U.S. Code Cong. and Adm. News, p. 2897.

1978 Acts. Senate Report No. 95–1118, see 1978 U.S. Code Cong. and Adm. News, p. 5235.

1982 Acts. Senate Report No. 97–275, see 1982 U.S. Code Cong. and Adm. News, p. 11.

Senate Report No. 97–494, House Conference Report No. 97–760 and Statements by Legislative Leaders, see 1982 U.S. Code Cong. and Adm. News, p. 781.

1996 Acts. House Report No. 104–820, see 1996 U.S. Code Cong. and Adm. News, p. 4348.

References in Text

The internal-revenue laws, referred to in subsec. (a)(1), are classified generally to Title 26, Internal Revenue Code.

Sections 8(g)(1) and 10(a)(1) of the Contract Disputes Act of 1978, referred to in subsec. (a)(2), are sections 8(g)(1) and 10(a)(1) of Pub.L. 95–563, Nov. 1, 1978, 92 Stat. 2387, 2388, which are classified to sections 607(g)(1) and 609(a)(1) of Title 41, Public Contracts.

Sections 6226, 6228(a), 7426, 7428, and 7429 of the Internal Revenue Code of 1986, referred to in subsec. (e), are classified to sections 6226, 6228(a), 7426, 7428, and 7429, respectively, of Title 26, Internal Revenue Code.

Effective and Applicability Provisions

1996 Acts. Amendment by Pub.L. 104–331 effective October 1, 1997, see section 3(d) of Pub.L. 104–331, set out as a note under section 1296 of this title.

Complete Annotation Materials, see Title 28 U.S.C.A.

1992 Acts. Amendment by Pub.L. 102–572 effective Oct. 29, 1992, see section 911 of Pub.L. 102–572, set out as a note under section 171 of this title.

1982 Acts. Amendment by Pub.L. 97–248 applicable to partnership taxable years beginning after Sept. 3, 1982, with provision for the applicability of the amendment to any partnership taxable year ending after Sept. 3, 1982, if the partnership, each partner, and each indirect partner requests such application and the Secretary of the Treasury or his delegate consents to such application, see section 407(a)(1) and (3) of Pub.L. 97–248, as amended, set out as a note under section 6221 of Title 26, Internal Revenue Code.

Amendment by Pub.L. 97–164 effective Oct. 1, 1982, see section 402 of Pub.L. 97–164, set out as a note under section 171 of this title.

1978 Acts. Amendment by Pub.L. 95–563 effective with respect to contracts entered into 120 days after Nov. 1, 1978 and, at the election of the contractor, with respect to any claim pending at such time before the contracting officer or initiated thereafter, see section 16 of Pub.L. 95–563, set out as a note under section 601 of Title 41, Public Contracts.

1970 Acts. Section 2 of Pub.L. 91–350 provided that:

"**(a)** In addition to granting jurisdiction over suits brought after the date of enactment of this Act [July 23, 1970], the provisions of this Act [amending this section and section 1491 of this title and section 724a of former Title 31, Money and Finance], shall also apply to claims and civil actions dismissed before or pending on the date of enactment of this Act if the claim or civil action is based upon a transaction, omission, or breach that occurred not more than six years prior to the date of enactment of this Act [July 23, 1970].

"**(b)** The provisions of subsection (a) of this section shall apply notwithstanding a determination or judgment made prior to the date of enactment of this Act that the United States district courts or the United States Court of Claims [now United States Court of Federal Claims] did not have jurisdiction to entertain a suit on an express or implied contract with a nonappropriated fund instrumentality of the United States described in section 1 of this Act."

1966 Acts. Section 203 of Title II of Pub.L. 89–719 provided that: "The amendments made by this title [amending this section and sections 1402 and 2410 of this title] shall apply after the date of the enactment of this Act [Nov. 2, 1966]."

1958 Acts. Amendment of section by Pub.L. 85–508 effective Jan. 3, 1959, upon admission of Alaska into the Union pursuant to Proc. No. 3269, Jan. 3, 1959, 24 F.R. 81, 73 Stat. c16, as required by sections 1 and 8(c) of Pub.L. 85–508, see notes set out under section 81A of this title and preceding former section 21 of Title 48, Territories and Insular Possessions.

Transfer of Functions

For transfer of authorities, functions, personnel, and assets of the Coast Guard, including the authorities and functions of the Secretary of Transportation relating thereto, to the Department of Homeland Security, and for treatment of related references, see 6 U.S.C.A. §§ 468(b), 551(d), 552(d) and 557, and the Department of Homeland Security Reorganization Plan of November 25, 2002, as modified, set out as a note under 6 U.S.C.A. § 542.

Savings Clause for Act Oct. 31, 1951

Act June 4, 1956, c. 363, 70 Stat. 246, which was formerly set out as a note under this section, and which conferred jurisdiction on district courts of certain actions to recover pay of employees who had been dismissed, was repealed by Pub.L. 89–554, § 8(a), Sept. 6, 1966, 80 Stat. 658.

Severability of Provisions

If any provision of section 101[a] [Title VIII] of Pub.L. 104–134, an amendment made by such Title, or the application of such provision or amendment to any person or circumstance is held to be unconstitutional, the remainder of such Title, the amendments made by such Title, and the application of the provisions of such Title to any person or circumstance not affected thereby, see section 101[a] [Title VIII, § 810] of Pub.L. 104–134, set out as a note under section 3626 of Title 18, Crimes and Criminal Procedure.

Termination of United States District Court for the District of the Canal Zone

For termination of the United States District Court for the District of the Canal Zone at end of the "transition period", being the 30–month period beginning Oct. 1, 1979, and ending midnight Mar. 31, 1982, see Paragraph 5 of Article XI of the Panama Canal Treaty of 1977 and sections 3831 and 3841 to 3843 of Title 22, Foreign Relations and Intercourse.

§ 1347. Partition action where United States is joint tenant

The district courts shall have original jurisdiction of any civil action commenced by any tenant in common or joint tenant for the partition of lands where the United States is one of the tenants in common or joint tenants.

(June 25, 1948, c. 646, 62 Stat. 933.)

§ 1348. Banking association as party

The district courts shall have original jurisdiction of any civil action commenced by the United States, or by direction of any officer thereof, against any national banking association, any civil action to wind up the affairs of any such association, and any action by a banking association established in the district for which the court is held, under chapter 2 of Title 12, to enjoin the Comptroller of the Currency, or any receiver acting under his direction, as provided by such chapter.

All national banking associations shall, for the purposes of all other actions by or against them, be deemed citizens of the States in which they are respectively located.

(June 25, 1948, c. 646, 62 Stat. 933.)

HISTORICAL AND STATUTORY NOTES

Exception as to Transfer of Functions

Functions vested by any provision of law in the Comptroller of the Currency, referred to in this section, were not included in the transfer of functions of officers, agencies and employees of the Department of the Treasury to the Secretary of the Treasury, made by 1950 Reorg. Plan No. 26, § 1, eff. July 31, 1950, 15 F.R. 4935, 64 Stat. 1280, set out in Appendix 1 to Title 5, Government Organization and Employees. See section 321(c)(2) of Title 31 Money and Fiance.

§ 1349. Corporation organized under federal law as party

The district courts shall not have jurisdiction of any civil action by or against any corporation upon the ground that it was incorporated by or under an Act of Congress, unless the United States is the owner of more than one-half of its capital stock.
(June 25, 1948, c. 646, 62 Stat. 934.)

§ 1350. Alien's action for tort

The district courts shall have original jurisdiction of any civil action by an alien for a tort only, committed in violation of the law of nations or a treaty of the United States.
(June 25, 1948, c. 646, 62 Stat. 934.)

HISTORICAL AND STATUTORY NOTES

Torture Victim Protection

Pub.L. 102–256, Mar. 12, 1992, 106 Stat. 73, provided that:
"Section 1.   Short Title.
"This Act may be cited as the 'Torture Victim Protection Act of 1991'.
"Sec. 2.   Establishment of civil action.
"(a) Liability.—An individual who, under actual or apparent authority, or color of law, of any foreign nation—
   "(1) subjects an individual to torture shall, in a civil action, be liable for damages to that individual; or
   "(2) subjects an individual to extrajudicial killing shall, in a civil action, be liable for damages to the individual's legal representative, or to any person who may be a claimant in an action for wrongful death.
"(b) Exhaustion of remedies.—A court shall decline to hear a claim under this section if the claimant has not exhausted adequate and available remedies in the place in which the conduct giving rise to the claim occurred.
"(c) Statute of limitations.—No action shall be maintained under this section unless it is commenced within 10 years after the cause of action arose.
"Sec. 3.   Definitions.
"(a) Extrajudicial killing.—For the purposes of this Act, the term 'extrajudicial killing' means a deliberated killing not authorized by a previous judgment pronounced by a regularly constituted court affording all the judicial guarantees which are recognized as indispensable by civilized peoples. Such term, however, does not include any such killing that, under international law, is lawfully carried out under the authority of a foreign nation.
"(b) Torture.—For the purposes of this Act—
   "(1) the term 'torture' means any act, directed against an individual in the offender's custody or physical control, by which severe pain or suffering (other than pain or suffering arising only from or inherent in, or incidental to, lawful sanctions), whether physical or mental, is intentionally inflicted on that individual for such purposes as obtaining from that individual or a third person information or a confession, punishing that individual for an act that individual or a third person has committed or is suspected of having committed, intimidating or coercing that individual or a third person, or for any reason based on discrimination of any kind; and
   "(2) mental pain or suffering refers to prolonged mental harm caused by or resulting from—
      "(A) the intentional infliction or threatened infliction of severe physical pain or suffering;
      "(B) the administration or application, or threatened administration or application, of mind altering substances or other procedures calculated to disrupt profoundly the senses or the personality;
      "(C) the threat of imminent death; or
      "(D) the threat that another individual will imminently be subjected to death, severe physical pain or suffering, or the administration or application of mind altering substances or other procedures calculated to disrupt profoundly the senses or personality."

§ 1351. Consuls, vice consuls, and members of a diplomatic mission as defendant

The district courts shall have original jurisdiction, exclusive of the courts of the States, of all civil actions and proceedings against—

   (1) consuls or vice consuls of foreign states; or

   (2) members of a mission or members of their families (as such terms are defined in section 2 of the Diplomatic Relations Act).

(June 25, 1948, c. 646, 62 Stat. 934; May 24, 1949, c. 139, § 80(c), 63 Stat. 101; Sept. 30, 1978, Pub.L. 95–393, § 8(a)(1), 92 Stat. 810.)

HISTORICAL AND STATUTORY NOTES

References in Text

Section 2 of the Diplomatic Relations Act, referred to in par. (2), is section 2 of Pub.L. 95–393, Sept. 30, 1978, 92 Stat. 808, which is classified to section 254a of Title 22, Foreign Relations and Intercourse.

Effective and Applicability Provisions

1978 Acts. Amendment by Pub.L. 95–393 effective at the end of the 90-day period beginning on Sept. 30, 1978, see section 9 of Pub.L. 95–393, set out as a note under section 254a of Title 22, Foreign Relations and Intercourse.

§ 1352. Bonds executed under federal law

The district courts shall have original jurisdiction, concurrent with State courts, of any action on a bond executed under any law of the United States, except matters within the jurisdiction of the Court of International Trade under section 1582 of this title.
(June 25, 1948, c. 646, 62 Stat. 934; Oct. 10, 1980, Pub.L. 96–417, Title V, § 506, 94 Stat. 1743.)

HISTORICAL AND STATUTORY NOTES

Effective and Applicability Provisions

1980 Acts. Amendment by Pub.L. 96–417 applicable with respect to civil actions commenced on or after the 90th day after Nov. 1, 1980, see section 701(c)(1)(B) of Pub.L. 96–417, as amended, set out as a note under section 251 of this title.

§ 1353. Indian allotments

The district courts shall have original jurisdiction of any civil action involving the right of any person, in whole or in part of Indian blood or descent, to any allotment of land under any Act of Congress or treaty.

The judgment in favor of any claimant to an allotment of land shall have the same effect, when properly certified to the Secretary of the Interior, as if such allotment had been allowed and approved by him; but this provision shall not apply to any lands held on or before December 21, 1911, by either of the Five Civilized Tribes, the Osage Nation of Indians, nor to any of the lands within the Quapaw Indian Agency.
(June 25, 1948, c. 646, 62 Stat. 934.)

§ 1354. Land grants from different states

The district courts shall have original jurisdiction of actions between citizens of the same state claiming lands under grants from different states.
(June 25, 1948, c. 646, 62 Stat. 934.)

§ 1355. Fine, penalty or forfeiture

(a) The district courts shall have original jurisdiction, exclusive of the courts of the States, of any action or proceeding for the recovery or enforcement of any fine, penalty, or forfeiture, pecuniary or otherwise, incurred under any Act of Congress, except matters within the jurisdiction of the Court of International Trade under section 1582 of this title.

(b)(1) A forfeiture action or proceeding may be brought in—

(A) the district court for the district in which any of the acts or omissions giving rise to the forfeiture occurred, or

(B) any other district where venue for the forfeiture action or proceeding is specifically provided for in section 1395 of this title or any other statute.

(2) Whenever property subject to forfeiture under the laws of the United States is located in a foreign country, or has been detained or seized pursuant to legal process or competent authority of a foreign government, an action or proceeding for forfeiture may be brought as provided in paragraph (1), or in the United States District court[1] for the District of Columbia.

(c) In any case in which a final order disposing of property in a civil forfeiture action or proceeding is appealed, removal of the property by the prevailing party shall not deprive the court of jurisdiction. Upon motion of the appealing party, the district court or the court of appeals shall issue any order necessary to preserve the right of the appealing party to the full value of the property at issue, including a stay of the judgment of the district court pending appeal or requiring the prevailing party to post an appeal bond.

(d) Any court with jurisdiction over a forfeiture action pursuant to subsection (b) may issue and cause to be served in any other district such process as may be required to bring before the court the property that is the subject of the forfeiture action.
(June 25, 1948, c. 646, 62 Stat. 934; Oct. 10, 1980, Pub.L. 96–417, Title V, § 507, 94 Stat. 1743; Oct. 28, 1992, Pub.L. 102–550, Title XV, § 1521, 106 Stat. 4062.)

[1] So in original. Probably should be capitalized.

HISTORICAL AND STATUTORY NOTES
Effective and Applicability Provisions

1992 Acts. Except as otherwise provided, amendment by Pub.L. 102–550 effective Oct. 28, 1992, see section 2 of Pub.L. 102–550, set out as a note under section 5301 of Title 42, The Public Health and Welfare.

1980 Acts. Amendment by Pub.L. 96–417 applicable with respect to civil actions commenced on or after the 90th day after Nov. 1, 1980, see section 701(c)(1)(B) of Pub.L. 96–417, as amended, set out as a note under section 251 of this title.

§ 1356. Seizures not within admiralty and maritime jurisdiction

The district courts shall have original jurisdiction, exclusive of the courts of the States, of any seizure under any law of the United States on land or upon waters not within admiralty and maritime jurisdiction, except matters within the jurisdiction of the Court of International Trade under section 1582 of this title.
(June 25, 1948, c. 646, 62 Stat. 934; Oct. 10, 1980, Pub.L. 96–417, Title V, § 508, 94 Stat. 1743.)

HISTORICAL AND STATUTORY NOTES
Effective and Applicability Provisions

1980 Acts. Amendment by Pub.L. 96–417 applicable with respect to civil actions commenced on or after the 90th day after Nov. 1, 1980, see section 701(c)(1)(B) of Pub.L. 96–417, as amended, set out as a note under section 251 of this title.

§ 1357. Injuries under Federal laws

The district courts shall have original jurisdiction of any civil action commenced by any person to recover damages for any injury to his person or property on account of any act done by him, under any Act of Congress, for the protection or collection of any of the revenues, or to enforce the right of citizens of the United States to vote in any State.
(June 25, 1948, c. 646, 62 Stat. 934.)

§ 1358. Eminent domain

The district courts shall have original jurisdiction of all proceedings to condemn real estate for the use of the United States or its departments or agencies.
(June 25, 1948, c. 646, 62 Stat. 935.)

§ 1359. Parties collusively joined or made

A district court shall not have jurisdiction of a civil action in which any party, by assignment or otherwise, has been improperly or collusively made or joined to invoke the jurisdiction of such court.

(June 25, 1948, c. 646, 62 Stat. 935.)

§ 1360. State civil jurisdiction in actions to which Indians are parties

(a) Each of the States listed in the following table shall have jurisdiction over civil causes of action between Indians or to which Indians are parties which arise in the areas of Indian country listed opposite the name of the State to the same extent that such State has jurisdiction over other civil causes of action, and those civil laws of such State that are of general application to private persons or private property shall have the same force and effect within such Indian country as they have elsewhere within the State:

State of	Indian country affected
Alaska	All Indian country within the State
California	All Indian country within the State
Minnesota	All Indian country within the State, except the Red Lake Reservation
Nebraska	All Indian country within the State
Oregon	All Indian country within the State, except the Warm Springs Reservation
Wisconsin	All Indian country within the State

(b) Nothing in this section shall authorize the alienation, encumbrance, or taxation of any real or personal property, including water rights, belonging to any Indian or any Indian tribe, band, or community that is held in trust by the United States or is subject to a restriction against alienation imposed by the United States; or shall authorize regulation of the use of such property in a manner inconsistent with any Federal treaty, agreement, or statute or with any regulation made pursuant thereto; or shall confer jurisdiction upon the State to adjudicate, in probate proceedings or otherwise, the ownership or right to possession of such property or any interest therein.

(c) Any tribal ordinance or custom heretofore or hereafter adopted by an Indian tribe, band, or community in the exercise of any authority which it may possess shall, if not inconsistent with any applicable civil law of the State, be given full force and effect in the determination of civil causes of action pursuant to this section.

(Added Aug. 15, 1953, c. 505, § 4, 67 Stat. 589, and amended Aug. 24, 1954, c. 910, § 2, 68 Stat. 795; Aug. 8, 1958, Pub.L. 85–615, § 2, 72 Stat. 545; Nov. 6, 1978, Pub.L. 95–598, Title II, § 239, 92 Stat. 2668; July 10, 1984, Pub.L. 98–353, Title I, § 110, 98 Stat. 342.)

HISTORICAL AND STATUTORY NOTES

Codifications

Subsec. (a) of this section was amended by Pub.L. 95–598, Title II, § 239, Nov. 6, 1978, 92 Stat. 2668, effective June 28, 1984, pursuant to Pub.L. 95–598, Title IV, § 402(b), Nov. 6, 1978, 92 Stat. 2682, as amended by Pub.L. 98–249, § 1(a), Mar. 31, 1984, 98 Stat. 116; Pub.L. 98–271, § 1(a), Apr. 30, 1984, 98 Stat. 163; Pub.L. 98–299, § 1(a), May 25, 1984, 98 Stat. 214; Pub.L. 98–325, § 1(a), June 20, 1984, 98 Stat. 268, set out as an Effective and Applicability Provisions note preceding section 101 of Title 11, Bankruptcy, by substituting "Alaska ...... All Indian country within the State" for "Alaska ...... All Indian country within the Territory".

Section 402(b) of Pub.L. 95–598 was amended by section 113 of Pub.L. 98–353 by substituting "shall not be effective" for "shall take effect on June 28, 1984", thereby eliminating the amendment by section 239 of Pub.L. 95–598, effective June 27, 1984, pursuant to section 122(c) of Pub.L. 98–353, set out as an Effective and Applicability Provisions note under section 151 of this title.

Section 121(a) of Pub.L. 98–353 directed that section 402(b) of Pub.L. 95–598 be amended by substituting "the date of enactment of the Bankruptcy Amendments and Federal Judgeship Act of 1984 [i.e. July 10, 1984]" for "June 28, 1984". This amendment was not executed in view of the prior amendment to section 402(b) of Pub.L. 95–598 by section 113 of Pub.L. 98–353.

Effective and Applicability Provisions

1984 Acts. Amendment by Pub.L. 98–353 effective July 10, 1984, see section 122(a) of Pub.L. 98–353, set out as a note under section 151 of this title.

Admission of Alaska as State

Admission of Alaska into the Union was accomplished Jan. 3, 1959 upon issuance of Proc. No. 3269, Jan. 3, 1959, 24 F.R. 81, 73 Stat. c16, as required by sections 1 and 8(c) of Pub.L. 85–508, July 7, 1958, 72 Stat. 339, set out as notes preceding former section 21 of Title 48, Territories and Insular Possessions.

Amendment of State Constitutions to Remove Legal Impediment; Effective Date

Section 6 of Act Aug. 15, 1953, provided that: "Notwithstanding the provisions of any Enabling Act for the admission of a State, the consent of the United States is hereby given to the people of any State to amend, where necessary, their State constitution or existing statutes, as the case may be, to remove any legal impediment to the assumption of civil and criminal jurisdiction in accordance with the provisions of this Act [adding section 1360 of this title and section 1162 of Title 18]: *Provided*, That the provisions of this Act shall not become effective with respect to such assumption of jurisdiction by any such State until the people thereof have appropriately amended their State constitution or statutes as the case may be."

Consent of United States to Other States to Assume Jurisdiction

Act Aug. 15, 1953, c. 505, § 7, 67 Stat. 590, which gave consent of the United States to any other State not having jurisdiction with respect to criminal offenses or civil causes of action, or with respect to both, as provided for in this section and section 1162 of Title 18, Crimes and Criminal Procedure, to assume jurisdiction at such time and in such manner as the people of the State shall, by legislative action, obligate and bind the State to assumption thereof, was repealed by section 403(b) of Pub.L. 90–284, Title IV, Apr. 11, 1968, 82 Stat. 79, such repeal not to affect any cession of jurisdiction made pursuant to such section prior to its repeal.

Retrocession by State of jurisdiction acquired by State pursuant to section 7 of Act Aug. 15, 1953, prior to its repeal, see section 1323 of Title 25, Indians.

§ 1361. Action to compel an officer of the United States to perform his duty

The district courts shall have original jurisdiction of any action in the nature of mandamus to compel an officer or employee of the United States or any agency thereof to perform a duty owed to the plaintiff.
(Added Pub.L. 87–748, § 1(a), Oct. 5, 1962, 76 Stat. 744.)

§ 1362. Indian tribes

The district courts shall have original jurisdiction of all civil actions, brought by any Indian tribe or band with a governing body duly recognized by the Secretary of the Interior, wherein the matter in controversy arises under the Constitution, laws, or treaties of the United States.
(Added Pub.L. 89–635, § 1, Oct. 10, 1966, 80 Stat. 880.)

§ 1363. Jurors' employment rights

The district courts shall have original jurisdiction of any civil action brought for the protection of jurors' employment under section 1875 of this title.
(Added Pub.L. 95–572, § 6(b)(1), Nov. 2, 1978, 92 Stat. 2457.)

HISTORICAL AND STATUTORY NOTES
Effective and Applicability Provisions
1978 Acts. Section 7 of Pub.L. 95–572 provided that:

"**(a)** Except as provided in subsection (b) of this section, the amendments made by this Act [enacting sections 1363 and 1875, renumbering as section 1364 prior section 1363, and amending sections 1863, 1865, 1866, 1869, and 1871 of this title] shall apply with respect to any grand or petit juror summoned for service or actually serving on or after the date of enactment of this Act [Nov. 2, 1978].

"**(b)** The amendment made by section 5 of this Act [to section 1871 of this title] shall apply with respect to any grand or petit juror serving on or after the sixtieth day following the date of enactment of this Act [Nov. 2, 1978]."

Prior Provisions
A prior section 1363 was renumbered 1366.

§ 1364. Direct actions against insurers of members of diplomatic missions and their families

(a) The district courts shall have original and exclusive jurisdiction, without regard to the amount in controversy, of any civil action commenced by any person against an insurer who by contract has insured an individual, who is, or was at the time of the tortious

act or omission, a member of a mission (within the meaning of section 2(3) of the Diplomatic Relations Act (22 U.S.C. 254a(3))) or a member of the family of such a member of a mission, or an individual described in section 19 of the Convention on Privileges and Immunities of the United Nations of February 13, 1946, against liability for personal injury, death, or damage to property.

(b) Any direct action brought against an insurer under subsection (a) shall be tried without a jury, but shall not be subject to the defense that the insured is immune from suit, that the insured is an indispensable party, or in the absence of fraud or collusion, that the insured has violated a term of the contract, unless the contract was cancelled before the claim arose.
(Added Pub.L. 95–393, § 7(a), Sept. 30, 1978, 92 Stat. 809, and amended Pub.L. 97–241, Title II, § 203(b)(4), Aug. 24, 1982, 96 Stat. 291; Pub.L. 100–204, Title I, § 138(a), Dec. 22, 1987, 101 Stat. 1347.)

HISTORICAL AND STATUTORY NOTES
Codifications
Two other sections 1364 were renumbered sections 1365 and 1366 of this title.

Effective and Applicability Provisions
1987 Acts. Section 138(b) of Pub.L. 100–204 provided that: "The amendment made by subsection (a) [amending subsec. (a) of this section] shall apply to the first tortious act or omission occurring after the date of enactment of this Act [Dec. 22, 1987]."

1982 Acts. Amendment by Pub.L. 97–241 effective Oct. 1, 1982, see section 204 of Pub.L. 97–241, set out as a note under section 4301 of Title 22, Foreign Relations and Intercourse.

1978 Acts. Section effective at the end of the 90 day period beginning on Sept. 30, 1978, see section 9 of Pub.L. 95–393, set out as a note under section 254a of Title 22, Foreign Relations and Intercourse.

§ 1365. Senate actions

(a) The United States District Court for the District of Columbia shall have original jurisdiction, without regard to the amount in controversy, over any civil action brought by the Senate or any authorized committee or subcommittee of the Senate to enforce, to secure a declaratory judgment concerning the validity of, or to prevent a threatened refusal or failure to comply with, any subpena or order issued by the Senate or committee or subcommittee of the Senate to any entity acting or purporting to act under color or authority of State law or to any natural person to secure the production of documents or other materials of any kind or the answering of any deposition or interrogatory or to secure testimony or any combination thereof. This section shall not apply to an action to enforce, to secure a declaratory judgment concerning the validity of, or to prevent a threatened refusal to comply with, any subpena or order issued to an officer or employee of the executive branch of the Federal Government acting within his or her official capacity, except that this section shall apply if the refusal to comply is based on the assertion of a personal privilege or objection and is not based on a governmental privilege or objection the assertion of which has been authorized by the executive branch of the Federal Government.

(b) Upon application by the Senate or any authorized committee or subcommittee of the Senate, the district court shall issue an order to an entity or person refusing, or failing to comply with, or threatening to refuse or not to comply with, a subpena or order of the Senate or committee or subcommittee of the Senate requiring such entity or person to comply forthwith. Any refusal or failure to obey a lawful order of the district court issued pursuant to this section may be held by such court to be a contempt thereof. A contempt proceeding shall be commenced by an order to show cause before the court why the entity or person refusing or failing to obey the court order should not be held in contempt of court. Such contempt proceeding shall be tried by the court and shall be summary in manner. The purpose of sanctions imposed as a result of such contempt proceeding shall be to compel obedience to the order of the court. Process in any such action or contempt proceeding may be served in any judicial district wherein the entity or party refusing, or failing to comply, or threatening to refuse or not to comply, resides, transacts business, or may be found, and subpenas for witnesses who are required to attend such proceeding may run into any other district. Nothing in this section shall confer upon such court jurisdiction to affect by injunction or otherwise the issuance or effect of any subpena or order of the Senate or any committee or subcommittee of the Senate or to review, modify, suspend, terminate, or set aside any such subpena or order. An action, contempt proceeding, or sanction brought or imposed pursuant to this section shall not abate upon adjournment sine die by the Senate at the end of a Congress if the Senate or the committee or subcommittee of the Senate which issued the subpena or order certifies to the court that it maintains its interest in securing the documents, answers, or testimony during such adjournment.

[(c) Repealed. Pub.L. 98–620, Title IV, § 402(29)(D), Nov. 8, 1984, 98 Stat. 3359]

(d) The Senate or any committee or subcommittee of the Senate commencing and prosecuting a civil action or contempt proceeding under this section may be represented in such action by such attorneys as the Senate may designate.

(e) A civil action commenced or prosecuted under this section, may not be authorized pursuant to the Standing Order of the Senate "authorizing suits by Senate Committees" (S. Jour. 572, May 28, 1928).

(f) For the purposes of this section the term "committee" includes standing, select, or special committees of the Senate established by law or resolution. (Added Pub.L. 95–521, Title VII, § 705(f)(1), Oct. 26, 1978, 92 Stat. 1879, § 1364, and amended Pub.L. 98–620, Title IV, § 402(29)(D), Nov. 8, 1984, 98 Stat. 3359; renumbered § 1365, Pub.L. 99–336, § 6(a)(1)(B), June 19, 1986, 100 Stat. 638; Pub.L. 104–292, § 4, Oct. 11, 1996, 110 Stat. 3460.)

HISTORICAL AND STATUTORY NOTES

Effective and Applicability Provisions

1984 Acts. Amendment by Pub.L. 98–620 not to apply to cases pending on Nov. 8, 1984, see section 403 of Pub.L. 98–620, set out as a note under section 1657 of this title.

1978 Acts. Section effective Jan. 3, 1979, see section 717 of Pub.L. 95–521, set out as a note under section 288 of Title 2, The Congress.

§ 1366. Construction of references to laws of the United States or Acts of Congress

For the purposes of this chapter, references to laws of the United States or Acts of Congress do not include laws applicable exclusively to the District of Columbia.
(Added Pub.L. 91–358, Title I, § 172(c)(1), July 29, 1970, 84 Stat. 590, § 1363; renumbered § 1364, Pub.L. 95–572, § 6(b)(1), Nov. 2, 1978, 92 Stat. 2456; renumbered § 1366, Pub.L. 99–336, § 6(a)(1)(C), June 19, 1986, 100 Stat. 639.)

HISTORICAL AND STATUTORY NOTES

Effective and Applicability Provisions

1970 Acts. Section effective first day of seventh calendar month which begins after July 29, 1970, see section 199(a) of Pub.L. 91–358, set out as a note under section 1257 of this title.

§ 1367. Supplemental jurisdiction

(a) Except as provided in subsections (b) and (c) or as expressly provided otherwise by Federal statute, in any civil action of which the district courts have original jurisdiction, the district courts shall have supplemental jurisdiction over all other claims that are so related to claims in the action within such original jurisdiction that they form part of the same case or controversy under Article III of the United States Constitution. Such supplemental jurisdiction shall include claims that involve the joinder or intervention of additional parties.

(b) In any civil action of which the district courts have original jurisdiction founded solely on section 1332 of this title, the district courts shall not have supplemental jurisdiction under subsection (a) over claims by plaintiffs against persons made parties under Rule 14, 19, 20, or 24 of the Federal Rules of Civil Procedure, or over claims by persons proposed to be joined as plaintiffs under Rule 19 of such rules, or seeking to intervene as plaintiffs under Rule 24 of such rules, when exercising supplemental jurisdiction over such claims would be inconsistent with the jurisdictional requirements of section 1332.

(c) The district courts may decline to exercise supplemental jurisdiction over a claim under subsection (a) if—

(1) the claim raises a novel or complex issue of State law,

(2) the claim substantially predominates over the claim or claims over which the district court has original jurisdiction,

(3) the district court has dismissed all claims over which it has original jurisdiction, or

(4) in exceptional circumstances, there are other compelling reasons for declining jurisdiction.

(d) The period of limitations for any claim asserted under subsection (a), and for any other claim in the same action that is voluntarily dismissed at the same time as or after the dismissal of the claim under subsection (a), shall be tolled while the claim is pending and for a period of 30 days after it is dismissed unless State law provides for a longer tolling period.

(e) As used in this section, the term "State" includes the District of Columbia, the Commonwealth of Puerto Rico, and any territory or possession of the United States.

(Added Pub.L. 101–650, Title III, § 310(a), Dec. 1, 1990, 104 Stat. 5113.)

HISTORICAL AND STATUTORY NOTES

References in Text

The Federal Rules of Civil Procedure, referred to in subsec. (b), are set out in this title.

Effective and Applicability Provisions

1990 Acts. Section 310(c) of Pub.L. 101–650 provided that: "The amendments made by this section [enacting this section] shall apply to civil actions commenced on or after the date of the enactment of this Act [Dec. 1, 1990]."

§ 1368. Counterclaims in unfair practices in international trade.

The district courts shall have original jurisdiction of any civil action based on a counterclaim raised pursuant to section 337(c) of the Tariff Act of 1930, to the extent that it arises out of the transaction or occurrence that is the subject matter of the opposing party's claim in the proceeding under section 337(a) of that Act.

(Added Pub.L. 103–465, Title III, § 321(b)(3)(A), Dec. 8, 1994, 108 Stat. 4946.)

HISTORICAL AND STATUTORY NOTES

References in Text

Section 337 of the Tariff Act of 1930, referred to in text, is section 337 of Act June 17, 1930, c. 497, Title III, 46 Stat. 703, which is classified to section 1337 of Title 19, Customs Duties.

Effective and Applicability Provisions

1994 Acts. Section applicable with respect to complaints filed under section 1337 of Title 19, Customs Duties, on or after the date on which the WTO Agreement enters into force with respect to the United States, Jan. 1, 1995, or in cases under section 1337 of Title 19 in which no complaint is filed, with respect to investigations initiated under such section on or after such date, see section 322 of Pub.L. 103–465, set out as a note under section 1337 of Title 19.

§ 1369. Multiparty, multiforum jurisdiction

(a) In general.—The district courts shall have original jurisdiction of any civil action involving minimal diversity between adverse parties that arises from a single accident, where at least 75 natural persons have died in the accident at a discrete location, if—

(1) a defendant resides in a State and a substantial part of the accident took place in another State or other location, regardless of whether that defendant is also a resident of the State where a substantial part of the accident took place;

(2) any two defendants reside in different States, regardless of whether such defendants are also residents of the same State or States; or

(3) substantial parts of the accident took place in different States.

(b) Limitation of jurisdiction of district courts.—The district court shall abstain from hearing any civil action described in subsection (a) in which—

(1) the substantial majority of all plaintiffs are citizens of a single State of which the primary defendants are also citizens; and

(2) the claims asserted will be governed primarily by the laws of that State.

(c) Special rules and definitions.—For purposes of this section—

(1) minimal diversity exists between adverse parties if any party is a citizen of a State and any adverse party is a citizen of another State, a citizen or subject of a foreign state, or a foreign state as defined in section 1603(a) of this title;

(2) a corporation is deemed to be a citizen of any State, and a citizen or subject of any foreign state, in which it is incorporated or has its principal place of business, and is deemed to be a resident of any State in which it is incorporated or licensed to do business or is doing business;

(3) the term "injury" means—

(A) physical harm to a natural person; and

(B) physical damage to or destruction of tangible property, but only if physical harm described in subparagraph (A) exists;

(4) the term "accident" means a sudden accident, or a natural event culminating in an accident, that results in death incurred at a discrete location by at least 75 natural persons; and

(5) the term "State" includes the District of Columbia, the Commonwealth of Puerto Rico, and any territory or possession of the United States.

(d) **Intervening parties.**—In any action in a district court which is or could have been brought, in whole or in part, under this section, any person with a claim arising from the accident described in subsection (a) shall be permitted to intervene as a party plaintiff in the action, even if that person could not have brought an action in a district court as an original matter.

(e) **Notification of judicial panel on multidistrict litigation.**—A district court in which an action under this section is pending shall promptly notify the judicial panel on multidistrict litigation of the pendency of the action.

(Added Pub.L. 107–273, Div. C, Title I, § 11020(b)(1)(A), Nov. 2, 2002, 116 Stat. 1826.)

HISTORICAL AND STATUTORY NOTES

Effective and Applicability Provisions

2002 Acts. Pub.L. 107–273, Div. C, Title I, § 11020(c), Nov. 2, 2002, 116 Stat. 1829, provided that: "The amendments made by subsection (b) [enacting this section and 28 U.S.C.A. §§ 1697 and 1785 and amending 28 U.S.C.A. §§ 1391 and 1441] shall apply to a civil action if the accident giving rise to the cause of action occurred on or after the 90th day after the date of the enactment of this Act [Nov. 2, 2002]."

CHAPTER 87—DISTRICT COURTS; VENUE

HISTORICAL AND STATUTORY NOTES

Codifications

Amendment by Pub.L. 104–331, § 3(b)(2)(B), Oct. 26, 1996, 110 Stat. 4069, which directed the addition of item 1413 to the end of chapter 37 of this title, was executed by adding item 1413 to the end of this chapter, as the probable intent of Congress.

The table of sections for chapter 87 was amended by Pub.L. 95–598, Title II, § 240(b), Nov. 6, 1978, 92 Stat. 2668, effective June 28, 1984, pursuant to Pub.L. 95–598, Title IV,

§ 402(b), Nov. 6, 1978, 92 Stat. 2682, as amended by Pub.L. 98–249, § 1(a), Mar. 31, 1984, 98 Stat. 116; Pub.L. 98–271, § 1(a), Apr. 30, 1984, 98 Stat. 163; Pub.L. 98–299, § 1(a), May 25, 1984, 98 Stat. 214; Pub.L. 98–325, § 1(a), June 20, 1984, 98 Stat. 268, set out as an effective dates note preceding section 101 of Title 11, Bankruptcy, by adding "1408, Bankruptcy appeals."

Section 402(b) of Pub.L. 95–598 was amended by section 113 of Pub.L. 98–353, Title 1, July 10, 1984, 98 Stat. 343, by substituting "shall not be effective" for "shall take effect on June 28, 1984," thereby eliminating the amendment by section 240(b) of Pub.L. 95–598, effective June 27, 1984, pursuant to section 122(e) of Pub.L. 98–353, set out as an Effective Date, note under section 151 of this title.

Section 121(a) of Pub.L. 98–353 directed that section 402(b) of Pub.L. 95–598 be amended by substituting "the date of enactment of the Bankruptcy Amendments and Federal Judgeship Act of 1984 [i.e. July 10, 1984]" for "June 28, 1984". This amendment was not executed in view of the prior amendment to section 402(b) of Pub.L. 95–598 by section 113 of Pub.L. 98–353.

Effective and Termination Dates

Pub.L. 105–304, Title V, §§ 502(c)(3), 505, Oct. 28, 1998, 112 Stat. 2917, 2918, provided that effective Oct. 28, 1998 and remaining in effect until the end of the 2-year period beginning on Oct. 28, 1998, the item relating to section 1400 is amended by inserting ", mask works, and designs" after "Patents and copyrights".

§ 1391. Venue generally

(a) A civil action wherein jurisdiction is founded only on diversity of citizenship may, except as otherwise provided by law, be brought only in (1) a judicial district where any defendant resides, if all defendants reside in the same State, (2) a judicial district in which a substantial part of the events or omissions giving rise to the claim occurred, or a substantial part of property that is the subject of the action is situated, or (3) a judicial district in which any defendant is subject to personal jurisdiction at the time the action is commenced, if there is no district in which the action may otherwise be brought.

(b) A civil action wherein jurisdiction is not founded solely on diversity of citizenship may, except as otherwise provided by law, be brought only in (1) a judicial district where any defendant resides, if all defendants reside in the same State, (2) a judicial district in which a substantial part of the events or omissions giving rise to the claim occurred, or a substantial part of property that is the subject of the action is situated, or (3) a judicial district in which any defendant may be found, if there is no district in which the action may otherwise be brought.

(c) For purposes of venue under this chapter, a defendant that is a corporation shall be deemed to reside in any judicial district in which it is subject to personal jurisdiction at the time the action is commenced. In a State which has more than one judicial district and in which a defendant that is a corporation is subject to personal jurisdiction at the time an action is commenced, such corporation shall be deemed to reside in any district in that State within which its contacts would be sufficient to subject it to personal jurisdiction if that district were a separate State, and, if there is no such district, the corporation shall be deemed to reside in the district within which it has the most significant contacts.

(d) An alien may be sued in any district.

(e) A civil action in which a defendant is an officer or employee of the United States or any agency thereof acting in his official capacity or under color of legal authority, or an agency of the United States, or the United States, may, except as otherwise provided by law, be brought in any judicial district in which (1) a defendant in the action resides, (2) a substantial part of the events or omissions giving rise to the claim occurred, or a substantial part of property that is the subject of the action is situated, or (3) the plaintiff resides if no real property is involved in the action. Additional persons may be joined as parties to any such action in accordance with the Federal Rules of Civil Procedure and with such other venue requirements as would be applicable if the United States or one of its officers, employees, or agencies were not a party.

The summons and complaint in such an action shall be served as provided by the Federal Rules of Civil Procedure except that the delivery of the summons and complaint to the officer or agency as required by the rules may be made by certified mail beyond the territorial limits of the district in which the action is brought.

(f) A civil action against a foreign state as defined in section 1603(a) of this title may be brought—

(1) in any judicial district in which a substantial part of the events or omissions giving rise to the claim occurred, or a substantial part of property that is the subject of the action is situated;

(2) in any judicial district in which the vessel or cargo of a foreign state is situated, if the claim is asserted under section 1605(b) of this title;

(3) in any judicial district in which the agency or instrumentality is licensed to do business or is doing business, if the action is brought against an agency or instrumentality of a foreign state as defined in section 1603(b) of this title; or

(4) in the United States District Court for the District of Columbia if the action is brought against a foreign state or political subdivision thereof.

(g) A civil action in which jurisdiction of the district court is based upon section 1369 of this title may be brought in any district in which any defendant resides or in which a substantial part of the accident giving rise to the action took place.

(June 25, 1948, c. 646, 62 Stat. 935; Oct. 5, 1962, Pub.L. 87–748, § 2, 76 Stat. 744; Dec. 23, 1963, Pub.L. 88–234, 77 Stat. 473; Nov. 2, 1966, Pub.L. 89–714, §§ 1, 2, 80 Stat. 1111; Oct. 21, 1976, Pub.L. 94–574, § 3, 90 Stat. 2721; Oct. 21, 1976, Pub.L. 94–583, § 5, 90 Stat. 2897; Nov. 19, 1988, Pub.L. 100–702, Title X, § 1013(a), 102 Stat. 4669; Dec. 1, 1990, Pub.L. 101–650, Title III, § 311, 104 Stat. 5114; Dec. 9, 1991, Pub.L. 102–198, § 3, 105 Stat. 1623; Oct. 29, 1992, Pub.L. 102–572, Title V, § 504, 106 Stat. 4513; Oct. 3, 1995, Pub.L. 104–34, § 1, 109 Stat. 293; Nov. 2, 2002, Pub.L. 107–273, Div. C, Title I, § 11020(b)(2), 116 Stat. 1827.)

HISTORICAL AND STATUTORY NOTES

References in Text

The Federal Rules of Civil Procedure, referred to in subsec. (e), are set out in this title.

Effective and Applicability Provisions

2002 Acts. Amendments by section 11020(b) of Pub.L. 107–273 shall apply to a civil action if the accident giving rise to the cause of action occurred on or after the 90th day after Nov. 2, 2002, see section 11020(c) of Pub.L. 107–273, set out as a note under 28 U.S.C.A. § 1369.

1992 Acts. Amendment by Pub.L. 102–572 effective Jan. 1, 1993, see section 1101(a) of Pub.L. 102–572, set out as a note under section 905 of Title 2, The Congress.

1988 Acts. Section 1013(b) of Title X of Pub.L. 100–702 provided that: "The amendment made by this section [amending this section] takes effect 90 days after the date of enactment of this title [Nov. 19, 1988]."

1976 Acts. Amendment by Pub.L. 94–583 effective 90 days after Oct. 21, 1976, see section 8 of Pub.L. 94–583, set out as a note under section 1602 of this title.

§ 1392.   Defendants or property in different districts in same State

Any civil action, of a local nature, involving property located in different districts in the same State, may be brought in any of such districts.

(June 25, 1948, c. 646, 62 Stat. 935; Oct. 1, 1996, Pub.L. 104–220, § 1, 110 Stat. 3023.)

[§ 1393.   Repealed.   Pub.L. 100–702, Title X, § 1001(a), Nov. 19, 1988, 102 Stat. 4664]

HISTORICAL AND STATUTORY NOTES

Section, Act June 25, 1948, c. 646, 62 Stat. 935, related to divisional venue in civil cases of a single defendant or defendants in different divisions.

Effective Date of Repeal

Section 1001(b) of Pub.L. 100–702 provided that "The amendments made by this section [repealing this section] take effect 90 days after the date of enactment of this Act [Nov. 19, 1988]."

§ 1394.   Banking association's action against Comptroller of Currency

Any civil action by a national banking association to enjoin the Comptroller of the Currency, under the provisions of any Act of Congress relating to such associations, may be prosecuted in the judicial district where such association is located.

(June 25, 1948, c. 646, 62 Stat. 935.)

HISTORICAL AND STATUTORY NOTES

Exception as to Transfer of Functions

Functions vested by any provision of law in the Comptroller of the Currency, referred to in this section, were not included in the transfer of functions of officers, agencies and employees of the Department of the Treasury to the Secretary of the Treasury, made by Reorg. Plan No. 26 of 1950, § 1, eff. July 31, 1950, 15 F.R. 4935, 64 Stat. 1280. See section 321(c)(2) of Title 31, Money and Finance.

§ 1395.   Fine, penalty or forfeiture

(a) A civil proceeding for the recovery of a pecuniary fine, penalty or forfeiture may be prosecuted in the district where it accrues or the defendant is found.

(b) A civil proceeding for the forfeiture of property may be prosecuted in any district where such property is found.

(c) A civil proceeding for the forfeiture of property seized outside any judicial district may be prosecuted in any district into which the property is brought.

(d) A proceeding in admiralty for the enforcement of fines, penalties and forfeitures against a vessel may be brought in any district in which the vessel is arrested.

(e) Any proceeding for the forfeiture of a vessel or cargo entering a port of entry closed by the President in pursuance of law, or of goods and chattels coming from a State or section declared by proclamation of the President to be in insurrection, or of any vessel or vehicle conveying persons or property to or from such State or section or belonging in whole or in part to a resident thereof, may be prosecuted in any district into which the property is taken and in which the proceeding is instituted.

(June 25, 1948, c. 646, 62 Stat. 936.)

HISTORICAL AND STATUTORY NOTES

Senate Revision Amendment

While section 3745(c) of Title 26, U.S.C., Internal Revenue Code, is one of the sources of this section, it was eliminated from the schedule of repeals by Senate amendment. Therefore, such section 3745(c) remains in Title 26. See 80th Congress Senate Report No. 1559.

Said section 3745(c) was subsequently repealed by Act May 24, 1949, c. 139, § 142, 63 Stat. 110.

§ 1396.   Internal revenue taxes

Any civil action for the collection of internal revenue taxes may be brought in the district where the liability for such tax accrues, in the district of the taxpayer's residence, or in the district where the return was filed.

(June 25, 1948, c. 646, 62 Stat. 936.)

HISTORICAL AND STATUTORY NOTES

Senate Revision Amendment

While section 3744 of Title 26, U.S.C., Internal Revenue Code [1939], is one of the sources of this section, it was eliminated from the schedule of repeals by Senate amendment. Therefore, it remains in Title 26 [I.R.C.1939]. See 80th Congress Senate Report No. 1559.

Said section 3744 was subsequently repealed by Act May 24, 1949, c. 139, § 142, 63 Stat. 110.

§ 1397.   Interpleader

Any civil action of interpleader or in the nature of interpleader under section 1335 of this title may be brought in the judicial district in which one or more of the claimants reside.

(June 25, 1948, c. 646, 62 Stat. 936.)

§ 1398.   Interstate Commerce Commission's orders

(a) Except as otherwise provided by law, a civil action brought under section 1336(a) of this title shall be brought only in a judicial district in which any of the parties bringing the action resides or has its principal office.

(b) A civil action to enforce, enjoin, set aside, annul, or suspend, in whole or in part, an order of the Interstate Commerce Commission made pursuant to the referral of a question or issue by a district court or by the United States Court of Federal Claims, shall be brought only in the court which referred the question or issue.

(June 25, 1948, c. 646, 62 Stat. 936; Aug. 30, 1964, Pub.L. 88–513, § 2, 78 Stat. 695; Jan. 2, 1975, Pub.L. 93–584, § 2, 88 Stat. 1917; Apr. 2, 1982, Pub.L. 97–164, Title I, § 130, 96 Stat. 39; Oct. 29, 1992, Pub.L. 102–572, Title IX, § 902(b)(1), 106 Stat. 4516.)

HISTORICAL AND STATUTORY NOTES

Effective and Applicability Provisions

1992 Acts. Amendment by Pub.L. 102–572 effective Oct. 29, 1992, see section 911 of Pub.L. 102–572, set out as a note under section 171 of this title.

1982 Acts. Amendment by Pub.L. 97–164 effective Oct. 1, 1982, see section 402 of Pub.L. 97–164, set out as a note under section 171 of this title.

1975 Acts. Amendment by Pub.L. 93–584 not applicable to actions commenced on or before the last day of the first month beginning after Jan. 2, 1975, and actions to enjoin or suspend orders of the Interstate Commerce Commission which are pending when this amendment becomes effective shall not be affected thereby, but shall proceed to final disposition under the law existing on the date they were commenced, see section 10 of Pub.L. 93–584, set out as a note under section 2321 of this title.

Abolition of Interstate Commerce Commission and Transfer of Functions

Interstate Commerce Commission abolished and functions of Commission transferred, except as otherwise provided in Pub.L. 104–88, to Surface Transportation Board effective Jan. 1, 1996, by sections 702 of Title 49, Transportation, and section 101 of Pub.L. 104–88, set out as a note under section 701 of title 49. References to Interstate Commerce Commission deemed to refer to Surface Transportation Board, a member or employee of the Board, or Secretary of Transportation, as appropriate, see section 205 of Pub.L. 104–88, set out as a note under section 701 of Title 49.

§ 1399. Partition action involving United States

Any civil action by any tenant in common or joint tenant for the partition of lands, where the United States is one of the tenants in common or joint tenants, may be brought only in the judicial district where such lands are located or, if located in different districts in the same State, in any of such districts.

(June 25, 1948, c. 646, 62 Stat. 936.)

§ 1400. Patents and copyrights, mask works, and designs

(a) Civil actions, suits, or proceedings arising under any Act of Congress relating to copyrights or exclusive rights in mask works or designs may be instituted in the district in which the defendant or his agent resides or may be found.

(b) Any civil action for patent infringement may be brought in the judicial district where the defendant resides, or where the defendant has committed acts of infringement and has a regular and established place of business.

(June 25, 1948, c. 646, 62 Stat. 936; Nov. 19, 1988, Pub.L. 100–702, Title X, § 1020(a)(5), 102 Stat. 4671; Oct. 28, 1998, Pub.L. 105–304, Title V, § 503(c)(1), (2), 112 Stat. 2917; Aug. 5, 1999, Pub.L. 106–44, § 2(a), 113 Stat. 223.)

HISTORICAL AND STATUTORY NOTES

Senate Revision Amendment

Title 17 of the United States Code was enacted into positive law by Act July 30, 1947, c. 391, 61 Stat. 652, and, in such enactment, section 35 of the prior title became section 111 of the new title, and all Acts from which sections of the prior title had been derived, were repealed. Therefore, this paragraph should read: "Based on Title 28, U.S.C., 1940 ed., § 109 (Mar. 3, 1911, c. 231, § 48, 36 Stat. 1100), and section 111 of Title 17, U.S.C., 1946 ed., Copyrights." By Senate amendment, section 111 of Title 17 U.S.C., is included in the schedule of repeals. See 80th Congress Senate Report No. 1559.

1988 Acts. House Report No. 100–889, see 1988 U.S. Code Cong. and Adm. News, p. 5982.

1998 Acts. House Conference Report No. 105–796 and Statement by President, see 1998 U.S. Code Cong. and Adm. News, p. 645.

Effective and Applicability Provisions

1998 Acts. Amendment by Pub.L. 105–304, effective Oct. 28, 1998, see section 505 of Pub.L. 105–304, set out as a note under section 1301 of Title 17, Copyrights.

§ 1401. Stockholder's derivative action

Any civil action by a stockholder on behalf of his corporation may be prosecuted in any judicial district where the corporation might have sued the same defendants.

(June 25, 1948, c. 646, 62 Stat. 936.)

§ 1402. United States as defendant

(a) Any civil action in a district court against the United States under subsection (a) of section 1346 of this title may be prosecuted only:

(1) Except as provided in paragraph (2), in the judicial district where the plaintiff resides;

(2) In the case of a civil action by a corporation under paragraph (1) of subsection (a) of section 1346, in the judicial district in which is located the principal place of business or principal office or agency of the corporation; or if it has no principal place of business or principal office or agency in any judicial district (A) in the judicial district in which is located the office to which was made the return of the tax in respect of which the claim is made, or (B) if no return was made, in the judicial district in which lies the District of Columbia. Notwithstanding the foregoing provisions of this paragraph a district court, for the convenience of the parties and witnesses, in the interest of justice, may transfer any such action to any other district or division.

(b) Any civil action on a tort claim against the United States under subsection (b) of section 1346 of this title may be prosecuted only in the judicial district where the plaintiff resides or wherein the act or omission complained of occurred.

(c) Any civil action against the United States under subsection (e) of section 1346 of this title may be prosecuted only in the judicial district where the property is situated at the time of levy, or if no levy is made, in the judicial district in which the event occurred which gave rise to the cause of action.

(d) Any civil action under section 2409a to quiet title to an estate or interest in real property in which an interest is claimed by the United States shall be brought in the district court of the district where the property is located or, if located in different districts, in any of such districts.

(June 25, 1948, c. 646, 62 Stat. 937; Sept. 2, 1958, Pub.L. 85–920, 72 Stat. 1770; Nov. 2, 1966, Pub.L. 89–719, Title II, § 202(b), 80 Stat. 1149; Oct. 25, 1972, Pub.L. 92–562, § 2, 86 Stat. 1176; Apr. 2, 1982, Pub.L. 97–164, Title I, § 131, 96 Stat. 39.)

HISTORICAL AND STATUTORY NOTES

Effective and Applicability Provisions

1982 Acts. Amendment by Pub.L. 97–164 effective Oct. 1, 1982, see section 402 of Pub.L. 97–164, set out as a note under section 171 of this title.

1966 Acts. Subsec. (c) of this section applicable after Nov. 2, 1966, see section 203 of Pub.L. 89–719, set out as a note under section 1346 of this title.

§ 1403.　Eminent domain

Proceedings to condemn real estate for the use of the United States or its departments or agencies shall be brought in the district court of the district where the land is located or, if located in different districts in the same State, in any of such districts.

(June 25, 1948, c. 646, 62 Stat. 937.)

§ 1404.　Change of venue

(a) For the convenience of parties and witnesses, in the interest of justice, a district court may transfer any civil action to any other district or division where it might have been brought.

(b) Upon motion, consent or stipulation of all parties, any action, suit or proceeding of a civil nature or any motion or hearing thereof, may be transferred, in the discretion of the court, from the division in which pending to any other division in the same district. Transfer of proceedings in rem brought by or on behalf of the United States may be transferred under this section without the consent of the United States where all other parties request transfer.

(c) A district court may order any civil action to be tried at any place within the division in which it is pending.

(d) As used in this section, the term "district court" includes the District Court of Guam, the District Court for the Northern Mariana Islands, and the District Court of the Virgin Islands, and the term "district" includes the territorial jurisdiction of each such court.

(June 25, 1948, c. 646, 62 Stat. 937; Oct. 18, 1962, Pub.L. 87–845, § 9, 76A Stat. 699; Oct. 19, 1996, Pub.L. 104–317, Title VI, § 610(a), 110 Stat. 3860.)

HISTORICAL AND STATUTORY NOTES

Effective and Applicability Provisions

1996 Acts. Section 610(c) of Pub.L. 104–317 provided that: "The amendments made by this section [amending this section and section 1406 of this title] apply to cases pending on the date of the enactment of this Act [Oct. 19, 1996] and to cases commenced on or after such date."

1962 Acts. Amendment of section by Pub.L. 87–845 effective Jan. 2, 1963, see section 25 of Pub.L. 87–845, set out as a note under section 14 of Title 18, Crimes and Criminal Procedure.

Termination of United States District Court for the District of the Canal Zone

For termination of the United States District Court for the District of the Canal Zone at end of the "transition period", being the 30–month period beginning Oct. 1, 1979, and ending midnight Mar. 31, 1982, see Paragraph 5 of Article XI of the Panama Canal Treaty of 1977 and sections 3831 and 3841 to 3843 of Title 22, Foreign Relations and Intercourse.

§ 1405.　Creation or alteration of district or division

Actions or proceedings pending at the time of the creation of a new district or division or transfer of a county or territory from one division or district to another may be tried in the district or division as it existed at the institution of the action or proceeding, or in the district or division so created or to which the county or territory is so transferred as the parties shall agree or the court direct.

(June 25, 1948, c. 646, 62 Stat. 937.)

§ 1406.　Cure or waiver of defects

(a) The district court of a district in which is filed a case laying venue in the wrong division or district shall dismiss, or if it be in the interest of justice, transfer such case to any district or division in which it could have been brought.

(b) Nothing in this chapter shall impair the jurisdiction of a district court of any matter involving a party who does not interpose timely and sufficient objection to the venue.

(c) As used in this section, the term "district court" includes the District Court of Guam, the District Court for the Northern Mariana Islands, and the District Court of the Virgin Islands, and the term "district" includes the territorial jurisdiction of each such court.

(June 25, 1948, c. 646, 62 Stat. 937; May 24, 1949, c. 139, § 81, 63 Stat. 101; Sept. 13, 1960, Pub.L. 86–770, § 1, 74 Stat. 912; Oct. 18, 1962, Pub.L. 87–845, § 10, 76A Stat. 699; Apr. 2, 1982, Pub.L. 97–164, Title I, § 132, 96 Stat. 39; Oct. 19, 1996, Pub.L. 104–317, Title VI, § 610(b), 110 Stat. 3860.)

HISTORICAL AND STATUTORY NOTES

Effective and Applicability Provisions

1996 Acts. Amendment by section 610(b) of Pub.L. 104–317 to apply to cases pending on Oct. 19, 1996, and to cases commenced on or after such date, see section 610(c) of Pub.L. 104–317, set out as a note under section 1404 of this title.

1982 Acts. Amendment by Pub.L. 97–164 effective Oct. 1, 1982, see section 402 of Pub.L. 97–164, set out as a note under section 171 of this title.

1962 Acts. Amendment of section by Pub.L. 87–845 effective Jan. 2, 1963, see section 25 of Pub.L. 87–845, set out as a note under section 14 of Title 18, Crimes and Criminal Procedure.

1960 Acts. Section 4 of Pub.L. 86–770 provided in part that: "The amendments made by sections 1 and 2 of this Act [adding subsec. (c) of this section and section 1506 of this title] shall apply to any case or proceeding pending on, or brought after, the date of enactment of this Act [Sept. 13, 1960] in the district courts or the Court of Claims."

Termination of United States District Court for the District of the Canal Zone

For termination of the United States District Court for the District of the Canal Zone at end of the "transition period", being the 30–month period beginning Oct. 1, 1979, and ending midnight Mar. 31, 1982, see Paragraph 5 of Article XI of the Panama Canal Treaty of 1977 and sections 3831 and 3841 to 3843 of Title 22, Foreign Relations and Intercourse.

§ 1407. Multidistrict litigation

(a) When civil actions involving one or more common questions of fact are pending in different districts, such actions may be transferred to any district for coordinated or consolidated pretrial proceedings. Such transfers shall be made by the judicial panel on multidistrict litigation authorized by this section upon its determination that transfers for such proceedings will be for the convenience of parties and witnesses and will promote the just and efficient conduct of such actions. Each action so transferred shall be remanded by the panel at or before the conclusion of such pretrial proceedings to the district from which it was transferred unless it shall have been previously terminated: *Provided, however*, That the panel may separate any claim, cross-claim, counter-claim, or third-party claim and remand any of such claims before the remainder of the action is remanded.

(b) Such coordinated or consolidated pretrial proceedings shall be conducted by a judge or judges to whom such actions are assigned by the judicial panel on multidistrict litigation. For this purpose, upon request of the panel, a circuit judge or a district judge may be designated and assigned temporarily for ser-

vice in the transferee district by the Chief Justice of the United States or the chief judge of the circuit, as may be required, in accordance with the provisions of chapter 13 of this title. With the consent of the transferee district court, such actions may be assigned by the panel to a judge or judges of such district. The judge or judges to whom such actions are assigned, the members of the judicial panel on multidistrict litigation, and other circuit and district judges designated when needed by the panel may exercise the powers of a district judge in any district for the purpose of conducting pretrial depositions in such coordinated or consolidated pretrial proceedings.

(c) Proceedings for the transfer of an action under this section may be initiated by—

    (i) the judicial panel on multidistrict litigation upon its own initiative, or

    (ii) motion filed with the panel by a party in any action in which transfer for coordinated or consolidated pretrial proceedings under this section may be appropriate. A copy of such motion shall be filed in the district court in which the moving party's action is pending.

The panel shall give notice to the parties in all actions in which transfers for coordinated or consolidated pretrial proceedings are contemplated, and such notice shall specify the time and place of any hearing to determine whether such transfer shall be made. Orders of the panel to set a hearing and other orders of the panel issued prior to the order either directing or denying transfer shall be filed in the office of the clerk of the district court in which a transfer hearing is to be or has been held. The panel's order of transfer shall be based upon a record of such hearing at which material evidence may be offered by any party to an action pending in any district that would be affected by the proceedings under this section, and shall be supported by findings of fact and conclusions of law based upon such record. Orders of transfer and such other orders as the panel may make thereafter shall be filed in the office of the clerk of the district court of the transferee district and shall be effective when thus filed. The clerk of the transferee district court shall forthwith transmit a certified copy of the panel's order to transfer to the clerk of the district court from which the action is being transferred. An order denying transfer shall be filed in each district wherein there is a case pending in which the motion for transfer has been made.

(d) The judicial panel on multidistrict litigation shall consist of seven circuit and district judges designated from time to time by the Chief Justice of the United States, no two of whom shall be from the same circuit. The concurrence of four members shall be necessary to any action by the panel.

(e) No proceedings for review of any order of the panel may be permitted except by extraordinary writ pursuant to the provisions of title 28, section 1651, United States Code. Petitions for an extraordinary writ to review an order of the panel to set a transfer hearing and other orders of the panel issued prior to the order either directing or denying transfer shall be filed only in the court of appeals having jurisdiction over the district in which a hearing is to be or has been held. Petitions for an extraordinary writ to review an order to transfer or orders subsequent to transfer shall be filed only in the court of appeals having jurisdiction over the transferee district. There shall be no appeal or review of an order of the panel denying a motion to transfer for consolidated or coordinated proceedings.

(f) The panel may prescribe rules for the conduct of its business not inconsistent with Acts of Congress and the Federal Rules of Civil Procedure.

(g) Nothing in this section shall apply to any action in which the United States is a complainant arising under the antitrust laws. "Antitrust laws" as used herein include those acts referred to in the Act of October 15, 1914, as amended (38 Stat. 730; 15 U.S.C. 12), and also include the Act of June 19, 1936 (49 Stat. 1526; 15 U.S.C. 13, 13a, and 13b) and the Act of September 26, 1914, as added March 21, 1938 (52 Stat. 116, 117; 15 U.S.C. 56); but shall not include section 4A of the Act of October 15, 1914, as added July 7, 1955 (69 Stat. 282; 15 U.S.C. 15a).

(h) Notwithstanding the provisions of section 1404 or subsection (f) of this section, the judicial panel on multidistrict litigation may consolidate and transfer with or without the consent of the parties, for both pretrial purposes and for trial, any action brought under section 4C of the Clayton Act.

(Added Pub.L. 90–296, § 1, Apr. 29, 1968, 82 Stat. 109, and amended Pub.L. 94–435, Title III, § 303, Sept. 30, 1976, 90 Stat. 1396.)

HISTORICAL AND STATUTORY NOTES
References in Text

The Federal Rules of Civil Procedure, referred to in subsec. (f), are set out in this title.

Section 4C of the Clayton Act, referred to in subsec. (h), is section 4C of Act Oct. 15, 1914, c. 323, as added by Pub.L. 94–435, Title III, § 301, Sept. 30, 1976, 90 Stat. 1394, which is classified to section 15c of Title 15, Commerce and Trade.

§ 1408.   Venue of cases under title 11

Except as provided in section 1410 of this title, a case under title 11 may be commenced in the district court for the district—

(1) in which the domicile, residence, principal place of business in the United States, or principal assets in the United States, of the person or entity that is the subject of such case have been located

for the one hundred and eighty days immediately preceding such commencement, or for a longer portion of such one-hundred-and-eighty-day period than the domicile, residence, or principal place of business, in the United States, or principal assets in the United States, of such person were located in any other district; or

(2) in which there is pending a case under title 11 concerning such person's affiliate, general partner, or partnership.

(Added Pub.L. 98–353, Title I, § 102(a), July 10, 1984, 98 Stat. 334.)

HISTORICAL AND STATUTORY NOTES
Effective and Applicability Provisions

1984 Acts. Section effective July 10, 1984, see section 122(a) of Pub.L. 98–353, set out as a note under section 151 of this title.

Prior Provisions

A prior section 1408, added by Pub.L. 95–598, Title II, § 240(a), Nov. 6, 1978, 92 Stat. 2668, which related to bankruptcy appeals, did not become effective pursuant to section 402(b) of Pub.L. 95–598, as amended, set out as an Effective and Applicability Provisions note preceding section 101 of Title 11, Bankruptcy.

§ 1409.   Venue of proceedings arising under title 11 or arising in or related to cases under title 11

(a) Except as otherwise provided in subsections (b) and (d), a proceeding arising under title 11 or arising in or related to a case under title 11 may be commenced in the district court in which such case is pending.

(b) Except as provided in subsection (d) of this section, a trustee in a case under title 11 may commence a proceeding arising in or related to such case to recover a money judgment of or property worth less than $1,000 or a consumer debt of less than $5,000 only in the district court for the district in which the defendant resides.

(c) Except as provided in subsection (b) of this section, a trustee in a case under title 11 may commence a proceeding arising in or related to such case as statutory successor to the debtor or creditors under section 541 or 544(b) of title 11 in the district court for the district where the State or Federal court sits in which, under applicable nonbankruptcy venue provisions, the debtor or creditors, as the case may be, may have commenced an action on which such proceeding is based if the case under title 11 had not been commenced.

(d) A trustee may commence a proceeding arising under title 11 or arising in or related to a case under title 11 based on a claim arising after the commencement of such case from the operation of the business of the debtor only in the district court for the district where a State or Federal court sits in which, under applicable nonbankruptcy venue provisions, an action on such claim may have been brought.

(e) A proceeding arising under title 11 or arising in or related to a case under title 11, based on a claim arising after the commencement of such case from the operation of the business of the debtor, may be commenced against the representative of the estate in such case in the district court for the district where the State or Federal court sits in which the party commencing such proceeding may, under applicable nonbankruptcy venue provisions, have brought an action on such claim, or in the district court in which such case is pending.

(Added Pub.L. 98–353, Title I, § 102(a), July 10, 1984, 98 Stat. 334.)

Amendment of Subsection (b)

Pub.L. 109–8, Title IV, § 410, Title XV, § 1501, Apr. 20, 2005, 119 Stat. 106, 216, provided that, except as otherwise provided, effective 180 days after April 20, 2005, and inapplicable with respect to cases commenced under Title 11 before the effective date, subsection (b) of this section is amended by inserting ", or a debt (excluding a consumer debt) against a noninsider of less than $10,000," after "$5,000", and by striking "$5,000" and inserting "$15,000".

HISTORICAL AND STATUTORY NOTES

Effective and Applicability Provisions

2005 Acts. Except as otherwise provided, amendments by Pub.L. 109–8 effective 180 days after April 20, 2005, and inapplicable with respect to cases commenced under Title 11 before the effective date, see Pub.L. 109–8, § 1501, set out as a note under 11 U.S.C.A. § 101.

1984 Acts. Section effective July 10, 1984, see section 122(a) of Pub.L. 98–353, set out as a note under section 151 of this title.

§ 1410. Venue of cases ancillary to foreign proceedings

(a) A case under section 304 of title 11 to enjoin the commencement or continuation of an action or proceeding in a State or Federal court, or the enforcement of a judgment, may be commenced only in the district court for the district where the State or Federal court sits in which is pending the action or proceeding against which the injunction is sought.

(b) A case under section 304 of title 11 to enjoin the enforcement of a lien against a property, or to require the turnover of property of an estate, may be commenced only in the district court for the district in which such property is found.

(c) A case under section 304 of title 11, other than a case specified in subsection (a) or (b) of this section, may be commenced only in the district court for the district in which is located the principal place of business in the United States, or the principal assets in the United States, of the estate that is the subject of such case.

(Added Pub.L. 98–353, Title I, § 102(a), July 10, 1984, 98 Stat. 335.)

Amendment of Section

Pub.L. 109–8, Title VIII, § 802(c)(4), Title XV, § 1501, Apr. 20, 2005, 119 Stat. 146, 216, provided that, except as otherwise provided, effective 180 days after April 20, 2005, and inapplicable with respect to cases commenced under Title 11 before the effective date, this section is amended to read as follows:

§ 1410. Venue of cases ancillary to foreign proceedings

A case under chapter 15 of title 11 may be commenced in the district court of the United States for the district—

(1) in which the debtor has its principal place of business or principal assets in the United States;

(2) if the debtor does not have a place of business or assets in the United States, in which there is pending against the debtor an action or proceeding in a Federal or State court; or

(3) in a case other than those specified in paragraph (1) or (2), in which venue will be consistent with the interests of justice and the convenience of the parties, having regard to the relief sought by the foreign representative.

HISTORICAL AND STATUTORY NOTES

References in Text

Chapter 15 of title 11, referred to in text, is 11 U.S.C.A. § 1501 et seq.

Effective and Applicability Provisions

2005 Acts. Except as otherwise provided, amendments by Pub.L. 109–8 effective 180 days after April 20, 2005, and inapplicable with respect to cases commenced under Title 11 before the effective date, see Pub.L. 109–8, § 1501, set out as a note under 11 U.S.C.A. § 101.

1984 Acts. Section effective July 10, 1984, see section 122(a) of Pub.L. 98–353, set out as a note under section 151 of this title.

§ 1411. Jury trials

(a) Except as provided in subsection (b) of this section, this chapter and title 11 do not affect any right to trial by jury that an individual has under applicable nonbankruptcy law with regard to a personal injury or wrongful death tort claim.

(b) The district court may order the issues arising under section 303 of title 11 to be tried without a jury.

(Added Pub.L. 98–353, Title I, § 102(a), July 10, 1984, 98 Stat. 335.)

Effective and Applicability Provisions

1984 Acts. Section, except subsec. (a), effective July 10, 1984, see section 122(a) of Pub.L. 98–353, set out as a note under section 151 of this title.

Subsec. (a) not applicable with respect to cases under Title 11, Bankruptcy, that are pending on July 10, 1984, or to proceedings arising in or related to such cases, see section 122(b) of Pub.L. 98–353, set out as a note under section 151 of this title.

§ 1412. Change of venue

A district court may transfer a case or proceeding under title 11 to a district court for another district, in the interest of justice or for the convenience of the parties.

(Added Pub.L. 98–353, Title I, § 102(a), July 10, 1984, 98 Stat. 335.)

HISTORICAL AND STATUTORY NOTES

Effective and Applicability Provisions

1984 Acts. Section effective July 10, 1984, see section 122(a) of Pub.L. 98–353, set out as a note under section 151 of this title.

§ 1413. Venue of cases under chapter 5 of title 3

Notwithstanding the preceding provisions of this chapter, a civil action under section 1346(g) may be brought in the United States district court for the district in which the employee is employed or in the United States District Court for the District of Columbia.

(Added Pub.L. 104–331, § 3(b)(2)(A), Oct. 26, 1996, 110 Stat. 4069.)

HISTORICAL AND STATUTORY NOTES

Codifications

Amendment by Pub.L. 104–331, § 3(b)(2)(A), which directed the addition of this section to the end of chapter 37 of this title, was executed by adding this section to the end of this chapter, as the probable intent of Congress.

Effective and Applicability Provisions

1996 Acts. Amendment by Pub.L. 104–331, § 3(b)(2)(B), effective October 1, 1997, see section 3(d) of Pub.L. 104–331, set out as a note under section 1296 of this title.

CHAPTER 89—DISTRICT COURTS; REMOVAL OF CASES FROM STATE COURTS

§ 1441. Actions removable generally

(a) Except as otherwise expressly provided by Act of Congress, any civil action brought in a State court of which the district courts of the United States have original jurisdiction, may be removed by the defendant or the defendants, to the district court of the United States for the district and division embracing the place where such action is pending. For purposes of removal under this chapter, the citizenship of defendants sued under fictitious names shall be disregarded.

(b) Any civil action of which the district courts have original jurisdiction founded on a claim or right arising under the Constitution, treaties or laws of the United States shall be removable without regard to the citizenship or residence of the parties. Any other such action shall be removable only if none of the parties in interest properly joined and served as defendants is a citizen of the State in which such action is brought.

(c) Whenever a separate and independent claim or cause of action within the jurisdiction conferred by section 1331 of this title is joined with one or more otherwise non-removable claims or causes of action, the entire case may be removed and the district court may determine all issues therein, or, in its discretion, may remand all matters in which State law predominates.

(d) Any civil action brought in a State court against a foreign state as defined in section 1603(a) of this title may be removed by the foreign state to the district court of the United States for the district and division embracing the place where such action is pending. Upon removal the action shall be tried by the court without jury. Where removal is based upon this subsection, the time limitations of section 1446(b) of this chapter may be enlarged at any time for cause shown.

(e)(1) Notwithstanding the provisions of subsection (b) of this section, a defendant in a civil action in a State court may remove the action to the district court of the United States for the district and division embracing the place where the action is pending if—

(A) the action could have been brought in a United States district court under section 1369 of this title; or

---

(B) the defendant is a party to an action which is or could have been brought, in whole or in part, under section 1369 in a United States district court and arises from the same accident as the action in State court, even if the action to be removed could not have been brought in a district court as an original matter.

The removal of an action under this subsection shall be made in accordance with section 1446 of this title, except that a notice of removal may also be filed before trial of the action in State court within 30 days after the date on which the defendant first becomes a party to an action under section 1369 in a United States district court that arises from the same accident as the action in State court, or at a later time with leave of the district court.

(2) Whenever an action is removed under this subsection and the district court to which it is removed or transferred under section 1407(j) has made a liability determination requiring further proceedings as to damages, the district court shall remand the action to the State court from which it had been removed for the determination of damages, unless the court finds that, for the convenience of parties and witnesses and in the interest of justice, the action should be retained for the determination of damages.

(3) Any remand under paragraph (2) shall not be effective until 60 days after the district court has issued an order determining liability and has certified its intention to remand the removed action for the determination of damages. An appeal with respect to the liability determination of the district court may be taken during that 60-day period to the court of appeals with appellate jurisdiction over the district court. In the event a party files such an appeal, the remand shall not be effective until the appeal has been finally disposed of. Once the remand has become effective, the liability determination shall not be subject to further review by appeal or otherwise.

(4) Any decision under this subsection concerning remand for the determination of damages shall not be reviewable by appeal or otherwise.

(5) An action removed under this subsection shall be deemed to be an action under section 1369 and an action in which jurisdiction is based on section 1369 of this title for purposes of this section and sections 1407, 1697, and 1785 of this title.

(6) Nothing in this subsection shall restrict the authority of the district court to transfer or dismiss an action on the ground of inconvenient forum.

(f) The court to which a civil action is removed under this section is not precluded from hearing and determining any claim in such civil action because the State court from which such civil action is removed did not have jurisdiction over that claim.

(June 25, 1948, c. 646, 62 Stat. 937; Oct. 21, 1976, Pub.L. 94–583, § 6, 90 Stat. 2898; June 19, 1986, Pub.L. 99–336, § 3(a), 100 Stat. 637; Nov. 19, 1988, Pub.L. 100–702, Title X, § 1016(a), 102 Stat. 4669; Dec. 1, 1990, Pub.L. 101–650, Title III, § 312, 104 Stat. 5114; Dec. 9, 1991, Pub.L. 102–198, § 4, 105 Stat. 1623; Nov. 2, 2002, Pub.L. 107–273, Div. C, Title I, § 11020(b)(3), 116 Stat. 1827.)

HISTORICAL AND STATUTORY NOTES
References in Text

Section 1407(j) of Title 28, referred to in subsec. (e)(2), does not exist.

Effective and Applicability Provisions

2002 Acts. Amendments by section 11020(b) of Pub.L. 107–273 shall apply to a civil action if the accident giving rise to the cause of action occurred on or after the 90th day after Nov. 2, 2002, see section 11020(c) of Pub.L. 107–273, set out as a note under 28 U.S.C.A. § 1369.

1986 Acts. Section 3(b) of Pub.L. 99–336 provided that: "The amendment made by this section [amending this section] shall apply with respect to claims in civil actions commenced in State courts on or after the date of the enactment of this section [June 19, 1986]."

1976 Acts. Amendment by Pub.L. 94–583 effective 90 days after Oct. 21, 1976, see section 8 of Pub.L. 94–583, set out as a note under section 1602 of this title.

§ 1442. Federal officers or agencies sued or prosecuted

(a) A civil action or criminal prosecution commenced in a State court against any of the following may be removed by them to the district court of the United States for the district and division embracing the place wherein it is pending:

(1) The United States or any agency thereof or any officer (or any person acting under that officer) of the United States or of any agency thereof, sued in an official or individual capacity for any act under color of such office or on account of any right, title or authority claimed under any Act of Congress for the apprehension or punishment of criminals or the collection of the revenue.

(2) A property holder whose title is derived from any such officer, where such action or prosecution affects the validity of any law of the United States.

(3) Any officer of the courts of the United States, for any act under color of office or in the performance of his duties;

(4) Any officer of either House of Congress, for any act in the discharge of his official duty under an order of such House.

(b) A personal action commenced in any State court by an alien against any citizen of a State who is, or at the time the alleged action accrued was, a civil officer of the United States and is a nonresident of such State, wherein jurisdiction is obtained by the State court by personal service of process, may be removed by the defendant to the district court of the United States for the district and division in which the defendant was served with process.

(June 25, 1948, c. 646, 62 Stat. 938; Oct. 19, 1996, Pub.L. 104–317, Title II, § 206(a), 110 Stat. 3850.)

§ 1442a.   Members of armed forces sued or prosecuted

A civil or criminal prosecution in a court of a State of the United States against a member of the armed forces of the United States on account of an act done under color of his office or status, or in respect to which he claims any right, title, or authority under a law of the United States respecting the armed forces thereof, or under the law of war, may at any time before the trial or final hearing thereof be removed for trial into the district court of the United States for the district where it is pending in the manner prescribed by law, and it shall thereupon be entered on the docket of the district court, which shall proceed as if the cause had been originally commenced therein and shall have full power to hear and determine the cause.

(Added Aug. 10, 1956, c. 1041, § 19(a), 70A Stat. 626.)

HISTORICAL AND STATUTORY NOTES

Codifications

Section was from the Uniform Code of Military Justice, Act May 5, 1950, c. 169, § 9, 64 Stat. 146, which was based on Article 117, Articles of War, Act June 4, 1920, c. 227, subch. II, § 1, 41 Stat. 811, as amended June 24, 1948, c. 625, Title II, § 242, 62 Stat. 642.

§ 1443.   Civil rights cases

Any of the following civil actions or criminal prosecutions, commenced in a State court may be removed by the defendant to the district court of the United States for the district and division embracing the place wherein it is pending:

(1) Against any person who is denied or cannot enforce in the courts of such State a right under any law providing for the equal civil rights of citizens of the United States, or of all persons within the jurisdiction thereof;

(2) For any act under color of authority derived from any law providing for equal rights, or for refusing to do any act on the ground that it would be inconsistent with such law.

(June 25, 1948, c. 646, 62 Stat. 938.)

§ 1444.   Foreclosure action against United States

Any action brought under section 2410 of this title against the United States in any State court may be removed by the United States to the district court of the United States for the district and division in which the action is pending.

(June 25, 1948, c. 646, 62 Stat. 938; May 24, 1949, c. 139, § 82, 63 Stat. 101.)

§ 1445.   Nonremovable actions

(a) A civil action in any State court against a railroad or its receivers or trustees, arising under sections 1–4 and 5–10 of the Act of April 22, 1908 (45 U.S.C. 51–54, 55–60), may not be removed to any district court of the United States.

(b) A civil action in any State court against a carrier or its receivers or trustees to recover damages for delay, loss, or injury of shipments, arising under section 11706 or 14706 of title 49, may not be removed to any district court of the United States unless the matter in controversy exceeds $10,000, exclusive of interest and costs.

(c) A civil action in any State court arising under the workmen's compensation laws of such State may not be removed to any district court of the United States.

(d) A civil action in any State court arising under section 40302 of the Violence Against Women Act of 1994 may not be removed to any district court of the United States.

(June 25, 1948, c. 646, 62 Stat. 939; July 25, 1958, Pub.L. 85–554, § 5, 72 Stat. 415; Oct. 17, 1978, Pub.L. 95–473, § 2(a)(3)(A), 92 Stat. 1465; Oct. 20, 1978, Pub.L. 95–486, § 9(b), 92 Stat. 1634; Sept. 13, 1994, Pub.L. 103–322, Title IV, § 40302(e)(5), 108 Stat. 1942; Dec. 29, 1995, Pub.L. 104–88, Title III, § 305(b), 109 Stat. 944; Oct. 11, 1996, Pub.L. 104–287, § 3, 110 Stat. 3388.)

HISTORICAL AND STATUTORY NOTES

References in Text

The Act of April 22, 1908, referred to in subsec. (a), popularly referred to as the [second] Employers' Liability Act, is Act Apr. 22, 1908, c. 149, 35 Stat. 65, as amended, which is classified generally to chapter 2 (section 51 et seq.) of Title 45, Railroads. For complete classification of this Act to the Code, see Short Title note set out under section 51 of Title 45 and Tables.

Section 40302 of the Violence Against Women Act of 1994, referred to in subsec. (d), means section 40302 of Pub.L. 103–322, the Violent Crime Control and Law Enforcement Act of 1994 (Title IV of such Act is the Violence Against Women Act of 1994), which is classified to section 13981 of Title 42, The Public Health and Welfare.

Effective and Applicability Provisions

1996 Acts. Amendment by section 3 of Pub.L. 104–287 effective on July 5, 1994, see section 8(1) of Pub.L. 104–287, set out as a note under section 5303 of Title 49, Transportation.

1995 Acts. Amendment by Pub.L. 104–88 effective Jan. 1, 1996, see section 2 of Pub.L. 104–88, set out as a note under section 701 of Title 49, Transportation.

1958 Acts. Amendment of section by Pub.L. 85–554 applicable only in the case of actions commenced after July 25,

1958, see section 3 of Pub.L. 85–554, set out as a note under section 1331 of this title.

§ 1446. Procedure for removal

(a) A defendant or defendants desiring to remove any civil action or criminal prosecution from a State court shall file in the district court of the United States for the district and division within which such action is pending a notice of removal signed pursuant to Rule 11 of the Federal Rules of Civil Procedure and containing a short and plain statement of the grounds for removal, together with a copy of all process, pleadings, and orders served upon such defendant or defendants in such action.

(b) The notice of removal of a civil action or proceeding shall be filed within thirty days after the receipt by the defendant, through service or otherwise, of a copy of the initial pleading setting forth the claim for relief upon which such action or proceeding is based, or within thirty days after the service of summons upon the defendant if such initial pleading has then been filed in court and is not required to be served on the defendant, whichever period is shorter.

If the case stated by the initial pleading is not removable, a notice of removal may be filed within thirty days after receipt by the defendant, through service or otherwise, of a copy of an amended pleading, motion, order or other paper from which it may first be ascertained that the case is one which is or has become removable, except that a case may not be removed on the basis of jurisdiction conferred by section 1332 of this title more than 1 year after commencement of the action.

(c)(1) A notice of removal of a criminal prosecution shall be filed not later than thirty days after the arraignment in the State court, or at any time before trial, whichever is earlier, except that for good cause shown the United States district court may enter an order granting the defendant or defendants leave to file the notice at a later time.

(2) A notice of removal of a criminal prosecution shall include all grounds for such removal. A failure to state grounds which exist at the time of the filing of the notice shall constitute a waiver of such grounds, and a second notice may be filed only on grounds not existing at the time of the original notice. For good cause shown, the United States district court may grant relief from the limitations of this paragraph.

(3) The filing of a notice of removal of a criminal prosecution shall not prevent the State court in which such prosecution is pending from proceeding further, except that a judgment of conviction shall not be entered unless the prosecution is first remanded.

(4) The United States district court in which such notice is filed shall examine the notice promptly. If it clearly appears on the face of the notice and any exhibits annexed thereto that removal should not be permitted, the court shall make an order for summary remand.

(5) If the United States district court does not order the summary remand of such prosecution, it shall order an evidentiary hearing to be held promptly and after such hearing shall make such disposition of the prosecution as justice shall require. If the United States district court determines that removal shall be permitted, it shall so notify the State court in which prosecution is pending, which shall proceed no further.

(d) Promptly after the filing of such notice of removal of a civil action the defendant or defendants shall give written notice thereof to all adverse parties and shall file a copy of the notice with the clerk of such State court, which shall effect the removal and the State court shall proceed no further unless and until the case is remanded.

(e) If the defendant or defendants are in actual custody on process issued by the State court, the district court shall issue its writ of habeas corpus, and the marshal shall thereupon take such defendant or defendants into his custody and deliver a copy of the writ to the clerk of such State court.

(f) With respect to any counterclaim removed to a district court pursuant to section 337(c) of the Tariff Act of 1930, the district court shall resolve such counterclaim in the same manner as an original complaint under the Federal Rules of Civil Procedure, except that the payment of a filing fee shall not be required in such cases and the counterclaim shall relate back to the date of the original complaint in the proceeding before the International Trade Commission under section 337 of that Act.

(June 25, 1948, c. 646, 62 Stat. 939; May 24, 1949, c. 139, § 83, 63 Stat. 101; Sept. 29, 1965, Pub.L. 89–215, 79 Stat. 887; July 30, 1977, Pub.L. 95–78, § 3, 91 Stat. 321; Nov. 19, 1988, Pub.L. 100–702, Title X, § 1016(b), 102 Stat. 4669; Dec. 9, 1991, Pub.L. 102–198, § 10(a), 105 Stat. 1626; Dec. 8, 1994, Pub.L. 103–465, Title III, § 321(b)(2), 108 Stat. 4946; Oct. 19, 1996, Pub.L. 104–317, Title VI, § 603, 110 Stat. 3857.)

HISTORICAL AND STATUTORY NOTES

References in Text

The Federal Rules of Civil Procedure, referred to in subsec. (a), are set out in this title.

Codifications

Section 10(a)(5)(A) of Pub.L. 102–198, which directed that subsec. (d) of this section be amended by substituting "removal" for "the removal", was executed by making such substitution at the first appearance of the term "the removal", as the probable intent of Congress.

1994 Acts

House Report No. 103–826 (Parts I and II) and Statement of Administrative Action, see 1994 U.S. Code Cong. and Adm. News, p. 3773.

Effective and Applicability Provisions

1994 Acts. Amendment by section 321(b)(2) of Pub.L. 103–465 applicable with respect to complaints filed under section 1337 of Title 19, Customs Duties, on or after the date on which the WTO Agreement enters into force with respect to the United States, Jan. 1, 1995, or in cases under section 1337 of Title 19 in which no complaint is filed, with respect to investigations initiated under such section on or after such date, see section 322 of Pub.L. 103–465, set out as a note under section 1337 of Title 19.

1977 Acts. Amendment by Pub.L. 95–78 effective Oct. 1, 1977, see section 4 of Pub.L. 95–78, set out as a note under section 3771 of Title 18, Crimes and Criminal Procedure.

§ 1447. Procedure after removal generally

(a) In any case removed from a State court, the district court may issue all necessary orders and process to bring before it all proper parties whether served by process issued by the State court or otherwise.

(b) It may require the removing party to file with its clerk copies of all records and proceedings in such State court or may cause the same to be brought before it by writ of certiorari issued to such State court.

(c) A motion to remand the case on the basis of any defect other than lack of subject matter jurisdiction must be made within 30 days after the filing of the notice of removal under section 1446(a). If at any time before final judgment it appears that the district court lacks subject matter jurisdiction, the case shall be remanded. An order remanding the case may require payment of just costs and any actual expenses, including attorney fees, incurred as a result of the removal. A certified copy of the order of remand shall be mailed by the clerk to the clerk of the State court. The State court may thereupon proceed with such case.

(d) An order remanding a case to the State court from which it was removed is not reviewable on appeal or otherwise, except that an order remanding a case to the State court from which it was removed pursuant to section 1443 of this title shall be reviewable by appeal or otherwise.

(e) If after removal the plaintiff seeks to join additional defendants whose joinder would destroy subject matter jurisdiction, the court may deny joinder, or permit joinder and remand the action to the State court.

(June 25, 1948, c. 646, 62 Stat. 939; May 24, 1949, c. 139, § 84, 63 Stat. 102; July 2, 1964, Pub.L. 88–352, Title IX, § 901, 78 Stat. 266; Nov. 19, 1988, Pub.L. 100–702, Title X, § 1016(c), 102 Stat. 4670; Dec. 9, 1991, Pub.L. 102–198, § 10(b), 105 Stat. 1626; Oct. 1, 1996, Pub.L. 104–219, § 1, 110 Stat. 3022.)

HISTORICAL AND STATUTORY NOTES

Exception to Subsection (d)

Section 3(c) of Act Aug. 4, 1947, c. 458, 61 Stat. 732, provided in part that the United States shall have the right to appeal from any order of remand entered in any case removed to a United States district court pursuant to the provisions of Act Apr. 12, 1926, c. 115, 44 Stat. 239. These Acts referred to herein relate to restrictions on land of the Five Civilized Tribes of Oklahoma and are set out as notes under section 355 of Title 25, Indians.

§ 1448. Process after removal

In all cases removed from any State court to any district court of the United States in which any one or more of the defendants has not been served with process or in which the service has not been perfected prior to removal, or in which process served proves to be defective, such process or service may be completed or new process issued in the same manner as in cases originally filed in such district court.

This section shall not deprive any defendant upon whom process is served after removal of his right to move to remand the case.

(June 25, 1948, c. 646, 62 Stat. 940.)

§ 1449. State court record supplied

Where a party is entitled to copies of the records and proceedings in any suit or prosecution in a State court, to be used in any district court of the United States, and the clerk of such State court, upon demand, and the payment or tender of the legal fees, fails to deliver certified copies, the district court may, on affidavit reciting such facts, direct such record to be supplied by affidavit or otherwise. Thereupon such proceedings, trial, and judgment may be had in such district court, and all such process awarded, as if certified copies had been filed in the district court.

(June 25, 1948, c. 646, 62 Stat. 940; May 24, 1949, c. 139, § 85, 63 Stat. 102.)

§ 1450. Attachment or sequestration; securities

Whenever any action is removed from a State court to a district court of the United States, any attachment or sequestration of the goods or estate of the defendant in such action in the State court shall hold the goods or estate to answer the final judgment or decree in the same manner as they would have been held to answer final judgment or decree had it been rendered by the State court.

All bonds, undertakings, or security given by either party in such action prior to its removal shall remain valid and effectual notwithstanding such removal.

All injunctions, orders, and other proceedings had in such action prior to its removal shall remain in full force and effect until dissolved or modified by the district court.

(June 25, 1948, c. 646, 62 Stat. 940.)

§ 1451. Definitions

For purposes of this chapter—

(1) The term "State court" includes the Superior Court of the District of Columbia.

(2) The term "State" includes the District of Columbia.

(Added Pub.L. 91–358, Title I, § 172(d)(1), July 29, 1970, 84 Stat. 591.)

HISTORICAL AND STATUTORY NOTES
Effective and Applicability Provisions

1970 Acts. Section effective the first day of the seventh calendar month which begins after July 29, 1970, see section 199(a) of Pub.L. 91–358, set out as a note under section 1257 of this title.

§ 1452. Removal of claims related to bankruptcy cases

(a) A party may remove any claim or cause of action in a civil action other than a proceeding before the United States Tax Court or a civil action by a governmental unit to enforce such governmental unit's police or regulatory power, to the district court for the district where such civil action is pending, if such district court has jurisdiction of such claim or cause of action under section 1334 of this title.

(b) The court to which such claim or cause of action is removed may remand such claim or cause of action on any equitable ground. An order entered under this subsection remanding a claim or cause of action, or a decision to not remand, is not reviewable by appeal or otherwise by the court of appeals under section 158(d), 1291, or 1292 of this title or by the Supreme Court of the United States under section 1254 of this title.

(Added Pub.L. 98–353, Title I, § 103(a), July 10, 1984, 98 Stat. 335, and amended Pub.L. 101–650, Title III, § 309(c), Dec. 1, 1990, 104 Stat. 5113.)

HISTORICAL AND STATUTORY NOTES
Effective and Applicability Provisions

1984 Acts. Section effective July 10, 1984, see section 122(a) of Pub.L. 98–353, set out as a note under section 151 of this title.

§ 1453. Removal of class actions

(a) **Definitions.**—In this section, the terms "class", "class action", "class certification order", and "class member" shall have the meanings given such terms under section 1332(d)(1).

(b) **In general.**—A class action may be removed to a district court of the United States in accordance with section 1446 (except that the 1–year limitation under section 1446(b) shall not apply), without regard to whether any defendant is a citizen of the State in which the action is brought, except that such action may be removed by any defendant without the consent of all defendants.

(c) **Review of remand orders.**—

(1) **In general.**—Section 1447 shall apply to any removal of a case under this section, except that notwithstanding section 1447(d), a court of appeals may accept an appeal from an order of a district court granting or denying a motion to remand a class action to the State court from which it was removed if application is made to the court of appeals not less than 7 days after entry of the order.

(2) **Time period for judgment.**—If the court of appeals accepts an appeal under paragraph (1), the court shall complete all action on such appeal, including rendering judgment, not later than 60 days after the date on which such appeal was filed, unless an extension is granted under paragraph (3).

(3) **Extension of time period.**—The court of appeals may grant an extension of the 60–day period described in paragraph (2) if—

(A) all parties to the proceeding agree to such extension, for any period of time; or

(B) such extension is for good cause shown and in the interests of justice, for a period not to exceed 10 days.

(4) **Denial of appeal.**—If a final judgment on the appeal under paragraph (1) is not issued before the end of the period described in paragraph (2), including any extension under paragraph (3), the appeal shall be denied.

(d) **Exception.**—This section shall not apply to any class action that solely involves—

(1) a claim concerning a covered security as defined under section 16(f)(3) of the Securities Act of 1933 (15 U.S.C. 78p(f)(3)) and section 28(f)(5)(E) of the Securities Exchange Act of 1934 (15 U.S.C. 78bb(f)(5)(E));

(2) a claim that relates to the internal affairs or governance of a corporation or other form of business enterprise and arises under or by virtue of the laws of the State in which such corporation or business enterprise is incorporated or organized; or

(3) a claim that relates to the rights, duties (including fiduciary duties), and obligations relating to or created by or pursuant to any security (as defined under section 2(a)(1) of the Securities Act of 1933 (15 U.S.C. 77b(a)(1)) and the regulations issued thereunder).

(Added Pub.L. 109–2, § 5(a), Feb. 18, 2005, 119 Stat. 12.)

HISTORICAL AND STATUTORY NOTES

References in Text

Section 16(f)(3) of the Securities Act of 1933, referred to in subsec. (d)(1), is May 27, 1933, c. 38, Title I, § 16(f)(3), 48 Stat. 84, as amended, which is classified to 15 U.S.C.A. § 78p(f)(3).

Section 28(f)(5)(E) of the Securities Exchange Act of 1934, referred to in subsec. (d)(1), is May 27, 1933, c. 38, Title I, § 2(f)(5)(E), 48 Stat. 74, as amended, which is classified to 15 U.S.C.A. § 78bb(f)(5)(E).

Section 2(a)(1) of the Securities Act of 1933, referred to in subsec. (d)(3), is May 27, 1933, c. 38, Title I, § 2(a)(1), 48 Stat. 74, as amended, which is classified to 15 U.S.C.A. § 77b(a)(1).

Effective and Applicability Provisions

2005 Acts. Amendments by Class Action Fairness Act of 2005, Pub.L. 109–2, Feb. 18, 2005, 119 Stat. 4, applicable to any civil action commenced on or after Feb. 18, 2005, see Pub.L. 109–2, § 9, set out as a note under 28 U.S.C.A. § 1332.

[CHAPTER 90—DISTRICT COURTS AND BANKRUPTCY COURTS] [OMITTED]

HISTORICAL AND STATUTORY NOTES

Codifications

Chapter 90, consisting of sections 1471 to 1482, which was added by Pub.L. 95–598, Title II, § 241(a), Nov. 6, 1978, 92 Stat. 2668, and which related to district courts and bankruptcy courts, did not become effective pursuant to section 402(b) of Pub.L. 95–598, as amended, set out as an Effective and Applicability Provisions note preceding section 101 of Title 11, Bankruptcy.

Transition to New Court System

Pub.L. 95–598, Title IV, § 409, Nov. 6, 1978, 92 Stat. 2687, as amended by Pub.L. 98–249, § 1(d), Mar. 31, 1984, 98 Stat. 116; Pub.L. 98–271, § 1(d), Apr. 30, 1984, 98 Stat. 163; Pub.L. 98–299, § 1(d), May 25, 1984, 98 Stat. 214; Pub.L. 98–325, § 1(d), June 20, 1984, 98 Stat. 268; Pub.L. 98–353, Title I, § 121(d), July 10, 1984, 98 Stat. 346, was repealed by Pub.L. 98–353, Title I, §§ 114, 122(a), July 10, 1984, 98 Stat.

343, 346, eff. July 10, 1984. The repealed section had provided for transfer to the new court system of 1) cases, and matters and proceedings in cases, under the Bankruptcy Act [former Title 11] pending at the end of Sept. 30, 1983, in the courts of bankruptcy continued under section 404(a) of Pub.L. 95–598, with certain exceptions, and 2) cases and proceedings arising under or related to cases under Title 11 pending at the end of July 9, 1984, in the courts of bankruptcy continued under section 404(a) of Pub.L. 95–598, and directed that civil actions pending on July 9, 1984, over which a bankruptcy court had jurisdiction on July 9, 1984, not abate, that actions not finally determined before Apr. 1, 1985, be removed to a bankruptcy court under this chapter, and that all law books, publications, etc., furnished bankruptcy judges as of July 9, 1984, be transferred to the United States bankruptcy courts under the supervision of the Director of the Administrative Office of the United States Courts.

CHAPTER 91—UNITED STATES COURT OF FEDERAL CLAIMS

§ 1491. Claims against United States generally; actions involving Tennessee Valley Authority

(a)(1) The United States Court of Federal Claims shall have jurisdiction to render judgment upon any claim against the United States founded either upon the Constitution, or any Act of Congress or any regulation of an executive department, or upon any express or implied contract with the United States, or for liquidated or unliquidated damages in cases not sounding in tort. For the purpose of this paragraph, an express or implied contract with the Army and Air Force Exchange Service, Navy Exchanges, Marine Corps Exchanges, Coast Guard Exchanges, or Exchange Councils of the National Aeronautics and Space Administration shall be considered an express or implied contract with the United States.

(2) To provide an entire remedy and to complete the relief afforded by the judgment, the court may, as an incident of and collateral to any such judgment, issue orders directing restoration to office or position, placement in appropriate duty or retirement status, and correction of applicable records, and such orders may be issued to any appropriate official of the United States. In any case within its jurisdiction, the court shall have the power to remand appropriate matters to any administrative or executive body or official with such direction as it may deem proper and just. The Court of Federal Claims shall have jurisdiction to render judgment upon any claim by or against, or dispute with, a contractor arising under section 10(a)(1) of the Contract Disputes Act of 1978, including a dispute concerning termination of a contract, rights in tangible or intangible property, compliance with cost accounting standards, and other nonmonetary disputes on which a decision of the contracting officer has been issued under section 6 of that Act.

[(3) Repealed. Pub.L. 104–320, § 12(a)(2), Oct. 19, 1996, 110 Stat. 3874]

(b)(1) Both the Unites [1] States Court of Federal Claims and the district courts of the United States shall have jurisdiction to render judgment on an action by an interested party objecting to a solicitation by a Federal agency for bids or proposals for a proposed contract or to a proposed award or the award of a contract or any alleged violation of statute or regulation in connection with a procurement or a proposed procurement. Both the United States Court of Federal Claims and the district courts of the United States shall have jurisdiction to entertain such an action without regard to whether suit is instituted before or after the contract is awarded.

(2) To afford relief in such an action, the courts may award any relief that the court considers proper, including declaratory and injunctive relief except that any monetary relief shall be limited to bid preparation and proposal costs.

(3) In exercising jurisdiction under this subsection, the courts shall give due regard to the interests of national defense and national security and the need for expeditious resolution of the action.

(4) In any action under this subsection, the courts shall review the agency's decision pursuant to the standards set forth in section 706 of title 5.

(c) Nothing herein shall be construed to give the United States Court of Federal Claims jurisdiction of any civil action within the exclusive jurisdiction of the Court of International Trade, or of any action against, or founded on conduct of, the Tennessee Valley Authority, or to amend or modify the provisions of the Tennessee Valley Authority Act of 1933 with respect to actions by or against the Authority.

(June 25, 1948, c. 646, 62 Stat. 940; July 28, 1953, c. 253, § 7, 67 Stat. 226; Sept. 3, 1954, c. 1263, § 44(a), (b), 68 Stat. 1241; July 23, 1970, Pub.L. 91–350, § 1(b), 84 Stat. 449; Aug. 29, 1972, Pub.L. 92–415, § 1, 86 Stat. 652; Nov. 1, 1978, Pub.L. 95–563, § 14(i), 92 Stat. 2391; Oct. 10, 1980, Pub.L. 96–417, Title V, § 509, 94 Stat. 1743; Apr. 2, 1982, Pub.L. 97–164, Title I, § 133(a), 96 Stat. 39; Oct. 29, 1992, Pub.L. 102–572,

Title IX, §§ 902(a), 907(b)(1), 106 Stat. 4516, 4519; Oct. 19, 1996, Pub.L. 104–320, § 12(a), 110 Stat. 3874.)

[1] So in original.

HISTORICAL AND STATUTORY NOTES

References in Text

The Contracts Disputes Act of 1978, referred to in subsec. (a)(2), is Pub.L. 95–563, Nov. 1, 1978, 92 Stat. 2383, which is classified principally to chapter 9 (section 601 et seq.) of Title 41, Public Contracts. Sections 6 and 10(a)(1) of such Act are classified to sections 605 and 609(a)(1), respectively, of Title 41. For complete classification of this Act to the Code, see Short Title note set out under section 601 of Title 41 and Tables.

The Tennessee Valley Authority Act of 1933, referred to in subsec. (b), is Act May 18, 1933, c. 32, 48 Stat. 58, as amended, which is classified generally to chapter 12A (section 831 et seq.) of Title 16, Conservation. For complete classification of this Act to the Code, see section 831 of Title 16 and Tables.

Effective and Applicability Provisions

1996 Acts. Section 12(b) of Pub.L. 104–320 provided that: "This section and the amendments made by this section [amending subsecs. (a)(3), (b), and (c) of this section] shall take effect on December 31, 1996 and shall apply to all actions filed on or after that date."

1992 Acts. Amendments by section 902(a) of Pub.L. 102–572 effective Oct. 29, 1992, see section 911 of Pub.L. 102–572, set out as a note under section 171 of this title.

Section 907(b)(2) of Pub.L. 102–572 provided that: "The amendment made by paragraph (1) [amending subsec. (a)(2) of this section] shall be effective with respect to all actions filed before, on, or after the date of the enactment of this Act [Oct. 29, 1992], except for those actions which, before such date of enactment, have been the subject of—

"(A) a final judgment of the United States Claims Court, if the time for appeal of that judgment has expired without an appeal having been filed, or

"(B) a final judgment of the Court of Appeals for the Federal Circuit."

1982 Acts. Amendment by Pub.L. 97–164 effective Oct. 1, 1982, see section 402 of Pub.L. 97–164, set out as a note under section 171 of this title.

1980 Acts. Amendment by Pub.L. 96–417 effective Nov. 1, 1980 and applicable with respect to civil actions pending on or commenced on or after such date, see section 701(a) of Pub.L. 96–417, as amended, set out as a note under section 251 of this title.

1978 Acts. Amendment by Pub.L. 95–563 effective with respect to contracts entered into 120 days after Nov. 1, 1978, and, at the election of the contractor, with respect to any claim pending at such time before the contracting officer or initiated thereafter, see section 16 of Pub.L. 95–563, set out as a note under section 601 of Title 41, Public Contracts.

1972 Acts. Section 2 of Pub.L. 92–415 provided that: "This Act [amending this section] shall be applicable to all judicial proceedings pending on or instituted after the date of its enactment [Aug. 29, 1972]."

1970 Acts. Amendment by Pub.L. 91–350 applicable to claims and civil actions dismissed before or pending on July 23, 1970, if the claim or civil action was based upon a transaction, omission, or breach that occurred not more than six years prior to July 23, 1970, notwithstanding a determination or judgment made prior to July 23, 1970, that the United States district courts or the United States Court of Claims did not have jurisdiction to entertain a suit on an express or implied contract with a nonappropriated fund instrumentality of the United States, see section 2 of Pub.L. 91–350, set out as a note under section 1346 of this title.

Transfer of Functions

For transfer of authorities, functions, personnel, and assets of the Coast Guard, including the authorities and functions of the Secretary of Transportation relating thereto, to the Department of Homeland Security, and for treatment of related references, see 6 U.S.C.A. §§ 468(b), 551(d), 552(d) and 557, and the Department of Homeland Security Reorganization Plan of November 25, 2002, as modified, set out as a note under 6 U.S.C.A. § 542.

Sunset Provisions

Section 12(d) of Pub.L. 104–320 provided that: "The jurisdiction of the district courts of the United States over the actions described in section 1491(b)(1) of title 28, United States Code [subsec. (b)(1) of this section] (as amended by subsection (a) of this section) shall terminate on January 1, 2001 unless extended by Congress. The savings provisions in subsection (e) [section 12(e) of Pub.L. 104–320, set out as a note under this section] shall apply if the bid protest jurisdiction of the district courts of the United States terminates under this subsection [this note]."

Savings Provisions

Section 12(e) of Pub.L. 104–320 provided that:

"**(1) Orders.**—A termination under subsection (d) [section 12(d) of Pub.L. 104–320, set out as a note under this section] shall not terminate the effectiveness of orders that have been issued by a court in connection with an action within the jurisdiction of that court on or before December 31, 2000. Such orders shall continue in effect according to their terms until modified, terminated, superseded, set aside, or revoked by a court of competent jurisdiction or by operation of law.

"**(2) Proceedings and applications.**—**(A)** a [sic] termination under subsection (d) shall not affect the jurisdiction of a court of the United States to continue with any proceeding that is pending before the court on December 31, 2000.

"**(B)** Orders may be issued in any such proceeding, appeals may be taken therefrom, and payments may be made pursuant to such orders, as if such termination had not occurred. An order issued in any such proceeding shall continue in effect until modified, terminated, superseded, set aside, or revoked by a court of competent jurisdiction or by operation of law.

"**(C)** Nothing in this paragraph prohibits the discontinuance or modification of any such proceeding under the same terms and conditions and to the same extent that proceeding could have been discontinued or modified absent such termination."

Study on Concurrent Jurisdiction

Section 12(c) of Pub.L. 104–320 provided that: "No earlier than 2 years after the effective date of this section [see section 12(b) of Pub.L. 104–320, set out as a note under this section], the United States General Accounting Office [now Government Accountability Office] shall undertake a study

regarding the concurrent jurisdiction of the district courts of the United States and the Court of Federal Claims over bid protests to determine whether concurrent jurisdiction is necessary. Such a study shall be completed no later than December 31, 1999, and shall specifically consider the effect of any proposed change on the ability of small businesses to challenge violations of Federal procurement law."

§ 1492.   Congressional reference cases

Any bill, except a bill for a pension, may be referred by either House of Congress to the chief judge of the United States Court of Federal Claims for a report in conformity with section 2509 of this title.

(June 25, 1948, c. 646, 62 Stat. 941; Oct. 15, 1966, Pub.L. 89–681, § 1, 80 Stat. 958; Apr. 2, 1982, Pub.L. 97–164, Title I, § 133(b), 96 Stat. 40; Oct. 29, 1992, Pub.L. 102–572, Title IX, § 902(a)(1), 106 Stat. 4516.)

HISTORICAL AND STATUTORY NOTES

Effective and Applicability Provisions

1992 Acts. Amendment by Title IX of Pub.L. 102–572 effective Oct. 29, 1992, see section 911 of Pub.L. 102–572, set out as a note under section 171 of this title.

1982 Acts. Amendment by Pub.L. 97–164 effective Oct. 1, 1982, see section 402 of Pub.L. 97–164, set out as a note under section 171 of this title.

[§ 1493.   Repealed. July 28, 1953, c. 253, § 8, 67 Stat. 226]

HISTORICAL AND STATUTORY NOTES

Section, Act June 25, 1948, c. 646, 62 Stat. 941, authorized the Court of Claims to give legal advice to the heads of executive departments in matters referred to it by such heads, if the Court had jurisdiction over such matters.

§ 1494.   Accounts of officers, agents or contractors

The United States Court of Federal Claims shall have jurisdiction to determine the amount, if any, due to or from the United States by reason of any unsettled account of any officer or agent of, or contractor with, the United States, or a guarantor, surety or personal representative of any such officer, agent or contractor, and to render judgment thereof,[1] where—

(1) claimant or the person he represents has applied to the proper department of the Government for settlement of the account;

(2) three years have elapsed from the date of such application without settlement; and

(3) no suit upon the same has been brought by the United States.

(June 25, 1948, c. 646, 62 Stat. 941; July 28, 1953, c. 253, § 9, 67 Stat. 226; Sept. 3, 1954, c. 1263, § 44(c), 68 Stat. 1242; Apr. 2, 1982, Pub.L. 97–164, Title I, § 133(c) (1), 96 Stat. 40; Oct. 29, 1992, Pub.L. 102–572, Title IX, § 902(a)(1), 106 Stat. 4516.)

1 So in original. Probably should be "thereon".

HISTORICAL AND STATUTORY NOTES

Effective and Applicability Provisions

1992 Acts. Amendment by Title IX of Pub.L. 102–572 effective Oct. 29, 1992, see section 911 of Pub.L. 102–572, set out as a note under section 171 of this title.

1982 Acts. Amendment by Pub.L. 97–164 effective Oct. 1, 1982, see section 402 of Pub.L. 97–164, set out as a note under section 171 of this title.

§ 1495.　Damages for unjust conviction and imprisonment; claim against United States

The United States Court of Federal Claims shall have jurisdiction to render judgment upon any claim for damages by any person unjustly convicted of an offense against the United States and imprisoned. (June 25, 1948, c. 646, 62 Stat. 941; Apr. 2, 1982, Pub.L. 97–164, Title I, § 133(c) (1), 96 Stat. 40; Oct. 29, 1992, Pub.L. 102–572, Title IX, § 902(a)(1), 106 Stat. 4516.)

HISTORICAL AND STATUTORY NOTES

Effective and Applicability Provisions

1992 Acts. Amendment by Title IX of Pub.L. 102–572 effective Oct. 29, 1992, see section 911 of Pub.L. 102–572, set out as a note under section 171 of this title.

1982 Acts. Amendment by Pub.L. 97–164 effective Oct. 1, 1982, see section 402 of Pub.L. 97–164, set out as a note under section 171 of this title.

§ 1496.　Disbursing officers' claims

The United States Court of Federal Claims shall have jurisdiction to render judgment upon any claim by a disbursing officer of the United States or by his administrator or executor for relief from responsibility for loss, in line of duty, of Government funds, vouchers, records or other papers in his charge. (June 25, 1948, c. 646, 62 Stat. 941; Apr. 2, 1982, Pub.L. 97–164, Title I, § 133(c)(1), 96 Stat. 40; Oct. 29, 1992, Pub.L. 102–572, Title IX, § 902(a)(1), 106 Stat. 4516.)

HISTORICAL AND STATUTORY NOTES

Effective and Applicability Provisions

1992 Acts. Amendment by Title IX of Pub.L. 102–572 effective Oct. 29, 1992, see section 911 of Pub.L. 102–572, set out as a note under section 171 of this title.

1982 Acts. Amendment by Pub.L. 97–164 effective Oct. 1, 1982, see section 402 of Pub.L. 97–164, set out as a note under section 171 of this title.

§ 1497.　Oyster growers' damages from dredging operations

The United States Court of Federal Claims shall have jurisdiction to render judgment upon any claim for damages to oyster growers on private or leased lands or bottoms arising from dredging operations or use of other machinery and equipment in making river and harbor improvements authorized by Act of Congress.

(June 25, 1948, c. 646, 62 Stat. 941; Apr. 2, 1982, Pub.L. 97–164, Title I, § 133(c), 96 Stat. 40; Oct. 29, 1992, Pub.L. 102–572, Title IX, § 902(a)(1), 106 Stat. 4516.)

HISTORICAL AND STATUTORY NOTES

Effective and Applicability Provisions

1992 Acts. Amendment by Title IX of Pub.L. 102–572 effective Oct. 29, 1992, see section 911 of Pub.L. 102–572, set out as a note under section 171 of this title.

1982 Acts. Amendment by Pub.L. 97–164 effective Oct. 1, 1982, see section 402 of Pub.L. 97–164, set out as a note under section 171 of this title.

§ 1498.　Patent and copyright cases

(a) Whenever an invention described in and covered by a patent of the United States is used or manufactured by or for the United States without license of the owner thereof or lawful right to use or manufacture the same, the owner's remedy shall be by action against the United States in the United States Court of Federal Claims for the recovery of his reasonable and entire compensation for such use and manufacture. Reasonable and entire compensation shall include the owner's reasonable costs, including reasonable fees for expert witnesses and attorneys, in pursuing the action if the owner is an independent inventor, a nonprofit organization, or an entity that had no more than 500 employees at any time during the 5–year period preceding the use or manufacture of the patented invention by or for the United States. Nothwithstanding [1] the preceding sentences, unless the action has been pending for more than 10 years from the time of filing to the time that the owner applies for such costs and fees, reasonable and entire compensation shall not include such costs and fees if the court finds that the position of the United States was substantially justified or that special circumstances make an award unjust.

For the purposes of this section, the use or manufacture of an invention described in and covered by a patent of the United States by a contractor, a subcontractor, or any person, firm, or corporation for the Government and with the authorization or consent of the Government, shall be construed as use or manufacture for the United States.

The court shall not award compensation under this section if the claim is based on the use or manufacture by or for the United States of any article owned, leased, used by, or in the possession of the United States prior to July 1, 1918.

A Government employee shall have the right to bring suit against the Government under this section except where he was in a position to order, influence, or induce use of the invention by the Government. This section shall not confer a right of action on any patentee or any assignee of such patentee with respect to any invention discovered or invented by a person while in the employment or service of the United States, where the invention was related to the official functions of the employee, in cases in which such functions included research and development, or in the making of which Government time, materials or facilities were used.

(b) Hereafter, whenever the copyright in any work protected under the copyright laws of the United States shall be infringed by the United States, by a corporation owned or controlled by the United States, or by a contractor, subcontractor, or any person, firm, or corporation acting for the Government and with the authorization or consent of the Government, the exclusive action which may be brought for such infringement shall be an action by the copyright owner against the United States in the Court of Federal Claims for the recovery of his reasonable and entire compensation as damages for such infringement, including the minimum statutory damages as set forth in section 504(c) of title 17, United States Code: *Provided*, That a Government employee shall have a right of action against the Government under this subsection except where he was in a position to order, influence, or induce use of the copyrighted work by the Government: *Provided, however*, That this subsection shall not confer a right of action on any copyright owner or any assignee of such owner with respect to any copyrighted work prepared by a person while in the employment or service of the United States, where the copyrighted work was prepared as a part of the official functions of the employee, or in the preparation of which Government time, material, or facilities were used: *And provided further*, That before such action against the United States has been instituted the appropriate corporation owned or controlled by the United States or the head of the appropriate department or agency of the Government, as the case may be, is authorized to enter into an agreement with the copyright owner in full settlement and compromise for the damages accruing to him by reason of such infringement and to settle the claim administratively out of available appropriations.

Except as otherwise provided by law, no recovery shall be had for any infringement of a copyright covered by this subsection committed more than three years prior to the filing of the complaint or counterclaim for infringement in the action, except that the period between the date of receipt of a written claim for compensation by the Department or agency of the Government or corporation owned or controlled by the United States, as the case may be, having authority to settle such claim and the date of mailing by the Government of a notice to the claimant that his claim has been denied shall not be counted as a part of the three years, unless suit is brought before the last-mentioned date.

(c) The provisions of this section shall not apply to any claim arising in a foreign country.

(d) Hereafter, whenever a plant variety protected by a certificate of plant variety protection under the laws of the United States shall be infringed by the United States, by a corporation owned or controlled by the United States, or by a contractor, subcontractor, or any person, firm, or corporation acting for the Government, and with the authorization and consent of the Government, the exclusive remedy of the owner of such certificate shall be by action against the United States in the Court of Federal Claims for the recovery of his reasonable and entire compensation as damages for such infringement: *Provided*, That a Government employee shall have a right of action against the Government under this subsection except where he was in a position to order, influence, or induce use of the protected plant variety by the Government: *Provided, however*, That this subsection shall not confer a right of action on any certificate owner or any assignee of such owner with respect to any protected plant variety made by a person while in the employment or service of the United States, where such variety was prepared as a part of the official functions of the employee, or in the preparation of which Government time, material, or facilities were used: *And provided further*, That before such action against the United States has been instituted, the appropriate corporation owned or controlled by the United States or the head of the appropriate agency of the Government, as the case may be, is authorized to enter into an agreement with the certificate owner in full settlement and compromise, for the damages accrued to him by reason of such infringement and to settle the claim administratively out of available appropriations.

(e) Subsections (b) and (c) of this section apply to exclusive rights in mask works under chapter 9 of title 17, and to exclusive rights in designs under chapter 13 of title 17 [17 U.S.C.A. § 1301 et seq.], to the same extent as such subsections apply to copyrights.

(June 25, 1948, c. 646, 62 Stat. 941; May 24, 1949, c. 139, § 87, 63 Stat. 102; Oct. 31, 1951, c. 655, § 50(c), 65 Stat. 727; July 17, 1952, c. 930, 66 Stat. 757; Sept. 8, 1960, Pub.L. 86–726, §§ 1, 4, 74 Stat. 855, 856; Dec. 24, 1970, Pub.L. 91–577, Title III, § 143(d), 84 Stat. 1559; Oct. 19, 1976, Pub.L. 94–553, Title I, § 105(c), 90 Stat. 2599; Apr. 2, 1982, Pub.L. 97–164, Title I, § 133(d), 96 Stat. 40; Nov. 19, 1988, Pub.L. 100–702, Title X, § 1020(a)(6), 102 Stat. 4671; Oct. 29, 1992, Pub.L. 102–572, Title IX, § 902(a), 106 Stat. 4516; Oct. 19, 1996, Pub.L. 104–308, § 1(a), 110 Stat. 3814; Dec. 16, 1997, Pub.L. 105–147, § 3, 111 Stat. 2680; Oct. 28, 1998, Pub.L. 105–304, Title V, § 503(d), 112 Stat. 2917.)

1 So in original. Probably should be "Notwithstanding".

HISTORICAL AND STATUTORY NOTES
References in Text

Hereafter, referred to in subsec. (b), probably means the date of enactment of Pub. L. 86–726 [which, among other changes, added subsec. (b)], which was approved on Sept. 8, 1960.

The copyright laws of the United States, referred to in subsec. (b), are classified generally to Title 17, Copyrights.

The "hereafter" set out at the beginning of subsec. (d) probably means after Dec. 24, 1970, the date of enactment of Pub.L. 91–577 which added subsec. (d).

Effective and Applicability Provisions

1998 Acts. Amendment by Pub.L. 105–304, effective Oct. 28, 1998, see section 505 of Pub.L. 105–304, set out as a note under section 1301 of Title 17, Copyrights.

1996 Acts. Section 1(b) of Pub.L. 104–308 provided that: "The amendment made by subsection (a) [amending subsec. (a) of this section] shall apply to actions under section 1498(a) of title 28, United States Code [subsec. (a) of this section], that are pending on, or brought on or after, the date of the enactment of this Act [Oct. 19, 1996]."

1992 Acts. Amendments by Title IX of Pub.L. 102–572 effective Oct. 29, 1992, see section 911 of Pub.L. 102–572, set out as a note under section 171 of Title 28, Judiciary and Judiciary Procedure.

1982 Acts. Amendment by Pub.L. 97–164 effective Oct. 1, 1982, see section 402 of Pub.L. 97–164, set out as a note under section 171 of this title.

1976 Acts. Amendment by Pub.L. 94–553 effective Jan. 1, 1978, see section 102 of Pub.L. 94–553, set out as a note preceding section 101 of Title 17, Copyrights.

1970 Acts. Amendment by Pub.L. 91–577 effective Dec. 24, 1970, see section 141 of Pub.L. 91–577, set out as a note under section 2321 of Title 7, Agriculture.

Waiver of Immunity for Members of Congress

Section 2 of Pub.L. 86–726 provided that: "Nothing in this Act [amending this section and section 2386 of Title 10, Armed Forces] shall be construed to in any way waive any immunity provided for Members of Congress under article I of section 6 of the Constitution of the United States."

§ 1499. Liquidated damages withheld from contractors under Contract Work Hours and Safety Standards Act [1]

The United States Court of Federal Claims shall have jurisdiction to render judgment upon any claim for liquidated damages withheld from a contractor or subcontractor under section 3703 of title 40.

(June 25, 1948, c. 646, 62 Stat. 942; Aug. 13, 1962, Pub.L. 87–581, Title II, § 202(a), 76 Stat. 360; Apr. 2, 1982, Pub.L. 97–164, Title I, § 133(e) (1), (2) (A), 96 Stat. 40, 41; Dec. 1, 1990, Pub.L. 101–650, Title III, § 325(b)(7), 104 Stat. 5121; Oct. 29, 1992, Pub.L. 102–572, Title IX, § 902(a)(1), 106 Stat. 4516; Aug. 21, 2002, Pub.L. 107–217, § 3(g)(3), 116 Stat. 1299.)

[1] So in original. Probably should read "Liquidated damages withheld from contractors".

HISTORICAL AND STATUTORY NOTES

References in Text

Contract Work Hours and Safety Standards Act, referred to in the section catchline, is Pub.L. 87–581, Title I, Aug. 13, 1962, 76 Stat. 357, as amended, which was classified generally

to subchapter II of chapter 5 of former Title 40, former 40 U.S.C.A. § 327 et seq., and was repealed and reenacted as chapter 37 of Title 40, 40 U.S.C.A. § 3701 et seq., by Pub.L. 107–217, §§ 1, 6(b), Aug. 21, 2002, 116 Stat. 1062, 1304.

Effective and Applicability Provisions

1992 Acts. Amendment by Title IX of Pub.L. 102–572 effective Oct. 29, 1992, see section 911 of Pub.L. 102–572, set out as a note under section 171 of Title 28, Judiciary and Judicial Procedure.

1982 Acts. Amendment by Pub.L. 97–164 effective Oct. 1, 1982, see section 402 of Pub.L. 97–164, set out as a note under section 171 of this title.

1962 Acts. Amendment of section by Pub.L. 87–581 effective 60 days after Aug. 13, 1962, but shall not affect contracts existing or thereafter entered into pursuant to invitations for bids outstanding on Aug. 13, 1962, see section 204 of Pub.L. 87–581, set out as a note under section 327 of former Title 40, Public Buildings, Property and Works.

Continued Jurisdiction Upon Claims Under Section 324 of Title 40

Pub.L. 87–581, Title II, § 202(a), Aug. 13, 1962, 76 Stat. 360 provided that: "The Court of Claims [now Court of Federal Claims] shall continue to have jurisdiction to render judgment upon any claim for a penalty withheld from a contractor or subcontractor under section 324 of title 40, United States Code [repealed], in connection with any contract subject to said section existing on the effective date of this Act [60 days after Aug. 13, 1962; see Pub.L. 87–581, Title II, § 204, Aug. 13, 1962, 76 Stat. 360, repealed Pub.L. 107–217, § 6(b), Aug. 21, 2002, 116 Stat. 1316], or thereafter entered into pursuant to invitations for bids that are outstanding at the time of the enactment of this Act [Aug. 13, 1962]."

§ 1500. Pendency of claims in other courts

The United States Court of Federal Claims shall not have jurisdiction of any claim for or in respect to which the plaintiff or his assignee has pending in any other court any suit or process against the United States or any person who, at the time when the cause of action alleged in such suit or process arose, was, in respect thereto, acting or professing to act, directly or indirectly under the authority of the United States.

(June 25, 1948, c. 646, 62 Stat. 942; Apr. 2, 1982, Pub.L. 97–164, Title I, § 133(e) (1), 96 Stat. 40; Oct. 29, 1992, Pub.L. 102–572, Title IX, § 902(a)(1), 106 Stat. 4516.)

HISTORICAL AND STATUTORY NOTES

Effective and Applicability Provisions

1992 Acts. Amendment by Title IX of Pub.L. 102–572 effective Oct. 29, 1992, see section 911 of Pub.L. 102–572 , set out as a note under section 171 of this title.

1982 Acts. Amendment by Pub.L. 97–164 effective Oct. 1, 1982, see section 402 of Pub.L. 97–164, set out as a note under section 171 of this title.

§ 1501. Pensions

The United States Court of Federal Claims shall not have jurisdiction of any claim for a pension.

(June 25, 1948, c. 646, 62 Stat. 942; Apr. 2, 1982, Pub.L. 97–164, Title I, § 133(e) (1), 96 Stat. 40; Oct. 29, 1992, Pub.L. 102–572, Title IX, § 902(a)(1), 106 Stat. 4516.)

HISTORICAL AND STATUTORY NOTES
Effective and Applicability Provisions

1992 Acts. Amendment by Title IX of Pub.L. 102–572 effective Oct. 29, 1992, see section 911 of Pub.L. 102–572, set out as a note under section 171 of this title.

1982 Acts. Amendment by Pub.L. 97–164 effective Oct. 1, 1982, see section 402 of Pub.L. 97–164, set out as a note under section 171 of this title.

§ 1502.   Treaty cases

Except as otherwise provided by Act of Congress, the United States Court of Federal Claims shall not have jurisdiction of any claim against the United States growing out of or dependent upon any treaty entered into with foreign nations.

(June 25, 1948, c. 646, 62 Stat. 942; May 24, 1949, c. 139, § 88, 63 Stat. 102; Apr. 2, 1982, Pub.L. 97–164, Title I, § 133(e) (1), 96 Stat. 40; Oct. 29, 1992, Pub.L. 102–572, Title IX, § 902(a)(1), 106 Stat. 4516.)

HISTORICAL AND STATUTORY NOTES
Effective and Applicability Provisions

1992 Acts. Amendment by Title IX of Pub.L. 102–572 effective Oct. 29, 1992, see section 911 of Pub.L. 102–572, set out as a note under section 171 of this title.

1982 Acts. Amendment by Pub.L. 97–164 effective Oct. 1, 1982, see section 402 of Pub.L. 97–164, set out as a note under section 171 of this title.

§ 1503.   Set-offs

The United States Court of Federal Claims shall have jurisdiction to render judgment upon any set-off or demand by the United States against any plaintiff in such court.

(June 25, 1948, c. 646, 62 Stat. 942; Apr. 2, 1982, Pub.L. 97–164, Title I, § 133(e) (1), 96 Stat. 40; Oct. 29, 1992, Pub.L. 102–572, Title IX, § 902(a)(1), 106 Stat. 4516.)

HISTORICAL AND STATUTORY NOTES
Effective and Applicability Provisions

1992 Acts. Amendment by Title IX of Pub.L. 102–572 effective Oct. 29, 1992, see section 911 of Pub.L. 102–572, set out as a note under section 171 of this title.

1982 Acts. Amendment by Pub.L. 97–164 effective Oct. 1, 1982, see section 402 of Pub.L. 97–164, set out as a note under section 171 of this title.

[§ 1504.   Repealed.   Pub.L. 97–164, Title I, § 133(f), Apr. 2, 1982, 96 Stat. 41]

HISTORICAL AND STATUTORY NOTES

Section, Act June 25, 1948, c. 646, 62 Stat. 942, directed that the Court of Claims [now Court of Federal Claims] have jurisdiction to review by appeal final judgments in the district courts in civil actions based on tort claims brought under section 1346(b) of this title if the notice of appeal filed in the district court had affixed to it a written consent on behalf of the appellees that the appeal be taken to the Court of Claims.

Effective Date of Repeal

Repeal effective Oct. 1, 1982, see section 402 of Pub.L. 97–164, set out as an Effective and Applicability Provisions of 1982 Amendments note under section 171 of this title.

§ 1505.   Indian claims

The United States Court of Federal Claims shall have jurisdiction of any claim against the United States accruing after August 13, 1946, in favor of any tribe, band, or other identifiable group of American Indians residing within the territorial limits of the United States or Alaska whenever such claim is one arising under the Constitution, laws or treaties of the United States, or Executive orders of the President, or is one which otherwise would be cognizable in the Court of Federal Claims if the claimant were not an Indian tribe, band or group.

(Added May 24, 1949, c. 139, § 89(a), 63 Stat. 102, and amended Apr. 2, 1982, Pub.L. 97–164, Title I, § 133(g), 96 Stat. 41; Oct. 29, 1992, Pub.L. 102–572, Title IX, § 902(a), 106 Stat. 4516.)

HISTORICAL AND STATUTORY NOTES
Effective and Applicability Provisions

1992 Acts. Amendment by Title IX of Pub.L. 102–572 effective Oct. 29, 1992, see section 911 of Pub.L. 102–572, set out as a note under section 171 of this title.

1982 Acts. Amendment by Pub.L. 97–164 effective Oct. 1, 1982, see section 402 of Pub.L. 97–164, set out as a note under section 171 of this title.

[§ 1506.   Repealed.   Pub.L. 97–164, Title I, § 133(h), Apr. 2, 1982, 96 Stat. 41]

HISTORICAL AND STATUTORY NOTES

Section, added Pub.L. 86–770, § 2(a), Sept. 13, 1960, 74 Stat. 912, provided that if a case within the exclusive jurisdiction of the district courts was filed in the Court of Claims [now Court of Federal Claims], the Court of Claims, if it were in the interest of justice, had to transfer such case to any district court in which it could have been brought at the time such case was filed, where the case would proceed as if it had been filed in the district court on the date it was filed in the Court of Claims.

Effective Date of Repeal

Repeal effective Oct. 1, 1982, see section 402 of Pub.L. 97–164, set out as a note under section 171 of this title.

§ 1507.   Jurisdiction for certain declaratory judgments

The United States Court of Federal Claims shall have jurisdiction to hear any suit for and issue a declaratory judgment under section 7428 of the Internal Revenue Code of 1986.

(Added Pub.L. 94–455, Title XIII, § 1306(b)(9)(A), Oct. 4, 1976, 90 Stat. 1720, and amended Pub.L. 97–164, Title I,

§ 133(i), Apr. 2, 1982, 96 Stat. 41; Pub.L. 99–514, § 2, Oct. 22, 1986, 100 Stat. 2095; Pub.L. 102–572, Title IX, § 902(a)(1), Oct. 29, 1992, 106 Stat. 4516.)

HISTORICAL AND STATUTORY NOTES

References in Text

Section 7428 of the Internal Revenue Code of 1986, referred to in text, is classified to section 7428 of Title 26, Internal Revenue Code.

Effective and Applicability Provisions

1992 Acts. Amendment by Title IX of Pub.L. 102–572 effective Oct. 29, 1992, see section 911 of Pub.L. 102–572, set out as a note under section 171 of this title.

1982 Acts. Amendment by Pub.L. 97–164 effective Oct. 1, 1982, see section 402 of Pub.L. 97–164, set out as a note under section 171 of this title.

1976 Acts. Section applicable with respect to pleadings filed with the United States Tax Court, the district court of the United States for the District of Columbia, or the United States Court of Claims more than 6 months after Oct. 4, 1976, but only with respect to determinations (or requests for determinations) made after Jan. 1, 1976, see section 1306(c) of Pub.L. 94–455, set out as a note under section 7428 of Title 26, Internal Revenue Code.

§ 1508.   Jurisdiction for certain partnership proceedings

The Court of Federal Claims shall have jurisdiction to hear and to render judgment upon any petition under section 6226 or 6228(a) of the Internal Revenue Code of 1986.

(Added Pub.L. 97–248, Title IV, § 402(c)(18)(A), Sept. 3, 1982, 96 Stat. 669, and amended Pub.L. 99–514, § 2, Oct. 22, 1986, 100 Stat. 2095; Pub.L. 102–572, Title IX, § 902(a)(2), Oct. 29, 1992, 106 Stat. 4516.)

HISTORICAL AND STATUTORY NOTES

References in Text

Sections 6226 and 6228(a) of the Internal Revenue Code of 1986, referred to in text, are classified to sections 6226 and 6228(a) of Title 26, Internal Revenue Code.

Effective and Applicability Provisions

1992 Acts. Amendment by Title IX of Pub.L. 102–572 effective Oct. 29, 1992, see section 911 of Pub.L. 102–572, set out as a note under section 171 of this title.

1982 Acts. Section applicable to partnership taxable years beginning after Sept. 3, 1982, with provision for the applicability of this section to any partnership taxable year ending after Sept. 3, 1982, if the partnership, each partner, and each indirect partner requests such application and the Secretary of the Treasury or his delegate consents to such application, see section 407(a)(1) and (3) of Pub.L. 97–248, set out as a note under section 6221 of Title 26, Internal Revenue Code.

§ 1509.   No jurisdiction in cases involving refunds of tax shelter promoter and understatement penalties

The United States Court of Federal Claims shall not have jurisdiction to hear any action or proceeding for any refund or credit of any penalty imposed under section 6700 of the Internal Revenue Code of 1986 (relating to penalty for promoting abusive tax shelters, etc.) or section 6701 of such Code (relating to penalties for aiding and abetting understatement of tax liability).

(Added Pub.L. 98–369, Div. A, Title VII, § 714(g)(2), July 18, 1984, 98 Stat. 962, and amended Pub.L. 99–514, § 2, Oct. 22, 1986, 100 Stat. 2095; Pub.L. 102–572, Title IX, § 902(a)(1), Oct. 29, 1992, 106 Stat. 4516.)

HISTORICAL AND STATUTORY NOTES

References in Text

Sections 6700 and 6701 of the Internal Revenue Code of 1986, referred to in text, are classified to sections 6700 and 6701, respectively, of Title 26, Internal Revenue Code.

Effective and Applicability Provisions

1992 Acts. Amendment by Title IX of Pub.L. 102–572 effective Oct. 29, 1992, see section 911 of Pub.L. 102–572, set out as a note under section 171 of this title.

1984 Acts. Section 714(g)(4) of Pub.L. 98–369 provided that: "The amendments made by this subsection [enacting this section and amending section 7422 of Title 26, Internal Revenue Code] shall apply to any claim for refund or credit filed after the date of the enactment of this Act [July 18, 1984]."

[CHAPTER 93—REPEALED]

[§§ 1541 to 1546.   Repealed. Pub.L. 97–164, Title I, § 134, Apr. 2, 1982, 96 Stat. 41]

HISTORICAL AND STATUTORY NOTES

Section 1541, Acts June 25, 1948, c. 646, 62 Stat. 942; June 2, 1970, Pub.L. 91–271, Title I, § 102, 84 Stat. 274; July 26, 1979, Pub.L. 96–39, Title X, § 1001(b)(4)(A), 93 Stat. 305; Oct. 10, 1980, Pub.L. 96–417, Title IV, § 401(a), Title V, § 501(23), (24), 94 Stat. 1740, 1742, gave the Court of Customs and Patent Appeals exclusive jurisdiction of appeals from all final decisions of the Court of International Trade and from interlocutory orders of the Court of International Trade granting, continuing, modifying, refusing, or dissolving injunctions, or refusing to dissolve or modify injunctions, and with discretion to entertain appeals from certain orders of the Court of International Trade. See section 1295(a)(5) of this title.

Section 1542, Acts June 25, 1948, c. 646, 62 Stat. 942; May 24, 1949, c. 139, § 89(b), 63 Stat. 102, gave the Court of Customs and Patent Appeals jurisdiction of appeals from decisions of the Board of Appeals and the Board of Interference Examiners of the Patent Office as to patent applications and interferences, at the instance of an applicant for a patent or any party to a patent interference, with such appeal by an applicant to waive his right to proceed under section 63 of

Title 35, and the Commissioner of Patents as to trade-mark applications and proceedings as provided in section 1071 of Title 15. See section 1295(a) (4) of this title.

Section 1543, Acts June 25, 1948, c. 646, 62 Stat. 943; Oct. 10, 1980, Pub.L. 96–417, Title IV, § 401(b) (1), 94 Stat. 1740, gave the Court of Customs and Patent Appeals jurisdiction to review final determinations of the United States International Trade Commission made under section 337 of the Tariff Act of 1930 relating to unfair trade practices in import trade. See section 1295(a) (6) of this title.

Section 1544, added Pub.L. 89–651, § 8(c) (1), Oct. 14, 1966, 80 Stat. 901, gave the Court of Customs and Patent Appeals jurisdiction to review, by appeal on questions of law only, findings of the Secretary of Commerce under headnote 6 to schedule 8, part 4, of the Tariff Schedules of the United

States (relating to importation of instruments or apparatus). See section 1295(a) (7) of this title.

Section 1545, added Pub.L. 91–577, Title III, § 143(a), Dec. 24, 1970, 84 Stat. 1558, gave the Court of Customs and Patent Appeals nonexclusive jurisdiction of appeals under section 71 of the Plant Variety Protection Act, classified to section 2461 of Title 7, Agriculture. See section 1295(a) (8) of this title.

Section 1546, added Pub.L. 96–417, Title IV, § 402(a), Oct. 10, 1980, 94 Stat. 1740, gave the Court of Customs and Patent Appeals all of the powers in law and in equity of, or conferred by statute upon, a court of appeals of the United States.

Effective Date of Repeal

Repeal effective Oct. 1, 1982, see section 402 of Pub.L. 97–164, set out as a note under section 171 of this title.

CHAPTER 95—COURT OF INTERNATIONAL TRADE

HISTORICAL AND STATUTORY NOTES

Prior Provisions

A prior Chapter 95—Customs Court, comprising sections 1581 and 1582, was omitted from the Code upon the general revision of this chapter by Pub.L. 96–417, Title II, § 201, Oct. 10, 1980, 94 Stat. 1728.

§ 1581. Civil actions against the United States and agencies and officers thereof

(a) The Court of International Trade shall have exclusive jurisdiction of any civil action commenced to contest the denial of a protest, in whole or in part, under section 515 of the Tariff Act of 1930.

(b) The Court of International Trade shall have exclusive jurisdiction of any civil action commenced under section 516 of the Tariff Act of 1930.

(c) The Court of International Trade shall have exclusive jurisdiction of any civil action commenced under section 516A of the Tariff Act of 1930.

(d) The Court of International Trade shall have exclusive jurisdiction of any civil action commenced to review—

(1) any final determination of the Secretary of Labor under section 223 of the Trade Act of 1974 with respect to the eligibility of workers for adjustment assistance under such Act;

(2) any final determination of the Secretary of Commerce under section 251 of the Trade Act of

1974 with respect to the eligibility of a firm for adjustment assistance under such Act; and

(3) any final determination of the Secretary of Commerce under section 271 of the Trade Act of 1974 with respect to the eligibility of a community for adjustment assistance under such Act.

(e) The Court of International Trade shall have exclusive jurisdiction of any civil action commenced to review any final determination of the Secretary of the Treasury under section 305(b)(1) of the Trade Agreements Act of 1979.

(f) The Court of International Trade shall have exclusive jurisdiction of any civil action involving an application for an order directing the administering authority or the International Trade Commission to make confidential information available under section 777(c)(2) of the Tariff Act of 1930.

(g) The Court of International Trade shall have exclusive jurisdiction of any civil action commenced to review—

(1) any decision of the Secretary of the Treasury to deny a customs broker's license under section 641(b)(2) or (3) of the Tariff Act of 1930, or to deny a customs broker's permit under section 641(c)(1) of such Act, or to revoke a license or permit under section 641(b)(5) or (c)(2) of such Act;

(2) any decision of the Secretary of the Treasury to revoke or suspend a customs broker's license or permit, or impose a monetary penalty in lieu thereof, under section 641(d)(2)(B) of the Tariff Act of 1930; and

(3) any decision or order of the Customs Service to deny, suspend, or revoke accreditation of a private laboratory under section 499(b) of the Tariff Act of 1930.

(h) The Court of International Trade shall have exclusive jurisdiction of any civil action commenced to review, prior to the importation of the goods involved, a ruling issued by the Secretary of the Treasury, or a refusal to issue or change such a ruling, relating to classification, valuation, rate of duty, marking, restricted merchandise, entry requirements, drawbacks, vessel repairs, or similar matters, but only if the party commencing the civil action demonstrates to the court that he would be irreparably harmed unless given an opportunity to obtain judicial review prior to such importation.

(i) In addition to the jurisdiction conferred upon the Court of International Trade by subsections (a)–(h) of this section and subject to the exception set forth in subsection (j) of this section, the Court of International Trade shall have exclusive jurisdiction of any civil action commenced against the United States, its agencies, or its officers, that arises out of any law of the United States providing for—

(1) revenue from imports or tonnage;

(2) tariffs, duties, fees, or other taxes on the importation of merchandise for reasons other than the raising of revenue;

(3) embargoes or other quantitative restrictions on the importation of merchandise for reasons other than the protection of the public health or safety; or

(4) administration and enforcement with respect to the matters referred to in paragraphs (1)–(3) of this subsection and subsections (a)–(h) of this section.

This subsection shall not confer jurisdiction over an antidumping or countervailing duty determination which is reviewable either by the Court of International Trade under section 516A(a) of the Tariff Act of 1930 or by a binational panel under article 1904 of the North American Free Trade Agreement or the United States–Canada Free–Trade Agreement and section 516A(g) of the Tariff Act of 1930.

(j) The Court of International Trade shall not have jurisdiction of any civil action arising under section 305 of the Tariff Act of 1930.

(Added Pub.L. 96–417, Title II, § 201, Oct. 10, 1980, 94 Stat. 1728, and amended Pub.L. 98–573, Title II, § 212(b)(1), Oct. 30, 1984, 98 Stat. 2983; Pub.L. 99–514, Title XVIII, § 1891(1), Oct. 22, 1986, 100 Stat. 2926; Pub.L. 100–449, Title IV, § 402(a), Sept. 28, 1988, 102 Stat. 1883; Pub.L. 103–182, Title IV, § 414(a)(1), Title VI, § 684(a)(1), Dec. 8, 1993, 107 Stat. 2147, 2219.)

Termination of Amendments

For provisions directing that, except for transition provisions relating to proceedings regarding protective orders and undertakings, and binational panel and extraordinary challenge committee reviews, the *amendment to this section by Title IV of Pub.L. 103–182 shall cease to have effect with respect to any country on the date on which such country ceases to be a NAFTA country, see 19 U.S.C.A. § 3451.*

Termination of United States–Canada Free–Trade Agreement

For provisions directing that the amendments made by Pub.L. 100–449, which amended this section, shall cease to have effect on the date on which the United States–Canada Free–Trade Agreement ceases to be in force, see section 501(c) of Pub.L. 100–449, set out in the note under 19 U.S.C.A. § 2112.

Articles 1906 and 2106 of the Agreement authorize either the United States or Canada to terminate the Agreement on 6–month notice if, at the end of the 7–year period following the date of the entry into effect of the Agreement, no agreement has been entered into between the United States and Canada on a substitute system of antidumping and countervailing duties.

HISTORICAL AND STATUTORY NOTES
References in Text

Sections 515 and 516 of the Tariff Act of 1930, referred to in subsecs. (a) and (b), respectively, are classified, respectively, to sections 1515 and 1516 of Title 19, Customs Duties.

The Trade Act of 1974, referred to in subsec. (d)(1) to (3), is Pub.L. 93–618, Jan. 3, 1975, 88 Stat.1978, as amended, which is classified principally to chapter 12 (section 2101 et seq.) of Title 19. Sections 223, 251, and 271 of the Trade Act of 1974 are classified to sections 2273, 2341, and 2371, respectively, of Title 19. For complete classification of this Act to the Code, see References in Text note set out under section 2101 of Title 19 and Tables.

Section 305(b)(1) of the Trade Agreements Act of 1979, referred to in subsec. (e), is classified to section 2515(b)(1) of Title 19, Customs Duties.

Sections 777(c)(2), 641(b), (c), (d), and 305 of the Tariff Act of 1930, referred to in subsecs. (f), (g), and (j), are classified to sections 1677f(c)(2), 1641, (b), (c), (d), and 1305, respectively, of Title 19, Customs Duties.

Section 499(b) of the Tariff Act of 1930, referred to in subsec. (g)(3), is classified to section 1499(b) of Title 19, Customs Duties.

Section 516A of the Tariff Act of 1930, referred to in subsec. (i), is classified to section 1516a of Title 19.

The United States–Canada Free–Trade Agreement, referred to in subsec. (i), was entered into on Jan. 2, 1988. The Agreement is not set out in the Code.

Effective and Applicability Provisions

1993 Acts. Amendment by section 414 of Pub.L. 103–182 effective on the date the North American Free Trade Agreement enters into force with respect to the United States [Jan. 1, 1994], but not to apply to any final determination described in section 1516a(a)(1)(B) or (2)(B)(i), (ii), or (iii) of Title 19, Customs Duties, notice of which is published in the Federal Register before such date, or to a determination described in section 1516a(a)(2)(B)(vi) of Title 19 notice of which is received by the Government of Canada or Mexico before such date, or to any binational panel review under the United States–Canada Free–Trade Agreement, or to any extraordinary challenge arising out of any such review that was commenced before such date, see section 416 of Pub.L. 103–182, set out as a note under section 3431 of Title 19.

Amendment by section 684(a)(1) of Pub.L. 103–182 effective Dec. 8, 1993, see section 692 of Pub.L. 103–182, set out as a note under section 58c of Title 19, Customs Duties.

1988 Acts. Amendment by Pub.L. 100–449 effective on the date the United States–Canada Free–Trade Agreement enters into force, (Jan. 1, 1989), and to cease to have effect on the date the Agreement ceases to be in force, see section 501(a), (c) of Pub.L. 100–449, set out in a note under section 2112 of Title 19, Customs Duties. [A Presidential Memorandum on the Canada–United States Free–Trade Agreement, dated Dec. 31, 1988, directing the Secretary of State to exchange notes with the Government of Canada to provide for the entry into force of the Agreement on Jan. 1, 1989, is set out in 24 Weekly Compilation of Presidential Documents 1688, Jan. 2, 1989.]

1984 Acts. Amendment by Pub.L. 98–573 to take effect on the close of the 180th day after Oct. 30, 1984, see section 214(d) of Pub.L. 98–573, set out as a note under section 1304 of Title 19, Customs Duties.

1980 Acts. Section effective on Nov. 1, 1980, and applicable with respect to civil actions pending on or commenced on or after such date, see section 701(a) of Pub.L. 96–417, as amended, set out as a note under section 251 of this title.

Subsecs. (d) and (g) to (i) of this section applicable with respect to civil actions commenced on or after Nov. 1, 1980, see section 701(b)(1)(A) of Pub.L. 96–417, as amended, set out as a note under section 251 of this title.

Transfer of Functions

For transfer of the functions, personnel, assets, and liabilities of the United States Customs Service of the Department of the Treasury, including the functions of the Secretary of the Treasury relating thereto, to the Secretary of Homeland Security, and for treatment of related references, see 6 U.S.C.A. §§ 203(1), 551(d), 552(d) and 557, and the Department of Homeland Security Reorganization Plan of November 25, 2002, as modified, set out as a note under 6 U.S.C.A. § 542.

Prior Provisions

A prior section 1581, Act June 25, 1948, c. 646, 62 Stat. 943, related to powers of the Customs Court generally and was omitted in the general revision of this chapter by Pub.L. 96–417. See section 1585 of this title.

Application of Amendments Relating to Accreditation of Private Laboratories

Section 684(b) of Pub.L. 103–182 provided that: "For purposes of applying the amendments made by subsection (a) [amending subsec. (g) of this section, and sections 2631, 2636, 2640 and 2642 of this title], any decision or order of the Customs Service denying, suspending, or revoking the accreditation of a private laboratory on or after the date of the enactment of this Act [Dec. 8, 1993] and before regulations to implement section 499(b) of the Tariff Act of 1930 [section 1499(b) of Title 19, Customs Duties] are issued shall be treated as having been denied, suspended, or revoked under such section 499(b)."

Prior History of Court

The United States Customs Court, the predecessor of the Court of International Trade, was omitted in the general revision of this chapter by Pub.L. 96–417.

The predecessor of the United States Customs Court was the Board of General Appraisers which was created by the Customs Administrative Act of June 10, 1890. The Board was under the administrative supervision of the Secretary of the Treasury.

From 1890 to 1926, the Board of General Appraisers had jurisdiction over all protests from decisions of the collectors of customs and appeals for reappraisement under sections 13 and 14 of the Customs Administrative Act of June 10, 1890, c. 407, 26 Stat. 136.

The Customs Court was established by Act May 28, 1926, c. 411, §§ 1, 2, 44 Stat. 669, sections 405a and 405b of Title 19, Customs Duties, and said act transferred to it all the jurisdiction and powers of the former Board of General Appraisers. The Tariff Act of June 1930, c. 497, Title IV, § 518, 46 Stat. 737, section 1518 of Title 19, continued the Customs Court as constituted on June 17, 1930 with, however, several important changes.

§ 1582. Civil actions commenced by the United States

The Court of International Trade shall have exclusive jurisdiction of any civil action which arises out of an import transaction and which is commenced by the United States—

    (1) to recover a civil penalty under section 592, 593A, 641(b)(6), 641(d)(2)(A), 704(i)(2), or 734(i)(2) of the Tariff Act of 1930;

    (2) to recover upon a bond relating to the importation of merchandise required by the laws of the United States or by the Secretary of the Treasury; or

    (3) to recover customs duties.

(Added Pub.L. 96–417, Title II, § 201, Oct. 10, 1980, 94 Stat. 1729, and amended Pub.L. 98–573, Title II, § 212(b)(2), Oct. 30, 1984, 98 Stat. 2983; Pub.L. 99–514, Title XVIII, § 1891(2), Oct. 22, 1986, 100 Stat. 2926; Pub.L. 103–182, Title VI, § 684(c), Dec. 8, 1993, 107 Stat. 2219.)

HISTORICAL AND STATUTORY NOTES

References in Text

Sections 592, 593A, 641(b)(2), 641(d)(2)(A), 704(i)(2), and 734(i)(2) of the Tariff Act of 1930, referred to in par. (1), are classified to sections 1592, 1593a, 1641(b)(6), 1641(d)(2)(A), 1671c(i)(2), and 1673c(i)(2) of Title 19, Customs Duties.

Effective and Applicability Provisions

1993 Acts. Amendment by section 684(c) of Pub.L. 103–182 effective Dec. 8, 1993, see section 692 of Pub.L. 103–182, set out as a note under section 58c of Title 19, Customs Duties.

1984 Acts. Amendment by Pub.L. 98–573 to take effect on the close of the 180th day after Oct. 30, 1984, see section

214(d) of Pub.L. 98–573, set out as a note under section 1304 of Title 19, Customs Duties.

1980 Acts. Section applicable with respect to civil actions commenced on or after the 90th day after Nov. 1, 1980, see section 701(c)(1)(A) of Pub.L. 96–417, as amended, set out as a note under section 251 of this title.

Prior Provisions

A prior section 1582, Acts June 25, 1948, c. 646, 62 Stat. 943; June 2, 1970, Pub.L. 91–271, Title I, § 110, 84 Stat. 278; July 26, 1979, Pub.L. 96–39, Title X, § 1001(b)(4)(B), 93 Stat. 305, related to the jurisdiction of the Customs Court and was omitted in the general revision of this chapter by Pub.L. 96–417.

§ 1583. Counterclaims, cross-claims, and third-party actions

In any civil action in the Court of International Trade, the court shall have exclusive jurisdiction to render judgment upon any counterclaim, cross-claim, or third-party action of any party, if (1) such claim or action involves the imported merchandise that is the subject matter of such civil action, or (2) such claim or action is to recover upon a bond or customs duties relating to such merchandise.

(Added Pub.L. 96–417, Title II, § 201, Oct. 10, 1980, 94 Stat. 1729.)

HISTORICAL AND STATUTORY NOTES

Effective and Applicability Provisions

1980 Acts. Section applicable with respect to civil actions commenced on or after Nov. 1, 1980, see section 701(b)(1)(A) of Pub.L. 96–417, as amended, set out as a note under section 251 of this title.

Prior Provisions

A prior section 1583, Act June 25, 1948, c. 646, 62 Stat. 943, related to certain cases of exclusive jurisdiction of the Customs Court and was repealed by Pub.L. 91–271, Title I, § 111, June 2, 1970, 84 Stat. 278.

§ 1584. Civil actions under the North American Free Trade Agreement or the United States–Canada Free–Trade Agreement

The United States Court of International Trade shall have exclusive jurisdiction of any civil action which arises under section 777(f) of the Tariff Act of 1930 and is commenced by the United States to enforce administrative sanctions levied for violation of a protective order or an undertaking.

(Added Pub.L. 100–449, Title IV, § 402(d)(1), Sept. 28, 1988, 102 Stat. 1884, and amended Pub.L. 103–182, Title IV, § 414(a)(2), Dec. 8, 1993, 107 Stat. 2147.)

Termination of Amendments

For provisions directing that, except for transition provisions relating to proceedings regarding protective orders and undertakings, and binational panel and extraordinary challenge committee reviews, the amendment to this section by Title IV of Pub.L. 103–182 shall cease to have effect with respect to any country on the date on which such country ceases to be a NAFTA country, see 19 U.S.C.A. § 3451.

Termination of United States–Canada Free–Trade Agreement

For provisions directing that the amendments made by Pub.L. 100–449, which enacted this section, shall cease to have effect on the date on which the United States–Canada Free–Trade Agreement ceases to be in force, see section 501(c) of Pub.L. 100–449, set out in the note under 19 U.S.C.A. § 2112.

Articles 1906 and 2106 of the Agreement authorize either the United States or Canada to terminate the Agreement on 6–month notice if, at the end of the 7–year period following the date of the entry into effect of the Agreement, no agreement has been entered into between the United States and Canada on a substitute system of antidumping and countervailing duties.

HISTORICAL AND STATUTORY NOTES

References in Text

Section 777(f) of the Tariff Act of 1930, referred to in text, is classified to section 1677f(f) of Title 19, Customs Duties.

Effective and Applicability Provisions

1993 Acts. Amendment by section 414 of Pub.L. 103–182 effective on the date the North American Free Trade Agreement enters into force with respect to the United States [Jan. 1, 1994], but not to apply to any final determination described in section 1516a(a)(1)(B) or (2)(B)(i), (ii), or (iii) of Title 19, Customs Duties, notice of which is published in the Federal Register before such date, or to a determination described in section 1516a(a)(2)(B)(vi) of Title 19 notice of which is received by the Government of Canada or Mexico before such date, or to any binational panel review under the United States-Canada Free-Trade Agreement, or to any extraordinary challenge arising out of any such review that was commenced before such date, see section 416 of Pub.L. 103–182, set out as a note under section 3431 of Title 19.

1988 Acts. Section effective on the date the United States–Canada Free–Trade Agreement enters into force (Jan. 1, 1989), and to cease to have effect on the date the Agreement ceases to be in force, see section 501(a), (c), of Pub.L. 100–449, set out in a note under section 2112 of Title 19, Customs Duties. [A Presidential Memorandum on the Canada–United States Free–Trade Agreement, dated Dec. 31, 1988, directing the Secretary of State to exchange notes with the Government of Canada to provide for the entry into force of the Agreement on Jan. 1, 1989, is set out in 24 Weekly Compilation of Presidential Documents 1688, Jan. 2, 1989.]

Prior Provisions

A prior section 1584, added Pub.L. 96–417, Title II, § 201, Oct. 10, 1980, 94 Stat. 1729, which provided that if a civil action within the exclusive jurisdiction of the Court of International Trade were commenced in a district court of the United States, the district court, in the interest of justice, would transfer such civil action to the Court of International

Trade, where such action proceeded as if it had been commenced in the Court of International Trade in the first instance, and that if a civil action within the exclusive jurisdiction of a district court, a court of appeals, or the Court of Customs and Patent Appeals were commenced in the Court of International Trade, the Court of International Trade, in the interest of justice, would transfer such civil action to the appropriate district court or court of appeals or to the Court of Customs and Patent Appeals where such action proceeded as if it had been commenced in such court in the first

instance, was repealed by Pub.L. 97–164, Title I, § 135, Apr. 2, 1982, 96 Stat. 41, eff. Oct. 1, 1982.

§ 1585.   Powers in law and equity

The Court of International Trade shall possess all the powers in law and equity of, or as conferred by statute upon, a district court of the United States. (Added Pub.L. 96–417, Title II, § 201, Oct. 10, 1980, 94 Stat. 1730.)

CHAPTER 97—JURISDICTIONAL IMMUNITIES OF FOREIGN STATES

§ 1602.   Findings and declaration of purpose

The Congress finds that the determination by United States courts of the claims of foreign states to immunity from the jurisdiction of such courts would serve the interests of justice and would protect the rights of both foreign states and litigants in United States courts. Under international law, states are not immune from the jurisdiction of foreign courts insofar as their commercial activities are concerned, and their commercial property may be levied upon for the satisfaction of judgments rendered against them in connection with their commercial activities. Claims of foreign states to immunity should henceforth be decided by courts of the United States and of the States in conformity with the principles set forth in this chapter. (Added Pub.L. 94–583, § 4(a), Oct. 21, 1976, 90 Stat. 2892.)

HISTORICAL AND STATUTORY NOTES

Effective and Applicability Provisions

   1976 Acts. Section 8 of Pub.L. 94–583 provided that: "This Act [enacting this chapter and section 1330 of this title, amending sections 1332, 1391, and 1441 of this title, and enacting provisions set out as notes under this section] shall take effect ninety days after the date of its enactment [Oct. 21, 1976]."

Separability of Provisions

   Section 7 of Pub.L. 94–583 provided that: "If any provision of this Act [enacting this chapter and section 1330 of this title, amending sections 1332, 1391, and 1441 of this title, and

enacting provisions set out as notes under this section and section 1 of this title] or the application thereof to any foreign state is held invalid, the invalidity does not affect other provisions or applications of the Act which can be given effect without the invalid provision or application, and to this end the provisions of this Act are severable."

Short Title

   1976 Acts. Authorization to cite Pub.L. 94–583, which enacted this chapter, as the "Foreign Sovereign Immunities Act of 1976", see section 1 of Pub.L. 94–583, set out as a note under section 1 of this title.

§ 1603.   Definitions

For purposes of this chapter—

   (a) A "foreign state", except as used in section 1608 of this title, includes a political subdivision of a foreign state or an agency or instrumentality of a foreign state as defined in subsection (b).

   (b) An "agency or instrumentality of a foreign state" means any entity—

     (1) which is a separate legal person, corporate or otherwise, and

     (2) which is an organ of a foreign state or political subdivision thereof, or a majority of whose shares or other ownership interest is owned by a foreign state or political subdivision thereof, and

     (3) which is neither a citizen of a State of the United States as defined in section 1332(c) and (e) of this title, nor created under the laws of any third country.

   (c) The "United States" includes all territory and waters, continental or insular, subject to the jurisdiction of the United States.

   (d) A "commercial activity" means either a regular course of commercial conduct or a particular commercial transaction or act. The commercial character of an activity shall be determined by reference to the nature of the course of conduct or particular transaction or act, rather than by reference to its purpose.

   (e) A "commercial activity carried on in the United States by a foreign state" means commercial

---

activity carried on by such state and having substantial contact with the United States.

(Added Pub.L. 94–583, § 4(a), Oct. 21, 1976, 90 Stat. 2892, and amended Pub.L. 109–2, § 4(b)(2), Feb. 18, 2005, 119 Stat. 12.)

HISTORICAL AND STATUTORY NOTES
Effective and Applicability Provisions

2005 Acts. Amendments by Class Action Fairness Act of 2005, Pub.L. 109–2, Feb. 18, 2005, 119 Stat. 4, applicable to any civil action commenced on or after Feb. 18, 2005, see Pub.L. 109–2, § 9, set out as a note under 28 U.S.C.A. § 1332.

1976 Acts. Section effective 90 days after Oct. 21, 1976, see section 8 of Pub.L. 94–583, set out as a note under section 1602 of this title.

§ 1604. Immunity of a foreign state from jurisdiction

Subject to existing international agreements to which the United States is a party at the time of enactment of this Act a foreign state shall be immune from the jurisdiction of the courts of the United States and of the States except as provided in sections 1605 to 1607 of this chapter.

(Added Pub.L. 94–583, § 4(a), Oct. 21, 1976, 90 Stat. 2892.)

HISTORICAL AND STATUTORY NOTES
References in Text

The time of enactment of this Act, referred to in text, probably means the time of enactment of Pub.L. 94–583, which was approved on Oct. 21, 1976.

Effective and Applicability Provisions

1976 Acts. Section effective 90 days after Oct. 21, 1976, see section 8 of Pub.L. 94–583, set out as a note under section 1602 of this title.

§ 1605. General exceptions to the jurisdictional immunity of a foreign state

(a) A foreign state shall not be immune from the jurisdiction of courts of the United States or of the States in any case—

(1) in which the foreign state has waived its immunity either explicitly or by implication, notwithstanding any withdrawal of the waiver which the foreign state may purport to effect except in accordance with the terms of the waiver;

(2) in which the action is based upon a commercial activity carried on in the United States by the foreign state; or upon an act performed in the United States in connection with a commercial activity of the foreign state elsewhere; or upon an act outside the territory of the United States in connection with a commercial activity of the foreign state elsewhere and that act causes a direct effect in the United States;

(3) in which rights in property taken in violation of international law are in issue and that property or any property exchanged for such property is present in the United States in connection with a commercial activity carried on in the United States by the foreign state; or that property or any property exchanged for such property is owned or operated by an agency or instrumentality of the foreign state and that agency or instrumentality is engaged in a commercial activity in the United States;

(4) in which rights in property in the United States acquired by succession or gift or rights in immovable property situated in the United States are in issue;

(5) not otherwise encompassed in paragraph (2) above, in which money damages are sought against a foreign state for personal injury or death, or damage to or loss of property, occurring in the United States and caused by the tortious act or omission of that foreign state or of any official or employee of that foreign state while acting within the scope of his office or employment; except this paragraph shall not apply to—

(A) any claim based upon the exercise or performance or the failure to exercise or perform a discretionary function regardless of whether the discretion be abused, or

(B) any claim arising out of malicious prosecution, abuse of process, libel, slander, misrepresentation, deceit, or interference with contract rights;

(6) in which the action is brought, either to enforce an agreement made by the foreign state with or for the benefit of a private party to submit to arbitration all or any differences which have arisen or which may arise between the parties with respect to a defined legal relationship, whether contractual or not, concerning a subject matter capable of settlement by arbitration under the laws of the United States, or to confirm an award made pursuant to such an agreement to arbitrate, if (A) the arbitration takes place or is intended to take place in the United States, (B) the agreement or award is or may be governed by a treaty or other international agreement in force for the United States calling for the recognition and enforcement of arbitral awards, (C) the underlying claim, save for the agreement to arbitrate, could have been brought in a United States court under this section or section 1607, or (D) paragraph (1) of this subsection is otherwise applicable; or

(7) not otherwise covered by paragraph (2), in which money damages are sought against a foreign state for personal injury or death that was caused by an act of torture, extrajudicial killing, aircraft sabotage, hostage taking, or the provision of material support or resources (as defined in section 2339A of title 18) for such an act if such act or provision of

material support is engaged in by an official, employee, or agent of such foreign state while acting within the scope of his or her office, employment, or agency, except that the court shall decline to hear a claim under this paragraph—

(A) if the foreign state was not designated as a state sponsor of terrorism under section 6(j) of the Export Administration Act of 1979 (50 U.S.C. App. 2405(j)) or section 620A of the Foreign Assistance Act of 1961 (22 U.S.C. 2371) at the time the act occurred, unless later so designated as a result of such act or the act is related to Case Number 1:00CV03110(EGS) in the United States District Court for the District of Columbia; and

(B) even if the foreign state is or was so designated, if—

(i) the act occurred in the foreign state against which the claim has been brought and the claimant has not afforded the foreign state a reasonable opportunity to arbitrate the claim in accordance with accepted international rules of arbitration; or

(ii) neither the claimant nor the victim was a national of the United States (as that term is defined in section 101(a)(22) of the Immigration and Nationality Act) when the act upon which the claim is based occurred.

(b) A foreign state shall not be immune from the jurisdiction of the courts of the United States in any case in which a suit in admiralty is brought to enforce a maritime lien against a vessel or cargo of the foreign state, which maritime lien is based upon a commercial activity of the foreign state: *Provided*, That—

(1) notice of the suit is given by delivery of a copy of the summons and of the complaint to the person, or his agent, having possession of the vessel or cargo against which the maritime lien is asserted; and if the vessel or cargo is arrested pursuant to process obtained on behalf of the party bringing the suit, the service of process of arrest shall be deemed to constitute valid delivery of such notice, but the party bringing the suit shall be liable for any damages sustained by the foreign state as a result of the arrest if the party bringing the suit had actual or constructive knowledge that the vessel or cargo of a foreign state was involved; and

(2) notice to the foreign state of the commencement of suit as provided in section 1608 of this title is initiated within ten days either of the delivery of notice as provided in paragraph (1) of this subsection or, in the case of a party who was unaware that the vessel or cargo of a foreign state was involved, of the date such party determined the existence of the foreign state's interest.

(c) Whenever notice is delivered under subsection (b)(1), the suit to enforce a maritime lien shall thereafter proceed and shall be heard and determined according to the principles of law and rules of practice of suits in rem whenever it appears that, had the vessel been privately owned and possessed, a suit in rem might have been maintained. A decree against the foreign state may include costs of the suit and, if the decree is for a money judgment, interest as ordered by the court, except that the court may not award judgment against the foreign state in an amount greater than the value of the vessel or cargo upon which the maritime lien arose. Such value shall be determined as of the time notice is served under subsection (b)(1). Decrees shall be subject to appeal and revision as provided in other cases of admiralty and maritime jurisdiction. Nothing shall preclude the plaintiff in any proper case from seeking relief in personam in the same action brought to enforce a maritime lien as provided in this section.

(d) A foreign state shall not be immune from the jurisdiction of the courts of the United States in any action brought to foreclose a preferred mortgage, as defined in the Ship Mortgage Act, 1920 (46 U.S.C. 911 and following). Such action shall be brought, heard, and determined in accordance with the provisions of that Act and in accordance with the principles of law and rules of practice of suits in rem, whenever it appears that had the vessel been privately owned and possessed a suit in rem might have been maintained.

(e) For purposes of paragraph (7) of subsection (a)—

(1) the terms "torture" and "extrajudicial killing" have the meaning given those terms in section 3 of the Torture Victim Protection Act of 1991;

(2) the term "hostage taking" has the meaning given that term in Article 1 of the International Convention Against the Taking of Hostages; and

(3) the term "aircraft sabotage" has the meaning given that term in Article 1 of the Convention for the Suppression of Unlawful Acts Against the Safety of Civil Aviation.

(f) No action shall be maintained under subsection (a)(7) unless the action is commenced not later than 10 years after the date on which the cause of action arose. All principles of equitable tolling, including the period during which the foreign state was immune from suit, shall apply in calculating this limitation period.

(g) **Limitation on discovery.—**

(1) **In general.—(A)** Subject to paragraph (2), if an action is filed that would otherwise be barred by section 1604, but for subsection (a)(7), the court, upon request of the Attorney General, shall stay any request, demand, or order for discovery on the

United States that the Attorney General certifies would significantly interfere with a criminal investigation or prosecution, or a national security operation, related to the incident that gave rise to the cause of action, until such time as the Attorney General advises the court that such request, demand, or order will no longer so interfere.

(B) A stay under this paragraph shall be in effect during the 12–month period beginning on the date on which the court issues the order to stay discovery. The court shall renew the order to stay discovery for additional 12–month periods upon motion by the United States if the Attorney General certifies that discovery would significantly interfere with a criminal investigation or prosecution, or a national security operation, related to the incident that gave rise to the cause of action.

(2) Sunset.—(A) Subject to subparagraph (B), no stay shall be granted or continued in effect under paragraph (1) after the date that is 10 years after the date on which the incident that gave rise to the cause of action occurred.

(B) After the period referred to in subparagraph (A), the court, upon request of the Attorney General, may stay any request, demand, or order for discovery on the United States that the court finds a substantial likelihood would—

(i) create a serious threat of death or serious bodily injury to any person;

(ii) adversely affect the ability of the United States to work in cooperation with foreign and international law enforcement agencies in investigating violations of United States law; or

(iii) obstruct the criminal case related to the incident that gave rise to the cause of action or undermine the potential for a conviction in such case.

(3) Evaluation of evidence.—The court's evaluation of any request for a stay under this subsection filed by the Attorney General shall be conducted ex parte and in camera.

(4) Bar on motions to dismiss.—A stay of discovery under this subsection shall constitute a bar to the granting of a motion to dismiss under rules 12(b)(6) and 56 of the Federal Rules of Civil Procedure.

(5) Construction.—Nothing in this subsection shall prevent the United States from seeking protective orders or asserting privileges ordinarily available to the United States.

(Added Pub.L. 94–583, § 4(a), Oct. 21, 1976, 90 Stat. 2892, and amended Pub.L. 100–640, § 1, Nov. 9, 1988, 102 Stat. 3333; Pub.L. 100–669, § 2, Nov. 16, 1988, 102 Stat. 3969; Pub.L. 101–650, Title III, § 325(b)(8), Dec. 1, 1990, 104 Stat. 5121; Pub.L. 104–132, Title II, § 221(a), Apr. 24, 1996, 110 Stat. 1241; Pub.L. 105–11, Apr. 25, 1997, 111 Stat. 22;

Pub.L. 107–77, Title VI, § 626(c), Nov. 28, 2001, 115 Stat. 803; Pub.L. 107–117, Div. B, Ch. 2, § 208, Jan. 10, 2002, 115 Stat. 2299.)

HISTORICAL AND STATUTORY NOTES

References in Text

Section 101(a)(22) of the Immigration and Nationality Act, referred to in subsec. (a)(7)(B)(ii), is classified to section 1101(a)(22) of Title 8, Aliens and Nationality.

The Ship Mortgage Act, 1920, referred to in subsec. (d), is section 30 of Act June 5, 1920, c. 250, 41 Stat. 1000, as amended, which was classified generally to chapter 25 (section 911 et seq.) of the Appendix to Title 46, Shipping, and was repealed by Pub.L. 100–710, Title I, § 106(b)(2), Nov. 23, 1988, 102 Stat. 4752, and reenacted by section 102(c) thereof as chapters 301 and 313 of Title 46, Shipping.

Section 3 of the Torture Victim Protection Act of 1991, referred to in subsec. (e)(1), is section 3 of Pub.L. 102–256, Mar. 12, 1992, 106 Stat. 73, set out in a note under section 1350 of this title.

Effective and Applicability Provisions

1997 Acts. Section 1 of Pub.L. 105–11 provided in part that the amendment of subsec. (a)(7)(B)(ii) by Pub.L. 105–11 is effective with respect to any cause of action arising before, on, or after April 25, 1997.

1996 Acts. Section 221(c) of Pub.L. 104–132 provided that: "The amendments made by this subtitle [amending this section and section 1610 of this title] shall apply to any cause of action arising before, on, or after the date of the enactment of this Act [Apr. 24, 1996]."

1988 Acts. Section 3 of Pub.L. 100–640 provided that: "The amendments made by this Act [amending this section and section 1610 of this title] shall apply to actions commenced on or after the date of the enactment of this Act [Nov. 9, 1988]."

1976 Acts. Section effective 90 days after Oct. 21, 1976, see section 8 of Pub.L. 94–583, set out as a note under section 1602 of this title.

Civil Liability for Acts of State Sponsored Terrorism

Pub.L. 104–208, Div. A, Title I, § 101(c) [Title V, § 589], Sept. 30, 1996, 110 Stat. 3009–172, provided that:

"**(a)** An official, employee, or agent of a foreign state designated as a state sponsor of terrorism designated under section 6(j) of the Export Administration Act of 1979 [section 2405(j) of the Appendix to Title 50, War and National Defense] while acting within the scope of his or her office, employment, or agency shall be liable to a United States national or the national's legal representative for personal injury or death caused by acts of that official, employee, or agent for which the courts of the United States may maintain jurisdiction under section 1605(a)(7) of title 28, United States Code [subsec. (a)(7) of this section] for money damages which may include economic damages, solatium, pain, and suffering, and punitive damages if the acts were among those described in section 1605(a)(7) [subsec. (a)(7) of this section].

"**(b)** Provisions related to statute of limitations and limitations on discovery that would apply to an action brought under 28 U.S.C. 1605(f) and (g) [subsecs. (f) and (g) of this section] shall also apply to actions brought under this section.

No action shall be maintained under this action [SIC] if an official, employee, or agent of the United States, while acting within the scope of his or her office, employment, or agency would not be liable for such acts if carried out within the United States."

§ 1606.   Extent of liability

As to any claim for relief with respect to which a foreign state is not entitled to immunity under section 1605 or 1607 of this chapter, the foreign state shall be liable in the same manner and to the same extent as a private individual under like circumstances; but a foreign state except for an agency or instrumentality thereof shall not be liable for punitive damages; if, however, in any case wherein death was caused, the law of the place where the action or omission occurred provides, or has been construed to provide, for damages only punitive in nature, the foreign state shall be liable for actual or compensatory damages measured by the pecuniary injuries resulting from such death which were incurred by the persons for whose benefit the action was brought.
(Added Pub.L. 94–583, § 4(a), Oct. 21, 1976, 90 Stat. 2894, and amended Pub.L. 105–277, Div. A, § 101(h) [Title I, § 117(b)], Oct. 21, 1998, 112 Stat. 2681–491; Pub.L. 106–386, Div. C, § 2002(f)(2), Oct. 28, 2000, 114 Stat. 1543; Pub.L. 107–297, Title II, § 201(c)(3), Nov. 26, 2002, 116 Stat. 2337.)

HISTORICAL AND STATUTORY NOTES
Effective and Applicability Provisions
1998 Acts. Amendment by section 117(b) of Pub.L. 105–277 to apply to any claim for which a foreign state is not immune under section 1605(a)(7) of this title arising before, on, or after Oct. 21, 1998, see Pub.L. 105–277, Div. A, § 101(h) [Title I, § 117(c)], set out as a note under section 1610 of this title.
1976 Acts. Section effective 90 days after Oct. 21, 1976, see section 8 of Pub.L. 94–583, set out as a note under section 1602 of this title.

Waiver of Exception to Immunity from Attachment or Execution
Provisions formerly authorizing the President to waive the requirements of section 117(b) of Pub.L. 105–277 [Div. A, § 101(h), Title I], (which amended this section) in the interest of national security, set out in Pub.L. 105–277, Div. A, § 101(h) [Title I, § 117(d)], Oct. 21, 1998, 112 Stat. 2681–491, which formerly appeared as a note under section 1610 of this title, were repealed by Pub.L. 106–386, Div. C, § 2002(f)(2), Oct. 28, 2000, 114 Stat. 1543.

§ 1607.   Counterclaims

In any action brought by a foreign state, or in which a foreign state intervenes, in a court of the United States or of a State, the foreign state shall not be accorded immunity with respect to any counterclaim—

    (a) for which a foreign state would not be entitled to immunity under section 1605 of this chapter had such claim been brought in a separate action against the foreign state; or

    (b) arising out of the transaction or occurrence that is the subject matter of the claim of the foreign state; or

    (c) to the extent that the counterclaim does not seek relief exceeding in amount or differing in kind from that sought by the foreign state.
(Added Pub.L. 94–583, § 4(a), Oct. 21, 1976, 90 Stat. 2894.)

HISTORICAL AND STATUTORY NOTES
Effective and Applicability Provisions
1976 Acts. Section effective 90 days after Oct. 21, 1976, see section 8 of Pub.L. 94–583, set out as a note under section 1602 of this title.

§ 1608.   Service; time to answer; default

(a) Service in the courts of the United States and of the States shall be made upon a foreign state or political subdivision of a foreign state:

    (1) by delivery of a copy of the summons and complaint in accordance with any special arrangement for service between the plaintiff and the foreign state or political subdivision; or

    (2) if no special arrangement exists, by delivery of a copy of the summons and complaint in accordance with an applicable international convention on service of judicial documents; or

    (3) if service cannot be made under paragraphs (1) or (2), by sending a copy of the summons and complaint and a notice of suit, together with a translation of each into the official language of the foreign state, by any form of mail requiring a signed receipt, to be addressed and dispatched by the clerk of the court to the head of the ministry of foreign affairs of the foreign state concerned, or

    (4) if service cannot be made within 30 days under paragraph (3), by sending two copies of the summons and complaint and a notice of suit, together with a translation of each into the official language of the foreign state, by any form of mail requiring a signed receipt, to be addressed and dispatched by the clerk of the court to the Secretary of State in Washington, District of Columbia, to the attention of the Director of Special Consular Services—and the Secretary shall transmit one copy of the papers through diplomatic channels to the foreign state and shall send to the clerk of the court a certified copy of the diplomatic note indicating when the papers were transmitted.

As used in this subsection, a "notice of suit" shall mean a notice addressed to a foreign state and in a form prescribed by the Secretary of State by regulation.

(b) Service in the courts of the United States and of the States shall be made upon an agency or instrumentality of a foreign state:

(1) by delivery of a copy of the summons and complaint in accordance with any special arrangement for service between the plaintiff and the agency or instrumentality; or

(2) if no special arrangement exists, by delivery of a copy of the summons and complaint either to an officer, a managing or general agent, or to any other agent authorized by appointment or by law to receive service of process in the United States; or in accordance with an applicable international convention on service of judicial documents; or

(3) if service cannot be made under paragraphs (1) or (2), and if reasonably calculated to give actual notice, by delivery of a copy of the summons and complaint, together with a translation of each into the official language of the foreign state—

    (A) as directed by an authority of the foreign state or political subdivision in response to a letter rogatory or request or

    (B) by any form of mail requiring a signed receipt, to be addressed and dispatched by the clerk of the court to the agency or instrumentality to be served, or

    (C) as directed by order of the court consistent with the law of the place where service is to be made.

(c) Service shall be deemed to have been made—

(1) in the case of service under subsection (a)(4), as of the date of transmittal indicated in the certified copy of the diplomatic note; and

(2) in any other case under this section, as of the date of receipt indicated in the certification, signed and returned postal receipt, or other proof of service applicable to the method of service employed.

(d) In any action brought in a court of the United States or of a State, a foreign state, a political subdivision thereof, or an agency or instrumentality of a foreign state shall serve an answer or other responsive pleading to the complaint within sixty days after service has been made under this section.

(e) No judgment by default shall be entered by a court of the United States or of a State against a foreign state, a political subdivision thereof, or an agency or instrumentality of a foreign state, unless the claimant establishes his claim or right to relief by evidence satisfactory to the court. A copy of any such default judgment shall be sent to the foreign state or political subdivision in the manner prescribed for service in this section.

(Added Pub.L. 94–583, § 4(a), Oct. 21, 1976, 90 Stat. 2894.)

HISTORICAL AND STATUTORY NOTES

Effective and Applicability Provisions

1976 Acts. Section effective 90 days after Oct. 21, 1976, see section 8 of Pub.L. 94–583, set out as a note under section 1602 of this title.

§ 1609. Immunity from attachment and execution of property of a foreign state

Subject to existing international agreements to which the United States is a party at the time of enactment of this Act the property in the United States of a foreign state shall be immune from attachment arrest and execution except as provided in sections 1610 and 1611 of this chapter.

(Added Pub.L. 94–583, § 4(a), Oct. 21, 1976, 90 Stat. 2895.)

HISTORICAL AND STATUTORY NOTES

References in Text

The time of enactment of this Act, referred to in text, probably means the time of enactment of Pub.L. 94–583, which was approved on Oct. 21, 1976.

Effective and Applicability Provisions

1976 Acts. Section effective 90 days after Oct. 21, 1976, see section 8 of Pub.L. 94–583, set out as a note under section 1602 of this title.

§ 1610. Exceptions to the immunity from attachment or execution

(a) The property in the United States of a foreign state, as defined in section 1603(a) of this chapter, used for a commercial activity in the United States, shall not be immune from attachment in aid of execution, or from execution, upon a judgment entered by a court of the United States or of a State after the effective date of this Act, if—

(1) the foreign state has waived its immunity from attachment in aid of execution or from execution either explicitly or by implication, notwithstanding any withdrawal of the waiver the foreign state may purport to effect except in accordance with the terms of the waiver, or

(2) the property is or was used for the commercial activity upon which the claim is based, or

(3) the execution relates to a judgment establishing rights in property which has been taken in violation of international law or which has been exchanged for property taken in violation of international law, or

(4) the execution relates to a judgment establishing rights in property—

    (A) which is acquired by succession or gift, or

    (B) which is immovable and situated in the United States: *Provided*, That such property is not used for purposes of maintaining a diplomatic or consular mission or the residence of the Chief of such mission, or

(5) the property consists of any contractual obligation or any proceeds from such a contractual obligation to indemnify or hold harmless the foreign state or its employees under a policy of automobile or other liability or casualty insurance covering the claim which merged into the judgment, or

(6) the judgment is based on an order confirming an arbitral award rendered against the foreign state, provided that attachment in aid of execution, or execution, would not be inconsistent with any provision in the arbitral agreement, or

(7) the judgment relates to a claim for which the foreign state is not immune under section 1605(a)(7), regardless of whether the property is or was involved with the act upon which the claim is based.

(b) In addition to subsection (a), any property in the United States of an agency or instrumentality of a foreign state engaged in commercial activity in the United States shall not be immune from attachment in aid of execution, or from execution, upon a judgment entered by a court of the United States or of a State after the effective date of this Act, if—

(1) the agency or instrumentality has waived its immunity from attachment in aid of execution or from execution either explicitly or implicitly, notwithstanding any withdrawal of the waiver the agency or instrumentality may purport to effect except in accordance with the terms of the waiver, or

(2) the judgment relates to a claim for which the agency or instrumentality is not immune by virtue of section 1605(a) (2), (3), (5), or (7), or 1605(b) of this chapter, regardless of whether the property is or was involved in the act upon which the claim is based.

(c) No attachment or execution referred to in subsections (a) and (b) of this section shall be permitted until the court has ordered such attachment and execution after having determined that a reasonable period of time has elapsed following the entry of judgment and the giving of any notice required under section 1608(e) of this chapter.

(d) The property of a foreign state, as defined in section 1603(a) of this chapter, used for a commercial activity in the United States, shall not be immune from attachment prior to the entry of judgment in any action brought in a court of the United States or of a State, or prior to the elapse of the period of time provided in subsection (c) of this section, if—

(1) the foreign state has explicitly waived its immunity from attachment prior to judgment, notwithstanding any withdrawal of the waiver the foreign state may purport to effect except in accordance with the terms of the waiver, and

(2) the purpose of the attachment is to secure satisfaction of a judgment that has been or may ultimately be entered against the foreign state, and not to obtain jurisdiction.

(e) The vessels of a foreign state shall not be immune from arrest in rem, interlocutory sale, and execution in actions brought to foreclose a preferred mortgage as provided in section 1605(d).

(f)(1)(A) Notwithstanding any other provision of law, including but not limited to section 208(f) of the Foreign Missions Act (22 U.S.C. 4308(f)), and except as provided in subparagraph (B), any property with respect to which financial transactions are prohibited or regulated pursuant to section 5(b) of the Trading with the Enemy Act (50 U.S.C. App. 5(b)), section 620(a) of the Foreign Assistance Act of 1961 (22 U.S.C. 2370(a)), sections 202 and 203 of the International Emergency Economic Powers Act (50 U.S.C. 1701–1702), or any other proclamation, order, regulation, or license issued pursuant thereto, shall be subject to execution or attachment in aid of execution of any judgment relating to a claim for which a foreign state (including any agency or instrumentality or such state) claiming such property is not immune under section 1605(a)(7).

(B) Subparagraph (A) shall not apply if, at the time the property is expropriated or seized by the foreign state, the property has been held in title by a natural person or, if held in trust, has been held for the benefit of a natural person or persons.

(2)(A) At the request of any party in whose favor a judgment has been issued with respect to a claim for which the foreign state is not immune under section 1605(a)(7), the Secretary of the Treasury and the Secretary of State should make every effort to fully, promptly, and effectively assist any judgment creditor or any court that has issued any such judgment in identifying, locating, and executing against the property of that foreign state or any agency or instrumentality of such state.

(B) In providing such assistance, the Secretaries—

(i) may provide such information to the court under seal; and

(ii) should make every effort to provide the information in a manner sufficient to allow the court to direct the United States Marshall's office to promptly and effectively execute against that property.

(3) Waiver.—The President may waive any provision of paragraph (1) in the interest of national security.

(Added Pub.L. 94–583, § 4(a), Oct. 21, 1976, 90 Stat. 2896, and amended Pub.L. 100–640, § 2, Nov. 9, 1988, 102 Stat. 3333; Pub.L. 100–669, § 3, Nov. 16, 1988, 102 Stat. 3969; Pub.L. 101–650, Title III, § 325(b)(9), Dec. 1, 1990, 104 Stat. 5121; Pub.L. 104–132, Title II, § 221(b), Apr. 24, 1996, 110 Stat. 1243; Pub.L. 105–277, Div. A, § 101(h) [Title I, § 117(a)], Oct. 21, 1998, 112 Stat. 2681–491; Pub.L. 106–386, Div. C, § 2002(g)(1), Oct. 28, 2000, 114 Stat. 1543; Pub.L. 107–297, Title II, § 201(c)(3), Nov. 26, 2002, 116 Stat. 2337.)

Complete Annotation Materials, see Title 28 U.S.C.A.

HISTORICAL AND STATUTORY NOTES

References in Text

The effective date of this Act, referred to in subsecs. (a) and (b), is 90 days after Oct. 21, 1976, see section 8 of Pub.L. 94–583, set out as an Effective and Applicability Provisions note under section 1602 of this title.

Effective and Applicability Provisions

1998 Acts. Pub.L. 105–277, § 101(h) [Title I, § 117(c)], provided that: "The amendments made by subsections (a) and (b) [amending this section and section 1606 of this title] shall apply to any claim for which a foreign state is not immune under section 1605(a)(7) of title 28, United States Code, arising before, on, or after the date of enactment of this Act [Oct. 21, 1998]."

1996 Acts. Amendment by Pub.L. 104–132 to apply to any cause of action arising before, on, or after Apr. 24, 1996, see section 221(c) of Pub.L. 104–132, set out as a note under section 1605 of this title.

1988 Acts. Amendment to this section by section 2 of Pub.L. 100–640, enacting subsec. (e) of this section, to apply to actions commenced on or after Nov. 9, 1988, see section 3 of Pub.L. 100–640, set out as a note under section 1605 of this title.

1976 Acts. Section effective 90 days after Oct. 21, 1976, see section 8 of Pub.L. 94–583, set out as a note under section 1602 of this title.

Treatment of Terrorist Assets

Pub.L. 107–297, Title II, § 201(a), (b), (d), Nov. 26, 2002, 116 Stat. 2337, provided that:

"**(a) In general.**—Notwithstanding any other provision of law, and except as provided in subsection (b) [of this note], in every case in which a person has obtained a judgment against a terrorist party on a claim based upon an act of terrorism, or for which a terrorist party is not immune under section 1605(a)(7) of title 28, United States Code, the blocked assets of that terrorist party (including the blocked assets of any agency or instrumentality of that terrorist party) shall be subject to execution or attachment in aid of execution in order to satisfy such judgment to the extent of any compensatory damages for which such terrorist party has been adjudged liable.

"**(b) Presidential waiver.**—

"**(1) In general.**—Subject to paragraph (2), upon determining on an asset-by-asset basis that a waiver is necessary in the national security interest, the President may waive the requirements of subsection (a) [of this note] in connection with (and prior to the enforcement of) any judicial order directing attachment in aid of execution or execution against any property subject to the Vienna Convention on Diplomatic Relations or the Vienna Convention on Consular Relations.

"**(2) Exception.**—A waiver under this subsection shall not apply to—

"**(A)** property subject to the Vienna Convention on Diplomatic Relations or the Vienna Convention on Consular Relations that has been used by the United States for any nondiplomatic purpose (including use as rental property), or the proceeds of such use; or

"**(B)** the proceeds of any sale or transfer for value to a third party of any asset subject to the Vienna Conven-

tion on Diplomatic Relations or the Vienna Convention on Consular Relations."

"**(d) Definitions.**—In this section [this note] the following definitions shall apply:

"**(1) Act of terrorism.**—The term 'act of terrorism' means—

"**(A)** any act or event certified under section 102(1) [Pub.L. 107–297, Title I, § 102(1), Nov. 26, 2002, 116 Stat. 2323, which is set out in a note under 15 U.S.C.A. § 6701]; or

"**(B)** to the extent not covered by subparagraph (A), any terrorist activity (as defined in section 212(a)(3)(B)(iii) of the Immigration and Nationality Act (8 U.S.C. 1182(a)(3)(B)(iii))).

"**(2) Blocked asset.**—The term 'blocked asset' means—

"**(A)** any asset seized or frozen by the United States under section 5(b) of the Trading With the Enemy Act (50 U.S.C. App. 5(b)) or under sections 202 and 203 of the International Emergency Economic Powers Act (50 U.S.C. 1701; 1702); and

"**(B)** Does not include property that—

"**(i)** is subject to a license issued by the United States Government for final payment, transfer, or disposition by or to a person subject to the jurisdiction of the United States in connection with a transaction for which the issuance of such license has been specifically required by statute other than the International Emergency Economic Powers Act (50 U.S.C. 1701 et seq.) or the United Nations Participation Act of 1945 (22 U.S.C. 287 et seq.); or

"**(ii)** in the case of property subject to the Vienna Convention on Diplomatic Relations or the Vienna Convention on Consular Relations, or that enjoys equivalent privileges and immunities under the law of the United States, is being used exclusively for diplomatic or consular purposes.

"**(3) Certain property.**—The term 'property subject to the Vienna Convention on Diplomatic Relations or the Vienna Convention on Consular Relations' and the term 'asset subject to the Vienna Convention on Diplomatic Relations or the Vienna Convention on Consular Relations' mean any property or asset, respectively, the attachment in aid of execution or execution of which would result in a violation of an obligation of the United States under the Vienna Convention on Diplomatic Relations or the Vienna Convention on Consular Relations, as the case may be.

"**(4) Terrorist party.**—The term 'terrorist party' means a terrorist, a terrorist organization (as defined in section 212(a)(3)(B)(vi) of the Immigration and Nationality Act (8 U.S.C. 1182(a)(3)(B)(vi))), or a foreign state designated as a state sponsor of terrorism under section 6(j) of the Export Administration Act of 1979 (50 U.S.C. App. 2405(j)) or section 620A of the Foreign Assistance Act of 1961 (22 U.S.C. 2371)."

Waiver of Exception to Immunity from Attachment or Execution

Pub.L. 105–277, Div. A, § 101(h) [Title I, § 117(d)], Oct. 21, 1998, 112 Stat. 2681–491, which had provided authority for the President to waive the requirements of section 117 of Pub.L. 105–277 [amending this section and section 1606 of this title and enacting provisions set out as notes under this section] in the interest of national security, was repealed by Pub.L. 106–386, Div. C, § 2002(g)(2), Oct. 28, 2000, 114 Stat. 1543; Pub.L. 107–297, Title II, § 201(c)(3), Nov. 26, 2002, 116 Stat. 2337.

§ 1611. Certain types of property immune from execution

(a) Notwithstanding the provisions of section 1610 of this chapter, the property of those organizations designated by the President as being entitled to enjoy the privileges, exemptions, and immunities provided by the International Organizations Immunities Act shall not be subject to attachment or any other judicial process impeding the disbursement of funds to, or on the order of, a foreign state as the result of an action brought in the courts of the United States or of the States.

(b) Notwithstanding the provisions of section 1610 of this chapter, the property of a foreign state shall be immune from attachment and from execution, if—

(1) the property is that of a foreign central bank or monetary authority held for its own account, unless such bank or authority, or its parent foreign government, has explicitly waived its immunity from attachment in aid of execution, or from execution, notwithstanding any withdrawal of the waiver which the bank, authority or government may purport to effect except in accordance with the terms of the waiver; or

(2) the property is, or is intended to be, used in connection with a military activity and

(A) is of a military character, or

(B) is under the control of a military authority or defense agency.

(c) Notwithstanding the provisions of section 1610 of this chapter, the property of a foreign state shall be immune from attachment and from execution in an action brought under section 302 of the Cuban Liberty and Democratic Solidarity (LIBERTAD) Act of 1996 to the extent that the property is a facility or installation used by an accredited diplomatic mission for official purposes.

(Added Pub.L. 94–583, § 4(a), Oct. 21, 1976, 90 Stat. 2897, and amended Pub.L. 104–114, Title III, § 302(e), Mar. 12, 1996, 110 Stat. 818.)

HISTORICAL AND STATUTORY NOTES

References in Text

The International Organizations Immunities Act, referred to in subsec. (a), is Act Dec. 29, 1945, c. 652, Title I, 59 Stat. 669, as amended, which is classified principally to section 288 et seq. of Title 22, Foreign Relations and Intercourse. For complete classification of this Act to the Code, see Short Title note set out under section 288 of Title 22 and Tables.

Section 302 of the Cuban Liberty and Democratic Solidarity (LIBERTAD) Act of 1996, referred to in subsec. (c), is Pub.L. 104–114, Title III, § 302, Mar. 12, 1996, 110 Stat. 815, which is classified to section 6082 of Title 22, Foreign Relations and Intercourse.

Effective and Applicability Provisions

1996 Acts. Amendment by section 302(e) of Pub.L. 104–114 effective Aug. 1, 1996, except as otherwise provided, see section 6085 of Title 22, Foreign Relations and Intercourse.

1976 Acts. Section effective 90 days after Oct. 21, 1976, see section 8 of Pub.L. 94–583, set out as a note under section 1602 of this title.

CHAPTER 99—GENERAL PROVISIONS

§ 1631. Transfer to cure want of jurisdiction

Whenever a civil action is filed in a court as defined in section 610 of this title or an appeal, including a petition for review of administrative action, is noticed for or filed with such a court and that court finds that there is a want of jurisdiction, the court shall, if it is in the interest of justice, transfer such action or appeal to any other such court in which the action or appeal could have been brought at the time it was filed or noticed, and the action or appeal shall proceed as if it had been filed in or noticed for the court to which it is transferred on the date upon which it was actually filed in or noticed for the court from which it is transferred.

(Added Pub.L. 97–164, Title III, § 301(a), Apr. 2, 1982, 96 Stat. 55.)

HISTORICAL AND STATUTORY NOTES

Effective and Applicability Provisions

1982 Acts. Section effective Oct. 1, 1982, see section 402 of Pub.L. 97–164, set out as a note under section 171 of this title.

PART V—PROCEDURE

CHAPTER 111—GENERAL PROVISIONS

§ 1651. Writs

(a) The Supreme Court and all courts established by Act of Congress may issue all writs necessary or appropriate in aid of their respective jurisdictions and agreeable to the usages and principles of law.

(b) An alternative writ or rule nisi may be issued by a justice or judge of a court which has jurisdiction. (June 25, 1948, c. 646, 62 Stat. 944; May 24, 1949, c. 139, § 90, 63 Stat. 102.)

HISTORICAL AND STATUTORY NOTES
Writ of Error

Act Jan. 31, 1928, c. 14, § 2, 45 Stat. 54, as amended Apr. 26, 1928, c. 440, 45 Stat. 466; June 25, 1948, c. 646, § 23, 62 Stat. 990, provided that: "All Acts of Congress referring to writs of error shall be construed as amended to the extent necessary to substitute appeal for writ of error."

§ 1652. State laws as rules of decision

The laws of the several states, except where the Constitution or treaties of the United States or Acts of Congress otherwise require or provide, shall be regarded as rules of decision in civil actions in the courts of the United States, in cases where they apply. (June 25, 1948, c. 646, 62 Stat. 944.)

§ 1653. Amendment of pleadings to show jurisdiction

Defective allegations of jurisdiction may be amended, upon terms, in the trial or appellate courts.

(June 25, 1948, c. 646, 62 Stat. 944.)

§ 1654. Appearance personally or by counsel

In all courts of the United States the parties may plead and conduct their own cases personally or by counsel as, by the rules of such courts, respectively, are permitted to manage and conduct causes therein. (June 25, 1948, c. 646, 62 Stat. 944; May 24, 1949, c. 139, § 91, 63 Stat. 103.)

§ 1655. Lien enforcement; absent defendants

In an action in a district court to enforce any lien upon or claim to, or to remove any incumbrance or lien or cloud upon the title to, real or personal property within the district, where any defendant cannot be served within the State, or does not voluntarily appear, the court may order the absent defendant to appear or plead by a day certain.

Such order shall be served on the absent defendant personally if practicable, wherever found, and also upon the person or persons in possession or charge of such property, if any. Where personal service is not practicable, the order shall be published as the court may direct, not less than once a week for six consecutive weeks.

If an absent defendant does not appear or plead within the time allowed, the court may proceed as if the absent defendant had been served with process within the State, but any adjudication shall, as regards the absent defendant without appearance, affect only the property which is the subject of the action. When a part of the property is within another district, but within the same state, such action may be brought in either district.

Any defendant not so personally notified may, at any time within one year after final judgment, enter his appearance, and thereupon the court shall set aside the judgment and permit such defendant to plead on payment of such costs as the court deems just.

(June 25, 1948, c. 646, 62 Stat. 944.)

---

§ 1656. Creation of new district or division or transfer of territory; lien enforcement

The creation of a new district or division or the transfer of any territory to another district or division shall not affect or divest any lien theretofore acquired in a district court upon property within such district, division or territory.

To enforce such lien, the clerk of the court in which the same is acquired, upon the request and at the cost of the party desiring the same, shall make a certified copy of the record thereof, which, when filed in the proper court of the district or division in which such property is situated after such creation or transfer shall be evidence in all courts and places equally with the original thereof; and, thereafter like proceedings shall be had thereon, and with the same effect, as though the case or proceeding had been originally instituted in such court.

(June 25, 1948, c. 646, 62 Stat. 944; Nov. 6, 1978, Pub.L. 95–598, Title II, § 242, 92 Stat. 2671.)

HISTORICAL AND STATUTORY NOTES

Codifications

This section, was amended by Pub.L. 95–598, Title II, § 242, Nov. 6, 1978, 92 Stat. 2671, effective June 28, 1984, pursuant to Pub.L. 95–598, Title IV, § 402(b), Nov. 6, 1978, 92 Stat. 2682, as amended by Pub.L. 98–249, § 1(a), Mar. 31, 1984, 98 Stat. 116; Pub.L. 98–271, § 1(a), Apr. 30, 1984, 98 Stat. 163; Pub.L. 98–299, § 1(a), May 25, 1984, 98 Stat. 214; Pub.L. 98–325, § 1(a), June 20, 1984, 98 Stat. 268, set out as an Effective and Applicability Provisions note preceding section 101 of Title 11, Bankruptcy, by inserting "or in a bankruptcy court" following "a district court".

Section 402(b) of Pub.L. 95–598 was amended by section 113 of Pub.L. 98–353, Title I, July 10, 1984, 98 Stat. 343, by substituting "shall not be effective" for "shall take effect on June 28, 1984", thereby eliminating the amendment by section 242 of Pub.L. 95–598, effective June 27, 1984, pursuant to section 122(c) of Pub.L. 98–353, set out as an Effective and Applicability Provisions note under section 151 of this title.

Section 121(a) of Pub.L. 98–353 directed that section 402(b) of Pub.L. 95–598 be amended by substituting "the date of enactment of the Bankruptcy Amendments and Federal Judgeship Act of 1984 [i.e. July 10, 1984]" for "June 28, 1984". This amendment was not executed in view of the prior amendment to section 402(b) of Pub.L. 95–598 by section 113 of Pub.L. 98–353.

§ 1657. Priority of civil actions

(a) Notwithstanding any other provision of law, each court of the United States shall determine the order in which civil actions are heard and determined, except that the court shall expedite the consideration of any action brought under chapter 153 or section 1826 of this title, any action for temporary or preliminary injunctive relief, or any other action if good cause therefor is shown. For purposes of this subsection, "good cause" is shown if a right under the Constitu-tion of the United States or a Federal Statute (including rights under section 552 of title 5) would be maintained in a factual context that indicates that a request for expedited consideration has merit.

(b) The Judicial Conference of the United States may modify the rules adopted by the courts to determine the order in which civil actions are heard and determined, in order to establish consistency among the judicial circuits.

(Added Pub.L. 98–620, Title IV, § 401(a), Nov. 8, 1984, 98 Stat. 3356.)

HISTORICAL AND STATUTORY NOTES

Codifications

Pub.L. 101–647, Title XXV, § 2527(b), Nov. 29, 1990, 104 Stat. 4877, purported to amend section 1657 of Title 18, Crimes and Criminal Procedure, by inserting "section 11, 12, or 13 of the Federal Deposit Insurance Act" after "consideration of any action brought under", which amendment could not be executed to the text of section 1657 of Title 18. Such amendment was probably intended to amend this section.

Effective and Applicability Provisions

1984 Acts. Section 403 of Pub.L. 98–620 provided that: "The amendments made by this subtitle [subtitle A of Title IV of Pub.L. 98–620, enacting this section, amending sections 596, 636, 1364, 2284, and 2349 of this title, sections 437g, 437h and 687 of Title 2, The Congress, section 552 of Title 5, Government Organization and Employees, sections 8, 136d, 136h, 136n, 136w, 194, 1366, 1600 and 1601 of Title 7, Agriculture, section 1464 of Title 12, Banks and Banking, sections 18a, 21, 45, 57a–1, 78k–1, 687a, 687c, 719h, 1415, 2003 and 2622 of Title 15, Commerce and Trade, sections 1463a, 1910, 3117, and 3168 of Title 16, Conservation, sections 1964 and 1966 of Title 18, Crimes and Criminal Procedure, sections 346a and 348 of Title 21, Food and Drugs, section 618 of Title 22, Foreign Relations and Intercourse, section 640d–3 of Title 25, Indians, sections 3310, 6110, 6363, 7609, 9010 and 9011 of Title 26, Internal Revenue Code, sections 110, 160, 660 and 1303 of Title 29, Labor, section 816 of Title 30, Mineral Lands and Mining, section 2022 of Title 38, Veterans' Benefits, section 3628 of Title 39, Postal Service, sections 300j–9, 504, 6508 and 8514 of Title 42, The Public Health and Welfare, sections 1062, 1349, 1652 and 2011 of Title 43, Public Lands, sections 355, 745, 1018 and 1205 of Title 45, Railroads, section 402 of Title 47, Telegraphs, Telephones, and Radio-telegraphs, section 2305 of Title 49 Appendix, Transportation, section 792a of Title 50, War and National Defense, sections 462 and 1984 of the Appendix to Title 50, repealing sections 1296 and 2647 of this title, section 28 of Title 15, Commerce and Trade, and section 3614 of Title 42, The Public Health and Welfare, and amending provisions set out as a note under section 2304 of Title 10, Armed Forces] shall not apply to cases pending on the date of the enactment of this subtitle [Nov. 8, 1984]."

§ 1658. Time limitations on the commencement of civil actions arising under Acts of Congress

(a) Except as otherwise provided by law, a civil action arising under an Act of Congress enacted after the date of the enactment of this section may not be commenced later than 4 years after the cause of action accrues.

(b) Notwithstanding subsection (a), a private right of action that involves a claim of fraud, deceit, manipulation, or contrivance in contravention of a regulatory requirement concerning the securities laws, as defined in section 3(a)(47) of the Securities Exchange Act of 1934 (15 U.S.C. 78c(a)(47)), may be brought not later than the earlier of—

(1) 2 years after the discovery of the facts constituting the violation; or

(2) 5 years after such violation.

(Added Pub.L. 101–650, Title III, § 313(a), Dec. 1, 1990, 104 Stat. 5114, and amended Pub.L. 107–204, Title VIII, § 804(a), July 30, 2002, 116 Stat. 801.)

HISTORICAL AND STATUTORY NOTES

References in Text

The date of the enactment of this section, referred to in text, is the date of enactment of this section by section 313(a) of Pub.L. 101–650, which was approved Dec. 1, 1990.

Effective and Applicability Provisions

2002 Acts. Pub.L. 107–204, Title VIII, § 804(b), July 30, 2002, 116 Stat. 801, provided that: "The limitations period provided by section 1658(b) of title 28, United States Code [subsec. (b) of this section], as added by this section [section 804 of Pub.L. 107–204, which amended this section], shall apply to all proceedings addressed by this section that are commenced on or after the date of enactment of this Act [July 30, 2002]."

1990 Acts. Section 313(c) of Pub.L. 101–650 provided that: "The amendments made by this section [enacting this section] shall apply with respect to causes of action accruing on or after the date of the enactment of this Act [Dec. 1, 1990]."

No Creation of Actions

Pub.L. 107–204, Title VIII, § 804(c), July 30, 2002, 116 Stat. 801, provided that: "Nothing in this section [Pub.L. 107–204, Title VIII, § 804, July 30, 2002, 116 Stat. 801, which amended this section and enacted provisions set out as a note under this section] shall create a new, private right of action."

§ 1659. Stay of certain actions pending disposition of related proceedings before the United States International Trade Commission

(a) Stay.—In a civil action involving parties that are also parties to a proceeding before the United States International Trade Commission under section 337 of the Tariff Act of 1930, at the request of a party to the civil action that is also a respondent in the proceeding before the Commission, the district court shall stay, until the determination of the Commission becomes final, proceedings in the civil action with respect to any claim that involves the same issues involved in the proceeding before the Commission, but only if such request is made within—

(1) 30 days after the party is named as a respondent in the proceeding before the Commission, or

(2) 30 days after the district court action is filed,

whichever is later.

(b) Use of Commission record.—Notwithstanding section 337(n)(1) of the Tariff Act of 1930, after dissolution of a stay under subsection (a), the record of the proceeding before the United States International Trade Commission shall be transmitted to the district court and shall be admissible in the civil action, subject to such protective order as the district court determines necessary, to the extent permitted under the Federal Rules of Evidence and the Federal Rules of Civil Procedure.

(Added Pub.L. 103–465, Title III, § 321(b)(1)(A), Dec. 8, 1994, 108 Stat. 4945.)

HISTORICAL AND STATUTORY NOTES

References in Text

Section 337 of the Tariff Act of 1930, referred to in text, is section 337 of Act June 17, 1930, c. 497, Title III, 46 Stat. 703, which is classified to section 1337 of Title 19, Customs Duties.

Effective and Applicability Provisions

1994 Acts. Section applicable with respect to complaints filed under section 1337 of Title 19, Customs Duties, on or after the date on which the WTO Agreement enters into force with respect to the United States, Jan. 1, 1995, or in cases under section 1337 of Title 19 in which no complaint is filed, with respect to investigations initiated under such section on or after such date, see section 322 of Pub.L. 103–465, set out as a note under section 1337 of Title 19.

CHAPTER 113—PROCESS

§ 1691. Seal and teste of process

All writs and process issuing from a court of the United States shall be under the seal of the court and signed by the clerk thereof.

(June 25, 1948, c. 646, 62 Stat. 945.)

HISTORICAL AND STATUTORY NOTES

Immunity from Seizure under Judicial Process of Cultural Objects Imported for Temporary Exhibition or Display

Presidential determination of cultural significance of objects and exhibition or display thereof in the national interest, see section 2459 of Title 22, Foreign Relations and Intercourse.

§ 1692. Process and orders affecting property in different districts

In proceedings in a district court where a receiver is appointed for property, real, personal, or mixed, situated in different districts, process may issue and be executed in any such district as if the property lay wholly within one district, but orders affecting the property shall be entered of record in each of such districts.

(June 25, 1948, c. 646, 62 Stat. 945.)

§ 1693. Place of arrest in civil action

Except as otherwise provided by Act of Congress, no person shall be arrested in one district for trial in another in any civil action in a district court.

(June 25, 1948, c. 646, 62 Stat. 945.)

§ 1694. Patent infringement action

In a patent infringement action commenced in a district where the defendant is not a resident but has a regular and established place of business, service of process, summons or subpoena upon such defendant may be made upon his agent or agents conducting such business.

(June 25, 1948, c. 646, 62 Stat. 945.)

§ 1695. Stockholder's derivative action

Process in a stockholder's action in behalf of his corporation may be served upon such corporation in any district where it is organized or licensed to do business or is doing business.

(June 25, 1948, c. 646, 62 Stat. 945.)

§ 1696. Service in foreign and international litigation

(a) The district court of the district in which a person resides or is found may order service upon him of any document issued in connection with a proceeding in a foreign or international tribunal. The order may be made pursuant to a letter rogatory issued, or request made, by a foreign or international tribunal or upon application of any interested person and shall direct the manner of service. Service pursuant to this subsection does not, of itself, require the recognition or enforcement in the United States of a judgment, decree, or order rendered by a foreign or international tribunal.

(b) This section does not preclude service of such a document without an order of court.

(Added Pub.L. 88–619, § 4(a), Oct. 3, 1964, 78 Stat. 995.)

HISTORICAL AND STATUTORY NOTES

Treaties and Conventions; Service Abroad of Judicial and Extrajudicial Documents in Civil or Commercial Matters; Observance On and After Feb. 10, 1969, by United States and Citizens and Persons Subject to Jurisdiction of United States

For text of Convention, see provisions set out as a note under Rule 4, Federal Rules of Civil Procedure, 28 U.S.C.A.

§ 1697. Service in multiparty, multiforum actions

When the jurisdiction of the district court is based in whole or in part upon section 1369 of this title, process, other than subpoenas, may be served at any place within the United States, or anywhere outside the United States if otherwise permitted by law.

(Added Pub.L. 107–273, Div. C, Title I, § 11020(b)(4)(A)(i), Nov. 2, 2002, 116 Stat. 1828.)

HISTORICAL AND STATUTORY NOTES

Effective and Applicability Provisions

2002 Acts. Amendments by section 11020(b) of Pub.L. 107–273 shall apply to a civil action if the accident giving rise to the cause of action occurred on or after the 90th day after Nov. 2, 2002, see section 11020(c) of Pub.L. 107–273, set out as a note under 28 U.S.C.A. § 1369.

CHAPTER 114—CLASS ACTIONS

§ 1711. Definitions

In this chapter:

(1) **Class.**—The term "class" means all of the class members in a class action.

(2) **Class action.**—The term "class action" means any civil action filed in a district court of the United States under rule 23 of the Federal Rules of Civil Procedure or any civil action that is removed to a district court of the United States that was originally filed under a State statute or rule of judicial procedure authorizing an action to be brought by 1 or more representatives as a class action.

(3) Class counsel.—The term "class counsel" means the persons who serve as the attorneys for the class members in a proposed or certified class action.

(4) Class members.—The term "class members" means the persons (named or unnamed) who fall within the definition of the proposed or certified class in a class action.

(5) Plaintiff class action.—The term "plaintiff class action" means a class action in which class members are plaintiffs.

(6) Proposed settlement.—The term "proposed settlement" means an agreement regarding a class action that is subject to court approval and that, if approved, would be binding on some or all class members.

(Added Pub.L. 109–2, § 3(a), Feb. 18, 2005, 119 Stat. 5.)

HISTORICAL AND STATUTORY NOTES

References in Text

Rule 23 of the Federal Rules of Civil Procedure, referred to in par. (2), is set out following the code sections of this title.

Effective and Applicability Provisions

2005 Acts. Enactment of this section by Class Action Fairness Act of 2005, Pub.L. 109–2, Feb. 18, 2005, 119 Stat. 4, applicable to any civil action commenced on or after Feb. 18, 2005, see Pub.L. 109–2, § 9, set out as a note under 28 U.S.C.A. § 1332.

Findings and Purposes

Pub.L. 109–2, § 2, Feb. 18, 2005, 119 Stat. 4, provided that:

"**(a) Findings.**—Congress finds the following:

"**(1)** Class action lawsuits are an important and valuable part of the legal system when they permit the fair and efficient resolution of legitimate claims of numerous parties by allowing the claims to be aggregated into a single action against a defendant that has allegedly caused harm.

"**(2)** Over the past decade, there have been abuses of the class action device that have—

"**(A)** harmed class members with legitimate claims and defendants that have acted responsibly;

"**(B)** adversely affected interstate commerce; and

"**(C)** undermined public respect for our judicial system.

"**(3)** Class members often receive little or no benefit from class actions, and are sometimes harmed, such as where—

"**(A)** counsel are awarded large fees, while leaving class members with coupons or other awards of little or no value;

"**(B)** unjustified awards are made to certain plaintiffs at the expense of other class members; and

"**(C)** confusing notices are published that prevent class members from being able to fully understand and effectively exercise their rights.

"**(4)** Abuses in class actions undermine the National judicial system, the free flow of interstate commerce, and

the concept of diversity jurisdiction as intended by the framers of the United States constitution, in that State and local courts are—

"**(A)** keeping cases of national importance out of Federal court;

"**(B)** sometimes acting in ways that demonstrate bias against out-of-State defendants; and

"**(C)** making judgments that impose their view of the law on other States and bind the rights of the residents of those States.

"**(b) Purposes.**—The purposes of this Act [the Class Action Fairness Act of 2005, which enacted this note, this chapter, and 28 U.S.C.A. § 1453, amended 28 U.S.C.A. §§ 1332, 1335, and 1603, and enacted provisions set out as notes under 28 U.S.C.A. §§ 1332, 2071, and 2074] are to—

"**(1)** assure fair and prompt recoveries for class members with legitimate claims;

"**(2)** restore the intent of the framers of the United States Constitution by providing for Federal court consideration of interstate cases of national importance under diversity jurisdiction; and

"**(3)** benefit society by encouraging innovation and lowering consumer prices."

[Enactment of this note by Class Action Fairness Act of 2005, Pub.L. 109–2, Feb. 18, 2005, 119 Stat. 4, applicable to any civil action commenced on or after Feb. 18, 2005, see Pub.L. 109–2, § 9, set out as a note under 28 U.S.C.A. § 1332.]

§ 1712.   Coupon settlements

(a) Contingent fees in coupon settlements.—If a proposed settlement in a class action provides for a recovery of coupons to a class member, the portion of any attorney's fee award to class counsel that is attributable to the award of the coupons shall be based on the value to class members of the coupons that are redeemed.

(b) Other attorney's fee awards in coupon settlements.—

(1) In general.—If a proposed settlement in a class action provides for a recovery of coupons to class members, and a portion of the recovery of the coupons is not used to determine the attorney's fee to be paid to class counsel, any attorney's fee award shall be based upon the amount of time class counsel reasonably expended working on the action.

(2) Court approval.—Any attorney's fee under this subsection shall be subject to approval by the court and shall include an appropriate attorney's fee, if any, for obtaining equitable relief, including an injunction, if applicable. Nothing in this subsection shall be construed to prohibit application of a lodestar with a multiplier method of determining attorney's fees.

(c) Attorney's fee awards calculated on a mixed basis in coupon settlements.—If a proposed settlement in a class action provides for an award of coupons to class members and also provides for equitable relief, including injunctive relief—

    (1) that portion of the attorney's fee to be paid to class counsel that is based upon a portion of the recovery of the coupons shall be calculated in accordance with subsection (a); and

    (2) that portion of the attorney's fee to be paid to class counsel that is not based upon a portion of the recovery of the coupons shall be calculated in accordance with subsection (b).

(d) Settlement valuation expertise.—In a class action involving the awarding of coupons, the court may, in its discretion upon the motion of a party, receive expert testimony from a witness qualified to provide information on the actual value to the class members of the coupons that are redeemed.

(e) Judicial scrutiny of coupon settlements.—In a proposed settlement under which class members would be awarded coupons, the court may approve the proposed settlement only after a hearing to determine whether, and making a written finding that, the settlement is fair, reasonable, and adequate for class members. The court, in its discretion, may also require that a proposed settlement agreement provide for the distribution of a portion of the value of unclaimed coupons to 1 or more charitable or governmental organizations, as agreed to by the parties. The distribution and redemption of any proceeds under this subsection shall not be used to calculate attorneys' fees under this section.

(Added Pub.L. 109–2, § 3(a), Feb. 18, 2005, 119 Stat. 6.)

HISTORICAL AND STATUTORY NOTES

Effective and Applicability Provisions

2005 Acts. Enactment of this section by Class Action Fairness Act of 2005, Pub.L. 109–2, Feb. 18, 2005, 119 Stat. 4, applicable to any civil action commenced on or after Feb. 18, 2005, see Pub.L. 109–2, § 9, set out as a note under 28 U.S.C.A. § 1332.

§ 1713. Protection against loss by class members

The court may approve a proposed settlement under which any class member is obligated to pay sums to class counsel that would result in a net loss to the class member only if the court makes a written finding that nonmonetary benefits to the class member substantially outweigh the monetary loss.

(Added Pub.L. 109–2, § 3(a), Feb. 18, 2005, 119 Stat. 7.)

HISTORICAL AND STATUTORY NOTES

Effective and Applicability Provisions

2005 Acts. Enactment of this section by Class Action Fairness Act of 2005, Pub.L. 109–2, Feb. 18, 2005, 119 Stat. 4, applicable to any civil action commenced on or after Feb. 18, 2005, see Pub.L. 109–2, § 9, set out as a note under 28 U.S.C.A. § 1332.

§ 1714. Protection against discrimination based on geographic location

The court may not approve a proposed settlement that provides for the payment of greater sums to some class members than to others solely on the basis that the class members to whom the greater sums are to be paid are located in closer geographic proximity to the court.

(Added Pub.L. 109–2, § 3(a), Feb. 18, 2005, 119 Stat. 7.)

HISTORICAL AND STATUTORY NOTES

Effective and Applicability Provisions

2005 Acts. Enactment of this section by Class Action Fairness Act of 2005, Pub.L. 109–2, Feb. 18, 2005, 119 Stat. 4, applicable to any civil action commenced on or after Feb. 18, 2005, see Pub.L. 109–2, § 9, set out as a note under 28 U.S.C.A. § 1332.

§ 1715. Notifications to appropriate Federal and State officials

(a) Definitions.—

    (1) Appropriate Federal official.—In this section, the term "appropriate Federal official" means—

        (A) the Attorney General of the United States; or

        (B) in any case in which the defendant is a Federal depository institution, a State depository institution, a depository institution holding company, a foreign bank, or a nondepository institution subsidiary of the foregoing (as such terms are defined in section 3 of the Federal Deposit Insurance Act (12 U.S.C. 1813)), the person who has the primary Federal regulatory or supervisory responsibility with respect to the defendant, if some or all of the matters alleged in the class action are subject to regulation or supervision by that person.

    (2) Appropriate State official.—In this section, the term "appropriate State official" means the person in the State who has the primary regulatory or supervisory responsibility with respect to the defendant, or who licenses or otherwise authorizes the defendant to conduct business in the State, if some or all of the matters alleged in the class action are subject to regulation by that person. If there is no primary regulator, supervisor, or licensing authority, or the matters alleged in the class action are not subject to regulation or supervision by that person, then the appropriate State official shall be the State attorney general.

(b) In general.—Not later than 10 days after a proposed settlement of a class action is filed in court, each defendant that is participating in the proposed settlement shall serve upon the appropriate State official of each State in which a class member resides and the appropriate Federal official, a notice of the proposed settlement consisting of—

(1) a copy of the complaint and any materials filed with the complaint and any amended complaints (except such materials shall not be required to be served if such materials are made electronically available through the Internet and such service includes notice of how to electronically access such material);

(2) notice of any scheduled judicial hearing in the class action;

(3) any proposed or final notification to class members of—

(A)(i) the members' rights to request exclusion from the class action; or

(ii) if no right to request exclusion exists, a statement that no such right exists; and

(B) a proposed settlement of a class action;

(4) any proposed or final class action settlement;

(5) any settlement or other agreement contemporaneously made between class counsel and counsel for the defendants;

(6) any final judgment or notice of dismissal;

(7)(A) if feasible, the names of class members who reside in each State and the estimated proportionate share of the claims of such members to the entire settlement to that State's appropriate State official; or

(B) if the provision of information under subparagraph (A) is not feasible, a reasonable estimate of the number of class members residing in each State and the estimated proportionate share of the claims of such members to the entire settlement; and

(8) any written judicial opinion relating to the materials described under subparagraphs (3) through (6).

(c) **Depository institutions notification.**—

(1) **Federal and other depository institutions.**—In any case in which the defendant is a Federal depository institution, a depository institution holding company, a foreign bank, or a non-depository institution subsidiary of the foregoing, the notice requirements of this section are satisfied by serving the notice required under subsection (b) upon the person who has the primary Federal regulatory or supervisory responsibility with respect to the defendant, if some or all of the matters alleged in the class action are subject to regulation or supervision by that person.

(2) **State depository institutions.**—In any case in which the defendant is a State depository institution (as that term is defined in section 3 of the Federal Deposit Insurance Act (12 U.S.C. 1813)), the notice requirements of this section are satisfied by serving the notice required under subsection (b) upon the State bank supervisor (as that term is defined in section 3 of the Federal Deposit Insurance Act (12 U.S.C. 1813)) of the State in which the defendant is incorporated or chartered, if some or all of the matters alleged in the class action are subject to regulation or supervision by that person, and upon the appropriate Federal official.

(d) **Final approval.**—An order giving final approval of a proposed settlement may not be issued earlier than 90 days after the later of the dates on which the appropriate Federal official and the appropriate State official are served with the notice required under subsection (b).

(e) **Noncompliance if notice not provided.**—

(1) **In general.**—A class member may refuse to comply with and may choose not to be bound by a settlement agreement or consent decree in a class action if the class member demonstrates that the notice required under subsection (b) has not been provided.

(2) **Limitation.**—A class member may not refuse to comply with or to be bound by a settlement agreement or consent decree under paragraph (1) if the notice required under subsection (b) was directed to the appropriate Federal official and to either the State attorney general or the person that has primary regulatory, supervisory, or licensing authority over the defendant.

(3) **Application of rights.**—The rights created by this subsection shall apply only to class members or any person acting on a class member's behalf, and shall not be construed to limit any other rights affecting a class member's participation in the settlement.

(f) **Rule of construction.**—Nothing in this section shall be construed to expand the authority of, or impose any obligations, duties, or responsibilities upon, Federal or State officials.

(Added Pub.L. 109–2, § 3(a), Feb. 18, 2005, 119 Stat. 7.)

HISTORICAL AND STATUTORY NOTES

References in Text

Section 3 of the Federal Deposit Insurance Act, referred to in subsecs. (a)(1)(B) and (c)(2), is Act Sept. 21, 1950, c. 967, § 2[3], 64 Stat. 873, as amended, which is classified to 12 U.S.C.A. § 1813. A Federal depository institution is defined in 12 U.S.C.A. § 1813(c)(4); a State depository institution, in 12 U.S.C.A. § 1813(c)(5); a depository institution holding company, in 12 U.S.C.A. § 1813(w)(1); a foreign bank, in 12 U.S.C.A. § 1813(s)(1); and State bank supervisor, in 12 U.S.C.A. § 1813(r)(1).

Effective and Applicability Provisions

2005 Acts. Enactment of this section by Class Action Fairness Act of 2005, Pub.L. 109–2, Feb. 18, 2005, 119 Stat. 4, applicable to any civil action commenced on or after Feb.

18, 2005, see Pub.L. 109–2, § 9, set out as a note under 28 U.S.C.A. § 1332.

CHAPTER 115—EVIDENCE; DOCUMENTARY

§ 1731.   Handwriting

The admitted or proved handwriting of any person shall be admissible, for purposes of comparison, to determine genuineness of other handwriting attributed to such person.

(June 25, 1948, c. 646, 62 Stat. 945.)

§ 1732.   Record made in regular course of business; photographic copies

If any business, institution, member of a profession or calling, or any department or agency of government, in the regular course of business or activity has kept or recorded any memorandum, writing, entry, print, representation or combination thereof, of any act, transaction, occurrence, or event, and in the regular course of business has caused any or all of the same to be recorded, copied, or reproduced by any photographic, photostatic, microfilm, micro-card, miniature photographic, or other process which accurately reproduces or forms a durable medium for so reproducing the original, the original may be destroyed in the regular course of business unless its preservation is required by law. Such reproduction, when satisfactorily identified, is as admissible in evidence as the original itself in any judicial or administrative proceeding whether the original is in existence or not and an enlargement or facsimile of such reproduction is likewise admissible in evidence if the original reproduction is in existence and available for inspection under direction of court. The introduction of a reproduced record, enlargement, or facsimile does not preclude admission of the original. This subsection[1] shall not be construed to exclude from evidence any document or copy thereof which is otherwise admissible under the rules of evidence.

(June 25, 1948, c. 646, 62 Stat. 945; Aug. 28, 1951, c. 351, §§ 1, 3, 65 Stat. 205, 206; Aug. 30, 1961, Pub.L. 87–183, 75 Stat. 413; Jan. 2, 1975, Pub.L. 93–595, § 2(b), 88 Stat. 1949.)

[1] Probably should be read as "section". Section formerly was subsec. (b) of this section.

§ 1733.   Government records and papers; copies

(a) Books or records of account or minutes of proceedings of any department or agency of the United States shall be admissible to prove the act, transaction or occurrence as a memorandum of which the same were made or kept.

(b) Properly authenticated copies or transcripts of any books, records, papers or documents of any department or agency of the United States shall be admitted in evidence equally with the originals thereof.

(c) This section does not apply to cases, actions, and proceedings to which the Federal Rules of Evidence apply.

(June 25, 1948, c. 646, 62 Stat. 946; Jan. 2, 1975, Pub.L. 93–595, § 2(c), 88 Stat. 1949.)

HISTORICAL AND STATUTORY NOTES
References in Text

The Federal Rules of Evidence, referred to in subsec. (c), are set out in this title.

§ 1734.   Court record lost or destroyed, generally

(a) A lost or destroyed record of any proceeding in any court of the United States may be supplied on application of any interested party not at fault, by substituting a copy certified by the clerk of any court in which an authentic copy is lodged.

(b) Where a certified copy is not available, any interested person not at fault may file in such court a verified application for an order establishing the lost or destroyed record.

Every other interested person shall be served personally with a copy of the application and with notice of hearing on a day stated, not less than sixty days after service. Service may be made on any nonresident of the district anywhere within the jurisdiction of the United States or in any foreign country.

Proof of service in a foreign country shall be certified by a minister or consul of the United States in such country, under his official seal.

If, after the hearing, the court is satisfied that the statements contained in the application are true, it shall enter an order reciting the substance and effect of the lost or destroyed record. Such order, subject to intervening rights of third persons, shall have the same effect as the original record.
(June 25, 1948, c. 646, 62 Stat. 946.)

§ 1735. Court record lost or destroyed where United States interested

(a) When the record of any case or matter in any court of the United States to which the United States is a party, is lost or destroyed, a certified copy of any official paper of a United States attorney, United States marshal or clerk or other certifying or recording officer of any such court, made pursuant to law, on file in any department or agency of the United States and relating to such case or matter, shall, on being filed in the court to which it relates, have the same effect as an original paper filed in such court. If the copy so filed discloses the date and amount of a judgment or decree and the names of the parties thereto, the court may enforce the judgment or decree as though the original record had not been lost or destroyed.

(b) Whenever the United States is interested in any lost or destroyed records or files of a court of the United States, the clerk of such court and the United States attorney for the district shall take the steps necessary to restore such records or files, under the direction of the judges of such court.
(June 25, 1948, c. 646, 62 Stat. 946.)

§ 1736. Congressional Journals

Extracts from the Journals of the Senate and the House of Representatives, and from the Executive Journal of the Senate when the injunction of secrecy is removed, certified by the Secretary of the Senate or the Clerk of the House of Representatives shall be received in evidence with the same effect as the originals would have.
(June 25, 1948, c. 646, 62 Stat. 947.)

HISTORICAL AND STATUTORY NOTES

Transfer of Functions

Any reference in any provision of law enacted before Jan. 4, 1995, to a function, duty, or authority of the Clerk of the House of Representatives treated as referring, with respect to that function, duty, or authority, to the officer of the House of Representatives exercising that function, duty, or

authority, as determined by the Committee on House Oversight of the House of Representatives, see section 2(1) of Pub.L. 104–14, set out as a note preceding section 21 of Title 2, The Congress.

§ 1737. Copy of officer's bond

Any person to whose custody the bond of any officer of the United States has been committed shall, on proper request and payment of the fee allowed by any Act of Congress, furnish certified copies thereof, which shall be prima facie evidence in any court of the execution, filing and contents of the bond.
(June 25, 1948, c. 646, 62 Stat. 947.)

§ 1738. State and Territorial statutes and judicial proceedings; full faith and credit

The Acts of the legislature of any State, Territory, or Possession of the United States, or copies thereof, shall be authenticated by affixing the seal of such State, Territory or Possession thereto.

The records and judicial proceedings of any court of any such State, Territory or Possession, or copies thereof, shall be proved or admitted in other courts within the United States and its Territories and Possessions by the attestation of the clerk and seal of the court annexed, if a seal exists, together with a certificate of a judge of the court that the said attestation is in proper form.

Such Acts, records and judicial proceedings or copies thereof, so authenticated, shall have the same full faith and credit in every court within the United States and its Territories and Possessions as they have by law or usage in the courts of such State, Territory or Possession from which they are taken.
(June 25, 1948, c. 646, 62 Stat. 947.)

§ 1738A. Full faith and credit given to child custody determinations

(a) The appropriate authorities of every State shall enforce according to its terms, and shall not modify except as provided in subsections (f), (g), and (h) of this section, any custody determination or visitation determination made consistently with the provisions of this section by a court of another State.

(b) As used in this section, the term—

(1) "child" means a person under the age of eighteen;

(2) "contestant" means a person, including a parent or grandparent, who claims a right to custody or visitation of a child;

(3) "custody determination" means a judgment, decree, or other order of a court providing for the custody of a child, and includes permanent and temporary orders, and initial orders and modifications;

(4) "home State" means the State in which, immediately preceding the time involved, the child lived with his parents, a parent, or a person acting as parent, for at least six consecutive months, and in the case of a child less than six months old, the State in which the child lived from birth with any of such persons. Periods of temporary absence of any of such persons are counted as part of the six-month or other period;

(5) "modification" and "modify" refer to a custody or visitation determination which modifies, replaces, supersedes, or otherwise is made subsequent to, a prior custody or visitation determination concerning the same child, whether made by the same court or not;

(6) "person acting as a parent" means a person, other than a parent, who has physical custody of a child and who has either been awarded custody by a court or claims a right to custody;

(7) "physical custody" means actual possession and control of a child;

(8) "State" means a State of the United States, the District of Columbia, the Commonwealth of Puerto Rico, or a territory or possession of the United States; and

(9) "visitation determination" means a judgment, decree, or other order of a court providing for the visitation of a child and includes permanent and temporary orders and initial orders and modifications.

(c) A child custody or visitation determination made by a court of a State is consistent with the provisions of this section only if—

(1) such court has jurisdiction under the law of such State; and

(2) one of the following conditions is met:

(A) such State (i) is the home State of the child on the date of the commencement of the proceeding, or (ii) had been the child's home State within six months before the date of the commencement of the proceeding and the child is absent from such State because of his removal or retention by a contestant or for other reasons, and a contestant continues to live in such State;

(B) (i) it appears that no other State would have jurisdiction under subparagraph (A), and (ii) it is in the best interest of the child that a court of such State assume jurisdiction because (I) the child and his parents, or the child and at least one contestant, have a significant connection with such State other than mere physical presence in such State, and (II) there is available in such State substantial evidence concerning the child's present or future care, protection, training, and personal relationships;

(C) the child is physically present in such State and (i) the child has been abandoned, or (ii) it is necessary in an emergency to protect the child because the child, a sibling, or parent of the child has been subjected to or threatened with mistreatment or abuse;

(D) (i) it appears that no other State would have jurisdiction under subparagraph (A), (B), (C), or (E), or another State has declined to exercise jurisdiction on the ground that the State whose jurisdiction is in issue is the more appropriate forum to determine the custody or visitation of the child, and (ii) it is in the best interest of the child that such court assume jurisdiction; or

(E) the court has continuing jurisdiction pursuant to subsection (d) of this section.

(d) The jurisdiction of a court of a State which has made a child custody or visitation determination consistently with the provisions of this section continues as long as the requirement of subsection (c)(1) of this section continues to be met and such State remains the residence of the child or of any contestant.

(e) Before a child custody or visitation determination is made, reasonable notice and opportunity to be heard shall be given to the contestants, any parent whose parental rights have not been previously terminated and any person who has physical custody of a child.

(f) A court of a State may modify a determination of the custody of the same child made by a court of another State, if—

(1) it has jurisdiction to make such a child custody determination; and

(2) the court of the other State no longer has jurisdiction, or it has declined to exercise such jurisdiction to modify such determination.

(g) A court of a State shall not exercise jurisdiction in any proceeding for a custody or visitation determination commenced during the pendency of a proceeding in a court of another State where such court of that other State is exercising jurisdiction consistently with the provisions of this section to make a custody or visitation determination.

(h) A court of a State may not modify a visitation determination made by a court of another State unless the court of the other State no longer has jurisdiction to modify such determination or has declined to exercise jurisdiction to modify such determination.

(Added Pub.L. 96–611, § 8(a), Dec. 28, 1980, 94 Stat. 3569, and amended Pub.L. 105–374, § 1, Nov. 12, 1998, 112 Stat. 3383; Pub.L. 106–386, Div. B, Title III, § 1303(d), Oct. 28, 2000, 114 Stat. 1512.)

HISTORICAL AND STATUTORY NOTES

Report on Effects of Parental Kidnapping Laws in Domestic Violence Cases

Pub.L. 106–386, Div. B, Title III, § 1303(a) to (c), Oct. 28, 2000, 114 Stat. 1512, provided that:

"(a) **In general.**—The Attorney General shall—

"(1) conduct a study of Federal and State laws relating to child custody, including custody provisions in protection orders, the Uniform Child Custody Jurisdiction and Enforcement Act adopted by the National Conference of Commissioners on Uniform State Laws in July 1997, the Parental Kidnaping Prevention Act of 1980 [Pub.L. 96–611, Dec. 28, 1980, 94 Stat. 3568] and the amendments made by that Act, and the effect of those laws on child custody cases in which domestic violence is a factor; and

"(2) submit to Congress a report describing the results of that study, including the effects of implementing or applying model State laws, and the recommendations of the Attorney General to reduce the incidence or pattern of violence against women or of sexual assault of the child.

"(b) **Sufficiency of defenses.**—In carrying out subsection (a) with respect to the Parental Kidnaping Prevention Act of 1980 [Pub.L. 96–611, Dec. 28, 1980, 94 Stat. 3568] and the amendments made by that Act [see Tables for classification], the Attorney General shall examine the sufficiency of defenses to parental abduction charges available in cases involving domestic violence, and the burdens and risks encountered by victims of domestic violence arising from jurisdictional requirements of that Act and the amendments made by that Act.

"(c) **Authorization of appropriations.**—There is authorized to be appropriated to carry out this section $200,000 for fiscal year 2001."

Congressional Findings and Declaration of Purpose

Section 7 of Pub.L. 96–611 provided that:

"(a) The Congress finds that—

"(1) there is a large and growing number of cases annually involving disputes between persons claiming rights of custody and visitation of children under the laws, and in the courts, of different States, the District of Columbia, the Commonwealth of Puerto Rico, and the territories and possessions of the United States;

"(2) the laws and practices by which the courts of those jurisdictions determine their jurisdiction to decide such disputes, and the effect to be given the decisions of such disputes by the courts of other jurisdictions, are often inconsistent and conflicting;

"(3) those characteristics of the law and practice in such cases, along with the limits imposed by a Federal system on the authority of each such jurisdiction to conduct investigations and take other actions outside its own boundaries, contribute to a tendency of parties involved in such disputes to frequently resort to the seizure, restraint, concealment, and interstate transportation of children, the disregard of court orders, excessive relitigation of cases, obtaining of conflicting orders by the courts of various jurisdictions, and interstate travel and communication that is so expensive and time consuming as to disrupt their occupations and commercial activities; and

"(4) among the results of those conditions and activities are the failure of the courts of such jurisdictions to give full faith and credit to the judicial proceedings of the other jurisdictions, the deprivation of rights of liberty and property without due process of law, burdens on commerce among such jurisdictions and with foreign nations, and harm to the welfare of children and their parents and other custodians.

"(b) For those reasons it is necessary to establish a national system for locating parents and children who travel from one such jurisdiction to another and are concealed in connection with such disputes, and to establish national standards under which the courts of such jurisdictions will determine their jurisdiction to decide such disputes and the effect to be given by each such jurisdiction to such decisions by the courts of other such jurisdictions.

"(c) The general purposes of sections 6 to 10 of this Act [enacting this section and sections 654(17) and 663 of Title 42, The Public Health and Welfare, amending section 655(a) of Title 42, and enacting provisions set out as notes under this section and sections 663 and 1305 of Title 42 and 1073 of Title 18, Crimes and Criminal Procedure] are to—

"(1) promote cooperation between State courts to the end that a determination of custody and visitation is rendered in the State which can best decide the case in the interest of the child;

"(2) promote and expand the exchange of information and other forms of mutual assistance between States which are concerned with the same child;

"(3) facilitate the enforcement of custody and visitation decrees of sister States;

"(4) discourage continuing interstate controversies over child custody in the interest of greater stability of home environment and of secure family relationships for the child;

"(5) avoid jurisdictional competition and conflict between State courts in matters of child custody and visitation which have in the past resulted in the shifting of children from State to State with harmful effects on their well-being; and

"(6) deter interstate abductions and other unilateral removals of children undertaken to obtain custody and visitation awards."

State Court Proceedings for Custody Determinations; Priority Treatment; Fees, Costs, and Other Expenses

Section 8(c) of Pub.L. 96–611 provided that: "In furtherance of the purposes of section 1738A of title 28, United States Code [this section], as added by subsection (a) of this section, State courts are encouraged to—

"(1) afford priority to proceedings for custody determinations; and

"(2) award to the person entitled to custody or visitation pursuant to a custody determination which is consistent with the provisions of such section 1738A [this section], necessary travel expenses, attorneys' fees, costs of private investigations, witness fees or expenses, and other expenses incurred in connection with such custody determination in any case in which—

"(A) a contestant has, without the consent of the person entitled to custody or visitation pursuant to a custody determination which is consistent with the provisions of such section 1738A [this section], (i) wrongfully removed the child from the physical custody of such person, or (ii) wrongfully retained the child after a visit or other temporary relinquishment of physical custody; or

"**(B)** the court determines it is appropriate."

§ 1738B.   Full faith and credit for child support orders

(a) General rule.—The appropriate authorities of each State—

(1) shall enforce according to its terms a child support order made consistently with this section by a court of another State; and

(2) shall not seek or make a modification of such an order except in accordance with subsections (e), (f), and (i).

(b) Definitions.—In this section:

"child" means—

(A) a person under 18 years of age; and

(B) a person 18 or more years of age with respect to whom a child support order has been issued pursuant to the laws of a State.

"child's State" means the State in which a child resides.

"child's home State" means the State in which a child lived with a parent or a person acting as parent for at least 6 consecutive months immediately preceding the time of filing of a petition or comparable pleading for support and, if a child is less than 6 months old, the State in which the child lived from birth with any of them. A period of temporary absence of any of them is counted as part of the 6–month period.

"child support" means a payment of money, continuing support, or arrearages or the provision of a benefit (including payment of health insurance, child care, and educational expenses) for the support of a child.

"child support order"—

(A) means a judgment, decree, or order of a court requiring the payment of child support in periodic amounts or in a lump sum; and

(B) includes—

(i) a permanent or temporary order; and

(ii) an initial order or a modification of an order.

"contestant" means—

(A) a person (including a parent) who—

(i) claims a right to receive child support;

(ii) is a party to a proceeding that may result in the issuance of a child support order; or

(iii) is under a child support order; and

(B) a State or political subdivision of a State to which the right to obtain child support has been assigned.

"court" means a court or administrative agency of a State that is authorized by State law to establish the amount of child support payable by a contestant or make a modification of a child support order.

"modification" means a change in a child support order that affects the amount, scope, or duration of the order and modifies, replaces, supersedes, or otherwise is made subsequent to the child support order.

"State" means a State of the United States, the District of Columbia, the Commonwealth of Puerto Rico, the territories and possessions of the United States, and Indian country (as defined in section 1151 of title 18).

(c) Requirements of child support orders.—A child support order made by a court of a State is made consistently with this section if—

(1) a court that makes the order, pursuant to the laws of the State in which the court is located and subsections (e), (f), and (g)—

(A) has subject matter jurisdiction to hear the matter and enter such an order; and

(B) has personal jurisdiction over the contestants; and

(2) reasonable notice and opportunity to be heard is given to the contestants.

(d) Continuing jurisdiction.—A court of a State that has made a child support order consistently with this section has continuing, exclusive jurisdiction over the order if the State is the child's State or the residence of any individual contestant unless the court of another State, acting in accordance with subsections (e) and (f), has made a modification of the order.

(e) Authority to modify orders.—A court of a State may modify a child support order issued by a court of another State if—

(1) the court has jurisdiction to make such a child support order pursuant to subsection (i); and

(2)(A) the court of the other State no longer has continuing, exclusive jurisdiction of the child support order because that State no longer is the child's State or the residence of any individual contestant; or

(B) each individual contestant has filed written consent with the State of continuing, exclusive jurisdiction for a court of another State to modify the order and assume continuing, exclusive jurisdiction over the order.

(f) Recognition of child support orders.—If 1 or more child support orders have been issued with regard to an obligor and a child, a court shall apply the following rules in determining which order to recognize for purposes of continuing, exclusive jurisdiction and enforcement:

(1) If only 1 court has issued a child support order, the order of that court must be recognized.

(2) If 2 or more courts have issued child support orders for the same obligor and child, and only 1 of the courts would have continuing, exclusive jurisdiction under this section, the order of that court must be recognized.

(3) If 2 or more courts have issued child support orders for the same obligor and child, and more than 1 of the courts would have continuing, exclusive jurisdiction under this section, an order issued by a court in the current home State of the child must be recognized, but if an order has not been issued in the current home State of the child, the order most recently issued must be recognized.

(4) If 2 or more courts have issued child support orders for the same obligor and child, and none of the courts would have continuing, exclusive jurisdiction under this section, a court having jurisdiction over the parties shall issue a child support order, which must be recognized.

(5) The court that has issued an order recognized under this subsection is the court having continuing, exclusive jurisdiction under subsection (d).

(g) Enforcement of modified orders.—A court of a State that no longer has continuing, exclusive jurisdiction of a child support order may enforce the order with respect to nonmodifiable obligations and unsatisfied obligations that accrued before the date on which a modification of the order is made under subsections (e) and (f).

(h) Choice of law.—

(1) In general.—In a proceeding to establish, modify, or enforce a child support order, the forum State's law shall apply except as provided in paragraphs (2) and (3).

(2) Law of State of issuance of order.—In interpreting a child support order including the duration of current payments and other obligations of support, a court shall apply the law of the State of the court that issued the order.

(3) Period of limitation.—In an action to enforce arrears under a child support order, a court shall apply the statute of limitation of the forum State or the State of the court that issued the order, whichever statute provides the longer period of limitation.

(i) Registration for modification.—If there is no individual contestant or child residing in the issuing State, the party or support enforcement agency seeking to modify, or to modify and enforce, a child support order issued in another State shall register that order in a State with jurisdiction over the nonmovant for the purpose of modification.

(Added Pub.L. 103–383, § 3(a), Oct. 22, 1994, 108 Stat. 4064, and amended Pub.L. 104–193, Title III, § 322, Aug. 22, 1996, 110 Stat. 2221; Pub.L. 105–33, Title V, § 5554, Aug. 5, 1997, 111 Stat. 636.)

HISTORICAL AND STATUTORY NOTES

Effective and Applicability Provisions

1997 Acts. Amendments by Pub.L. 105–33 made by sections 5531 to 5556 to take effect as if included in the enactment of Title III of the Personal Responsibility and Work Opportunity Reconciliation Act of 1996 (Pub.L. 104–193, Aug. 22, 1996, 110 Stat. 2105), except for amendments made by section 5532(b)(2) (amending section 608(a)(3)(A) of Title 42, The Public Health and Welfare), see section 5557 of Pub.L. 105–33, set out as a note under section 608 of Title 42, The Public Health and Welfare.

1996 Acts. For effective date of Title III of Pub.L. 104–193, see section 395(a) to (c) of Pub.L. 104–193, set out as a note under section 654 of Title 42, The Public Health and Welfare.

Congressional Findings and Declaration of Purpose

Section 2 of Pub.L. 103–383 provided that:

"**(a) Findings.**—The Congress finds that—

"**(1)** there is a large and growing number of child support cases annually involving disputes between parents who reside in different States;

"**(2)** the laws by which the courts of different jurisdictions determine their authority to establish child support orders are not uniform;

"**(3)** those laws, along with the limits imposed by the Federal system on the authority of each State to take certain actions outside its own boundaries—

"**(A)** encourage noncustodial parents to relocate outside the States where their children and the custodial parents reside to avoid the jurisdiction of the courts of such States, resulting in an increase in the amount of interstate travel and communication required to establish and collect on child support orders and a burden on custodial parents that is expensive, time consuming, and disruptive of occupations and commercial activity;

"**(B)** contribute to the pressing problem of relatively low levels of child support payments in interstate cases and to inequities in child support payments levels that are based solely on the noncustodial parent's choice of residence;

"**(C)** encourage a disregard of court orders resulting in massive arrearages nationwide;

"**(D)** allow noncustodial parents to avoid the payment of regularly scheduled child support payments for extensive periods of time, resulting in substantial hardship for the children for whom support is due and for their custodians; and

"**(E)** lead to the excessive relitigation of cases and to the establishment of conflicting orders by the courts of various jurisdictions, resulting in confusion, waste of judicial resources, disrespect for the courts, and a diminution of public confidence in the rule of law; and

"**(4)** among the results of the conditions described in this subsection are—

"**(A)** the failure of the courts of the States to give full faith and credit to the judicial proceedings of the other States;

"**(B)** the deprivation of rights of liberty and property without due process of law;

"**(C)** burdens on commerce among the States; and

"**(D)** harm to the welfare of children and their parents and other custodians.

"**(b) Statement of policy.**—In view of the findings made in subsection (a), it is necessary to establish national standards under which the courts of the various States shall determine their jurisdiction to issue a child support order and the effect to be given by each State to child support orders issued by the courts of other States.

"**(c) Purposes.**—The purposes of this Act [enacting this section and a provision set out as a note under section 1 of this title] are—

"**(1)** to facilitate the enforcement of child support orders among the States;

"**(2)** to discourage continuing interstate controversies over child support in the interest of greater financial stability and secure family relationships for the child; and

"**(3)** to avoid jurisdictional competition and conflict among State courts in the establishment of child support orders."

§ 1738C. Certain acts, records, and proceedings and the effect thereof

No State, territory, or possession of the United States, or Indian tribe, shall be required to give effect to any public act, record, or judicial proceeding of any other State, territory, possession, or tribe respecting a relationship between persons of the same sex that is treated as a marriage under the laws of such other State, territory, possession, or tribe, or a right or claim arising from such relationship.

(Added Pub.L. 104–199, § 2(a), Sept. 21, 1996, 110 Stat. 2419.)

§ 1739. State and Territorial nonjudicial records; full faith and credit

All nonjudicial records or books kept in any public office of any State, Territory, or Possession of the United States, or copies thereof, shall be proved or admitted in any court or office in any other State, Territory, or Possession by the attestation of the custodian of such records or books, and the seal of his office annexed, if there be a seal, together with a certificate of a judge of a court of record of the county, parish, or district in which such office may be kept, or of the Governor, or secretary of state, the chancellor or keeper of the great seal, of the State, Territory, or Possession that the said attestation is in due form and by the proper officers.

If the certificate is given by a judge, it shall be further authenticated by the clerk or prothonotary of the court, who shall certify, under his hand and the seal of his office, that such judge is duly commissioned and qualified; or, if given by such Governor, secre-

tary, chancellor, or keeper of the great seal, it shall be under the great seal of the State, Territory, or Possession in which it is made.

Such records or books, or copies thereof, so authenticated, shall have the same full faith and credit in every court and office within the United States and its Territories and Possessions as they have by law or usage in the courts or offices of the State, Territory, or Possession from which they are taken.

(June 25, 1948, c. 646, 62 Stat. 947.)

§ 1740. Copies of consular papers

Copies of all official documents and papers in the office of any consul or vice consul of the United States, and of all official entries in the books or records of any such office, authenticated by the consul or vice consul, shall be admissible equally with the originals.

(June 25, 1948, c. 646, 62 Stat. 947.)

§ 1741. Foreign official documents

An official record or document of a foreign country may be evidenced by a copy, summary, or excerpt authenticated as provided in the Federal Rules of Civil Procedure.

(June 25, 1948, c. 646, 62 Stat. 948; May 24, 1949, c. 139, § 92(b), 63 Stat. 103; Oct. 3, 1964, Pub.L. 88–619, § 5(a), 78 Stat. 996.)

HISTORICAL AND STATUTORY NOTES

Treaties and Conventions; Taking of Evidence Abroad in Civil or Commercial Matters; Observance On and After Oct. 7, 1972, by United States and Citizens and Persons Subject to Jurisdiction of United States

For text of Convention, see provisions set out as a note under section 1781 of this title.

[§ 1742. Repealed. Pub.L. 88–619, § 6(a), Oct. 3, 1964, 78 Stat. 996]

HISTORICAL AND STATUTORY NOTES

Section, Act June 25, 1948, c. 646, 62 Stat. 948, related to authentication and certification of copies of documents relating to land titles, by persons having custody of such of any foreign government or its agents, certification by an American minister or consul that they be true copies of the originals, the recording of such copies in the office of the General Counsel for the Department of the Treasury, and to the evidentiary value of such copies.

§ 1743. Demand on postmaster

The certificate of the Postmaster General or the Government Accountability Office of the mailing to a postmaster of a statement of his account and that payment of the balance stated has not been received shall be sufficient evidence of a demand notwithstanding any allowances or credits subsequently made. A copy of such statement shall be attached to the certificate.

(June 25, 1948, c. 646, 62 Stat. 948; July 7, 2004, Pub.L. 108–271, § 8(b), 118 Stat. 814.)

HISTORICAL AND STATUTORY NOTES

Change of Name

"Government Accountability Office" substituted for "General Accounting Office" in text on authority of Pub.L. 108–271, § 8(b), cited in the credit to this section and set out as a note under 31 U.S.C.A. § 702, which provided that any reference to the General Accounting Office in any law, rule, regulation, certificate, directive, instruction, or other official paper in force on July 17, 2004, to refer and apply to the Government Accountability Office.

Transfer of Functions

The office of Postmaster General of the Post Office Department was abolished and all functions, powers, and duties of the Postmaster General were transferred to the United States Postal Service by Pub.L. 91–375, § 4(a), Aug. 12, 1970, 84 Stat. 773, set out as a note under section 201 of Title 39, Postal Service.

§ 1744. Copies of United States Patent and Trademark Office documents, generally

Copies of letters patent or of any records, books, papers, or drawings belonging to the United States Patent and Trademark Office and relating to patents, authenticated under the seal of the United States Patent and Trademark Office and certified by the Under Secretary of Commerce for Intellectual Property and Director of the United States Patent and Trademark Office, or by another officer of the United States Patent and Trademark Office authorized to do so by the Director, shall be admissible in evidence with the same effect as the originals.

Any person making application and paying the required fee may obtain such certified copies.

(June 25, 1948, c. 646, 62 Stat. 948; May 24, 1949, c. 139, § 92(c), 63 Stat. 103; Nov. 29, 1999, Pub.L. 106–113, Div. B, § 1000(a)(9) [Title IV, § 4732(b)(15)(B), (C)], 113 Stat. 1536, 1501A–584.)

HISTORICAL AND STATUTORY NOTES

Effective and Applicability Provisions

1999 Acts. Amendment by Pub.L. 106–113 [§ 4732], effective 4 months after Nov. 29, 1999, see Pub.L. 106–113 [§ 4731], set out as a note under section 1 of Title 35.

Change of Name

Patent Office and Commissioner of Patents redesignated Patent and Trademark Office and Commissioner of Patents and Trademarks, respectively, by section 3 of Pub.L. 93–596, Jan. 2, 1975, 88 Stat. 1949, set out as a note under section 1 of Title 35, Patents.

Transfer of Functions

The functions of all officers of the Department of Commerce and all functions of all agencies and employees of such Department, were, with a few exceptions, transferred to the Secretary of Commerce, with power vested in him to author-

ize their performance or the performance of any of his functions by any of such officers, agencies, and employees, by 1950 Reorg. Plan No. 5, §§ 1, 2, eff. May 24, 1950, 15 F.R. 3174, 64 Stat. 1263, set out in Appendix 1 to Title 5, Government Organization and Employees. The Patent Office [now Patent and Trademark Office], referred to in this section, is an agency of the Department of Commerce, and the Commissioner of Patents [now Commissioner of Patents and Trademarks], referred to in this section, is an officer of such Department.

§ 1745. Copies of foreign patent documents

Copies of the specifications and drawings of foreign letters patent, or applications for foreign letters patent, and copies of excerpts of the official journals and other official publications of foreign patent offices belonging to the United States Patent and Trademark Office, certified in the manner provided by section 1744 of this title are prima facie evidence of their contents and of the dates indicated on their face.

(June 25, 1948, c. 646, 62 Stat. 948, § 1746; renumbered § 1745 and amended May 24, 1949, c. 139, § 92(d), (e), 63 Stat. 103; Oct. 3, 1964, Pub.L. 88–619, § 7(a), 78 Stat. 996; Nov. 29, 1999, Pub.L. 106–113, Div. B, § 1000(a)(9) [Title IV, § 4732(b)(16)], 113 Stat. 1536, 1501A–585.)

HISTORICAL AND STATUTORY NOTES

Effective and Applicability Provisions

1999 Acts. Amendment by Pub.L. 106–113 [§ 4732], effective 4 months after Nov. 29, 1999, see Pub.L. 106–113 [§ 4731], set out as a note under section 1 of Title 35.

Change of Name

Patent Office redesignated Patent and Trademark Office by section 3 of Pub.L. 93–596, Jan. 2, 1975, 88 Stat. 1949, set out as a note under section 1 of Title 35, Patents.

Prior Provisions

A prior section 1745, Act June 25, 1948, c. 646, 62 Stat. 948, related to printed copies of patent specifications and drawings, prior to repeal by Act May 24, 1949, c. 139, § 92(d), 63 Stat. 103.

§ 1746. Unsworn declarations under penalty of perjury

Wherever, under any law of the United States or under any rule, regulation, order, or requirement made pursuant to law, any matter is required or permitted to be supported, evidenced, established, or proved by the sworn declaration, verification, certificate, statement, oath, or affidavit, in writing of the person making the same (other than a deposition, or an oath of office, or an oath required to be taken before a specified official other than a notary public), such matter may, with like force and effect, be supported, evidenced, established, or proved by the unsworn declaration, certificate, verification, or statement, in writing of such person which is subscribed by him, as true under penalty of perjury, and dated, in substantially the following form:

---

(1) If executed without the United States: "I declare (or certify, verify, or state) under penalty of perjury under the laws of the United States of America that the foregoing is true and correct. Executed on (date).

(Signature)".

(2) If executed within the United States, its territories, possessions, or commonwealths: "I declare (or certify, verify, or state) under penalty of perjury

that the foregoing is true and correct. Executed on (date).

(Signature)".

(Added Pub.L. 94–550, § 1(a), Oct. 18, 1976, 90 Stat. 2534.)

HISTORICAL AND STATUTORY NOTES

Prior Provisions

A prior section 1746 was renumbered section 1745 of this title by Act May 24, 1949.

CHAPTER 117—EVIDENCE; DEPOSITIONS

HISTORICAL AND STATUTORY NOTES

Deposition in Admiralty Cases

Prior to the general unification of civil and admiralty procedure and the rescission of the Admiralty Rules on July 1, 1966, Revised Statutes, §§ 863 to 865, as amended, which related to depositions de bene esse, when and how taken, notice, mode of taking, and transmission to court, provided as follows:

"Sec. 863. The testimony of any witness may be taken in any civil cause depending in a district court by deposition de bene esse, when the witness lives at a greater distance from the place of trial than one hundred miles, or is bound on a voyage to sea, or is about to go out of the United States, or out of the district in which the case is to be tried, and to a greater distance than one hundred miles from the place of trial, before the time of trial, or when he is ancient and infirm. The deposition may be taken before any judge of any court of the United States, or any clerk of a district court, or any chancellor, justice, or judge of a supreme or superior court, mayor or chief magistrate of a city, judge of a county court or court of common pleas of any of the United States, or any notary public, not being of counsel or attorney to either of the parties, nor interested in the event of the cause. Reasonable notice must first be given in writing by the party or his attorney proposing to take such deposition, to the opposite party or his attorney of record, as either may be nearest, which notice shall state the name of the witness and the time and place of the taking of his deposition; and in all cases in rem, the person having the agency or possession of the property at the time of seizure shall be deemed the adverse party, until a claim shall have been put in; and whenever, by reason of the absence from the district and want of an attorney of record or other reason, the giving of the notice herein required shall be impracticable, it shall be lawful to take such depositions as there shall be urgent necessity for taking, upon such notice as any judge authorized to hold courts in such district shall think reasonable and direct. Any person may be compelled to appear and depose as provided by this section, in the same manner as witnesses may be compelled to appear and testify in court.

"Sec. 864. Every person deposing as provided in the preceding section [R.S. § 863] shall be cautioned and sworn to testify the whole truth, and carefully examined.

"His testimony shall be reduced to writing or typewriting by the officer taking the deposition, or by some person under his personal supervision, or by the deponent himself in the officer's presence, and by no other person, and shall, after it has been reduced to writing or typewriting, be subscribed by the deponent. [As amended May 23, 1900, c. 541, 31 Stat. 182.]

"Sec. 865. Every deposition taken under the two preceding sections [R.S. §§ 863, 864] shall be retained by the magistrate taking it, until he delivers it with his own hand into the court for which it is taken; or it shall, together with a certificate of the reasons as aforesaid of taking it and of the notice, if any, given to the adverse party, be by him sealed up and directed to such court, and remain under his seal until opened in court. But unless it appears to the satisfaction of the court that the witness is then dead, or gone out of the United States, or to a greater distance than one hundred miles from the place where the court is sitting, or that, by reason of age, sickness, bodily infirmity, or imprisonment, he is unable to travel and appear at court, such deposition shall not be used in the cause."

R.S. §§ 863 to 865, as amended, quoted above, were applicable to admiralty proceedings only. Proceedings in bankruptcy and copyright are governed by Rule 26 et seq. of Federal Rules of Civil Procedure. See also Rules of Bankruptcy Procedure set out in Title 11, Bankruptcy.

§ 1781. Transmittal of letter rogatory or request

(a) The Department of State has power, directly, or through suitable channels—

(1) to receive a letter rogatory issued, or request made, by a foreign or international tribunal, to transmit it to the tribunal, officer, or agency in the United States to whom it is addressed, and to receive and return it after execution; and

(2) to receive a letter rogatory issued, or request made, by a tribunal in the United States, to transmit it to the foreign or international tribunal, officer, or agency to whom it is addressed, and to receive and return it after execution.

(b) This section does not preclude—

(1) the transmittal of a letter rogatory or request directly from a foreign or international tribunal to the tribunal, officer, or agency in the United States to whom it is addressed and its return in the same manner; or

(2) the transmittal of a letter rogatory or request directly from a tribunal in the United States to the foreign or international tribunal, officer, or agency to whom it is addressed and its return in the same manner.

(June 25, 1948, c. 646, 62 Stat. 949; Oct. 3, 1964, Pub.L. 88–619, § 8(a), 78 Stat. 996.)

TREATIES AND CONVENTIONS
CONVENTION ON THE TAKING OF EVIDENCE ABROAD IN CIVIL OR COMMERCIAL MATTERS

The States signatory to the present Convention,

Desiring to facilitate the transmission and execution of Letters of Request and to further the accommodation of the different methods which they use for this purpose.

Desiring to improve mutual judicial co-operation in civil or commercial matters.

Have resolved to conclude a Convention to this effect and have agreed upon the following provisions—

*   *   *   *   *   *   *

CHAPTER I—LETTERS OF REQUEST
Article 1

In civil or commercial matters a judicial authority of a Contracting State may, in accordance with the provisions of the law of that State, request the competent authority of another Contracting State, by means of a Letter of Request, to obtain evidence, or to perform some other judicial act.

A Letter shall not be used to obtain evidence which is not intended for use in judicial proceedings, commenced or contemplated.

The expression "other judicial act" does not cover the service of judicial documents or the issuance of any process by which judgments or orders are executed or enforced, or orders for provisional or protective measures.

Article 2

A Contracting State shall designate a Central Authority which will undertake to receive Letters of Request coming from a judicial authority of another Contracting State and to transmit them to the authority competent to execute them. Each State shall organize the Central Authority in accordance with its own law.

Letters shall be sent to the Central Authority of the State of execution without being transmitted through any other authority of that State.

Article 3

A Letter of Request shall specify—

(a) the authority requesting its execution and the authority requested to execute it, if known to the requesting authority;

(b) the names and addresses of the parties to the proceedings and their representatives, if any;

(c) the nature of the proceedings for which the evidence is required, giving all necessary information in regard thereto;

(d) the evidence to be obtained or other judicial act to be performed.

Where appropriate, the Letter shall specify, inter alia—

(e) the names and addresses of the persons to be examined;

(f) the questions to be put to the persons to be examined or a statement of the subject-matter about which they are to be examined;

(g) the documents or other property, real or personal, to be inspected;

(h) any requirement that the evidence is to be given on oath or affirmation, and any special form to be used;

(i) any special method or procedure to be followed under Article 9.

A Letter may also mention any information necessary for the application of Article 11.

No legalization or other like formality may be required.

Article 4

A Letter of Request shall be in the language of the authority requested to execute it or be accompanied by a translation into that language.

Nevertheless, a Contracting State shall accept a Letter in either English or French, or a translation into one of these languages, unless it has made the reservation authorized by Article 33.

A Contracting State which has more than one official language and cannot, for reasons of internal law, accept Letters in one of these languages for the whole of its territory, shall, by declaration, specify the language in which the Letter or translation thereof shall be expressed for execution in the specified parts of its territory. In case of failure to comply with this declaration, without justifiable excuse, the costs of translation into the required language shall be borne by the State of origin.

A Contracting State may, by declaration, specify the language or languages other than those referred to in the preceding paragraphs, in which a Letter may be sent to its Central Authority.

Any translation accompanying a Letter shall be certified as correct, either by a diplomatic officer or consular agent or by a sworn translator or by any other person so authorized in either State.

Article 5

If the Central Authority considers that the request does not comply with the provisions of the present Convention, it shall promptly inform the authority of the State of origin which transmitted the Letter of Request, specifying the objections to the Letter.

Article 6

If the authority to whom a Letter of Request has been transmitted is not competent to execute it, the Letter shall be sent forthwith to the authority in the same State which is competent to execute it in accordance with the provisions of its own law.

Article 7

The requesting authority shall, if it so desires, be informed of the time when, and the place where, the proceedings will take place, in order that the parties concerned, and their representatives, if any, may be present. This information shall be sent directly to the parties or their representatives when the authority of the State of origin so requests.

Article 8

A Contracting State may declare that members of the judicial personnel of the requesting authority of another Contracting State may be present at the execution of a Letter of Request. Prior authorization by the competent authority designated by the declaring State may be required.

Article 9

The judicial authority which executes a Letter of Request shall apply its own law as to the methods and procedures to be followed.

However, it will follow a request of the requesting authority that a special method or procedure be followed, unless this is incompatible with the internal law of the State of execution or is impossible of performance by reason of its internal practice and procedure or by reason of practical difficulties.

A Letter of Request shall be executed expeditiously.

Article 10

In executing a Letter of Request the requested authority shall apply the appropriate measures of compulsion in the instances and to the same extent as are provided by its internal law for the execution of orders issued by the authorities of its own country or of requests made by parties in internal proceedings.

Article 11

In the execution of a Letter of Request the person concerned may refuse to give evidence in so far as he has a privilege or duty to refuse to give the evidence—

(a) under the law of the State of execution; or

(b) under the law of the State of origin, and the privilege or duty has been specified in the Letter, or, at the instance of the requested authority, has been otherwise confirmed to that authority by the requesting authority.

A Contracting State may declare that, in addition, it will respect privileges and duties existing under the law of States other than the State of origin and the State of execution, to the extent specified in that declaration.

Article 12

The execution of a Letter of Request may be refused only to the extent that—

(a) in the State of execution the execution of the Letter does not fall within the functions of the judiciary; or

(b) the State addressed considers that its sovereignty or security would be prejudiced thereby.

Execution may not be refused solely on the ground that under its internal law the State of execution claims exclusive jurisdiction over the subject-matter of the action or that its internal law would not admit a right of action on it.

Article 13

The documents establishing the execution of the Letter of Request shall be sent by the requested authority to the requesting authority by the same channel which was used by the latter.

In every instance where the Letter is not executed in whole or in part, the requesting authority shall be informed immediately through the same channel and advised of the reasons.

Article 14

The execution of the Letter of Request shall not give rise to any reimbursement of taxes or costs of any nature.

Nevertheless, the State of execution has the right to require the State of origin to reimburse the fees paid to experts and interpreters and the costs occasioned by the use of a special procedure requested by the State of origin under Article 9, paragraph 2.

The requested authority whose law obliges the parties themselves to secure evidence, and which is not able itself to execute the Letter, may, after having obtained the consent of the requesting authority, appoint a suitable person to do so. When seeking this consent the requested authority shall indicate the approximate costs which would result from this procedure. If the requesting authority gives its consent it shall reimburse any costs incurred; without such consent the requesting authority shall not be liable for the costs.

CHAPTER II—TAKING OF EVIDENCE BY DIPLOMATIC OFFICERS, CONSULAR AGENTS AND COMMISSIONERS

Article 15

In a civil or commercial matter, a diplomatic officer or consular agent of a Contracting State may, in the territory of another Contracting State and within the area where he exercises his functions, take the evidence without compulsion of nationals of a State which he represents in aid of proceedings commenced in the courts of a State which he represents.

A Contracting State may declare that evidence may be taken by a diplomatic officer or consular agent only if permission to that effect is given upon application made by him or on his behalf to the appropriate authority designated by the declaring State.

Article 16

A diplomatic officer or consular agent of a Contracting State may, in the territory of another Contracting State and within the area where he exercises his functions, also take the evidence, without compulsion, of nationals of the State in which he exercises his functions or of a third State, in aid of proceedings commenced in the courts of a State which he represents, if—

(a) a competent authority designated by the State in which he exercises his functions has given its permission either generally or in the particular case, and

(b) he complies with the conditions which the competent authority has specified in the permission.

Complete Annotation Materials, see Title 28 U.S.C.A.

A Contracting State may declare that evidence may be taken under this Article without its prior permission.

Article 17

In a civil or commercial matter, a person duly appointed as a commissioner for the purpose may, without compulsion, take evidence in the territory of a Contracting State in aid of proceedings commenced in the courts of another Contracting State if—

(a) a competent authority designated by the State where the evidence is to be taken has given its permission either generally or in the particular case; and

(b) he complies with the conditions which the competent authority has specified in the permission.

A Contracting State may declare that evidence may be taken under this Article without its prior permission.

Article 18

A Contracting State may declare that a diplomatic officer, consular agent or commissioner authorized to take evidence under Articles 15, 16 or 17, may apply to the competent authority designated by the declaring State for appropriate assistance to obtain the evidence by compulsion. The declaration may contain such conditions as the declaring State may see fit to impose.

If the authority grants the application it shall apply any measures of compulsion which are appropriate and are prescribed by its law for use in internal proceedings.

Article 19

The competent authority, in giving the permission referred to in Articles 15, 16 or 17, or in granting the application referred to in Article 18, may lay down such conditions as it deems fit, *inter alia*, as to the time and place of the taking of the evidence. Similarly it may require that it be given reasonable advance notice of the time, date and place of the taking of the evidence; in such a case a representative of the authority shall be entitled to be present at the taking of the evidence.

Article 20

In the taking of evidence under any Article of this Chapter persons concerned may be legally represented.

Article 21

Where a diplomatic officer, consular agent or commissioner is authorized under Articles 15, 16 or 17 to take evidence—

(a) he may take all kinds of evidence which are not incompatible with the law of the State where the evidence is taken or contrary to any permission granted pursuant to the above Articles, and shall have power within such limits to administer an oath or take an affirmation;

(b) a request to a person to appear or to give evidence shall, unless the recipient is a national of the State where the action is pending, be drawn up in the language of the place where the evidence is taken or be accompanied by a translation into such language;

(c) the request shall inform the person that he may be legally represented and, in any State that has not filed a declaration under Article 18, shall also inform him that he is not compelled to appear or to give evidence;

(d) the evidence may be taken in the manner provided by the law applicable to the court in which the action is pending provided that such manner is not forbidden by the law of the State where the evidence is taken;

(e) a person requested to give evidence may invoke the privileges and duties to refuse to give the evidence contained in Article 11.

Article 22

The fact that an attempt to take evidence under the procedure laid down in this Chapter has failed, owing to the refusal of a person to give evidence, shall not prevent an application being subsequently made to take the evidence in accordance with Chapter I.

CHAPTER III—GENERAL CLAUSES

Article 23

A Contracting State may at the time of signature, ratification or accession, declare that it will not execute Letters of Request issued for the purpose of obtaining pretrial discovery of documents as known in Common Law countries.

Article 24

A Contracting State may designate other authorities in addition to the Central Authority and shall determine the extent of their competence. However, Letters of Request may in all cases be sent to the Central Authority.

Federal States shall be free to designate more than one Central Authority.

Article 25

A Contracting State which has more than one legal system may designate the authorities of one of such systems, which shall have exclusive competence to execute Letters of Request pursuant to this Convention.

Article 26

A Contracting State, if required to do so because of constitutional limitations, may request the reimbursement by the State of origin of fees and costs, in connection with the execution of Letters of Request, for the service of process necessary to compel the appearance of a person to give evidence, the costs of attendance of such persons, and the cost of any transcript of the evidence.

Where a State has made a request pursuant to the above paragraph, any other Contracting State may request from that State the reimbursement of similar fees and costs.

Article 27

The provisions of the present Convention shall not prevent a Contracting State from—

(a) declaring that Letters of Request may be transmitted to its judicial authorities through channels other than those provided for in Article 2;

(b) permitting, by internal law or practice, any act provided for in this Convention to be performed upon less restrictive conditions;

(c) permitting, by internal law or practice, methods of taking evidence other than those provided for in this Convention.

Article 28

The present Convention shall not prevent an agreement between any two or more Contracting States to derogate from—

(a) the provisions of Article 2 with respect to methods of transmitting Letters of Request;

(b) the provisions of Article 4 with respect to the languages which may be used;

(c) the provisions of Article 8 with respect to the presence of judicial personnel at the execution of Letters;

(d) the provisions of Article 11 with respect to the privileges and duties of witnesses to refuse to give evidence;

(e) the provisions of Article 13 with respect to the methods of returning executed Letters to the requesting authority;

(f) the provisions of Article 14 with respect to fees and costs;

(g) the provisions of Chapter II.

Article 29

Between Parties to the present Convention who are also Parties to one or both of the Conventions on Civil Procedure signed at the Hague on the 17th of July 1905 [99 British Foreign and State Papers 990] and the 1st of March 1954 [286 UNTS 265], this Convention shall replace Articles 8–16 of the earlier Conventions.

Article 30

The present Convention shall not affect the application of Article 23 of the Convention of 1905, or of Article 24 of the Convention of 1954.

Article 31

Supplementary Agreements between Parties to the Conventions of 1905 and 1954 shall be considered as equally applicable to the present Convention unless the Parties have otherwise agreed.

Article 32

Without prejudice to the provisions of Articles 29 and 31, the present Convention shall not derogate from conventions containing provisions on the matters covered by this Convention to which the Contracting States are, or shall become Parties.

Article 33

A State may, at the time of signature, ratification or accession exclude, in whole or in part, the application of the provisions of paragraph 2 of Article 4 and of Chapter II. No other reservation shall be permitted.

Each Contracting State may at any time withdraw a reservation it has made; the reservation shall cease to have effect on the sixtieth day after notification of the withdrawal.

When a State has made a reservation, any other State affected thereby may apply the same rule against the reserving State.

Article 34

A State may at any time withdraw or modify a declaration.

Article 35

A Contracting State shall, at the time of the deposit of its instrument of ratification or accession, or at a later date, inform the Ministry of Foreign Affairs of the Netherlands of the designation of authorities, pursuant to Articles 2, 8, 24 and 25.

A Contracting State shall likewise inform the Ministry, where appropriate, of the following—

(a) the designation of the authorities to whom notice must be given, whose permission may be required, and whose assistance may be invoked in the taking of evidence by diplomatic officers and consular agents, pursuant to Articles 15, 16 and 18 respectively;

(b) the designation of the authorities whose permission may be required in the taking of evidence by commissioners pursuant to Article 17 and of those who may grant the assistance provided for in Article 18;

(c) declarations pursuant to Articles 4, 8, 11, 15, 16, 17, 18, 23 and 27;

(d) any withdrawal or modification of the above designations and declarations;

(e) the withdrawal of any reservation.

Article 36

Any difficulties which may arise between Contracting States in connection with the operation of this Convention shall be settled through diplomatic channels.

Article 37

The present Convention shall be open for signature by the States represented at the Eleventh Session of the Hague Conference on Private International Law.

It shall be ratified, and the instruments of ratification shall be deposited with the Ministry of Foreign Affairs of the Netherlands.

Article 38

The present Convention shall enter into force on the sixtieth day after the deposit of the third instrument of ratification referred to in the second paragraph of Article 37.

The Convention shall enter into force for each signatory State which ratifies subsequently on the sixtieth day after the deposit of its instrument of ratification.

Article 39

Any State not represented at the Eleventh Session of the Hague Conference on Private International Law which is a Member of this Conference or of the United Nations or of a specialized agency of that Organization, or a Party to the Statute of the International Court of Justice[1] may accede to the present Convention after it has entered into force in accordance with the first paragraph of Article 38.

The instrument of accession shall be deposited with the Ministry of Foreign Affairs of the Netherlands.

The Convention shall enter into force for a State acceding to it on the sixtieth day after the deposit of its instrument of accession.

The accession will have effect only as regards the relations between the acceding State and such Contracting States as will have declared their acceptance of the accession. Such declaration shall be deposited at the Ministry of Foreign Affairs of the Netherlands; this Ministry shall forward, through diplomatic channels, a certified copy to each of the Contracting States.

The Convention will enter into force as between the acceding State and the State that has declared its acceptance of the accession on the sixtieth day after the deposit of the declaration of acceptance.

Article 40

Any State may, at the time of signature, ratification or accession, declare that the present Convention shall extend to all the territories for the international relations of which it is responsible, or to one or more of them. Such a declaration shall take effect on the date of entry into force of the Convention for the State concerned.

At any time thereafter, such extensions shall be notified to the Ministry of Foreign Affairs of the Netherlands.

The Convention shall enter into force for the territories mentioned in such an extension on the sixtieth day after the notification indicated in the preceding paragraph.

Article 41

The present Convention shall remain in force for five years from the date of its entry into force in accordance with the first paragraph of Article 38, even for States which have ratified it or acceded to it subsequently.

If there has been no denunciation, it shall be renewed tacitly every five years.

Any denunciation shall be notified to the Ministry of Foreign Affairs of the Netherlands at least six months before the end of the five year period.

It may be limited to certain of the territories to which the Convention applies.

The denunciation shall have effect only as regards the State which has notified it. The Convention shall remain in force for the other Contracting States.

Article 42

The Ministry of Foreign Affairs of the Netherlands shall give notice to the States referred to in Article 37, and to the States which have acceded in accordance with Article 39, of the following—

(a) the signatures and ratifications referred to in Article 37;

(b) the date on which the present Convention enters into force in accordance with the first paragraph of Article 38;

(c) the accessions referred to in Article 39 and the dates on which they take effect;

(d) the extensions referred to in Article 40 and the dates on which they take effect;

(e) the designations, reservations and declarations referred to in Articles 33 and 35;

(f) the denunciations referred to in the third paragraph of Article 41.

IN WITNESS WHEREOF the undersigned, being duly authorized thereto, have signed the present Convention.

DONE at The Hague, on the 18th day of March 1970, in the English and French languages, both texts being equally authentic, in a single copy which shall be deposited in the archives of the Government of the Netherlands, and of which a certified copy shall be sent, through the diplomatic channel, to each of the States represented at the Eleventh Session of the Hague Conference on Private International Law. [Signatures omitted.]

Convention on the taking of evidence abroad in civil or commercial matters. Done at The Hague March 18, 1970; entered into force for the United States October 7, 1972. TIAS 7444; 23 UST 2555

States which are parties:

Argentina [1]
Australia [1a]
Barbados [1b]
China, Hong Kong Special Administrative Region only [1c]
Cyprus [1d]
Czech Republic [1e]
Denmark [1f]
Estonia [1g]
Finland [2]
France [2a]
Federal Republic of Germany [2b]
Israel [2c]
Italy [2d]
Latvia [2e]
Luxemburg [2f]
Mexico [2g]
Monaco [2h]
Netherlands [2i]
Norway [3]
Poland [3a]
Portugal [3b]
Singapore [3c]
Slovak Republic [3d]
South Africa [3e]
Spain [3f]
Sweden [3g]
Switzerland [3h]
United Kingdom [3i]
United States [4]
Venezuela [5]

---

[1] *Notification pursuant to Article 42 of the Convention*

In conformity with Article 39, paragraph 2, the instrument of accession by the **Argentine Republic** to the above-mentioned Convention was deposited with the Ministry of Foreign Affairs of the Kingdom of the Netherlands on 8 May 1987.

The instrument of accession of the Argentine Republic contains the following reservation, referred to in Article 33, first paragraph, of the Convention:

"La República Argentina excluye totalmente la applicación de las disposiciones del párrafo 2° del artículo 4°, así como las del capítulo II."

(Translation)

"The Argentine Republic totally excludes the application of the provisions of paragraph 2 of Article *4*, as well as those of Chapter II.";

and the following declaration regarding Article 23 of the Convention:

"La República Argentina no cumplirá los exhortos que tengan por objeto un procedimiento conocido en Los Estados del "Common Law", por el nombre de "pre-trial discovery of documents (exhibicion de documentos antes del juicio)."

(Translation)

"The Argentine Republic will not execute Letters of Request issued for the purpose of obtaining pre-trial discovery of documents as known in the Common Law Countries."

Furthermore, the instrument contains the declaration annexed to this notification.

In accordance with paragraph 3 of Article 39, the Convention will enter into force for the Argentine Republic on 7 July 1987.

According to Article 39, paragraph 4 of the Convention, the accession will have effect only as regards the relations between the Argentine Republic and such Contracting States as will have declared their acceptance of the accession. Such declarations shall be deposited at the Ministry of Foreign Affairs of the Kingdom of the Netherlands.

The Hague 20, May 1987

"The Argentine Republic excludes the extension of the application of the Convention on the taking of evidence abroad in civil or commercial matters, adopted at The Hague on March 18, 1970, to the Malvinas, South Georgia, and South Sandwich Islands, which was notified by the United Kingdom of Great Britain and Northern Ireland to the Ministry of Foreign Affairs of the Kingdom of the Netherlands on November 23, 1979, and reaffirms its rights of sovereignty over the Malvinas, South Georgia and South Sandwich Islands, which form an integral part of its national territory."

The General Assembly of the United Nations has adopted resolutions 2065 (XX), 3160 (XXVIII), 31/49, 37/9, 38/12, 39/6, 40/21 and 41/40 in which the existence of a dispute of sovereignty is recognized in reference to the Malvinas Islands, and it urges the Argentine Republic and the United Kingdom of Great Britain and Northern Ireland to maintain negotiations with the purpose of finding a peaceful and definitive solution to the dispute as soon as possible, with the good offices of the Secretary General of the United Nations, who will inform the General Assembly of the progress that has been accomplished.

In like manner, "the Argentine Republic excludes the June 19, 1986 approval formulated by the United Kingdom of Great Britain and Northern Ireland for the Malvinas, South Georgia and South Sandwich Islands with respect to the accession of the Principality of Monaco to the aforementioned Convention." (Translation provided by the Division of Language Services, Department of State)

In accordance with Article 35 of the Convention the Government of the Argentine Republic designated the following competent authority:

Ministerio de Relaciones Exteriores y Culto

Reconquista 1088

Buenos Aires.

In accordance with Article 39 the Convention will enter into force between

Argentina and the United States of
America . . . . January 30, 1988
Finland . . . . 6 April 1990
Sweden . . . . 20 November 1987
Israel . . . . 23 November 1987
Denmark . . . . 7 December 1987
France . . . . 11 January 1988
United Kingdom of Great Britain and
Northern Ireland . . . . 11 April 1988
    also for Anguilla, the Cayman Islands, the Falklands, Gibraltar, Guernsey, Hong Kong, the Isle of Man, South Georgia and South Sand-

wich Islands and the Sovereign Base Areas of Akrotiri and Dhekelia in the islands of Cyprus)
Czechoslovakia . . . . 11 April 1988
Federal Republic of Germany . . . . 21 June 1988
Jersey . . . . 9 September 1988
Spain . . . . 28 August 1994
Switzerland . . . . 13 January 1995

1a *Notification pursuant to Article 42 of the Convention.*

In conformity with Article 39, paragraph 2, the instrument of accession by Australia to the above-mentioned Convention was deposited with the Ministry of Foreign Affairs of the Kingdom of the Netherlands on 23 October 1992.

The instrument of accession of Australia contains the following reservation and declarations:

Pursuant to Article 33, it excludes the operation of paragraph 2 of Article 4.

The Government of Australia hereby declares, for and on behalf of Australia, that:

—pursuant to Article 2, the Secretary to the Attorney–General's Department of the Commonwealth of Australia will be its Central Authority;

—pursuant to Article 8, members of the judicial personnel of the requesting authority of another Contracting State may be present at the execution of a Letter of Request, subject to prior authorisation by the judicial authority executing the Letter of Request;

—pursuant to Article 15, evidence may be taken by a diplomatic officer or consular agent only if permission to that effect is given upon application to the Secretary of the Attorney–General's Department of the Commonwealth of Australia;

—pursuant to Article 16, the Secretary to the Attorney–General's Department of the Commonwealth of Australia will be its competent authority for the purposes of that Article and is empowered to specify conditions with respect to any permission given under that Article; and

—pursuant to Article 23, it will not execute Letters of Request issued for the purpose of obtaining pre-trial discovery of documents as known in Common Law Countries.

—pursuant to Article 24, it designates the Registrars of the State and Territory Supreme Courts as additional authorities.

—pursuant to Article 40, the Convention extends to all the territories for the international relations of which it is responsible.

In accordance with paragraph 3 of Article 39, the Convention will enter into force for Australia on 22 December 1992.

According to Article 39, paragraph 4, of the Convention the accession will have effect only as regards the relations between Australia and such Contracting States as will have declared their acceptance of the accession. Such declarations shall be deposited at the Ministry of Foreign Affairs of the Kingdom of the Netherlands.

The following States have declared their acceptance of Australia's accession to the Convention: Aruba, Cyprus, Finland, the Federal Republic of Germany, Luxembourg, the Kingdom of the Netherlands (for the Kingdom in Europe), Norway, Switzerland, the United States of America.

In accordance with Article 39 the Convention will enter into force between Australia and

the United States of America . . . . 22 August 1993
France . . . . 27 March 1993
Denmark . . . . 12 April 1993
the United Kingdom of Great Britain and
Northern Ireland . . . . 20 April 1993
Cyprus . . . . 19 June 1993
the Federal Republic of Germany . . . . 3 July 1993
Luxembourg . . . . 9 February 1993
the Kingdom of the Netherlands . . . . 14 February 1993
   (for the Kingdom in Europe)
Aruba . . . . 19 July 1993
Finland . . . . 23 July 1993

Sweden .... 1 March 1994
Norway .... 18 June 1994
Spain .... 28 August 1994
Italy ....16 January 1996
Slovak Republic .... 20 May 1996
Czech Republic .... 31 May 1996

1b *Notification in conformity with Article 42, sub. e, of the Convention.*

By a Letter of 2 September 1982, received at The Ministry of Foreign Affairs of the Kingdom of the Netherlands on 29 September 1982, Barbados informed the Depositary in accordance with Article 35 of the above-mentioned Convention of the following: ".... for the purpose of the said Convention, the Central Authority is the Registrar of the Supreme Court of Barbados."

In accordance with Article 39 the Convention will enter into force between Barbados and

Spain .... 28 August 1994
Switzerland ....13 January 1995

1c "The Embassy of the People's Republic of China in the Kingdom of the Netherlands

"No. He Wai Fa (97)–53 .... (Translation)

The Hague, June 10, 1997

"Your Excellency,

"In accordance with the Joint Declaration of the Government of the People's Republic of China and the Government of the United Kingdom of Great Britain and Northern Ireland on the Question of Hong Kong signed on 19 December 1984 (hereinafter referred to as the "Joint Declaration"), the People's Republic of China will resume the exercise of sovereignty over Hong Kong with effect from 1 July 1997. Hong Kong will, with effect from that date, become a Special Administrative Region of the People's Republic of China and will enjoy a high degree of autonomy, except in foreign and defence affairs which are the responsibilities of the Central People's Government of the People's Republic of China.

"It is provided both in Section XI of Annex I to the Joint Declaration, 'Elaboration by the Government of the People's Republic of China of its Basic Policies Regarding Hong Kong', and Article 153 of the Basic Law of the Hong Kong Special Administrative Region of the People's Republic of China, which was adopted on 4 April 1990 by the National People's Congress of the People's Republic of China, that international agreements to which the People's Republic of China is not a party but which are implemented in Hong Kong may continue to be implemented in the Hong Kong Special Administrative Region.

"In accordance with the above provisions, I am instructed by the Minister of Foreign Affairs of the People's Republic of China to make the following notification:

"The Convention on Taking of Evidence Abroad in Civil or Commercial Matters done at the Hague on 18 March 1970 (hereinafter referred to as the 'Convention'), by which the Government of the Kingdom of the Netherlands is designated as the depository, which applies to Hong Kong at present, will continue to apply to the Hong Kong Special Administrative Region with effect from 1 July 1997. The Government of the People's Republic of China also makes the following declarations:

"1. With reference to the provisions of Article 16 of the Convention, the diplomatic officer or consular agent of the other Contracting State will not be permitted to take the evidence of nationals of the People's Republic of China or of a third State in the Hong Kong Special Administrative Region.

"2. It declares, in accordance with Article 23 of the Convention, the Hong Kong Special Administrative Region will not execute the 'Letters of Request issued for the purpose of obtaining pre-trial discovery of documents'. The 'Letters of Request issued for the purpose of obtaining pre-trial discovery of documents' for the purposes of the foregoing Declaration include any Letter of Request which requires a person:

"1) to state what documents relevant to the proceedings to which the Letter of Request relates are, or have been, in his possession, custody or power; or

"2) to produce any documents other than particular documents specified in the Letter of Request as being documents appearing to the requested Court to be, or to be likely to be, in his possession, custody or power.

"3. In accordance with Article 24 of the Convention, it designates the Registrar of the High Court of the Hong Kong Special Administrative Region as an Other Authority competent to receive Letters of Request for execution in the Hong Kong Special Administrative Region; in accordance with Article 17 of the Convention, it designates the Administrative Secretary of the Government of Hong Kong Special Administrative Region as the competent authority for the Hong Kong Special Administrative Region.

"4. In accordance with Article 4 and 33 of the Convention, the Hong Kong Special Administrative Region will not accept a Letter of Request in the French Language.

"Within the above ambit, responsibility for the international rights and obligations of a party to the Convention will be assumed by the Government of the People's Republic of China...."

1d *Notification in conformity with Article 42, sub e. of the Convention.*

After having designated the Central Authority on 3 May 1984 (see Notification No. 2/1984) the Government of Cyprus informed the Ministry of Foreign Affairs of the Kingdom of the Netherlands of the following on 15 May 1984:

"The Republic of Cyprus makes the following declarations:

"1. Under Article 2 the Ministry of Justice is designated as the Competent Authority .

"2. Under Article 16 the Ministry of Justice is designated as the Competent Authority.

"3. Under Article 17 the Ministry of Justice is designated as the Competent Authority.

"4. In accordance with Article 18 the Republic of Cyprus declares that a diplomatic officer, consular agent or commissioner authorized to take evidence under Articles 15, 16 or 17 may apply to the Competent Authority for appropriate assistance to obtain such evidence by compulsion as prescribes by the law for internal proceedings, provided that the requesting Contracting State has made a declaration affording reciprocal facilities under Article 18.

"5. In accordance with Article 23, the Government of the Republic of Cyprus declares that the Republic of Cyprus will not execute Letters of Request issued for the purpose of obtaining pre-trial discovery of documents. The Government of the Republic of Cyprus further declares that the Republic of Cyprus understands 'Letters of Request issued for the purpose of obtaining pre-trial discovery of documents' for the purposes of the foregoing declaration as including any Letter of Request which requires a person:

"a. to state what documents relevant to the proceedings to which the Letter of Request relates are, or have been, in his possession, custody or power; or

"b. to produce any documents other than particular documents specified in the Letter of Request as being documents appearing to the requested court to be, or likely to be, in his possession, custody or power.

"The Republic of Cyprus makes the following reservations:

"1. In accordance with Article 8 the Republic of Cyprus declares that members of the judicial personnel of the requesting authority may be present at the execution of a Letter of Request.

"2. In accordance with the provisions of article 33 the Republic of Cyprus will not accept a Letter of Request in French."

According to the depositary the declaration under 5 and the reservation under 2 should have been made at the time of accession. The States which have declared to accept Cyprus' accession to the Convention, namely: the Federal Republic of Germany, Finland, France, Israel, Italy, the Kingdom of the Netherlands, Luxembourg, Portugal, the United Kingdom of Great Britain and Northern Ireland, Sweden and Czechoslovakia, are requested to inform the Ministry of Foreign Affairs of the Kingdom of the Netherlands whether they accept the declaration and the reservation concerned.

Complete Annotation Materials, see Title 28 U.S.C.A.

Notification pursuant to Article 42 of the Convention

The following State declared its acceptance of the accession of Cyprus to the above-mentioned Convention:

the United States of America .... 1 December 1987

In accordance with Article 39 the Convention will enter into force between Cyprus and

the United States of America .... 30 January 1988
Spain .... 10 July 1994
Switzerland................................. 13 January 1995

1e By notification dated January 28, 1993 the Czech Republic communicated the following: "In accordance with the valid principles of international law and to the extent defined by it, the Czech Republic, as a successor state created as a result of the division of the Czech and Slovak Federal Republic, considers itself bound, as of January 1, 1993, i.e. the date of the division of the Czechoslovak federation, by multilateral international treaties to which the Czech and Slovak Federal Republic was a party on that date, including reservations and declarations to their provisions made earlier by Czechoslovakia", which are as follow:

(Translation)

"The Socialist Republic of Czechoslovakia declares, with reference to Article 16 of the Convention on the taking of evidence abroad in civil or commercial matters, concluded at The Hague on 18 March 1970, that evidence may be taken in accordance with Chapter II without its prior permission provided the principle of reciprocity is applied.

"The Socialist Republic of Czechoslovakia also declares, in connection with Article 18 of the said Convention, that a diplomatic officer, consular agent or commissioner authorized to take evidence under Articles 15, 16 and 17, may request the competent Czechoslovak court or the Czechoslovak state notary to carry out procedural action and that such a diplomatic officer, consular agent or commissioner will transmit the dossier to that court or notary through the intermediary of the Minister of Justice of the Czech Socialist Republic in Prague or the Minister of Justice of the Slovak Socialist Republic in Bratislava, provided the principle of reciprocity is applied.

"The Socialist Republic of Czechoslovakia wishes to state, in connection with Article 40 of the Convention according to all states the right to declare that the convention shall be applicable to all territories for the international relations of which it is responsible, that keeping certain countries in a state of dependence is in its opinion contrary to the spirit and objectives of the United Nations Declaration of 14 December 1960 on the granting of independence to colonial countries and peoples, which declares the necessity for a speedy and unconditional end to colonialism in all its forms.".

By notification contained in Note dated May 28, 1978, the Minister of Justice of the Czech Socialist Republic and the Minister of Justice of the Slovak Socialist Republic have been designated as central authorities in accordance with Articles 2 and 24 of the Convention.

1f With the following reservations:

"**1)** Availing itself of the provisions laid down in Article 33, the Danish Government hereby declares, in accordance with Article 4, that Denmark will not accept Letters of Request which are sent in French.

"**2)** Availing itself of the provisions laid down in Article 33, the Danish Government hereby declares, in accordance with Article 17, that Denmark will not accept the taking of evidence by commissioners."

And with the following declarations in accordance with Article 35:

"*Article 2*

"The Ministry of Justice is hereby designated as Central Authority.

"*Article 4*

"Letters of Request may be sent in Norwegian and Swedish, and Denmark accepts no obligation to return evidence taken in other languages than Danish.

"*Article 8*

"Members of the judicial personnel of the requesting authority of another contracting State may be present at the execution of a Letter of Request if they have obtained prior authorization from the competent Danish authority.

"*Article 15*

"A diplomatic officer or consular agent may take evidence if he has been authorized to do so by the Ministry of Justice.

"*Article 16*

"The Ministry of Justice will issue authorizations to take evidence.

"*Article 23*

"Letters of Request issued for the purpose of obtaining pre-trial discovery of documents may not be executed in Denmark.

"*Article 27a*

"As has been the case hitherto, Letters of Request may be transmitted directly to the competent Danish court by the consular agents of foreign States."

Additional declaration of July 23, 1980:

"The declaration made by the Kingdom of Denmark in accordance with article 23 concerning 'Letters of Request issued for the purpose of obtaining pre-trial discovery of documents' shall apply to any Letter of Request which requires a person:

"**a)** to state what documents relevant to the proceedings to which the Letter of Request relates are, or have been, in his possession, other than particular documents specified in the Letter of Request;

or

"**b)** to produce any documents other than particular documents which are specified in the Letter of Request, and which are likely to be in his possession."

1g The Permanent Bureau of the Hague Conference on private international law presents its compliments to the Diplomatic Missions of the Member States and to the National Organs and has the honour to inform them that, by instrument deposited on 2 February 1996 with the Ministry of Foreign Affairs of the Kingdom of the Netherlands.

the *Republic of Estonia*

acceded to the above-mentioned Convention.

The instrument of accession contains the following declarations:

"1) on the basis of Article 8 the judges of the pursuing state have the right to participate in the process operation subject to the preceding consent of the Ministry of Justice of the Republic of Estonia;

"2) on the basis of Article 11, a person may refuse to participate in the taking of evidence or process operation, in case he has the right or commitment to it in accordance with the laws of his home-state;

"3) on the basis of Article 23 the Republic of Estonia fulfills a requisition where the producing of the documents or its copy is requested if it corresponds to the following requirements:

"a) process has been launched;

"b) documents have been reasonably identified according to the dates, the contents or other information;

"c) circumstances have been indicated giving ground to presume that the documents are in the property, possession of the person or known to him."

According to Articles 16 and 17 of the Convention the competent authority designated to give its permission is the *Ministry of Justice of the Republic of Estonia.*

In accordance with the terms of Article 39, paragraph 3, the Convention will enter into force for the *Republic of Estonia* on *2 April 1996.*

According to Article 39, paragraph 4, of the Convention the accession will have effect only as regards the relations between the Republic of Estonia and such Contracting States as will have declared their acceptance of the accession. Such declaration shall be deposited with the Ministry of Foreign Affairs of the Kingdom of the Netherlands.

In accordance with Article 39 the Convention entered into force between Estonia and

Luxembourg . . . . 18 June 1996
Denmark . . . . 22 June 1996
Slovak Republic . . . . 25 June 1996
Israel . . . . 30 June 1996
Germany . . . . 2 July 1996
Italy . . . . 6 July 1996
Finland . . . . 5 August 1996
Netherlands (for the Kingdom in Europe
and Aruba) . . . . 16 August 1996
Poland . . . . 14 September 1996
United Kingdom . . . . 21 February 1997
   (Dependent Territories Anguilla,
   Cayman Islands, Channel Islands,
   Sovereign Base Areas of Cyprus,
   Falkland Islands, Gibraltar, Isle of
   Man)
Cyprus . . . . 16 March 1997
Sweden . . . . 13 April 1997
Singapore . . . . 4 May 1997
Spain . . . . 25 May 1997

2 With the following reservation and declaration:

Reservation:

"In conformity with Article 33, Finland enters a reservation to paragraph 2 of Article 4 to the effect that Letters of Request in the English or French languages will not be accepted."

Declaration:

"**1.** In Finland the Ministry of Justice (as of 6/1/82) shall be the Central Authority referred to in Article 2.

"**2.** Swedish is the second official language of Finland. Finland will therefore in accordance with paragraph 1 of Article 4 accept Letters of Request in the Swedish language. The answer shall be given in the Swedish language if in connection with the Letter of Request this has been specifically requested.

"**3.** A member of the judicial personnel of the requesting authority may in accordance with Article 8 be present at the execution of a Letter of Request, provided that the Finnish Ministry of Justice has given its consent.

"**4.** The evidence referred to in Articles 16 and 17 of the Convention may be taken without the prior permission of the Finnish authorities.

"**5.** Finland is not going to execute Letters of Request referred to in Article 23 issued for the purpose of obtaining pre-trial discovery of documents as known in Common Law countries."

Notification in conformity with Article 42, paragraph e, of the Convention

By note dated 11 December 1980 and received at the Ministry of Foreign Affairs of the Kingdom of the Netherlands on 12 December 1980 the Government of Finland informed the Ministry of the withdrawal in part of the reservation to Article 4, paragraph 2, of the above-mentioned Convention made at the time of ratification and declared that it hereafter accepts the Letters of Request done in or translated into the English language. In accordance with Article 35, sub. c, the Government of Finland made the following declaration:

"By accepting Letters of Request in English, the Republic of Finland does not undertake to execute the request, or transmit the evidence thus obtained in the English language; nor to have translated the documents which establish the execution of the Letter of Request.".

Furthermore the Government of Finland modified the declaration concerning Article 23 of the above-mentioned Convention made at the time of ratification. The modified declaration is worded as follows:

"The declaration made by the Republic of Finland in accordance with Article 23 concerning 'Letters of Request issued for the purpose of obtaining pre-trial discovery of documents' shall apply only to Letters of Request which require a person:

"**a)** to state what documents relevant to the proceedings to which the Letter of Request relates are, or have been, in his possession, custody or power;

"**b)** to produce any documents other than particular documents specified in the Letter of Request, which are likely to be in his possession, custody or power.".

2a With the following declarations:

With respect to the first paragraph of Article 40 of the Convention, France declares that the Convention shall apply to all the Territory of the French Republic.

In conformity with the provisions of Article 33, the French Government declares:

That, in application of the second paragraph of Article 4, it will execute only Letters in French or accompanied by a translation in French.

That, in application of Article 23, it will not execute Letters of Request issued for the purpose of obtaining pre-trial discovery of documents as known in Common Law countries;

In conformity with the provisions of Article 2, the Ministry of Justice, Civil Division of International Judicial Assistance, 13 Place Vendôme, Paris (1er), is designated as the Central Authority to the exclusion of any other authority.

In conformity with the provisions of Article 16, the Ministry of Justice, Civil Division of International Judicial Assistance, 13 Place Vendôme, Paris (1er), is designated as the competent authority to give permission to diplomatic officers or consular agents of a Contracting State to take the evidence, without compulsion, of persons other than nationals of that State in aid of proceedings commenced in the courts of a State which they represent.

That permission, which shall be given for each specific case and shall be accompanied by special conditions when appropriate, shall be granted under the following general conditions:

1. Evidence shall be taken only within the confines of the Embassies or Consulates;

2. The date and time of taking the evidence shall be notified in due time to the Civil Division of International Judicial Assistance so that it may have the opportunity to be represented at the proceedings;

3. Evidence shall be taken in premises accessible to the public;

4. Persons requested to give evidence shall be served with an official instrument in French or accompanied by a translation into French, and that instrument shall mention:

   a. That evidence is being taken in conformity with the provisions of The Hague Convention of March 18, 1970 on the Taking of Evidence Abroad in Civil or Commercial Matters and relates to legal proceedings pending before a jurisdiction specifically designated by a Contracting State;

   b. That appearance is voluntary and failure to appear will not give rise to criminal proceedings in the State of origin;

   c. That the parties to the trial are consenting or, if not, the grounds of their objections;

   d. That in the taking of evidence the person concerned may be legally represented;

   e. That a person requested to give evidence may invoke a privilege or duty to refuse to give evidence.

A copy of these requests shall be transmitted to the Ministry of Justice.

5. The Civil Division of International Judicial Assistance shall be kept informed of any difficulty.

In conformity with the provisions of Article 17, the Ministry of Justice, Civil Division of International Judicial Assistance, 13 Place Vendôme, Paris (1er), is appointed as the competent authority to give permission to persons duly appointed as commissioners to proceed, without compulsion, to take any evidence in aid of proceedings commenced in the courts of a Contracting State.

This permission, which shall be given for each specific case and shall be accompanied by special conditions when appropriate, shall be granted under the following general conditions:

1. Evidence shall be taken only within the Embassy confines;

2. The date and time of taking the evidence shall be notified in due time to the Civil Division of International Judicial Assistance so that it may have the opportunity to be represented at the proceedings;

3. Evidence shall be taken in premises accessible to the public;

4. Persons requested to give evidence shall be served with an official instrument in French or accompanied by a translation in French, and that instrument shall mention:

    a. That evidence is being taken in conformity with the provisions of The Hague Convention of March 18, 1970 on the Taking of Evidence Abroad in Civil or Commercial Matters and relates to legal proceedings pending before a jurisdiction specifically designated by a Contracting State;

    b. That appearance is voluntary and failure to appear will not give rise to criminal proceedings in the State of origin;

    c. That the parties to the trial are consenting and, if not, the grounds of their objections;

    d. That in the taking of evidence the person concerned may be legally represented;

    e. That a person requested to give evidence may invoke the privilege and duty to refuse to give evidence.

A copy of these requests shall be transmitted to the Ministry of Justice.

5. The Civil Division of International Judicial Assistance shall be kept informed of any difficulty.

The request for permission transmitted by the requesting authority to the Ministry of Justice shall specify:

1. The motives that led to choosing this method of taking evidence in preference to that of a Letter of Request, considering the judiciary costs incurred;

2. The criteria for appointing commissioners when the person appointed does not reside in France.

The French Government declares that, in application of the provisions of Article 8, members of the judicial personnel of the requesting authority of a Contracting State may be present at the execution of a Letter of Request.

———

The Permanent Bureau of the Hague Conference on private international law presents its compliments to the Diplomatic Missions of the Member States and to the National Organs and has the honour to inform them that, by a letter received at the Ministry of Foreign Affairs of the Kingdom of the Netherlands on 19 January 1987, in accordance with Article 34 of the Convention, *France* has modified its declaration regarding Article 23 as follows:

The declaration made by the French Republic in accordance with Article 23 relating to Letters of Request issued for the purpose of obtaining pre-trial discovery of documents does not apply when the requested documents are enumerated limitatively in the Letter of Request and have a direct and precise link with the object of the procedure. (*Translation*)

The Permanent Bureau avails itself of this opportunity to renew to the Diplomatic Missions of the Member States and to the National Organs an assurance of its highest consideration and esteem.

2b "**A.** The Government of the Federal Republic of Germany makes the following declarations in accordance with paragraph 1 of Article 33 of the Convention of 18th March 1970:

"The Federal Republic of Germany makes the reservation provided for in the first sentence of paragraph 1 of Article 33 of the Convention excluding the application of the provisions of paragraph 2 of Article 4 of the Convention. Letters of Request to be executed under Chapter 1 of the Convention must, in accordance with paragraphs 1 and 5 of Article 4 of the Convention, be in the German language or be accompanied by a translation into that language.

"The Federal Republic of Germany declares in accordance with the option provided for in the first sentence of paragraph 1 of Article 33 of the Convention to make a reservation excluding the application of the provisions of Chapter II of the Convention that the taking of evidence by diplomatic officers or consular agents is not permissible in its territory if German nationals are involved.

"**B.** The Government of the Federal Republic of Germany makes the following declarations pursuant to Article 35 of the Convention of 18th of March 1970:

"(1) The authority competent to execute a Letter of Request shall be the local court (Amtsgericht) in whose district the official act is to be performed.

Letters of Request shall be addressed to the Central Authority of the Land in which the respective request is to be executed. Germany has deposited the following revised list of Central Authorities designated in accordance with Article 2 of the Convention:

Baden-Württemberg	Justizministerium Baden-Württemberg Schillerplatz 4 70173 Stuttgart
Bavaria	Bayerisches Staatsministerium der Justiz Justizpalast Prielmayerstrasse 7 80335 München
Berlin	Senatsverwaltung für Justiz von Berlin Salzburger Strasse 21–25 10825 Berlin
Brandenburg	Ministerium der Justiz des Landes Brandenburg Heinrich-Mann-Allee 107 14460 Potsdam
Bremen	der Präsident des Landsgerichts Domsheide 16 28195 Bremen
Hamburg	Präsident des Amtsgerichts Hamburg Sievekingplatz 1 20335 Hamburg
Hesse	Hessisches Ministerium der Justiz Luisenstrasse 13 65185 Wiesbaden
Lower Saxony	der Niedersächsisches Justizministerium Am Waterlooplatz 1 30169 Hannover
Mecklenburg —Western Pomerania	Ministerium für Justiz, Bundes–und Europa- angelegen heiten des Landes Mecklen- burg-Vorpommern Demmlerplatz 14 19053 Schwering
Northrhine-Westphalia	Präsident des Oberlandesgerichts Düsseldorf Cecilienallee 3 40474 Düsseldorf
Rhineland-Palatinate	Ministerium der Justiz Ernst-Ludwig Strasse 3 55116 Mainz
Saarland	Ministerium der Justiz des Saarlandes Zähringerstrasse 12 66119 Saarbrücken
Saxe	Sächsisches Staatsministerium

	der Justiz
	Archivstrasse 1
	01097 Dresden
Saxe–Anhalt	Ministerium des
	Justiz
	des Landes Sachsen
	–Anhalt
	Wilhelm-Höpfner-
	Ring 6
	39116 Magdeburg
Schleswig-Holstein	Der Justizminister des
	Landes Schleswig-
	Holstein
	Lorentzdamm 35
	24103 Kiel
Thuringe	Thüringer Justizministerium
	Alfred-Hess-Strasse 8
	99094 Erfurt

"**(2)** Pursuant to Article 8 of the Convention, the Government of the Federal Republic of Germany declares that members of the requesting court of another Contracting State may be present at the execution of a Letter of Request by the local court if prior authorization has been given by the Central Authority of the Land where the request is to be executed.

"**(3)** The taking of evidence by diplomatic officers or consular agents pursuant to paragraph 1 of Article 16 of the Convention which involves nationals of a third State or stateless persons shall be subject to permission from the Central Authority of the Land where the evidence is to be taken. Pursuant to paragraph 2 of Article 16 of the Convention, permission shall not be required if the national of the third State is also a national of the State of the requesting court.

"**(4)** A commissioner of the requesting court may not take evidence pursuant to Article 17 of the Convention unless the Central Authority of the Land where the evidence is to be taken has given its permission. Such permission may be made subject to conditions. The local court in whose district official acts would have to be performed by virtue of a Letter of Request in the same matter shall be entitled to control the preparation and the actual taking of the evidence. Under the second sentence of Article 19 of the Convention, a member of the court may be present at the taking of the evidence.

"**(5)** The Federal Republic of Germany declares in pursuance of Article 23 of the Convention that it will not, in its territory, execute Letters of Request issued for the purpose of obtaining pre-trial discovery of documents as known in Common Law countries."

2c *Notification in conformity with Article 42, paragraph e, of the Convention*

In accordance with Article 35 of the Convention Israel notified by a Note dated April 17, 1980 and received at the Ministry of Foreign Affairs of the Kingdom of the Netherlands on April 25, 1980, that the Central Authority designated by the State of Israel in accordance with Article 2 of the above-mentioned Convention, is the Director of Courts, 19 Jaffa Road, Jerusalem.

2d *Notification in conformity with Article 42, subs. a and e, of the Convention*

The Italian Republic deposited its instrument of ratification of the above-mentioned Convention with the Ministry of Foreign Affairs of the Kingdom of the Netherlands on 22 June 1982, in accordance with Article 37, paragraph 2, of the Convention.

In accordance with Article 38, paragraph 2, the Convention will enter into force for Italy on 21 August 1982.

At the time of the deposit of the instrument of ratification the Italian Government notified the Ministry of Foreign Affairs of the following:

Translation

"**(1)** The Italian Government declares, in accordance with Article 8, that members of the judicial personnel of the requesting authority of another Contracting State may be present at the execution of a Letter of Request, subject to prior authorization by the competent authority designated by the Italian State under (4) paragraph 2 below.

"**(2)** The Italian Government declares, in accordance with Article 18, that a diplomatic officer, consular agent or commissioner who is taking evidence under Article 15, 16 or 17, may apply to the Authority designated by the Italian State under (4) paragraph 2 below, for appropriate assistance to obtain the evidence by compulsion.

"**(3)** The Italian Government declares, in accordance with Article 23, that it will not execute Letters of Request issued for the purpose of obtaining pre-trial discovery of documents as known in Common Law countries.

"**(4)** In accordance with Article 35 the Italian Government designates the Ministry of Foreign Affairs pursuant to Article 2 as the Central Authority which will undertake to receive Letters of Request coming from a judicial authority of another Contracting State and to transmit them to the authority competent to execute them.

"In accordance with the abovementioned Article the Italian Government designates the Court of Appeal within whose jurisdiction proceedings are to take place as the authority competent to:

"—authorize foreign judicial personnel to be present at the execution of a Letter of Request, pursuant to Article 8;

"—authorize foreign diplomatic officers, consular agents or commissioners to take evidence under Article 16 or 17;

"—grant the judicial assistance provided for in Article 18."

2e In accordance with Article 2 the following Central Authority has been designated by Latvia:

Ministry of Justice

Brivibas Boulevard 34

LV-1536, Riga

Tel: 282607

Fax: 285575

In accordance with Article 39, paragraph 5, the Convention will enter into force between Latvia and

Luxembourg	15 July 1995
Finland	21 August 1995
United Kingdom of Great Britain and Northern Ireland	12 September 1995
United States	24 October 1995
Germany	11 November 1995
Italy	16 January 1996
Australia	20 January 1996
Norway	27 January 1996
Israel	27 February 1996
Slovak Republic	20 May 1996
Denmark	22 June 1996
Netherlands(for the Kingdom in Europe and Aruba)	16 August 1996
Singapore	4 May 1997
Spain	25 May 1997

2f *Notification in accordance with Article 42, subs. a and e, of the Convention*

In accordance with Article 37, paragraph 2, Luxemburg deposited on 26 July 1977 its instrument of ratification of the Convention with the Ministry of Foreign Affairs of the Kingdom of the Netherlands.

In conformity with Article 38, paragraph 2, the Convention shall enter into force for Luxemburg on 24 September 1977.

On the occasion of the deposit of the said instrument of ratification the Government of Luxemburg made the following declarations and reservations (translation):

"—In accordance with Article 2 the Parquet Général is designated as the Central Authority.

"—In pursuance of Article 4, paragraph 4, Letters of Request in German shall also be accepted.

Complete Annotation Materials, see Title 28 U.S.C.A.

"—In pursuance of Article 23, Letters of Request issued for the purpose of obtaining pre-trial discovery of documents as known in Common Law countries shall not be executed.

"—In accordance with the provisions of Article 16, the Parquet Général is designated as the authority competent to authorise the diplomatic officers or consular agents of a Contracting State to take, without compulsion, the evidence of persons other than the nationals of the State in aid of proceedings commenced in the courts of the State which they represent.

"This authorisation, which is given in each specific case and to which specific conditions, where appropriate, are attached, is granted under the following general conditions:

"**1**—The evidence shall be taken only within the precincts of an Embassy or Consulate.

"**2**—The Parquet Général shall be given reasonable advance notice of the time, date and place of the taking of evidence so that it can, if it wishes, be represented.

"**3**—A request to a person to appear shall, in accordance with the regulations, be in the form of an official document in French or German or accompanied by an [sic] translation into one of these languages stating:

"**a)** that the evidence is to be taken in accordance with the provisions of the Convention on the taking of evidence abroad in civil or commercial matters concluded at The Hague on 18 March 1970, and in the framework of a judicial procedure followed in a jurisdiction designated by a Contracting State;

"**b)** that the appearance is voluntary and that no prosecution in the requesting State will result from failure to appear;

"**c)** that the parties to the action, where appropriate, consent to the taking of the evidence or are opposed to it for reasons to be given;

"**d)** that the person requested to appear may be legally represented;

"**e)** that the person requested to appear may invoke a privilege or a duty to refuse to give evidence.

"—In accordance with the provisions of Article 17, the Parquet Général is designated as the authority competent to authorise persons designated in accordance with the regulations as commissioners to take evidence, without compulsion, in aid of proceedings commenced in the courts of another Contracting State.

"This authorisation, which is given in the particular case and to which specific conditions, where appropriate, are attached, is granted under the following general conditions:

"**1**—The Parquet Général shall be given reasonable advance notice of the time, date and place of the taking of evidence so that it can, if it wishes, be represented.

"**2**—A request to a person to appear shall, in accordance with the regulations, be in the form of an official document in French or German or accompanied by a translation into one of these languages stating:

"**a)** that the evidence is to be taken in accordance with the provisions of the Convention on the taking of evidence abroad in civil or commercial matters concluded at The Hague on 18 March 1970, and in the framework of a judicial procedure followed in a jurisdiction designated by a Contracting State;

"**b)** that the appearance is voluntary and that no prosecution in the requesting State will result from failure to appear;

"**c)** that the parties to the action, where appropriate, consent to the taking of the evidence or are opposed to it for reasons to be given;

"**d)** that the person requested to appear may be legally represented;

"**e)** that the person requested to appear may invoke a privilege or a duty to refuse to give evidence.

"—In pursuance of Article 8, members of the judicial personnel of the requesting authority of a Contracting State may be present at the execution of a Letter of Request."

2g In conformity with Article 39, paragraph 2, the instrument of accession by the United Mexican States to the above-mentioned Convention was deposited with the Ministry of Foreign Affairs of the Kingdom of the Netherlands on 27 July 1989.

The instrument of accession of the United Mexican States contains the declarations and reservations the text of which together with a translation in English is annexed to this notification.

In accordance with paragraph 3 of Article 39, the Convention will enter into force for the United Mexican States on 25 September 1989.

According to Article 39, paragraph 4, of the Convention the accession will have effect only as regards the relations between the United Mexican States and such Contracting States as will have declared their acceptance of the accession. Such declarations shall be deposited at the Ministry of Foreign Affairs of the Kingdom of the Netherlands.

Unofficial translation

A) TRANSMISSION AND EXECUTION OF LETTERS OF REQUEST

  1. *Central Authority (Article 2)*
    Name: Secretaría de Relaciones Exteriores,
                   Dirección General de Asuntos Jurídicos.
    Address: Ricardo Flores Magón No. 1
    Telephone: 782-34-40
    Telex: 01762090
  2. *Language requirements (Article 4)*
    2.1 The United Mexican States does hereby make a special reservation related to the provisions of paragraph 2 of Article 4, and declares in accordance with paragraph 4 of the same Article, that letters of request sent to its Central Authority or judicial authorities shall be written in the spanish language or shall otherwise be accompanied by a translation into said language.

B) TAKING OF EVIDENCE ABROAD BY DIPLOMATIC OFFICERS, CONSULAR AGENTS AND COMMISSIONS (CHAPTER II)

  3.   The United Mexican States makes a special and complete reservation concerning the provisions contained in Articles 17 and 18 of this Chapter in relation to the "commissioners" and the use of measures to compulsion by diplomatic officers and consular agents.

C) FORMULATION OF PRE–TRIAL DISCOVERY OF DOCUMENTS

  4.   With reference to Article 23 of the Convention, the United Mexican States declares that according to Mexican law, it shall only be able to comply with letters of request issued for the purpose of obtaining the production and transcription of documents when the following requirements are met:
    a)   that the judicial proceeding has been commenced;
    b)   that the documents are reasonably identifiable as to date, subject and other relevant information and that the request specifies those facts and circumstances that lead the requesting party to reasonable belief that the requested documents are known to the person from whom they are requested or that they are in his possession or under his control or custody;
    c)   that the direct relationship between the evidence or information sought and the pending proceeding be identified.

D) OTHER TRANSMISSION CHANNEL TO THE JUDICIAL AUTHORITIES DIFFERENT FROM THOSE PROVIDED FOR IN ARTICLE 2

  5.   In regard to Article 27, paragraph a) of the Convention, the United Mexican States does hereby declare that the letters of request may be transmitted to its judicial authorities not only through the Central Authority but also through diplomatic or consular channels or through judicial channels (directly sent from the foreign court to the Mexican Court), providing that in the latter case all requirements relating to legalization of signatures are fulfilled.

  6.   In regard to Article 32 of the Convention, the United Mexican States informs that it is a State Party to the Inter-american Convention on the Taking of Evidence Abroad,

signed in Panama on January the thirtieth, nineteen hundred and seventy-five, as well as to its Additional Protocol signed in La Paz, Bolivia, on May the twenty-fourth, nineteen hundred and eighty-four.

In accordance with Article 39 the Convention will enter into force between the United Mexican States and

Norway	20 November 1989
Israel	17 December 1989
the United States of America	24 December 1989
Argentina	25 December 1989
Finland	16 January 1990
Denmark	22 January 1990
the United Kingdom of Great Britain and Northern Ireland	16 March 1990

    (also for Anguilla, the Cayman Islands, the Falkland Islands, Gibraltar, Guernsey, Hong Kong, the Isle of Man, Jersey, South Georgia and the South Sandwich Islands and the Sovereign Base Areas of Akrotiri and Dhekelia in the Island of Cyprus)

the Federal Republic of Germany	23 March 1990
Czechoslovakia	2 April 1990
the Kingdom of the Netherlands	16 April 1990

    (for the Kingdom in Europe)

Aruba	18 May 1991
Sweden	17 April 1990
Portugal	14 October 1991
Spain	29 June 1994
Switzerland	13 January 1995
Italy	25 May 1996

2h *Notification in conformity with Article 42, sub c and e, of the Convention*

In accordance with Article 39, paragraph 2, the Principality of Monaco deposited its instrument of accession to the above-mentioned Convention with the Ministry of Foreign Affairs of the Kingdom of the Netherlands on 17 January 1986, with the following declarations and reservations:

Translation

1. In accordance with article 2, the Directorate of Judicial Services, MC 98025 MONACO CEDEX, is designated as the Central Authority.

2. Under article 4, paragraph 2, only Letters of Request drawn up in French or accompanied by a translation in that language shall be accepted.

3. Under article 23, Letters of Request issued for the purpose of obtaining pre-trial discovery of documents shall not be executed.

4. In accordance with articles 16 and 17, the Directorate of Judicial Services is designated as a competent authority for the purpose of authorising, as appropriate:

—the consular authorities of a Contracting State to take the evidence without compulsion of persons other than nationals of that State and in aid of proceedings commenced in a court of the State which they represent, or

—persons duly designated as commissioners to take evidence without compulsion in aid of proceedings commenced in a court of the Contracting State.

Such authorisation, which shall be granted for each particular case and may contain specific conditions, shall be subject to the following general conditions:

a) evidence shall be taken solely on the premises of consulates when the latter are situated within the Principality, and in other cases in the Palais de Justice of Monaco;

b) the Directorate of Judicial Services shall be informed of the date and time of the taking of the evidence in time to permit the Directorate to be represented, and, if necessary, to provide courtroom accommodation at the Palais de Justice of Monaco;

c) the persons concerned in the taking of evidence shall be duly summoned by an official document drawn up in French or accompanied by a translation in that language; this document shall indicate:

—that the taking of the evidence in question is being conducted in accordance with the provisions of the Hague Convention of 18 March 1970 on the Taking of Evidence Abroad in Civil or Commercial Matters, and that the procedure constitutes part of legal proceedings pursued under the specially designated jurisdiction of a Contracting State;

—that appearance is voluntary and non-appearance would not entail legal proceedings in the requesting State;

—that the person concerned in the taking of evidence may be represented by a lawyer or defense counsel;

—that the parties in the proceedings, should they be instituted, give their consent, and if not the document shall state the reasons for their opposition;

—that the person concerned in the taking of evidence may apply to be exempted or barred from testifying.

A copy of the summonses shall be sent to the Directorate of Judicial Services, which is also to be kept informed of any difficulties.

Pursuant to Article 39, paragraph 3, the Convention will enter into force for the Principality of Monaco on 18 March 1986.

The accession will have effect only as regards the relations between Monaco and such Contracting States as will have declared their acceptance of the accession.

Notification pursuant to Article 42 of the Convention

In accordance with Article 39 the Convention will enter into force between Monaco and

the United States of America	January 30, 1988
The Kingdom of the Netherlands (Kingdom in Europe)	14 July 1986
Portugal	14 October 1991
Spain	29 June 1994
Switzerland	13 January 1995

2i *Notification in conformity with Article 42, sub a and e, of the Convention.*

"The Kingdom of the Netherlands deposited on 8 April 1981, in accordance with Article 37, paragraph 2, of the Convention its instrument of ratification for the Kingdom in Europe of the above-mentioned Convention.

"Upon the deposit of the instrument of ratification the Government of the Kingdom of the Netherlands has made the following declarations

Translation

"In the Netherlands the Convention shall be applied as follows:

"*Article 2*

"The Public Prosecutor at The Hague District Court is designated as the Central Authority.

"*Article 4*

"Letters of Request will be accepted in Dutch, German, English or French, or if they are accompanied by a translation into one of these languages.

"The Netherlands does not undertake to translate documents for the execution of a Letter of Request.

"*Article 8*

"Members of the judicial personnel of another Contracting State may be present at the execution of a Letter of Request provided that the court which is responsible for execution authorises this and provided that any conditions which the court may impose are respected.

"*Article 11*

"Only the court which is responsible for executing the Letter of Request shall be competent to decide whether any person concerned by the execution has a privilege or duty to refuse to give evidence under the law of a State other than the State of origin; no such privilege or duty exists under Dutch law.

"*Article 14*

"Fees paid to experts and interpreters and costs occasioned by the use of a special procedure requested by the State of origin under Article 9, paragraph 2 of the Convention shall be borne by the State of origin.

"Article 16

"In the Netherlands, no prior permission is required for the taking of evidence as provided for in Article 16.

"Article 17

"The permission referred to in Article 17 must be requested from the President of the District Court in the area in which evidence is to be taken. If evidence is to be taken from witnesses or experts, the area in question will be that in which the witnesses or experts, or the majority of them reside. If the President gives permission, he may impose any conditions which he considers necessary to ensure that the evidence is taken in proper manner. He may decide that the evidence should be taken at the court, under the supervision of a judge designated by him. Permission will only be granted if the following conditions are met:

"**a**) the witness or expert concerned must have been duly summoned; the summons must be in Dutch or must be accompanied by a Dutch translation and must contain:

"—the facts of the case and a summary of the proceedings in connection with which the evidence is to be taken, and details of the court which has requested the evidence;

"—a statement to the effect that there is no obligation for the witness or expert to appear, and that if he refuses to appear, to take an oath, to give his word of honour or to give evidence, he will not incur any penalty or measure of any kind, either in the Netherlands or in the State where the proceedings have been instituted;

"—a statement to the effect that the person concerned may be legally represented;

"—a statement to the effect that in so far as the person concerned has a privilege or duty to refuse to give evidence, he may do so;

"—a statement to the effect that the commissioner will reimburse expenses incurred by the witness or expert in connection with his appearance to give evidence.

"**b**) A copy of the summons must be forwarded to the President.

"**c**) The request for permission must state the reasons why the taking of evidence has been entrusted to a commissioner and it must state the commissioner's official status unless he is a lawyer competent to practise in the Netherlands.

"**d**) The costs of taking the evidence, i.e., the expenses of the witnesses, experts or interpreters, must be reimbursed in full.

"Article 23

"The Netherlands will not execute Letters of Request issued for the purpose of obtaining pre-trial discovery of documents as known in Common Law countries.

"For the purposes of Article 23 of the Convention, "Letters of Request issued for the purpose of obtaining pre-trial discovery of documents as known in Common Law countries", which the Netherlands will not execute, are defined by the Government of the Kingdom of the Netherlands as being any Letters of Request which require a person:

"**a.** to state which of the documents which are of relevance to the proceedings to which the Letter of Request relates have been in his possession, custody or power; or

"**b.** to produce any document other than particular documents specified in the Letter of Request as being documents which the court which is conducting the proceedings believes to be in his possession, custody or power.

"Article 26

"The Netherlands will request that any State of origin which has made a request pursuant to paragraph 1 of Article 26 should reimburse the fees and costs to which this paragraph refers.

"In accordance with Article 38, paragraph 2, the Convention will enter into force for the Kingdom of the Netherlands (the Kingdom in Europe) on 7 June 1981."

In accordance with Article 40, paragraph 2, the Kingdom of the Netherlands declared on 28 May 1986 that the Convention shall extend to Aruba.

In conformity with Article 40, paragraph 3, the Convention will enter into force for Aruba on 27 July 1986.

The Permanent Bureau of the Hague Conference on private international law presents its compliments to the Diplomatic Missions of the Member States and to the National Organs and has the honour to inform them that, in accordance with Article 2 of the above-mentioned Convention, the

Kingdom of the Netherlands

has designated the *"Procureur-Generaal in Aruba van het Gemeenschappelijk Hof van Justitie van de Nederlandse Antillen en Aruba"* (the Attorney-General in Aruba of the joint Court of Justice of the Netherlands Antilles and of Aruba) as Central Authority for *Aruba*.

The Convention is being applied in Aruba subject to the same declarations as made upon ratification of the Convention on 8 April 1981 by the Kingdom of the Netherlands for the Kingdom in Europe. In addition, in conformity with Article 4, paragraphs 3 and 4, Aruba will not accept Letters of Request in French, unless accompanied by a translation into Dutch, English, or Spanish.

The Permanent Bureau avails itself of this opportunity to renew to the Diplomatic Missions of the Members States and to the National Organs an assurance of its highest consideration and esteem.

3 With the following reservation:

"In conformity with article 33, Norway enters a reservation to paragraph 2 of article 4 to the effect that Letters of Request in the French language will not be accepted."

And with the following declarations:

"**I.** The Royal Ministry of Justice and Police is designated as the Central Authority with reference to article 2 and as the Competent Authority with reference to articles 15, 16 and 17.

"**II.** With reference to article 4, paragraph 3, the Kingdom of Norway declares that letters in the Danish or Swedish languages can be sent to the Central Authority.

"**III.** By accepting Letters of Request in another language than the Norwegian, the Kingdom of Norway does not undertake to execute the request, or transmit the evidence thus obtained in this other language; nor to have translated the documents which establish the execution of the Letter of Request.

"**IV.** By virtue of article 15, evidence can be taken by diplomatic officers or consular agents only if, upon application, prior permission to that effect has been granted.

"**V.** By virtue of article 23, the Kingdom of Norway declares that it will not execute Letters of Request issued for the purpose of obtaining pre-trial discovery of documents as known in Common Law countries."

The declaration made by the Kingdom of Norway in accordance with article 23 concerning "Letters of Request issued for the purpose of obtaining pre-trial discovery of documents" shall apply only to Letters of Request which require a person

a) to state what documents relevant to the proceedings to which the Letter of Request relates, are, or have been, in his possession, other than particular documents specified in the Letter of Request; or

b) to produce any documents other than particular documents which are specified in the Letter of Request, and which are likely to be in his possession.

3a The Permanent Bureau of the Hague Conference on private international law presents its compliments to the Diplomatic Missions of the Member States and to the National Organs and has the honour to inform them that, by instrument deposited on 13 February 1996 with the Ministry of Foreign Affairs of the Kingdom of the Netherlands,

the *Republic of Poland*

acceded to the above-mentioned Convention.

./. The instrument of accession contains a reservation, the text of which is attached.

Translation

Articles 23 et 33 will not be applicable within the territory of the Republic of Poland.

./. The instrument of accession was accompanied by the following declarations and reservations, the text of which is also attached.

Translation

Declarations

Article 2, Paragraph I—the Central Authority designated to receive requests for service coming from another Contracting State shall be the Ministry of Justice.

Article 8—the Authority designated to complete a certificate of service in the republic of Poland shall be the Ministry of Justice.

Article 24 and Article 27, sub-paragraph a—other authorities (in addition to the Central Authority) designated to receive requests for service shall be the voivodship courts.

Reservations

Article 23—the Republic of Poland declares, that it will not execute Letters of Request issued for the purpose of obtaining "pre-trial discovery of documents" as known in common law countries.

Article 33—the Republic of Poland excludes the application on its territory:

—the provisions of Article 4, paragraph 2,

—the provisions of Chapter II, excluding provisions of Article 15.

In accordance with paragraph 3 of Article 39, the Convention will enter into force for the *Republic of Poland* on *13 April 1996*.

According to Article 39, paragraph 4, of the Convention the accession will have effect only as regards the relations between the Republic of Poland and such Contracting States as will have declared their acceptance of the accession. Such declarations shall be deposited with the Ministry of Foreign Affairs of the Kingdom of the Netherlands.

In accordance with Article 39, paragraph 5, the Convention will enter into force between Poland and

Luxembourg	2 June 1996
Denmark	22 June 1996
Slovak Republic	25 June 1996
Israel	30 June 1996
Finland	5 August 1996
Netherlands (for the Kingdom in Europe and Aruba)	16 August 1996
Sweden	13 April 1997
Singapore	4 May 1997
Spain	25 May 1997

3b With the following reservations and declarations:

(Translation)

"**a**) In accordance with Article 33 of the Convention, the Portuguese State makes the following reservations:

"**1.** exclusion of the application of paragraph 2 of Article 4;

"**2.** exclusion of the application of Chapter II, with the exception of Article 15.

"**b**) In accordance with Articles 15 and 23 of the Convention, the Portuguese State makes the following declarations:

"**1.** The Portuguese State declares that the evidence as referred to in Article 15, can only be taken if permission to that effect is given by the appropriate authority designated by it upon application made by the diplomatic or consular agent;

"**2.** The Portuguese State declares that it will not execute Letters of Request issued for the purpose of obtaining pre-trial discovery of documents as known in Common Law Countries.

"**c**) With regard to Articles 2 and 15 of the Convention, the competent Portuguese authority will be the Director-General of the Judiciary Department ("Direccào-Geral dos Serviços Judiciários") of the Ministry of Justice.".

3c In accordance with Article 39, paragraph 3, the Convention shall enter into force for the Republic of Singapore on December 26, 1978.

Notification in accordance with Convention Article 42(c) and (e):

On October 27, 1978, the Ministry of Foreign Affairs of the Kingdom of the Netherlands received the instrument of accession of the Republic of Singapore to the Convention on the Taking of Evidence Abroad in Civil and Commercial Matters in accordance with Article 39, Paragraph 2, of the aforesaid Convention.

At the time of its accession the Government of the Republic of Singapore made the following reservations:

"**(i)** The entire Chapter II of the Convention is not applicable to the Republic of Singapore; and

"**(ii)** With regard to Article 4, paragraph 2, the Republic of Singapore will not accept a Letter of Request in a language other than English, since this language is the one used by the judicial personnel in Singapore."

In accordance with Article 23 the Government of the Republic of Singapore has declared that the Republic of Singapore will not execute Letters of Request issued for the purpose of obtaining pre-trial discovery of documents as known in Common Law countries.

The Government of the Republic of Singapore has further declared that it understands "Letters of Request issued for the purpose of obtaining pre-trial discovery of documents" for the purposes of the foregoing declaration as including any Letter of Request which requires a person:

(**a**) to state what documents relevant to the proceedings to which the Letter of Request relates are, or have been, in his possession, custody or power; or

(**b**) to produce any documents other than particular documents specified in the Letter of Request as being documents appearing to the requested court to be, or likely to be, in his possession, custody or power. It is also understood that the reference to civil or commercial actions in the Convention does not include tax matters for the Republic of Singapore.

In accordance with Article 39, paragraph 3, the Convention shall enter into force for the Republic of Singapore on December 26, 1978.

The accession shall be effective only for relations between the Republic of Singapore and contracting States that declare that they accept this accession.

Notification in conformity with Article 42, paragraph e, of the Convention:

In accordance with Article 35 of the Convention Singapore notified the Ministry of Foreign Affairs of the Kingdom of the Netherlands by a Note dated August 4, 1979, that the Central Authority which will undertake to receive Letters of Request referred to in Article 2 of the Convention, is the Registrar of the Supreme Court.

In accordance with Article 39, paragraph 5, the Convention will enter into force between Singapore and

Spain	28 August 1994
Switzerland	13 January 1995
United States	24 October 1995

3d By notification dated March 15, 1993 the Slovak Republic communicated the following: "In accordance with relevant principles and norms of international law and to extent defined by it, the Slovak Republic, as a successor State, born from the division of the Czech and Slovak Federal Republic, considers itself bound, as of January 1, 1993, i.e. the date of the division of the Czechoslovak Federation, by multilateral international treaties to which the Czech and Slovak Federal Republic was a party at that date, including reservations and declarations in respect of provisions made earlier by Czechoslovakia, as well as objections by Czechoslovakia in respect of reservations made by other treaty parties", which are as follows: [Same declarations and reservations, *mutatis mutandis,* under Czech Republic, see footnote 1e].

The Slovak Republic has designated in accordance with Articles 2 and 8 [of the Convention] the following Central Authority:

Ministerstvo spravodlivosti Slovenskej republiky

Zupne namestie 13, 813 11 Bratislava

Slovak Republic

fax: (00427) 5316035

3e The Permanent Bureau of the Hague Conference on private international law presents its compliments to the Diplomatic Missions of the Member States and to the National Organs and has the honour to inform them that, by instrument deposited on 8 July 1997 with the Ministry of Foreign Affairs of the Kingdom of the Netherlands,

the *Republic of South Africa*

acceded to the above-mentioned Convention.

The instrument of accession contains the following reservations, designation of authorities and declarations:

"1. Reservations

"That the Republic of South Africa excludes the following in terms of Article 33 of the Convention, namely—

"(a) the application of the provision of paragraph 2 of Article 4 of the Convention, which provides that a Letter of Request shall be accepted in French; and

"(b) the application of the provisions of Articles 15 and 16 of Chapter II of the Convention.

"2. Designation of authorities

"That the Republic of South Africa designates—

"(a) the Director General of the Department of Justice as Central Authority in terms of Article 2 of the Convention and as the competent authority referred to in Article 8 of the Convention; and

"(b) the division of the High Court of South Africa that has jurisdiction as the competent authority referred to in Articles 17 and 18 of the Convention

"3. Declarations

"That the Republic of South Africa makes the following declarations under the Convention:

"(a) For the purposes of paragraph 4 of Article 4 of the Convention, a Letter of Request, if not in English, may also be sent to the Central Authority in any of the following languages: Sepedi, Sesotho, Setswana, siSwati, Tshivenda, Xitsonga, Afrikaans, isiNdebele, isiXhosa and isiZulu.

"(b) Members of the judicial personnel of the requesting authority of another Contracting State may, after authorisation by the competent authority referred to in Article 8 of the Convention, be present at the execution of a Letter of Request as contemplated in that article.

"(c) Evidence may not be taken in terms of Article 17 of the Convention without the prior permission of the competent authority referred to in that Article.

"(d) A commissioner authorised to take evidence under Article 17 of the Convention may, in terms of Article 18 of the Convention, apply to the competent authority referred to in that Article to obtain the evidence by compulsion, subject to the measures of compulsion which are appropriate and prescribed by South African law for use in internal proceedings.

"(e) Letters of Request issued for the purpose of obtaining pre-trial discovery of documents as known in Common Law countries, will not be executed as provided for in Article 23."

In accordance with the terms of Article 39, paragraph 3, the Convention will enter into force for the *Republic of South Africa* on 6 *September 1997.*

According to Article 39, paragraph 4, of the Convention the accession will have effect only as regards the relations between the Republic of South Africa and such Contracting States as will have declared their acceptance of the accession. Such declaration shall

be deposited with the Ministry of Foreign Affairs of the Kingdom of the Netherlands.

In accordance with Article 38, paragraph 5, the Convention will enter into force between the United States of America and South Africa on November 1, 1997.

3f *Notification pursuant to Article 42 of the Convention*

In accordance with Article 37, paragraph 2, of the above-mentioned Convention Spain deposited its instrument of ratification with the Ministry of Foreign Affairs of the Kingdom of the Netherlands on 22 May 1987.

The instrument of ratification contains the following reservation:

"De conformidad con el artículo 33 en relación con el artículo 4.°, párrafo 2, España no aceptará comisiones rogatorias que no estén redactadas en español o acompañadas de una traducción.

Translation

In accordance with Article 33 in relation with Article 4, paragraph 2, Spain will not accept Letters of Request which are not drawn up in Spanish or accompanied by a translation.

and the following declarations:

"**a)** La Autoridad Central española a que se refiere el artículo 2 será: El Ministerio de Justicia.-Secretaría General Técnica.-(San Bernardo, 45. 28015 MADRID), con exclusión de cualquier otra Autoridad.

"**b)** Previa autorización del Ministerio de Justicia español, un Juez del Estado requirente podrá intervenir en el cumplimiento de una comisión rogatoria, de conformidad con el artículo 8.

"**c)** De conformidad con los artículos 16 y 17, la prueba podrá ser practicada, sin necesidad de autorización previa de la Autoridad española, en los locales de la Representación diplomática o consular del Estado requirente.

"**d)** A tenor del artículo 23, España no acepta las comisiones rogatorias derivadas del procedimiento 'pre-trial discovery of documents' conocido en los países del 'Common Law'.".

Translation

"**a)** The Spanish Central Authority is: "La Direccion General de Codificacion y Cooperacion Juridica Internacional, Ministerio de Justicia e Interior", with exclusion of any other Authority.

"**b)** With prior authorization of the Spanish Ministry of Justice, a Judge of the requesting State may intervene in the execution of a Letter of Request, in accordance with Article 8.

"**c)** In accordance with Articles 16 and 17, the evidence may be taken, without prior permission of the Spanish Authority, in the premises of the diplomatic or consular representation of the requesting State.

"**d)** Pursuant to Article 23 Spain does not accept Letters of Request derived from the "pre-trial discovery of documents" procedure known in Common Law countries."

The Convention will enter into force for Spain on 21 July 1987.

3g With the following declarations:

(Translation)

—That, in pursuance of Article 4, para. 4, Letters of Request in the Danish and Norwegian languages will be accepted;

—That, in pursuance of Article 8, members of the judicial personnel of the requesting authority of another Contracting State may be present at the execution of a Letter of Request without prior authorisation;

—That, in pursuance of Article 15, para. 2, a diplomatic officer or consular agent may only take evidence if permission to do so has been granted by the competent Swedish authority;

—That, in pursuance of Article 23, Letters of Request issued for the purpose of obtaining pre-trial discovery of documents as known in Common Law countries will not be executed;

—That documents provided by Sweden which establish that a Letter of Request has been executed will be in the Swedish language only.

Ministry of Foreign Affairs, Stockholm, has been designated as the Central Authority referred to in Article 2 and also as the Competent Authority referred to in Article 15–17.

Additional declaration on July 11, 1980:

"The Swedish Government understands 'Letters of Request issued for the purpose of pre-trial discovery of documents' for the purposes of the foregoing Declaration as including any Letter of Request which requires a person:

"**a)** to state what documents relevant to the proceedings to which the Letter of Request relates are, or have been, in his possession, custody or power; or

"**b)** to produce any documents other than particular documents specified in the Letter of Request, which are likely to be in his possession, custody or power."

3h *Notification pursuant to Article 42 of the Convention*

In accordance with Article 37, paragraph 2, of the above-mentioned Convention *Switzerland* deposited its instrument of ratification with the Ministry of Foreign Affairs of the Kingdom of the Netherlands on 2 November 1994.

The instrument of ratification contains the following reservation and declarations:

Translation

"Re Article 1

"1. With regard to Article 1, Switzerland takes the view that the Convention applies exclusively to the Contracting States. Moreover, regarding the conclusions of the Special Commission which met in The Hague in April 1989, Switzerland believes that, whatever the opinion of the Contracting States on the exclusive application of the Convention, priority should in any event be given to the procedures provided for in the Convention regarding requests for the taking of evidence abroad.

"Re Articles 2 and 24

"2. In accordance with Article 35, first paragraph, Switzerland designates the cantonal authorities listed in the annex as Central Authorities as referred to in Articles 2 and 24 of the Convention. Requests for the taking of evidence or the execution of any other judicial act may also be addressed to the Federal Justice and Police Department in Bern, which will forward them to the appropriate Central Authority.

"Re Article 4, second and third paragraphs

"3. In accordance with Articles 33 and 35, Switzerland declares, with regard to Article 4, second and third paragraphs, that Letters of Request and any accompanying documents must be in the language of the authority requested to execute them, i.e. in German, French or Italian, or accompanied by a translation into one of these languages, depending on the part of Switzerland in which the documents are to be executed. The documents confirming execution will be drawn up in the official language of the requested authority (cf. annex).

"Re Article 8

"In Accordance with Article 35, second paragraph, Switzerland declares, with regard to Article 8, that members of the judicial personnel of the requesting authority of another Contracting State may be present at the execution of a Letter of Request provided they have obtained prior authorization from the executing authority.

"Re Articles 15, 16 and 17

"In accordance with Article 35, Switzerland declares that evidence may be taken according to Articles 15, 16 and 17 subject to prior authorization by the Federal Justice and Police Department. A request for authorization must be addressed to the Central Authority in the canton where the evidence is to be taken.

"Re Article 23

"In accordance with Article 23, Switzerland declares that Letters of Request issued for the purpose of obtaining pre-trial discovery of documents will not be executed if:

"a. the request has no direct and necessary link with the proceedings in question; or

"b. a person is required to indicate what documents relating to the case are or were in his/her possession or keeping or at his/her disposal; or

"c. a person is required to produce documents other than those mentioned in the request for legal assistance, which are probably in his/her possession or keeping or at his/ her disposal; or

"d. interests worthy of protection of the concerned persons are endangered".

The list of Central Authorities for the Cantons is attached.

Autorités centrales cantonales			Annexe
Cantons	Langue(s) officielle(s) (a=allemand) (f=français) (i=italien)	Adresses	Numéros de téléphone
Appenzell Ausserrhoden	a	Kantonsgericht Appenzell A.Rh., 9043 Trogen	071/ 94 24 61
Appenzell Innerrhoden	a	Kantonsgericht Appenzell I.Rh., 9050 Appenzell	071/ 87 95 51
Aargau	a	Obergericht des Kantons Aargau, 5000 Aarau	064/ 21 19 40
Basel-Landschaft	a	Obergericht des Kantons Basel-Landschaft, 4410 Liestal	061/925 51 11
Basel-Stadt	a	Appellationsgericht Basel-Stadt, 4054 Basel	061/267 81 81
Bern	a/f	Justizdirektion des Kantons Bern, 3011 Bern	031/633 76 76
Fribourg	f/a	Tribunal cantonal, 1700 Fribourg	037/ 25 39 10
Genéve	f	Parquet du Procureur général, 1211Genéve 3	022/319 21 11
Glarus	a	Obergericht des Kantons Glarus, 8750 Glarus	058/ 61 15 32
Graubünden	a	Justiz-, Polizei- und Sanitäts-departement Graubünden, 7001 Chur	081/ 21 21 21
Jura	f	Département de la Justice, 2800 Delémont	066/ 21 51 11
Luzern	a	Obergericht des Kantons Luzern,	041/ 24 51 11

Cantons	Langue(s) officielle(s) (a=allemand) (f=français) (i=italien)	Adresses	Numéros de téléphone
Neuchâtel	f	6002 Luzern Département de Justice, 2001 Neuchâtel	038/ 22 31 11
Nidwalden	a	Kantonsgericht Nidwalden, 6370 Stans	041/ 63 79 50
Obwalden	a	Kantonsgericht des Kantons Obwalden, 6060 Sarnen	041/ 66 92 22
St. Gallen	a	Kantonsgericht St. Gallen, 9001 St. Gallen	071/ 21 31 11
Schaffhausen	a	Obergericht des Kantons Schaffhausen, 8201 Schaffhausen	053/ 82 74 22
Schwyz	a	Kantonsgericht Schwyz, 6430 Schwyz	043/ 24 11 24
Solothurn	a	Obergericht des Kantons Solothurn, 4500 Solothurn	065/ 21 73 11
Tessin	i	Tribunale di appello, 6901 Lugano	091/ 21 51 11
Thurgau	a	Obergericht des Kantons Thurgau, 8500 Frauenfeld	054/ 22 31 21
Uri	a	Gerichtskanzlei Uri, 6460 Altdorf	044/ 4 22 44
Valais	f/a	Tribunal cantonal, 1950 Sion	027/ 22 93 93
Vaud	f	Tribunal cantonal, 1014 Lausanne	021/313 15 11
Zug	a	Obergericht des Kantons Zug, Rechtshilfe, 6300 Zug	042/ 25 33 11
Zürich	a	Obericht des Kantons Zürich, Rechtshilfe, 8023 Zürich	01/257 91 91

3i *Notification in conformity with Article 42, under a and e, of the Convention:*

In accordance with Article 37, paragraph 2, the United Kingdom of Great Britain and Northern Ireland deposited on July 16, 1976 its instrument of ratification with the Ministry of Foreign Affairs of the Netherlands.

In conformity with Article 38, paragraph 2, the Convention shall enter into force for the United Kingdom on September 14, 1976.

The instrument of ratification mentioned above, contains the following reservation:

". . . in accordance with the provisions of Article 33 the United Kingdom will not accept a Letter of Request in French."

On the occasion of the deposit of the said instrument of ratification the Government of the United Kingdom of Great Britain and Northern Ireland made the following declarations:

"**1.** In accordance with Article 8 Her Majesty's Government declare that members of the judicial personnel of the requesting authority may be present at the execution of a Letter of Request.

"**2.** In accordance with Article 18 Her Majesty's Government declare that a diplomatic officer, consular agent or commissioner authorised to take evidence under Articles 15, 16 and 17 may apply to the competent authority designated hereinbefore for appropriate assistance to obtain such evidence by compulsion provided that the Contracting State whose diplomatic officer, consular agent or commissioner makes the application has made a declaration affording reciprocal facilities under Article 18.

"**3.** In accordance with Article 23 Her Majesty's Government declare that the United Kingdom will not execute Letters of Request issued for the purpose of obtaining pre-trial discovery of documents. Her Majesty's Government further declare that Her Majesty's Government understand "Letters of Request issued for the purpose of obtaining pre-trial discovery of documents" for the purposes of the foregoing Declaration as including any Letter of Request which requires a person:—

"**a.** to state what documents relevant to the proceedings to which the Letter of Request relates are, or have been, in his possession, custody, or power; or

"**b.** to produce any documents other than particular documents specified in the Letter of Request as being documents appearing to the requested court to be, or to be likely to be, in his possession, custody or powers.

"**4.** In accordance with Article 27 Her Majesty's Government declare that by the law and practice of the United Kingdom the prior permission referred to in Articles 16 and 17 is not required in respect of diplomatic officers, consular agents or commissioners of a Contracting State which does not require permission to be obtained for the purposes of taking evidence under Articles 16 and 17."

In accordance with Article 35 of the Convention, the Government of the United Kingdom made the following designations:

1. Under Article 2: the Foreign and Commonwealth Office.

2. Under Article 16: the Foreign and Commonwealth Office.

3. Under Article 17: the Foreign and Commonwealth Office.

4. Under Article 18: the Senior Master of the Supreme Court (Queen's Bench Division) for England and Wales; the Crown Agent for Scotland, for Scotland; the Master (Queen's Bench and Appeals). The address of the Master (Queen's Bench and Appeals) is Royal Courts of Justice, Belfast 1.

5. Under Article 24: the Senior Master of the Supreme Court (Queen's Bench Division) in England and Wales; the Crown Agent for Scotland, for Scotland; the Master (Queen's Bench and Appeals). The address of the Master (Queen's Bench and Appeals) is Royal Courts of Justice, Belfast 1.

Extension to Gibraltar.—

In accordance with Article 40, Paragraph 3, the Convention shall enter into force for Gibraltar on January 20, 1979.

The extension declaration contains the following reservation: "In accordance with the provisions of Article 4 and Article 33 of the Convention, Gibraltar will not accept a Letter of Request in French."

In accordance with Article 35 of the Convention the following designations have been made:

"(a) Under Articles 16 and 17 of the Convention, the Deputy Governor is designated as the competent authority for Gibraltar;

"(b) Under Article 18 of the Convention, the Registrar of the Supreme Court of Gibraltar is designated as the competent authority;

"(c) Under Article 24 of the Convention, the Deputy Governor is designated as an additional authority competent to receive Letters of Request for execution in Gibraltar."

[For declarations see the original note.]

Notification in conformity with Article 42, subs. d and e, of the Convention

By a letter dated November 20, 1978, and received at the Ministry of Foreign Affairs of the Kingdom of the Netherlands on November 21, 1978, the Ambassador of the United Kingdom of Great Britain and Northern Ireland at The Hague, referring to the deposit on July 16, 1976 of the instrument of ratification of the above-mentioned Convention by the United Kingdom of Great Britain and Northern Ireland, declared in accordance with article 40 that the Convention shall extend to Gibraltar. The Convention shall enter into force for Gibraltar on January 20, 1979.

The declaration of extension contains the following reservation:

". . . in accordance with the provisions of Article 4 and Article 33 of the Convention, Gibraltar will not accept a Letter of Request in French."

In accordance with Article 35 of the Convention the following designations have been made:

a) under Articles 16 and 17 of the Convention the Deputy Governor is designated as the competent authority for Gibraltar;

b) under Article 18 of the Convention, the Registrar of the Supreme Court of Gibraltar is designated as the competent authority;

c) under Article 24 of the Convention, the Deputy Governor is designated as an additional authority competent to receive Letters of Request for execution in Gibraltar, and the following declarations:

1. In accordance with Article 8, members of the judicial personnel of the requesting authority may be present at the execution of a Letter of Request in Gibraltar.

2. In accordance with Articles 18, a diplomatic officer, consular agent or commissioner authorised to take evidence under Articles 15, 16 and 17 of the Convention may apply to the competent authority in Gibraltar designated hereinbefore for appropriate assistance to obtain such evidence by compulsion provided that the Contracting State whose diplomatic officer, consular agent or commissioner makes the application has made a declaration affording reciprocal facilities under Article 18.

3. In accordance with Article 23, Gibraltar will not execute Letters of Request issued for the purpose of obtaining pre-trial discovery of documents. The Government of Gibraltar understands "Letters of Request issued for the purpose of obtaining pre-trial discovery of documents" for the purposes of the foregoing Declaration as including any Letter of Request which requires a person:

a) to state what documents relevant to the proceedings to which the Letter of Request relates are, or have been, in his possession, custody or power; or

b) to produce any documents other than particular documents specified in the Letter of Request as being documents appearing to the requested court to be, or likely to be, in his possession, custody or power.

4. In accordance with Article 27, by the law and practice of Gibraltar the prior permission referred to in Articles 16 and 17 of the Convention is not required in respect of diplomatic officers, consular agents or commissioners of a Contracting State which does not require permission to be obtained for the purposes of taking evidence under Articles 16 or 17.

Extension to Sovereign Base Areas of Akrotiri and Dhekelia in the Island of Cyprus.—

"The Convention shall enter into force for the Sovereign Base Areas of Akrotiri and Dhekelia in the Island of Cyprus on August 24, 1979."

The declaration of extension contains the following reservation:

". . . in accordance with the provisions of Article 4 and Article 33 of the Convention, the Sovereign Base Areas will not accept a Letter of Request in French.".

In accordance with Article 35 of the Convention the following designations have been made:

a) under Articles 16 and 17 of the Convention the Chief Officer, Sovereign Base Areas, is designated as the competent authority for the Sovereign Base Areas;

b) under Article 18 of the Convention, the Senior Registrar of the Judge's Court of the Sovereign Base Areas of Akrotiri and Dhekelia is designated as the competent authority;

c) under Article 24 of the Convention, the Senior Registrar of the Judge's Court of the Sovereign Base Areas of Akrotiri and Dhekelia is designated as an additional authority competent to receive Letters of Request for execution in the Sovereign Base Areas.

and the following declarations:

1. In accordance with Article 8, members of the judicial personnel of the requesting authority may be present at the execution of a Letter of Request in the Sovereign Base Areas.

2. In accordance with Article 18, a diplomatic officer, consular agent or commissioner authorised to take evidence under Articles 15, 16 and 17 of the Convention may apply to the competent authority in the Sovereign Base Areas designated hereinbefore for appropriate assistance to obtain such evidence by compulsion provided that the Contracting State whose diplomatic officer, consular agent or commissioner makes the application has made a declaration affording reciprocal facilities under Article 18.

3. In accordance with Article 23, the Sovereign Base Areas will not execute Letters of Request issued for the purpose of obtaining pre-trial discovery of documents. The Administration of the Sovereign Base Areas understands "Letters of Request issued for the purpose of obtaining pre-trial discovery of documents" for the purposes of the foregoing Declaration as including any Letter of Request which requires a person:

a) to state what documents relevant to the proceedings to which the Letter of Request relates are, or have been, in his possession, custody or power; or

b) to produce any documents other than particular documents specified in the Letter of Request as being documents appearing to the requested court to be, or likely to be, in his possession, custody or power.

4. In accordance with Article 27, by the law and practice of the Sovereign Base Areas the prior permission referred to in Articles 16 and 17 of the Convention is not required in respect of diplomatic officers, consular agents or commissioners of a Contracting State which does not require permission to be obtained for the purposes of taking evidence under Articles 16 or 17.

Extension to Falkland Islands and Dependencies.—

Notification in conformity with Article 42, subs. d and e, of the Convention

By a letter dated November 23, 1979, and received at the Ministry of Foreign Affairs of the Kingdom of the Netherlands on November 26, 1979, the Ambassador of the United Kingdom of Great Britain and Northern Ireland at The Hague, referring to the deposit on July 16, 1976 of the instrument of ratification of the above-mentioned Convention by the United Kingdom of Great Britain and Northern Ireland, declared in accordance with Article 40 that the Convention shall extend to the Falkland Islands and Dependencies.

The Convention shall enter into force for the Falkland Islands and Dependencies on January 25, 1980.

The declaration of extension contains the following reservation:

". . . in accordance with the provisions of Article 4 and Article 33 of the Convention, the Falkland Islands and Dependencies will not

---

accept a Letter of Request in French." In accordance with Article 35 of the Convention the following designations have been made:

a) under Articles 16, 17 and 18 of the Convention the Judge of the Supreme Court of the Falkland Islands, is designated as the competent authority for the Falkland Islands and Dependencies;

b) under Article 24 of the Convention, the Governor of the Falkland Islands and its dependencies is designated as an additional authority competent to receive Letters of Request for execution in the Falkland Islands and Dependencies.

and the following declarations:

1. In accordance with Article 8, members of the judicial personnel of the requesting authority may be present at the execution of a Letter of Request in the Falkland Islands and Dependencies.

2. In accordance with Article 18, a diplomatic officer, consular agent or commissioner authorised to take evidence under Articles 15, 16, and 17 of the Convention may apply to the competent authority in the Falkland Islands and Dependencies designated hereinbefore for appropriate assistance to obtain such evidence by compulsion provided that the Contracting State whose diplomatic officer, consular agent or commissioner makes the application has made a declaration affording reciprocal facilities under Article 18.

3. In accordance with Article 23, the Falkland Islands and Dependencies will not execute Letters of Request issued for the purpose of obtaining pre-trial discovery of documents.

The Governor of the Falkland Islands and its Dependencies understands "Letters of Request issued for the purpose of obtaining pre-trial discovery of documents" for the purposes of the foregoing declaration as including any Letter of Request which requires a person:

a) to state what documents relevant to the proceedings to which the Letter of Request relates are, or have been, in his possession, custody or power; or

b) to produce any documents other than particular documents specified in the Letter of Request as being documents appearing to the requested court to be, or likely to be, in his possession, custody or power.

4. In accordance with Article 27, by the law and practice of the Falkland Islands and Dependencies the prior permission referred to in Articles 16 and 17 of the Convention is not required in respect of diplomatic officers, consular agents or commissioners of a Contracting State which does not require permission to be obtained for the purposes of taking evidence under Article 16 or 17.

Extension to Isle of Man.—

Notification in conformity with article 42, subs. d and e, of the Convention

By a letter dated April 16, 1980, and received at the Ministry of Foreign Affairs of the Kingdom of the Netherlands on April 16, 1980, the Ambassador of the United Kingdom of Great Britain and Northern Ireland at The Hague, referring to the deposit on July 16, 1976 of the instrument of ratification of the above-mentioned Convention by the United Kingdom of Great Britain and Northern Ireland, declared in accordance with article 40 that the Convention shall extend to the Isle of Man.

The Convention shall enter into force for the Isle of Man on June 15, 1980.

The declaration of extension contains the following reservation:

". . . in accordance with the provisions of Article 4 and Article 33 of the Convention, the Isle of Man will not accept a Letter of Request in French."

In accordance with Article 35 of the Convention the following designations have been made:

a) under Articles 16, 17 and 18 of the Convention Her Majesty's First Deemster and Clerk of the Rolls is designated as the competent authority for the Isle of Man;

b) under Article 24 of the Convention, Her Majesty's First Deemster and Clerk of the Rolls is designated as an additional authority

competent to receive Letters of Request for execution in the Isle of Man.

and the following declarations:

1. In accordance with Article 8, members of the judicial personnel of the requesting authority may be present at the execution of a Letter of Request in the Isle of Man.

2. In accordance with Article 18, a diplomatic officer, consular agent or commissioner authorised to take evidence under Article 15, 16 and 17 of the Convention may apply to the competent authority in the Isle of Man designated hereinbefore for appropriate assistance to obtain such evidence by compulsion provided that the Contracting State whose diplomatic officer, consular agent or commissioner makes the application has made a declaration affording reciprocal facilities under Article 18.

3. In accordance with Article 23, the Isle of Man will not execute Letters of Request issued for the purpose of obtaining pre-trial discovery of documents.

The Government of the Isle of Man understands "Letters of Request issued for the purpose of obtaining pre-trial discovery of documents" for the purposes of the foregoing declaration as including any Letter of Request which requires a person:

a) to state what documents relevant to the proceedings to which the Letter of Request relates are, or have been, in his possession, custody or power; or

b) to produce any documents other than particular documents specified in the Letter of Request as being documents appearing to the requested court to be, or likely to be, in his possession, custody or power.

4. In accordance with Article 27, by the law and practice of the Isle of Man the prior permission referred to in Articles 16 and 17 of the Convention is not required in respect of diplomatic officers, consular agents or commissioners of a Contracting State which does not require permission to be, obtained for the purposes of taking evidence under Article 16 or 17.

Extension to Cayman Islands.—

Notification in conformity with Article 42, subs. d and e, of the Convention

By letter dated 16 September 1980 and received at the Ministry of Foreign Affairs of the Kingdom of the Netherlands on that same date, the Ambassador of the United Kingdom of Great Britain and Northern Ireland at The Hague referring to the deposit on 16 July 1976 of the instrument of ratification of the above-mentioned Convention by the United Kingdom of Great Britain and Northern Ireland declared in accordance with Article 40 that the Convention shall extend to the Cayman Islands.

The Convention will enter into force for the Cayman Islands on 15 November 1980.

The declaration of extension contains the following reservation:

". . . in accordance with the provisions of Article 4 and Article 33 of the Convention, ... the Cayman Islands will not accept a Letter of Request in French".

In accordance with Article 35 of the Convention the following designations have been made:

a) Under Articles 16 and 17 of the Convention, the Attorney General is designated as the competent authority for the Cayman Islands;

b) Under Article 18 of the Convention, the Clerk of the Grand Court is designated as the competent authority;

c) Under Article 24 of the Convention, His Excellency the Governor is designated as an additional authority competent to receive Letters of Request for execution in the Cayman Islands.

and the following declarations:

1. In accordance with Article 8, members of the judicial personnel of the requesting authority may be present at the execution of a Letter of Request in the Cayman Islands.

2. In accordance with Article 18, a diplomatic officer, consular agent or commissioner authorised to take evidence under Articles 15, 16

and 17 of the Convention may apply to the competent authority in the Cayman Islands designated hereinbefore for appropriate assistance to obtain such evidence by compulsion provided that the Contracting State whose diplomatic officer, consular agent or commissioner makes the application has made a declaration affording reciprocal facilities under Article 18.

3. In accordance with Article 23, the Cayman Islands will not execute Letters of Request issued for the purpose of obtaining pre-trial discovery of documents. The Government of the Cayman Islands understand "Letters of Request issued for the purpose of obtaining pre-trial discovery of documents" for the purposes of the foregoing declaration as including any Letter of Request which requires a person:

    a) to state what documents relevant to the proceedings to which the Letter of Request relates are, or have been, in his possession, custody or power; or

    b) to produce any documents other than particular documents specified in the Letter of Request as being documents appearing to the requested court to be, or likely to be, in his possession, custody or power.

4. In accordance with Article 27, by the law and practice of the Cayman Islands the prior permission referred to in Articles 16 and 17 of the Convention is not required in respect of diplomatic officers, consular agents or commissioners of a Contracting State which does not require permission to be obtained for the purposes of taking evidence under Article 16 or 17.

Extension to Guernsey.—

Notification in accordance with Article 42, subs. d and e, of the Convention

With reference to the deposit of its instrument of ratification of the above-mentioned Convention on 16 July 1985 the Government of the United Kingdom of Great Britain and Northern Ireland declared by letter of 13 November 1985 which was received by the Ministry of Foreign Affairs of the Kingdom of the Netherlands on 19 November 1985, in accordance with Article 40, second paragraph, that the Convention shall extend to Guernsey.

In accordance with Article 35 the Government of the United Kingdom furthermore declared that:

"**(a)** under Articles 8 and 25 of the Convention, the Bailiff, Deputy Bailiff, any Jurat of the Royal Court of Guernsey, the Chairman or a Jurat of the Court of Alderney and the Seneschal (or Deputy) of the Court of the Seneschal of Sark are designated as the competent authorities for Guernsey;

"**(b)** under Article 23 of the Convention, Guernsey will not execute Letters of Request issued for the purpose of obtaining pretrial discovery of documents.".

In accordance with Article 40, third paragraph, the Convention will enter into force for Guernsey on 18 January 1986.

Extension to Anguilla.—

Notification pursuant to Article 42, paragraph c, d and e, of the Convention

In accordance with Article 40, paragraph 2, the Kingdom of Great Britain and Northern Ireland declared, by a Letter dated 1 July 1986, received at the Ministry of Foreign Affairs on 3 July 1986, that the present Convention shall extend to Anguilla.

In accordance with Article 35, of the Convention, the following designations have been made:

"**a.** Under Articles 16, 17 and 18 of the Convention the Registrar of the East Caribbean Supreme Court is designated as the competent authority for Anguilla.

"**b.** Under Article 24 of the Convention, the Governor of Anguilla is designated as an additional authority competent to receive Letters of Request for execution in Anguilla."

and the following declarations:

" . . . . in accordance with the provisions of Articles 4 and 33 of the Convention, Anguilla will not accept a Letter of Request in French.

"In accordance with Article 8, members of the juridical personnel of the requesting authority may be present at the execution of a Letter Request in Anguilla.

In accordance with Article 18, a diplomatic officer, consular agent or commissioner authorized to take evidence under Articles 15, 16 and 17 of the Convention may apply to the competent authority in Anguilla designated above for appropriate assistance to obtain such evidence by compulsion provided that the contracting State whose diplomatic officer, consular agent or commissioner makes (sic) the application has made a declaration affording reciprocal facilities under Article 18.

In accordance with Article 23, Anguilla will not execute Letters of Request issued for the purpose of obtaining pre-trial discovery of documents. Anguilla understands 'Letters of Request issued for the purpose of obtaining pre-trial discovery of documents' for the purposes of the foregoing declaration as including any Letter of Request which requires a person:

"**i.** to state what documents relevant to the proceedings to which the Letter of Request relates are, or have been, in his possession, custody or power; or

"**ii.** to produce any documents other than particular documents specified in the Letter of Request as being documents appearing to the requested court to be, or likely to be, in his possession, custody or power.

In accordance with Article 27, by the law and practice of Anguilla the prior permission referred to in Articles 16 and 17 of the Convention is not required in respect of diplomatic officers, consular agents or commissioners of a Contracting State which does not require permission to be obtained for the purposes of taking evidence under Articles 16 or 17."

4 With the following designations and declarations:

In accordance with Article 40, the Convention entered into force for Anguilla on 1 September 1986.

The United States Department of Justice, Washington, D.C., 20530, is designated as the Central Authority referred to in Article 2 of the Convention.

Under paragraph 2 of Article 4 of the United States has agreed to accept a Letter of Request in or translated into French. The United States wishes to point out that owing to the necessity of translating such documents into English it will take the Central Authority longer to comply with a Letter of Request in or translated into French than with a similar request received in English.

In accordance with paragraph 3 of Article 4 the United States declares that it will also accept Letters of Request in Spanish for execution in the Commonwealth of Puerto Rico.

In accordance with Article 8 the United States declares that subject to prior authorization members of the judicial personnel of the requesting authority of another Contracting State may be present at the execution of a Letter of Request. The Department of Justice is the competent authority for the purposes of this Article.

The United States declares that evidence may be taken in the United States under Articles 16 and 17 without its prior permission.

In accordance with Article 18 the United States declares that a diplomatic or consular officer or a commissioner authorized to take evidence under Articles 15, 16 or 17 may apply for appropriate assistance to obtain the evidence by compulsion. The competent authority for the purposes of Article 18 is the United States district court of the district in which a person resides or is found. Such court may order him to give his testimony or statement or to produce a document or thing for use in a proceeding in a foreign tribunal. The order may direct that the testimony or statement be given, or the document or other thing be produced, before a person appointed by the court.

In accordance with Article 40 the United States declares that the Convention shall extend to Guam, Puerto Rico and the Virgin Islands.

In accordance with the provisions of Article 39 of the Convention, the United States declared its acceptance of the accessions by Argentina, Barbados, Cyprus, Monaco, and Singapore.

Complete Annotation Materials, see Title 28 U.S.C.A.

5 In accordance with Article 2 [of the Convention] Venezuela designated the following Central Authority: el ministerio de Relaciones Exteriores.

In accordance with Article 39, paragraph 5, the Convention will enter into force between Venezuela and

Cyprus	29 April 1994
United Kingdom of Great Britain and Northern Ireland	15 August 1994*
Sweden	3 September 1994
Germany	21 October 1994
Denmark	27 November 1994
Spain	6 February 1995
Finland	11 March 1995
Italy	16 January 1996
Australia	20 January 1996
Israel	19 March 1996
Slovakia	20 May 1996

* The Permanent Bureau of the Hague Conference on private international law presents its compliments to the Diplomatic Missions of the Member States and to the National Organs and has the honour to inform them that, by a Note dated 9 February 1995 and received on 21 February 1995, the Embassy of the United Kingdom of Great Britain and Northern Ireland informed the Ministry of Foreign Affairs of the Kingdom of the Netherlands that the acceptance of Venezuela's accession to the Convention, set out in the Embassy's Note of 14 June 1994 (see L.c. A No 51/L.c. ON No 47 dated 26 July 1994) was also in respect of the territories for the international relations of which the United Kingdom is responsible and to which the application of the Convention has been extended.

The Embassy also informed that, unless otherwise stated, in future the acceptance by the United Kingdom of the accession of any State to the Convention shall also be acceptance in respect of all the territories for the international relations of which the United Kingdom is responsible and to which the application of the Convention has been extended.

Annotations to the Convention

"Report of the U.S. Delegation on the Evidence Convention", 8 Int'l Legal Materials 804 (1969).

Amram, "Explanatory Report on the Convention on the Taking of Evidence Abroad in Civil and Commercial Matters—Message from the President of the United States", Sen.Exec. A, 92nd Cong., 2d Sess. (Feb. 1, 1972).

Edwards, "Taking of Evidence Abroad in Civil or Commercial Matters", 18 Int'l and Comp.L.Q. 646 (1969).

Amram, "U.S. Ratification of the Hague Convention on the Taking of Evidence Abroad" 67 Am.J. Int'l L. (1973).

Model for Letters of Request Recommended for Use in Applying the Hague Convention of 18 March 1970 on the Taking of Evidence Abroad in Civil or Commercial Matters

Request for International Judicial Assistance Pursuant to the Hague Convention of 18 March 1970 on the Taking of Evidence in Civil or Commercial Matters

N.B. Under the first paragraph of article 4, the Letter of Request shall be in the language of the authority requested to execute it or be accompanied by a translation into that language. However, the provisions of the second and third paragraphs may permit use of other languages.

In order to avoid confusion, please spell out the name of the month in each date.

I.   *(Items to be included in all Letters of Request.)*

     1.   Sender   _____*(identity and address)*_____

     2.   Central Authority of the Requested State   _____*(identity and address)*_____

     3.   Person to whom the executed request is to be returned   _____*(identity and address)*_____

II.   *(Items to be included in all Letters of Request.)*

     4.   In conformity with article 3 of the Convention, the undersigned applicant has the honour to submit the following request:

     5.   a.   Requesting judicial authority (article 3, a)   _____*(identity and address)*_____

         b.   To the competent authority of (article 3, a)   _____*(the requested State)*_____

     6.   Names and addresses of the parties and their representatives (article 3, b)

         a.   Plaintiff

---

　　　b.　Defendant　　　　　　　　　　_____
　　　　　　　　　　　　　　　　　　　_____

　　　c.　Other parties　　　　　　　_____
　　　　　　　　　　　　　　　　　　　_____
　　　　　　　　　　　　　　　　　　　_____

7.　Nature and purpose of the　　　_____
　　proceedings and summary　　　　_____
　　of the facts (article 3, c)　　　_____

8.　Evidence to be obtained or　　　_____
　　other judicial act to be per-　　_____
　　formed (article 3, d)　　　　　　_____

III.　*(Items to be completed where applicable.)*

9.　Identity and address of any　　_____
　　person to be examined (article　_____
　　3, e)　　　　　　　　　　　　　　_____

10.　Questions to be put to the
　　persons to be examined or
　　statement of the subject-　　　_____*(or see attached list)*_____
　　matter about which they　　　　_____
　　are to be examined (article 3, f)　_____

11.　Documents or other proper-
　　ty to be inspected (article　　_____*(specify whether it is to be*
　　3, g)　　　　　　　　　　　　*produced, copied, valued, etc.)*_____
　　　　　　　　　　　　　　　　　_____

12.　Any requirement that the
　　evidence be given on oath　　_____*(In the event that the evi-*
　　or affirmation and any spe-　*dence cannot be taken in the man-*
　　cial form to be used (article　*ner requested, specify whether it*
　　3, h)　　　　　　　　　　　　*is to be taken in such manner as*
　　　　　　　　　　　　　　　　provided by local law for the form-
　　　　　　　　　　　　　　　　*al taking of evidence.)*_____

13.　Special methods or proce-　　_____
　　dure to be followed (arti-　　　_____
　　cles 3, i and 9)
14.　Request for notification of
　　the time and place for the
　　execution of the Request　　　_____
　　and identity and address　　　_____
　　of any person to be notified　_____
　　(article 7)
15.　Request for attendance or
　　participation of judicial
　　personnel of the requesting　_____
　　authority at the execution　　_____
　　of the letter of Request
16.　Specification of privilege
　　or duty to refuse to give　　　_____
　　evidence under the law of　　_____
　　the State of origin (article　　_____
　　11, b)　　　　　　　　　　　　_____

17. The fees and costs incurred which are reimbursable under the second paragraph of article 14 or under article 26 of the Convention will be borne by

_____(identity and address)_____
_____
_____
_____

_____

IV. *(Items to be included in all Letters of Request.)*

18. Date of request

_____

19. Signature and seal of the requesting authority

_____
_____

TREATIES AND CONVENTIONS

INTER–AMERICAN CONVENTION ON LETTERS ROGATORY

The Governments of the Member States of the Organization of American States, desirous of concluding a convention on letters rogatory, have agreed as follows:

I. USE OF TERMS

Article 1

For the purposes of this Convention the terms "exhortos" and "cartas rogatorias" are synonymous in the Spanish text. The terms "letters rogatory", "commissions rogatoires", and "cartas rogatórias" used in the English, French and Portuguese texts, respectively, cover both "exhortos" and "cartas rogatorias".

II. SCOPE OF THE CONVENTION

Article 2

This Convention shall apply to letters rogatory, issued in conjunction with proceedings in civil and commercial matters held before the appropriate judicial or other adjudicatory authority of one of the States Parties to this Convention, that have as their purpose:

a. The performance of procedural acts of a merely formal nature, such as service of process, summonses or subpoenas abroad;

b. The taking of evidence and the obtaining of information abroad, unless a reservation is made in this respect.

Article 3

This Convention shall not apply to letters rogatory relating to procedural acts other than those specified in the preceding article; and in particular it shall not apply to acts involving measures of compulsion.

III. TRANSMISSION OF LETTERS ROGATORY

Article 4

Letters rogatory may be transmitted to the authority to which they are addressed by the interested parties, through judicial channels, diplomatic or consular agents, or the Central Authority of the State of origin or of the State of destination, as the case may be.

Each State Party shall inform the General Secretariat of the Organization of American States of the Central Authority competent to receive and distribute letters rogatory.

IV. REQUIREMENTS FOR EXECUTION

Article 5

Letters rogatory shall be executed in the States Parties provided they meet the following requirements:

a. The letter rogatory is legalized, except as provided for in Articles 6 and 7 of this Convention. The letter rogatory shall be presumed to be duly legalized in the State of origin when legalized by the competent consular or diplomatic agent;

b. The letter rogatory and the appended documentation are duly translated into the official language of the State of destination.

Article 6

Whenever letters rogatory are transmitted through consular or diplomatic channels or through the Central Authority, legalization shall not be required.

Article 7

Courts in border areas of the States Parties may directly execute the letters rogatory contemplated in this Convention and such letters shall not require legalization.

Article 8

Letters rogatory shall be accompanied by the following documents to be delivered to the person on whom process, summons or subpoena is being served:

a. An authenticated copy of the complaint with its supporting documents, and of other exhibits or rulings that serve as the basis for the measure requested;

b. Written information identifying the judicial or other adjudicatory authority issuing the letter, indicating the time-limits allowed the person affected to act upon the request, and warning of the consequences of failure to do so;

c. Where appropriate, information on the existence and address of the court-appointed defense counsel or of competent legal-aid societies in the State of origin.

Article 9

Execution of letters rogatory shall not imply ultimate recognition of the jurisdiction of the judicial or other adjudicatory authority issuing the letter rogatory or a commitment to recognize the validity of the judgment it may render or to execute it.

V. EXECUTION
Article 10

Letters rogatory shall be executed in accordance with the laws and procedural rules of the State of destination.

At the request of the judicial or other adjudicatory authority issuing the letter rogatory, the authority of the State of destination may execute the letter through a special procedure, or accept the observance of additional formalities in performing the act requested, provided this procedure or the observance of those formalities is not contrary to the law of the State of destination.

Article 11

The authority of the State of destination shall have jurisdiction to determine any issue arising as a result of the execution of the measure requested in the letter rogatory.

Should such authority find that it lacks jurisdiction to execute the letter rogatory, it shall ex officio forward the documents and antecedents of the case to the authority of the State which has jurisdiction.

Article 12

The costs and other expenses involved in the processing and execution of letters rogatory shall be borne by the interested parties.

The State of destination may, in its discretion, execute a letter rogatory that does not indicate the person to be held responsible for costs and other expenses when incurred. The identity of the person empowered to represent the applicant for legal purposes may be indicated in the letter rogatory or in the documents relating to its execution.

The effects of a declaration in forma pauperis shall be regulated by the law of the State of destination.

Article 13

Consular or diplomatic agents of the States Parties to this Convention may perform the acts referred to in Article 2 in the State in which they are accredited, provided the performance of such acts is not contrary to the laws of that State. In so doing, they shall not perform any acts involving measures of compulsion.

VI. GENERAL PROVISIONS
Article 14

States Parties belonging to economic integration systems may agree directly between themselves upon special methods and procedures more expeditious than those provided for in this Convention. These agreements may be extended to include other States in the manner in which the parties may agree.

Article 15

This Convention shall not limit any provisions regarding letters rogatory in bilateral or multilateral agreements that may have been signed or may be signed in the future by the States Parties or preclude the continuation of more favorable practices in this regard that may be followed by these States.

Article 16

The States Parties to this Convention may declare that its provisions cover the execution of letters rogatory in criminal, labor, and "contentious-administrative" cases, as well as in arbitrations and other matters within the jurisdiction of special courts. Such declarations shall be transmitted to the General Secretariat of the Organization of American States.

Article 17

The State of destination may refuse to execute a letter rogatory that is manifestly contrary to its public policy ("ordre public").

Article 18

The States Parties shall inform the General Secretariat of the Organization of American States of the requirements stipulated in their laws for the legalization and the translation of letters rogatory.

VII. FINAL PROVISIONS
Article 19

This Convention shall be open for signature by the Member States of the Organization of American States.

Article 20

This Convention is subject to ratification. The instruments of ratification shall be deposited with the General Secretariat of the Organization of American States.

Article 21

This Convention shall remain open for accession by any other State. The instrument of accession shall be deposited with the General Secretariat of the Organization of American States.

Article 22

This Convention shall enter into force on the thirtieth day following the date of deposit of the second instrument of ratification.

For each State ratifying or acceding to the Convention after the deposit of the second instrument of ratification, the Convention shall enter into force on the thirtieth day after deposit by such State of its instrument of ratification or accession.

Article 23

If a State Party has two or more territorial units in which different systems of law apply in relation to the matters dealt with in this Convention, it may, at the time of signature, ratification or accession, declare that this Convention shall extend to all its territorial units or only to one or more of them.

Such declaration may be modified by subsequent declarations, which shall expressly indicate the territorial unit or units to which the Convention applies. Such subsequent declarations shall be transmitted to the General Secretariat of the Organization of American States, and shall become effective thirty days after the date of their receipt.

Article 24

This Convention shall remain in force indefinitely, but any of the States Parties may denounce it. The instrument of denunciation shall be deposited with the General Secretariat of the Organization of American States. After one year from the date of deposit of the instrument of denunciation, the Convention shall no longer be in effect for the denouncing State, but shall remain in effect for the other States Parties.

Article 25

The original instrument of this Convention, the English, French, Portuguese and Spanish texts of which are equally authentic, shall be deposited with the General Secretariat of the Organization of American States. The Secretariat shall notify the Member States of the Organization of American States and the States that have acceded to the Convention of the signatures, deposits of instruments of ratification, accession, and denunciation as well as of reservations, if any. It shall also transmit the information mentioned in the second paragraph of Article 4 and in Article 18 and the declarations referred to in Articles 16 and 23 of this Convention.

IN WITNESS WHEREOF the undersigned Plenipotentiaries, being duly authorized thereto by their respective Governments, have signed this Convention.

DONE AT PANAMA CITY, Republic of Panama, this thirtieth day of January one thousand nine hundred and seventy-five.

[Signatures omitted]

Inter–American Convention on Letters Rogatory.

Done at Panama January 30, 1975; entered into force for the United States August 27, 1988.

States which are parties:

Argentina*

Brazil*

Chile[1],*

Columbia*

Costa Rica

Ecuador[2],*

El Salvador[3]

Guatemala[4],*

Honduras

Mexico[5],*

Panama*

Paraguay*

Peru*

Spain[6]

United States[7]

Uruguay[8],*

Venezuela[9],*

* The United States has a treaty relationship only with those countries which are a party to the Convention and the Additional Protocol.

---

[1] (Declaration made at the time of ratification, according to Article 16 of the Convention)

The instrument of ratification corresponding to this Convention contains the declaration "that its provisions cover the execution of letters rogatory in criminal, labor, and contentious-administrative cases, as well as in arbitrations and other matters within the jurisdiction of special courts".

(Provided information in accordance with Article 4)

The Central Authority to receive and distribute letters rogatory is the Ministry of Foreign Affairs of the Republic of Chile (May 7, 1987).

[2] On 23 April 1984 sent information (Note No. 89-OEA/84), appointing the Asesoría Técnico-Jurídica of the Ministry of Foreign Affairs of Ecuador as the "Central Authority, to carry out the functions entrusted to it in the Inter-American Convention on Letters Rogatory."

[3] Reservation to application of Article 7.

(Provided information in accordance with Articles 4 and 18)

In El Salvador the Supreme Court of Justice is the competent central authority for receiving and distributing Letters Rogatory. The requirements exacted for legalization and translation of Letters Rogatory are those prescribed in Article 261 of the Code of Civil Procedures and Articles 388, 389, 391 and 392 of the Bustamente Code . . . (The text of the articles is omitted).

[4] (Provided information in accordance with Article 4)

The Central Authority competent to transmit, receive and distribute letters rogatory is the Supreme Court of Justice (October 21, 1987)

[5] With the interpretative declaration made at the time of signature.

"It is the interpretation of the Government of Mexico that Article 9 of this Convention refers to the international validity of foreign judgments."

(Provided information in accordance with Article 4)

The Central Authority competent to receive and distribute letters rogatory is the Secretariat of Foreign Affairs of Mexico.

[6] (Provided information in accordance with Article 4)

The Central Authority competent to receive and distribute letters rogatory is the General Technical Secretariat of the Ministry of Justice (Secretaría General Técnica), whose address is: San Bernardo 47, Madrid 28015, Spain (April 14, 1988).

[7] (Reservations made at the time of ratification)

"1. Pursuant to Article 2(b) of the Inter–American Convention on Letters Rogatory, letters rogatory that have as their purpose the taking of evidence shall be excluded from the rights, obligations and operation of this Convention between the United States and another State Party.

"2. In ratifying the Inter–American Convention on Letters Rogatory, the United States accepts entry into force and undertakes treaty relations only with respect to States which have ratified or acceded to the Additional Protocol as well as the Inter–American Convention, and not with respect to States which have ratified or acceded to the Inter–American Convention alone."

(Provided information in accordance with Articles 4 and 18)

Pursuant to Article 4 of the Convention and Article 2 of the Additional Protocol, the Government of the United States wishes to inform the Secretary General that the Department of Justice is the Central Authority competent to receive and distribute letters rogatory. The mailing address for these purposes is:

Office of International Judicial Assistance

Civil Division

Department of Justice

Todd Building Room 1234

550 11th Street, N.W.

Washington, D.C. 20530 (*)

Pursuant to Article 18 of the Convention, the Government of the United States wishes to inform the Secretary General that letters rogatory to be executed in the United States must be translated into the English language.

(*) Phone: (202) 724–7455

[8] (Provided information in accordance with Article 4)

On 30 August 1985 sent information (Note No. 961/85) appointing the Ministry of Education and Culture "Asesoría Autoridad Central de Cooperación Jurídica Internacional" as the "Central Authority" provided for in Article 4 of the Convention.

[9] (Reservation made at the time of ratification)

With reservation to letter b) of Article 2 of the Convention.

(Provided information in accordance with Article 4)

The Central Authority competent to receive and distribute letters rogatory is the Ministry of Foreign Affairs of the Republic of Venezuela (11 December 1984).

ADDITIONAL PROTOCOL TO THE INTER–AMERICAN CONVENTION ON LETTERS ROGATORY

The Governments of the Member States of the Organization of American States, desirous of strengthening and facilitating international cooperation in judicial procedures as provided for in the Inter–American Convention on Letters Rogatory done in Panama on January 30, 1975, have agreed as follows:

I. SCOPE OF PROTOCOL

Article 1

This Protocol shall apply only to those procedural acts set forth in Article 2(a) of the Inter–American Convention on Letters Rogatory, hereinafter referred to as "the Convention". For the purposes of this Protocol, such acts shall be understood to mean procedural acts (pleadings, motions, orders, and subpoenas) that are served and requests for information that are made by a judicial or other adjudicatory authority of a State Party to a judicial or administrative authority of another State Party and are transmitted by a letter rogatory from the Central Authority of the State of origin to the Central Authority of the State of destination.

II. CENTRAL AUTHORITY

Article 2

Each State Party shall designate a central authority that shall perform the functions assigned to it in the Convention and in this Protocol. At the time of deposit of their instruments of ratification or accession to this Protocol, the States Parties shall communicate the designations to the General Secretariat of the Organization of American States, which shall distribute to the States Parties to the Convention a list containing the designations received. The Central Authority designated by a State Party in accordance with Article 4 of the Convention may be changed at any time. The State Party shall inform the above-mentioned Secretariat of such change as promptly as possible.

III. PREPARATION OF LETTERS ROGATORY

Article 3

Letters rogatory shall be prepared on forms that are printed in the four official languages of the Organization of American States or in the languages of the State of origin and of the State of destination and conform to Form A contained in the Annex to this Protocol.

Letters rogatory shall be accompanied by the following:

a. Copy of the complaint or pleading that initiated the action in which the letter rogatory was issued, as well as a translation thereof into the language of the State of destination;

b. Untranslated copy of the documents attached to the complaint or pleading;

c. Untranslated copy of any rulings ordering issuance of the letter rogatory;

d. Form conforming to Form B annexed to this Protocol and containing essential information for the person to be served or the authority to receive the documents; and

e. Certificate conforming to Form C annexed to this Protocol on which the Central Authority of the State of destination shall attest to execution or non-execution of the letter rogatory.

The copies shall be regarded as authenticated for the purposes of Article 8(a) of the Convention if they bear the seal of the judicial or other adjudicatory authority that issued the letter rogatory.

A copy of the letter rogatory together with Form B and the copies referred to in items a, b, and c of this Article shall be delivered to the person notified or to the authority to which the request is addressed. One of the copies of the letter rogatory and the documents attached to it shall remain in the possession of the State of destination; the untranslated original, the certificate of execution and the documents attached to them shall be returned to the Central Authority of the State of origin through appropriate channels.

If a State Party has more than one official language, it shall, at the time of signature, ratification or accession to this Protocol, declare which language or languages shall be considered official for the purposes of the Convention and of this Protocol. If a State Party comprises territorial units that have different official languages, it shall, at the time of signature, ratification or accession to this Protocol, declare which language or languages in each territorial unit shall be considered official for the purposes of the Convention and of this Protocol. The General Secretariat of the Organization of American States shall distribute to the States Parties to this Protocol the information contained in such declarations.

IV. TRANSMISSION AND PROCESSING OF LETTERS ROGATORY

Article 4

Upon receipt of a letter rogatory from the Central Authority in another State Party, the Central Authority in the State of destination shall transmit the letter rogatory to the appropriate judicial or administrative authority for processing in accordance with the applicable local law.

Upon execution of the letter rogatory, the judicial or administrative authority or authorities that processed it shall attest to the execution thereof in the manner prescribed in their local law, and shall transmit it with the relevant documents to the Central Authority. The Central Authority of the State Party of destination shall certify execution of the letter rogatory to the Central Authority of the State Party of origin on a form conforming to Form C of the Annex, which shall not require legalization. In addition, the Central Authority of the State of destination shall return the letter rogatory and attached documents to the Central Authority of the State of origin for delivery to the judicial or other adjudicatory authority that issued it.

V. COSTS AND EXPENSES

Article 5

The processing of letters rogatory by the Central Authority of the State Party of destination and its judicial or administrative authorities shall be free of charge. However, this State Party may seek payment by parties requesting execution of letters rogatory for those services which, in accordance with its local law, are required to be paid for directly by those parties.

The party requesting the execution of a letter rogatory shall, at its election, either select and indicate in the letter rogatory the person who is responsible in the State of destination for the cost of such services or, alternatively, shall attach to the letter rogatory a check for the fixed amount that is specified in Article 6 of this Protocol for its processing by the State of destination and will cover the cost of such services or a document proving that such amount has been transferred by some other means to the Central Authority of the State of destination.

The fact that the cost of such services ultimately exceeds the fixed amount shall not delay or prevent the processing or execution of the letter rogatory by the Central Authority or the judicial or administrative authorities of the State of destination. Should the cost exceed that amount, the Central Authority of the State of destination may, when returning the executed letter rogatory, seek payment of the outstanding amount due from the party requesting execution of the letter rogatory.

Article 6

At the time of deposit of its instrument of ratification or accession to this Protocol with the General Secretariat of the Organization of American States, each State Party shall attach a schedule of the services and the costs and other expenses that, in accordance with its local law, shall be paid directly by the party requesting execution of the letter rogatory. In addition, each State Party shall specify in the above-mentioned schedule the single amount which it considers will reasonably cover the cost of such services, regardless of the number or nature thereof. This amount shall be paid when the person requesting execution of the letter rogatory has not designated a person responsible for the payment of such services in the State of destination but has decided to pay for them directly in the manner provided for in Article 5 of this Protocol.

The General Secretariat of the Organization of American States shall distribute the information received to the States Parties to this Protocol. A State Party may at any time notify the General Secretariat of the Organization of American States of changes in the above-mentioned schedules, which shall be communicated by the General Secretariat to the other States Parties to this Protocol.

Article 7

States Parties may declare in the schedules mentioned in the foregoing articles that, provided there is reciprocity, they will not charge parties requesting execution of letters rogatory for the services necessary for executing them, or will accept in complete satisfaction of the cost of such services either the single fixed amount specified in Article 6 or another specified amount.

Article 8

This Protocol shall be open for signature and subject to ratification or accession by those Member States of the Organization of American States that have signed, ratified, or acceded to the Inter–American Convention on Letters Rogatory signed in Panama on January 30, 1975.

This Protocol shall remain open for accession by any other State that accedes or has acceded to the Inter–American Convention on Letters Rogatory, under the conditions set forth in this article.

The instruments of ratification and accession shall be deposited with the General Secretariat of the Organization of American States.

Article 9

This Protocol shall enter into force on the thirtieth day following the date on which two States Parties to the Convention have deposited their instruments of ratification or accession to this Protocol.

For each State ratifying or acceding to the Protocol after its entry into force, the Protocol shall enter into force on the thirtieth day following deposit by such State of its instrument of ratification or accession, provided that such State is a Party to the Convention.

Article 10

If a State Party has two or more territorial units in which different systems of law apply in relation to matters dealt with in this Protocol, it may, at the time of signature, ratification or accession, declare that this Protocol shall extend to all its territorial units or only to one or more of them.

Such declaration may be modified by subsequent declarations that shall expressly indicate the territorial unit or units to which this Protocol applies. Such subsequent declarations shall be transmitted to the General Secretariat of the Organization of American States, and shall become effective thirty days after the date of their receipt.

Article 11

This Protocol shall remain in force indefinitely, but any of the States Parties may denounce it. The instrument of denunciation shall be deposited with the General Secretariat of the Organization of American States. After one year from the date of deposit of the instrument of denunciation, the Protocol shall no longer be in effect for the denouncing State, but shall remain in effect for the other States Parties.

Article 12

The original instrument of this Protocol and its Annex (Forms A, B and C), the English, French, Portuguese and Spanish texts of which are equally authentic, shall be deposited with the General Secretariat of the Organization of American States, which will forward an authenticated copy of the text to the Secretariat of the United Nations for registration and publication in accordance with Article 102 of its Charter. The General Secretariat of the Organization of American States shall notify the Member States of that Organization and the States that have acceded to the Protocol of the signatures, deposits of instruments of ratification, accession and denunciation, as well as of reservations, if any. It shall also transmit to them the information mentioned in Article 2, the last paragraph of Article 3, and Article 6 and the declarations referred to in Article 10 of this Protocol.

IN WITNESS WHEREOF the undersigned Plenipotentiaries, being duly authorized thereto by their respective Governments, have signed this Protocol.

DONE AT MONTEVIDEO, Republic of Uruguay, this eighth day of May, one thousand nine hundred and seventy-nine.

[Signatures omitted]

ANNEX TO THE ADDITIONAL PROTOCOL
TO THE INTER–AMERICAN CONVENTION ON LETTERS ROGATORY
FORM A
LETTER ROGATORY [1]

1	2
REQUESTING JUDICIAL OR OTHER ADJUDICATORY AUTHORITY Name Address	CASE: DOCKET No.:

3	4
CENTRAL AUTHORITY OF THE STATE OF ORIGIN Name Address	CENTRAL AUTHORITY OF THE STATE OF DESTINATION Name Address

5	6
REQUESTING PARTY Name Address	COUNSEL TO THE REQUESTING PARTY Name Address

PERSON DESIGNATED TO ACT IN CONNECTION WITH THE LETTER ROGATORY

Name

Address

Is this person responsible for costs and expenses?

YES ☐   NO ☐

*If not, check in the amount of
_____ is attached
*Or proof of payment is attached

The Central Authority signing this letter rogatory has the honor to transmit to you in triplicate the documents listed below and, in conformity with the Protocol to the Inter–American Convention on Letters Rogatory:

* A.   Requests their prompt service on:

_____

_____

_____

The undersigned authority requests that service be carried out in the following manner:

* (1).   In accordance with the special procedure or additional formalities that are described below, as provided for in the second paragraph of Article 10 of the above-mentioned Convention; or

_____

_____

_____

* (2).   By service personally on the identified addressee or, in the case of a legal entity, on its authorized agent; or

* (3). If the person or the authorized agent of the entity to be served is not found, service shall be made in accordance with the law of the State of destination.

* B.   Requests the delivery of the documents listed below to the following judicial or administrative authority:

Authority _____

_____

* C.   Requests the Central Authority of the State of destination to return to the Central Authority of the State of origin one copy of the documents listed below and attached to this letter rogatory, and an executed Certificate on the attached Form C.

Done at _____ this _____ date of _____, 19___.

_____   _____

Signature and stamp of the   Signature and stamp of the
judicial or other adjudicatory   Central Authority of the
authority of the State of origin   State of origin

Title or other identification of each document to be delivered:

_____

(Attach additional pages, if necessary.)

1 Complete the original and two copies of this form; if A(1) is applicable, attach the original and two copies of the translation of this item in the language of the State of destination.
* Delete if inapplicable.

ANNEX TO THE ADDITIONAL PROTOCOL
TO THE INTER–AMERICAN CONVENTION ON LETTERS ROGATORY

FORM B

ESSENTIAL INFORMATION FOR THE ADDRESSEE 1

To   (Name and address of the person being served)_____

You are hereby informed that (Brief statement of nature of service) _____

_____

A copy of the letter rogatory that gives rise to the service or delivery of these documents is attached to this document. This copy also contains essential information for you. Also attached are copies of the complaint or pleading initiating the action in which the letter rogatory was issued, of the documents attached to the complaint or pleading, and of any rulings that ordered the issuance of the letter rogatory.

ADDITIONAL INFORMATION

I*

FOR SERVICE

A.   The document being served on you (original or copy) concerns the following:

_____

B.   The remedies sought or the amount in dispute is as follows:

_____

C.   By this service, you are requested:

_____

D.   *   In case of service on you as a defendant you can answer the complaint before the judicial or other adjudicatory authority specified in Form A, Box 1 (State place, date and hour):

_____

     *   You are being summoned to appear as: _____

*   If some other action is being requested of the person served, please
describe: _____
_____
_____
_____

E.   If you fail to comply, the consequences might be: _____
_____
_____

F.   You are hereby informed that a defense counsel appointed by the Court or the following legal
aid societies are available to you at the place where the proceeding is pending.
Name: _____

Address: _____
_____

The documents listed in Part III are being furnished to you so that you may better understand
and defend your interests.

II *

FOR INFORMATION FROM JUDICIAL OR ADMINISTRATIVE AUTHORITY

To: _____
_____

(Name and address of the judicial or administrative authority)

You are respectfully requested to furnish the undersigned authority with the following information:
_____
_____
_____
_____

The documents listed in Part III are being furnished to you to facilitate your reply.

III

LIST OF ATTACHED DOCUMENTS

_____
_____
_____
_____
_____
_____

(Attach additional pages if necessary.)

Done at _____ this _____ day of _____, 19___

_____   _____
Signature and stamp of the   Signature and stamp of
judicial or other adjudicatory   the Central Authority
authority of the State of origin   of the State of Origin

1 Complete the original and two copies of this form in the language of the State of origin and two
copies in the language of the State of destination.
* Delete if inapplicable.

ANNEX TO THE ADDITIONAL PROTOCOL
TO THE INTER–AMERICAN CONVENTION ON LETTERS ROGATORY

FORM C

CERTIFICATE OF EXECUTION1

To: _____
_____

(Name and address of judicial or other adjudicatory authority that issued the letter rogatory)

In conformity with the Additional Protocol to the Inter–American Convention on Letters Rogatory, signed at Montevideo on May 8, 1979, and in accordance with the attached original letter rogatory, the undersigned Central Authority has the honor to certify the following:

* A.　That one copy of the documents attached to this Certificate has been served or delivered as follows:

　　　Date: _____

　　　At (Address) _____

By one of the following methods authorized by the Convention.

　　*(1)　In accordance with the special procedure or additional formalities that are described below, as provided for in the second paragraph of Article 10 of the above-mentioned Convention, or

　　　　_____
　　　　_____
　　　　_____

　　*(2)　By service personally on the identified addressee or, in the case of a legal entity, on its authorized agent, or

　　*(3)　If the person or the authorized agent of the entity to be served was not found, in accordance with the law of the State of destination: (Specify method used)

　　　　_____
　　　　_____
　　　　_____
　　　　_____

*B.　That the documents referred to in the letter rogatory have been delivered to:

　　　Identity of person _____
　　　_____

　　　Relationship to the addressee _____
　　　　　　　　　　　　　　　(family, business or other)

　　　_____
　　　_____

*C.　That the documents attached to the Certificate have not been served or delivered for the following reason(s):

　　　_____
　　　_____
　　　_____

*D.　In conformity with the Protocol, the party requesting execution of the letter rogatory is requested to pay the outstanding balance of costs in the amount indicated in the attached statement.

　　　Done at _____ the _____ day of _____ 19___

_____
Signature and stamp of Central Authority of the State of destination

Where appropriate, attach originals or copies
of any additional documents proving service
or delivery, and identify them.
1 Complete the original and one copy in the language of the State of destination.
* Delete if inapplicable.

Additional Protocol to the Inter–American Convention on Letters Rogatory, with Annex. Done at Montevideo May 8, 1979; entered into force for the United States August 27, 1988.

States which are parties:

Argentina*
Brazil*
Chile*
Columbia*
Ecuador [1]*
Guatemala*
Mexico [2]*
Panama [2a]*
Paraguay*
Peru*
United States [3]
Uruguay [4]*
Venezuela*

* The United States has a treaty relationship only with those countries which are a party to the Convention and the Additional Protocol.

[1] On 23 April 1984 sent information (Note No. 89-OEA/84), appointing the Asesoría-Técnico-Jurídica of the Ministry of Foreign Affairs of Ecuador as the "Central Authority", to carry out the functions entrusted to it in the Additional Protocol to the Inter-American Convention on Letters Rogatory.

[2] In accordance with the provisions stipulated in Article 2 of the Additional Protocol to the Inter-American Convention on Letters Rogatory relative to the designation of a central authority, I notify Your Excellency that this shall be the Secretariat of Foreign Affairs of Mexico (9 March 1983).

[2a] (Provided information in accordance with Article 2 of the Protocol)

On October 4, 1991, Panama designated the Ministry of Foreign Affairs as the Central Authority competent pursuant to the functions of article 2 of the Protocol.

[3] (Reservations made at the time of ratification)

"1. Pursuant to Article 2(b) of the Inter-American Convention on Letters Rogatory, letters rogatory that have as their purpose the taking of evidence shall be excluded from the rights, obligations and operation of this Convention between the United States and another State Party.

"2. In ratifying the Inter-American Convention on Letters Rogatory, the United States accepts entry into force and undertakes treaty relations only with respect to States which have ratified or acceded to the Additional Protocol as well as the Inter-American Convention, and not with respect to States which have ratified or acceded to the Inter-American Convention alone."

(Provided information in accordance with Article 2)

Pursuant to Article 4 of the Convention and Article 2 of the Additional Protocol, the Government of the United States wishes to inform the Secretary General that the Department of Justice is the Central Authority competent to receive and distribute letters rogatory. The mailing address for these purposes is:

> Office of International Judicial Assistance
> Civil Division
> Department of Justice
> Todd Building Room 1234
> 550 11th Street, N.W.
> Washington, D.C. 20530
> Phone: (202) 724–7455

(Declarations made at the time of ratification)

Pursuant to Article 6 of the Additional Protocol, the Government of the United States declares that the United States reserves the right to charge a total of twenty-five dollars for performance of the services referred to therein.

Pursuant to Article 7 of the Additional Protocol, the Government of the United States declares that the aforementioned charge shall be waived on a reciprocal basis for the execution of a letter rogatory emanating from any State Party to both the Convention and Additional Protocol and may be otherwise waived as appropriate.

[4] (Declaration made at the time of ratification)

With the declaration made at the time of signature.

The scope of public order:

Uruguay wishes to state that it expressly ratifies the line of thought enunciated in Panama at CIDIP–I reaffirming its genuine Pan American spirit and its clear and positive decision to contribute with its ideas and endorsement to the successful development of the legal community.

This line of thinking and conduct has been evidenced in undoubtable form by the unreserved ratification by Uruguay of all the Conventions of Panama, approved by law number 14,534 in 1976.

In line with the foregoing, Uruguay gives its affirmative vote to the formula regarding public order. Nevertheless, Uruguay wishes to state expressly and clearly that, in accordance with the position it maintained in Panama, its interpretation of the aforementioned exception refers to international public order as an individual juridical institution, not necessarily identifiable with the internal public order of each state.

Therefore, in the opinion of Uruguay, the approved formula conveys an exceptional authorization to the various States Parties to declare in a nondiscretionary and well-founded manner that the precepts of foreign law are inapplicable whenever these concretely and in a serious and open manner offend the standards and principles essential to the international public order on which each individual state bases its legal individuality.

(Provided information in accordance with Articles 2, 6 and 7)

For the purposes indicated in articles six and seven of the above-cited Protocol, I wish to state that the single fixed amount of the cost of the services necessary for execution of the letter rogatory will be twenty readjustable units or its equivalent in currency. Also the schedule of the services that must be paid directly by the interested party will be limited to the possibility of resorting to the need for the services of appraisers, experts and other assistants in the case affected.

On 30 August 1985 sent information (Note No. 961/85) appointing the Ministry of Education and Culture "Asesoría Autoridad Central de Cooperación Jurídica Internacional" as the "Central Authority" provided for in Article 2 of the Protocol.

§ 1782. Assistance to foreign and international tribunals and to litigants before such tribunals

(a) The district court of the district in which a person resides or is found may order him to give his testimony or statement or to produce a document or other thing for use in a proceeding in a foreign or international tribunal, including criminal investigations conducted before formal accusation. The order may be made pursuant to a letter rogatory issued, or request made, by a foreign or international tribunal or upon the application of any interested person and may direct that the testimony or statement be given, or the document or other thing be produced, before a person appointed by the court. By virtue of his appointment, the person appointed has power to administer any necessary oath and take the testimony or statement. The order may prescribe the practice and procedure, which may be in whole or part the practice and procedure of the foreign country or the international tribunal, for taking the testimony or statement or producing the document or other thing. To the extent that the order does not prescribe otherwise, the testimony or statement shall be taken, and the document or other thing produced, in accordance with the Federal Rules of Civil Procedure.

A person may not be compelled to give his testimony or statement or to produce a document or other thing in violation of any legally applicable privilege.

(b) This chapter does not preclude a person within the United States from voluntarily giving his testimony or statement, or producing a document or other thing, for use in a proceeding in a foreign or international tribunal before any person and in any manner acceptable to him.

(June 25, 1948, c. 646, 62 Stat. 949; May 24, 1949, c. 139, § 93, 63 Stat. 103; Oct. 3, 1964, Pub.L. 88–619, § 9(a), 78 Stat. 997; Feb. 10, 1996, Pub.L. 104–106, Div. A, Title XIII, § 1342(b), 110 Stat. 486.)

HISTORICAL AND STATUTORY NOTES

References in Text

The Federal Rules of Civil Procedure, referred to in subsec. (a), are set out in this title.

§ 1783.   Subpoena of person in foreign country

(a) A court of the United States may order the issuance of a subpoena requiring the appearance as a witness before it, or before a person or body designated by it, of a national or resident of the United States who is in a foreign country, or requiring the production of a specified document or other thing by him, if the court finds that particular testimony or the production of the document or other thing by him is necessary in the interest of justice, and, in other than a criminal action or proceeding, if the court finds, in addition, that it is not possible to obtain his testimony in admissible form without his personal appearance or to obtain the production of the document or other thing in any other manner.

(b) The subpoena shall designate the time and place for the appearance or for the production of the document or other thing. Service of the subpoena and any order to show cause, rule, judgment, or decree authorized by this section or by section 1784 of this title shall be effected in accordance with the provisions of the Federal Rules of Civil Procedure relating to service of process on a person in a foreign country. The person serving the subpoena shall tender to the person to whom the subpoena is addressed his estimated necessary travel and attendance expenses, the amount of which shall be determined by the court and stated in the order directing the issuance of the subpoena.

(June 25, 1948, c. 646, 62 Stat. 949; Oct. 3, 1964, Pub.L. 88–619, § 10(a), 78 Stat. 997.)

HISTORICAL AND STATUTORY NOTES

References in Text

The Federal Rules of Civil Procedure, referred to in subsec. (b), are set out in this title.

§ 1784.   Contempt

(a) The court of the United States which has issued a subpoena served in a foreign country may order the person who has failed to appear or who has failed to produce a document or other thing as directed therein to show cause before it at a designated time why he should not be punished for contempt.

(b) The court, in the order to show cause, may direct that any of the person's property within the United States be levied upon or seized, in the manner provided by law or court rules governing levy or seizure under execution, and held to satisfy any judgment that may be rendered against him pursuant to subsection (d) of this section if adequate security, in such amount as the court may direct in the order, be given for any damage that he might suffer should he not be found in contempt. Security under this subsection may not be required of the United States.

(c) A copy of the order to show cause shall be served on the person in accordance with section 1783(b) of this title.

(d) On the return day of the order to show cause or any later day to which the hearing may be continued, proof shall be taken. If the person is found in contempt, the court, notwithstanding any limitation upon its power generally to punish for contempt, may fine him not more than $100,000 and direct that the fine and costs of the proceedings be satisfied by a sale of the property levied upon or seized, conducted upon the notice required and in the manner provided for sales upon execution.

(June 25, 1948, c. 646, 62 Stat. 949; Oct. 3, 1964, Pub.L. 88–619, § 11, 78 Stat. 998.)

§ 1785.   Subpoenas in multiparty, multiforum actions

When the jurisdiction of the district court is based in whole or in part upon section 1369 of this title, a subpoena for attendance at a hearing or trial may, if authorized by the court upon motion for good cause shown, and upon such terms and conditions as the court may impose, be served at any place within the United States, or anywhere outside the United States if otherwise permitted by law.

(Added Pub.L. 107–273, Div. C, Title I, § 11020(b)(4)(B)(i), Nov. 2, 2002, 116 Stat. 1828.)

HISTORICAL AND STATUTORY NOTES

Effective and Applicability Provisions

2002 Acts. Amendments by section 11020(b) of Pub.L. 107–273 shall apply to a civil action if the accident giving rise to the cause of action occurred on or after the 90th day after Nov. 2, 2002, see section 11020(c) of Pub.L. 107–273, set out as a note under 28 U.S.C.A. § 1369.

Prior Provisions

A prior section 1785, Act June 25, 1948, c. 646, 62 Stat. 950, relating to the privilege against self-incrimination on examination under letters rogatory (see section 1782(a) of this title), was repealed by Pub.L. 88–619, § 12(a), Oct. 3, 1964, 78 Stat. 998.

CHAPTER 119—EVIDENCE; WITNESSES

§ 1821. Per diem and mileage generally; subsistence

(a)(1) Except as otherwise provided by law, a witness in attendance at any court of the United States, or before a United States Magistrate Judge, or before any person authorized to take his deposition pursuant to any rule or order of a court of the United States, shall be paid the fees and allowances provided by this section.

(2) As used in this section, the term "court of the United States" includes, in addition to the courts listed in section 451 of this title, any court created by Act of Congress in a territory which is invested with any jurisdiction of a district court of the United States.

(b) A witness shall be paid an attendance fee of $40 per day for each day's attendance. A witness shall also be paid the attendance fee for the time necessarily occupied in going to and returning from the place of attendance at the beginning and end of such attendance or at any time during such attendance.

(c)(1) A witness who travels by common carrier shall be paid for the actual expenses of travel on the basis of the means of transportation reasonably utilized and the distance necessarily traveled to and from such witness's residence by the shortest practical route in going to and returning from the place of attendance. Such a witness shall utilize a common carrier at the most economical rate reasonably available. A receipt or other evidence of actual cost shall be furnished.

(2) A travel allowance equal to the mileage allowance which the Administrator of General Services has prescribed, pursuant to section 5704 of title 5, for official travel of employees of the Federal Government shall be paid to each witness who travels by privately owned vehicle. Computation of mileage under this paragraph shall be made on the basis of a uniformed table of distances adopted by the Administrator of General Services.

(3) Toll charges for toll roads, bridges, tunnels, and ferries, taxicab fares between places of lodging and carrier terminals, and parking fees (upon presentation of a valid parking receipt), shall be paid in full to a witness incurring such expenses.

(4) All normal travel expenses within and outside the judicial district shall be taxable as costs pursuant to section 1920 of this title.

(d)(1) A subsistence allowance shall be paid to a witness when an overnight stay is required at the place of attendance because such place is so far removed from the residence of such witness as to prohibit return thereto from day to day.

(2) A subsistence allowance for a witness shall be paid in an amount not to exceed the maximum per diem allowance prescribed by the Administrator of General Services, pursuant to section 5702(a) of title 5, for official travel in the area of attendance by employees of the Federal Government.

(3) A subsistence allowance for a witness attending in an area designated by the Administrator of General Services as a high-cost area shall be paid in an amount not to exceed the maximum actual subsistence allowance prescribed by the Administrator, pursuant to section 5702(c)(B) of title 5, for official travel in such area by employees of the Federal Government.

(4) When a witness is detained pursuant to section 3144 of title 18 for want of security for his appearance, he shall be entitled for each day of detention when not in attendance at court, in addition to his subsistence, to the daily attendance fee provided by subsection (b) of this section.

(e) An alien who has been paroled into the United States for prosecution, pursuant to section 212(d)(5) of the Immigration and Nationality Act (8 U.S.C. 1182(d)(5)), or an alien who either has admitted belonging to a class of aliens who are deportable or has been determined pursuant to section 240 of such Act (8 U.S.C. 1252(b) [1]) to be deportable, shall be ineligible to receive the fees or allowances provided by this section.

(f) Any witness who is incarcerated at the time that his or her testimony is given (except for a witness to whom the provisions of section 3144 of title 18 apply) may not receive fees or allowances under this section, regardless of whether such a witness is incarcerated at the time he or she makes a claim for fees or allowances under this section.

(June 25, 1948, c. 646, 62 Stat. 950; May 10, 1949, c. 96, 63 Stat. 65; May 24, 1949, c. 139, § 94, 63 Stat. 103; Oct. 31, 1951, c. 655, § 51(a), 65 Stat. 727; Sept. 3, 1954, c. 1263, § 45, 68 Stat. 1242; Aug. 1, 1956, c. 826, 70 Stat. 798; Mar. 27, 1968, Pub.L. 90–274, § 102(b), 82 Stat. 62; Oct. 27, 1978, Pub.L. 95–535, § 1, 92 Stat. 2033; Dec. 1, 1990, Pub.L. 101–650, Title III, §§ 314(a), 321, 104 Stat. 5115, 5117; Oct. 14, 1992, Pub.L. 102–417, § 2(a)–(c), 106 Stat. 2138; Sept. 30, 1996, Pub.L. 104–208, Div. C, Title III, § 308(g)(5)(E), 110 Stat. 3009–623.)

¹ So in original. Reference in parenthesis should probably be "(8 U.S.C. 1229a)".

HISTORICAL AND STATUTORY NOTES

References in Text

Clause (B) of section 5702(c) of title 5, referred to in subsec. (d)(3), was redesignated clause (2) by Pub.L. 96–54, § 2(a)(36), Aug. 14, 1979, 93 Stat. 383. Thereafter subsec. (c) of section 5702 of Title 5, which related to conditions under which an employee could be reimbursed for actual and necessary expenses of official travel when the maximum per diem allowance was less than these expenses, was struck out in its entirety, and subsec. (e) of that section was redesignated as subsec. (c) thereof, by Pub.L. 99–234, Title I, § 102, Jan. 2, 1986, 99 Stat. 1756. Both amendments were made without any conforming amendments to this section.

Effective and Applicability Provisions

1996 Acts. Amendment by section 308(g)(5)(E) of Div. C of Pub.L. 104–208, effective, with certain exceptions and subject to certain transitional rules, on the first day of the first month beginning more than 180 days after Sept. 30, 1996, see section 309 of Pub.L. 104–208, set out as a note under section 1101 of Title, Aliens and Nationality.

1992 Acts. Section 2(d) of Pub.L. 102–417 provided that: "The amendments made by this section [amending this section] shall be effective on and after the date of the enactment of this act [Oct. 14, 1992] and shall apply to any witness who testified before such date and has not received any fee or allowance under section 1821 of title 28, United States Code [this section], relating to such testimony."

1978 Acts. Section 2 of Pub.L. 95–535 provided that: "The amendments made by this Act [amending this section] shall take effect on October 1, 1978, or on the date of enactment [Oct. 27, 1978], whichever occurs later."

1968 Acts. Amendment by Pub.L. 90–274 effective 270 days after Mar. 27, 1968, except as to cases in which an indictment has been returned or a petit jury empaneled prior to such effective date, see section 104 of Pub.L. 90–274, set out as a note under section 1861 of this title.

Change of Name

"United States magistrate judge" substituted for "United States magistrate" in text pursuant to section 321 of Pub.L. 101–650, set out as a note under 28 U.S.C.A. § 631.

Severability of Provisions

If any provision of Division C of Pub.L. 104–208 or the application of such provision to any person or circumstances is held to be unconstitutional, the remainder of Division C of Pub.L. 104–208 and the application of the provisions of

Division C of Pub.L. 104–208 to any person or circumstance not to be affected thereby, see section 1(e) of Pub.L. 104–208, set out as a note under section 1101 of Title 8, Aliens and Nationality.

Payment of Fact Witness Fee to Incarcerated Person Prohibited

Pub.L. 102–395, Title I, § 108, Oct. 6, 1992, 106 Stat. 1841, provided that: "Notwithstanding 28 U.S.C. 1821 [this section], no funds appropriated to the Department of Justice in fiscal year 1993 or any prior fiscal year, or any other funds available from the Treasury of the United States, shall be obligated or expended to pay a fact witness fee to a person who is incarcerated testifying as a fact witness in a court of the United States, as defined in 28 U.S.C. 1821(a)(2) [subsec. (a)(2) of this section]."

Similar provisions were contained in the following prior appropriations Acts:

Pub.L. 102–140, Title I, § 110, Oct. 28, 1991, 105 Stat. 795.

Pub.L. 102–27, Title II, § 102, Apr. 10, 1991, 105 Stat. 136.

§ 1822. Competency of interested persons; share of penalties payable

Any person interested in a share of any fine, penalty or forfeiture incurred under any Act of Congress, may be examined as a witness in any proceeding for the recovery of such fine, penalty or forfeiture by any party thereto. Such examination shall not deprive the witness of his share.

(June 25, 1948, c. 646, 62 Stat. 950.)

[§ 1823. Repealed. Pub.L. 91–563, § 5(a), Dec. 19, 1970, 84 Stat. 1478]

HISTORICAL AND STATUTORY NOTES

Section, Acts June 25, 1948, c. 646, 62 Stat. 950; May 24, 1949, c. 139, § 95, 63 Stat. 103; Oct. 5, 1949, c. 601, 63 Stat. 704; July 7, 1952, c. 581, 66 Stat. 439; July 28, 1955, c. 424, § 3, 69 Stat. 394, related to payment of witness fees to officers and employees of the United States, and is now covered by sections 5515, 5537, 5751, and 6322 of Title 5, Government Organization and Employees.

§ 1824. Mileage fees under summons as both witness and juror

No constructive or double mileage fees shall be allowed by reason of any person being summoned both as a witness and a juror.

(June 25, 1948, c. 646, 62 Stat. 951.)

§ 1825. Payment of fees

(a) In any case in which the United States or an officer or agency of the United States is a party, the United States marshal for the district shall pay all fees of witnesses on the certificate of the United States attorney or assistant United States attorney, and in the proceedings before a United States magistrate judge, on the certificate of such magistrate judge, except that any fees of defense witnesses, other than experts, appearing pursuant to subpoenas issued upon approval of the court, shall be paid by the United States marshal for the district—

(1) on the certificate of a Federal public defender or assistant Federal public defender, in a criminal case in which the defendant is represented by such Federal public defender or assistant Federal public defender, and

(2) on the certificate of the clerk of the court upon the affidavit of such witnesses' attendance given by other counsel appointed pursuant to section 3006A of title 18, in a criminal case in which a defendant is represented by such other counsel.

(b) In proceedings in forma pauperis for a writ of habeas corpus, and in proceedings in forma pauperis under section 2255 of this title, the United States marshal for the district shall pay, on the certificate of the district judge, all fees of witnesses for the party authorized to proceed in forma pauperis, except that any fees of witnesses for such party, other than experts, appearing pursuant to subpoenas issued upon approval of the court, shall be paid by the United States marshal for the district—

(1) on the certificate of a Federal public defender or assistant Federal public defender, in any such proceedings in which a party is represented by such Federal public defender or assistant Federal public defender, and

(2) on the certificate of the clerk of the court upon the affidavit of such witnesses' attendance given by other counsel appointed pursuant to section 3006A of title 18, in any such proceedings in which a party is represented by such other counsel.

(c) Fees and mileage need not be tendered to a witness upon service of a subpoena issued on behalf of the United States or an officer or agency of the United States, upon service of a subpoena issued on behalf of a defendant represented by a Federal public defender, assistant Federal public defender, or other attorney appointed pursuant to section 3006A of title 18, or upon service of a subpoena issued on behalf of a party authorized to proceed in forma pauperis, if the payment of such fees and mileage is to be made by the United States marshal under this section.

(June 25, 1948, c. 646, 62 Stat. 951; Sept. 2, 1965, Pub.L. 89–162, 79 Stat. 618; Nov. 14, 1986, Pub.L. 99–651, Title I, § 104, 100 Stat. 3645; Dec. 1, 1990, Pub.L. 101–650, Title III, § 321, 104 Stat. 5117.)

HISTORICAL AND STATUTORY NOTES

Effective and Applicability Provisions

1986 Acts. Amendment to this section by section 104 of Pub.L. 99–651 to take effect one hundred and twenty days after Nov. 14, 1986, see section 105 of Pub.L. 99–651, set out

as a note under section 3006A of Title 18, Crimes and Criminal Procedure.

Change of Name

"United States magistrate judge" substituted for "United States magistrate" in text pursuant to section 321 of Pub.L. 101–650, set out as a note under 28 U.S.C.A. § 631.

§ 1826. Recalcitrant witnesses

(a) Whenever a witness in any proceeding before or ancillary to any court or grand jury of the United States refuses without just cause shown to comply with an order of the court to testify or provide other information, including any book, paper, document, record, recording or other material, the court, upon such refusal, or when such refusal is duly brought to its attention, may summarily order his confinement at a suitable place until such time as the witness is willing to give such testimony or provide such information. No period of such confinement shall exceed the life of—

(1) the court proceeding, or

(2) the term of the grand jury, including extensions,

before which such refusal to comply with the court order occurred, but in no event shall such confinement exceed eighteen months.

(b) No person confined pursuant to subsection (a) of this section shall be admitted to bail pending the determination of an appeal taken by him from the order for his confinement if it appears that the appeal is frivolous or taken for delay. Any appeal from an order of confinement under this section shall be disposed of as soon as practicable, but not later than thirty days from the filing of such appeal.

(c) Whoever escapes or attempts to escape from the custody of any facility or from any place in which or to which he is confined pursuant to this section or section 4243 of title 18, or whoever rescues or attempts to rescue or instigates, aids, or assists the escape or attempt to escape of such a person, shall be subject to imprisonment for not more than three years, or a fine of not more than $10,000, or both. (Added Pub.L. 91–452, Title III, § 301(a), Oct. 15, 1970, 84 Stat. 932, and amended Pub.L. 98–473, Title II, § 1013, Oct. 12, 1984, 98 Stat. 2142.)

§ 1827. Interpreters in courts of the United States

(a) The Director of the Administrative Office of the United States Courts shall establish a program to facilitate the use of certified and otherwise qualified interpreters in judicial proceedings instituted by the United States.

(b)(1) The Director shall prescribe, determine, and certify the qualifications of persons who may serve as certified interpreters, when the Director considers certification of interpreters to be merited, for the hearing impaired (whether or not also speech impaired) and persons who speak only or primarily a language other than the English language, in judicial proceedings instituted by the United States. The Director may certify interpreters for any language if the Director determines that there is a need for certified interpreters in that language. Upon the request of the Judicial Conference of the United States for certified interpreters in a language, the Director shall certify interpreters in that language. Upon such a request from the judicial council of a circuit and the approval of the Judicial Conference, the Director shall certify interpreters for that circuit in the language requested. The judicial council of a circuit shall identify and evaluate the needs of the districts within a circuit. The Director shall certify interpreters based on the results of criterion-referenced performance examinations. The Director shall issue regulations to carry out this paragraph within 1 year after the date of the enactment of the Judicial Improvements and Access to Justice Act.

(2) Only in a case in which no certified interpreter is reasonably available as provided in subsection (d) of this section, including a case in which certification of interpreters is not provided under paragraph (1) in a particular language, may the services of otherwise qualified interpreters be used. The Director shall provide guidelines to the courts for the selection of otherwise qualified interpreters, in order to ensure that the highest standards of accuracy are maintained in all judicial proceedings subject to the provisions of this chapter.

(3) The Director shall maintain a current master list of all certified interpreters and otherwise qualified interpreters and shall report periodically on the use and performance of both certified and otherwise qualified interpreters in judicial proceedings instituted by the United States and on the languages for which interpreters have been certified. The Director shall prescribe, subject to periodic review, a schedule of reasonable fees for services rendered by interpreters, certified or otherwise, used in proceedings instituted by the United States, and in doing so shall consider the prevailing rate of compensation for comparable service in other governmental entities.

(c)(1) Each United States district court shall maintain on file in the office of the clerk, and each United States attorney shall maintain on file, a list of all persons who have been certified as interpreters by the Director in accordance with subsection (b) of this section. The clerk shall make the list of certified interpreters for judicial proceeding available upon request.

(2) The clerk of the court, or other court employee designated by the chief judge, shall be responsible for securing the services of certified interpreters and otherwise qualified interpreters required for proceedings initiated by the United States, except that the United States attorney is responsible for securing the services of such interpreters for governmental witnesses.

(d)(1) The presiding judicial officer, with the assistance of the Director of the Administrative Office of the United States Courts, shall utilize the services of the most available certified interpreter, or when no certified interpreter is reasonably available, as determined by the presiding judicial officer, the services of an otherwise qualified interpreter, in judicial proceedings instituted by the United States, if the presiding judicial officer determines on such officer's own motion or on the motion of a party that such party (including a defendant in a criminal case), or a witness who may present testimony in such judicial proceedings—

(A) speaks only or primarily a language other than the English language; or

(B) suffers from a hearing impairment (whether or not suffering also from a speech impairment)

so as to inhibit such party's comprehension of the proceedings or communication with counsel or the presiding judicial officer, or so as to inhibit such witness' comprehension of questions and the presentation of such testimony.

(2) Upon the motion of a party, the presiding judicial officer shall determine whether to require the electronic sound recording of a judicial proceeding in which an interpreter is used under this section. In making this determination, the presiding judicial officer shall consider, among other things, the qualifications of the interpreter and prior experience in interpretation of court proceedings; whether the language to be interpreted is not one of the languages for which the Director has certified interpreters, and the complexity or length of the proceeding. In a grand jury proceeding, upon the motion of the accused, the presiding judicial officer shall require the electronic sound recording of the portion of the proceeding in which an interpreter is used.

(e)(1) If any interpreter is unable to communicate effectively with the presiding judicial officer, the United States attorney, a party (including a defendant in a criminal case), or a witness, the presiding judicial officer shall dismiss such interpreter and obtain the services of another interpreter in accordance with this section.

(2) In any judicial proceedings instituted by the United States, if the presiding judicial officer does not appoint an interpreter under subsection (d) of this section, an individual requiring the services of an interpreter may seek assistance of the clerk of court or the Director of the Administrative Office of the

United States Courts in obtaining the assistance of a certified interpreter.

(f)(1) Any individual other than a witness who is entitled to interpretation under subsection (d) of this section may waive such interpretation in whole or in part. Such a waiver shall be effective only if approved by the presiding judicial officer and made expressly by such individual on the record after opportunity to consult with counsel and after the presiding judicial officer has explained to such individual, utilizing the services of the most available certified interpreter, or when no certified interpreter is reasonably available, as determined by the presiding judicial officer, the services of an otherwise competent interpreter, the nature and effect of the waiver.

(2) An individual who waives under paragraph (1) of this subsection the right to an interpreter may utilize the services of a noncertified interpreter of such individual's choice whose fees, expenses, and costs shall be paid in the manner provided for the payment of such fees, expenses, and costs of an interpreter appointed under subsection (d) of this section.

(g)(1) There are authorized to be appropriated to the Federal judiciary, and to be paid by the Director of the Administrative Office of the United States Courts, such sums as may be necessary to establish a program to facilitate the use of certified and otherwise qualified interpreters, and otherwise fulfill the provisions of this section and the Judicial Improvements and Access to Justice Act, except as provided in paragraph (3).

(2) Implementation of the provisions of this section is contingent upon the availability of appropriated funds to carry out the purposes of this section.

(3) Such salaries, fees, expenses, and costs that are incurred with respect to Government witnesses (including for grand jury proceedings) shall, unless direction is made under paragraph (4), be paid by the Attorney General from sums appropriated to the Department of Justice.

(4) Upon the request of any person in any action for which interpreting services established pursuant to subsection (d) are not otherwise provided, the clerk of the court, or other court employee designated by the chief judge, upon the request of the presiding judicial officer, shall, where possible, make such services available to that person on a cost-reimbursable basis, but the judicial officer may also require the prepayment of the estimated expenses of providing such services.

(5) If the Director of the Administrative Office of the United States Courts finds it necessary to develop and administer criterion-referenced performance examinations for purposes of certification, or other examinations for the selection of otherwise qualified interpreters, the Director may prescribe for each examination a uniform fee for applicants to take such examination. In determining the rate of the fee for each examination, the Director shall consider the fees charged by other organizations for examinations that are similar in scope or nature. Notwithstanding section 3302(b) of title 31, the Director is authorized to provide in any contract or agreement for the development or administration of examinations and the collection of fees that the contractor may retain all or a portion of the fees in payment for the services. Notwithstanding paragraph (6) of this subsection, all fees collected after the effective date of this paragraph and not retained by a contractor shall be deposited in the fund established under section 1931 of this title and shall remain available until expended.

(6) Any moneys collected under this subsection may be used to reimburse the appropriations obligated and disbursed in payment for such services.

(h) The presiding judicial officer shall approve the compensation and expenses payable to interpreters, pursuant to the schedule of fees prescribed by the Director under subsection (b)(3).

(i) The term "presiding judicial officer" as used in this section refers to any judge of a United States district court, including a bankruptcy judge, a United States magistrate judge, and in the case of grand jury proceedings conducted under the auspices of the United States attorney, a United States attorney.

(j) The term "judicial proceedings instituted by the United States" as used in this section refers to all proceedings, whether criminal or civil, including pretrial and grand jury proceedings (as well as proceedings upon a petition for a writ of habeas corpus initiated in the name of the United States by a relator) conducted in, or pursuant to the lawful authority and jurisdiction of a United States district court. The term "United States district court" as used in this subsection includes any court which is created by an Act of Congress in a territory and is invested with any jurisdiction of a district court established by chapter 5 of this title.

(k) The interpretation provided by certified or otherwise qualified interpreters pursuant to this section shall be in the simultaneous mode for any party to a judicial proceeding instituted by the United States and in the consecutive mode for witnesses, except that the presiding judicial officer, sua sponte or on the motion of a party, may authorize a simultaneous, or consecutive interpretation when such officer determines after a hearing on the record that such interpretation will aid in the efficient administration of justice. The presiding judicial officer, on such officer's motion or on the motion of a party, may order that special interpretation services as authorized in section 1828 of this title be provided if such officer determines that the provision of such services will aid in the efficient administration of justice.

(*l*) Notwithstanding any other provision of this section or section 1828, the presiding judicial officer may appoint a certified or otherwise qualified sign language interpreter to provide services to a party, witness, or other participant in a judicial proceeding, whether or not the proceeding is instituted by the United States, if the presiding judicial officer determines, on such officer's own motion or on the motion of a party or other participant in the proceeding, that such individual suffers from a hearing impairment. The presiding judicial officer shall, subject to the availability of appropriated funds, approve the compensation and expenses payable to sign language interpreters appointed under this section in accordance with the schedule of fees prescribed by the Director under subsection (b)(3) of this section.

(Added Pub.L. 95–539, § 2(a), Oct. 28, 1978, 92 Stat. 2040, and amended Pub.L. 100–702, Title VII, §§ 702–710, Nov. 19, 1988, 102 Stat. 4654–4657; Pub.L. 101–650, Title III, § 321, Dec. 1, 1990, 104 Stat. 5117; Pub.L. 104–317, Title III, § 306, Title IV, § 402(a), Oct. 19, 1996, 110 Stat. 3852, 3854.)

HISTORICAL AND STATUTORY NOTES

References in Text

The date of the enactment of the Judicial Improvements and Access to Justice Act, referred to in subsec. (b)(1), is the date of enactment of Pub.L. 100–702, which was approved Nov. 19, 1988.

The Judicial Improvements and Access to Justice Act, referred to in subsec. (g)(1), is Pub.L. 100–702, Nov. 19, 1988, 102 Stat. 4642. For complete classification of this Act to the Code, see Short Title note set out under section 1 of this title and Tables.

The effective date of this paragraph, referred to in subsec. (g)(5), probably means the date of enactment of Pub.L. 104–317, which was approved Oct. 19, 1996.

Effective and Applicability Provisions

1988 Acts. Section 712 of Title VII of Pub.L. 100–702 provided that: "This title [amending subsecs. (a) to (e) and (g) to (k) of this section and enacting provisions set out as notes under this section and section 1 of this title] shall become effective upon the date of enactment [Nov. 19, 1988]."

1978 Acts. Section effective 90 days after Oct. 28, 1978, see section 10(b) of Pub.L. 95–539, set out as a note under section 602 of this title.

Change of Name

"United States magistrate judge" substituted for "United States magistrate" in text pursuant to section 321 of Pub.L. 101–650, set out as a note under 28 U.S.C.A. § 631.

Short Title

1978 Acts. For Short title of Pub.L. 95–539 as "Court Interpreters Act", see section 1 of Pub.L. 95–539, set out as a note under section 1 of this title.

Impact on Existing Programs

Section 711 of Title VII of Pub.L. 100–702 provided that: "Nothing in this title [amending subsecs. (a) to (e) and (g) to (k) of this section and enacting provisions set out as notes under this section and section 1 of this title] shall be construed to terminate or diminish existing programs for the certification of interpreters."

Payment for Contractual Services

Section 402(b) of Pub.L. 104–317 provided that: "Notwithstanding sections 3302(b), 1341, and 1517 of title 31, United States Code [sections 3302(b), 1341, and 1517 of Title 31, Money and Finance], the Director of the Administrative Office of the United States Courts may include in any contract for the development or administration of examinations for interpreters (including such a contract entered into before the date of the enactment of this Act [Oct. 19, 1996]) a provision which permits the contractor to collect and retain fees in payment for contractual services in accordance with section 1827(g)(5) of title 28, United States Code [subsec. (g)(5) of this section]."

§ 1828.   Special interpretation services

(a) The Director of the Administrative Office of the United States Courts shall establish a program for the provision of special interpretation services in criminal actions and in civil actions initiated by the United States (including petitions for writs of habeas corpus initiated in the name of the United States by relators) in a United States district court. The program shall provide a capacity for simultaneous interpretation services in multidefendant criminal actions and multidefendant civil actions.

(b) Upon the request of any person in any action for which special interpretation services established pursuant to subsection (a) are not otherwise provided, the Director, with the approval of the presiding judicial officer, may make such services available to the person requesting the services on a reimbursable basis at rates established in conformity with section 9701 of title 31, but the Director may require the prepayment of the estimated expenses of providing the services by the person requesting them.

(c) Except as otherwise provided in this subsection, the expenses incident to providing services under subsection (a) of this section shall be paid by the Director from sums appropriated to the Federal judiciary. A presiding judicial officer, in such officer's discretion, may order that all or part of the expenses shall be apportioned between or among the parties or shall be taxed as costs in a civil action, and any moneys collected as a result of such order may be used to reimburse the appropriations obligated and disbursed in payment for such services.

(d) Appropriations available to the Director shall be available to provide services in accordance with subsection (b) of this section, and moneys collected by the Director under that subsection may be used to reimburse the appropriations charged for such services. A presiding judicial officer, in such officer's discretion, may order that all or part of the expenses shall be apportioned between or among the parties or shall be taxed as costs in the action.

(Added Pub.L. 95–539, § 2(a), Oct. 28, 1978, 92 Stat. 2042, and amended Pub.L. 97–258, § 3(g), Sept. 13, 1982, 96 Stat. 1065.)

HISTORICAL AND STATUTORY NOTES
Effective and Applicability Provisions

1978 Acts. Section effective 90 days after Oct. 28, 1978, see section 10(b) of Pub.L. 95–539, set out as a note under section 602 of this title.

CHAPTER 121—JURIES; TRIAL BY JURY

§ 1861. Declaration of policy

It is the policy of the United States that all litigants in Federal courts entitled to trial by jury shall have the right to grand and petit juries selected at random from a fair cross section of the community in the district or division wherein the court convenes. It is further the policy of the United States that all citizens shall have the opportunity to be considered for service on grand and petit juries in the district courts of the United States, and shall have an obligation to serve as jurors when summoned for that purpose.

(June 25, 1948, c. 646, 62 Stat. 951; Sept. 9, 1957, Pub.L. 85–315, Part V, § 152, 71 Stat. 638; Mar. 27, 1968, Pub.L. 90–274, § 101, 82 Stat. 54.)

HISTORICAL AND STATUTORY NOTES
Effective and Applicability Provisions

1968 Acts. Section 104 of Pub.L. 90–274 provided that: "This Act [amending this section and sections 1821, 1862–1869, and 1871 of this title, repealing section 867 of Title 48, Territories and Insular Possessions, and enacting provisions set out as notes under this section] shall become effective two hundred and seventy days after the date of enactment [Mar. 27, 1968]: *Provided* That this Act shall not apply in any case in which an indictment has been returned or petit jury empaneled prior to such effective date."

Short Title

1978 Acts. Pub.L. 95–572, § 1, Nov. 2, 1978, 92 Stat. 2453, provided that: "This Act [which enacted sections 1363 and 1875 of this title, renumbered as section 1364 prior section 1363 of this title, amended sections 1863, 1865, 1866, 1869, and 1871 of this title, and enacted provisions set out as a note under section 1363 of this title] may be cited as the 'Jury System Improvements Act of 1978'."

1968 Acts. Section 1 of Pub.L. 90–274 provided: "That this Act [amending this section and sections 1821, 1862–1869, and 1871 of this title, repealing section 867 of Title 48, Territories and Insular Possessions, and enacting material set out as notes under this section] may be cited as the 'Jury Selection and Service Act of 1968'."

§ 1862. Discrimination prohibited

No citizen shall be excluded from service as a grand or petit juror in the district courts of the United States or in the Court of International Trade on account of race, color, religion, sex, national origin, or economic status.

(June 25, 1948, c. 646, 62 Stat. 952; Mar. 27, 1968, Pub.L. 90–274, § 101, 82 Stat. 54; Oct. 10, 1980, Pub.L. 96–417, Title III, § 302(c), 94 Stat. 1739.)

HISTORICAL AND STATUTORY NOTES
Effective and Applicability Provisions

1980 Acts. Amendment by Pub.L. 96–417 effective on Nov. 1, 1980 and applicable with respect to civil actions pending on or commenced on or after such date, see section 701(a) of Pub.L. 96–417, as amended, set out as a note under section 251 of this title.

1968 Acts. Amendment by Pub.L. 90–274 effective 270 days after Mar. 27, 1968, except as to cases in which an indictment has been returned or a petit jury empaneled prior to such effective date, see section 104 of Pub.L. 90–274, set out as a note under section 1861 of this title.

§ 1863. Plan for random jury selection

(a) Each United States district court shall devise and place into operation a written plan for random selection of grand and petit jurors that shall be designed to achieve the objectives of sections 1861 and 1862 of this title, and that shall otherwise comply with the provisions of this title. The plan shall be placed into operation after approval by a reviewing panel consisting of the members of the judicial council of the circuit and either the chief judge of the district whose plan is being reviewed or such other active district judge of that district as the chief judge of the district may designate. The panel shall examine the plan to ascertain that it complies with the provisions of this title. If the reviewing panel finds that the plan does not comply, the panel shall state the particulars in which the plan fails to comply and direct the district court to present within a reasonable time an alternative plan remedying the defect or defects. Separate plans may be adopted for each division or combination of divisions within a judicial district. The district court may modify a plan at any time and it shall modify the plan when so directed by the reviewing panel. The district court shall promptly notify the panel, the Administrative Office of the United States Courts, and the Attorney General of the United States, of the initial adoption and future modifications of the plan by filing copies therewith. Modifications of the plan made at the instance of the district court shall become effective after approval by the panel. Each district court shall submit a report on the jury selection process within its jurisdiction to the Administrative Office of the United States Courts in such form and at such times as the Judicial Conference of the United States may specify. The Judicial Conference of the United States may, from time to time, adopt rules and regulations governing the provisions and the operation of the plans formulated under this title.

(b) Among other things, such plan shall—

(1) either establish a jury commission, or authorize the clerk of the court, to manage the jury selection process. If the plan establishes a jury commission, the district court shall appoint one citizen to serve with the clerk of the court as the jury commission: *Provided, however,* That the plan for the District of Columbia may establish a jury commission consisting of three citizens. The citizen jury commissioner shall not belong to the same political party as the clerk serving with him. The clerk or the jury commission, as the case may be, shall act under the supervision and control of the chief judge of the district court or such other judge of the district court as the plan may provide. Each jury commissioner shall, during his tenure in office, reside in the judicial district or division for which he is appointed. Each citizen jury commissioner shall receive compensation to be fixed by the district court plan at a rate not to exceed $50 per day for each day necessarily employed in the performance of his duties, plus reimbursement for travel, subsistence, and other necessary expenses incurred by him in the performance of such duties. The Judicial Conference of the United States may establish standards for allowance of travel, subsistence, and other necessary expenses incurred by jury commissioners.

(2) specify whether the names of prospective jurors shall be selected from the voter registration lists or the lists of actual voters of the political subdivisions within the district or division. The plan shall prescribe some other source or sources of names in addition to voter lists where necessary to foster the policy and protect the rights secured by sections 1861 and 1862 of this title. The plan for the District of Columbia may require the names of prospective jurors to be selected from the city directory rather than from voter lists. The plans for the districts of Puerto Rico and the Canal Zone may prescribe some other source or sources of names of prospective jurors in lieu of voter lists, the use of which shall be consistent with the policies declared and rights secured by sections 1861 and 1862 of this title. The plan for the district of Massachusetts may require the names of prospective jurors to be selected from the resident list provided for in chapter 234A, Massachusetts General Laws, or comparable authority, rather than from voter lists.

(3) specify detailed procedures to be followed by the jury commission or clerk in selecting names from the sources specified in paragraph (2) of this subsection. These procedures shall be designed to ensure the random selection of a fair cross section of the persons residing in the community in the district or division wherein the court convenes. They shall ensure that names of persons residing in each of the counties, parishes, or similar political subdivisions within the judicial district or division are placed in a master jury wheel; and shall ensure that each county, parish, or similar political subdivision within the district or division is substantially proportionally represented in the master jury wheel for that judicial district, division, or combination of divisions. For the purposes of determining proportional representation in the master jury wheel, either the number of actual voters at the last general election in each county, parish, or similar political subdivision, or the number of registered voters if registration of voters is uniformly required throughout the district or division, may be used.

(4) provide for a master jury wheel (or a device similar in purpose and function) into which the names of those randomly selected shall be placed. The plan shall fix a minimum number of names to be placed initially in the master jury wheel, which shall be at least one-half of 1 per centum of the total number of persons on the lists used as a source of names for the district or division; but if this number of names is believed to be cumbersome and unnecessary, the plan may fix a smaller number of names to be placed in the master wheel, but in no event less than one thousand. The chief judge of the district court, or such other district court judge as the plan may provide, may order additional names to be placed in the master jury wheel from time to time as necessary. The plan shall provide for periodic emptying and refilling of the master jury wheel at specified times, the interval for which shall not exceed four years.

(5)(A) except as provided in subparagraph (B), specify those groups of persons or occupational classes whose members shall, on individual request therefor, be excused from jury service. Such groups or classes shall be excused only if the district court finds, and the plan states, that jury service by such class or group would entail undue hardship or extreme inconvenience to the members thereof, and excuse of members thereof would not be inconsistent with sections 1861 and 1862 of this title.

(B) specify that volunteer safety personnel, upon individual request, shall be excused from jury service. For purposes of this subparagraph, the term "volunteer safety personnel" means individuals serving a public agency (as defined in section 1203(6) of title I of the Omnibus Crime Control and Safe Streets Act of 1968) in an official capacity, without compensation, as firefighters or members of a rescue squad or ambulance crew.

(6) specify that the following persons are barred from jury service on the ground that they are exempt: (A) members in active service in the Armed Forces of the United States; (B) members of the fire or police departments of any State, the District of Columbia, any territory or possession of the United States, or any subdivision of a State, the District of Columbia, or such territory or possession; (C) public officers in the executive, legislative, or judicial branches of the Government of the United States, or of any State, the District of Columbia, any territory or possession of the United States, or any subdivision of a State, the District of Columbia, or such territory or possession, who are actively engaged in the performance of official duties.

(7) fix the time when the names drawn from the qualified jury wheel shall be disclosed to parties and to the public. If the plan permits these names to be made public, it may nevertheless permit the chief judge of the district court, or such other district court judge as the plan may provide, to keep these names confidential in any case where the interests of justice so require.

(8) specify the procedures to be followed by the clerk or jury commission in assigning persons whose names have been drawn from the qualified jury wheel to grand and petit jury panels.

(c) The initial plan shall be devised by each district court and transmitted to the reviewing panel specified in subsection (a) of this section within one hundred and twenty days of the date of enactment of the Jury Selection and Service Act of 1968. The panel shall approve or direct the modification of each plan so submitted within sixty days thereafter. Each plan or modification made at the direction of the panel shall become effective after approval at such time thereaf-

ter as the panel directs, in no event to exceed ninety days from the date of approval. Modifications made at the instance of the district court under subsection (a) of this section shall be effective at such time thereafter as the panel directs, in no event to exceed ninety days from the date of modification.

(d) State, local, and Federal officials having custody, possession, or control of voter registration lists, lists of actual voters, or other appropriate records shall make such lists and records available to the jury commission or clerks for inspection, reproduction, and copying at all reasonable times as the commission or clerk may deem necessary and proper for the performance of duties under this title. The district courts shall have jurisdiction upon application by the Attorney General of the United States to compel compliance with this subsection by appropriate process.

(June 25, 1948, c. 646, 62 Stat. 952; Mar. 27, 1968, Pub.L. 90–274, § 101, 82 Stat. 54; Apr. 6, 1972, Pub.L. 92–269, § 2, 86 Stat. 117; Nov. 2, 1978, Pub.L. 95–572, § 2(a), 92 Stat. 2453; Nov. 19, 1988, Pub.L. 100–702, Title VIII, § 802(b), (c), 102 Stat. 4657, 4658; Oct. 29, 1992, Pub.L. 102–572, Title IV, § 401, 106 Stat. 4511.)

HISTORICAL AND STATUTORY NOTES

References in Text

Section 1203(6) of title I of the Omnibus Crime Control and Safe Streets Act of 1968, referred to in subsec. (b)(5)(B), is section 1203(6) of Pub.L. 90–351, Title I, as added Pub.L. 96–157, § 2, Dec. 27, 1979, 93 Stat. 1220, which is classified to section 3796b(6) of Title 42, The Public Health and Welfare.

The date of enactment of the Jury Selection and Service Act of 1968, referred to in subsec. (c), is the date of enactment of Pub.L. 90–274, which was approved on Mar. 27, 1968.

Effective and Applicability Provisions

1992 Acts. Amendment by Pub.L. 102–572 effective Jan. 1, 1993, see section 1101(a) of Pub.L. 102–572, set out as a note under section 905 of Title 2, The Congress.

1978 Acts. Amendment by Pub.L. 95–572 applicable with respect to any grand or petit juror summoned for service or actually serving on or after Nov. 2, 1978, see section 7(a) of Pub.L. 95–572, set out as a note under section 1363 of this title.

1968 Acts. Amendment by Pub.L. 90–274 effective 270 days after Mar. 27, 1968, except as to cases in which an indictment has been returned or a petit jury empaneled prior to such effective date, see section 104 of Pub.L. 90–274, set out as a note under section 1861 of this title.

Refilling of Master Jury Wheel Not Later Than September 1, 1973; Refilling of Qualified Jury Wheel Not Later Than October 1, 1973; Retroactive Effect

Sections 3 and 4 of Pub.L. 92–269 provided that:

"Sec. 3. (a) Each judicial district and each division or combination of divisions within a judicial district, for which a separate plan for random selection of jurors has been adopted pursuant to section 1863 of title 28, United States Code [this section], other than the District of Columbia and the districts of Puerto Rico and the Canal Zone, shall not later than September 1, 1973, refill its master jury wheel with names obtained from the voter registration lists for, or the lists of actual voters in, the 1972 general election.

"**(b)** The District of Columbia and the judicial districts of Puerto Rico and the Canal Zone shall not later than September 1, 1973, refill their master jury wheels from sources which include the names of persons eighteen years of age or older.

"**(c)** The qualified jury wheel in each judicial district, and in each division or combination of divisions in a judicial district for which a separate plan for random selection of jurors has been adopted, shall be refilled from the master jury wheel not later than October 1, 1973.

"**Sec. 4.** **(a)** Nothing in this Act [amending this section and section 1865 of this title] shall affect the composition of any master jury wheel or qualified jury wheel prior to the date on which it is first refilled in compliance with the terms of section 3.

"**(b)** Nothing in this Act shall affect the composition or preclude the service of any jury empaneled on or before the date on which the qualified jury wheel from which the jurors' names were drawn is refilled in compliance with the provisions of section 3."

§ 1864. Drawing of names from the master jury wheel; completion of juror qualification form

(a) From time to time as directed by the district court, the clerk or a district judge shall publicly draw at random from the master jury wheel the names of as many persons as may be required for jury service. The clerk or jury commission may, upon order of the court, prepare an alphabetical list of the names drawn from the master jury wheel. Any list so prepared shall not be disclosed to any person except pursuant to the district court plan or pursuant to section 1867 or 1868 of this title. The clerk or jury commission shall mail to every person whose name is drawn from the master wheel a juror qualification form accompanied by instructions to fill out and return the form, duly signed and sworn, to the clerk or jury commission by mail within ten days. If the person is unable to fill out the form, another shall do it for him, and shall indicate that he has done so and the reason therefor. In any case in which it appears that there is an omission, ambiguity, or error in a form, the clerk or jury commission shall return the form with instructions to the person to make such additions or corrections as may be necessary and to return the form to the clerk or jury commission within ten days. Any person who fails to return a completed juror qualification form as instructed may be summoned by the clerk or jury commission forthwith to appear before the clerk or jury commission to fill out a juror qualification form. A person summoned to appear because of failure to return a juror qualification form as instructed who personally appears and executes a juror qualification form before the clerk or jury commission

may, at the discretion of the district court, except where his prior failure to execute and mail such form was willful, be entitled to receive for such appearance the same fees and travel allowances paid to jurors under section 1871 of this title. At the time of his appearance for jury service, any person may be required to fill out another juror qualification form in the presence of the jury commission or the clerk or the court, at which time, in such cases as it appears warranted, the person may be questioned, but only with regard to his responses to questions contained on the form. Any information thus acquired by the clerk or jury commission may be noted on the juror qualification form and transmitted to the chief judge or such district court judge as the plan may provide.

(b) Any person summoned pursuant to subsection (a) of this section who fails to appear as directed shall be ordered by the district court forthwith to appear and show cause for his failure to comply with the summons. Any person who fails to appear pursuant to such order or who fails to show good cause for noncompliance with the summons may be fined not more than $100 or imprisoned not more than three days, or both. Any person who willfully misrepresents a material fact on a juror qualification form for the purpose of avoiding or securing service as a juror may be fined not more than $100 or imprisoned not more than three days, or both.

(June 25, 1948, c. 646, 62 Stat. 952; Mar. 27, 1968, Pub.L. 90–274, § 101, 82 Stat. 57; Nov. 19, 1988, Pub.L. 100–702, Title VIII, § 803(a), 102 Stat. 4658.)

HISTORICAL AND STATUTORY NOTES

Effective and Applicability Provisions

1968 Acts. Amendment by Pub.L. 90–274 effective 270 days after Mar. 27, 1968, except as to cases in which an indictment has been returned or a petit jury empaneled prior to such effective date, see section 104 of Pub.L. 90–274, set out as a note under section 1861 of this title.

§ 1865. Qualifications for jury service

(a) The chief judge of the district court, or such other district court judge as the plan may provide, on his initiative or upon recommendation of the clerk or jury commission, or the clerk under supervision of the court if the court's jury selection plan so authorizes, shall determine solely on the basis of information provided on the juror qualification form and other competent evidence whether a person is unqualified for, or exempt, or to be excused from jury service. The clerk shall enter such determination in the space provided on the juror qualification form and in any alphabetical list of names drawn from the master jury wheel. If a person did not appear in response to a summons, such fact shall be noted on said list.

(b) In making such determination the chief judge of the district court, or such other district court judge as the plan may provide, or the clerk if the court's jury selection plan so provides, shall deem any person qualified to serve on grand and petit juries in the district court unless he—

(1) is not a citizen of the United States eighteen years old who has resided for a period of one year within the judicial district;

(2) is unable to read, write, and understand the English language with a degree of proficiency sufficient to fill out satisfactorily the juror qualification form;

(3) is unable to speak the English language;

(4) is incapable, by reason of mental or physical infirmity, to render satisfactory jury service; or

(5) has a charge pending against him for the commission of, or has been convicted in a State or Federal court of record of, a crime punishable by imprisonment for more than one year and his civil rights have not been restored.

(June 25, 1948, c. 646, 62 Stat. 952; Mar. 27, 1968, Pub.L. 90–274, § 101, 82 Stat. 58; Apr. 6, 1972, Pub.L. 92–269, § 1, 86 Stat. 117; Nov. 2, 1978, Pub.L. 95–572, § 3(a), 92 Stat. 2453; Nov. 19, 1988, Pub.L. 100–702, Title VIII, § 803(b), 102 Stat. 4658; Nov. 13, 2000, Pub.L. 106–518, Title III, § 305, 114 Stat. 2418.)

HISTORICAL AND STATUTORY NOTES

Effective and Applicability Provisions

1978 Acts. Amendment by Pub.L. 95–572 applicable with respect to any grand or petit juror summoned for service or actually serving on or after Nov. 2, 1978, see section 7(a) of Pub.L. 95–572, set out as a note under section 1363 of this title.

1968 Acts. Amendment by Pub.L. 90–274 effective 270 days after Mar. 27, 1968, except as to cases in which an indictment has been returned or a petit jury empaneled prior to such effective date, see section 104 of Pub.L. 90–274, set out as a note under section 1861 of this title.

§ 1866. Selection and summoning of jury panels

(a) The jury commission, or in the absence thereof the clerk, shall maintain a qualified jury wheel and shall place in such wheel names of all persons drawn from the master jury wheel who are determined to be qualified as jurors and not exempt or excused pursuant to the district court plan. From time to time, the jury commission or the clerk shall publicly draw at random from the qualified jury wheel such number of names of persons as may be required for assignment to grand and petit jury panels. The jury commission or the clerk shall prepare a separate list of names of persons assigned to each grand and petit jury panel.

(b) When the court orders a grand or petit jury to be drawn, the clerk or jury commission or their duly designated deputies shall issue summonses for the required number of jurors.

Each person drawn for jury service may be served personally, or by registered, certified, or first-class mail addressed to such person at his usual residence or business address.

If such service is made personally, the summons shall be delivered by the clerk or the jury commission or their duly designated deputies to the marshal who shall make such service.

If such service is made by mail, the summons may be served by the marshal or by the clerk, the jury commission or their duly designated deputies, who shall make affidavit of service and shall attach thereto any receipt from the addressee for a registered or certified summons.

(c) Except as provided in section 1865 of this title or in any jury selection plan provision adopted pursuant to paragraph (5) or (6) of section 1863(b) of this title, no person or class of persons shall be disqualified, excluded, excused, or exempt from service as jurors: *Provided,* That any person summoned for jury service may be (1) excused by the court, or by the clerk under supervision of the court if the court's jury selection plan so authorizes, upon a showing of undue hardship or extreme inconvenience, for such period as the court deems necessary, at the conclusion of which such person either shall be summoned again for jury service under subsections (b) and (c) of this section or, if the court's jury selection plan so provides, the name of such person shall be reinserted into the qualified jury wheel for selection pursuant to subsection (a) of this section, or (2) excluded by the court on the ground that such person may be unable to render impartial jury service or that his service as a juror would be likely to disrupt the proceedings, or (3) excluded upon peremptory challenge as provided by law, or (4) excluded pursuant to the procedure specified by law upon a challenge by any party for good cause shown, or (5) excluded upon determination by the court that his service as a juror would be likely to threaten the secrecy of the proceedings, or otherwise adversely affect the integrity of jury deliberations. No person shall be excluded under clause (5) of this subsection unless the judge, in open court, determines that such is warranted and that exclusion of the person will not be inconsistent with sections 1861 and 1862 of this title. The number of persons excluded under clause (5) of this subsection shall not exceed one per centum of the number of persons who return executed jury qualification forms during the period, specified in the plan, between two consecutive fillings of the master jury wheel. The names of persons excluded under clause (5) of this subsection, together with detailed explanations for the exclusions, shall be forwarded immediately to the judicial council of the circuit, which shall have the power to make any appropriate order, prospective or retroactive, to redress any misapplication of clause (5) of this subsection, but otherwise exclusions effectuated under such clause shall not be subject to challenge under the provisions of this title. Any person excluded from a particular jury under clause (2), (3), or (4) of this subsection shall be eligible to sit on another jury if the basis for his initial exclusion would not be relevant to his ability to serve on such other jury.

(d) Whenever a person is disqualified, excused, exempt, or excluded from jury service, the jury commission or clerk shall note in the space provided on his juror qualification form or on the juror's card drawn from the qualified jury wheel the specific reason therefor.

(e) In any two-year period, no person shall be required to (1) serve or attend court for prospective service as a petit juror for a total of more than thirty days, except when necessary to complete service in a particular case, or (2) serve on more than one grand jury, or (3) serve as both a grand and petit juror.

(f) When there is an unanticipated shortage of available petit jurors drawn from the qualified jury wheel, the court may require the marshal to summon a sufficient number of petit jurors selected at random from the voter registration lists, lists of actual voters, or other lists specified in the plan, in a manner ordered by the court consistent with sections 1861 and 1862 of this title.

(g) Any person summoned for jury service who fails to appear as directed shall be ordered by the district court to appear forthwith and show cause for his failure to comply with the summons. Any person who fails to show good cause for noncompliance with a summons may be fined not more than $100 or imprisoned not more than three days, or both.

(June 25, 1948, c. 646, 62 Stat. 952; May 24, 1949, c. 139, § 96, 63 Stat. 103; Mar. 27, 1968, Pub.L. 90–274, § 101, 82 Stat. 58; Dec. 11, 1970, Pub.L. 91–543, 84 Stat. 1408; Nov. 2, 1978, Pub.L. 95–572, § 2(b), 92 Stat. 2453; Jan. 12, 1983, Pub.L. 97–463, § 2, 96 Stat. 2531; Nov. 19, 1988, Pub.L. 100–702, Title VIII, § 801, 102 Stat. 4657.)

HISTORICAL AND STATUTORY NOTES

Effective and Applicability Provisions

1978 Acts. Amendment by Pub.L. 95–572 applicable with respect to any grand or petit juror summoned for service or actually serving on or after Nov. 2, 1978, see section 7(a) of Pub.L. 95–572, set out as a note under section 1363 of this title.

1968 Acts. Amendment by Pub.L. 90–274 effective 270 days after Mar. 27, 1968, except as to cases in which an indictment has been returned or a petit jury empaneled prior to such effective date, see section 104 of Pub.L. 90–274, set out as a note under section 1861 of this title.

§ 1867. Challenging compliance with selection procedures

(a) In criminal cases, before the voir dire examination begins, or within seven days after the defendant

discovered or could have discovered, by the exercise of diligence, the grounds therefor, whichever is earlier, the defendant may move to dismiss the indictment or stay the proceedings against him on the ground of substantial failure to comply with the provisions of this title in selecting the grand or petit jury.

(b) In criminal cases, before the voir dire examination begins, or within seven days after the Attorney General of the United States discovered or could have discovered, by the exercise of diligence, the grounds therefor, whichever is earlier, the Attorney General may move to dismiss the indictment or stay the proceedings on the ground of substantial failure to comply with the provisions of this title in selecting the grand or petit jury.

(c) In civil cases, before the voir dire examination begins, or within seven days after the party discovered or could have discovered, by the exercise of diligence, the grounds therefor, whichever is earlier, any party may move to stay the proceedings on the ground of substantial failure to comply with the provisions of this title in selecting the petit jury.

(d) Upon motion filed under subsection (a), (b), or (c) of this section, containing a sworn statement of facts which, if true, would constitute a substantial failure to comply with the provisions of this title, the moving party shall be entitled to present in support of such motion the testimony of the jury commission or clerk, if available, any relevant records and papers not public or otherwise available used by the jury commissioner or clerk, and any other relevant evidence. If the court determines that there has been a substantial failure to comply with the provisions of this title in selecting the grand jury, the court shall stay the proceedings pending the selection of a grand jury in conformity with this title or dismiss the indictment, whichever is appropriate. If the court determines that there has been a substantial failure to comply with the provisions of this title in selecting the petit jury, the court shall stay the proceedings pending the selection of a petit jury in conformity with this title.

(e) The procedures prescribed by this section shall be the exclusive means by which a person accused of a Federal crime, the Attorney General of the United States or a party in a civil case may challenge any jury on the ground that such jury was not selected in conformity with the provisions of this title. Nothing in this section shall preclude any person or the United States from pursuing any other remedy, civil or criminal, which may be available for the vindication or enforcement of any law prohibiting discrimination on account of race, color, religion, sex, national origin or economic status in the selection of persons for service on grand or petit juries.

(f) The contents of records or papers used by the jury commission or clerk in connection with the jury selection process shall not be disclosed, except pursuant to the district court plan or as may be necessary in the preparation or presentation of a motion under subsection (a), (b), or (c) of this section, until after the master jury wheel has been emptied and refilled pursuant to section 1863(b)(4) of this title and all persons selected to serve as jurors before the master wheel was emptied have completed such service. The parties in a case shall be allowed to inspect, reproduce, and copy such records or papers at all reasonable times during the preparation and pendency of such a motion. Any person who discloses the contents of any record or paper in violation of this subsection may be fined not more than $1,000 or imprisoned not more than one year, or both.

(June 25, 1948, c. 646, 62 Stat. 953; Sept. 2, 1957, Pub.L. 85–259, 71 Stat. 583; Mar. 27, 1968, Pub.L. 90–274, § 101, 82 Stat. 59.)

HISTORICAL AND STATUTORY NOTES

Effective and Applicability Provisions

1968 Acts. Amendment by Pub.L. 90–274 effective 270 days after Mar. 27, 1968, except as to cases in which an indictment has been returned or a petit jury empaneled prior to such effective date, see section 104 of Pub.L. 90–274, set out as a note under section 1861 of this title.

§ 1868. Maintenance and inspection of records

After the master jury wheel is emptied and refilled pursuant to section 1863(b)(4) of this title, and after all persons selected to serve as jurors before the master wheel was emptied have completed such service, all records and papers compiled and maintained by the jury commission or clerk before the master wheel was emptied shall be preserved in the custody of the clerk for four years or for such longer period as may be ordered by a court, and shall be available for public inspection for the purpose of determining the validity of the selection of any jury.

(June 25, 1948, c. 646, 62 Stat. 953; Mar. 27, 1968, Pub.L. 90–274, § 101, 82 Stat. 60.)

HISTORICAL AND STATUTORY NOTES

Effective and Applicability Provisions

1968 Acts. Amendment by Pub.L. 90–274 effective 270 days after Mar. 27, 1968, except as to cases in which an indictment has been returned or a petit jury empaneled prior to such effective date, see section 104 of Pub.L. 90–274, set out as a note under section 1861 of this title.

§ 1869. Definitions

For purposes of this chapter—

(a) "clerk" and "clerk of the court" shall mean the clerk of the district court of the United States, any authorized deputy clerk, and any other person authorized by the court to assist the clerk in the performance of functions under this chapter;

(b) "chief judge" shall mean the chief judge of any district court of the United States;

(c) "voter registration lists" shall mean the official records maintained by State or local election officials of persons registered to vote in either the most recent State or the most recent Federal general election, or, in the case of a State or political subdivision thereof that does not require registration as a prerequisite to voting, other official lists of persons qualified to vote in such election. The term shall also include the list of eligible voters maintained by any Federal examiner pursuant to the Voting Rights Act of 1965 where the names on such list have not been included on the official registration lists or other official lists maintained by the appropriate State or local officials. With respect to the districts of Guam and the Virgin Islands, "voter registration lists" shall mean the official records maintained by territorial election officials of persons registered to vote in the most recent territorial general election;

(d) "lists of actual voters" shall mean the official lists of persons actually voting in either the most recent State or the most recent Federal general election;

(e) "division" shall mean: (1) one or more statutory divisions of a judicial district; or (2) in statutory divisions that contain more than one place of holding court, or in judicial districts where there are no statutory divisions, such counties, parishes, or similar political subdivisions surrounding the places where court is held as the district court plan shall determine: *Provided,* That each county, parish, or similar political subdivision shall be included in some such division;

(f) "district court of the United States", "district court", and "court" shall mean any district court established by chapter 5 of this title, and any court which is created by Act of Congress in a territory and is invested with any jurisdiction of a district court established by chapter 5 of this title;

(g) "jury wheel" shall include any device or system similar in purpose or function, such as a properly programed electronic data processing system or device;

(h) "juror qualification form" shall mean a form prescribed by the Administrative Office of the United States Courts and approved by the Judicial Conference of the United States, which shall elicit the name, address, age, race, occupation, education, length of residence within the judicial district, distance from residence to place of holding court, prior jury service, and citizenship of a potential juror, and whether he should be excused or exempted from jury service, has any physical or mental infirmity impairing his capacity to serve as juror, is able to read, write, speak, and understand the English language, has pending against him any charge for the commission of a State or Federal criminal offense punishable by imprisonment for more than one year, or has been convicted in any State or Federal court of record of a crime punishable by imprisonment for more than one year and has not had his civil rights restored. The form shall request, but not require, any other information not inconsistent with the provisions of this title and required by the district court plan in the interests of the sound administration of justice. The form shall also elicit the sworn statement that his responses are true to the best of his knowledge. Notarization shall not be required. The form shall contain words clearly informing the person that the furnishing of any information with respect to his religion, national origin, or economic status is not a prerequisite to his qualification for jury service, that such information need not be furnished if the person finds it objectionable to do so, and that information concerning race is required solely to enforce nondiscrimination in jury selection and has no bearing on an individual's qualification for jury service.

(i) "public officer" shall mean a person who is either elected to public office or who is directly appointed by a person elected to public office;

(j) "undue hardship or extreme inconvenience", as a basis for excuse from immediate jury service under section 1866(c) (1) of this chapter, shall mean great distance, either in miles or traveltime, from the place of holding court, grave illness in the family or any other emergency which outweighs in immediacy and urgency the obligation to serve as a juror when summoned, or any other factor which the court determines to constitute an undue hardship or to create an extreme inconvenience to the juror; and in addition, in situations where it is anticipated that a trial or grand jury proceeding may require more than thirty days of service, the court may consider, as a further basis for temporary excuse, severe economic hardship to an employer which would result from the absence of a key employee during the period of such service;

(k) "publicly draw", as referred to in sections 1864 and 1866 of this chapter, shall mean a drawing which is conducted within the district after reasonable public notice and which is open to the public at large under the supervision of the clerk or jury commission, except that when a drawing is made by means of electronic data processing, "publicly draw" shall mean a drawing which is conducted at a data processing center located in or out of the district, after reasonable public notice given in the district for which juror names are being drawn, and which is open to the public at large under such supervision of the clerk or jury commission as the Judicial

Conference of the United States shall by regulation require; and

(l) "jury summons" shall mean a summons issued by a clerk of court, jury commission, or their duly designated deputies, containing either a preprinted or stamped seal of court, and containing the name of the issuing clerk imprinted in preprinted, type, or facsimile manner on the summons or the envelopes transmitting the summons.

(June 25, 1948, c. 646, 62 Stat. 953; Oct. 16, 1963, Pub.L. 88–139, § 2, 77 Stat. 248; Mar. 27, 1968, Pub.L. 90–274, § 101, 82 Stat. 61; July 29, 1970, Pub.L. 91–358, Title I, § 172(b), 84 Stat. 590; Sept. 29, 1972, Pub.L. 92–437, § 1, 86 Stat. 740; Nov. 2, 1978, Pub.L. 95–572, §§ 3(b), (4), 92 Stat. 2453; Nov. 6, 1978, Pub.L. 95–598, Title II, § 243, 92 Stat. 2671; Nov. 14, 1986, Pub.L. 99–650, § 3, 100 Stat. 3641; Nov. 19, 1988, Pub.L. 100–702, Title VIII, §§ 802(a), 804, 102 Stat. 4657, 4658.)

HISTORICAL AND STATUTORY NOTES

References in Text

The Voting Rights Act of 1965, referred to in subsec. (c), is Pub.L. 89–110, Aug. 6, 1965, 79 Stat. 437, as amended, which is classified generally to subchapters I–A (Section 1973 et seq.), I–B (Section 1973aa et seq.), and I–C (Section 1973bb et seq.) of chapter 20 of Title 42, The Public Health and Welfare. For complete classification of this Act to the Code, see Short Title note set out under section 1973 of Title 42 and Tables.

Codifications

Subsec. (f) of this section was amended by Pub.L. 95–598, Title II, § 243, Nov. 6, 1978, 92 Stat. 2671, effective June 28, 1984, pursuant to Pub.L. 95–598, Title IV, § 402(b), Nov. 6, 1978, 92 Stat. 2682, as amended by Pub.L. 98–249, § 1(a), Mar. 31, 1984, 98 Stat. 116; Pub.L. 98–271, § 1(a), Apr. 30, 1984, 98 Stat. 163; Pub.L. 98–299, § 1(a), May 25, 1984, 98 Stat. 214; Pub.L. 98–325, § 1(a), June 20, 1984, 98 Stat. 268, set out as an Effective and Applicability Provisions note preceding section 101 of Title 11, Bankruptcy, by inserting "chapter 6 of title 28, United States Code," following "chapter 5 of title 28, United States Code,".

Section 402(b) of Pub.L. 95–598 was amended by section 113 of Pub.L. 98–353, Title I, July 10, 1984, 98 Stat. 343, by substituting "shall not be effective" for "shall take effect on June 28, 1984", thereby eliminating the amendment by section 243 of Pub.L. 95–598, effective June 27, 1984, pursuant to section 122(c) of Pub.L. 98–353, set out as an Effective and Applicability Provisions note under section 151 of this title.

Section 121(a) of Pub.L. 98–353 directed that section 402(b) of Pub.L. 95–598 be amended by substituting "the date of enactment of the Bankruptcy Amendments and Federal Judgeship Act of 1984 [i.e. July 10, 1984]" for "June 28, 1984". This amendment was not executed in view of the prior amendment to section 402(b) of Pub.L. 95–598 by section 113 of Pub.L. 98–353.

Effective and Applicability Provisions

1986 Acts. Section 4(a) of Pub.L. 99–650 provided in part that: "The provisions of this Act [amending this section] shall take effect 180 days after the date of enactment of this Act [Nov. 14, 1986]".

1978 Acts. Amendment by Pub.L. 95–572 applicable with respect to any grand or petit juror summoned for service or actually serving on or after Nov. 2, 1978, see section 7(a) of Pub.L. 95–572, set out as a note under section 1363 of this title.

1972 Acts. Section 2 of Pub.L. 92–437 provided that: "This Act [amending subsec. (h) of this section] shall take effect on the sixtieth day after the date of its enactment [Sept. 29, 1972]".

1970 Acts. Amendment by Pub.L. 91–358 effective the first day of the seventh calendar month which begins after July 29, 1970, see section 199(a) of Pub.L. 91–358, set out as a note under section 1257 of this title.

1968 Acts. Amendment by Pub.L. 90–274 effective 270 days after Mar. 27, 1968, except as to cases in which an indictment has been returned or a petit jury empaneled prior to such effective date, see section 104 of Pub.L. 90–274, set out as a note under section 1861 of this title.

Termination of United States District Court for the District of the Canal Zone

For termination of the United States District Court for the District of the Canal Zone at end of the "transition period", being the 30–month period beginning Oct. 1, 1979, and ending midnight Mar. 31, 1982, see Paragraph 5 of Article XI of the Panama Canal Treaty of 1977 and sections 3831 and 3841 to 3843 of Title 22, Foreign Relations and Intercourse.

§ 1870. Challenges

In civil cases, each party shall be entitled to three peremptory challenges. Several defendants or several plaintiffs may be considered as a single party for the purposes of making challenges, or the court may allow additional peremptory challenges and permit them to be exercised separately or jointly.

All challenges for cause or favor, whether to the array or panel or to individual jurors, shall be determined by the court.

(June 25, 1948, c. 646, 62 Stat. 953; Sept. 16, 1959, Pub.L. 86–282, 73 Stat. 565.)

§ 1871. Fees

(a) Grand and petit jurors in district courts appearing pursuant to this chapter shall be paid the fees and allowances provided by this section. The requisite fees and allowances shall be disbursed on the certificate of the clerk of court in accordance with the procedure established by the Director of the Administrative Office of the United States Courts. Attendance fees for extended service under subsection (b) of this section shall be certified by the clerk only upon the order of a district judge.

(b)(1) A juror shall be paid an attendance fee of $40 per day for actual attendance at the place of trial or hearing. A juror shall also be paid the attendance fee for the time necessarily occupied in going to and returning from such place at the beginning and end of such service or at any time during such service.

(2) A petit juror required to attend more than thirty days in hearing one case may be paid, in the discretion of the trial judge, an additional fee, not exceeding $10 more than the attendance fee, for each day in excess of thirty days on which he is required to hear such case.

(3) A grand juror required to attend more than forty-five days of actual service may be paid, in the discretion of the district judge in charge of the particular grand jury, an additional fee, not exceeding $10 more than the attendance fee, for each day in excess of forty-five days of actual service.

(4) A grand or petit juror required to attend more than ten days of actual service may be paid, in the discretion of the judge, the appropriate fees at the end of the first ten days and at the end of every ten days of service thereafter.

(5) Certification of additional attendance fees may be ordered by the judge to be made effective commencing on the first day of extended service, without reference to the date of such certification.

(c)(1) A travel allowance not to exceed the maximum rate per mile that the Director of the Administrative Office of the United States Courts has prescribed pursuant to section 604(a)(7) of this title for payment to supporting court personnel in travel status using privately owned automobiles shall be paid to each juror, regardless of the mode of transportation actually employed. The prescribed rate shall be paid for the distance necessarily traveled to and from a juror's residence by the shortest practical route in going to and returning from the place of service. Actual mileage in full at the prescribed rate is payable at the beginning and at the end of a juror's term of service.

(2) The Director shall promulgate rules regulating interim travel allowances to jurors. Distances traveled to and from court should coincide with the shortest practical route.

(3) Toll charges for toll roads, bridges, tunnels, and ferries shall be paid in full to the juror incurring such charges. In the discretion of the court, reasonable parking fees may be paid to the juror incurring such fees upon presentation of a valid parking receipt. Parking fees shall not be included in any tabulation of mileage cost allowances.

(4) Any juror who travels to district court pursuant to summons in an area outside of the contiguous forty-eight States of the United States shall be paid the travel expenses provided under this section, or actual reasonable transportation expenses subject to the discretion of the district judge or clerk of court as circumstances indicate, exercising due regard for the mode of transportation, the availability of alternative modes, and the shortest practical route between residence and court.

(5) A grand juror who travels to district court pursuant to a summons may be paid the travel expenses provided under this section or, under guidelines established by the Judicial Conference, the actual reasonable costs of travel by aircraft when travel by other means is not feasible and when certified by the chief judge of the district court in which the grand juror serves.

(d)(1) A subsistence allowance covering meals and lodging of jurors shall be established from time to time by the Director of the Administrative Office of the United States Courts pursuant to section 604(a)(7) of this title, except that such allowance shall not exceed the allowance for supporting court personnel in travel status in the same geographical area. Claims for such allowance shall not require itemization.

(2) A subsistence allowance shall be paid to a juror when an overnight stay is required at the place of holding court, and for the time necessarily spent in traveling to and from the place of attendance if an overnight stay is required.

(3) A subsistence allowance for jurors serving in district courts outside of the contiguous forty-eight States of the United States shall be allowed at a rate not to exceed that per diem allowance which is paid to supporting court personnel in travel status in those areas where the Director of the Administrative Office of the United States Courts has prescribed an increased per diem fee pursuant to section 604(a)(7) of this title.

(e) During any period in which a jury is ordered to be kept together and not to separate, the actual cost of subsistence shall be paid upon the order of the court in lieu of the subsistence allowances payable under subsection (d) of this section. Such allowance for the jurors ordered to be kept separate or sequestered shall include the cost of meals, lodging, and other expenditures ordered in the discretion of the court for their convenience and comfort.

(f) A juror who must necessarily use public transportation in traveling to and from court, the full cost of which is not met by the transportation expenses allowable under subsection (c) of this section on account of the short distance traveled in miles, may be paid, in the discretion of the court, the actual reasonable expense of such public transportation, pursuant to the methods of payment provided by this section. Jurors who are required to remain at the court beyond the normal business closing hour for deliberation or for any other reason may be transported to their homes, or to temporary lodgings where such lodgings are ordered by the court, in a manner directed by the clerk and paid from funds authorized under this section.

(g) The Director of the Administrative Office of the United States Courts shall promulgate such regulations as may be necessary to carry out his authority under this section.

(June 25, 1948, c. 646, 62 Stat. 953; May 24, 1949, c. 139, § 97, 63 Stat. 103; July 14, 1949, c. 333, 63 Stat. 411; Sept. 7, 1957, Pub.L. 85–299, 71 Stat. 618; Sept. 2, 1965, Pub.L. 89–165, 79 Stat. 645; Mar. 27, 1968, Pub.L. 90–274, § 102(a), 82 Stat. 62; Nov. 2, 1978, Pub.L. 95–572, § 5, 92 Stat. 2454; Dec. 1, 1990, Pub.L. 101–650, Title III, § 314(b), 104 Stat. 5115; Oct. 29, 1992, Pub.L. 102–572, Title IV, § 402, 106 Stat. 4511.)

HISTORICAL AND STATUTORY NOTES

Effective and Applicability Provisions

1992 Acts. Amendment by Pub.L. 102–572 effective Jan. 1, 1993, see section 1101(a) of Pub.L. 102–572, set out as a note under section 905 of Title 2, The Congress.

1978 Acts. Amendment by Pub.L. 95–572 applicable with respect to any grand or petit juror serving on or after the sixtieth day following Nov. 2, 1978, see section 7(b) of Pub.L. 95–572, set out as a note under section 1363 of this title.

1968 Acts. Amendment by Pub.L. 90–274 effective 270 days after Mar. 27, 1968, except as to cases in which an indictment has been returned or a petit jury empaneled prior to such effective date, see section 104 of Pub.L. 90–274, set out as a note under section 1861 of this title.

Refreshment of Jurors

Pub.L. 101–162, Title IV, Nov. 21, 1989, 103 Stat. 1012, provided in part: "That for fiscal year 1990 and hereafter, funds appropriated under this heading [Courts of Appeals, District Courts and Other Judicial Services and Fees of Jurors and Commissioners] shall be available for refreshment of jurors."

§ 1872. Issues of fact in Supreme Court

In all original actions at law in the Supreme Court against citizens of the United States, issues of fact shall be tried by a jury.

(June 25, 1948, c. 646, 62 Stat. 953.)

§ 1873. Admiralty and maritime cases

In any case of admiralty and maritime jurisdiction relating to any matter of contract or tort arising upon or concerning any vessel of twenty tons or upward, enrolled and licensed for the coasting trade, and employed in the business of commerce and navigation between places in different states upon the lakes and navigable waters connecting said lakes, the trial of all issues of fact shall be by jury if either party demands it.

(June 25, 1948, c. 646, 62 Stat. 953.)

§ 1874. Actions on bonds and specialties

In all actions to recover the forfeiture annexed to any articles of agreement, covenant, bond, or other specialty, wherein the forfeiture, breach, or nonperformance appears by default or confession of the defendant, the court shall render judgment for the plaintiff for such amount as is due. If the sum is uncertain, it shall, upon request of either party, be assessed by a jury.

(June 25, 1948, c. 646, 62 Stat. 953.)

§ 1875. Protection of jurors' employment

(a) No employer shall discharge, threaten to discharge, intimidate, or coerce any permanent employee by reason of such employee's jury service, or the attendance or scheduled attendance in connection with such service, in any court of the United States.

(b) Any employer who violates the provisions of this section—

(1) shall be liable for damages for any loss of wages or other benefits suffered by an employee by reason of such violation;

(2) may be enjoined from further violations of this section and ordered to provide other appropriate relief, including but not limited to the reinstatement of any employee discharged by reason of his jury service; and

(3) shall be subject to a civil penalty of not more than $1,000 for each violation as to each employee.

(c) Any individual who is reinstated to a position of employment in accordance with the provisions of this section shall be considered as having been on furlough or leave of absence during his period of jury service, shall be reinstated to his position of employment without loss of seniority, and shall be entitled to participate in insurance or other benefits offered by the employer pursuant to established rules and practices relating to employees on furlough or leave of absence in effect with the employer at the time such individual entered upon jury service.

(d)(1) An individual claiming that his employer has violated the provisions of this section may make application to the district court for the district in which such employer maintains a place of business and the court shall, upon finding probable merit in such claim, appoint counsel to represent such individual in any action in the district court necessary to the resolution of such claim. Such counsel shall be compensated and necessary expenses repaid to the extent provided by section 3006A of title 18, United States Code.

(2) In any action or proceeding under this section, the court may award a prevailing employee who brings such action by retained counsel a reasonable attorney's fee as part of the costs. The court may tax a defendant employer, as costs payable to the court, the attorney fees and expenses incurred on behalf of a prevailing employee, where such costs were expended by the court pursuant to paragraph (1) of this subsection. The court may award a prevailing employer a reasonable attorney's fee as part of the costs only if the court finds that the action is frivolous, vexatious, or brought in bad faith.

(Added Pub.L. 95–572, § 6(a)(1), Nov. 2, 1978, 92 Stat. 2456, and amended Pub.L. 97–463, § 1, Jan. 12, 1983, 96 Stat. 2531.)

HISTORICAL AND STATUTORY NOTES
Effective and Applicability Provisions

1978 Acts. Section applicable with respect to any grand or petit juror summoned for service or actually serving on or after Nov. 2, 1978, see section 7(a) of Pub.L. 95–572, set out as a note under section 1363 of this title.

§ 1876. Trial by jury in the Court of International Trade

(a) In any civil action in the Court of International Trade which is to be tried before a jury, the jury shall be selected in accordance with the provisions of this chapter and under the procedures set forth in the jury selection plan of the district court for the judicial district in which the case is to be tried.

(b) Whenever the Court of International Trade conducts a jury trial—

(1) the clerk of the district court for the judicial district in which the Court of International Trade is sitting, or an authorized deputy clerk, shall act as clerk of the Court of International Trade for the purposes of selecting and summoning the jury;

(2) the qualifications for jurors shall be the same as those established by section 1865(b) of this title for jurors in the district courts of the United States;

(3) each party shall be entitled to challenge jurors in accordance with section 1870 of this title; and

(4) jurors shall be compensated in accordance with section 1871 of this title.

(Added Pub.L. 96–417, Title III, § 302(a), Oct. 10, 1980, 94 Stat. 1739.)

HISTORICAL AND STATUTORY NOTES
Effective and Applicability Provisions

1980 Acts. Section applicable with respect to civil actions commenced on or after Nov. 1, 1980, see section 701(b)(1)(C) of Pub.L. 96–417, as amended, set out as a note under section 251 of this title.

§ 1877. Protection of jurors

(a) Subject to the provisions of this section and title 5 of the United States Code, subchapter 1 of chapter 81, title 5, United States Code, applies to a Federal grand or petit juror, except that entitlement to disability compensation payments does not commence until the day after the date of termination of service as a juror.

(b) In administering this section with respect to a juror covered by this section—

(1) a juror is deemed to receive monthly pay at the minimum rate for grade GS–2 of the General

Schedule unless his actual pay as a Government employee while serving on court leave is higher, in which case monthly pay is determined in accordance with section 8114 of title 5, United States Code, and

(2) performance of duty as a juror includes that time when a juror is (A) in attendance at court pursuant to a summons, (B) in deliberation, (C) sequestered by order of a judge, or (D) at a site, by order of the court, for the taking of a view.

(Added Pub.L. 97–463, § 3(1), Jan. 12, 1983, 96 Stat. 2531.)

§ 1878.   Optional use of a one-step summoning and qualification procedure

(a) At the option of each district court, jurors may be summoned and qualified in a single procedure, if the court's jury selection plan so authorizes, in lieu of the two separate procedures otherwise provided for by this chapter. Courts shall ensure that a one-step summoning and qualification procedure conducted under this section does not violate the policies and objectives set forth in sections 1861 and 1862 of this title.

(b) Jury selection conducted under this section shall be subject to challenge under section 1867 of this title for substantial failure to comply with the provisions of this title in selecting the jury. However, no challenge under section 1867 of this title shall lie solely on the basis that a jury was selected in accordance with a one-step summoning and qualification procedure authorized by this section.

(Added Pub.L. 100–702, Title VIII, § 805(a), Nov. 19, 1988, 102 Stat. 4658, and amended Pub.L. 102–572, Title IV, § 403(a), Oct. 29, 1992, 106 Stat. 4512.)

HISTORICAL AND STATUTORY NOTES

Effective and Applicability Provisions

1992 Acts. Amendment by Pub.L. 102–572 effective Jan. 1, 1993, see section 1101(a) of Pub.L. 102–572, set out as a note under section 905 of Title 2, The Congress.

Savings Provisions

Section 403(c) of Pub.L. 102–572 provided that: "For courts participating in the experiment authorized under section 1878 of title 28, United States Code [this section] (as in effect before the effective date of this section [see Effective and Applicability Provisions of 1992 Amendments note set out under this section]), the amendment made by subsection (a) of this section [amending this section] shall be effective on and after January 1, 1992."

CHAPTER 123—FEES AND COSTS

HISTORICAL AND STATUTORY NOTES

Change of Name

"United States magistrate judge" substituted for "United States magistrate" in text pursuant to section 321 of Pub.L. 101–650, set out as a note under 28 U.S.C.A. § 631. Previously, United States commissioners, referred to in text, were replaced by United States magistrates pursuant to Pub.L. 90–578, Oct. 17, 1968, 82 Stat. 1118. See chapter 43 of Title 28, 28 U.S.C.A. § 631 et seq.

§ 1911.   Supreme Court

The Supreme Court may fix the fees to be charged by its clerk.

The fees of the clerk, cost of serving process, and other necessary disbursements incidental to any case before the court, may be taxed against the litigants as the court directs.

(June 25, 1948, c. 646, 62 Stat. 954.)

§ 1912.   Damages and costs on affirmance

Where a judgment is affirmed by the Supreme Court or a court of appeals, the court in its discretion may adjudge to the prevailing party just damages for his delay, and single or double costs.

(June 25, 1948, c. 646, 62 Stat. 954.)

§ 1913.   Courts of appeals

The fees and costs to be charged and collected in each court of appeals shall be prescribed from time to time by the Judicial Conference of the United States. Such fees and costs shall be reasonable and uniform in all the circuits.

(June 25, 1948, c. 646, 62 Stat. 954.)

JUDICIAL CONFERENCE SCHEDULE OF FEES

Court of Appeals Miscellaneous Fee Schedule

(Issued in accordance with 28 U.S.C. § 1913)

(eff. 01/01/2005)

Following are fees to be charged for services provided by the courts of appeals. No fees are to be charged for services rendered on behalf of the United States, with the exception of those specifically prescribed in items 2, 4 and 5. No fees under this schedule shall be charged to federal agencies or programs which are funded from judiciary appropriations, including, but not limited to, agencies, organizations, and individuals providing services authorized by the Criminal Justice Act, 18 U.S.C. § 3006A, and Bankruptcy Administrator programs.

(1) For docketing a case on appeal or review, or docketing any other proceeding, $250. A separate fee shall be paid by each party filing a notice of appeal in the district court, but parties filing a joint notice of appeal in the district court are required to pay only one fee. A docketing fee shall not be charged for the docketing of an application for the allowance of an interlocutory appeal under 28 U.S.C. § 1292(b), unless the appeal is allowed.

(2) For every search of the records of the court and certifying the results thereof, $26. This fee shall apply to services rendered on behalf of the United States if the information requested is available through electronic access.

(3) For certifying any document or paper, whether the certification is made directly on the document, or by separate instrument, $9.

(4) For reproducing any record or paper, 50 cents per page. This fee shall apply to paper copies made from either: (1) original documents; or (2) microfiche or microfilm reproductions of the original records. This fee shall apply to services rendered on behalf of the United States if the record or paper requested is available through electronic access.

(5) For reproduction of recordings of proceedings, regardless of the medium, $26, including the cost of materials. This fee shall apply to services rendered on behalf of the United States if the reproduction of the recording is available electronically.

(6) For reproduction of the record in any appeal in which the requirement of an appendix is dispensed with by any court of appeals pursuant to Rule 30(f), F.R.A.P., a flat fee of $71.

(7) For each microfiche or microfilm copy of any court record, where available, $5.

(8) For retrieval of a record from a Federal Records Center, National Archives, or other storage location removed from the place of business of the court, $45.

(9) For a check paid into the court which is returned for lack of funds, $45.

(10) Fees to be charged and collected for copies of opinions shall be fixed, from time to time, by each court, commensurate with the cost of printing.

(11) The court may charge and collect fees commensurate with the cost of providing copies of the local rules of court. The court may also distribute copies of the local rules without charge.

(12) The clerk shall assess a charge for the handling of registry funds deposited with the court, to be assessed from interest earnings and in accordance with the detailed fee schedule issued by the Director of the Administrative Office of the United States Courts.

(13) Upon the filing of any separate or joint notice of appeal or application for appeal from the Bankruptcy Appellate Panel, or notice of the allowance of an appeal from the Bankruptcy Appellate Panel, or of a writ of certiorari, $5 shall be paid by the appellant or petitioner.

(14) The court may charge and collect a fee of $200 per remote location for counsel's requested use of videoconferencing equipment in connection with each oral argument.

(15) For original admission of attorneys to practice, $150 each, including a certificate of admission. For a duplicate certificate of admission or certificate of good standing, $15.

ELECTRONIC PUBLIC ACCESS FEE SCHEDULE (eff. 1/1/05)

As directed by Congress, the Judicial Conference has determined that the following fees are necessary to reimburse expenses incurred by the judiciary in providing electronic public access to court records. These fees shall apply to the United States unless otherwise stated. No fees under this schedule shall be charged to federal agencies or programs which are funded from judiciary appropriations, including, but not limited to, agencies, organizations, and individuals providing services authorized by the Criminal Justice Act, 18 U.S.C. § 3006A, and bankruptcy administrator programs.

I. For electronic access to court data via dial up service: sixty cents per minute. For electronic access to court data via a federal judiciary Internet site: eight cents per page, with the total for any document, docket sheet, or case-specific report not to exceed the fee for thirty pages- provided however that transcripts of federal court proceedings shall not be subject to the thirty-page fee limit. Attorneys of record and parties in a case (including *pro se* litigants) receive one free electronic copy of all documents filed electronically, if receipt is required by law or directed by the filer. No fee is owed under this provision until an account holder accrues charges of more than $10 in a calendar year. Consistent with Judicial Conference policy, courts may, upon a showing of cause, exempt indigents, bankruptcy case trustees, individual researchers associated with educational institutions, courts, section 501(c)(3) not-for-profit organizations and pro bono ADR neutrals from payment of these fees. Courts must find that parties from the classes of persons or entities listed above seeking exemption have demonstrated that an exemption is necessary in order to avoid unreasonable burdens and to promote public access to information. Any user granted an exemption agrees not to sell for profit the data obtained as a result. Exemptions may be granted for a definite period of time and may be revoked at the discretion of the court granting the exemption.

II. For printing copies of any record or document accessed electronically at a public terminal in the courthouse: ten cents per page. This fee shall apply to services rendered on behalf of the United States if the record requested is remotely available through electronic access.

III. For every search of court records conducted by the PACER Service Center, $20.

JUDICIAL CONFERENCE POLICY NOTES

Courts should not exempt local, state or federal government agencies, members of the media, attorneys or others not members of one of the groups listed above. Exemptions should be granted as the exception, not the rule. A court may not use this exemption language to exempt all users. An exemption applies only to access related to the case or purpose for which it was given.

The electronic public access fee applies to electronic court data viewed remotely from the public records of individual cases in the court, including filed documents and the docket sheet. Electronic court data may be viewed free at public terminals at the courthouse and courts may provide other local court information at no cost. Examples of information that can be provided at no cost include: local rules, court forms, news items, court calendars, opinions, and other information—such as court hours, court location, telephone listings—determined locally to benefit the public and the court.

Miscellaneous Fee Schedules
Registry Fund Fees

Effective June 12, 1989, a fee will be assessed for handling funds deposited in noncriminal proceedings with the court and held in interest bearing accounts or instruments pursuant to 28 U.S.C. § 2041 and Federal Rules of Civil Procedure rule 67. For new accounts, i.e., investments made on or after June 12, 1989, the fee will be equal to the first 45 days income earned on the deposit. Each subsequent deposit of new principal in the same case or proceeding will be subject to the fee. Reinvestment of prior deposits will not be subject to the fee. For existing accounts, i.e., investments held by the court prior to June 12, 1989, a fee will be assessed equal to the first 45 days of income earned beginning 30 days after June 12, 1989. Subsequent deposits of new principal in the same account will be subject to the fee. Subsequent reinvestment of existing deposits will not be subject to the fee.

The fee will apply only once to each sum deposited regardless of the length of time deposits are held and will not exceed income actually earned on the account.

The fee does not apply in the District Courts of Guam, Northern Mariana Islands, the Virgin Islands, the United States Claims Court, or other courts whose fees are not set under 28 U.S.C. §§ 1913, 1914, and 1930.

Registry Fund Fees—Item 12
(55 F.R. 42867, October 24, 1990)

Effective December 1, 1990, the registry fee assessment provisions were revised and converted from a one-time charge equal to all income earned in the first 45 days of the investment to a charge of 10 percent of the income earned while funds are held in the court registry. Additionally, the fee was extended to any funds placed in the court's registry and invested regardless of the nature of the action underlying the deposit.

The new method will not be applied on investments in cases from which a fee has been exacted based on the prior method (interest earned in the first 45 days the funds were invested or the first 45 days following July 12, 1989). The new method will also not be applied in cases where the investment instrument has a maturity date greater than one year, but where a fee under the prior method applies but has not been deducted.

The fee does not apply in the District Courts of Guam, the Northern Mariana Islands, the Virgin Islands, the United States Claims Court, or any other federal court whose fees are not set under 28 U.S.C. §§ 1913, 1914, and 1930.

Registry Fund Fees—Item 12
(56 F.R. 56356, November 4, 1991)

Effective February 3, 1992, the registry fee assessment provisions are revised and converted from a charge equal to 10 percent of the income earned while funds are held in the court's registry to a variable rate based on the amount deposited with the court and, in certain cases, the length of time funds are held in the court's registry.

The revised fee will be a fee of 10 percent of the total income received during each income period from investments of less than $100,000,000 of registry funds in income-bearing accounts. On investments exceeding $100,000,000 the 10 percent fee shall be reduced by one percent for each increment of $50,000,000 over the initial $100,000,000. For those deposits where funds are placed in the registry by court order for a time certain, for example, by the terms of an adjudicated trust, the fee will be further reduced. This further reduction will amount to 2.5 percent for each five-year interval or part thereof. The total minimum fee to be charged will be no less than two percent of the income on investments.

The following table sets out the fee schedule promulgated by this notice:

REGISTRY—SCHEDULE OF FEES

[% of income earned]

Amount of deposit *	0–5 yrs.	>5–10 yrs.	>10–15 yrs.	>15 yrs.
less than 100M	10	7.5	5.0	2.5
100M–<150M	9	6.5	4.0	2.0
150M–<200M	8	5.5	3.0	2.0
200M–<250M	7	4.5	2.0	2.0
250M–<300M	6	3.5	2.0	2.0
300M–<350M	5	2.5	2.0	2.0
350M–<400M	4	2.0	2.0	2.0
400M–<450M	3	2.0	2.0	2.0
over 450M	2	2.0	2.0	2.0

The new fee applies to all earnings applied to investments on and after the effective date of this change, except for earnings on investments in cases being administered under the provisions of the May 11, 1989 notice [54 FR 20407], i.e., to which the fee equal to the first 45 days income is applicable.

The fee, as modified herein, will continue to apply to any case where the court has authorized the investment of funds placed in its custody or held by it in trust in its registry regardless of the nature of the underlying action.

The fee does not apply in the District Court of Guam, the Northern Mariana Islands, the Virgin Islands, the United States Claims Court, or any other Federal court whose fees are not set under 28 U.S.C. §§ 1913, 1914, and 1930.

HISTORICAL AND STATUTORY NOTES

Court Fees for Electronic Access to Information

Pub.L. 102–140, Title III, § 303, Oct. 28, 1991, 105 Stat. 810, as amended Pub.L. 104–317, Title IV, § 403(b), Oct. 19, 1996, 110 Stat. 3854; Pub.L. 107–347, Title II, § 205(e), Dec. 17, 2002, 116 Stat. 2915, provided that:

"**(a)** The Judicial Conference may, only to the extent necessary, prescribe reasonable fees, pursuant to sections 1913, 1914, 1926, 1930, and 1932 of title 28, United States Code [this section and sections 1914, 1926, 1930, and 1932 of this title], for collection by the courts under those sections for access to information available through automatic data processing equipment. These fees may distinguish between classes of persons, and shall provide for exempting persons or classes of persons from the fees, in order to avoid unreasonable burdens and to promote public access to such information. The Director of the Administrative Office of the United States Courts, under the direction of the Judicial Conference of the United States, shall prescribe a schedule of reasonable fees for electronic access to information which the Director is required to maintain and make available to the public.

"**(b)** The Judicial Conference and the Director shall transmit each schedule of fees prescribed under paragraph (a) to the Congress at least 30 days before the schedule becomes effective. All fees hereafter collected by the Judiciary under paragraph (a) as a charge for services rendered shall be deposited as offsetting collections to the Judiciary Automation Fund pursuant to 28 U.S.C. 612(c)(1)(A) [section 612(c)(1)(A) of this title] to reimburse expenses incurred in providing these services."

[Amendment by Pub.L. 107–347, § 205, effective 120 days after Dec. 17, 2002, see section 402(a) of Pub.L. 107–347, set out as a note under 44 U.S.C.A. § 3601.]

Similar provisions were contained in the following prior appropriation Act:

Pub.L. 101–515, Title IV, § 404, Nov. 5, 1990, 104 Stat. 2132.

§ 1914. District court; filing and miscellaneous fees; rules of court

(a) The clerk of each district court shall require the parties instituting any civil action, suit or proceeding in such court, whether by original process, removal or otherwise, to pay a filing fee of $250, except that on application for a writ of habeas corpus the filing fee shall be $5.

(b) The clerk shall collect from the parties such additional fees only as are prescribed by the Judicial Conference of the United States.

(c) Each district court by rule or standing order may require advance payment of fees.

(June 25, 1948, c. 646, 62 Stat. 954; Nov. 6, 1978, Pub.L. 95–598, Title II, § 244, 92 Stat. 2671; June 19, 1986, Pub.L. 99–336, § 4(a), 100 Stat. 637; Oct. 18, 1986, Pub.L. 99–500, Title I, § 101(b) [Title IV, § 407(a)], 100 Stat. 1783–39, 1783–64, and Oct. 30, 1986, Pub.L. 99–591, Title I, § 101(b) [Title IV, § 407(a)], 100 Stat. 3341–39, 3341–64; Oct. 19, 1996, Pub.L. 104–317, Title IV, § 401(a), 110 Stat. 3853;

Pub.L. 108–447, Div. B, Title III, § 307(a), Dec. 8, 2004, 118 Stat. 2895.)

JUDICIAL CONFERENCE SCHEDULE OF FEES

District Court Miscellaneous Fee Schedule

[The Judicial Conference of the United States, at its session on March 7–9, 1979, set forth the schedule of fees to be charged in the United States district courts pursuant to this section. That new schedule became effective on October 1, 1979. At its March 1987 meeting, the Judicial Conference amended the schedule of fees to be effective May 1, 1987. Amendments to this revision of the schedule of fees were adopted at the September, 1988 and March, 1990 meetings of the Judicial Conference. At its 1991 meeting, the Judicial Conference amended its schedule of fees to be effective Feb. 3, 1992. At its March 1991 meeting, the Judicial Conference amended the schedule of fees to be effective Oct. 19, 1992, with later implementation. At its March, 1993 meeting, the Judicial Conference amended its schedule of fees to be effective May 6, 1993. At its September, 1993 meeting, the Judicial Conference amended its schedule of fees to be effective October 1, 1993. At its 1994 meeting, the Judicial Conference amended its schedule of fees to be effective January 1, 1995. At its March 15, 1995 meeting, the Judicial Conference amended its schedule of fees to be effective April 18, 1995, and at its 1996 meetings it adopted amendments to be effective April 1, 1996 and December 18, 1996. At its 1997 meeting, the Judicial Conference amended its schedule of fees to be effective January 1, 1998. At its 1999 meeting, the Judicial Conference amended its schedule of fees to be effective October 1, 1999. The Judicial Conference subsequently adopted amendments to its fee schedule effective February 1, 2001. At its March 2001 meeting, the Judicial Conference amended its schedule of fees to be effective July 1, 2001. The Judicial Conference adopted amendments to its fee schedule effective November 1, 2003. The Judicial Conference at its March 16, 2004 meeting adopted amendments to its fee schedule to be effective June 1, 2004.]

[The Administrative Office of the United States Courts provided for Registry Fund Fees effective June 12, 1989.]

Following are fees to be charged for services provided by the district courts. No fees are to be charged for services rendered on behalf of the United States, with the exception of those specifically prescribed in items 2, 4 and 5. No fees under this schedule shall be charged to federal agencies or programs which are funded from judiciary appropriations, including, but not limited to, agencies, organizations, and individuals providing services authorized by the Criminal Justice Act, 18 U.S.C. § 3006A, and Bankruptcy Administrator programs.

(1) For filing or indexing any document not in a case or proceeding for which a filing fee has been paid, $39.

(2) For every search of the records of the district court conducted by the clerk of the district court or a deputy clerk, $26 per name or item searched. This fee shall apply to services rendered on behalf of the United States if information requested is available through electronic access.

(3) For certification of any document or paper, whether the certification is made directly on the document or by separate instrument, $9. For exemplification of any document or paper, twice the amount of the fee for certification.

(4) For reproducing any record or paper, $.50 per page. This fee shall apply to paper copies made from either: (1) original documents; or (2) microfiche or microfilm reproductions of the original records. This fee shall apply to services rendered on behalf of the United States if the record or paper requested is available through electronic access.

(5) For reproduction of recordings of proceedings, regardless of the medium, $26, including the cost of materials. This fee shall apply to services rendered on behalf of the United States, if the reproduction of the recording is available electronically.

(6) For each microfiche sheet of film or microfilm jacket copy of any court record, where available, $5.

(7) For retrieval of a record from a Federal Records Center, National Archives, or other storage location removed from the place of business of the court, $45.

(8) For a check paid into the court which is returned for lack of funds, $45.

(9) For an appeal to a district judge from a judgment of conviction by a magistrate in a misdemeanor case, $32.

(10) For original admission of attorneys to practice, $50 each, including a certificate of admission. For a duplicate certificate of admission or certificate of good standing, $15.

(11) The court may charge and collect fees commensurate with the cost of providing copies of the local rules of court. The court may also distribute copies of the local rules without charge.

(12) The clerk shall assess a charge for the handling of registry funds deposited with the court, to be assessed from interest earnings and in accordance with the detailed fee schedule issued by the Director of the Administrative Office of the United States Courts.

(13) For filing an action brought under Title III of the Cuban Liberty and Democratic Solidarity (LIBERTAD) Act of 1996, P.L. 104–114, 110 Stat. 785 (1996), $5,431. (This fee is in addition to the filing fee prescribed in 28 U.S.C. § 1914(a) for instituting any civil action other than a writ of habeas corpus.)

ELECTRONIC PUBLIC ACCESS FEE SCHEDULE (eff. 1/1/05)

As directed by Congress, the Judicial Conference has determined that the following fees are necessary to reimburse expenses incurred by the judiciary in providing electronic public access to court records. These fees shall apply to the United States unless otherwise stated. No fees under this schedule shall be charged to federal agencies or programs which are funded from judiciary appropriations, including, but not limited to, agencies, organizations, and individuals providing services authorized by the Criminal Justice Act, 18 U.S.C. § 3006A, and bankruptcy administrator programs.

I. For electronic access to court data via dial up service: sixty cents per minute. For electronic access to court data via a federal judiciary Internet site: eight cents per page, with the total for any document, docket sheet, or case-specific report not to exceed the fee for thirty pages- provided however that transcripts of federal court proceedings shall not be subject to the thirty-page fee limit. Attorneys of record and parties in a case (including *pro se* litigants) receive one free electronic copy of all documents filed electronically, if receipt is required by law or directed by the

filer. No fee is owed under this provision until an account holder accrues charges of more than $10 in a calendar year. Consistent with Judicial Conference policy, courts may, upon a showing of cause, exempt indigents, bankruptcy case trustees, individual researchers associated with educational institutions, courts, section 501(c)(3) not-for-profit organizations and pro bono ADR neutrals from payment of these fees. Courts must find that parties from the classes of persons or entities listed above seeking exemption have demonstrated that an exemption is necessary in order to avoid unreasonable burdens and to promote public access to information. Any user granted an exemption agrees not to sell for profit the data obtained as a result. Exemptions may be granted for a definite period of time and may be revoked at the discretion of the court granting the exemption.

II. For printing copies of any record or document accessed electronically at a public terminal in the courthouse: ten cents per page. This fee shall apply to services rendered on behalf of the United States if the record requested is remotely available through electronic access.

III. For every search of court records conducted by the PACER Service Center, $20.

JUDICIAL CONFERENCE POLICY NOTES

Courts should not exempt local, state or federal government agencies, members of the media, attorneys or others not members of one of the groups listed above. Exemptions should be granted as the exception, not the rule. A court may not use this exemption language to exempt all users. An exemption applies only to access related to the case or purpose for which it was given.

The electronic public access fee applies to electronic court data viewed remotely from the public records of individual cases in the court, including filed documents and the docket sheet. Electronic court data may be viewed free at public terminals at the courthouse and courts may provide other local court information at no cost. Examples of information that can be provided at no cost include: local rules, court forms, news items, court calendars, opinions, and other information—such as court hours, court location, telephone listings—determined locally to benefit the public and the court.

Registry Fund Fees—Item 13
(54 F.R 20407, May 11, 1989)

Effective June 12, 1989, a fee will be assessed for handling funds deposited in noncriminal proceedings with the court and held in interest bearing accounts or instruments pursuant to 28 U.S.C. § 2041 and Federal Rules of Civil Procedure rule 67. For new accounts, i.e, investments made on or after June 12, 1989, the fee will be equal to the first 45 days income earned on the deposit. Each subsequent deposit of new principal in the same case or proceeding will be subject to the fee. Reinvestment of prior deposits will not be subject to the fee. For existing accounts, i.e., investments held by the court prior to June 12, 1989, a fee will be assessed equal to the first 45 days of income earned beginning 30 days after June 12, 1989. Subsequent deposits of new principal in the same account will be subject to the fee. Subsequent reinvestment of existing deposits will not be subject to the fee.

The fee will apply only once to each sum deposited regardless of the length of time deposits are held and will not exceed income actually earned on the account.

The fee does not apply in the District Courts of Guam, Northern Mariana Islands, the Virgin Islands, the United States Claims Court, or other courts whose fees are not set under 28 U.S.C. § 1914.

Registry Fund Fees—Item 13
(55 F.R. 42867, October 24, 1990)

Effective December 1, 1990, the registry fee assessment provisions were revised and converted from a one-time charge equal to all income earned in the first 45 days of the investment to a charge of 10 percent of the income earned while funds are held in the court registry. Additionally, the fee was extended to any funds placed in the court's registry and invested regardless of the nature of the action underlying the deposit.

The new method will not be applied on investments in cases from which a fee has been exacted based on the prior method (interest earned in the first 45 days the funds were invested or the first 45 days following July 12, 1989). The new method will also not be applied in cases where the investment instrument has a maturity date greater than one year, but where a fee under the prior method applies but has not been deducted.

The fee does not apply in the District Courts of Guam, Northern Mariana Islands, the Virgin Islands, the United States Claims Court, or any other federal court whose fees are not set under 28 U.S.C. §§ 1913, 1914, and 1930.

Registry Fund Fees—Item 13
(56 F.R. 56356, November 4, 1991)

Effective February 3, 1992, the registry fee assessment provisions are revised and converted from a charge equal to 10 percent of the income earned while funds are held in the court's registry to a variable rate based on the amount deposited with the court and, in certain cases, the length of time funds are held in the court's registry.

The revised fee will be a fee of 10 percent of the total income received during each income period from investments of less than $100,000,000 of registry funds in income-bearing accounts. On investments exceeding $100,000,000 the 10 percent fee shall be reduced by one percent for each increment of $50,000,000 over the initial $100,000,000. For those deposits where funds are placed in the registry by court order for a time certain, for example, by the terms of an adjudicated trust, the fee will be further reduced. This further reduction will amount to 2.5 percent for each five-year interval or part thereof. The total minimum fee to be charged will be no less than two percent of the income on investments.

The following table sets out the fee schedule promulgated by this notice:

REGISTRY—SCHEDULE OF FEES

[% of income earned]

Amount of deposit *	0–5 yrs.	>5–10 yrs.	>10–15 yrs.	>15 yrs.
less than 100M	10	7.5	5.0	2.5
100M–<150M	9	6.5	4.0	2.0
150M–<200M	8	5.5	3.0	2.0
200M–<250M	7	4.5	2.0	2.0
250M–<300M	6	3.5	2.0	2.0
300M–<350M	5	2.5	2.0	2.0
350M–<400M	4	2.0	2.0	2.0

Amount of deposit *	0–5 yrs.	>5–10 yrs.	>10–15 yrs.	>15 yrs.
400M–<450M	3	2.0	2.0	2.0
over 450M	2	2.0	2.0	2.0

* Except where otherwise authorized by the Director, each deposit into any account is treated separately in determining the fee.

The new fee applies to all earnings applied to investments on and after the effective date of this change, except for earnings on investments in cases being administered under the provisions of the May 11, 1989 notice [54 FR 20407], i.e., to which the fee equal to the first 45 days income is applicable.

The fee, as modified herein, will continue to apply to any case where the court has authorized the investment of funds placed in its custody or held by it in trust in its registry regardless of the nature of the underlying action.

The fee does not apply in the District Court of Guam, the Northern Mariana Islands, the Virgin Islands, the United States Claims Court, or any other Federal court whose fees are not set under 28 U.S.C. §§ 1913, 1914, and 1930.

HISTORICAL AND STATUTORY NOTES

Codifications

Pub.L. 99–591 is a corrected version of Pub.L. 99–500.

Effective and Applicability Provisions

2004 Acts. Pub.L. 108–447, Div. B, Title III, § 307(c), Dec. 8, 2004, 118 Stat. 2895, provided that: "This section [amending subsec. (a) of this section and subsecs. (a) and (b) of 28 U.S.C.A. § 1931] shall take effect 60 days after the date of the enactment of this Act [Dec. 8, 2004]."

1996 Acts. Section 401(c) of Pub.L. 104–317 provided that: "This section [amending this section and section 1931 of this title] shall take effect 60 days after the date of the enactment of this Act [Oct. 19, 1996]."

1986 Acts. Section 4(c) of Pub.L. 99–336 provided that: "The amendments made by this section [amending this section and provisions of the District of Columbia Code not classified to this Code] shall apply with respect to any civil action, suit, or proceeding instituted on or after the date of the enactment of this Act [June 19, 1986]."

1978 Acts. Amendment by Pub.L. 95–598 effective Oct. 1, 1979, see section 402(c) of Pub.L. 95–598, set out as a note preceding section 101 of Title 11, Bankruptcy.

Court Fees for Electronic Access to Information

Judicial Conference to prescribe reasonable fees for collection by courts under this section for access to information available through automatic data processing equipment and fees to be deposited in Judiciary Automation Fund, see section 303 of Pub.L. 102–140, set out as a note under section 1913 of this title.

§ 1915.   Proceedings in forma pauperis

(a)(1) Subject to subsection (b), any court of the United States may authorize the commencement, prosecution or defense of any suit, action or proceeding, civil or criminal, or appeal therein, without prepayment of fees or security therefor, by a person who submits an affidavit that includes a statement of all assets such prisoner possesses that the person is unable to pay such fees or give security therefor. Such affidavit shall state the nature of the action, defense or appeal and affiant's belief that the person is entitled to redress.

(2) A prisoner seeking to bring a civil action or appeal a judgment in a civil action or proceeding without prepayment of fees or security therefor, in addition to filing the affidavit filed under paragraph (1), shall submit a certified copy of the trust fund account statement (or institutional equivalent) for the prisoner for the 6–month period immediately preceding the filing of the complaint or notice of appeal, obtained from the appropriate official of each prison at which the prisoner is or was confined.

(3) An appeal may not be taken in forma pauperis if the trial court certifies in writing that it is not taken in good faith.

(b)(1) Notwithstanding subsection (a), if a prisoner brings a civil action or files an appeal in forma pauperis, the prisoner shall be required to pay the full amount of a filing fee. The court shall assess and, when funds exist, collect, as a partial payment of any court fees required by law, an initial partial filing fee of 20 percent of the greater of—

(A) the average monthly deposits to the prisoner's account; or

(B) the average monthly balance in the prisoner's account for the 6–month period immediately preceding the filing of the complaint or notice of appeal.

(2) After payment of the initial partial filing fee, the prisoner shall be required to make monthly payments of 20 percent of the preceding month's income credited to the prisoner's account. The agency having custody of the prisoner shall forward payments from the prisoner's account to the clerk of the court each time the amount in the account exceeds $10 until the filing fees are paid.

(3) In no event shall the filing fee collected exceed the amount of fees permitted by statute for the commencement of a civil action or an appeal of a civil action or criminal judgment.

(4) In no event shall a prisoner be prohibited from bringing a civil action or appealing a civil or criminal judgment for the reason that the prisoner has no assets and no means by which to pay the initial partial filing fee.

(c) Upon the filing of an affidavit in accordance with subsections (a) and (b) and the prepayment of any partial filing fee as may be required under subsection (b), the court may direct payment by the United States of the expenses of (1) printing the record on appeal in any civil or criminal case, if such printing is required by the appellate court; (2) preparing a transcript of proceedings before a United States magistrate judge in any civil or criminal case, if such transcript is required by the district court, in the case of proceedings conducted under section 636(b) of this title or under section 3401(b) of title 18, United States Code; and (3) printing the record on appeal if such printing is required by the appellate court, in the case of proceedings conducted pursuant to section 636(c) of this title. Such expenses shall be paid when authorized by the Director of the Administrative Office of the United States Courts.

(d) The officers of the court shall issue and serve all process, and perform all duties in such cases. Witnesses shall attend as in other cases, and the same remedies shall be available as are provided for by law in other cases.

(e)(1) The court may request an attorney to represent any person unable to afford counsel.

(2) Notwithstanding any filing fee, or any portion thereof, that may have been paid, the court shall dismiss the case at any time if the court determines that—

(A) the allegation of poverty is untrue; or

(B) the action or appeal—

(i) is frivolous or malicious;

(ii) fails to state a claim on which relief may be granted; or

(iii) seeks monetary relief against a defendant who is immune from such relief.

(f)(1) Judgment may be rendered for costs at the conclusion of the suit or action as in other proceedings, but the United States shall not be liable for any of the costs thus incurred. If the United States has paid the cost of a stenographic transcript or printed record for the prevailing party, the same shall be taxed in favor of the United States.

(2)(A) If the judgment against a prisoner includes the payment of costs under this subsection, the prisoner shall be required to pay the full amount of the costs ordered.

(B) The prisoner shall be required to make payments for costs under this subsection in the same manner as is provided for filing fees under subsection (a)(2).

(C) In no event shall the costs collected exceed the amount of the costs ordered by the court.

(g) In no event shall a prisoner bring a civil action or appeal a judgment in a civil action or proceeding under this section if the prisoner has, on 3 or more prior occasions, while incarcerated or detained in any facility, brought an action or appeal in a court of the United States that was dismissed on the grounds that it is frivolous, malicious, or fails to state a claim upon which relief may be granted, unless the prisoner is under imminent danger of serious physical injury.

(h) As used in this section, the term "prisoner" means any person incarcerated or detained in any facility who is accused of, convicted of, sentenced for, or adjudicated delinquent for, violations of criminal law or the terms and conditions of parole, probation, pretrial release, or diversionary program.

(June 25, 1948, c. 646, 62 Stat. 954; May 24, 1949, c. 139, § 98, 63 Stat. 104; Oct. 31, 1951, c. 655, § 51(b), (c), 65 Stat. 727; Sept. 21, 1959, Pub.L. 86–320, 73 Stat. 590; Oct. 10, 1979, Pub.L. 96–82, § 6, 93 Stat. 645; Dec. 1, 1990, Pub.L. 101–650, Title III, § 321, 104 Stat. 5117; Apr. 26, 1996, Pub.L. 104–134, Title I, § 101[(a)] [Title VIII, § 804(a), (c) to (e)], 110 Stat. 1321–73, 1321–74, 1321–75; renumbered Title I May 2, 1996, Pub.L. 104–140, § 1(a), 110 Stat. 1327.)

HISTORICAL AND STATUTORY NOTES
Change of Name

"United States magistrate judge" substituted for "United States magistrate" in text pursuant to section 321 of Pub.L. 101–650, set out as a note under 28 U.S.C.A. § 631.

Severability of Provisions

If any provision of section 101[a] [Title VIII] of Pub.L. 104–134, an amendment made by such Title, or the application of such provision or amendment to any person or circumstance is held to be unconstitutional, the remainder of such Title, the amendments made by such Title, and the application of the provisions of such Title to any person or circumstance not affected thereby, see section 101[a] [Title VIII, § 810] of Pub.L. 104–134, set out as a note under section 3626 of Title 18, Crimes and Criminal Procedure.

§ 1915A. Screening

(a) Screening.—The court shall review, before docketing, if feasible or, in any event, as soon as practicable after docketing, a complaint in a civil action in which a prisoner seeks redress from a governmental entity or officer or employee of a governmental entity.

(b) Grounds for dismissal.—On review, the court shall identify cognizable claims or dismiss the complaint, or any portion of the complaint, if the complaint—

    (1) is frivolous, malicious, or fails to state a claim upon which relief may be granted; or

    (2) seeks monetary relief from a defendant who is immune from such relief.

(c) Definition.—As used in this section, the term "prisoner" means any person incarcerated or detained in any facility who is accused of, convicted of, sentenced for, or adjudicated delinquent for, violations of criminal law or the terms and conditions of parole, probation, pretrial release, or diversionary program.

(Added Pub.L. 104–134, Title I, § 101[(a)][Title VIII, § 805(a)], Apr. 26, 1996, 110 Stat. 1321–75; renumbered Title I Pub.L. 104–140, § 1(a), May 2, 1996, 110 Stat. 1327.)

HISTORICAL AND STATUTORY NOTES
Severability of Provisions

If any provision of section 101[a] [Title VIII] of Pub.L. 104–134, an amendment made by such Title, or the application of such provision or amendment to any person or circumstance is held to be unconstitutional, the remainder of such Title, the amendments made by such Title, and the application of the provisions of such Title to any person or circumstance not affected thereby, see section 101[a] [Title VIII, § 810] of Pub.L. 104–134, set out as a note under section 3626 of Title 18, Crimes and Criminal Procedure.

§ 1916. Seamen's suits

In all courts of the United States, seamen may institute and prosecute suits and appeals in their own names and for their own benefit for wages or salvage or the enforcement of laws enacted for their health or safety without prepaying fees or costs or furnishing security therefor.

(June 25, 1948, c. 646, 62 Stat. 955.)

§ 1917. District courts; fee on filing notice of or petition for appeal

Upon the filing of any separate or joint notice of appeal or application for appeal or upon the receipt of any order allowing, or notice of the allowance of, an appeal or of a writ of certiorari $5 shall be paid to the clerk of the district court, by the appellant or petitioner.

(June 25, 1948, c. 646, 62 Stat. 955.)

§ 1918. District courts; fines, forfeitures and criminal proceedings

(a) Costs shall be included in any judgment, order, or decree rendered against any person for the violation of an Act of Congress in which a civil fine or forfeiture of property is provided for.

(b) Whenever any conviction for any offense not capital is obtained in a district court, the court may order that the defendant pay the costs of prosecution.

(June 25, 1948, c. 646, 62 Stat. 955.)

§ 1919. Dismissal for lack of jurisdiction

Whenever any action or suit is dismissed in any district court, the Court of International Trade, or the Court of Federal Claims for want of jurisdiction, such court may order the payment of just costs.

(June 25, 1948, c. 646, 62 Stat. 955; Oct. 10, 1980, Pub.L. 96–417, Title V, § 510, 94 Stat. 1743; Oct. 29, 1992, Pub.L. 102–572, Title IX, § 908(a), (b)(1), 106 Stat. 4519.)

HISTORICAL AND STATUTORY NOTES
Effective and Applicability Provisions

1992 Acts. Amendment by Title IX of Pub.L. 102–572 effective Oct. 29, 1992, see section 911 of Pub.L. 102–572, set out as a note under section 171 of this title.

1980 Acts. Amendment by Pub.L. 96–417 applicable with respect to civil actions commenced on or after Nov. 1, 1980, see section 701(b)(1)(E) of Pub.L. 96–417, as amended, set out as a note under section 251 of this title.

§ 1920. Taxation of costs

A judge or clerk of any court of the United States may tax as costs the following:

(1) Fees of the clerk and marshal;

(2) Fees of the court reporter for all or any part of the stenographic transcript necessarily obtained for use in the case;

(3) Fees and disbursements for printing and witnesses;

(4) Fees for exemplification and copies of papers necessarily obtained for use in the case;

(5) Docket fees under section 1923 of this title;

(6) Compensation of court appointed experts, compensation of interpreters, and salaries, fees, expenses, and costs of special interpretation services under section 1828 of this title.

A bill of costs shall be filed in the case and, upon allowance, included in the judgment or decree.

(June 25, 1948, c. 646, 62 Stat. 955; Oct. 28, 1978, Pub.L. 95–539, § 7, 92 Stat. 2044.)

HISTORICAL AND STATUTORY NOTES

Effective and Applicability Provisions

1978 Acts. Amendment by Pub.L. 95–539 effective Oct. 28, 1978, see section 10(a) of Pub.L. 95–539, set out as a note under section 602 of this title.

§ 1921. United States marshal's fees

(a)(1) The United States marshals or deputy marshals shall routinely collect, and a court may tax as costs, fees for the following:

(A) Serving a writ of possession, partition, execution, attachment in rem, or libel in admiralty, warrant, attachment, summons, complaints, or any other writ, order or process in any case or proceeding.

(B) Serving a subpoena or summons for a witness or appraiser.

(C) Forwarding any writ, order, or process to another judicial district for service.

(D) The preparation of any notice of sale, proclamation in admiralty, or other public notice or bill of sale.

(E) The keeping of attached property (including boats, vessels, or other property attached or libeled), actual expenses incurred, such as storage, moving, boat hire, or other special transportation, watchmen's or keepers' fees, insurance, and an hourly rate, including overtime, for each deputy marshal required for special services, such as guarding, inventorying, and moving.

(F) Copies of writs or other papers furnished at the request of any party.

(G) Necessary travel in serving or endeavoring to serve any process, writ, or order, except in the District of Columbia, with mileage to be computed from the place where service is returnable to the place of service or endeavor.

(H) Overtime expenses incurred by deputy marshals in the course of serving or executing civil process.

(2) The marshals shall collect, in advance, a deposit to cover the initial expenses for special services required under paragraph (1)(E), and periodically thereafter such amounts as may be necessary to pay such expenses until the litigation is concluded. This paragraph applies to all private litigants, including seamen proceeding pursuant to section 1916 of this title.

(3) For purposes of paragraph (1)(G), if two or more services or endeavors, or if an endeavor and a service, are made in behalf of the same party in the same case on the same trip, mileage shall be computed to the place of service or endeavor which is most remote from the place where service is returnable, adding thereto any additional mileage traveled in serving or endeavoring to serve in behalf of the party. If two or more writs of any kind, required to be served in behalf of the same party on the same person in the same case or proceeding, may be served at the same time, mileage on only one such writ shall be collected.

(b) The Attorney General shall from time to time prescribe by regulation the fees to be taxed and collected under subsection (a). Such fees shall, to the extent practicable, reflect the actual and reasonable cost of the service provided.

(c)(1) The United States Marshals Service shall collect a commission of 3 percent of the first $1,000 collected and 1½ percent on the excess of any sum over $1,000, for seizing or levying on property (including seizures in admiralty), disposing of such property by sale, setoff, or otherwise, and receiving and paying over money, except that the amount of commission shall be within the range set by the Attorney General. if [1] the property is not disposed of by marshal's sale, the commission shall be in such amount, within the range set by the Attorney General, as may be allowed by the court. In any case in which the vessel or other property is sold by a public auctioneer, or by some party other than a marshal or deputy marshal, the commission authorized under this subsection shall be reduced by the amount paid to such auctioneer or other party. This subsection applies to any judicially ordered sale or execution sale, without regard to whether the judicial order of sale constitutes a seizure or levy within the meaning of State law. This subsection shall not apply to any seizure, forfeiture, sale, or other disposition of property pursuant to the applicable provisions of law amended by the Comprehensive Forfeiture Act of 1984 (98 Stat. 2040).

(2) The Attorney General shall prescribe from time to time regulations which establish a minimum and maximum amount for the commission collected under paragraph (1).

(d) The United States marshals may require a deposit to cover the fees and expenses prescribed under this section.

(e) Notwithstanding section 3302 of title 31, the United States Marshals Service is authorized, to the extent provided in advance in appropriations Acts—

(1) to credit to such Service's appropriation all fees, commissions, and expenses collected by such Service for—

(A) the service of civil process, including complaints, summonses, subpoenas, and similar process; and

(B) seizures, levies, and sales associated with judicial orders of execution; and

(2) to use such credited amounts for the purpose of carrying out such activities.

(June 25, 1948, c. 646, 62 Stat. 955; Sept. 9, 1950, c. 937, 64 Stat. 824; Aug. 31, 1962, Pub.L. 87–621, § 1, 76 Stat. 417; Nov. 10, 1986, Pub.L. 99–646, § 39(a), 100 Stat. 3600; Nov. 18, 1988, Pub.L. 100–690, Title VII, § 7608(c), 102 Stat. 4515; Nov. 29, 1990, Pub.L. 101–647, Title XII, § 1212, 104 Stat. 4833.)

1 So in original. Probably should be capitalized.

HISTORICAL AND STATUTORY NOTES

References in Text

The Comprehensive Forfeiture Act of 1984, referred to in subsec. (c)(1), is chapter III (sections 301 to 322) of Title II of Pub.L. 98–473, Oct. 12, 1984, 98 Stat. 2040, as amended. For complete classification of this Act to the Code, see Short Title of 1984 Amendments note set out under section 1961 of Title 18, Crimes and Criminal Procedure, and Tables.

Effective and Applicability Provisions

1986 Acts. Section 39(b) of Pub.L. 99–646 provided that: "The amendments made by this section [amending this section] shall take effect 30 days after the date of enactment of this Act [Nov. 10, 1986]."

1962 Acts. Section 3 of Pub.L. 87–621 provided that: "This Act [amending this section] shall become effective ninety days after enactment [Aug. 31, 1962]."

Collection and Disposition of Fees and Expenses for Services

Pub.L. 101–162, Title II, Nov. 21, 1989, 103 Stat. 997, provided in part: "That notwithstanding the provisions of title 31 U.S.C. 3302 [section 3302 of Title 31, Money and Finance], for fiscal year 1990 and hereafter the Director of the United States Marshals Service may collect fees and expenses for the services authorized by 28 U.S.C. 1921 as amended by Public Law 100–690 [this section], and credit

such fees to this appropriation to be used for salaries and other expenses incurred in providing these services."

§ 1922. Witness fees before United States magistrate judges

The fees of more than four witnesses shall not be taxed against the United States, in the examination of any criminal case before a United States magistrate judge, unless their materiality and importance are first approved and certified to by the United States attorney for the district in which the examination is had.

(June 25, 1948, c. 646, 62 Stat. 956; Oct. 17, 1968, Pub.L. 90–578, Title IV, § 402(b)(2), 82 Stat. 1118; Dec. 1, 1990, Pub.L. 101–650, Title III, § 321, 104 Stat. 5117.)

HISTORICAL AND STATUTORY NOTES

Change of Name

"United States magistrate judge" substituted for "United States magistrate" in text pursuant to section 321 of Pub.L. 101–650, set out as a note under 28 U.S.C.A. § 631. Previously, United States commissioners, referred to in text, were replaced by United States magistrates pursuant to Pub.L. 90–578, Oct. 17, 1968, 82 Stat. 1118. See chapter 43 of Title 28, 28 U.S.C.A. § 631 et seq.

§ 1923. Docket fees and costs of briefs

(a) Attorney's and proctor's docket fees in courts of the United States may be taxed as costs as follows:

$20 on trial or final hearing (including a default judgment whether entered by the court or by the clerk) in civil, criminal, or admiralty cases, except that in cases of admiralty and maritime jurisdiction where the libellant recovers less than $50 the proctor's docket fee shall be $10;

$20 in admiralty appeals involving not over $1,000;

$50 in admiralty appeals involving not over $5,000;

$100 in admiralty appeals involving more than $5,000;

$5 on discontinuance of a civil action;

$5 on motion for judgment and other proceedings on recognizances;

$2.50 for each deposition admitted in evidence.

(b) The docket fees of United States attorneys and United States trustees shall be paid to the clerk of court and by him paid into the Treasury.

(c) In admiralty appeals the court may allow as costs for printing the briefs of the successful party not more than:

$25 where the amount involved is not over $1,000;

$50 where the amount involved is not over $5,000;

$75 where the amount involved is over $5,000.

(June 25, 1948, c. 646, 62 Stat. 956; June 18, 1954, c. 304, 68 Stat. 253; Nov. 6, 1978, Pub.L. 95–598, Title II, § 245, 92 Stat. 2671.)

HISTORICAL AND STATUTORY NOTES

Codifications

Section 408(c) of Pub.L. 95–598, Nov. 6, 1978, 92 Stat. 2687, as amended by Pub.L. 98–166, Title II, § 200, Nov. 28, 1983, 97 Stat. 1081; Pub.L. 98–353, Title III, § 323, July 10, 1984, 98 Stat. 358; Pub.L. 99–429, Sept. 30, 1986, 100 Stat. 985; Pub.L. 99–500, § 101(b) [title II, § 200], Oct. 18, 1986, 100 Stat. 1783–39, 1783–45, and Pub.L. 99–591, § 101(b) [Title II, § 200], Oct. 30, 1986, 100 Stat. 3341–39, 3341–45; Pub.L. 99–554, Title III, § 307(a), Oct. 27, 1986, 100 Stat. 3125, which provided for the deletion of any references to United States Trustees in this title at a prospective date, was repealed by Pub.L. 99–554, Title III, § 307(b), Oct. 27, 1986, 100 Stat. 3125.

[For effective date of repeal, see section 302 of Pub.L. 99–554, set out as a note under section 581 of Title 28.]

Effective and Applicability Provisions

1978 Acts. Amendment by Pub.L. 95–598 effective Oct. 1, 1979, see section 402(c) of Pub.L. 95–598, set out as a note preceding section 101 of Title 11, Bankruptcy.

§ 1924. Verification of bill of costs

Before any bill of costs is taxed, the party claiming any item of cost or disbursement shall attach thereto an affidavit, made by himself or by his duly authorized attorney or agent having knowledge of the facts, that such item is correct and has been necessarily incurred in the case and that the services for which fees have been charged were actually and necessarily performed.

(June 25, 1948, c. 646, 62 Stat. 957.)

§ 1925. Admiralty and maritime cases

Except as otherwise provided by Act of Congress, the allowance and taxation of costs in admiralty and maritime cases shall be prescribed by rules promulgated by the Supreme Court.

(June 25, 1948, c. 646, 62 Stat. 957.)

§ 1926. Court of Federal Claims

(a) The Judicial Conference of the United States shall prescribe from time to time the fees and costs to be charged and collected in the United States Court of Federal Claims.

(b) The court and its officers shall collect only such fees and costs as the Judicial Conference prescribes. The court may require advance payment of fees by rule.

(June 25, 1948, c. 646, 62 Stat. 957; Apr. 2, 1982, Pub.L. 97–164, Title I, § 139(p)(1), 96 Stat. 44; Oct. 29, 1992, Pub.L. 102–572, Title IX, § 902(b), 106 Stat. 4516.)

JUDICIAL CONFERENCE SCHEDULE OF FEES

United States Court of Federal Claims Fee Schedule

[The Federal Courts Improvement Act of 1982 [Pub.L. 97–164, Apr. 2, 1982, 96 Stat. 25] added a new Sec. 1926 to Title 28, United States Code [this section], authorizing the Judicial Conference to prescribe from time to time the fees and costs to be charged and collected in the United States Claims Court [now Court of Federal Claims]. A fee schedule was approved, effective October 1, 1982. At its March 1987 meeting, the Judicial Conference amended the schedule of fees to be effective May 1, 1987. Amendments to this revision of the schedule of fees were adopted at the September, 1988 and March, 1990 meetings of the Judicial Conference. The Judicial Conference amended the schedule of fees at its September, 1992 meeting to be effective Nov. 15, 1992. The Judicial Conference amended the schedule of fees at its March 15, 1995 meeting to be effective April 18, 1995. The Judicial Conference amended the schedule of fees at its 1996 meeting to be effective April 15, 1996. The Judicial Conference amended the schedule of fees at its 1999 meeting to be effective October 1, 1999. The Judicial Conference subsequently adopted amendments to its fee schedule effective February 1, 2001. The Judicial Conference amended the schedule of fees at its March 2001 meeting to be effective July 1, 2001 The Judicial Conference adopted amendments to its fee schedule effective November 1, 2003. The Judicial Conference at its March 16, 2004 meeting adopted amendments to its fee schedule to be effective June 1, 2004.]

Following are fees to be charged for services provided by the United States Court of Federal Claims. No fees are to be charged for services rendered on behalf of the United States, with the exception of those specifically prescribed in items 2 and 8. No fees under this schedule shall be charged to federal agencies or programs which are funded from judiciary appropriations, including, but not limited to, agencies, organizations, and individuals providing services authorized by the Criminal Justice Act, 18 U.S.C. § 3006A, and Bankruptcy Administrator programs.

(1) For filing a civil action or proceeding, $150.

(2) For reproducing any record or paper, $.50 per page. This fee shall apply to paper copies made from either: (a) original documents; or (b) microfiche or microfilm reproductions of the original records. This fee shall apply to services rendered on behalf of the United States if the record or paper requested is available through electronic access.

(3) For certification of any document or paper, whether the certification is made directly on the document or by separate instrument, $9. For exemplification of any document or paper, twice the amount of the charge for certification.

(4) For admission of attorneys to practice, $50 each, including a certificate of admission. For a duplicate certificate of admission or certificate of good standing, $15.

(5) For receipt of a monthly listing of court orders and opinions, $19 per year.

(6) The court may charge and collect fees commensurate with the cost of providing copies of the local rules of court. The court may also distribute copies of the local rules without charge.

(7) For a check paid into the court which is returned for lack of funds, $45.

(8) For every search of the records of the Court of Federal Claims conducted by the clerk of the court or a deputy clerk, $26 per name or item searched. This fee shall apply to services rendered on behalf of the United States if the information requested is available through electronic access.

ELECTRONIC PUBLIC ACCESS FEE SCHEDULE (eff. 1/1/05)

As directed by Congress, the Judicial Conference has determined that the following fees are necessary to reimburse expenses incurred by the judiciary in providing electronic public access to court records. These fees shall apply to the United States unless otherwise stated. No fees under this schedule shall be charged to federal agencies or programs which are funded from judiciary appropriations, including, but not limited to, agencies, organizations, and individuals providing services authorized by the Criminal Justice Act, 18 U.S.C. § 3006A, and bankruptcy administrator programs.

I. For electronic access to court data via dial up service: sixty cents per minute. For electronic access to court data via a federal judiciary Internet site: eight cents per page, with the total for any document, docket sheet, or case-specific report not to exceed the fee for thirty pages- provided however that transcripts of federal court proceedings shall not be subject to the thirty-page fee limit. Attorneys of record and parties in a case (including *pro se* litigants) receive one free electronic copy of all documents filed electronically, if receipt is required by law or directed by the filer. No fee is owed under this provision until an account holder accrues charges of more than $10 in a calendar year. Consistent with Judicial Conference policy, courts may, upon a showing of cause, exempt indigents, bankruptcy case trustees, individual researchers associated with educational institutions, courts, section 501(c)(3) not-for-profit organizations and pro bono ADR neutrals from payment of these fees. Courts must find that parties from the classes of persons or entities listed above seeking exemption have demonstrated that an exemption is necessary in order to avoid unreasonable burdens and to promote public access to information. Any user granted an exemption agrees not to sell for profit the data obtained as a result. Exemptions may be granted for a definite period of time and may be revoked at the discretion of the court granting the exemption.

II. For printing copies of any record or document accessed electronically at a public terminal in the courthouse: ten cents per page. This fee shall apply to services rendered on behalf of the United States if the record requested is remotely available through electronic access.

III. For every search of court records conducted by the PACER Service Center, $20.

JUDICIAL CONFERENCE POLICY NOTES

Courts should not exempt local, state or federal government agencies, members of the media, attorneys or others not members of one of the groups listed above. Exemptions should be granted as the exception, not the rule. A court may not use this exemption language to exempt all users. An exemption applies only to access related to the case or purpose for which it was given.

The electronic public access fee applies to electronic court data viewed remotely from the public records of individual cases in the court, including filed documents and the docket sheet. Electronic court data may be viewed free at public terminals at the courthouse and courts may provide other local court information at no cost. Examples of information that can be provided at no cost include: local rules, court forms, news items, court calendars, opinions, and other information—such as court hours, court location, telephone listings—determined locally to benefit the public and the court.

HISTORICAL AND STATUTORY NOTES

Effective and Applicability Provisions

1992 Acts. Amendment by Pub.L. 102–572 effective Oct. 29, 1992, see section 911 of Pub.L. 102–572, set out as a note under section 171 of this title.

1982 Acts. Amendment by Pub.L. 97–164 effective Oct. 1, 1982, see section 402 of Pub.L. 97–164, set out as a note under section 171 of this title.

Court Fees for Electronic Access to Information

Judicial Conference to prescribe reasonable fees for collection by courts under this section for access to information available through automatic data processing equipment and fees to be deposited in Judiciary Automation Fund, see section 303 of Pub.L. 102–140, set out as a note under section 1913 of this title.

§ 1927. Counsel's liability for excessive costs

Any attorney or other person admitted to conduct cases in any court of the United States or any Territory thereof who so multiplies the proceedings in any case unreasonably and vexatiously may be required by the court to satisfy personally the excess costs, expenses, and attorneys' fees reasonably incurred because of such conduct.

(June 25, 1948, c. 646, 62 Stat. 957; Sept. 12, 1980, Pub.L. 96–349, § 3, 94 Stat. 1156.)

§ 1928. Patent infringement action; disclaimer not filed

Whenever a judgment is rendered for the plaintiff in any patent infringement action involving a part of a patent and it appears that the patentee, in his specifications, claimed to be, but was not, the original and first inventor or discoverer of any material or substantial part of the thing patented, no costs shall be included in such judgment, unless the proper disclaimer has been filed in the United States Patent and Trademark Office prior to the commencement of the action.

(June 25, 1948, c. 646, 62 Stat. 957; Nov. 29, 1999, Pub.L. 106–113, Div. B, § 1000(a)(9) [Title IV, § 4732(b)(17)], 113 Stat. 1536, 1501A–585.)

HISTORICAL AND STATUTORY NOTES

Effective and Applicability Provisions

1999 Acts. Amendment by Pub.L. 106–113 [§ 4732], effective 4 months after Nov. 29, 1999, see Pub.L. 106–113 [§ 4731], set out as a note under section 1 of Title 35.

Change of Name

Patent Office redesignated Patent and Trademark Office by section 3 of Pub.L. 93–596, Jan. 2, 1975, 88 Stat. 1949, set out as a note under section 1 of Title 35, Patents.

§ 1929. Extraordinary expenses not expressly authorized

Where the ministerial officers of the United States incur extraordinary expense in executing Acts of Congress, the payment of which is not specifically provided for, the Attorney General may allow the payment thereof.

(June 25, 1948, c. 646, 62 Stat. 957.)

§ 1930. Bankruptcy fees

(a) Notwithstanding section 1915 of this title, the parties commencing a case under title 11 shall pay to the clerk of the district court or the clerk of the bankruptcy court, if one has been certified pursuant to section 156(b) of this title, the following filing fees:

(1) For a case commenced under chapter 7 or 13 of title 11, $155.

(2) For a case commenced under chapter 9 of title 11, equal to the fee specified in paragraph (3) for filing a case under chapter 11 of title 11. The amount by which the fee payable under this paragraph exceeds $300 shall be deposited in the fund established under section 1931 of this title.

(3) For a case commenced under chapter 11 of title 11 that does not concern a railroad, as defined in section 101 of title 11, $800.

(4) For a case commenced under chapter 11 of title 11 concerning a railroad, as so defined, $1,000.

(5) For a case commenced under chapter 12 of title 11, $200.

(6) In addition to the filing fee paid to the clerk, a quarterly fee shall be paid to the United States trustee, for deposit in the Treasury, in each case under chapter 11 of title 11 for each quarter (including any fraction thereof) until the case is converted or dismissed, whichever occurs first. The fee shall be $250 for each quarter in which disbursements total less than $15,000; $500 for each quarter in which disbursements total $15,000 or more but less than $75,000; $750 for each quarter in which disbursements total $75,000 or more but less than $150,000; $1,250 for each quarter in which disbursements total $150,000 or more but less than $225,000; $1,500 for each quarter in which disbursements total $225,000 or more but less than $300,000; $3,750 for each quarter in which disbursements total $300,000 or more but less than $1,000,000; $5,000 for each quarter in which disbursements total $1,000,000 or more but less than $2,000,000; $7,500 for each quarter in which disbursements total $2,000,000 or more but less than $3,000,000;

$8,000 for each quarter in which disbursements total $3,000,000 or more but less than $5,000,000; $10,000 for each quarter in which disbursements total $5,000,000 or more. The fee shall be payable on the last day of the calendar month following the calendar quarter for which the fee is owed.

(7) In districts that are not part of a United States trustee region as defined in section 581 of this title, the Judicial Conference of the United States may require the debtor in a case under chapter 11 of title 11 to pay fees equal to those imposed by paragraph (6) of this subsection. Such fees shall be deposited as offsetting receipts to the fund established under section 1931 of this title and shall remain available until expended.

An individual commencing a voluntary case or a joint case under title 11 may pay such fee in installments. For converting, on request of the debtor, a case under chapter 7, or 13 of title 11, to a case under chapter 11 of title 11, the debtor shall pay to the clerk of the district court or the clerk of the bankruptcy court, if one has been certified pursuant to section 156(b) of this title, a fee of the amount equal to the difference between the fee specified in paragraph (3) and the fee specified in paragraph (1).

(b) The Judicial Conference of the United States may prescribe additional fees in cases under title 11 of the same kind as the Judicial Conference prescribes under section 1914(b) of this title.

(c) Upon the filing of any separate or joint notice of appeal or application for appeal or upon the receipt of any order allowing, or notice of the allowance of, an appeal or a writ of certiorari $5 shall be paid to the clerk of the court, by the appellant or petitioner.

(d) Whenever any case or proceeding is dismissed in any bankruptcy court for want of jurisdiction, such court may order the payment of just costs.

(e) The clerk of the court may collect only the fees prescribed under this section.

(Added Pub.L. 95–598, Title II, § 246(a), Nov. 6, 1978, 92 Stat. 2671, and amended Pub.L. 98–353, Title I, § 111(a), (b), July 10, 1984, 98 Stat. 342; Pub.L. 99–500, Title I, § 101(b) [Title IV, § 407(b)], Oct. 18, 1986, 100 Stat. 1783–64; Pub.L. 99–554, Title I, §§ 117, 144(f), Oct. 27, 1986, 100 Stat. 3095, 3097; Pub.L. 99–591, Title I, § 101(b) [Title IV, § 407(b)], Oct. 30, 1986, 100 Stat. 3341–64; Pub.L. 101–162, Title IV, § 406(a), Nov. 21, 1989, 103 Stat. 1016; Pub.L. 102–140, Title I, § 111(a), Oct. 28, 1991, 105 Stat. 795; Pub.L. 103–121, Title I, § 111(a)(1), (b)(1), Oct. 27, 1993, 107 Stat. 1164; Pub.L. 104–91, Title I, § 101(a), Jan. 6, 1996, 110 Stat. 11, as amended Pub.L. 104–99, Title II, § 211, Jan. 26, 1996, 110 Stat. 37; Pub.L. 104–208, Div. A, Title I, § 101(a) [Title I, § 109(a)], Sept. 30, 1996, 110 Stat. 3009–18; Pub.L. 106–113, Div. B, § 1000(a)(1) [Title I, § 113], Nov. 29, 1999, 113 Stat. 1535, 1501A–20; Pub.L. 106–518, Title I, §§ 103 to 105, Nov. 13, 2000, 114 Stat. 2411.)

Amendment of Subsection (a)

Pub.L. 109–8, Title IV, § 418(1), Title XV, § 1501, Apr. 20, 2005, 119 Stat. 108, 216, provided that, except as otherwise provided, effective 180 days after April 20, 2005, and inapplicable with respect to cases commenced under Title 11 before the effective date, subsection (a) of this section is amended by striking "Notwithstanding section 1915 of this title, the" and inserting "The".

Amendment of Subsection (a)(1)

Pub.L. 109–8, Title III, § 325(a)(1), Title XV, § 1501, Apr. 20, 2005, 119 Stat. 98, 216, provided that, except as otherwise provided, effective 180 days after April 20, 2005, and inapplicable with respect to cases commenced under Title 11 before the effective date, subsection (a)(1) is amended to read as follows:

(1) For a case commenced under—

    (A) chapter 7 of title 11, $200; and

    (B) chapter 13 of title 11, $150.

Amendment of Subsection (a)(3)

Pub.L. 109–8, Title III, § 325(a)(2), Title XV, § 1501, Apr. 20, 2005, 119 Stat. 98, 216, provided that, except as otherwise provided, effective 180 days after April 20, 2005, and inapplicable with respect to cases commenced under Title 11 before the effective date, subsection (a)(3) is amended by striking "$800" and inserting "$1000".

Enactment of Subsection (f)

Pub.L. 109–8, Title IV, § 418(2), Title XV, § 1501, Apr. 20, 2005, 119 Stat. 109, 216, provided that, except as otherwise provided, effective 180 days after April 20, 2005, and inapplicable with respect to cases commenced under Title 11 before the effective date, subsection (f) of this section is enacted to read as follows:

(f)(1) Under the procedures prescribed by the Judicial Conference of the United States, the district court or the bankruptcy court may waive the filing fee in a case under chapter 7 of title 11 for an individual if the court determines that such individual has income less than 150 percent of the income official poverty line (as defined by the Office of Management and Budget, and revised annually in accordance with section 673(2) of the Omnibus Budget Reconciliation Act of 1981) applicable to a family of the size involved and is unable to pay that fee in installments. For purposes of this paragraph, the term "filing fee" means the filing fee required by subsection (a), or any other fee prescribed by the Judicial Conference under subsections (b) and (c) that is payable to the clerk upon the commencement of a case under chapter 7.

(2) The district court or the bankruptcy court may waive for such debtors other fees prescribed under subsections (b) and (c).

(3) This subsection does not restrict the district court or the bankruptcy court from waiving, in accordance with Judicial Conference policy, fees prescribed under this section for other debtors and creditors.

JUDICIAL CONFERENCE SCHEDULE OF FEES

Bankruptcy Court Miscellaneous Fee Schedule

[The Judicial Conference of the United States at its session on March 7–9, 1979, set forth the schedule of fees to be charged in bankruptcy courts pursuant to this section. That schedule became effective on October 1, 1979. At its sessions in March and September 1980, March, 1981, March, 1987, and March and September, 1988, the Judicial Conference amended the schedule of fees. The Administrative Office of the United States Courts provided for Registry Fund Fees effective June 12, 1989. At its September, 1989 meeting, the Judicial Conference again amended the schedule of fees, such amendments effective pursuant to 1989 Judicial Conference Statement. The schedule of fees was again amended by the Judicial Conference at its March, 1990 and September, 1990 meetings. At its 1991 meeting, the Judicial Conference amended the schedule of fees to be effective Feb. 3, 1992. At its March 1991 meeting the Judicial Conference adopted Item 23 to be effective Oct. 19, 1992, with later implementation. At its September, 1992 meeting the Judicial Conference amended Item 8 to be effective Dec. 1, 1992. At its March, 1993 meeting the Judicial Conference amended its fee schedule effective May 6, 1993. At its September, 1993 meeting the Judicial Conference amended its fee schedule to be effective November 8, 1993. At its 1994 meeting, the Judicial Conference amended its fee schedule to be effective January 1, 1995. At its September, 1995 meeting the Judicial Conference amended its fee schedule to be effective November 9, 1995, and at its 1996 meetings it adopted amendments to be effective April 1, 1996 and October 28, 1996. At its 1997 meeting the Judicial Conference amended its fee schedule to be effective January 1, 1998. At its 1999 meeting the Judicial Conference amended its fee schedule to be effective October 1, 1999. The Judicial Conference subsequently adopted amendments to its fee schedule effective February 1, 2001. At its March 2001 meeting the Judicial Conference amended its fee schedule to be effective July 1, 2001. The Judicial Conference adopted amendments to its fee schedule effective January 1, 2002; and effective November 1, 2003. The Judicial Conference at its March 16, 2004 meeting adopted amendments to its fee schedule to be effective June 1, 2004.]

Following are fees to be charged for services provided by the bankruptcy courts. No fees are to be charged for services rendered on behalf of the United States, with the exception of those specifically prescribed in items 1, 3, and 5, or to bankruptcy administrators appointed under Public Law No. 99–554, § 302(d)(3)(I). No fees under this schedule shall be charged to federal agencies or programs which are funded from judiciary appropriations, including, but not limited to, agencies, organizations, and individuals providing services authorized by the Criminal Justice Act, 18 U.S.C. § 3006A.

(1) For reproducing any record or paper, $.50 per page. This fee shall apply to paper copies made from either: (1) original documents; or (2) microfiche or microfilm reproductions of the original records. This fee shall apply to services

rendered on behalf of the United States if the record or paper requested is available through electronic access.

(2) For certification of any document or paper, whether the certification is made directly on the document or by separate instrument, $9. For exemplification of any document or paper, twice the amount of the charge for certification.

(3) For reproduction of recordings of proceedings, regardless of the medium, $26, including the cost of materials. This fee shall apply to services rendered on behalf of the United States, if the reproduction of the recording is available electronically.

(4) For amendments to a debtor's schedules of creditors, lists of creditors, matrix, or mailing lists, $26 for each amendment, provided the bankruptcy judge may, for good cause, waive the charge in any case. No fee is required when the nature of the amendment is to change the address of a creditor or an attorney for a creditor listed on the schedules or to add the name and address of an attorney for a listed creditor.

(5) For every search of the records of the bankruptcy court conducted by the clerk of the bankruptcy court or a deputy clerk, $26 per name or item searched. This fee shall apply to services rendered on behalf of the United States if the information requested is available through electronic access.

(6) For filing a complaint, a fee shall be collected in the same amount as the filing fee prescribed in 28 U.S.C. § 1914(a) for instituting any civil action other than a writ of habeas corpus. If the United States, other than a United States trustee acting as a trustee in a case under title 11, or a debtor is the plaintiff, no fee is required. If a trustee or debtor in possession is the plaintiff, the fee should be payable only from the estate and to the extent there is any estate realized. If a child support creditor or its representative is the plaintiff, and if such plaintiff files the form required by § 304(g) of the Bankruptcy Reform Act of 1994, no fee is required.

(7) For filing or indexing any document not in a case or proceeding for which a filing fee has been paid, $39.

(8) In all cases filed under title 11, the clerk shall collect from the debtor or the petitioner a miscellaneous administrative fee of $39. This fee may be paid in installments in the same manner that the filing fee may be paid in installments, consistent with the procedure set forth in Federal Rule of Bankruptcy Procedure 1006.

(9) Upon the filing of a petition under chapter 7 of the Bankruptcy Code, the petitioner shall pay $15 to the clerk of the court for payment to trustees serving in cases as provided in 11 U.S.C. § 330(b)(2). An application to pay the fee in installments may be filed in the manner set forth in Federal Rule of Bankruptcy Procedure 1006(b).

(10) Upon the filing of a motion to convert a case to chapter 7 of the Bankruptcy Code, the movant shall pay $15 to the clerk of court for payment to trustees serving in cases as provided in 11 U.S.C. § 330(b)(2). Upon the filing of a notice of conversion pursuant to section 1208(a) or section 1307(a) of the Code, $15 shall be paid to the clerk of the court for payment to trustees serving in cases as provided in 11 U.S.C. § 330(b)(2). If the trustee serving in the case before the conversion is the movant, the fee shall be payable only from the estate that exists prior to conversion.

(11) For filing a motion to reopen a Bankruptcy Code case, a fee shall be collected in the same amount as the filing fee prescribed by 28 U.S.C. § 1930(a) for commencing a new case on the date of reopening, unless the reopening is to correct an administrative error or for actions related to the debtor's discharge. The court may waive this fee under appropriate circumstances or may defer payment of the fee from trustees pending discovery of additional assets. If payment is deferred, the fee shall be waived if no additional assets are discovered.

(12) For each microfiche sheet of film or microfilm jacket copy of any court record, where available, $5.

(13) For retrieval of a record from a Federal Records Center, National Archives, or other storage location removed from the place of business of the court, $45.

(14) For a check paid into the court which is returned for lack of funds, $45.

(15) For docketing a proceeding on appeal or review from a final judgment of a bankruptcy judge pursuant to 28 U.S.C. § 158(a) and (b), the fee shall be the same amount as the fee for docketing a case on appeal or review to the appellate court as required by Item 1 of the Courts of Appeals Miscellaneous Fee Schedule. A separate fee shall be paid by each party filing a notice of appeal in the bankruptcy court, but parties filing a joint notice of appeal in the bankruptcy court are required to pay only one fee. If a trustee or debtor in possession is the appellant, the fee should be payable only from the estate and to the extent there is any estate realized.

(16) For filing a petition ancillary to a foreign proceeding under 11 U.S.C. § 304, the fee shall be the same amount as the fee for a case commenced under chapter 11 of title 11 as required by 28 U.S.C. § 1930(a)(3).

(17) The court may charge and collect fees commensurate with the cost of providing copies of the local rules of court. The court may also distribute copies of the local rules without charge.

(18) The clerk shall assess a charge for the handling of registry funds deposited with the court, to be assessed from interest earnings and in accordance with the detailed fee schedule issued by the Director of the Administrative Office of the United States Courts.

(19) When a joint case filed under § 302 of title 11 is divided into two separate cases at the request of the debtor(s), a fee shall be charged equal to the current filing fee for the chapter under which the joint case was commenced.

(20) For filing a motion to terminate, annul, modify, or condition the automatic stay provided under § 362(a) of title 11, a motion to compel abandonment of property of the estate pursuant to Rule 6007(b) of the Federal Rules of Bankruptcy Procedure, or a motion to withdraw the reference of a case or proceeding under 28 U.S.C. § 157(d), a fee shall be collected in the amount of the filing fee prescribed in 28 U.S.C. § 1914(a) for instituting any civil action other than a writ of habeas corpus. No fee is required for a motion for relief from the co-debtor stay or for a stipulation for court approval of an agreement for relief from a stay. If a child support creditor or its representative is the movant, and if such movant files the form required by § 304(g) of the Bankruptcy Reform Act of 1994, no fee is required.

(21) For docketing a cross appeal from a bankruptcy court determination, the fee shall be the same amount as the fee for docketing a case on appeal or review to the appellate

court as required by Item 1 of the Courts of Appeals Miscellaneous Fee Schedule. If a trustee or debtor in possession is the appellant, the fee should be payable only from the estate and to the extent there is any estate realized.

ELECTRONIC PUBLIC ACCESS FEE SCHEDULE (eff. 1/1/05)

As directed by Congress, the Judicial Conference has determined that the following fees are necessary to reimburse expenses incurred by the judiciary in providing electronic public access to court records. These fees shall apply to the United States unless otherwise stated. No fees under this schedule shall be charged to federal agencies or programs which are funded from judiciary appropriations, including, but not limited to, agencies, organizations, and individuals providing services authorized by the Criminal Justice Act, 18 U.S.C. § 3006A, and bankruptcy administrator programs.

I. For electronic access to court data via dial up service: sixty cents per minute. For electronic access to court data via a federal judiciary Internet site: eight cents per page, with the total for any document, docket sheet, or case-specific report not to exceed the fee for thirty pages- provided however that transcripts of federal court proceedings shall not be subject to the thirty-page fee limit. Attorneys of record and parties in a case (including *pro se* litigants) receive one free electronic copy of all documents filed electronically, if receipt is required by law or directed by the filer. No fee is owed under this provision until an account holder accrues charges of more than $10 in a calendar year. Consistent with Judicial Conference policy, courts may, upon a showing of cause, exempt indigents, bankruptcy case trustees, individual researchers associated with educational institutions, courts, section 501(c)(3) not-for-profit organizations and pro bono ADR neutrals from payment of these fees. Courts must find that parties from the classes of persons or entities listed above seeking exemption have demonstrated that an exemption is necessary in order to avoid unreasonable burdens and to promote public access to information. Any user granted an exemption agrees not to sell for profit the data obtained as a result. Exemptions may be granted for a definite period of time and may be revoked at the discretion of the court granting the exemption.

II. For printing copies of any record or document accessed electronically at a public terminal in the courthouse: ten cents per page. This fee shall apply to services rendered on behalf of the United States if the record requested is remotely available through electronic access.

III. For every search of court records conducted by the PACER Service Center, $20.

JUDICIAL CONFERENCE POLICY NOTES

Courts should not exempt local, state or federal government agencies, members of the media, attorneys or others not members of one of the groups listed above. Exemptions should be granted as the exception, not the rule. A court may not use this exemption language to exempt all users. An exemption applies only to access related to the case or purpose for which it was given.

The electronic public access fee applies to electronic court data viewed remotely from the public records of individual cases in the court, including filed documents and the docket sheet. Electronic court data may be viewed free at public terminals at the courthouse and courts may provide other local court information at no cost. Examples of information that can be provided at no cost include: local rules, court forms, news items, court calendars, opinions, and other information—such as court hours, court location, telephone listings—determined locally to benefit the public and the court.

STATEMENT RESPECTING 1988 AMENDMENTS FROM ADMINISTRATIVE OFFICE OF UNITED STATES COURTS

The Director of the Administrative Office of the United States Courts in a memorandum to the Chief Judges of the United States Courts of Appeals, United States District Courts, and United States Bankruptcy Courts, dated April 19, 1988, provided in part that: "The amendment establishing a fee for filing a petition ancillary to a foreign proceeding under § 304 of the Bankruptcy Code will become effective May 1, 1988. The amendment expanding the exemption for services rendered 'to the United States' to include services rendered to bankruptcy administrators simply expresses a policy which has been in effect since the creation of the bankruptcy administrator program by Congress in the Bankruptcy Judges, United States Trustees and Family Farmer Bankruptcy Act of 1986. [Pub.L. No. 99–554, § 302(d)(3)(I).]"

Statement from 1989 Meeting of Judicial Conference

The Judicial Conference, at the September 20, 1989 meeting, provided in part that Item 21 takes effect on December 21, 1989. The Conference further provided that: "The remaining fees, Items 20 and 22, take effect on January 11, 1990, pending approval of the Appropriations Committees."

Registry Fund Fees—Item 19
(54 FR 20407, May 11, 1989)

Effective June 12, 1989, a fee will be assessed for handling funds deposited in noncriminal proceedings with the court and held in interest bearing accounts or instruments pursuant to 28 U.S.C. § 2041 and Federal Rules of Civil Procedure rule 67. For new accounts, i.e., investments made on or after June 12, 1989, the fee will be equal to the first 45 days income earned on the deposit. Each subsequent deposit of new principal in the same case or proceeding will be subject to the fee. Reinvestment of prior deposits will not be subject to the fee. For existing accounts, i.e., investments held by the court prior to June 12, 1989, a fee will be assessed equal to the first 45 days of income earned beginning 30 days after June 12, 1989. Subsequent deposits of new principal in the same account will be subject to the fee. Subsequent reinvestment of existing deposits will not be subject to the fee.

The fee will apply only once to each sum deposited regardless of the length of time deposits are held and will not exceed income actually earned on the account.

The fee does not apply in the District Courts of Guam, Northern Mariana Islands, the Virgin Islands, the United States Claims Court, or other courts whose fees are not set under 28 U.S.C. § 1930.

Registry Fund Fees—Item 19
(55 F.R. 42867, October 24, 1990)

Effective December 1, 1990, the registry fee assessment provisions were revised and converted from a one-time charge equal to all income earned in the first 45 days of the investment to a charge of 10 percent of the income earned while funds are held in the court registry. Additionally, the fee was extended to any funds placed in the court's registry and invested regardless of the nature of the action underlying the deposit.

The new method will not be applied on investments in cases from which a fee has been exacted based on the prior method (interest earned in the first 45 days the funds were invested or the first 45 days following July 12, 1989). The new method will also not be applied in cases where the investment instrument has a maturity date greater than one year, but where a fee under the prior method applies but has not been deducted.

The fee does not apply in the District Courts of Guam, the Northern Mariana Islands, the Virgin Islands, the United States Claims Court, or any other federal court whose fees are not set under 28 U.S.C. §§ 1913, 1914, and 1930.

Registry Fund Fees—Item 19
(56 F.R. 56356, November 4, 1991)

Effective February 3, 1992, the registry fee assessment provisions are revised and converted from a charge equal to 10 percent of the income earned while funds are held in the court's registry to a variable rate based on the amount deposited with the court and, in certain cases, the length of time funds are held in the court's registry.

The revised fee will be a fee of 10 percent of the total income received during each income period from investments of less than $100,000,000 of registry funds in income-bearing accounts. On investments exceeding $100,000,000 the 10 percent fee shall be reduced by one percent for each increment of $50,000,000 over the initial $100,000,000. For those deposits where funds are placed in the registry by court order for a time certain, for example, by the terms of an adjudicated trust, the fee will be further reduced. This further reduction will amount to 2.5 percent for each five-year interval or part thereof. The total minimum fee to be charged will be no less than two percent of the income on investments.

The following table sets out the fee schedule promulgated by this notice:

REGISTRY—SCHEDULE OF FEES

[% of income earned]

Amount of deposit *	0–5 yrs.	>5–10 yrs.	>10–15 yrs.	>15 yrs.
less than 100M	10	7.5	5.0	2.5
100M–<150M	9	6.5	4.0	2.0
150M–<200M	8	5.5	3.0	2.0
200M–<250M	7	4.5	2.0	2.0
250M–<300M	6	3.5	2.0	2.0
300M–<350M	5	2.5	2.0	2.0
350M–<400M	4	2.0	2.0	2.0
400M–<450M	3	2.0	2.0	2.0
over 450M	2	2.0	2.0	2.0

* Except where otherwise authorized by the Director, each deposit into any account is treated separately in determining the fee.

The new fee applies to all earnings applied to investments on and after the effective date of this change, except for earnings on investments in cases being administered under the provisions of the May 11, 1989 notice [54 FR 20407], i.e., to which the fee equal to the first 45 days income is applicable.

The fee, as modified herein, will continue to apply to any case where the court has authorized the investment of funds placed in its custody or held by it in trust in its registry regardless of the nature of the underlying action.

The fee does not apply in the District Court of Guam, the Northern Mariana Islands, the Virgin Islands, the United States Claims Court, or any other Federal court whose fees are not set under 28 U.S.C. §§ 1913, 1914, and 1930.

HISTORICAL AND STATUTORY NOTES

References in Text

Chapter 7, 11, 12, or 13 of title 11, referred to in text, is 11 U.S.C.A. § 701 et seq., 11 U.S.C.A. § 1101 et seq., 11 U.S.C.A. § 1201 et seq., or 11 U.S.C.A. § 1301 et seq., respectively.

Chapter 7 of title 11, referred to in subsec. (f)(1), is 11 U.S.C.A. § 701 et seq.

Section 673(2) of the Omnibus Budget Reconciliation Act of 1981, referred to in subsec. (f)(1), is Pub.L. 97–35, Title VI, § 673(2), Aug. 13, 1981, as added Pub.L. 105–285, Title II, § 201, Oct. 27, 1998, 112 Stat. 2729, which is classified to 42 U.S.C.A. § 9902(2).

Codifications

Pub.L. 99–591 is a corrected version of Pub.L. 99–500.

Section 101(a) of Pub.L. 104–91, as amended by section 211 of Pub.L. 104–99, provided in part that section 111(a) of the General Provisions for the Department of Justice in Title I of the Departments of Commerce, Justice, and State, the Judiciary, and Related Agencies Appropriations Act, 1996 (H.R. 2076) as passed by the House of Representatives on Dec. 6, 1995, was enacted into permanent law. Such section 111(a) of H.R. 2076 amended subsec. (a)(6) of this section. See 1996 Amendments note set out under this section.

Effective and Applicability Provisions

2005 Acts. Except as otherwise provided, amendments by Pub.L. 109–8 effective 180 days after April 20, 2005, and inapplicable with respect to cases commenced under Title 11 before the effective date, see Pub.L. 109–8, § 1501, set out as a note under 11 U.S.C.A. § 101.

1999 Acts. Amendment by Pub.L. 106–113, [§ 113], effective 30 days after Nov. 29, 1999, see Pub.L. 106–113, [§ 113], set out as a note under section 589a of this title.

1993 Acts. Section 111(a) of Pub.L. 103–121 provided in part that amendment by section 111(a)(1) of Pub.L. 103–121, amending subsec. (a)(1) of this section, is effective 30 days after Oct. 27, 1993.

Section 111(b) of Pub.L. 103–121 provided in part that amendment by section 111(b)(1) of Pub.L. 103–121, amending subsec. (a)(3) of this section, is effective 30 days after Oct. 27, 1993.

1991 Acts. Amendment by Pub.L. 102–140 effective 60 days after the date of the enactment of Pub.L. 102–140, which was approved Oct. 28, 1991, see section 111(a) of Pub.L. 102–140, set out as a note under section 589a of this title.

1986 Acts. Amendment by Pub.L. 99–554 effective 30 days after Oct. 27, 1986, except as otherwise provided for, see section 302(a) of Pub.L. 99–554, set out as a note under section 581 of this title.

Amendment by Pub.L. 99–554, § 117(4), not to become effective in or with respect to certain specified judicial districts until, or apply to cases while pending in such district before, the expiration of the 270-day period beginning 30 days after Oct. 27, 1986, or of the 30-day period beginning on the date the Attorney General certifies under section 303 of Pub.L. 99–554 the region specified in a paragraph of section 581(a) of Title 28, as amended by section 111(a) of Pub.L. 99–554, that includes such district, whichever occurs first, see section 302(d)(1) of Pub.L. 99–554, set out as a note under section 581 of this title.

Amendment by Pub.L. 99–554, § 117(4), not to become effective in or with respect to certain specified judicial districts until, or apply to cases while pending in such district before, the expiration of the 2-year period beginning 30 days after Oct. 27, 1986, or of the 30-day period beginning on the date the Attorney General certifies under section 303 of Pub.L. 99–554 the region specified in a paragraph of section 581(a) of Title 28, as amended by section 111(a) of Pub.L. 99–554, that includes such district, whichever occurs first, see section 302(d)(2) of Pub.L. 99–554, set out as a note under section 581 of this title.

Amendment by Pub.L. 99–554, § 117(4), not to become effective in or with respect to judicial districts established for the States of Alabama and North Carolina until, or apply to cases while pending in such district before, such district elects to be included in a bankruptcy region established in section 581(a) of Title 28, as amended by section 111(a) of Pub.L. 99–554, or Oct. 1, 2002, whichever occurs first, and, except as otherwise provided for, with respect to cases under chapters 7, 11, 12, and 13 of Title 11 commenced before 30 days after Oct. 27, 1986, and pending in a judicial district in the States of Alabama or North Carolina before any election made under section 302(d)(3)(A) of Pub.L. 99–554 by such district becomes effective or Oct. 1, 2002, whichever occurs first, amendments by Pub.L. 99–554 not to apply until Oct. 1, 2003, or the expiration of the 1-year period beginning on the date such election becomes effective, whichever occurs first, and further, in any judicial district in Alabama or North Carolina not making the election described in section 302(d)(3)(A) of Pub.L. 99–554, any person appointed under regulations issued by the Judicial Conference to administer estates in cases under Title 11 authorized to establish, etc., a panel of private trustees, and to supervise cases and trustees in cases under chapters 7, 11, 12, and 13 of Title 11, until amendments by sections 201 to 231 of Pub.L. 99–554 effective in such district, see section 302(d)(3)(A) to (F), (H), (I) of Pub.L. 99–554, set out as a note under section 581 of this title.

Deposit in the general receipts of the Treasury of funds collected as a result of the amendments made by section 117 of Pub.L. 99–554 in a judicial district in the States of Alabama or North Carolina under section 1930(a) of Title 28 before the date the amendments made by sections 201 to 231 of Pub.L. 99–554 take effect in such districts, and notwithstanding section 589a of Title 28, see section 302(d)(3)(G) of Pub.L. 99–554, set out as a note under section 581 of this title.

Amendment by Pub.L. 99–554, § 117(4), except as otherwise provided, with respect to cases under chapters 7, 11, 12, and 13 of Title 11 commenced before 30 days after Oct. 27, 1986, and pending in a judicial district referred to in section 581(a) of Title 28, as amended by section 111(a) of Pub.L.

99–554, for which a United States trustee is not authorized before 30 days after Oct. 27, 1986 to be appointed, not applicable until the expiration of the 3-year period beginning on Oct. 27, 1986, or of the 1-year period beginning on the date the Attorney General certifies under section 303 of Pub.L. 99–554 the region specified in a paragraph of such section 581(a) that includes, such district, whichever occurs first, see section 302(e)(1), (2) of Pub.L. 99–554, set out as a note under section 581 of this title.

Rule of construction regarding fees for cases under Title 11 for any conduct or period occurring before section 1930(a)(6) of Title 28 becomes effective in the district in which such case is pending, see section 302(e)(3) of Pub.L. 99–554, set out as a note under section 581 of this title.

1984 Acts. Amendment by Pub.L. 98–353 effective July 10, 1984, see section 122(a) of Pub.L. 98–353, set out as a note under section 151 of this title.

1979 Acts. Section effective Oct. 1, 1979, see section 402(c) of Pub.L. 95–598, set out as a note preceding section 101 of Title 11, Bankruptcy.

Use of Increased Receipts

Pub.L. 109–8, Title III, § 325(e), Apr. 20, 2005, 119 Stat. 99, provided that:

"**(1) Judges' salaries and benefits.**—The amount of fees collected under paragraphs (1) and (3) of section 1930(a) of title 28, United States Code, during the 5-year period beginning on the date of enactment of this Act [Apr. 20, 2005], that is greater than the amount that would have been collected if the amendments made by subsection (a) had not taken effect shall be used, to the extent necessary, to pay the salaries and benefits of the judges appointed pursuant to section 1223 of this Act [amending 28 U.S.C.A. § 152 and enacting provisions set out as notes under 28 U.S.C.A. §§ 1 and 152].

"**(2) Remainder.**—Any amount described in paragraph (1), which is not used for the purpose described in paragraph (1), shall be deposited into the Treasury of the United States to the extent necessary to offset the decrease in governmental receipts resulting from the amendments made by subsections (b) and (c)."

Effective and Applicability Provisions of 1989 Amendments; Miscellaneous Fees

Section 406(a) of Pub.L. 101–162 provided in part that: "Pursuant to section 1930(b) of title 28 [subsec. (b) of this section] the Judicial Conference of the United States shall prescribe a fee of $60 on motions seeking relief from the automatic stay under 11 U.S.C. section 362(b) [section 362(b) of Title 11, Bankruptcy] and motions to compel abandonment of property of the estate. The fees established pursuant to the preceding two sentences shall take effect 30 days after the enactment of this Act [Nov. 21, 1989]."

Accrual and Payment of Quarterly Fees in Chapter 11 Cases After Jan. 27, 1996; Confirmation Status of Plans

Section 101(a) of Pub.L. 104–91, as amended Pub.L. 104–99, Title II, § 211, Jan. 26, 1996, 110 Stat. 37; Pub.L. 104–208, Div. A, Title I, § 101(a) [Title I, § 109(d)], Sept. 30, 1996, 110 Stat. 3009–19, provided, in part: "That, notwithstanding any other provision of law, the fees under 28 U.S.C. 1930(a)(6) [subsec. (a)(6) of this section] shall accrue and be payable from and after January 27, 1996, in all cases (including, without limitation, any cases pending as of that date), regardless of confirmation status of their plans."

Collection and Disposition of Fees in Bankruptcy Cases

Section 404(a) of Pub. L. 101–162 provided that: "For fiscal year 1990 and hereafter, such fees as shall be collected for the preparation and mailing of notices in bankruptcy cases as prescribed by the Judicial Conference of the United States pursuant to 28 U.S.C. 1930(b) [subsec. (b) of this section] shall be deposited to the 'Courts of Appeals, District Courts, and Other Judicial Services, Salaries and Expenses' appropriation to be used for salaries and other expenses incurred in providing these services."

Court Fees for Electronic Access to Information

Judicial Conference to prescribe reasonable fees for collection by courts under this section for access to information available through automatic data processing equipment and fees to be deposited in Judiciary Automation Fund, see section 303 of Pub.L. 102–140, set out as a note under section 1913 of this title.

Issuance of Notices to Creditors and Other Interested Parties

Section 403 of Pub.L. 101–162 provided that: "Notwithstanding any other provision of law, for fiscal year 1990 and hereafter, (a) The Administrative Office of the United States Courts, or any other agency or instrumentality of the United States, is prohibited from restricting solely to staff of the Clerks of the United States Bankruptcy Courts the issuance of notices to creditors and other interested parties. (b) The Administrative Office shall permit and encourage the preparation and mailing of such notices to be performed by or at the expense of the debtors, trustees or such other interested parties as the Court may direct and approve. (c) The Director of the Administrative Office of the United States Courts shall make appropriate provisions for the use of and accounting for any postage required pursuant to such directives."

Report on Bankruptcy Fees

Section 111(d) of Pub.L. 103–121 provided that:

"(1) **Report required.**—Not later than March 31, 1998, the Judicial Conference of the United States shall submit to the Committees on the Judiciary of the House of Representatives and the Senate, a report relating to the bankruptcy fee system and the impact of such system on various participants in bankruptcy cases.

"(2) **Contents of report.**—Such report shall include—

"(A)(i) an estimate of the costs and benefits that would result from waiving bankruptcy fees payable by debtors who are individuals, and

"(ii) recommendations regarding various revenue sources to offset the net cost of waiving such fees; and

"(B)(i) an evaluation of the effects that would result in cases under chapters 11 and 13 of title 11, United States Code [sections 1101 et seq. and 1301 et seq., respectively, of Title 11, Bankruptcy], from using a graduated bankruptcy fee system based on assets, liabilities, or both of the debtor, and

"(ii) recommendations regarding various methods to implement such a graduated bankruptcy fee system.

"(3) **Waiver of fees in selected districts.**—For purposes of carrying out paragraphs (1) and (2), the Judicial Conference of the United States shall carry out in not more than six judicial districts, throughout the 3–year period beginning on October 1, 1994, a program under which fees payable under section 1930 of title 28, United States Code [this section], may be waived in cases under chapter 7 of title 11, United States Code [section 701 et seq. of Title 11], for debtors who are individuals unable to pay such fees in installments.

"(4) **Study of graduated fee system.**—For purposes of carrying out paragraphs (1) and (2), the Judicial Conference of the United States shall carry out, in not fewer than six judicial districts, a study to estimate the results that would occur in cases under chapters 11 and 13 of title 11, United States Code [sections 1101 et seq. and 1301 et seq., respectively, of Title 11], if filing fees payable under section 1930 of title 28, United States Code [this section], were paid on a graduated scale based on assets, liabilities, or both of the debtor."

§ 1931. Disposition of filing fees

(a) Of the amounts paid to the clerk of court as a fee under section 1914(a) or as part of a judgment for costs under section 2412(a)(2) of this title, $190 shall be deposited into a special fund of the Treasury to be available to offset funds appropriated for the operation and maintenance of the courts of the United States.

(b) If the court authorizes a fee under section 1914(a) or an amount included in a judgment for costs under section 2412(a)(2) of this title of less than $250, the entire fee or amount, up to $190, shall be deposited into the special fund provided in this section.

(Added Pub.L. 99–500, Title I, § 101(b) [Title IV, § 407(c)], Oct. 18, 1986, 100 Stat. 1783–64, and Pub.L. 99–591, Title I, § 101(b) [Title IV, § 407(c)], Oct. 30, 1986, 100 Stat. 3341–64, and amended Pub.L. 101–162, Title IV, § 406(d), Nov. 21, 1989, 103 Stat. 1016; Pub.L. 102–572, Title III, § 301(b), Oct. 29, 1992, 106 Stat. 4511; Pub.L. 104–317, Title IV, § 401(b), Oct. 19, 1996, 110 Stat. 3853; Pub.L. 108–447, Div. B, Title III, § 307(b), Dec. 8, 2004, 118 Stat. 2895.)

HISTORICAL AND STATUTORY NOTES

Codifications

Pub.L. 99–591 is a corrected version of Pub.L. 99–500.

Effective and Applicability Provisions

2004 Acts. Amendments by Pub.L. 108–447, Div. B, § 307(b), shall take effect 60 days after December 8, 2004, see Pub.L. 108–447, Div. B, § 307(c), set out as a note under 28 U.S.C.A. § 1914.

1996 Acts. Amendment by section 401(b) of Pub.L. 104–317 effective 60 days after Oct. 19, 1996, see section 401(c) of Pub.L. 104–317, set out as a note under section 1914 of this title.

1992 Acts. Amendment by Pub.L. 102–572 effective Jan. 1, 1993, see section 1101(a) of Pub.L. 102–572, set out as a note under section 905 of Title 2, The Congress.

Disposition of Miscellaneous Fees

Pub.L. 106–518, Title I, § 102, Nov. 13, 2000, 114 Stat. 2411, provided that: "For fiscal year 2001 and each fiscal year thereafter, any portion of miscellaneous fees collected as prescribed by the Judicial Conference of the United States under sections 1913 [this section], 1914(b), 1926(a), 1930(b), and 1932 of title 28, United States Code, exceeding the amount of such fees in effect on September 30, 2000, shall be deposited into the special fund of the Treasury established under section 1931 of title 28, United States Code [this section]."

Collection and Deposit of Miscellaneous Bankruptcy Fees

Section 406(b) of Pub.L. 101–162, as amended Pub.L. 103–121, Title I, § 111(a)(3), (b)(4), Oct. 27, 1993, 107 Stat. 1164; Pub.L. 106–113, Div. B, § 1000(a)(1) [Title I, § 113], Nov. 29, 1999, 113 Stat. 1535, 1501A–20; Pub.L. 106–518, Title II, § 209(a), Nov. 13, 2000, 114 Stat. 2415; Pub.L. 109–8, Title III, § 325(c), Apr. 20, 2005, 119 Stat. 99, provided that: "All fees as shall be hereafter collected for any service not of a kind described in any of the items enumerated as items 1 through 7 and as items 9 through 18, as in effect on November 21, 1989, of the bankruptcy miscellaneous fee schedule prescribed by the Judicial Conference of the United States under section 1930(b) of title 28, United States Code [28 U.S.C.A. § 1930(b)], 31.25 of the fees collected under section 1930(a)(1)(A) of that title [28 U.S.C.A. § 1930(a)(1)(A)], 30.00 percent of the fees collected under section 1930(a)(1)(B) of that title [28 U.S.C.A. § 1930(a)(1)(B)], and 25 percent of the fees collected under section 1930(a)(3) of that title [28 U.S.C.A. § 1930(a)(3)] shall be deposited as offsetting receipts to the fund established under section 1931 of that title [this section] and shall remain available to the Judiciary until expended to reimburse any appropriation for the amount paid out of such appropriation for expenses of the Courts of Appeals, District Courts, and other Judicial Services and the Administrative Office of the United States Courts. The Judicial Conference shall report to the Committees on Appropriations of the House of Representatives and the Senate on a quarterly basis beginning on the first day of each fiscal year regarding the sums deposited in said fund."

[For termination, effective May 15, 2000, of provisions relating to a quarterly report to the Committees on Appropriations of the House of Representatives and the Senate in section 406(b) of Pub.L. 101–162, as amended, set out as a note above, see Pub.L. 104–66, § 3003, as amended, set out as a note under 31 U.S.C.A. § 1113 and page 12 of House Document No. 103–7.]

[Amendment of this note by Pub.L. 106–113, [§ 113], effective 30 days after Nov. 29, 1999, see Pub.L. 106–113, [§ 113], set out as a note under section 589a of this title.]

[Pub.L. 106–518, Title II, § 209(b), Nov. 13,, 2000, 114 Stat. 2415, provided that: "The amendment made by subsection (a) [amending this note] shall not apply with respect to fees collected before the date of enactment of this Act [Nov. 13, 2000]."

[Section 111(a) of Pub.L. 103–121 provided in part that amendment of this note by section 111(a)(3) of Pub.L. 103–121 is effective 30 days after Oct. 27, 1993.]

[Section 111(b) of Pub.L. 103–121 provided in part that amendment of this note by section 111(b)(4) of Pub.L. 103–121 is effective 30 days after Oct. 27, 1993.]

[Amendment of this note by Pub.L. 109–8, § 325(c), effective during 2–year period beginning on Apr. 20, 2005, see Pub.L. 109–8, § 325(d), set out as a note under 28 U.S.C.A. § 589a.]

Disposition of Fees

Section 404 of Pub.L. 104–317 provided that:

"**(a) Disposition of attorney admission fees.**—For each fee collected for admission of an attorney to practice, as prescribed by the Judicial Conference of the United States pursuant to section 1914 of title 28, United States Code [section 1914 of this title], $30 of that portion of the fee exceeding $20 shall be deposited into the special fund of the Treasury established under section 1931 of title 28, United States Code [this section]. Any portion exceeding $5 of the fee for a duplicate certificate of admission or certificate of good standing, as prescribed by the Judicial Conference of the United States pursuant to section 1914 of title 28, United States Code [section 1914 of this title], shall be deposited into the special fund of the Treasury established under section 1931 of title 28, United States Code [this section].

"**(b) Disposition of bankruptcy complaint filing fees.**— For each fee collected for filing an adversary complaint in a bankruptcy proceeding, as established in Item 6 of the Bankruptcy Court Miscellaneous Fee Schedule prescribed by the Judicial Conference of the United States [set out under section 1930 of this title] pursuant to section 1930(b) of title 28, United States Code [section 1930(b) of this title], the portion of the fee exceeding $120 shall be deposited into the special fund of the Treasury established under section 1931 of title 28, United States Code [this section].

"**(c) Effective date.**—This section shall take effect 60 days after the date of the enactment of this Act [Oct. 19, 1996]."

§ 1932.[1] Judicial Panel on Multidistrict Litigation

The Judicial Conference of the United States shall prescribe from time to time the fees and costs to be charged and collected by the Judicial Panel on Multidistrict Litigation.

(Added Pub.L. 104–317, Title IV, § 403(a)(1), Oct. 19, 1996, 110 Stat. 3854.)

1 Another section 1932 is set out post.

JUDICIAL CONFERENCE SCHEDULE OF FEES

Judicial Panel on Multidistrict Litigation Fee Schedule

[The Judicial Conference of the United States issued pursuant to this section the schedule of the fees to be charged and collected by the Judicial Panel on Multidistrict Litigation effective October 1, 1999. The Judicial Conference at its March 2001 meeting adopted amendments to its fee schedule to be effective July 1, 2001. The Judicial Conference adopted amendments to its fee schedule effective January 1, 2002; and effective November 1, 2003. The Judicial Conference at its March 16, 2004 meeting adopted amendments to its fee schedule to be effective June 1, 2004.]

Following are fees to be charged for services provided by the Judicial Panel on Multidistrict Litigation. No fees are to be charged for services rendered on behalf of the United

States, with the exception of those specifically prescribed in items 1 and 3. No fees under this schedule shall be charged to federal agencies or programs which are funded from judiciary appropriations, including, but not limited to, agencies, organizations, and individuals providing services authorized by the Criminal Justice Act, 18 U.S.C. § 3006A.

(1) For every search of the records of the court conducted by the clerk of the court or a deputy clerk, $26 per name or item searched. This fee shall apply to services rendered on behalf of the United States if the information requested is available through electronic access.

(2) For certification of any document or paper, whether the certification is made directly on the document or by separate instrument, $9.

(3) For reproducing any record or paper, $.50 per page. This fee shall apply to paper copies made from either: (1) original documents; or (2) microfiche or microfilm reproductions of the original records. This fee shall apply to services rendered on behalf of the United States if the record or paper requested is available through electronic access.

(4) For retrieval of a record from a Federal Records Center, National Archives, or other storage location removed from the place of business of the court, $45.

(5) For a check paid into the Panel which is returned for lack of funds, $45.

ELECTRONIC PUBLIC ACCESS
FEE SCHEDULE (eff. 1/1/05)

As directed by Congress, the Judicial Conference has determined that the following fees are necessary to reimburse expenses incurred by the judiciary in providing electronic public access to court records. These fees shall apply to the United States unless otherwise stated. No fees under this schedule shall be charged to federal agencies or programs which are funded from judiciary appropriations, including, but not limited to, agencies, organizations, and individuals providing services authorized by the Criminal Justice Act, 18 U.S.C. § 3006A, and bankruptcy administrator programs.

I. For electronic access to court data via dial up service: sixty cents per minute. For electronic access to court data via a federal judiciary Internet site: eight cents per page, with the total for any document, docket sheet, or case-specific report not to exceed the fee for thirty pages- provided however that transcripts of federal court proceedings shall not be subject to the thirty-page fee limit. Attorneys of record and parties in a case (including *pro se* litigants) receive one free electronic copy of all documents filed electronically, if receipt is required by law or directed by the filer. No fee is owed under this provision until an account holder accrues charges of more than $10 in a calendar year. Consistent with Judicial Conference policy, courts may, upon a showing of cause, exempt indigents, bankruptcy case trustees, individual researchers associated with educational institutions, courts, section 501(c)(3) not-for-profit organizations and pro bono ADR neutrals from payment of these fees. Courts must find that parties from the classes of persons or entities listed above seeking exemption have demonstrated that an exemption is necessary in order to avoid unreasonable burdens and to promote public access to information. Any user granted an exemption agrees not to sell for profit the data obtained as a result. Exemptions may be granted

for a definite period of time and may be revoked at the discretion of the court granting the exemption.

II. For printing copies of any record or document accessed electronically at a public terminal in the courthouse: ten cents per page. This fee shall apply to services rendered on behalf of the United States if the record requested is remotely available through electronic access.

III. For every search of court records conducted by the PACER Service Center, $20.

JUDICIAL CONFERENCE POLICY NOTES

Courts should not exempt local, state or federal government agencies, members of the media, attorneys or others not members of one of the groups listed above. Exemptions should be granted as the exception, not the rule. A court may not use this exemption language to exempt all users. An exemption applies only to access related to the case or purpose for which it was given.

The electronic public access fee applies to electronic court data viewed remotely from the public records of individual cases in the court, including filed documents and the docket sheet. Electronic court data may be viewed free at public terminals at the courthouse and courts may provide other local court information at no cost. Examples of information that can be provided at no cost include: local rules, court forms, news items, court calendars, opinions, and other information—such as court hours, court location, telephone listings—determined locally to benefit the public and the court.

§ 1932.[1]   Revocation of earned release credit

In any civil action brought by an adult convicted of a crime and confined in a Federal correctional facility, the court may order the revocation of such earned good time credit under section 3624(b) of title 18, United States Code, that has not yet vested, if, on its own motion or the motion of any party, the court finds that—

(1) the claim was filed for a malicious purpose;

(2) the claim was filed solely to harass the party against which it was filed; or

(3) the claimant testifies falsely or otherwise knowingly presents false evidence or information to the court.

(Added Pub.L. 104–134, Title I, § 101[(a)][Title VIII, § 809(a)], Apr. 26, 1996, 110 Stat. 1321–76; renumbered Title I Pub.L. 104–140, § 1(a), May 2, 1996, 110 Stat. 1327.)

1 Another section 1932 is set out ante.

HISTORICAL AND STATUTORY NOTES
Severability of Provisions

If any provision of section 101[a] [Title VIII] of Pub.L. 104–134, an amendment made by such Title, or the application of such provision or amendment to any person or circumstance is held to be unconstitutional, the remainder of such Title, the amendments made by such Title, and the application of the provisions of such Title to any person or circumstance not affected thereby, see section 101[a] [Title VIII, § 810] of Pub.L. 104–134, set out as a note under section 3626 of Title 18, Crimes and Criminal Procedure.

CHAPTER 125—PENDING ACTIONS AND JUDGMENTS

§ 1961. Interest

(a) Interest shall be allowed on any money judgment in a civil case recovered in a district court. Execution therefor may be levied by the marshal, in any case where, by the law of the State in which such court is held, execution may be levied for interest on judgments recovered in the courts of the State. Such interest shall be calculated from the date of the entry of the judgment, at a rate equal to the weekly average 1–year constant maturity Treasury yield, as published by the Board of Governors of the Federal Reserve System, for the calendar week preceding.[1] the date of the judgment. The Director of the Administrative Office of the United States Courts shall distribute notice of that rate and any changes in it to all Federal judges.

(b) Interest shall be computed daily to the date of payment except as provided in section 2516(b) of this title and section 1304(b) of title 31, and shall be compounded annually.

(c)(1) This section shall not apply in any judgment of any court with respect to any internal revenue tax case. Interest shall be allowed in such cases at the underpayment rate or overpayment rate (whichever is appropriate) established under section 6621 of the Internal Revenue Code of 1986.

(2) Except as otherwise provided in paragraph (1) of this subsection, interest shall be allowed on all final judgments against the United States in the United States Court of Appeals for the Federal circuit,[2] at the rate provided in subsection (a) and as provided in subsection (b).

(3) Interest shall be allowed, computed, and paid on judgments of the United States Court of Federal Claims only as provided in paragraph (1) of this subsection or in any other provision of law.

(4) This section shall not be construed to affect the interest on any judgment of any court not specified in this section.

(June 25, 1948, c. 646, 62 Stat. 957; Apr. 2, 1982, Pub.L. 97–164, Title III, § 302(a), 96 Stat. 55; Sept. 13, 1982, Pub.L. 97–258, § 2(m)(1), 96 Stat. 1062; Jan. 12, 1983, Pub.L. 97–452, § 2(d)(1), 96 Stat. 2478; Oct. 22, 1986, Pub.L. 99–514, § 2, Title XV, § 1511(c)(17), 100 Stat. 2095, 2745; Oct. 29, 1992, Pub.L. 102–572, Title IX, § 902(b)(1), 106 Stat. 4516; Dec. 21, 2000, Pub.L. 106–554, § 1(a)(7) [Title III, § 307(d)(1)], 114 Stat. 2763, 2763A–636.)

[1] So in original. The period probably should not appear.
[2] So in original. Probably should be "Circuit,".

HISTORICAL AND STATUTORY NOTES

References in Text

Section 6621 of the Internal Revenue Code of 1986, referred to in subsec. (c)(1), is section 6621 of Title 26, Internal Revenue Code.

Codifications

Amendment of subsec. (b) by Pub.L. 97–452, substituting "section 1304(b) of title 31" for "section 1302 of the Act of July 27, 1956 (31 U.S.C. 724a)" was executed without reference to the intervening amendment by Pub.L. 97–258, as the probable intent of Congress.

Effective and Applicability Provisions

1992 Acts. Amendment by Pub.L. 102–572 effective Oct. 29, 1992, see section 911 of Pub.L. 102–572, set out as a note under section 171 of this title.

1986 Acts. Amendment by section 1511(c)(17) of Pub.L. 99–514 applicable for purposes of determining interest for periods after Dec. 31, 1986, see section 1511(d) of Pub.L. 99–514, set out as a note under section 47 of Title 26, Internal Revenue Code.

1982 Acts. Section 2(m) of Pub.L. 97–258 provided in part that the amendment to subsec. (b) would be effective on Oct. 1, 1982.

Amendment by Pub.L. 97–164 effective Oct. 1, 1982, see section 402 of Pub.L. 97–164, set out as a note under section 171 of this title.

Calculation of Interest

The method of calculation of interest on money judgments in civil cases recovered in district courts changed as of December 21, 2000, the date of enactment of Pub.L. 106–554, § 1(a)(7) [Title III, § 307(d)(1)] which amended subsec. (a) of this section. It was formerly calculated at a rate equal to the coupon issue yield equivalent (as determined by the Secretary of the Treasury) of the average accepted auction price for the last auction of fifty-two week United States Treasury bills (for past rates, see Table set out below). It is now calculated at a rate equal to the weekly average 1-year constant maturity Treasury yield, as published by the Board of Governors of the Federal Reserve System. For information regarding weekly releases, see *www.federalreserve.gov*.

52–WEEK T–BILL RATE TABLE OF CHANGES

Date of Auction	Equivalent Coupon Issue Yield
12/11/74	7.07%
01/08/75	6.80%
02/05/75	5.61%
03/05/75	5.99%
04/02/75	6.92%
04/30/75	6.84%
05/28/75	6.17%
06/24/75	6.72%
07/24/75	7.27%
08/20/75	7.89%

Date of Auction	Equivalent Coupon Issue Yield	Date of Auction	Equivalent Coupon Issue Yield
09/17/75	7.90%	06/18/80	8.08%
10/18/75	7.07%	07/16/80	8.25%
11/13/75	6.40%	08/13/80	9.75%
12/10/75	6.88%	09/10/80	10.93%
01/07/76	5.92%	10/08/80	13.33%
02/04/76	5.92%	10/30/80	13.67%
03/03/76	6.29%	11/26/80	14.97%
03/31/76	6.13%	12/23/80	13.49%
04/29/76	5.98%	01/22/81	14.68%
05/26/76	6.72%	02/19/81	14.39%
06/23/76	6.47%	03/19/81	12.76%
07/21/76	6.25%	04/16/81	14.63%
08/19/76	5.97%	05/14/81	16.70%
09/15/76	5.89%	06/11/81	14.82%
10/13/76	5.41%	07/09/81	15.57%
11/09/76	5.49%	08/07/81	16.60%
12/08/76	4.95%	09/03/81	17.26%
01/05/77	4.97%	10/01/81	16.55%
02/02/77	5.65%	10/29/81	14.84%
03/02/77	5.52%	11/25/81	11.58%
03/30/77	5.44%	12/23/81	14.02%
04/27/77	5.45%	01/21/82	14.92%
05/25/77	5.71%	02/18/82	14.87%
06/22/77	5.72%	03/18/82	14.03%
07/20/77	5.98%	04/15/82	14.30%
08/17/77	6.49%	05/13/82	13.64%
09/14/77	6.55%	06/10/82	13.61%
10/12/77	7.07%	07/08/82	13.79%
11/09/77	6.98%	08/05/82	12.41%
12/07/77	6.99%	09/02/82	11.32%
01/04/78	6.99%	09/30/82	10.41%
02/01/78	7.29%	10/28/82	9.29%
03/01/78	7.34%	11/24/82	9.07%
03/29/78	7.36%	12/23/82	8.75%
04/26/78	7.58%	01/20/83	8.65%
05/24/78	7.97%	02/17/83	8.99%
06/21/78	8.27%	03/17/83	9.16%
07/19/78	8.43%	04/14/83	8.98%
08/16/78	8.50%	05/12/83	8.72%
09/13/78	8.59%	06/09/83	9.59%
10/12/78	8.90%	07/07/83	10.25%
11/08/78	10.17%	08/09/83	10.74%
12/06/78	10.17%	09/01/83	10.58%
01/03/79	10.51%	09/29/83	9.98%
01/31/79	10.21%	11/01/83	9.86%
02/28/79	10.40%	11/23/83	9.93%
04/04/79	10.09%	12/22/83	10.10%
04/25/79	10.10%	01/19/84	9.87%
05/23/79	10.01%	02/16/84	10.11%
06/20/79	9.63%	03/15/84	10.60%
07/18/79	9.70%	04/12/84	10.81%
08/15/79	10.05%	05/15/84	11.74%
09/12/79	10.88%	06/07/84	12.08%
10/10/79	12.83%	07/10/84	12.17%
11/07/79	13.18%	08/02/84	11.93%
12/05/79	11.98%	08/30/84	11.98%
01/02/80	12.25%	09/27/84	11.36%
01/30/80	12.45%	10/25/84	10.33%
02/27/80	15.28%	11/27/84	9.50%
03/26/80	16.46%	12/20/84	9.08%
04/23/80	11.45%	01/17/85	9.09%
05/21/80	9.02%	02/14/85	9.17%

Date of Auction	Equivalent Coupon Issue Yield	Date of Auction	Equivalent Coupon Issue Yield
03/14/85	10.08%	12/14/89	7.66%
04/11/85	9.15%	01/11/90	7.74%
05/14/85	8.57%	02/13/90	7.97%
06/06/85	7.70%	03/08/90	8.36%
07/09/85	7.60%	04/05/90	8.32%
08/01/85	8.18%	05/03/90	8.70%
08/29/85	7.91%	05/31/90	8.24%
09/26/85	7.87%	06/28/90	8.09%
10/24/85	8.08%	07/26/90	7.88%
11/26/85	7.87%	08/23/90	7.95%
12/19/85	7.57%	09/20/90	7.78%
01/16/86	7.85%	10/26/90	7.51%
02/13/86	7.71%	11/15/90	7.28%
03/13/86	7.06%	12/13/90	7.02%
04/10/86	6.31%	01/10/91	6.62%
05/13/86	6.56%	02/12/91	6.21%
06/05/86	7.03%	03/07/91	6.46%
07/08/86	6.35%	04/04/91	6.26%
07/31/86	6.18%	05/02/91	6.07%
08/28/86	5.63%	05/30/91	6.09%
09/25/86	5.79%	06/27/91	6.39%
10/23/86	5.75%	07/25/91	6.26%
11/20/86	5.77%	08/22/91	5.68%
12/23/86	5.93%	09/19/91	5.57%
01/15/87	5.75%	10/17/91	5.42%
02/12/87	6.09%	11/14/91	4.98%
03/12/87	6.04%	12/12/91	4.41%
04/09/87	6.30%	01/09/92	4.02%
05/12/87	7.02%	02/06/92	4.21%
06/04/87	7.00%	03/05/92	4.58%
07/02/87	6.64%	04/02/92	4.55%
08/04/87	6.98%	04/30/92	4.40%
09/01/87	7.22%	05/28/92	4.26%
09/30/87	7.88%	06/25/92	4.11%
10/22/87	6.90%	07/23/92	3.51%
11/19/87	6.93%	08/20/92	3.41%
12/17/87	7.22%	09/17/92	3.13%
01/14/88	7.14%	10/15/92	3.24%
02/11/88	6.59%	11/17/92	3.76%
03/10/88	6.71%	12/10/92	3.72%
04/07/88	7.01%	01/07/93	3.67%
05/05/88	7.20%	02/04/93	3.45%
06/02/88	7.59%	03/04/93	3.21%
06/30/88	7.54%	04/06/93	3.37%
07/28/88	7.95%	04/30/93	3.25%
08/25/88	8.32%	05/27/93	3.54%
09/22/88	8.04%	06/24/93	3.54%
10/20/88	8.15%	07/22/93	3.58%
11/17/88	8.55%	08/19/93	3.43%
12/15/88	9.20%	09/16/93	3.40%
01/12/89	9.16%	10/14/93	3.38%
02/15/89	9.32%	11/16/93	3.57%
03/09/89	9.43%	12/09/93	3.61%
04/06/89	9.31%	01/06/94	3.67%
05/04/89	9.15%	02/03/94	3.74%
06/01/89	8.85%	03/03/94	4.22%
06/29/89	8.16%	03/31/94	4.51%
07/27/89	7.75%	04/28/94	5.02%
08/24/89	8.27%	5/26/94	5.28%
09/21/89	8.19%	6/23/94	5.31%
10/19/89	7.90%	7/21/94	5.49%
11/16/89	7.69%	8/18/94	5.67%

Date of Auction	Equivalent Coupon Issue Yield	Date of Auction	Equivalent Coupon Issue Yield
9/15/94	5.69%	6/22/99	5.163%
10/13/94	6.06%	7/20/99	4.966%
11/10/94	6.482%	8/17/99	5.224%
12/08/94	7.22%	9/14/99	5.285%
1/5/95	7.34%	10/13/99	5.411%
2/2/95	7.03%	11/9/99	5.471%
3/2/95	6.57%	12/7/99	5.670%
3/30/95	6.41%	1/4/00	5.997%
4/27/95	6.28%	2/1/00	6.287%
5/25/95	5.88%	2/29/00	6.197%
6/22/95	5.53%	5/31/00	6.375%
7/20/95	5.70%	8/29/00	6.241%
8/17/95	5.89%	11/28/00	6.052%
9/14/95	5.52%		
10/12/95	5.62%		
11/15/95	5.45%		
12/7/95	5.35%		
1/4/96	5.16%		
2/1/96	4.89%		
2/29/96	5.25%		
4/2/96	5.46%		
4/25/96	5.60%		
5/23/96	5.62%		
6/20/96	5.89%		
7/18/96	5.81%		
8/15/96	5.67%		
9/12/96	5.90%		
10/10/96	5.64%		
11/7/96	5.49%		
12/5/96	5.45%		
1/2/97	5.61%		
1/30/97	5.64%		
2/27/97	5.67%		
3/26/97	6.00%		
4/24/97	6.06%		
5/22/97	5.88%		
6/19/97	5.65%		
7/17/97	5.56%		
8/14/97	5.58%		
9/11/97	5.60%		
10/9/97	5.49%		
11/6/97	5.42%		
12/4/97	5.468%		
1/6/98	5.341%		
1/29/98	5.232%		
2/26/98	5.407%		
3/26/98	5.391%		
4/23/98	5.407%		
5/21/98	5.434%		
6/18/98	5.413%		
7/16/98	5.375%		
8/18/98	5.271%		
9/15/98	4.730%		
10/13/98	4.242%		
11/9/98	4.616%		
12/8/98	4.513%		
1/5/99	4.545%		
2/2/99	4.584%		
3/2/99	4.918%		
3/30/99	4.732%		
4/27/99	4.727%		
5/25/99	4.879%		

§ 1962.   Lien

Every judgment rendered by a district court within a State shall be a lien on the property located in such State in the same manner, to the same extent and under the same conditions as a judgment of a court of general jurisdiction in such State, and shall cease to be a lien in the same manner and time. This section does not apply to judgments entered in favor of the United States. Whenever the law of any State requires a judgment of a State court to be registered, recorded, docketed or indexed, or any other act to be done, in a particular manner, or in a certain office or county or parish before such lien attaches, such requirements shall apply only if the law of such State authorizes the judgment of a court of the United States to be registered, recorded, docketed, indexed or otherwise conformed to rules and requirements relating to judgments of the courts of the State. (June 25, 1948, c. 646, 62 Stat. 958; Nov. 29, 1990, Pub.L. 101–647, Title XXXVI, § 3627, 104 Stat. 4965.)

HISTORICAL AND STATUTORY NOTES

Effective and Applicability Provisions

1990 Acts. Amendment by section 3627 of Pub.L. 101–647 effective 180 days after Nov. 29, 1990, see section 3631 of Pub.L. 101–647, set out as a note under section 3001 of this title.

§ 1963.   Registration of judgments for enforcement in other districts

A judgment in an action for the recovery of money or property entered in any court of appeals, district court, bankruptcy court, or in the Court of International Trade may be registered by filing a certified copy of the judgment in any other district or, with respect to the Court of International Trade, in any judicial district, when the judgment has become final by appeal or expiration of the time for appeal or when ordered by the court that entered the judgment for good cause shown. Such a judgment entered in favor of the United States may be so registered any time after judgment is entered. A judgment so registered shall have the same effect as a judgment of the district court of the district where registered and may be enforced in like manner.

A certified copy of the satisfaction of any judgment in whole or in part may be registered in like manner in any district in which the judgment is a lien.

The procedure prescribed under this section is in addition to other procedures provided by law for the enforcement of judgments.

(June 25, 1948, c. 646, 62 Stat. 958; Aug. 23, 1954, c. 837, 68 Stat. 772; July 7, 1958, Pub.L. 85–508, § 12(*o*), 72 Stat. 349; Nov. 19, 1988, Pub.L. 100–702, Title X, § 1002(a), (b)(1), 102 Stat. 4664; Nov. 29, 1990, Pub.L. 101–647, Title XXXVI, § 3628, 104 Stat. 4965; Oct. 19, 1996, Pub.L. 104–317, Title II, § 203(a), 110 Stat. 3849.)

HISTORICAL AND STATUTORY NOTES
Effective and Applicability Provisions

1990 Acts. Amendment by section 3628 of Pub.L. 101–647 effective 180 days after Nov. 29, 1990, see section 3631 of Pub.L. 101–647, set out as a note under section 3001 of this title.

1988 Acts. Section 1002(c) of Title X of Pub.L. 100–702 provided that: "The amendments made by this section [amending this section and repealing section 1963A of this title] take effect 90 days after the date of enactment of this title [Nov. 19, 1988]."

1958 Acts. Amendment by Pub.L. 85–508 as effective Jan. 3, 1959, upon admission of Alaska into the Union pursuant to Proc. No. 3269, Jan. 3, 1959, 24 F.R. 81, as required by sections 1 and 8(c) of Pub.L. 85–508, see notes set out under section 81A of this title and preceding section 21 of Title 48, Territories and Insular Possessions.

[§ 1963A.   Repealed.   Pub.L. 100–702, Title X, § 1002(b)(2), Nov. 19, 1988, 102 Stat. 4664]

HISTORICAL AND STATUTORY NOTES

Section, added Pub.L. 96–417, Title V, § 511(a), Oct. 10, 1980, 94 Stat. 1743, provided for registration of judgments of the Court of International Trade. See section 1963 of this title.

Effective Date of Repeal

Section repealed 90 days after Nov. 19, 1988, see section 1002(c) of Pub.L. 100–702, set out as a note under section 1963 of this title.

§ 1964.   Constructive notice of pending actions

Where the law of a State requires a notice of an action concerning real property pending in a court of the State to be registered, recorded, docketed, or indexed in a particular manner, or in a certain office or county or parish in order to give constructive notice of the action as it relates to the real property, and such law authorizes a notice of an action concerning real property pending in a United States district court to be registered, recorded, docketed, or indexed in the same manner, or in the same place, those requirements of the State law must be complied with in order to give constructive notice of such an action pending in a United States district court as it relates to real property in such State.

(Added Pub.L. 85–689, § 1(a), Aug. 20, 1958, 72 Stat. 683.)

HISTORICAL AND STATUTORY NOTES
Effective and Applicability Provisions

1958 Acts. Section 2 of Pub.L. 85–689 provided that: "The amendments made by this Act [adding this section] shall only be effective with respect to actions commenced in United States district courts more than one hundred and eighty days after the date of enactment of this Act [Aug. 20, 1958]."

CHAPTER 127—EXECUTIONS AND JUDICIAL SALES

§ 2001.   Sale of realty generally

(a) Any realty or interest therein sold under any order or decree of any court of the United States shall be sold as a whole or in separate parcels at public sale at the courthouse of the county, parish, or city in which the greater part of the property is located, or upon the premises or some parcel thereof located therein, as the court directs. Such sale shall be upon such terms and conditions as the court directs.

Property in the possession of a receiver or receivers appointed by one or more district courts shall be sold at public sale in the district wherein any such receiver was first appointed, at the courthouse of the county, parish, or city situated therein in which the greater part of the property in such district is located, or on the premises or some parcel thereof located in such county, parish, or city, as such court directs, unless the court orders the sale of the property or one or more parcels thereof in one or more ancillary districts.

(b) After a hearing, of which notice to all interested parties shall be given by publication or otherwise as the court directs, the court may order the sale of such realty or interest or any part thereof at private sale for cash or other consideration and upon such terms and conditions as the court approves, if it finds that the best interests of the estate will be conserved thereby. Before confirmation of any private sale, the court shall appoint three disinterested persons to appraise such property or different groups of three appraisers each to appraise properties of different classes or situated in different localities. No private sale shall be confirmed at a price less than two-thirds of the appraised value. Before confirmation of any private sale, the terms thereof shall be published in such newspaper or newspapers of general circulation as the court directs at least ten days before confirmation. The private sale shall not be confirmed if a bona fide offer is made, under conditions prescribed by the court, which guarantees at least a 10 per centum increase over the price offered in the private sale.

(c) This section shall not apply to sales and proceedings under Title 11 or by receivers or conservators of banks appointed by the Comptroller of the Currency.

(June 25, 1948, c. 646, 62 Stat. 958; May 24, 1949, c. 139, § 99, 63 Stat. 104.)

§ 2002.   Notice of sale of realty

A public sale of realty or interest therein under any order, judgment or decree of any court of the United States shall not be made without notice published once a week for at least four weeks prior to the sale in at least one newspaper regularly issued and of general circulation in the county, state, or judicial district of the United States wherein the realty is situated.

If such realty is situated in more than one county, state, district or circuit, such notice shall be published in one or more of the counties, states, or districts wherein it is situated, as the court directs. The notice shall be substantially in such form and contain such description of the property by reference or otherwise as the court approves. The court may direct that the publication be made in other newspapers.

This section shall not apply to sales and proceedings under Title 11 or by receivers or conservators of banks appointed by the Comptroller of the Currency.

(June 25, 1948, c. 646, 62 Stat. 959; May 24, 1949, c. 139, § 100, 63 Stat. 104.)

§ 2003.   Marshal's incapacity after levy on or sale of realty

Whenever a United States marshal dies, is removed from office, or the term of his commission expires, after levying on realty or any interest therein under a writ of execution issued by a court of the United States, and before sale or other final disposition thereof, like process shall issue to the succeeding marshal and the same proceedings shall be had as if such contingency had not occurred.

Whenever any such contingency arises after a marshal has sold any realty or interest therein and before a deed is executed, the court may, on application by the purchaser, or the plaintiff in whose action the sale was made, setting forth the facts of the case and the reason why the title was not perfected by such marshal, order the succeeding marshal to perfect the title and execute a deed to the purchaser, upon payment of the purchase money and unpaid costs.

(June 25, 1948, c. 646, 62 Stat. 959; May 24, 1949, c. 139, § 101, 63 Stat. 104.)

§ 2004.   Sale of personalty generally

Any personalty sold under any order or decree of any court of the United States shall be sold in accordance with section 2001 of this title, unless the court orders otherwise.

This section shall not apply to sales and proceedings under Title 11 or by receivers or conservators of banks appointed by the Comptroller of the Currency.

(June 25, 1948, c. 646, 62 Stat. 959.)

§ 2005.   Appraisal of goods taken on execution

Whenever State law requires that goods taken on execution be appraised before sale, goods taken under execution issued from a court of the United States shall be appraised in like manner.

The United States marshal shall summon the appraisers in the same manner as the sheriff is required to summon appraisers under State law.

If the appraisers fail to attend and perform their required duties, the marshal may sell the goods without an appraisal. Appraisers attending and performing their duties, shall receive the fees allowed for appraisals under State law.

(June 25, 1948, c. 646, 62 Stat. 959.)

§ 2006.   Execution against revenue officer

Execution shall not issue against a collector or other revenue officer on a final judgment in any proceeding against him for any of his acts, or for the recovery of any money exacted by or paid to him and subsequently paid into the Treasury, in performing his official duties, if the court certifies that:

    (1) probable cause existed; or

    (2) the officer acted under the directions of the Secretary of the Treasury, the Director, Bureau of Alcohol, Tobacco, Firearms, and Explosives, Department of Justice, or other proper Government officer.

When such certificate has been issued, the amount of the judgment shall be paid out of the proper appropriation by the Treasury.

(June 25, 1948, c. 646, 62 Stat. 960; Nov. 25, 2002, Pub.L. 107–296, Title XI, § 1112(l), 116 Stat. 2277.)

HISTORICAL AND STATUTORY NOTES

Effective and Applicability Provisions

2002 Acts. Amendment to this section by Pub.L. 107–296 effective 60 days after Nov. 25, 2002, see Pub.L. 107–296, § 4, set out as a note under 6 U.S.C.A. § 101.

§ 2007. Imprisonment for debt

(a) A person shall not be imprisoned for debt on a writ of execution or other process issued from a court of the United States in any State wherein imprisonment for debt has been abolished. All modifications, conditions, and restrictions upon such imprisonment provided by State law shall apply to any writ of execution or process issued from a court of the United States in accordance with the procedure applicable in such State.

(b) Any person arrested or imprisoned in any State on a writ of execution or other process issued from any court of the United States in a civil action shall have the same jail privileges and be governed by the same regulations as persons confined in like cases on process issued from the courts of such State. The same requirements governing discharge as are applicable in such State shall apply. Any proceedings for discharge shall be conducted before a United States magistrate judge for the judicial district wherein the defendant is held.

(June 25, 1948, c. 646, 62 Stat. 960; Oct. 17, 1968, Pub.L. 90–578, Title IV, § 402(b)(2), 82 Stat. 1118; Dec. 1, 1990, Pub.L. 101–650, Title III, § 321, 104 Stat. 5117.)

HISTORICAL AND STATUTORY NOTES

Change of Name

"United States magistrate judge" substituted for "United States magistrate" in text pursuant to section 321 of Pub.L. 101–650, set out as a note under 28 U.S.C.A. § 631. Previously, United States commissioners, referred to in text, were replaced by United States magistrates pursuant to Pub.L. 90–578, Oct. 17, 1968, 82 Stat. 1118. See chapter 43 of Title 28, 28 U.S.C.A. § 631 et seq.

CHAPTER 129—MONEYS PAID INTO COURT

§ 2041. Deposit of moneys in pending or adjudicated cases

All moneys paid into any court of the United States, or received by the officers thereof, in any case pending or adjudicated in such court, shall be forthwith deposited with the Treasurer of the United States or a designated depositary, in the name and to the credit of such court.

This section shall not prevent the delivery of any such money to the rightful owners upon security, according to agreement of parties, under the direction of the court.

(June 25, 1948, c. 646, 62 Stat. 960; Sept. 13, 1982, Pub.L. 97–258, § 2(g)(4)(C), 96 Stat. 1061.)

HISTORICAL AND STATUTORY NOTES

Registry Administration Account

Pub.L. 100–459, Title IV, Oct. 1, 1988, 102 Stat. 2211, provided in part: "That any funds hereafter collected by the Judiciary as a charge for services rendered in administering accounts kept in a court's registry shall be deposited into a separate account entitled 'Registry Administration Account' in the Treasury of the United States. Such funds shall remain available to the Judiciary until expended to reimburse any appropriation for the amount paid out of such appropriation for expenses of the Courts of Appeals, District Courts and Other Judicial Services and the Administrative Office of the United States Courts."

§ 2042. Withdrawal

No money deposited under section 2041 of this title shall be withdrawn except by order of court.

In every case in which the right to withdraw money deposited in court under section 2041 has been adjudicated or is not in dispute and such money has remained so deposited for at least five years unclaimed by the person entitled thereto, such court shall cause such money to be deposited in the Treasury in the name and to the credit of the United States. Any claimant entitled to any such money may, on petition to the court and upon notice to the United States attorney and full proof of the right thereto, obtain an order directing payment to him.

(June 25, 1948, c. 646, 62 Stat. 960; Sept. 13, 1982, Pub.L. 97–258, § 2(g)(4)(D), 96 Stat. 1061.)

§ 2043. Deposit of other moneys

Except for public moneys deposited under section 2041 of this title, each clerk of the United States courts shall deposit public moneys that the clerk collects into a checking account in the Treasury, subject to disbursement by the clerk. At the end of each accounting period, the earned part of public moneys accruing to the United States shall be deposited in the Treasury to the credit of the appropriate receipt accounts.

(Added Pub.L. 97–258, § 2(g)(4)(E), Sept. 13, 1982, 96 Stat. 1061.)

§ 2044. Payment of fine with bond money

On motion of the United States attorney, the court shall order any money belonging to and deposited by or on behalf of the defendant with the court for the purposes of a criminal appearance bail bond (trial or appeal) to be held and paid over to the United States attorney to be applied to the payment of any assessment, fine, restitution, or penalty imposed upon the defendant. The court shall not release any money deposited for bond purposes after a plea or a verdict of the defendant's guilt has been entered and before sentencing except upon a showing that an assessment, fine, restitution or penalty cannot be imposed for the offense the defendant committed or that the defendant would suffer an undue hardship. This section shall not apply to any third party surety.

(Added Pub.L. 101–647, Title XXXVI, § 3629(a), Nov. 29, 1990, 104 Stat. 4966.)

CHAPTER 131—RULES OF COURTS

§ 2071. Rule-making power generally

(a) The Supreme Court and all courts established by Act of Congress may from time to time prescribe rules for the conduct of their business. Such rules shall be consistent with Acts of Congress and rules of practice and procedure prescribed under section 2072 of this title.

(b) Any rule prescribed by a court, other than the Supreme Court, under subsection (a) shall be prescribed only after giving appropriate public notice and an opportunity for comment. Such rule shall take effect upon the date specified by the prescribing court and shall have such effect on pending proceedings as the prescribing court may order.

(c)(1) A rule of a district court prescribed under subsection (a) shall remain in effect unless modified or abrogated by the judicial council of the relevant circuit.

(2) Any other rule prescribed by a court other than the Supreme Court under subsection (a) shall remain in effect unless modified or abrogated by the Judicial Conference.

(d) Copies of rules prescribed under subsection (a) by a district court shall be furnished to the judicial council, and copies of all rules prescribed by a court other than the Supreme Court under subsection (a) shall be furnished to the Director of the Administrative Office of the United States Courts and made available to the public.

(e) If the prescribing court determines that there is an immediate need for a rule, such court may proceed under this section without public notice and opportunity for comment, but such court shall promptly thereafter afford such notice and opportunity for comment.

(f) No rule may be prescribed by a district court other than under this section.

(June 25, 1948, c. 646, 62 Stat. 961; May 24, 1949, c. 139, § 102, 63 Stat. 104; Nov. 19, 1988, Pub.L. 100–702, Title IV, § 403(a)(1), 102 Stat. 4650.)

HISTORICAL AND STATUTORY NOTES

Effective and Applicability Provisions

1990 Acts. Section to take effect 180 days after Nov. 29, 1990, see section 3631 of Pub.L. 101–647, set out as a note under section 3001 of this title.

HISTORICAL AND STATUTORY NOTES

Senate Revision Amendment

By Senate amendment, all provisions relating to the Tax Court were eliminated. Therefore, section 1111 of Title 26, U.S.C., Internal Revenue Code, was not one of the sources of this section as finally enacted. However, no change in the text of this section was necessary. See 80th Congress Senate Report No. 1559.

1949 Acts. This amendment clarifies section 2071 of Title 28, U.S.C., by giving express recognition to the power of the Supreme Court to prescribe its own rules and by giving a better description of its procedural rules.

1988 Acts. House Report No. 100–889, see 1988 U.S. Code Cong. and Adm. News, p. 5982.

Effective and Applicability Provisions

1988 Acts. Section 407 of Title IV of Pub.L. 100–702 provided that: "This title [enacting sections 332(d)(4), 604(a)(19) [redesignated (a)(20)], 2071(b)–(f), and 2072–2074 of this title; amending sections 331, 332(d)(1), 372(c)(11), 636(d), 2071(a) [formerly designated 2071], and 2077(b) of this title and sections 460n–8 of Title 16, Conservation and 3402 of Title 18, Crimes and Criminal Procedure; redesignating as 604(a)(23) former section 604(a)(18) of this title; repealing former section 2072 and section 2076 of this title and sections 3771 and 3772 of Title 18; and enacting provisions set out as notes under this section] shall take effect on December 1, 1988."

1983 Acts. Pub.L. 97–462, § 4, Jan. 12, 1983, 96 Stat. 2530, provided: "The amendments made by this Act [which amended Rule 4 of the Federal Rules of Civil Procedure, added Form 18–A, Appendix of Forms, enacted provisions set out as notes under this section, and amended section 951 of Title 18, Crimes and Criminal Procedure] shall take effect 45 days after the enactment of this Act [Jan. 12, 1983]."

Savings Provisions

Section 406 of Title IV of Pub.L. 100–702 provided that: "The rules prescribed in accordance with law before the effective date of this title [Dec. 1, 1988] and in effect on the date of such effective date [Dec. 1, 1988] shall remain in force until changed pursuant to the law as amended by this title [see Effective and Applicability Provisions of 1988 Amendments note under this section]."

Short Title

1983 Acts. Pub.L. 97–462, § 1, Jan. 12, 1983, 96 Stat. 2527, provided: "That this Act [which amended Rule 4 of the Federal Rules of Civil Procedure, enacted Form 18–A, Appendix of Forms, enacted provisions set out as notes under this section, and amended section 951 of Title 18, Crimes and Criminal Procedure] may be cited as the 'Federal Rules of Civil Procedure Amendments Act of 1982'."

Rulemaking Authority of Supreme Court and Judicial Conference

Pub.L. 109–2, § 8, Feb. 18, 2005, 119 Stat. 14, provided that: "Nothing in this Act [the Class Action Fairness Act of 2005, which enacted this note and 28 U.S.C.A. §§ 1453 and 1711 to 1715, amended 28 U.S.C.A. §§ 1332, 1335, and 1603, and enacted provisions set out as notes under 28 U.S.C.A. §§ 1332, 1711, and 2074] shall restrict in any way the authority of the Judicial Conference and the Supreme Court to propose and prescribe general rules of practice and procedure under chapter 131 of title 28, United States Code [this chapter]."

[Enactment of this note by Class Action Fairness Act of 2005, Pub.L. 109–2, Feb. 18, 2005, 119 Stat. 4, applicable to any civil action commenced on or after Feb. 18, 2005, see Pub.L. 109–2, § 9, set out as a note under 28 U.S.C.A. § 1332.]

Admiralty Rules

The Rules of Practice in Admiralty and Maritime Cases, promulgated by the Supreme Court on Dec. 20, 1920, effective Mar. 7, 1921, as revised, amended, and supplemented, were rescinded, effective July 1, 1966, in accordance with the general unification of civil and admiralty procedure which became effective July 1, 1966. Provision for certain distinctively maritime remedies were preserved however in the Supplemental Rules for Certain Admiralty and Maritime Claims, Rules A to F, Federal Rules of Civil Procedure.

Tax Court Rulemaking Not Affected

Section 405 of Title IV of Pub.L. 100–702 provided that: "The amendments made by this title [see Effective and Applicability Provisions of 1988 Amendments note set out under this section] shall not affect the authority of the Tax Court to prescribe rules under section 7453 of the Internal Revenue Code of 1986 [section 7453 of Title 26, Internal Revenue Code]."

§ 2072. Rules of procedure and evidence; power to prescribe

(a) The Supreme Court shall have the power to prescribe general rules of practice and procedure and rules of evidence for cases in the United States district courts (including proceedings before magistrate judges thereof) and courts of appeals.

(b) Such rules shall not abridge, enlarge or modify any substantive right. All laws in conflict with such rules shall be of no further force or effect after such rules have taken effect.

(c) Such rules may define when a ruling of a district court is final for the purposes of appeal under section 1291 of this title.

(Added Pub.L. 100–702, Title IV, § 401(a), Nov. 19, 1988, 102 Stat. 4648, and amended Pub.L. 101–650, Title III, §§ 315, 321, Dec. 1, 1990, 104 Stat. 5115, 5117.)

HISTORICAL AND STATUTORY NOTES

Effective and Applicability Provisions

1988 Acts. Section effective Dec. 1, 1988, see section 407 of Pub.L. 100–702, set out as a note under section 2071 of this title.

Change of Name

"United States magistrate judge" substituted for "United States magistrate" in text pursuant to section 321 of Pub.L. 101–650, set out as a note under 28 U.S.C.A. § 631.

Prior Provisions

A prior section 2072, Acts June 25, 1948, c. 646, 62 Stat. 961; May 24, 1949, c. 139, § 103, 63 Stat. 104; July 18, 1949, c. 343, § 2, 63 Stat. 446; May 10, 1950, c. 174, § 2, 64 Stat. 158; July 7, 1958, Pub.L. 85–508, § 12(m), 72 Stat. 348; Nov. 6, 1966, Pub.L. 89–773, § 1, 80 Stat. 1323, which authorized the Supreme Court to prescribe rules of civil procedure, was repealed by Pub.L. 100–702, Title IV, §§ 401(a), 407, Nov. 19, 1988, 102 Stat. 4648, 4652, effective Dec. 1, 1988.

Admiralty Rules

The Rules of Practice in Admiralty and Maritime Cases, promulgated by the Supreme Court on Dec. 20, 1920, effective Mar. 7, 1921, as revised, amended, and supplemented, were rescinded, effective July 1, 1966, in accordance with the general unification of civil and admiralty procedure which became effective July 1, 1966. Provision for certain distinctively maritime remedies were preserved however, in the Supplemental Rules for Certain Admiralty and Maritime Claims, Rules A to F, Federal Rules of Civil Procedure, this title.

Applicability to Virgin Islands

Rules of civil procedure promulgated under this section as applicable to the District Court of the Virgin Islands, see section 1614 of Title 48, Territories and Insular Possessions.

§ 2073. Rules of procedure and evidence; method of prescribing

(a)(1) The Judicial Conference shall prescribe and publish the procedures for the consideration of proposed rules under this section.

(2) The Judicial Conference may authorize the appointment of committees to assist the Conference by recommending rules to be prescribed under sections 2072 and 2075 of this title. Each such committee shall consist of members of the bench and the professional bar, and trial and appellate judges.

(b) The Judicial Conference shall authorize the appointment of a standing committee on rules of practice, procedure, and evidence under subsection (a) of this section. Such standing committee shall review each recommendation of any other committees so appointed and recommend to the Judicial Conference rules of practice, procedure, and evidence and such changes in rules proposed by a committee appointed under subsection (a)(2) of this section as may be necessary to maintain consistency and otherwise promote the interest of justice.

(c)(1) Each meeting for the transaction of business under this chapter by any committee appointed under this section shall be open to the public, except when the committee so meeting, in open session and with a majority present, determines that it is in the public interest that all or part of the remainder of the meeting on that day shall be closed to the public, and states the reason for so closing the meeting. Minutes of each meeting for the transaction of business under this chapter shall be maintained by the committee and made available to the public, except that any portion of such minutes, relating to a closed meeting and made available to the public, may contain such deletions as may be necessary to avoid frustrating the purposes of closing the meeting.

(2) Any meeting for the transaction of business under this chapter, by a committee appointed under this section, shall be preceded by sufficient notice to enable all interested persons to attend.

(d) In making a recommendation under this section or under section 2072 or 2075, the body making that recommendation shall provide a proposed rule, an explanatory note on the rule, and a written report explaining the body's action, including any minority or other separate views.

(e) Failure to comply with this section does not invalidate a rule prescribed under section 2072 or 2075 of this title.

(Added Pub.L. 100–702, Title IV, § 401(a), Nov. 19, 1988, 102 Stat. 4649, and amended Pub.L. 103–394, Title I, § 104(e), Oct. 22, 1994, 108 Stat. 4110.)

HISTORICAL AND STATUTORY NOTES

Effective and Applicability Provisions

1994 Acts. Amendment by Pub.L. 103–394 effective on Oct. 22, 1994, and not to apply with respect to cases commenced under Title 11 of the United States Code before Oct. 22, 1994, see section 702 of Pub.L. 103–394, set out as a note under section 101 of Title 11, Bankruptcy.

1988 Acts. Section effective Dec. 1, 1988, see section 407 of Pub.L. 100–702, set out as a note under section 2071 of this title.

Separability of Provisions

If any provision of or amendment made by Pub.L. 103–394 or the application of such provision or amendment to any person or circumstance is held to be unconstitutional, the remaining provisions of and amendments made by Pub.L. 103–394 and the application of such provisions and amendments to any person or circumstance shall not be affected thereby, see section 701 of Pub.L. 103–394, set out as a note under section 101 of Title 11, Bankruptcy.

Prior Provisions

A prior section 2073, Acts June 25, 1948, c. 646, 62 Stat. 961; May 24, 1949, c. 139, § 104, 63 Stat. 104; May 10, 1950,

c. 174, § 3, 64 Stat. 158, which empowered the Supreme Court to prescribe, by general rules, the practice and procedure in admiralty and maritime cases in the district courts, was repealed by Pub.L. 89–773, § 2, Nov. 6, 1966, 80 Stat. 1323, which provided in part that the repeal of section 2073 should not operate to invalidate or repeal rules adopted under the authority of such section prior to the enactment of Pub.L. 89–773, which rules should remain in effect until superseded by rules prescribed under the authority of former section 2072 of this title as amended by Pub.L. 89–773. See sections 2071 to 2074 of this title.

More Complete Information Regarding Assets of the Estate

Pub.L. 109–8, Title IV, § 419, Apr. 20, 2005, 119 Stat. 109, provided that:

"**(a) In general.**—

"**(1) Disclosure.**—The Judicial Conference of the United States, in accordance with section 2075 of title 28 of the United States Code and after consideration of the views of the Director of the Executive Office for United States Trustees, shall propose amended Federal Rules of Bankruptcy Procedure and in accordance with rule 9009 of the Federal Rules of Bankruptcy Procedure [set out in Title 11] shall prescribe official bankruptcy forms directing debtors under chapter 11 of title 11 of United States Code [11 U.S.C.A. § 1101 et seq.], to disclose the information described in paragraph (2) by filing and serving periodic financial and other reports designed to provide such information.

"**(2) Information.**—The information referred to in paragraph (1) is the value, operations, and profitability of any closely held corporation, partnership, or of any other entity in which the debtor holds a substantial or controlling interest.

"**(b) Purpose.**—The purpose of the rules and reports under subsection (a) [of this note] shall be to assist parties in interest taking steps to ensure that the debtor's interest in any entity referred to in subsection (a)(2) [of this note] is used for the payment of allowed claims against debtor."

Standard Form Disclosure Statement and Plan

Pub.L. 109–8, Title IV, § 433, Apr. 20, 2005, 119 Stat. 110, provided that: "Within a reasonable period of time after the date of enactment of this Act [Apr. 20,. 2005], the Judicial Conference of the United States shall prescribe in accordance with rule 9009 of the Federal Rules of Bankruptcy Procedure official standard form disclosure statements and plans of reorganization for small business debtors (as defined in section 101 of title 11, United States Code, as amended by this Act), designed to achieve a practical balance between—

"(1) the reasonable needs of the courts, the United States trustee, creditors, and other parties in interest for reasonably complete information; and

"(2) economy and simplicity for debtors."

Uniform Reporting Rules and Forms for Small Business Cases

Pub.L. 109–8, Title IV, § 435, Apr. 20, 2005, 119 Stat. 111, provided that:

"**(a) Proposal of rules and forms.**—The Judicial Conference of the United States shall propose in accordance with section 2073 of title 28 of the United States Code [this section] amended Federal Rules of Bankruptcy Procedure, and shall prescribe in accordance with rule 9009 of the Federal Rules of Bankruptcy Procedure [set out in Title 11] official bankruptcy forms, directing small business debtors to file periodic financial and other reports containing information, including information relating to—

"(1) the debtor's profitability;

"(2) the debtor's cash receipts and disbursements; and

"(3) whether the debtor is timely filing tax returns and paying taxes and other administrative expenses when due.

"(b) **Purpose.**—The rules and forms proposed under subsection (a) [of this note] shall be designed to achieve a practical balance among—

"(1) the reasonable needs of the bankruptcy court, the United States trustee, creditors, and other parties in interest for reasonably complete information;

"(2) a small business debtor's interest that required reports be easy and inexpensive to complete; and

"(3) the interest of all parties that the required reports help such debtor to understand such debtor's financial condition and plan the such debtor's future."

§ 2074. Rules of procedure and evidence; submission to Congress; effective date

(a) The Supreme Court shall transmit to the Congress not later than May 1 of the year in which a rule prescribed under section 2072 is to become effective a copy of the proposed rule. Such rule shall take effect no earlier than December 1 of the year in which such rule is so transmitted unless otherwise provided by law. The Supreme Court may fix the extent such rule shall apply to proceedings then pending, except that the Supreme Court shall not require the application of such rule to further proceedings then pending to the extent that, in the opinion of the court in which such proceedings are pending, the application of such rule in such proceedings would not be feasible or would work injustice, in which event the former rule applies.

(b) Any such rule creating, abolishing, or modifying an evidentiary privilege shall have no force or effect unless approved by Act of Congress.

(Added Pub.L. 100–702, Title IV, § 401(a), Nov. 19, 1988, 102 Stat. 4649.)

HISTORICAL AND STATUTORY NOTES

Effective and Applicability Provisions

1988 Acts. Section effective Dec. 1, 1988, see section 407 of Pub.L. 100–702, set out as a note under section 2071 of this title.

Prior Provisions

A prior section 2074, Act July 27, 1954, c. 583, § 1, 68 Stat. 567, which empowered the Supreme Court to prescribe rules for review of decisions of the Tax Court of the United States, was repealed by Pub.L. 89–773, § 2, Nov. 6, 1966, 80 Stat. 1323, which provided in part that the repeal of section 2074 of this title should not operate to invalidate or repeal rules adopted under the authority of such section prior to the enactment of Pub.L. 89–773, which rules should remain in effect until superseded by rules prescribed under the author-

ity of former section 2072 of this title as amended by Pub.L. 89–773. See sections 2071 to 2074 of this title.

Amendments to Civil Rules Proposed March 27, 2003

Pub.L. 109–2, § 7, Feb. 18, 2005, 119 Stat. 13, provided that: "Notwithstanding any other provision of law, the amendments to rule 23 of the Federal Rules of Civil Procedure, which are set forth in the order entered by the Supreme Court of the United States on March 27, 2003, shall take effect on the date of enactment of this Act [Feb. 18, 2005] or on December 1, 2003 (as specified in that order), whichever occurs first."

[Enactment of this note by Class Action Fairness Act of 2005, Pub.L. 109–2, Feb. 18, 2005, 119 Stat. 4, applicable to any civil action commenced on or after Feb. 18, 2005, see Pub.L. 109–2, § 9, set out as a note under 28 U.S.C.A. § 1332.]

Amendments to Criminal Rules Proposed April 29, 2002

Pub.L. 107–273, Div. C, Title I, § 11019(a), Nov. 2, 2002, 116 Stat. 1825, provided that: "The proposed amendments to the Federal Rules of Criminal Procedure that are embraced by an order entered by the Supreme Court of the United States on April 29, 2002, shall take effect on December 1, 2002, as otherwise provided by law, but with the amendments made in subsection (b) [amending Rule 16 of the Federal Rules of Criminal Procedure]."

Amendments to Criminal Rules Proposed April 29, 1994

Pub.L. 103–322, Title XXIII, § 230101, Sept. 13, 1994, 108 Stat. 2077, provided that:

"(a) **Modification of proposed amendments.**—The proposed amendments to the Federal Rules of Criminal Procedure which are embraced by an order entered by the Supreme Court of the United States on April 29, 1994, shall take effect on December 1, 1994, as otherwise provided by law, but with the following amendments:

"(b) **In general.**—Rule 32 of the Federal Rules of Criminal Procedure is amended by—

"(1) striking 'and' following the semicolon in subdivision (c)(3)(C);

"(2) striking the period at the end of subdivision (c)(3)(D) and inserting '; and';

"(3) inserting after subdivision (c)(3)(D) the following:

" '(E) if sentence is to be imposed for a crime of violence or sexual abuse, address the victim personally if the victim is present at the sentencing hearing and determine if the victim wishes to make a statement or present any information in relation to the sentence.';

"(4) in subdivision (c)(3)(D), striking 'equivalent opportunity' and inserting in lieu thereof 'opportunity equivalent to that of the defendant's counsel';

"(5) in the last sentence of subdivision (c)(4), striking 'and (D)' and inserting '(D), and (E)';

"(6) in the last sentence of subdivision (c)(4), inserting 'the victim,' before 'or the attorney for the Government.'; and

"(7) adding at the end the following:

" '(f) **Definitions.**—For purposes of this rule—

" '(1) "victim" means any individual against whom an offense has been committed for which a sentence is to be imposed, but the right of allocution under subdivision (c)(3)(E) may be exercised instead by—

" '(A) a parent or legal guardian if the victim is below the age of eighteen years or incompetent; or

" '(B) one or more family members or relatives designated by the court if the victim is deceased or incapacitated;

if such person or persons are present at the sentencing hearing, regardless of whether the victim is present; and

" '(2) "crime of violence or sexual abuse" means a crime that involved the use or attempted or threatened use of physical force against the person or property of another, or a crime under chapter 109A of title 18, United States Code.'

"(c) **Effective date.**—The amendments made by subsection (b) [amending Rule 32 of the Federal Rules of Criminal Procedure] shall become effective on December 1, 1994."

Amendments to Civil Rules Proposed April 30, 1991

Pub.L. 102–198, § 11, Dec. 9, 1991, 105 Stat. 1626, provided that:

"(a) **Technical amendment.**—Rule 15(c)(3) of the Federal Rules of Civil Procedure for the United States Courts, as transmitted to the Congress by the Supreme Court pursuant to section 2074 of title 28, United States Code [this section], to become effective on December 1, 1991, is amended by striking 'Rule 4(m)' and inserting 'Rule 4(j)'.

"(b) **Amendment to Forms.**—Form 1–A, Notice of Lawsuit and Request for Waiver of Service of Summons, and Form 1–B, Waiver of Service of Summons, included in the transmittal by the Supreme Court described in subsection (a), shall not be effective and Form 18–A, Notice and Acknowledgment for Service by Mail, abrogated by the Supreme Court in such transmittal, effective December 1, 1991, shall continue in effect on or after that date."

Amendments to Civil Rules Proposed April 28, 1982

Pub.L. 97–462, § 5, Jan. 12, 1983, 96 Stat. 2530, provided: "The amendments to the Federal Rules of Civil Procedure [Rule 4], the effective date [Aug. 1, 1982] of which was delayed [to Oct. 1, 1983] by the Act [Pub.L. 97–227] entitled 'An Act to delay the effective date of proposed amendments to rule 4 of the Federal Rules of Civil Procedure', [proposed by the Supreme Court of the United States and transmitted to the Congress by the Chief Justice on Apr. 28, 1982], approved August 2, 1982 (96 Stat. 246), shall not take effect."

Pub.L. 97–227, Aug. 2, 1982, 96 Stat. 246, provided: "That notwithstanding the provisions of section 2072 of title 28, United States Code, [section 2072 of this title] the amendments to rule 4 of the Federal Rules of Civil Procedure as proposed by the Supreme Court of the United States and transmitted to the Congress by the Chief Justice on April 28, 1982, shall take effect on October 1, 1983, unless previously approved, disapproved, or modified by Act of Congress.

"Sec. 2. This Act shall be effective as of August 1, 1982, but shall not apply to the service of process that takes place between August 1, 1982, and the date of enactment of this Act [Aug. 2, 1982]."

Amendments to Criminal Rules and Rules of Evidence Proposed April 30, 1979; Postponement of Effective Date

Pub.L. 96–42, July 31, 1979, 93 Stat. 326, provided: "That notwithstanding any provision of section 3771 or 3772 of title 18 of the United States Code [section 3771 or 3772 of Title 18, Crimes and Criminal Procedure] or of section 2072, 2075, or 2076 of title 28 of the United States Code [sections 2072, 2075 and 2076 of this title] to the contrary—

"(1) the amendments proposed by the United States Supreme Court and transmitted by the Chief Justice on April 30, 1979, to the Federal Rules of Criminal Procedure affecting rules 11(e)(6), 17(h), 32(f), and 44(c), and adding new rules 26.2 and 32.1, and the amendment so proposed and transmitted to the Federal Rules of Evidence affecting rule 410, shall not take effect until December 1, 1980, or until and then only to the extent approved by Act of Congress, whichever is earlier; and

"(2) the amendment proposed by the United States Supreme Court and transmitted by the Chief Justice on April 30, 1979, affecting rule 40 of the Federal Rules of Criminal Procedure shall take effect on August 1, 1979, with the following amendments:

"(A) In the matter designated as paragraph (1) of subdivision (d), strike out 'in accordance with Rule 32.1(a).'

"(B) In the matter designated as paragraph (2) of subdivision (d), strike out 'in accordance with Rule 32.1(a)(1)'."

Approval and Effective Date of Amendments Proposed November 20, 1972 and December 18, 1972

Pub.L. 93–595, § 3, Jan. 2, 1975, 88 Stat. 1949, provided that: "The Congress expressly approves the amendments to the Federal Rules of Civil Procedure [Rules 30(c), 32(c), 43 and 44.1] and the amendments to the Federal Rules of Criminal Procedure [Rules 26, 26.1 and 28], which are embraced by the orders entered by the Supreme Court of the United States on November 20, 1972, and December 18, 1972, and such amendments shall take effect on the one hundred and eightieth day beginning after the date of the enactment of this Act [Jan. 2, 1975]."

Approval and Effective Date of Rules Governing Section 2254 Cases and Section 2255 Proceedings for United States District Courts

Pub.L. 94–426, § 1, Sept. 28, 1976, 90 Stat. 1334, provided: "That the rules governing section 2254 cases in the United States district courts and the rules governing section 2255 proceedings for the United States district courts, as proposed by the United States Supreme Court, which were delayed by the Act entitled 'An Act to delay the effective date of certain proposed amendments to the Federal Rules of Criminal Procedure and certain other rules promulgated by the United States Supreme Court' (Public Law 94–349), are approved with the amendments set forth in section 2 of this Act and shall take effect as so amended, with respect to petitions under section 2254 and motions under section 2255 of title 28 of the United States Code [sections 2254 and 2255 of this title] filed on or after February 1, 1977."

Amendments to Rules of Evidence Proposed on April 29, 1994

Pub.L. 103–322, Title IV, § 40141, Sept. 13, 1994, 108 Stat. 1918, provided that:

"(a) **Modification of proposed amendment.**—The proposed amendments to the Federal Rules of Evidence that are embraced by an order entered by the Supreme Court of the United States on April 29, 1994, shall take effect on December 1, 1994, as otherwise provided by law, but with the amendment made by subsection (b).

"(b) Rule.—Rule 412 of the Federal Rules of Evidence is amended to read as follows:

" 'Rule 412. Sex Offense Cases; Relevance of Alleged Victim's Past Sexual Behavior or Alleged Sexual Predisposition

" '(a) Evidence generally inadmissible.—The following evidence is not admissible in any civil or criminal proceeding involving alleged sexual misconduct except as provided in subdivisions (b) and (c):

" '(1) Evidence offered to prove that any alleged victim engaged in her sexual behavior.

" '(2) Evidence offered to prove any alleged victim's sexual predisposition.

" '(b) Exceptions.—

" '(1) In a criminal case, the following evidence is admissible, if otherwise admissible under these rules:

" '(A) evidence of specific instances of sexual behavior by the alleged victim offered to prove that a person other than the accused was the source of semen, injury or other physical evidence;

" '(B) evidence of specific instances of sexual behavior by the alleged victim with respect to the person accused of the sexual misconduct offered by the accused to prove consent or by the prosecution; and

" '(C) evidence the exclusion of which would violate the constitutional rights of the defendant.

" '(2) In a civil case, evidence offered to prove the sexual behavior or sexual predisposition of any alleged victim is admissible if it is otherwise admissible under these rules and its probative value substantially outweighs the danger of harm to any victim and of unfair prejudice to any party. Evidence of an alleged victim's reputation is admissible only if it has been placed in controversy by the alleged victim.

" '(c) Procedure to determine admissibility.—

" '(1) A party intending to offer evidence under subdivision (b) must—

" '(A) file a written motion at least 14 days before trial specifically describing the evidence and stating the purpose for which it is offered unless the court, for good cause requires a different time for filing or permits filing during trial; and

" '(B) serve the motion on all parties and notify the alleged victim or, when appropriate, the alleged victim's guardian or representative.

" '(2) Before admitting evidence under this rule the court must conduct a hearing in camera and afford the victim and parties a right to attend and be heard. The motion, related papers, and the record of the hearing must be sealed and remain under seal unless the court orders otherwise.'

"(c) Technical amendment.—The table of contents for the Federal Rules of Evidence is amended by amending the item relating to rule 412 to read as follows:

" '412. Sex Offense Cases; Relevance of Alleged Victim's Past Sexual Behavior or Alleged Sexual Predisposition:

" '(a) Evidence generally inadmissible.

" '(b) Exceptions.

" '(c) Procedure to determine admissibility.' "

Congressional Approval Requirement for Proposed Rules of Evidence for United States Courts and Amendments to Federal Rules of Civil Procedure and Criminal Procedure; Suspension of Effectiveness of Such Rules

Pub.L. 93–12, Mar. 30, 1973, 87 Stat. 9, provided: "That notwithstanding any other provisions of law, the Rules of Evidence for United States Courts and Magistrates, the Amendments to the Federal Rules of Civil Procedure, and the Amendments to the Federal Rules of Criminal Procedure, which are embraced by the orders entered by the Supreme Court of the United States on Monday, November 20, 1972, and Monday, December 18, 1972, shall have no force or effect except to the extent, and with such amendments, as they may be expressly approved by Act of Congress."

Postponement of Effective Date of Proposed Rules and Forms Governing Proceedings Under Sections 2254 and 2255 of this Title

Pub.L. 94–349, § 2, July 8, 1976, 90 Stat. 822, provided: "That, notwithstanding the provisions of section 2072 of title 28 of the United States Code [section 2072 of this title], the rules and forms governing section 2254 [section 2254 of this title] cases in the United States district courts and the rules and forms governing section 2255 [section 2255 of this title] proceedings in the United States district courts which are embraced by the order entered by the United States Supreme Court on April 26, 1976, and which were transmitted to the Congress on or about April 26, 1976, shall not take effect until thirty days after the adjournment sine die of the 94th Congress, or until and to the extent approved by Act of Congress, whichever is earlier."

§ 2075. Bankruptcy rules

The Supreme Court shall have the power to prescribe by general rules, the forms of process, writs, pleadings, and motions, and the practice and procedure in cases under title 11.

Such rules shall not abridge, enlarge, or modify any substantive right.

The Supreme Court shall transmit to Congress not later than May 1 of the year in which a rule prescribed under this section is to become effective a copy of the proposed rule. The rule shall take effect no earlier than December 1 of the year in which it is transmitted to Congress unless otherwise provided by law.

(Added Pub.L. 88–623, § 1, Oct. 3, 1964, 78 Stat. 1001, and amended Pub.L. 95–598, Title II, § 247, Nov. 6, 1978, 92 Stat. 2672; Pub.L. 103–394, Title I, § 104(f), Oct. 22, 1994, 108 Stat. 4110.)

Amendment of Section

Pub.L. 109–8, Title XII, § 1232, Title XV, § 1501, Apr. 20, 2005, 119 Stat. 202, 216, provided that, except as otherwise provided, effective 180 days after April 20, 2005, and inapplicable with respect to cases commenced under Title 11 before the effective date, this section is amended by adding at the end the following:

The bankruptcy rules promulgated under this section shall prescribe a form for the statement required under section 707(b)(2)(C) of title 11 and may provide general rules on the content of such statement.

HISTORICAL AND STATUTORY NOTES

Effective and Applicability Provisions

2005 Acts. Except as otherwise provided, amendments by Pub.L. 109–8 effective 180 days after April 20, 2005, and inapplicable with respect to cases commenced under Title 11 before the effective date, see Pub.L. 109–8, § 1501, set out as a note under 11 U.S.C.A. § 101.

1994 Acts. Amendment by Pub.L. 103–394 effective on Oct. 22, 1994, and not to apply with respect to cases commenced under Title 11 of the United States Code before Oct. 22, 1994, see section 702 of Pub.L. 103–394, set out as a note under section 101 of Title 11, Bankruptcy.

1978 Acts. Amendment by Pub.L. 95–598 effective Nov. 6, 1978, see section 402(d) of Pub.L. 95–598, set out as a note preceding section 101 of Title 11, Bankruptcy.

Separability of Provisions

If any provision of or amendment made by Pub.L. 103–394 or the application of such provision or amendment to any person or circumstance is held to be unconstitutional, the remaining provisions of and amendments made by Pub.L. 103–394 and the application of such provisions and amendments to any person or circumstance shall not be affected thereby, see section 701 of Pub.L. 103–394, set out as a note under section 101 of Title 11, Bankruptcy.

Additional Rulemaking Power

Pub.L. 95–598, Title IV, § 410, Nov. 6, 1978, 92 Stat. 2687, provided that: "The Supreme Court may issue such additional rules of procedure, consistent with Acts of Congress, as may be necessary for the orderly transfer of functions and records and the orderly transition to the new bankruptcy court system created by this Act [see Tables for complete classification of Pub.L. 95–598]."

Applicability of Rules to Cases Under Title 11

Pub.L. 95–598, Title IV, § 405(d), Nov. 6, 1978, 92 Stat. 2685, provided that: "The rules prescribed under section 2075 of title 28 of the United States Code and in effect on September 30, 1979, shall apply to cases under title 11, to the extent not inconsistent with the amendments made by this Act, or with this Act [see Tables for complete classification of Pub.L. 95–598], until such rules are repealed or superseded by rules prescribed and effective under such section, as amended by section 248 of this Act."

Rules Promulgated by Supreme Court

Pub.L. 98–353, Title III, § 320, July 10, 1984, 98 Stat. 357, provided that: "The Supreme Court shall prescribe general rules implementing the practice and procedure to be followed under section 707(b) of title 11, United States Code [section 707(b) of Title 11, Bankruptcy]. Section 2075 of title 28, United States Code [this section], shall apply with respect to the general rules prescribed under this section."

[§ 2076.   **Repealed. Pub.L. 100–702, Title IV, § 401(c), Nov. 19, 1988, 102 Stat. 4650]**

HISTORICAL AND STATUTORY NOTES

Section, added Pub.L. 93–595, § 2(a)(1), Jan. 2, 1975, 88 Stat. 1948, and amended Pub.L. 94–149, § 2, Dec. 12, 1975, 89 Stat. 806, related to Federal Rules of Evidence prescribed by the Supreme Court and amendment thereof. See sections 2072 to 2074 of this title.

Effective Date of Repeal

Section repealed effective Dec. 1, 1988, see section 407 of Pub.L. 100–702, set out as a note under section 2071 of this title.

§ 2077. Publication of rules; advisory committees

(a) The rules for the conduct of the business of each court of appeals, including the operating procedures of such court, shall be published. Each court of appeals shall print or cause to be printed necessary copies of the rules. The Judicial Conference shall prescribe the fees for sales of copies under section 1913 of this title, but the Judicial Conference may provide for free distribution of copies to members of the bar of each court and to other interested persons.

(b) Each court, except the Supreme Court, that is authorized to prescribe rules of the conduct of such court's business under section 2071 of this title shall appoint an advisory committee for the study of the rules of practice and internal operating procedures of such court and, in the case of an advisory committee appointed by a court of appeals, of the rules of the judicial council of the circuit. The advisory committee shall make recommendations to the court concerning such rules and procedures. Members of the committee shall serve without compensation, but the Director may pay travel and transportation expenses in accordance with section 5703 of title 5.

(Added Pub.L. 97–164, Title II, § 208(a), Apr. 2, 1982, 96 Stat. 54, and amended Pub.L. 100–702, Title IV, § 401(b), Nov. 19, 1988, 102 Stat. 4650; Pub.L. 101–650, Title IV, § 406, Dec. 1, 1990, 104 Stat. 5124.)

HISTORICAL AND STATUTORY NOTES

Effective and Applicability Provisions

1990 Acts. Amendment by section 406 of Pub.L. 101–650 effective 90 days after Dec. 1, 1990, see section 407 of Pub.L. 101–650, set out as a note under section 332 of this title.

1988 Acts. Amendment by Pub.L. 100–702 effective Dec. 1, 1988, see section 407 of Pub.L. 100–702, set out as a note under section 2071 of this title.

1982 Acts. Section effective Oct. 1, 1982, see section 402 of Pub.L. 97–164, set out as a note under section 171 of this title.

CHAPTER 133—REVIEW—MISCELLANEOUS PROVISIONS

§ 2101. Supreme Court; time for appeal or certiorari; docketing; stay

(a) A direct appeal to the Supreme Court from any decision under section 1253 of this title, holding unconstitutional in whole or in part, any Act of Congress, shall be taken within thirty days after the entry of the interlocutory or final order, judgment or decree. The record shall be made up and the case docketed within sixty days from the time such appeal is taken under rules prescribed by the Supreme Court.

(b) Any other direct appeal to the Supreme Court which is authorized by law, from a decision of a district court in any civil action, suit or proceeding, shall be taken within thirty days from the judgment, order or decree, appealed from, if interlocutory, and within sixty days if final.

(c) Any other appeal or any writ of certiorari intended to bring any judgment or decree in a civil action, suit or proceeding before the Supreme Court for review shall be taken or applied for within ninety days after the entry of such judgment or decree. A justice of the Supreme Court, for good cause shown, may extend the time for applying for a writ of certiorari for a period not exceeding sixty days.

(d) The time for appeal or application for a writ of certiorari to review the judgment of a State court in a criminal case shall be as prescribed by rules of the Supreme Court.

(e) An application to the Supreme Court for a writ of certiorari to review a case before judgment has been rendered in the court of appeals may be made at any time before judgment.

(f) In any case in which the final judgment or decree of any court is subject to review by the Supreme Court on writ of certiorari, the execution and enforcement of such judgment or decree may be stayed for a reasonable time to enable the party aggrieved to obtain a writ of certiorari from the Supreme Court. The stay may be granted by a judge of the court rendering the judgment or decree or by a justice of the Supreme Court, and may be conditioned on the giving of security, approved by such judge or justice, that if the aggrieved party fails to make application for such writ within the period allotted therefor, or fails to obtain an order granting his application, or fails to make his plea good in the Supreme Court, he shall answer for all damages and costs which the other party may sustain by reason of the stay.

(g) The time for application for a writ of certiorari to review a decision of the United States Court of Appeals for the Armed Forces shall be as prescribed by rules of the Supreme Court.

(June 25, 1948, c. 646, 62 Stat. 961; May 24, 1949, c. 139, § 106, 63 Stat. 104; Dec. 6, 1983, Pub.L. 98–209, § 10(b), 97 Stat. 1406; June 27, 1988, Pub.L. 100–352, § 5(b), 102 Stat. 663; Oct. 5, 1994, Pub.L. 103–337, Div. A, Title IX, § 924(d)(1)(C), 108 Stat. 2832.)

HISTORICAL AND STATUTORY NOTES

Effective and Applicability Provisions

1988 Acts. Amendment by section 5(b) of Pub.L. 100–352, which substituted "section 1253" for "sections 1252, 1253 and 2282" in subsec. (a), effective ninety days after June 27, 1988, except that such amendment not to apply to cases pending in the Supreme Court on such effective date or affect the right to review or the manner of reviewing the judgment or decree of a court which was entered before such effective date, see section 7 of Pub.L. 100–352, set out as a note under section 1254 of this title.

1983 Acts. Amendment by Pub.L. 98–209 effective on the first day of the eighth calendar month beginning after Dec. 6, 1983, see section 12(a)(1) of Pub.L. 98–209, set out as a note under section 801 of Title 10, Armed Forces.

§ 2102. Priority of criminal case on appeal from State court

Criminal cases on review from State courts shall have priority, on the docket of the Supreme Court, over all cases except cases to which the United States is a party and such other cases as the court may decide to be of public importance.

(June 25, 1948, c. 646, 62 Stat. 962.)

[§ 2103. Repealed. Pub.L. 100–352, § 5(c), June 27, 1988, 102 Stat. 663]

HISTORICAL AND STATUTORY NOTES

Section, Acts June 25, 1948, c. 646, 62 Stat. 962; Sept. 19, 1962, Pub.L. 87–669, § 1, 76 Stat. 556, provided that appeal from State court or from a United States court of appeals improvidently taken be regarded as petition for writ of certiorari.

Effective Date of Repeal

Repeal of section effective ninety days after June 27, 1988, except that such repeal not to apply to cases pending in the Supreme Court on such effective date or affect the right to review or the manner of reviewing the judgment or decree of a court which was entered before such effective date, see section 7 of Pub.L. 100–352, set out as a note under section 1254 of this title.

§ 2104. Reviews of State court decisions

A review by the Supreme Court of a judgment or decree of a State court shall be conducted in the same manner and under the same regulations, and shall have the same effect, as if the judgment or decree reviewed had been rendered in a court of the United States.

(June 25, 1948, c. 646, 62 Stat. 962; June 27, 1988, Pub.L. 100–352, § 5(d)(1), 102 Stat. 663.)

HISTORICAL AND STATUTORY NOTES

Effective and Applicability Provisions

1988 Acts. Amendment by section 5(d)(1) of Pub.L. 100–352 effective ninety days after June 27, 1988, except that such amendment not to apply to cases pending in the Supreme Court on such effective date or affect the right to review or the manner of reviewing the judgment or decree of a court which was entered before such effective date, see section 7 of Pub.L. 100–352, set out as a note under section 1254 of this title.

§ 2105. Scope of review; abatement

There shall be no reversal in the Supreme Court or a court of appeals for error in ruling upon matters in abatement which do not involve jurisdiction.

(June 25, 1948, c. 646, 62 Stat. 963.)

§ 2106. Determination

The Supreme Court or any other court of appellate jurisdiction may affirm, modify, vacate, set aside or reverse any judgment, decree, or order of a court lawfully brought before it for review, and may remand the cause and direct the entry of such appropriate judgment, decree, or order, or require such further proceedings to be had as may be just under the circumstances.

(June 25, 1948, c. 646, 62 Stat. 963.)

§ 2107. Time for appeal to court of appeals

(a) Except as otherwise provided in this section, no appeal shall bring any judgment, order or decree in an action, suit or proceeding of a civil nature before a court of appeals for review unless notice of appeal is filed, within thirty days after the entry of such judgment, order or decree.

(b) In any such action, suit or proceeding in which the United States or an officer or agency thereof is a party, the time as to all parties shall be sixty days from such entry.

(c) The district court may, upon motion filed not later than 30 days after the expiration of the time otherwise set for bringing appeal, extend the time for appeal upon a showing of excusable neglect or good cause. In addition, if the district court finds—

(1) that a party entitled to notice of the entry of a judgment or order did not receive such notice from the clerk or any party within 21 days of its entry, and

(2) that no party would be prejudiced,

the district court may, upon motion filed within 180 days after entry of the judgment or order or within 7 days after receipt of such notice, whichever is earlier, reopen the time for appeal for a period of 14 days from the date of entry of the order reopening the time for appeal.

(d) This section shall not apply to bankruptcy matters or other proceedings under Title 11.

(June 25, 1948, c. 646, 62 Stat. 963; May 24, 1949, c. 139, §§ 107, 108, 63 Stat. 104; Nov. 6, 1978, Pub.L. 95–598, Title II, § 248, 92 Stat. 2672; Dec. 9, 1991, Pub.L. 102–198, § 12, 105 Stat. 1627.)

HISTORICAL AND STATUTORY NOTES

Senate Revision Amendment

By Senate amendment, all provisions relating to the Tax Court were eliminated. Therefore, section 1142 of Title 26, U.S.C., Internal Revenue Code, was not one of the sources of this section as finally enacted. However, no change in the text of this section was necessary. See 80th Congress Senate Report No. 1559.

1949 Acts. This amendment to section 2107 of Title 28, U.S.C., restores the former 15-day limitation of time within which to appeal from an interlocutory order in admiralty.

This amendment eliminates as surplusage the words "in any such action, suit or proceeding," from the fourth paragraph of section 2107 of Title 28, U.S.C., and corrects a typographical error in the same paragraph.

1991 Acts. House Report No. 102–322, see 1991 U.S. Code Cong. and Adm. News, p. 1303.

Codifications

This section was amended by Pub.L. 95–598, Title II, § 248, Nov. 6, 1978, 92 Stat. 2672, effective June 28, 1984, pursuant to Pub.L. 95–598, Title IV, § 402(b), Nov. 6, 1978, 92 Stat. 2682, as amended by Pub.L. 98–249, § 1(a), Mar. 31, 1984, 98 Stat. 116; Pub.L. 98–271, § 1(a), Apr. 30, 1984, 98 Stat. 163; Pub.L. 98–299, § 1(a), May 25, 1984, 98 Stat. 214; Pub.L. 98–325, § 1(a), June 20, 1984, 98 Stat. 268 [set out as an Effective and Applicability Provisions note preceding section 101 of Title 11, Bankruptcy], by adding "or the bankruptcy court" following "district court" and by striking out the final paragraph relating to nonapplicability to bankruptcy matters or other proceedings under Title 11.

Section 402(b) of Pub.L. 95–598 was amended by section 113 of Pub.L. 98–353, Title I, July 10, 1984, 98 Stat. 343, by substituting "shall not be effective" for "shall take effect on June 28, 1984", thereby eliminating the amendment by section 248 of Pub.L. 95–598, effective June 27, 1984, pursuant to section 122(c) of Pub.L. 98–353, set out as an Effective Date note under section 151 of this title.

Section 121(a) of Pub.L. 98–353 directed that section 402(b) of Pub.L. 95–598 be amended by substituting "the date of enactment of the Bankruptcy Amendments and Federal Judgeship Act of 1984 [i.e. July 10, 1984]" for "June 28, 1984". This amendment was not executed in view of the prior amendment to section 402(b) of Pub.L. 95–598 by section 113 of Pub.L. 98–353.

§ 2108. Proof of amount in controversy

Where the power of any court of appeals to review a case depends upon the amount or value in controversy, such amount or value, if not otherwise satisfactorily disclosed upon the record, may be shown and ascertained by the oath of a party to the case or by other competent evidence.

(June 25, 1948, c. 646, 62 Stat. 963.)

§ 2109. Quorum of Supreme Court justices absent

If a case brought to the Supreme Court by direct appeal from a district court cannot be heard and determined because of the absence of a quorum of qualified justices, the Chief Justice of the United States may order it remitted to the court of appeals for the circuit including the district in which the case arose, to be heard and determined by that court either sitting in banc or specially constituted and composed of the three circuit judges senior in commission who are able to sit, as such order may direct. The decision of such court shall be final and conclusive. In the event of the disqualification or disability of one or more of such circuit judges, such court shall be filled as provided in chapter 15 of this title.

In any other case brought to the Supreme Court for review, which cannot be heard and determined because of the absence of a quorum of qualified justices, if a majority of the qualified justices shall be of opinion that the case cannot be heard and determined at the next ensuing term, the court shall enter its order affirming the judgment of the court from which the case was brought for review with the same effect as upon affirmance by an equally divided court.

(June 25, 1948, c. 646, 62 Stat. 963.)

[§ 2110. Repealed. Pub.L. 97–164, Title I, § 136, Apr. 2, 1982, 96 Stat. 41]

HISTORICAL AND STATUTORY NOTES

Section, Act June 25, 1948, c. 646, 62 Stat. 964; May 24, 1949, c. 139, § 109, 63 Stat. 105, provided that appeals to the Court of Claims in tort claims cases, as provided in section 1504 of this title, be taken within 90 days after the entry of the final judgment of the district court.

Effective Date of Repeal

Repeal effective Oct. 1, 1982, see section 402 of Pub.L. 97–164, set out as a note under section 171 of this title.

§ 2111. Harmless error

On the hearing of any appeal or writ of certiorari in any case, the court shall give judgment after an examination of the record without regard to errors or defects which do not affect the substantial rights of the parties.

(Added May 24, 1949, c. 139, § 110, 63 Stat. 105.)

§ 2112. Record on review and enforcement of agency orders

(a) The rules prescribed under the authority of section 2072 of this title may provide for the time and manner of filing and the contents of the record in all proceedings instituted in the courts of appeals to enjoin, set aside, suspend, modify, or otherwise review or enforce orders of administrative agencies, boards, commissions, and officers. Such rules may authorize the agency, board, commission, or officer to file in the court a certified list of the materials comprising the record and retain and hold for the court all such materials and transmit the same or any part thereof to the court, when and as required by it, at any time prior to the final determination of the proceeding, and such filing of such certified list of the materials comprising the record and such subsequent transmittal of any such materials when and as required shall be deemed full compliance with any provision of law requiring the filing of the record in the court. The record in such proceedings shall be certified and filed in or held for and transmitted to the court of appeals by the agency, board, commission, or officer concerned within the time and in the manner prescribed by such rules. If proceedings are instituted in two or more courts of appeals with respect to the same order, the following shall apply:

(1) If within ten days after issuance of the order the agency, board, commission, or officer concerned receives, from the persons instituting the proceedings, the petition for review with respect to proceedings in at least two courts of appeals, the agency, board, commission, or officer shall proceed in accordance with paragraph (3) of this subsection. If within ten days after the issuance of the order the agency, board, commission, or officer concerned receives, from the persons instituting the proceedings, the petition for review with respect to proceedings in only one court of appeals, the agency, board, commission, or officer shall file the record in that court notwithstanding the institution in any other court of appeals of proceedings for review of that order. In all other cases in which proceedings have been instituted in two or more courts of appeals with respect to the same order, the agency, board, commission, or officer concerned shall file the record in the court in which proceedings with respect to the order were first instituted.

(2) For purposes of paragraph (1) of this subsection, a copy of the petition or other pleading which institutes proceedings in a court of appeals and which is stamped by the court with the date of filing shall constitute the petition for review. Each agency, board, commission, or officer, as the case may be, shall designate by rule the office and the officer who must receive petitions for review under paragraph (1).

(3) If an agency, board, commission, or officer receives two or more petitions for review of an order in accordance with the first sentence of paragraph (1) of this subsection, the agency, board, commission, or officer shall, promptly after the expiration of the ten-day period specified in that sentence, so notify the judicial panel on multidistrict litigation authorized by section 1407 of this title, in such form as that panel shall prescribe. The judicial panel on multidistrict litigation shall, by means of random selection, designate one court of appeals, from among the courts of appeals in which petitions for review have been filed and received within the ten-day period specified in the first sentence of paragraph (1), in which the record is to be filed, and shall issue an order consolidating the petitions for review in that court of appeals. The judicial panel on multidistrict litigation shall, after providing notice to the public and an opportunity for the submission of comments, prescribe rules with respect to the consolidation of proceedings under this paragraph. The agency, board, commission, or officer concerned shall file the record in the court of appeals designated pursuant to this paragraph.

(4) Any court of appeals in which proceedings with respect to an order of an agency, board, commission, or officer have been instituted may, to the extent authorized by law, stay the effective date of the order. Any such stay may thereafter be modified, revoked, or extended by a court of appeals designated pursuant to paragraph (3) with respect to that order or by any other court of appeals to which the proceedings are transferred.

(5) All courts in which proceedings are instituted with respect to the same order, other than the court in which the record is filed pursuant to this subsection, shall transfer those proceedings to the court in which the record is so filed. For the convenience of the parties in the interest of justice, the court in which the record is filed may thereafter transfer all the proceedings with respect to that order to any other court of appeals.

(b) The record to be filed in the court of appeals in such a proceeding shall consist of the order sought to be reviewed or enforced, the findings or report upon which it is based, and the pleadings, evidence, and proceedings before the agency, board, commission, or officer concerned, or such portions thereof (1) as the rules prescribed under the authority of section 2072 of this title may require to be included therein, or (2) as the agency, board, commission, or officer concerned, the petitioner for review or respondent in enforcement, as the case may be, and any intervenor in the court proceeding by written stipulation filed with the agency, board, commission, or officer concerned or in the court in any such proceeding may consistently with the rules prescribed under the authority of section 2072 of this title designate to be included therein, or (3) as the court upon motion of a party or, after a prehearing conference, upon its own motion may by order in any such proceeding designate to be included therein. Such a stipulation or order may provide in an appropriate case that no record need be filed in the court of appeals. If, however, the correctness of a finding of fact by the agency, board, commission, or officer is in question all of the evidence before the agency, board, commission, or officer shall be included in the record except such as the agency, board, commission, or officer concerned, the petitioner for review or respondent in enforcement, as the case may be, and any intervenor in the court proceeding by written stipulation filed with the agency, board, commission, or officer concerned or in the court agree to omit as wholly immaterial to the questioned finding. If there is omitted from the record any portion of the proceedings before the agency, board, commission, or officer which the court subsequently determines to be proper for it to consider to enable it to review or enforce the order in question the court may direct that such additional portion of the proceedings be filed as a supplement to the record. The agency, board, commission, or officer concerned may, at its option and without regard to the foregoing provisions of this subsection, and if so requested by the petitioner for review or respondent in enforcement shall, file in the court the entire record of the proceedings before it without abbreviation.

(c) The agency, board, commission, or officer concerned may transmit to the court of appeals the original papers comprising the whole or any part of the record or any supplemental record, otherwise true copies of such papers certified by an authorized officer or deputy of the agency, board, commission, or officer concerned shall be transmitted. Any original papers thus transmitted to the court of appeals shall be returned to the agency, board, commission, or officer concerned upon the final determination of the review or enforcement proceeding. Pending such final determination any such papers may be returned by the court temporarily to the custody of the agency, board, commission, or officer concerned if needed for the transaction of the public business. Certified copies of any papers included in the record or any supplemental record may also be returned to the agency, board, commission, or officer concerned upon the final determination of review or enforcement proceedings.

(d) The provisions of this section are not applicable to proceedings to review decisions of the Tax Court of the United States or to proceedings to review or enforce those orders of administrative agencies, boards, commissions, or officers which are by law reviewable or enforceable by the district courts.

(Added Pub.L. 85–791, § 2, Aug. 28, 1958, 72 Stat. 941, and amended Pub.L. 89–773, § 5(a), (b), Nov. 6, 1966, 80 Stat. 1323; Pub.L. 100–236, § 1, Jan. 8, 1988, 101 Stat. 1731.)

HISTORICAL AND STATUTORY NOTES
Effective and Applicability Provisions

1988 Acts. Section 3 of Pub.L. 100–236 provided that: "The amendments made by this Act [amending subsec. (a) of this section and section 1369(b) of Title 33, Navigation and Navigable Waters] take effect 180 days after the date of the enactment of this Act [Jan. 8, 1988], except that the judicial panel on multidistrict litigation may issue rules pursuant to subsection (a)(3) of section 2112 of title 28, United States Code (as added by section 1) [subsec. (a)(3) of this section], on or after such date of enactment."

Savings Provisions

Section 5(c) of Pub.L. 89–773 provided that: "The amendments of section 2112 of title 28 of the United States Code [this section] made by this Act shall not operate to invalidate or repeal rules adopted under the authority of that section prior to the enactment of this Act [Nov. 6, 1966], which rules shall remain in effect until superseded by rules prescribed under the authority of section 2072 of title 28 of the United States Code [section 2072 of this title] as amended by this Act."

§ 2113. Definition

For purposes of this chapter, the terms "State court", "State courts", and "highest court of a State" include the District of Columbia Court of Appeals.

(Added Pub.L. 91–358, Title I, § 172(a)(2)(A), July 29, 1970, 84 Stat. 590.)

HISTORICAL AND STATUTORY NOTES
Effective and Applicability Provisions

1970 Acts. Section effective the first day of the seventh calendar month which begins after July 29, 1970, see section 199(a) of Pub.L. 91–358, set out as a note under section 1257 of this title.

PART VI—PARTICULAR PROCEEDINGS

CHAPTER 159—INTERPLEADER

§ 2361. Process and procedure

In any civil action of interpleader or in the nature of interpleader under section 1335 of this title, a district court may issue its process for all claimants and enter its order restraining them from instituting or prosecuting any proceeding in any State or United States court affecting the property, instrument or obligation involved in the interpleader action until further order of the court. Such process and order shall be returnable at such time as the court or judge thereof directs, and shall be addressed to and served by the United States marshals for the respective districts where the claimants reside or may be found.

Such district court shall hear and determine the case, and may discharge the plaintiff from further liability, make the injunction permanent, and make all appropriate orders to enforce its judgment.

(June 25, 1948, c. 646, 62 Stat. 970; May 24, 1949, c. 139, § 117, 63 Stat. 105.)

†